THE
WIZARD CLIP
HAUNTING

Nineveh's Crossing

August 18, 2023

Character Comments

"If I knew it was going to be hell on earth, I would have said 'no'."

— MARY ANN LIVINGSTON (née Babbitt)
Revolutionary War widow

"I am resolute in my judgment: Richard McSherry is a hypocrite, a double liar, a fraud, and he will not marry my daughter, Anastasia, so help me God."

— RICHARD LILLY
Conewago Planter

"Far more work than I anticipated or prayed for."

— RICHARD MCSHERRY
Irish bachelor who married well

"Men are not all the same. Thank God."

— ANASTASIA MCSHERRY (née Lilly)
Richard McSherry's wife

"That such attention has been given to a renegade priest is abhorrent."

— REV. ANTONIO DE SEDELLA, OFM Cap.
Louisiana Franciscan Superior

"My appreciation to Mister Livingston for taking my advice, allowing me to assist, and employing General Gates' former slaves. An honorable man."

— JOHN ADAMS
U.S. Minister to England/U.S. President

"Many of the Catholic faith are misled into strange mysteries, but I am glad they are residents in our fair town. They are good citizens."

— JONATHAN HAGER, JR
Son of Hagerstown founder

"He will make a good seaman, whether on land or water. Mighty glad he was aboard. America is better for it."

— CAPTAIN JOHN WERNER
American merchant ship Eagle

"Never have I met a layman as well educated or a priest as rebellious."

— REV. JOHN CARROLL, S.J.
United States Superior and Bishop

"Next time there will be blood and bones to pay. Gaspar does not relent."

— JOSÉ GASPAR
Legendary Florida pirate

"I am a good Catholic girl...not a hussy. But nothing is forever."

— LETITIA MCCARTNEY
Irish siren

ISBN-13: 978-1-7329735-3-4 Hardback (6" x 9")
ISBN-13: 978-1-7329735-4-1 Paperback (6" x 9")
ISBN-13: 978-1-7329735-7-2 (Paperback 5.5 x 8.5 Book 1)
ISBN-13: 978-1-7329735-8-9 (Paperback 5.5 x 8.5 Book 2)
ISBN-13: 978-1-7329735-9-6 (Paperback 5.5 x 8.5 Book 3)
ISBN-13: 978-1-7329735-6-5 (Electronic PDF)
ISBN-13: 978-1-7329735-5-8 (Electronic ePub)

Library of Congress Control Number: 2023930749

Printed in the United States of America

This is a work of historical fiction. Many of the events, names are taken from historical records then enhanced by the author's imagination. The author makes no claim that anything in this story is true, but others have claimed that much is.

Bible Quotations on the Part Title pages are in memory of Matthew Carey, an Irish journalist who was jailed in England for criticizing the British government for its persecution of Catholics. He fled to America in 1784, and in 1790, the time of the story chronicled in this novel, he published the first non-King James Version of the English Bible in the United States—the Douay-Rheims Version English Bible. Translated to English from the Latin Vulgate it was first published in Rome by the English College (NT in 1582, OT in 1610). The original Douay-Rheims employed a heavy Latinate vocabulary and was hard to read. In later years several new editions were released, some based on the King James Version text rigorously checked for readability and consistency with the Vulgate. The quotations herein are from the Douay-Rheims 1899 American Edition (DRA).

Distributed by:

Nineveh's Crossing
www.NinevehsCrossing.com
Novi, Michigan USA

Early Reader Comments

The Wizard Clip Haunting combines the best of both worlds. It accurately shares the known facts of the Wizard Clip with exciting fiction of what may have been. I felt as if I were there. I laughed, cried, celebrated and mourned with the characters. A riveting novel. (K.M.)

Rich in American History, it's a dynamite story told well. (A.R.)

This is the first "modern" story (meaning written after 1950) that I had read in ages that I actually wanted to finish. The storyline is fascinating, the changing point of view adds intrigue, the writing is very good, with excellent pacing that compels one to continue reading. And it does this without the use of Hardy Boy cliffhangers. (M.R.)

After an extensive 10 year research into the life of Prince-Priest Demetrius A. Gallitzin (1770-1840), including his personal involvement in the Wizard Clip Hauntings, you can imagine my fascination in how this novel delightfully brings to life the initial facts and the formation and integration of the many complex personalities involved. The character development is excellent as is the high suspense and drama leading up to the Wizard and his clipping! (Betty Seymour, Loretto, PA)

A colossus of historical fiction. The reader is given a glimpse of New World pragmatism shredded by otherworldly forces it denies, and the Ancient Faith sweeping in to rescue surprised saints. (J.W.)

I'm captivated by The Wizard Clip. From the very beginning the characters sprung to life and I was there with them, and I cried when...(spoiler)...I think every waking moment will be spent reading this. (K.M.)

The Wizard Clip Haunting is a wonderful historical horror novel dealing with religion, the devil and his demons and a group of people who are interesting characters in a story I wasn't quite expecting. Yes it is a horror story with the devil and demons playing their part at trying to deceive and rid the world of those who are good. The pull of good and evil with guardians and demons is as old as religion and one that most never tire of reading or hearing. I'm one where good needs to win, and it does here, but how it happens is interesting and the ending ties all the different characters together in what was happening and needed to be done to set things right. Even if you are not religious, this book based in religion is well worth the time to read just for the characters, the suspense of what will happen next, and how it will all be resolved. (B.M.)

If you're looking for a novel that has action, adventure, drama, and other worldly interactions, you'll enjoy this Historical Fiction on the first documented exorcism in the US. I was so impressed with the novel, I looked up some of the main characters and the events the book is based on. The story and the characters are enthralling, you'll love it. (S.R.)

Contents

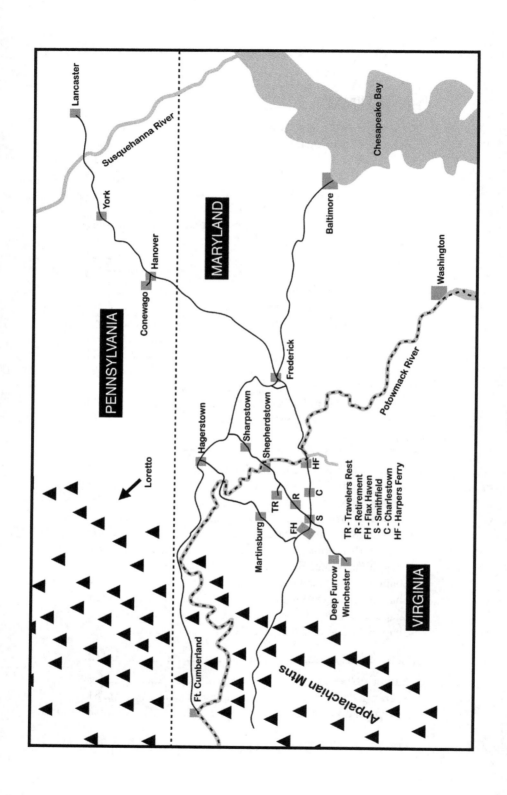

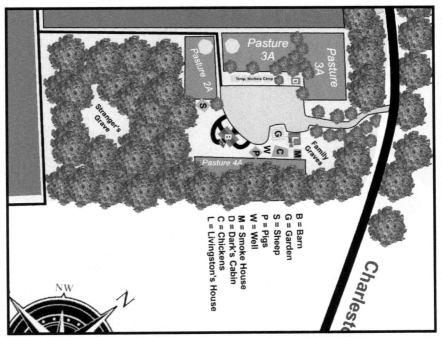

B = Barn   G = Garden
S = Sheep
P = Pigs
W = Well
M = Smoke House
D = Dark's Cabin
C = Chickens
L = Livingston's House

Adam Livingston's 350A Smithfield, Virginia Farm

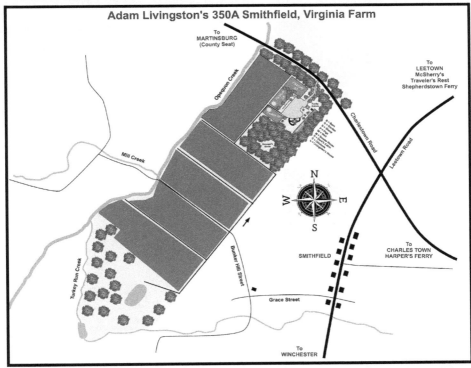

for

JAIME ANTONIO SOTELO

an expat Filipino and emigrant to Australia who
first told me about the Mystery of the Wizard Clip in 2012.

THE

WIZARD CLIP
HAUNTING

A True Early American Ghost Story

Stanley D. Williams

Nineveh's Crossing

* An asterisk precedes a letter or paragraph indicating a documented historical source for all or part of what follows, e.g., most of the letters between Fr. Denis Cahill and Bishop John Carroll are real and not imagined. Also, an asterisk precedes the first mention of a name or place indicating a documented historical (or legendary) person or place that is not immediately known to common history, e.g., *George Washington* is not asterisked, but *Richard Lilly* is. While none of what the author ascribes to such persons or places can be relied on as true, nonetheless much of it evidently did happen.

Your minister would laugh heartily if you should relate to him the above facts; for with wise men of our enlightened age, he has peremptorily decided that miracles, &c., are no longer necessary, and of course they have ceased. Since when I did not learn; nor did I ever find any passage in Scripture which authorizes the belief that miracles should ever cease altogether, or that evil spirits should never have it any more in their power to molest the bodies and property of men, as they used to do during the life time of our Saviour, and even after his resurrection. (Acts v. 16.)

—Rev. Prince Demetrius Augustine Gallitzin
(aka Fr. Smith)

Part One:
Progenitor

That which hath been made, the same continueth:
the things that shall be, have already been:
and God restoreth that which is past.
I saw under the sun
in the place of judgment wickedness,
and in the place of justice iniquity.
And I said in my heart:
God shall judge both the just and the wicked,
and then shall be the time of every thing.

(Ecclesiastes 3:15–17)

Chapter 1
Nudged by a Divine Impulse

1

April 23, 1821.

Two-thousand feet up an Allegheny mountainside the warm setting sun gave way to the cool dawn of night. Even higher, a thin waxing crescent moon broke through the overcast to back-light stands of spruce, balsam, and fir. Weaving its way through the warp and weft of valleys and high pastures, a cool breeze flew past the pinnacle of a small frame church and a matching rectory that together stood guard over the young village of *Loretto.

Inside the rectory was the austere study of a master bibliophile. The fragrance of pulp, fiberboard, and leather emanated from hundreds of volumes perfectly cataloged, but rarely read, on oak shelves that reached to the ceiling along every wall.

At a walnut secretary hutch, its front pulled down to create a writing surface, sat Loretto's founder, the *Reverend (Prince) Demetrius Augustine Gallitzin, a thin, fifty-year-old man in a black cassock with thick, white, wavy hair falling in gentle curls to his shoulders. For some minutes he sat erect and still, staring into space. The grand arch of his Aristotelian nose set off his high cheek bones and recessed cheeks, his complexion ruddy. He appeared gaunt, almost malnourished if not for the deep-set, piercing blue eyes revealing an alert mind. Once a Russian prince, he carried his aristocracy humbly, and preferred to be addressed by his parishioners simply as Fr. Smith.

Looking down at the blank parchment on his desk, he knew that in twenty years he would not remember, but now he did. Yet the events he had been ordered to recount haunted him, for they documented an infestation some actors in the story would like to forget. Fluent in French, Russian, Dutch, and now English, words were not foreign to him, nor were his well-used quills. Although a sharp knife lay about ready to sharpen the quills, finding the right words required wit.

As if nudged by a divine impulse, his right hand reached out, turned-up the lamp's wick, uncovered his inkwell, and at once his left hand grasped a favorite quill, submerged its nib in the pool of lampblack, and began the long journey.

2

Octave of Easter, Monday - 23 April 1821
St. Michael Catholic Church
Loretto, Pennsylvania
The *Most Reverend Ambrose Maréchal
Archbishop of Baltimore, Maryland

My Lord Maréchal,

In 1797, your once-removed predecessor, *John Carroll, directed me to travel from my residence in *Conewago, Pennsylvania to *Smithfield, Virginia. I was to investigate what neither of us believed—extraordinary stories emanating from an ordinary village about an ordinary man and his experiences with Spiritism. After three months of investigation, I was soon converted to a full belief of them. No lawyer in a court of justice did more than I, nor procured more than your unworthy servant.

As you have recalled, and indeed it is true, I wrote a careful account of these matters at that time and gave it to a then trustworthy acquaintance. But like a good book loaned, it never returned, and all manner of requests have only succeeded in securing its mysterious disappearance.

Therefore, at your request, here is an account of those events, which neither of us wish to be lost to time but no doubt will be forgotten. It seems, too, that the stories may finally have come to their natural end with the recent passing of Mr. Adam Livingston. I will, therefore, write a full, orderly, and accurate account of what I have experienced, what I have discovered, and what the passage of time has revealed of those most strange and mysterious occurrences. While a curiosity to many, they were intolerable to a few.

The story begins during the upheaval in North America for control of land between the British and the French. In the British Colonies between 1756–1763 it was called the French and Indian War. In Europe it was the Seven-Year War, though to some it continues to this day. The conflict created uncertainties throughout Pennsylvania and Virginia, which were British Colonies then and commonwealths of the United States today.

But there was a second and overlapping theater of turmoil that influenced the actors and agencies of our story. It was the entrenched hatred of European kings and political leaders for the Catholic Church. The hostility of the day were missionaries of the Society of Jesus, Jesuits, which detractors considered the Association of Satan. In England the haters found their excuse for belligerency in the 1605 Gunpowder Plot, or the Jesuit Treason as some called it. It was the alleged attempt by dissident Catholics to assassinate Protestant King James I. Led by *Robert Catesby and the likes of *Guy Fawkes, its discovery and the execution of its ring leaders is celebrated still, both in the U.K. and here at the infamous Guy Fawkes bonfires traditionally lit on the evening of the fifth of November.

In other countries, such as Portugal, France, and Spain the hatred stemmed from the economic success Jesuit missionaries enjoyed in the New World, and their reluctance to turn over their acquired wealth to the royal treasuries of their sponsoring countries. Jesuit achievement, or arrogance, depending on one's persuasion, was rewarded by their suppression and exile from the New World, which was demanded by kings and acquiesced to by Pope Clement XIV. Their reduction farming communes were closed down and their chapels leveled, but not necessarily in an orderly fashion, unless conflagrations set by royal armies are considered orderly. Anything of value was confiscated and given to the "poor"—as royal coffers were proclaimed to be.

Such were the global forces, the colonial values, the royal bigotries, and the social undercurrents in which Adam Livingston and Fr. Denis Cahill found themselves.

What follows is not one story but four, woven into a single fabric no doubt by Providence prompted by the purveyors of Perdition. The first story regards the *thirty-five acres of land in Smithfield, next to the *Opequon Creek, which you have considered significant but which the courts count as trivial. It is, as you have been told, sufficiently large and situated for the support of a priest, although it supports no one today. The second is the story of a resourceful but tragic farmer, *Adam Livingston. Some claim he was of the Lutheran persuasion but that is an exaggeration; for it is no exaggeration to say he was of no persuasion whatsoever. The third is the story of a heroic pioneering priest, *Denis Cahill, who found and forged a heroic missionary path in the early days of the nation but has since evidently lost his way. The fourth is of a supernatural demonic spirit, which the locals to this day call the *Clipping Wizard, and the town whence it came was known as Smithfield, but is today known as Wizard Clip or Clip Town. There are elements of this fourth narrative that you may suspect are inventions of my imagination. Yet, I assure you I am not known to imagine much of anything but God's grace that comes to the undeserved, and his mercy that prohibits what is deserved.

Your Servant,
Fr. Smith

Chapter 2
Nor Did He Curse God

1

June, 1760.

Leaving the main road, the vagrant tied up his horse under the Opequon Creek bridge, climbed up the bank, crawled through thick brush, and walked the perimeter of the thirty-five acre property. It took a good hour as he was careful to stay out of sight. Except for a plentiful source of water from the creek that ran along the northwest boundary, the land was barren, untended, and seemingly useless, without hint of even a tobacco crop. How could a man exist without livestock, poultry, tobacco or even a barn? There had to be a reason, a good reason—no doubt he had hidden a treasure. How else could Alexander Mayfield have paid in gold for a sack of supplies at the Winchester general store?

The paradox made the vagrant grit his teeth and clench his fists. This had been a chance to change the trajectory of his life. *Damn!* Easily riled, he grabbed a fallen branch, and swung it hard against the trunk of a large tree. The blow reverberated up the stick, through his arms, and shook his torso until his eyes slammed shut. When he opened them, he was left with a crooked walking stick. *Small consolation.*

Returning to the road with his newly acquired staff, Silas Cain started up the winding cart path to the cabin. The path was hidden from the main road by wild brush and a grove of unkempt fruit trees. For that he was glad, and instinctually quickened his pace, thumping the heavy stick at rocks along the path.

Mayfield's modest, one story cabin was constructed of squared-off logs and cement chink, atop a fieldstone foundation. There was a small porch with just enough room for two rocking chairs, one either side of the door. A flintlock rifle leaned against the cabin next to the door. There was a sweater draped over one of the chairs and next to it a few dishes and a jug, probably of home-made brew. It looked as if there used to be two persons living in the cabin, but now there was only Mayfield and he spent a lot of time in that one rocking chair next to the rifle. *Be careful.*

As he drew near, Silas tried to look presentable. A thirty-year-old Virginian, Cain was more than your common vagrant. He was a British army deserter having spent six months under George Washington's command in a contingent of *Brigadier-General John Forbes' 6,000 strong force. Cain had joined up looking for action. But he quickly grew tired of building Forbes' 300-mile-long supply road across the Allegheny Mountains. The road would later support an attack on the French at Fort Duquesne. That was two years ago, and since then

Cain had led a depraved life of corruption, thievery, and murder. It bothered him not in the least.

Saddled with a Sicilian complexion, pointed chin, high but flat cheekbones, and a monstrous nose he was shunned by every village he visited. Ostensibly looking for a job, he would case the community, break in, steal, murder if he had to, and escape with whatever treasure or food he could find. He would have made a good pirate, but sea-faring piracy was out of fashion.

Such a life was getting old, and Cain was feeling the need to settle down and stop running. Yet even when he seriously applied to proprietors or farm owners there was no work. Perhaps it was because his thick, black, unkempt hair, stubble beard, and deep-set black eyes made him appear dangerous. At least he had that going for him.

Just south of the cabin Cain caught sight of Mayfield down on all fours. He was digging by hand in a small garden.

Cain strutted onto the property and pulled up short of the garden. He leaned on his stick, and raised the old man. "You Alexander Mayfield?"

Mayfield looked up, grabbed a long-handled hoe that had been lying next to him, slowly rose to his feet and stared at the visitor. "Who's asking? You lost?"

"I aren't lost, old man," Cain said.

Mayfield stood erect, protected as it were behind a row of radish plants and the hoe he held across his chest.

Cain took a moment to size the old man up—fair complexion, couldn't spend too much time outside, probably spent it inside counting his gold—age spots on his bald head—tangled, white hair hung over his ears that melded into a beard. That beard! He must trim it with a dull knife, once he combed the dried food out of it, which of late he hadn't. Short, stoutly built, probably not someone to tangle with in years past or perhaps even now. An old-school, stiff upper lip, proper English gentleman who believed in God, but only as far as he could stretch his hoe. "You a hermit or something?" said Cain.

"What is it to likes of you?"

"Hard living alone, aren't it?"

"Been jest fine for years, since the Missus died. 'Fore that it was hard."

"I'm interested in yer land. Like to buy it from ya."

"Not fer sale. Leave me. Got radishes to attend. They don't like company."

"But I'll pay you a good price, if we kin negotiate."

Mayfield stepped out of his garden; the hoe still held across his body. "Told you git. I aren't good at negotiating wid nobody fer nothin'. What's wrong with yer head? Ya sick?"

"I'm Silas Cain. New to the area, looking for land to work."

"Well, Mister Cain. This here is my land and I'm workin' it."

"Not lookin' too good. You could use some help, it seems."

Mayfield's squared off stance and his squinty eyes lookin' Cain up and down were insulting. "No need of assistance—or slave labor. Now I've work to do, insofar as you point out I have no assistance."

"The ground's practically barren. I looked it over just this day. Why ya pretend to farm it?"

The old man glared. "Why is that any business of yours? It is mine to do with as I please. Now, git, or da'ya need persuasion?" At that Mayfield gripped his hoe until his knuckles turned white.

"It's not for farming' is it, old man? Yer holding a secret 'bout it," Cain said.

"What's there to keep secret?" said Mayfield. "You've walked the land. I watched you. Don't think I didn't. I've got no fences. Perhaps it might produce more if morons like you weren't trespassing on my crops."

"Crops! Those weeds, old man. Ya don't know what yer doing, and I kin do it better."

"With heaven as my judge, why should I care what you can do?"

"I buy it from ya. Sell it ta me. It not worth anything to ya. Dollar a acre. How many ya got?"

"A dollar per? I paid two-fifty per for these thirty-five, and I'll not part wid one of 'em, especially to insulters. Git off my land. I'm done wid ya."

Cain's brow dug valleys and his neck stiffened as he gripped his walking stick and glared at the old man who had grunted and turned back to hoeing his garden. *There was something hid here, and he was going to have it.* "Look, mister, I was just trying to be friendly. I'm not a claim jumper or anythin'."

Mayfield turned and advanced on Cain, his eyes narrowed, and the hoe now held higher with two white-knuckled fists.

"Okay. Okay. I going. No need to get all rankled-like." Cain kept his eye on Mayfield and stepped backward careful not to trip over one of the many rocks protruding from the ground. When Mayfield went back to gardening, Cain turned, put his back to the old man, and slogged down the path toward the road. He noticed a footpath through the brush that shortened the distance to the bridge and his horse. But his walk slowed. He was listening, pondering his options.

Suddenly, a small rock stung him hard in the back of the head—a perfect strike, from a sling shot? Cain whirled to confront the old man.

But Mayfield was in his garden, again on all fours, and turned away.

A bird or tree squirrel? Cain searched the sky, trees, and ground. Nothing!

Mad, he turned quickly to go, but his boot slipped into a rut. He lost his balance and fell. Stretching out his arm toward the ground to break the fall, the edge of a black obsidian rock cut his palm wide open.

At once. Blood. Everywhere.

Hatred boiled over. Grabbing the tail of his shirt, he jammed it into this palm and tightened his fist to stem the flow of blood. He couldn't ride back to town this way. The old man must have bandages. Picking up his walking stick, Cain turned back toward the cabin.

As he turned, a thorny branch whipped into Cain's face and cut his lower lip. The taste of blood, the perfect exacerbation.

A few steps more and a hole suddenly appeared under Cain's pounding step, twisting his ankle, wrenching his spirit, and fueling his temper.

But there was more. A swarm of biting flies attacked Cain's exposed head and neck. Frustrated, he swatted wildly at the stinging parasites with his fist, then with his stick, striking his ear with stinging effect.

To escape, Cain ran toward the cabin, one hand in a fisted bandage restrained by his shirt tail, the other holding the stick and his injured ear.

As he ran, an invisible boot kicked Cain in the shin. He gasped for air, but there was none. Twisting and turning, the pain and agony only fueled his ire. He hobbled as best he could back to the old man and yelled: "Sir. Kind, sir! Yer cursed land attacked me. I am in need. Help me. Please, help me!"

Limping and lamenting, Cain came at Mayfield. One arm was swinging fiendishly as if it had been mostly severed from his shoulder. The other arm flailed about, the walking stick circling savagely over his head. Mayfield, seeing the visitor in torment, jumped to his feet and ran to Cain's aid, this time without his long-handled hoe.

For Cain there was but a split second of reflection of the original plan which had moments ago fled his consciousness, but now flooded back with clarity and vile. His adrenaline rushed so mightily that all his pain and impairment disappeared. Suddenly and instinctively, Cain, with his walking stick, viciously and repeatedly struck the side of Mayfield's head.

Immediately, Mayfield fell in a heap to the earth. Blood spurted and drained from the old man's ear, only to be swiftly sucked into the virgin Virginia soil.

Cain stood over Mayfield's body, trying to understand what had just happened. The old man did not seem to be breathing. Good. But while the deed was done, it went nothing like Cain had planned, at least not as he had hoped. Mayfield had no time to scream. Nor did he curse God before he died.

2

Cyn Namrasit, Order of Paroled Sub-Demons (OPSD), hovered invisibly about the scene. Below Cyn, Alexander Mayfield lay motionless on the cool earth now being warmed by blood draining from his left ear—blood that would curse the land. Standing over Mayfield, Silas Cain breathed heavily. His wide-open eyes darted left and right, his bloody hand wrapped tightly in the tail of his shirt.

Cyn spastically swirled in self-reproach, a veil of devastation blanketed his belligerency. Like Cain's darting eyes that searched for a cause, Cyn's damned essence searched for a hell-bound effect. But the scintillation in the continuum told Cyn that Mayfield's soul was not on its way to Perdition.

The consequences were devastating, not for Cain, or Mayfield, but for Cyn. Again, he had inadvertently assisted in sending yet another soul to that intermediate place that demons feared. For although it wasn't Heaven, it *was* Glory's vestibule and thus cut off from demonic influence.

Damn them all and Alexander Mayfield, Cyn cursed even as he hoped.

Jutting toward the dimensional crack to challenge the angel's claim, Cyn stopped short. Last time he attempted the jump, his scar-laced hide was ripped open by the sharp edges of the discontinuity. It required fire, painful fire, to anneal his hide shut again.

Cyn plunged back to the temporal scene to figure out what needed to be done. His plan had failed, miserably failed. While he relished the powers of suggestion and psychokinetics granted him, he had grown too confident. He was not yet the knighted demon he believed himself to be. Well, he was once, but that was before his last bust. Now on parole to live an abusive existence, he had fallen into a habit of anxious aggression to motivate his targets. Perhaps Cain was too agreeable to suggestions. He did respond rather well. Cyn had enjoyed pulling his strings like a marionette. The joy of seeing his ghoulish behavior acted out in one human toward another was nothing short of orgasmic. But there was a consequence to everything. Sub-demons still operated in a realm of natural cause and effect, the connections between which he and his kind could not revise. Cyn feared the consequences he now faced, much like last time.

Would his impatient supervisor send him back for remedial training yet again? He doubted it. What good would it do? He didn't learn last time. Too impulsive, too aggressive, too impatient. But wasn't that the idea?

He felt anger, the wrong kind, he was sure. It wasn't aimed at others, but rather at himself from a more powerful and dangerous place. He wanted to run and hide. But where could that possibly be? He wasn't clever enough to invent a new dimension for himself alone.

Perhaps if he suggested a punishment for this stupidity, his master would let him exercise some control over the next decade of existence. Remedial hell was no fun. At once it was drowning, choking, bloody anguish, and death by fire while falling into a canyon of sharp obsidian rocks. The purpose, of course, was to experience pain, not to relieve it. Perhaps he could conjure a self-imposed penance, an exile that would avoid the temporal retribution for being an idiot.

No sooner had he considered the consequences of his rash behavior and had planned an inconspicuous exit, then Mayfield's corpse moved. Cyn didn't have a heart, but if he had one, it would have stopped in ecstasy.

Cyn got down close, allowing his essence to surround Mayfield's body, and hoped for a spark of life. If he could get Mayfield breathing again, he might have a chance to save his hide. He whispered to Cain: *Help the man. Awaken him. Cajole, then taunt. Make him mad, angry.* Cyn had to do this right. Then he could revisit his plan and execute it—*Mayfield must curse God just before he dies.* That was the plan. Cyn would be hailed as a hero. Perhaps it was still possible to take this fool to Hell and fleece that atrocious angel of victory. Yes, that was his chance. All he needed to do was to get him breathing again, let him soak in the pain, real, deep pain, get him to curse the Almighty, and then Cain can kill him again...for good.

3

Cain gawked at his malevolent deed sprawled on the ground before him. From Mayfield's left temple blood poured profusely, but just as quickly was sucked up by the earth. The panic that coursed through Cain's body was bittersweet. His spine quivered as it always did when he killed, but there was fear, too. Turning to the right and left, his eyes darted about. Had he been seen? Had anyone noticed?

He glared down at Mayfield's body and stabbed at it with his stick. He looked dead, but was he? Mayfield's face was in the dirt. Cain stooped down to get a closer look. The pallor had turned blue, but the man's nostrils repeatedly flared then collapsed as black vapor streamed in and out—the corpse was still breathing. In fact, the sooty vapor also pulsed in and out of the man's half-opened mouth.

Cain gasped, and his head jerked back. From the side of Mayfield's mouth, a miniature tornado of dirt rose into the air. *Odd.* Standing up, Cain took his stick and rolled Mayfield's body onto its back, whereupon the swirl of dirt transformed itself into a jet of dark vapor that alternately pushed air into and then sucked it out of Mayfield's gaping mouth. At the same time his chest began to repeatedly expand and contract. A drool of blood on Mayfield's lips pumped in and out with the gusts of air. Cain narrowed his eyes on the man's face. Might the man rise from the dead as if by some wizardly force?

Cain's brain fogged over. What he saw made no sense. His eyebrows pinched the bridge of his nose, and his teeth bit into both lips. This was no time to be squeamish. Refocusing, he looked around, and dug the biggest rock he could find out of the ground. It was a granite boulder. With both hands he raised the boulder over Mayfield's head. The jets of vapor seemed to increase in intensity and speed. Mayfield's chest rose farther. *What are you waiting for? You want him to get up and fight back?* Surging with anger, Cain brought his arms down and rammed the boulder squarely onto Mayfield's nose, crushing it and flattening his face.

Alexander Mayfield was certainly now dead. His chest stopped moving and the jets and puffs of sooty smoke disappeared, strangely enough, into the ground.

Cain relaxed, but clarity of thought had not returned. He began to lament the usual gap in his planning. For minutes he paced around the body trying to visualize his options. How was he going to dispose of the body, for the bloody mess was out in the open, as was the killing. The longer he stood there, the better the odds he'd be found out.

He could leave everything as it is, and go back to his horse the way he came probably undetected. But that would accomplish nothing and put him right back at the beginning of the day. His life would be no different. Something had to change.

Guilt? He felt none. Guilt was something for lesser men. Life was hard enough to regret the dismissal of those that dismissed him. But he hated this part of the recurring story—although he considered himself smart and clever, he never knew what to do with the body.

Of course, he could bury it. Yes, that's what he'll do. But there are problems with that as well. Getting the body to that clump of trees behind the cabin was only half the battle; he'd get his horse to help with that. He also had to dig a grave deep enough that ravishing animals would not claw off a hand or foot and drag it across the road in broad daylight. Cain hated work. Especially hard manual work like digging graves. His lungs took a deep breath. *Might as well get on with it.*

He looked around...there was a stable across the yard; a shovel could be found there. Next, he needed to get his horse, then the rest wouldn't be so bad.

4

Silas Cain climbed out of the shallow hole. The rocks he had pulled from it were piled to one side. He pulled Mayfield's body into the hastily dug grave. As the body dropped awkwardly into the earthen tomb, black steam rose like a dark mist out of the hole, coalesced into a spinning funnel several feet high, and drilled itself into the middle of the rock pile. Cain jumped back. The funnel was otherworldly, choreographed, and quick. With his shovel he fearfully nudged the top rocks aside. There were a variety: granite, agate, sandstone, and a box like stone of chiseled black obsidian. But there was no indication where the spinning funnel of smoke had gone.

A half-hour later, as dusk fell, he finished covering the grave with dead brush and arranged the rocks into a cairn as a hastily built memorial, the least he could do. Stepping back, he leaned on the shovel, and gazed at the cairn. Sadness overtook him. Why, he wondered? Was he mad to be sad, or sad that he was no longer mad? Killing always confused him.

A cool evening breeze wove through the trees. Cain sucked the fresh air into his lungs as if on the foredeck of his uncle's barque driving into a wind. But there was no cool saltwater breeze to savor. Just the musky, August dust. Rubbing the dust from his eyes he looked at his hands...no blood? By now, the body and its blood were feeding worms and other subterranean vermin.

Casually he returned to the site of the killing by the house as if nothing was amiss. He dug up the bloodied ground, and scattered it among the outlying shrubs.

With Mayfield out of the way, excitement returned to his demeanor. It was time to do what he came for. He tied his horse to a tree with a long rein near a patch of grass, found a bucket of water for the animal, and turned toward the cabin, at last.

Mayfield may have been a terrible farmer, but he was orderly. It took but a few minutes to find the property's claim with a full description of Mayfield's thirty-five acres and its history. King Charles II had granted the land to Lord Fairfax as a political payoff for Fairfax's support during the English civil war. Fairfax then surveyed the land, subdivided it for speculation, deeded 600 acres to Mayfield's uncle, Andrew Mayfield, who in turn granted thirty-five acres to his nephew.

It took much longer than expected, but after several tries by lamp light, Cain eventually forged a bill of sale, a new document renewing the claims but in his own name...with witnesses, no less. Stoking the dying embers in the fireplace he burned the original claim, and with a bottle of found brandy, celebrated his new acquisition. He was now the proud owner of thirty-five acres of Virginia land—a first for Silas Cain.

5

My Despised Cyn Namrasit:

You should be commended if it wasn't for the condemnation you bring upon your temporal presence. You are commended for the fraud and murder you have affected. Such things usurp the common order, while increasing man's selfish reliance on himself and never the Almighty...always our goal. Keep vigilant for opportunities to affect more of the same. However, for your temporal impatience which prevented your mark from cursing the Creator before his death, you are condemned; reports are Alexander Mayfield easily slipped into Glory. Tsk! Tsk!

For this failure you will be returned to a remedial state, and your physical presence will be coffined here on this cursed land where Mayfield's humble blood soaks the earth. Here your sooty presence will remain until you learn the patience of fools befitting our nature, and the land is once again occupied. Until then your spirit may roam wherever and whenever your deceptive influence is required, for there is much to do.

Future intelligence has apprised that this place will next be occupied by a German farmer from Lancaster, Pennsylvania. He is Adam Livingston. Since he is likely next to touch your presence, he is your next mark. Your goal is to usher him into Perdition the moment he curses God.

Livingston is already a weakened and vulnerable man who finds little consolation in the Creator's religion. He claims to have no faith, but he overstates the case. His faith is trivial but still significant against the backdrop of eternity. We must push him away until he cannot return. Fortunately, unto his misfortune, Livingston is self-reliant and almost irredeemably arrogant. He does have a weakness for attractive Presbyterian women, no doubt because he was raised by unattractive Lutherans. He works a small farm in York. He thinks it was a gift from his father-in-law but it's a trap. To that end, go and influence him even further toward egotistical pride and those around him to a similar path. Of course, you must go disembodied since your physical presence must remain here. If our intelligence is correct, and Livingston comes here to live and farm, you may be able to manipulate him to lift your coffin from its grave. Such an auspicious moment would reconstitute your physical presence and aid your effectiveness. Then you must reveal to Livingston the subtle and persuasive detriments of your nature we so highly esteem.

Now, there is a complication that will challenge your bilocation faculty, although in the spiritual state such is eased. Future intelligence also tells us that Livingston's eternal destiny is to be determined by a child shortly to be conceived in Dublin, Ireland. The parents are Francis and Alice Cahill. Francis is nominally Protestant, but Alice is secretly and devoutly Catholic. We do not know if the child will be male or female. Neither do we know how or when the Cahill child and Livingston's paths will cross. For us, it is fortunate that to be Catholic in Ireland is illegal; and if you're a priest it's certain death. Thus, a place to begin, and a simple task it would seem, is to prevent this Cahill child from being baptized. Divining the future meeting of these two persons is not possible but do what you can to prevent it at all costs. Now, be not hasty but clever. Go forth, far and wide, in what ways you can, promote pride and arrogance, and other evil upon those regions of earth to which you have been charged. Hell depends on you.

Eternally yours,
Master of Derelicts

Chapter 3
Count On It

1

May 6, 1766.

Francis David Cahill was a large man with a square face, strong arms, and a gentle spirit. It was evening as he checked the windows of his small, thatched-roof cottage and made sure they were closed and the curtains drawn tight. He also made sure the two doors were latched and barred. With the house secured, Francis joined the group of friends crowded into the tiny gathering room.

Although he was not a very religious man, this night he prayed silently that the cover of darkness would protect his wife, Alice, the infant in her arms, a few of their trusted friends, and most of all his childhood mentor, Father Killian Doyle. Their voices were hushed as all eyes were on the tiny baby with the red tuft of hair, which Alice cradled close to her breasts.

Alice was a slight but strong-framed woman with round full breasts, a pale oval face, blue doe eyes, a thin, pointed nose, and rich auburn hair she tied in a bun.

Francis reached out and gently stroked the arm of the sleeping infant. Alice smiled up at her brawny husband and kissed his fingers. Francis wished his hands were cleaner, but the calluses and cracks of a mine laborer were always going to be lined with grime.

Fr. Killian faced the small group. He was a slight man, older than the others, dressed in shabby clothes with a green linen clerical stole draped about his neck. His eyes were clear, blue, and bright. He gazed sweetly at Francis and Alice and in a familiar Irish lilt asked them, "What do ye name this child?"

"Denis," said Alice with a contented smile.

Fr. Killian turned to the father. "Francis?"

"Aye, Father. It is Denis Francis we name him."

"After Saint Denis of Paris, Father," said Alice.

Killian smiled, "Ah, a good name, but a martyr for the faith. You not wishing his beheadin', 're ye?"

"No, Father. Not that," said Francis gravely.

"Aye, then a great warrior of valor that name makes him," said Fr. Killian.

Francis glanced admirably at his old mentor. *Why does he smile as if there's not a care in the world? We're all in danger he must know, grave danger.*

"Francis, it is okay...that you are not Catholic, although I know that Alice wishes you were, especially after all these years. But we are here in the sight of God and he will bless you and your son for this courageous act."

Francis' lower lip was at work as he attempted to quell his nerves, "Aye, Father. I thank you."

Alice leaned lovingly against her husband's bulk and pulled little Denis close to her breasts.

The priest turned back to the small book of rites in his hands, studied it for a moment, then looked back to the parents. "Francis, Alice, what do you ask of the Church of God?"

"The faith," the couple said quietly in unison just as they had rehearsed.

"What does the faith offer thee?"

"Eternal life," they both said.

Francis held within him an avalanche of emotion that defied his understanding. For eighteen years he and Alice had prayed unceasingly for a child. Their prayers had always been answered, or so it seemed. Alice had conceived five children but was never able to carry any of them to a live birth. With each child Francis feared Alice might not conceive; then he feared she might die in childbirth only for her to deliver a dead baby. It was always heartbreaking. They had buried each child in the town's cemetery, usually without a burial rite since there were no Catholic priests on the island.

Denis Francis was the first to be born alive and healthy. Over the past week as Francis anticipated the illegal gathering, he often caught himself holding his breath; and his appetite had nearly disappeared. To forestall danger on the job from weakness, he had forced himself to eat. He was happy and proud to have arranged for the baptism of his son, if only because he loved his eternally optimistic and always smiling Alice. Now Francis feared in a different way, not just for Alice's life, but for the life of his friend, Fr. Killian. With an increase in his fear, so his hearing had improved. When a cart rolled past his cottage on the cobblestones outside a covered window, his body tensed in trepidation that death might yet be at the door. As it was, Francis paid slight attention to the rite. He had to be attentive to what could still transpire and what possible action he would take if trouble arose.

The last time he had seen Fr. Killian was at his wedding in a small Capuchin chapel in the hills west of Dublin. Francis thought the wedding was a secret. But evidently it wasn't. Word got out, and shortly after their private Mass, the Brits burned the chapel to the ground for violating the penal code against all things Catholic. Nonetheless, he was a man of his word, and despite the danger, he had promised to baptize and raise any children they had in the Roman faith. Twenty years ago, he had learned that making such a promise was the only way he could make the red-haired beauty his wife. But it took two years to convince himself, and Alice, that he'd be true to his word.

True, he was not a religious man, but he was a romantic. He believed his life was at the service of his wife, and the mystical Emerald Isle he cherished. He disagreed with the boisterous and often raucous Protestants at the mine. They believed that Catholic papists should all be run out of the country or hanged.

Wasn't it enough that Catholics could not own land, or a business, or run for parliament, or hold any official position in the government? Did they also have to leave this sacred green isle?

Fr. Killian continued the baptism rite. *"We now pray for this child who will have to face the world with its temptations and fight the devil in all his cunning. Father in heaven, your Son died and rose again to save us. By his victory over sin and death, cleanse this child from the stain of original sin. Strengthen him with the grace of Christ and watch over him at every step in life's journey. We ask this through Christ our Lord. Amen."*

"Fight the devil!" Fr. Killian had said. Francis worried that little Denis would not have to wait too long to do that. As soon as Denis was born, Francis sent a simple message with a trusted seaman to his mentor in Brest, a French port. To there, years ago, Fr. Killian had escaped. The message read: "Would you come visit our new family?"

Killian came immediately on the return ship to Dublin. He knew that a child, indeed a miracle child, had been born to his friends Francis and Alice Cahill, and that a covert baptism was needed. Hidden in a small bag along with some food would be a book of rites and his stole, the only indication that the otherwise shabby looking old man was an incognito Catholic priest.

The rite continued far too long, thought Francis. The longer it took the greater the opportunity for detection. He could not imagine what evils would befall them all if this illegal event were discovered. He had considered booking passage for the three of them on a ship to Brest. But on his meager earnings that was out of the question.

Fr. Killian blessed the water that Alice had provided in a beat-up tin basin, and then took the infant from his mother.

Immediately, as if the tyke was willing himself to be awake for the auspicious moment, little Denis' eyes flew open and gazed up into Fr. Killian's eyes. So caught up he was in the sudden appearance of the old priest's benevolent face, the babe cooed a greeting.

Holding the infant in his left arm with his hand supporting the baby's neck and head over the basin, Fr. Killian used his right hand to gather successive handfuls of water and cascade them over little Denis' scalp and the small tuft of red hair. *"Denis Francis Cahill, ego te baptízo in nómine Patris...et Fílii...et Spíritus Sancti. Amen."*...(I baptize you in the name of the Father...and the Son... and the Holy Spirit.)

"Are we done now, Father?"

"Not quite, Francis. There's no reason to rush these things."

"Aye, that is where ye are wrong, Killian. The devil is at the door and I'll not soften until yer back safely on the Stella Maris."

The old priest nodded, seemingly unworried. He took out a vial of sacred chrism, opened it, and wetted a finger in the oil. Then, making the sign of the cross in oil on the crown of the child's head, Fr. Killian anointed young Denis:

"*Deus omnípotens, Pater Dómini nostri Iesu **Christi**...*The God of power and Father of our Lord Jesus Christ has freed you from sin."

The prayers went on, seemingly forever, which only served Francis as a reminder of one reason he wasn't Catholic...they never stopped praying. *How do you ever get any work done?*

When the baptism was finally over and even before the guests had left, Francis persuaded Fr. Killian to say his quick goodbyes, and be escorted the eight blocks to the docks. Once there, Francis would see that the priest was sequestered on the Stella Maris. He had already paid the Catholic-friendly captain for the priest's passage. Then, sometime before dawn with the outgoing tide, the ship would slip away from the quay and the danger would pass.

But a safe exit from rabid hooligans operating with impunity under the guise of fulfilling the king's anti-Catholic penal laws was not to be.

As Francis and Killian stepped into the night and shut the door behind them, a dark fume of smoke passed lazily over the waning crescent moon. Neither Francis nor Killian noticed the fume, yet they both experienced a premonition of danger.

Francis carried an unlit lantern. They navigated their way toward the quay along the narrow streets mostly by the lights in the windows of closed-up cottages. They steered clear of a noisy pub, crossed through a cemetery, passed a ship repair yard, and finally turned down an alley toward the quay. At the end of the alley was a pub where sailors bided their time. Above the roof of the pub Francis could see the two masts of the Stella Maris. The ninety-seven foot yankee rigged, freight-schooner's masts and yards were outlined against the moonlit clouds that hung over the Irish Sea. The closer they got to the ship the more Francis was relieved that he would see his mentor of many years safely to the ship.

As they turned the final corner next to the pub and began to cross the last hundred feet to the ship's boarding ramp, they were greeted by an unwanted sight. Francis' quick pace suddenly slowed. Keeping his eyes sharp and wide open, he pulled his cap down over this forehead so as not to be recognized.

Loitering near the ship's boarding ramp, in the light of the pub's open door, were five men that Francis instantly recognized as the self-appointed enforcers of Britain's penal laws. These were men with blood on their hands, pro-government Protestant vigilantes who spent their free time getting drunk and plotting revenge on Catholics. They were especially hostile toward priests.

Francis reached out, took Fr. Killian's arm, and pulled them both to a stop. There was nothing peculiar in the dress or behavior of Fr. Killian that would announce him as a Catholic cleric. But there was something about the way the men suddenly and purposefully turned toward Francis and his friend in the dark that announced they knew who Killian Doyle was. Perhaps they also knew why he was in Dublin.

Fr. Killian was Irish, and years earlier had been chased off the island because he was a priest who wore his Catholicism on his sleeve as a badge of honor. There would be those who would have recognized him. Perhaps a member of the Stella Maris crew knew the priest was violating the law by returning to Ireland and had alerted the anti-Catholic ruffians. Here they were, clubs in hand, waiting for the priest to return from his calling.

The five men, all large and hell-bent, lined up abreast and dared Francis and Fr. Killian to run their blockade to the ship's ramp.

Francis scanned the ship's deck looking for crew, mate, or captain that might come to their aid, but the deck was clear. He had expected a few mates to be loading cargo right up until the tide eased the ship out of the canal towards the sea. But there was no one.

He turned his head to the door of the quay-side pub. The rambunctious noise inside had quieted down. Another half-dozen men edged their way out of the door, defiant looks on their faces, to watch what was about to happen.

How many other ways were there off the island, thought Francis? He surveyed the possibilities—perhaps a dozen. But it was too late.

"Killian, let's go," said Francis as he pulled on Fr. Killian's sleeve getting him to retreat into the darkness of the ally.

"No, Francis. The ship is just there. Captain Terry will see me safe on board," said Fr. Killian.

But before Francis could answer, there as a voice behind them. "Francis! Why you bring a popish priest to our town?"

Francis and Fr. Killian turned. Behind them, blocking their exit to the ally, were three men he knew well. Each held a menacing club in his grasp.

Francis cowered, hunched down in defense, trying to hold still the darkened lantern. "He's, no...not, a priest, Sal. He's a friend going back, now to...to France."

"Francis, there's no need of that." Fr. Killian turned to the men with bars and clubs as if offering the sign of peace at Mass. "Aye, I am a priest and happy for it. God is my guide and judge."

The hooligans closed in. One called out, bolstered and emboldened from the evening's alcohol, "Git him, boys. No popish witch on these here sacred isles, I say."

Francis saw the flash of white hatred in the group's eyes as he and Fr. Killian were encircled. The clubs raised and swung in attack. Francis no more ducked one club but at once two others hit him squarely on the back and the side of his head. Instantly, he fell to the cobblestone quay. Warm blood ran down his neck. As he dropped, he caught sight of Fr. Killian receiving the greater number of deadly blows to his head and chest until he crumpled to the quay's deck. Once down the thugs viciously kicked the priest in the ribs and groin. Finding his prayer book, they ripped out its pages. The green linen stole was yanked from his coat pocket and tied around his neck, then pulled tight suffocating him.

There was no yelling or screams, just the sound of lethal blows from wooden clubs to skin, bones, and skull. Crippled and in the way, Francis was shoved and pushed from the pile, then forgotten as if already dead.

Nearly exhausted, the vigilante Irishmen each gave Fr. Killian one last savage kick or cruel boot to the head. Then, covered in sweat with the drunken drool of mad dogs frothing from their gasping mouths, they backed away and surveyed their *good deed*. Finally, too spent to howl even verbal insults, they staggered back toward the pub—sweat, blood, and saliva dripped from their hands and faces. Entering the pub, they raised their clubs and fists in the air, saluting their demonic victory, and cheered each other as if their football team had just scored a goal to win the match.

Francis raised his head as best he could. Through his own sweat and blood, he trembled at the sight of the hooligans filing into the pub. Fresh ale was already being poured to cheers of celebration.

Not sure he could bear the sight, he nonetheless forced his eyes to focus on the lifeless pile of his childhood mentor and friend, dead on the quay, a few feet from the ship that would have carried him safely home.

Behind, on the ship, a tall and broad-shouldered man, dressed like the ship's captain, stood silent and still near the aft rail, his form silhouetted against the moonlit clouds beyond.

Francis dragged his body to Fr. Killian's and managed to sit up and hold Fr. Killian's head in his lap. He tried in vain to push hair, blood, and spit from his friend's eyes. Francis openly sobbed. Gasping for breath he rested his cut forehead on the beaten skull of the priest. "Father! Father! Forgive me. I did not know. I did not know. But I should have."

Raising his head to look at the peaceful crescent moon now covered by a cloud, he yelled through what he now realized were broken teeth, "*God where is your vengeance? Kill the bastards or I will. I swear by Saint Peter. Why are you silent and just stand by while this holy man is, is...*"

Suddenly, there was a tug on his coat lapel. He stopped his wailing demand for vengeance and looked down into the face and the eyes of the beaten pulp of a man in his lap. The priest was still alive.

Through broken cheek bones and blood, Fr. Killian smiled up at Francis. "Francis? I made it. I kin't sin anymore. I'm all right, now." Fr. Killian coughed up dark gruel and blood. His breathing was labored and short. "Do you hear me, Francis? I made it. I kin't sin anymore."

Francis looked at the priest in astonishment, not understanding what the priest was trying to say between his last breaths.

"Pray...for me, Francis. I will...pray for him...for little Denis.... Yes? Count... on it. Hey? I kin watch over him...I be there for him. Fret not...dear friend." With a shallow smile on his thin lips Fr. Killian took his last gasp of breath, even as his eyes focused one last time on the mine laborer who tried to make sense of it all, the father of Denis Francis Cahill.

As the men's eyes connected, and Francis gripped the priest with all his remaining strength, as if to prevent life from slipping out of his body, Fr. Killian's body relaxed, and the ruddy skin quickly drained of blood. One moment the priest was full of life, and the next whitened, empty, and soulless.

For the longest time Francis held his friend's body in his arms like the Madonna held her Son after his crucifixion.

He sat there, exhausted, not knowing what to do. He was alone...all alone. Or so it seemed.

Then, as the cloud slipped away from the moon, allowing the quay to once again be engulfed in soft light, he heard a voice—at least he thought he did: "I can see it all now, Francis. I will intercede for little Denis. Fear not."

Francis felt nothing but overwhelming guilt and remorse. How could he have let this happen? His dear Alice would be fearfully saddened and perhaps never forgive him for bringing Fr. Killian back to the city's quay. He should have known better.

He had been crying for more than an hour. But now his tear ducts were dry. Tears no longer came.

Reverently laying his friend's head on the cobblestone, Francis tried to stand, but he found it difficult.

Then a supportive arm and another, under his, raised him up. Two crew members from the Stella Maris helped him onto the ship. Captain Terry stood by the ramp and waved four other men off the ship. They scrambled to Fr. Killian's dead body, hoisted it onto their husky frames and followed Francis onto the ship.

Captain Terry's surgeon patched up Francis as much as he could. In the early morning hours the deck crew saw Francis away from the quay and onto the streets back to his home. Captain Terry also put a bag of money in Francis' pocket equal to what he had previously paid for Fr. Killian's passage. Terry, although not Catholic, was smart enough to know he didn't need a curse on his ship for taking profit for the passage of a martyred priest. The captain promised Francis to deliver Fr. Killian's body to his order in France.

Before dawn, the Stella Maris slipped its lines and drifted away from the quay with the outgoing tide and its sacred cargo.

As Francis staggered the last few blocks to his home, he relived the weight of the tragedy. He wished it had been him that had died and not the good priest. But for some unexplained reason Francis did not feel the deep remorse he thought he should have. Surely, as soon as he entered his house and his wife's bedroom where she would be asleep with the child, he would have to tell her what happened.

Remarkably, he felt a sliver of hope, as if, despite the murder and his own injuries, things would be good. But he could not explain why.

He stood outside the back door to his house but a moment, not wanting to track the blood of the encounter onto his doorstep. He looked up at the moon now fading into the morning sky. There were no clouds. There was a fresh breeze. The Stella Maris would be well on its way by now, and safe from the miseries of Dublin's evil.

As he reached for the door's latch, he had a vision of taking Alice away on a ship as well. What if the anti-Catholic sentiment took her life? He had not known that to happen to any woman, although some outspoken Catholic men had been hanged in the woods. They had openly confronted groups such as those that had killed Killian. Would they kill sweet Alice if they knew? He shivered—some of them probably did know. But what would he do in France? He did not know the language and there he would not likely find work, unless for slave wages. Still there was something in his mind that he wanted to better understand, as if Killian was already at work in the supernatural realm.

The sun was coming up and he would need rest. No work today. He would send a friend to the mine to substitute for him. He pushed the door open, but it was barred. A moment later, he heard the bar being removed and the door opened revealing Alice, very much awake. She flung herself into his arms. She had been crying.

2

Word had traveled back to Alice that Fr. Killian had been murdered and that her husband had been beat-up but spared. Frightened more for her son's life than her own she had barred herself in the cottage, extinguished the lamps, and prayed. *Where was God?*

That little Denis had cooed himself to sleep in her arms was a divine consolation. Perhaps God was around, but not near enough for her. She had kept a lookout for Francis and when he came around the corner in one piece, albeit a bit bloody, she thanked God and unbarred the door.

When he entered the cottage, she could not restrain herself in holding his large frame in her frail arms and soothing every hate-filled wound with her loving kisses. The surgeon had done a good job, but she would do even better.

Shortly, Francis sent her out to find his friend Michael and ask him to take his place at the mine. She did and returned without delay.

While he ate a large bowl of warm porridge and goat's milk, he recounted the attack, the kindness of the captain, and handed over to Alice the bag of money. He apologized profusely for not being more religious and sensitive to her needs. But she had never thought of him otherwise. Together, they decided the bag of money was sacred and would be reserved for something special.

When Francis was done talking, she could not shake from her mind what Fr. Killian had last said: "*I will pray for him, for Denis. Count on it. I can watch over him now. I'll be there for him. Do not fret.*"

But when it got right down to it, she was scared. She loved Ireland and her friends, but at what cost? She feared for her son the most. Being the mother of a young child changes everything. Francis, even with such a Catholic name, was safe. Technically, he was Protestant, although Fr. Killian's murder caused Francis to confess that he was embarrassed to be one.

Could they go to France where they didn't know the language and where Francis would have to work for a pittance? Here he had a good, stable job. Would they be safer to move out of the city and further south where hooligans were fewer, but compassionate friends more distant? And what about work? Mine labor paid a lot better than farm labor.

By keeping her Catholicism under wraps, they had been safe these past tumultuous years. Unless they started holding meetings and causing a religious ruckus their lives were probably not in danger. Since there were only elections at the beginning of a new reign not much was likely to change.

But it was the Act to Restrain Foreign Education of 1695, one of a series of Penal Laws, that bothered Alice the most. She was barred from sending little Denis overseas for an education. The Protestant-controlled Irish Parliament was afraid foreign educated children would come back to Ireland as adults and, as had happened in the past, attempt to overthrow the government by seditions and open rebellion. The punishment for sending Denis to, say, France for schooling would result in the loss and forfeit of all their goods, chattels, trusts, lands, tenements, and all hereditary privileges for the rest of their natural lives. Not that she or Francis had any such trappings—rents, annuities, trusts, lands, tenements, or heritage. They didn't. They lived month-to-month, and only then, she was convinced, by the grace of God.

Months later, as little Denis grew, he often would wake from a nap and begin to fuss. Alice loved the spontaneity of such moments. She was needed. She was a mother, and she loved it. She put down her mending and stepped quickly to the cradle in their bedroom. As soon as she appeared and looked down at him, his little legs and feet kicked with delight and the dimples in his chin appeared with a little laugh. A quick check of his wool diaper proved him still dry. "Good boy," she congratulated him. "Are we hungry?" As if he understood perfectly, little Denis puckered his lips and made that all familiar sucking sound that sent Alice's milk aflow. "Yes, darling, you're empty and Mama's full. Let's fix that." Picking him up in her arms, little Denis' eyes grew wide with the adventure of flight and then awe as he landed on her soft, full breasts. Wrapping a blanket about him, she cradled her son in a rocker, opened her dress, and satisfied both their needs.

As mother and child gazed at each other, Alice relaxed. The turmoil of her mind about their future made peace with the realization that neither of them were in any immediate danger. In fact, they were probably safe for a number of years. She would begin his education, teaching him to read, write, and speak properly. After all she was the one with an education, not Francis, although he could read a little. When it came time for more formal classroom experience there was an underground hedge school taught by a good man her mother had told her about. He might even be a Catholic priest in disguise as her mother suspected. Brave man. At any rate she was determined to keep Denis out of the government's Protestant boarding schools.

When Francis came home from the mines, he was usually tired. But after little Denis joined their family, she noticed an extra alertness in Francis' step and eyes. In the evenings he spent "man-time" with their son, which, at first, worried Alice. Francis would rough house with the boy making the child alternatively laugh and cry. She had been gentle with their son all through the day..."training him in the way he should go"...and then came this burst of energy from the giant in the boy's life. After a while, however, it became obvious that little Denis looked forward to Francis' return from the mines. The babe seemed to love the tumbling, and throwing, and teasing. He was always begging for more.

One night, after Francis cleaned up from work, something different happened. Little Denis had been rocking back and forth on the floor trying to understand the mechanics of crawling, when Francis picked up the boy, put him on his big lap, and sat before the fireplace just staring at the child. Meanwhile, Denis, looking for activity, kept busy climbing the mountain that was his father to inspect and pull at lips, eyes, nose and ears. Occasionally, Francis would look over at her, as if he wanted to say something. But he didn't. Instead, he'd go back to tickling little Denis' belly, causing the child to wiggle furiously. Alice was sure the child would fall head-first onto the stone floor, and often he did tumble. But never did he fall onto anything but his father's soft, outstretched hands.

At first such father-son play caused her to panic. After a while, however, she realized Francis was too careful to ever let Denis fall and hurt himself. She forced herself to relax...but only until the next time little Denis took flight.

At supper, Francis quietly held his son on his lap, and played at putting food in the child's mouth, which little Denis wisely spit out.

"'Tis not what the tyke's expectin'" Alice said.

Francis took his big finger, rescued the bean full of drool as it came out of the baby's mouth, and shoved it in his own and chewing wildly...showed the child how it was done. Little Denis stared wide-eyed. Francis would then open his mouth wide as if to swallow his son whole, "Notice, my son. 'Tis gone."

"Stay that," Alice teased. "He's likin' to try it an' choke to his grave."

"Aye, that he might." Francis chuckled.

"What's come over ye?"

"Me, Lass?"

"You's not what I was expectin'...tonight."

Francis got quiet and gently cradled little Denis with both of his large arms. "I had me a talk with Michael today...about Killian. He was angry, wanted to kill someone 'imself."

"But he's not Catholic."

"No. But he's a good non-conformist, if you askin' me."

"What's he belivin' in, then?"

"Nothin' that he tells me."

"What then did you talk 'bout?"

Francis was quiet again.

"Out with it, now," Alice teased.

Francis took a breath, held it for a moment. "Michael thinks there's probably somethin' special about our little Denis. Thinks he should be dedicated t'God or somethin', insofar as a holy priest gave his life for him."

Alice thought about that. "Does Michael know what Fr. Killian said about praying for Denis from heaven?"

"Aye, I told Michael that."

The couple were quiet for a long time, when it was that Alice started to weep.

"Alice? What matter?"

There was another long silence between them. Alice collected her thoughts. "Do you remember the story from the Bible I've always found a favorite, 'bout Samuel and his mother?"

"Ah, 'haps not. You're the scholar of the two of us. I lucky to read."

"But you've heard it, I'm sure. She was barren. Like me. And she, like me, prayed that God would give her a child...a living child. She prayed so much that the priest thought she was high on the bottle and told her to put away her wine...except she wasn't. She was praying. You remember me praying for a child, Francis?"

"Oh, Lass! Of course, I do. I do," his voice quavered. "That is why Killian came. It was a miracle we both thinks."

"Well, Samuel's mother was so grateful that she did something any mother would find impossible. As soon as Samuel was weaned, she took him to the Temple, dedicated him to God, and left him there to be raised as a priest. She brought him food now and then, but he never again slept at home. She saw very little of him after that, it's possible."

Alice noticed Francis' deep frown as he pulled little Denis closer. "Aye, I do recall the story now that you tell it. But, Alice, I'm not thinkin' I'm likin' what yer suggestin.'"

"Francis, I'm not suggestin' we give Denis away to anyone. But I think Michael may be right."

"What is it you mean?"

"We should dedicate him to God, and perhaps also to the Church...that he would one day be a priest."

"What?! And be killed like Killian? Not in my lifetime."

"Then, let it be him that decides it, when the time is right. But we can raise him with that in mind."

"I don't think Michael had that at all in mind."

"Perhaps not." Alice smoothed her skirt and looked around; she felt her tears still wet. "Do you remember the name of Samuel's mother?" She looked deep into her husband's eyes, willing him to recall.

He remembered. "It was Hannah."

Alice nodded...

...and Francis cried.

It was then, they both knew that God would protect their child, and do something great with him—the son of Francis David and Alice Hannah Cahill.

3

My Despised Cyn:

We don't give wreaths for participation, although we've been successful in getting humans to. We have been excellent at promoting mediocrity.

What a sorry mess you are as a demonic influence—an honorable title for your peers we suppose—but you have pilfered it for a laughingstock. What does it matter that another priest is murdered in his meekness? Yes, it upsets a few, and allows the haters to crow. But the priest's soul is in Glory, not Perdition where all should be. Where is your loyalty, fool?

The only thing here worth celebrating is that we now know the Cahill child is male, and that there's a fearful humility in his mother to dedicate him to God—that means the priesthood, which we must prevent. Can you do that? If so, the Devil be God! To allow this Cahill child to become a priest would be irreversible, even if we push him into some dark sin.

Again, the laws of Ireland are on our side for there are no Catholic seminaries on the Green Isle. For Denis Cahill to be a priest he would have to be educated outside, perhaps in France or Spain. How he ends up outside Ireland is going to be a stretch for his parents, for they would lose everything as your peers so wonderfully accomplished one-hundred years ago with the Act to Restrain Foreign Education. What a beautiful act of national, arrogant pride we have got the Irish into.

For the time being you can do little there. Get back to Pennsylvania and see if you can further disintegrate your mark's faith. Damn his humble wife, *Esther, a pain in Hell's rear. Perhaps we should dare to petition for her demise.

Eternally yours,
Master of Shadows

Part Two: Decision

Let no man say when he is tempted, I am tempted of God:
for God cannot be tempted with evil, neither tempteth he any man.
But every man is tempted, when he is drawn away
by his own concupiscence, and is enticed.
Then when lust hath conceived, it bringeth forth sin,
and sin when it is finished, bringeth forth death.
Err not my dear brethren.
Every good giving and every perfect gift is from above,
and cometh down from the Father of lights,
with whom is no variableness, neither shadow of turning.

(James 1:13–17)

Chapter 4
Something's Happened

1

November 3, 1787.

Adam Livingston was not bold or brash, but he was an exceptional farmer. The first American-born son of German immigrant *Johann Lieberstein, both father and son were flax planters and producers. From the middle seventeenth century, German settlers came to Pennsylvania and either brought with them the knowledge of flax production or learned it once they came. So prevalent were German flax farmers and producers during that time that in 1691 the founder of Germantown, Pennsylvania, *Francis Pastorius, designed the flax symbol into the town's seal.

Like many first-generation Americans, Adam experimented with planting and harvesting schedules, seeds from Europe, crop rotation, and irrigation. Like others, he generously shared his discoveries with other farmers to advance the production and quality of flax products. But there was a difference—Adam was more diligent and persistent than his peers, and he was more curious and more willing to take risks.

All men possess a variety of virtues and flaws, but they're not distributed evenly. Virtues to one man are flaws to another. Adam virtuously believed he was ultimately responsible and accountable for the care and yield his land produced. But that was also his flaw. He had no control over what made a seed sprout, the sun to shine, the soil to be mineralized, or how much or when it rained. Yet Adam believed that he alone was responsible for the quality and quantity of his harvest. He believed this even when hail, frost, and drought killed his plants. Some would call his worldview a denial of reality, an agnostic view of Providence, or fatal arrogance. But Adam Livingston didn't see it that way. He didn't ask God for good soil or seed, nor did he thank God for rain and sun. When crops failed, he didn't shake his fist at heaven. He believed every farmer could improve their yields if only they would work hard, discipline their regimen, and think. In short, he gave no quarter to the supernatural.

Adam's wife, however, believed differently. Esther believed a farmer's yield was directly proportional to his faith in a God who was sovereign over the natural laws of sun, rain, and soil. Since her husband was successful, she believed he had faith in God, or in the universal laws God controlled, or in the common sense and self-discipline with which God had blessed him. She was right to a degree.

An objective observer could conclude that Adam and Esther believed the same; they gazed at their common valley from different mountain tops: Esther saw that God provided, where Adam saw that man must labor to benefit. Those were the two equal sides of the same equation, the necessary collaboration of the natural and the supernatural. Some called it Providential Causality—that the effects seen in the natural realm were caused by what cannot be seen in the supernatural realm.

There were ways, however, that Adam encountered the supernatural. On occasion he would experience extraordinary premonitions of evil, which came to him as dreams, or visions. He had grown up as a child with these experiences. To him they were commonplace and not evidence of another realm. He could be in the field harvesting grain when suddenly, for several seconds, disturbing images and sounds would besiege his mind. They came in pairs, perhaps hours apart. He couldn't explain them; he just accepted them. It some quarters Adam Livingston would be known as a mystic, although a reluctant one.

When he tried to explain his visions to Esther she listened, but just as often she discounted them, concluding that, well, he *had* spent the entire day in the sun...what do you expect? But then days or hours later something happened that correlated with the vision. One evening a premonition came to him while working in the barn. In a sudden flash Adam saw a nondescript inferno and heard the wail of alarmed animals. It scared him and he feared that his barn might be on fire. He spent some minutes searching through the barn and on the outside for an open flame, or a lantern that may have fallen over. But he found nothing. Later, before he left for the night, he triple-checked that the lanterns in the barn were fully extinguished. Then, days later he heard that a neighbor's barn had burned down in the middle of that same night. A lantern had been left burning and an animal knocked it over into the straw. Adam was devastated and wondered to himself if there was any way he could have warned his friend. Such times unnerved Esther, for she always desired to see the good in tragic events, but sometimes that was not possible. She often considered Adam too pessimistic and morose, but those were also traits that were compatible with an obsession for detail and his success as a farmer. After he told her about the barn burning, she said, quite seriously, "Maybe God's angels are trying to tell you something...something you're supposed to know."

There came a time, however, several times, when she was forced to give credibility to Adam's gift...as unwelcome as it was. Three times he fell into a deep depression for days but would not tell her why. The first two times were followed by her own devastating still births two years apart. They mourned for weeks after each. He finally told Esther about the premonitions. The first was of a child's tragic death in a carriage accident, and a year later he imagined being present when a crying infant was buried alive. He confessed he was afraid to tell her, since both premonitions had scared him. She told him he was right; she didn't want to know.

Their third attempt for children resulted in a baby girl they named Amy.

Amy was a precious child, always happy, giggling, smiling, recognizing man and beast, and she was starting to talk a bit. They were happy as a family, finally.

When the tyke was perhaps seven months old, Adam experienced a third and terrifying premonition. It was in a dream he could remember clearly, and it haunted him. The dream was not clear, there were no faces, but it was of a funeral for a small child. He was at the funeral, but Esther wasn't. He had no idea it was *his* child.

Three days later their little Amy died in her sleep. He lamented not telling Esther before in case there was something he or she could have done. When they held the funeral, Esther was so grief stricken she did not attend, although he did.

Long after they buried Amy, one evening after Esther returned to the house after praying at the graves, he told her about the dream. She stared at him in disbelief, and then told him what he didn't want to hear:

"You should have told me."

"But you didn't want to know," he reminded her.

"I do now."

"What would you have done?"

She thought for a long time. "I don't know. Maybe God would have told me something."

"If he wanted to tell you something, he could have, don't you think?" It was one of his rare attacks on her religion. She was the one with the bucket load of faith, not him. Why was he responsible? Why blame him if God was trying to communicate with her? It was just another reason Adam distanced himself from religion.

He disliked the premonitions. They certainly made no sense. Why would God pick him as the messenger? If they were attempts to get him to save his own children, they were failures. With three children dead and buried, all that was left was the guilt. He could never rid himself of the sense that he could have done something.

Were the premonitions a challenge to a duel with a belligerent from another time or place? He could not envision participating in a duel or fight. He wasn't given to anger, nor was he aggressive, or confrontational. He was thoughtful. He made efforts to avoid conflict, which at times upset Esther. She believed that one had to fight on behalf of justice and the vulnerable. The Revolutionary War made sense to her; he wished it had never happened, although he understood why it did. It was one of those things where seeking justice was often unjust. Yet, regarding the deaths of his own children, the guilt lingered. He was a man who claimed responsibility for the outcome of things under his control, and it certainly seemed as if the lives of his children fell under his control, in some way. Some would argue that premonitions about the future were a gift. Adam came to consider them a curse—the deaths of his three children provided the evidence.

2

Notwithstanding Adam's rejection of Providence, over the next eight years the grace that falls on all men fell on Adam and Esther Livingston. In 1779, in the midst of the Revolutionary War and the death that engulfed the colonies, a healthy and robust girl was born to them, and miraculously survived. In the coming years the child even avoided the dreadful childhood diseases that took so many young children. Adam was afraid to name her at first for fear she would die before her first birthday. But Esther insisted and said out of faith they should name her Eve—their first born with promise. That turned out to be true. Before Eve was two she was talking in complete sentences and demonstrated a insatiable curiosity about everything around her. When Esther read to her, Eve never fell asleep but always wanted her mother to read more, even if it was the genealogies from the Bible that droned on forever with unpronounceable names. It seemed Eve loved the sound of words and how they fit together.

Two years later in 1781 a second child was born whom Adam wanted to name Henry, although there was not a Henry in any of Adam's lineage, at least that he could remember. Why, Esther wanted to know. Why not John after Adam's father, at least? Adam's only response was that he wanted his first son to have an American name, not a German name, a name that was somewhat different, and a name he could yell at the top of his voice when his son needed to come in from the fields for dinner. And "HEN-RRR-Y" had a ring about it that felt good when Adam said it, or so he finally convinced Esther. Henry turned out to be the opposite of Eve—non interested in much, non-verbal until he was three, rambunctious to a fault, and always on the go, even in his sleep. Many times in the morning they would find Henry asleep feet from his crib, in another room, downstairs, or even on the stairs head-down, but always on the floor and sprawled out on his stomach.

They kept trying to have more children, but none came. That saddened Esther; she had wanted a baker's dozen. The only consolation was that with her apparent barren condition, there were also no further miscarriages, still births, or early childhood deaths. So, she poured herself into Eve who was a sponge, and encouraged Adam to teach Henry everything about the farm. Adam was more than willing, but unlike Eve who enjoyed mimicking her mama in everything, Henry preferred finding a pile of straw in the barn, sprawling out and falling asleep.

3

In 1787, with the harvest in and winter fast approaching, Adam reflected on the yield. It had been above average, just like last fall. His diligent experimentation with crop rotation and planting had again yielded a record per acre. He had discovered that flax grew best when it was planted on grain stubble. But with a small fifty acre farm, forty of which were tillable, he still would not be able to compete at market. He would show off his harvest and a few individuals would express admiration. But he would not bring home a flush of cash because larger farms with inferior product set the market price, and the price was always less than what his crop was worth, or so he reasoned.

Adam's six-year-old son, Henry, had spent the afternoon with him and the day laborers as they moved the dry flax stalks into the barn. Father and son, aside from age, could not have been more different. At forty-eight, Adam carried a muscular build of normal height with an angular face and long rounded nose. His deep-set brown eyes and high forehead were at ease with his coal-black hair, combed straight back. The bushy and tightly curled salt-n-pepper beard covered his neck down to the top of his overalls. Henry, on the other hand, was a still-growing, lanky boy, with a round face and light brown, unruly hair that carried over his ears in gentle waves. Adam was a man unafraid of work; he found meaning and purpose in it. Henry, however, hated anything associated with the concept or requiring the use of the word "work" to describe it. Nonetheless, throughout the day Henry had been asking questions, seemingly about everything related to flax planting and how it was transformed into a salable product. So, after the laborers left, Adam took Henry into the barn and explained the involved process. He was anxious for his son to learn the trade, although six was a bit young to do the laborious work.

Taking a handful of flax stalks Adam led Henry to one of several flax breaks—a three-inch square timber about three feet long mounted horizontally on a stand. Carved in the top of the stationary timber lengthwise were two deep grooves which produced three knife-like blades sticking up. On top of this was a mating timber with a round handle at one end and an iron hinge at the other. It had a one-inch deep groove in it with two knife-like blades sticking down. Henry held the bunch of stalks across the stationary break, and Adam slammed the hinged break down on the stalks, breaking them where the top knives buried themselves into the opposing grooves. Once the top timber lifted, Henry shoved the stalks further into the break, and his father would slam the knife-like contraption down again. As they continued this the outer rim of the stalks, called *shives*, broke into small sections, and fell to the floor. The strong, flexible flax fiber inside the stalks was unaffected by the break. Adam watched his son to see if he was paying attention. True to character, Henry looked a little bored and no doubt would soon forget the day's events.

But that was not to be on this day.

Adam slammed the break's knife down once more. Suddenly, with the *bang* of the break, a premonition—a flash of pale yellow and white cloth fluttered before his eyes. With the image he heard a woman's gasp for breath, and then soft logs falling to a wooden floor. At once there was also something he had never before experienced—a thin voice laid over what sounded like a cauldron of bats streaking from their cave in search of food. The voice was quick and sudden, compressed in time, and over with in a flash: "*Stalks break, shives be buried, the fiber never.*" It wasn't really a sound, but a fleeting thought that invaded his mind. It sounded like a gentleman's challenge. He froze. He played the image and the words over in his mind: *Stalks break, shives be buried, the fiber never.* The prediction was clear enough that he wanted to take some action. But what?

"What's wrong, Papa?" Henry asked.

Adam didn't move for a few seconds, then: "Nothing, son, nothing." But something was wrong, that's for sure, and yet he was unsure what that something was.

Adam turned to Henry and explained that getting the stalks totally removed from the valuable fibers, required two more steps.

Adam had Henry bring the bunch of broken flax stalks to a scutching board. This was simply a vertical flat board about six inches wide that was mounted securely on the barn's floor. Adam helped Henry hold the stalks, so they hung down vertically along the board. Then with a large wooden-like knife Adam repeatedly struck and scraped the stalks, attempting to drive out the remaining broken shives to the floor.

Henry asked, "We done yet?"

"Not quite, there's one more step. But you might like this one."

"I doubt it," said the ever-ready Henry.

Adam led Henry to yet another device nailed to a work-bench. It looked like a bunch of nails arranged in a square about five inches on a side, with the sharp tips pointing into the air. "Hold the flax bunch at the base of the stalks, then pull the stalks through the bed of nails."

Henry tried but he was not strong enough, so Adam helped. As they pulled, the remaining pieces of the stalk surrounding the central fibers were pulled off, revealing the thin, blonde, flexible flax fibers ready for spinning.

As soon as the thin fibers were exposed Henry cried out, "Hey, that's what Mama uses in the spinner."

"That's right. To make thread so she can weave linen cloth and make our clothes."

Henry's eyes lit up like Adam had never seen before. "You mean our clothes are made from all that stuff?" he said pointing across the barn to the piles of flax stalks that nearly reached the roof line.

"Well, some of it. After we process all *that stuff,* we'll take most of it to market in York, and sell it so others can make clothes, towels, blankets, table coverings, and all sorts of other things."

Henry's mouth was hanging open as his eyes flipped back and forth between the pile of dry stalks and the small bunch of fibers in Adam's clenched fist.

Adam took a deep breath, inhaling a bit of flax dust. He coughed it out and smiled broadly. His son just might catch on to this yet, or so he hoped.

"This is a lot of work, isn't it?" Henry said suddenly with scorn.

Adam's countenance fell. That was not the reaction he hoped for. Henry would have new overalls in the spring, and he would be happy about them, but not about the work to produce them. Maybe next year.

He studied Henry's frame and face, wondering again if he took after Esther or himself. He could never see the resemblance, although others claimed Henry took after Esther. Once again, he decided Henry took after neither. For Esther was just as industrious as he was, if not more so.

Each year Esther asked Adam to hold back more than the ten-percent tithe of the harvest for her good works. Surprisingly, his heart raced with satisfaction as he realized with enjoyment the good work both he and Esther would be able to accomplish during the winter. He would, of course, with the help of his laborers, process the flax. That would take a long time, but it was productive work. She would take the ten percent he set aside, spin it into yarn and thread, and bleach or dye some of the yarn skeins. Both would take turns on the loom and weave the linen cloth, although she was much better at it than he. With the woven cloth she sewed children's clothes, which he would then take to her Presbyterian church for distributing to the dirt-poor immigrants that arrived in larger numbers every year. He was sure there must have been someone like Esther that helped his indentured parents when they first came to the colonies from Germany. He was indebted.

And so, he and Esther were a team and he loved that about their marriage. She said it was God's work. He knew better. It was *their* work. If it was God's work, there wouldn't be any poor immigrants to begin with. If God was around there wouldn't have been a war that had killed both her aunt and uncle when they refused food and lodging to a squad of British Red Coats. That nothing was perfect in this world fueled his skepticism about God being around.

Sometimes he went to church with Esther. He didn't mind it so much. He was a good man, and his wife, whom he loved with all his heart, was even a better woman.

He was daydreaming about Esther's beauty and elegance, when suddenly the premonition hit again. This time it was louder, clearer, and sure. It was the same image, the same sounds, the same voice, the same words, but shorter: "*Break. Bury. Never.*" If the past was any indication, something dark was present. He grew tense.

4

Henry heard the running feet first and nudged his father. At once, they both turned to the barn door that was still open for the wagons that had brought in the loads of flax. Adam's eight-year-old daughter, Eve, appeared. She was out of breath, her eyes wide with fear and her cheeks were flush like she had seen a ghost. "PAPA! SOMETHING'S HAPPENED. COME! COME QUICK!"

Panic rose from someplace deep within Adam. He immediately made the connection to the premonition as he had never done before. He stopped breathing and stared at his surprisingly intelligent, tough daughter who seemed always to possess calm confidence. He had never seen her frantic or alarmed, until now. Her uncharacteristic behavior had nailed his boots to the barn floor in fear.

She repeated her plea. "Papa! Come, please! Something's happened to Mama." This time Adam saw her tears, twisted mouth, and contorted muscles. She turned and ran back to the house.

That pulled the nails out of his shoes. Adam dropped the fistful of flax and ran after her. "Where, daughter?"

"Gathering hall," she yelled, turning back to him as she ran ahead.

The gathering hall was the largest room in their house. In it was a large fireplace for warmth during the winter, a spinner, a loom, a china cabinet, a linen dresser, and a long wood-plank table. Esther spent most of her time in the gathering hall spinning, weaving, sewing, and cooking. Of late, she was hand-stitching shirts, pants, and dresses for the poor children that lived near her church in York. Her hand-sewing skills were the envy of many women. There was a natural proportion and tightness to her even hems, straight seams, and billowy ruffles. Esther was proud to fashion clothing out of hearty linen that would last for generations. Adam was always amazed at how swiftly she could stitch a garment even as she baked and prepared meals. He felt very lucky to have married such a woman. Now, with Eve coming of age, Esther was passing on her skills. He had hope for the future.

Their two-story frame farmhouse stood apart from the barn about fifty yards. The barn and the house took up two acres, next to which was a three-acre pasture for their four horses and sheep, and pens for the goats, sow, and piglets. Beyond that there were the forty acres for crops.

Eve ran ahead of Adam, up the front porch stairs and into the house; Henry followed. At forty-eight years of age, Adam found it disheartening that he couldn't catch up. Eve stopped at the front door and held it open for him. He jumped up the porch steps two-at-a-time.

He expected that Esther had burned herself in the fireplace, perhaps preparing a stew for supper, and that she'd be standing there, perhaps holding her burned wrist, a smile on her face. *"Relax, Adam, I'm all right. I just singed my wrist. Eve, don't scare your father like that."* Esther was a slender woman of average height with a long face, pointed chin, small mouth with thin lips, and piercing close-set brown eyes framed by a massive crop of curly auburn hair that she wore down. She had been a tomboy as a child, keeping up with her four brothers, two older, two youngins. She tended the sheep and cows her family kept, fed the chickens, and chased piglets in the mud. She feared nothing, and one time at the age of ten she brought home a harmless three-foot long scarlet milk snake causing her mother to run for the barn and a shovel. The snake survived to slither away, and so did Esther's mother.

When Adam mounted the porch and entered the foyer, Esther didn't appear. He did hear the plaintive meow of Esther's long-haired calico cat, Cleopatra. Following Eve, Adam turned left into the gathering hall.

"Papa, over here," Eve said with a fright as she stood trembling behind the large wood-planked table at the back of the room near the door that led down to the summer kitchen. After breakfast, the table had been cleared and was now covered with patterns and pieces of cut neutral colored cloth for a small girl's dress in the making. Next to the cut cloth were shears, a pin cushion, and bobbins of white thread.

When Adam maneuvered around the furniture, he saw his wife lying on the floor in a clump. She was wearing her favorite pale-yellow work dress and her knit shawl around her shoulders. Cleopatra was crouched next to Esther's head, as if to warm her fallen mistress. There was no rhyme or reason to how her torso, arms, and legs laid askew next to the chair in which she had evidently been sitting. A needle, thread, and half-finished seam lay loose in her hands. Her neck was twisted awkwardly to one side. Her long, dark auburn hair partially obscured her face. Her body dead still. It was as if a life-size rag doll, with no backbone, or *any* bones for that matter, had been dropped in the chair and then flopped to the floor.

Adam knelt at Esther's side, pushed her hair aside and turned her face toward him. Her white muffin mop cap had fallen over her eyes. He pushed it back. Her eyes were closed. Her face relaxed, no scratches. "Esther!" He gently shook her shoulders, trying to revive her.

Eve took the needle, thread, and unfitted garment from her mother's hands, folded them neatly and put them on the table, then knelt on the other side, "Is she breathing?"

Adam put his ear next to Esther's partially opened mouth. "Yes, but a little."

'Papa, what's wrong with Mama?" asked Henry, who stood over them. There was worry in his voice.

Adam just shook his head.

"He don't know," Eve said, her voice shaking.

Adam straightened Esther's legs and arms and ran his hands over them searching for broken bones. None. Her skin color was rugged as usual. He felt for a pulse, but his calloused fingers weren't much good for that.

"Let's get her to bed," he said. Adam gently put his arms under his much smaller wife, lifted her easily and carried her out of the room. Eve ran ahead of him to the foyer and the staircase. Esther was like a rag doll as Adam carried her up the stairs. Once in the upstairs hall, Eve opened the door to the master bedroom, Adam followed and gently laid Esther on their bed.

He took off her cap. Eve helped him remove her shoes. She just lay there, not moving except for the slight rise and fall of her chest. They covered her with a linen blanket, and he took a wet cloth and wiped her face and hands. But there was no response. Not a groan, not a whimper.

"Esther? Esther, please wake up," Adam said, worry in his voice.

But she didn't.

Henry's boots scampered up the stairs and into the room. When he saw his mother lying in bed as if she was dead, he stopped, stared, and started to cry. Eve came to him, put an arm around him, and with her voice breaking said, "Henry, it's okay. Mama's going to be just fine." There was a pause. She looked at Papa. "Right, Papa?"

"I better go get the doctor. If she wakes, stay with her. You and Henry will be all right, won't you?"

Eve didn't answer at first. Then she just nodded. There were tears in her eyes, like Henry's. Adam thought, *she doesn't believe what she just told Henry. Mama might not be all right.*

Adam realized Esther's breathing was quick and shallow. How could he leave Esther for even a minute? It would be a good hour before he could come back with Doc Evans, provided the good man was even around and not off on another call.

"Eve. Henry. I'm going to go get Doctor Evans. I'll be gone at least an hour. Do not worry. I'm going ta saddle up."

"Papa, can I come with ya?" asked Henry.

Thinking about it for a moment, Adam crouched down and met his son's eyes. "Not this time, son. I'm going to ride hard and fast."

"I can ride with you, not on the pony."

"I'd be afraid of you fallin' off son. No, you stay here."

"Please?"

Eve spoke up, "Henry, I need you to help me do something very important while papa is getting the doctor, okay?"

Adam looked at her, not understanding.

Henry didn't understand either, "What's that? Weed the garden?" he asked sarcastically misreading her intent and trying at all costs to avoid work.

"No, silly." She looked at Papa for permission. But she didn't ask. "We're goin' to pray," she said.

Adam gazed at her a moment. He felt like rebuking her, but decided it was better just to nod as if to say, "*Yes, please pray.*"

A moment later Adam was down the stairs, out of the house, and running toward the corral.

5

Eve, realizing she must act adult-like, went calmly to the front window of Mama's bedroom and watched Papa bridle and saddle Calvin, his favorite shire stallion. They owned two black shires with white feathering on all four legs. Papa used the horses for plowing and pulling. Both were sweethearts and gentle, but Calvin was Adam's pet, always craving a bit more attention than Luther, the gelding. Cleopatra jumped up into Eve's lap, licked her hand a few times, then investigated Eve's face and meowed. Henry stood at Eve's side and leaned against her as the three of them watched Papa and Calvin canter out of the yard.

As soon as Papa was out of sight, Eve felt relieved, and her muscles relaxed. She was glad Papa had left so quickly to get help. She turned from the window and went to Mama's side. She wondered why Henry kept looking out the window.

"Papa's going to be a while, Henry."

He said nothing.

"Are you going to pray with me for Mama?" she asked Henry.

"Do I have to?"

What's wrong with this boy? Does he have anything better to do? "I guess not. But what else is there to do?" she said more than a bit miffed.

"I'm hungry."

Such a selfish boy. She stared at his back and waited.

Henry finally turned around and said, "She probably just needed a nap. Let her sleep and let's eat." But his tone was unsure, his voice quavered, and his eyes were red and wet. He had kept his back to Eve because he was crying and afraid.

Yet, Eve was just as afraid, but she hid it better than he could. Years of practice, she figured. She walked slowly to him, put her arm around his shoulder and walked him back to the bed. "Let's pray for Mama, okay?" she asked gently.

He just nodded and looked down at his sleeping Mama.

Eve lowered herself to her knees resting her elbows on her mom's bedside, and gently pulled her brother down next to her. Her head was barely above the comforter on which her mother rested. Henry buried his face in the side of the bed, and Cleo jumped up on the bed and curled up next to Esther's breast.

Eve closed her eyes and prayed. "Dear God. We are very sad right now. Something bad has happened to Mama. Papa went to get the doctor, but we don't have to wait for him. You can make Mama well right now. Would you do that? Please? We're so afraid...so is Papa."

She stopped and glanced at her brother, who was staring off into space. She put her head back down. "And please get Henry to pray, too."

She peeked, Henry had put his head down and closed his eyes. She continued, "Please make Mama well so she can cook our food, spin the flax, weave the cloth, and make clothes for those that are poor. Don't you need her to do those things? I'm learning, but I'm too young and I don't know much about all that. And Henry is always hungry. We gotta feed Henry so he can grow big and strong like Papa. Please wake Mama up so she can be a good mother again. We love her so much." She stopped and wondered what she had forgotten to say. "Oh, and we love you, too, God. Amen."

6

Eve had fallen asleep on the floor, next to Mama's bed and Henry next to her. She had refused to fix him anything to eat although he asked politely several times. She figured if Mama couldn't eat, they shouldn't.

The sound of Doc Evan's buggy and Calvin trotting to a stop outside the front porch woke her. She sat up quickly when she heard the two men step onto the front porch and enter the house. It was dark outside and in the room. She realized she had not lit any of the lanterns in the bedroom. About the time she regained her bearings and found the tinder box on the dresser, Papa came into the room with a bright lantern followed by Doc Evans.

Papa set the bright lantern on the side table next to Mama's side of the bed, then lit the lantern that was already there and put it higher-up on the dresser. Finally, he lit the lantern on the side table on his side of the bed. Immediately, Doc Evans sat next to Mama and started to examine her. Adam lifted the still sleeping Henry off the floor and laid him on the foot of the bed. "Eve? Were you asleep? Did you eat? I'm sorry I was gone so long."

"I guess, on the floor, there," she said sleepily. "No, we didn't eat." She glanced at Henry, who was shivering. Taking a blanket off the chest at the foot of the bed she draped it over her brother. It was only then that she realized she was cold, too. Looking about, she found Mama's shawl on a chair and pulled it snug around her shoulders.

Doc Evans said nothing as he leaned over Mama, touching her face, neck, and hand. Papa leaned over Doc's shoulders but only for a moment before they both raised up.

Papa sat down hard on the bed and began to weep.

Doc Evans turned to Eve. "Eve, did your mother stir, wake, or make any sound at all while your papa was gone?"

"What's wrong, Mister Evans? Is Mama all right?"

Doc Evans lifted the lantern over Mama and while prying her eye open with one hand, passed the lantern back and forth over her face. Closing Mama's eye lid, he put the lantern down, and laid his hands on Mama's neck for another moment or two before turning to Eve who stood next to her weeping papa. "Eve, I am sorry to tell you this, but your mother has passed on. She is no longer with us."

Papa had been weeping quietly, but when Doc Evans said what he just did, Papa could no longer hold it in. As big and as strong as he was, he suddenly wrapped his arms around his knees, curled up into a ball and burst out crying like a little baby who had lost his mother.

Eve did the same.

7

My Despised Cyn:

Petitioning the Almighty to take Livingston's wife was a gamble. That he permitted it—uncommon. Letting her pass so easily into Glory, our detriment. But it opens doors to the rest of the family. Don't pass this up. Make sure he fully blames the Almighty for her demise. This should be easy in his weakened state. Consider how rigorously your peers attached him to a mortal. Their logic was impeccable: she was a believer, he put his trust in her, thus faith in the Almighty was needless. So, when she was gone, his soul was vacant, and fools like you rush in. Delightful!

There's also the precious corruption we've been able to promulgate that when bad things happen they're so caught up in selfish anguish they refuse to see the obvious. We just tell them it must be the "Will of God." What an idiotic, sentimental interpretation of Isaiah's words that the Almighty's ways are not their ways. If they only knew the truth. Since the Protestant Reformation their faith is so without reason they become irrepressibly gullible and blame their own mistakes, often rooted in pride, on Him. Thankfully we've been blessed with marks so easily deluded.

And to sugarcoat it, they rarely remember to thank the Almighty for what is good, true, or beautiful. Thus, your chances of turning Livingston's heart from lukewarm, to cold, to raging anger excites us. Get inside his head. Lie to him as is our perfection. How could a loving God ever allow this to happen? Show him the foolishness of reliance on angels and glory's riffraff.

You asked about petitioning for his daughter. Don't go there. The Almighty has his limits, and we risk *ourselves* ending up in Perdition.

Worry if you will, you are on your way. Keep up the pressure. We think he has no chance against your devices.

Eternally yours,
Master of Death

Chapter 5
The Leaves Failed to Flinch

1

November 5, 1787.

Eve Livingston stepped out of the farmhouse's front door and onto the porch. It was a cool afternoon. She wrapped her mother's favorite knit shawl about her shoulders, the one she wore the day she died. A collection of twenty or so buggies and horses were tied up around the perimeter of the yard and near the corral. The breeze was fresh with the rooty odor of horses after a good trot. That was especially true now that it was turning colder, and their hair was getting longer. In the corners of the porch hay dust swirled in eddies. Papa had asked Stephen, a day-laborer, to see that the guests' horses were watered, fed, and secure. Stephen had spread small piles of hay on the ground in front of each horse and they were all contentedly nibbling at their share, and a few greedily eyeing their neighbor's. Horses can be so piggy at times.

Eve smiled at Luther and Calvin, social beasts that they were, trying to make friends with their visiting peers and share in the fresh hay if they could get their noses through the corral fence. Pickles, their pony, and Sizemore, their gelded paint, were more skittish and stood at a distance watching the menagerie.

Not far from her mind, however, was how she should understand her mother's sudden death. Was it punishment for something secret that Eve didn't know about? Just before Mama collapsed, Eve remembered sensing a wave of cold dread flow past her, like a cold draft that made her skin crawl. It was a cool day, but the fireplace was warming the room, and no one had opened the door. Mother felt the coldness too, Eve noticed she shivered and pulled her shawl around her just before she fell off her chair. Eve again pulled the shawl tighter around her shoulders and scanned the yard. All seemed well enough. With a heavy heart she stepped back into the house and shut the door.

Inside, she glanced up the staircase, then down the hall that led to the back-door. To the right was the parlor and warming fireplace. There, a few women milled around a table at the far end. To her left through an archway was the gathering hall with a cooking fireplace. In contrast to the rough-hewn timber and white plaster walls of both the parlor and gathering hall, finely turned and finished European furniture graced the rooms' orderly perimeters.

She entered the gathering hall. A dozen neighbors and a few children sat or chatted quietly in the afternoon light as an old man she could not see chanted a prayer in cadence with the rhythmic sound of the large flying shuttle loom.

The loom was surround by baskets of flax thread, woolly yarn, and a collection of plain but tightly woven linen cloth that had yet to be hemmed. Between the loom and the fireplace was a spinning wheel.

Papa worked the loom. She stopped near him to watch. Someday she wanted to be tall enough and strong enough to weave. He wore clean overalls, and a white collared shirt that set off his black hair and grey-speckled beard. He was focused, working hard, sweating at the brow a bit. His rugged face could not hide the tears that fell from his usually alert eyes.

Sheesh-smack—the shuttle flew through the shed, across the loom, pulling the weft to the left. *Thump-thump*—Papa pulled the beater against the weft twice and the whole loom shuttered. *Flutter-thwack*—his feet fumbled across the treadles as the heddles opened and closed the multiple threads of the warp. Then, again with a jerk of the shuttle chord—*sheesh-smack*—the shuttle flew through the shed to the right. *Thump-thump*—another row of thread was added to the weave.

But Papa was not smooth and graceful like Mama. When Mama wove, the loom barely moved. But when Papa wove, especially today, he was waging war and the loom was his instrument of destruction. Each depression of a treadle was like a cannon ball dropping. Each pick of the shuttle was like the firing of a musket. When he pulled the beater, the whole loom shook, and she was sure the loom inched toward the front door a smidgen more. With each pick of the shuttle, she couldn't stop her muscles from twitching. So strongly did Papa pull on the shuttle chords, she thought the flying shuttle would leave its track and fly clear across the room shattering Mama's china. It's a wonder the loom didn't break. It was always this way with Papa. But tonight, it was worse—his choreography driven by deep bitterness.

Yet, she found herself mesmerized by the call of the loom and the response of the old man's lament. She turned now and saw him, in the nook between the archway and the front window behind the loom. He sat on a woven chair, hunched over, his pure white beard hanging over his hands that rested on a walking stick like Papa's shillelagh. His eyes were closed, and he swayed with the rhythm of the loom and his chanted verse. For a thin man he had a thick, weathered voice that dug deep as he sustained the minor-key notes through the loom's *thwacks*, *smacks*, and *thumps*. The mixture of sounds gave her the impression of a draft horse like Luther pulling Papa's walk-behind plow and carving a deep furrow of sadness into a muddy field.

Flutter-thwack - O, Lord...
Sheesh-smack - Look at...
Thump-thump - My affliction...affliction
Flutter-thwack - For the enemy...
Sheesh-smack - Has triumphed...
Thump-thump - Over me...O, me
Flutter-thwack - Lo, Lo...

Sheesh-smack - O, Lord...
Thump-thump - And see...O, see
Flutter-thwack - How worthless...
Sheesh-smack - I have...
Thump-thump - Become...O, come
Flutter-thwack - Is it nothing...
Sheesh-smack - To you...
Thump-thump - Who pass by? ...pass by?

She finally relented and retreated from the noisy loom and stood next to her brother some feet away. Eve was embarrassed for Henry. Standing together they must have caused everyone in the room to wonder if they were related. Henry stuck his hands deep in his pockets, a sure sign that his terrible twos had carried over into his spoiled sixes. His hair was normally brown and wavy, but it hadn't been combed in days. His dirty overalls, torn flannel shirt, and muddy boots were in stark contrast to her clean white dress and a perfectly tied black linen bow in her long, carefully brushed, blonde hair. She pulled the shawl tighter around her shoulders. There was a fire in the fireplace to her right, but for some reason she was shivering.

Behind them stood half a dozen neighbors who came to pay their respects. The group stood quietly and watched Adam weep as he awkwardly banged away at the loom.

How badly she wanted to reach out and wrap her arms around Papa, and just hold him still. She remembered how just a few days ago when he sat next to the glowing fireplace late at night, and Mama was busy in the wash house, she sat on his lap, rested her head against his chest and let it ride up and down as he breathed. He usually smelled like the fresh flax, or the slight pungent scent of the barn. She loved all those things. They reminded her of home, of heaven, of the earth, and all that was good and beautiful.

But tonight, it was all different. Papa was not happy. He had not come in and hugged her warm and loving mother as he usually did. Eve wished she could change places with Mama. But she couldn't it seemed, so she stood silently, bowed her head, and prayed.

Abruptly, Adam stopped weaving. He retrieved the shuttle and examined it. The spindle was probably empty. He ran his hand lovingly over the wrap of linen on the take-up beam on which his tears had fallen.

Mrs. Wilks, an older woman who stood near Eve, broke from the group. Eve followed her. The woman stood behind Adam, Eve to the side, her shoulders drooped and her eyes squeezed shut to hold back the tears.

Mrs. Wilks lightly laid her hand on Adam's shoulder. He jerked up and looked directly at Eve. Gazing back at Papa, she felt tears falling down her cheeks. Papa twisted somewhat and gazed about the room.

"That's enough, Adam," Mrs. Wilks said softly. "You have plenty. Are you sure this is what we should use?"

Adam, still stroking the cloth, said, "Yes, I'm sure. She should have it." He took shears...*clank, clank, clank*...cut the warps from the loom, tied them off, pulled the rest of the cloth from the warp's take up beam, and cut and tied-off those ends as well. Gathering up the bundled cloth from his lap, he brought it to his face, breathed its fresh scent, wiping his eyes as he did, then handed the bundle of linen to Mrs. Wilks.

She recruited another woman and together they reverently folded the cloth. "Adam, this is an extraordinary satin-linen weave. It's luxurious. Was this from the flax you harvested?"

Adam nodded.

"And Mama spun the threads, too," said Eve.

As Mrs. Wilks turned from the loom, other grown-ups crowded around to examine the linen. It was exquisite, smooth, and had a sheen even in the dim light of the lanterns that lit the room. One could tell, however, where the awkward Adam had picked up the weave after Esther had left off days earlier. It seemed everyone had to touch Mama's satin-linen and hold it up to the lamp light. It was a tight weave. They were all impressed. She knew it was the best. Mama always wove the best of anyone around.

Adam put out his hands, palms up, and Mrs. Wilks laid the folded bundle in them. Adam looked across the room, "Henry? Come here, son."

Henry lowered his eyes as if he were being called out to the woodshed for a beating. But he came slowly to his papa and stood next to Eve.

Adam held out the cloth to them. "Daughter. Son. This is for your mother. Take it to her. It is our love for her, even as it's her goodness and love for us."

Eve adjusted the shawl over her neck and then stuck out her forearms. "Henry, stick out your arms like this," she said.

Henry looked at his sister's arms and shook his head to register his discontent at being told what to do. But he did it and stuck out his arms.

"Good boy, son," Adam said. He draped the cloth over the four arms to form as it were an altar.

"Okay, Henry," Eve said, "now we're going to take this to Mama. Okay?"

Henry looked at Eve with suspicion but well enough matched her slow walk out of the gathering hall and toward the parlor. Eve flashed a thin smile at Mrs. Wilks who nodded her approval. Eve glanced back. The other adults were formed up behind and following them like a royal procession. She imagined she was carrying a silk pillow on which rested a crown for the coronation of a queen.

2

Adam watched the procession leave the gathering hall where he sat on the loom's bench. Although there were at least two dozen people in the house, he felt alone and tired. But it was time. He feared what was coming. Taking up his shillelagh, a knob-headed fighting stick that was always within arm's reach unless he was working in the barn or fields, he rotated his torso over his knees, raised up from his perch, and lumbered toward the foyer.

He looked back at the room he had built for Esther. At the rear was a large cooking fireplace made from fieldstone she had requested for winter cooking. She liked cooking and baking here in the winter because she would be in the gathering hall with him and the children. The summer kitchen was too cold in the winter since Adam had never sealed it against the weather. To make the house even more appealing for her, he had plastered the walls inside of the post-and-beam structure. The room was not only large but functional and warm. He loved the room, or at least he once did. He never minded splitting the firewood or stacking it near the four fireplaces for the winter. Once he got the fire going, he loved to sit across the room and watch Esther settle down by the hearth and tell stories to the children. Once the kids were in bed, he would watch her spin, mend his overalls, make shirts, or weave. It was her room, and now she was in the other room, never to enter this one again.

Turning his back on the gathering hall he padded through the foyer, past the central stairs, and into the parlor now crowded with neighbors.

As he entered, they parted for him. At the far end, two women, their backs to him, were busy leaning over the supper table they had taken out of the gathering hall and placed at the end of this room. Between him and the women stood Eve and Henry holding the cloth, their backs to him, waiting.

How could he eat at that table ever again? How could he even live in this house any longer? He had always thought of it as Esther's house for she had helped him design and build it. She loved it, and he her. Now what was he to do? He stepped further into the room toward the women on whom he fixed his swollen gaze. Then he stopped. Overlapping both hands on the knob of his shillelagh, he locked his arms and leaned forward on the stick to rest.

After a moment the women stood aside. There, laid out on the table was his Esther, or at least her body. He felt numb. He couldn't keep his eyes off the woman he had loved, still loved. The women had worked several hours preparing her for burial. To one side on a washstand was a basin of soap, water, and several used linen wash cloths. They had undressed her, washed her body, fixed her hair, and put on her Sunday best. He was surprised how perfect her curly auburn hair looked, draped over her shoulders. How he loved to nuzzle that hair after they had made love. He was going to miss her voluptuous breasts and big smile. Her lips were so thin, he often kissed her slightly up-turned nose; he joked that it was easier to find. She'd giggle and then grab the back of his head and kiss him proper-like. But now the giggling and kissing were gone, as was the rugged, vivacious beauty. Now she was white-as-a-ghost, and the smile was gone, too. But the ladies had done a respectful enough job and for that he was grateful. They had even put a small wooden cross on a chain around her neck. She liked going to divine services. He had stopped going with her a year or so ago. He didn't see the sense in it. Now, her sudden passing had proved him right about God. What good was a god that took your love away?

As he approached the table, he saw wide white ribbons adorning her hair, neck, waist, and wrists—to chase off the devils, he had been told. *Stupid superstitions.* No more harm could be done to her now. Why bother? Although, the cross around her neck was a nice touch.

Oh, Esther, you look so, so...dignified. Yes, that was it. Dignity was all that was left. The goodness and the beauty were gone.

The two women took the linen from Eve and Henry, stretched it out lengthwise along the table next to Esther. Two men stepped forward and lifted Esther's upper body slightly and the women slid the linen under her. Lifting her torso and legs the women repeated the procedure until Esther was lying entirely on the cloth. They were getting close to the end now. He felt a bitter-sweet surge, at once wanting this moment to never end, and not wanting to wait until it was.

The kids stepped back a bit and then he saw it. On the floor, between him and the table was a plain, pine coffin, the lid removed. Two other men joined the first two, and with two on each side they gripped the cloth under Esther, lifted her up and away from the table, then gently lowered her squarely into the coffin. As soon as her body was positioned, they lifted the coffin and put it up on the table. He must commend Jack Wares, the village carpenter; the coffin was a perfect fit.

The women, then, as if they had done it a hundred times, reverently covered Esther's body with the abundant tails of the rich linen, wrapping her body like a present, except for her face. *Her face. Take a good look. You won't see this much longer.* A cold rush exploded in his groin, raced to his neck, and down his arms. Suddenly, he was transfixed. Her face suddenly took on a warm, eerie luminescence, as if there were hot coals just beneath her pale skin. It didn't last long, but later he would claim he saw her smile.

Foster Richardson, an acquaintance from Esther's church whose land was north of the Livingston farm, stepped up. Adam, eager to gaze on living flesh, turned and stared at Foster. The man avoided Adam's gaze, and shook his head slightly at those behind him who seem to have urged him on. Something awkward was brewing. Foster leaned over and whispered in Adam's ear, "Adam, are we to expect either Rev. Webster or Rev. Brauer to conduct the service?"

Adam winced and turned his face back to Esther in the box. Two men had picked up the coffin's cover and were standing ready with hammers and nails. They were watching Adam for a signal. After a moment he took a breath, turned to Foster, and said just loud enough for the others to hear, "I told Webster and Brauer to stay away. Didn't want a Presbyterian, or Lutheran, or any others like 'em. Esther was a good woman. I don't need some so-called men of God to tell me that."

Murmuring rose as he expected. But there was also a current of agreement. A woman started a hymn. It had been a long time since he had been in church, but he recognized it immediately as one of the later verses from Luther's *A Mighty Fortress is our God.* He listened to the woman's remarkably strong and resonant voice.

> *And though this world, with devils filled,*
> *should threaten to undo us,*
> *we will not fear, for God has willed*
> *his truth to triumph through us.*
> *The prince of darkness grim,*
> *we tremble not for him;*
> *his rage we can endure,*
> *for lo! his doom is sure;*
> *one little word shall fell him.*

It sounded as if the entire room began to sing. The men with the coffin's lid kept waiting for his cue. He held up a finger, suggesting they wait a moment longer. They nodded and backed off a bit.

As the hymn continued, Adam took his children by the hand, and led them to the coffin's side. He lifted Henry up and let him first stand on the table and then crouch down by the coffin's side. Eve dragged over a chair and stood on the seat. The three of them looked on their mother for the last time.

He had once lusted for his woman, so he leaned in and placed a gentle kiss on her pale lips. He inhaled, searching for a hint of her scent, a trace of the feminine musky rose that caused him to melt into her arms when she smiled at him in the candlelight of their bed. Instead, he inhaled only death and a hint of lavender soap. He recoiled and wiped his mouth with the back of his hand.

Henry looked at his papa for permission. Adam nodded, and Henry leaned over his mom and kissed her cheek. Then Eve leaned over and kissed Esther's forehead, praying softly, "Mama, pray for us. We'll pray for you."

Wishing things were different he finally straightened, pulled the last piece of linen over Esther's face, leaving the long locks of her auburn hair still visible. Then, he stepped back in resignation.

Henry jumped down to the floor and Eve abandoned her chair.

Adam's chest tightened. This is it, the end of life as he knew it. He nodded to the men with the top, backed away and took up a position to fix his eyes on his wife's face, now covered with a cloth of grace.

"Papa? Pick me up so I can see," Henry said coming to Adam's side.

Adam picked him up and held him in his right arm. Eve came and leaned into him on his left, and around her he put his arm. He wanted to remember every pore, every freckle, and every strand of Esther's dark auburn hair. She had a bit of Irish in her, although Adam denied it to his British friends. As the lid came down, he forced himself to think only of her goodness.

Then the hammers went to work. *Bang. Bang. Bang. Bang.* There was no embalming. The coffin was not sealed. Such was the custom.

Adam glanced at the wall behind the coffin. There hung a large mirror with a distinctive frame. It had been covered over with a black cloth as some arcane superstitious Christian tradition demanded. He was glad in a way. It prevented him from looking into his own eyes and peering past his soul at the being who had allowed this to happen.

Under his breath he uttered a curse at God who had taken this woman from him. Abruptly and with resolution, he put Henry down. He turned away, intent on forgetting and forging a new life without the little faith he had acquired under Esther's watch.

Adam stepped quickly from the room to the foyer. He pulled his children with him through the entry door to the porch where they would wait for the coffin.

The four men who had previously lifted Esther's body into the coffin now stretched leather straps under the wooden box and carried it out the door. Those in the room placed a kiss on the coffin's top as it passed by. The group then lit candles and followed the procession out of the house into the cool of the early evening.

As they followed the coffin to the family plot, the women who had prepared Esther for burial chanted a medieval requiem for the dead.

> *Wondrous sound the trumpet flingeth,*
> *Through earth's sepulchers it ringeth,*
> *All before the throne it bringeth.*
> *Death is struck and nature quaking,*
> *All creation is awaking,*
> *To its judge an answer making.*
> *Lo the book exactly worded,*
> *Wherein all hath been recorded,*
> *Thence shall judgment be awarded.*

3

A few miles from the Livingston farm a crowd of revelers gathered for a bonfire in a vacant field. It was a once a year celebration. The Reverend Frederick Brauer watched from the edges of the crowd. He hunched into his jacket and pulled down the brim of his black felt hat. A gregarious, middle-aged Lutheran minister of some size and formidable temperament, Brauer wanted to leave and not be seen. Guy Fawkes Day celebrations usually devolved into crude behavior and drunken reverie, despite the children present.

Looking about, Brauer saw what he came for. Four men holding aloft oil torches ignited the massive stack of timber. One of the torch bearers was his deacon, a man he otherwise respected. Brauer was disappointed.

Staying on the fringe of the crowd, Brauer moved to intercept his deacon at the water buckets. There, under a clump of small trees, the buckets stood ready to dampen an inadvertent brush fire and to extinguish the torches.

With a blazing torch still in hand, Deacon Lucas Witt, a slight man with a full beard and heavy coat, stood back as the kindling caught fire and worked its way up the ten-foot stack of logs piled in the center of a clearing.

With hundreds of revelers and children, Lucas cheered the beginning of the extemporaneous party. When he cut a path to the buckets, Brauer was waiting.

"Lucas!"

Witt submerged his torch and looked up. "Reverend! Why you here?" Witt looked a bit surprised if not embarrassed at the appearance of his minister.

"I should be asking that of you," said Brauer. "You were going to ride with me out to Adam Livingston's. You forget?"

Witt reacted with a blank grin and then shook his head. "No, I didn't ferget."

He turned to gaze at the flames that now soared thirty feet and more into the cool night sky. Mothers were pulling their children back to safety. Brauer shifted his eyes from the deacon to the fire.

Was Witt using the bonfire as an excuse to avoid an awkward visitation with his pastor? Was he just looking for free beer and a warm bonfire? Or, was he here to celebrate the discovery of Guy Fawkes in the undercroft of the House of Lords guarding two tons of fused gunpowder 182 years ago today?

Brauer was sure the history had been forgotten, and the bonfire was only an excuse to express their hate for and intimidate the few Catholics that lived nearby in York.

"You fought in the war, didn't you, Lucas?"

"Yep, ended up in the Virginia Rifle Regiment. Sharpshooter."

"General Washington banned these Guy Fawkes bonfires, didn't he?"

Lucas partly turned back to Brauer but kept his eyes on the teens dancing around the inferno. "Reckon so, minister. We're hopin' to make up for some of that tonight. Damn papists. Got no use fer 'em."

"A lot of Catholics fought and died in the war, Lucas."

"Not as many as should've, if yer askin' me. Idolaters! They got no rights in my min."

Wincing, a sadness came over Brauer. He said no more. Continuing the conversation was futile. Instead, he started to brainstorm titles for next Sunday's sermon and cut a path back to his horse.

All of this reminded him of how a few months ago he had been in Philadelphia, just after the new U.S. Constitution had been signed. He was there with a delegation of other ministers who were concerned that the new Constitution did nothing to protect their freedom of assembly, speech, or religion. They were fearful that the religious persecution still popular in Europe would find new life here. There had been some promises by the delegates for a central bill of rights apart from those in a few of the states. But how that might happen was part of an on-going and chaotic debate. Politicians were good at making promises, but lousy at keeping them.

Their ministerial contingent in Philadelphia had met *Charles Carroll, one of the signers of the Declaration of Independence, and his cousin, *Daniel Carroll, who signed the Constitution. Both were wealthy Maryland planters. In fact, it was reported that Charles had, with his own money, partly funded the war effort against Britain. Being that he was the wealthiest of any man in the Thirteen Colonies when the war began, he had everything to lose, including his head. Under Maryland laws, until the Constitution was ratified and put into effect, and because both Daniel and Charles were Roman Catholic, they were not allowed to hold public office or even vote. Clearly their willingness to sacrifice their lives and livelihoods for freedom from the king's tyranny was enough for Maryland's electorate to disregard their own laws and trust them as delegates. Brauer could only hope that the citizens here in Pennsylvania would be as noble.

Other men and women from Brauer's congregation were at the bonfire and they, like Lucas, were surprised but glad to see their minister. Did any of them realize the dangerous tradition they were preserving? It was religious persecution that drove settlers from Europe to the colonies. Did these revelers realize the new Constitution, as signed, meant that the religious majority in political power could punish dissenters of another faith? There was no guarantee of individual rights. There was talk of a Bill of Rights, but nothing yet. It was the problem they had all just escaped from. It was why General Washington had stopped his troops from staging Guy Fawkes bonfires. Had they learned nothing from the past? He would pray and preach more on religious tolerance. The consequence otherwise would be as bloody as the war they had just survived.

As the heat of the massive pyre reached the perimeter of the festivities, Rev. Brauer's spotted appaloosa mare pulled at the grazing rope that reined it to a tree. Eager to depart and avoid what was coming next, Brauer untied his steed and calmly stroked the horse's neck to calm its nerves. He checked the saddle's billet strap, adjusted the reins, stepped into the stirrup, pulled on the horn, and swung his bulk up into the saddle.

No sooner had he dropped into the saddle than a reveler who recognized the minister, but not the minister the reveler, ran to the appaloosa's side, grabbed the horse's bridle, and over the crescendo of noise that now included the discharging of firearms, clamored for Brauer's attention.

"Minister, where off? We's 'bout to see the anti-Christ up in flames, and fireworks is comin.'"

Brauer scanned the bonfire and the horde around it. Incredibly, the fire was so large it appeared to engulf those closest to it, *a preview of hell*, he thought. There was the sermon topic: *Are you the fuel for your own bonfire?* Then he saw it. To one side, hanging from a long-cantilevered pole, was an effigy of Pope Pius VI, vestments, miter cap, *et al.* The resemblance was remarkable and frightening.

"Fair sir," Brauer said. "I am late for the wake of a dear parishioner's wife and a quest to save his soul. My blessings to your friends. Do try not to wake the devil. He may come and join you. Now, if you don't mind." Brauer tugged at his reins,

The man let go of the bridle and waved the minister adieu.

Brauer thanked him with a nod, pulled the horse's nose away, and cantered into the night under a crescent moon.

4

As Adam returned with his friends and neighbors from burying his wife, he gazed up at the waning crescent moon. It was the end of an age. In a few days the moon would begin to rise with the sun—the beginning of a new day, a new age. He wanted to believe that everything would be all right. He inhaled the evening's freshness, and repeatedly jabbed his shillelagh on the ground as if to dig out a firmer foundation. *Mourn modesty. Tomorrow the sun will rise and so must ye.*

As they entered the foyer, Adam noticed a Pennsylvania Packet newspaper had been left by one of his guests on the console table. He didn't subscribe to a newspaper; friends would drop by editions after a while. He got some news late, but he didn't mind so much. To keep current, he would mostly read the broadsides when he went into the village or into York. The edition on the console table was folded to an article on page two. He picked it up and read:

> PHILADELPHIA. The United States...In GENERAL ASSEMBLY. Saturday, September 29, 1787. WHEREAS the Convention of Deputies from the several states composing the union, lately held in this city, have published a constitution for the future government of the United States, to be submitted to conventions of deputies chosen in each state by the people thereof, under the recommendation of its legislature, for their assent and ratification. —Charles Thomson, Secretary.

Adam relaxed and took a deep, satisfying breath. It was true, the Articles of Confederation, which had been ratified in 1781, were being replaced by this new constitution. The sun would rise on the new country, as well. It would be nice to live for the moment, to forget the past, and not burden the future too much.

While Adam and the pallbearers backfilled the grave, others had returned to the house, moved the wood-planked supper table back to the gathering hall, washed it down, spread a clean linen over it, and laid out a spread of food they had brought. When he got back to the house, he went around the room, shaking everyone's hand, holding it a little longer or squeezing it a little harder, looking each in the eye and thanking them for coming. He was glad some would stay the night to keep him company and leave to their distant homes in the morning's light.

Emotionally exhausted, Adam sat with his back to the entrance and faced the fireplace's warmth. A copper pitcher of coffee warmed on a hook when Eve was not pouring the brew into mugs for their guests.

His eyes skimmed the room. Esther's touch was everywhere, especially in her handcrafted lace, embroidery, hand towels, and linens. But there were also his father's rugs, and his mother's needlepoint—evidence of his family's legacy in textiles. For the first time today, he felt some pride. He sat up straight and shifted his shoulders back a bit. He glanced at the glass jar filled with flax seed which sat on the mantelpiece. It was a gift from his grandfather to his father, or so he had been told—a reminder that every part of the flax plant was useful, even the oil from the seed.

Adam turned to look at the loom he had built out of walnut, cherry, and oak for Esther, making improvements over the years, like adding the flying shuttle which doubled her productivity. Tears formed in his eyes and he imagined his Esther sitting at the loom singing a hymn in rhythm to the percussive sounds of her weaving.

"Do you want this, Papa?"

He turned back toward the fireplace. Eve held out a steaming cup of coffee and a faint smile. "Yes," he said.

"Are you feeling better now?"

He took the mug, sipped the brew, and warmed his hands around it. "Now that I have your warm coffee, I do. Thank you." He put his nose into the cup and inhaled the invigorating aroma and drank some more.

"Can Henry and I stay up and be with you and the others?" Eve asked. "It'd be awfully hard to sleep with all these people here. And I can help serve food and coffee, and clean up."

Adam raised his face to his attentive daughter and fell into her generous eyes. "Eve, stay up if you like and do whatever seems best to you. Perhaps your mother may even pay us a visit."

Eve leaned over and hugged Papa. "Thank you, Papa." But a dark expression suddenly swept across her face. "Do you mean Mama might come back and visit us like a ghost or a spirit?"

Adam grimaced. He had not meant to scare her, but only assure her of Esther's love. He pondered what to say. "There are no such things as ghosts, or haunting spirits, Eve. What I meant was…." But he wasn't sure exactly what he meant. "I mean she might come back to us…in a dream. A pleasant dream." Adam smiled at his daughter, but he could see that the cloud still hung over her pretty little head.

She lowered her voice and leaned in a bit. "I've heard grown-ups say that sometimes the dead send their spirits back to haunt us, to warn us about hell."

"Never you mind such things. Besides, if there is a hell, I'm sure your Mama has no inkling of what it's like to warn you."

"Oh, I don't think Mama's in hell."

"Good, then there's nothing to worry about," he said.

But Eve was not convinced.

Adam changed the subject. "Henry's awfully quiet. Do you suppose he's not well?"

Eve turned quickly to see Henry in a corner behind them, sitting on the floor and leaning against a cabinet. He rolled a small log back and forth between his knees. "He's okay, Papa. There are no other boys here his age, and he's just wondering what's going to happen."

"Yes, we all are wondering that." He squeezed his eyes, forcing out a tear that had been demanding its freedom.

She took his coffee cup, put it aside, sat on his lap, hugged him long and hard, and breathed into his soft beard. "Mama. Oh, Mama. Don't scare us. But do come and help us. Send your angels to guard over us."

As Adam returned his daughter's hug, he peered over her shoulder at Henry. At that moment, Henry looked up and met his papa's inquisitive eyes. Nothing was said, but it was as if he had given Henry a hug, too. After a moment, Henry stopped rolling his log and smiled back at his papa. Adam wrinkled his forehead and raised an eyebrow as if to ask his son, *You okay?* Henry shrugged his shoulders and nodded, *Yeah, I'm okay, I guess.* Like a secret handshake, Henry crossed his eyes and tilted his head back like a passed-out drunk. At that Adam laughed out loud.

Eve suddenly pulled back from her hug. "What's so funny," she asked.

"Your brother is making faces at me," he said.

She twisted around to look at Henry, at which Henry took two fingers and stuck them up his nose at her. "He's so rude," she said, as she got up from her father's lap.

"He's a boy," Adam said.

Florence Worthington caught Adam's eye. With her was her ever-present husband, Alfred. They were the proprietors of the general store at Wrightsville, the village on the Susquehanna Adam frequented. They stepped over to Adam, her head held high and proper; Alfred was the quiet one. "Mister Livingston, I want to commend you on the behavior of your children. They are very mature for such a time." She turned to Alfred as if to ask permission to speak further, but she didn't wait for his nod. She turned back to Adam. "Would you like to come to the village this week for supper? Bring your children, of course."

"Thank you kindly, Missus Worthington…and Alfred." Adam bowed slightly out of respect. "My children are good workers and loyal. They get their loyalty from their Irish mother and their hard work from the Liebersteins."

Adam paused to collect his thoughts. He was used to speaking to the head of households and not their wives. Not sure he wanted to dress up for dinner, travel two hours one way with Calvin and Luther pulling a buggy, spend a couple hours with the Worthington's and then back another two hours. It would be an all-day excursion, and a day away from work. Might be good for business, however. They were successful merchants.

He turned to Alfred and put Florence to his side. "Alfred. I must tell you that your generosity exceeds my own in what you did last night."

"'Twas, not me, dear neighbor. It was but my gentle Florence who watched over your missus through the night. She's a stalwart soul...Florence is. She loved dear Esther. She could hardly part, and thus appreciated the custom, as it were."

Florence would not be left out. She stepped back in front of Adam and asserted her right as an adult. When she did, Alfred released a shallow smile and gave her room

"Esther will be missed by all of us," said Florence. "The least I could do was show her the dignity that she showed all of us, by being with her those dark hours." Florence smiled as if talking to a dear friend, "We spent the time chatting of the time two years ago she and you brought your linen to sell in our store and she stayed with me a couple days showing me how to weave and I taught her how to preserve."

Surely, he remembered the trip and the generosity the Worthington's showed them two harvests ago. But he wondered how to respond to this business about chatting with a corpse through the night. They were kind friends and business associates, and they were staying the night. But what a ridiculous thought this fool woman had in her head. It was true that friends of the deceased paid them respect by watching over their dead bodies the night of their death and before their preparation for burial. But Esther was dead. Gone. You can't talk to a corpse. You can't chat and reminisce with it.

Adam was tempted to ignore Florence and address Alfred like any decent man would and should. Yet Alfred seemed to have acquiesced to the inappropriate acts and irrational thoughts of the woman. That's one thing Esther was not guilty of. In the presence of men, she was polite and never barged in when logic was holding court. Such was the authority of a man over his household.

Adam stiffened, and against his better judgment turned to Alfred's spouse. "My dear Missus Worthington. She was dead." Adam said nothing more but did allow himself to stare at the woman as if she was a disobedient farm hand and needed to get in touch with reality.

Florence, finding no offense in Adam's brusque manner, didn't lose a beat and presented herself as the higher species. "Ah, but Mister Livingston, perhaps she was dead in her body. But her soul was very much with us." At this Florence smiled broadly and looked about the room as if to watch Esther's ghost float by. Then, staring at the ceiling as if talking to Esther's angel, "Esther is still very much with us."

Florence then turned abruptly back to Adam and lost the smile, as if she were a schoolmarm reprimanding a rebellious student. "And it was with her soul I conversed, Mister Livingston. And it was for her soul I prayed. All. Night. Long."

Adam was not swayed by Florence's theatrics. He straightened his spine, attempting to rise to his full seated stature and gaze down at her as if she were an alien species worthy of study. But she didn't flinch. Her posture remained erect and her gaze steady.

He liked the woman. She ran a good store, kept it orderly and the prices fair while her husband visited and showed patrons where stuff was shelved, stacked, or barreled. Alfred knew what to order for the men; she ordered for the women. But it was Florence who did the bookkeeping. Alfred would rather be playing checkers. She was pleasant enough to look at, but what spunk. He glanced at Alfred who smiled through thin, clamped lips to his friend as if to say, "You picked this battle and I'm in no position to start a civil war in my home."

Adam scoffed. For a moment he was speechless, having gotten no help from Alfred. "Needin' doin' any of that," Adam said to Mrs. Worthington. He decided it was time to change the subject. "Missus Worthington, I do apologize for not having your order for spun-flax ready. As you may know we've had a bit of a problem this week."

"Apology accepted, Mister Livingston," she said, then decided to rub it in. "We could sure use it, but last night Esther explained it all to me." She smiled, underscoring her sorcery.

It was as if God was rubbing it in. But this was his house, his life, and God had taken his wife. He still had two children to watch over. What authority did these friends of his have to bluster about their faith or his lack of it? Faith could not bring back the dead. Oh, but how he wished he could have control over life, death, and the spiritual realm, if it existed.

He pondered. What *could* he control? As the last few hours had proved, he could hardly control his reactions. Did he have dominion over his own life? Did he not have jurisdiction over his home? It seemed he did not. Yet he was determined that he would. He would not be broken like the stalks of his harvest in a flax-break. He would be self-sufficient and as strong as the fiber within, and he would weave a robust and resilient tapestry, regardless of religion.

At that moment the front door opened, and a host of voices greeted a late comer. The new arrival distracted Adam, but it did not distract Florence Worthington. "Esther was a woman of deep faith, Mister Livingston, you know...."

"Aye, so she said," Adam interrupted. He did not want to talk about religion or faith anymore. But at the moment he had no such control over his life.

"Adam!" A sharp, controlled, and polished voice cut through the din like musket fire.

Adam instantly recognized the voice, and he was none too happy about it. His countenance dropped. His eyes slowly closed, and he clamped his lips so tight they turned white. Before turning to the man who had just crashed the party, Adam finished speaking to Florence. "Thank you, Missus Worthington, for your patience. I'll have your spun-flax next week at the latest."

Suddenly, his body jerked forward. Adam turned to greet the lumberjack of a man who had just slapped him on the back as if they were at a pub drinking beer and telling tall tales of hilarity.

Florence and Alfred lowered their heads and turned away from Adam and the gregarious Lutheran cleric, Frederick Brauer.

Brauer nodded at the retreating duo as he shook Adam's shoulder. "Hobnobbing with Presbyterian pagans, I see," he said loud enough for the Worthingtons to hear.

Adam's blood ran black against Brauer. "They are here because they are my friends," said Adam, who had disliked the minister from the first time they had met. Brauer was loud, over-bearing, arrogant, and pious to a fault, both in person and in the pulpit. After two Sunday services he could take it no longer and stopped attending church. "What are you doing here, Frederick?"

"We familiar now, are we? If I didn't see ya at your wife's wake I wouldn't see you at all."

"And why is it that you should?"

"Adam! Adam! There is no need to turn away from faith. Your wife was a saint. And you can be, too. Shall I hear your confession?"

"I need no such fancy. I should hear God's. Or perhaps yours. Where was God when my dear Esther…." But he couldn't finish the thought. "Where were you?"

"God and I have been where we always are. Where were *you*, dear friend?"

Adam scoffed. "Friend?" He gazed across the room at his neighbors, who stood erect in his defense. He thought, they're probably all on their way to hell if this minister has any say. All he heard was the crackle of burning logs in the fireplace. He leaned into Brauer but spoke loud enough for others to hear: "I have no need of you or God."

There was a soft gasp, and then the room fell silent.

"Or, so you say. Adam, harden not your heart. There be consequences."

Adam stared him down, even as he caught a sense of unease among his friends. He was sure they were friends, and not ones to turn aside in a man's time of discontent. But perhaps they were more fundamentalist than he figured, as in "our way or no way." Up until that moment he sensed that they were with him. They were Reformed, Methodist, Lutheran, Church of England, and some, like him, at least as of a moment ago, of no particular faith at all. But with his claim that he had no need of the Almighty he sensed a shift.

Seeing that his time had prematurely expired, Rev. Brauer turned and left as abruptly as he had come.

Watching the man leave, Adam unclenched the fist at his side.

In the shadow of Brauer's exit, the din of the conversations in the room took on a different sound. There was more movement and less chatter. There was a sense of restlessness.

Before long, friends of many years were cutting their stay short, saying their good-nights, and leaving. That it was late and only a moon's sliver lit the roads didn't matter.

Before long only Adam, Eve, and Henry were left alone in the house that became quiet and somber. There were no overnight guests.

Eve's eyes were half closed as she roused Henry from the corner of the room where he had fallen asleep. Adam, not accustomed to putting them to bed, watched Eve lead her half sleep-walking brother up the stairs.

Now alone in the gathering hall, Adam slowly lowered himself into the chair before the fire. A moment later he quickly got back up to stoke the fire. He debated burning another log. If Esther had been here, he would not have hesitated to put two logs on the fire and sit with her on the love seat.

They would talk of the day's events and plans for the next. She would stroke his hand and talk kindly to him of his labors in the fields and tell him about how his children were growing up and loved him.

Often as not, she would show her appreciation for his hard work and lead him to bed. As she caressed him under the covers, she would tell him how she loved him for being a strong man. Then she would kid him about being a stubborn man. But that was good, she would say, because he was stubborn about how much he loved her and relied on her to get him and the family through the day. Then he would take her in his arms, and in his gentle, stubborn, and strong way make love to her. She loved it…at least she told him that. He loved her for saying it. Life was hard, but Esther made it worthwhile.

But that was not going to happen tonight.

He was surprised at the darkness of sorrow that occupied his heart and left him causeless. If Esther had been sick for months…if it had slowly overtaken her…if it had been painful…if it had been a protracted illness…then he could have been prepared for her passing. But none of that happened, and he wasn't prepared.

His shoulders dropped as he rested his elbows on his knees and stared into the mesmerizing embers. A shallow melancholy engulfed him and the room. He wondered, when it was his turn, how would he pass?

He decided the embers, as they were, would last till morning. He climbed the stairs and entered the children's room. They were already asleep, but he took time to tuck the covers around them. He returned downstairs, put on his coat and hat, took up his shillelagh, and drifted out the front door.

5

Feeling very much alone and beat down, Adam walked across his farm to the small grove of oaks that stood guard over the family graves.

There in a clearing was Esther's freshly covered grave, next to the graves of their two still-born children whom they had never named and little Amy's grave. He sat on an old, weathered stool that Esther had brought out years ago when little Amy had died in her sleep. Esther would sit for a while during the week and pray for their souls, and for her own strength. Now, Adam sat on the stool and faced Esther's grave. But he didn't pray. The idea came to his mind that he should rail at the perversity and absurdity of it all.

The thoughts came easily to him. It wasn't that he doubted God's existence, though he often said as much, but rather that God doubted Adam's right to exist. Esther had found him worthy, but God was finding him worthless. If God didn't need him, he could do without the Almighty. Of German descent, he was industrious and stubborn enough to get over "God" and rely on the one thing on which he could trust—himself. He knew how to farm, how to make linen and how to trade and make things work. He was proud of all that and the resourcefulness instilled in him by his father.

He could do just about anything without anyone else. Yes, that was it. At least that is what he told himself. He caught himself gazing at the pile of dirt in front of him and conjured up a vision of Esther standing before him in her white sleeping gown, the moon shining through it, her femininity visible in her delicate and robust silhouette, her long auburn hair blowing in the breeze.

Damn you, God! I sure don't need you or your gifts. Where did that idea come from, he thought? Surely Esther was a gift he had felt he needed, even now. What a beautiful gift. How could he think otherwise?

Suddenly, fear, overcame him. Fear of what? Himself? Of God? Of the Devil? Hell? If there was no God, there was no hell. He was sure of that. Yet, if he was honest, he was fearful of not knowing, especially in comparison to Esther's conviction that there was a God and a Heaven. If Esther was right, then there was no need to fear. But Esther was dead. Did that make her wrong? *Yes, she was dead wrong, and wrong as she is dead,* came the thought.

He let loose and openly cried, knowing that no one could hear him. Oh, that Esther might hear. He had not been taken totally by surprise when their children were born dead. That was sometimes the case, and he had always been prepared. But he was not prepared for Esther's death...at only thirty-eight years of age.

He gasped for air and wiped flowing tears from his cheeks. He repeatedly tightened and relaxed his grip on his shillelagh, trying to get a handle on his predicament.

He thought back to his ride to get Doc Evans, and chasing him down at two other appointments, and then the ride back to the farm. All the time clinging to hope that she would be awake and smiling when he returned. But when he and Doc Evans walked in, her mouth was open, her breath gone, her skin white and cold.

That was when he heard the screech owl.

Doc had swung the warm flame of the lantern above, her pupils dilated, black, unresponsive. He had gripped her hand, but it was cold. She had left him a shed skin, a cold sarcophagus.

Angry and tense, he rose from the stool and glared at her grave.

Screech—the owl again.

Cold revenge pummeled his frame. He flipped the blackthorn shillelagh into the air, grasped the narrow end with both hands and liberated the cudgel knob.

Then, tightening his grip he widened his stance and narrowed his eyes. Slowly he swung the club back and forth, gauging its weight and letting the momentum of the pendulum build. Suddenly, the muscles in his face, neck, arms, and legs went taunt. He reared back, extended his arms, and willed every ounce of adrenaline into his fibrous muscles and *smashed* the loaded knob into the largest of the oaks. He willed the tree to crumble under the massive force of his loathing. But the tree didn't topple...the leaves failed to flinch...though a few flecks of bark flew into the air.

But there was an effect, however. The impact resonated bitterly through the blackthorn grain and shattered his shillelagh into countless pieces that flew into the night, leaving him with a splintered stub. Further, the force ricocheted into his hands, forearms, and shoulders with such magnitude that he was sure to feel the pain for weeks.

Casting aside the splintered stub, he massaged his hands and trudged back to the barn. He was sure the children had not watered nor fed the animals before crawling into bed. Well, they had an excuse.

6

My Despised Cyn:

If we gave out medals for accomplishments, and if you had a chest to pin them on, you'd be loaded, if only temporarily. The last few days might be considered your crowning achievement. What celebration there was down here when Livingston echoed our motto: "Damn...God!" Indeed. No one needs Him. Your work is paying off. Oh, that all your peers should be as successful!

Perhaps, now that your mark seems to be committed to our policy of revenge, we can influence him to drag along his daughter, his son, and a few others.

And what about engineering some lust, greed, and retribution of everything around him. Let's put some icing on this cake.

Now that your mark is firmly within our sights...get your despised spirit down to New Orleans. Your failure at preventing what we feared in the life of Denis Cahill is about to receive some help from your peers. They've been hard at work to up-end advances made by our enemies in the middle of that God-forsaken, devil-inhabited swamp.

Perhaps you can augment their efforts. It is soon to get very warm down there...just like home.

Arrogantly yours,
Master of Broken

Chapter 6
Connected to Eternity

1

March 21, 1788.

A blustery southern gale descended across the northern reaches of the Gulf of Mexico. Sliding into the Mississippi delta, it threaded its way through cypress swamps and strafed sluggish bayous before reaching its destination—the New Orleans stockade. There, it swirled about the quay, rolled a few brigs, tipped a Spanish man-of-war, and jostled dozens of long boats that had brought grain, livestock, and textiles from the center of the continent to this busy seaport. Having announced its arrival, the warm, salty air climbed the bustling quay, veered past *Governor Esteban Rodríguez Miró's mansion, and tore into the open villa windows of *Vicente Jose Núñez, the army paymaster.

Being a devout man, and it being Good Friday, Núñez had lit dozens of liturgical candles before his home altar. The candles had not cost a fortune but burning them was nonetheless unfortunate. Gusts of wind hold a certain authority over candle flames, which early in the afternoon made the short leap from Núñez's altar to the floor-to-ceiling curtains behind. Whereupon, under the authority of the laws of convection, the flames engulfed the curtains and ignited the timbers of the cypress ceiling. Within minutes, the authority of combustion channeled the fire through the ceiling and ignited the cedar shake roof. Because wind only increases a fire's fury, flames vaulted easily from one roof to another.

Two short blocks from Núñez's villa, Fr. Denis Cahill, now a Franciscan Capuchin dressed in the obligatory black habit robe and knotted white cincture belt, was in the sacristy of the *Church of St. Louis. He was preparing to assist Fr. Antoine, their superior, at the Good Friday service with other friar-priests. There rose an unusual commotion in the streets and then in the nave. Fr. Antoine, who had already vested, nodded for Fr. Cahill, still in his black robe, to see what was amiss.

Fr. Cahill was neither tall nor short, but his relaxed disposition, erect posture, open face, and piercing blue eyes gave one the impression that he could see over the heads of most people. His thin red beard and ready smile gave him a youngish appeal that charmed the ladies. He stepped into the nave. A dozen or so parishioners were sitting on benches ready for Good Friday services, but all were looking behind them at the entrance. Outside, citizens were running back and forth on the plaza and screaming. More surprising was the sudden appearance of the stout and rotund Governor Miró who waddled up the side aisle as fast as his stubby legs would take him toward the sacristy. Fr. Cahill met him where the aisle met the south transept.

"Why aren't you ringing the bells?" yelled Miró. "The city's on fire!"

At that moment Cahill recognized the taste of burnt creosote oil on his tongue, and the sweet aroma of smoked cypress. His eyes flew to the south facing windows. There, towering above the prison and guardhouse were the roaring flames of roofs on fire. His chest tightened attempting to restrain his pounding heart.

A hand suddenly gripped Fr. Cahill's shoulder. It was his tall, gaunt, stern-faced superior, Fr. Antoine, officially known as *Père Antoino de Sedella, Order of Franciscans Minor, Capuchins. As the forty-year-old spiritual leader of Louisiana, Fr. Antoine had a reputation of being rigid. After France sold the Louisiana colony to Spain, Fr. Antoine had been sent from the Spanish courts of the Inquisition to New Orleans to regularize the Catholics in the colony and quell their inclination for scandal and sacrilege. It helped that Fr. Antoine's hair was pure white, flatly styled, and crowned a full but shaggy red-grey beard that set off his beady turquoise eyes which bore through whomever he happened to be interrogating.

"There will be no bells, Governor," said Fr. Antoine.

"But why?" Miró asked in a panic.

An elderly sexton with anxious eyes ran up to Fr. Antoine, who glared at the sexton and sharply shook his head, then calmly turned back to Miró. "Why you ask? Because I have ordered that no bells shall ring. It's Good Friday. We never ring the bells on Good Friday. This is a day of reflection and contemplation. It can't be disturbed."

"Forgive my insolence, my Lord, but if the church burns down won't that disturb the reverence?" Miró glared at the prelate. "Damn it. The city is on fire. You must sound the alarm."

Fr. Antoine stood erect, unmoved, his voice deliberate, "Your responsibility is the city, mine is the faith and the church."

"But the people must be alerted."

Fr. Antoine glared out the entrance at the panicked citizens.

"Fire is its own alarm, and it seems as if the citizens are alarmed enough."

Governor Miró was flabbergasted, and so was Fr. Cahill who looked around the nave—everyone had run out to save their homes, if that was possible. *So much for not disturbing contemplative reverence of prayer.* Adrenaline flushed through his veins. Brushing a biting insect from his perspiring brow, he turned to his superior. "Father, we are Franciscans."

Fr. Antoine's countenance softened. The friars knew him to be compassionate, and not interested in the oppression brought about by the Inquisition except to achieve political favors so he could help the poor, those imprisoned, and especially the women and children of African slaves. "Yes, Fr. Cahill, we are needed. Do you know the Louvieres?" There was urgency in his voice.

"Yes, Jean and Dolucila, and their children."

"Then go quickly. They will need help." Suddenly, Fr. Antoine pulled off his vestments and irreverently tossed them aside. "Lead the way Governor. The people will need food, shelter, and drink. Let's get the stores out of the warehouses and onto the Plaza." The two men that were most responsible for the citizens of New Orleans ran out the Church to lead the relief.

In turn, Fr. Cahill ran to the north exit behind the sanctuary that led directly to the friary. His memory surveyed his cell. There was little there—a cot with two blankets, a small dresser for his few clothes, a washbasin, a table, and above it on a shelf his breviary and Bible. On the table some paper, a quill and ink well and some letters he had begun to write to his parents in Ireland. Although there was a momentary feeling of loss as he considered the letters, there was nothing he needed to save. He could lose it all. As he turned a corner that led to the exit, he almost knocked down Brother Luke, the Order's librarian whose arms carried, presumably to safety, a bundle of church documents scavenged from Fr. Antoine's office. Fr. Cahill stepped aside to let Brother Luke exit first and then, tightening the cincture around his black habit, he stepped outside the church and ran toward Royal Street.

To get to the Louviere's dwelling he would have to take one of the three streets that led away from the church northwest into the heart of the colony. But every one of them, St. Peter Street, Orleans Street, and St. Ana Street were packed with citizens and their overloaded carts of possessions coming directly at him. The people flowed around the sides of the church to the large open space of the plaza in front of the church. It was orderly chaos.

Fr. Cahill glanced to his left. Just a street away, the flames ravaged everything in sight and the wind was blowing toward him. That meant the prison and guard quarters, the church and the friary were next to be consumed by the inferno. He needed to move quickly, but the frightened populace blocked his way. There were men and women, young and old, babes in arms, toddlers, and teens, fathers trying to keep their families together, and mothers frantically counting heads. Among all these were Europeans, mostly French, some Spanish, blacks both free and slave, and Cajuns—the French settlers from Nova Scotia who were forced to emigrate to New Orleans when the British kicked them out of Acadia in the Northeast Territories thirty years before.

A chill of dread excitement filled Fr. Cahill as he pressed himself into the counter-flowing crowd along Royal Street which, if he continued in this southwestern direction, would take him directly into the advancing fire.

Because the pioneer city had no fire department, nor even plans for a bucket brigade, the rising flames were quickly plunging the city into hell. Screams of panic filled his ears, while secret stashes of gunpowder exploded more than a few homes into smithereens. Normally a fearless man of strong faith and intelligence, Fr. Cahill's mind ran in circles. What could anyone do at such a time as this? Seminary had not trained him for conflagrations, except for those found in purgatory or hell...that now visited them.

2

Instinctively, he turned right off Royal Street and headed northwest into the city along Orleans Street, his blue eyes focusing on the faces running toward him. He dodged families, animals, children, and the occasional cart. He probably seemed mad, for he was running the wrong way. Such was the life of a priest, he thought, always running into danger rather than away from it, always facing death and confronting demons. He gazed longingly at this mass of humanity in crisis. Was this why he became a priest? To run into fires and risk one's life? He thought about his parents who had shipped him out of Ireland at sixteen when Catholic families were still threatened by Protestant mobs. But here that was not the case. Here there were other dangers: the unforgiving storms at sea, the mysterious diseases that indiscriminately killed hundreds in epidemics, and the mad hallucinatory demonic practices from the islands. As he ran, he saw the results of such dangers—mothers and fathers with no spouses, and even children without parents. Then there were the slaves, ripped from the heart of their villages in Africa—all children of some mother and father, long ago lost but not forgotten.

In two blocks he turned southwest along Dauphine Street toward the tenements where the poor crowded together in apartments they called home.

When he came to the rows of substandard buildings, his heart ached. The fire had spread too quickly, and it was already feeding off these dry thatched roofs. Destruction was imminent—family, home, protection, all gone in minutes, on Good Friday no less. Despair and longing filled him.

Fr. Cahill wept, but the tears were dried quickly by the hot blast of flames that surrounded. He stopped. What should he do?

Then he saw them. Dolucila and Jean, in the doorway of their building. Fr. Cahill shoved his way through the crowd toward them.

Dolucila was a black freewoman from the West Indies and Jean, her husband, a fiercely independent Frenchman from Nova Scotia. Both carried their muscular frames with pride of long, hard manual labor. Jean had once been broad-shouldered and Dolucila was big-breasted and broad-hipped. Defying social norms, they had been married in the St. Louis Church just three years before. Fr. Cahill was taken by their love for each other and how they protected their children in face of the vile rejection by most everyone else in the city due to their mixed race.

He watched as Dolucila ran from their tenement carrying the infant Maria to the safety of the street. But Jean, trying to follow his wife, and crippled with splints on one leg, dropped to the wooden porch in a coughing fit brought on by the smoke pouring from the entrance.

Dolucila turned in panic and in the shrill of her West Indies dialect, "Jean!

Upstairs! The children! *The children!"*

Jean, however, was overcome by smoke, and couldn't climb stairs if he had to. He struggled to breathe as smoke flowed freely out the top of the doorway.

Fr. Cahill was alarmed. Dolucila and Jean had three children, and only the youngest was out of the house. That meant Sabine, one year of age, and Julian, three years old, were still trapped in the house.

He ran to Dolucila and momentarily grabbed her upper arm to let her know he was there. Dolucila looked up with hope to the young, handsome priest; the light of the flames highlighted his wavy auburn hair, chiseled face, and red stubble beard. "Oh, Father! They upstairs!"

Fr. Cahill instantly felt a dark force beckoning him into the inferno. Fear overtook him, even as it drew him into the flames. The children were in the house and needed to be rescued, but to enter the engulfed house was madness. *Oh, but you'll be a hero,* came the thought. *Yes, you may get burned a little, but imagine how you will be celebrated.* The thoughts poured into his consciousness…but they were foreign, alien, and had nothing to do with his sensibilities. He shook them off and prayed instead: *Saint Eustachius, Holy Saint Denis, protect your children and me, not for my glory but for God's.*

Fr. Cahill ran to Jean and dragged him off the porch away from the house and lowered him to the ground at Dolucila's feet. Surprised by his own bark, Fr. Cahill yelled: "Dolucila, get further away. I'll get the children."

Filling his lungs with fresh air, Fr. Cahill placed the edge of his robe over his mouth, ducked into the doorway, under the smoke, and dashed into the flaming structure, his flapping robes teasing the demonic blaze.

The flames had not yet worked their way onto the first floor. The smoke was coming from the downdraft through the house caused by the breech in the roof. While the cypress wood was almost impervious to rot, it was still soft and light in weight and burned quickly, giving off a sweet, intoxicating aroma like pine incense.

Fr. Cahill's heart raced. *This is madness.* But concern for the children drove him to the stairs. Keeping his head below the layer of smoke that poured down, his youthful legs pumped up the narrow staircase. He had been here before. He knew the way, but never at night, never in dense smoke and fire, never in near panic. Was this his calling? Was he ready for this? Is this what he wanted…what God wanted?

On his hands and knees he crawled to the children's room, if he could remember where it was. It was only yesterday that he was in this apartment, but not upstairs. *Have mercy, O God. Are you there? Are you going to help me find their room? Are they going to find air to breathe?*

Then he heard the children's cry. Two voices, a boy calling for "Papa!" and a little girl crying between severe coughs. A smile broke under the cloth that covered his mouth.

Good. He crawled faster and rounded the corner of the room's entrance.

There were the children. Julian, the three-year-old boy, was sitting on the floor calling out. But his one-year-old sister, Sabine, was still in her slatted bed, unable to get below the smoke. She was coughing and gasping for breath. The boy recognized Fr. Cahill and put out his stubby little arms.

3

Dolucila Louviere sat on the ground next to Jean who cried as they watched their home and few possessions burn. They gripped each other's hands, staring at the burning building, pressing little Maria protectively between them. The three people they most cared for in the world, besides Maria, were in their burning home—little Sabine, toddler Julian, and a young Irish priest who had showed them so much love over the last year.

She was surprised when her crippled husband jumped up unable to contain his elation. A black robe like an evil spirit had emerged from the now almost black smoke that surrounded the house. Fr. Cahill dragged Julian by an arm, and in his arms he carried the tiny Sabine, whose burning and watery eyes had already latched on to her mother's.

Clutching Maria, Dolucila ran to hug the children and the strong, courageous priest with the red beard and blue eyes. She took the little girl from Fr. Cahill's arms. "Sabine! Sabine! Are you all right? My precious little girl!" Dolucila checked Sabine all over. She was not all right. She was gasping for air between coarse coughs.

She watched as Fr. Cahill led the boy to his father, who with tears in his eyes had sat back down on the ground and embraced his son. "Julian! Oh, thank Jesus!" Jean looked up to Fr. Cahill with gratitude. "Thank you, Father! Thank you!" Under her breath, Dolucila echo Jean's thanksgivings.

Fr. Cahill said, "Quickly, let's get away from here. Come! Come! We will find safety on the plaza." Dolucila was worried about Sabine, but she knew they had to move before the fire closed off the street. Fr. Cahill led them away from the approaching flames three blocks to the northeast, then turned southeast down St. Philippe Street toward the quay. A throng of a dozen other families joined them. Looking southwest along Bourbon and Royal Streets, the raging fires had burned out and collapsed many a building. The destruction was breathtaking and Dolucila cried. She cried for the families alive but with no homes. She cried for the children that had died, and she cried for the children who were alive but were now motherless and fatherless.

When they arrived at the quay and doubled back to the Plaza, Dolucila was shocked to see that all the structures behind the untouched upwind government buildings had been reduced to ashes. Amidst rising columns of smoke only blackened brick chimneys stood guard like executioners.

Dolucila and her family followed Fr. Cahill to a clear space on the grass. She knew Sabine needed clean air, and where they were now was as good as anyplace, but the turbulent southern winds, which had spread the fire, occasionally wafted smoke their way. Suddenly Sabine began to vomit. The little girl kept coughing amidst her vomiting and crying, and rubbing her nose as if to remove the hot smoke she had inhaled.

She knew that Fr. Cahill was a young priest. Could he pray for Sabine's healing? She wondered if he had ever been in such a tragedy as this. Would it be presumptuous to ask? He was a priest, after all, and priests had special powers, or so she had always believed. She watched him. He was a calm and determined young man, unafraid of entering a burning house. She saw him growing into a great warrior of valor. "Fr. Cahill, you bless little Sabine? Please, Father. Pray for her. You're priest. You know God. God will hear you and heal her," she said hoping for a miracle.

For a moment it appeared as if Fr. Cahill was unsure of himself, as if he despised his youth. He furrowed his brow and cast his eyes down at Sabine. She hoped this kind priest would not say he had never done such a thing or didn't know how. She hoped he was a saint, and that he would miraculously heal her Sabine.

Without hesitation, Fr. Cahill kneeled at Dolucila's side, placed both of his hands on Sabine's little curly topped head, bowed his head, and prayed loud enough for all those around to hear the familiar Latin prayer. Dolucila and Jean prayed with him:

> Ave Maria, gratia plena,…
> *Hail Mary, full of grace,*
> *The Lord is with you*
> *Blessed are you among women,*
> *And blessed is the fruit of your womb, Jesus.*
> *Holy Mary, Mother of God*
> *Pray for us now, and in the*
> *Moment of our death. Amen.*

Hearing the prayer in Latin in the middle of great tragedy gave Dolucila hope. When they had finished the prayer, Dolucila caught her breath and stared down at her little girl cradled in her arms. Sabine was quiet and coughed only slightly. *Was she healed? That quick?* Oh, *thank you, Mother Mary. Thank you, Jesus.*

For a few moments worry and fear left her, but she could not yet feel joy. Little Sabine's face was still pale, and her eyes were not clear and happy as she had been before. Dolucila quickly pulled down her top and offered a full breast to the child. She noticed Fr. Cahill suppressing a grin and turning away. Sabine took the offered nipple and started to suck. Dolucila felt her milk drop and her hopes rise.

At that moment the hundreds of people who had huddled in safety around her became suddenly quiet and still. As she held Sabine to her bosom, she looked up and followed their gaze. The Church of St. Louis, the building upon which the plaza was centered, was fully engulfed in flames. This surprised Dolucila. She knew well that fire was always a danger to settlements like New Orleans because everything, from the structural framing to the exterior and interior sheathing, was constructed from wood. But she had heard from old timers that the church would never burn because sixty years earlier the church had been constructed in an entirely new way by French engineer Adrien DePauger. Instead of traditional construction that used only flammable wood, DePauger built the church walls with stacks of mortared bricks that would not burn. But now Dolucila could see that the six-by-six-foot square sections of mortared bricks were held in place by squared-off wooden beams, and that each wall had been further braced in place by more wooden beams, and that all the wooden beams were on fire.

Yet, what had caught everyone's attention was the bell tower. It was leaning, more and more each second. Its base was frightfully ablaze. She stared transfixed at the rising flames as she anticipated the tower's collapse. In a few moments, it did fall, to the side, like the dismasting of a ship following a volley of cannon fire. When the bell tower fell, everyone heard the bell clang. It was an ugly, muted tone...the first time ever on a Good Friday.

Within seconds, the *coup de grâce*. The interior beams of the Church fell. Then, with no lateral support, the four walls of the church fell quickly in on top of one another. The ground shook, and with it fiery eruptions of embers and debris rose into the air mingled with an immense cloud of smoke and debris that rode the gusts of southern wind to the north. Dolucila sensed the sad pall of the people around her, and for herself—she wondered if she would ever see anything quite so dispiriting. Ironically, she would later discover that the only venerable objects that survived the conflagration were those already dead—the dozen or so bodies of former pastors and politicians that had been buried under the Church in cement crypts.

4

What horror! Fr. Cahill thought, as the Church collapsed in a cloud of sparks, soot, and smoke. If only he had the power to stop a raging fire or to heal the mortally ill—the authority to change people's lives. He imagined the immense good that he could do. But he doubted he had authority over diseases, catastrophes, demons, or death. Maybe the only power he had was over *his* future.

His mind flashed back to when he first arrived in Spain at sixteen, having been sent there by his parents to escape the Protestant persecution in Dublin. They had hoped he would become a priest. Wanting to please his parents, whom he loved very much, Denis was determined to comply.

But he was only there a week when he met a pretty young lady that caused him to question his intentions. They had a whirlwind romance—at least in their minds. They became close in an intellectual sort of way. Nothing physical. But he remembered the spark in Rosette's eye when he stole a glance at her and caught her smiling at him. He would turn away quickly, but she didn't. He recalls the teasing they gave each other about who caught the other looking.

Then came a very sad day when he finally told her his plans—he was entering the seminary to be a priest. He couldn't understand her sadness at first. He looked for her often after that, but she had disappeared. One day, he sought out the girl's mother and inquired of Rosette's whereabouts. With an abrupt and dismissive air, the mother had said, "Rosette has gone to the country to stay with an aunt. Good-bye." With that the mother stuck her nose in the air, turned, and walked off.

After the rebuff, Denis fell into a depression. But once his studies began in earnest the doubts he had about his vocation slowly disappeared. There was something mystical and authoritative about the priesthood, which appealed to his sense of purpose. Going forward, he rarely looked back.

As he looked down on little Sabine suffering, he contemplated his apparent lack of authority over temporal things. He enjoyed being with children. He wondered if he had made the right choice. Perhaps he should have pursued Rosette, married her, and had children. He studied little Sabine. She had not fed at her mother's breast for very long. As the Church walls had tumbled, Dolucila had pulled up her blouse. As the swollen debris cloud rose into the sky, so too had the child's swollen eyes given rise to more crying. The prayer had not worked. He could not imagine the fear that Jean and Dolucila were feeling. Jean was looking up at him as if expecting a miracle. *What could he, a lowly priest, do?*

Fr. Cahill searched the crowd for his superior. Fr. Antoine would know what to do. But no other priest was in sight. At a loss, Fr. Cahill leaned over and stroked little Sabine's back as she heaved and tried to breath. Clearly, her lungs were not right. "Sabine, darling, it is all right. God is with you," said Fr. Cahill.

Jean, sitting on the ground, took Sabine from his wife and held the infant in his arms. He looked up at Fr. Cahill. "She will be well, yes, Father? God will heal her through your prayer?" It was a question, not a statement of faith. "God can do that through you, Father?" Yet another question. "I believe, Father. Is that right, Father? Will our little Sabine be good?"

What could Fr. Cahill do but agree? "Yes, Jean, God will heal little Sabine. Just have faith. God can do anything."

"Yes, but, Father," Jean protested, "it is you. You are Christ here with us. Your prayers are like his. You can heal little children like he did, no?"

"Yes. Yes," said Fr. Cahill. What else could he say at a time like this? God was God, after all, and while a priest was supposedly the vicar of Christ, he was only a priest—a priest with some authority, but only some.

By now a small crowd of other mothers and fathers had gathered to watch the unfolding drama. Sabine's coughs had subsided, her heaves were weaker, as well, but the color in her face was fading.

"Ask the Blessed Mother, Father...again, pray to Mary, Father," said Dolucila.

Fr. Cahill nodded. Again, he laid his hands on the child's curly hair and prayed, this time in English. "Blessed Mother, we ask you to work through me, your Son's priest. Please ask the Holy Spirit to come, visit us, and heal little Sabine...make her well. Your Son has given power to his priests here for a time... like this. We pray to you. We bless you. We ask you to intercede to your Son on our behalf. Hail Mary, full of grace. Blessed art thou among women, and blessed is the fruit of your womb, Jesus. Holy Mary, Mother of God, pray for us sinners now and at the hour of our death. Amen."

Miraculously, when he finished the prayer there was a hush over the small crowd. Little Sabine was no longer coughing, or heaving, or even crying. It was indeed a miraculous thing.

But then Dolucila, who was holding the child, began to weep. They were not tears of joy. It was a long, quiet moment before Jean, Fr. Cahill, and the others realized that little Sabine was not moving. She wasn't even breathing. Sabine had died. She had gone to be with Jesus—perfectly healed. But how could he tell Dolucila such a thing?

5

Fr. Cahill wandered through the crowd of bundled families. Many reached out to him. He gripped their hands and blessed them, although the events of the past few hours had left him dry. He found himself just going through the motions.

He came upon an old woman sitting alone on a bare patch of earth staring seemingly into space. He went to console her, as a son would console a mother. But when he lifted his hand to impart a blessing, she grabbed it, pulled it down, and would not let go. With her other hand she pointed in the direction she had been gazing, and said, "Look, Father!"

Fr. Cahill turned where the old woman pointed. All he saw beyond the people on the plaza was the smoldering ruins of the fiery plague that had wiped out everything in its path. He kept looking in the direction she was pointing, but he saw nothing more. He glanced back at the woman. Tears were now in her eyes. She let go of his hand, crossed herself, and murmured a prayer.

He looked again. Then he realized she was pointing to what was missing— the Church of St. Louis. There, but a few hours ago, he was preparing to assist Fr. Antoine at Good Friday services. It had been the center of the friar's life of prayer and service. Now, it was gone, gutted, destroyed. All that was left were stubble walls and smoking rubble. No sooner had he relived its final collapse, but he noticed that the two-story friary that he had called home just north of the church was gone as well. To the south, the prison and guard house were also gone. Everything from Conti Street to Dauphine Street and from Conti Street past Du Maine Street had been leveled in the wind-swept blaze—eighteen blocks. In three-quarters of an hour, eighteen blocks, about three-quarters of the colony, had been incinerated. Only those buildings that fronted the water—the Customs House, the tobacco warehouses, the Governor's Building, the Storehouse, the Royal Hospital, and the Ursuline Convent—had been saved, most likely due to the direction of the aggravating winds. Sadness and despair engulfed him, and he wept.

Partly in a daze, he crossed Chartres Street to the edge of the Church's collapsed walls and stared in wonder. As dusk settled on a tragic Good Friday, it dawned on him that Easter Sunday was but the other side of Saturday. The catastrophe here was not unlike the original nearly 2,000 years ago in Palestine. The lack of hope he now experienced must have been similar back then.

With all the suffering that surrounded him, what approached from the south, down the middle of Chartres street, was hard to imagine. Naked but for a dirty loin cloth came a bounding and unsteady Cajun. He was screaming wildly, as if arguing with a haunting demon—first there was a cry of celebration, then an equally loud vulgar epitaph. He sounded like two crazed drunkards arguing incoherently, each trying to outdo the other. His arms thrashed about just as wildly at nothing. The brown, sweaty skin of the man's gut and limbs were taut and muscular, probably from a combination of starvation and opium; and his long, tangled, greasy hair resembled a whaling ship's oily deck mop.

Mesmerized by the reveler's antics, Fr. Cahill held his ground. The crazed man stopped directly in front of the young priest and glared; his bloodshot eyes jumped back and forth like an insect caught in a spider's web. As the reveler leaned unsteadily into Fr. Cahill and tried to lock onto the priest's eyes, Fr. Cahill stepped back. The stench of the reveler's breath and body ensured he was safe from malaria—no biting insect dare approach. Silently, as if to gather whatever wits he had left, the reveler scowled at the priest, then turned and surveyed what was left of the gutted church. He turned back to the priest and then swiveled to the ruins again, as if trying to make a connection between the standing man and the fallen ruins.

Suddenly, the man wailed in laughter and mockery unable to contain himself, "'Bout time you whoring papists got your due!" He squared his body at Fr. Cahill as if to attack. His chest and shoulders displayed an elaborate tattoo of interwoven crescent moons. The man cursed into Fr. Cahill's face. "Guess this proves the power of yer goddamned, pissing, black magic, idol worship." He broke into prolonged laughter that was both hysterical and grotesque, his raspy voice taking on the low, guttural resonance of a bottomless pit.

Although a priest, Fr. Cahill was not the forgiving sort. Compassionate? Yes. Forgiving? No. His anger boiled, but discipline cooled. Having learned to give evil space, he stepped back. In Europe he had run-ins with anti-clerics, but this was the first time in Louisiana, the first with a possessed lunatic.

Fr. Cahill studied the man's intricately interlaced, crescent moon tattoos and his perspiring ash-smeared face. The man appeared to have just stepped out of a blazing inferno, except his skin was neither burned nor cut. Clearly, he was mad, perhaps freshly inebriated by a hallucinatory delicacy from the islands.

"On your way to a fire?" said Fr. Cahill.

"Burn in hell, priest!"

"That I may, but it seems you'll join me," Fr. Cahill rejoined.

The half-naked reveler spit in Fr. Cahill's face, laughed grotesquely, coughed up more phlegm, spat at the Church's burnt rubble, then teetered off to play in his sandbox of ashes.

Calmly as he could manage, Fr. Cahill raised the sleeve of his robe and wiped the spittle from his face. He looked for meaning in the encounter. The man's appearance wasn't that unusual for these parts. Drug induced states and demonic trances were common in the islands. Although, in these parts, the vitriol toward the Church was new to him. He recalled how the governor had tried to keep such chaos from the colony, but it was hard to police what disembarked from a ship. Like rats and the plague, dark supernatural forces could also find their way into the populace, and Fr. Cahill worried. The consequences were far reaching.

Fr. Cahill teetered on the edge of despair. He looked at his hands. At twenty-two, he was too young to be shaking. But the combination of the fire, losing the Church and the friary, Sabine's death, and now this drugged-up reveler unnerved him. Had his faith taught him nothing? What had he missed? Was he cut out to be a priest?

His mouth was dry, as no doubt were the mouths of many others. What of the well? It was a deep well and the water was drinkable. Perhaps that's what he should do while sorting out his thoughts.

He crossed quickly to the friary's rubble next to the Church. The well was undisturbed, but he needed vessels. The debris from the friary's kitchen was disheartening, but not too far from the fallen wall were several large copper cannisters. The embers were too hot for his sandaled soles, but he found a stick that was, remarkably unburned. With the stick he knocked the metal containers and some drinking cups to the edge of the ruins. He picked up a cup, but immediately dropped it. The copper was still hot. Going to the well, he retrieved a bucket, filled it with water, and brought it to the hot copper containers and poured water over their exteriors to cool them. Then, after drinking a couple of cups of water himself, he was able to fill the cannisters and busied himself carrying water to the families on the plaza. He found purpose in quenching the thirst of the destitute, and reconnecting mothers with their wandering children.

Fr. Antoine and the Governor had unlocked the storehouse which, being near the water, was untouched by the flames. From it they directed guards and soldiers to bring tents, cots, and blankets to the plaza, for it would be weeks and months before homes could be rebuilt. Owners of the buildings untouched by the fire took in families whose homes were lost. At the far northeast edge of the colony, where the fire had not reached, the hospital and Ursuline Convent were busy tending to the sick and injured. New Orleans would come back, and the builders who had been eager to build with bricks instead of wood would be heeded.

But would the Church be heeded when it was most needed? In his short time as priest he had become both frustrated and disappointed. He was frustrated that the Church's authority, based in natural law and common sense, had been spurned by kings, queens, and those in secular authority. At the same time, he was disappointed that the Church, now and again, refused to abandon human traditions, which while piously symbolic, were ultimately detrimental to a community. He perceived that the latter was the cause of the former. He didn't have a problem with God. He had a problem with the Church refusing to use its authority to do what was right for the common good, thus undermining its authority when it was time for the community to heed a moral imperative.

In short, he would have rung the church bell. Why was the Church content in supplying catastrophe relief instead of preventing or mitigating the catastrophe in the first place?

He thought back to his own family in Dublin who still lived in fear. His mother was probably still secretly a Catholic and his father a tolerant Protestant who, while he believed the pope was evil, nevertheless loved Denis' mother, a papist. Denis had been with his father and his drinking buddies when his father had lied about his mother's religion. Denis learned early that had his father done anything else he would have been mercilessly persecuted for marrying a papist. At the very least he probably would have lost his job at the mine and the family ended up destitute. What authority did the Church have to stop such things or the British penal laws that allowed such a curse? Evidently, none. Yet, the Church claimed to represent the source of power in the universe.

He thought of the hundreds of New Orleans residents who were, at that moment, seeking the docks for safety from the fire, just as he had been told Fr. Killian had sought the safety of the docks in Dublin to board a ship out of Ireland. Most of the people of New Orleans did get to the wharf in time. But Fr. Killian never did, and the Church never even protested.

Growing up he had learned about the Jesuit Suppression. In the last fifty years the Society of Jesus, a religious order of well-educated priests, had become known for their successful plantations in the New World that educated and protected industrious Native Indians from their warring peers. The large haciendas and reductions also served to imbue civilization and a productive work ethic into the native populations while protecting them from swindling foreign merchants and gold hungry European kings. Consequently, Jesuits did not hesitate to be involved in a country's economic intrigue or pronounce God's judgments on kings for taking mistresses. Being educated in France, Spain, and Portugal as

he was, Fr. Cahill learned that many kings resented the Jesuits, not just the order's success, wealth, and property, but the papacy's moral supervision, via the
Jesuits, over their countries. As Fr. Cahill recalled the stories, in 1759, Portugal,
followed by France, Spain, and other sovereign states, gave the papacy a choice:
either the Jesuit order would be suppressed by the pope, with their wealth and
possession confiscated by the states (in payment for their supposed meddling),
or the states would confiscate all Church property. Fr. Cahill was pretty sure
England's Henry VIII had influenced the Jesuit Suppression when he persuaded
the British Parliament, in 1534, to steal from the Church all its property and
holdings and let him head up the new Church of England.

When Fr. Cahill first came to New Orleans, he remembered asking about
the decorative vestments and gold altar vessels the Capuchins used. Such finery was unheard of in Capuchin monasteries where vows of poverty were tak-
en seriously. Fr. Antoine explained that in 1768 when the Suppression hit the
American continents, the Jesuits were forced to shut down the large plantation
just outside New Orleans' western perimeter. There, the Jesuit blackrobes and
their local help prospered. They grew sugar, tobacco, and oranges. As the Jesuits
got on the boat to leave for their exile in the Papal States, they gave their rich
vestments and gold altarware to the Capuchin friars as a farewell blessing. After
their departure and the plantation's failure, the economy suffered much. There
was less to trade, less employment, and the Indian tribes that worked the plantation took to wandering, drinking, immorality, and fighting. To Fr. Cahill, the
Church had capitulated at every turn. In so doing, the hierarchy demonstrated
in practical terms that they had no authority whatsoever. It was no wonder why
evil became ubiquitous in the palaces of empires and the streets of common
society.

If his faith had any meaning at all, something was very wrong. What *should*
he do about it? What *would* he do? He had made temporary vows as Capuchin
but had not yet made solemn vows. That was to happen next month. He wondered what he *could* do.

6

As Fr. Cahill contemplated history past, he considered how little effect the
Church was having on history present. Earlier in the day he had brought water
to the guards who were clearing debris from the ruins of their Guard House
quarters. The capitán had not hesitated to corner the young priest, shoving his
ceremonial halberd against Fr. Cahill's throat.

"Damn priest! I hear about Fr. Antoine. He did not ring the church's bell.
We needed to alert the town, to come and fight fire. But you wouldn't ring bell.
We think you should be hung. What you think? Hey?"

Fr. Cahill had heard the charge, and while it was true that the church bells
are never rung on Good Friday, by his recognizance there was another reason.

Pushing the dull halberd from this throat with his fingers he continued to offer the guards water.

"It is true, Capitán. The church bells are never rung on Good Friday. It is a day of sadness, not celebration. But early this morning there was another reason. Did you not notice? Did you see? Were you there?"

The capitán lowered his intensity. "I wont there. Another told me. He swore you not ring the bell."

Fr. Cahill handed water to the capitán, who took it but did not drink. "And he failed to tell you why. Is that right, Capitán?"

"He not say." Turning to the other guards, the capitán laughed, "What be a reason, priest. There is no."

"If your guard had opened his eyes," Fr. Cahill said, "he would have seen the reason. The church tower was engulfed in flames, and the rope that rang the bell had caught fire and had dropped from the belfry. So, Capitán, if you needed to ring the bell, why didn't *you*? You are a man of authority and courageous. No? Didn't you have an extra rope? Perhaps you should have climbed into flaming belfry to attach a new rope. Hey?!"

"You a liar, papist."

"And you, Capitán, could be excommunicated for what you have failed to do," whispered the priest.

"Ya can't excommunicate a pagan." laughed the capitán. "It fact. You have no authority over any soul. Heh?"

"You may be right," said Fr. Cahill."

It was no use arguing. Fr. Cahill had made his point and so had the capitán. Fr. Cahill ripped the cup out of the capitán's hand, spilling water on his uniform. Fr. Cahill glared at the capitán, temping him to raise his halberd. But the capitán did not. Fr. Cahill left. Others elsewhere were thirsty and would drink.

The more Fr. Cahill thought about it, the problem was clear. It wasn't that God had abandoned people, but that the Church, and by extension its priests, had abandoned their duty, their calling, and their authority…if the Church or its priests had any to begin with.

His spine shivered with the thought. If he could not be sure about the Church and what it taught, could he be sure of anything? He turned to gaze behind as if stalked by doubt. Unconsciously, he brushed flecks of red soil from his habit as if the soil of reality discolored the loyalty of his vows to serve the poor. He blinked at the dirt falling from his robes, watching it mingle with the dried earth under his sandals.

He had promised obedience to his local superior, the pastor of the St. Louis Church, Fr. Antoine. When there was an opportunity he would confess his frustration and ask for advice.

Some had more authority than others, he thought. Charles III, King of Spain, would be glad that he had appointed capable men to manage the colony. When the tragedy struck, Governor Esteban Miró and civil administrator

Martin Navarro were quick to act. They quickly brought stability to the colony, thus protecting the king's investment. It appeared to Fr. Cahill that by nature both men were compassionate, generous, and proactive. They borrowed from the royal treasury, gave money to those that needed it the most, and immediately sent a ship to Philadelphia for grain to avert famine. Fr. Cahill had heard that they had also sent requests up the Mississippi to farmers and merchants to accelerate shipments of needed products like lumber and nails down to New Orleans. The guards erected tents on the plaza for the homeless masses. Within a day, every resident of New Orleans had shelter. Of course, there were several hundred buildings still standing, so families, businesses, the hospital, and the Ursuline nuns took in many. By quick and efficient action, Miró and Navarro knew their authority and thwarted the evil that besieged the colony's gates. Fr. Cahill wished the church could act so decisively.

Of course, the friars elected to stay in tents on the plaza near the ruins of the St. Louis Church so they could be easily found by the populace. But it would be a long time before life could return to any semblance of normality. Mass on Easter Sunday and the months after were held in the open air on the Plaza. Fr. Antoine's emphasis on serving the poor, which now included three-fourths of the colony, meant that clearing the ruins of the church and friary were at the bottom of the "return-to-normalcy" list. Besides, with the occasional hurricane that threatened the colony with high winds and flood waters, it was also important to build a more substantial structure, perhaps one that was fireproof, if that was possible.

Through the spring and into the summer, Fr. Cahill and the other friars were constantly busy. Little Sabine was only one of many deaths attributed to the fire, which included all the prisoners in the jail which no one made an attempt to rescue. Afterwards, however, the rate of baptisms, confirmations, and confessions increased. There were also more communicants at daily and Sunday Mass, as people were reminded of their mortality. When food began to arrive in the colony from the river and eventually bags of grain from the United States, Governor Miró asked the Capuchins to administer the distribution with the able-bodied assistance of the guard. Thus, the friars were occupied for many months with feeding the hungry and general shepherding of the flock as adjustments were made by all to the new, confusing, and often difficult way of life.

Late one afternoon, just outside the grain dispensary, at a provisionally erected three-sided cypress lean-to, Fr. Cahill was confronted by the mother of five children. Madeleine-Rose Seibold was a short woman who more than made up for her lack of stature with the personality of a 24-gun warship. She had repeatedly demanded more than her family's share of the grain rations. Fr. Cahill understood her concern insofar as her oldest was a young man who had just passed through adolescence and alone was consuming as much as the rest of the family put together. But Fr. Cahill also knew the boy was slothful and avoided the restoration work crews who were given double rations. Several times Fr. Cahill suggested her son, Augusta, join a work crew if he wanted more rations, but she would have nothing to do with it.

"You did not give Augusta the fair amount of our allotment when he came this afternoon," the broad-hipped Madeleine Seibold shouted. "I have seven mouths to feed, have you no sense of my need?"

"Madeleine," said Fr. Cahill, "you know that is not true. He received full measure due your family. And for sustaining the lie I will expect you in the confessional tomorrow." He smiled unflinchingly at the squat gunship who had just broadsided him.

"Never mind your own measures," she challenged. "You are required to measure what the governor says. He is the boss, not you. You are but a priest. You must listen to him. You do not make the rules. We have stomachs to fill. We do not care if you want to starve. That is your business. We will enter heaven on full stomachs, which is our right."

Fr. Cahill lowered his voice and his gaze for a moment's reflection. Then he leaned into the woman's eyes and carefully started, again, what she refused to hear. "Madeleine. God is for those with stomachs for him, not for those who believe God must stomach them. You will get no more grain this week. If you want more, since your husband is invalid, Augusta can work like other able-bodied men and earn a greater share."

"That is ignorant, priest. You know Augusta is a bad worker. He cannot do these silly works for others. He is his own man."

"Precisely my point," said Fr. Cahill. "He makes his decisions and is paid accordingly."

She shot back, "You have no authority to do this. We are citizens, you are but a visitor. We are French, you areSpanish. My family has been here for generations. We are important. We must be sustained. God gives us rights and the Church must obey the governor. Give us more."

"No. Go away, Madam. Perhaps God will give you what you believe you deserve at the proper time." Fr. Cahill turned his back on her, his own anger rising.

It was warm, but that did not explain the perspiration that streamed from the pores under his robe. The muscles of his mouth and chin strained against his jawbone. The assumption that the Church worked for the governor caused his bowels to boil.

He had to do something. Working for a church that had little real authority was not what he signed up for. It made little sense that the state controlled and directed the Church's mission. The authority of the state for the temporal good of society was one thing, but when it came to giving society purpose the Church needed to reclaim its role—a role earnestly connected to eternity.

He found Fr. Antoine saying his office in the ruins of the friary. When his superior was done, Fr. Cahill would confess that life as a Capuchin in New Orleans was incompatible with reason. He wanted more authority to see the sovereignty of the Church at work. He had a sense of what he might do, but telling his superior his deepest fears would come first.

7

My Despised Cyn:

I so love a fire. It reminds me of home. Cavorting around the conflagration was rewarding as it ushered so many into Condemnation, and unfortunately a few into Glory. Nonetheless, a luscious time of reward for our efforts. Seeing the church building reduced to rubble, while essentially meaningless in the long run, provides a lasting metaphor for the loss of hope, which hopefully will be decimated in the long run. That's what counts.

I was looking for your contribution to the mess. Nice try to immolate Cahill. Unfortunately, Saint Eustachius and Saint Denis were on duty. Do saints ever sleep? Did you try to personify yourself with the naked Cajun? It did have a resemblance.

We are concerned with Cahill's desire to quit his order. Does he think he can simply walk into the United States? That's a long walk...ah, but perhaps he won't make it. Clever! Recall that it is in our interest to keep him from Livingston. The more this damn priest thinks he can do better in the States, the more problematic our prospects become. You may continue to sow blame about his priestly work in New Orleans, but if he just shifts geographically and not loyalty, then he's just as dangerous.

Perhaps suggesting he ditch the whole priesthood thing. Is there an opportunity to foster lust? That's always fertile ground. Do recall, that Cahill occasionally entertains the thought that he was called to the priesthood by his mother, not the Creator. It may well have been the only option his arrogant parents gave him.

Have you looked in on Livingston lately? The death of his wife is paying dividends. He's desperate. Perhaps he's closer to Perdition than we suspected, although it's a quandary to our intelligence how he gets to Virginia. Do some digging and manipulating to that end. Your future depends on it.

Eternally yours,
Master of Ruinous

Chapter 7
With Gritted Teeth and Bowed Head

1

June, 1788.

With the death of his wife late last year, Adam Livingston was faced with a serious dilemma, and he had but months to resolve it. Although working a small farm made his produce less competitive, thus providing only a modicum of cash to keep the operation afloat, there had been one advantage—no mortgage. If he was diligent he could break even without losing the farm. But with Esther's death, there was a catch.

Eastern Pennsylvania German farmers typically passed down their farms from father to first son, as Adam was. But such inheritance "gifts" were not "free." They had sizable mortgages attached, not with the banks but with siblings. It worked like this: The oldest son would inherit the farm and all the lands associated with it, but there would be a mortgage payable to his siblings if the siblings worked the land under the eldest son's guidance. Until the mortgage was paid off, the eldest was tied to the land and charged with generating its prosperity for the benefit of his brothers and sisters. The arrangement ensured that the land would stay in one piece, in the family, and thus improve its efficiency. Dividing up the land into smaller portions for each of the children undercut the benefit of scale and created less sustainable portions which the water and woodland resources of a larger farm provided. Further, to strengthen the tie between first son and the siblings, the mortgage was larger than the land was worth. This fostered initiative in the oldest, and loyalty among the younger.

But that is not what happened to Adam. When he and Esther were prepared to marry, Adam's father was not prepared to part with his land. Johann Lieberstein was still healthy and had no plans to divest himself of the land, the work, or the sizable flax and linen business he had created. Johann wanted his son Adam to work with him and run the flax processing plant. But Adam wanted to work a farm of his own. A disagreement ensued between stalwart father and stubborn son and nothing transpired at the time.

The solution that allowed Adam and Esther to marry and be on their own came from Esther's father, Aaron Murphy, a skilled Irish blacksmith from York. Aaron had never worked a farm, but he took a side interest in land speculation popular at the time. Over time, Aaron, the thrifty village smithy, had purchased a fifty acre plat of improved land and gave it as a dowry of sorts to his daughter to do with as she saw fit.

From Adam's perspective, the catch was that the fifty acres had been deeded to Esther, not to him. Aaron Murphy didn't trust Germans, or their offspring, and he was not overly excited about Esther marrying one, so Aaron insisted that the property be left only in Esther's name and that under no circumstances was it to pass to Adam. It was intended as her security against the temperamental German Liebersteins, as he saw them. Because Adam's love for Esther was strong, Adam forbore his father-in-law's prejudice. But he could not have foreseen that Esther would have died so soon. Now, with Esther dead something had to be done.

Adam could not easily negotiate the deed because both of Esther's parents had died two years earlier in the *Great Pumpkin Flood along the Eastern Susquehanna River, so-called because of the great many pumpkins that floated away, all the way to the Atlantic. A York judge ended up adjudicating the agreement but refused to change any of the major provisions. Fortunately, the peculiarities of the deed were such that Adam could sell the land and take half the proceeds, while the other half would be divided among Esther's surviving siblings. But the land could never be his. The judge had given him a year to dispose of the farm and move on. He knew it was unfair, but he had no equity, and thus no leverage to negotiate. That was the predicament which caused Adam to sit on a bench and stare into space outside the barn with chickens pecking at his feet. He shuffled his boot in the dirt like the chickens scratching the ground, nervously trying to dig out a rut or path forward that made sense.

He liked the simplicity of the small farm. With a few hired workers he would plant, cultivate, harvest, and process the flax and other goods his family needed. At the same time, however, he had few goods to trade for other necessities that the farm didn't provide naturally.

A small farm also provided him flexibility to experiment with plant rotation and harvesting of flax and other crops that his father would never have allowed. Adam didn't fully accept the German ways of planting or harvesting that his father had brought from Europe. Here the soil was different, the climate was different, and there were new ideas that he wanted to try. His innovations proved successful, and his peers were impressed with the quality of his plants and his yields per acre. Then, suddenly, the love of his life, and the land representing her goodness, was taken from him. He was blindsided by it all, and his shoulders slumped as he watched his chickens peck out a bare existence—an omen.

While the stock of German farmers could be beat down, it could not be trampled. Time was of the essence. He could get more for the land just before harvest than at any other time. Now that the fields were planted, he must act.

After breakfast one morning, he told his children, "I'm going to be gone for the rest of the day."

Henry immediately piped up, "Can I go with you, Pa? Where'ya going?"

"Not today. You need to stay and help Eve. Do you think you'll be able to do that? Will you be a grown-up boy and help do that?"

Henry shed a small tear but nodded his willingness to try. That kind of reaction didn't make Adam feel any better. He looked over at Eve who was busy putting things away, and caught a sad-filled glint in her eye as if to say to Papa, *do you need to go?*

Adam appreciated his daughter's grown-up attitude. But she was not even a young woman. She was still a child of eight, although a very mature one.

He let go of Henry's shoulders, relenting to their sadness. "Let's all go together. Daughter, Henry and I are gonna hitch up the buggy. It may be cold. Get clothes for all of us. If I take both you with me, it will be a longer trip...but perhaps a good one for us to get away."

Eve smiled immediately and wiped away a tear. "Where we goin', Pa?"

It was then that it struck Adam how out of sense he was. Where they needed to go wasn't an hour or two's ride, but a good day or more. To think he was about to set off and leave them for days—foolish man. "To your grandparents in Lancaster. Now, bring some food in a basket and several days of clothes. We'll stay at a tavern for the night. We have a long journey. But before we go, I need to ride over and have a word with Clinton. He'll be watching the animals and Cleopatra while we're gone."

Eve and Henry both smiled as Henry pulled himself into his papa's arms for a hug. Eve put away the crockery, spread out the fire to die on its own, and ran upstairs to help Henry pack for a trip that would change their lives forever.

By late morning Calvin was pulling the covered buggy with the family and supplies along the road due east to Lancaster. Six hours later and twenty-four miles farther, they stopped at a tavern for the night.

The next day at mid-morning they arrived at the mile-wide Susquehanna River. They engaged *Wright's Ferry for twelve-pence to cross the shallow rapids aboard a platform balanced on two large dugout canoes pulled by four surefooted, experienced mules across the river.

Later that day around dusk, the buggy and its occupants arrived at Johann Lieberstein's large farm and flax processing plant just outside Lancaster.

Looking about the farm and plant, Adam could not help but recall how far his father had come. When his parents first immigrated to the New World, they had bartered their Atlantic passage by indenturing themselves as domestic servants until their passage had been paid off in labor. They came as twenty-year-old newlyweds. Johann had brought with him several years of experience as an apprentice in his grandfather's flax processing plant in Germany, and Susan was an efficient young spinner and weaver. Isaiah Smith, the captain of their ship, the eighty-ton square rigged schooner, Grey Pigeon, sold their indentured contract to the owner of a flax processing plant in Germantown, Pennsylvania. It was a quick arrangement, for Johann and Susan both spoke German and knew the flax business.

Although they lived in poverty and squalor for four years, they had been valuable to the plant owner. Just as importantly, the owner had been an honest man and released them from their indentureship as originally agreed.

It did not take long after that, with such experience in both the Old and New World, for Johann to become one of the largest flax growing and processing planters in the colonies. Although other planters sold their harvest to Johann to process, he also owned 2,000 acres on which he grew flax. But Adam recalled that his father was not a very efficient farmer. Johann had rejected the more modern theories of crop rotation and planting a cover crop to keep the land productive year-after-year. When a crop failed from lack of ground nutrients, Johann would fallow the field for a year or two. That is what rankled Adam. The old man would not listen to reason or even look around to what other productive farms were doing.

Lieberstein, like other German farmers in Pennsylvania, saw no good coming from owning slaves. German industrious ideology relied more on motivation by personal accountability than collective tyranny. They believed that prosperity and productivity came from hard work and right behavior. Consequently, it was common to see the owner's family laboring in the fields along with hired day laborers.

After the harvest, processing the flax would take months. But in the late winter the processed flax would be in much demand by textile factories along the East Coast.

Over the years Johann's entire family became expert weavers on looms the family owned for personal and small custom commercial projects. Adam was one of those well-trained weavers, although he preferred field work. He did not like spending his days dealing with the tedium and noise of multiple looms inside a dusty building.

When Adam pulled their wagon up to his father's sprawling, two-story stone house, it was but moments before his father, mother, and Margaret, the one sister still at home and unmarried, ran out to greet them.

But upon settling her eyes on the family climbing down from the wagon, Adam's mother began to cry. At first, Adam didn't understand. But then he remembered. When he and the children had come last year after Harvest, it was the first time that Esther was not with them. Further, he had not written ahead. He and the children just came, in part to mourn. At that time Susan knew there could be only one reason that Adam had come with his children but without Esther. Now the memory of that first visit and the shock of not seeing Esther get down from the wagon returned to haunt her. Susan had loved Esther as one of her own children, and discovering that the undiagnosed illness had taken her crushed Susan's heart. There were too many young women like Esther that had died in recent years.

This time, when greeting his father, there was no bravado as there had been on previous trips. In earlier years Adam's experimentation with combinations of flax seed variations, crop rotations, planting, and harvesting times were reasons to come home and flaunt his success. He was always trying to encourage his father to rebel against the unproven farming traditions of Europe and embrace the newer ideas.

But Johann had been adamant. He had told his son, "Why should I listen to you when I am the rich merchant known throughout the colonies for our linens? You are barely able to pay your bills because you so foolishly ran off. You are the rebel."

Whenever his father went off on such a tirade it saddened Adam, and it took days for Adam to convince himself that his father was just jealous and stubborn. Adam knew that his father's operation could never sustain itself on fifty acres using the old techniques of exhausting the land and then letting it lie fallow for a year or two. There had to be a mechanism to restore the land so it could be profitable every year.

So, when Adam came home this time, it was with gritted teeth and bowed head. It wasn't because Adam was wrong about his farming techniques. No, that was not it. The embarrassment stemmed from having lost the entire operation providentially through this wife's premature death.

Adam knew that had he listened to his father, in all probability he would be closer to inheriting his father's entire operation, which he could then modify to improve its productivity. But at the time he had not wanted to wait that long, nor did he want to wait that long now. His father was far from retiring.

After a late supper, during which the conversation covered the peaks and valleys of the last months, Adam asked his father for time alone. Susan cared for the children and put them in the spare bedrooms. Adam and Johann put on coats and went outside to the porch and sat on a couple of weathered, maple rockers.

Adam had been rehearsing his concession speech during the long trip. Now it was time to deliver. Unable to rock back and relax, he planted his feet on the porch floor and leaned toward his papa.

"Father, I want to ask your forgiveness. The last months, and days…my well has run dry. In my working to gain everything, I have lost everything."

"Ja, 'aven't just lost yer Frau, 'ave you?"

"No. I have also lost all that I have labored for—our farm. Do you not recall the deed?"

"Ja! It was a bad deed, son. Aber Sie wouldn't listen. Yer love fer Esther vas too strong."

"Is that possible?"

Johann thought about that. "Ja. Obwohl, perhaps nicht in your case."

"What?"

"She was yer muse, yer inspiration. I know I have been cold and short with ya before. Reports of yer experiments ut growing an' all were too much to bear. Lookin' for a 'etter way have you? Lo, I 'ave paid attention, 'nd I've heard. Yer a smart lad I've learned, and I'm proud of ya. Ja!"

"Where have you heard? I have never gone to the Philadelphia market as you do."

"Ya. That's true. But thought many times I'd see ya there soon. Reports of your work, much to my bemusement, has gotten around. I'm proud of ya!"

Adam just stared at his father, not believing what he was hearing.

Johann continued. "'Tis reported that yer getting highest return per acre of any flax producer in the country."

Adam was speechless. Rather than his father turning on him, he was being complimented. "Why have I not known this?" asked Adam.

His father chuckled and smiled knowingly at his son. "Ya! Reason is simple. To keep yer price down. If ye knew ye was doing as well as ye were, ye could demand higher prices. They want ye to think you're being outproduced. Buyers want to pay less, not more."

Tears came to Adam's eyes. He had no idea. But then reality hit him. What difference did any of this make unless he was going to come to work for his father and put his knowledge to good use? Yes, that's what he'd do if his father would have him.

Adam composed himself and set about again to concede his failure, at least about the deed, and his willingness to subjugate himself to his father. "Father, would you take me back, let me move here to Lancaster county with my children and work for you? Perhaps I could improve your yields."

Johann rocked back on his chair and smiled, but not in an *I told you so* sort of way. He looked at his son to gauge his sincerity. Then he shook his head *no*. "Son, ye shall not work fer me."

Adam was shaken. He had burned his bridges with his father and now he was lost. What would he do? He took a deep breath and held it, not knowing if he could breathe or not. Anxiety built in his chest. Where would he work or farm? What was to become of his children?

Johann said, "Ye know I've done well. We are nicht the largest flax producer in the union, but ve are nearly the largest. I don't need yer knowledge about how to improve me yield. I already know. Ye taught me…how yer rotating yer crops and yer attention to seeding, son, your secrets are out.

Adam was scared, now. In a flash he recalled talking to traders and buyers at York. He remembered sharing with them what he was doing and what he wasn't. What worked and didn't. As he thought about it, things that had formerly confused him when taking his product to market now became clear. No one ever questioned the quality of his processed flax. He was always able to sell at the highest bid price, though the price was never as high as he thought the product deserved. His quantities were so low and his overall revenue so minimal that he felt lucky to make ends meet.

With a furrowed forehead he turned to his papa. "So, what can I do? I have no farm. I have no place for my family to live. If you won't have me, where will I go?"

Johann stared at his son for a long time, the expression on his face blank, untelling. Finally...

"O! That's easy, son. Gather up yer things and go south to Virginia. There's a valley there that is rich, the farms are big, and the demand for flax and linen is ever on the rise. Ye'll do fine."

Emotionally distraught, disoriented and muddle-minded, Adam said, "Pa, what are you talking about?"

Johann laughed at his son's bewilderment. He laughed so loud that Margaret came out on the porch to see what was going on.

"What's so funny?" asked Margaret. She was holding back a quiet smile as if in on a joke.

But Adam did not get it. He narrowed his eyes at his sister and then tightened his lips and turned again to his father as if he was the brunt of a joke.

Suddenly, Margaret glared at her father. "You, didn't! Papa! That's mean!"

Johann gazed up at his daughter and shrugged his shoulders begging for forgiveness.

She turned to Adam. "He didn't tell you yet, did he?"

If Adam was not already distraught, now he was confused, "Tell me what?"

Margaret sat down on a stool, "All right, Papa. I'm going to sit here until you level with Adam as you did with me." She turned to Adam. "You have alternatives." She smiled and turned back to her father. "Right, Papa? Tell him."

"He may not like it, daughter," said their father.

"He may like it better, Papa," said Margaret.

The father nodded, and then at length explained. Yes, Adam could come back and work for the family business, and rightfully inherit it once Johann decided to retire. If Adam did that, he would inherit the business and land but with the traditional mortgage he would owe to Margaret, provided she continue to work at the farm and processing plant as she did now. This scenario did, however, involve several complications. First, Adam would not be his own boss, and he would not be able to continue all of the farming innovations he had begun. Second, his father was physically robust and would be farming for a couple more decades. Adam didn't want to wait that long to steer his destiny as he had these last thirteen years on *Esther's farm*...that's what he needed to call it now. Third, Margaret was betrothed to Johann's top supervisor, Paul Heller, and there would no doubt be some competition and perhaps conflict between Adam and forth coming brother-in-law should Adam return to the business. Fourth, when his father retired and Adam took over the farm, he would take on a large mortgage which he would pay to Margaret as long as she, Paul, or their children worked at the farm.

Most of this Adam knew but let his father outline the major points; Margaret filled in the details. Coming back to work for his father and eventually take over the operation was his right, his birthright. If he refused, as he had done once before, the operation would pass to Margaret, and then she would owe to Adam a portion of the property's income but only if he stayed and worked for her, which was not going to happen. If he left home, he would forfeit the birthright. The more Adam listened, the more he wanted to get away. It was a strange feeling and made no sense. Here his father was explaining how "all this could be yours" someday, and it felt like a premonition, an evil one, without the strange visions or sounds. The more they talked the more it all sounded like the quivering of bat wings. He could not imagine submitting to his father's way of thinking for the next ten years or longer. The alternative was to move out west where land was cheap and the opportunity perhaps cheaper. His life, again, felt cursed. Evidently, Johann recognized Adam's lack of enthusiasm for reclaiming his birthright. Adam noticed that Margaret was enthusiastic about Adam's lack of it. Made sense.

Without much hesitation Johann started in on the alternative, although Adam had his doubts. *It was in Virginia of all places.*

Like so many others, Johann Lieberstein had dabbled in land speculation. Unknown to Adam until now, his father had purchased 350 acres of farmland in the rich Shenandoah Valley to the southwest, in Virginia. Johann owned the land free and clear, but had never visited the place. Supposedly it was rich, virgin farmland, unimproved, and adjacent to a major creek or small river. Johann offered his son a deal, which Margaret was anxious for Adam to take. Johann would sell Adam the land at a favorite son price…in a roundabout way. Using the land as collateral, Adam would acquire a mortgage from an investor or bank and pay off his father in a lump sum at the time of sale. While this carried a financial burden which risked the farm's success, especially sight unseen, the advantage was that Adam could develop the farm from scratch however he saw fit. The disadvantage was that if Adam defaulted on the loan, due to bad crops or his own incapacity, the bank would own the land, not anyone in Adam's family.

When his father was done with his pitch, along with commentary from Margaret, Adam was dazed. He felt some excitement at the prospect, but there was a great tension in his gut. That the Virginia land was *unimproved* meant there was not even a squatter's cabin present. *Was the land really farmable? Was it cleared of trees? There was a creek, but could it be used for irrigation? What did Paul think about either of the plans? If Adam took the first option and worked with his father, could he and Paul work together? Or was Adam better off going southwest by himself? Did Margaret and Paul want to go southwest and leave him here alone? What did his father want? What did Margaret want? Most importantly, what did he really want?*

That evening, Adam took Henry for a ride on Calvin around his father's farm to contemplate his future. He was no longer young. At forty-nine, starting a new farm from scratch would not be easy. He had married late in life, his children were younger than most, and while the prospects of moving to Virginia seemed intriguing, he was unsure what moving to the Shenandoah Valley would mean, although he had heard it was exceptional farmland. Would he be required to hire slaves to work the new farm? Virginia was a slave state, unlike Pennsylvania. Would he need to get remarried, in essence taking on a new partner to run the house and raise and educate the children? He had his doubts about that. While he had cast God aside, Esther was still fresh in his heart.

He and Henry stopped at a pond to water Calvin and explore the rocky bank. He picked up a stone and skipped it across the water showing Henry how it was done. Adam had not lost his touch. The flat sandstone skipped so far it slammed into a rock on the far shore and exploded into pieces. At that instant Adam was stunned by an image that likewise exploded before his eyes. It was a family sitting down to dinner, but it was a strange dinner. Everyone was eating from bowls of pale blue flax petals. They were stuffing them into their mouths and reaching for more. The faces of the family, which he could not make out, were smeared with blue powder as the petals rubbed off on their faces. There was also a weird sound like they were chewing on something crunchy. The vision was a premonition like he had had many times before. But what did it mean? Usually his visions foreshadowed something bad which was to happen in the future. But what could devouring blue flax petals mean? The image gave him the impression that the flax market would be glutted and they'd have to eat flax pedals to survive. That didn't make sense. But how could an abundance of flax be bad? He wondered what the petals tasted like. But he wondered more why these visions came to him.

"What's wrong, Papa?"

"Oh…I guess I was just getting a little hungry."

"But we just ate. You looked like you had seen a ghost."

"No. No, nothing like that," Adam said.

"But your face is all funny looking."

"What do you mean?!" asked Adam.

"You were smiling, then frowning, then smiling again," said Henry. "It was scary."

Adam smiled at his son and laughed to himself. A larger farm in the fertile Shenandoah Valley would be challenging, he decided. He wondered what his first flax harvest would be like. He could not deny there could be opportunity, although the mortgage he'd be taking on was sobering. He had never had such a debt. Many others did, but many others also lost their farms because of it. Then again, it was possible that the land in Virginia might help him achieve a long-sought goal. He longed for the flax he brought to market to be of such a high-quality that it would be *his* crop that set the season's premium price, not a competitor's from a larger but inferior crop.

Adam thought about a second goal that was related to the first. The Shenandoah farm might allow him to prove to himself and others what Esther had long teased him about. She was always thanking God for the success of the farm. He would tell her, "It's not God, it's our hard work. It's the testing and seed trials I do. It's the right crop-rotation. It's our self-discipline to get up before dawn every morning so we have time to till, plant, cultivate, harvest, and process our crops. It's us being responsible for everything. I ain't waiting on God."

Now, with Esther gone, sad as it was, a new farm was an opportunity to prove to the world, if not to Esther *in absentia*, that his success had nothing to do with religion, faith, or God. Esther would often refer to the realm of the supernatural where good angels and evil demons slugged it out for our souls. She'd claim that the farm was but a pawn used to influence our decisions. To Adam that was all poppycock. Farming had nothing to do with the supernatural. Proving that on the lush virgin farmland of the Shenandoah Valley could be worth the effort.

As he hoisted Henry up into Calvin's saddle, two other goals came to mind. He very much would like to leave a debt-free working farm to Henry, and for Eve, to teach her how to weave like her mother. Not that Adam knew exactly how that was done. Yes, he had learned the mechanics, but what Esther did was an art—a mysterious art.

The next morning Adam talked again with his father and Margaret. He told them he would move south and buy the land his father owned in the Shenandoah Valley. It was definitely closer to home than moving out west to Ohio.

Riding into Lancaster, they paid a visit to Johann's bank. The loan officer Johann knew was willing to deal with Adam, and postdated the agreement for October when Adam would move to Virginia. Once there, the Lancaster bank would sell the indenture to a Virginia bank, which would hold the mortgage and to which Adam would be indebted. Johann agreed to sell the Virginia property to his son for 1,000 pounds sterling, which was a modest twenty-five percent over what Johann had paid for it. The bank estimated that the property was currently worth close to 1,800 pounds sterling and more by the time October rolled around. The amount gave Adam pause, but the bank agreed that the loan could be paid back over ten years, at five percent interest. The annual payments would be about 120 pounds sterling. It still sounded like a lot, but Adam realized he could modify the terms as they went along, since the land was valued so much higher than his loan would be. At worse he'd just pay the interest, which for the first year was about fifty pounds sterling.

Adam left the bank with his father's quit claim deed to the Shenandoah property and an indenture dated six months hence (October 1, 1788) when the sale would commence. Until then he had to put the York farm in order, take in the harvest, find a buyer, execute the sale, and pack up his belongings.

He wondered if George Eshelman, his York neighbor, really did want Esther's farm as he had so often hinted. He would find out.

2

Friday, October 10, 1788.

Eighteen years ago, this fall, on the fifty acres deeded from Esther's father, Adam and some friends tore down the claim shack that no one had ever lived in, built a two-story frame house, and erected the pole barn. Then came the happy day of his marriage to Esther on December 1, 1770.

But that era of his life was now over. He had decided to move to Virginia with the remnant of his family. Esther would remain behind in the quiet glen, her grave next to the three other graves.

Those were sad times. He had wept bitterly for days after each of his children's burials. But nothing had compared to the day Esther died. Her passing had kicked him in the groin and purged his soul of hope. Her freshly covered grave, within eyesight of his farm work, was a daily distraction. For weeks after her death a simple glance at her grave would bring tears, and often after the kids were put to bed he would sit by her grave and grieve.

Each morning he was grateful for his eight-year-old daughter, Eve. For it was she, so much like her mother in disposition, who incited him to do what farmers had to do. Her seemingly inexhaustible energy and initiative even motivated lazy Henry, at age six, to get his hands dirty mucking out barn stalls. Henry hated work, but he hated more the wrath of his older sister.

The days, weeks, and months passed, as Adam, Eve, and Henry, with the help of many day laborers, brought in the harvests and set the farm aright for its next owner.

As he labored in preparation for the move, Adam recalled the years of experimentation with crop rotation to maximize his yields. He had divided his forty tillable acres into four oddly shaped parcels through which he rotated his crops. In early April he had planted a crop of flax in the parcel he called Creek Field that was situated mostly along the creek. Harvested in July, the flax was processed for its fiber throughout August and early September. He had taken the fiber bundles to market in late September, selling them to spinners and weavers. Normally, he would have held back some for Esther, but not now. As soon as the flax was mowed and cleared his laborers immediately planted buckwheat in the same field. The buckwheat would replenish some of the nutrients removed by the flax. The buckwheat would be ready to harvest in early November, but it would not fetch much at market, so its value was more as a cover crop to replenish the soil.

Chestnut Field was named after the seven chestnut trees at the south end which provided the family with nutty snacks and several bushels to sell at market. It had been planted this past year with oats, which were mowed, threshed, and winnowed in August and taken to market in September along with the flax. While he was at market, his laborers had gathered up the oat straw and baled it for winter bedding for barn animals should the next owner need it.

In Fence Field, which was along the split-rail fence, Adam had planted a crop of cover clover for grazing.

Granite Field, named after a granite boulder too large to move, had been planted with equal amounts of turnips and sweet potatoes. Now, at the beginning of October, they had just finished harvesting and taking to market what they could.

As was true every year after going to market, Adam was flush with cash. But this year he only took payment in gold, not the state's paper currency or trade credit. He was moving to Virginia and Pennsylvania money would depreciate as soon as he crossed the border where only Virginia money would be in circulation. Gold, on the other hand, was good anywhere.

George Eshelman was Adam's neighbor, a good farmer who worked 220 acres adjacent to Livingston's property. For the last five years George had been after Adam to sell the fifty acres to him. George had even offered to hire Adam to work the larger combined farm as a supervisor. But Adam was his own man, as was George. Eshelman, a man in his early forties, worked the land that had been granted to his father by some long-forgotten British earl in exchange for some long-forgotten political plot hatched years before in England. George's light-hearted temperament complimented Livingston's melancholy and the two men liked each other. So, when Adam and the children had returned from his father's last June, Adam was quick to pay George a visit and begin negotiations. George was all too happy to oblige.

There was some legal stickiness that Adam wrangled through the courts with the help of Frank Sylvester, a barrister from York. Adam wanted to separate the sale of the land from the sale of the buildings, livestock, implements, and the remaining harvest of buckwheat. He had argued that the original deed, in Esther's name, was only to the land, and it was only the land's value that should be split between him and Esther's estate. Adam, at his own expense and effort, had constructed all the buildings that were on the property, built up the livestock herds and flocks, and had made most of the implements. Thus, Adam was allowed to retain one hundred percent of the revenue from his contributions to the land's value, thus maximizing the revenue he would take to Virginia. As expected, there was some wrangling over the value of the various assets but in the end the deal was done. Eshelman would pay the Murphy estate the half of the land-sale due them, leaving the rest to be paid to Adam.

Mid-morning, George arrived by horseback with a heavy leather satchel. With him, Adam walked about the property and buildings and reviewed the various buildings' contents and implements that came with the farm's sale. An hour later, Frank Sylvester showed up in his carriage driven by a coachman who also served as Frank's security. Eve appeared and offered to care for Frank's gelding and let it graze with George's horse. The coachman undid the horse's harness and Eve confidently led it to the corral. Adam then invited George and Frank into the house to finalize the sale.

It felt strange for Adam to climb the porch steps for the last time and enter the almost empty house. Housewares had been carefully packed in wooden crates. The furniture, including the loom which had been dissembled and wrapped in blankets, had all been packed into one of the two Conestoga wagons standing in the yard with hired drivers and mule teams. There was also Adam's freight wagon that he had covered with canvas over a frame of hickory bows in which the family would ride with food, camping gear, tack and saddles. The freight wagon would be pulled by Calvin and Luther. Their milk cow, Bethany, was be hitched to the rear of Adam's freight wagon. Pickles and Sizemore, their pony and paint, good pals that they were, were tethered together at the rear of the front Conestoga wagon on short leads, and the two drivers' personal horses were tethered to the rear of the second Conestoga.

As Adam, George, and Frank entered the gathering hall, they removed their hats but kept on their coats, for it was cool now that October had arrived. Most of the heavier furniture, like the table in the gathering hall, would remain behind. It was at that table, the one Adam had made for Esther and on which she had been laid out, that Adam, George, and Frank sat down to finalize their agreement. As he sat at the table for the last time, Adam's emotions and memories were awhirl, for this table had been witness to eighteen years of his life, thousands of meals with his young family, and Esther's death and burial.

Nonetheless, Adam looked forward to this final act on the York property that would spirit him away on a new adventure. As terms of the sale, George Eshelman would pay Adam Livingston in Spanish gold escudos, which ranged in denominations from half- to eight-escudos. The two-escudo coin was the common gold doubloon. The one-escudo was equal to the Spanish silver dollar, or piece-of-eight, the most common and stable coinage in the colonies and now the States. Adam wanted little to do with the various paper notes or currencies that each state had been issuing. Each note had a different underlying value relating to the British pound sterling, which was the de facto reference for currency. But without a federal monetary and coinage policy the value fluctuation of the paper currency was volatile. Many thought the paper money would be soon worthless like the Continentals, which had been issued to finance the war and most recently had been used for fireplace kindling. No, it was gold that he wanted. In a pinch he could always melt down the Spanish gold into bullion and ensure that it would retain its value.

From a leather satchel Frank produced four copies of the indenture sales agreement and the deed, three newfangled fountain pens, and a small wooden box. "Gentlemen, here are the indentures for the sales agreement and the deed. Adam, you've agreed to sell your fifty acres, buildings, implements, and this house, and your livestock, et cetera, for 550-pound sterling to be paid in Spanish gold. Is that correct? Here look over the inventory." Frank handed copies of the bill of sale to Adam and George.

Adam took a few minutes to look over the inventory and terms. "Aye, this is right. I agree."

Frank continued, "I've taken the liberty of reconstituting the deed according to current statutes so that it corresponds to recent state and county requirements. Please examine these copies, especially the description and map of the surveyed land, and the payment terms. Once signed, each of you will retain one copy of the signed sales agreement and deed, as will my office. I will file the fourth copy of both with the York County Land Office. They will, in turn, issue to you, George, a patent giving you clear title to the land. There are no mortgage terms, this being a cash sale to which you have both agreed."

Adam didn't study the map as closely as George. Their lands were adjacent, and the land had been surveyed and marked with iron stakes only recently when both men were present. As they studied the documents, Frank opened the wooden box and set up a portable balance scale with calibrated counterweights.

Seeing the indentured agreements, the deeds, and the balance scale Adam had a flash of seller's remorse. His face tightened and he was a bit surprised to discover he was holding his breath. He wondered if he was doing the right thing. It wasn't as if he hadn't thought about this moment day and night for the past few months. It took him a long time to get to this moment, especially since he wanted to bring in the harvest. But the time had come. It was now or never.

Taking a deep breath and shaking off the moment's tension, Adam signed the four copies of the two documents, as did George. Finally, Frank witnessed the signatures with his own. By now Eve and Henry had come into the room and stood behind their father watching the transaction.

George produced the large satchel he had brought and had protectively carried around the farm. Unfastening the straps from one of the satchel's compartments, he poured onto the table a large pile of Spanish gold doubloons. From another compartment, he dumped a smaller pile of half-escudos, also known as quarter-doubloons.

Meanwhile, Frank performed a few hand calculations on paper. "Mister Eshelman, the 550 pound sterling is equivalent to 733 and one-third doubloons. Let's start with the 733. If it's agreeable to Mister Livingston, we won't weigh every one of your coins but a sampling. If you'll create stacks of ten coins each, Adam will select at random a selection of those stacks, and we'll weigh each until Adam is satisfied. We'll need seventy-three stacks of ten plus a stack of three. Each stack should weigh two troy ounces and just under two-tenths. Let's see how close we are."

George began making stacks of ten doubloons. Meantime, Frank set up his scale. In the right tray he placed a two-ounce counterweight and a tenth-ounce counterweight. "Ten doubloons should weigh in at just over two ounces plus a tenth," Frank said. Adam selected the first stack of ten doubloons and slid it to Frank who placed them in the left pan. The scale tipped to reveal that the coins were slightly heavier than the two and a tenth ounce counterweight. "Excellent," Frank said. "That is exactly what we should expect. These ten are respectable coins. Adam, pass me another stack."

Frank repeated the test for a total of ten stacks of coins all with similar results. "Frank," said Adam, "I'll accept the rest as equivalent to these 100 coins we've tested."

"Good. Then please, with George's assistance, ensure that you have a total of 733 coins, and place them in front of you. Then we will continue."

Adam and George counted for a few minutes until Adam was satisfied that he had in front of him 733 authentic gold doubloons. During that time Frank made a few calculations on a piece of paper.

"Now," continued Frank, "the one-third doubloon is equivalent to five shillings. Do you have that separately, Mister Eshelman, or do we need to cut a doubloon in thirds."

Frank smiled, "Yes, I have that." Frank produced his pocketbook and counted out five shillings and pushed them across to Adam. George then removed the extra and unnecessary coins he had brought, putting them in a smaller bag he produced from the larger satchel.

Frank tallied the number and denomination of the coins on the bill of sale that George had presented for payment. Then, Adam and George witnessed the tally with their signatures.

Frank continued, "Now for the Murphy estate we need to take fifty percent of the 500-pound sterling for land sale alone, which is 250-pound sterling or...," Frank stopped for a moment to make calculations. "Three-hundred, thirty-three and a third doubloons, from those in front of you, Adam.

Adam objected, "You mean I can't keep all this?"

Frank, the barrister and bean-counter that he was, didn't see the humor. "No, Adam, the terms of your...."

But Adam interrupted. "Frank, just kidding. Although it would be nice to keep all of this." Adam laughed with George, but Adam took note that Frank didn't even smile. *Okay, no more jokes with the barrister,* he thought. Here you go, Frank, you have someplace to put these?" Adam began to push across the table thirty-three stacks of doubloons, plus the five shillings.

Frank double-checked the count and carefully placed them in a large pocket of his own satchel. Meanwhile, Adam double counted to ensure there were still forty stacks of ten still on his side of the table.

Frank made more notations on the bottom of the bills of sale, and had both Adam and George signed the documents. Frank then placed the Murphy funds in a leather pouch, made sure Adam and Frank had their copies of their agreements, packed up his scale, and returned everything to his large satchel. "That's it, gentlemen. Mister Eshelman, the land is yours. Adam, the gold is yours. Just one more thing. My fee." From his satchel he pulled two bills, one for buyer and one for seller. "As discussed earlier my fee for this is a flat ten shillings split between you; six shillings credit, five shillings currency, or four shillings cash which is a gold quarter-doubloon."

Adam opened his pocketbook and dug out a quarter-doubloon as did George and slid the coins across the table. Frank signed the bills paid, gave them receipts, and pocketed the gold.

"Thank you for your business, gentlemen," said Frank. "Take care of what is rightfully yours, both of you."

George then pushed across the table the now empty leather satchel in which he had brought the coins. "Here, Adam, take this pouch with the coins. You'll need something substantial. I've used this when I've returned from market. You'll note that the pouch when closed and sealed with these straps is impervious to most things except liquid, and there's an extra pocket on the side for documents. So, for your trip south put this at the bottom of a barrel of grain or fruit. Thieves will never look for it there should such an unfortunate event occur."

Adam smiled and took the pouch. "I'm much obliged, George. I must admit I had not considered such a thing." Adam put the coins into the pouch, as well as his copy of the sales agreement, the deed, and Frank's bill in the side pocket after George demonstrated how to lace the satchel tight.

"Dust won't get in there now," said George.

Adam, holding the satchel close to his chest, exchanged pleasantries with George and Frank as he walked them out the front door. Frank's coachman had already harnessed up the gelding after its rest and feeding in the corral. Frank got into the carriage, shook hands with Adam and George one last time, and the carriage trotted out of the yard.

George turned to Adam. "Well, my friend, all is in order that I can tell. I want to thank you muchly for this opportunity. I'll take good care of your land, I will."

"Yah. Yours now. You've coveted it long enough, Mister Eshelman," said Adam.

George chuckled. Adam had shown his respect for their friendship all these years by calling him "Mister," a title that George had repeatedly told Adam was unnecessary. But Adam respected George and was glad to leave on good terms. One never knows what may lie in the future and good friends in old places may be needed.

While George visited with the two Conestoga wagon drivers, Adam, still holding the satchel close, took a quick last tour through the house. Over the last few days two of his day laborers had helped Adam pack the three wagons for the trip south. There was one thing he had not packed but had kept hidden in his bedroom. Making sure everyone else was out of the house, he shut the door to his bedroom, shoved the bed frame he was leaving behind a foot from the windows, loosened a now accessible floorboard, slid the board aside, and lifted out a metal strong box. It was here that Adam had kept the bulk of his cash most recently from his trips to market, as well as other currency and his all-important accounts ledger. Kneeling on the floor behind the frame, he opened the box. Seeing the glimmering gold gave Adam an instant feeling of satisfaction, but he didn't linger. There would be time later to enter the day's transaction in the ledger, count the money, and reconcile the accounts. He quickly transferred the gold and the residual currency and coin along with the ledger book into his new robust satchel George had given him. Holding the now empty strong box and much heavier satchel in one arm, he stood up, pushed the floorboard back in place with his boot, and heaved his hip against the bed frame to slide it back in place.

As Adam descended the stairs, he patted his coat pocket for his pocket-book. It was there, and no doubt had enough coin to get them to the Potow-mack, if not Smithfield. So, he could take George's advice and put the satchel at the bottom of a fruit barrel in his wagon.

He was about to step out the front door and leave the house for the last time when Eve ran into the house and launched herself up the stairs. "Eve? What doing?"

Henry jumped onto the porch at that moment. "Papa, the men say they're ready. They say everything is secure and the teams are ready. Are you?"

Adam looked at his son as if he'd never heard him talk like a grown-up before. Then he turned his attention back up the stairs.

"I be missing you already, now," said George.

At that moment, Eve came down the stairs carrying a small crate with a cloth thrown over the top and Cleopatra sitting on top of it all. "What that, Daughter?" Adam was surprised at the crate and the cat, having assured him-self that the house was empty of all their goods. But Eve kept on going with the crate and slid it into the back of the covered freight wagon. Cleopatra sensing the import of the entire affair jumped readily into the wagon and found a cav-ern between crates in which to curl up. "Eve?" Adam walked after her, finally helping her slide the crate into the back of the wagon and securing it. He lifted the cover, "What is this?"

"Mother's table coverings we never used."

"But we have trunks full of..."

Eve interrupted him. "These are special. She saved these apart for special occasions, do you not recall the embroidery?"

Adam couldn't remember. "Where were they then, that only now...."

"I had stored them at the back of the storage nook between my bedroom and the eaves, do you remember it? They were the ones I helped her spin and weave, and she told me to keep them safe for when I was older."

Adam was taken back. He had forgotten about the "hole in the wall" and these special linens. He pricked his memory of how much Eve had become like Esther, and how Esther had left Eve a dowry that could not be replaced. "In-deed, Daughter. I am very glad you remembered."

Eve crawled through the canvas opening into the back of the freight wag-on and further straightened and secured the crates and barrels of housewares.

Adam checked that the rear drop-down table he had rigged at the back of the wagon with iron hinges and chains was secure and roped off so nothing would fall out. Then he pushed his son around the side of the wagon and toward the driving bench. "Okay, Henry, get up there."

Adam checked the harnesses to Calvin and Luther, went back and chatted with the drivers of the Conestoga wagons, checked on Pickles, Sizemore, and Bethany, and marveled at the two four-mule teams that would pull their belongings in the Conestoga wagons to Virginia. Until three years ago there were no mules in the country. In 1785, King Charles III of Spain made George Washington a gift of two male and *two female sought-after Andalusian donkeys. One of the males died on the voyage from Spain, but the remaining male was bred with female horses. These mule-teams were the second-generation result—half horse, half donkey. Strong, smart animals that could go days without water and eat very little, and you could graze them anywhere. He was excited to have found these teams for the journey.

Adam mounted the front seat of his freight wagon, the smaller of the three, and sat next to his son who held the reins. He checked his rucksack, his Brown Bess musket, and his Kock flintlock pistol: all were secure and hidden just behind his driving bench, along with a powder and ball case. His new shillelagh was handy and stuck in the sideboard where it could be quickly retrieved.

In the back of the wagon Adam opened the apple barrel, dumped the apples into a canvas pocket that had formed over several crates, laid the satchel into the bottom of the barrel, and asked Eve to replace the apples.

Crawling back onto the driving bench and ensuring that Eve and Henry were present and accounted for, he released the brake, gave the reins a stiff snap, and Calvin and Luther pulled the wagon out of the yard for the last time. The Conestoga wagons followed.

George yelled after his friend, "God with you now." But Adam just smiled and waved off the blessing.

It would be a short day of traveling before they stopped in Newport for the night. Maybe there, he'd have time to balance his ledger.

3

My Despised Cyn:

Finding ways for humans to distrust each other is always a joy. I hope you took note of what those that came before you were able to arrange. It was deliciously devious that Esther's father never trusted Adam or his father, Johann Lieberstein, when in fact it was Aaron Murphy, Esther's father, who was duplicitous. For it was his pride-filled refusal to put the 50 acres in Adam and Esther's name that restricted Adam from expanding his farm or selling it at an advantage. Now, under duress, the price has been reduced. Bigotry and lies alway has a way of diminishing returns, which rends relationships. Whenever and wherever you can, try to do the same.

I am glad that our Future Intelligence was accurate; so often it is not. Our agents are so Machiavellian; they'll say anything to appear in control. The plot of land, as you now know, which you arranged for Cain to steal from Mayfield, is part of the Johann Lieberstein land grant to his son. That means your work is about to converge and bear rot, though our adversaries might hope for fruit. Feel free to imbue in Livingston the worry so prevalent to our kind, but consider the benefits to yourself and your peers of him arriving safely, until at least he is able to uncover your confinement.

Congratulations, too, for triggering Eshelman's absentmindedness about what's in that satchel. It should prove to our advantage in a short while.

Eternally yours,
Master of Woebegone

Chapter 8
Papists, Thieves, and Scoundrels

1

Adam was used to making long-term goals, but some gave him pause. He sat on the driving bench holding the reins as Calvin and Luther pulled the wagon. He hoped they were up to the journey. Indeed, he hoped *he* was up to the journey. He liked challenges, but his arms and legs weren't always in favor of what his head told them to do. He anticipated forging rivers, outsmarting thieves, and keeping his children out of danger. His heart sped and slowed as his mind flopped to and fro. The weather wasn't cold, but he shivered, nonetheless.

When they arrived at Smithfield, what then? It was unlikely there were any structures on the property. Would there be tillable land, or would it be rock strewn? Would there be tree stands for building a home and barn? If not, how far away would he need to transport hardware and lumber?

All he could do was to slap the reins now and then and keep the beasts on the road—one hoof in front of the next. He tried to relax and keep an eye on Henry, half afraid his rambunctious son would fall off the wagon...and be happy about it. And Eve? She seemed to be his salvation. Stalwart like her mother, he glanced at her in wonder. She returned his gaze, stoic like, never perturbed. Taking each mile as it came. He was grateful. "Are you content, daughter...that we are finally on the road to a future?"

She looked at him wondering what kind of strange question that was. The question could not be answered in a practical sense. "What future, Papa? Do you know what's to happen?"

Adam kept his attention on the team. "You may know better than your papa. I imagine things at times. Like not having enough money for the seed, or the wagons getting washed down the river in a flood. That sort of thing."

"Do you think that could happen?" she asked a bit fearful.

"I'm trying to figure it out. You know the dreams I sometimes have. I had one about a child's funeral before your baby sister died. But I didn't know that it was going to be Amy, or when, or how. I never know enough to stop it."

Eve was quiet for a time. "Have you had a dream about the wagons and a flood?"

"No, so that doesn't seem to be a real possibility."

She pressed: "Or about us not having money to buy seed?"

"Not that either," said Adam.

"What then?" she asked.

"I knew a woman was going to die before your mother did. But I didn't know it was her, or when. It's like someone is trying to warn me. But I don't know what to do about it. I miss your mother; she seemed to always know what to say or do."

Eve moved closer to Papa, and looped her arm through his, laying her head on this dusty shoulder. "Yes, me too," she said. After a pause he felt her arm squeeze his. "Mama, please pray for us. I think we're going to need it."

The Pennsylvania Freight Company in York had rented Adam the two Conestoga wagons and mule teams, and had arranged for two team drivers, or teamsters, to drive the teams of mules and wagons to Virginia. The wagon master, responsible for the safety of the trip and for contracting a return load if there was one to be found, was forty-year-old Revolutionary War veteran Michael McCoy. He was a large, red-bearded, confident man with a pleasant disposition. Michael had suggested they hire 20-year-old Jimmy Knight to be the second teamster. Jimmy had long black hair and appeared to be a bit nervous, as if this might be his first overland trip. Adam watched the men work together as they packed and balanced the loads. Jimmy was taking direction and advice from Michael, but not always so readily. Adam decided that Jimmy was probably Michael's apprentice, although Jimmy had not been introduced that way and Adam had contracted them separately.

The newly designed *Conestoga wagons had been built by the Mennonites near Adam's father in Lancaster County. Designed for carrying heavy loads the wagons were handcrafted from oak and poplar. Their curved bottoms kept the load from shifting on rough terrain, and their slanted front and backs could be lowered to form ramps for loading and unloading. The inside seams were pitched with tar to prevent leakage when the wagons dipped their bottoms into the water during river crossings, though he doubted they would float due to the weight of their loads. The steel rimmed wheels were very wide, too, so there was less chance of getting stuck in mud or a slough. They were marvelous new inventions, Adam thought.

Along with the wagon teamsters came a map of his journey, such as it was. Adam knew it was only approximately right. According to their calculations, the trip would take eleven days and cover just over one hundred miles. On average, that was about nine miles each day, which included time to rest, water, and feed the teams several times a day.

Their destination was to the southwest and a place called Smithfield, Virginia. Settled by *John Smith in 1734, the village was adjacent to the 350 acres his father had sold him. Adam studied the map. By leaving in October there would be little rain on the journey, if any. They would cross countless streams that should be either shallow or dry. There were two river crossings that would require a ferry.

The second crossing, at Harper's Ferry, worried him the most. It was across the Potowmack River just before it joined the Shenandoah River. There would be rapids and deep water. There were stories of ferries dumping their loads into rivers and lives lost. He sucked in his breath and tried not to visualize all his earthly belongings being washed down the Potowmack into the muddy Chesapeake. He thought about it, but there was no premonition. Good, he thought.

Repressing his fear, he focused on the immediate road ahead, and again checked on the whereabouts of Henry. He was sleeping in the back on a pile of bedding and linen. And Eve? She sat next to him reading a book. How she could do that on a bumpy seat was beyond him. Young eyes!

He needed to rest the horse and mule teams every three to five hours, so once they reached the town limits of Newport and while it was still light he found a place to pull off for the night next to a meadow where the animals could graze and sleep.

Newport had been settled by *Alexander Parker after he was given the land grant for his Revolutionary War service. Just outside of town was a well-known iron forge at Spring Grove operated by a man who knew his father. Adam wanted to learn about the iron forging process, but they had left the York area too late, and this being the first night out he didn't want to leave the wagons. There would be much to adjust and settle after camping for the night.

With help from his children, Michael, and Jimmy they set up a corral with ropes for the livestock, pitched their tents, and cooked a meal. With supper complete, Adam reviewed the journey ahead with Michael and Jimmy, and then they turned in for the night. He checked on Eve and Henry; both were properly tucked into their bedrolls at the far end of their tent. Taking a lantern Adam crawled into his wagon.

First, he checked the load to make sure nothing had jostled loose and containers were tightly closed. Second, he closed the back of the wagon's cover to keep out bugs, dew, and rain if it should come, and pulled the front cover mostly closed. He would close it up completely when he turned in to the tent.

Then, digging into the apple barrel he pulled out the money satchel and set it next to his lantern on top of a crate with a flat top. Opening the satchel, he removed his accounting ledger and opened it up to his most recent entries. Next, he took out the farm's bill of sale and Frank's bill and entered them into the ledger. Finally, he removed as quietly as he could the gold doubloons from his market sales and the farm sale, and the paper currency he had left over. Carefully, he counted everything, confirming an earlier approximation that he had 550 gold doubloons worth 413-pound sterling. His pocketbook change was a wild assortment of denominations including Pennsylvania currency, shillings, pence, a few farthings, a handful of quarter-doubloons, a single gold guinea and a half dozen half-crowns, altogether worth about twenty-pound sterling.

Counting gold doubloons was satisfying work, but he knew the pile of gold was misleading. He feared it wasn't enough until his crops from the new farm were taken to market. He also lamented the lack of a national monetary policy that allowed so many kinds of coins and currencies. There were thirteen state notes, each valued differently against the pound sterling. Add to that the confusion created by various foreign coinage, denominations, and evaluations. Altogether, there were at least fifty different currencies and coinages in circulation. It was too confusing. He was happy to have insisted on gold for the recent harvest and land sale. He was in a fair position, but he didn't have enough to fully establish the farm, especially with the mortgage hanging over his head for ten years; and then there was the trivial matter, which wasn't so trivial, of the fee for the deed to be transferred from his father to himself. He'd do that at the Berkeley County Land Office after they arrived.

Wondering if there was a better place to hide the satchel than at the bottom of an apple barrel, he lifted a few tarps, and considered a few other containers. Then he thought of the tragedy he would face if upon crossing the Potowmack the wagon could fall off the ferry and be lost in the river. His possessions were one thing, but this satchel was filled with his life savings. He picked the satchel off the floor of the wagon, wondering if it would float. It was a silly reaction, considering that the satchel, which was now empty, probably would float. But with over 500 gold doubloons inside, regardless of their weight—and doubloons were light compared to pieces of eight— he was sure he'd never see the money again. He bounced the satchel in his hands imagining its buoyancy on top of the water, being tossed here and there by the rushing waves of the rapids near where they would cross.

Suddenly, he stopped his reverie. Something wasn't right. He jiggled the satchel again and heard only the leather straps hitting the side. But then he turned the satchel on end and shook it again. This time he heard it. There were coins still in the satchel. He gazed at the stacks of doubloons and other coins on the crate top. According to his ledger he wasn't missing any money; all was accounted for. Except for a discovered arithmetic error, his books easily reconciled. He shook the satchel again. There were coins inside.

Laying the satchel on a nearby crate so as not to disturb the stacks of money, he opened the satchel wide, held up the lantern and gazed into the two large compartments, and then the four smaller ones on the outside. Each was empty. He put his hand into each compartment and felt for coins perhaps caught under a wrinkle in the material. Nothing.

But when he shook the bag a certain way, there were clearly at least a dozen coins, and they sounded like gold coins. He turned the bag around and examined the outside. Nothing unusual.

When loading up the satchel after the sale, George Eshelman had held the largest of the two top-loading compartments open and Adam and placed the stacks inside. Adam put his hand back in the compartment and felt the leather bottom carefully. There were bumps, curved ribs…the shape of coins. Was there a false bottom? He felt carefully around the four edges. One of the long edges was sewn tight into the seam. The other three edges, however, were not sewn but tucked tightly into the corners of the bag's bottom. The edges fit so snugly that they appeared to be sewn into the corner seams, but they weren't…it was a flap. The three loose edges of the thick leather formed a false bottom. The fit was so tight he had to claw at the edges with his fingernail. Finally, the edge rose from the faux seam enough for him to pry it open. Before he could look in, he felt the coins. They didn't exactly feel like doubloons. He pulled the false bottom open enough and angled the satchel to allow light into the compartment. He looked in. At least a dozen *double* doubloons, each worth four gold escudos, had been hidden in the bottom of the satchel. He pulled them out carefully two at a time and put them on the crate. When he was done, there were fourteen gold double doubloons, each worth four escudos, or two times larger and heavier than a two escudo or regular gold doubloon.

He was thrilled with the discovery. This made a difference. He was worried about having enough money, and here it was…another twenty-one-pound sterling.

He felt light-headed. Again, it wasn't much, but then he had rarely cast his eyes on double doubloons. They were a rare sight. He stacked them in his hand and felt their weight. They weren't as heavy as pieces of eight made from silver, but then this was gold, and it was his. *Possession was nine-tenths of the law*, he thought. *George did not need to know. Let's keep them hidden.* He slipped them back under the hidden flap at the bottom of the satchel's main compartment and didn't even bother recording their existence in his ledger. It would be his little secret.

Putting the rest of the coin and ledger back in the satchel, he laced it up tight, and shoved it back in the apple barrel out of sight and out of mind. The apples went on top, except for one that became his midnight snack.

2

Saturday, October 11, 1788.

The next day they drove hard to get to Hanover before dusk. The teams were exhausted. At the Trotter Livery on Frederick Street, Adam arranged to have all fifteen animals brushed, watered, and fed, and have the wagons secured and guarded. Then the group dined and stayed overnight a short walk down the street at *Caspar Reinecker's Inn. Caspar had the reputation as a promoter and wasted no time telling the travelers about the times Thomas Jefferson also dined and spent the night at the inn on April 12, 1776. Evidently, Jefferson was on his way from Monticello to Philadelphia where he would draft the Declaration of Independence. Then, on his return, some months later, Jefferson lodged again at Reinecker's on September 5.

Adam was skeptical and bristled at Caspar's bravado. The food was good, but not that good. It was a teaching moment he decided and afterwards in their room, gave a lecture to his children about how to recognize habitual liars.

3

October 12, 1788.

The next morning was Sunday. Eve tried to get Papa to read a letter that had been tacked to the wall near the door exiting the Inn, supposedly signed by Jefferson, thanking Caspar for the "excellent food" and "outstanding hospitality." But Adam would have no part of it and refused to acknowledge the letter's existence.

The group headed for the livery to hitch up the mule teams, horses, and cow. In so doing, Adam noticed something amiss with Calvin—he was limping.

Samuel Trotter, the proprietor and local farrier, stopped Adam as he led the horses to the wagon. "Excuse me, Mister Livingston. Can I have a word with thee?"

Adam, distracted by Calvin's limp, immediately turned to Trotter.

"First, thank you for stopping with your teams last night. We were glad to oblige with our services. Might you be passing this way again, soon?"

"Not I," said Adam, "But McCoy and Knight here may be as they'll be returning to York, maybe with a fresh load in a week or two, not sure."

"Either way, Mister Livingston, when we were brushing this shire of yours, maybe you've noticed, too, his left hind limp."

Adam nodded for the man to go on.

"I looked at him this morning after Peter pointed it out to me. Look here." Trotter lifted Calvin's left hind foot, bent it back at the knee, and drew it up between his legs onto his leather apron.

Adam took one glance and he saw immediately that the iron shoe was half missing. The hard drive into Hanover had taken its toll.

Adam felt miserable. He realized that he had violated one of his own strict rules, "Care for your beasts like you care for your children." He had not done that. He had not checked Calvin's or Luther's shoes before they left. How stupid he felt.

"He'll need at least one new shoe, he will, before he'll be any good to ya," said Trotter. "If you've got time, I'd suggest at least both hind hoofs be newly shod."

Immediately Adam checked Calvin's front hoofs and Trotter came along. Then they moved on to check Luther. After a few minutes Adam agreed with Trotter's recommendation and asked him to reshoe the hind hoofs on both horses. Moving to the mules that Jimmy and Michael were preparing to harness up, the four men checked the mule's hoofs as well.

"Mister Livingston," said Michael, "we made sure they all had new shoes before we came to your place. They should be fine. That was part of our agreement."

So it was. The shoes on all the mules were sound and their hoofs healthy.

But Adam was tense. All this was going to slow down the trip.

Having two horses reshod, even just the hinds, would take three to four hours since the shoes would have to be custom fitted.

He asked Trotter how long and how much it would cost. Trotter was quick with a reply. The price was fair and the time was what he expected.

So, when it became clear that their journey would be halted for half-a-day or more, Michael McCoy approached Adam.

"Mister Livingston, sir? I be a Catholic from Ireland if you rightly know. Last night in the tavern I hear say that there be a beautiful new church just north of us about a mile. They say it's quite large and beautiful. If it not too inconvenient, since it's been a while for me, and we're here for a bit, would ye mind if I go up to Mass? I'm sure you and your children would be welcome too, and Jimmy might go, though I don't know."

Adam stiffened at the request and stared at the man a moment. He was a good enough driver, as was his partner, Jimmy Knight. Neither ever complained, and they cared for their beasts well. He could hardly say no. There was nothing else for either of the men to do for hours.

"Papa?" It was Eve, who had been standing next to her father. "We should go to church, too, like Mister McCoy says."

They're ganging-up on me, Adam laughed to himself. There was nothing for him to do…might as well do some sight-seeing. But go inside a pagan Catholic church, as much as he was angry at God, was out of the question.

"Please, Papa, can I go with Mister McCoy and Jimmy?" Eve persisted.

Adam turned to his son. "You want to go with Eve, Mister McCoy and Mister Knight to church?"

"I wouldn't be wanting it if ya made me," said Henry. "Ya making me?"

Adam laughed at the face his son was making, like he was being made to eat swine gut before it was stuffed with spiced meat.

"Mister McCoy," Adam said, "it's fine by me, and I don't mind if Eve tags along, although I'll walk up there with you. But so you know, I haven't a need to step inside no pagan temple."

McCoy held his lip at the slight. "Thank ye. I'll go find Jimmy and tell him what we're gonna do."

The farrier overheard their conversation and interrupted. "Gentlemen, Conewago Chapel, which you're taking about, is three to four mile outside of town. Take my wagon out back. I'll lend you a horse while I work on these shoes."

Adam was pleased, and he told the farrier that; so he and the children, Michael, and Jimmy piled into the farrier's wagon and cantered out of town. In the process, Adam noticed that Jimmy was a bit stiff about the plans, but he said nothing.

The Conewago Chapel was a new, two-and-a-half story brownstone Catholic Church that had been finished only a year or two earlier. It featured a west-facing, Federal style entrance, and attached to its south side was an equally impressive three story rectory for missionary priests.

Adam bristled with jealousy at the sight of the church. It was bigger than any church he and Esther had ever attended. Eve happily went along with Michael inside for Mass, but neither he nor Henry went in. Neither did Jimmy darken the church door. Jimmy finally revealed his reticence of the field trip by expressing some shadowy anti-Catholic sentiment.

Two hours later, the Mass over, Michael and Eve came out of the church smiling.

"Well?" her father inquired. "You seem to be in one piece. I guess they didn't sacrifice you to their idols." Adam was serious, but Eve laughed.

"No, Papa, but there was blood, or at least I was told. It's very beautiful. There wasn't regular music like at Mama's church. Michael says it's called...." She turned to Michael for the word.

"Chanting," said Michael. "It's like singing but with fewer notes."

"But the strange part," Eve continued, "everything was in some strange language."

"Latin," Michael interjected again.

"I didn't understand a thing," Eve said.

Michael gave her a sad look.

"Okay, so he told me what some of it was about."

"Now, not all was in Latin, missy," Michael reminded her.

"Oh, okay. There was the sermon. I understood that, but it was awfully short."

"Enough," said Adam. "Let's get back to the livery and hitch up the teams. We have a way to go if we don't want our journey to take forever."

Adam looked about for Jimmy, who was already sitting in the wagon, arms crossed like an impatient five-year-old. Michael swung himself up next to Jimmy, at which time Adam caught Jimmy turn away and scowl. Michael seemed to be in his normally good mood, but Jimmy was stiff and mad about something. This tensed Adam and he became alert. He knew how men could be, holding grudges against each other that had nothing to do with either. He wondered what had come over Jimmy.

When they got back to the livery and Adam had thanked the proprietor for the wagon's use, he was told it'd be another hour or so before Luther was ready, but Calvin was newly shod and could be harnessed whenever it was convenient. Adam took the opportunity to help Michael and Jimmy harness up the mule teams, and when that was done, he asked Jimmy for help harnessing up Calvin.

As Adam slipped the collar over Calvin's head, Jimmy held down the horse's ears. Then, together, they laid out the rest of the harness on the horse's back. "What's in your bonnet, Jimmy?" asked Adam. "Ever since we rode out to Conewago it seems you've been miffed 'bout somethin'."

Jimmy hesitated as he straightened the back and breeching straps. "Is not e'ry day your wagon master tells ya to go to hell," Jimmy said. "Damn papists love to judge the rest of us thinkin' it makes 'em better."

Jimmy draped Calvin's breeching over his rump and pulled down the loin straps as Adam positioned and buckled the girth and tightened the bellyband. "I've been told that many times in my life, the hell part," said Adam. "But why'd he say such a thing? Michael seems a sensible man."

"Like I says, it's the papist way of belittling ya. That's why I hate 'em so much. So pious, and they just ain't. Know what I mean?"

Jimmy was getting worked up and that wasn't good for getting the work done. So, Adam backed off. "I'll have talkin' to him, Jimmy. Thanks for your help. Much obliged."

"I likes me job, and the animals. Travelin' ain't too bad either."

And with that Jimmy looped Calvin's tail through the crupper, and Adam threaded the traces and reins through their respective terrets. Jimmy asked, "No bearing rein?"

"No, hate 'em, probably more than you hate papists. Too much attitude and not enough honest work."

Jimmy laughed. "That's be right by me, Mister Livingston."

Michael, meanwhile, was checking the Conestoga wagon loads, axles, and wheels. Adam was still in awe of the wagons' wide rear rims. They were probably seven or eight inches wide and not likely to get stuck in mud; more likely they'd glide right over it, he thought.

"Everything all right, Michael?" Adam asked.

"Seems to be. These wagons are nearly new."

"We'll be ready to go shortly, as soon as Luther gets his hinds on."

"That be fine. We're ready to go, now, I reckon," said Michael. "Somethin' botherin' ya, sir?"

Adam hesitated. "Just had a talk with Jimmy. You notice his attitude since we returned from Conewago?"

Michael was reluctant to answer. "Jimmy has a problem with the Irish and with Catholics, and I'm proud to be both. Since you suggested we all go to Conewago because I wanted to attend church, he's been threatening to blackmail me with lies to you sir, to undermine my leadership of our small team."

"He said you told him he was going to hell."

"Is that all he told you?" asked Michael. "Did he also lie to ya about me stealing things from your wagons?"

Adam suddenly felt his anger rise. "Have you? What have you taken?"

"I haven't taken anything, sir. And if I had, where would I put it. We each have one bag with a change of clothes and our personal items. You can search both at any time, the way I see it. But I don't want to accuse Jimmy of what I have no real knowledge of. But he's threatened to tell you I have stolen from you, and for that I told him he'd go to hell if he did. I suspect he's waiting for the right time to say something to you."

Adam was mad, if not at one of his drivers for stealing from him, then at the discord that threatened the smoothness of the journey. Michael looked up and past Adam with a scowl. Adam turned to see Jimmy leaning against the covered farm wagon casting about a smirk. Adam figured he better get this resolved before they went any further. "Mister Knight, come here."

Jimmy swaggered over and stood with his legs spread apart and his fingers in his belt as if he was ready for a fight. "Yes, sir. What can I do for you Mister Livingston?" he said in a jocular sort of way.

"Michael here has accused you of threatening him by some blackmail scheme. What do you have to say 'bout that?"

"The papist's a damn cheat, a thief, and a scoundrel, sir. And I can prove it."

Michael interrupted. "Watch yourself, Jimmy. This ain't goin' to go well for you."

"Oh, yeah? You going to stop me?" Jimmy was quick to continue: "Mister Livingston, you would do well to check out his rucksack. You'll find what I saw him take of yours."

As soon as Jimmy said that, Michael lunged at him. Jimmy jumped back as Adam stepped between them. "Let's have a look, Michael," said Adam. "Let me see your rucksack. You won't mind, will you?"

"Not at all!" Michael was infuriated at the accusation. He broke off his attack of Jimmy, turned to the wagon he was driving, climbed up on the tongue behind the wheel mule, and pulled out an old leather rucksack with multiple straps holding it tightly closed. He handed it to Adam. "Here you go sir, take a look."

Adam looked at Jimmy who wore a big smirk. Adam carried the rucksack to the front of his wagon, set it on the floor of the driving bench and proceeded to unlace the straps. The sack had several pockets on the side and bottom, but Adam opened the top first. All he saw at first was a clean change of clothes and a book. He stuck his hand down the side and moved it around as if looking for something easily recognized by touch. Suddenly he stopped, then carefully pulled out a beautifully engraved flintlock pistol. It was about a foot long with a polished brass grip, tip, and trigger guard, delicately engraved and fitted onto a walnut stock with carved scrolling behind the tang.

Adam glanced at Michael, who always carried his pistol in a leather pouch on his belt. "You have two pistols, Michael?" Adam asked, bemused.

"No, I only own one, and that one ain't mine." Michael answered with deep anger in his voice as he glared at Jimmy.

Adam glared at Jimmy and then looked carefully at the gun in his hand. "You're right. This is not yours. It's mine—the Kock of Mayntz pistol my father gave me as a wedding gift." Adam turned back to Jimmy, who was still smirking like a silly jackass.

Suddenly, Michael lost it. "You damn fool." Michael lunged at Jimmy as he whipped out his Dutch Dragoon pistol, grabbed it around the barrel, and swung the menacing iron-tipped grip at Jimmy who tried to dodge the attack. But Michael was faster, striking Jimmy on his left collar bone with a crack.

Jimmy immediately collapsed to the ground whereupon Michael jumped on top of the smaller man and commenced slugging him in the head and torso alternatively with the gun and fist. Jimmy struggled to strike back, but he was at a great disadvantage. Michael sat astride Jimmy, beating him mercilessly. Blood flowed from Jimmy's nose and onto the ground, and yet Michael did not let up.

Adam quickly laid the Kock on the driving floor of his wagon, reached behind his seat and grabbed his shillelagh.

Gripping the fighting stick he shouted at the men, "Stop it you two! McCoy, get off him. Now, I tell you. Get off!"

But neither man responded. At some point Jimmy managed to push Michael off but they continued to scrap, rolling in the dirt, throwing punches at each other but mostly missing.

By now Trotter, Henry, and Eve had all gathered around. After some wallowing, Michael returned to his superior position and started to strangle Jimmy. "Hell is imminent for you, fool."

Adam hesitated no longer. He cocked his shillelagh above his head, and with one swift swing, the knob of his shillelagh struck Michael in the head, knocking him out cold and causing the big man to flop as if dead atop Jimmy.

Trotter and Adam rolled Michael over onto his back and off Jimmy. Adam, worried that he had killed Michael, checked his breathing and pulse. Thankfully, Michael was just stunned.

Jimmy staggered to his feet, his face a bloody mess. Unable to stand, he sat back on the ground with a thud.

About that time the proprietor's wife, Rebecca Trotter, appeared on the scene. "Sam," she said, "get him inside."

As if a foot soldier who had just been given orders by a general, the farrier helped Jimmy get to his feet and into the nearby house.

Adam was an emotional wreck. His Germanic nature sought order and function. But theft was the opposite of order, and the fight was function inside out.

Now that the fight had ceased, at least for the time being, Adam took a series of deep breaths and started pacing back and forth between his wagon and the mules. After a moment....

"I didn't steal your pistol, Mister Livingston." Michael's groggy voice came from behind.

Adam whirled around from his pacing swinging his shillelagh in frustration.

Michael rubbed the lump on the side of his head as he eyed the shillelagh with caution and struggled to sit up. "That fool did it to get back at me fer me being Catholic. And it was he who put your pistol in my rucksack. I didn't see him do it, but that's what I figure."

"Aye. I know that. It came to be obvious," said Adam more than a bit angry.

"But you acted like it wasn't. And to take it out on me for not knowing what I could plainly see, you tried to kill him, you did. What for? Yer pride?"

Michael put his head between his knees, still rubbing the lump. He glanced around. "Where's he at?"

"Trotters took him inside to mend him."

"I didn't kill him?"

"No."

"Lucky bastard."

"You're the lucky bastard that I didn't kill you," said Adam.

"Not sure 'bout that. I suspect it's quieter in a grave."

"Are all Catholics this violent?"

"No, only the ones whose sisters have been raped and brothers murdered by Protestants. We should be the ones protesting."

Such a revelation caused Adam to pause.

"Mister Livingston, I'm sorry to put you to this inconvenience, but I'll not be having Mister Knight anymore on this trip. I do not trust him to do right by you or me."

"That's some claim for a man that could be sent to jail for attempted murder."

"It was self-defense."

"In your mind! I'm not sure I want either of you to accompany me further. I have no patience for this sort of scrapping."

"Please note, sir, that I was severely provoked, I was libeled, my livelihood threatened, and my honor mocked. And why? Because I am Catholic. I had even hand-picked Mister Knight for this trip. I was generous to him. For him to turn on me in such a manner...." Michael hesitated.

Adam waited patiently, stopped swinging his shillelagh, and held it firmly behind his back out of sight.

Michael continued. "...unprovoked by me, or my treatment of him, was— well, I'm between on this. In a sense he had it all coming to him in justice, but in another sense, my discipline or chastisement was over the mark."

Adam turned toward the farrier's house. There was no sign of Jimmy or the Trotters.

"I owe you an apology, Mister Livingston. If not for almost killing my vassal, then drawing you into the problem by hiring him in the first place."

Michael stood up, unsteadily at first, then squared his shoulders to Adam. "I'm ready to continue, Mister Livingston, and bring your property safely to Smithfield, if you'll let me. But first I need to inform Mister Knight that he won't be coming along."

"How will you manage that? You can't drive two wagons yourself."

Michael nodded. "That is true. But I met someone this morning at the chapel that can drive the second wagon, if he is willing. But it will take me an hour to find him and arrange it if you'd be patient for me."

"What guarantee do I have that I should go along with this, that your second choice is better than your first?"

"You know me to be an honest man who has little patience for wrongdoing, and thus I can be trusted to do you honor. You certainly will trust the man I bring to you if I can find him. Reserve your decision until you meet him. Will you, sir?"

Adam narrowed his eyes at Michael and crossed his arms. He gripped the shillelagh across his chest like a king's scepter, the symbol of power and authority. He was at a loss about what to do. If he said no and fired both men, he would be without assistance in finding new drivers and having two children in his keep. On the other hand, if he said yes, he was opening himself up for another episode with Michael—a man with a hot temper. What was clear and sad at once, was that he did not want Jimmy Knight anywhere near his wagons.

Adam raised his eyebrows, bit his lip, and said, "Okay, let's meet this man. Then I give you my answer...or not. But let me deal with Jimmy."

"Thank you, sir," said Michael, who then dusted off his clothes, saddled up his horse, and in a few minutes was riding toward Conewago.

Adam went to the Conestoga wagon Jimmy and been driving, pulled out his rucksack and bedroll, opened all the pockets, padded down the bedroll, and searched for contraband, but found none. He then grabbed Jimmy's saddle that was in the Conestoga he was driving, and set Jimmy's rucksack, bedroll, and saddle on the farrier's porch. Adam then went into the farrier's house.

Jimmy sat in a chair at their supper table as Mrs. Trotter finished up mending his face and wounds. It would be months before his smirk returned. Mister Trotter stood ready a few yards away, watching Rebecca's every move, ready to jump at her command.

"Missus Trotter, I am much obliged for your assistance," Adam said. "And I apologize for this most unfortunate incident. Here is something for your trouble." He handed her a half-escudo.

She said nothing but smiled and took the gold coin.

"Jimmy, can you walk?" asked Adam.

"Yeah, I can walk," Jimmy said begrudgingly.

"Let's go outside and have a talk." He turned to the farrier. "Mister Trotter, you're an honorable man and I'll spread the word about your hospitality and service. You did a good job on my horses, and I am forever in your debt. I'll settle up with you before we leave in the next hour or two."

"That will be fine, Mister Livingston. I'm sorry, too, for the trouble you've had, but we are glad to help. That is what we're here for."

"Let's go, Jimmy." Adam led a hobbling Jimmy Knight out the front door to the porch and then down a few steps to the yard.

No sooner had Jimmy's boot hit the dirt, than he challenged Adam, "Where's the damned papist?" But Jimmy stopped when he saw his possessions on the edge of the porch. His body flinched and stiffened.

"Michael's whereabouts is no longer your business." Adam said. "What you need to be concerned with is where you're at and where you need to git." Adam handed him a half-escudo. "Take this and go wherever you want, I don't care. Your horse is in the corral. York is but a half-day's ride, I figure."

Jimmy scowled at the coin in his hand and angrily said, "You givin' me leave? We bargained for eight escudos each. This is a pittance; it ain't right."

"It's right and just, Jimmy. You defrauded Michael and me. Rightly I owe you nothing. We're far from our destination and close enough for you to walk home, although you've got a horse. I'm being generous by giving you that half-escudo and not calling the sheriff. Now git before Michael returns and finishes what he started."

Adam could see Jimmy wasn't happy. But in Adam's way of figuring it, the apprentice teamster had gotten off easy for what he had done. Jimmy glared at Adam for a few seconds wanting to say something more, but wisely held his tongue. He limped over to lift his sack, roll, and saddle, which he did with a bit of pain, then trudged to the corral. Adam kept an eye on him until he was riding out of the yard and turned down the road toward York.

At that point Adam felt a sudden release of tension and coughed. His mouth was dry.

He walked to the well, pumped himself a few handfuls of cool water, and washed off his face. Drying his face on his dirty sleeve, he turned his attention back to something really important, his children. He would find them, reassure them, and then check on their cow, maybe milk her a bit, and visit Pickles and Sizemore, if the kids weren't already riding them around the corral.

An hour later, two men and their horses trotted into the yard. One was Michael on his black mustang. The other rode erect atop a handsome chestnut mare. He was a tall and trim man in hunting attire. On his head he wore a distinctive black round cap in which was stuck a red feather. But the most remarkable thing about the man was in a scabbard under the man's leg. It was the longest musket Adam had ever seen. Peter took the reins of the two horses and they dismounted to greet Adam.

"Mister Livingston," said Michael, 'this here is Private *Charles Smith, of the 1st Pennsylvania Regiment, a local war hero who fought the British under the command of *Colonel Edward Hand."

Adam shook the man's hand. "Mister Smith. Glad to meet you. I have met Edward Hand, I think. Doesn't he own the *Rock Ford Plantation not far from Lancaster? My father's farm is there."

"Yes, that's him. Colonel Hand was a fine leader. I think he also practices medicine in that fine town, if I'm not mistaken," said Charles. From his accent Adam noticed immediately that Charles Smith was clearly French in ancestry.

"Where were you born, Mister Smith?"

"Alsace, France, sir, not far from Germany. My parents immigrated here when I was fifteen. I think they were sorry to see France lose territory over here and wanted to get some of it back for themselves. My father was a miller. I have turned out to be a rifleman and a teamster."

"That's a mighty long gun you have there," Adam said pointing to the scabbard on his saddle.

"Yep, it's almost too long for carryin' on horseback. It was made in Lancaster by a German craftsman just before the war broke out. It has served me well. I can hit a rabbit at 250 yards, though it takes a while to reload. It has a rifled barrel, spins the ball. But, Michael here says you might need me to drive one of your Conestogas here for a few days. Is that right?"

"Aye. The trip may take two weeks at the rate we're going about it. I am resettling in Smithfield, Virginia, a day or two west of the Potowmack."

"That I can do. After my sharpshooting days during the war, I was a driver for the army's supply trains, until just recently. Be glad to help for a fair wage and food."

"I can offer you eight gold escudos on delivery plus grub along the way, if that's agreeable."

"Aye, that's fair. Michael here says you're a good man, so I am ready."

At that "good man" comment, Adam gazed at Michael and the lump on the side of his head. Michael returned the gaze by taking a sudden interest in his boots. "Then let's get going. Michael will orient you. Michael?"

Michael looked up. "I see you've harnessed up Luther, so I'm sure we can be ready in less than an hour, soon as I get Charles settled."

"Good," said Adam. The men shook hands and got to work.

After the teams were harnessed, Adam noticed Samuel Trotter was watching them from the livery with his receipt book in hand. *Probably wonders when I'm going to open my pocketbook*, he thought. "Mister Trotter?" Adam called across the yard. Mister Trotter left the livery entrance and walked toward Adam. "We're about ready, and I don't think we'll be needin' any more provisions from you, so let's settle up. What do I owe you?"

Trotter showed Adam the tab of stabling and feeding their fifteen animals, plus livery services, and the horseshoes. Adam scanned it, nodded his head and read the total, "One-pound, six-shilling and one-pence Pennsylvania money. Right?"

"That would be acceptable, Mister Livingston."

Adam looked at the man carefully. He could tell that he'd take silver or gold, but didn't want Pennsylvania currency, even if they were still in Pennsylvania. "Well, Mister Trotter, I don't like currency, nor do I care much for Pennsylvania money, these days. Will one and three-quarters gold doubloons do and make things a-right?"

Sam Trotter looked down at his receipt book, did some mental calculations, his lips moving slightly as he did so. Finally, he looked up and smiled, "Yes, sir. That would be generous of you."

Adam nodded, opened his pocketbook, dug out a gold doubloon and a three-quarter doubloons, and put them in Trotter's open palm.

"Thank you very much, Mister Livingston," Trotter said, "and for the tip you gave the Missus. Sorry you had issues while visiting us."

"It wasn't you, of course. Was it?" Adam teased.

"No, not rightly."

Adam turned to go but Trotter had more to say.

"Mister Livingston, if you don't mind, I know you said you were moving to Virginia, the other side of Harper's Ferry, but I'm curious why you're taking this southern route and not the newer and improved, so the governor says, Philadelphia Wagon Trail from Lancaster, Gettysburg, and Hagerstown? There be plenty of blacksmiths, turners, wood workers and provisions along that route, more so than this route to Frederick. This time of year, being dry like it is, while the fording will be easy, there will be less water in the streams for this host of horses and mules you got."

"You would recommend the northern wagon road?"

"Yes, you could leave here and go straight west...well, north a little...for Gettysburg and not be out of your way much."

Adam thought about it, then shook his head. "Mister Trotter, I've not traveled either route, but I've talked to more than a few who have come up from Hagerstown to York from whence I came. The reports are that the Wagon Road is not all it's talked-up to be. It's a rough journey they all say. I've heard many times if a wagon is stuck along the road going south, and because of all the herds of cattle, sheep, and swine being brought up to market at Lancaster and Philadelphia, why there may be twenty to thirty wagons waiting for the one poor man to fix his wheel or replace an axle. They also say there be no walking-alongside the wagons insofar as the road is dusty and heavily soiled with animal stools the whole way. The scent I hear is at times asphyxiatin'. But this southern route, which was used quite a bit until a few years ago, is now much quieter and peaceful. And I understand the road is still there, not hard to follow."

"What about provisions," asked Trotter. "There are numerous taverns and merchants long the new road but very few now-days south."

"That may be, but we're provisioned for three weeks, and I expect it will take us only half that long to get to Charles Town, even with this delay at your fine establishment. But thank you much for the advice."

The men said their farewells once again, and within the hour Adam and his posse were back on the road, albeit by then it was mid-afternoon.

4

My Despised Cyn:

Great job fostering narcissistic greed in your mark. And excellent work causing Eshelman to forget the extra gold in the satchel. Regardless, Livingston has fallen for the trap, and now has endeared himself to our way of thinking. Perhaps we can use that extra gold for some devious purpose that will further entrench him.

At Hanover, I was rooting for Jimmy until Michael attacked him. At that point I recognized that, once again, you had overplayed your hand. Jimmy's valid and visible hatred of Catholics was so obvious that it never would have fooled Livingston. We have not done ourselves any favors by allowing Michael McCoy to head up the teams. Named after one of our greatest arch enemies, McCoy's likely to become an ongoing nuisance. We must be better liars. Unfortunately, it is nearly impossible to defraud truth in the end. Truth has a way of not changing, whereas our lies can change constantly. Being so clever isn't so clever in the end. So, you got a little delay out of Livingston's journey, but in the end, Livingston stuck with the Catholic. So, what good did all that foolery do?

Livingston is soon to come to his land in Virginia and will discover the consequences of your work years ago with Cain and Mayfield. Of course, if you're in luck, for Providence will not avail you mercy, Livingston may even find something dear to you. May his chest-pounding pride lead you to freedom.

Eternally yours,
Master of Bigotry

Chapter 9
With a Rock

1

Adam was not a happy farmer. For one thing he was not farming. For another he disliked the constant struggle to hire and manage laborers. Earth, water, and crops rarely argued with him. He wasn't sure who to blame for the latest human fiasco. Was it Michael for believing in a God whom Adam liked less and less? Was it Jimmy for hating those that found comfort in religion? Or was it himself?

One thing for sure, and he took pride in this: The problems of the last days were due to his own negligence. Had he properly shod Luther and Calvin before they left the York farm, Michael would not have attended Mass, Jimmy would still be on the job, and the whole team would be twelve miles closer to Smithfield. Adam knew he was fully capable of doing better, and he determined he would.

Looking for encouragement, he reminded himself that making this trip in October was the right decision. It had been a dry week and that was good. Dry roads, not mud, would help them make up for lost time. Even today, they could make the seven miles to Littleton before dusk if they didn't stop and rest the teams. But for Michael and Charles, it meant dust, thus the bandanas they wore across their faces.

There was another downside to the dry conditions made evident when they came to Plum Creek just southwest of Hanover. The creek was dry. To his right he saw the cattails of the swamp that in wetter seasons fed the creek. Today its grasses were high and dry and the mudflats cracked. Traveling in the fall was not good for watering their livestock. He may have wished that he had taken Trotter's suggestion and detoured to the newer Philadelphia Wagon Road.

As long as they made progress, however, he was content and his children kept him busy along the way. Eve, always curious, continuously asked questions about the countryside or what they would do or find in Virginia. At times she would take the reins and seemed to relish learning how to drive the team. Adam wondered how she would hold up in a new household without her mother. He felt her strong constitution would ultimately fail being left alone in the house all day with Henry to contend with while he worked the fields.

Henry too was learning to rein the team, but he complained that his arms hurt, or they got tired, or his butt was sore, or his legs ached. It was always something. Adam knew it wasn't any of those things. Rather, something was awry with Henry's basic constitution. His perpetual malaise tested Adam's patience. Whose kid was he? Neither Eve, nor his own brothers, or his parents were lazy. While Henry complained that the horses wouldn't do what he wanted, Eve just pulled harder and harder until the horse responded. But Henry had a point. Adam could never figure out why the two horses just didn't stay on the road but every once in a while would head off into a field as if their work for the day was done.

"Look, Henry," Adam would try to explain, "all your life is going to be like this. You decide to go down a particular path, but something pulls your attention in another direction and you get lost in the field of briars or beans. You have to focus on the road ahead, and continually make adjustments, pulling this way or that, until you reach your goal."

And what would his dear son say? "What path do I have to take to get some food?"

At the end of their fifth day, after winding through hills mostly on a slight downgrade, indicating they were getting close to a waterway, they came to the Monocacy River, the largest of Maryland's tributaries to the Potowmack. The Monocacy would be their first ferry crossing.

When Adam's wagon came off the last rise before descending to the ferry's landing, he both sucked in his breath and felt a sense of calm. The river was clearly deep at this point and flowing quickly. That made him cautious. But the river was perhaps only one-hundred feet wide.

Eve sat next to Adam with Cleopatra in her lap. She gazed at the river ahead. "How are we going to get across that?" There was a touch of trepidation in her voice.

Adam glanced at her and realized she could not yet see the ferry, for it was on the other side of the river and hidden behind a line of trees on the near bank. But the landing on this side was visible and a few wagons and horses with their riders were waiting their turn to cross. He was tempted to tease her, since she had probably never seen a ferry of this kind before and didn't see one now. It was a rope ferry with two ropes tied to large trees on either side of the river. A careful eye could make out the impressions of the ferry's loading ramps on the river's bank and the wheel ruts from wagons that disappeared, supposedly into the river's depths, when they mounted the ferry's ramp. He pointed to the two ropes tied to the near side. "See those large ropes tied to those two trees?"

Eve leaned slightly forward and held on, for the wagon was navigating a few hilly ruts as it came closer to the landing. "Yes, I see them."

"Well," Adam said with deadpan seriousness, "when the signal is given, we drive the wagon directly into the water between those ropes. The wagon will float for a bit before it fills up and sinks, so we must work fast. You and Henry will grab one rope and I'll grab the other. As the horses swim across, we pull on the two ropes and the wagon will follow the horses across. But we must pull quickly or else the wagon will sink. The Conestoga wagons however are designed to float like boats, so they won't sink. Just possibly our wagon."

Adam watched her reaction out of the side of his eyes. Her face turned white, and she grabbed her father's coat sleeve and squeezed. The wagon was rocking a bit so he couldn't tell, but he suspected she wasn't breathing either. Suddenly, from behind him Henry spoke up. He was standing behind the driving seat and holding onto the cover's frame.

"Eve don't believe that. Papa's teasing."

Eve turned to her brother and demanded, "What do you mean?"

Henry answered in the same deadpan as his father. "The truth is, the wagon won't float at all. It will sink to the bottom right away."

Adam kept one eye on her as she looked quickly between Papa and brother. She must have caught a twinkle somewhere because she quickly caught on.

"You both are absolutely terrible. And neither of you can lie very good at all. The least you could do is keep a straight face." She was mad, but she looked back at the river and the ropes. "So, how do we get across?"

Just then the ferry came into view as it returned from the other shore. Adam nodded in the direction and she stared for the longest time.

The ferry was constructed of what appeared to be four large wooden canoes, that acted as long floats underneath a deck made of tightly fitted wooden planks that ran across the four canoes. Adam figured they were nailed to the gunnels of the canoe-shaped floats. Around the perimeter of the deck was a four-inch-high frame that prevented wagon wheels from sliding off the deck and into the river. Fastened to the frame were vertical posts through which thin ropes were passed to act as lifelines on the side of the ferry for passengers to hold onto. At each end of the ferry was a wide wooden ramp that was hinged on the deck and raised upright as the ferry crossed the river. At the farthest outside tips of each ramp a long pole was tied that allowed the two ferrymen at once to lift or lower the ramp. When lifted for passage across the river, the inside end of the poles had rope loops that hooked to a cleat on the side of the ferry, keeping the ramp upright. The bottoms of both ends of the ferry were sloped up away from the water to approximate the shape of the river's bank. So, when the ferry ran upon the bank a bit, the operators would drop the ramp and allow wagons, people, and animals to disembark. As Adam had thought, there were two big men who were pulling on the ropes that were tied to the trees. The ropes where threaded through steel deadeyes mounted on vertical braces at on the four corners of the ferry. The men would walk to the end of the ferry in the direction they wanted to go, grab hold of the rope, and pull on it as they walked to the rear of the ferry. Of course, the rope would not move, but the ferry would as the men's feet pushed against the ferry deck, allowing the ferry to slide along the rope to the opposite bank. At the same time, the current was pushing the ferry downstream; but the ropes, in their rove through the deadeyes, kept the ferry from doing so more than a foot or two until the ferry landed on the other side.

Eve watched the operation with amazement. As the ferry arrived at the landing and hit the shore, the ferrymen pulled ever harder to get the ferry against the shore. Then they grabbed smaller ropes that were tied to the big ropes close to shore. These smaller ropes were tied to cleats on the ferry that prevented the current from dragging the ferry away from shore. Then they released rope loops at the end of the ramp poles, lowered the ramp to the shore, and allowed people and wagons to disembark.

Adam guided his wagon onto the landing. There were three other wagons ahead of him plus a bevy of horses and riders. His group added three more wagons and a baker's dozen more animals. It appeared that the ferry was just long enough for one Conestoga and a team of four, so it would take several hours before they would all be on the other side. Adam grabbed three leather buckets and gave one to Eve and another to Henry; together they walked to the river and filled them with water for Calvin and Luther. Henry took his bucket to Pickles, their pony. Adam and Eve made repeated trips for Sizemore, their paint, and their cow, Bethany. Meanwhile, Michael and Charles did the same for their mule teams and their personal horses at the back of the train.

"Gentlemen," Adam said to the teamsters, "once on the other side we will stop for supper at the tavern up the hill, and after that we should try to drive for another three hours until dusk." The men agreed.

When their turn came, Adam paid the local ferriage of thirteen shillings, four pence for his train of wagons and animals. Then one wagon at a time they crossed the Monocacy River. Four hours later they camped just inside the city limits of Frederick.

A day out of Frederick, the wagon trail wound as it bent sharply around one four-hundred-foot mound after another. Thankfully, the road went around each rather than over the top of each. There were, however, ruts from erosion and mud pits along the road. During the rainy periods wagon wheels were swallowed by mud pits. Over the past days Adam had seen the broken debris of more than one wagon wheel that had been left behind. Each time they passed such a site, Adam checked to see if the spare wheel for his wagon was still attached to its side. It was. Curiously, his worry-wart personality never failed to check the security of the spare wheels on each of the Conestogas as well.

Finally, they came to Catoctin Creek. Adam was glad it was the fall for the creek's ford was easily passable being a foot deep at the most with a clear rocky bottom and only sixty to eighty feet wide. Either side of the ford small rocks protruded above the surface creating a small rapids effect, but for the most part the ford had been cleared of such obstructions. The crossing was uneventful except for pauses to let the animals dip their heads into the cool mountain stream and drink their fill. He could imagine this being a fast-flowing rapids in the spring and difficult for even a ferry to get safely across. The crude map he carried indicated that several miles downstream it emptied into the Potowmack.

After fording Catoctin Creek, the road climbed thirty feet to a ridge before its descent to the Potowmack River basin. At the top of the rise they stopped for the night and camped the train so as to take in the view looking west—a beautiful vista of the Potowmack River valley and the much smaller Shenandoah River valley. In the distance through a blue haze he could make out two massive tree-topped mountain ranges as they rose fourteen-hundred feet above the river. It was an amazing sight for a farmer who preferred flat land. As far as the eye could see to the north and south there were mountains rising to the sky—the Appalachians, as the Indians called them. But before him, the powerful and persistent waters of the Potowmack had punched two large gaps in the mountains as if they were butter, which allowed its water to flow hundreds of more miles to the ocean. He wondered how long it had taken the river to cut that gap. On either side of the gaps right up to where he sat on his wagon, leaves on oaks and maples were turning red, orange, and yellow against the green spruce and tall standing firs. The Potowmack flowed toward them and gleamed in the reflected setting sunlight. Ahead of him, the road descended some four-hundred feet to the basin. The road would then snake along the north shore of the Potowmack to Harper's Ferry where the Shenandoah River emptied into the Potowmack.

The next afternoon they pulled close to the Potowmack ferry landing, there was little space for a landing due to the steep rise of a rocky wall that rose four-hundred feet almost straight up. If the other side of the valley was any indication, at the top of the wall to his right the mountain would moderate its slope and rise a thousand more feet to a tree-topped ridge.

The same three wagons that were ahead of him at Catoctin Creek were now waiting along the rocky wall for their turn to cross the river. There was just enough room for the arriving ferry's load to disembark and pass them. In the spring, Adam wondered if when the water was high, the road, let alone the landing, existed at all.

While they waited, they braked and chocked their wagons, for they had stopped on a slight incline. Adam, his children, Michael, and Charles all walked down to inspect the ferry and talk with the ferrymen.

The actual ferry was twice the length of the one at Catoctin Creek, and resembled ones he had been on back east. They had wood fences on both sides to keep people from falling overboard. But it was still not long enough for two Conestogas and their teams of four. So, again it would take them several trips and several hours to get across.

Charles pointed out an innovation none of the men had seen before. The main means of propulsion across the river was a cable stretched tightly between the two shores which was wrapped around the small hub of a large six-foot wheel mounted on the side of the ferry. A ferryman stood on an outboard platform and turned the wheel by hand. The leverage he gained by the large outside diameter of the wheel easily turned the smaller hub, which then pulled the ferry across the river on the cable.

Adam asked the cost of the service. It was higher here, eight pence per man, beast, or wheel. It was only five pence per at Monocacy. But this was a larger operation and more dangerous. Both Adam and the ferryman had to do some figuring with his fifteen animals and three wagons (each with four wheels). They finally both decided it as 256 pence, or one pound, one shilling, and four pence.

"Will a gold guinea do it fer ya?" Adam asked, although he knew it was a shave less than what was being asked, although it was gold and not silver or currency.

"Sir, I don't know. Just workin' for the lady. Guess, to be safe I'd rather just have the twenty-one shilling and four-pence, I know that's a right."

Adam dug through his pocketbook. I have only twelve shillings left. "How about two-crowns instead of the twenty shillings?"

The man twisted his nose.

"They're *silver* half-crowns," Adam said, holding the coins up for the man to see, "worth half-pound each."

"Mister, you may be right and generous, but I just don't know me money that well."

Charles came up to the two men. "Need change, Mister Livingston?"

"Yep, ten shillings for a half-crown?"

Charles opened his pocketbook and scratched around. "Yes, sir." He handed Adam the ten shillings and took the half-crown. Adam in turn gave the happy ferryman the twenty-one shillings and four pence for the ferriage.

"Can we get over this evening, still?" asked Adam.

"'Tis the end of the day fer us. We can take one of yer wagons now, and the other two in the morning, if you like," said the ferryman.

Adam was disappointed but didn't press the point. It made no sense to rush a man doing a job that threatens their safety. "No, we will go together one after the other tomorrow morning."

The ferryman turned to go but Adam stopped him. "Who's the lady you work for? Doesn't *Robert Harper run the ferry?"

"Oh, no sir. Mister Harper passed away, oh, I guess it was nearly six year ago. Had no children. So, *Miss Sarah Wager, Mister Harper's niece, now runs the ferry 'n' the tavern across in Shenandoah Falls."

With that the ferryman invited the two buggies and riders behind Adam to get on the ferry for the last trip of the day.

Adam had hoped they could all have stayed at the inn and had a good meal. They'd just have to settle for whatever they could rustle up over a campfire. He consoled himself. They had come a long way without a breakdown if he didn't call the Hanover affair a breakdown. At any rate all were safe. Michael and Charles told Adam they'd get a fire going and tend to the livestock, and Adam promised to milk Bethany in a bit, for what it was worth, and it probably wouldn't be worth much.

His children came out of the wagon and he told them what was going on. They were disappointed, too. This close, and still not far enough. Adam took a long look at the crossing and the swiftly moving water. He had worried that this crossing would jeopardize everything he owned. He had imagined his wagon falling off the ferry and his possessions, money, and even his children being washed down the river. It was sundown as he studied the eight-hundred foot crossing and what he saw surprised him. Indeed, there were places that appeared to be very deep. But there were also numerous large, flat limestone rocks that created a steppingstone path across the river, provided one had a twenty foot stride. Curiously, where the ferry was pulled across, there were no rocks. Could they have been blasted away to allow the ferry's smooth passage? He didn't know. But the chance of the ferry tipping over was slight, not because of the protruding limestone rocks, which would prevent the ferry from slipping downstream, but because the ferry's floats, those canoe-shaped hulls, were so widely spaced. He watched as the ferry made its last trip to its overnight dockage in Virginia as it carried a few horses, their riders, and the two buggies. There was not the slightest tipping. He could sleep comfortably now.

Henry had taken to throwing rocks in the river, while Eve leaned up against her father, putting Adam between her and Henry, just in case Henry's rock flinging went awry and one flew sideways at her. One of the stones did come off his hand sideways but ended up skipping a good hundred feet into the river.

"Are we almost there, Papa?" she finally asked.

"Indeed, we are, daughter. That town across the river is Shenandoah Falls. You see it's at the bottom of a hill. Luther and Calvin and the mule teams will have to work hard tomorrow morning pulling us up that hill, which I'm pretty sure the road switchbacks behind those buildings. After that we'll be on a plateau, and by this time tomorrow we could be at our new home, a town called Smithfield."

"I didn't think we'd be living in a town. You still going to be a farmer?"

"Of course. Our farm is going to be seven times larger than the one we sold to Mister Eshelman. It lies just next to the village of Smithfield, which is very small. In fact, it doesn't even have a market."

"Seven times larger?" Eve's eyes got bigger.

Henry tried to pick up a rock bigger than he could lift.

"How you going to farm all that?" Eve asked. "You'll have to hire a lot of workers."

Adam recognized his daughter's insight. "I sure hope so. The problem is, I reckon it'll be two years before we can do any farming at all. First, we must build a cabin to live in this winter, and maybe a shed to store our goods. These wagons and teams need to be returned to York. Then, in the spring, we'll build a real house, and then a barn, clear the field, build fences, dig a well, buy livestock, and put up your loom."

"My loom!?"

"Yes. Once we put it back together in our new home, your mother's loom will be yours. You want to learn to weave, don't you?"

"Oh, yes. Like mother. I already know how to spin." With that realization Eve's eyes focused on the land across the river. Adam could see hope rise in her expression—there was something to look forward to in her future.

Adam also focused on the land across the river. For he saw something he had known about, but now for the first time realized it would be a big problem—it was when Eve had said, *"You'll have to hire a lot of workers."* Indeed, he might have a problem hiring a lot of workers. "Watch your brother, Eve. Don't let him fall into the river. I'll be right back."

Adam went behind the wagons where Michael had started the campfire. Charles had the horses and mules on long reins on a grazing line stretched along the foliage and grass beneath the cliff, and two-by-two were leading them to the feed troughs on the back of the Conestogas.

"Michael, can I ask you something?"

"Sure, thing, Mister Livingston. You must be feelin' pretty good being this far. We only got maybe one more day to do, don't we?"

"Yes, that's what I reckon, too." Adam paused to change the subject as he looked across the river at a group of people milling behind the tavern. "You've been in and out of Virginia quite a bit haven't you?"

"Yes, many times over the last, oh, ten years. The Shenandoah Valley is especially rich, right where's you're heading. You'll have a fertile farm, I'd say."

Adam nodded. "I have those hopes too. You know, soon after we crossed Mason and Dixon's line into Maryland, I noticed a lot of slaves working in the fields, and very few free men, although some of the Africans I saw working may not be slaves but free. Yet, the further we've traveled south, these past days, it seems to me that I have seen fewer and fewer freemen and more slaves, although I don't know if the Africans are free, indentured, or slaves. But I would think most are slaves. Adam moved between the wagons and pointed to the milling of men behind the tavern. "Look there, behind the tavern. What is that you see?"

Michael joined Adam between the wagons and gazed toward the tavern in the low light.

There was a group of white men, some dressed as farmers, others dressed up with ties, pointing and seemingly haggling over a group of black men, who were in shackles. "Those Africans are definitely not freemen," said Adam.

"No, they are not," said Michael. "That is a local slave market. Shenandoah Falls is a major commercial center, this being the main route between Maryland and Virginia. See that shed further back from the tavern with no windows?"

"Yes," said Adam.

"Notice the woman in the doorway watching the men?"

Adam nodded his head.

"That's where the slaves will be kept overnight until the sales are finalized and then, probably tomorrow, shipped across the river to where we're standing and off to their new owners. The men and women are sold separately, even though they may be married. I suspect that in a few minutes the men will be taken back inside the shed and the women will then be brought out for examination."

Adam said, "Or, maybe the women have already gone through the indignity and that woman we're seeing is watching what's to happen to her husband."

"Yeah," said Michael, "that may be."

Adam turned away and dropped his head. "Michael, I detest slavery in all its forms. As did my father. I'm having a terrible argument deep within me right now. What am I doing establishing a large farm in a state that relies so much on slave labor? That seems to be a question I should be asking, but haven't. Secondly, am I going to have trouble finding free men to work my farm? For I will not buy, hire, or rent enslaved persons."

Michael was silent for a moment as he considered Adam's dilemma. "Mister Livingston, I have to be honest with you. I have been wondering that very thing this whole trip. Franklyn Sidwell, my agent back in York, told me a bit about you and assured me that you were an honorable man. He said you were an upright son of German immigrants, hardworking, and trustworthy. And that although you were no abolitionist, you got along just fine without slaves."

Adam nodded. "Frank was right, I have not been an active abolitionist, but I am an outspoken supporter, as was my father, of the *Abolition Act and very glad when the Pennsylvania assembly passed it into law some years back. Even happier when they closed those loopholes earlier this year. But what I want to ask: Do you have much knowledge about the availability of day laborers, not slaves, where I'm goin'? Am I goin' to be able to find labor to work my farm; it's modestly large—three-hundred-fifty acres, though I won't be planting all of that."

"Yes, sir. I think that's going to be a problem for you. The further south you go, white men git lazier. They seem to take manual labor as an insult. I don't take to that line of thinking, and that's why I live and operate out of York."

Adam's face and countenance fell as if one of his Conestoga wagons had just fallen off the ferry and floated down the river with all his hopes and dreams.

"Mister Livingston, are you familiar with manumission and Virginia's laws regulating it?"

Adam narrowed his eyes and gazed at Michael. "I know what manumission is, but nothing of Virginia's slavery laws. Why?"

Michael said, "Manumission in Virginia was illegal...until eighty-two. Now it's legal and the owner doesn't need permission for the state legislature to free a slave or slaves. Supposedly, there's a clause in the law that requires manumitted slaves to leave the state within one year. But since the act was passed six years ago, I've not heard of it being enforced."

Adam was uncomfortable with what Michael was suggesting—buy slaves and set them free, hoping they'd stick around and still work for you. "How's that supposed to work. If I buy a slave to work for me, and manumit him, how's he supposed to keep working for me?"

"Indentures can work," said Michael. "Especially if done in front of a magistrate."

That was a lot more complicated than Adam wanted to consider. It was especially problematic because most of the labor he needed was seasonal—during planting and harvest. What Michael was suggesting was a year-round commitment.

Suddenly, they were interrupted by Henry's scream. A second later, Eve ran to her father. "Papa, come quickly, Henry needs you."

Adam and Michael and behind them Charles came running to the river's shore. Adam felt sure that Henry, his wayward ward, had fallen into the river. But something quite the opposite had occurred. Henry was struggling to grab a large fish in the river's shallow bank.

"It's a bass," said Charles. "Grab it Henry, it won't bite."

Henry couldn't quite get his little hands around the big squirmy fish, so Adam reached out and grabbed it and held it up for all to see. It was a heavy and healthy-looking fish. But Adam didn't know what to do with it.

"Let's cook it," said Charles. "It will taste good, although one is hardly enough for all of us. But we could make chowder by adding Bethany's milk and some potatoes, beans, 'n' carrots to it."

The five humans in the group looked at each other with this new kind of event as if to ask one another for permission.

"Wait a minute," said Adam, putting his son on the spot. "Just how did you come upon this?"

But Henry didn't know. He twisted his nose and shrugged his shoulders.

"I'll tell you," said Eve. "He hit it...with a rock."

"On purpose?" asked Adam.

"I don't suppose so," Eve said. "He just threw this big rock in the river to make a splash, and next thing he knew that fish flew up into the air and ended up at his feet splashing and scaring us. Can you really eat that?"

"Oh, yes," said Charles. "Come. I'll show you how it's done."

The group walked to the campfire where Charles gave a cooking lesson in the making of bass chowder. Adam felt a flutter in his belly, not unlike the flopping around of that fish. There was hope for Henry yet, even if it was accidental.

2

My Despised Cyn:

What have you been doing? Have wayward villagers distracted you? Or did I miss your translation to and from New Orleans? How are matters in the swamp?

I do wish you could persuade your mark to buy some slaves. Oh, how that would simplify our duty. But should he buy some slaves and later manumit them, perhaps there's some skulduggery to make him sorry for doing it. Surely, someone near him in Virginia will object. We've worked hard at keeping Virginia a slave state. Allowing manumissions there was a mistake and your peers are paying the price by being enslaved themselves.

Is there a way for your mark to lose a wagon in the Shenandoah rapids, perhaps the wagon with his money? That would help our cause and draw him into our decrepit end.

Eternally yours,
Master of Manipulation

Chapter 10
Discrepancy

1

Saturday, October 18, 1788.

The next morning the men fed and harnessed the teams while Eve, with some help from Henry, packed up the campsite. While they waited for the ferry, Adam surveyed the landing. During the night a southern wind had dumped rain onto their campsite, and had driven water over the landing, soaking the ground and leaving some standing water. Adam walked the landing. His boots easily sunk several inches into the bank at the place where the wagon wheels would mount the ferry's ramp. Adam realized he didn't weigh nearly as much as the wheels of the loaded wagons. He imagined the smaller front wheels of his wagon sinking into the muck and not being able to span the breach onto the ramp without something breaking. What they needed was something to firm up the soft earth where the ferry would drop its ramp.

He felt anxious. Yet, if it was any consolation, he had experienced no premonition about this day. Did that mean they would cross over without incident? He hoped so but he didn't know.

He turned to the Conestogas and his teamsters. "Michael? Charles? We may have a problem. Can I distract you for a few minutes?"

The men followed Adam to the landing, and he demonstrated the problem by stepping on the soft ground and seeing the heel of his boot disappear. But neither man seemed too concerned.

"I don't think that's going to be a problem for the Conestogas," said Michael.

Adam was not assured. "Well, maybe not for the big Conestoga wheels as wide and big as they are, but my wagon's front wheels are a lot thinner and smaller. They'll sink right in and get stuck."

"Could be," said Michael.

Michael was about to say something else when they heard the otherwise very quiet ferry quickly approaching the landing site where they were standing. They stepped away as the ferry came to rest on the bank with its burden of horses, men, and a loaded cargo wagon. As soon as the ferry pushed against the shore, Adam noticed that the ferryman operating the wheel secured it so the ferry could not float away. The pull-cable wrapped around the wheel's hub kept the ferry pushed against the shore, and the overhead pulleys kept the ferry from floating downstream. In time, the ferrymen lowered the ramp, and indeed it didn't reach far enough to span the soggy ground, just as Adam had suspected.

But on-board the ferry deck, neither the horses, their riders, nor the wagon moved to disembark. In fact, Adam noticed that the riders were holding their steeds back as if they too saw the problem.

But that wasn't it. As soon as the ramp was dropped the ferrymen walked to the back of the ferry on the up-stream side and lifted two long, wooden planks. They carried them forward, off the ramp, and placed each plank on top of the soft ground, side-by-side, next to the ramp, and then stomped them down with their boots. Due to their surface area the boards sunk into the ground only a fraction of an inch. The men went back onto the ferry and brought more of the same kind of planks onto shore and continued to build the breach over the soft ground. Two more trips and the planks formed a short but effective wood-plank roadbed from the ramp to solid ground. Then the riders, their horses, and the heavy wagon safely came off the ferry and went on their way up the road.

Michael spoke first. "That's what I was about to say. Notice those planks have been used before. I believe they keep them high and dry on the home shore and if it rains like it did last night, they simply bring them over on the first load. It's common practice. But this is nothing compared to what I've seen after a major storm. The ground is so muddy and soft that one layer of boards like this is not enough. Maybe someday they'll build a small but permanent wharf or quay. I've suggested it to a few ferrymen, but so far, I've never seen one."

After the arriving load disembarked, the ferrymen told Adam to come ahead and drive his wagon down the very center of the ferry so that his wagon's wheels ran on top of a set of longitudinal boards the length of the deck. Adam complied, and his wheels fit perfectly onto the boards, centering the wagon's weight on the ferry's deck. One of the ferrymen helped by taking Calvin's bridle and leading the horse all the way forward. "Sir," said the ferryman to Adam, "please set your brake and chocks, and rein in your team slightly. And it might help some if ya'll come down and hold your horses' bridles, so they'll be content. We don't need a horse panicking. The trip can be a little tippy."

"Eve? Go up and stand between Calvin and Luther so they can see you. And pet them, tell them it's all right. Henry, you stay put."

"Okay," Eve said, "but they did fine the last time without us."

"Well, let's do as they say. This is a bigger and perhaps more dangerous crossing."

With that Adam got down from his perch and helped Eve to the ferry deck. She went forward, and he went behind to check on Bethany, bringing her up a little tighter to the wagon to make room for a few single riders and their mounts that came onto the ferry at the rear. He looked back to shore and Michael and Charles gave him a high sign that all was well. He looked down on the planks that extended the ramp. All were high and dry.

When all was settled, the ferrymen lifted the ramp and secured it. One of the ferrymen stepped over the lifelines and onto the outside platform to unlock the wheel and turn it toward the opposite shore, and indeed the ferry began to move. As they started across, the other ferryman addressed those on board. "Okay folks, please hold on to your steed or the lifelines on the side. It will be just a tad bumpy this morning due to the rain we had last night. The river is alive and feeling her oats."

At that moment Adam glanced at Eve. She stood between Calvin and Luther holding onto their bridles and facing forward...but her head was bowed.

Crossing the Potowmack was anxious but uneventful, for which Adam was glad. Once across, Adam noticed Eve bowed her head once again and said loud enough for him to hear, "Mama, thank you for sending angels to protect us. Don't stop praying for us. Amen."

He had hoped to arrive at his property by the end of the day, but that was looking less likely. It had taken them nearly three hours to get all his wagons and livestock across the river, and longer to get up the hill from Shenandoah Falls, and onto the road to Charles Town. Neither did Adam count on the sounder of perhaps two-hundred head of swine they encountered hogging the road just outside Shenandoah Falls. Even though it had rained the night before, the dust kicked up by the sounder, along with the noise, and the disturbance underfoot made Calvin and Luther jumpy. It was a nuisance. but Adam and his train drove through.

It was late afternoon when they arrived in Charles Town. At the ferryman's suggestion, Adam stopped at the *Washington Tavern* for the night. The Tavern was near the corner of the main east-west and north-south roads in the middle of Charles Town. The east-west road, which originated in Shenandoah Falls, would take them all the way to Smithfield. In Charles Town the road was named Washington Street. They found the tavern and turned north to get behind the tavern to where the livery was supposed to be situated. As they turned Adam noticed signs at the intersection that announced they were turning off Washington Street and onto George Street. How did it happen that the two main streets in town were named after the Revolutionary War general? But the names piled up. As if it wasn't enough that the Washington Tavern faced Washington Street; they discovered the livery, on George Street, was named *George's Stables*. The livery proprietor was a man named Manchester, who went by Chester. Adam asked him about the street names.

"This here area was settled by Charles Washington, the general's youngest brother," said Chester, as he checked Luther's and Calvin's hoofs. "He lives jist south of here 'bout half-a-mile, big white house. Calls it *Happy Retreat*." Chester laughed at the name and shook his head. "Couple year ago, Virginia Assembly agreed ta acquire 80-acres from him and he laid out this town fir 'em, named the streets after his relatives. This here George, over thar Samuel, his brother, and beyond that, second street over is Mildred...his wife." Chester chuckled again. "Don't ye see? His brother was closer to him than his wife, I reckon." Chester mopped his brow with a dirty rag. "It was George that surveyed this whole territory, all the way up the Potowmack...hired by Lord Fairfax, they says."

"Even over in Smithfield?" asked Adam.

"Most definitely, Smithfield," said Chester. "Not sure George slept there, but he trod all over this area."

2

It was mid-morning, Sunday, October 19, 1788, when Adam and his train headed west and passed through the north end of the tiny village of Smithfield. About noon they came upon the bridge that crossed the Opequon Creek. They had arrived; it took just ten days. According to the map and deed his father had given him, the bridge and the road were the major landmark at the north corner of his property. His property was on his left and it stretched southwest about a mile and a half.

He found an old wagon trail that entered the property from the road, although it was overgrown with shrub and backed up by a row of trees. Adam told the kids to stay put, as he jumped to the ground, signaled to Michael and Charles that they had arrived, and walked around front to Calvin and Luther.

He stroked their necks with affection. "Calvin. Luther. I want to thank you both for bringing us this far." He pointed into the land where there was plenty of grass for grazing, "This here is our new home, and it looks as if you're in for a good supper. Let me walk you in."

With that, Adam took Calvin's bridle and led the horses and wagon through the overgrowth and onto the property. The wagon path was rocky. He made a note to relay the rocks with flat sandstone in a tight pattern that would provide a solid all-weather roadbed. The path wandered in an "S" curve just a bit, with tall wild-growing shrubs hiding the road from the land, and the land from the road. He thought a colonnade of oak or ash would look better and more welcoming, although replanting fruit trees along the path would be inviting in spring with their blossoms.

Adam was euphoric. They had made it. The journey was not long for some, but it was long enough for him. Instinctively, he smiled broadly and looked behind him. The kids, sitting high on the wagon's drive bench, craned their necks to look around their new home. Michael's and Charles' Conestogas were close behind.

He caught the men's eyes and saluted them. Michael saluted him back and Charles doffed his hat and gave a loud "Whoop!"

As he led his team off the wagon path and around the last shrub, they came to a large open area without trees. It was an old wagon yard. Unexpectedly, just beyond the yard sat a small, one story cabin constructed of squared-off and chinked logs. It appeared to sit on a stone foundation and was covered by a shake roof that wasn't in too bad of shape. Centered on the front was a small plain porch without a railing. There had been a three-step stoop; the stringers were still present, but the treads had rotted away. Centered on the porch was a door into the cabin, which swung open in the breeze.

For Adam, the cabin was a surprise that sent a warm tingling through his limbs. He had expected at most the ruins of a never-inhabited squatter's shack. Yet, the cabin appeared to be sturdily built, and it meant they might not have to start from scratch.

He led his team to pull the wagon close to the cabin's front porch. He might be assuming too much, but maybe, just maybe they could sleep the night with a roof over their heads. Michael and Charles pulled their wagons to the side and out of the way, dismounted, and started to explore the land.

Calvin and Luther seemed to know they had arrived, for both horses started to snort and stomp like they wanted loose. Adam figured it was the smell of water flowing along Opequon Creek, which they could not see, but they could hear and smell.

"Men," announced Adam, "let's get these animals into the field to graze. Eve, take Henry and some buckets to the creek over there, and see if you can safely get at the water."

"Mister Livingston?" yelled Charles. "You might not need to do that, look here." Charles pointed to a clump of shrubs on the north side of the cabin. Pushing the branches out of the way a cement cistern atop a stone foundation appeared. Adam looked up and saw that the cabin's roof was designed in such a way that all the rainwater that fell onto the roof ran through a trough into the cistern which was covered by a copper cover hammered into the shape of a cone. Lifting it up, Adam confirmed that the cistern was full of water, hundreds of gallons no doubt. On the side of the cistern and near the bottom was a wooden plug, that indeed was leaking. What a pleasant surprise it was. He put his hand into the water. It was cool. Tasting his fingers, the water was sweet.

Charles said, "Mister Livingston, look where you're standing."

Adam looked around him. He was standing in front of the cistern by the plug. He stepped back and noticed that there was a depression in the ground. Clearing away some of the weeds revealed a ten-foot oval dry-pond defined by cement chinked rocks surrounding the depression's perimeter with the cistern's plug hanging over one edge.

"Mister Livingston, let's get that plug out, you may have yourself a watering hole."

"Let me ready a new plug," said Michael. "I don't think that one will come out in one piece. Later we can fit it with a stopper vale."

Adam retrieved an axe for Michael, who readied a new plug from a small oak sapling. When Michael's new plug was ready, Adam used the axe to pry out the old plug. It didn't want to come out at first, but soon it did, and with it a mighty stream of clear water began to fill the depression.

Eve was standing nearby with Henry. "Papa," she said, "it's just like Meribah in the Bible."

"What!?" Adam said.

"You remember, Mama used to tell us the story when we'd bring water from the well. There was no water for the children of Israel when they were in the desert. God told Moses to tell the rock to give forth water, but he was mad and hit the rock with his staff. Water came out all right, but as punishment Moses never got into the Promised Land."

Adam looked at his daughter bewildered, trying to make sense of the story. He hadn't spoken to or hit the cistern. He had just pried out the plug. Now the little watering hole was full of water, and the horses and the mules had their eyes on it, twisting in their harnesses, wanting to be loosed. "Michael, see if your plug works, then let's get our livestock over here."

Michael took his plug, pushed it in against the flood of water. It sprayed him pretty good, but after hammering the plug home, the water stopped, and the pond was full.

"Papa look!" said Eve. She pointed to the edge of the pond. There was Cleopatra, Esther's cat, lapping happily at the water.

The men undid their teams' harnesses and led them to the water…they did not have to make them drink.

About fifty yards behind them, half-hidden by overgrowth, Adam found a dilapidated stable of modest size. It wasn't big enough for all their livestock, but it would do fine for Bethany for the time being. They just needed some straw for bedding. For feeding there was plenty of grass in the meadow between them and the Opequon Creek which, upon inspection, turned out to be more like a river. It was a good twenty-feet wide with a four-foot embankment, and flowing rapidly.

After the teams were cared for, everyone wanted to explore the cabin. Adam took a sturdy crate from his wagon to make a step up to the porch. The porch was a bit unsteady, but solid enough that one or two could stand on it at a time. Entering the open door that was swinging on rusty hinges, Adam saw that it was a one-room cabin, with a door that went out the back. Four windows, two broken and open. Birds had nested in the rafters and, no doubt, rodents under the floorboards. He found a door to a crawl space, probably a root cellar, but he was afraid to open it and look in. The place was a shamble, and filled with dust, animal droppings, and artifacts of the previous resident. A door at the rear, which was swollen shut, didn't want to open until push came to shove. It led to an outhouse that was still erect but probably unusable.

As he stood in the center of the dilapidated building his shoulders drooped even as his spirits soared. He had anticipated the need to build a new structure immediately for the winter for his family and their necessities. That work was now shortened considerably. The cabin was sturdy enough that in a week it would be ready for habitation, along with the privy. They had a water supply, with the cistern and the nearby creek. There was also the remnant of a well which he needed to check out. They'd fix up the stable for their livestock, maybe they could even start the foundation of the large two-story house he planned, and the three-level barn.

Once the surprise of the cabin and cistern wore off, Adam began to wonder if this land was indeed virgin farmland as his father was told. He examined his father's deed. There was no indication of a cabin or the stable. He became suspicious and wondered if there was going to be an issue when he got to the land office in Martinsburg. The deed said his property was in three parcels, but together roughly formed a rectangular with the short side of the rectangle about a half-mile long along the Charles Town road. From there it ran back a mile and a half to the southwest, bounded by Turkey Creek. Another road, Bunker Hill Street, bisected the property connecting the south end of Smithfield with the Opequon Creek ford.

A few minutes later he had jumped onto Calvin's bare back with only a bridle and reins and trotted along the road from the bridge to the southeast an estimated half-mile. He scanned the side of the road for a cairn that might mark the southeast corner of his property. It took a few back and forth passes before he spotted the cairn under a pile of weeds. It was an older cairn of flat interlocking stones with two arms, one pointing along the road back to the bridge, and the other pointing perpendicular from the road to the southwest. That seemed about right. Adam grinned and sat straighter on Calvin's back believing all was right. He also took note that this corner of the property was at the top of a hill that ran back into his land, on top of which was a significant stand of soft and hard timber directly to the southwest with a clearing to the northeast...not a bad place for a house and barn. The land indeed looked fertile.

Walking Calvin back along the road, he was about halfway when he suddenly stopped and slid off Calvin. There by the side of the road was another boundary corner, similarly positioned like the first one, but much newer and larger. He wondered how he had missed it before. It was clearly a corner boundary marker of interlocking field stones with one arm pointing like the first cairn to the southwest and the other arm pointing back to the bridge. But it was far short of where the deed suggested the corner of his land should be. He paced around it, clenched his jaw and shook his head. He looked around from where he stood. He could see the cabin they had found through the scrub bush and a few trees. Yes, this was probably the corner boundary for whatever stake was associated with that cabin, and it was far different from what his deed claimed. A ache suddenly found the back of his neck which he twisted in an attempt to exorcise it. But the tension was not going to go away anytime soon. Tomorrow he'd go to Martinsburg and pay a visit to the land survey office. Hopefully, they would know what's going on with the two corner markers. His shoulders slumped; he was expecting a fight.

When he returned to the wagons, he said nothing. Tonight, they would camp as they had been doing for the past week, build a fire and reminisce the journey.

The next morning Michael and Charles agreed to stay on for several weeks and help Adam get settled. With the children's help they started to clean out the cabin and stable. Meanwhile, Adam rode Calvin to the Berkeley County seat in Martinsburg to register the deed…and resolve the dilemma for the two corner markers.

3

In the land supervisor's office, Adam stood over a small-scale plat map of Smithfield and the surrounding farms' property lines. Also on the table were the two deeds, his father's quit claim deed, and the county's. Across from Adam was the county's land agent, Fritz Ivery, a fifty-year-old man with gold rimmed glasses, sandy-grey hair to his shoulders and a grey handlebar mustache yellowed on the ends. The county's restless surveyor, Cornwall Sutton, stood nearby in his mud boots. At twenty-five years, Sutton was slender, not very tall, and muscular. Ivery's office manager was the brains of the operation, Jane Ivery, his elder daughter, who held a stack of files near the doorway to the meeting room they occupied.

Adam said, "This is not what's in my father's deed." Adam waved his copy of the deed at Ivery before setting it back down on the table next to the land office's plat of the land. According to Adam's copy of the deed there were three parcels that comprised the half-mile wide by mile-and-a-half long property of three-hundred-fifty acres. Together it was bounded to the northwest by the Opequon Creek, to northeast by the Charles Town Wagon Road, to southwest along the V-shaped Turkey Run Creek, and to the southeast along a straight line with a surveyed length of 458 poles between the Charles Wagon Road and Turkey Run Creek that ran at 38.75 degrees true north.

But according to the land office's records a thirty-five-acre section of the property, which coincided with the northern corner of Adam's land and whose corner boundary corresponded with the second cairn he had found, was in some sort of legal limbo. Adam's headache had returned in full force.

The discrepancy which the land office could not explain only added to his earlier frustration with the office's inefficient and plagued filing system, which eventually regurgitated the conflicting deeds. Adam felt cheated. He had brought ample proof and a quit claim deed from his father for the transfer of the land. He even had an old-style indenture agreement that physically matched the indents of the copy in the land office. But still the land office would not issue him a patent to the land, which would allow the transfer of the deed from Johann to Adam.

He was not the explosive type. But his emotions ran over into his head and he felt the sweat pool behind his neck, down the sides of his face, and under his beard.

"Gentlemen, you had better explain this to me and how we're going to rectify what is clearly stated in this indenture that I carry. For I'm pretty sure a magistrate is going to side with my father's agreement and not whatever you're making noise about."

Adam looked hard between Ivery and Sutton.

"You're right, Mister Livingston. What we are facing is not your father's intention. But there is a problem, as Mister Sutton will explain," said Ivery, who then glared at Sutton. It seemed to Adam, however, that Sutton wasn't too keen on being the fall guy.

Cornwall Sutton came to the table and explained the issue. "Mister Livingston, in addition to my survey work, I'm the clerk responsible for maintaining the land patents and subsequent deeds in our county." He pointed to the small-scale plat map. "This here outlines the land your father bequeathed to you all right. It's almost exactly 350 acres. But we can't deliver to you clear title because of this." Sutton put out his hand to Jane who hand him a file. Sutton opened the file and unfolded a deed. "Here is a deed for thirty-five acres that lies at the north end of your property along the Charles Town Road, and it includes the improved cabin that was at one time occupied."

Adam took the county's recorded deed and studied it, then dubiously compared its description of the land with the deed from his father. The deed Sutton handed to him did describe the front thirty-five acres of the land described in Adam's deed. But it made no mention of his father, King George, or *Thomas Fairfax (the sixth Lord Fairfax) who had inherited the original patent from Charles II. The deed from Adam's father traced the ownership of the property from King George to Johann Lieberstein. The county's deed did, however, mention an Alexander Mayfield who sold the land to one Silas Cain in 1760. "Who are these Mayfield or Cain fellas. Are they around?" asked Adam.

"We can find no record of them…either one of them," said Sutton.

"Adam compared the deeds side-by-side. "Doesn't it seem strange that the deed given me by my father is witnessed by a magistrate and the script is that of a learned hand, but this deed from the county has none of the characteristics of education."

Sutton and Ivery were quiet for a moment or two as they exchanged looks. Ivery finally spoke, "Indeed. And it raises questions as to its authenticity. But here's the second problem. The Mayfield-Cain deed is legally registered with this office. It is a legal document, just as your indentured deed is. This is not your fault. Suppose it's our fault, but by individuals before us."

Adam asked, "How am I to interpret this? What's the resolution?"

It was quiet for a few moments before Ivery took a deep breath, glanced at Sutton, and then to Jane, who spoke for the first time.

"Do you want me to check now, Father?"

"Yes. See if he can see us," said Ivery.

And with that Jane put down the stack of files on her father's desk and walked briskly out of the office. A moment later they heard the front door of the land office open and close.

"Mister Livingston," said Ivery, "bear with us. We're going to try to resolve this quickly if Judge Argyle is available. His office and chambers are across the street in the county courthouse. I assume you want to resolve this as soon as possible, insomuch as you've just arrived on the land and want to improve it."

"Yes, that is my intention. But I'm disturbed by this whole affair."

"Yes, we understand, and had we known the situation before you arrived, we might have had a solution beforehand. If it's any consolation, while we wait for Jane to return, here is what we suspect happened. Alexander Mayfield had somehow acquired squatter's rights, or perhaps he had been granted a form of headrights to this little parcel of land. We think he was a tenant of Lord Fairfax some forty to fifty years ago. But no deed or sale was ever recorded with the Virginia colony. Maybe he was just a squatter and there was no deed, or agreement. Whatever paperwork existed has been lost to history. At some point, perhaps as early as 1760, Mayfield met Cain and they drafted this deed together which Silas Cain (by the appearance of the deed) legally registered with this office. You see, both signatures are on the document."

Adam picked up the registered deed. "Yes, I see there are two signatures on the document, and it's been witnessed by, looks like, William Fairfax. But it also says," and Adam read the document aloud to the other men in the room, "appeared before me one Silas Cain, as representing both seller and buyer, this day...and so forth. There's no mention of this Alexander Mayfield appearing. As I mentioned a moment ago, this does not look like any document that came from an official office. The paper isn't square, there is no indenture, and the ink is flawed and spotty. It appears a fraud. Why can't you see that?"

Before Ivery or Sutton could answer, the front door opened, footsteps could be heard approaching the office across the wood planked floor, and Jane entered the inner office. The men turned and looked to her.

"Gentlemen, the judge will see you now."

"How was he?" asked her father.

"The usual," she replied. "Gruff. Upset. It seems his wife is stirring up rumors again, and threatening to sue the neighbors."

"As I expected. Okay, let's get over there. Jane, bring the rest of the files."

Ivery collected the deeds off the table, Jane the files, Sutton the maps, and Adam his father's paperwork, and they all followed Jane out of the office and across the street.

The meeting with Judge Jordan Argyle didn't take long; he needed to put together a posse and look for his wife.

On the way back to the land office, Adam tried to contain his anger. If Judge Argyle ever ran for county magistrate again, Adam would oppose him. Sutton had explained to the judge that the land did not need another survey. There was no question about where the boundaries lay. But the condition the judge set for dissolving the Mayfield-Cain deed was that the land be surveyed again by a reputable company, after which a new deed would be drafted, which the judge would witness, and then be registered in the county office. Adam argued that the Mayfield-Cain deed was an obvious forgery, yet Argyle blindly referred to it as a legally registered deed. By agreeing to dissolve the "registered deed" all Argyle required was a re-survey; that logically would do nothing to prove the deed authentic or a forgery.

Adam was fuming. Then, to add fuel to the fire, after they left the judge, Sutton revealed that the "reputable company" the land office was instructed to use was Christian Fox Surveyors—Judge Argyle's son-in-law.

"Can he do that, force you to use his son-in-law's firm?" bellowed Adam.

Ivery answered, "No, he can't, and we won't, which is one reason we don't like to go to him for much of anything. Except we can move things along faster with his signature."

Back in the land office, Adam begrudgingly asked, "All right. How much?"

Ivery was ready with an answer. "Sutton, here, will ride out to your property and look around. That will constitute our survey to legally satisfy ourselves that the original deed, the one your father passed on to you, agrees with what is there. When that is done, we'll draft a new deed, get Argyle's signature on it, and bring it to you. Five pounds should cover all of that; and it will make your property whole."

Adam was frustrated but came to accept this new reality. He recalled that five-pound sterling was about a quarter of the extra gold he found at the bottom of George's satchel. It was a lot, he didn't want to part with it, and he didn't think he should, but he also realized this would only be the beginning of the unplanned expenses he would face. He reckoned he might as well get on the proper side of the local system. "Okay," he said. "Draft a letter to the effect that this problem is going to disappear when I pay you the five pounds."

"Yes, we'll do that right away. Jane, will you start that?"

"I'll just need clarification of some wording first," said Jane.

With that Adam opened his satchel. He was glad he brought along some gold just in case…like this, to buy back part of his own land.

Before he left Martinsburg, Adam found the tavern and sat down at the secretary desk, where writing paper, quills, ink, wax, and a seal were available. The local letter writer tried to cajole Adam into paying him to write his letter, but Adam told the old man he knew how to read and write and thank-you-very-much I'll write my own. *Poor fellow trying to earn a decent living.* But this letter was going to be more personal. He sat at the table, took quill, and paper, and wrote to his father of all that had happened since arriving. Most of the short letter was about the thirty-five acres that he had to repurchase, although his father's deed clearly stated otherwise. In closing, he was generous with praise for his father's choice of land by the creek and how there was a small cabin on the property that they would use until they could build their new home. Finally, he closed by directing his father to send return mail to the tavern in Charles Town which was much closer to the new farm than Martinsburg.

That night the moon was nearly full. After everyone had turned in and his kids had fallen asleep, Adam collected all the extra gold he had brought with him, including the extra Eshelman gold, and placed it in a small lockable strong box. With a shovel he headed off into the woods. Doing this in the dark without a lantern would avoid attracting undue attention. Deep in the woods he found a large elm with a distinctive horizontal and twisted limb about 8-feet off the ground, which pointed to a dense colony of maple leaf shrubs. Getting between the shrubs was difficult in the dark, but once there it seemed the ground was hidden from sight. He dug a hole for the strong box, deposited the box in it, covered over the hole, and then scavenged several field stones to pile on top. Eventually he might come to trust the bank in Charles Town, but not now. This way if he needed it, he could retrieve his gold much easier.

4

My Despised Cyn:

Well, that was dull. No sudden flash flood to wash the family into the Atlantic. Can you only effect his dreams and imagination and not reality? What good are you? Yes, I know...I know, you need to be physically present to do that sort of thing. In time, we trust. Livingston is not far from your coffin, as it lies under that misplaced and obscure cairn.

Isn't there some way to quiet the girl down with all her humble prayers and weak Biblical illustrations? It's disheartening to see and hear. If she keeps it up, she's likely to have some negative effect on our efforts.

I fear the incorporation of the United States into a mostly functioning union will be a constant irritation to our goals. Notice how easily Livingston negotiated the confusion about the Mayfield property. In any other country of the world, we would have been happy when the fists and swords started to fly. But no fists, no swords here, just a damn regular process of decision making and abiding by laws. Distasteful. No chance for chaos, even if the judge's solution was self-centered. Imagine the chaos without judgment. Judges need to go fishing more often and step away from their responsibility. That way we can introduce frustration in the people who think they have been unjustly treated. We need to remove the recourse for even a sense of objectivity and fairness. That is our calling.

Now, do get your spiritual sense along, as Denis Cahill is about to make a decision that we'd like to prevent. Our goal is to keep him in New Orleans. We do not want him coming to the United States. Get your decrepitness down there.

Eternally yours,
Master of Frustration

Part Three: Passage

And the Lord said to Abram:
Go forth out of thy country, and from thy kindred,
and out of thy father's house,
and come into the land which I shall shew thee.
And I will make of thee a great nation,
and I will bless thee, and magnify thy name,
and thou shalt be blessed.

(Genesis 12:1–2)

Chapter 11
Killing Instinct

1

It was six months after the New Orleans Good Friday fire. The friars and many of the families still lived in tents on the Plaza while their homes were rebuilt. Although the ruins of the church and presbytery had been cleared away, there was no schedule for rebuilding the landmark structures.

Fr. Cahill made his way from his tent on the Plaza to the wharf. It was his turn to hear confessions from seamen. As he approached the corner of the Plaza where the small penance tent was erected, his eyes scanned the busy wharf. There were nine merchant ships under American, French, Spanish, Portuguese, and British flags loading or unloading cargo. At the far end was *La Feroz* (The Ferocious), an old Spanish war galleon that was antiquated and inadequate for fighting sea battles, so it was billeted as barracks for soldiers.

Upstream, behind the ocean-going vessels, were dozens of flatboats that had floated down from the interior of the continent to trade their produce. While the flat boats were efficient at floating down the mighty Mississippi, they were useless going upstream. Once in New Orleans they were disassembled, and their wood sold for lumber or fuel.

There were a thousand souls that worked along the long wharf, attempting to improve the quality of life for New Orleans inhabitants. But there was one area of activity that, in Capuchin minds, negated all the rest. What made it most distressing was that it took place every day, including Sundays, only five hundred feet from the church and presbytery property.

Until a few years earlier, the trading of slaves had taken place under cover in the privately owned coffeehouses, saloons, or in one of the warehouses set up as a slave pen a block or two behind the wharf.

Slave traders realized, however, how the spectacle of public auctions raised the price of their commodities. So, a platform had been erected at the downriver side of the wharf where men, women, and child slaves were displayed, inspected, and sold like soulless animals.

Often, the white European plantation owners were invited up onto the high platform to inspect the debased merchandise that the auctioneer prodded, poked, and manhandled.

The purchasers were scattered among the crowd, which was composed mostly of curiosity seekers dressed in their Sunday finery. Many were either coming from or going to Mass. Some brought their children, who tried to outdo each other by ridiculing and mocking the downtrodden on display.

Fr. Cahill stopped short of the confession tent and forced himself to stare at the sight. Although even a quick look often haunted his dreams, he needed to pray devoutly for the black families experiencing this horror. He needed to pray that the practice found its end.

As he watched the auction from afar, he thought about how, as a Capuchin priest, he was not altogether different from the slaves, at least symbolically. His black habit that covered him head to toe was nearly the same color as the Africans' and some Indians' skin. The habit's rough texture reminded him of the many scars and callouses that the skin of slaves exhibited. Then there was his habit's cincture, a long, white, corded rope that tied around the waist. The cincture helped keep his sack robe closed on gusty days, and the three knots in the rope that hung from his waist represented his voluntary vows, the three cornerstones of the Franciscan order—Poverty, Chastity, and Obedience. The vows to him were entirely voluntary, but to slaves the same were forced upon them on threat of death. Finally, his cincture was made of rope, which symbolically bound him to his master, Christ, who reminded him to love and serve others. But the ropes that bound slaves to their masters and plantations were not symbolic but literally articles of hate and oppression.

Staring at the auction, something unexpected caught his eye. His eyes narrowed at the sight of a respectably dressed gentleman in tailored blue linen coat with tails and a purple satin top hat worn by the upper crust of society. The man was perhaps thirty years of age and if met on the street one would be tempted to bow in respect for his high station. But what Fr. Cahill witnessed was not something worthy of respect.

The man strode from the notary's desk near the auction platform toward the gangplank of a Spanish trading brig. Before him he whipped and shoved a slave he had just purchased. Fr. Cahill had seen slaves being lashed until blood ran freely from their back; the scars on the backs of men and women were a common sight. Yet he never witnessed such overt hatred and abuse. At first, he averted his eyes knowing not what else to do. But he was drawn back by something he had not seen before.

Sustaining the blows, from the otherwise proper appearing gentleman, was not a man, or a woman,...but a boy...a boy no more than ten years of age—a dark-skinned Chitimacha Indian, whose hands were tied behind his back, his ankles in shackles and chain.

When the boy fell to the ground, the "gentleman" kicked the lad in the ribs until the boy got up and struggled again toward the vessel. As the boy turned his back to get on the ship, Fr. Cahill could see blood seeping through the lad's thin muslin shirt.

It was bad enough that the evils of slavery had been practiced by warring Indian and African tribes who enslaved their enemies for the past thousand years. But then came the European profiters who exploited and expanded slave trade across the seas. It was not new that entire families were enslaved, including the children. Fr. Cahill had known this, but he had not seen the brutality until this moment. His blood boiled at the sight. He shook with repulsion, and he feared for all mankind. Seeing what he had never seen before, and understanding its consequences cut into his composure and opened his calloused eyes. His natural instincts told him that somewhere there was a mother crying, sobbing uncontrollably for her son. The father of the boy, probably a warrior, was most likely dead somewhere in the cypress swamp—food for alligators.

And the boy? He was probably headed for one of the islands never to be seen again by his mother or tribe. Fr. Cahill quickly scanned the slaves lined up on the auction stand. Was there an Indian mother there? No. All were African men in various states of health, their futures bleak.

He prayed an *Our Father* for the boy's safety as he watched him being kicked into the hold of the ship. Fr. Cahill considered running onto the ship and offering himself in the boy's place.

But he was interrupted.

2

A decently dressed British seaman, about thirty years of age, approached the tent, probably a first mate of a nearby brig.

"Father, can you hear my confession?"

Fr. Cahill turned to the sailor, "Yes. *Salve filius emus*...hello, my son."

"Salve, Pater," the man said.

Fr. Cahill donned his purple confessional stole, and the two men ducked into the small, off-white canvas tent. The tent was no more than an awning to block out the sun with a thin muslin sheet acting as a screen separating the men. On one side Fr. Cahill sat on a chair turned sideways so his left ear was directed toward where the man knelt, facing the sheet from the other side.

Making the sign of the cross toward the sheet, Fr. Cahill began, "In nomine Patris, et Filii, et Spiritus Sancti...*In the name of the Father, and the Son, and the Holy Ghost. Amen.*"

"Bless me, Father, for I have sinned. It has been six months since my last confession. And these are my sins. I have committed fornication with a woman of the street when our vessel was in Havana. In my position as an officer of the deck I have mistreated those under my command and whipped a man at the mast for his dereliction of duty which was just, but I did it with anger and hatred toward him for his disrespect of my person. For these and all the sins of my past life, I ask pardon of God, penance, and absolution from you, Father."

Fr. Cahill knew that where there was smoke, there had to be fire. "Have you also borne fornication in your heart, my son?"

"Well, that is obvious, Father. Many times. It is a difficult curse to be at sea for months without such thoughts, and when in port more so. It is natural, is it not?"

"Yes. But it is still a sin, and you are not alone in this."

The man cracked a smile. "Father, you do not need to confess to me."

"My son, I am not asking you for absolution. You are asking me, and our Savior in heaven."

"Yes. I confess my immoral thoughts, as well."

"Is that all you have to confess? Is there no drunkenness, or idleness in your heart? Do you doubt God, or put power and money before your Lord?"

"I am not guilty of grave sin in those areas, but such do navigate through my mind at times. My captain exceeds his authority as does our king. But I am an obedient servant of his Majesty. I was formerly a naval officer-of-the-line and know my place."

"Very well, my son. Keep up the good work for God, not the king."

"Aye, but the king is a defender of God, Father."

"Only at times, my son. Do not confuse the two."

The seaman was silent at this.

"For you penance...are you a praying man?"

"Yes, Father, I am."

"Then, for your penance, I want you to do two things. Before you leave port, find an old woman, perhaps a widow, and go out of your way to pay her some generous kindness. But not money. Do something that humbles yourself for her. Secondly, the man you whipped. Is he still in your command, will he be shipping out with you?"

"I believe so. He has a wife and family in Ireland."

"Ah, I am Irish, too, if you have caught my tongue."

"Aye, I have, Father."

"Then, seek him out, and likewise pay some honor by being of service to him in some way that proves your sincerity of heart and forgiveness for his disrespect. He has paid for his crime, has he not?"

"Aye, I can do that, and will, Father."

"Good; now say a good Act of Contrition such that the Lord will see the true disposition of your heart and forgive you."

In sincerity the man prayed in Latin, "*O my God, I am heartily sorry for having offended Thee, and I detest all my sins because I dread the loss of heaven and the pains of hell. But most of all because they offend Thee, who art all good and worthy of all my love. And I firmly resolve, with the help of Thy grace, to confess my sins, to do penance, and to amend my life. Amen.*"

Cahill was impressed. The man's Latin was near perfect. Making the sign of the cross over the man on the other side of the screen, Fr. Cahill intoned, likewise in Latin, "*May our Lord Jesus Christ absolve you; and by His authority I absolve you from every bond of excommunication and interdict, so far as my power allows and your needs require. Thereupon, I absolve you of your sins in the name of the Father, and the Son, and the Holy Spirit. Amen. Now, may the Passion of Our Lord Jesus Christ, the merits of the Blessed Virgin Mary and of all the saints, and whatever good you do or evil you endure, merit for you the remission of your sins, the increase of grace, and the reward of everlasting life. Amen."*

The seaman, with head bowed, crossed himself, then kissed his thumb which was crossed over his index finger. "Gratias ago tibi, Pater."

Standing tall outside the tent, as if relieved of his burden, the seaman reflected a moment then dug into his coat pocket and withdrew a coin. He stepped around the sheet, took Fr. Cahill's hand, shook it and deposited in the coin in the priest's palm.

Before Cahill could object, the merchant mariner was gone.

3

The coin given Fr. Cahill was an embarrassment to be sure. Paying for one's sins to be forgiven never did work. Cahill had the sense, however, that this was not a bribe or payment for absolution. It was an offering of thanksgiving, an extra penance. So, Fr. Cahill reverently gave God thanks, then studied the coin of which he had not seen many before. The George III 1787 silver shilling was relatively new. He looked at it for a moment, turned it over in his fingers and studied the relief letters around the back of the coin's perimeter. There, in raised relief, was the traditional *F.D.—Fidei Defensor.

What a lie, Cahill thought. What hypocrisy.

He had often bristled when defenders of European monarchies claimed that their kings and queens were "Fidei Defensor"—*Defenders of the Catholic Faith*. Cahill marveled that the inscription was still on the British Empire's coins even as he unconsciously rubbed the coin between his fingers as if trying to wear off the abbreviated inscription.

He recalled how two hundred years earlier Pope Leo X had bestowed upon Britain's King Henry VIII the "Fidei Defensor" title in recognition of his 1521 *Defense of the Seven Sacraments* against Luther and the Protestants. Cahill recalled how the document not only defended marriage as sacred but also the papacy as supreme.

And what did King Henry do?

Nine years later he rebelled against the papacy for not granting an annulment with Catharine of Aragon so he could marry his mistress, Anne Boleyn. Then, he had parliament oversee the confiscation of all Catholic property in England. He exiled or arrested the monks, friars, and priests for treason. Then Henry set himself up as the head of the Church, declared his marriage with Catharine annulled, and he married Anne. It was adulterous lunacy. What authority did Henry have? His own ego? Who does he think he is? Obviously he thinks he's God. But God was not fooled, Cahill thought. Lies have consequences. God, not the king, should be in charge. What the world needed was a humble theocracy, not an arrogant monarchy.

Flipping the coin over and over in his fingers, a trick he had learned from a Spanish peasant during seminary, he recalled how the papacy wasn't fooled either. No sooner had Henry reneged on his defense of the pope than Pope Clement VIII reneged on Henry's title. In the Church's eyes Henry was no longer "F.D." But what did Henry care? Now he was head of the Church of England and rolled parliament over his fingers, like the coin Fr. Cahill flipped on his.

Fr. Cahill stared at the F.D. once more. It was not the pope's F.D, he thought. It was rather the British parliament's F.D. pressed by Henry to reinstate it as if it carried the same significance. As Cahill put the coin in his waist-purse he could not figure why the world was so blind and dumb about what had happened.

4

Fr. Cahill got up from his chair and stepped out of the tent. The sun had peeked out from behind the clouds, and the winds had clocked to the northwest bringing a cooling breeze to the otherwise humid and overcast summer day.

Nearby the captain of the American brig Eagle stood among bales of wheat and barrels of pig loins, discussing the loading of his ship with a cargo walloper and an agent. Fr. Cahill knew the cargo walloper, Michael Lewis, a trim Cajun man of perhaps eighteen with little education but a good heart. The agent Cahill had seen frequently at the wharf but did not know. Fr. Cahill's attention was on the sharply tailored, short, but poised, clean-shaven, straight-backed merchant marine captain.

There you go, he thought. The Americans were to him proof that his discontent with the rest of the world was justified. The same Europeans that in their arrogant omniscience titled their monarchs "Defenders of the Faith" also claimed that the American revolutionaries would self-destruct within a year of their founding. Never mind that the rag-tag army of the colonies had defeated the best-known, best-trained, and best-supplied army in the world. No, America was to be reckoned with.

Momentarily, a mate of the Eagle walked up to the captain and handed him four books. In turn, the captain handed two books to each of the two men with whom he was talking. The books looked new. They had brown bindings, maroon covers, and gold imprints on their fronts, although he couldn't read what it said from his distance. They also featured gold filigree trim front and back. *Important books,* he guessed.

When Fr. Cahill saw the faces of the two men light up at their gift, he became intensely interested in what they were. He loved to read, but books in New Orleans, especially new ones, were rare.

The captain noticed Fr. Cahill looking at him, nodded his respect and said something to the men, seemingly about Fr. Cahill. As the American captain hurriedly left and walked briskly back to the Eagle, Cahill made his way to the men who looked admirably at their gifts. What was also evident is that Michael Lewis, not knowing how to read, had no idea what to do with his volumes.

Fr. Cahill caught Michael's eye and as they stepped to greet each other, the agent, clearly on a timely errand, waved his departure.

"Good 'ay, Father," said Michael.

Fr. Cahill could see the curiosity in Michael's face, as if the good priest was going to accuse him of some moral offense of which the cargo walloper was ignorant. "Good day, Michael. What do you have there?" said Father Cahill gesturing to the books.

"I have no idea, Father. You knows I kin't read, and dis very kind Capt'in gave me both of these, 'en Mister Monroe. But..."

"May I see them"?

"Shar," said Michael handing the books over.

The books were beautifully trimmed in gold with sewn bindings. Fr. Cahill could not believe his luck. Or was it Providence? Yes, that was it. His hands trembled as he read aloud the title of the book on top:

THE FEDERALIST: A COLLECTION OF ESSAYS WRITTEN IN FA-VOUR OF THE NEW CONSTITUTION, AS AGREED UPON BY THE FEDERAL CONVENTION SEPTEMBER 17, 1787 IN TWO VOLUMES, INCLUDING THE FULL TEXT OF THE PROPOSED CONSTITU-TION.

"What d'fedal'st?" Michael asked.

Even before Fr. Cahill came to North America he had heard of the fledgling experiment in democracy and its rumored design based on the premise that all men were created equal. It was pretty clear that the writers of the Declaration of Independence were saying that the British king was no better than a colonial farmer. In the eyes of their creator, the two should be afforded equal respect and dignity. But in Fr. Cahill's thinking, the concept went far beyond king versus farmer; it should be extended to slaves. In God's eyes a slave owner was no better than the person enslaved. The two should be afforded equal respect and dignity, which of course, if it were to happen, would eradicate slavery.

But what about women? In God's eyes they were certainly deserving of equal respect and dignity. The church may be run by men, thanks to Eve's lack of gardening skills, but certainly the Virgin Mary was exalted higher than any man, priest, or pope. Thinking about this made his head hurt, but it all underscored Michael's question, "What d'fedal'st?"

A federalist, of course, was someone who believed in the distribution of power and not an all powerful central government. There would be no king in the United States. A federalist believed the states were as important as the central government, and that the states and the federal government had to work together for the common good. That meant there had to be fairness and reciprocity—a contracted agreement between the various levels of governance. For such reasons it was called the *United* States. He had read everything he could about the new society. Whenever he had a chance, he would corner an American and ask them if what he as a young seminarian was reading was true.

Now, in the Spanish-owned Louisiana port of New Orleans, he was hearing much more, directly from hundreds of American citizens who traveled down the Mississippi to trade. What a unique place New Orleans had become over the last fifty years. United States farmers and manufacturers along the Ohio and Mississippi Rivers built flatboats to carry their products down to New Orleans. There, they loaded their produce and manufactured goods onto merchant sailing vessels that would take their products to America's East Coast markets where eighty percent of their new country's population lived.

It was thousands of miles longer than freighting products over the Allegheny Mountains, but the river and ocean route was much cheaper and the sailing merchants had readily established markets in Boston, New York, Philadelphia, Williamsburg, and even Havana. Consequently, Spanish-governed New Orleans received timely news about America, both from the heartland farmers via the flatboatmen, and from the crews of sailing vessels that arrived almost daily from America's East Coast.

For Fr. Cahill, the promise of an American's freedom from government control and the attending persecutions over the Church was invigorating. Fr. Cahill reasoned it should be the other way around, as it was centuries earlier. The church should control and even prosecute the state for its immoral offenses.

He remembered not too long ago that his eyes had literally glistened with joy when he read in a Boston newspaper that the U.S. Constitution had been ratified on June 21, although it was too early to tell how well the legal contraption would work. That day, Fr. Antoine and Brother Luke had asked why he was so happy. Fr. Cahill made some off-handed comment about the weather. But the news had given him a high, brisk step. He told himself that the world would be watching with eager anticipation...as would he. His interest in the news about America was addictive, and he wondered if he should carry his obsession into the confessional.

And now this. *The Federalist* would explain it all, or at least he hoped it would. He had read several of the first essays when they appeared in New York newspapers the previous year. But he felt deprived that he had not seen the later essays. And yet, here they all were, in two volumes. Or so he hoped.

"Michael," the priest said, "these two volumes are a collection of essays or writings that the supporters of the new U.S. Constitution wrote, in an effort to get it ratified."

"What d'rats done w'd it?"

"No. Ratified or Ratify. To ratify means to accept and put into law, which just happened months ago. I've been trying to learn all I can of what's going on in America and of their new Constitution."

"You tell me what happen'g?"

"Can I borrow these, so I can read them. Then I promise I'll tell you."

"Fin w'd me. You kin keep 'em if you want. I can't use 'em for nothing."

The cargo walloper hesitated for a moment, trying to remember something— "Oh, Father, d'American capt'n aks you come d'America. Say they need priests. Capt'n he want to confess, but he can't leave 'is ship while loading. I must git back, now, Father. Will you excuse me?"

"Certainly, Michael. You go. God bless you."

As Michael scurried back to the Eagle to finish packing its hold, Fr. Cahill followed at a slower pace. He stood near the brig's gangway and hoped to catch the captain's eye. He held the two books in his arms across his chest and let his eyes marvel at the grandness of the seasoned vessel and the large American flag flying off its stern.

It wasn't long before the captain caught sight of him, and after giving instructions to a mate, hurried off the ship to greet Fr. Cahill. The brig's captain was a short, stocky, and muscular appearing man, probably in his mid-thirties. Fr. Cahill took note of his piercing eyes and long aristocratic nose. He wore no cap. His dark hair, bleached by the sun in light brown streaks, was already thinning at the sides. But he was a fashionable man, no doubt. He wore a dark blue frock coat and a common ruffled linen shirt, white stockings, and flat work shoes with leather buckles.

"Father, I am Captain Werner Johns of the brig Eagle, an old but salty vessel almost ready for retirement. Ya think? Look at her. But she has several more voyages before that, I reckon. I see you have the books I gave to my walloper. He said he would give them to someone who could read. He's a good lad. You know him?"

"Yes. He is Michael Lewis, a good young man. I have promised to read these for him and explain the U.S. Constitution to him. I know something about it, having read the first two Federalist Papers in newsprint. But I'm anxious to read the rest. These are a great gift. Your generosity is a grace."

"I told the wallop...er, Michael, that we need priests in America. You should come if you are able. Catholics in the United States, and there are many, do not have priests as they should. We don't even have a bishop. It's a terrible situation, even as we continue to be persecuted in an off-handed way by those loyal to the Crown, Guy Fawkes and all. But the people are hungry. Can you possibly come?"

Fr. Cahill was dumb-founded, and he just stared at the somewhat shorter man. Euphoria filled his spirit for a moment. He realized that he would love to go, but a priest is not free to go off somewhere on his own, especially not a religious order priest, such as himself. There were the vows of obedience, chastity and poverty. His pause to think of an answer prompted Captain Johns to say more.

"If I could, I would *press* you, but I'm sure God would not bless my voyage and perhaps even damn it if I did such a thing. But there is this other thing. The Eagle is shy a chaplain because I won't have a Protestant. I'm a loyal papist, which does not please some of my crew. But if you will come, I can pay you as crew, if you can be ready by the time we sail, in a day or two it seems. We're awaiting some flatboats to arrive. And if you then come, I will then have time to confess." He said this last with a twinkle in his eye.

Fr. Cahill was struck. Oh, if he was only free and able, he would go. He looked down at the three knots of his cincture. "Will your confession take that long, Captain? Are you suggesting it may take days and we will need to take breaks for food and sleep?"

It was a joke, and the captain threw back his head in hearty laughter. "No, no, father. I am not a big sinner. But long voyages take a toll. I would have a priest on board all the time if I had my way."

"Then is it that big a matter?" Fr. Cahill took his confessional stole from his pocket, kissed the cross embroidered on it, and laid it around his neck.

Captain Johns' eyes got big, and then he looked behind him at his crew loading the brig, and back to the priest. "Aye, it will not take that long." He gestured to an island of crates and barrels that were stacked on the wharf a few feet out of the hearing of his loading crew.

Fr. Cahill walked to the crate and sat down, and Captain Johns next to him. Keeping their voices low, Fr. Cahill led Captain Johns through the rite.

After a few brief minutes, Fr. Cahill gave the captain absolution, and the captain broke into a bold smile as if he had just completed a long and successful voyage. He stood up, gave the priest a quick bow. "Father, what is your name, I must know it. You have done me a great service."

"I am Denis Cahill of Ireland, now a Capuchin here in the Spanish colony."

"Denis Cahill. I will remember that. We are headed to Baltimore. Again, I pray you would consider coming to America. We need priests desperately."

Pensive for a moment, he finally answered, "I would love to come, if God wills it. May your voyage be safe and prosperous. I will pray for you."

"And I for you, Fr. Denis Cahill. Thank you." The captain grabbed Fr. Cahill's hands, and shook them as if he was raising the brig's anchor. With that the captain hurried back to his ship.

Fr. Cahill watched him go, glanced over the ship one last time, gazed at the large American Flag flying off the ship's stern, and finally returned to his humble confessional awning.

5

After a late supper with the brothers, Fr. Cahill took a stroll along the wharf with a purpose. He noticed the Eagle was still at its berth, but that was not his destination. He was headed further down the wharf where the slavers were docked.

He casually approached the Spanish brig onto which the slaver's captain in the blue tailcoat had imprisoned the young American Indian boy. Painted on her prow was the name Crescent, and indeed she was flying the Spanish merchant ensign from the top of her mizzen.

Fr. Cahill's instinct was to ask permission to see the captain in his quarters, kill the man in some brutal way, then rescue the boy. He was sure God would forgive him if not reward him for the a virtuous act. Armed marines guarded the midship gangplank and there were guards on the bowsprit and taffrail along with additional lookouts posted halfway up the top.

Cahill approached the aft guard, a tall but harmless looking Spanish soul perhaps with some French blood. He had obviously been to sea for many years. His hair was dark, long, and wet from sweat. Two week's growth of beard hung from his face and an iron belaying pin protruded rudely from his waist—a ready weapon.

"A sturdy going barque, she is," the tiny priest said to the massive guard who suspiciously eyed Fr. Cahill up and down. It was then that Fr. Cahill recalled that bloody rescues had not been part of his seminary training. He quickly gave up his plan to kill the captain and rescue the Indian lad and at once he asked God to forgive him for his cowardice.

"Thar she a's, priest. But dat's der a brig. D'barque is much bigger—three masts. That her' Crescent only two. But thall her' run wit small crew."

"Departing tomorrow, are you?"

"Aye. Cap' Français. D'Paris of d'Nu Wo'ld."

"A cruel place, Santa Dominque. I've been there," related the priest.

"Aye. But captain, he a very rich man, he say prices good. We all git rich." The sailor's deep laugh and broad smile bared his mostly missing teeth. At the same time the iron belaying pin came loose from the man's trousers and fell. A swift swipe and his gnarled hand grasped the pin before it hit the ground. He jammed it back into the front of his trousers with a vulgar gesture.

Cahill pictured this man disembarking at Cap' Français on Santa Dominque and couldn't avoid the foreboding desolation that engulfed him. Santa Dominque was anything but a saintly place. Its cruelty toward slaves was legendary. Voodoo was rampant and chaos reigned just outside the rich plantations where slaves were flogged to death and buried in mass graves. There were rumors of rebellion. But it was unlikely the island's slaves, black in the north and mulatto in the south, could agree on enough to forge an effective rebellion against the European landowners.

Fr. Cahill began praying for the boy and all the other slaves that were clearly headed toward the worst time of their lives and perhaps a cruel death. Perhaps God would be merciful and sink the ship before it arrived. He prayed mercy on the cargo as he walked away, his head downcast.

Later that night, Fr. Cahill stayed up as late as he could reading by lamplight about what the U.S. Constitution would do and not, or at least what the supporters hoped it would do or not.

An obvious omission from the Constitution document itself was how the government was going to protect the religious rights of its citizens. The Constitution only stipulated how the government would be elected and structured, its checks and balances, how the governed would determine who would lead them, and what kind of laws it could pass. But there was nothing about religious liberty.

He was at first disappointed. But upon further reading, some of the essays freely spoke about the importance of religious liberty. They tried to put to rest the concern that the Constitution, as written, was a road map to religious tyranny.

Fr. Cahill hoped that the principles of religious and civil liberties would likely be strengthened with a series of constitutional amendments that were rumored to soon follow.

He was not naive, however, about how rules and legislative whims could change the pursuit of liberty in a fortnight. He was an Irishman whose parents told frequent stories about the repressive anti-Catholic penal laws of their childhood that allowed priests to be hunted down and hanged from the nearest tree.

While the penal laws of Ireland and England had been recently relaxed, it was still technically unlawful for Catholic families to own land, vote, run for parliament, or be promoted to positions of public leadership. Laws shifted violently like the winds of a hurricane shifted direction as the eye passed overhead. One of the problems was that the people of England and Ireland, although they both had publicly elected parliaments, did not govern themselves—King George III did. Also, there were no checks or balances that helped ensure a fair and just system of laws.

Hopefully, the United States Constitution, which divided the powers of government, would not fall into the same dark cavern, unless one of those divisions of powers abdicated their sacred responsibility or carried it out corruptly.

6

My Despised Cyn:

Don't you love how we can equivocate and confuse the masses. I love the story about how Henry VIII no longer defends the faith, but still used the "Fidei Defensor" title. He can do that, you know, since he is now his own pope. Equivocation is one of our greatest tools to fool humanity into thinking they're in control. Yes, we strive to elevate their pride and arrogance, but at our glorious core is a lie or a deceit. Because with pride and arrogance, it becomes easy to camouflage what is true—we simply state over-and-over the opposite. After a while the repetition of lies becomes so familiar it seduces like silk that so easily hides lascivious sewage. The Devil may be a liar, but who can tell the difference between a lie and the truth when their life hangs in the balance. He who wields the sword, wields the truth...don't forget that. In the case of Livingston, he wields the sword of his own domicile. Yes, he's his own pope; he determines what is true or false—arrogance is such a productive tool. We must keep reminding humanity that there is no objective truth. How else do you suppose we stay in control for so long? Will the United States fall into the same fallacious mire? Of course, it will. Fools all. We must keep working the lie that the Church and objective morality are irrelevant.

And that's just what Cahill is going to discover very soon when one of our heroes, William Sloan, darkens his confessional. I'm sure you'll do just fine with this one since Sloan is already the epitome of a self-sufficient, prideful moralist.

Eternally yours,
Master of Slavery

Chapter 12
Cold Trim Binding

1

Fr. Cahill was busy with a long string of seamen and officers seeking penance before their ships departed. Instead of lunch, he decided to fast and opened his breviary and began his Afternoon Office. It was a respite from hearing the bawdy and sometimes disgusting sins of unprincipled men who traveled the world, rarely saw their wives, almost never attended Mass, and often found their grog more satisfying than prayer.

No sooner had he begun reading, *"God, come to my assistance. —Lord, make haste to help me..."* than a deep baritone voice of some authority came from the other side of the muslin sheet.

"Father, I need absolution before my ship departs for Santa Dominque."

Fr. Cahill put down his breviary and turned to the sheet. Now, the sheet was not entirely opaque. It was muslin, and since the sun was out and Fr. Cahill sat in the shade, he could easily see who was kneeling just beyond. Normally, he refrained from looking, since anonymity for the priest was as desirable as for the penitent. But he felt a spiritual nudge—and looked.

His first reaction was repulsion...then anger. But this was a confessional, though a makeshift one, and discipline had taught him that despite his own sin, the rite was sacred and was to be entered into devoutly by both the penitent and the priest.

Instinctually, he quietly asked forgiveness for his judgment of the man that knelt before him...although he wasn't sure his prayer had been heard, perhaps because he uttered the confession insincerely. Nonetheless, he began as required. Making the sign of the cross toward the man, Fr. Cahill began, "In nomine Patris, et Filii, et Spiritus Sancti. Amen."

"Father, I need absolution before we depart." It was a command, not a request.

Cahill did not know immediately how to respond. The man was at least twenty years older, but if the church was right, he was still a *son* of God. If the Church was wrong, the man in Fr. Cahill's thinking was Satan's bastard. Cahill willed his voice even. "My son, what do you ask of the Church?"

"I need absolution! Said that, already." There was no hint of a request in the man's tone, no confession of sin, nor nuance of contrition.

Cahill wondered if the man had ever darkened a confessional before, or if he was Catholic at all. "The Lord is ready to give you his mercy. How long has it been since your last confession?"

"I dunno. I don't keep count." The man chuckled at his own joke, such as it was.

Cahill chilled a bit and thought before he continued. "Are you Catholic, my son?"

"Hell, yes, priest. What do you think I'm doing here? Playing with my gobbler? Com'on let's get on with it!"

Cahill cautioned himself—this was not going to end well. "And what do you have to confess to Christ and the Church? For what do you seek God's mercy?"

"Ah, well, let's see. I'm a greedy son-of-a-whore. But I'm a good negotiator. I get what I want, you see. But that's good 'cause my crew gits its cut, cause they're loyal. I cuss a lot. But I don't drink or mess with women—dangerous lot. I get mean, but only with those dat deserve it." There was a long pause. Finally, "Guess that's it."

Now it was Fr. Cahill's turn to inject a long silence, as if he were contemplating the obvious but unwanted response. So, he decided to postpone the inevitable and query once more. "Is there nothing else? Do you love God?"

"Sure. Guess I love the Almighty."

"Do you love your fellow human beings?"

"What you mean by dat?"

"Are you kind to them and show God's mercy to others as God has shown to you?"

"If'n they deserve it," the man snapped.

"Have you mistreated another human being? Have you beat anyone? Have you flogged them?"

"Not real people."

"Do you own slaves?"

"What's this all about? Of course, I own slaves. Hell, the Church owns slaves. Nothing wrong with that."

"The Church does not own slaves, my son. We are but slaves for those in the world."

"Hell, you say. Where you from? You're not from here, are ya? Don't sound like it much. Why, d'Ursulines they've got twenty-some slaves. They're down at the auction this wharf almost every time I've been here. Slavin' part of this here culture and the Church approves it."

Fr. Cahill's mind raced. He knew well the Ursuline nuns, who lived and worked out of the large convent at the northeast corner of the colony. *They did own twenty four slaves. But the slaves at the convent were protected, sheltered, fed, kept safe and taught to read and write, all inside the convent grounds. Mostly the slaves were families of African descent. The nuns had searched out husbands, wives, and children that had been separated by the slavers, brought them together within the safety of the convent property, instructed them in the faith, baptized those that were not, and saw to it that they had sacramental marriages. Over the years many were emancipated. The Africans they kept may have been slaves in a legal sense, but not in the sense of being treated as sub-human, nor were they debased servants. Instead, they were cared for as one would care for a dependent child. They were given an education, and responsibilities for building up the convent and keeping the sisters' ministry alive and functional. Fr. Cahill disapproved strongly of slavery, especially when men, women, and children were treated with indignity as chattel or a tradable resource. But here in New Orleans, and other places in the world, cities could not be built without slaves—mankind had fallen so deeply into sin that corruption had seeped into every aspect of society and culture. To eradicate slavery in all its forms would take hundreds of years, if not thousands, and only then with the sacrificial and concerted effort of an entire civilization. *Civilization. What a strange and ironic word.*

The Ursuline vocations were charged with saving souls, whether enslaved or free, not beating them to death or condemning them to Perdition. Fr. Cahill had seen the Ursulines' baptism records of nearly one-thousand free and enslaved souls that went back fifty years. The Jesuits had acted as the Ursulines' superiors, until they left under the Suppression. Now spiritual leadership fell to Fr. Antoine, and the Capuchins, including himself. Did that make him a slave holder, or the overseer of those that owned slaves? This bothered him. What if he was in charge? What would he do? Would he simply wake up one morning and free his slaves? Where would they go? How would they feed, clothe, and shelter themselves? Clearly it was the Church's responsibility to care for the poor, which displaced African slaves clearly were. In such a way the Church should have *owned* more slaves and treated them with the utmost dignity, Fr. Cahill reasoned. Indeed, the Jesuits did much the same thing on their reduction missions as they attempted to protect native Americans from slavery at the hands of Spanish and French armies and from slaughter by neighboring tribes.

Fr. Cahill drew a deep slow breath. "My, son, you are a malicious hater of the men and children under your care. It is not that you're a slaver, you're a sinner."

"Do not judge me, Father. Jesus said that."

Fr. Cahill intended a breezy tone, but he came back with gale force. "You want absolution? I get to judge. Jesus said that. The Church binds by virtue of this confessional what is to be bound. What is loosed is loosed. What is forgiven is forgiven. What is not forgiven is not forgiven. All of this by God's command, not man's. Yesterday, I saw you beat a young Chitimacha boy you had bought and kick him into the hold of your ship the Crescent. I believe you intend to sell him in Saint Dominque, where you do not care what happens to him. You will collect your money, and the boy will likely die. His blood will be on your hands. You know this. Do you not want to confess this intention and undo it before you have completed the evil and set sail?"

There was silence on the other side of the sheet, except for the man's deep and rapid breathing. Then the man let out a torrent of hatred at the priest.

"I will confess no such thing to you, or another God damned priest. I am Master William Sloan of Charleston, South Carolina, a respected trader, and a rich man. I will have your hide, your life, your sanctimonious pride and hang it from the nearest limb like the niggers who have run from their owners. You are a bastard, and if you will not give me absolution, I will give you what you deserve."

"Mister Sloan, it is not I that absolves, but God who forgives and extends mercy. I am but his slave and emissary. It is your heart that condemns you, not me. From me, this day, you will not receive absolution. If you were to suddenly turn from this path and confess, I doubt I would see anything but your pride and arrogance. I refuse you absolution, for...Hell is your destiny. Therefore, by virtue of Christ's command I bind you to it until you heart is truly contrite and pure. May God have mercy on your soul. Go in the turmoil your heart has bred, and reflect on this."

And with that, Master William Sloan, the man in the blue tails and commander of the Crescent, quickly departed, swearing his revenge on the priest.

2

There are consequences to every action. Fr. Cahill had informed Mister Sloan of the natural consequences if he continued in his evil ways. But there are also consequences that flow the other way. When Master Sloan left Fr. Cahill's confessional, it wasn't to return to his ship. No, he went directly to one of his closest acquaintances, a man with whom he often shared supper and with whom he spent many evenings telling tall tales—some even true. Master Sloan went directly to Louisiana Governor Esteban Rodriguez Miro, the acting mayor of New Orleans—friend of the king, and general of the king's Louisiana army.

Fr. Cahill did not know that, at least not right away. He heard a few more confessions and was about to return to the presbytery tent when Fr. Antoine arrived with a scowl on his face. One look and Fr. Cahill instantly knew why. *That was fast*, he thought.

Fr. Antoine addressed the younger cleric in a serious tone. "Am I to understand that the king has sent a new inquisitor to be in our midst? I did not know this. Why did you not inform me of your new calling?"

His superior didn't wait for Cahill to respond but continued to explain. Master Sloan had gone to his friend the governor and described in colorful terms that "the Capuchins had begun a purge of all sinners from the colony." Fr. Antoine stopped and repeated the way the governor had put that phrase to him, "A *purge* of *all* sinners from the colony." Fr. Antoine paused, looked aside, and then said most seriously, "What a delightful concept."

"The man is an unrepentant scoundrel," Cahill replied. "He didn't ask for God's mercy, he demanded it as a slave master would order cruelty upon one of his slaves. He showed no contriteness, but belligerence."

"Yes, I believe you. That was no doubt your first encounter with a *self-esteemed* trader of human flesh and peddler of self-importance. There are many such rogues." The Capuchin superior paused. "And I agree with you that Hell has a special place reserved for Master and Commander Sloan."

Fr. Cahill started to offer a defense, "Father, I...."

But his superior held up a hand to stop him, "Denis...we are called to be salt and light to the society in which we are placed. That does not mean we are called to inaugurate a theocracy for the Church."

"Who we bind, they are bound," said Denis.

"They are bound before they open their mouths by their own conscience," said Fr. Antoine. "God does not need our proclamation for it to be so, Denis. We must practice the works of mercy, even when the recipients of those works are odious to it."

"In other words," Denis countered, "we should deceive and act as if their pride is acceptable."

"That is not what I said. We are called to minister the truth with kindness, not assault."

"So, I should have absolved Master Sloan even if his sins are not confessed?"

"The words of the rite are sacred," said Fr. Antoine, "but they are not sovereign. The Holy Spirit utters what is true to the Father." The superior cracked a sly smile. "Even between clenched teeth no doubt."

"So, the governor and king are above the Church."

"Of course not. But the Church can afford to be tolerant and compassionate and not demand what the state demands. We can give sway—like the mast of a ship in a storm. If it is too stiff it will break and the ship will wallow, or perhaps sink, altogether. It is not perfection we are ministering to a miserable people, but miserly perfection to the imperfect. We must work with the government and not publicly oppose it. We must invite slave traders to dine with us so they can see our good works and come to emulate them."

"My Lord...," Cahill began, again.

"Why do you address me that way? It is inappropriate. You know the rule. Come, let us walk the wharf."

Denis stowed his stole, stood, left the tent, and walked submissively next to and a little behind his superior, the man who when he first came to New Orleans was referred to as *the inquisitor and judge* for his legalistic manner. Denis pushed, "Then you would prefer an address that suggested we are equals?" said Cahill.

"We are all equal in the eyes of God."

"Even the bondmen and bondwomen?" asked Denis, "Are they equal to their masters? What part does freedom play in our ministry among the poor?"

"Before God, we are equal, but not before man," said Fr. Antoine. "And neither is man equal with God. There is a hierarchy, is there not? Look around you."

Along the wharf Denis paid attention to the individuals and their relationships. He had never noticed before but most of the faces in New Orleans were black Africans. Some were Creoles for sure, the consequence of French slave owners taking African mistresses and common law wives during the French period. Many of the second and third generation Creoles were free. There were also Cajuns, the offspring of French Canadians exiled from New Scotland who resettled in New Orleans. It was a mixed lot. But the Negro was dominant in number and at the bottom of the "equal" ladder according to Spanish law and common practice.

Fr. Antoine broke the silence. "Perhaps this will help if you consider that the slave culture helps the Church win souls. If everyone was free and independent, they would look only to themselves for guidance and not to those in authority over them. That is what I fear for the United States. Their so-called Declaration of Independence imbues the idea that among men everyone is equal. It doesn't work like that. What if the pope were to declare that all laymen, priests, religious superiors, and bishops were equal? The people are necessary for the work of God, but there's an order. They can't all be their own pope, can they? The Protestants have tried that and look where it has gotten them. They all disagree with each other on the fundamentals of faith and morality. Why, they can't even agree on what constitutes baptism, communion, marriage, heaven, hell, death, or the last judgment. Hierarchies and authority are good, natural, and necessary for propagating truth and avoiding relativism. Authority within the Church isn't for exerting power. Leave that to the slavers. As pastors our responsibility is the delivery of God's mercy; that is, we need to avoid condemnation when it is deserved, while delivering God's Grace. Yes, even the sacraments when they are not deserved. We are not rulers. We are imperfect handmaids of the Lord."

The superior was on a roll. It was a good homily, thought Denis.

"It is not that we are equal," Fr. Antoine continued. "We are not. But that we are all *equally worthy of salvation*, regardless of our station in life. We must work out our own salvation with fear and trembling in accordance with the natural hierarchy in which we are settled as humans. In our case that natural hierarchy, here in the settlement of New Orleans, includes the king of Spain, his officials, and his laws. *Render to Caesar*. That must be our understanding."

The argument was subtle and well put. But in the end it frustrated Denis. To him, life as a priest in the hierarchy of the Church was at the service of the truth. But what service was the Church providing when it enabled the Jesuit repression? And wasn't the Church complicit in the Devil's work when it pronounced absolution over an unrepentant, abusive, slaver—as it seemed Fr. Antoine was suggesting? In truth, such actions would not and could not force God's hand; so, against the backdrop of eternity there was no injustice. But, in Denis' mind such policies and actions temporally pushed God aside and cooperated with demons.

3

From the plaza, Fr. Cahill stopped and turned toward the mighty Mississippi, and watched the sea of humanity crisscrossing the wharf between ships, warehouses, flatboats, and the ramps that led into the city.

Agents exchanged bills of lading with first mates who directed dockhands where to stow the cargo, while slaves did the heavy lifting. At first glance the scene was chaotic. But on closer inspection the loading and unloading of ships was orderly and efficient.

Cahill admitted to himself that without an authoritative hierarchy there would be chaos, and nothing would be accomplished. Progress would come to a standstill and the goods that fed and clothed a country would cease to flow.

He gazed at the Crescent which had been docked with its bow pointing upstream. The ship was about to set sail. Dockhands and mates had secured one end of a long warp, or spring line, to the far port side of the bow, led it around the aft of the boat, and then forward, on the wharf, to the boat's midships. There, a crew of twenty men pulled tension on the line. With an amazing display of coordination, directed by commands shouted by the first mate, the starboard dock lines were at once cast off and pulled aboard. Immediately, the twenty men on the wharf heaved the spring line which pulled the bow to port and into the river's current. The heaving effect also pulled the boat's stern forward so that it did not engage the docked ship to its rear. Then, just as the current caught the bow and the boat turned without help from the dock crew, a final command to the rigging crew balancing on the main top yard horses unfurled the tops and topgallant sails which caught the land breeze, and the ship was gracefully away downriver toward the Gulf.

"Beautiful, just beautiful isn't it, Father?" asked Fr. Antoine. "Did you notice the order and efficiency of the hierarchical commands that allowed the ship to get underway? All those ropes, who knows what to pull or which way? Simply amazing to see it happen so effortlessly. The key, need I point out, is the hierarchal order of persons and their following the ship's rules. Into the stream and on to its next port. Simply amazing."

Fr. Cahill waited a moment, then offered a rejoinder to his superior. "And on that ship, if you noticed leaning against the aft rail, was William Sloan, who has chained slaves in the hold. Once they are so elegantly and no doubt efficiently warped onto the wharf at Cap Français, Master Sloan's young Chitimacha slave boy will be sold to a plantation where an overseer will eventually bring upon him abuse and death. Yes, the authority aboard the ship is a beautiful thing."

Fr. Cahill took notice that Fr. Antoine stiffened halfway through his rejoinder and was silent for a good time after.

The superior finally broke the silence, looking downcast. "I didn't know the object of your altercation with Master Sloan was a boy, nor that he was Chitimacha."

The two priests continued to talk as they walked back to Fr. Antoine's tent on the Plaza. There, Fr. Antoine asked Fr. Cahill to sit with him a bit more.

When they got settled, Fr. Antoine gave him a new assignment. "I have a request of the governor," said Fr. Antoine. "He wants you to take a break from being seen in public. He feels your continual presence and militant religious attitude to change the customs of the colony is disruptive to the common good."

Fr. Cahill's eyes bore down on Fr. Antoine as if he were the devil incarnate. Gripping his folded hands, the flesh under his fingers went white. He tried to control his reaction, but his heart beat faster, and his breathing grew intense. He was even surprised at the intensity in his voice. "*He* can't be serious."

Fr. Antoine was gentle but honest, his voice clear and without judgment. "He, the governor, asks for prudence, and I have agreed. For the foreseeable future I am asking you to stay in the background. No confessions, no public masses or baptisms, even at the Ursulines. No communication with anyone other than your brothers in the Presbytery. Cloister yourself for a time of reflection and prayer."

Fr. Cahill was speechless. This was the worst of all horrors. He stood abruptly and walked to the tent opening. The entrance flap had been tied back allowing a breeze, but the young priest began to sweat uncontrollably. In the thirty seconds he stood in the tent's entrance the back of his Capuchin habit soaked through. The anger he felt prevented the breeze from doing its work. This was an embarrassment almost too much to bear. He wasn't a monk; he was a friar. Monks were called to cloister themselves with contemplative work and prayer. Friars were called to go out into the world and evangelize it with their works. The words purported to St. Francis flooded his mind: "Preach the Gospel at all times and when necessary use words." Okay, so he liked to use words. Yes, harsh cutting words, to put sinners in their place, to elevate the Church to its rightful place of authority. How else can it bind or loose, forgive or retain?" His eyes watered over as he stood helplessly staring out at the world yet standing in the shade of authority. He spoke: "Am I prevented from leaving my tent or literally appearing in public at Mass, or walking the streets to say my office?"

"No," replied Fr. Antoine. "Considering we have no building, church, or even a kitchen, that would be impractical. I just ask that you speak with no one unless absolutely necessary. When you must speak to another, do so with humility. Full deference should be your style."

Cahill could feel himself breathe deeply and slowly, gathering his wits, adjusting to this new order. "Yes, Father. But my work. What shall I do?"

"Help Brother James in the cooking tent. I just suggest that you don't sample the food as much as Brother James is ought to do. Soon we'll need a sailmaker for his New Year's habit."

Fr. Cahill smiled, deeply appreciating Fr. Antoine's humor and gentleness.

"I have made only temporary vows, Father," Cahill said.

"Yes. A time of evaluating your agreeableness to the order. I understand.

Nothing is out of the ordinary here. Work and pray, Denis. God will lead you." With that Fr. Antoine gripped Fr. Cahill's shoulder for encouragement, slipped past him, and left the tent.

4

Obedience, chastity, and poverty are the evangelical counsels that religious orders such as the Capuchins believe lead to perfection, especially as the counsels applied to the Capuchin's ministry to the poor. The chastity part, while primarily meaning the avoidance of sexual relations consistent with one's vocation, more broadly meant fostering honorable relationships with everyone, not just the poor.

But to Fr. Cahill the issue was about authority. Who was able to supernaturally bind and loose? Father Cahill was convinced it was only the Church, while Fr. Antoine was content with letting the ruling government have a say in the process.

Fr. Antoine had reminded Fr. Cahill that it was Jesus who told his disciples to render to Caesar the things that are Caesar's. Fr. Cahill reminded Fr. Antoine that it was the pope that crowned kings and excommunicated some.

To Fr. Antoine's thinking, authority was anyone that was over you, sacred or secular. You had a duty to obey, regardless. Fr. Cahill, on the other hand, only wanted to obey God—the way Fr. Cahill heard God—not the way the governor or king understood the Almighty. Cahill was willing to listen to his superior, but when the superior listened to the sectarian rulers to make decisions…well, that's where Fr. Cahill drew the line.

He reasoned that authority was given by God to the Church alone—to bind and loose with impunity and infallibly, as Christ had prophesied. Giving authority to anyone else robbed not just the Church of its duty but robbed the individual of the freedom to obey.

What he was beginning to see with the Capuchins in New Orleans, and the Church in general, starting with the pope, was inconsistent in how it interpreted the evangelical councils and how they were practiced. One of the reasons he joined the Capuchins was because of how they saw poverty as the great equalizer. It was a mark of poverty, and thus equality, with the order that you could not tell the difference between an ordained priest or a non-ordained brother, although both were called brothers. In like manner Capuchin superiors did not force their friars and brothers to perform tasks they found disagreeable but discussed and adjusted the tasks around the friary to suit the abilities and skills of its members. What infuriated Fr. Cahill was how the order claimed equality among men, but then bowed in deference to secular rulers, thus giving the king or his governors the authority to rule over the work of the friars. Due to this thinking, neither the church of St. Louis nor the Presbytery were rebuilt, Fr. Cahill was prohibited from publicly practicing the sacraments, and the Church essentially approved the slavery by its silence if not also endorsing the giving of absolution to the vilest of men. Then there's the whole debacle with the suspension of the Jesuits when the pope buckled to the demands of kings. Such decisions destroyed the Church's credibility.

The contradictions and inconsistencies about how he should live his life sent him into a deep depression. Saint Ignatius of Loyola called it desolation—being at the edge of hell's doorstep and looking in. Fr. Cahill feared a loss of faith. He certainly felt desolate when he saw the Creek boy being whipped. Where was God? Perhaps God did not exist. Why does the *Almighty* sideline his power and fail to intercede in the lives of men who were so unjustly tormented?

Desolation also came from not knowing how this life was supposed to work. He was more than willing to suffer for another if there was some concrete way of seeing the deliverance. But was there? Everything seemed to be so ethereal and invisible.

It wasn't enough for the temporary Capuchin to be told time and again in seminary and in homilies that our purpose for suffering for the salvation of the world is connected to the most unjust act ever—the death of God's Son on the cross. In Fr. Cahill's mind that did not count. How could a mortal man feel that his suffering had purpose just because the immortal Christ, the son of God, gave up his life for a few hours? Christ knew he was going to come back from the dead. For Christ, wasn't it like being bedridden with abdominal pain for a few days knowing that with rest and water you'd be okay?

How does three days of suffering and death, willfully given into by the most omnipotent and omniscient force in the universe compare to forty or more years of powerless, hopeless, purposeless torture? Jesus held in his hand the ability to enact complete and eternal revenge on his killers. What chance does the slave have of enduring the whip day after day? The comparison was ridiculous and meaningless. It sounded good, but reason made it cruel.

Ruminating about such things caused Fr. Cahill to lose his appetite. He had fasted at mid-day, and now supper was fast approaching, but he was not hungry. It was easy to fast when faced with incontrovertible contradictions of faith.

A professor in seminary had once said that embracing the desolations with humility made one stronger, and more robust in his faith. Fr. Cahill doubted it. But then he was doubting just about everything right now.

Clearly, he had to find the paradox in the apparent contradictions or go mad. He wished at least one Jesuit had been around. Talking to a member of an order that had lost more missionaries to massacres in the New World than were alive when they were exiled might have brought some understanding. Who else could compare? Who else understood the sufferings under Spanish rule in New Orleans?

At that moment, he stepped away from Fr. Antoine's tent, glanced toward the burned-out St. Louis church, and saw his answer—Sister Saint Angele walked past the ruins with another Ursuline nun. Sister Angele, the former

Marguerite Félicité Calder, was part Creole. Her father was from Scotland who by way of France had come to New Orleans as an early plantation owner. Master Calder took a fancy to Marguerite's mother, who became his slave, housekeeper, and eventually his common law wife. They had several children, and all were educated by the Ursuline nuns.

In their plantation's home and at the convent's school, Marguerite learned to speak both English and French. So, in Cahill's occasional but official capacity of celebrating Mass at the Ursuline convent, the Irish priest had struck up a friendship with Sister Angele.

Although she was slightly older than Fr. Cahill, he found her smart, articulate, spiritually sensitive, and sexually attractive. But in the latter case neither were so inclined to push aside their vows of chastity. At the moment it was her spiritual sensitivity and analytical mind that nudged him to seek her out.

When he caught up to them, Sister Angele, and Sister Saint Louis de Gonzague were walking back to the convent from some errand of mercy for a family they had taken in during the great fire. He obtained their permission to walk and visit with them on their return. When they arrived at the convent, he asked their superior's permission to privately counsel with Sister Angele, which he received. Over the next hour, in the convent parlor, he poured out his heart to the Creole nun and his dilemma of being a Capuchin in New Orleans.

She said little to him after he was done. But she was clear and direct about what he should do. She suggested that he should follow the Ursulines' lead of faith and action. The Ursuline founders had sailed from France to an alien settlement and established a missionary work without the leadership of priest, bishop, or king. It had been dangerous, dirty, uncomfortable, and unpredictable. But their work had expanded. Surprisingly, they found a way to counter the government's approval of slavery by buying slaves, training them, baptizing them, and emancipating them. It was through the Ursulines that the first African men and women of Louisiana obtained their legal freedom. Her advice to Fr. Cahill was to do the same: *Eschew secular authority, take physical action, embrace risk, and do something you're totally unprepared for.*

As he departed, she said, "Do not be afraid. Go set people free. You will be a good priest and father to the repentant."

5

Thursday, October 23, 1788.

Under Brother Andrew's guidance, Fr. Cahill helped prepare supper, served it up, and ate with the other brothers. After cleaning up the make-shift kitchen, he spoke with Fr. Antoine briefly about his meeting with Sister Angele. Then he took his usual night walk along the wharf to pray his Evening Office and examine his conscience.

Under the light of torches, he saw wallopers transfer bundles of grain from a nearby flatboat that had floated down from the Ohio Valley. The grain was being packed aboard a Boston bound ship tied up at the wharf. A waning half-moon backlit the ship's rigging. The juxtaposition reminded Fr. Cahill of the entrepreneurial spirit that characterized the United States. The grain's long journey on flatboats from Ohio, down the Mississippi, then by sailing vessel up the East Coast to New England, was a circuitous route. Yet, it was the cheapest and faster way of getting mid-continent product to market, and even to Europe. To Fr. Cahill it illustrated how the United States shone like a harvest moon on an otherwise desolate night after a devastating blight.

His night walk took an uncharacteristic turn through the city. He passed warehouses, slave pens, and trading company offices where a few lamps were still burning, and where men spoke in dark corners.

Along Roiale Street he listened to the cacophony of the ribald songs that emanated from saloons, and he sustained the jeers directed at him by unsavory seamen on their last drunk before risking their lives once again at sea.

Much later he returned to the plaza and walked through the ruins of the St. Louis Church. He passed the new construction of the government's headquarters, the Cabildo. The king always came first.

Glancing at the line of docked ships, Fr. Cahill noticed that a Dutch brig had taken the Crescent's spot along the wharf. His eyes scanned the dark flowing river beyond, across which the moon had risen. It was a chaotic and melancholy scene. A strong wind blew uncommonly toward the southwest which bucked the northeast flowing current. The opposing fetch created a rogue turbulence across the third-of-a-mile-wide serpentine river. One could not tell which way the river flowed as the tops of white caps staged a coup against the mighty Mississippi's current. The confluence of nature's compelling forces broke up the river's reflection of the waning moon to create a demonic desolation upon the water. Peace was not at hand. He was mesmerized by the scene, for it mirrored his own inner turmoil.

Suddenly, Fr. Cahill caught his breath, and his heart raced. In the middle of the river a flatboat was attempting to cross the river to safety on the wharf. Flatboats were no more than rafts with steering oars. They had no method of propulsion except for their long steering oars, relying mostly on the current's press against the hull, or the windage of their topside. Like most, this flatboat was built close to the water with a tall cabin that stretched across its breadth and covered the rear half of its cargo deck. Atop the cabin, at the rear, a helmsman wrapped his arms around the long steering oar. He swayed left and right attempting to guide the boat's travel if not propel it. Two other men also stood on the cabin roof but forward a bit and to the sides. Their arms were likewise wrapped around long sweeping oars as they leaned their bodies fore and aft helping the helmsman steer and propel the boat and avoid obstacles.

As the crew struggled to direct the flatboat through the chaotic waves, giant white caps drenched their faces, obstructed their progress, and deposited more and more water aboard, causing the boat to sink deeper into the river. There were no hard-goods or grain aboard. The cargo of this boat consisted of eight people: three white men, an old black woman, a middle-aged black man and woman, and two white teenagers, a girl and a boy. As the flatboat gyrated through the water and sunk deeper, the group stared indifferently forward, as if their safety was never in jeopardy.

After a minute Fr. Cahill realized the flatboat crew was making no progress, yet the boat was close to sinking. He ran onto the wharf to alert a warp crew to throw out a line or take a warp line to the imperiled flatboat by small boat. But the wharf was uncharacteristically vacant, no one was around.

He moved closer to the water where waves crashed against the sea wall and drenched him. He looked again at the three crew on the cabin roof. The helmsman was dressed like a Capuchin friar with a long black habit and a white rope cincture. The man on the port sweeping oar was a bearded farmer; he was stout, strong, and wore overalls. The third man on the starboard sweeping-oar was dressed like a parish priest. All three were soaking wet as they hung onto their oars for fear that the next wave would wash them overboard. As the boat came closer, the white caps grew larger, and took the shape of crescent moons which repeatedly cascaded over the trio.

Fr. Cahill called out to them...they looked up...locked eyes with him...and suddenly the boat, the long oars, the passengers, and the crew all disappeared in a burst of black dust. Left behind were only the crescent-shaped white caps that quickly melded back into random waves that objected to the current.

Distraught at what he had just witnessed, Fr. Cahill stood transfixed on the wharf contemplating the vision. *Could the helmsman on the steering oar have been himself? What could that mean?*

As he entered his tent and prepared for bed, a strange faculty invaded his mind. Suddenly, he found himself looking down on his body, watching himself get undressed, pray his Compline, blow out the lantern, slip under the mosquito netting and pull it closed. In the dark he could see that his eyes were wide open. It would be a while before sleep overtook him, if it did at all this night.

He had the sense that perhaps America was in his near future, and that he was on the front lines of history. He knew himself to be a man full of faith and courage, but was that enough? He recalled how old hatreds could not be swept away with the passing of a constitution. He envisioned Catholic priests wherever they lived being chased, harassed, hung, drawn, and quartered.

He bristled that most of Europe considered American revolutionaries misguided members of a lunatic political fringe that would soon be forgotten to history. Yet, it had been twelve years since the lunatic fringe had defeated the world's best army. Since then, a permanency seemed to blanket the country.

In America the Church might be able to exercise its God-given authority without obstruction. Indeed, the United States may have a government that understands that strong moral convictions, properly formed by religious principles, were the necessary shrouds and stays of a political vessel's rigging capable of withstanding history's rogue waves and gales. He wanted a church that would seek social justice without a secular authority looking over its shoulder. He didn't mind taking vows of obedience, chastity, and poverty, but declaring such vows for political efficacy was disordered.

Sr. Angele's idea had taken hold. Fr. Cahill finally closed his eyes, but his mind was running before the wind.

6

The next morning, a canopy of clouds covered the New Orleans colony as a cool wind swept over the wharf from the north, straining dock lines and beckoning the brigs, barques, and schooners *bon voyage*. The sun, hidden from sight, looked for an opportunity to warm the cold landscape.

Fr. Antoine, having finished morning prayers, bent his head low and entered his tent. A solemn mood had possessed him for weeks; he was desperate to rebuild the St. Louis church, except the basic physical needs of the community were still unmet and Governor Miro's demands to expend all energy on essentials and leave the non-essentials for another day held him back. His debate with Fr. Cahill the day before about church versus civic responsibilities haunted him. Cahill was right, a friar's responsibility was first to the church... as long as one ignored the Church's dependency on the civic governor for food and shelter.

At that moment Fr. Cahill entered his tent. Fr. Antoine was not pleased to see him. No time to even sit down. But he did, sit down that is, and then looked up at his not entirely welcomed visitor. Fr. Cahill's posture was peculiarly stiff.

"My Lord, I have come to ask your blessing," began Cahill.

"You know I detest such titles, why do you insist? You have my regards, though not always my approval. What do you want, my son?"

Cahill reflected for a moment, his eyes gazing straight ahead and not down at his superior. Inwardly, Fr. Antoine groaned; outwardly he stiffened, waiting for the indictment. *Out with it, man.*

Cahill finally opened his mouth, but nothing came out for a few seconds. Then, "I would like your blessing to leave the order. God is calling me to the United States as a missionary."

Fr. Antoine repressed an immediate swell of anger, although he could not repress the bile that caused him to jump to his feet. He did not hesitate to lash out: "The devil, Denis! Why do you insist on being contrary? Where is your charity, your obedience? Have you lost your mind? Where could God possibly be calling you without my awareness, my solicitude, my voice?"

Fr. Cahill retained his composure and his line of sight. There was a slight tear in the tent's side through which daylight, although not sunlight, slithered. But he said nothing. His request had been made.

Fr. Antoine had little patience for the Irish upstart. "To even have such thoughts is the epitome of disobedience. Do you intend to wrap yourself in the American revolutionary's Gadsden flag, flop onto the ground like a snake before the pope and throw a tantrum like a three-year-old? Such insolence!"

Denis dared to continue: "We should be leading, not following. Authentic authority is only from God, through the Church, to the state. Instead, we have bowed to the secular rulers. We have it backwards."

"Authority! Indeed, authority is about obedience, Denis." The superior was now yelling. "Yes, me to the pope, and you to me. We are not bowing to the state but to God. Did not Jesus remind his disciples to render to Caesar the things that are Caesar's? Yes, it is the pope that crowns kings. Authority is that which you must obey, to anyone that is over you, sacred or secular. I have a duty to obey the pope, and he tells me to obey my secular authority for the sake of peace. Likewise, you have the same duty to obey. To reject order is to invite chaos, rebellion, and more death."

But as it was, and Fr. Antoine knew this, they were not in Rome, they were not even in Spain. They were but a few day's walk from the pioneering borders of the United States of America. The temptation to flee one set of problems in hope that the new problems would be less of a problem was overwhelming. If he were to be honest, Fr. Antoine had also thought of abdicating his responsibility and sneaking into the United States. But Fr. Antoine was a man of discipline and kept such wicked thoughts suppressed.

"You want to join the rebels and receive their eventual fate in hell for rebelling against the king?" he asked. "Go ahead, but don't ask the Church to save your neck. You are a priest forever, but you are an ungrateful, rebellious priest. You will get no money from me for whatever you intend. Go ruin your life if you must. You are no use to us here. You are on your own." Angry, Fr. Antoine gathered his robes, whipped them close to his body and dashed from his tent.

6

After his superior stormed out of the tent, Fr. Cahill didn't move. He continued to contemplate the tear in the tent wall, willing it larger so the sliver of daylight would brighten and illumine his path. Emotionally, he was at once disappointed and relieved. He had hoped for a touch of understanding or intellectual discussion, not a rant. But the decision was now clear...at least to leave. He had been dismissed. Did he need some sort of document or license to prove it?

His body tried to shake off the adrenaline brought on by Fr. Antoine's rebuke and his new though undetermined status; but the chemical rush would take hours to wear off, not seconds. He turned and left the tent, shielding his eyes from the bright sun that had found a crack in the clouds. The dark tent had dilated his eyes and it would be some minutes before he could see clearly without squinting.

Catholic missionary priests had been coming to the North American continent since the mid-sixteenth century. Many were killed by Indians who feared the black robes of the Jesuits were a prognostication of evil. But now, with the political courage of America's founders, more Christian missionaries would come, especially Catholic priests whose lives and ministries were eminently threatened in their native countries. Had he stayed in Spain there was no doubt he would have been imprisoned or had a change in mind—with the assistance of a guillotine.

Would the United States be any different? He had heard rumors of Guy Fawkes celebrations and how priests were harassed, and no doubt killed. But the stories were anecdotal and if the rule of law had any effect, religious persecution would be in decline, or so he rationalized. Having taken a vow of poverty he had no money, and Fr. Antoine had made it clear no money was coming from the order.

He was tempted to panic, but panic had never been part of his make-up. Stubborn determination, free will, and choices were more to his liking. But his choices were limited. He smiled, took a deep breath, and looked about as if the answer to his dilemma was stalking him. As he looked about, a small laughing child ran toward him, having escaped the grasp of his doting mother chasing the truant toddler. Thinking the child was running to him, Fr. Cahill crouched down to greet the tyke. But the kid ignored the priest and ran past, giggling and snorting in delight of his newly gained freedom to roam and live outside the confines of the authority over him. The mother, unable to keep up, gestured wildly at Fr. Cahill, who was more than willing to find something good and safe to do. Trotting after the wayward ward, Fr. Cahill swooped-up the bliss-filled boy and brought him kicking and laughing back to his mother, who by now was laughing as well. Crossing herself, she did all but kiss Fr. Cahill's sandaled feet for his fatherly feat.

"Thank you. Bless you, Father." Then, to her child, whom she hugged for dear life, "Oh, my dear Salvador, what has gotten into you, running away like that from your mother as if you know where you were going? You would get lost." Then to the priest again, "Oh, Father, what would I do without you? Will you bless me and mischievous Salvador? Please, *señor?*"

Fr. Cahill smiled, placed his hands on the mother's veiled head and on the squirming child's curly black locks. Instantly, the child stopped trying to break free and gazed in wonderment at the priest. Fr. Cahill blessed the madonna and child, "*Benedictio Dei omnipotentis, Patris, et Filii, et Spiritus Sancti, descendat super vos, et maneat semper. Amen.*"

The mother bowed a thanksgiving to the priest that had rescued her child and departed in the direction they came. Fr. Cahill reflected. I am not running from. I'm running to. I am still a priest. May God speed and use me. *Benedictio Dei omnipotentis, Patris, et Filii, et Spiritus Sancti, descendat super vos, et maneat semper. Amen*...he intoned under his breath, blessing himself.

Sustaining a life changing event— being dismissed by one's superior—required contemplation. He would spend more time today in prayer. He turned toward the burned city, took a small breviary from his habit's pocket, bowed his cappella romano covered head, and decided to recite all the day's prayers as he walked through what was left of the colony. Psalm 90 was first:

> *Lord, you have been our dwelling place throughout all genera-tions. Before the mountains were born or you brought forth the whole world, from everlasting to everlasting you are God. You turn people back to dust, saying, "Return to dust, you mortals." A thousand years in your sight are like a day that has just gone by, or like a watch in the night. Yet you sweep people away in the sleep of death— they are like the new grass of the morning: In the morning it springs up new, but by evening it is dry and withered.*

He was a waif among humanity's ruins, coaxing an existence from smoke and ashes...unworthy of life, let alone a shaman in a world of hurt. His heart thundered, and his eyes glistened with unwelcome tears. Who was he to en-counter life as he had, or to be given the opportunity of the future? He longed to empty his soul and let the Spirit fill him with purpose.

He turned southwest along Dauphine Street toward the tenements. The fire's destruction had been complete. He recalled his own tears the day he came to find Dolucila and Jean and rescued Julian and dear predestined Sabine. The burned-out tenements had been mostly cleared, and reconstruction had begun, although the shortage of lumber slowed the task. He stopped to watch the prog-ress, such as it was. Jean saw the priest first and hobbled into the street to offer his respect; shortly behind him came Dolucila. They took Fr. Cahill's hands and kissed them.

"How is it with you and your dear children?" the priest inquired.

"Well as can be," said Jean. His eyes filled with hope of a good word from Fr. Cahill. But it would not be today.

"Where are you staying while...?"

Jean tugged the priest's arm around the construction, then pointed.

Behind the buildings, in a little patch of nothingness, a tent was erected. Stashed next to it were wooden crates with their food and belongings, or what was left of them. Fr. Cahill nodded his head. "And the children, Maria and Ju-lian? What of them?"

"They are fine and happy," said Dolucila, her gleaming eyes taking in the young priest with near adoration. "Have you come to bless us, Father?"

"No, but I will do so. Let us find the children."

They walked to the tent behind the construction. There, children were playing happily with discarded blocks of wood, oblivious to their wretched condition. Fr. Cahill marveled at their resilience and wished his own situation could be perceived as simply as they did theirs. He talked with them a bit then gathered them together to lay hands on them and pray. He was surprised as ten other adults and children from nearby huddled around him as well. He smiled at each, asked their names, and prayed over each.

Dolucila showed Fr. Cahill the lock of Sabine's hair she had kept in her prayer book. She cried when she touched it and asked Fr. Cahill to bless the hair and pray for the little girl's soul. He did not hesitate.

When he was done, he ushered Dolucila and Jean aside, took off his hat, and in a low voice told them what had transpired. "So, it seems to be the will of God that I will be leaving the colony and going to the United States to find God's purpose for my life."

The announcement at once brought fear to Dolucila's face and confusion to Jean's. There were words of entreatment, but in the end, it was Fr. Cahill who asked for their blessing. A priest had never asked them for such a thing, and it took some convincing before he bowed his head, and they placed their hands on his arms and took his hand and whispered an *Our Father* over their beloved priest.

When done, Jean looked with great concern into Fr. Cahill's eyes. "How will you go, Father? It is dangerous?"

Later, Fr. Cahill made his way around the colony, breviary in hand, head still bowed, he wondered what the answer was to Jean's question. Just how does a poor priest leave New Orleans? A man, especially a priest, does not just walk out of New Orleans alone and expect to get to a distant destination safely. The roads and canals, such as they were, through miles of cypress swamps were populated by thieves and murderers to say nothing of ravenous alligators, venomous snakes, and malaria-carrying mosquitoes. He needed someone to travel with, preferably a group of trusted men who had made the trip before and who were hopefully armed.

Fortunately, there were groups of flatboatmen that left the New Orleans stockade almost daily and traveled in groups the great distance to the north. Many of them carried with them the profits of their entire year's labor. It would take weeks on horseback or months on foot to return the thousand or so miles back home. He wondered if he could dress as a commoner, pull a donkey packed with supplies, clothing, a few books, and a tent.

But the other problem he faced is he didn't know exactly where he was headed. Major cities were along the seacoast, not inland, and if he was to establish a mission, he'd need patrons with some money to fund the churches he might want to build.

The trek overland gave him pause and much doubt. The longer it took, and it would take months to reach the heart of the population in the northeast, the more things could go wrong. He might never reach a city where he could minister. Further concerning was that after separating from his would-be traveling companions as they would branch off to their homes in the western rural parts of the young nation, he'd be on his own.

It was about then, in such contemplation, that he passed the guardhouse at the north gate, next to the bastion called Fort St. John. The gates were open, so he walked outside the city along the road that led to St. John's Bayou and Lake Pontchartrain. Two-hundred yards beyond the stockade he stopped at the city cemetery where he prayed the rest of his office.

7

The next morning, with resolve and hope in his step, Fr. Cahill dressed in his habit, packed his few belongings, a Mass kit, his Roman Missal, clothes, breviary, and the two volumes of the Federalist Papers, into a black cowhide suitcase given to him by the Ursulines. He fastened the belt straps around the suitcase and was about to lift it off his bed, when suddenly he stopped.

At that moment he remembered his promise to Michael Lewis—to read and explain the Federalist Papers. He was not someone to forget such a promise, but he had, and he felt bad. Immediately, he put down the suitcase, undid the straps, opened it wide, removed the two volumes, and then strapped the case shut again.

Leaving his own tent, he stopped at the tents of a few of his Capuchin brothers and made his good-byes. Then he went to the tent nearest the burned down church. The flaps were tied back, and at a table at the entrance where the light was best, sat their librarian, Brother Luke, with several books and parchments spread out before him. He looked up in surprise at Fr. Cahill holding his suitcase, wearing his cappella romano, and carrying the two volumes of the Federalist Papers.

"Leaving us so soon?" snarked Brother Luke.

"I am, right away," said Fr. Cahill, and he held out the two beautifully clad volumes to Brother Luke.

Luke gazed at the volumes as if they were a treasure chest filled with gold doubloons. "For me?"

"Yes, with one condition."

In awe Luke took the books, set one down with reverence on his table and opened the other. "These are beautiful. I've never seen anything like this. Where could you have possibly been gifted these?"

"Would you believe from a cargo walloper who can't read."

"I don't believe you," said Brother Luke still smitten by the gifts in front of him.

Fr. Cahill briefly told him how the books came to him at the wharf between confessions.

Brother Luke shook his head in disbelief. "If only I was there at the time."

"Well, it doesn't matter, because in essence you were. Here they are. They're yours."

Brother Luke lowered his head and at once peered up at the priest, "And what are the conditions of this gift?"

"That you read them, understand them, and then sit with Michael Lewis and explain them to him. You know the cargo walloper whom I mean?"

Brother Luke didn't hesitate. "Yes, I know the young man. Very diligent and generous. So, he cannot read? Is that it?"

"Right, and these were a gift from the captain to him, then to me, and now me to you. But as you notice, I am leaving, and I had promised to Michael to do..."

"...what you are now asking of me," Brother Luke finished the sentence.

"Yes. Will you?"

"Most assuredly! Indeed! I have considered, or perhaps God has put it on my heart, that Michael Lewis is of such a character that he might become one of us, someday. But to do so, he must learn to read, at least."

Now it was time for Fr. Cahill to be astonished. Indeed, Michael had impressed him with his devoutness to the faith, and in that instant Fr. Cahill confessed to God that his prejudice against the uneducated young man was to cast him aside as being unworthy of the Franciscan order. "Brother Luke, that is a wonderful idea. Michael may indeed be called, and perhaps these volumes can be useful in that discernment."

"Then this is the will of God, and I will do it," Brother Luke said with a gleam in his eyes as he took up the two volumes and turned them over, admiring the gold trim binding once again.

When Fr. Cahill left Brother Luke's tent, his suitcase and his heart were lighter. He quickened his pace to the wharf where he hoped Captain Werner Johns of the U.S. merchant ship Eagle would welcome him aboard.

8

My Despised Cyn:

It is with deep displeasure that this Cahill fellow is on his way to the United States and no doubt sponsored by Werner Johns. Whichever one of your peers is responsible for harassing Johns is surely guilty of dereliction of duty. Perhaps we can do something to conjure up a storm and prevent the boat from ever reaching the Florida Straits, but then there are pirates in the Straits, as our back up...if they're not too drunk to do their job. I'll see what some of your cohorts can do if they're not napping on a beach.

What was going on at the wharf the other night? Was Cahill seeing a vision? It wasn't from us. Damn those angels. *Your young men shall see visions and dream dreams.* That has always been one of our weaknesses.

May Hell bless and prosper William Sloan; we need more like him. We should take encouragement from his observations, although distorted. For we have done well in the slow but insidious destruction of the Church. The promotion of falsehoods in seemingly insignificant increments and getting Christians to embrace small compromises for the sake of peace has been our secret weapon. We deserve some sort of prize. Look at our accomplishments: popes and bishops are at our beck and call because they fear the state to whom they supposedly have licensed God's power to rule. Yet we're able to totally suppress the entire Jesuit order out of envy by the kings, and fear by the pope. It's a luscious irony that we work so well across civilizations, cults, and customs.

And then we have pigeons like Fr. Antoine, who luckily for us understands the consequences of disobeying the local governor but has little fear of God. He's been a good student. We are good at what we do, though it takes time and great patience.

Now if we only could control those damn Ursuline nuns as easily. They are dangerous. Unfortunately, they have now imbued in Cahill their worldview—take action, embrace risk, and do something you're totally unprepared for.

Perhaps we can be better prepared than he.

Eternally yours,
Master of Hatred

Chapter 13
Lost Before Christmas

1

Michael and Charles helped Adam and the children set up a temporary camp near the well which needed a little fixing to make it functional. But the water that eventually came up from the bottom was clear and cool.

It was more work to clean out the small cabin, patch its roof, clear the cellar, repair windows, and make the cottage habitable. Of course, a fresh latrine was dug, and the old privy repaired and moved over it. Making the small stable usable was easily accomplished by bracing the walls and patching a few holes in the roof; livestock are not fussy about their accommodations. Until a corral fence could be erected, the livestock were left to wander the nearby meadow. Barrels of household living items from the wagons were moved into the cabin, but there wasn't enough room for everything.

*John Smith II helped Adam find and rent a decent barn nearby in Smithfield into which the men stored the rest of the household goods until a full-size house and barn could be built next summer. The empty wagons were then used for trips first to Charles Town, and then to Martinsburg, for supplies, lumber, nails, hardware, food stuffs, feed, and hay. When things were straightened away, Adam paid Michael and Charles and they started back to Pennsylvania with the Conestoga wagons and the mules. With the lighter load they should make the journey back in less than a week, although Michael intended to stop in Charles Town and see if there wasn't a load they could pick up to make the return profitable.

Adam felt good about their quaint log cottage, for the winter was fast approaching. With the children's help they started clearing the dead wood from the woods and stacking it for winter heat. Both Henry and Eve were a big help, carrying the chopped pieces and stacking them in boxed rows under a shelter they had built. During the evenings, with the children in tow, he walked the land.

The Opequon Creek was cut deep into the land, which meant it would require some ingenuity to use it directly for irrigation, but neither was it likely to overflow during the spring rains. Turkey Creek, at the rear of the property, which fed the Opequon, would be more useful. Most of the land was free of trees, but there would be field stones to pull. They would be repurposed for foundations, paths, and fences. The pond in back was large and shallow. Water from Turkey Creek flowed through it, making it perfect for retting his flax.

All the while he kept thinking of where he would get laborers to do the field work and construction. It was time to get acquainted with their neighbors and ask about the local labor pool.

With their temporary home secured, albeit small, Adam, the children, and Cleopatra celebrated by baking a dozen loaves of bread and took them to the neighbors as a way of introducing themselves. There was not much in Smithfield. An old man, Feltsbarron was his name, ran a livery, but the steeds looked older than their keeper, and Adam took quick note that his forge was cold and had been so for some time.

John Smith II (the son of Smithfield's founder now deceased), and his missus lived in what might be considered a mansion by local standards, but it was mostly show and little substance. The place had the pretense of being rambling, but the rambling vines would soon take over. Smith didn't seem mindful of the place. He claimed to be a land speculator, proud of it, or so it seemed. The missus was quiet and kept her eyes to the floor and offered them no hospitality, taking the loaf of bread with a faint smile and hiding it in the kitchen.

The real disappointment for Adam, however, came when they took their buggy to adjacent farms and witnessed slaves by the dozens in the field. This was not a surprise for Adam; it was Virginia, after all. The farm closest to them, just north of the Opequon, was owned by Gregory McCullough. He was married with four strong looking teenage sons and a pleasant daughter Eve's age. He had over 500 acres, or so the man said, and grew wheat, corn, tobacco, and soybeans, but not flax. He had a stable of horses and donkeys, farm wagons and implements for harvesting, and went to market in Charles Town for both buying and selling, he said. But what took the wind from Adam's sails was the worn-looking shack of a dormitory behind the barn around which a few elderly black ladies congregated while small children, too small to work, played in a field. Gregory caught Adam staring at the building, next to which was a wooden water pump and well.

"I've got me eighteen slaves to work the field, counting the old nannies and children ya see there. Unfortunately, only nine of 'em any good. Would love to git me rid of some of 'em. I'm not much into disciplining them as some are. Perhaps, if you know to use a whip, I might sell you a few of them cheap. Yer goin' to need a dozen or so to work yer land, what you got 'bout 300 acres o'er there?"

"Less than that for farming, I reckon," said Adam.

Adam detested slavery as did his father. Staring at the broken-down dormitory prompted Adam to adjust his thinking—he didn't detest slavery as much as he detested slave owners who detested slaves. His heart ached for the old women and the children, who seemed happy enough. Their living quarters were unfit for humans, but perhaps they were well fed. *There was no use telling the man what he really thought.* Adam didn't say much after that. Shortly after handing over their loaf of bread, Adam excused his family and left.

In one way or another the other landowners in the vicinity were the same, except to the northeast along the Leetown Road. Leetown was like Smithfield in that it wasn't really a town but a scattered collection of estates, but not all were farmers. One place along the south side of the Leetown Road appeared to be a large tract of land and wood, with a large stone house; but no one was home, nor were there any livestock. Oddly, the land was not fenced off, except for a hedge row next to the road and a modest corral next to a small stable for horses. Next to the stable, under a sturdy lean-to shelter, was a handsome closed carriage to be driven by a coachman. The house had been recently built, perhaps no more than ten years earlier. Adam and the children walked around the two-story stone house looking for the owners or sign of them.

What they found instead, just east of the house, was a walk-through garden of low hedges and arbors in the shape of a narrow cross or a cathedral with transepts. The neatly trimmed, three-foot-high hedges stood in for the cathedral's walls. At the entrance, which was closest to the house, was a fountain, or what could have been a fountain had there been any water in it. Past the fountain, one could walk into the nave of the cathedral garden between the parallel row of hedges. After walking through the center of the nave, past occasional benches along the side and under arbors that reminded one of flying buttresses, one came to the crossing. In the center of the crossing was a full-size marble statue of a woman in flowing robes and veil over her head, her face and eyes cast down, but her arms extended slightly upward. From the crossing one could walk left into the south transept, or right into the north transept, or behind the statue into the chancel. The hedges encircling the crossing were planted in a perfect circle around the statue, except for openings to the nave, transepts, and chancel. Between the crossing's openings and along the curved hedges were benches. The ends of the nave, transepts, and chancel were open, allowing passage in or out of the garden. But what was most remarkable about the garden were the ten towering iron arbors reminiscent of flying buttresses that arched over the hedges. At the base of each arbor, rose bushes had been planted. At the time, they had lost most of their blossoms due to the fall and approaching winter. So far, the rose bushes had grown two or three feet up the arbors. Adam wanted to come back in several years during the summer after the roses had climbed all the way over the arches and were in bloom; it would be beautiful. Eve marveled at the garden as well, and with Henry ran through all the paths, in and out of the garden, several times. Eve even found reason to stand on a bench in the crossing and twirl, her arms out-stretched, as if celebrating something otherworldly.

Leetown had a somewhat unique origin, Adam learned from the neighbors that were home. Three former British military officers lived there. The town was named after *General Charles Lee who, when war broke out with Britain, had wanted Washington's job as commander in chief. But Congress favored Washington, so Lee took on several commands under Washington, some successful. Eventually, Lee was court-martialed for a serious failure in the battle of Monmouth. After the war, Lee moved from his estate in Leetown, which he called *Prato Rio or Hopewell, to Philadelphia, where he died six years later in

1782. Still living were *Generals Adam Stephen and *Horatio Gates. Stephen had built a hunting lodge east of Leetown on the Opequon, which he called The Bower, but now lived in Martinsburg. Horatio Gates, however, was living down the road a few miles at his farming plantation called *Travelers Rest.

When Adam and his children arrived at Travelers Rest, they had two loaves of bread left. Gates' Plantation was a working farm, and slaves were aplenty. Adam noticed, however, that they were better cared for than McCullough's slaves. Still, Adam was not sure he wanted to engage with a general of the Revolutionary Army who owned slaves.

Pulling up in their wagon, there were two other covered carriages nearby, their steeds being groomed by a groomsman at the nearby stable. A well-dressed and healthy looking teenage slave boy greeted Adam and the children. He took Calvin's reins and directed Adam and the children up the steep stoop onto a large porch of the white stone house. Eve carried a loaf of bread.

Adam knocked on the door, whereupon a male servant opened the door and invited them into the foyer. The floor was covered with imported rugs, tapestries hung on the walls lining the staircase, and there was a white marble statue of some naked woman in the foyer. Adam suspected they were calling on a neighbor over their rank.

Momentarily, a matronly woman walked into the foyer and greeted Adam and the children. "Good day to you sir, and children. I'm *Mary Valens, General Gates' wife. How can I be of service to you?" Adam recognized the strong British accent in the woman's voice, a recent immigrant from Britain no doubt.

"Good day to you Madam," said Adam. "I am Adam Livingston, a planter recently arrived in Smithfield with my children. We've just established ourselves there on a plantation situated on the Opequon. I beg your forgiveness, but my dear wife died earlier in the year. Subsequently, my father bequeathed a large tract of land here. And that is what prompted our move to these parts. May I introduce my children? This is Henry. Henry, bow politely for the lady. And my daughter, Eve."

With that, Eve curtsied and produced the wrapped loaf of bread as a gift. "For your household, Missus Gates, although it's not much for such a large house, I suspect."

Adam stared at his daughter in wonder. *Where did she learn to curtsy? Certainly not from me.* But he was proud of her civility and good manners. Not bad for a farm girl.

"Pa?" said Henry. "We got another loaf, if the horse ain't ate it up."

Adam glanced at his son. "So we do son. Go get it." The servant went to open the door, but Henry beat him to it. Then running out of the house, Henry tripped and fell on the threshold, but got up in a flash and flew off the porch. Adam likewise stared after his son: *Whatever refinement Eve had established Henry had destroyed in an instant.*

When Adam turned back, a bit embarrassed, Mrs. Gates was smiling. She took the loaf from Eve and said, "Thank you very much. This is very kind of you. Just a moment, please." With that, the very proper Mary Valens handed the loaf to a girl-servant wearing a kitchen apron, then walked briskly out of the foyer into what appeared to be a library, partly closing the door, but not completely. Adam could hear men's voices in the library discussing something that sounded important. Properly, he turned from listening to look at a nearby tapestry.

Momentarily, Henry toddled back into the house, the door being opened this time by the servant, and Mary Valens returned from the library.

"Here, Madam," said Henry, "fresh baked yesterday, just for you and yer slaves. I managed to rescue it from our horse before he ate it." Adam held his breath as Henry handed the loaf to Mary Valens who chuckled in good humor.

"Why thank you, young man," she said, giving the second loaf to the girl-servant and gesturing the girl back to the kitchen. Mrs. Gates then turned to Adam. "Would you like to meet the general? Come this way. You too, children," and she waved the trio into the library.

The library was a modest room, perhaps fifteen feet square with as high a ceiling. It was lined with bookshelves interrupted by a window that looked out on the front of the house and lit by a candled chandelier by night. There were four Georgian leader wing chairs sided by small tables topped with books. The four chairs faced the center of the room and jumping from two of them were men of obvious distinction indicated by their long waist coats worn over frock shirts, knee breeches, stockings, and buckled shoes. They were older men, one shorter and stouter than the other, who was tall and lean. The shorter man, who was bald on top but had very curly grey-white hair on the sides that worked its way down onto his mutton chops, stood back with his hands clasped behind his back. The taller man, his pure white hair falling in curls over his ears, offered his hand to Adam.

"Mister Livingston? I am General Horatio Gates, retired, and my friend here is Minister *John Adams, who has recently returned as our country's ambassador to Britain, where he's been dueling with King George."

"Not literally, sir," said John Adams to Adam with a mischievous grin. "The man doth exaggerate to humor me. Your first name is Adam, sir?"

"Yes, Minister Adams," rejoined Adam with a smile. Such a fine last name you have. I admire it."

"And your first name, *un beau nom.*"

Adam squinted at the French.

"A fine name, sir," said John Adams. "French."

The men smiled.

But Adam Livingston was aware that he was perhaps out-classed, and glancing at his children, who thankfully were not pulling books off shelves out of boredom, tried to excuse himself. "Gentleman, we are new in the area, and we just brought by some loaves of bread as a greeting."

Mary Valens spoke. "General, Mister Adams, we will enjoy the bread for supper this evening, I assure you. They are, how do you say, "Belles miches de pain?""

John Adams laughed and addressed Adam and the children, "Indeed. She said they are *fine loaves of bread*." He then adjusted his attitude and took a serious tone to Adam. "Sir, if I may inquire, where have you come from? I do not distinguish a Virginia dialect as my dear friend the general is apt to have."

"We are from York...Pennsylvania, sir," said Adam.

"Yes, I detected as much," said John Adams. "It is not far to the north, but north enough that I will dare to ask your opinion of the very conversation in which the general and I have been engaged."

Adam glanced at the general, who sighed deeply at the smaller man.

"A little debate if you may, but a polite one." Adams quizzed Adam to see if the newly arrived planter was game.

"If you desire, sir," said Adam.

John Adams began: "I have been trying to persuade my friend here..." Adams gestured to the general, "...to adopt a business model that would improve his profitability, and simultaneously free his slaves, all seventy-four of them."

"And he's not much succeeding," added the general.

At that the two waistcoated gentlemen fell silent and gazed at their new guest for a response.

But Adam, more than aware that these were classically trained gentlemen of what would nominally have been America's aristocracy, if America had such a class, was mute. He had his opinion and his moral compass, that he knew, but sharing that with such learned men pulled him up short and speechless.

2

But pulled up short and speechless wasn't part of Eve Livingston's personality. She politely opined: "How can it possibly be that the color of a person's skin indicates they are more or less human, and thus rightful members of society? For in my young life I have seen many a so-called 'slave,' and the darkness of their skin varies widely. There was one African I witnessed that was much whiter than any of us in this room, and yet she was enslaved. Why is that? And what about women? My mama was smarter than my papa, and even he has said so." She turned her gaze to Papa, whose eyes avoided hers and instead found the paisley upholstery of a nearby stool a sudden curiosity. Eve went on, "I dare say the brain of slaves is smarter than any whites, for reason that they have to tolerate so much abuse. A less intelligent creature would go wild, but slaves bare it for they must see the importance of it that others don't."

Eve stopped and waited for a response.

"My dear young lady," said the general as he attempted to mount a defense, "no slave can read, nor do they have the capacity to do numbers. If you owned slaves you would know that, but since you don't you can be forgiven for such ignorance, and impudence."

"Horatio, you know that is not true," said John Adams. "In your own division, before the Battle of Camden..."

"Do not remind me," said Gates.

"But you recounted to me how, what's his name, Bert..."

"Albert. *Albert Pinion."

"Yes, yes. You said he was a British fellow. But an African."

At this point Gates withdrew, turned, and stepped to a side table where decanters of spirits were available, and poured himself a dark green-looking liquid into a crystal glass, and took a sip, ignoring the conversation.

John Adams smiled and turned to Eve, "You are right young lady. Said Albert Pinion was a freed African slave who not only taught himself to read but was a brilliant Army scout and sometimes spy who could also read French. Something that came in handy to the general here during the French and Indian war. General Gates' French isn't that stellar."

"I would like to teach slaves to read and write, sir," said Eve. She turned to Mary Valens who was listening amused and obviously taken with the outspoken Eve Livingston. "Do you have slaves that would like to read and write, Madam? I can teach them, I'm sure."

All were silent for a moment as Adam, Minister Adams, and Mary Valens looked at Eve with astonishment, if not also admiration. Mary Valens looked to her husband and he to her. He was outnumbered, and he knew it. After a moment Mary Valens turned and gazed admirably at Eve, but spoke to Adam Livingston. "Mister Livingston, you have an outspoken but brilliant daughter."

"She has my heart, Madam, and on this topic my mind as well," said Adam.

"So, you do not intend for Africans to help run your farm," said Mary Valens. It wasn't a question, but Mary Valens looked to Adam as if it was.

Adam slowly nodded. "Yes, Madam that is my hope. But it seems that there are few laborers in this area, much as I was used to hiring in York. I must admit I'm in somewhat a quandary."

Mary Valens turned to the general. "General? There's the offer you've been looking for, haven't you? You've been doing a heap of complaining lately about Sam and his wife, what's her name."

There was a long pause, for only Mary Valens and General Gates knew the story here. General Gates paced a bit, glancing at his friend, John, who by now was rocking back on his heels, acutely interested in what was about to happen.

Eve didn't think much of it when Papa, General Horatio Gates, and John Adams took a stroll outside to discuss "business." She had already been distracted by the intricate tapestries in the foyer, inlaid wood floors, and leaded glass that adorned doors and some windows. When the men went off to do their business, Mary Valens offered to give Eve and Henry a tour of the house. Eve was all up for that, although Henry wanted to tag along with his Pa.

The tour started in the foyer and Eve and Henry found out about the naked lady carved hundreds of years ago from marble, or was it granite? It was brought to Travelers Rest from Greece, or was it Italy? Then there were the tapestries from China, or was it Egypt? There were paintings from a country she had never heard of before, let alone pronounced. Mary Valens spoke several languages, or so it seemed. They did learn that General Gates' first wife had died some years before, and that Mary Valens was his second...and that all the art in the house, including the naked lady, were from her father's estate. So, Mary Valens was rich, and General Gates, well, they discovered he wasn't the most famous general of all times, but in fact was fired by General Washington halfway through the Revolutionary War. Not that Eve cared one way or the other. Regardless, for nearly an hour Eve and Henry were tutored in Western Civilization, foreign languages, Greek (or was it Italian) culture, and the arts.

Eve loved to learn, but this was all so much and so fast. Her mind swirled with excitement, but sadness too, for she could not possibly remember a tenth of what Mary Valens told them, and yet Eve wanted to remember it all.

As the tour continued, Eve's heart raced with excitement. Yet almost every minute she was pulled back to reality by Henry's picking something up and playing with it. Eve could tell Henry's behavior made Mary Valens nervous, so Eve was constantly taking the object, worth thousands of gold doubloons no doubt, from Henry and putting it back, then smiling apologies to their docent.

When they were done, Eve could not help but ask, "Missus Gates, is there a way I could come back and visit you again? All of this is so interesting, and I've never been to a real school, and I've never even read a book about any of this. Oh, please, perhaps I can clean for you?"

"Oh child! That's not necessary. We have servants that do all of that. But yes, you are invited anytime." Mary Valens then cast an evil eye at mischievous Henry as if to let Eve know that Henry was welcome *to stay at home* if such an occasion arose.

And with that the Livingston visit to Travelers Rest was over.

As Adam drove the wagon back to Smithfield, Eve was disappointed that Papa didn't say a word about whatever the discussion with General Gates and John Adams had been about. He only remarked how smart the men were, and how he was going back to visit them again in the morning...something about a business arrangement. Could Eve and Henry return with him, she wanted to know—she was anxious for another Mary Valens tour. But Papa said no, tomorrow she and Henry would stay behind.

Eve felt badly about that last part and found herself falling into silence and a deep pout.

As Calvin pulled their wagon onto their land, she broke out of her mostly self-induced slump. "Papa, how long are you going to be gone tomorrow and what are Henry and I to do?"

"Well, Bethany needs milking, of course. And while you're at it, we're going to need to give her a new name. Bethany will no longer suit her. You and Henry might think one up."

"Why's that?" asked Eve. "We've always called her Bethany. Why, she won't come if we call her anything else."

"Jus' pull on her rope," said Henry. Stupid cow don't know her name. Call her cow."

"That's rude," said Eve. "Let's think. What does she look like?"

"I always thought she looked like a bunch of moons," said Henry, "with all those white spots on her."

"That's it, Papa!" said Eve. "We'll call her Moon Beam."

Adam laughed. "Moon Beam it is."

"But why?" asked Eve. "Why does Bethany need a new name?"

"That will have to wait until tomorrow," said her father.

3

Eve noted that Papa was unusually quiet the next morning as they ate breakfast. She also found it curious that he took the wagon and not his horse to visit the Gates Plantation. She and Henry busied themselves during his absence. Well, she busied herself. Henry was off exploring the bank of the creek. He could be irritating, and she often wondered what her reaction would be if he fell in and drowned. He had been gone a good hour before she started to worry. A hawk caught her eye as it landed in a tree in the direction of the creek and glared down at the ground across a meadow to where there was a clearing near the creek surrounded by trees.

Suddenly, her heart crept into her throat. Before she knew what she was doing, she ran toward that clearing next to the wide and deep creek where just days earlier they had all reconnoitered, thinking it might be a good place from which to fish.

As she ran, she scanned the meadow and clearing just ahead. When she neared the clearing, she yelled, "HENRY! HENRY? Where are you?"

There was no answer. It was unnervingly quiet.

"HENRY! HENRY?" she called out.

Again, silence except for the wind, birds, the chatter of squirrels, and the fast-flowing water along the creek bed.

Her heart started to race as panic crowded in.

Unconsciously, she ran faster until she reached the clearing and stopped dead, suddenly realizing the steep bank that dropped four to six feet to the water was at her feet. Another step and she would have been in the water and carried along by the current.

Cautiously, she stepped back while craning her neck over the bank's rim looking for some sign of her brother. But she saw nothing. She started looking for signs that he had even been there. As far as she knew he was back exploring

Turkey Creek, although that was a long hike from their cottage.

Suddenly, she was struck on the head by an acorn, and then another in fast succession.

Angry at the squirrels she had seen running about, she looked up into the tree behind her and saw the culprit. Her response was immediate. From head to toe her muscles went taunt, blood rushed into her face, and her fists clenched.

"HENRY! Get down from there."

"Awe, c'mon, sis. I thought that was a pretty good shot," as he threw another acorn at her. She batted it away in furry and stomped to the tree trunk as he climbed down out of the oak.

"You gave me a fright," she snapped. "Thought you might have fallen in and drowned yourself"

Jumping to the ground he said, "There's a beach, by the way, over there," said Henry pointing downstream. "C'mon, let me show you."

Eve followed her brother around the edges of the meadow, around some brush and a few trees, and there by the Charles Town Road, next to the bridge, the side of the road had washed out and become a rocky path that led to a rocky beach of sorts next to the creek. Horse prints in the mud told her riders had brought their horses down here to water. Henry picked up a flat stone and skipped it across the water. She followed the stone as it skipped all the way across and landed on the far bank.

There, on the far bank, much to their surprise, were three African farm workers, two women and a man, in shabby clothes, kneeling by the water, lapping up water from the creek with their hands. The two young white kids on one side of the creek and the three African slaves on the other side froze in place and stared at each other for a moment, before the African man hustled the women away from the creek, up the far bank, and into the field beyond.

Eve was shaken. She immediately scanned the far side of the creek and along the underside of the bridge. *Were there others that had sneaked away from their work to get a drink of water?* "C'mon, Henry, we should get back. We don't want to be missing when Pa returns."

"Were those slaves from that farm?" asked Henry.

"Pretty sure they were. Probably from the McCullough's. Let's go."

Up the wadi they scrambled and headed back to the cabin they called home.

It was early afternoon that Eve heard Papa's wagon pull into the yard. She hurried outside followed by Henry. Sitting next to Papa on the driver's bench was a muscular African man in a loose work shirt, and canvas pants held up by suspenders. Obviously a slave, the man had a square face, clear eyes, shaved head, short neck, large shoulders, and he sat taller than Papa, and Papa was no small man. Behind the African man, sitting on a crate was an African woman, smaller than the man, with a scarf tied over her curly jet-black hair. She wore a shawl around her shoulders and was dressed otherwise in a plain cotton dress. She looked tired and appeared to have been crying. What created confusion in

Eve's mind was that both the man and the woman were also smiling, broadly.

Nonetheless, Eve's heart leaped in anger and confusion at Papa.

She found herself holding her breath, and unconsciously crossed her arms, digging her fingers into opposite biceps. Narrowing her eyes at Papa, she avoided the Africans and walked to his side of the wagon as he dismounted. But before she should speak, he did.

"Eve? Henry? Come here, lad."

Henry, too, looked confused and was reluctant to approach his papa. But Adam reached out and grabbed the shoulder straps of his son's bib overalls and pulled the boy next to him.

Eve looked over at her brother. His hands were stuck deep in his overall pockets and his arms clenched to his sides. The African man had smiled broadly at her and then moved to the back of the wagon to help the woman down. There were also half a dozen crates in the back of the wagon.

"Papa," said Eve in a severe whisper. "You said you would never own slaves."

Adam smiled at his daughter, but said nothing in reply; he stood his ground and gently placed his arms around Eve's shoulders while he kept a firm, upward grip on Henry's suspenders, preventing him from going anywhere. Momentarily, the African man and woman came around from the backside of the wagon to meet the children. Adam spoke first. "Eve. Henry. I'd like you to meet Mister Sam and Missus Bethany Dark. You should, from this time forward, call them either Mister Dark or Missus Dark."

Eve was familiar enough with slaves to know that no one called slaves mister or missus.

Suddenly, Henry dared to ask the big question as he stared at the two Africans before him, "Are you gonna be our slaves?"

At that Sam and Bethany's smiles turned solemn. They said nothing but simply bowed their heads in submission and glanced at Adam.

"No, son, Mister and Missus Dark are not our slaves and never will be."

The smiles returned in force to Sam and Bethany's face and their eyes gleamed with tears.

"What are you, then?" asked Eve, still staring at the couple as if they were part of a window display at a store.

Adam was silent and simply nodded at Sam.

Taking the cue, Sam gripped his wife's hand and said with tears in his eyes, "Thank to your Missta, and Missta Adams, dis mornin' when we wokes up, we *were* slaves on de Travelers Rest Plantation. But as we's stand here now, we's free. We's Freedmen. Yer Missta has manumitted us." Sam pulled a piece of paper out of his pocket, unfolded it, and showed it to Eve. "I dunt know wad dat say. I kin't read. But Missta Adams, he tell us dat your papa has paid for our freedom, and das hired us to help ya work yer farm and care for yer farm. If that okay with you chil'en."

Eve was suddenly overcome with a flush of emotion she could not understand.

She looked to Papa and saw his smile, then back to Mr. and Mrs. Dark, who let their tears flow freely. Mrs. Dark gripped her husband's muscular arms to keep upright. Eve took the paper from Mr. Dark and read it.

> *This Indenture made this 30th Day of October in the Year of our Lord one thousand seven hundred and eighty-eight, between Adam Livingston Esquire of Smithfield in the County of Berkeley and State of the Virginia, on the One Part; and Samuel and Bethany Dark a negro-man and his wife on the Other part --*
>
> *Witnesseth, that the said Adam Livingston at once grants unto Samuel and Bethany Dark their freedom, with full liberty to depart from his family and service if they shall so be inclined.*
>
> *Further, at once, Adam Livingston as an employer offers to them, Samuel and Bethany Dark, an indenture to labor as freemen, to earn a wage, to acquire goods, and enjoy the rights of other free persons by the faithful performance of certain services hereafter to be performed for a certain time, which the said Sam and Bethany Dark in their part of this covenant hereinafter contained, hath promised and engaged to perform for eight years, through the 30th day of October, in the year of our Lord one thousand seven hundred and ninety-six in exchange for a fair wage less living expenses if provided by Adam Livingston, and the said Adam Livingston will give them the said Samuel and Bethany, in exchange for their labor, good and sufficient meat, drink, apparel and washing and lodging during the aforesaid term of eight years, but will also at the end of said term give them each, such clothes as shall be proper and suitable for them. Their wage to be determined solely by Adam Livingston, shall be off-set of the indebtedness Adam Livingston incurred to purchase their freedom from their former state and for their upkeep.*
>
> *The said Samuel and Bethany Dark on their part, do by these present, covenant and agree with the aforesaid Adam Livingston Esquire in manner and form following, that is to say, that they, the said Samuel and Bethany Dark, will well and truly serve him, the said Adam Livingston, in doing the usual business of his family with cheerfulness and fidelity without murmuring, or contradicting the just and reasonable orders of him the said Adam (or his wife if he should marry) for and during and unto the full end and term of eight years from the day of this date of these present; and that during the*

whole of said term of eight years as aforesaid, they, the said Samuel and Bethany Dark, will behave themselves in all respects towards Adam Livingston and his whole family, as a good and faithful servant ought to do. Particularly that they will not at any time when they are singularly or together sent out on errands stay longer than they ought to do -- that they will not at any time go out on evenings into company without letting their employer know their whereabouts nor keep up the family beyond the usual hour of bed-time, but will come home in proper season so as not in any way to disturb the family -- that they will get up early in the morning and perform duties agreed upon-- and that they will behave themselves during the whole of the said term of eight years above mentioned, with sobriety and good temper, agreeable to the true intent and meaning -- of the foregoing Covenant and Agreement.

In Witness whereof the Parties to these Presents have hereunto set their Hands and Seals interchangeably, the Day and Year first above written:

Sam and Bethany Dark
Adam Livingston, Esq.

Signed Sealed and delivered in the presence of us:

John Adams, Esq.
Mary Valens Gates

As she read the indenture agreement, Eve became more and more excited. She had never read anything like this before. Although she wanted to stop and ask questions of Papa, she decided to do that later, assuming he had a copy. She just didn't want to stop reading.

The more she read, the more she grew faint for she was breathing very deeply and purposefully. When she finished her hands were trembling, and she handed the indenture back to Sam...er, Mister Dark, and putting on a pleasant smile said, "Welcome to the family, Mister and Missus Dark. Do you want me to teach you both to read?"

That got the Darks nodding and crying all the more.

4

For Adam, the first and second order of business after bringing Sam and Bethany to his land was to get them temporarily settled into his own cottage and then build them a cabin of their own. In his head, he had already laid out where his main residence, the barn, corral, and other outbuildings would be located. He also had selected a field where there were few trees, but which was near the well, for building several cabins to house workers. So, once he shared his plans with Sam, they set about scouting the property for the proper timber and stones.

Sam was a good fit for Adam who was used to delegating tasks to workers with common sense and a clear head. The problem that Sam created for General Gates was that Sam was a self-starter and had his own ideas about how things should be done. Further, Sam's ideas were typically better than the field supervisors he worked under, and that caused a lot of turmoil. Gates told Adam that Sam didn't take orders well, which was obviously a concern for Adam. Mary Valens, who was not a great fan of owning slaves but didn't oppose it, pointed out to John Adams and her husband that Sam and Bethany were a bad fit for their plantation. It seemed ironic, but Mary Valens understood human nature. Slaves that were well "seasoned" didn't think for themselves and would cause her husband's supervisors less aggravation. In her household duties, Bethany was much like her husband. She did things her own way, not the way she was told. After a while, Mary Valens discovered that Bethany knew better how to get things done than she did herself. Mary Valens came to like that about Bethany, but the general never did. So, John Adams had suggested that Adam Livingston quietly question the supervisors as to what their problem with Sam was; that is, for Adam to get the supervisors to share very specific issues of how Sam was a contrarian. What John Adams suspected, and what Adam Livingston confirmed, was that Sam had more gumption and common sense than the field supervisors. John Adams thought such might be the case from his years of knowing Gates during the war. In government, as well as on his plantation, Gates was known for his inefficiency and lack of progress. In fact, had it not been for Mary Valens' riches, the plantation might have fallen into bankruptcy, which is what John Adams thought might happen in the not-too-distant future. The source of the problem was that Gates was not the best at assigning platoon commanders during the war. Gates favored people that agreed with him and turned aside field commanders that thought for themselves. It was probably the reason Gates was fired as an under-general. He kept losing battles.

After a week or so working side-by-side with Sam, Adam discovered that Mary Valens and John Adams were right. Sam usually had a better idea, and Adam had no problem letting Sam do it his own way. Work got done faster, and usually better.

Adam and Sam toured the property taking an inventory of what trees to use for the new cabin, and where flat-sided stones might be collected or shaped for the floor. As they worked Adam made mention that he was going to need more men than Sam to work the farm. Did Sam know where he could hire day workers as he had done in York? The casual comment seemed to light a fire under Sam.

"Missta Livingston, sir, I knows whah dere at least one fine worker. But I's 'fraid to mention it, as I not sure of his exact whereabouts, but I 'ear rumors."

"Who, Sam?"

"He be my younger bro'her, though I don't know his odder name. Not sure wad my own, if you's know my meanin's."

A wave of regret and embarrassment coursed through Adam as he realized, stupidly, that "Dark" was not Sam's real name, but his slave name. Of course it was.. Sam was dark skinned, darker than most.

Adam stopped in his tracks, faced Sam, and looked up at him, for Sam was a least a hand taller.

"You don't know what your family's name is?"

"No sir. My mama and papa 'en dey mama and papa were slaves too, and I don'ts remember wad last names dey had, as I was taken from dem as a child, and give de name Sam Dark. Me bro'her was wid me for a while, but back two year or so, he were sold to a family. I think the name is Colloughs."

A pang of reality hit Adam in his throat. He looked at Sam harder. "Do you mean, McCullough? Is it McCullough?"

Sam stared at the ground for a moment, thinking. "Yas, sir, do believe that it. McCulloughs. Does you's know dem?"

A broad smile came over Adam. He grabbed Sam's arm and turned him toward the Opequon creek that was about fifty yards to their north.

"Do you see that farmland, the other side of the creek?" Adam said.

"Yas, sir."

"Well, that is the McCullough farm. The very day I first met General Gates and your name was mentioned, I had also met Gregory McCullough. He offered to sell me some of his slaves. He doesn't have many and he says most are lazy and not worth much. He offered to sell them to me cheap. What kind of worker is your brother? What did you say his name was?"

Sam was now making long strides toward the creek wanting to see better across it. "I call 'em Nwanne (new-AN-nay)."

An unease creeped upon Adam. *What kind of tinder box had he just opened?* Becoming alert to what might be across the creek, he quickened his pace to keep up with Sam, although it occurred to him that he could in no way out match Sam's stride. What Sam wanted to do he would do. He hoped common sense would prevail.

5

One morning several days later, Adam harnessed up Luther to the wagon and revisited Gregory McCullough under the pretense of buying one of his slaves. McCullough had his supers lined up a half-dozen in the yard for Adam's inspection. Adam looked them over and felt nothing but compassion for them, as he hung his head and shook it in rejection. Secretly, he wanted to buy them all from McCullough. But he didn't have the money or facilities to pull off such an altruistic deed. He told McCullough he wanted just one strong male, hoping to be led to Nwanne. McCullough rode around the farm with Adam and pointed out a few of the slaves he was willing to unload. Nwanne was not hard to identify, even though McCullough had avoided pointing him out. He was indeed physically like his brother, Sam—dark skin, muscular, similar facial features, but a bit smaller. Of course, McCullough didn't want to sell Nwanne, for he was one of the better workers, though the sores on his body and his general unhealthy constitution were hardly convincing arguments. But they were arguments that Adam used to convinced McCullough that Nwanne wasn't much use to him, but he could be to Adam...sick as he seemed to be. McCullough tried again to get Adam to buy some of his "lazier" properties. But Adam was persistent, and the men finally settled on a price.

McCullough took Adam inside to his office where he produced a blank bill of sale, filled it out in duplicate, both men signed the documents, Adam paid in gold, making Nwanne officially an enslaved person of Adam Livingston. Adam didn't want to sign the document, but realized he had to or there would be trouble with McCullough. Afterward, Adam folded the bill of sale and put it into his overall pocket. At first, he thought he might later burn it. Then he realized there would be county and state records that would need to be reconciled, and the purchase of Nwanne would have to be recorded at the courthouse in Martinsburg. John Adams had promised to see to the registration of Sam and Bethany's sale and their subsequent manumission.

While the sales agreement was being tended to, a supervisor led Nwanne back to his dormitory. When Adam and McCullough exited the house, Nwanne returned carrying a crate of personal effects. He was downcast and obviously attached to some of the other slaves. One was a young woman who seemed to have eyes for Nwanne. But a field supervisor swung his stick and they all scattered back to their jobs, although the young woman looked back a few times in sadness, and Adam noticed how Nwanne looked after her.

Adam's blood boiled. He was more an abolitionist than he thought. For the time being he hardened his exterior and looked away, pretending not to care. He fought against his inner impulses and tried to act like an autocratic slave lord. It seemed to work, although Adam knew himself to be a terrible actor.

McCullough instructed Nwanne to slide his crate into Adam's wagon and crawl up into the cargo space. McCullough then took a stretch of rope and bound Nwanne's arms behind his back and his wrists to the tie-down bullseye on the side of the wagon. Adam watched with distaste but said nothing to continue the subterfuge. But before he knew it, McCullough had bound tight Nwanne's ankles as well.

Adam stepped in. "Greg, that's not necessary."

"You've never owned a slave before, you said. You're going to have to keep this one tied up for a while and season him to your way of operatin.'"

"Well, let me do it then. Cut that rope off his ankles. The man needs some ability to maneuver."

"Yer foolish if you ask me." McCullough glared at Adam.

But Adam held his ground and simply nodded at the tied ankles as if waiting for McCullough to do as he asked.

Disgruntled, McCullough unsheathed a glistening knife and began to pry open the knot that secured the rope around Nwanne's ankles. Adam watched, afraid that McCullough might needlessly...or purposely...cut Nwanne's leg. It was a sunny day about noon when this took place. As McCullough turned his knife to pry open the knot, the shiny blade, for an instant, reflected the sun directly into Adam's eyes. Adam shut his eyes and turned away, but it was too late...with the sun's bright rays came a terrifying vision, a premonition that occupied all his senses. What he saw was a raging inferno of a building so totally consumed he could not recognize what it was or where. The whole vision, as before, was time compressed, but suddenly there was a catastrophic explosion that turned everything white. It felt like his skin would burn off his face, the heat was so intense. And then there was the mysterious, unintelligible screaming of a woman. What scared Adam the most was the searing heat of his face, as if he had tried to walk into the fire to feed it dry wood. Adam put his hands over his eyes, fell to the ground, and gasped for breath. Almost as soon as the vision began it was over, leaving Adam nonetheless shocked and nearly invalid on the ground.

"What happened?" asked McCullough, looking down at Adam while working out the knot.

Adam shook his head in a daze, "I'm not sure. The sun hit the edge of your knife, and ..." He dared not say anything about what he saw; McCullough would think he was crazy and renege on the sale. "You need help, old man?" McCullough teased.

Adam shook his head again, trying to rid himself of what he had seen and heard, but not really wanting to forget it. "No, I'm okay. I'm not sure what happened, but...well, that's a mighty shiny knife you got there," he joked. Adam stood and brushed himself off about the time McCullough pulled the rope off Nwanne's ankles.

"Satisfied now?" McCullough asked. "Sure you okay?"

"Yeah! Yeah!" Adam said, brushing off his clothes. Adam gazed at Nwanne sitting in the cargo bay of his wagon, his back to the side where his hands were tied to a deadeye, his eyes wide, watching Adam's every move with some suspicion, as if his new owner was crazed, possessed, or both.

Adam gathered himself and stumbled to his wagon, checked on the ropes that bound Nwanne, trying to catch Nwanne's eye and nonverbally offering him some hope, while at the same time not showing his hand to McCullough.

Nwanne finally looked up at Adam and saw something that made him relax a bit and crack a smile. But Adam shook his head ever so slightly as if to tell Nwanne not to let on, but to play along. Nwanne did, and put on a good show of resistance, looking Adam in the eye all the time as if he knew something without knowing anything.

Finally, they were on the road, Calvin pulling them along at a good pace away from McCullough's place. Adam kept playing back the vision over and over in his mind, wanting desperately to know what it meant, but nothing came to him.

It was two miles from McCullough's yard before they pulled onto the path to Adam's property. The shadow of the trees and tall wild-growing shrubs hid the road from the land, and the land from the road. Adam halted the wagon and set the brake.

Adam looked around and felt confident that no one could see them. He relaxed that this part of the plan had gone easily. Tying off Calvin's reins he swiveled his legs over the driver's bench and landed his boots on the wagon floor next to Nwanne, who was watching Adam's every move. He's probably worried what's next, thought Adam. "Nwanne, I'm going to unbind you, for I do not want the person you are about to meet to see you like this."

Nwanne was weak and Adam suspected also disheartened being treated as he had been, expecting nothing much of a change in his future. "Who dat, sir? Will I knows dis person?"

"Yes, I suspect you will. No, I don't suspect it. I know you will. Let's get you unfettered. I'm sorry you had to put up with this."

Nwanne's mouth fell open as if he was not sure to be happy or afraid. He let Adam get the ropes off his hands, arms, and legs, which were convoluted and tight.

Damn that McCullough, thought Adam, and he worked harder and quicker to get the ropes off Nwanne. Having finally finished, Adam coiled and stacked the rope under the seat. It was cursed rope. Perhaps someday it could be redeemed...or burned.

Or burned. *What did the burning premonition have to do with rope, or with Nwanne? Each time he played the vision back he grew fearful, as if he was attacked by an unseen and all-powerful force.*

Adam climbed out of the load deck and onto the drive bench, scooting to the left. "Okay, Nwanne," said Adam. "Sit up here with me. Your life is about to change."

"Yas, sir," said Nwanne weakly. There was a sliver of hope in his voice as he climbed up and over the bench and sat down.

"Do you know how to drive a wagon?"

"I do dat fer Missta McCullough, in de field."

"Good, you're in the driver's seat now. Take those reins." Adam pointed to the beast hitched to the wagon. "That there is Calvin, one of my favorite steeds. Be kind and gentle with him. Now drive us the rest of the way into my place. Oh, and release the brake, there."

Nwanne's eyes got bigger and bigger the more Adam talked. But looking around, he grabbed the reins like a seasoned driver, released the brake, and slapping the reins ever so cautiously said, "Let's go home, Missta Calvin. Missta Livingston here thinks someone waitin' fer us."

Adam smiled. He liked Nwanne. And as the wagon lurched forward, Adam felt intensely happy. *So far, so good.* Nwanne was indeed a bit like his brother—give him the reins and a little guidance and he'll do well. Adam sat back confidently in the seat and gazed at Nwanne's worn boots braced against the footrest. *Yes, new boots would be in order, too.*

The wagon left the S-curve of the entrance and entered the yard proper in front of the small cabin. Adam directed Nwanne to pull the wagon up by the front and stop. Compared to McCullough's farm, the little cabin and the absence of a barn, the place looked sparse. Adam noticed Nwanne looking around with suspicion. There had not been time nor place before they left McCullough's to explain everything to Nwanne. Besides, he wanted to surprise the man. He was not to be disappointed.

From behind, suddenly, came a loud WHOOP! "NWANNE! NWANNE!," yelled Sam, grinning widely as he came running from the small stable he had been clearing.

Nwanne turned in shock at hearing his brother. When he saw Sam smiling ear to ear, he was so surprised he froze on the seat as if he had seen a ghost. As Sam got closer, Adam noticed that Nwanne began to shake with excitement. But still he didn't move until Sam came to the side of the wagon and literally pulled his brother down and into his arms. Sam was crying, and soon Bethany and Eve came from inside the cabin to see what was going on. Henry had been in the stable and, taking his time, shuffled across the dusty yard to watch the celebration as if this was a common occasion.

Sam stood back and held Nwanne at arms-length. "Nwanne, lil' bro'her, looks at me. Let me see you's. Wad you's think of dis? We have wanted dis fo so long, and now we have it."

Bethany stepped off the porch and with a big smile welcomed Nwanne with a hug, and that brought on a smile from Nwanne. "It is good to see you, Nwanne," she said. "Are you okay? You look tired." She lovingly brushed her soft hands across his face, feeling the sores as if trying to rub a healing salve into them.

"Yas, I dink so," said Nwanne. "Wad is dis? Do you's now works for dis man, Livingston?"

"Yes," she said, "but it is different. We are not slaves. No longer. Neither are you."

"In time, Bethany," said Adam. "Technically, Nwanne is still enslaved."

Immediately, Sam glared at Adam. He whispered angrily at Adam, "He is not free? You's told me..."

"In time, Sam. There's been no time. But yes, he will be."

Nwanne looked at Adam as if he was not sure he should smile, be confused, or be upset like his brother had suddenly become.

"Wad is dis?" Sam asked.

Adam suddenly felt anxious that things could get out of control. He had wanted to make this reunion a surprise for both men, but now he was wondering if he should have told Nwanne what was going on sooner, and Sam too, for there was no one like Minister John Adams at the McCullough farm to create the manumission papers.

Adam gestured toward the repaired swinging door on the cabin, "Let's all go inside and sit down. I will explain everything. Eve, can you get some milk for Nwanne, here? Nwanne would you like some fresh milk?"

"Milk!? Oh, yes, dat would be so good. I have not milk in a very long time."

Sam gestured aggressively at Adam demanding a quick explanation.

As Nwanne, followed Bethany inside along with Eve, Adam held Sam back.

"Sam, it will happen exactly as I said. I bought Nwanne from McCullough, but McCullough thinks Nwanne is still an enslaved person, and technically he is, until we draft the manumission document, which we will do yet today. But remember, Nwanne must agree to the terms of the manumission just as you did, and I didn't have time to explain all of that to him, especially not in front of McCullough. I was not fortunate to have a John Adams with us, as we did with General Gates. Now, let's go in and explain all this to him. He's going to be surprised, so your presence is very important. He trusts you."

So, it was that over the next several hours a lot happened. Nwanne indeed did agree to a similar indenture agreement like Sam and Bethany had agreed to. Adam and Eve made a copy of the indenture Sam and Bethany had signed. With tears in his eyes Nwanne made his mark on the manumission document after which Sam, Bethany, and Eve all signed as witnesses.

Adam was surprised when Sam and Bethany crudely printed "*Sam Dark*" and "*Bethany Dark*" as signatures on the paper, which Eve had been teaching them how to do—first steps toward reading and writing which up until now they had been forbidden to learn. It was signing their names in block letters that convinced Nwanne this was all very real, and he could not stop crying for a long time.

While Eve prepared dinner for all, with a little nuisance help from Henry, and a lot of help from Bethany, Sam took Nwanne to the creek for a bath and a fresh set of clothes which Sam provided from his several sets General Gates permitted him to take.

Then they all settled down to dinner of chicken, potatoes, and beans, and a surprise bag of licorice Adam had picked up in Charles Town.

Still Nwanne cried through it all, sitting next to Sam who put his arm frequently around his brother's shoulders and hugged him as if they never had.

Until Sam and Bethany's cabin was built, the sleeping arrangements for the next few weeks would be tight, as they would all sleep inside the one room cottage in makeshift beds, although when the weather was warm enough Sam and Nwanne slept on the porch. But now, being early November, that was not often.

Adam made a second trip to Martinsburg to register the bills of sale and manumission agreements for Nwanne and to ensure the Darks' manumission was registered. The expense was minimal. As the registrations were being recorded, he realized that while General Gates knew the Darks were manumitted, McCullough did not know of Nwanne's manumission. He wondered if that was going to be a problem.

To alleviate the crowded sleeping conditions in the cabin, he worked extra hard to guide Sam, Bethany, and Nwanne in the design and building of the cabin they would call home.

Earlier, Adam and Sam had staked out locations for the new barn, Adam's eventual house, the crew cabins, where the Darks would live, as well as a sheep pen and building, hog pen and shed, a smoke house, and a garden. All of these would congregate near the well at the northeast corner of the property where there was a well that still needed to be fully rejuvenated with new walls and a pump mechanism.

Before the group started felling trees and preparing them for building, Adam spent the better part of a day with Sam, Bethany, and Nwanne discussing the design and construction of their cabin-house. Because Nwanne was now with them, the Darks' cabin would have to be larger, and Adam decided that the cabin to be built for them would be their home for as long as they worked for him. He made it clear that he was not going to restrict within reason the kind of cabin, its size or design, except that they had to finish it before bad weather set in, which gave them only a month or two to close the building in.

The group decided on a 12-foot x 30-foot cabin with a center-peaked, cedar-shake shingled roof, with bedrooms at either end, each with stone fireplaces, and a great room with a cooking fireplace in the center at the rear. A 4-foot x 14-foot woodshed with a cellar would be attached at the rear, and there would be a full-length porch with a lean-to roof in front. They would first lay a flat-stone foundation with mortar to seal the stones, on top of which would go two crisscrossed layers of wooden planks for insulation. Adam would buy the lumber and supplies for the floor, doors, and windows. The walls would be constructed from notched pine timbers felled on the property. The cabin would be built with its rear against a stand of trees for a windbreak, but the front would face what would become the center courtyard for the new Livingston compound of buildings.

With the plans made and drawn on scraps of paper, the team began clearing and leveling the building site, collecting stones, and identifying trees. It would take all their time over the next weeks to rough in the cabin and make it habitable. Little did they know that the hard labor would be lost before Christmas.

6

My Despised Cyn:

Gregory McCullough and his supervisors deserve medals for their delusional conceit. Don't you just love it? McCullough especially—arrogance on a stick.

But McCullough is going to need your help; we must put a dent in Livingston's altruistic sentiments about slavery. If we don't, Livingston will disrupt what we've managed to keep alive in Virginia. Enslavement has benefited our cause tremendously over the millennia and we must keep it so here in the New World. It will be the death of us to see it abolished. Of course, if it is abolished in a physical sense, we should influence the political sentiment to enslave the lower class in a way that seems beneficial to them but represses their initiative and independence. Dependence is the watch word...we need to always elicit dependence of the lower class on the upper class in a way that controls their lives as if eternally enslaved. That will, of course, breed class welfare if not class warfare, and our cause will be championed.

I'm not excited about Livingston and his girl stumbling across the Leetown garden. How long can we keep those two families apart? It seems that St. Michael and our enemies are about; oh...if we could only see them.

General Gates is a wimp for listening to John Adams and allowing Livingston to manumit the Darks. Free will is such a deterrent. We need control not freedom, especially over that snitty girl of his. She's going to be the wreck of us if we can't silence her. If you can't influence the right minds, I might have to do it for you.

Now, do you have any idea what happened when Livingston fell to the ground at McCulloughs? It was as if he saw something, something revealed to him by our enemies. If we could only perceive their presence, yet unless they deliberately break into our dimension, we have no indication. But something is amiss and I don't like it. Do you recall the discussion he had with his daughter a while back about his dreams and knowing beforehand that his children and wife were to die, but not knowing enough to stop it? It's like he's being warned. What did he see? Maybe he'll tell his kid, then we can find out. We must find out.

Meantime that Cahill fellow in New Orleans is about to make a decision that will weigh catastrophically against us. Get your imperceptible presence down there. Do something. Maybe a shipwreck, pirates...anything.

Eternally yours,
Master of Deceit

Chapter 14
Laborer in the Field

1

On the evening of Oct. 25, 1778, the United States merchant ship Eagle was moored at the New Orleans wharf. She was a 150-foot long, forty-eight-foot beam, two-masted, square-rigged snow-brig. The fore and main masts supported aloft four yards, each a little narrower than the ship. Respectively, from bottom to top, the masts carried the fore and main course sails, above those the lower tops'ls, the upper tops'ls, and finally, the topgallant sails. The absence of a royal or skysail above the topgallants meant fewer lines, and fewer spare spars to clutter the deck. Stepped immediately behind the main mast was a shorter mast called the snow mast. The snow-brig evolved from the larger three-masted ship where the mizzen mast was slowly moved forward and shortened until it was attached to the main mast top, one-third of the way up. The snow mast did not have a yard, but rather a boom that nominally carried only a gaff sail which aided in beating to windward. The Eagle was big and strong, but not swift. Cargo rated at 350 tonnage roughly meant it had capacity for 3,500 cubic feet of cargo. When Fr. Cahill arrived, the Eagle was set low in the water, evidence that she was using every bit of her cargo capacity.

Captain Johns was thrilled to see Fr. Cahill with his luggage...and welcomed him aboard, taking him to his own cabin and offering him the mate's bunk. "You will eat with me here, as well, Father. I am most blessed that you have joined our voyage. Will you conduct Mass in my cabin on the eve of our departure?"

"I will be glad to." But there was doubt in Fr. Cahill's eyes. "How long before we depart?"

"We will be set to sail tonight before we turn in, but we leave just before sun-up tomorrow morning," said the captain.

"Then I must first go ashore and purchase some provisions," said the priest.

"For what? You will eat with me at table."

"I was thinking of a bottle of port and bread for communion. In my haste I was negligent, even for myself." Fr. Cahill hesitated. "But..."

"You have nothing, do you?" The captain went to his locker, reached into a bag, and handed a coin to Fr. Cahill. "Buy enough wine for a three-week voyage, but bread for only a week. Thomas, our cook, will provide you with bread after that. Though very few of the crew are of the faith, it might be only six or ten for Mass each day."

The priest looked at the coin in his hand. It was a double gold Spanish doubloon. He doubted he had ever held a coin of such value. But he gripped it with his fist, and simply said, "Aye, Captain. That I will do and be back shortly." With that Fr. Cahill skipped out of the cabin and ran down the gangplank to the shops along the wharf.

Fr. Cahill was overjoyed. He could not believe his luck at meeting Captain Johns and being berthed in the captain's quarters. Now this, gold to buy communion wine, though he was old enough to know that all that glitters is not gold. He would be cautious, for where there is light, shadows lurk.

Nonetheless, he smiled and nearly laughed all the way to the wine and bread merchants, even as he realized that he'd need enough left over to tip a lad to help him back to the ship with the case of port he was about to buy.

So it was that Fr. Cahill situated himself aboard the merchant ship Eagle and prepared to depart for the United States of America. He would seek out his next adventure once he arrived in Baltimore. He had no way of knowing, however, that adventure would find him long before they arrived.

In preparation for Mass, Fr. Cahill used the table in Captain Johns' cabin as an altar. From his Mass kit, he set out corporal linen, his small crucifix, paten, chalice, and purificator linens. He poured a small amount of wine into his chalice and tore off part of a loaf of bread, placing it onto the paten. Standing aside he opened his missal and reviewed the day's readings. All the while there was a cacophony of foot traffic above his head on the poop deck as the crew prepared to get the ship ready for departure in the morning.

The door opened and a trim sailor of thirty or so with a short red beard poked his head in and surveyed the room. His bright eyes opened wide when they landed on Fr. Cahill standing by the aft windows with his missal. Donald Irish, first mate, turned his head outward and yelled, "Aye, Captain, priest is here."

Out of sight came the reply, "Very well, carry on."

Irish glanced at the altar set for Mass, quickly smiled at the priest, and leaving the door open retreated onto the quarterdeck.

Unsure of the protocol or what to expect, Fr. Cahill stood in his place, stared at the open door, and listened to the noise of sailors lowering crates into the hold, coiling lines, hoisting yards, creaking timbers, and a growling sucking sound from deep within the hull.

Moments later Captain Johns, Irish, and four other men, all sweaty and covered with grime, entered the cabin, and presented themselves for inspection by removing their caps and holding them respectfully over their midsection. Without ado they arranged themselves in an arc around the altar as if they had been mustered for roll call.

The cacophony continued above as Fr. Cahill celebrated Mass in Latin. He did not need to prompt his maritime congregation for the responses. They were quick and devout. The gospel from Matthew he read in English:

After he had finished all his sayings in the hearing of the peo-
ple, he entered Capernaum. Now a centurion had a servant who
was sick and at the point of death, who was highly valued by
him. When the centurion heard about Jesus, he sent to him elders
of the Jews, asking him to come and heal his servant. And when
they came to Jesus, they pleaded with him earnestly, saying, "He is
worthy to have you do this for him, for he loves our nation, and he
is the one who built us our synagogue." And Jesus went with them.
When he was not far from the house, the centurion sent friends,
saying to him, "Lord, do not trouble yourself, for I am not worthy
to have you come under my roof. Therefore, I did not presume to
come to you. But say the word, and let my servant be healed. For
I too am a man set under authority, with soldiers under me: and
I say to one, 'Go,' and he goes; and to another, 'Come,' and he
comes; and to my servant, 'Do this,' and he does it." When Jesus
heard these things, he marveled at him, and turning to the crowd
that followed him said, "I tell you, not even in Israel have I found
such faith." And when those who had been sent returned to the
house, they found the servant well.

"Laus tibi, Christe," said Fr. Cahill.

"Per Evangélica dicta, deleántur nostra delicata," the sailors responded.

After communion and just before the final blessing, there was a ruckus outside the cabin on the quarter deck. Voices suddenly called out, "A-HOY! AVAST! A-LOFT!" followed by the scampering of feet, and the loud noise of a heavy timber falling to the deck. Captain Johns immediately jumped out the door. Cahill heard the commotion and panicked voices.

"NETHERS! CASSIDY?" yelled Captain Johns.

"Aye, sir, all here," said the second mate, Kyle Nethers. "Cassidy in the rig. Bowline slipped."

"Bowlines don't slip, they're tied wrong," countered Johns with disdain.

Cahill watched the shocked looks on the men's faces that were waiting for the final blessing. But they didn't wait. Anxious, each quickly approached and thanked him, then quickly shuffled out of the cabin to their duty. Fr. Cahill stuck his head out the cabin door to see what had happened. Only feet from where he stood, the main-topgallant yard, nearly as wide as the ship and fitted with all its gear and a furled sail in its gaskets, had fallen. It was lying in a tangle of ropes in the middle of the quarterdeck. Captain Johns paced back and forth looking for someone to keel haul. Nethers, appearing responsible, was busy cleaning up the mess and giving orders to untangle and coil lines.

"Mister Woodcraft!" cried Captain Johns.

"Here, sir." An older but husky man with a full white beard and a limp in his left leg climbed up from the waist of the ship wearing a carpenter's apron.

"Report, if you will, Woodcraft." Johns caught Donald Irish's eyes who was on his hands and knees pouring over the yard, its gear, and sail. "I've only two spare timbers in the channels, and we haven't even left the wharf," snarled the captain.

"Aye, sir." Woodcraft now gazed at the fallen timber. "Why this is the yard I just refitted with new parrel beads. It should have been into its gear by now."

"Yes, yes! But what of it now!? Can it sail!? Or are we to do without our main topgallant, yet again?"

Nethers finally had the quarter deck clear of the tangle of brace, tack, sheet, foot rope, Flemish horse, jackstays, gaskets, and clewlines. He had coiled and seized them all apart from the others, allowing Woodcraft to examine what had recently left his workshop below. Johns paced as Woodcraft smoothed his hands over the surface of the yard and tugged on slings and blocks: "Mates, turn her over," ordered Woodcraft.

Several of the crew lifted the half-ton spar and turned it over. Woodcraft, again, ran his hands over every square inch, feeling the edges of his handiwork. "No splinters, the fillet smooth. The blocks, slings, bunts, and seizings are okay. She seems to be ready for a fair breeze in her tops. It's a miracle, she's not damaged. I say, let her fly, Captain."

Johns eyed his crew, then looked aloft at Karl Cassidy hanging on a rat line at the lower main's top. "Anyone here know how to tie a bowline?" he shouted.

Cahill looked around at the faces of the men. First there was fear. Johns was not happy. If they couldn't lift a yard into place while tied to the wharf, what of being at sea with the boat reeling about like a wild thing? But shortly the men, knowing their skipper a bit better than Cahill, began to snicker and laugh. But not too much.

"Carry on Mister Irish. Perhaps they need your guidance, as usual."

Irish barked, "Cassidy, send that halyard down properly now."

So it was that Fr. Cahill became acquainted with the crew and their regimen. At the end of the yard affair, the captain was a bit stiff but there was a quaint smile on his face that told the priest everything was all right. Fr. Cahill stood back in the cabin's doorway enough to be out of the way but watched as the crew tied a yoke onto the heavy yard, which must have been thirty feet long, seized on the halyard, lifted it into place ninety feet into the rigging, attached the lifts, the parrel beads around the mast, and then hanked on the brace, tack, and sheet lines. It was a well-organized effort, all led by first mate Donald Irish, who, when the accident had happened, happened to be in prayer at Mass.

Amid the deck chaos Fr. Cahill wondered if he had fallen in with a cabal of American incompetents, incapable of performing a simple nautical task at dockside. Indeed, there was some of that. But seeing the command and competence of Captain Johns and his first mate, Irish, gave Fr. Cahill a sense of security that the voyage was in good hands. Or so he told himself.

Upon seeing the topgallant yard attached to the main mast hauled into its gear, the sail unfurled and the clewlines, tack, and sheets run down and attached to their belaying pins on the rails, Fr. Cahill retreated to the cabin to purify and stow his Mass kit.

2

The day began at 6:40 a.m. when Fr. Cahill woke to a boson whistle piping the crew to stations. He recalled there would be no breakfast until they were underway. But he did not know the reason. Before long he climbed to the poop deck and leaned against the port aft rails to watch the crew ready the Eagle for departure

It was about 7:00 a.m. when the orders came fast but orderly from Captain Johns on the poop: "*Man the main and fore, upper lower tops'ls. Slack braces, clews and sheets.*" On that command it seemed the entire crew jumped into motion. Half of the crew scampered quickly up ratlines into the rigging, while others removed coils of line from the starboard and port belaying pins and flaked the coils on the deck so they could run free. Up in the rigging, the lads stopped at the lower main's cross tree and waited.

After a moment, "*Haul the halyards.*" Two teams of men, one on the forecastle deck and one on the quarter deck where the two masts were stepped, hauled hard on lines that were rove through blocks at the base of each mast. Looking aloft, Fr. Cahill saw the fore and main upper tops'l yards rise slowly into position. "*Belay halyards,*" bellowed Johns, followed quickly with, "*Loose gaskets all, topgallants, upper, lower tops'ls, stays'ls, and courses. Haul the clews.*"

At that, most of the lads on the deck joined their comrades in the rigging, and within seconds crews were laid out on the yards, loosening the gaskets that held the sails tight to the yards. When the gaskets were untied, the sails fell "into their gear." The sails, however, did not fill since those few men still on the deck were tauting up the tops'ls clews and buntlines, and thus the sails were folded into bights near the yardarms, held there by buntlines that were woven through bullseyes sewn into the canvas sails. Even in a strong wind they would not hold wind but flap like folded-up towels on a clothesline.

"*Aye, there. Good work, all. Prepare to cast off. Man the tops'ls, stays'ls and jigger.*" Descending from the rig, the crew responded quickly. While some manned lines at the belaying pins, others went to the bow, waist, and stern rails. Fr. Cahill noticed there were also hands on the wharf ready to untie the dock lines at the bow and another crew at the stern line—a whole gang of them were holding on to the stern line still partially wrapped around two bollards.

"*Haul the bowlines, sheet home t' stays'ls,*" came the order. The dock hands untied and released the bow dock lines and the deck crew hauled them onto the boat. Others of the deck crew unfurled the two stays'ls and sheeted them home. They immediately filled with air and pulled the bow away from the wharf. "*Hold tight the stern, let her turn...turn...turn.*" Since the Eagle's bow was docked facing upstream, when her bow lines were cast off, the morning breeze filled the staysails and pulled the bow out from the wharf, turning the ship downstream. When the turn was halfway around, "*Sheet home the tops'ls, haul stern lines forward.*" Suddenly the four tops'ls were filled and pulling the ship out from the wharf, but much to Cahill's surprise, the gang of perhaps twelve on the wharf were hauling the Eagle's stern lines upstream, which had the effect of pulling the stern away from the ship behind her that was still tied to the wharf. When the Eagle's stern made enough upstream progress that her stern was where her waist had been moments ago..."*Haul the stern lines. Thank you, gentlemen. Much obliged.*" Johns waved heartily to the land crew, who waved back, as the stern deck crew hauled in the stern lines and coiled them on the deck. "*Haul, t' spanker, if you will. Haul her all the way and sheet her home.*" With the spanker hauled out and sheeted home, the brig got underway enough to give her steerage, allowing the helm to bear left, which brought the stern fully around and maneuvered gently out into the Mississippi.

Thus, the Eagle departed New Orleans and embarked on her ninety-six nautical-mile journey to the Gulf of Mexico.

Ten minutes later, when the Eagle was clear of the port, "*Sheet home the topgallants. Attention the brace Mister Irish, we'll be splitten hairs next few. Some bracin' and turning we be doing.*"

"*Aye, Captain. Man the braces and main courses,*" cried Irish.

Fr. Cahill noticed that the helmsman, Miquel Cortez, a squarely-built Spaniard with quick eyes, a black stocking cap, and canvas trousers and coat, was taking orders from a gentleman dressed much better than the rest of the crew. "That's port pilot, Henry Javits," said Captain Johns who was suddenly standing next to his ship's chaplain. "He knows these waters and the location of shoals better than most. We pay him and others like him to join us on our trip upriver and now, down. Just before we head into the Gulf, he'll leave us. Port pilots, such as he, have an overnight cottage and a cutter near the main passages to the Gulf. We will pass it on our way out and leave Mister Javits there."

Before long, the large fore and main courses were set, and the Eagle was pulling on all sails. Fr. Cahill turned to Captain Johns when things quieted down. "When I came to New Orleans it took us three days to come up the river. I was told the wind and the current were not in our favor and we anchored each night and waited for favorable winds, but only during daylight did we make way upstream. What do you expect going down river, will you do the same?"

"The wind will be in our favor today. My goal is to get into the Gulf waters before it gets too dark to navigate by sight," said Captain Johns. "That is why the early start, even before breakfast."

It was at that moment that Mister Irish piped the crew to breakfast. The crew answered with a cheer and headed to the wardroom.

"More to your question," said Captain Johns, "now that we have a fresh breeze and are under a full set of sails, we will know in a few moments." He nodded aft.

At the aft rail second mate Kyle Nethers along with two other men were preparing to drop the log. "We will do this every hour during our entire voyage," said the captain. The log consisted of a triangular chip of wood about six inches on a side, leaded down on its two bottom corners, which was attached at its top vertex to the thin log line stored on a reel containing 150 fathoms of thin line. A fathom being 6 feet, the reel contained 900 feet of line. Every 7 fathoms (42 feet) along the line there was a large knot, and halfway between the large knots was a smaller knot. The sailor with the reel faced the stern and used both hands to firmly hold a rod threaded through the center of the reel allowing the line to unreel. Nethers tossed the wood chip into the water. The chip landed in the water and stood upright due to its leaded corners, essentially marking a stationary point in the water. As the ship sailed forward, the line was pulled off the reel. After a few seconds unreeling, enough time for the chip to stabilize in the water, a small red rag tied to the line flew past the rail. At that moment Nethers yelled, "TURN," and a third seaman turned over a thirty-second hourglass. At the same moment Nethers started counting the large and small knots that were pulled astern. "ONE...half...TWO...half...THREE...half...FOUR...half...FIVE...half...SIX..." About that time the hourglass ran out of sand, and the seaman holding the glass yelled "STOP." The number of knots and half knots pulled into the sea gave Nethers the ship's speed...just over six knots.

"Carry on, Mister Nethers. Come with me, Father." On his way off the poop, Johns stopped to speak with Cortez and his ever-present pilot. "Anything I should know gentlemen? Mister Irish in the waist there will see to it that the stacks are braced around for your turns. Do let him know before you need them braced up."

"Aye, Captain. Will do," answered Nethers.

Johns turned to Cortez and the pilot. "I'll see to it that breakfast is brought to you in a few minutes."

In the cabin, Captain Johns pulled out a large, hardbound book that when opened was nearly a foot tall and a foot and a half wide. It was the ship's log. Johns also unrolled a chart of the Mississippi delta, weighted down the corners, opened a leather case, and retrieved dividers. Passing his finger over the chart he traced the river to the Gulf. "The Mississippi is nearly a half-mile wide all the way to the opening of the *Pass A Loutre*, a channel through the delta we will take to the Gulf. It's ninety-six nautical miles from where we were docked to the open Gulf. If we maintain our speed at six-plus knots, and if that represents our speed made good over ground..." Johns worked a calculation on paper, "...it will take us sixteen hours. That would mean we'd pass through the *Pass A Loutre* in the dark, and I won't do that. If that's the case we would anchor in the river for the night. But attending our journey is the current of the river, which adds just over one knot to our speed over ground. That makes our speed made good about 7.4 knots, at least until we get to the entrance to *Pass A Loutre*." He stopped again to run a calculation. "So, if the wind and speed are maintained we'll get to the Gulf in just under thirteen hours." He picked up his Almanac and flipped to a table, scanning down its columns. "Counting twilight, we have just thirteen hours to make it. Daylight alone is only eleven hours and thirteen minutes. We left the docks and got up to speed quickly, let's say it was 7:00 hours, which, I recall, was just a few minutes before sunrise. Thirteen hours later would mean 20:00 hours, and that would mean..." he checked the Almanac again "...the last hour of our trip would be in total blackness, which I cannot risk." Johns leaned over the ship's log and entered the time of departure, code for the weather, the speed at seven knots "made good," blotted his entry, and left the book open on the table. "Let us pray for an increase in winds once we get into the main part of the delta. It's either that, or we spend a fitful night at anchor battling the largest mosquitoes known to man and beast."

Fr. Cahill said, "I will say my office this morning for that very request, Captain. It is a valid intention for the safety and health of all. When I arrived in New Orleans, several in our ship's company acquired malaria, no doubt from the vermin we were exposed to at anchor those two nights during our trip upriver."

"If we have a wind at anchor, the chance of flying vermin will be less," said Johns. "But let's not plan on that. I must see if we can get up more canvas and trim what we have. Excuse me." Johns left the cabin to Fr. Cahill who studied the chart for a few minutes, and then found his breviary and settled down to pray.

3

On the deck, Captain Johns found his first and second mate and informed them of their need to pick up at least another knot over ground. The easterly breeze would pick up and back to the north as they got closer to the Gulf, but that wasn't going to be enough. They needed more canvas. The mates set the crew to work. Within a half-hour they had spread a large flying jib off the bow, added a top stays'l to the fore mast, the main topmast, and main top gallant. Stays'ls were triangular fore-aft running sails rigged between two masts and the squared rigged sails. Eagle was now as fully rigged as possible. When Mister Nethers and his crew next dropped the log, they were clipping along at seven-knots through the water, which meant 8.2 knots made good. If they could maintain that speed, they'd get to open waters before dark.

"Mister Irish, Mister Cortez, please do everything to square our rig to the changing wind and cut corners off the river where possible. Can you help us with that, Mister Javits?"

"Yes, we can, Captain," answered Javits, "there are only a few more shoals to worry about and we will avoid them."

"I'll keep an active watch on the braces, Captain," said Irish.

Two hours later, Nethers and his log crew determined the ship was hauling

7.5 knots through the water, and all seemed well. But in the mid-afternoon, the breeze began to die, and their progress slowed. Most of the day their bearing was southerly, but when they came to bear east into the *Pass A Loutre*, it was just two hours before dark with another sixteen nautical miles to go before open waters. Captain Johns faced a dilemma. He asked Mister Javits to join him in his cabin for a look at the chart.

"If we drop you off, here, two miles into the Pass at the head of the Southwest Pass, which I do not intend to take..."

"And you are right not to," said Javits, "for it is very shoaly and has silted up near its mouth, where it is only a fathom at high tide."

The captain continued, "Can you give me advice to reach out to open water? Can I take this pass here that turns south, out of *Pass A Loutre* at the east end, for it is more direct for me? Though there is this island near the surface halfway down that branch. Is it above or below water now, and will I see it an hour after sunset? What of it?"

Javits was quick with his advice. "Do not take what we call the *Pass A Loutre's* South Pass; the island you point to is above the water for sure, but there are shoals at the mouth, and you'd need to go slow and take soundings. Take the North Pass. You have several advantages. One, it gets deep quickly and there are no shoals. Second, the bearing is straight. From the head of the Southwest Passage here, where I will join my cutter, you'll be on a straight east-northeast bearing until you come to the South Pass to the right and the North Pass forks to the left. It will be light enough to navigate. Stay in the center. Take the North Pass. No shoals. You need only to split the islands visible. You'll be on a northeast by east bearing. Stay on that for two nautical miles past the last island starboard. That will take you beyond a surface island half-mile to starboard. At that point you have open water to the south and you can bear it."

"And the current?"

"Oh, it will be less that what you have now. Running only quarter-knot at best."

It was clear to Johns he would not get to open water before it was pitch black.

When it came time for Javits to leave, the pilot cutter came along side. The Eagle crew dropped a tow line which the cutter tied on. The Eagle towed the much smaller cutter along as Javits climbed down the side on a rope ladder and dropped into his boat. The tow line was let loose, hauled aboard the Eagle with the rope ladder, and the cutter came about and headed back to their cabin on what was called Pilot Island.

When Javits left them, Johns set a lead crew in the bow to give soundings continuously for the next few hours, and he relieved Cortez at the wheel. Irish directed the watch to trim the braces and sheets every few minutes, for the wind was now coming out of the north, almost directly on their port, and the sail stacks were braced around to 45 degrees Their speed slowed, but Johns wasn't worried. If it got too dark, they would just have to drop anchor and wait until morning; but as long as he could see the shoreline to starboard and port, they would press on. He sent a sailor with good night eyes into the foretop to ensure the ship stayed in the center of the channel.

An hour later they lit the oil lamp in the binnacle so they could read the compass rose in the twilight. Irish hung a large lamp off the bow and stern, in case another ship in the dark approached them.

As the Eagle passed what Johns thought to be the last island to port, night fell dramatically. They had left twilight nearly half an hour ago, and now there was no seeing land either side of the ship. But there would be one more island to leeward, or starboard, which the ship could possibly hail if they gave too much leeway. "Nethers!" called Johns.

"Yes, sir, right behind you."

"Let's make it three, not two nautical miles northeast by east. What is our speed right now?

Nethers' crew dropped the log. After a minute, "Six and a half, captain."

"That means thirty minutes on this tack before we turn. Mark the time, Nethers."

Nethers brought the ship's clock to the poop deck near the binnacle.

"Mister Irish, take the helm steady on northeast by north. Cheat it north. Bear it close."

Johns went to the fore-port chains, a small platform that jutted out from either side of the ship left and right of the masts to give the mast shrouds added purchase. Standing on the platform outside the rail was Allan Curtis heaving the lead line forward, letting out line as the lead sank to the bottom and hauling it in as the ship moved forward. When the line was vertical and taut, Curtis took note of the markers woven into the line that were still above the water, and called out what he saw. "By the mark, three." They were in eighteen feet of water, and the ship drew twelve, or two fathoms.

The markers woven into the lead line at various lengths of the line above the lead weight were different strips of colored cloth or leather depending on the depth. The Eagle's lead was marked with two leather strips at two fathoms, three leather strips at three fathoms, a white cloth at five fathoms, a red cloth at seven fathoms, and a red and white strip of cloth at ten fathoms.

"Keep it up, Curtis, our safety depends on you," said Johns.

"Aye, Captain." Curtis again heaved the lead forward and drew it taut as the ship passed over the lead on the bottom. "By the deep, half, three," he shouted out.

It was getting deeper. Any depth two and a half fathoms or greater was safe, but the deeper the better. A moment later: "By the mark half, three." Curtis saw the captain standing on the forecastle deck near him. "We're getting way, Captain, deeper it is. The swells are longer, too."

"I see it, Curtis, keep it up. Thank you for all of us."

"By the deep, four."

Moments later Johns found Fr. Cahill reading his breviary by lamplight in the cabin. Johns entered their dead-reckoning position in the ship's log. As he did, he felt Irish turn on their new course southeast, and heard the stacks being braced around on their new bearing as the ship smoothed its motion and ran before the northerly wind.

They had made it safely out of the delta. But they hadn't yet made it safely to Baltimore.

4

Everyday near noon, when the sun was visible, Johns could be found on the poop deck between the wheel and the aft rail peering through his quadrant at the sun. Through an arrangement of mirrors and smoked glass he would turn a knob that rotated a brass arm attached to one of the mirrors, and through the telescopic eyepiece progressively align the edge of the rising sun with the horizon. At some point the sun no longer rose higher in the sky and Johns stopped adjusting the angle of the mirror. At that moment he would exclaim, "MARK!" Nearby, third mate Dana Boatman noted the time on the ship's chronograph. Johns lowered the quadrant and studied the indicator at the end of the brass arm which pointed to a protractor gradient marked off in degrees. The indicator told him the highest angle of the sun over the horizon—local noon. Comparing the angle of the sun over the horizon with an Almanac table of dates and the tilt of the Earth with respect to the sun gave Johns the ship's latitude, at least within the limits of his ability to site the sun at noon on the deck of a rolling ship. In a similar fashion, the ship's chronograph would tell him how many hours, minutes, and seconds he was west of Greenwich, England, to which the ship's chronograph was synchronized. Again, consulting a table in the Almanac, he was able to determine the ship's longitude. On this day, Johns logged their approximate position as 26 degrees 21 minutes north, 85 degrees 38 minutes west. Pricking his chart with dividers and marking it with a pencil, he was surprised that they were halfway to their waypoint at the west end of the Florida Straits, which was thirty miles off Havana and clear of the shoals surrounding the Florida archipelago. Since they left the Mississippi's *Pass A Loutre* channel they had covered 240 nautical miles on their southeast course, made possible by a west northwest 15–20 knot breeze directly on her port beam. This allowed the Eagle to make a good 10–12 knots over ground as she headed south-southeast for the Straits of Florida under blue skies and puffy white clouds.

But Captain Johns didn't believe the fresh breeze alone accounted for the nearly record-setting distance under the keel. To him, their speed was also explained by a three-knot loop current that swirled north through the gap between the Yucatán Peninsula and Cuba, flowed past the Mississippi delta, then looped eastward to Florida's west coast, which in turn forced the loop back south toward Cuba.

On the Eagle's way to New Orleans he had taken advantage of the same current. After leaving the western passage through the Florida Straits he had not steered northwest directly toward New Orleans but rather further west to catch the loop current as it flowed north to the mouth of the Mississippi. That route, although longer, had been faster. Now, by steering east and then south, the ship's record-making progress confirmed his theory.

While he was pleased at the confirmation of his loop-current theory, making fast progress had its downside. Checking the charts, he estimated their arrival at the dangerous Florida archipelago islands and shoals in ten hours. The islands reached over 100 miles westward into the Gulf and were a true hazard, especially at night when they were invisible. He wanted them well off to port before turning east, and the best way to do that was to steer south until the beacon fires on the mountains behind Havana were visible on the horizon. Then he could set a course east before hailing the Florida archipelago on his port and follow them around to the mainland of Florida's southern coast. He surely did not want Cayo Hueso (Key West) or its sister islands coming up on his bow or starboard in the dark.

Since the ship was making top speed under full sail, he could not push the Eagle faster and arrive at the archipelago before dark. If anything, he'd like to slow her down. The faster they went the more his groaning boat would leak. He already had two men rotating on the bilge pump which produced that bittersweet sucking sound deep within the hull. The irritating sound meant the ship would be afloat another day, but it also meant the sea was a constant threat of sinking the ship if the pump should fail, although they had the means to repair it.

Such thoughts coursed through his mind as he left his cabin and climbed to the helm on the poop deck. As soon as he arrived, he found his excuse to slow down. Behind the ship to the north, near the horizon where he expected to see a blue-green gleam, he saw only a menacing grey-black gloom. The wind was currently coming out of the northeast at 15–20 knots, and the Eagle's mast stacks were turned nearly square to it. But the sky to the north told Johns the wind would back to the north and increase.

"Mister Irish," Johns called to his first mate standing near the helm. "Have you looked sternboard?"

"Aye, Captain, I have," came the reply with a smile.

Johns grimaced at his first mate who was bored by fair weather passages.

"All hands on deck, Mister Irish."

"Aye, Aye, sir," Irish replied with a touch of relish.

Absent a bosun, for theirs was a civilian crew, Irish took a bosun pipe from his pocket and piped ATTENTION and ALL HANDS ON DECK. Within seconds the crew assembled on the quarterdeck and waist to await orders. The crew was modest for a ship this size, twenty-five altogether—captain (Johns), three mates (Irish, Nethers, and Boatman), a cook (Tille), a carpenter (Wood-craft), the cabin boy (Forbes), and eighteen sailors. There was no surgeon, al-though Nethers was their go-to medicine man when the need arose. The call for All Hands meant everyone. Fr. Cahill made an appearance as well, but nothing was expected of the priest...except prayer.

"*Weather approaching*," Captain Johns addressed the crew in a loud voice. "*We will douse the topgallants, upper tops'ls, and courses, leaving up the lower tops'ls. One at a time men, starting forward.*"

Before the next command, Johns looked around to ensure Fr. Cahill was out of the way. The ship's chaplain was standing at the windward aft taffrail. Fr. Cahill had told the captain earlier that he enjoyed watching the men work the large ship and the complexity of lines at the captain's command. He remarked that he wished the Church would work toward a common goal as the crews did on sailing ships. When the crew efficiently followed a captain's or mate's orders the ship made ready and ordered progress through what was often a chaotic sea. Hierarchy and authority, said Fr. Cahill, brought progress and safety to ex-tremely complex things. Without a hierarchy, things like ships and churches, to say nothing of families or governments, devolved, leading to anarchy. Johns agreed that a benevolent and intelligent authority and an efficient hierarchy was always a blessing.

Well, let's see just how ready and ordered my crew really is, thought Captain Johns as he stood on the poop and surveyed his ship and crew.

Johns shouted, "*Man the fore topgallant gear.*" The fore topgallant sail was the topmost sail on the foremast. On deck, men moved quickly to various sta-tions around the foremast and the rails where they removed coiled lines from belaying pins and flaked the lines on the deck so they would run free.

"*Ease t' topgallant halyard. Clew down. Round braces in,*" barked the cap-tain.

Acting as one, the crew eased out the fore topgallant halyard allowing the yardarm to slide down the fore mast until it came to rest in its lifts just above the upper tops'l yard. At the same time crews on both sides of the deck took slack out of the clewlines which were attached to the lower corners of the sail, which also helped to pull down the yard. Similarly, the braces (attached to the ends of the yardarm and which positioned the slant of the yard with respect to the ship's centerline), and the sheets (attached to the bottom corners of the sail which kept the billowed sail at the same angle as the yard), were kept taut to keep the yard from swinging until the lifts (ropes tied to the upper topgallant mast), stopped the yard from falling further.

"*Clews up,*" shouted Captain Johns.

The sheets were flaked and allowed to run free—as the clewlines (attached to the bottom outside corners of the sail), the leechlines (attached to the leech or outside edges of the sail), and the buntlines (attached to the foot of the sail) were hauled—lifting the corners, leech, and foot of the sail toward the yardarm.

The buntlines drew up the foot of the sail through sewn-in bullseyes that flaked the sail neatly into bights (or folds) as the sail came up into its gear just below the yardarm. Slack in the halyard was then removed and belayed to support the center of the yard. The end result was a neatly folded-up sail in several bights that hung harmlessly just below the yard. The wind whipped the bottom of these sail bights, but any drive from the sail was removed.

The dousing of the fore upper tops'l, the sail just below the fore topgallant, proceeded next without delay. While these top two sails on the foremast were being doused, four members of the deck crew doused the inner and outer jibs at the ship's bow. When that was done the same crew hustled to the rear of the ship and double reefed the spanker that was boomed out on the snow-mast. The double-reefed spanker would help to balance the ship's helm, assisting the helmsman to stay on course.

After the foremast's top two sails were doused in similar manner, one-by-one, the other sails were doused—the fore course, the main topgallant and upper tops'l, and finally the main course. When all this was done, only the fore and main lower tops'l were drawing wind and driving the boat forward. Throughout the dousing operation, the boat's speed had steadily dropped from seven-knots through the water to three.

As soon as the sails were doused, teams of men were sent up the rat lines to each yard to furl the sails. Starting with the foremast sails, four men climbed to the topgallant yard, four to the upper tops'l yard, and eight to the course yard. To lay-out on their respective yards, the men faced the ship's stern, stood on the horse ropes, and pressed their torsos against the yard. They were then able to scoot out onto the yard until they were evenly spaced along it, two on each side of the topgallant and upper tops'l, and four each on either side of the much larger fore course sail. Then, leaning over the yard, the men grabbed bights of sail and pulled them up onto the yard, one after the other. The last bight to pull up was the foot, which they used as a pouch into which the rest of the sail was rolled and stuffed. This left the smooth foot of the sail as the cover over the entire sail as it sat on top of the yard. Then with gasket lines they secured the rolled-up sail neatly onto the jackstay atop the yard. With all three sails on the foremast thus furled, the team moved to the mainmast and repeated the operation.

"Mister Irish, whoever you have on the pumps, double it. And oil the pumps, please," called Captain Johns. "We can't have them fail. If that wind backs anymore, and I suspect it will to Force 6 or 7, we're going to have more water flowing in the rudder post with following seas."

"Captain, already on that," answered Irish. "Smith, Foster, Carter, and Pinkett are rotating at the pumps. I'll attend to the oiling myself, right away." Irish climbed down off the poop and scurried below, happy to be busily applied. He loved heavy weather. *Damn fool*, thought Johns.

As the captain predicted, the sky got darker, the wind backed further to the north, and increased in speed; and as the wind's direction shifted, the crew automatically braced the yards so the sails were perpendicular to the wind's direction, which at present was nearly behind them. Captain Johns felt the ship pick up speed under his feet even as the apparent wind disappeared with each shift of wind direction and bracing round of the mast stacks. For now they were moving before the wind rather than at an angle to it. He also heard the hull groan as pressure on the masts and hull shifted. Thankfully, the crew was out of the rigging and safely back on deck, but the wind notched back another point, and rose to gale Force 8, which was nearly forty knots. This windstorm meant business. Moments later the aged, 450-ton wooden snow-brig was surfing down waves seeking its destiny.

Johns changed course a point to starboard in anticipation of what was next and nodded to Nethers in the waist who ordered the yards braced accordingly. Johns then took out his eyeglass, wiped the objective lens, braced himself on the aft taffrail and pointed the eyeglass astern. What he saw neither surprised nor shocked him. In the distance roaring toward them was a solid wall of white beneath the black sky. It was not harmless fog or mist. It was a shock wave of blown sea water that had left the surface and was flying toward the Eagle at Force 10. It was not a strong breeze or even a strong gale. It was a storm.

Irish wasn't back from the pumps, so Johns jumped to the poop rail and yelled over the increasing wind, "*Secure the deck. Double reef the tops'ls. Careful mates, she's goin' t' blow.*" Then he turned quickly to Fr. Cahill. "Father, it's time you went to our cabin, secure anything loose, and hang on...and a prayer or two would be appropriate. We're in for a ride."

Fr. Cahill glanced back at the fast-approaching wall of wind, crossed himself, and climbed off the poop.

Captain Johns watched as Fr. Cahill climbed down and Irish climbed up wearing a rain slicker and handed Johns his own. Irish then stood next to the helmsman, Daniel Forester, to lend a hand when the time came.

"Steer southeast by south, mates," said Johns. "That should take us well west of the islands until we see, or hear, God-forbid, the Cuban coast. Then it's due east."

"Aye, Captain," Irish and Forester responded in unison. Forester, who was helming, glanced at the compass binnacle and made a slight correction with the large wooden-spoked wheel. Irish gazed back at their fast-approaching nemesis trying to discern its true nature.

In the ship's waist, Nethers supervised the reefing affair: "*Man the fore lower tops'l to reef.*" At the starboard and port belaying pins crewmen loosened the lower tops'l clewlines and leech lines while others prepared to haul on the reef tackles. A team of six climbed the ratlines fifty feet to the fore lower tops'l yard and laid out on it, three to a side.

The fore and main lower topsi'ls were the only square sails on the ship that could be reefed. There were two reef points on the sails, each with multiple reef gaskets sewn into reinforced bullseyes spaced horizontally along the sail. Shortening the sails to the first reef point would remove twenty-five percent of the sail's area. A second reef would remove fifty percent.

When all were ready, Nethers continued: "*Slack clews and leeches mates. Haul reef tackles to their second.*"

The clewlines and leech lines came off their starboard and port pins all but a turn as the four men, one on each line, slacked their lines carefully against the force of the wind as the reef tackles were hauled up to the yard. The men on the yard grabbed the second reef gaskets, pulled up the slack sail above the reef point, furled it into the extra sail and prepared to tie down the reef point gaskets to the jackstay.

Suddenly, the Force 10 wall of wind and water hit the ship's hull and rigging, creating a thunderous roar. The hull lurched, creaked, and groaned under the supernatural pressure. Seaman Bud Sally, a likable enough young man of twenty, was on the lee side of the lower tops'l yard. He had just loosened his grip on the jack stay to haul a double handful of sail to tuck it into its roll. But doing so left him momentarily vulnerable, for he was braced against the yard with only his gut and his feet on the horse rope. The sudden onslaught of wind billowed the untucked canvas sail below him with such force that it flew up into his shoulders and face driving him backwards. That, coupled with the slight roll of the ship to leeward, set him off balance. He had but a fraction of a second to grab the jackstay. But the billowed canvas had covered over what he intended to grab. Like a chunk of insignificant sea foam at the mercy of the wind, he flew backward off the yard and into the air. The sixty-foot fall to the forecastle's deck would typically break a man's arm or leg. But when you fall headfirst, the crew plans your funeral on the way down.

Captain Johns' stomach spasmed as he watched Bud Sally fall headfirst to the deck. Keeping one eye on the ship and the mates running to Sally's aid, he was distressed to see Sally's limp body carried into the fo'c'sle. His own life passed in front of him as he recalled one after the other the previous six times sailors had died on his ships. Seven total now. Would they stop?

Johns braced himself against the forward poop rail. He felt faint before he forcibly relaxed and let his heart pump blood into his head to keep upright and in command.

The crew aloft doubled their efforts. The lives of everyone on ship depended on shortening sail as fast and safely as possible. As soon as the fore lower tops'l was reefed the crew scrambled down the fore ratlines to the deck, across the deck, and up the main ratlines to reef the main lower tops'l.

The further backing of the wind didn't surprise Johns, but the combination of that and its increased speed concerned him. Even with a balanced ship under a second reef on just the two lower tops'l, the storm-level winds pushed them forward at ten knots and there was the added leeway to port which in a few hours would also be a lee shore hidden under the water—*shoals surrounding those damn islands.*

He turned to Forrester and Irish, both now on the helm. "How's she weathering, boys?" Before they answered he turned back forward and gazed aloft through the driven mist. The ship's pendant was pointing due south, a point to starboard, but the courses were squared off.

"Easy to windward, Captain," came Irish's reply.

"Ease her off, then, follow the wind...that'll take us safe westward, if the swells stay moderate.

"Aye Captain," and with that Johns could feel the boat shift under his feet, and with it the harder pull on the hull by the sails and masts.

The longer they stayed on this tack, the swells would grow from the sustained winds and the longer fetch as they moved south. It would not be long before the vessel was surfing down mountains. If the swells raised the aft of the ship far enough, the water passing over the rudder that gave them steerage would be lost. All it would then take was a nudge from an errant wave and the ship would turn suddenly sideways. Such a broach would be catastrophic, and the ship would likely capsize.

With each new swell that ran down upon them from the north, the snow-brig plowed into the backsides of the fetched swell and the aft rose farther and farther into the air. Forrester and Irish, both on the wheel, were having a time of it now, for each swell raised the rudder farther out of the water.

One swell caused Captain Johns' heart to get caught in his throat. He grabbed the rail as the ship heeled to port and slid sideways down a swell.

"*Starboard, two points,*" he called out. "*Nethers, brace stacks.*" With the ship steering now south-southwest, the yards, clews and rigging had to be twisted to keep the wind square to the two reefed sails. On a heaving deck that now was heeling to leeward, with wave tops washing over the deck, this was no easy task. Nethers and his crew however jumped, for their lives depended on their quick actions. The boat had already turned and the pendant at the top of the mizen mast revealed how far they had to adjust the yards to affect the trim. Although there were only two yards, one on each mast that carried sails, all the yards on each mast were tied together by virtue of the sheets, which were secured at the base of the masts. To affect the trim, the sheets for both masts would be loosened by four men, two on each mast, one for each sheet, in coordination with the eight other men who loosed and hauled the braces at the rail. The braces trimmed the yards around, and once adjusted to Nethers' satisfaction, the sheets and braces would again be trimmed tight and secured by the belaying pins. Altogether it took but a few minutes. The shift generated a lot of noise, as Nethers shouted commands against the noise of the wind in the rigging. All along, the waves washed the deck, and the general all-around creaking of timbers that made up the heavy ship offered little peace.

5

Below the poop deck in the captain's cabin, Fr. Cahill struggled to keep his equilibrium. The tossing of the ship, lack of fresh air, and views out the aft windows of wave after wave assaulting the ship kept him tense and exhausted. At the same time, he was thankful the conditions were not worse. He recalled his Atlantic crossing when storms and a confused sea raged for over a week. In the midst of that storm, he was sure he would perish.

He was in the middle of an unrelenting vomit episode when the knock of destiny banged on the door. Third mate Nethers swung the door open and braced himself within the jam. "Father?"

Fr. Cahill was kneeling over a bucket requisitioned for such times. His face was drained of blood and his eyes were barely opened as his torso convulsed one last time and his pale faced dove into the pail. "Yes?" came the thin echo of a voice lost in the occasion.

"Captain wants to commit seaman Sally, if you're able."

Cahill cringed at the idea of performing a funeral at sea when the attendees might be swept into the sea before the deceased. Imagine the cruel irony of a ship left with only a corpse, and only because it was lying low while the others were standing by the rail in respect.

Cahill jerked his head from the bucket and forced himself to suppress a spasm. He wiped his face and mouth with a rag appropriated before nature took its course.

With his eyes still on the pail as if ready to plunge his head into it at any moment, Fr. Cahill nodded his approval and faintly replied, "And perhaps myself at the same time...'twill save the captain time." Getting to his feet and attempting to stand in one place with the rolling floor, Cahill eyed Nethers. "Why now? Should we not wait until it can be done with a semblance of dignity?"

"Bad luck...morale. Crew don't want to slog over a dead man while tending to their duties. Reminds them of what could happen to them."

Cahill nodded. "Where?"

"Windward. Fo'c'sle," said Nethers, his feet bracing fore and aft to stop himself from falling into the cabin with the pitching deck. "It be just you and the pallbearers. Too dangerous for the whole crew."

Of course, Fr. Cahill thought. *I'm the courageous one with my face vomiting my life away; it's only logical that I should risk my life to bury a dead man.*

Taking a moment to reconnoiter, Fr. Cahill found his book of rituals and stumbled out of the cabin. Nethers helped him down the ladder to the waist, and holding onto his upper arm guided Fr. Cahill across the sea swept deck, past the main mast, and up the fo'c's'le ladder. Captain Johns met them and grasped Fr. Cahill's other arm, helping him up to the fo'c's'le and across the pitching deck between the foremast and capstan. There, Bud Sally's body was wrapped head to toe in a discarded sailcloth tied on with old, frayed ropes. The mummy-wrapped body lay on a wooden plank with lines looped through holes in the side for pallbearers to grasp. An iron casting was tied around the body's ankles. Disregarding the deck's flexing and groaning with every swell, a large portion of the crew stood nearby. They held onto stays, shrouds, belaying pins, and lines. With Nethers holding his port arm and Captain Johns his starboard, Fr. Cahill was able to hold his book of rituals and read the burial rite. As loud as he could, he intoned the Scripture and prayers that commended Bud Sally to God's mercy and grace. He finished with a prayer:

> Almighty God,
> you created the earth and shaped the vault of heaven;
> you fixed the stars in their places.
> When we were caught in the snares of death
> you set us free through Baptism;
> in obedience to your will
> our Lord Jesus Christ
> broke the fetters of hell and rose to life,
> bringing deliverance and resurrection
> to those who are his by faith.
> In your mercy look upon this grave,
> so that your servant may sleep here in peace;
> and on the day of judgment raise him up
> to dwell with your Saints in paradise.
> Through Christ our Lord. Amen.

When he was done, six sailors came forward, carried the plank to the windward rail and slid Bud Sally's body to his eternal rest.

Fr. Cahill was surprised by how deeply he was affected by the short ritual. Tears had come to his eyes during the final prayer, making it hard to read. Gone was the nauseous feeling and there was a lightness to his heart. Although the deck was heaving like it did before, he found himself slipping out of Captain Johns' and Nethers' grip, and he walked confidently across the moving deck to the rail without need of support, like a seasoned seaman, which he was not. There he prayed over the sea, begging God again to have mercy on Bud Sally, and to bring the ship safely to Baltimore. After some moments of contemplation at the rail he turned to see most of the ship's crew reverently staring at him, all dipping their heads slightly toward him out of respect. He bowed his head to them and making the sign of the cross three times blessed them. He was surprised as every one of them, even the non-Catholics which he knew most of them to be, crossed themselves as well and headed back to their stations or into the fo'c'sle cabin.

Later in the captain's cabin, Fr. Cahill reflected on what had just happened. There was something almost supernatural in his spirit's consolation, as if his priestly participation in the burial had buoyed his body to the third heaven. Gone...completely gone was the desire to heave, or even the squeamishness of being on a heaving ship. What he had done was not difficult. He had simply read some prayers and verses of encouragement to those still living. Yes, he had been sincere. There was a sense that he had fulfilled some grand calling and accomplished some purpose for the sake of the universe. He had never felt like that before. It was like receiving an unearned reward, a grace, or perhaps more accurately a visitation by a heavenly being.

He cried—a spiritual consolation of deep contentment. He had read about such experiences many times but could not recall ever experiencing one himself. He took a deep breath of air as if to test the feeling's authenticity, for it might dissipate, this sense of fulfillment, if he were to just replenish the oxygen depleted in his lungs. The sense of satisfaction and fulfillment was still there.

Fr. Cahill was bracing himself in the corner of a built-in window seat when the captain entered the cabin.

"Father, how are you? Are you feeling better?"

"Quite well, sir," said Fr. Cahill with a chuckle. "Although I am sitting here wondering why, considering our situation."

"Father, what happened with you out there this afternoon? After the service which you so kindly held, you were a different man, like coming into your own. Got your sea legs, it appears to me."

"I've been contemplating that a fair amount over the past hour or so. I do not mean to patronize you, dear Captain, but in demonstrating respect for your dear fallen crew member, you did me an honor. You and even the non-Catholics on board showed me respect as a priest that I have never experienced before. It was as if I was realizing my calling for the first time since my ordination. It's frightening in a way."

"Perhaps this voyage for you is one of self-discovery."

"I think it is, but discovery of what? What is in my future?"

"Your service to Bud Sally and the confidence you give to my crew by your very presence is most agreeable, Father. I want you to know that simply making yourself available brings peace to everyone on board. I pray your ministry in the United States is as fruitful and filled with such goodness."

Fr. Cahill paused for a moment to study the captain's face for signs of stress on which the ship's seemingly precarious situation might possibly be revealed. But the captain's face was serene, even as the ship groaned and tossed. "And how are you, or perhaps I should ask how is the ship feeling?" Fr. Cahill asked. "It seems to be groaning in this weather."

"Ah, the Eagle. She flies, Father, with your blessings no doubt. That groaning of timbers is her deep breaths of pleasure. She is secure and fairly dry, although the pumps need constant attention. The weather has steadied, and so we are trimmed and making fine progress. Let me show you."

The captain's table was nailed to the floor for obvious reasons, and although the chairs were safely stowed, Captain Johns produced a chart of the Gulf of Mexico, clamped it to the table, and taking a rule, dividers, and parallels, added to his earlier dead reckoning plots, drawing this time a larger circle than before, indicating the Eagle's approximate position.

"I was unable today to take a noon fix with the clouds so thick and the ship vomiting on every wave, but we are about here." He stabbed his thumb on the map northwest of the Florida archipelago. "At dusk we will turn southeast, and around the start of the middle watch, or midnight, we will turn due east. We hope to run past the Los Martires islands (Florida Keys) in the dead of night avoiding nuisance pirates that still prowl the Florida Straits."

6

*José Gaspar grasped the aft rail of his ship as he stared south toward Cuba. It was near midnight and except for a few torches and lanterns aboard, it was pitch black all around. It was possible, however, that his first mate, Rodrigo Lopez, who was in the main top, might catch a glimpse of a signal fire on a mountain top or two in Cuba, across the Florida Straits.

At once Gaspar was both bored and anxious. Paranoia caused his eyes to restlessly dart about the dark waters, into his ship's rigging, at the men lying on deck trying to sleep, and at the flicker of lanterns. Finally, he purposefully gazed up at Lopez in the main top. Moonlight revealed Lopez with an eyeglass dutifully raised scanning the horizon for a vessel to raid.

The day before, he had directed his crew to bring Floriblanca, his pirated 160-foot galleon, to anchor a half-mile off the south shore of Cay Hueso, the most westward Los Martires islands of the Florida archipelago. Now, in the lee of the island they would avoid the fetch building up on the north side. A northern gale had prevented them from returning to their island base further north on Florida's west coast. It was a good move for late that same afternoon the gale built into a fierce storm that surely would have driven the wind-susceptible Floriblanca galleon, with its high topsides, into a coral reef, tearing its hull to shreds. But even on the leeward side, the wind was so strong they had to row out a second anchor from the stern to embed it on the beach. Eight hours later, the wind dropped to a moderate gale and he ordered the beach anchor retrieved in hopes they might make a rapid departure if an opportunity presented itself that night.

Nonetheless, the northern gale ripped through rigging producing a loud, irritating hum that shook the entire ship. He wondered how his men, scattered about the deck, could sleep with that sound and the hull's resonance. But it was necessary they rest on deck for at a moment's notice they had to be in the rigging to set sail, man the guns, board a prize, and do what pirates do—plunder, rape, and murder—before Davey Jones collects his due. His attention was drawn to the aft-port belaying pin rack and the port-main-brace that was vibrating rapidly. Gaspar lowered himself from the poop to the quarter deck, tugged on the brace to reduce its vibrations, and tightened the line's wrap around the pin. But the tightening didn't do much to dampen the sound that was using the hull as a sounding board.

It had been over a week since his crew's last raid on a merchant vessel—it had been a bust. The small Portuguese brig carried only grain and wood. Not a jewel, nor a piece of eight, nor a gold coin on board. Yet this captain and crew had all the luxuries of freedom, respectability, trade and profit that Gaspar and his buccaneers were denied. Motivated by murderous envy, Gaspar and his men killed the entire crew of twelve, then cut off the hands of the captain and let him bleed out. The captain wallowed in pain and his own blood in the ship's waist as they stripped the vessel of anything worth taking—ropes, food, hardware, sailcloth, carpenter tools, and a very nice sextant. Returning to the Floriblanca, they turned broadside to the brig, and used it for target practice until the raped ship, its bloody bodies, and the cargo were all consigned to the devil's abyss.

He feared a revolt of his buccaneers if he didn't keep them busy with violence, treasure, grog, and strumpets. The irony was lost on them, but not him. The violence would eventually kill those that perpetrated it, the treasure could never be spent without first being captured and hung, the grog deadened their nerves and ability to remember, and the strumpets...well, not everything was ironic. Yet, he was aware of the thin line he walked, hoping to avoid what he had orchestrated five years earlier aboard this very ship. Then, he and a cadre of his men mutinied their abusive Captain Miguel Espinosa. Near the coast of France, they had thrown him overboard without his hands attached. After sailing aimlessly for a week, they decided to come to Florida, set up base on an uninhabited island, and pillage merchant ships, kill the crews unless they wanted to join their rapscallion tribe, and ransom the captured important women or keep captive the unimportant ones as concubines.

Merchant ships were easy targets since most were not armed with sufficient cannon, or personnel to fire them. But now and then he had to attack a warship and fight marines to the death just to resupply his ammunition and military hardware like cannonballs, gunpowder, shots, muskets, chains, and lost swords. Such raids always resulted in lost men, and he could only hope to recruit more from those he raided by dangling either death or gold in front of their greedy eyes.

Tonight, however, they had an advantage. The wind was behind them and they could approach a vessel in the dark without being seen. Granted there were risks associated with pirating at night — they might attack a well-equipped and manned naval vessel with more than the twenty-four twelve-pounders that armed Floriblanca, and they might not even know it until it was too late. War ships were usually much larger than merchant ships, but their silhouette on the water with the moon behind them usually provided an accurate gauge beforehand of what kind of ship they were attacking. However, it was also harder to gauge speed and distance at night. The moon was waning in its last quarter; their night light was dimming. So, unless they happened upon a ship tonight, all bets were off for a night raid until a waxing moon again illuminated the waters two weeks from now.

Hopefully, Lopez with his good night vision would find them a prize. The success of any raid depended a great deal on his judgment.

Gaspar didn't wait long.

"Captain!" called out Lopez. "*Eastbound merchant brig. Hull-down. Beam reach, full sail. Twenty-thirty miles.*"

Gaspar laughed out loud and pounded the rail with his fist. "*Rise and shine scalawags,* he yelled. "*It's payday. Man the capstan, prepare to weigh anchor. Into the rig. Loose t' damn gaskets. Standby clewlines.*"

7

The Eagle, again under full sail since the northern winds had abated, was an hour into the middle watch when first mate Donald Irish, in the upper-fore-top, sighted the signal fires on the mountain behind Havana. The upper-fore-top was sixty-five feet above the water line, and the signal fire was atop of 950-foot mountain. That put the Eagle about forty miles off Havana. Captain Johns ordered a course correction from south-south-east to due east. When the snow-brig turned, it went from an even keel with wind behind her to heeling to starboard as she came onto a beam-reach. But she also picked up speed, and now was making good at nine knots and sometimes better. In two hours she would be thirty miles off the southern tip of the Florida Archipelago. It would be daylight in seven hours, and in twenty hours the Eagle would begin her turn northward toward Baltimore.

Johns had planned the transit by night, at high speed, and far enough from the Archipelago to go unnoticed from shore-based pirates, but there was no getting around the risk. For one thing, a waning moon behind them provided a hull-down silhouette to any attacking ship from the north. The risk was increased because the Eagle would not see an attacking ship until it was nearly upon them. The next five hours until dawn would prove critical. Irish was in the upper-foremast-top until dawn keeping a watch to the north for any sign of sails, wakes, or the occulting of stars or their reflections in the water. Fortunately, the Eagle was on a port-beam reach, so the stacks were braced to starboard and would not block his view.

Now that they had made the turn, it was time to prepare one last thing. "*Mister Nethers!*"

Nethers had been trimming the sails from his vantage on the rear quarter deck. He belayed a line and climbed to the poop deck.

"Aye, Captain."

"I want all the guns manned and ready in one hour. Unless we're trimming braces, men should be at their guns.

"Loads?"

"Chain-shot in the chasers. Round in the waist. Canister on the quarters. And a round or two of *dry* practice if you will."

"Aye, Captain, we're on it."

Over the next hours there was warlike activity on the decks as guns were rolled into position, lashed down with blocks and tackle, rams, swaps, ammunition, and powder were both loaded into the guns and positioned next to them. Each team practiced their gun cleaning, loading, hauling, and dry firing at full speed at least twice.

Fr. Cahill watched the activity and when the captain seemed to be settled, he approached. "Anything I can do, Captain?"

"Yes, bless the boat and the men. They go through this drill every time we make this passage, so they will not take it too seriously, although it's usually in daylight that we do it. In daylight there is plenty of warning if a strange boat approaches. Yet the weather and moon conditions are such tonight that I have a premonition to be extra cautious. Your presence may make the difference."

Fr. Cahill immediately went to the cook and acquired an empty leather canteen, attached a line, and filled it with sea water. In the captain's quarters he dug out his book of rites, prayed over the water, which ideally was already saturated with salt. He then proceeded to make the rounds to each of the gun crews, the helmsman, and the captain...and sprinkled each with what was now Holy Water. The crew, even those who were not Catholic, crossed themselves as he visited, blessed, and sprinkled each.

When he was done and the guns were set, Captain Johns ordered that all lamps be extinguished except the binnacle lamp that was enclosed and lit the compass rose. Johns stood near the helm where both Dana Boatman and Miguel Cortez stood watch and took turns on the helm.

With preparations made, and nothing else to do, they waited and prayed that they would pass through the Straits without incident. But Captain Johns was unusually tense. To ease the feeling and keep his mind alert, he walked the deck, visiting each gun station and encouraging the men to stay alert and ready, although most of them were reclined and a few tried to catch some sleep; Johns let them.

No sooner had he returned to the poop than he heard a strange but familiar humming of wind through rigging coming from the north as if riding on the wind. It was a sound one might hear at an anchorage with other ships nearby. Except they were miles from any anchorage.

Moments later, Irish thumped five times on the foremast with a belaying pin, the signal that a ship had been sighted and was approaching off the port beam. His thumping automatically alerted the crew; they came awake and ready. A moment after, suddenly to port the light of a cannon blast illuminated the horizon and silhouetted the prowl of a large Spanish galleon bearing down on them, perhaps two-hundred yards distance. A fraction of a second later the sound of the blast reached them. The sailors aboard the Eagle knew this was no drill. A moment later, a large splash was heard just aft of the Eagle.

Johns' orders came fast, and on top of each other. *"Helm hard right. Brace around. When steady, chasers, FIRE at the centerline, on first crest.*

Immediately both Boatman and Cortez rotated the large wooden wheel to the right, turning the Eagle downwind to run before their pursuers. The trim crew immediately left their guns, loosened lines, braced around the stacks and trimmed crewlines and sheets with lightning speed. As soon as the turn was complete and the boat rose on a crest, the two chasers, canons mounted on the aft, exploded with nearly simultaneous BOOMS sending their double 14-pound chain linked charges flying end-over-end through the air at their attacker's center line.

At the moment the chasers fired, Captain Johns noticed that the galleon turned from pursuing them and took to an east bearing, thus presenting their starboard broadside to the Eagle. This was not good. Johns quickly counted eight long-guns, deadly 24-pounders each, run out through open doors aimed at the Eagle. If the galleon got off a volley, the Eagle would be done for.

Johns had forgotten, however, that when the chasers were fired, the galleon's profile was narrow, giving the chaser gunners a difficult target to hit, but when the galleon turned sideways to get off a broadside, the chain-shot's trajectory flew at a much larger target. At the same time the Eagle had turned downwind, which presented the galleon with a narrow target. She was no longer a 150-foot wide boat, but a 48-foot narrow boat, although a direct hit on her rigging would be more devastating since it would be compact and lined up down her centerline. It could be devastating.

In the seconds it took the chain-shot to traverse the distance between the two boats, the galleon had turned sideways, and again there were two simultaneous events. First, both the chain shots hit the galleon. One chain-shot hit halfway up the upper bow stays, tearing them away from the foremast. The second hit the tip of the bowsprit tearing it completely off the galleon's bow, destroying the primary forward purchase of the stays on the foremast. The galleon heeled momentarily to its port due to the leverage of both chain shots' impact on the upper stays and bowsprit. At the very second the galleon heeled, all eight guns of its broadside lit up the night sky with a barrage of fire accompanied by a deafening and cascading explosion, as the eight guns sent shot flying toward the Eagle.

Just before the galleon's shot reached the Eagle, Johns saw the foremast of the galleon topple to the cheers of his whole crew. A split second later the shots from the galleon arrived. They had been obviously all aimed at the Eagle's waterline, intended to hole the hull, and stop her movement. But the slight heeling of the galleon just before her cannons blazed changed the trajectory of the broadside shot. It was too high. Two of the balls put holes in the Eagle's lower tops'ls and the others which were also way above the hull flew harmlessly into the water either side and beyond the Eagle.

"*Helm, hard left, due east. Brace around,*" yelled Johns.

Boatman and Cortez responded instantly, and Nethers' stack crew was only a second behind them to trim the sails, bringing the Eagle back on a fast beam reach. Within a minute the Eagle was again flying east at ten knots, leaving the crippled galleon behind, tangled in her stays and severed bowsprit.

The entire crew of the Eagle rose in a cheer as they sailed off safely into the dark of night.

Johns was thrilled with the result. It was miraculous in a way. He thought of something Benjamin Franklin had written recently: Success is when preparation meets opportunity.

He found himself astonished as he looked back at the torches being lit on the galleon to inspect her damage and make repairs. He thought that if the Eagle had been a war vessel, he would round about and sink the galleon. But now, no doubt, they would repair the galleon and be a threat in the Straits into the future.

But the Eagle was not out of danger yet. It would be four more hours to daylight and hours more before they were out of the Straits. He could only pray that the galleon was the last pirate they'd see tonight. When he had the time, he would make a full written account and make sure the new U.S. Navy, formed just last year, got a copy. He hoped they could give chase and put an end to pirating.

8

Having avoided more pirates, although campfires among the Los Martires told of their presence, the Eagle made its way up the Atlantic coastline without further incident. At least no one else died, and the bad weather they encountered only added to Fr. Cahill's confidence and character.

As the Eagle approached Baltimore, Fr. Cahill had a lot on his mind — what would he do when he landed in Baltimore?

The option was to seek out the local ordinary, or bishop, submit himself for evaluation, and offer his services as a priest in whatever capacity the bishop required. Of course, that had not worked out so well in New Orleans, but Fr. Cahill believed that was the problem—the Church's subservience to the state. He hoped nothing like that ever happened in the United States. Perhaps the Bill of Rights that had been talked about was the solution, provided it had teeth.

One day, after a squall had thrown the Eagle off course a few miles, Fr. Cahill asked if Captain Johns knew any of the bishops in the United States. The captain laughed out loud. "There are no bishops. That's why the United States is so appealing. If the bishops in Europe are any example, their only usefulness involves politics and administration. You put a bishop in charge anywhere and everything, and I mean everything falls apart. The United States doesn't need a bishop. No, there is none. Thank God."

Fr. Cahill was shocked by Captain Johns' answer. How could there even be a Church in the United States without a bishop? The Church couldn't exist without bishops, or so his seminary studies led him to believe. Nonetheless, there had to be someone in charge. Who could that be? The president? God forbid. He asked Captain Johns, "Could the United States fall into the same perilous political pit from which the colonies had just escaped...from King George?"

"No, that is not likely," said Johns. "Neither the president nor any other government official has say over anyone's practice of religion. Do not worry about that."

"Okay, so there's no bishop," reflected Cahill. "What do you suggest I pursue?"

Captain Johns was quick with an answer. "Become an independent missionary priest, convert souls, and teach people how to battle the atheistic and anticlerical bigotry that perforates our new nation."

How depressing that sounds, thought Fr. Cahill. *But, of course, that is what he would say. As captain of a ship, he is an independent merchant who must on occasion battle pirates—the atheists of the high seas. He can take on whatever cargo he believes has value, and sail to wherever he believes he can sell the cargo for a profit. The ship may be owned by investors, but all they care about is a cut of the profit. How their captain goes about it is not their concern. It is the independent captain's responsibility.*

That Johns was Catholic, Cahill thought ironic. Merchant sea captains with their entrepreneurial spirit and independence were analogous to Protestantism, not Catholicism. Protestants did what they wanted without oversight of their belief, practice, or interpretation of the Bible, which seemed fairly similar to merchant sea captains. Catholics were under authority regarding nearly everything...then it hit him.

By leaving his order in New Orleans he was acting like a Protestant, rejecting the authority over him. He was thinking like a Protestant...but all he wanted to do was exercise the authority given to the Church and practice the sacraments under Christ's authority. He was confused for a few sea miles, and he walked the deck thinking through his actions, which he now feared might have been Machiavellian, where the end justifies the means. He shuttered at the thought.

In the waist, as he leaned against the windward rail, an errant spray of seawater drenched his entire body. *Is God trying to tell me something or baptize me into a new way of thinking?* But his thoughts were no clearer, just saltier. He became aware that he might be rationalizing his decisions, making them morally invalid. Circumstances have a way of doing that. Did he become a priest because he was called, or because the priesthood was the only option at the time? Was he being called to be a missionary priest by God, or a sea captain? Was God using Captain Johns, or was the Devil? Was his pursuit of being an independent, missionary priest because he was called, or was it the only rational option open to him at the time? How does one know the difference? Perhaps that is how God calls some to a particular ministry...it's the only thing reasonable to pursue at the time.

Missionary priests, by definition, are independent, he thought, even if they are sent by a bishop in a faraway country. Communicating with the bishop on a daily basis would be impossible. The priest is on his own. Bishops, like investors in a merchant ship, only care about the return, which is spiritual. Yet, there was also the temporal side to his existence, for it was in the temporal state that he existed. He needed food, shelter and clothing, and such things normally require money. He wasn't a disembodied spirit flitting around at will to do whatever wherever he wanted—as much as that sounded attractive.

He considered approaching charities. Would they want to employ a chaplain? The chaplains of charities he had known were all volunteers. Whatever he considered, the prospects seemed bleak. He found himself pacing endlessly on the deck wondering and worrying about his future. He prayed about his situation, asking God for advice, but no apparent answer came. He prayed, but fell asleep praying the Rosary—only to wake when the ship lurched in heavy seas reminding him to finish the next decade.

As the Eagle tacked up the Chesapeake and anchored in the bay awaiting warps to pull her into a berth, Fr. Cahill finally came upon a decision, though a tentative one and not much of any decision at all. Baltimore was known as a community of merchants ready to sell anything, including dirt, to men and their families preparing to move west. Word had it that you could buy anything in Baltimore, even a birthright to the king's fortune. Sailors had also told him there were more Catholics in the city than in the surrounding countryside, and that these same said Catholics were men of integrity, many with thriving businesses, plantations, and fortunes. There were even a few Catholic *Irishmen*, he was told.

Although the presence of Catholic Irishmen was not all that encouraging; he was one such man and knew of what an Irish man was capable. Such thoughts gave him hope, if not also a sinister smirk. Irish men, like his father, were loyal laborers. One normally doesn't associate a priest with physical labor, but he was young, and while not accustomed to manual labor, his body was able. He was also advantaged in that when he disembarked the Eagle, he did not come with an indentured contract to work off under bondage to a landowner. Captain Johns made it clear that Fr. Cahill's only payment for transit was to be true to his calling as a priest in the new land, wherever God may lead. Indeed, Johns paid him a fee for his services as chaplain.

When Fr. Cahill considered these things, a flush of hope came over him like a warm, fresh-water bath, which he would soon need. He would labor until God led. In so doing he would learn about the people, and minister to them in their needs as he was able. After all, a priest is a laborer in the field. It was that simple.

9

My Despised Cyn:

You were useless. What kind of sub-demonic creature are you that you avoid boarding a sea-bound vessel in your spiritual state? Sure, it's difficult maintaining your equilibrium. But you manage well enough on a spinning globe, lurching through space. What's another four-dimensions of tortuous motion? This is why you never advanced, and why, in your physical state, you were weaponized only with shears...without pointy tips...and if you're physically reconstituted, even those will likely be forbidden.

And yet, over the centuries, your higher-level peers have managed to hang, quarter, drown, stab, and slice up not a few sailors into Condemnation. Yes, it is true, one storm at sea, if it is severe enough, will prepare an entire crew for Glory. It can put fear of the Creator in them. It may seem odd that shipwrecked sailors, with no hope of survival, turn to the Almighty who doesn't seem mighty enough to save their foolish hides. It's something written on their souls, which damned as we try, is impossible to erase.

And when you put a priest on board, especially one that is as robust and seemingly fearless as Cahill, the results are frightful. Even the pagans start to pray as they dump corpses overboard, ironically to be irreverently sliced, diced, and devoured by creatures too vicious for them to contemplate. At least we have full control over part of creation. But still their faith grows...out of fear.

Did you think cavorting on Cay Hueso, a non-gyrating land mass that it is, would inspire Gaspar to be of some use to us? You should know by now that you must constantly be in our agent's head. On his own, Gaspar is of little use to us. He's only been a dull light working on our behalf over the last five years because one of your peers has been doing a decent job. It's been wonderful to count the many humans he's assisted in consigning to the deep and to Condemnation. I hope he has many years ahead of him, though it seems he's no match for a vessel with a priest on board. Imagine what you could have done had you been aboard the Eagle. You possibly could have fully prevented Cahill from getting to the United States and Adam Livingston. It's appalling how susceptible you are to motion sickness. How is that possible?

Now that Cahill is in the United States, thanks to your cowardice, we must prevent him from finding Livingston. There must be someone we can find that trades in hate.

Eternally yours,
Master of Tempests

Chapter 15
No Use for Papists

1

*William McSherry was of handsome and rugged appearance, with reced-ing red hair and a full beard that hid a square chin. His dress was practical, not fashionable, for he ran a successful hardware business. It was near the wharf in Baltimore and open every day of the week simply because citizens needed the products he sold every day. Mister McSherry, as he was known by Baltimoreans, had never been known to darken the door of a church, nor did he attend balls, or public events that might require him to buy a ruffled shirt, waist coat, silk stockings, or a powdered wig. His customers who knew him expected to find him in a clean frock shirt without ruffles, linen pants, and comfortable work boots. He wore a bibbed leather apron to protect himself from the inevitable dirt acquired from unloading the dark reaches of a ship's hold, stacking lumber on carts, shoveling pounds of oily nails into buckets, or sweeping up after cus-tomers and workers.

He was a shrewd businessman who negotiated carefully. He was known to be fair with all, but not overly generous. He was a bachelor of whom it was ru-mored that he was born in Ireland and at eighteen left with his twin brother for Jamaica. There, the rumor insisted, they earned a sizable fortune as land-based trader-merchants buying and selling hardware cargo from passing ships. They were not fond of the British, and so when the colonialists in America defeated the British and established the United States, their curiosity of the new country and personal ambitions knew no bounds.

Their deliberation in business and in their lives allowed them to slowly gather information about the American experiment in governance. Trade from the United States increased, and when they were assured that the new country was stable and expanding, they decided to be part of it. In 1786 they sold their business in Jamaica, took their accumulated gold, and came to the United States to seek their second fortune, or so rumor had it.

Most doubted the rumor. William worked too hard to be rich, and no one had ever seen his brother. But that his business was a success was not in ques-tion. Banks readily loaned to him, and within eighteen months of opening his small store, he had acquired most of the city block behind his store, which be-came a large and busy lumber yard. William McSherry was a legend in his own time—it was said he would sell you anything, even a bag of dirt.

The business had expanded so fast that he could not find reliable employees fast enough. There were always people who wanted a job, but they didn't want to do the prerequisite work, at least not the way William wanted it done. Then there were always the pious men who came looking for a job but refused to work on Sunday. William had no patience for lazy workers. There was an effort underway to outlaw business on Sundays, and William was vocal at city council meetings to object to it. His voice was respected, for there was hardly anyone that didn't rely on McSherry Hardware and Lumber to supply them some fancy tool or a crate of goods at the drop of a hat...even on Sunday.

It was late in the day as customers filed through the store aisles picking out last minute merchandise and squabbling over supplies. A ship's steward haggled with William over the cost of a spool of rope, and a matronly woman decided to test the resilience of a skillet by banging on its bottom with a hammer. It was not a quiet business, but William saw to it that it was profitable—the woman was told she had to purchase the now dented skillet.

In the midst of this, a weary looking man of odd appearance walked into the store. He stood near the entrance and looked around as if he was not just bewildered but exhausted. The suitcase told William he had just disembarked from a boat, except this was no sailor. William had to look twice at the floor-length, black hooded habit, round black parson's hat, and a white knotted rope belt cinched around his waist before he realized who the man was—a *damned priest. What can he possibly want?* William wanted to turn away and avoid the man, but that wasn't his style. So, he put on his big boy pants and approached the priest, who appeared to be in need of salvation.

"Hello, Reverend," William said with a touch of distain. "Wha'cha looking for? McSherry's probably got it as long as it's not heaven or hell."

The priest, who stood as if he had been on his feet all day, put down the suitcase. "I've come looking for the proprietor. Are you him by chance?"

"By chance, indeed. I'm William McSherry. Welcome to McSherry Hardware and Lumber. Where you come from, priest?"

"Earlier today from the U.S. merchant ship Eagle, after a two-week voyage from New Orleans."

"Ah, Captain Johns. I've met the man," said William. "Runs a good ship, I hear. You arrived safely, I see."

The priest put on a smile. "Another merchant told me that I could get just about anything here."

"Just about," said William, "except bread, a bunk, and ah...female companionship."

The priest grimaced at the attempt of a joke, but otherwise ignored it. "I've spent the day looking for employment. I must have spoken to over twenty proprietors. I'm able-bodied, can read, write, and do numbers, and I also speak Spanish and a little Latin, but not sure the latter would be of any use here," he added with a smile as he glanced about the store.

"And Irish, I take it," William responded to the priest's lilt.

The priest laughed and responded in a Dublin accent, "Aye leaid, that I am when the conversation warrants."

William smiled. This bloke was okay, but he had never been approached by a priest looking for a job. Usually, they had their work cut out for them. "Don't you have a parish to tend to?"

"That is my goal, to be perfectly honest. With your last name, perhaps you are Catholic? From Ireland? There does not seem to be a parish nearby."

"Was Catholic. Got tired of it," said William. "Left it to my brother, but he's no-wheres near here," said William. "And nope, there's no Roman church any-where near here that I know of."

"Well, I guess that's why I need regular employment. Perhaps if I had a job, in my spare time I could start a parish. Early this morning as our ship docked, the captain paid me for my services as a chaplain aboard, so I'm not likely to be a burden for anyone. I passed some boarding houses earlier today that I can stay at. Mister McSherry, I can work to prove my worth to you, until you can pay me."

William laughed. "Reverend, you would not want to stay at any of the boarding houses nearby, unless you have a fondness for a particular type of woman. Do you?"

The priest blushed. "No, I assure you. Do you know of a Catholic family nearby?"

William realized getting rid of this priest wasn't going to be easy. If only his brother was nearby. *Richard (McSherry) was always looking for a priest for one of his projects. It had been Richard's obsession with Catholicism that caused them to separate after touring the country for six months. Knowing that there was a need for a hardware concern near the wharf was good reason for William to return there. Richard, for his part, longed for the open country, though he missed his brother at times. They made a good deal of money togeth-er in Jamaica. But all good things come to an end.

"I don't suppose, padre, you're available to work on Sundays. This here es-tablishment is open seven days a week to serve the people and ships of this great city." William watched the priest's face drop. *Good, maybe that sealed it and I won't have to deal with this guy. What do I have that would satisfy a priest, anyhow?*

The priest just shook his head. "Thank you, Mister McSherry. I'll look else-where. Good day." With that the priest picked up his bag and walked out of the store.

William instantly felt guilty for treating a priest so abruptly. *But what was he supposed to do, feed and clothe him until the Second Coming?* Not that he be-lieved any of that malarkey. He thought about chasing after him, but customers were lined up at the checkout and Davey, his clerk who always had difficulty making change from Spanish pieces of eight to British sterling, was holding up the works. William stepped behind the counter and told Davey to watch again how it was done. After a while, between the two, the customers were taken care of and William relaxed, picked up a broom and handed it to Davey. "Go brush off the walk, will you?"

"No problem," Davey said.

William watched as Davey took the broom and walked out front where there were benches on the boardwalk backed up to the store windows. That's when his eye, through the storefront window, caught the priest in his black parson's hat sitting on one of his benches. He didn't mind that so much. That's what the benches were for—for travelers to rest a bit before moving on. And the priest was clearly in need of a rest. Looking for a job all day in that heavy robe and carrying a suitcase can be brutal.

Having cashed out several customers William felt a tinge of guilt. The priest was in need, and he was in the business of providing just about anything to everyone. Why couldn't he have been more helpful? Well, he knew why.

William wiped his hands on his apron, took a quick look around the store, then walked outside and sat on the bench next to the priest to rest a bit himself. "Too bad my brother isn't here. He'd like to meet you. What's your name?"

The priest, surprised by William's sudden appearance, smiled. "I am Fr. Denis Cahill, Capuchin, Order of Franciscans Minor. Tell me about your brother."

"Well, Fr. Cahill, Richard is my twin, but we're only alike in appearance. We were born in Ireland like you. He's minutes older than me. We left home together at eighteen and joined a trading firm run by an uncle in Jamaica. After a few years the uncle retired and went back home, leaving us in charge. We hated the British. Still do. So, when the British were chased out of this country, after a while we found a willing buyer for our business in Jamaica, sold out, and came here looking for what's next. But over the years my brother, Richard, got more religious and I got less. We were into hardware and supplies in Jamaica and I know the business well, so after we toured America, from New York to Georgia, he settled down to do some land speculating out west, and I came back here to start this business. Believe it or not, there wasn't a hardware or lumber supplier near the wharf. I thought it was crazy that there wasn't, so here I am. Meanwhile, Richard is off in Virginia...and here's the thing. Last time I talked to him—he was here a few months ago—he was looking for a Catholic priest. He wants to start Catholic societies and churches out where he lives. I think he's nuts, but maybe you could help him. He's more Catholic than the pope, by the way." William could see that the idea excited his bench mate. "You don't have a horse, do you?"

Fr. Cahill shook his head, as William eyed the suitcase. "Do you ride?"

"I have not been on a horse for two years. But yes, I get along well with the beasts. I went to school in Spain and we rode regularly to our preaching assignments. Can you recommend a livery? I don't have much money, but perhaps...."

William cut him off. "Here's an offer if you're interested. Richard lives in a little village called Leetown, the other side of the Potowmack."

"What's Potowmack?" asked Fr. Cahill.

"It's a major river that divides us from the western part of Maryland. Richard comes here every few months to buy supplies. It's terribly out of his way. I think he comes in some vain hope to save my soul. Anyway, I've been putting aside a few items that he'll want. What if I outfit you with a horse and a pack mule, and whatever else you need to make the trip west, and you take the stuff to him. I'm pretty sure he'd like to meet you, and maybe he could help you."

"How far is it?" asked Fr. Cahill.

"The route is not direct...about 100 miles. It will take you a week or so."

"Do I pay you something for this generosity?" asked Fr. Cahill.

William thought about that for a moment, although he would never take money from a priest. He didn't much care for the Church, but neither did he want to invite God's wrath. "No. Just give over the horse and mule to Richard. He'll see that they get back to me."

At that point William noticed Fr. Cahill's sleight of hand. It looked like he was putting a Rosary back into his habit's pocket.

"Mister McSherry, I will take you up on your offer, and I will do something in return for you."

"What's that?"

"All the way to Leetown, that is every day until I meet your brother..." At this point Fr. Cahill smiled broadly, as if to tease the hardware maven. "I will pray for your soul."

At first McSherry frowned, but then they both laughed heartily. They had a deal.

2

Fr. Cahill was amazed at the mysterious way God appeared to be working. Here was a man who had supposedly rejected the faith, but nonetheless was going out of his way to connect him with a Catholic man in search of a priest. *Why had it taken him all day to find William McSherry?*

That evening, William found a home that provided Fr. Cahill board and room for a small fee, for which Fr. Cahill gladly paid.

It took half of the next day for William McSherry and his staff to outfit Fr. Cahill for the trip west. Fr. Cahill would ride a spotted gelding named Sassafras. Lashed to Sassafras' saddle would be a long lead to a compliant pack mule the livery owner called Ebenezer. The mule would carry large leather saddle bags stuffed with Richard's favorite imported goods. Running a world trade business for years in Jamaica, William and Richard had acquired a taste for the best the world had to offer, at least those that stopped in Jamaica. Thus, William carefully packed Richard's favorites: cannisters of tea from China, bottles of Madeira wine from Portugal and sherry from Spain, tins of chocolate from Germany, cinnamon from India, Jamaican coffee, licorice from Greece, a box of starch from Poland, and several bags of sugar from Antigua. Fr. Cahill wondered about the starch from Poland since everything else was edible. "Wait until you meet Richard, then you'll understand," said William with a touch of derision.

It seemed to Fr. Cahill that all these imported goods were likely the real reason Richard made the two-hundred-mile round-trip to Baltimore's harbor district several times a year. Nonetheless, Fr. Cahill decided he would still pray for William's soul during the trip.

Ebenezer also carried feed for both herself, Sassafras, and Fr. Cahill, and camping gear should overnight accommodations at a tavern be unavailable. For clothing, Fr. Cahill preferred to wear his Capuchin robe hitched up around his waist but agreed to wear heavy linen pants and leather boots to protect against chaff from riding astride.

William recommended he change out of his habit and not wear the parson's hat for his safety since he would be traveling alone. Fr. Cahill thought that if people knew he was a priest they would treat him with respect on the road, or he might be called on to minister to someone in need. That was his calling, after all.

William disagreed, but not for the reasons Fr. Cahill considered. "It doesn't matter who you are, priest or farmer," said William. "Although, if you look like a banker, you may attract more thieves than if you're a farmer. But in your case, the danger is not likely going to be thieves. Nothing a priest is likely to be packing will be thought of as having any value. What you're more in danger of attracting are the anti-Catholic element. Before the war most of the British colonies had some sort of Penal Laws against Catholicism, including life imprisonment if you were discovered to be a priest. That was true in New York up to just a few years ago. General Washington has tried to stop all that, but it persists in individuals. So, the route on that map I've given you will keep you on the busy roads where you won't be alone and vulnerable. I don't suppose you'd take a gun, would you?"

"No, I have a better weapon," said Fr. Cahill as he took the Rosary from his pocket.

William glanced at the Rosary. "You goin' to strangle a bad guy with that? Or tie him up until the sheriff arrives?"

More derision, thought Fr. Cahill. *He understands…just doesn't believe.* "I'll be fine. But I honor your generosity and concern." The priest smiled and pocketed the Rosary.

3

Fr. Cahill left the Baltimore harbor area Friday morning, November 7. On the trail, he found Sassafras a friendly beast as long has he had an apple in his hand. Ebenezer wasn't interested in the fruit, but if fed and watered on a regular basis, she was mostly compliant, unless she was napping while standing on all fours.

William had reviewed with Fr. Cahill the route from Baltimore east along the main wagon trail fifty-five miles to Fredrick, Virginia, then slightly south about twenty-five miles to Harper's Ferry. After crossing the Potowmack into Virginia, it was only fifteen miles through Charles Town to Smithfield where he was to turn north and take the Mecklenburg road another three miles to Leetown. There, hopefully, Fr. Cahill would find Richard McSherry. If Richard wasn't at home, which was possible because he traveled a fair amount, Fr. Cahill should seek lodging with a nearby neighbor until William returned. He was warned that Leetown was barely a village. There were no stores there, nor was there a livery or even a tavern, just a collection of farms and estates spread widely along the main road.

Fr. Cahill ran the distances through his mind. He figured if he could stay on the road for ten hours a day, and average two to three miles each hour, the trip would take him just four days. In bad weather, or some other unexpected delay, probably five days. Reviewing his stores, he was confident there would be no problem. As a priest, he would say his office while on horseback each morning, and then in camp celebrate Mass each evening.

As Sassafras and Ebenezer climbed the first slight rise out of the harbor area, a surge of confidence swept through him. He contemplated his good Providence to be in the United States pursuing what appeared to be God's plan for his life, although he had no idea what that plan really was.

Instinctively, he took out his Rosary, and decided to pray a Rosary in thanksgiving. Surely it was the Blessed Mother who interceded for him to the Lord who sent an angel to get William McSherry's attention and put him on a horse and on his way. He only wished everything in life could be so readily known.

But he wondered why evil also seemed to come so readily. There was the killing of the priest that baptized him, the New Orleans fire, the Gulf Storm, and the death of Bud Sally. He also had other questions. Was his leaving New Orleans God's will or just his arrogant attitude about the relationship of Church and state? He wished he knew God's will better. He once asked his confessor how a priest could know a particular decision he was about to make was in God's will or not? Or if a particular decision was a good one or not? His confessor at the time was an elderly Capuchin, white hair, stooped over a bit, wise, and always carried a sly smile on the corner of his lips. Denis Cahill, not yet ordained, wanted the magic formula that would reveal God's will. There had to be a spiritual answer to the eternal questions mankind had always asked themselves. *Is this something I should be doing, or not? Is this God's will or mine?* The old priest simply smiled and said, "Well, sometimes you just have to do it, and see if it works out. Maybe it will. Maybe it won't." After that, and after he was ordained, Fr. Cahill realized that just because priests have the wherewithal to effect a miracle at the altar doesn't make them clairvoyant or even wise. One could hope otherwise, but it just wasn't so. In seminary he had been told time and again that once ordained he would be a priest forever. He doubted that, too.

Fr. Cahill spent his second night in a lodge above a tavern just east of Fredrick Town. Passing through the town on day three, he made note of the cosmopolitan nature of the people. While mostly German, there were European settlers from France, Spain, Italy, and England. It seemed like a natural place to establish a house of religion along this well-traveled National Road. Tempted to stop, his load of goods promised for Richard McSherry kept him going.

Riding a horse and leading a pack mule wasn't the most comfortable way to travel but he felt better if he sat erect in the saddle. The trousers and boots William provisioned for him helped guard against what he assumed were nonetheless going to be saddle sores long after his journey ended. He kept looking back at Ebenezer to make sure the load was secure. The large saddle bags helped, but there were a few things still tied on with ropes, and he wasn't as good at knots as William's outfitting staff. He worried that something was going to come loose.

It was mid-afternoon when Fr. Cahill forded the nearly dry Wye Creek southwest of Fredrick Town.

Coming up the hill from Wye Creek he came upon a rugged pioneering village of a dozen small log homes and a winding dirt road surrounded by small hills. Walking toward him from the village was a funeral procession. Out of respect he stopped, dismounted, and stood by the side of the road. In the very front were two men with muskets at the ready. He wondered what they were about, having never seen an armed funeral. Behind the armed guards was an adolescent boy who had been crying but bravely held aloft a procession standard topped with a crucifix. *Was this a Catholic procession? It must be.* The boy was followed by a middle-aged man also in grief holding tight the hands of two young teen girls. One of the girls steeled herself against emotion and held her head high. But the other girl's head was downcast. Then there was a woman, tearless but focused, who held chest high a small picture of the Blessed Mother. Following her was a plain wooden coffin held on the shoulders of four men. As the coffin came upon Cahill, he genuflected and crossed himself.

He was surprised coming upon what was obviously a Catholic funeral procession. He looked about—there was no priest. At the rear was a lone elderly matron. When she saw Fr. Cahill her eyes widened. Fr. Cahill noticed that she was gripping a Rosary, her old fingers white at the knuckles.

"STOP! STOP!" she yelled at the procession in front of her. It did, and the men, even those carrying the casket, turned as much as they could to see what had happened. The matron came close to Fr. Cahill, "Sir, are you by chance a Roman priest?" There was a Germanic lilt to her voice.

"I am. I'm Fr. Denis Cahill, Franciscan, Capuchin," he said with a distinct Irish brogue.

"You are Irish. We are German. Father have mercy on us." The woman began to cry out loud and explain rapidly. He had to concentrate to understand her thick accent. "My daughter was murdered. The mother of three children and a good husband. We are Roman. Men from the town raped and killed her because she demanded they stop profaning the Holy Mother. We go to bury her now. We fear they will come and kill us, too. There is no Catholic priest or church anywhere near us. No sacraments. Please, father, will you say a Mass for her...at her grave. Please father. I have been begging God to send us a priest. Here you are; God has sent you!"

Fr. Cahill took the old woman's hands that held her Rosary. "Madam, I am not afraid. What is your name?"

"I am Anna-Monica Kaiser."

"Yes, I will say Mass and bless all of you, Anna-Monica. A good name you have."

"Thank you, Father." She fell to her knees and kissed his hands. The others having heard their conversation, also knelt and crossed themselves, except for the casket bearers who simply bowed their heads and crossed themselves.

"Come, get up," Fr. Cahill said. "I will go with you to where you will bury your martyred daughter. We will celebrate Mass. Come! Come now. I will go with you. Lead the way."

At first the group was utterly silent and still. One of the men with a musket came to Fr. Cahill, took his hand and arm, and shook it heartily in thanks. "Father, she was my sister. Marie, her name." The man turned and tugged on the man's shirt that held the two teen girls and pulled him to Fr. Cahill. "This is Mark, and his daughters Janie and Kathryn. He was a good husband and is a good father."

Mark was in shock as he just stared at Fr. Cahill. Through tears he just nodded his head and smiled.

Fr. Cahill instinctively put his hand on Mark's head, making the sign of the cross with his thumb on the man's forehead, and then the same on the two girls. "Is this your son, Mark?" Fr. Cahill gestured at the youth holding the processional crucifix, who stood back.

"Yes, this is Robert Folger, my only son."

Fr. Cahill reach out, put his hand on Robert's head and also signed the cross. Fr. Cahill held up his hands in a blessing to all. Most were still on their knees. "May Almighty God, who gives us life and even in death eternal life, bless you and protect you, now in our sorrow, and tomorrow in hope. Amen. In the name of the Father +, Son +, and Holy Ghost +".

The group together said, "Amen."

"Now, let us go and celebrate Mass and bury Marie. It is Sunday, the Lord's day."

The deceased's brother took Sassafras and Ebenezer's lead and walked with Fr. Cahill. They arrived at a small secluded burial ground behind a hill. Sassafras and Ebenezer were put on long tethers and allowed to feed nearby. Fr. Cahill unpacked his Mass kit, opened one of the bottles of wine intended for Richard, and celebrated Mass on top of Marie's coffin. After Mass was concluded and just before the casket was lowered on ropes by the bearers, Fr. Cahill led the villagers in the *Memorare*. They assured him they knew the prayer. He was thrilled that they knew it in Latin.

> Memorare, O piissima Virgo Maria...
> *Remember, O most gracious Virgin Mary,*
> *that never was it known that anyone*
> *who fled to thy protection, implored thy help,*
> *or sought thy intercession, was left unaided.*
> *Inspired by this confidence, I fly unto thee,*
> *O Virgin of virgins, my Mother.*
> *To thee do I come, before thee I stand, sinful and sorrowful.*
> *O Mother of the Word Incarnate, despise not my petitions,*
> *but in thy mercy hear and answer me.*
> *Amen.*

After the casket was covered with soil, most of the villagers returned home in a reverent but somber mood. Fr. Cahill was joined by Marie's family, who walked back to the main road with him.

"Father," said Mark, "where are you going?"

"I'm going to Leetown in Virginia. It is..."

Mark interrupted him. "General Charles Lee lived there. Why are you going there?"

"I am on a mission for God, it appears," said Fr. Cahill. "I met a man in Baltimore who asked me to take supplies to a man who lives there, his brother."

"General Lee was known and liked," said Mark. "I fought in his regiment at the Battle of Monmouth. It did not go well. I and many of my friends were captured and held by the British for almost a year until there was a prisoner exchange. Marie and I already had Robert. After I came home our two girls were born. General Lee was court-martialed. I think he died a few years back."

"I'm glad you made it back to your family safely and that God has further blessed you with two beautiful daughters." Fr. Cahill again touched in blessing the heads of the girls.

"It was the Holy Mother," said Mark. "She prayed for us. Marie prayed a Rosary every day I was gone, or so she said. I believe her, of course. But she is gone now." Mark could not hold back the tears.

"She is with the Blessed Mother now, I am sure," said Fr. Cahill. "She was here when she was most needed, to pray for your safe return and to give you two beautiful daughters."

"But it is dangerous for them here. We hope things will get better. But..." his voice trailed off.

Fr. Cahill thought to change the subject. "Do you know the way to Leetown? I have instructions, but the closer I get I've been told to ask advice."

Mark collected his thoughts, "I've been to Virginia several times, although never to Leetown. But I will tell you, this is not the right way to go...through Harper's Ferry at Shenandoah. Do you know the National Road out of Fredrick Town?"

"Yes, I was on it for a while, but the brother of the man I'm to see told me to take the trail to Harper's Ferry."

"Some say that is the way to go, but it is not nearly as well marked or provisioned as the National Road, which I take to Margaretville, and then take the southern road to Sharpsburg, Mecklenburg, and soon you'll come directly to Leetown. The advantage is that at Mecklenburg you can ford the Potowmack any time of year. It's wide and very shallow. But at the ferry crossing at Shenandoah, the river is deep and often so dangerous the ferry can't cross in the rapids. Crossing at the ford will not cost you a farthing. I have no idea what the ferrymen charge nowadays, but it isn't cheap."

Fr. Cahill thought about Mark's recommendation. It seemed like good advice. After a little more information, Mark showed him a short cut that headed due north. So, Fr. Cahill set out to follow Mark's directions. It was dusk before he was back on the National Road heading northwest. Soon, he came to a tavern where there was also lodging and a livery, and so he stayed the night.

The next morning he got an early start. The road had recently been improved, and both William and Mark were right about one thing—there was plenty of company on the road, with provision establishments every few miles.

Dusk came before he got to Margaretville, so he camped for the night along the road with a few other families.

Early the next morning he rose early and got into Margaretville mid-morning, asked directions, and soon was on the southwest trail toward the Potowmack ford at Mecklenburg which he hoped to reach before nightfall and stay at a lodge there.

He was feeling calm and confident of the trip so far, although he felt a blister coming on under his left thigh where the saddle rubbed him wrong. He found himself standing more and more on his left stirrup, which only aggravated some hidden hip nerve that rendered a sharp pain in his buttock.

Finally, he stopped, unpacked a blanket, and situated it on the saddle for additional padding. That was some help, but the blanket was not strapped on, so it slid. More adjustments were necessary.

4

It was a cool Tuesday, November 11, as Fr. Cahill stopped once again to adjust the saddle and his padding. As he dismounted, the hem of his black habit fell over his pants and boots. If the habit didn't identify him as a priest, the round, wide brimmed parson's hat, or galero, would. That he was traveling alone into the interior except for a heavily packed mule drew attention, although for the last half-hour he had seen no one.

He was rummaging around inside one of Ebenezer's packs looking for a leather belt or rope when he glanced up to see four horsemen in their twenties and thirties come over a rise toward him. He glanced up as they passed, smiled, and waved. But they didn't smile back. In fact, the rider that passed closest to him, the oldest of the four, snarled and spit at him.

Suddenly, he felt vulnerable—four against one was no odds. But when the four kept on in the direction of Margaretville Fr. Cahill relaxed, although a couple of them glanced back at him. He decided, wisely, that the saddle sores would just have to get worse. Quickly he cinched up the pack, got back in the saddle, and prodded Sassafras into a trot away from the men; but getting a mule to trot was not so easy.

His encounters with anti-Catholic individuals in New Orleans and William's warning of such individuals here in the United States caused him to take out his Rosary and start praying another decade or two, even though he had said his office and five decades earlier. Prayer with his Rosary was his only weapon. *No, Richard, I'm glad I don't have a gun. Thank you.*

There was a crude village sign along the road, "Welcome to Sharpsburg." Someone had attached a second shingle below the official sign that had scrawled on it in white paint, "Where all the Burrs are sharp," with the initials "R.B." carved below like a signature. He chuckled at the add-on shingle. At the same time he heard the trotting hoofs of four horses approach from behind.

His instincts were right; the four horsemen had returned, and he suspected without good intentions. They reigned in their steeds and followed Fr. Cahill's pack mule through the village. Sharpsburg wasn't much. There was a tavern, a livery, a sheriff's office, and a few cabins scattered about. The last building on the right was a small general store with a barber chair in the front window. The store did not seem to have any customers, but through the window Fr. Cahill saw a man laying back in the barber chair with a towel wrapped about his face and the barber sweeping the floor. That was it. Sharpsburg was kind of dull, he thought, except for the four horsemen on his tail, which sharpened his attention. Briefly, he considered stopping for a shave. He did need one, but the cost had always forced him to shave himself.

He tried to ignore his pursuers even as he urged Sassafras on a bit faster. But there was a limit to how fast Ebenezer was going go for she was carrying the heavier burden.

Once out of town, the trail rounded a bend, and the game was up. Two of the four came either side of him. The man on his left, the older of the four, grabbed Sassafras' reigns and pulled the horse to a stop.

Cahill's heart raced. He looked around at the two men behind him. They had come alongside Ebenezer and had taken hold of her lead as well. All four were clean shaven, the two behind were smiling and were a bit younger than the two on either side of him The weather being cool they all wore heavy trail coats and hats. Fr. Cahill couldn't tell what their occupation might be, except now they clearly meant to be disruptors.

"Good-day and God speed, gentlemen," said Fr. Cahill, his voice shaking a bit. "What can I do for you?"

The four laughed. The older of the four, or so it seemed, a slightly heavy-set man nearing forty, was quick to speak. "It's what we're gonna do for you, ya damned papist."

Fr. Cahill gazed at the man's face. His black eyes were deep-set and fierce. His teeth had not been entirely in his mouth for some time. Between his white neckerchief and his brown flannel shirt, Fr. Cahill caught sight of a tattoo that looked eerily similar to the crescent moon tattoos of that crazed reveler in New Orleans. The man's angst was real, and Fr. Cahill froze in his saddle.

5

Will Canning jerked the gelding's reins out of the priest's hands, but the gelding, realizing something was seriously wrong, began to buck and kick. At first, Will found it entertaining that the priest was bucked so vigorously that one instant he was flying into the air and the next he was being slammed into his saddle. *He held onto that saddle horn pretty good,* thought Will. But then, Will realized the damn horse was trying to swing his rear end around to kick him.

"Look out, Will," Sid yelled.

"I got it, shut up," Will yelled back, as he yanked down on the gelding's reins and bit. But the horse kept at it, twisting and kicking so viciously and almost connecting with Will's head a couple times, that Will let go and jumped out of the way.

Free, the priest's gelding charged ahead with the priest still holding on for dear life. Edgar, one of Will's sidekicks who was used to cutting out cattle, nudged his stallion into action. The stallion, by instinct, leaped ahead, cut off the gelding, and forced it into a stand of prickly shrub. The gelding agitated twice now, reared up, and threw the priest from his saddle to the ground with a thud.

The four men laughed. "Whoa, there, cowpoke," said Sid. "Guess that hors-ey didn't like ya much."

Will promptly dismounted, gave his horse's reins to Edgar, grasped the gelding's hanging reins, and jerked them down, forcing the rebellious steed to stop its contortions and back up further into the brush. The gelding again tried to rear back as fear filled its eyes, but Will, who had broken more than one wild horse by scaring it nearly to death, fearlessly forced it down with a vicious tug.

"Red! Here! Take these," snapped Will, handing the gelding's reins to the kid with the red hair. "I got me some work to do."

Will had been around preachers long enough to know that the pope was the anti-Christ, the Virgin Mary was the whore of Babylon, and that priests were the insidious instigators of idolatry. The Bible was real clear about not making graven images and bowing down to them, but Catholics loved their idols and worshiped that whore whom Jesus rebuked at the wedding feast by calling her "woman." It was important to rid the land of these tools of Satan before it was too late. Getting the chance to corner a priest and beat the hell out of him was a dream come true. He would not be denied such just pleasure.

Getting back to his feet, the priest wore a black robe over his trousers which now unfurled from his waist all the way to his ankles. It made him look like a woman. "That's a pretty little black dress you got there priest; you confused or sometin?" Will came at the priest, fists clenched, malevolence in his eyes. The priest backed away, still stunned after falling off his horse, and backed into the flank of Sid's horse. Sid yanked hard left on his reins, causing his horse to suddenly jolt its hindquarters in the opposite direction, tossing the unsuspecting priest like a rag doll at Will. *God I love this,* Will thought, and welcomed the flung priest with his fist, driving it deep into the priest's gut. With his air displaced, and no doubt some of his guts, the priest promptly doubled over and fell to the ground.

"But maybe he's not a priest," yelled Red, the youngest of the four.

"Oh, he's Roman all right, lookie here." Will leaned over and with his right hand tried to rip the Rosary out of the priest's fist. But the priest had such a firm grip on the thin chain that its sharp edges cut a slash across Will's hand, releasing a spew of blood. Will screamed at the sharp pain, but the sight of his own blood enraged him all the more. With the priest bent over, Will kicked at the priest's head. The priest blocked most of the swift moving boot with his arm, but the force sent him tumbling deep into the brush. "Go home, you piece of shit, wherever you come from. We got no use for papists in this here country."

Will's hand was badly bleeding. Quickly, he pulled off his white neckerchief and wrapped the dust-laden cloth around his bleeding hand, tucking in the ends to make a makeshift bandage. Then, tucking the injured hand to his chest, he used his left hand to pick up a rock and hurl it at the priest's head. It connected, knocking the priest out, smashing his nose, and creating a long slash above his ear from which warm, red blood flowed over his head and covered his face. But Will wasn't done with the papal invader. Taking up a stick he beat the downed priest with all his might, spouting hate-filled epithets, building up a mad sweat, as he used all his energy to slam the papist's arms, legs, and back. He wanted the man dead.

Will's sidekicks glanced at each other as if to say, this has gone far enough. Edgar took the hint and maneuvered his horse between Will and the priest. But Will screamed at Edgar, "God damn it Edgar, get out of my way, let me do my duty." In his rabid state, Will tried to shove Edgar's horse out of the way, but the stallion was too big and ornery, and on its own lunged at Will.

"Will, that's enough! Stop it already," yelled Red.

"Just shut your yap, Red. Get your damn horse away from me, Edgar, if you know what's good for ya," said Will, "or I'll practice on you next."

"No, you won't, Will," said Edgar, "that's enough. Stop. He done nothin' to you. You got that cut to yourself. Let's go."

"He's the devil's apostle, I telling' ya. They pray to idols, worship that whore of Babylon. They gonna corrupt the entire land if we let 'em. Eradicate them I say."

The priest laid in a pile of twisted arms and legs in the shrubs as if dead.

"Jesus, Will," said Sid. "You probably killed the guy. Let's get out of here."

Will, exhausted and finding it hard to stand, collected his breath, and looked for a way to get in another wallop at the priest, but Edgar would have none of it.

"Take his horse, at least," said Will.

"And this pack mule," said a smiling Red, who already had the mule's reins in hand. "Probablys got stuff in there worth sumpt'in, you think guys?"

"I doubt it," said Sid.

Will staggered back to his horse and managed to climb into the saddle. "Let's go. Sid, hang back. Make sure no one follows. C'mon Red, bring the ass, makes no sense to leave it here."

Will took one last look at his object of hatred. The priest's body lay motionless; blood covered his head and face. He might well be dead. Luckily, the body was almost out of sight, thrown back off the road into a growth of vines and thorny shrub, with that damn string of beads still in his grasp.

Pulling along a frightened gelding and mule, they took the main trail back toward sleepy Sharpsburg, where they were known, but sure that no one would dare to ask where they found the fine gelding and pack mule.

6

My Despised Cyn:

I suppose you had to wait until you had some accomplices to dissuade Cahill from his calling. Will Canning was a good choice—bigoted, fearless, and a virtually untouchable local authority.

Good of you too to pull some punches. We want Cahill to curse God before he dies, or at least leave the priesthood. We don't win points by sending another priest to Glory. Glad you've learned that lesson.

But you must stay on him. I doubt it will take one vicious attack to change his mind. Conjure up a few more. This man seems robust, which does not bode well for our purposes. We might try something more subtle, like subterfuge or seduction. Maybe both.

Yes, it was a good idea to confiscate his supplies. They were intended for Richard McSherry who needs to be deprived. It's likely now the supplies will never get to him. Like a good military intervention, we must continue to disrupt the enemy's supply chain.

Eternally yours,
Master of Disasters

Chapter 16
Many Moons Ago

1

The shop on the edge of Sharpsburg was small and neatly organized, like the barber, a diminutive merchant with a large heart. He cleaned his straight razor, put it aside, then poured hot water over a soft towel and wrapped his customer's face with a sweet-smelling scent that always made the store smell nice for an hour after. "So, what were you doing up in Hagerstown? Some filly up there getting your attention finally?"

The customer, laying back in the chair with his face covered with the warm towel, chuckled. "David, you need to marry Sarah proper-like."

"Find me a priest. Besides, been married once before. But you...well, you need to pay the price like the rest of us," said David, as he swept up his customer's hair that had fallen around the chair. "Now tell me, what's in Hagerstown that gets you up there so often?"

The customer smiled again, although David didn't notice. "Oh, you know, the usual. Visited some of my tenants up that way. And there is a lady in Hagerstown."

"See! See! I was right," exclaimed David, throwing the fallen hair into a dust bin.

"No. No. This lady, she's a widow and old enough to be my mother. She wants to start a society there and has enlisted my help in the effort."

"You don't say?!" David took off the towel wrap, brushed the last few loose hairs off his customer's shoulders and chest, and raised the chair. There you go, all done."

Richard McSherry stepped out of the chair, took a small silver coin from his vest pocket, and gave it to the very appreciative David McKee, the only barber he considered of any worth between Hagerstown and Winchester. Richard could easily afford to have a barber trim his wavy dark auburn hair, trim his goatee, and shave the rest of his face and neck. He turned to the mirror (such as it was) hanging on David's wall. Richard disliked looking at himself, but believed he had a duty to keep up what some had described as his fine personal appearance. Thus, he dressed carefully in the fashion of his day, with a starched collar, lace ruffles, waistcoat, linen trousers, and boots with silver buckles. His only reason was to present himself as a gentleman whose opinion might be considered. He eschewed the grey powdered wigs unless invited to some formal occasion. His brother back in Baltimore had insisted he wear one to a ball to which they were both invited upon first coming to the United States and meeting some dignitaries. William carried a line of the "puffy-dos" as Richard called them, and made sure Richard was provided with the latest style. But Richard was more interested in being genial and kind in manners, exercising generosity and providing elegant hospitality to his guests. Although the latter was somewhat out of his league since he did not live in a city nor did he have a hospitable wife to be hospitable.

"Richard, I do appreciate your business. I know you need not darken the threshold of my shop and chair."

"I'm glad to do it when I pass by David, if for no other reason than I relish your prayers for my mission."

"You have them. Just not sure how acceptable your mission would be in these parts."

"This I know...be careful," said Richard as he donned his coat and hat.

Outside Richard untied his horse, a dark chestnut thoroughbred stallion he called Romeo. The steed stood 17-hands and exhibited a pure white diamond on his forehead. The Maryland breeder told Richard that the horse was the great, great grandson of Bulle Rock, the first thoroughbred imported to the American colonies in 1730. It was a claim Richard doubted, but Romeo did have all the qualities of a pure breed—strong, smart, purpose-driven, spirited and loyal.

Richard swung up into Romeo's saddle and began his two-hour trot to Mecklenburg where he would stay overnight with friends before a more leisurely ride to Retirement, his estate in Leetown. But as he trotted out of Sharpsburg four men on horseback entered the small village. They were leading behind an empty-saddled gelding that was resisting its lead, and a well-ladened pack horse. He recognized the lead-man, Will Canning, Sharpsburg's sheriff. Richard tipped his hat to the group, but they ignored him, although Will gazed at Richard suspiciously. Will didn't know Richard, but Richard knew Will by reputation. He was the local instigator of the annual anti-Catholic Guy Fawkes bonfire. David McKee feared Will Canning would someday discover the town's barber was a devout papist, although a secretive one.

At first Richard thought it odd that the men refused to acknowledge him, another traveler, especially when he, a gentleman, acknowledged them. But something else bothered him about the posse, but he couldn't put his mind exactly to it. So, he ignored the *faux pas* and gave way for Romeo to trot on. Richard's unease, however, would not pass, and he racked his brain for the contradiction.

Not far out of the village, after rounding a turn, Richard came upon a buggy with an elderly man and woman aboard, and a man on horseback. Both had stopped in the middle of the trail and were staring off into the scrub. As soon as they saw Richard approaching on a trot, the two broke apart. The buggy came toward him while the rider headed further down the road. As the buggy approached him, he slowed to a walk and then a stop, and held out his hand for the buggy to stop. It did. Inside was an older man dressed with some distinction, and a well-wrapped matron, no doubt his wife. Richard looked down at them and tipped his hat as if to speak, but the man spoke first.

"A bloody body, dead, no doubt. Blood everywhere," said the man, who Richard recognized as the Anglican priest from the Margaretville Society.

"Very troubling...disgusting," said the man's wife as she clutched at her shawl pulling it tight around her neck.

Richard smiled and said, "Are you Rev. and Missus Bebbington?"

The old man lit up. "Yes. Are you a member of our society whom we have not met?" asked the man.

"Yes," smiled the woman, her countenance suddenly transformed. "Please tell us who you are. Have we met?"

"I believe we have once," said Richard. "I am Richard McSherry of Leetown. I'm a..." he hesitated for a moment not wanting to create unease. "I am a layman from another religious society and in some past gathering I believe we met...in Margaretville. I believe by a creek. It was a reception."

"Oh, yes," the Bebbingtons said in unison.

"It was at our outreach picnic this past summer," Mrs. Bebbington said.

Richard wanted no more small talk. "Did you check on the man, or body? Are you sure...the person is deceased?"

"Didn't want to get mixed up in such a thing," said Rev. Bebbington.

Richard pressed: "And what about the other man, the rider I saw stopped with you."

"Don't know him, Mister McSherry," said Mrs. Bebbington. "But if you know what's good for you, you'll pass it quickly like the other fellow did and let the wolves take care of the business. Terrible. Terrible."

Richard was left speechless, and suddenly became anxious to check on the body himself. "Well, good-day to both of you. I guess it's up to me to check." Without further salutation, Richard prodded Romeo into a canter.

When Richard arrived at the spot on the wagon trail where the Bebbington's buggy and the lone rider had stopped, he saw a great amount of blood on the trail. That led to the marks of a scuffle and horse-trampled grass and brush... and then his eyes fell on the bloody body in the brush. It was a body dressed in a black robe but wearing riding pants and boots underneath. This was no accident. It was the work of thieves...vicious thieves.

Anger rushed through his veins as he became more alert to his surroundings. The thieves could still be around, although that was doubtful since the Bebbingtons had not been attacked. Romeo, too, sensed danger. Richard could feel the stallion's muscles tighten as his ears perked up and started twisting about.

Reaching into his right saddle bag, Richard retrieved his double-barrel Blair pistol. It was a tool he admired both for its ivory-handled beauty and its defensive utility. Traveling as much as he did, he practiced with it regularly, cleaned it often, and kept powder, pad, and ball loaded in both barrels. He had brandished it several times to ward off danger, but thank God he had never fired it against an attacker. Being always prepared was a trait of his upbringing, but it was also reinforced in Jamaica, where pirates and thieves were common-place. He and his brother had discovered that if thieves knew you were bold and prepared, they tended to stay away, desiring instead to prey on the weak and vulnerable. Evidently, the poor bloke in the brush was one of the latter. Keeping up his guard, Richard dismounted, and went quickly to the man in the weeds.

The man's fist gripped a bloody Rosary. *Catholic!* Richard felt the man's arms and legs...nothing broken. Then Richard made an awful discovery; the man was wearing a clerical habit over his riding pants and boots, and partially covering his bloodied face was a galero or parson's hat. *This was a priest.* "Jesus! Jesus!" Richard said out loud, begging the angels to close in.

Richard's hands trembled as adrenaline pumped through his veins quick-ening his breath, pulse, and movements. His hands felt the man's neck. It was warm, and there was a pulse. *God help us, he's alive. But, God, why did you allow this?"*

Sticking the pistol in the back of his waist-belt, he carefully pulled the priest from the brush and into the open. The man moaned. He was surely alive, but badly beaten. Romeo's head craned down next to Richard smelling the situation and snorting at the disgust of it all. "Yes, Romeo, we have an answer to prayer, but a tragic one it seems."

Romeo backed up to give Richard more room, nipping at Richard's head as if to say, *he needs air, give him room to breathe.* Romeo's close presence told Richard the thieves were nowhere close. If they were, Romeo's heightened senses would let him know of the danger. The stallion's ears nevertheless were twitching every which way and his nostrils were flailing. But the horse was calm and kept his eyes on the priest and Richard's attempt to pull to him out of the thorns and undercover.

After getting the priest to lay flat on the crushed grasses, Richard stood and dug through a saddle bag. From it he pulled one of his white ruffled shirts and a canteen. He began to wash the priest's face of the blood. There was a nasty gash across his head, something had hit it, and his head was swollen; but the blood had clotted, and it was no longer bleeding.

Though it was cool, Richard's face was red and perspired with rage. Barely corralled hostile thoughts invaded his mind. *God, is this how you answer my prayer for a priest? You almost kill him on the way? What kind of God are you that would allow this? Angels in heaven how could you be silent?*

Richard tipped his canteen to the man's lips ever so slowly, trying to get moisture into the man's mouth, which was partially agape. That did it. Suddenly the man coughed and hacked, though his eyes were still partly held closed with dried blood that had dripped from his forehead.

"Father! Father!" Richard called out. "Are you all right?" *What a stupid* question. *Of course, you're not.* He tipped the canteen again to the priest's lips. "Here. Drink. It's water." But the man only sputtered and spat out the water; yet he was groaning louder now, almost talking. *Keep trying Richard.*

Richard felt the man's cheek and checked for broken bones again, especially around his neck. The only time the man responded was when Richard applied pressure to his left arm, leg, or chest. *Perhaps fractured. Hopefully, just badly bruised. Got to get him to safety. But he's in no shape to ride or be draped over a horse. It's going to be dusk soon. How'd he get here? Where is he from?*

Frustration, not fear, filled Richard with angst as he kept trying to give the priest water and replace his dazed delirium with sobering clarity.

Gently, Richard shook the man. *If his bones are not broken and he can hold his balance he can ride in the saddle and I can walk. If only he could regain consciousness.* But he didn't.

Richard finally retrieved canvas gloves and a small hatchet from his camp roll. Thirty minutes later Richard had rigged a stretcher made from two small trees to drag behind Romeo. He used vines to lace between the two poles so he could suspend a blanket on which the priest could lie. As he dragged the priest onto the stretcher, the pain clearly brought the man around, and his eyes opened, but his speech was slurred and incoherent. Richard tied the man onto the stretcher.

He next had to decide where he was going to take his patient. Sharpsburg was the closest town, but with a Catholic priest in tow he did not want to engage the sheriff, who David McKee had warned was radically hostile toward Catholics. Richard thought to himself, *just imagine the Sharpsburg sheriff running into a Catholic priest on the road.* That's when it hit him—what had bothered him about Will Canning and his posse's snub on the road. Could it be that the horse and that pack mule the posse had led into town belonged to this priest? Either they had found the animals wandering alone in the wild, or it was...and then it hit him again. A rush of excitement stopped him as he stared down at the priest on the stretcher and the dried blood on the wagon trail he had first noticed. The blood on the trail was not the priest's blood, it was too far from where the priest had been. He looked over at the Rosary that the priest still held in his hands. He had not cleaned the blood from it, and now he knelt next to the stretcher and examined the Rosary carefully. There was dried blood all over it, and what appeared to be pieces of torn flesh. He tried to pry open the priest's hands, but he held the Rosary tightly. Then the priest grunted. Richard looked at the priest's unshaven face now looking back at Richard, the freshly shaved gentleman.

"He tried to take my weapon," the priest mumbled, and he opened his hand that was holding the Rosary allowing Richard to take it. It was a beautiful mother-of-pearl Rosary, the kind a mother would have. Richard took the priest's hand and wiped the blood from it, looking for a wound. There was none. The blood on his hand and the Rosary was not the priest's. It belonged to the thief.

Then Richard remembered: When Will Canning rode past Richard he held his right hand close to his body. Around his hand was a white neckerchief...a white neckerchief soaked in red blood. Will Canning, the sheriff, had tried to take this priest's Rosary, but the priest hadn't let him, and the Rosary cut open Will's hand. While there was no justice in beating this priest, there was justice in Will Canning cutting open his hand on a Rosary of all things. Will Canning had met his match, the Holy Mother of God. *Don't mess with Mary* the saying goes.

Richard looked the priest in the eyes. "What's your name?"

The priest could not talk well, but he was awake and had a question of his own, though his speech was slurred. "Are you Catholic?"

"I am," said Richard. "And I am here to help you. What's your name?"

"Den-is...Ca-hill."

Richard recognized the lilt. "Ireland?"

"Somewhat. New Orleans."

"Are you a priest?"

"Capuchin."

"Father, I have prayed for years for a Catholic priest to come to us, but never did I imagine it would be this way. I am so sorry."

"I am on my way somewhere...not here," said the priest, his thoughts still not clearly forming.

Disappointment set in.

"Sorry," said the priest, "Can't remember where...I was to go."

Richard decided to change subjects, "The man who tried to take your Rosary, was he wearing a white neckerchief, brown shirt, a little heavy set?"

The priest stared at Richard blankly, his eyes wandering, thinking. Finally, he nodded. "There were four."

Richard's blood ran cold. There was no doubt now about what happened.

"Where is Sassafras and Eb'nezer?"

"Who?" asked Richard.

"Horse...mule."

Richard could not believe what he was hearing but the story came together. "They are not here, but I think I can find them. How do you feel? I am going to pull you to a home, a Catholic home where you can heal. You're on a stretcher. Is that okay?"

The priest nodded, tried to smile. "Mother's Rosary?"

"Absolutely, here." Richard wound the Rosary loosely around the priest's hand and closed it over the thin silver chain and pearls." Fr. Cahill gripped the Rosary tight.

"Bless you," said the priest weakly and then closed his eyes.

Richard felt relieved. Some success. Clearly the man was in a lot of pain. Hopefully, David would know how to reach a doctor. But the priest was alive and with the angels' help, if they cared to, the priest would survive. He thanked God for being able to save this man, even though he may not be the answer to years of his prayers.

2

Romeo seemed to understand Richard's urgency and purpose as the stallion dutifully pulled the priest carefully and confidently over back fields, around logs, up hills, and across creek beds. The massive stallion was unusually gentle as he responded to Richard's direction along the unorthodox route, for they avoided the normal trails, roads, and Sharpsburg proper.

An hour later, at dusk, Richard and Romeo pulled up to the rear of David and Sarah McKee's home. Richard had not yet dismounted before the diminutive but elegant Sarah came running out the back door wringing her hands, as she so often did. She wore a long, plain dress, accented by a bright blue ribbon which was woven into her long black and grey mixed hair tied in a tight braid that hung past her waist. She had been looking for David to come home from closing the store when she recognized Richard and Romeo coming unusually slowly down the road, turning in by the garden, and ending up behind the house. It was an unusual place for guests to stop. She greeted Richard, concerned that he was all right due to his unusual arrival...when she saw the stretcher and man lying on it.

Richard briefly explained the circumstances of finding the priest. Within minutes he and Sarah, with help from Romeo, managed to get the priest into the house and onto a bed in the guest room. While Richard cared for Romeo in the McKee's barn, Sarah removed the priest's boots and soiled clothes, cleaned his wounds, covered him with warm blankets, and helped him drink a mug of warm chicken broth. The priest thanked her with his exhausted eyes, seemed better for it, and quickly fell asleep.

Before David arrived home, Richard filled Sarah in on everything he knew. She told Richard to make himself at home; but that she was going to hurry David home. He sometimes stayed late to clean up or stock shelves.

"Do you or David know of a nearby doctor?" asked Richard.

"David might, but I do not trust white doctors," said Sarah. "They know little what is good. They want to bleed the sick for any reason. But we know it is our blood that keeps us alive. Why would you remove that which gives life? They are stupid men, Richard. Not good. I will treat the priest. Do not bleed him. He bleed enough. He will be fine. I will get David."

With that she rushed out of the back, ran to the barn, and seconds later galloped out on a beautiful cream-colored palomino, riding bareback, without even a bridle. Richard marveled at Sarah's efficiency and spunk and understood fully why David had settled in with her. She was a full-bread Chickahominy who met David when he was an Indian trader for the English before the war. She was a chief's daughter and had admired David for his fair dealings with her father over the years. When David took an interest, the chief was more than willing to give his willing daughter to David along with his blessing and a dowry. But David was then Catholic, and the wedding had never been regularized by a priest, so they had lived together as common law husband and wife ever since.

It was after dusk when Sarah returned. A few minutes later David, also on horseback, arrived. Even with a saddle he could not match her on bareback.

After quietly checking on the priest, the three talked quietly just outside the guest room.

"The only doctor I know of nearby that I would trust is Kalvin Sullivan in Mecklenburg," said David.

Richard nodded. "I know him. I'll ride there first thing in the morning and either bring him back, or some medicine."

"Well, brave men you all are," said a stern-faced Sarah, "This white doctor not have good medicine. I not trust white doctor with battle wounds as these. I think you let me make priest better. I know how. Already prepared is goldenseal paste, but before I will clean his wounds deep with little lye in wine. He will be good. I know how. I not wait for doctor, too late then. I know how. Warm food help, soup, too."

Although they talked in whispers, and Sarah was trying to be quiet, they were suddenly interrupted.

"My horse and mule. I had...I was taking."

They turned in shock at the priest who was trying to sit up and talk. Sarah hurried to his side. "Do you want food, eat, water, wine? You stay in bed, I fix your wounds."

But the priest was too tired, he just shook his head. "There was wine," he whispered before he let his head fall back against the pillow. For a moment he stared up at pretty Sarah, then closed his eyes.

"I'm sure I can locate his horse and mule," said Richard. "Will Canning and his boys have them."

David turned to Richard. "Oh, Richard, you're playing with the king's men. Not good!"

"It's worth a look. The four of them brought a horse and mule directly into town. I saw them after I left your shop. It's dark now. We also have a new moon. It will be plenty dark."

Richard left the McKee's house and by starlight and with Romeo's good night vision, found his way to the edge of Sharpsburg. By stealth Romeo took him slowly to a shallow stand of birch behind the sheriff's office. There, as he suspected, were five horses and a mule. One horse was separated from the others. Packs were still on the mule, although it appeared some unpacking had been done. Lantern light streamed through the rear window of the office by the rear door. There was the muffled laughter of men who had been drinking...the priest's wine no doubt.

Leaving Romeo in the stand of birch and his double-barreled Blair tucked into his belt, he walked quietly behind a shed that was near the hitching post. The last thing he wanted to do was spook the horses, which he was sure to do if he came too close too quickly to the tied up animals, particularly since his scent would not be familiar to them. At first he had no idea which was Cahill's horse. But when he got closer he saw that one of the horses had large saddle bags and a camp pack on the back. The others only had day saddles. The priest's horse and the mule were tied up next to each other at the end of the hitching post nearest him. That made it a little easier.

He was about to get a closer look when the door at the back of the sheriff's office suddenly opened and two men toppled out of the door, clearly drunk. Then a third, and finally Will Canning himself came out and leaned against the back-lit door jamb with what looked like a bottle of wine in his hand.

Richard instantly panicked, worried that he or his steed would be detected. He jumped back behind the shed, held his breath, and then gazed toward the stand of birch to check on Romeo. It was too dark to see. He chanced a look through the shadows of the dim light coming from the open door.

"All right boys," said Will. "Get some rest, see ya tomorrow."

The three unhitched their horses and eventually got into their saddles, although it was a good trick in their inebriated state. "Nice wine tasting party, Will. Thanks for the invite," one of the boys snickered.

"What 'bout the mule, here?" teetered another.

"I'll get to it in a minute. Got paperwork to attend to."

And after a bit more give and take the three boys wandered off with their horses leaving Will to close the door and go back inside. That left Will's horse tied to the building's roof pillar, a good ten feet from the priest's horse and mule tied at a rail attached to the shed.

Richard waited and plotted how he was going to do what came next. With his left hand he opened the flap on his left coat pocket and produced an apple. With his right he grasped his Blair holding it low at his side. Slowly he inched along the shed toward the mule and put the apple under the mule's nose. The animal immediately took the apple and chomped away. This got the horse's attention, a gelding Richard surmised. Untying the mule, Richard was able to step in front and hand an apple to the gelding's greedy and hungry mouth. As the gelding chomped, Richard untied its reins with one hand, keeping his Blair at the ready, one eye on the reins, and the other on the office door. The mule's pack was still open, but nothing seemed to be ready to fall out, so he left it unstrapped.

Slowly Richard led the two beasts back into the darkness and the stand of birch. The gelding seemed more than willing to follow Richard into the unknown.

He was most nervous now, almost shaking, worrying what would happen if Will decided it was time to close up the office and head for home with his horse and the stolen property. Richard prayed under his breath for an angel or something to keep the sheriff occupied for a few moments longer.

Suddenly, the office door opened, and Will appeared in the door holding a lantern.

Richard froze and prayed none of the animals, who were now forty feet or so from the hitching post snorted, stomped, or whinnied.

Will left the office door open, carried the lantern a few steps to the front of the shed that Richard now saw was detached from the office building. Will tried to open the shed's door, but the door was stuck or locked.

"Damn it, com'n," Will said, as he jerked the door handle. But the door wouldn't yield.

Meanwhile the lantern that Will held partly aloft easily illuminated Richard and the rear end of the beasts he held on their reins. Richard held his breath and marveled that Will didn't see that the horse and mule were no longer hitched at the rail but rather with a man dressed in fancy clothes in the middle of the field in plain sight.

Richard was scared and readied the pistol, stepping slightly away from the mule so he might get off a clean shot if Will suddenly spotted him. Or should he run for it, for Will clearly did not have a firearm with him. But Richard was not a fighting man, and if things came to blows, Richard, though a bit younger, was no match for the sheriff.

The stuck door came unstuck, and the lantern entered the door revealing the inside to be a privy. Will closed the door behind him. Richard hoped Will's business would take more than a minute or two. He quickly walked the horse and mule to Romeo who greeted his master with a polite snort, as if to approve of their new company.

Holding tight the reins of the mule and horse, Richard mounted Romeo and ordered him to lead them to safety, further back into the stand of trees. The farther away they got, the harder they would be able to be spotted if Will should come looking. Richard hoped no lantern would be bright enough to reveal their presence.

But Will did not come out any time soon, and after moving back into the wild a few hundred feet, Richard stopped to secure the mule and horse's reins to either side of his saddle and let Romeo with his better eyesight get them back to the trail that would return them to the McKees.

Richard, however, was not out of the woods, figuratively or literally. For now, he worried what he was going to do when he got back to the McKees'. Their house wasn't far enough away that come morning the sheriff would get together his boys, fan out, and find them.

By the time he and Romeo found their way back to the McKee's, Richard's anxiety surfaced in short breaths and a shaky rein. He still didn't know what to do. Something told him he had to get the animals out of the vicinity by morning, but where? Especially since now he was convinced they belonged to the priest. But where was the priest headed?

As soon as he returned with the goods from his first experience as a thief, although a *just* one, David congratulated him, told him that the priest was still asleep, and that good Sarah was keeping an eye on him.

David suggested they put the animals in the barn where they could be out of sight, fed and watered, and even get some sleep if that was needed. So, that's what they did, lighting a few lanterns in the barn when they got there.

"Did the priest wake up long enough to tell you anything about where he was headed or where he was from?" asked Richard.

"No, nothing," said David. Gesturing to the saddle bagged horse and pack mule, "Is this all his?"

"I'm pretty sure, less some bottles of wine that I suspect you'll find in the sheriff's office. Let's get them unburdened."

Richard and David removed the saddle, bags, and packs, and led the animals to a trough and bail of hay. The animals took right to it; they were hungry after their ordeal.

"Shall we see what's in the packs?" asked David. "Might give us a clue."

"Yes, let's. I think there must've been wine in this pack. It was open when I got there, and Will and his boys were pretty drunk on it." Richard went on to explain what had happened and how he retrieved the animals.

Richard unstrapped the partially empty pack and looked inside. He pulled out a bottle of Madeira wine from Portugal wrapped in familiar paper. David reached in and unwrapped a bottle of sherry from Spain. "David, these are two of my favorites. How is that possible?"

"Well, they are the favorites of many, Richard. Don't be so sure God likes you *that* much."

But Richard didn't hear what David had said; he was folding and unfolding the paper packing material. It looked very familiar.

Meanwhile, David moved to the second pack that was sitting in the straw. He opened it, and started to remove one item after another: "A bag of sugar from Antigua, licorice from Greece, cinnamon from India, German chocolates, and here's an odd thing: what is this?"

Richard was still mesmerized by the packing paper, and now a rush of *déjà vu* took hold. He came over to where David held a box with foreign writing on it. David had opened it up and taken a whiff as if it were another food item. "Ugh, it's powder...smells disgusting," said David. "What do you suppose this is?" He handed it to Richard.

Richard took the smallish box, gazed at it, and the other items and...and suddenly began to weep. It was but a moment later that he collapsed to his knees on the floor and sobbed uncontrollably.

David was more than bewildered.

While Richard was kneeling on the floor unable to speak or even see through his tears, Sarah came running into the barn with an astonished look on her face. "David! David!" she yelled. But when she saw Richard in his fine clothes crumbled on the straw floor, sobbing, she stopped. "What happened?"

David shrugged. He didn't know.

Richard was closing the box of white powder with the strange lettering on the side. "It's from Poland. It's from Poland," he kept saying while gasping for breath between sobs.

"What is?" David said.

"Starch. It's starch from Poland!" Richard exclaimed.

Sarah and David just stared at each other. They had never seen such a sight. A man crying over starch.

Finally, Richard rose to his feet, handed the box of starch to Sarah, and stumbled to the saddle bags he had removed from the horse and placed over a pen railing. He opened one side of the bag and looked through it, but not finding what he wanted, he turned the bag around, and opened the other side. There, he pulled out a piece of paper, unfolded it, and studied it but a second before he began to sob again. This time with spasms of screams that were seemingly uncontrolled, all the while waving the paper in the air like a flag of surrender, a frantic flag of surrender, and falling to his knees again in tears and great sobs.

Sarah took the paper from him, glanced at it, but because she didn't read so well, gave it to David. David held the paper, turned it around to read it right side up, and immediately began to tremble. To Sarah he explained, "This is a piece of paper from McSherry's Hardware and Lumber. That's Richard's brother, William's establishment in Baltimore. I buy goods from him. I know him. This is his handwriting. And his is a map and directions to the residence of Richard McSherry...in Leetown."

"That's what I just found out," said Sarah. "The priest is talking. His name is Denis Cahill, and he's on his way to find Richard McSherry."

And with that Richard got to his feet, bounded out of the barn, and ran to the house.

David gazed at the unwrapped goods they had taken from the pack. He took Sarah in his arms, hugged her, and said, "God sure does work in strange ways."

3

Since settling in the United States, Richard McSherry had prayed for a priest to serve in the towns and villages where he had invested in farms and speculated on land. That Fr. Cahill was from Ireland, which Richard sorely missed, was a bonus.

After two days of healing in the McKee household, Fr. Cahill was ready to travel again. In the dead of night, with Richard riding Romeo, and Fr. Cahill on Sassafras with Ebenezer carrying what remained of the supplies, the two stole off for Mecklenburg and Thomas Shepherd's Packhorse Ford. They had chosen a crescent moonlit night, crossed the Potowmack after midnight, and arrived safely an hour later at the Virginian estate of *Gabriel Menghini and his wife Ruth. Gabriel ran a tavern and boarding house in Mecklenburg, and while he had not expected Richard to arrive in the middle of the night, he was glad to see his good friend and especially a Catholic priest in tow.

The next morning was Saturday. Richard rose early, saddled Romeo, and spent the day canvasing the homes and families in the area. That evening, David and Sarah McKee arrived, and with the Menghinis, Richard, and a few close friends they celebrated Fr. Cahill's rescue and recovery—although it was far from complete. By the roaring fireplace the group reveled in Fr. Cahill's stories of the New Orleans fire, storms in the Gulf of Mexico, the burial at sea, the run-in with pirates, William McSherry's outfitting of Fr. Cahill, the impromptu funeral Mass near Wye Creek, the Sharpsburg attempt on Fr. Cahill's life, Richard's rescue of Fr. Cahill, stealing back his horse and mule, their speculation of bringing Sheriff Canning to justice, and the party's expectation of the next day, Sunday; it was to be a historic day for Mecklenburg.

On Sunday morning, November 16, 1788, buggies and saddled horses started to arrive ferrying families dressed in their Sunday best. They brought pots of food and wine with them, and the men re-arranged furniture in the gathering hall. They put a table near the fireplace, which Ruth covered with an ironed white linen cloth and six candle sticks. Scattered about the room facing the table were the Menghinis' collection of fine-turned chairs from Europe and a few local craftsmen. When Sarah came down the grand staircase from their guest room, everyone greeted her with compliments on her Chickahominy themed dress, wondering where she bought it. She was polite but finally had to explain that her Chickahominy mother had made it from deer hide, many moons ago. They were quiet after that. She just smiled; it was an important dress for an important day, the day her marriage to David would be regularized by the Church. It would be the first ever Catholic Mass to be celebrated in Mecklenburg, Virginia, and the first regular Mass celebrated by Fr. Cahill in the United States, if he didn't count those on board the Eagle, or the impromptu funeral Mass near Wye Creek.

The happy and romantic exchange of David's and Sara's vows in the middle of Mass went smoothly. After Mass the families shared the food they had brought and talked excitedly about the future. If Fr. Cahill agreed with Richard's plan to establish a circuit of societies in the area, the group vowed to establish a regular society in Mecklenburg. Fr. Cahill would come once a month and celebrate Mass. This was quickly fulfilling Richard's dream.

For some reason that Richard had never understood, the local Catholics disliked the name of their town, Mecklenburg. They had already met and had petitioned the state to change the town's name to Shepherd's Town, not only in honor of the town's founder, but also because the name had Christian significance. So it was that the Shepherd's Town Catholic Society, which met in the Menghinis' gathering hall, was founded, long before there was a Shepherd's Town.

4

My Despised Cyn:

Damn it. Who knew Richard McSherry was hiding under that towel? All your plans and our hopes dashed. Even the supplies lost, except a couple bottles of whatever Canning and his goons were drowning their glee in. Why could Will not see Richard and the ass in plain sight? Could you not prompt him to open his eyes instead of the privy door? Did you see the enemy about? I did not. It is not fair that we cannot see what we should. We are too easily blinded by pride.

Now, we need to plan. Things are getting away from us. McSherry's Retirement is but a few miles from Livingston's new farm. They will undoubtedly meet unless we can seriously distract one or the other. Prayers of the enemy are being answered, and we can't hear them or discern the path they take. It is most disturbing.

Even the work of a distant peer on David McKee and his Indian wife has been undone. We thought it good they were unmarried, and David had fallen into fornication. A lot of good that work did us. Now, fully restored.

But there are other things we must attend. Your effort to elicit lust in Nwanne is beginning to pay dividends. Have you noticed his distraction of late? If not, drift over to Livingston's and see for yourself. Perhaps there's a way to capitalize on human frailty.

Eternally yours,
Master of Wretched

Chapter 17
Much To Do

1

Nwanne Dark was mostly fulfilled in his new life. He felt energized and alive as he worked alongside Sam and Adam. They were building a simple log cabin with three rooms and two lofts, but to him it felt like a mansion. He would share the cabin with his brother and wife. When he was a slave at McCullough's plantation, he shared a cabin with eighteen others; and he shared a room with nine men. There was no privacy. Now he would have a room of his own. At McCullough's there were few decisions he could make for himself, including going to toilet. There he felt subhuman, like a dog on a leash. Now he would be his own person.

By the end of the second week in December they had the cabin closed-in with chinking, windows, doors, and a roof. He and Sam smiled with satisfaction. Walking into the small building gave them a sense of security and accomplishment. At McCullough's he would stack firewood for the main house where the family and supervisors lived, but as slaves they were not allowed to stack more than a few logs for their own small fireplaces. There he was not motivated, except by fear, to find wood for McCullough. But now, finding and stacking dried wood for their fireplaces was an exciting and freeing affair.

All the while Nwanne longed for what his brother had, a loving female companion—a wife. When he was enslaved and treated harshly, there were moments when he shared his hard life with a young woman he was sure he loved. Her name was Annenew (Ann-NEW). He knew very little about Annenew's past. Separate quarters for males and females, though some were married, made life difficult. The journey from McCullough's farm to the Livingstons' was bittersweet. Sweet because it meant freedom, although he didn't realize that at first. Bitter because he was separated from Annenew's smile and occasional friendship. The day after his arrival on Livingston's farm his attention was increasingly drawn to the Opequon Creek; Annenew lived just the other side. He felt a surge of hope because the chance of seeing her was no longer remote. In his free time, he was able to wander about, which always took him to the creek's bank. He would gaze across in hope that he would see friends or even Annenew. It was unusual that McCullough's slaves were able to steal away to the creek to take a break from field work or to bathe. So, he rarely saw any sign of life; and now that it was December and the harvest was in, the chances were less. His walks along the creek turned into times of sadness and disappointment. He told this to Sam, but Sam thought he was nuts. Sam would remind him: *better to be free and absent in love, than to be in love and absent in freedom.* Nwanne thought about talking to Mister Livingston about Annenew but dared not involve his new owner, who had paid a hefty price for his freedom. Sam's focus was on getting them a home of their own. Living with Adam and his children in their small temporary cabin was becoming difficult for all.

The day came when Mister Livingston performed a thorough inspection of the cabin. He showed Nwanne, Sam, and Bethany how to seal up small gaps in the construction to prevent cold air from leaking into their living quarters. They darkened the cabin and looked for daylight that sneaked inside through visible gaps and cracks, and he demonstrated with a candle flame where cold air could sneak in through invisible gaps and leaks. Most were around windows and door jams. He then showed them how to fill the gaps, cracks, and stop the leaks with thinned chinking, wood scraps, gobs of warm wax, and thin strips of felt...all to keep the cabin warm. Both Nwanne and Sam were impressed with Mister Livingston's concern for their comfort and health since none of their previous owners ever made such an effort. The four adults worked hard for most of the day sealing the cabin. They finished late afternoon, after which Nwanne and Sam built the first fires in the three fireplaces. The cabin warmed quickly, and that evening the Darks moved in, along with a few pieces of furniture they had collected.

By the end of the next day, Nwanne saw to it that the woodshed, attached to the back of the cabin and closed off from the weather, was filled with wood for winter burning. But there was still dry wood that was cut and split. So, with the wagon he and Sam brought a large load and stacked firewood under the front porch roof, leaving space for light to enter their bedroom windows. They now had plenty of firewood to keep the cabin warm and for cooking during the winter.

Relationships between Adam and the Darks had been a bit tense because of their close living arrangements, but after the Darks moved into their new quarters, rapport became congenial again. Bethany still did most of her cooking with Eve in the main cabin where Adam and his children lived, but she cooked enough food for herself, Sam and Nwanne, and used the fireplace in the new cabin to reheat the food. As time passed, Nwanne noticed that Bethany kept more and more food in their cabin so as not to bother the Livingstons.

One evening, as Nwanne again wandered along the creek, he caught sight of a young teen slave boy he knew from McCullough's. Cecil was dipping a pail into the creek and preparing to carry it off. A muscular and reliant lad, Cecil was wearing traditional canvas pants, a pull over sweater, and a cap. Years earlier he had been separated from his mother by a "bill of sale." Cecil worked during the day for the McCullough supervisors. When evening came, he helped an old woman he called Granny, although not his grandmother. She was too old to work or even carry a bucket of water, and was considered a burden by McCullough. The slaves saw to it that she was cared for.

Excited to see life on the other side of the creek, Nwanne called out, "Cecil!" At first the boy jumped from shock as if he had been found out by a field boss and was about to be whipped. But Nwanne called out again, in a loud whisper, "Cecil, it is Nwanne! Over here!" The boy jerked around, looking for the voice. Nwanne, feeling hopeful once again, moved to a place directly across the creek when the boy suddenly saw him.

"Bro'her!" the boy replied in shock. "You'd be gone. What'ca doing dere? Tryin' ta come back?"

Evidently Nwanne's peers didn't know that he had been sold to the farm just southeast of the creek. Usually, when a slave was sold he or she was taken far away never to be seen again. "No! No! Dis de place I sold to, 'cept everythin' better now."

Cecil stared at Nwanne a moment, though still holding the bucket of water at his side. "You's different. New clothes, 'n that hat, brand new."

Nwanne indeed had a new wide brim felt hat that kept the sun off and the warmth in. "Yes, de hat and clothes are from Missta Livingston. He nice man and his children good, too." Nwanne was smiling broadly and was very happy to have found Cecil, for he knew that Cecil knew Annenew. "Cecil! How's yer granny?"

"What you's mean? You know she old. Dat why I fetch her water in dis leaky tin."

"Tell her I remember her and hope her comfort," said Nwanne.

"You's want come back? Your masta treating yous bad? Don't look like it," said Cecil.

"Oh, no, no. Everythin' good, good. You's know Annenew, you's tell her you's saw me…here?"

"Oh, yes. I tell her. She cry some, since yous gone."

Nwanne lost his smile. "Tell her I want to sees her. Maybe she comes to creek with you's to get water?"

Cecil didn't say anything. He looked down at the bucket that had leaked a good portion of the water as he stood there talking to Nwanne.

"Tell her I'm manumitted. Free. My brother Sam is here wid his wife, and we builds nice cabin in wid we live. Three fireplaces, it warm, and we have much food is we want. Will you tell Annenew that? Tell her, I love her." As Nwanne spoke tears welled up and drained from his eyes, and his heart beat harder. "You go Cecil before yous missed. Yous do not want to get whipped for being gone too long."

"What is manumitted?" Cecil said.

"I am no more slave. I free."

"But you are there. Does your owner work you? Why are you there?" asked Cecil.

"Yes, I work here. But I am no beaten or whipped. I am paid money and live with my bro'her and his wife. It much different. It good. Missta Livingston who bought me, freed me. I work for him now. He good to me."

Cecil gazed at Nwanne but said nothing. He didn't seem to understand. Finally, he said, "I must go, Granny worry. I tell Annenew for you." With that Cecil leaned into the creek, filled the bucket once again, looked back in alarm at Nwanne and ran off into the field beyond.

Nwanne was euphoric. He might see Annenew again. But then he felt sad, for he didn't arrange for Cecil to bring Annenew to the creek, and he didn't know when Cecil might return. Without thinking he found himself searching the far side of the creek bank, up and down the creek, looking for a supervisor or any other person who might have seen or heard their exchange. Seeing no one he made his way back to the cabin but could not stop glancing back toward the creek and the spot along the bank he and Cecil had talked. He would return to that same spot often, he decided.

That night Bethany served up a warm meal of biscuits and rabbit stew as Nwanne excitedly told Sam and Bethany about his meeting with Cecil. Bethany was happy about the encounter, but Sam turned sullen, and shook his head. Sam explained that he understood Nwanne wanted to see Annenew, but worried about McCullough finding out that Nwanne had been manumitted. It could bring beatings for the slaves McCullough still owned. Sam explained, "From wad you tell me 'bout McCullough and de supers, if dey think their slaves know you manumitted, they whip you's friends just so dey not think of bein' free."

Nwanne turned sullen, his eyes cast down. He didn't have an answer, and now he worried for Cecil and Annenew.

Over the coming week, Nwanne drifted daily by the "visitation spot" as he called it, where he had met Cecil. But he never saw Cecil or Annenew or any other slaves. One day, however, he saw two McCullough supervisors scouring the far creek bank, one hitting the bushes with his musket and another with a couple of hounds straining on long leashes. Nwanne figured they were looking for a slave that was at the creek without permission. Fearful that he'd be seen and taken for an escaped slave, Nwanne hid by sliding slowly into the shrubs and laying low. As the men came closer and directly across the creek from where Nwanne hid, he recognized one of the men, Dean Boy, an especially malevolent supervisor who had whipped Nwanne on one occasion. Not wanting to aggravate the man which could be carried back to Annenew, Nwanne kept hidden until the men and dogs were out of sight, and then he hustled back to his cabin.

The next morning Sam and Nwanne took the wagon to Charles Town for supplies. Adam had established an account with several merchants in Charles Town where Sam was known to work on the Livingston farm. By early afternoon, Sam and Nwanne had returned with a wagon full of materials and were unloading the bulk of them into their new cabin, as the smaller cabin, that Adam and the children occupied, was already packed tight. As Nwanne and Sam unloaded supplies, Bethany and Eve were cooking in the smaller cabin and Adam and Henry were mucking out the small stable.

Nwanne noticed right away when three men rode onto the property and up to the Livingston cabin. Although it was 800 feet from the Darks' cabin, he could see clearly who the men were. The man on the largest of the animals wore a distinctive brown corduroy coat and black hat with red trim. Nwanne's blood ran cold and his pulse quickened. His first instinct was to run, but he stood his ground. Bethany appeared at the door with Eve at her side. Eve spoke first and pointed to the stable. Without dismounting, the three men steered their steeds to the stable where Adam made an appearance.

"Who ya suppose dat is?" said Sam.

Nwanne had just heaved a 50-pound bag of flour onto his shoulder. "Dat der, in the black hat and red ribbon is Missta Gregory McCullough, my former masta, and two his supers. Dey one with dey dirty white hat dey calls Dean Boy. A bad man." Nwanne suddenly felt weak, as if his legs were to collapse under him as the fifty-pound sack of flour suddenly became heavier. He still feared those men, as if he was still their slave, or was about to be again. He looked to Sam, who was staring at the men. "Ya suppose dis has anything ta do with what ya told dat Cecil fellow the other day?"

"Dat's what I'm wonderin'," said Nwanne. But Nwanne was beyond wonder. He was shaking, scared that his freedom was about to come to an end, as if there was some mistake in the bill of sale. Something bad was happening for sure, especially with the way Mister Livingston was standing and gesturing and the way he was keeping his Henry behind him. Then Nwanne saw Mister Livingston look toward and gesture at him and Sam. The three men on horseback turned in their saddles and looked their way and at their cabin.

"Best we stay busy," said Sam.

"Good idea," said Nwanne as he carried the 50-pound sack of flour into the cabin.

2

With a shovel firmly in hand, Adam stood his ground and kept Henry behind him. Gregory McCullough and his two hands were in an impatient mood; they had not come in peace. That they were armed with muskets and pistols was all he needed to be on his guard. Adam shot back, "It doesn't seem to be any of your business, neighbor."

"It does when it affects my production," said McCullough leaning forward in his saddle as if to get in Adam's face. "You've violated a sacred oath, Livingston, that this here state of Virginia and all its landowners and planters have striven to abide by long before you made your appearance, and I won't have it. Just how many slaves you have here? I sold you one, but I've seen three already."

"I tell you I own no slaves and never will," said Adam.

"Then how many darks you got?"

"None of your business, as I said before." Adam didn't trust McCullough, or his hands, and he wished he wasn't standing his ground holding just a shovel; he'd left his shillelagh in the cabin. But he was going to let them know what he thought was right. He glanced at McCullough's two sidekicks, who were staring back at the Darks' cabin and exchanging looks. Adam's anger was rising. "That's their cabin, built it themselves, and they can cook what they want, and eat what they want, and come and go as they want. They're freemen. I'm even paying them a wage. I'd like to know what you're gonna do about that." It wasn't a question.

"We've got a plantation to run," snapped McCullough, "and when you think you can manumit your slaves and not affect the well-being of my operation, it's everything to me. My slaves are on the verge of rebellion because of you, and now they're all demanding I do the same. Well, hell if I will. I about wore out one of my hands here," he gestured to the man in the white hat "whipping them back into place. They keep at it and they'll be dead, lazy bastards."

Adam raised the shovel across his chest, a weak threat, but one nonetheless. "Get off my land, McCullough. You're in no position to judge any man or your slaves and certainly not me." Adam considered pulling the man off his horse and beating him bloody. He was beginning to regret ever coming to Virginia.

"I'd advise you neighbor," said McCullough, "not to register that manumission, if you know what's good for you."

"God damn, you, McCullough. I already have, and if I could, I would manumit every one of your slaves."

McCullough was more than angry now. "You'll be sorry, Livingston, and I'll see to it. C'mon fellas, this place is damned, if you ask me."

And with that McCullough and his supervisors rode off in a gallop of spite... and that's when it happened, again. Adam was staring at the hind end of the three horses galloping off when the premonition struck. Fire! A blazing inferno, the same image he had experienced weeks before at McCullough's. This time the vision was silent, no screaming woman, but it was clear, and it lasted as long as the departing McCulloughs were visible. As soon as their horses disappeared behind the trees marking the entrance to his property, the inferno dissipated. Adam wasn't sure how long he froze to the spot staring after the men. Henry didn't seem to notice, but Adam took firm notice.

"Sure glad they left, Papa. I don't much like them."

Adam handed the shovel to Henry. "Son, put this back in the stable, I'm going to talk to Sam and Nwanne."

Henry did as he was told and caught up with his father. "Can I come, Pa?"

"Yes!" said Adam. "Best you know what's happening around this God forsaken place."

The veins in Adam's neck were bulging and his pace quickened as he marched across the yard. Correlating the two visions with McCullough and Nwanne was easy, but the implications were hardly obvious. Something was warning him that danger was near. He had to get to the bottom of what was happening, although to those around him what was happening was nothing unusual. When he arrived at the Darks' cabin the wagon was nearly empty and Sam and Nwanne came attentively to Adam as he approached. He knew they had seen the confrontation.

But before Adam could speak, Nwanne jumped in: "Missta Livingston, sir, I sorry for any problem I caused, please don't send me back to that man. I'll work twice as hard, I will." Adam tried to speak but Nwanne was on a nervous tear, and it was confession time. "I had jist wanted to tell my freedom to my woman friend, Annenew. At the creek I met a youngin boy I know, Cecil. I told him to tell Annenew that I had been manumitted."

Adam gazed at Nwanne for a moment and then shook his head. "Well, that does explain something. But that ain't it. Did you hear what Gregory McCullough was saying to me?"

"No, sir," interjected Sam. "Ma bro'her has a guilty conscience, fo no reason I knows."

Adam waved off the chatter. "Just so you both know, once and for all. I'm not going to un-manumit either of you, even if I could do such a thing. And I don't think I can. And I am not angry with either of you, nor with you Nwanne for whatever you told whomever. Though it is true, Gregory McCullough is upset that I've manumitted you. He reckoned he was selling you to another slave owner. I never told him otherwise, and you both know that is not what I am, nor will I ever be. I detest slavery. But McCullough found out about your manumission, or rather his boys found out...most likely from the merchants in Charles Town where you both trade for me. Evidently, you showed Mister Riser at the general store your manumission papers. Have you had any problems in Charles Town that I should know about? Has anyone questioned your manumission, your freedom?"

Sam and Nwanne glanced at each other and shook their heads.

"No, sir. None of dat," said Sam. "Everyone dey been respectful to us and I don't think Nwanne has ever been asked to see his manumission, have you?"

"No," said Nwanne, "now you mention it; how do they even know I free?"

"Because you're wid me," said Sam. "We look alike, and they've seen my papers before."

Adam knew this was probably true. Adam looked down at his son who was looking up and following with keen interest. "Well! Here is what we have to deal with. McCullough, and his two hands, whoever they are..."

"One, the dirty white hat one, is called Dean Boy—a bad man," said Nwanne.

At this Nwanne flinched and tears flowed into his big eyes. He turned away from Sam and Adam as if not wanting them to see him cry.

Adam put out a hand and gripped Nwanne's shoulder, "I understand. I'm sorry. But you should know what he said to me." Adam paused for a moment. "McCullough said he was going to get even for my disrupting his operation by manumitting both of you, and probably Bethany, too. We have to be watchful."

Adam was hoping McCullough's thugs would just calm down and forget it all. That's what grown-ups would do; but of course, gaining in years doesn't mean one gains in wisdom; there are a lot of old fools in the world. "Look," Adam said with some disappointment, "if either of you need to go into town, make sure I'm with you. Don't leave the property alone. That's not an order. You're free to go, but I'm just saying, my presence could mean your safety. Something tells me we have to be extra vigilant."

Sam and Nwanne looked to each other and nodded agreement with Adam. "We need to warn Bethany, too" said Sam.

"And Eve," said Adam.

Henry had been quiet, but now it was his turn: "Nah, you don't have to worry about Eve. No one's going to hurt her without getting hurt back. I know."

At that the grown men laughed, and Adam put his arm around his son and gave him a man hug. But as Adam left with Henry, he turned back and gazed at the Darks' cabin for a long time and the logs stacked on the front porch. He wasn't sure why he did that, but there was something nagging at him. He felt danger close at hand but could not see it.

3

A few days later Adam, Nwanne, and Sam made a trip to Charles Town for supplies. While Sam loaded up the wagon, Adam dropped by the tavern to see if his father had written back since his first letter sent from Martinsburg. Indeed, there was a letter from his father and another that he was not expecting. He ordered a brew and sat down at a table to read both. His father's letter expressed deep condolences for the problem with the deed and the strange case of the thirty-five acres that Adam had to resurvey and pay a fee. As he opened the second letter the tavern proprietor set a mug of brew in front of him, but Adam never touched it. The letter was from George Eshelman. He wanted to know if Adam happened to find fourteen gold double-doubloons in the false bottom of the satchel George had given to Adam when they closed the deal on the Pennsylvania property.

Guilty as charged, Adam thought. He had been found out. Or had he? He flapped the letter back and forth in his hand, nervous, not knowing what to do with it. He could just ignore it and pretend he never got the letter. How did George even know to send it to Charles Town and not somewhere else? His breathing intensified. He was in the habit of making friendly eye contact with anyone walking close to his table. But now he found himself wishing he was invisible. He had the sense that if anyone looked at him they would know the contents of the letter he was flapping in his hand. He stopped the letter from flapping. He didn't look around and meet the glances of others, but he was sure everyone was staring at him—*we the jury have reached a verdict your honor.* How had he been found out?

Ignoring the mug, he walked to a corner secretary desk where writing paper, quills, ink, a blotter, and sealing wax were available. Sitting down he took paper and quill and wrote a letter.

George Eshelman
Manchester Township
York County, Pennsylvania.

My Dear George.

How good it is to hear from you, now that we are settling here in Virginia. Thank you for asking about our care. We are doing fine. We have obtained the land I told you about, hired help, and are looking forward to the livestock auction in Mecklenburg, soon.

Adam pauses to consider this next pen strokes.

I am so sorry to hear that you have misplaced the gold coin you had been saving for such a time as you are now facing. No, I do not have it. The amount we agreed on for my property, now yours, was exactly what was included in the satchel.

Another long pause. *Should he say more?*
No.

Sincerely,
Adam Livingston.

Adam folded and sealed the letter, addressed it, took a pence from his pocket and handed both to the tavern proprietor, and quickly took his leave.

4

It was a week before Christmas in the middle of the night. A light snow had fallen, and the Livingstons and the Darks were in their cabins asleep. Well, that wasn't entirely true. Adam was experiencing a recurring nightmare: A whirlwind was blowing his teamless, covered wagon across the prairie at a dangerous speed. His children were aboard screaming for help. Helpless and frantic, he ran yards behind the runaway wagon desperately trying to catch it and save his children. In bed, his body was jerking and sweating something fierce as he sprinted in his sleep. The noise of Adam thrashing woke Eve. In the soft glow of the fireplace embers she watched Papa's contorting body. All she could do was pray, for she feared waking him.

In the Darks' cabin it was Nwanne who was unable to sleep. He too was dreaming, but it was a pleasant dream. When he was a slave under McCullough, he had longed to taste the pig barbecues that he smelled roasting on a spit over the supervisor's fire Saturday evenings after the harvest. That is what he was enjoying in his sleep, a sweet dream it was of the luscious taste of ham and bacon.

But it seemed to him that the supervisors were roasting their pig a bit too much, for what he smelled no longer made him salivate, but rather cringe at the bitter taste in his mouth. It occurred to him that they had forgotten the pig and were simply enjoying the fire without the meat, or instead they had a wet pine log in the spit. What a waste he thought. He inhaled once again hoping this time to smell the sweet fat of the animal which would no doubt lull him back to sleep. But this time, there was a harsh stinging in his nostrils and lungs, like a sharp knife dragged through his nose and down his throat.

When he opened his eyes expecting darkness, what he saw instead was a roasting pit with an out-of-control blazing fire just outside his bedroom window. Every time he took a breath, he came more fully awake with a burning in his lungs. Finally, he realized that this was no barbecue unless he was the pig on the spit.

The cabin was ablaze, or at least the pile of dry wood stacked on the front porch. He stumbled out of bed, stood up, breathed, and crashed to the floor. He had to escape, but his limbs were shaking, and his breath was raw. Keeping below the layer of smoke, he frantically crawled out of his bedroom, into the gathering hall, and banged on the door to Sam and Bethany's room, slamming it open. Sam jumped up from bed in fright.

"FIRE!" screamed Nwanne as best he could, his throat still raw. "Front porch! Down! Stay down! Smoke!"

Indeed, smoke was circling the ceiling inside the bedroom, which Nwanne could not understand if the fire was outside. But then he noticed that the windows in the front of the house had been broken, and the fire had already spread; the shake roof above them was ablaze.

Nwanne crawled to the front door, but when he went to grab the latch it was so hot he let go. He could hardly speak, the smoke was so thick it stung his eyes. Nwanne crawled to the rear door that led to the walk-through woodshed. Right behind him, Sam dragged Bethany by her night clothes. Warm cinders glowed in the hall fireplace waiting to be awoken for breakfast coffee. Nwanne reached for the rear door handle. It was cold. He opened it. Darkness. He crawled to the exterior door. That latch was cold as well. He opened the door. Cold air blasted him. As he looked out, it was dark, except for the reflected light from the fire on the front porch that illuminated the snow on the trees and ground. Shoving the door all the way open, he tumbled to the ground behind the house. Sam and Bethany followed. The three scrambled to their feet and gasped air repeatedly until their lungs were clear. In their bare feet on the light snow they ran to the front of the cabin.

The entire front porch and roof were engulfed in flames, and the green timbers of the logs that made up the cabin's front wall sizzled with steam. The buckets they used to carry water were inside the cabin, and the well-bucket was in the repaired well hundreds of feet away, too far and too small to do any good against the roaring blaze. All they could do was look around them and see if anything else was in danger of catching fire.

Nwanne was devastated, yet wanting desperately to do something.

"Go to Missta Livingston, Nwanne," yelled Sam.

Bethany hung onto Sam with all her strength as Nwanne ran off to the Livingston cabin in his bare feet over the snow. He had no more run onto the cabin's small porch than Adam threw the door open and ran outside in his bed clothes He looked startled at the Darks' cabin going up in flames and then to Nwanne, "Sam, Bethany?"

"Out. Safe," said Nwanne.

Eve and Henry stumbled out onto the small porch and looked at the inferno to their southeast. "What happened?!" Eve cried.

"Your clothes?" Adam looked at Nwanne.

Nwanne just shook his head and gestured at the cabin.

Adam ran back inside, stepped into his boots that were by the door, and took off running as best he could to the fire.

When he got there, there was nothing anyone could do.

"Sam, Nwanne come with me," yelled Adam as he ran to the back of the house. The fire had not yet spread to the rear. "What can we get out through the rear door?"

"By da hearth," said Bethany, "There's a bag of flour."

"Open the door and let the smoke pour out," said Adam.

Sam opened the door, and the smoke poured out. A moment later Nwanne ran in, keeping low. He could see from the light of the fire in front and above in the roof. He looked about quickly. He might have only one chance to grab anything and get out. There was the fifty-pound bag of flour that had been only slightly used. *Bethany could use that*, he thought. He closed the top as best he could and heaved it up to his shoulders. But as soon as he did, he could feel the flour pouring out of the opening he had not fully secured and dumping onto the floor behind him. He turned around to see how much had fallen out. But his twisting only caused the flour to spill in a torrent, which raised a massive cloud of flour dust into the air. The fringe of the dust cloud caught the edge of a flame. Suddenly there was a loud noise, a blinding flash, and everything went white.

5

Sam had not felt good about his brother running into the burning building, but there was little he could do. Nwanne had been in the cabin only a moment when suddenly a brutal and blinding white explosion blew out the back wall out of the cabin and knocked Sam, Bethany, Adam, and the children to the ground. The blast was so massive it blew out most of the fire that had raged across the roof, and the cabin's front. There were still flames on the perimeters, but the inferno was suddenly gone, leaving behind smoking timbers and debris.

Sam was first to his feet after the blast. Seeing that the back wall was blown apart at the door, and that the flames were mostly out, he rushed in to tend to Nwanne. But when Sam found Nwanne there was nothing to tend to. Nwanne was slumped against the back wall as if a gigantic hammer had pounded him flat. His clothes on the top half of his body were burned off, and the skin from his head to his waist was charred black. Blood dripped from his mouth, eyes, and nose, and his arms were bent backwards. Sam was so shocked by what he saw he could hardly breathe. "NWANNE!" he cried and collapsed on the floor next to Nwanne's lifeless body.

Adam came in, saw Sam on his knees, and thinking something was wrong grabbed him by the shoulders. But Sam was sobbing. Then Adam saw Nwanne's body contorted and bloodied against the wall. Adam screamed: "NO!" But no amount of screaming or crying was going to bring Nwanne back.

After some time, Adam pulled Sam to his feet, "Let's get out of here, Sam. C'mon."

The two men stumbled outside to Bethany and the children. Sam was fully in tears as he embraced Bethany.

That's when Bethany screamed.

6

Adam stumbled out of the burned cabin pushing Sam in front of him. He felt numb believing he had condemned Nwanne to death for suggesting they try to get out what they could.

That's when Bethany screamed.

Adam stopped cold and glared at Bethany as if she had just emerged from the pit of hell. Sam had her enveloped in his arms. The scream! It was the scream he had heard during the premonition at McCullough's. The realization was brutal. He stopped breathing and turned sharply to the cabin—the inferno. It was the inferno in his vision. McCullough! Nwanne! His whole body shook. He stumbled back, so severe was the shock. Eve came to him and hugged him. She too was crying. But Adam was scared to hell. He had foreseen all of this. Weeks earlier. It was a warning. Yet he had done nothing.

Adam directed the group back to the small cabin where they spent the rest of the night, but none of them slept. Adam built a strong hearth fire, Bethany baked rolls and brewed coffee, and Adam broke open a bottle of Madeira wine.

Late in the morning after the sun broke through the dreary clouds, Adam directed Bethany and the children to stay in the cabin and not come near the Darks' cabin. Adam gave Sam a pair of socks and a pair of leather overboots to wear, as well as a sweater and overalls.

As yet, Adam did not have a burial plot on his land, but now there was a need. Further, Sam wanted to make a strong coffin for his brother. Adam readily agreed. There was lumber left over from planking the Darks' cabin, so Adam directed Sam to do his best with the supplies they had. Meanwhile, Adam reconnoitered the property and decided the best place for a family plot was atop the hill into which he had decided to build his home and the barn. When Adam showed Sam the spot, Sam broke down in tears. For here was a white man who had just agreed to bury an African in his family plot, as if he were a loved one.

Adam and Sam took shovels, dug a deep grave on top the hill, and with a blanket dragged Nwanne's corpse to the hole next to where Sam had placed the new coffin. They put Nwanne's charred body in the box. Sam nailed it shut, and they lowered it into the hole. Adam steeled his nerves and wanted to get the burial business over with in short order. But Sam wanted to be religious and pray over the body before they covered it. Adam could hardly object. Afterwards, Sam constructed a wooden cross from broken branches and stuck it in a cairn of rocks over the grave.

On the way back to the burned-out cabin, Adam's mind turned to justice. "Sam, did you see or hear anything last night that might lead us to what started the fire?"

Sam didn't answer right away, but Adam saw that he was thinking over events or replaying a dream. "I'm been thinking it was t' McCulloughs, like you Missta Livingston. But I remember nothing until Nwanne slammed open our door 'n woke us. Sure glad he did, but dis is a hard day, Missta Livingston. I don't know how I'm gonna get through it."

"If the McCulloughs did this," said Adam, "they would have left tracks in the snow, I'm thinking. Help me look out front and around the grounds."

But when the men examined the grounds around the cabin where heat had not melted the snow, all the way out to the road, they found the snow so thick that any tracks that might have been there were now covered by new snow.

A good deal of the cabin's interior and exterior walls were still in tact, by virtue of the explosion and the green logs. But the front porch, the roof over it, and the dry wood that had been stacked on the porch were gone; only ash remained. Traipsing through the debris, however, did reveal that metal objects like cooking pots, hardware, and some clothes were salvageable. Sam found his boots. Bethany's were scorched, but still usable. Between them, they picked up a few items and headed back to the small cabin, where Adam gathered the group around.

"We've buried Nwanne, and we've surveyed the grounds looking for indications that the McCulloughs started the fire. But we found nothing. The snow covered their tracks. Nonetheless, I'm going to the Martinsburg sheriff to report what I know of the threats, the fire, and Nwanne's death. While I'm gone, keep a sharp eye out for anyone and protect yourself. Sam, I'm going to leave you my musket, powder, and balls. Do you know how to use it?"

"Yas, sir, I do."

"Good, I'll take my pistol and shillelagh. While I'm gone, please go through the ruins and salvage everything you can find, hardware, clothes, pots, whatever. We'll start to rebuild first good weather day we get. And if it isn't obvious, Sam, you and Bethany are back living with us. Eve, make them welcome."

As calm and controlled as Adam seemed to the others, he was seething inside. Adam kept turning over and over in his mind—*McCullough did this; he wanted to kill Nwanne, Sam, and Bethany. McCullough had to be brought to justice.* Adam wasn't sure it was justice he wanted; revenge would do. But how to achieve either was beyond him. He was also disturbed about the visions that suddenly came to him unannounced. They clearly announced something, but he never knew what.

7

In Martinsburg Adam waited several hours for Sheriff Watterson, who was out investigating a robbery. When Watterson returned, Adam told him about coming to the area a few months back from Pennsylvania, his purchase of Sam, Bethany and Nwanne, manumitting them, and registering the same with the office next door. Adam also recounted Gregory McCullough's threatening visit followed weeks later by the fire that led to Nwanne's death.

Watterson challenged Adam: "What proof do you have that McCullough was responsible for the fire? It could have been a spark from the fireplace. Such things happen all the time."

"It started outside on the porch. The entire front of the cabin was destroyed as well as the front of the roof, but the logs around the fireplace were virtually untouched, as was the woodshed in the back which was near the fireplace," countered Adam.

"Maybe it was lightning," said Watterson.

"Have you ever seen lightening when it was snowing?"

"Was it? Snowing?"

"Yes, come down and see for yourself," said Adam.

"Well, I'm kind of busy right now."

It was obvious to Adam that Watterson wasn't interested.

"Look, Mister Livingston. I'm sorry for your loss," Watterson said without a great deal of conviction. "But this here is Virginia Country. Slavery is a good thing for our farmers. Without them, why our economy would sink, and we'd be facing a hard time to compete in the markets for our goods."

"I thought manumission was legal in Virginia. Your county clerk thinks so."

"Now, Mister Livingston, don't get all riled up..."

"Why not? A crime was committed that resulted in the death of a human being."

"You mean a former slave, don't you?"

"Yes. Why does that matter?"

Well, because slaves or former slaves, they're not, as the United States Constitution states, fully human; they're only three-fifths human. So, it's not like you've lost as much as you claim."

Adam could see this was useless. The man was cut from the same cloth as McCullough.

"Mister Livingston," Watterson went on, "if you'd just conduct your affairs like other Virginians, you're not likely to have any other problems. Isn't that right?"

Adam wanted to haul this sheriff back to Pennsylvania and put *him* on trial. "I'm getting to the point where I'm sorry I came to Virginia."

"Well, sir, you're welcome to go back where you came from. Now if you don't mind, I've got other business to attend to than a cabin burning down and not quite a person having been stupid enough to run inside the place when it was engulfed in flames."

Adam got up and left without bothering to thank the man for his time. Watterson was not getting Adam's vote, if indeed votes were even counted in this county. He also figured, sadly, it was no use filing suit in court. The courts would probably claim he had no standing, which only meant there was no justice for the crime. Where there is no adjudication, there is no justice.

Late in the afternoon, on the way back to his farm, he passed the McCullough plantation. How he wished he was less principled. He would have used McCullough for pistol practice. Perhaps the best he could do was best McCullough in the marketplace, but they would rarely complete except in a few cash crops. Then he fancied a folly: Perhaps through a third-party Adam could buy McCullough's slaves, manumit them and put him out of business.

8

Adam insisted that every decent weather day throughout the winter they rebuild the Darks' cabin. Everyone helped, including Bethany, Eve, and Henry. He conjured up hope where he could find it. Many of the green logs or parts of them were salvageable by cutting off the burnt portion and splicing in new logs. While the green logs would shrink with age requiring additional chinking, it was their resilience to burning that proved their value...but at such a terrible cost, thought Adam.

He still wondered what had caused the explosion. Days later, in talking to a merchant in Charles Town, Adam and Sam learned that grain or processed grain, like bags of flour, were not just flammable but could explode if the dust was mixed with air and exposed to a flame. This was something Adam didn't know, although he recalled hearing tales of flax grain burning under the right conditions. Amidst the ruins of the cabin, they found remnants of the flour sack, but no flour except for what they decided was flour ash about the floor where Nwanne's body was found. Did he die trying to save the sack of flour for Bethany? He considered the possibility and felt humiliated at the idea that a man had died at his suggestion for something as easily replaced as flour. He wanted to crawl into a dark hole and disappear. Tears came easily, and for weeks after, whenever he thought of all this, a flood of shame besieged him.

Sam wanted to build the second bedroom and replace the furniture just as Nwanne had wanted it. Erasing Nwanne's memory from his brother's mind was not an option, and Adam understood. There may come a time when the extra room would make sense, possibly if Sam and Bethany had children. He didn't mention that idea, but he suspected he didn't need to. They also would no longer store extra firewood on the porch, but rather store it under a lean-to shed a hundred feet behind the cabin into the wood a few steps from the new privy, so when one visited the privy, one could easily bring back an armful of wood.

Adam channeled his shame and anger into making the new cabin with Sam as good as they could, with fewer air leaks and straighter lines. He found it satisfying and honorable work.

On bad weather days he spent time designing his future house that would be built to the southeast of the Darks' cabin. It would have two floors, plus a cellar, and be constructed with posts and beams, allowing large, open rooms. He would also erect a large barn. Clearly, he was going to need help, and enlisted the support of John Smith's connections. But there was still no way he would allow any slave to work on his buildings unless he could find a way to afford to buy them and manumit them. But his gold would last just so long, and there was at least another year of development before he could raise livestock, plant, and harvest.

Adam often thought his life and land were cursed. Yet, he persevered. They finished rebuilding the Darks' cabin by late January, at which time Adam shifted his attention to finishing the design of his own home and the barn that would be built during the following summer. There was much to do.

9

My Despised Cyn:

Finally, some injustice in our favor, and no doubt at the behest of your many attempts to tempt and influence Nwanne's lust (which we must always refer to as love), Cecil's stupidity ('tis so smart of us), McCullough's greed (the more the merrier), Dean Boy's bigotry (double standards always make me double over), and the subtle suggestion to Bethany that something dispensable like flour is indispensable. That's the way to do it. Suggestions that seem intelligent but ultimately are fatal through ignorance. How would they know flour dust is explosive? Good work!

Nwanne's soul hasn't checked in, so we're not sure of his final rest. When this sort of thing happens, purgation is at fault, which means he's lost to Perdition. Hope that isn't so, but we're blocked from knowing.

At least Livingston will likely cease to be manumitting slaves. We were worried he might start a rebellion, although a war over slaves can't be all bad. There's an idea. Imagine the slavers and abolitionists fighting a war over slaves? That has a nice sound to it. I'm going to run it down the flagpole and see if anyone below salutes.

Eternally yours,
Master of Revenge

Chapter 18
She was Lying Just a Little

1

Miss *Anastasia Lilly was the sixth and middle child of eleven born to *Richard Lilly and wife *Mary Ellen (nee Elder) of Conewago, Pennsylvania. At sixteen Anastasia was intelligent, determined, and attractive. Her trim, slight frame, delicate features, piercing blue eyes, and rust-red, curly hair, which she always wore pulled back, entranced everyone that met her, especially the men. Anastasia didn't particularly like being the proverbial middle child, but it did have its advantages. Astute and observant, she had learned much from her two older sisters and three older brothers, who had all left home by their eighteenth birthday. That left her the oldest, and by default the nanny of her five younger brothers, ages fourteen to eight. Her mother, Mary Ellen, had her hands full making or repairing clothing, weaving, and managing the family's food supply from a large garden next to the house. Mary Ellen was helped by *Hannah, their house slave, a strong but small woman who was born into slavery from slaves imported to Virginia some thirty years earlier.

Growing up with eight brothers and a gruff father gave Anastasia confidence around the male species. When she turned fourteen, men started coming by the plantation to court her, but she had no interest in men that came from outside her family, for within the family she had all the masculinity she could handle. Beginning with her farmer father, Richard, she found the men in her family not particularly given to cleanliness, cordiality, or hospitality. As nanny, she attempted to instill in her five younger brothers an appreciation for personal appearance, etiquette, and demeanor. But as soon as their father came in the door caked with mud from the fields, her influence was abandoned and she fell into a state of temporary depression.

The only time any of the men in her life cleaned up and acted proper was when the entire family (including their four slaves) went to Mass at *Conewago Chapel. When the whole compliment of eleven children showed up, the family filled two full pews at the Chapel, for which her father paid a semi-annual pewage fee...about which he bitterly complained until the next payment was due. At least, he argued, the Lilly family name plate at the end of the two pews should have been larger for all that he was paying. But then, as the sexton pointed out, the name 'LILLY' had only five letters, most of which were skinny, as compared to the 'GILDERHOFTENSTEIN' name plate with seventeen letters many of which were fat and nearly required a wider pew.

From a young age Anastasia had been attracted to the Mass, if only because it was logical and orderly. The priests and altar servers always wore clean, pressed vestments, and the whole affair was choreographed like an elegant, grand dance infused with etiquette and dignity. It was the contrast with home-life that attracted her to the Church. Where life at home was often chaotic, rude, and dirty, life in the Church was structured, respectful, and hospitable.

Anastasia liked their slaves, but she disliked slavery. It seemed in contradiction to what the Church was all about. She had heard that the Jesuit Order, who had started Conewago Chapel, owned at least a thousand slaves at some large plantation in Maryland. This disturbed her and she often argued with her father that slavery was wrong. Her father argued back that without slaves he would not be able to work the farm and put food on the table. She looked forward to the day when she turned eighteen, and like her older brothers and sisters found a way to leave home and forge her own path. Her two older sisters, *Elanore Ann, now thirty-two and a mother herself, and *Mary Beth, now twenty-one, had married at eighteen and were happy as far as she could tell. But Anastasia could not imagine herself being married. She wondered if Elanore and Mary Beth were putting up a happy front just to escape their chaotic home. How horrible if that were true. Anastasia had plenty of potential suitors, but none that she could stand, as they were all too much like her brothers. *Now, if there was a polite and proper priest with starched cuffs who bathed daily*...but no, that was not an option and she felt repulsed that such an idea had come to mind. Priests did not marry, under any circumstances.

But then, shortly after she turned sixteen, something of a miracle occurred. Uncle *Arnold Elder, her mother's younger brother from Hagerstown, paid the family a visit. This was unusual. She had remembered him visiting only once before when she was ten or eleven. At that time he had brought his new bride, *Clotilda Phoebe (nee Green), to their home for a short visit. He was a handsome, outgoing man, and his pretty but shy bride was much younger. That seemed normal, as most men, her mother had explained to her, must establish themselves and be earning an income before they can marry and have the wherewithal to afford a homestead and a family. It was not unusual for wives to be twenty years younger than their husbands, although Mama was only seven years younger than Papa.

Occasionally, Mama and Arnold would exchange letters. After reading one of his letters, Mama would always speak highly of Arnold in a most general way. But apart from the rare comment or visit, Anastasia knew nothing about him except that he was different than her father and brothers. Uncle Arnold was a gentleman and dressed like one, too. That caught her attention.

The hint of a miracle came the first night of Uncle Arnold's visit during dinner at the large wood plank table in the gathering hall—a large but cozy room with a stone fireplace at one end, and a small loom at the other. It was a cold evening, and while the fireplace warmed the room, five oil lanterns lit the table down the center. Dinner was chaotic as usual except when grace was said.

282 ○ *Stanley D. Williams*

At the 'Amen,' all hands reached for whatever could be reached for. She watched Uncle Arnold, who seemed both surprised and amused by the flailing of arms and food. He just sat back until everyone had their plates filled, then carefully helped himself while he joked with Ma and Pa and told them how his business was doing and how he couldn't keep up with the many orders they were receiving.

As he talked, Anastasia noticed there was something a little different about Uncle Arnold that made her curious. She was used to visiting men gazing at her, and she had come to understand that she was attractive, although she was anything but vain about it. Uncle Arnold, like other men, would look at her, and let his gaze settle on her for a moment or two longer than just a passing glance. It made her a little uncomfortable, but his gaze was different than other men who visited their home. Other men let their eyes scrutinize her body, especially her breasts, which weren't particularly large like her mother's, but she had filled out nicely and felt womanly in that respect. Yet Uncle Arnold never let his eyes drop from her eyes. It was like he was trying to read her mind. She liked that about him.

Not being a shy child, what girl could be with eight brothers, she decided to find out a bit more about this uncle, though social convention frowned on a young woman of sixteen initiating conversation with an older man. But convention was not part of Anastasia's constitution.

She made eye contact with him and asked, "Uncle, what business are you talking about?"

He held her gaze for a moment, then smiled, and nodded out of respect for her question. "Anastasia, I own a textile factory. It's a small one, but we're growing and it's a very interesting enterprise."

Anastasia glanced at her father for permission to continue the interrogation. Her father was chewing on a chicken leg, the skin of which dripped over both hands as he gnawed on it; but he winked and nodded at her as if it was okay to continue.

"What's a textile factory?"

Her mother and father made some non-verbal sound as if it were either a good question or a dumb one, she couldn't tell. When she looked back at Uncle Arnold, he smiled, wiped his mouth with a handkerchief, not the tablecloth like her brothers were given to do, and waited until his mouth was empty before speaking. She couldn't help herself from staring wide-eyed at him when he did that, or not doing what she had expected, for she could not remember ever a man emptying his mouth before speaking. *Surely this is a strange and perhaps a good man. But he's already married. Oh, my, what a thought!* She quickly put the idea aside. After all, he was old enough to be her father, although that never stopped her sisters.

"We buy raw material from plantations like wool, flax, and some cotton, spin it to make yarns and threads...then we design and weave cloth or rugs.

From the cloth we make linens, blankets, and sell bolts of the cloth to others who design and make clothing."

Anastasia's eyes lit up. Her mother had a small loom to make simple clothing like socks, shawls, blankets, and tablecloths. But she had never considered that there were factories with many people that did it. "Do you have a lot of people spinning and weaving?"

"In a way. All total we have just twenty, not counting myself. There are some that process the raw materials, others that spin, and others that weave, and we have clerks who do the buying the selling."

Uncle Arnold was now looking at her with increased interest as if he was going to turn the tables and ask her a question, but she was trying to put his factory into perspective. "My brothers all work the farm with my father...along with *Jack and *Shadwell our slaves and a boy slave, *Henry. Sometimes I help if I don't have chores in the house. Do your children work in your factory? Are there just men, or do women work there, too?"

Uncle Arnold glanced at Ma and Pa with a smile, and they smiled back, as if they were sharing a secret. They almost laughed out loud.

"What!?" asked Anastasia. "What's so funny?"

Hannah started to clear the table and her mother got up to help her with a load of dishes. "Boys, take your dishes to the pitch, and then you're excused," said her mother. "Richard, you done?"

Richard nodded, and wiped his hands and face with the apron of the tablecloth.

"Good," said Mary Ellen. "Hannah, I'll leave the rest to you."

"Yes'm," said Hannah as she gathered more dishes.

"Ana, go to the parlor with Uncle Arnold and your father. I'll be there momentarily."

Anastasia's heart jumped into her throat. *What's this about?* It sounded strangely familiar, like other times when a man would visit and she was asked to retire to the parlor with her parents and the man. But this felt different, though oddly the same. She looked at her father, who was looking back at her with a contrived grimace. He shrugged and held up his hands as if to say, "Just wait. Be patient." But then he dropped his gaze along with the soiled tablecloth, a fine linen weave she noticed that would take Hannah a good thirty minutes to scrub clean again.

2

The Lilly parlor was a formal sitting room for greeting guests and for quiet but serious conversations. There was a bar with several different wines and stemware. There was a leather love seat, and near the window was a table that now held plants but could be brought to the center for table games. It was also the room where Ma showed off her exquisite needlework, mostly upholstered into the padded seat of wooden chairs, but also in a pillow on the love seat. It was where Ana's sisters were courted by their men-friends. A sliding door to the foyer could be closed completely or opened partially, providing various degrees of privacy.

Once in the parlor, with the sliding door wide open, her father poured a drink from a decanter into a wine glass for Uncle Arnold, "Sherry? From Spain."

Uncle Arnold accepted graciously. "I didn't think farmers drank sherry."

"Only if we have reason to celebrate," her father said, and winked at Ana.

The comment and the wink surprised Ana, but not as much as what came next. She watched as he poured a quarter glass for himself, or so she thought. But instead of putting the bottle down and picking up the glass to drink himself, he offered her the glass. "Anastasia?"

Ana didn't know whether to accept or decline. Pa had never offered her anything stronger than what she drank daily with her meals—small beer. He brewed his own beer, of course, like other farmers, and then made small beer for the children by diluting it with boiled or distilled water. The undiluted, or strong beer and porter, was reserved for himself, her older brothers, her mother, and guests. The imported sherry, like the wine, was purchased and served only for special occasions. Her father continued to hold out the glass. She looked at Uncle Arnold, who was waiting to sample his own drink until Papa had poured himself a glass. But that had not yet happened, and Uncle Arnold was now, again, gazing into Ana's eyes as if wondering what she would do.

Just then—

"RICHARD! NO! She's just a child."

Ana turned to see Mama ramrod straight at the parlor entrance, with her eyebrows in the middle of her forehead and her mouth agape. Pa looked at Ma and gestured with the glass toward Uncle Arnold's direction as if to say, "Is there a better time?"

Ma looked back at the tableau: the glass being held out to Ana, who stared at Uncle Arnold for permission, who looked at Richard with amusement, who gazed at his wife perplexed at her objection.

After several seconds, Ma relented. "All right! All right! I suppose you're right. Go ahead. Ana, welcome to our world."

Cautiously, Ana took the glass and stared into it at the swirling auburn liquid, not unlike a priest who stared into the cup during the consecration at Mass.

She suddenly felt older, as if she had entered a special society. A shiver ran up her spine, since none of this rite, or so it seemed, had been expected or explained to her. She looked at her mother for some explanation, but all Ma did was shake her head and sit with drooped shoulders on a chair upholstered with one of her needlepoint cushions. Her father lifted the bottle to Mama as if to ask if she wanted a glass, but mother simply waved it off, and raised a perturbed eyebrow at her brother. Pa finally poured himself a full glass.

Not sure what to expect or if she should say anything, Ana took a whiff of the sherry and then a sip. It was warm and rich in her mouth, fruity in flavor. She smiled a thanks at her father.

"Well, brother," said her mother at last. "Here we are."

"Yes," said Uncle Arnold. "And glad to be here. Let me begin by saying how thankful I am that you invited me."

"We didn't invite you," Ma shot back with a smile. "You invited yourself. Which is fine. I'm glad to see you once every other year or so."

Uncle Arnold turned to Ana who by now had decided to sit on a straight-back chair with a needlepoint cushion of a chicken and her eggs. As she adjusted herself on the needlework she wondered if the eggs would crack or hatch.

"Anastasia," her uncle began, "you asked if my children helped in our factory."

Ana was feeling the sherry warm her inners, but she perked up and gazed at her uncle for his answer.

"Well, unfortunately, Phoebe and I have been unable to have children. We've tried, but only once did she get pregnant, and then a few months later the baby was lost. We named him Louie. He's buried behind our home. So, no children of ours to help in the factory."

"Do you have slaves then?" Anastasia asked.

Before he answered, Uncle Arnold looked at his brother-in-law as if to ask permission to offend. "No, we have no slaves. I'm a devout abolitionist. The black man, or white for that matter, are our brothers, not our servants, unless we pay them a wage for such services. They are free in my mind. I do employ darks who were former slaves and others, and I pay them a wage. The textile industry is such that I can do that." He paused to let that sink in.

Ana suddenly liked Uncle Arnold more. She sat on the edge of her chair listening. She glanced at her father who was concentrating on finishing his full glass of sherry.

Uncle Arnold continued. "The problem I have is that our business has expanded, which is a great problem to have. But there are some tasks for which I need to hire individuals whom I can trust. People that are good at figures, and detail, and who are naturally organized. Such people are very hard to find. I'm here because your mother tells me that *you* are very good at all those things. She says you are also a good writer, know grammar well, and are hospitable to strangers."

Anastasia's eyes began to collect tears. Her heart beat heavily. Suddenly she wanted to drink all her sherry in one gulp. But she just sat there with her mouth agape.

"Your mother also says you are a religious person who never misses Mass and you go to confession regularly; and that you are a person that can be trusted with a lot of responsibility. So, I'm here to ask you, with your parents' blessing, if you might have an interest in moving to Hagerstown and living with Phoebe and me and keeping track of accounts for the factory. The work would entail meeting with planters, buying their raw materials, keeping track of how much material is purchased, tracking how it moves through the factory, and recording how much product it yields. Of course, I'll train you. It requires organization, figures, and paying attention to detail. About half of the work is with figures at a desk, about one-quarter of the work is dealing with planters, and finally, walking through the factory taking inventory, counting materials, finished products, and estimating yields and such. In addition to room and board with us, I will pay you a fair wage and you can do with the money as you wish. Betsy and I also have several gentle horses you can use when you're not working." At this Arnold stopped, and took a long sip of his sherry.

Ana was excited beyond belief. Her hand holding the sherry glass began to shake, but she quickly stilled it with her other hand. Being the precocious sort, she was surprised that she was caught speechless. She knew what she wanted to say, but she didn't know if she had permission to say it, although she sat there in her parent's parlor with a glass of sherry given to her by her father with her mother's approval. She looked at her mother, who was quietly staring at her folded hands in her lap. "Mother?"

Ma looked up sharply but didn't smile. "Yes, Ana?" Ana saw that her mother's eyes were wet. "Yes, Ana, what is it?" she asked gently.

"Who will care for my brothers?" Ana said.

Ma was silent for a moment. She glanced down at her hands, which now revealed a small needle point handkerchief that she gripped tightly. "Ana, John is fourteen and James twelve." She forced a smile. "Neither is as grown-up as you, but they ably help your father in the fields day after day. I'm sure they will manage. And, of course, there is Ignatius, Henry and Junior. You're my last girl, Ana. I love you dearly. But God has also given me five strong lads to love after you leave."

"Junior isn't so strong, Mama. What about him?"

"He'll be okay. We've always trusted him to God, we will continue to do so." Ma dabbed at her eyes with the small handkerchief.

"Uncle Arnold," Ana asked, "how far away is Hagerstown?"

"About forty miles, a long day's journey on a walking horse."

Ana looked to her father, who through tight lips forced a willing smile. He said nothing, which was about as much as her mother had just said. They would miss her, especially her mother, who would be left with all men not easy to get along with. Anastasia stared at the nearly empty glass of sherry in her hands. What Uncle Arnold was offering was just the sort of thing she had longed for, but she would also have to face some unknowns. Was she old enough to do it? Evidently her mother, father, and uncle all thought so. But she wasn't so sure. She loved her family. Would she miss them, especially her mother? *O God, what am I to do?* She had been quiet a long time and probably looked frightened if not overwhelmed at the prospect.

"What do you say, Ana? Do you have any questions that I can answer?" her uncle asked.

Ana finally looked up and willed her voice to speak. "When can I start?"

3

The next day Anastasia Lilly moved with her uncle to Hagerstown to work at his Hagerstown textile factory. Aunt Phoebe welcomed her like a long-lost daughter. She had a room of her own, no brothers to take care of, and access to a chestnut mare named Podunk. The work was agreeable and suited her curiosity, intelligence, and capability. She learned quickly, and Uncle Arnold seemed happy with her progress.

But there were a couple of problems. The first was that there was no Catholic Chapel anywhere near Hagerstown. Ana found that distressing. She was so used to going to Mass, sometimes daily, and to confession at least twice a month. Uncle Arnold was Catholic like her mother and father, but in a very relaxed way. He didn't care if he missed Mass, and about confession he told her, "It's none of a priest's business." He tried, in a nice way, to tell her not to worry about it: "God knows it's not your fault you can't attend Mass."

But she saw it differently—it *was* her fault. *She* moved away from Conewago Chapel; the Chapel didn't move away from her. Over time Anastasia became depressed about missing Mass and confession. One day she expressed to her uncle her regret about missing Mass, and that she may need to return home. This distressed Arnold. Upon further questioning her it did seem that the lack of a Catholic presence in Hagerstown was the issue. It wasn't home sickness, although Anastasia expressed that it was a kind of homesickness—she always thought of the Church as her spiritual home.

This lit a fire under Uncle Arnold. Anastasia had become invaluable to him. He begged her to stick it out and let him talk to the city manager, *Jonathan Hager, Jr. who was himself a religious man, although not a Catholic. A week later, Uncle Arnold sought her out. "Anastasia, I have some good news for you, I think."

Ana put aside her work and gave him her attention.

"Jonathan Hager, Jr., the son of Hagerstown's founder, controls most of the land around the town through rents or outright ownership. He's a religious and honest man, German Reformed. As you know, there are numerous churches in town, including Reformed, Lutheran, Methodist, and Church of England. But there is no Catholic Church. I expressed our need for a Catholic Chapel to Mister Hager, even if it was a log chapel and not beautifully built with high steeples like the others. I told him that I needed to attract and retain good employees like you and that a Catholic Church would help do that. Not only did he understand your need and mine, but he told me that just within the last month he had been contacted by a land baron he knows, a Catholic, who is trying to find a priest to make a regular circuit stop in Hagerstown."

"Oh, that's wonderful, Uncle," said Anastasia. "Did he say when that would be?"

"No. He wasn't sure. But he revealed that he was more than ready to help make that happen if the priest suddenly shows up. He said, 'Hagerstown will be richer for having a Catholic Church and not just Protestant churches, and I will do my best to help that happen.' That's what he said. Sorry it's not going to happen right away, but sounds like it's in the works. Maybe you should pray for that."

Anastasia felt a rush of joy and a tingling throughout her body. "Yes, I will. That gives me hope. Thank you, Uncle. Thank you. I'll be patient."

"Good, and thank you," replied her uncle with a smile and a pat on her shoulder.

With this report, Ana felt a wave of peace come over her. She hoped it wouldn't take too long. She was eager to go to confession and confess her lack of respect for her parents who tried to marry her off, and thus her desire to leave home when she was eighteen without getting married. Then it suddenly occurred to her that she was sixteen, had left home two years sooner than her sisters, and she was not getting married. That was better than what she had hoped for. Why was she feeling guilty for receiving a miraculous answer to prayer? At least, that's the way she interpreted it. Tonight, she would pray a Rosary in thanksgiving and she would pray one each successive night until she was able to return to Mass and confession.

But there was another problem that was not so easily solved. Some of the men at the factory, both young and old, seemed much too interested in her. Her uncle had tried to put that to rest, but evidently there was no quenching male interest in a pretty and seemingly available young filly. She had muted their attention somewhat by opening her mouth and revealing she was more than just pretty—she was also probably smarter than they were. She also made it clear that she had no interest in their attention, although she would appreciate their respect as she respected them. If that didn't do it, as it had not done in more than one case, she made it immediately known that she was not interested in marriage or courting. As soon as she said such a thing, she knew she had to go to confession. She was lying, if only just a little.

Chapter 19
Threat of Death

1

It was Sunday, January 11, 1789 at Richard McSherry's Retirement estate in Leetown, Virginia. Fr. Denis Cahill had fully recovered from his injuries suffered at the hands of Will Canning, the Sharpsburg sheriff, and had just celebrated Mass in Richard's large and plush stone home with a dozen other Catholics. After saying goodbye to their guests, Fr. Cahill donned a heavy coat provided by Richard, as was everything else, and retired to the Rosary garden next to the house to pray and reflect.

The garden consisted of low hedges that outlined the form of a Christian cathedral or cross. Ten tall arbors arched over the four entrances and the paths inside the cross. Richard had told Fr. Cahill that in summer the ten arbors exploded with hundreds of red rose blossoms. One could walk inside the hedged garden from one arbor to the next and recite the "Hail, Mary" while meditating on the related mystery of Christ's life. There were also benches wide enough for two to sit and pray or converse while enjoying the rose bouquet that was said to relax and clear the mind. Today, however, well into January, a cold northwest wind blew through the arbors where there were no blossoms. It must be lovely in the summer, thought Fr. Cahill. He would have to return then.

He walked the path through the center of the cross and recalled the first time Richard had given him an explanation for his garden's design. Fr. Cahill was dumbfounded that he had fallen in with a well-to-do Catholic bachelor who was devout enough to spend years cultivating such a garden. He felt deep appreciation to Richard and to God for bringing him here. Today, despite the cold wind, the sun was warm and the sky clear. But his future was foggy, if not clouded over with doubt.

The Will Canning caning was the dark cloud that hung over Fr. Cahill. Although he was willing to forgive, as Christ had forgiven his executioners, Richard McSherry was not ready to forgive the injustice. In fact, McSherry harbored a bitterness that teetered on revenge. Fr. Cahill knew this because Richard had told him so in confession a week ago. It was a reasonable response, and not a grave sin, or so Fr. Cahill had told the penitent. "Just don't do violence against the man or your soul will be in jeopardy. As it is," Fr. Cahill continued, "Will Canning's soul is already in jeopardy. We don't need both of you in Hell."

This was the first of many honest exchanges between the men, and Fr. Cahill was glad that his host expressed no displeasure at being corrected by a priest. It bolstered Fr. Cahill's assurance that something higher and more important was at stake and at work.

In June of last year the new U.S. Constitution was ratified. Yesterday, January 10, was the last day for voting in the new U.S. Federal elections. The new government was set to take power March 4. He was aware that Article VI, Section 2 of the new Constitution required that the election of officials be free of any religious test. There were also ten Constitutional Amendments that further secured religious freedom; but these were not yet ratified. Fr. Cahill prayed that the new Constitution and Amendments worked as they were intended and did not return the country into chaos, a chaos that was predicted to erupt any day in France. That the United States' strange experiment in government had gotten this far, although it had cost much, left him in awe. It was safe to say that his run-in with anti-Catholic sentiment was a warning that all was not safe.

After Fr. Cahill had recovered sufficiently, Richard explained how he had prayed for a Catholic priest to come to the region and establish a circuit between the towns where Richard had land investments. It was part of Richard's plan to attract Catholic settlers to the region. There were also hundreds, if not thousands of Catholics in the area who needed a priest so they could attend Mass and have access to the sacraments.

Richard had asked Fr. Cahill to pray about being that priest. Fr. Cahill said he would not pray about it; he would do it. The Providential circumstances that had brought him from New Orleans to Richard's home in Leetown were miraculous. He was sure God and the Holy Mother would be upset if he questioned the miraculousness of it all. So, in the morning he and Richard would leave on a tour that would introduce Fr. Cahill to five Shenandoah Valley towns where Richard wanted to establish Catholic societies and parishes. Fr. Cahill knew little about these towns, but Richard had assured him that there were faithful Catholics in each that longed to have regular access to the sacraments. Thus, from behind dark clouds of doubt, the sun began to shine.

Due to the time of year and the possibility of inclement weather, for it was winter and there were literally dark clouds about, the two men traveled in Richard's closed carriage pulled by two horses and driven by a hired coachman from Charles Town. The closed carriage also gave the men opportunity to talk and lay plans for establishing the circuit. As Richard tried to explain and Fr. Cahill was to discover, each town had its peculiarities and personalities that would need to be assuaged.

They stayed at least two days in each town and made sure they met with the local sheriff and mayors to be sure there would not be trouble starting a Catholic society in the town. They wanted to avoid the difficulties that would have arisen in Sharpsburg. But the mayors and sheriffs weren't ready to give their assurance that a Catholic presence, even if only for a day during Fr. Cahill's occasional visits, was going to be openly welcome. They nonetheless gave their assent that they had a right to do so. Staying at least a couple of days in each town also allowed the men time to get out an announcement that Mass would be celebrated before they left town, usually in the home of their host. Fr. Cahill braced for some show of open hostility surrounding the Mass celebrations, but none appeared and all was congenial.

Richard and Fr. Cahill had first traveled the twenty miles south to Winchester where they met with a Mrs. Felicity McGuire, a widow who had land holdings sufficient to donate a lot in town to build a chapel, but she didn't have the money to construct the building. Fr. Cahill had hoped that the richness of American society would allow for the immediate construction of a church with a tall steeple as he had so often seen on Protestant churches. Being turned down so quickly to build a fine church was a disappointment. It created in Fr. Cahill some immediate humility. But encouragement came when she offered her home for Mass whenever Fr. Cahill could come. She was gracious and welcoming.

In Martinsburg, they dined with *Mrs. Albert Lodsdon, another widow. But here in Martinsburg the lay of the land was a bit different, since Richard owned most of the empty lots which he had purchased over the last few years. Consequently, when they met with the town leaders they also stopped at the clerk's office and Richard signed over a deed for a lot to the newly formed Martinsburg Catholic Society. But, as before, until they had money to build, Mass would be held fortnightly in Mrs. Lodsdon's gathering hall, or so was the plan that Mrs. Lodsdon persisted in getting from the men before they left.

In Shepherd's Town, Gabriel Menghini had already agreed to house Fr. Cahill when he came and held Mass in their large hall. But on their visit this time a surprise awaited them. *Thomas Shepherd, Jr., son of the town's founder, and the proprietor of a tavern and inn in town, came to supper and said he was disappointed that he had missed the Mass and marriage of David and Sarah McKee. He had been in Martinsburg registering deeds. He was looking forward to the morrow when they would celebrate Mass again and arranged for Fr. Cahill to hear his confession beforehand. This made Fr. Cahill feel more than welcome, and he found himself sitting a bit straighter after that. But there was more. For the building of a chapel, he would donate to the Catholic Church a four-acre parcel of land on a hill that overlooked the town and the bend in the Potowmack River. When the time was right and society outgrew the Menghinis' hall, which was large, Thomas said he would tithe the inn's income to help fund construction of a modest chapel on the hill. *No steeple*, thought Fr. Cahill, *but neither did it sound like Mister Shepherd wanted a log cabin church sitting on the hill overlooking the town and his tavern.* Fr. Cahill was ashamed for this introspective cynicism, so he immediately and gratefully thanked Mister Shepherd for the offer and hoped they would be able to take advantage of it sooner than later.

They passed through Hagerstown on their way to Chambersburg, the farthest of the towns to which Fr. Cahill would travel. There they met Charles Hartley, a perpetually enthusiastic blacksmith, who said his entire family would

292 ○ Stanley D. Williams

come to Mass, but that he wasn't sure of anyone else. How big was his family? Counting the little ones and his elder married children, fourteen. Where would they meet? That would be a problem, since everyone in Chambersburg was poor and lived in smaller houses or cabins. They finally agreed that Mass could be held in his blacksmith shop. After all, reasoned Charles, the shop was big enough for several horses to be reshod at once. Fr. Cahill felt an immediate revulsion at the thought, for at that moment they were standing in the middle of what would be the nave and were attempting to avoid stepping in the solid and liquid horse deposits that littered the floor. Fr. Cahill could not help looking around and evaluating Charles' offer, which Charles noticed, and quickly added that he would clean the place up first. Fr. Cahill managed to nod, smile, and say, "Thank you." Nonetheless, he tried to imagine spreading a white altar linen cloth over the bent-up and rusty iron worktable that sat next to the largest anvil he had ever seen in his life. Then, again, conforming souls to God's word wasn't much different from heating iron in a forge and hammering it into a useful shape. Inspiration for a homily no doubt.

As he and Richard rode away from Chambersburg, Fr. Cahill had another embarrassing thought. The first Christian church, where Jesus Christ was first worshipped, was no better than Charles Hartley's shop. Fr. Cahill wondered if Mary and Joseph felt revulsion when offered the lowly stable that first Christmas day? Did they have to muck out a stall first before spreading straw for the Savior's birth? God worked in strange and wonderful ways.

Returning to Hagerstown, they stayed at a tavern-inn the night before meeting with Richard's connection there, Jonathan Hager, Jr., son of the town's founder. The trip from Chambersburg was cold and sleety. Richard had stopped to rig blankets on the backs of his horses, which they seemed to appreciate. When they arrived at the Hagerstown Inn few other travelers were on the road. They found themselves alone, warming their travel-worn bodies by the inn's fireplace while sampling some port the innkeeper had recommended.

Despite the questionable situation in Chambersburg, Fr. Cahill confessed his appreciation to Richard. "Mister McSherry, you have exceeded all expectations and requirements of a saint here on earth."

Richard stretched out his legs and with a touch of cynical dubiety said, "Oh, how's that?"

"Why, everywhere we go, or just about, the people are overflowing with generosity and are anxious to build a Catholic church. This is every priest's dream." Fr. Cahill knew he was stretching the truth of his feelings, but sipping port while sitting before a warm fire on a cold winter's night did that to a man.

Richard took a slow sip of his wine and rejoined, "Well, don't get your hopes up quite yet."

"I'm serious, Richard. When I agreed to your five-year plan of declining support, I wondered if five years would be long enough before I could build congregations and churches and thus support myself through religious industry. But so far, I think we'll be able to build churches in one or two years, and you'll be free of my sponsorship after three years at most."

Richard bit his lip and slowly shook his head.

Fr. Cahill saw this and became perplexed. "What? You don't think so? You have doubts?"

"Oh, I have no doubts...I know. Five years won't be long enough. Perhaps I should confess that when I cut that deal with you I knew it was unrealistic. I apologize, although there's room for hope."

"How can you possibly think that, after land and money has been offered?"

"Because you, we, the Church doesn't have the money...yet. Land is easy to donate. It costs the land holders very little to claim that they've donated an acre or a hector of land to a church. They believe just saying that will attract additional responsible buyers for the vacant lots they can sell or rent at a premium. Which is exactly what I'm trying to do with you, except my motivations are religious not gold. But until you have the money to build...I mean have the money in your purse, it won't happen."

"Why, won't people give money to build a church? How much do we need?"

Richard took a moment to ponder before replying, "Ten pounds from a well-to-do merchant or inn keeper is a nothing. You're going to need a thousand pound subscription every year. The real problem is that the United States, which is very young, consists of people from all ranks who are struggling to exist. This is especially true of Catholics who are still persecuted and pushed aside in many ways. I am afraid that in such a society most Catholics will see such a sacrificial observance of the faith as unneeded and unnecessary. They will reason that they have already sacrificed enough simply by being Catholic. On the other hand, religion to Protestants is tolerated and seems to be a necessity, if the size and grandeur of their churches is any gage."

Fr. Cahill was not liking this discussion. "What are we to do then?"

Richard went on to explain: "Construction in a town can be expensive and there are investors with lots near the lots we've been given who will not want a church built near them. I do think the presence of churches increases land values. But many, many opposing individuals believe the opposite. For such persons I think it's the inherent evil in their hearts. There's something evil in their lives they work hard to cover up, and a church nearby they fear will uncover it. It's always been that way."

"What about your land at Retirement?" asked Fr. Cahill.

"We can hold Mass at Retirement, of course, but it's too far from a major population center to attract a large enough group who could afford or would want to build a church."

Fr. Cahill's chest tightened as a deep disappointment descended. His hopes and dreams were being crushed by the very same man who had sponsored those same hopes and dreams. After a long pause, Fr. Cahill asked, "What then are we going to do?"

"We're waiting for tomorrow," said Richard. "I think tomorrow will bring us some hope, if not an answer."

2

Richard had purposely organized their tour so Hagerstown would be last to visit. Yet, he feared the stay in Hagerstown would offend his spartan-like priest. Hagerstown was not only the hub of social sophistication and exaggerated culture in western Maryland, but also the crossroads of trade and enterprise between the Blue Mountains and the seaboard. It was where the most intelligent and industrious German families and craftsmen had settled. Every imaginable kind of business professional or craftsman that had successfully transplanted their European trade to the New World could be found in Hagerstown. There were tanners, coopers, bookbinders, millers, attorneys, weavers, bankers, gunsmiths, hatters, merchants, physicians, saddlers, scriveners, spinners, cabinet makers, tavern-keepers, teachers, and tin-plate makers. The town enjoyed the recognition and trade from the wealthiest of families along the eastern shore. Consequently, men and women alike had become accustomed to fine clothing, courtly attire of lace and ruffles, powdered hair, and silk hose for the men. Ladies particularly were given to costly dresses, black lace, fancy hats, and a bewildering assortment of silk and satin wardrobes pulled tight about the waist with long trains. Richard found it off-putting and in contradiction to his spiritual interests of helping the unfortunate. Though as a concession to the culture he had packed his own collection of ruffled shirts, waist-coats, and silk stockings to wear with his buckled shoes as occasion required in an effort to persuade. His one refusal to the culture, however, was to wear one of those damned powdered wigs. He had a few but despised them, choosing to keep them hidden.

Hagerstown had an upside, however, as far as his vision for Fr. Cahill was concerned. More so than any of the other towns in the Shenandoah Valley, here was the opportunity to find patronage for the Church. Beneath the haughty and materialistic exterior and extravagance was an interest in spiritual matters. Such was evidenced by the presence of eight Protestant denominations, some with grand facades and spires...and a few without. Methodists, Reformed, Moravian, Congregationalist, Quaker, Mennonites, Anabaptists, and Church of England were all here. He hoped that the presence of a Catholic priest would foster a greater spiritual willingness to help the poor rather than parade the fool, and thus establish in Hagerstown a Catholic Society.

To that end, Richard hoped to parlay his good business relationship with the son of the town's founder, Jonathan Hager, Jr. The son had managed his late father's land holdings and businesses since his father's untimely death fourteen years earlier. The Hagers, as well as being one of the richest families in the valley, were also one of the most religious. The reports of Jonathan Sr., which Richard had heard were glowing, if not legendary. In fact, Richard had never heard a negative thing said of the town's generous founder or his late wife, Elizabeth. Richard concluded that everything he had heard was true, because Jonathan Jr., in Richard's experience, was not just gentlemanly, but honest, industrious, and astute.

Richard introduced Fr. Cahill to Jonathan at *Hager's Rest, the Hagers' large, two-story white fieldstone home south of the town. After greeting his visitors in the foyer, Jonathan ushered the men into the parlor where they all found a place to sit in the sea of upholstered French chairs and embroidered cushions. The parlor was a museum of his father's military and political achievements and connections. There were ceremonial as well as blood-stained swords, paintings, lamps, dueling pistols, and furniture collected from travel, as well as gifts from both British and American notables. Of particular interest was a surveyor's sun compass on a polished walnut base from General George Washington. It was Washington who had originally surveyed part of the 10,000 acres that Jonathan currently owned and managed.

"My father was a very generous man, Fr. Cahill," said Jonathan. "He was also very religious, which I hope I am as well...not just in name but in actual deed. As Mister McSherry may have told you, I have agreed to donate land to the Catholic Church, should such a society find root here in Hagerstown. My father donated land to build the Reformed Church in town, although he was not a member at the time." Jonathan paused for a moment as if remembering something painful.

"That's where your father died, wasn't it? In building it?" asked Richard.

"It was at the mill. I was twenty at the time. He not only donated the land but had also purchased the lumber to be used. He was supervising the cutting of a large log at the mill he co-owned when a log rolled off a platform and crushed him." Jonathan took a moment to collect his thoughts. Then he reached back to his desk and picked up a worn Bible. "This was my father's German Lutheran Bible, though he wasn't Lutheran. He despised them, in fact. Didn't much care for Luther for some reason. But he loved the Bible."

Jonathan opened the leather cover and wiped his eyes a bit with his fingers. "Right after my mother died, when I was ten, he gave me this Bible and wrote inside. Although he loved the vocal sound of thick German, he loved more to write in English."

Jonathan turned the Bible so Richard and Fr. Cahill could see the inscription, then turned it back and read aloud:

> *O, my child, lay rightly to heart the words of this hymn, and do right and fear God and keep His commandments. And if you have anything, do not forget the poor, and do not exalt yourself in pride and haughtiness above your fellowmen. For you are not better than the humblest before God's eyes, and perhaps not as good. And so, if you have no fear of God within you, all is in vain. My child, keep this in remembrance

of your father, and live according to it, and it will go well with you here while you live, and there eternally.

"My father used to say, '*What God does is well done.*' He said that when my mom died. He loved her. Spent sixteen years together and he never married again. I don't always understand how God works. Sometimes it's frustrating. But ever since he died building a church, I've wanted to honor my father by donating land to a church."

Jonathan stopped, put the Bible back on his desk, and looked at his guests and smiled. "Just to let you know. I don't intend to die in the process."

The three chuckled.

"Not to drastically change the subject," began Richard, "but this just occurred to me. Remind me, what is your wife's name?"

"Mary. *Mary Magdalene," said Jonathan.

"That doesn't sound like a Reformed name," said Richard. "Is she Catholic by chance?"

"Oh, no. German-Reformed. My wife is the daughter of *Major Christopher Orndorff of Sharpsburg. They have a large plantation there."

Richard and Fr. Cahill glanced at each other.

Jonathan went on, unaware of his guests' recollection. To Richard, Jonathan was sort of a troubadour not liking to pass up the opportunity to tell a good story. "As was the practice after the war, *officers would often stop at the Orndorff's commodious home and be received and entertained. It was like the unofficial post-war Army headquarters. In 1776, I was captured by the British and spent seven years as a prisoner of war in Nova Scotia. In my absence I was elevated to Colonel. On my return home, here in Hagerstown in November '83, I stopped with others at the Orndorff home and met his youngest daughter, Mary. I guess I was luckier than some. The month before I arrived, probably in October of 1783, Mary had been proposed to, through her father, by none other than the disgraced General Horatio Gates. I guess Gates' first wife, Elizabeth, had died that summer. Mary tells me he proposed marriage only hours after seeing her pass him in the hall. He never talked to her. She was fifteen at the time and marriage to a man forty-years her senior didn't sit well. Her father declined for her. At least I took a few weeks in the effort, but then I was only ten years her senior. We were married a few weeks later."

"Do her parents still reside in Sharpsburg?" asked Richard.

"Yes, they do," said Jonathan.

"Do you happen to know the sheriff there, a Will Canning?" asked Richard with some directness.

"Richard?!" interjected Fr. Cahill, looking at him as if the question was improper.

Richard glanced at Fr. Cahill with a wry smile, and then turned back to Jonathan, "A distant acquaintance, that's all."

"No, never met the man," said Jonathan.

"Just as well," Richard said, smiling at Fr. Cahill, who by now looked as if he had been visited upon by the Holy Ghost. Richard turned back to Jonathan: "Why don't we name the church in honor of your wife's namesake, "Saint Mary Magdalene?"

Jonathan thought about that for a moment. "Would you name a Catholic church after Magdalene before naming it after Jesus' Mother?" asked the astute Protestant.

"No, we would not," interjected Fr. Cahill. "We would name the first church in the area after the Mother of God, and perhaps later, a second church after Magdalene."

"I stand corrected," said Richard with a smile. *"St. Mary's Catholic Church then?"

"Fine by me," said Jonathan, and I'm sure my wife would be so honored... indirectly of course."

3

Fr. Cahill was now convinced that God had called him to America, and that his coming was not a selfish passion or effort to escape the political tragedy that he called New Orleans. He could not have imagined that Catholic Richard McSherry and Protestant Jonathan Hager (along with his wife, Mary Magdalene) could conspire together in such a gentlemanly manner for the benefit of a somewhat renegade Catholic priest. By the time he and Richard headed back to Leetown, Jonathan had deeded over to Richard's newly formed *Shenandoah Catholic Society* a vacant frame house on a quarter-acre lot in town, which would serve as a rectory for several priests. Richard had expressed the hope to find at least two additional priests to assist Fr. Cahill in the work.

Fr. Cahill chose to call the property *Magdala*. Jonathan thought it a wonderful name and assured Fr. Cahill that his Mary would be much pleased. The name, of course, would be registered with the county clerk and be used throughout the community. But it wasn't just a name of a property to Fr. Cahill. Mary of Magdala's name is found in the Gospels more often than most of the Apostles because she was a devout follower of Christ, as should be the priests that reside there. Magdala was also a fishing village on the western shore of the Sea of Galilee; the priests would be fishing for souls, of course. Lastly, although Fr. Cahill wasn't sure how it applied, Magdalene became a follower of Christ *after* he cast out of her seven demons; Fr. Cahill hoped demons were not in his future.

Magdala was a two-story, post-and-beam house vacated by renters who had stopped paying rent and skipped town. Jonathan offered it at a discount for it was run down, as well as believing that having priests live in it and care for it would only increase the value of the properties around it, or so he hoped. Upon entering Magdala's front door, the foyer opened on the left through an archway to the gathering hall. In the center of the foyer was a staircase to the second floor, and to the right was the parlor. On the second floor, accessible from the central hall, were four rooms, each with an integrated stone fireplace whose chimney was integrated with the fireplaces on the first floor. Richard explained his idea that three of the rooms would serve as priest or guest quarters; and the fourth room would be set aside as an oratory or chapel where the Blessed Sacrament would be reserved. Richard's plan was to find several priests to ride circuits out of Hagerstown; but eventually they would settle in a single commu-nity when there were enough practicing Catholics to support them. This was all acceptable to Fr. Cahill. Richard would have made a good bishop, thought Fr. Cahill; he was good at finding priests and assigning them parish boundaries.

On the first floor the parlor was only half the depth of the house. It was a sitting room for greeting guests. At the back of the parlor was a door that led to a separate kitchen and cooking fireplace. The parlor stretched halfway across the house behind the central staircase, with a door that entered the rear of the gathering hall. The front of the gathering hall, of course, led through an archway back to the foyer.

The gathering hall was ideal for celebrating Mass. It wasn't a church, but it would serve as one until money could be raised to build a proper St. Mary's church on the lots at *the corner of Washington and Walnut Streets that Jona-than Hager had also donated to the fledgling Catholic society.

Before they left Hagerstown, Richard had arranged for Magdala to be cleaned, repaired, minimally furnished, and provided with linens. He also or-dered a confessional screen to be built for the hall, one made to Fr. Cahill's specifications—one short return wall with a translucent screen, but not fully enclosed for either priest or penitent. Fr. Cahill was slightly claustrophobic, ac-customed as he was to the similarly designed confessional tents on the wharf in New Orleans where there was a screen but otherwise there were no walls.

Meanwhile, Richard and Fr. Cahill returned to Retirement where they had a glass of Madeira and made final arrangements for the new circuit and cir-cuit-riding priest. Richard arranged to buy Sassafras and Ebenezer from his twin brother, William. Sassafras was given to Fr. Cahill for his personal mare, and Ebenezer was sold at the Charles Town livery to begin funding Denis' sponsorship. Fr. Cahill made up a circuit schedule which Richard posted in the newspapers at Winchester, Shepherd's Town, Martinsburg, Chambersburg, and Hagerstown. The schedule would allow Fr. Cahill to attend services in each town twice a month where he would hear confessions, confer baptisms, cele-brate Mass, and provide instruction.

In late January Richard helped Fr. Cahill move into Magdala, at which time Jonathan Hager hosted an open house to welcome the town's first Catholic priest. Out of loyalty to the Hagers many came, including city officials and busi-ness owners. But some came not to pay their respects but to incite resentment at the presence of Catholicism into the neighborhood. Jonathan took note of these and let the belligerents know that while they were free to express their opinions, proper deportment was required unless they expected to be deported from the vicinity. He was no dictator, but favorite son status was a privilege, not a right, and he was the favorite son enforcer.

Fr. Cahill made his joy evident by writing Jonathan and Mary weekly a note of appreciation telling of his activities and asking if there was anything he could ever do for them besides pray, which he told them he did for them daily.

4

By mid-February, Fr. Cahill had completed his first circuit with Sassafras. Both Richard and Jonathan strongly recommended that, for his safety, he travel incognito, without his parson's hat or robe, and never at night. This Fr. Cahill began to do, although Sassafras had proven fully capable of a gallop when the occasion required a swift departure. The circuit took ten days when he heard only confessions and celebrated Mass. When he added days for spiritual direction and instruction it took longer. Weather began to warm significantly in March, allowing easier travel, although rain made things excessively messy at times. In April, at the request of some landowners out west, he began to travel the sixty miles one way to the head of the National Road in Fort Cumberland once a month to hear confessions and celebrate Mass and deliver other sacraments as needed, such as baptism, confirmation, anointing, and matrimony.

If there was something to tie a priest emotionally to the community, it was hearing confessions—a bitter-sweet affair. The sweetness came with his pronouncement of absolution, for he was the instrument through which God absolved sin and eternal punishment. However, listening to the accounts of sins committed was depressing, even if the penitents only referred to the number of the commandment violated. *"Father, I committed numbers 2, 4, 6 and 7, respectively 3, 2, 1, and 4 times this month. Am I going to hell?"* Fr. Cahill was tempted to respond: *"Only if you persist in 2, 4, 5, and 7 and throw in 1, 3, 5, 8, 9 and 10 for good measure."* Men were always lusting and committing adultery. He disliked listening to those confessions for no other reason than admiring beautiful women was his own weakness and occasionally made him question his vocation as a chaste priest. Thankfully, the gazing was short lived, and he had never acted on the temptations. A few admitted to killing someone in their past or stealing from a neighbor or the business where they worked. Women were fond of gossip and lying about neighbors out of revenge or jealousy. Some wanted to go into long narrative details. He stopped them, usually before they started. Such stories stuck in the mind and were distractions to his own spiritual life, although they did provide great fodder for sermons. Very few suffered from scrupulosity—oh, how he wished more had such a problem. It was a malady from which Martin Luther evidently suffered.

Ironically, there was a local politician, *Beej Galloway, who wrote editorials for the Hagerstown Herald in support of the Constitution. He was an honest and good man, though he was guilty of lying that he was Protestant. It humored Fr. Cahill that Beej would come to confession at least twice a month and not confess his lying about being Protestant, but rather his invective language against another Maryland politician and notable attorney, *Luther Martin. Martin was an appointed Maryland representative to the Continental Congress, but due to his lawyering duties never attended a single session. Instead, claimed Beej, Luther Martin wrote essays and made ungrammatical and often disorganized speeches against the Constitution and its Federalist design. Beej's contention was that had Martin attended to his duties as a delegate of the people he would not have been so despicable a character. It turned out that Beej's problem was envy. Beej had wanted to be a delegate, but the Maryland legislature passed him over in favor of Martin. Fr. Cahill started to read both men's essays and agreed with Beej—Martin was a despicable man. He told Beej he could not absolve this apparent sin of language against Martin because it was not a sin. He also told Beej that indeed Martin needed to be publicly rebuked and Beej should keep it up. On this point Beej suffered from scrupulosity and he had to stop lying about being Protestant, come to Mass, and come out as Catholic. His penance was ten Hail Marys for every time he publicly implied he was Protestant and not Catholic. Either that or he should stop coming to a Catholic priest for confession.

As much as he disliked hearing confessions, he had to admit the sessions energized him. He felt a modest thrill at being able to confidently hear a person's inner moral thoughts and guide them to something more becoming a Christian. It was a powerful role for a priest, but also humbling. For listening to tales of sin, and providing absolution for them, had the effect of strengthening Fr. Cahill's resolve to be true to his vocation and avoid even the appearance of sin. But he was vulnerable.

As soon as Fr. Cahill started celebrating public Mass in Hagerstown, a beautiful young lady with fair skin, a trim figure, alert blue eyes, and rust-red hair, started to attend. She never missed a Mass, and always sat on a bench near the front. Her comportment was modest and humble, and yet her posture was erect. She carried a Roman Missal, but rarely opened it; she knew the Latin parts of the Mass verbatim. On Sundays she dressed fashionably with ruffles, silks, and a lace reticule. Whenever he celebrated weekday Mass and opened it to the public she was there, often dressed down, for she was going to work after. But nonetheless, her appearance was neat and organized, and she greeted others with a beguiling and pleasant smile There were few young women her equal in these things. Fr. Cahill also admired her for being not given to society; her name was never mentioned in those columns of the Herald that teetered on rabid gossip.

Perhaps it was her curly red hair that she bundled behind her head that raised feelings of nostalgia and caused Fr. Cahill to think she was Irish. He had to admit that her innocent beauty attracted him. But he quickly put that out of his mind, although he was curious to know more about her. Upon greeting her as she left the service, her accent was clearly mid-American. No immigrant. He managed to ask her name; it was Anastasia Lilly, and she worked for her uncle at Hagerstown Textile. While Fr. Cahill didn't inquire right away, there was no indication she was married, for she always came alone, walking to and from Magdala. It was also obvious that she was not being ignored. Whenever he caught sight of her coming or going, there were men, both young and old, that could not help but stop and gaze at her. Later he was astonished to discover she was not betrothed or married. She could not be more than sixteen years of age, but she carried herself like a confident and much older woman.

The first time Fr. Cahill made confession available in Hagerstown, Anastasia came. Typically, Fr. Cahill sat in a chair behind the screen and did not look at the penitents lined up behind the screen. Bue he knew whom each voice belonged to from greeting them otherwise after Mass or talking with them during the week. When he heard Anastasia's voice, he became concerned, and he momentarily held his breath, wishing her away. This was one aspect of hearing confessions that was uncomfortable—for he had a repressed weakness for feminine beauty. So far, he had worked diligently and successfully to keep lascivious thoughts at bay. He was serious about his priestly and Capuchin vows of poverty, obedience, and chastity. He also prayed a lot. But when said beauties came to confession and confessed sexual sins, even if it was by the numbers, he had to work to suppress the immoral-tinted thoughts that came after. What could he do but focus on the task at hand?

Anastasia's voice through the screen was as singular as she was peculiar in Hagerstown society. She confessed of being too fastidious with figures (she managed accounts), too obsessed with being modest (so not to unduly attract the attention of men), too concerned with being separated from her parents and brothers (although she was apart from them with their blessing), too content that no man was courting her (single life satisfied her and she had told more than a few men that she had no interest in marriage or children), and too upset with her father for owning slaves (one of the reasons she had wanted to leave home). Then she lowered the boom: She wondered if it was too religious to pray a Rosary every day for her family and five younger brothers back in Conewago?

Fr. Cahill was well-nigh speechless. Who was this woman, this angel, this saintly child? In as gentle a way as he could, he expressed that none of what she had confessed could be considered even venial sins. Nonetheless, at her request, he gave her absolution for all her sins, even the ones she could not remember. But he refused to give her a penance, except to tell her to keep praying her Rosary for all the needs that God revealed to her. She promised she would. With that he gave her his blessing. He was tempted, however, to ask her to bless him.

When she left that first time, Fr. Cahill noticed that his own face was perspiring, though it was a cold day in February, and the fireplace had nearly gone out from lack of attention.

5

Fr. Cahill advertised that the Christ Mass would be celebrated at Magdala beginning at midnight on Christmas, Friday, December 25. Later, mid-morning, there would also be a regular Mass. The advertisement told confirmed Catholics planning to attend to fast from food and drink from sundown on Christmas Eve, December 24. A waxing gibbous half-moon would light their way to church that night, but it would set during Mass and the walk or ride home would be darker and that lanterns would be necessary to light their way.

The weather had been accommodating with a little wind but no snow. Though it was near freezing in temperature, the fireplace kept the room toasty and an early arrival volunteered to keep it supplied with seasoned logs. There were lantern sconces around the perimeter of the room, two on either side of the ambo, and of course the six candles on the altar were lit and burning. Fr. Cahill hoped the good weather would encourage people to come, even though Mass was scheduled for midnight. So, he was pleased when Magdala's hall was filled, half with individuals he had never met.

What a joyful Christmas, he thought as he waited in his new vestments at the back of the hall and greeted the arrivals. The new vestments were a gift from Richard. With every new arrival, especially children that came with their family, he could not help but break out in a large smile. Perhaps too enthusiastically, he reached out and shook everyone's hand, including the ladies, even if they did not offer to do so.

The midnight Christ Mass went smoothly, although he could not help but notice that not everyone knew the correct verbal responses or always when to stand, kneel, or sit. But he guided them in all these things and was gentle and happy that such an important Mass would be celebrated by so many in his modest hovel of a chapel. He celebrated Mass again later at mid-morning, after which he had been invited to multiple family dinners. Out of respect, he tried to make an appearance at all.

All in all, it was an emotional high for Fr. Cahill. Everyone was welcoming and happy, although there were a few women who he felt had become too elaborate in their Christmas outfits complete with fancy hats, sashes and silks, and layers of colors that could not be unseen. He was kind, but he found his eyes searching for something more mundane to admire. Consequently, after the very busy and generally joyous day, he went to bed exhausted, but fulfilled. He had met many new people and was encouraged that his ministry had been accepted by the people of Hagerstown.

But not everything that glitters is gold, he reminded himself.

Unless he was swinging wildly from a hammock on a sailing vessel battling a storm-swept sea, Fr. Cahill normally slept well. On the night after Christmas, however, he slept fitfully. He kept waking to strange sounds. Once he noticed the fire in his room's fireplace had nearly gone out, and he spent some minutes getting it going again with fresh logs. Another time it sounded to him as if there were people walking on the roof, or that branches were falling from trees and hitting the side of the house. But when he checked, there was no windstorm that explained such noise. Occasionally, over the years he would experience visions or dreams at night—dreams of his boyhood at home in Ireland with his mother and father doing pleasant things. When, on rare occasions, he experienced dreadful dreams of violence or ugly confrontations with belligerents, he would take out his Rosary, hold it close to his heart, cover himself completely with his bedding, and pray the Rosary until he fell back asleep, which was almost immediately. But on this night, there were dark fellows wandering around his bed, or floating above it, and murmuring vile threats of which he would only sense the tone but not the actual words.

He finally rose from bed later than normal, and not entirely rested. He felt a tad fearful, but being a man of robust temperament, he generally did not fear even desperate figures like the crazed reveler in New Orleans, or Will Canning. So, he couldn't decide why it was, especially after such a good day of celebrations with friends.

At that moment he belched and wondered if it wasn't an overindulgence in the good food he had been offered, and having been offered it ate it. Yes, that must be it. He wasn't used to eating as much as he had on Christmas day.

So, he washed, dressed, and prepared to do some study and prepare the homily he would preach on the circuit that would start the day after next.

As he moved around the house, he noticed that the street in front of Magdala was a bit busier than normal. But he put it out of his mind, until he noticed through a window a group of men led by Jonathan Hager walking quickly to his front door. A moment later there was a modest pounding at the door. He became worried, and his muscles tensed. Going to the door, he unbarred, unlatched, and opened it.

Jonathan Hager was there with two others, and they were not happy. Jonathan was dressed for the weather with heavy coat and his riding hat, an old black felt cocked hat affair that he often wore with a short, powdered wig, but the hat had been donned, crookedly he noted, without the bother of the wig.

"My very dear Father Cahill, I am troubled and very unhappy for this entirely unbecoming incident. I heartily apologize and my associates here will make amends and correct the situation forthwith as soon as we have your permission. Jonathan stared at Fr. Cahill as if he expected an immediate response, but Fr. Cahill had no idea what he was talking about. Fr. Cahill simply stood where he was and gazed at the three men as if reading a public posting trying to figure out what the big words were that the posting so indelicately had used.

Jonathan looked back as his associates and then at Fr. Cahill, now demanding with his eyes a response. But Fr. Cahill just stared ahead with his brow forming deep ridges of cluelessness.

"My dear sir!" said Jonathan, as he stepped back and gestured to his right.

Fr. Cahill looked in the direction of Jonathan's gesture, but all he saw were perhaps seven men and women in the street staring at the front of Magdala in stunned consternation.

At that point Jonathan gently reached forward, took Fr. Cahill's arm, and pulled him out onto the porch. Suddenly, Fr. Cahill saw what the commotion was about. There hanging from the front edge of his porch, tied to one of the support beams, was a life-sized stuffed doll. It took but a moment before he realized that it was an effigy. Without bothering to don a coat or hat, Fr. Cahill immediately stepped out onto the porch, down the two steps to the front, then turned to look back at the hanging object. At first, he was shocked and stepped back out of repulsion and surprise. Clearly, the creator of this concoction was no artist. Made from old white sheets, stained with red paint, and stuffed with straw, it hung from a noose snugged about the effigy's neck. There was no telling who it was supposed to represent except for the scrawled sign hanging around the neck: "Death to pope and papists."

It was not just Jonathan that expressed his regret, several of the neighbors did the same. Emotionally, Fr. Cahill felt sad, if not numb. If it hadn't been for the many town people that just yesterday had demonstrated respect and love for the Church in the two Masses he celebrated, he might have feared for his life.

Fr. Cahill began to shiver in the cold, but he just stood there and stared at the sight. After a moment, Jonathan signaled his associates to climb up on a crate they had brought and with a knife cut down the figure and haul it off. "We'll burn it at the dump, Father," said Jonathan. "Again, I'm very sorry, and if we can find out who did this, I'll deal with them personally. Are you all right?"

Fr. Cahill took Jonathan's forearm and hand and gripped it tightly. "I'm fine. We had a very good turnout for Midnight and then Christmas day Masses, by the way. Everyone was very kind and generous. I'm very thankful for you, your concern and sense of justice. This must have happened during the night. I did not sleep well, and this must have wakened me, but I did not know what it was."

Jonathan did not appear content, and instinctively defended his town: "Honestly, while I've heard of this stuff happening in other places, I've never known it to happen here. I just can't believe this is anyone that lives here."

Fr. Cahill was now shaking, from what he thought was the cold.

Jonathan said, "You better get inside, it's too cold out here without coat and hat."

Fr. Cahill nodded, thanked Jonathan again, ran back inside, and shut the door.

Moving to the fireplace, which he had stoked moments before, Fr. Cahill rotated his body before the fire like a pig on a rotisserie to warm up. But the shaking continued. It was then that he faced the reality that it was not just the cold, but the threat of death that had shocked him. He would have to be on his guard. He also realized that his fitful night's rest was not just some invisible demon sent to scare him. Next time he experienced a fitful sleep he would rise from his bed and...and...do what? He wasn't sure. Maybe he would go out onto the porch and preach. Yes, that would scare off his detractors...and the demons.

6

My Despised Cyn:

We are most unfortunate that we've been unable to turn Jonathan Hager. He is too principled of a man. I wish there was a way we could compromise his values. That a Catholic Society has been established in the heart of Western Maryland's narcissistic culture, which we have worked hard for many years to establish, is not good. These people with their fancy hats, spats, and bone stays don't need public reminders of objective, moral laws. They need freedom of expression, of society, and freedom to do whatever they please...which is another way of saying what we please. How else can the unchangeable natural laws of creation be destroyed, and souls carted off to Perdition? Never lose sight of that goal. We must perceive and succeed at all costs.

I see you've somewhat perfected the art of inducing nightmares from gluttony. But an effigy, Cyn? Is that the best you can do? A stuffed doll on a rope. Is that supposed to spread panic, foment dread, or cast aspersion on the Church? I hardly think so. As you see, it only created sympathy for Cahill and the Church. Perhaps effigies worked during your Dark Middle Age assignments. But these are so-called sophisticated folk, although thankfully self-centered. They take whores, not dolls; they buy ribbons, not ropes; they wear fancy hats, not gibbets. Yes, they have base passions that can be compromised, but not directly. You must tweak their pride, with what appeals to their base passions—greed, lust, self—the usual things.

Sit back and watch them feed off their arrogance; if they only knew what we were up to in the name of love.

Eternally yours,
Master of Hopelessness

Part Four: Courtships

For the lips of a strange woman
are like a honeycomb dropping,
and her throat is smoother than oil.
But her end is bitter as wormwood,
and sharp as a two-edged sword.
Her feet go down into death,
and her steps go in as far as hell.

(Proverbs 5:3–5)

Chapter 20
Things Be Different

1

Adam called his new farm "Flax Haven." Like his ancestors, growing flax had been a spiritual undertaking, although he had since given up being spiritual. Nonetheless, growing, harvesting, processing, and producing flax by-products were attractive to his German nature. Flax was strong, robust, and versatile. It was the miracle product of nature used for clothing, construction, and food. Throughout history, linens made from flax (not cotton, silk, or other fibers) were used for altar cloths, temple curtains, priestly robes, and the table coverings of kings. Whereas other fibers would rot and decay, flax-linen would last unscathed for thousands of years. When grown long and strong, then woven tightly without rag, the resulting linens were associated with purity. There was a sense that association with flax-linen brought one closer to creation, to God, and invited miracles. In short, flax revolutionized civilization.

Livingston's flax farming, in Pennsylvania and now in Virginia, produced three main products: flax fibers for cloth, flax seed that was ground for flour, and flax seed that was pressed for cooking oil and paint. Livingston planted his fiber fields densely so that the flax stalks would grow tall and straight. For his seed crop he planted the flax thinly so that the stalks would branch and produce more and bigger seed pods. To ensure a robust harvest, he rotated his flax fields with more mundane cash crops of corn, beans, oats, potatoes, or barley. There was also winter wheat and a root like sweet potatoes. Then, every five years he would furlough the fields with clover to let them recover.

But he kept coming back to flax, and every year, one or two of his fields would produce the best flax in the county. His late wife, Esther, had adored the flax he harvested and would turn out linens that were the envy of their neighbors. Now, in Virginia, he hoped that Eve would learn to spin and weave like her mother.

Livingston had learned to never replant his own flaxseed. Instead, he imported seed from Holland. For some reason, perhaps the more robust northern European climate, Holland produced seed that was able to grow long, strong fibers for the finest cloth. It was not ragged like some seeds from eastern Europe. Importing seed, however, was more costly than growing your own. Flax being an annual, seeds had to be planted every spring. Raising flax was not hard labor, but it was long and at times backbreaking, especially during weeding and harvest when the weeds or the crop had to be pulled by hand from the ground. But it was rewarding, if not financially, then spiritually, or so Eve kept reminding her papa.

In the spring of 1789 Adam, Sam, and Henry staked out five fields of 29–40 acres each. Through John Smith II, Adam found the day labor he required. Although Virginia was a slave state, there were still enough men (and a few women) who were absent the initiative and discipline to run a farm, but they were willing to work the fields for a day at a time. Sometimes they were only good for two days at a stretch, but he easily kept track of their labor and production and paid them at the end of each day. He found a few supervisors, too, that he paid weekly at a higher rate.

Anxious to get crop in the ground, but not having the time to clear and prepare all 175 acres, Adam chose two of the fields that required the least preparation and clearing. He would plant one field with beans and one with flax. His crew went to work clearing the two fields of the small trees and rocks and digging irrigation and draining ditches to ensure the soil was well-drained and capable of being supplied water from the creeks when needed. Then with Luther and Calvin leading the way, they deep plowed and graded the two fields.

The flax had to be seeded early in the morning on a windless day because the seeds were so small. Adam had, over the years, developed a rhythm and pattern of scattering the seed so that it was evenly dispersed. So, he seeded the flax fields with a few men supplying him with fresh seed and grading over the spots after they were seeded. With the fields planted, he turned his attention to construction.

During the winter, mostly on bad weather days, and in the evenings after helping Sam rebuild their cabin, Adam had designed his house, barn, and outbuildings. He found builders from Charles Town and Martinsburg that brought crews and camped out on his property to speed along construction. All the while, Sam proved to be invaluable. His work ethic was Germanic, his wisdom trustworthy, and Adam often asked him to supervise major efforts.

Although Adam was primarily a vegetable farmer, there was also the need to be both self-sufficient and provide cash products for the market in Charles Town. Here is where Eve and Henry, with some guidance from Sam and Bethany, paid off. Adam acquired two dozen chickens, which gave them a daily supply of eggs, and a small pen of pigs, thus pork and bacon would be harvested next year. They now had an additional milk cow which the kids called Bottom. Moon Beam seemed to enjoy the company. At least the milk was sweeter.

By late summer the two-story plus cellar house and the three-level barn were roughed in, although both were far from finished. The house had been built into the side of a hill and over the top of a clear-water spring, providing a source of clean water inside the house and cool storage for the family's stock of roots and vegetables. The barn also was built into the side of the same hill, with a wagon ramp dug down to the lower level, and on the opposite side, on top of the hill, a wagon ramp of soil and flat field stone was built up to the third level.

With the house and barn roughed in and closed-up, they moved out of the small Mayfield cabin, tore it down along with the small stable, and salvaged the lumber. Clearing the stone foundations of the Mayfield cabin, stable, and cairns in the vicinity would have to wait. Otherwise, they set aside acreage along the Opequon Creek and the Charles Town Road for clover and grass for their livestock. Eventually Adam would surround them with peach, pear, and apple trees. Immediately southwest of the compound were seventeen acres of woodland for birds, bees, small mammals, and a source of firewood and lumber. Running along the Opequon and behind the woods were the five large produce fields. Clearing these fields was an on-going task. At the far southeast end of the property, bounded by Turkey Creek, was a pond that provided supplementary water for irrigation and for retting the flax, along with seventy more acres of scattered soft and hard woods.

2

In late summer Adam harvested his beans and quickly sold them for much desired cash at the market in Charles Town. It wasn't much, but it was a beginning, and he was glad to be back to market with a crop after a year's absence.

The long process of harvesting and processing his flax began a month after the flax's blue blooms began to appear. That the field he had selected to grow his flax was a virgin field may have had something to do with it, but when the blossoms appeared he could not remember as lush a field of blue at any time in Pennsylvania. The color and heights of the stalks warmed Adam's heart. Here was something worth his labor.

His crew of ten, which varied day-to-day, began the back breaking job of pulling the flax out of the ground by hand, root and all. The flax stalks with roots intact were tied together in bundles and stood upright (stooked) in the fields for a week until dry. The stooked bundles were then carted off to the barn for threshing or rippling whereby the top of the dry bundles were pulled through a comb of nails to deseed the stalks. The pulled seeds would drop to a clean linen sheet lying on the floor. Adam would eventually press this seed into oil, some of which he would keep for their own cooking, and the rest to be sold at market.

After rippling, the stalks were hauled off to the back of the property to the pond fed by Turkey Creek. Here the stalks were laid in the pond's shallows and held down by stones. The slow flowing water cleaned the stalks while the woody portion of the stalk decomposed in the sun, air, and water for a week or two.

When the outer stalks were sufficiently soft, they were collected and taken back to the field to dry in the open air once again. Once dry, the harvest was moved to the third level of the barn. There the tedious and winter-long process of processing flax was done by hand, one small bundle at a time—*breaking* the stalks into small shives, *scutching* the stalks to separate the stalk from the robust flax fiber, and *hackling* to clean the fiber of the last remnant of the straw shives. What remained were the super strong, supple, and golden gloss fibers ready for spinning and weaving.

By late winter of 1790 Adam was ready to take his flax products to market. He would take the seed to a miller to be ground into flour, meal, and pressed into linseed oil. The market for flour and oil was stronger in Martinsburg, but Charles Town was closer.

The market for his flax stalks was a bigger concern. There was not much of a market in northeastern Virginia and so he expected less competition and thus higher prices for his fibers. In York and points east, there were ready flax markets and tons shipped overseas to Ireland. Growers also varied in the species of flax grown and how far along they processed their flax before taking it to market. Some would sell their pulled and stooked crop to processors; others would process only the seeds and leave the retting, breaking, scutching, and hackling to others. Adam, on the other hand, prided himself in producing long, golden, clean flax fibers ready for spinning. Yes, it took more work, but the price offered by spinners and weavers was higher. He saved some of the fibers back for Eve to spin and weave but carefully bundled the rest for delivery.

The thirty-five-acre crop was an excellent one—nearly five tons of fiber. He was surprised and thrilled with the result. He attributed the record yield to several things: the fertile and virgin Shenandoah Valley soil, his use of Holland seed, his attention to planting and harvesting at the right time, and ensuring the land was well drained and irrigated.

Maybe his life wasn't cursed after all. But now, he was going to have to rent a freight wagon or a Conestoga wagon to get the flax to a buyer. The five tons should get him close to 125 dollars, or forty-five-gold guineas, which he had heard was the current market price. That, with the 90 dollars the bean harvest brought him, would suit him well until next harvest. Making these estimates made renting the Conestoga a little easier. He looked forward to market and the weaver he had been directed to in Hagerstown, Maryland.

3

Anastasia was still upset about the effigy hanging at Magdala, although it had been two months since. Mister Hager still had no idea who was responsible. There was a rumor that it was some bigoted men from a nearby town who had seen Fr. Cahill's Christ Mass announcement. There was also the fear that the perpetrators could have burned down Magdala since they arrived and departed without detection.

She liked Fr. Cahill but worried about him. He was young, handsome, happy, and had a charming Irish lilt to his voice. He was kind in confession, too, although she thought him wrong to inform her she had no obligation to confess what out of obligation she continued to confess.

Since Fr. Cahill had come and the Hagerstown Catholic Society had been founded, she no longer thought about leaving her job. She liked her job. It made her feel productive and appreciated. The tasks were not difficult, but they none-theless challenged her intellect and resourcefulness. She spent most of her time in the office up-front, which was partitioned off from the warehouse and factory proper. The office was a spartan space which she decorated with flowers when they were in bloom. There were a few windows that looked out on the front yard and which let in light; and there was a fireplace with a stash of wood that workmen brought in each morning. In the center of the room were four heavy plank tables for evaluating product, and a large, counter-balance scale on the floor next to a large door that led to the noisy factory of whirling spinners and loud slapping looms.

Anastasia enjoyed overseeing the routing of raw materials through the factory and how they were turned into beautiful and practical rugs, curtains, and fabric bolts for clothing. Everyday she found herself excited to take her inventory checklist to the factory floor and record what had been spun and woven in the last twenty-four hours. She found satisfaction in tracking the product as it was produced and marveled at the creativity of the designers and weavers. To her the cacophonic clanging and chatter of the looms was an energetic and satisfying rhythm—it was the sound of progress—she despised indolence. Sometimes the attention men paid to her was a benefit for the weavers were mostly men who were eager to satisfy her curiosity and teach her the weaving craft—she had an insatiable thirst for knowledge.

It was late in the day of the first week in March 1790 that a Conestoga wagon pulled by a team of two gigantic black shires arrived in the front yard of the factory. Both horses carried a rider. The left horse, the traditional wheel horse, carried a large black man, and the right carried an older white man with a black beard. By the way the wagon sat on its axles Ana knew that the wagon was loaded with several tons of raw material. She was pleased with herself that just after a few months on the job she could almost guess what the wagons were loaded with, and she guessed that this Conestoga was loaded with freshly processed flax. But she was also scared a bit. Over the past months she had met a lot of farmers who had come to sell their harvest but had left disappointed.

Instinctively she donned her coat, tied on a hat, and went out into the yard to meet the farmer and his slave who was driving the team. "Good afternoon, gentlemen," she addressed the two. She was being a bit forward by addressing them both the same way, but that was her way of demanding a bit of dignity for slaves. She figured that if she treated slaves with the same dignity as the owner or supervisors, maybe they'd start doing the same.

She was surprised by what came next. The slave spoke first and didn't dip his head to avoid eye contact as every other slave had done.

"Good-day, Miss," said the big black slave as he tipped his hat with a smile and looked directly at her.

She met his gaze and smiled back. *What was this?* He looked to the white man who was dismounting from his shire.

"Hello, Miss," said the white man. "I'm Adam Livingston, a planter starting up a farm in Smithfield, Virginia, a day's drive south of you. Can I see the owner? I've got a load of flax to market."

Mister Livingston was about fifty she thought, a bit taller than she, with broad shoulders and a full, curly black beard with grey in patches near his temples. His face was angular and strong with deep set brown eyes and high forehead mostly hid by his round, box hat.

"Glad to meet you, Mister Livingston. I'm Anastasia Lilly, the accounts manager here. Mister Arnold Elder, my uncle, is the owner of Hagerstown Textile. I'll be glad to help you. What do you have for us?"

"I'm glad to meet you. I have a daughter, probably a few years younger than you, whom I've left in charge of our farm." Adam laughed a bit. "I think your uncle and I would get along well, giving over our industry to the capable young women in our lives."

The compliment made Anastasia blush. She had never met a man as old as Mister Livingston who was so willing to accept her as his equal in business. She stood erect and accepted his comment at face value.

"Let me introduce my field manager, Sam Dark," said Adam gesturing to the African who was still astride the team's drive horse. "Sam's a very adept man, who with his wife have their home on my land and I am glad to have them in my employ." Catching Anastasia's eye, Adam winked at her, acknowledging his confidence in her judgment that Sam was *not* a slave.

At that Anastasia felt attracted to Adam Livingston as a child felt attached to a good parent. Here was a man she might well be able to call father, for it appeared that Mister Livingston did not own slaves. Sam was a freeman, and his nod and smile at Anastasia confirmed it once again.

Anastasia walked to the back of the Conestoga and climbed up to examine the load. Underneath the canvas cover, tied in small hand-sized lashings which were in turn tied in large bundles, was fully processed and polished flax stalks. The work that this wagon-full represented was amazing to her, as it must have taken all winter to break, scutch, and hackle this much. "Do you know how much you have here, Mister Livingston, in weight?" she asked.

"I estimate five tons."

Anastasia climbed down. "Would you please untie a representative bundle and bring it into our office. I am going to get my uncle."

"Sam, help me here," said Adam.

Anastasia found her uncle working with a weaver to repair one of the larger rug looms. He came to the office, where Adam and Sam were untying a large bundle of flax on one of the evaluation tables. Anastasia made the introductions. Adam explained where his farm was, and how he had moved into the Shenandoah Valley after farming near York, Pennsylvania. This was his first crop from his new farm. He was surprised and pleased with the quality and quantity of the yield compared to his experience near York.

Uncle Arnold didn't say much but evaluated the stalks, measured their length, about twenty-five inches, put a stalk into a device that clamped either end of a single stalk, and then turned a wheel that was geared to the clamps which pulled the stalk until it broke. The number of turns of the crank told Uncle Arnold how strong the stalk was. Uncle Arnold also massaged the stalk between his fingers, tasted and chewed the stalk, smelled it, held the stalk up to a lantern light, and finally took a knife to the stalk and scraped it to test its abrasion resistance.

"Mister Livingston," Uncle Arnold finally said, "if this bundle is any example of what's in your wagon, it is fine flax that you've brought us. Understand, we would test samples throughout our intake of your product. You say you have about five tons of this quality, and Ana with the help of our team would be weighing bundle by bundle so we both would have an accurate accounting of it. But you must know that we've had an extremely productive season for flax, even up in Pennsylvania where we've had growers bring us their crop since last fall. I can't speak for the entire country, of course, but while your crop is very well processed, and appears clean, strong, resilient and has a good luster and abrasion characteristics, I can only offer you about nineteen dollars a ton...and I suspect that is not what you've been expecting."

There it was, thought Anastasia. What she feared. But based on what she had seen in the market since last fall, what Uncle Arnold had just said was very true and the price fair.

4

Adam was devastated. He had expected a price of twenty-five dollars a ton. His demeanor fell uncontrollably as he sucked in his breath. Hopes dashed! "You're right, Mister Elder, that is not what I was expecting, or planning, and it does not seem right. I haven't sold my flax crops for that little in years, especially since I know this crop is, as you say, a very fine crop indeed. It is processed, clean, and ready for spinning. I'm a second-generation flax grower and while I've been out of the market for a year moving, this just doesn't seem right, or fair."

"I've been in the textile business for a long time, too," said Elder, "and my father before me. Two years ago, I was paying twenty-two dollars a ton for flax, not nearly as good as yours. But the market has fallen apart in the last six months, for the growing seasons have been ideal and the yield for every crop is so high that supply exceeds our demand." Elder turned to his niece. "Ana, bring along your product inventory, will you? Mister Livingston, Sam, come with me for a spell. I want to show you what I'm up against."

The proprietor led the group into the factory, where a cacophony of sounds from spinners and weavers greeted their ears. There were three parts to the small operation, one for flax, another for wool, and a third for cotton. In each there were spinners, which created bobbins of thread, and then looms of various sizes and types weaving cloth. At the back of the factory was where Elder warehoused the completed bolts of cloths, rugs, and curtain drapery on rolls. In fact, the warehouse portion of the building was encroaching on the weavers. There seemed to be an overabundance of finished materials, including a portion set aside with threads and yarn on small spindles that were stacked high.

"All through this past winter, and even up until today with your flax, we cannot sell everything we are producing. We have a glut of product as you see. Normally, this area is only half this full. Ana, let me see that book."

Ana opened the book to a specific page and handed it to her uncle.

"Normally, at this time of year, we have a thirty-day supply of bolt cloth, a fifteen-day supply of thread and yarn, and a forty-five-day supply of floor coverings, like these rugs on these rolls over here. But right now," he ran his finger through columns in the record book, "we have a sixty-five-day supply of cloth, a thirty-five-day supply of our spool products, and a nearly four-month supply of rugs. We should stop making rugs, I see. As it is, our prices are down twenty-five percent from last year at this time, and we're still having difficult moving everything. There's so much."

Adam's shoulders slumped as he shook his head in defeat. This was the only textile factory within a reasonable distance of Smithfield. He couldn't just go to the next town, unless he wanted to cart his material to York, which was nearly a week's travel away, and there was no guarantee that prices would be better there. But there had to be a reason for all this, rather than just the weather. It was in his nature to reject such anomalies and look for a reason he could control.

"Mister Elder, it can't be just the weather, is it?"

"For the time being, I think it is," said Elder. "I don't expect this same market next year. It's unusual though I've seen similar years, just not as good or severe, depending on your perspective, of course. You saw that bag of cotton up front? The raw cotton product is cheap to produce, especially down south."

"You mean with slave labor," Adam interjected.

"Well, yes. But my point is that cotton is still not easy to make into cloth. We were given those two bags of raw cotton to see if we could come up with a way to easily remove the seed, so it could be spun. But it's maddening trying to pull the seeds out. If someone can come up with a way to make it cheaper to use, then there's going to be a glut of flax that we've never seen before. But I don't see that happening anytime soon."

Adam was happy about that, except it sounded more like a doom's day prophecy he didn't need to hear. Growing cotton and sending slaves into his fields to pick it was not something he wanted to fathom. A shiver ran up his spine and down his legs at the thought of not being able to farm flax and having to plant cotton instead.

"Is that the best you can do, Mister Elder, the $19 a ton?"

"Yes, I'm afraid it is. I'm sorry. As you see, I have my own problems to deal with and our cash flow is not strong right now."

"I'm sorry, too, Mister Livingston," offered Anastasia with a smile.

To Adam they both seemed like good and sincere persons.

Anastasia continued: "We still would like to do business with you. Uncle, if I may...?" She flipped her inventory book over a few pages and showed her uncle an entry. He studied it for a moment and nodded to her. "Mister Livingston," Anastasia continued, "we'd like to buy your flax. You should know that the price my uncle offered you, $19 a ton, is a $1.50 higher than the last several loads we've purchased." She turned to her uncle.

"Mister Livingston," Arnold continued, "it appears you have an exceptional product. And Anastasia is right, we want to buy your flax. Please accept our offer and our apologies to what extent it makes sense."

That was it. Adam sold his load of processed flax to the Hagerstown Textile operation, but his feelings about growing flax were suddenly mixed. This was not the most encouraging trip to market he had ever made. Now he began to worry about the reception he'd find in Charles Town or Martinsburg with his flax meal and linseed oil. More than likely those markets were depressed as well.

He quickly, if only as a reflex, signed the agreement with Anastasia and was paid forty gold guineas, with ten percent held back until the entire load of flax was processed into the factory operations and with periodic test of the load's quality.

Sam drove the Conestoga into the rear yard and Elder's workers unloaded the wagon into the building within the hour.

The next morning, after spending the night in the upper rooms of a Hagerstown tavern connected to a livery, Adam and Sam returned to Charles Town to return the wagon and then ride back home on Calvin and Luther. As they rode they talked.

"You's know somethin' Missta Livingston," said Sam at one point, "next year yours yield or quality may not be good as dis year. Yet, ya might just make more money. Things have a way of workin' out dat way, strange as it seems."

Adam laughed at the truth of Sam's comment. "Yes, I suppose that's the way it could be."

"I be prayin' for the harvest, Missta Livingston, as I's been doing all along. Things be fine. The Almighty see ta dat."

Adam wasn't so convinced about the Almighty taking care of him. As far as Adam was concerned, it was the Almighty that killed his wife in the prime of her life. "So, Sam, how do you figure the Almighty was taking care of your brother? Seems to me the Almighty isn't all mighty, or he doesn't really care."

Sam waited only a beat. "No, sir. That's not the way it is. De ways I sees it, Miss Bethany and me...Nwanne's in ah better place. He was a slave all his life until you bought him and manumitted him. Dat was a great gift. But maybe you's didn't know, but Nwanne's heart was broken when you's bought him. Good as wad you did was. For he had set his heart on marryin' that slave girl back at McCulloughs. He loved her more than we knows. 'En when you's took Nwanne away, he never did see her again. He told us, Bethany and me, he miss her somethin' bad, but he didn't want to tell you for fear you'd not think him grateful for manumitting him. De way it was, he would never have seen Annenew again, as long as he live. He wanted to go back to McCullough just to be with Annenew and help her and protect her as much as he could. But Nwanne gone now, in a better place, and he probably not missing Annenew. He be prayin' God to free Annenew, that is what Bethany and me thinks. So, de Almighty did care fer him, my bro'her. And maybe Annenew, too. We see."

Adam shook his head. He refused to argue with Sam. Although Sam was younger, he had seen more life and death than Adam would ever see, and yet Sam revealed no bitterness at the life he had been dealt. Adam sucked in his breath. He didn't like all this God-talk. "Sam, you have my respect, but I still don't think it happens that way."

"Well, you jist wait Missta Livingston. Things be different."

Adam nodded and sent Sam a patronizing smile. Indeed, he would wait.

Perhaps next year would be better. Rotating his crops gave him options. The bean market was not depressed, nor were corn, beans, oats, potatoes, barley, winter wheat, or sweet potatoes. On the long trip back to Charles Town he remembered how various crops all had their droughts and their yields. That was the business side of crop rotation. You spread your risk and in the end things worked out.

But he worried about cotton suddenly being able to be processed quickly. He had never grown cotton, but it was easy to grow and grew plentifully. It was also easy to spin and make into comfortable clothes.

Then he laughed. "Sam, you know what they say about flax and cotton?"

"No sir, but I figure ya'll gonna tell me."

"Cotton's comfy for clans, but linen's the luxury of legions."

Sam looked sideways at Adam. "Never heard dat before. You jist make that up?"

5

My Despised Cyn:

Do you see how the uncertainties of farming can play into our hands? Farmers count on forces beyond their control to grow crops—soil and weather. Then they hope that other forces like pestilence and market demand, which are also beyond their control, don't hinder the sale price. Usually anything beyond a farmer's control is attributed to the Creator, especially in bad years—they blame it on God. Why can't Livingston do that? Is he so arrogant that he'll take the hit for a bad crop, too? He may be of a character we've not encountered before.

But I do hope you have made the connection that is sure to haunt the future of your assignment—Anastasia Lilly. Insights into the future fail us here, but it appears that she will have some impact on our efforts. Her priest is Denis Cahill, and she has just purchased flax from Livingston's Flax Haven. Is this just coincidence? I sense it is not. We may be faced with Flax Hell.

Perhaps you need to drop in on Miss Anastasia from time to time, drive a few hat pins into that skull of hers.

Eternally yours,
Master of Devastation

Chapter 21
The Bride Wore White

1

It was April 1790. After working for Uncle Arnold at Hagerstown Textile for a year and three months, and saving her earnings, although she did indulge in a few fancy hats, Anastasia was feeling all grown-up. Living with her uncle and aunt did save money since they refused to take anything for room or board, explaining that free room and board was part of the deal. Aunt Phoebe also treated her like the adult daughter she never had, although Auntie would occasionally hint that Anastasia might consider accepting the proposal of one of the fourteen men that had come courting her over the last year. Yet, when Ana recited a list of the men and what was wrong with each, Aunt Phoebe agreed that none were worth the effort. Anastasia was also able to attend Mass whenever Fr. Denis celebrated in Hagerstown, which was irregularly several times a month due to his circuit schedule. But she was also most satisfied with being able to go to confession at least once a month, although she thought Fr. Denis a bit strange in his counsel.

He kept telling her that what she confessed were not sins, not even venial sins, and that she was being scrupulous—which in itself might be a sin, but hardly worthy of penance, or so Father claimed. What she confessed were sins to her, of course. Maybe she was telling him wrong. She had decided that next time, which was this afternoon, she would confess that she was *obsessed* with perfection. She was sure that was a sin—not the perfection, but the obsession. Yes, she knew Jesus told his followers to "be perfect as he was perfect." But she also understood the concept of hyperbole to make a point. *Obviously, no one can be perfect and certainly she wasn't.* Why, just this last week she had discovered at least two errors in her figures, and she had made a third error in counting. Such sins required she go back into the noisy factory three...no four times to correct it. This counting business was an obsession.

Yet, if Fr. Denis still didn't think that was a sin, then she had a surprise for him. She had discovered a real doozy to confess, and she was sure she would no doubt be given a sizable penance, which she would accept with extreme humility. *Oh, wait! Was that a sin? Being extremely humble—was she proud of being humble? Pretty sure that was a sin. She would confess that, too.*

At the allotted time she entered Magdala's foyer and took a seat in a chair along the wall. There were two women ahead of her. Curious, she could not think of ever seeing a man at confession. As she entered the foyer the older women looked up at her, smiled, and then bowed their heads once again. The waiting line had been moved to the foyer because when they were lined up in the gathering hall near Fr. Denis' confessional screen, those waiting could make out what was being confessed, even though the penitent and Fr. Denis spoke in whispered tones. Before long Fr. Denis was hearing confessions of gossip; and when he traced down the source, he was shocked to discover it was from those waiting in line at his confessional. The women were hearing what was being said, then passing it around town. So, he moved the lineup of chairs to the foyer, and moved the confessional screen in the gathering hall as far away as possible from the archway that led to the foyer. Even then, if one had keen hearing, and it's amazing how keen a woman's hearing can become in such situations, catch phrases could still be made out. It was not hard to fill in the blanks, especially when the penitent walked out through the foyer and you saw who it was. Anastasia was sure as soon as the weather got warmer, the line of chairs would be on the front porch. That way the whole town could see who was going to confession. Further, with a sandglass or timepiece at their disposal, an observer could time the duration between Magdala exits and determine who was the biggest sinner in town. *That could be a problem,* she thought.

When her time came she entered the gathering hall, walked to the confessional, and kneeled before the screen.

Fr. Denis began, "In nomine Patris, et Filii, et Spiritus Sancti. Amen," and Anastasia crossed herself.

"Bless me, Father, for I have sinned. It's been..."

"Wait!" said the voice from the other side of the screen.

She stopped.

Fr. Denis let out a long sigh. "Are you sure you have sinned, Anastasia?"

"Oh, yes, Father. I'm very sure. God has convicted me and that is why I have come to ask the Church's pardon."

There was another long pause. Then, another sigh. Finally: "Very well, my daughter: In nomine Patris, et Filii, et Spiritus Sancti. Amen."

"Bless me, Father, for I have sinned. It is two weeks since my last confession, and these are my sins: I have been obsessed, really obsessed with making my figures for my uncle correct. I count wrong and have to go back into the factory and recount, even when I write down what I counted, I don't trust what I wrote down and have to go back and check, even again." She paused. "It's my *obsession,* Father...with wanting to be perfect." She paused again...then quickly added: "And I was rude to Mister Harrison when he asked for my hand."

"How were you rude?"

"I said, no. I told him I have no interest in marriage. I'm sure I didn't smile at him, or curtsy as you're supposed to do. I just told him, no, and that he should leave and not to think about me ever again."

"Was the tone of your voice harsh or angry?"

Softly she said, "I tried to be gentle. I felt bad to turn him down. He's a very polite man, and perhaps he should be married. But I'm sure he's been turned down many times. It's so sad."

"How do you know he's been turned down many times?"

"I just can't imagine any woman saying, yes."

"Why is that?"

Ana didn't want to say. If she answered truthfully, she was sure she would commit a sin of extreme rudeness. If she lied, well, that would clearly be a sin.

"Why, Anastasia?"

She took a slow, deep breath. "Because...I don't think...he ever bathes."

"Ahhh. Is this Frank Harrison, the cobbler?

"Yes."

"Well, yes, that may be the case with Mister Harrison. Anything else?"

"Yes. I'm humble."

"How's that?"

"I'm *proud* that I'm humble. I'm pretty sure that's a sin of pride. Isn't it?"

Fr. Denis intoned: "Indeed. You may have sinned."

"But I have another one. You'll be happy with this."

"I'll be happy that you've sinned?" said Fr. Denis.

"But you don't like me to confess things that you think aren't sins," Ana said. "So, I'm trying to please you, and find an actual sin...that is, a sin I should confess."

"Are we obsessed here with a perfect confession?" asked Fr. Denis.

"Is that a sin?"

"I don't think so. Go ahead, how have you sinned," Fr. Denis' voice conveyed some doubt.

"I lied, a great many times."

There was a long pause on the other side of the screen. "A great many times? How did you lie, my child?"

I told Mister Harrison...and every one of the other men that has asked for my hand, more than I can count, that I'm not interested in marriage, or having children."

"And that is a lie?"

"Well, yes!" she said with some surprise, as if a priest should know that every young woman wants to be married and have children.

"Let me understand, Anastasia, you *do* want to be married...and have children?"

This time her voice was soft, and she let out a tiny sob, "Yes."

There was a long pause, then very gently Fr. Denis asked again: "Anything else, Ana?"

"No, I don't think so," and she fell back into the ritual. "For these and all the sins of my past life, I ask pardon of God, penance, and absolution from you, Father."

"Okay. Good," said Fr. Denis. "Now let me understand something. Is it true you believe that counting perfectly for your uncle, even being obsessed about it, is a sin?"

"If I obsess about it, yes."

"So, you must believe that *counting with errors, or being imperfect* in your job is *acceptable* and not a sin."

Ana paused to think that one through. It did present a dilemma. "Well, I guess he does expect the count to be perfect."

"I'm sure he does," said Fr. Denis. "But when you seek to be perfect you think you are imperfect, or that seeking perfection in counting is a sin?"

Ana was confused. "I guess, I don't know."

Fr. Denis continued. "On the other hand, when it comes to a man courting you, seeking perfection in the man is a good thing. It's not a sin. Is that what you believe? Or, is it that you should readily accept the obvious imperfections and your incompatibility with a particular man, and agree to matrimony?"

Anastasia had been caught in a contradiction of sorts. "Oh, dear." she confessed.

"Ana, God calls us to be perfect in those areas that are within our capacity. But he knows we cannot be perfect in everything. We must try to use good judgment and absolutely try our best, such as trying hard to get the count perfect, even when you must go back again and again. That is something you *can* do. The sin of obsession, on the other hand, involves our attempt to be perfect in areas that are beyond our capacity, when we try again and again to achieve something that only God can do. Such as the selection of your prospective husband…if marriage is what God has called you to."

"So, you're saying," Anastasia repeated thoughtfully, "that I probably should seek with all my heart and mind to do my numbers perfect for my uncle, but that to expect my husband to be perfect, is an imperfection…a sin?"

"Something like that," said Fr. Denis.

With a palatable despondency Anastasia spoke quietly to herself, "So my husband, if I were to marry, is going to be someone that…right now…I would not like at all."

"Ana! I didn't say that," corrected Fr. Denis. "I suspect, if you are to marry, that the imperfection in your judge of character will lead you to believe that the man you are to marry will be perfect, and that in his imperfection, he will think you are perfect."

"How can that possibly work, Father?"

"My child, with a perfect God all imperfect things are perfectly possible."

She would have to think about that one for a while.

"Now say a good Act of Contrition."

It took her a moment to realize that the rite was over. Slowly she recited the prayer asked of her. It was a favorite:

> *O my God, I am heartily sorry for having offended Thee, and I*
> *detest all my sins because I dread the loss of heaven and the pains*

of hell. But most of all because they offend Thee, who art all Good and worthy of all my love. And I firmly resolve, with the help of Thy grace, to confess my sins, to do penance, and to amend my life. Amen.

Glad to have gotten all that off her heart, Fr. Denis imparted absolution:

Dominus noster Jesus Christus te absolvat; et ego... May our Lord Jesus Christ absolve you; and by His authority I absolve you from every bond of excommunication (suspension) and interdict, so far as my power allows and your needs require. + Thereupon, I absolve you from your sins in the name of the Father, and of the Son, + and of the Holy Spirit. Amen

As was always the case for Anastasia, after hearing the words of Fr. Denis' absolution she felt elated. "Thank you, Father."

"Go in peace."

"But father, wait. My penance. You forgot to give me a penance for my sins."

"I did not forget. You don't need a penance."

Anastasia started to object, but Fr. Denis cut her off.

"Hearing your confession is penance enough...for both of us. Now, get out of here," he said. She detected the smile in his voice.

Hesitantly, Anastasia rose from the kneeler, then with a light heart marched out of the gathering hall, through the foyer, and into the street, not worrying one bit about who might see her. She was free.

What she didn't know was that because of this confession, her life of udder freedom was about to change.

2

Two months later, in early May, Richard McSherry made his rounds via buggy as landlord of various properties in and around Hagerstown. As necessary he looked in on tenants, collected rents, signed over deeds, purchased properties, and ordered repairs. He was always careful to coordinate his visit with Fr. Denis' circuit travels so he could pay a visit to Magdala and see his friend, the "priest under contract," as he jokingly referred to Fr. Denis.

When Richard arrived at Magdala, he walked right in as if he owned the place, which in a technical sense he did. But before he took three steps into the foyer, an older, rotund woman, of slight stature and high energy, bounded out of the parlor and blocked his path. She wore a full apron over a house dress and a head scarf of a pattern that matched neither dress nor apron. Glaring up at the Irish bachelor she demanded, "Who this?" Her eyes peered up at the rather tall man as if he had no business being there and she owned the place, which she did, in a manner of speaking and of which Richard was about to discover.

"Who are you?" Richard snapped back, with a big smile on his face, for meeting new and interesting people for him was always a joy.

"You first, who barge in my domain unannounced," she shot back while wiping her hands on the apron.

Richard laughed out loud, *who was this wonderful woman, and can we have a dozen like her?*

"I am Richard McSherry, Fr. Denis' sponsor and title holder to this domain of *yours.*"

The woman was suddenly a burst of sunshine and happiness. "OH! OH! Mister McSherry, I so long to meet you. You are my much welcome." Without hesitation, invitation, or request she grabbed Richard like he was her returning Prodigal Son and hugged him with a big laugh.

Richard absorbed the hug and then, with some effort, pulled her off, held her at arm's length and asked, "Now, who are you?"

"OH! OH! Mister McSherry. I am Priest Keeper."

"Really?" said Richard. "Well, that's wonderful, does the 'priest keeper' have a real name?"

At that moment Fr. Denis trotted down the staircase. "Richard! So, glad to see you. I see you've met indeed my priest keeper. This is Immacolata Rosso, whom I have hired out of your generosity and the offering boxes, to care for Magdala and feed me. She lives with her elderly sister, also a widow, a short walk away. She's a wonderful caregiver and everyone in Hagerstown loves her."

In that way Richard discovered Magdala's Immacolata, an older but very capable Italian widow. Of prodigious taste and middle, Immacolata worked for very little, ensured that Fr. Denis had time to visit parishioners, study, pray, and do other priestly things. As Richard discovered, Immacolata Rosso loved being known as the "Priest Keeper." Her goal, as she told Richard, was to fatten up the skinny Irish priest so he will be healthy enough to get into heaven. She was convinced that all Saints were fat and well fed, as was her husband before his untimely death of a heart attack. "It was God's will," she said, "that I have time now to care for first priest of Hagerstown."

That night Richard and Fr. Denis caught up over supper cooked and served by a very happy and anxious to please Mrs. Rosso.

After supper they settled down before the fireplace to enjoy a bottle of sherry, for Richard was anxious to hear of the progress Fr. Denis was making among his circuit of Catholic societies.

Immacolata had cleaned up supper and was about to leave for the night, when Fr. Denis excused himself to talk to his keeper in whispers by the door. When Fr. Denis returned, he put aside the storytelling and clothed his demeanor is a serious tone.

"Richard, I want you to meet someone from the city about an endeavor I want to pursue. Something here in Hagerstown has been brought to my attention. It's highly confidential and of a strategic nature. I am glad you have come when you did. Can you spend another night and dine with me and this individual tomorrow night, here at Magdala as we have dined tonight?"

"Of course, Father. Is it Jonathan Hager we're to meet? What is it? You have my attention now."

"No, no. Not tonight. No, the person is much more important than Mister Hager. But tonight, I am too tired. This other party needs to hear what I have to say at the same time as you. It has major consequences for the future. Tonight, I am well-kept, as you might say," holding up his mostly empty glass of sherry. "I have asked Immacolata to have supper ready at the beginning of the first watch, or about six bells as we have recently become acquainted."

Richard knew he meant six in the evening. The recently installed clock tower in town struck its deeply resonant Spanish cast bell on the hour. It was helpful during the day to keep the town on schedule, but it was waking people up at night, especially when at midnight it struck twelve times.

"Is there trouble brewing? Another effigy in the making, I pray not?"

"No, no. Not of that nature. But one of great consequence, of which I'm not sure to fear or be joyous over. Let us not talk any more about it now, as my mind is slipping, and before my mouth slips, too, I need yet to observe my office before sleep overtakes me."

Richard was intrigued since he knew everyone in town of any significance. Or, at best he thought he did. But the confidence and earnestness of which Fr. Denis spoke kept Richard calm. So, they finished their sherry and turned in for the night.

3

The next day Richard busied himself visiting renters and associates, timing his return to Magdala just as the town clock struck six. *A marvelous acquisition that clock,* he thought. If only he could get a hold of one of those pocket watches that were gaining popularity in Europe. Yet, because each watch was handmade and very expensive, he supposed he could do without the timepiece. Besides, no one else he knew or did business with could afford one. Further, rumor was you had to reset them every day to local sun time. He guessed the traditional 'early-mid-late,' 'morning-afternoon-evening,' would have to do, unless you have a town clock, with two clock keepers, who both evidently had sundials perfectly stationed on their windowsills with a cloudless corridor to the noon sun. Not sure how the clocks were going to keep time in winter with a perpetually overcast sky. It sounded very mystical.

Nonetheless it was six o'clock, as they were wont to say, so he went straight to his room and put aside his leather satchel of documents and pocketbook of rents collected. Since he had been rummaging around in some foul field and he was to meet a town dignitary "more important than Mister Hager," he changed into clean silk socks and off-white linen breeches, high collar white shirt, ruffled cravat, and double-breasted blue waistcoat. He would wear no wig, they were so fake, and the colored powder got into everything to say nothing of the dusting of one's clothes.

But back to the boots. All he had for footwear were his riding boots, which were good for mucking around unimproved land, but not entirely appropriate for supper with a city or bank official. He felt disappointed that he had left his buckled shoes back at Retirement. He quickly took a damp cloth and wiped the mud off the boots and tried to buff them to some level of respectability.

He was brushing dust off his powder blue waist coat, *probably wig dust*, he thought, when he heard the front door open and Immacolata welcoming in a man and a woman. He stopped and listened, wondering if this was their guest. It was then that he realized he had not heard from Fr. Denis or heard him in his room. When he was ready, he left his room, walked across the hall, and knocked on Denis' door. "Father, you in there? I smell a roast or something cooking downstairs. You about ready?"

But no answer came.

Well, he must be downstairs.

4

Anastasia was charmed that Uncle Arnold invited her to a supper with Fr. Denis to discuss a future order of altar linens for use in the various home churches on Fr. Denis' circuit. When they arrived, Immacolata greeted them in the foyer and ushered them into the parlor where a supper table was set...for two. Ana was suddenly embarrassed and felt out of place. Clearly the supper was intended for Fr. Denis and Uncle Arnold and she was not supposed to attend. But Uncle Arnold didn't seem to be concerned that the table was for two and not three. Perhaps he didn't notice. But then neither did Immacolata who always seemed to know more about what's going on than the people themselves. Gracious, as always, she invited them to sit on the love seat while she got the food ready, disappearing into the kitchen at the back of the parlor.

"Uncle, are you sure I'm invited? The table is set for only two," asked Anastasia.

"Oh! Well, I, ah...thought I had told Fr. Denis you were coming...but perhaps I forgot. Immacolata can set another place. No worry."

"But she may not have prepared food for three," objected Anastasia.

"What do you mean, you eat like a morning dove," her uncle joked. "You can have some of mine."

At that moment she heard steps coming down the stairs and stood up to greet Fr. Denis. Except the footsteps sounded heavier and farther apart, as if the person was in no rush and wearing riding boots. She had never seen Fr. Denis in riding boots. Uncle Arnold remained seated, so she turned to him and gestured that he should stand out of respect for the priest. But he gestured her concern away, and at that moment the riding boots came down the steps, seemed to walk into the gathering hall where they stopped for a moment, and then walked back toward the parlor, and entered.

5

The first thing...perhaps the only thing, Richard McSherry saw upon entering the parlor was a beautiful, erect, young creature wearing a fancy lime-green hat beneath which were two doe, blue eyes, and a thin, delicate smile all framed with a mass of naturally curly rust-red hair, pulled back. The creature had started to curtsy, but stopped when she saw him, as if she was expecting someone else. Then after gazing at him for a moment, her mouth fell open, she dipped her head and curtsied deeply, and he bowed back, still unable to look away. She wore a plain yellow dress with a high choke-collar and lime-green necktie of the same silk ribbon that matched her hat, and that tightly encircled her naturally trim waist—without, he suspected, one of those damn corsets that distorted the female form like a medieval tourniquet. She wore no hoop under her petticoat, which teased at the bottom of her skirt with delicate white ruffles. *The dress fit her perfectly, or perhaps she was just perfect.* He could not decide which. At once she was plain but stunning, innocent but mature, childlike but well-mannered, and his heart stopped whenever his gaze passed over her.

Richard finally forced his eyes to look at the young woman's companion, a man of about his own age. *This must be the city dignitary of some importance that I was to meet*, he thought. But the man was not dressed as such, but rather wore a drab suit of common wool and a plain shirt as a commoner or perhaps a merchant. *Was she his daughter? What a contrast the two made.*

At that moment Immacolata entered from the kitchen with a bowl of greens and placed it in the middle of the table, which he now saw was set for two.

He spoke up: "Immacolata, Father Cahill. Do you expect him soon?"

"Oh! Oh! Mister McSherry," gushed Immacolata, "good to see you again. I have good supper for you."

"Yes. Thank you," Richard said, as his eyes again wandered to the young creature of whom he was anxiously waiting for an introduction, even as she gazed back at him looking confused and out of place. "And Fr. Denis, Immacolata? Where is he?"

Immacolata stopped and looked up at the ceiling as if Fr. Denis was going to float down into the room at any moment. "I'm not entirely sure, Mister McSherry, but I think he rode to Fort Cumberland this afternoon."

"Fort Cumberland!" gasped Richard. "That's sixty miles away. We're supposed to have supper tonight..." Suddenly, Richard caught himself and turned to the man who seemed to be sitting comfortably on the love seat paying attention to the dialogue and blocking, as if he was watching a stage play. Richard leaned toward the man, bowed, and offered his hand. "Sir, I am Richard McSherry of Leetown, Virginia. I suspect that Fr. Denis intended for us, you and me that is, to sup with him tonight to discuss something of significant importance regarding the future, but I know not what. Perhaps you might enlighten me?"

The man stood up and pressed his lips together as if to prevent unintended words from escaping. He bowed to Richard. "Mister McSherry, I am Arnold Elder, owner and merchant of Hagerstown Textiles. We purchase flax, wool, and cotton, but not silk, and make bolt cloth, rugs, and spindles of yarn and thread." He smiled politely at Richard, stood still as if ready for inspection, and said nothing more.

To Richard the man had delivered the line as if he was at a country fair, standing on a soap box, pitching his business to passersby as if he might be ready to buy a rug. Richard collected himself and said graciously, "Mister Elder, I have ridden past your factory many times. So glad to make your acquaintance. Do you know…?"

But Arnold held up his hand to stop Richard from going on. "Let me introduce you to my niece, Anastasia Lilly, of Conewago, Pennsylvania. Anastasia lives with my wife and me here in Hagerstown and is our account manager at Hagerstown Textiles."

Richard lit up, adroitly turned to Anastasia, and bowed again, as she curtsied to Richard. "I'm most enchanted to make your acquaintance, Miss Lilly." His eyes riveted on hers.

"And of you likewise, Mister McSherry." The creature spoke…beguilingly. Then, perhaps out of turn, she twisted her mouth into a sardonic smile, "But I am disappointed that you are not my priest, whom we were to meet here tonight for supper. But now, we are to find out…" Anastasia peered at Immacolata, "…is nowhere nearby. Is that right, Madam Priest Keeper?"

Immacolata shrugged her shoulders, shook her head, swung her hips a bit, as if to ask for forgiveness and replied, "I don't know Miss Lilly, I'm just here to serve you supper."

Anastasia's brow furrowed at her uncle, who held up his hands in defense.

But they were interrupted. "Okay, that's enough," said Immacolata taking charge. "Arnold, you come with me to the kitchen. We will eat there. Mister McSherry, Miss Lilly, enjoy the supper, I made it especially for the two you." With that Mrs. Rosso left for the kitchen.

"I have one more task," said Arnold. Whereupon he turned to the table, lifted an already opened but uncorked bottle of wine, and poured it into the two empty stemware glasses on the table. He put down the bottle, picked up the glasses, and handed one to Richard and one to Anastasia. "Enjoy. I'll be in there." He pointed to the kitchen door, and toddled off.

6

Anastasia Lilly was a smart young woman. But this was new territory. Her first response was anger. No one had asked if she wanted to have supper with a

330 O *Stanley D. Williams*

strange man in her priest's parlor. The idea sounded scandalous. Then she wondered if celibate priests are secretly trained to be matchmakers. She sincerely hoped that was not the case, but here was evidence that it might be.

Perhaps Aunt Phoebe had something to do with this, but she didn't think her aunt could keep a secret, and this was a big secret. And Uncle Arnold's imagination was limited to fabric designs; otherwise, he played everything straight by the book. But here she was with a wine glass in her hand facing an obviously befuddled, strange, attractive, and by the way he was dressed, rich man...also holding a wine glass, which at this point began to shake. The man was nervous, and clearly out of his comfort. He kept looking at her, then his wine glass, then opening his mouth to speak, then closing it. It quickly became clear to Anastasia that this rendezvous was not his idea nor was he aware of it until it happened. That left one person...okay, two persons. Either Immacolata...no, it couldn't be...she wouldn't try to match up two people she barely knows. But there was one person that knew them both well. That meant *it was the priest, in the parlor, with a wine bottle.* Except the priest had conveniently skipped town...or so they were told.

It was true they were chaperoned by her uncle...yes, he was in on this...and Immacolata, who probably was just the cook, not one of the conspirators. She wondered if Mister McSherry was Catholic? Only one way to find out.

"So, Mister McSherry," began Anastasia a little miffed, "I think we've both been tricked, by a priest no less."

Richard searched her face for an answer, but clearly did not know what to say. "Denis...er, Fr. Denis, asked me to come to supper tonight to meet with a town dignitary about some future project he was considering."

"And Uncle Arnold asked if I wanted to tag along to have supper with Fr. Denis about a future linen order he was going to place," rejoined Anastasia.

Richard thought about that, smiled a little and said, "Who do priests confess to? They need another priest, don't they?"

"I think that's the way it works," she said. "When was your last confession, Mister McSherry?"

He bowed slightly to her, "Please, call me Richard."

She nodded and smiled.

"Two months ago, when I was here last," Richard said as he put his other hand on his wine glass to stop it from shaking. Then, after steadying it, he took a sip. "Hmmm, Madeira, Portugal, 1775 perhaps. Communion wine." Richard shook his head in light disappointment. "He could have asked. I would have gotten him something...dryer."

So, he's Catholic, she thought. *Okay, off to a good start.* She took a sip of her wine as well. "Yep, that's his communion wine," she giggled and took another sip.

Immacolata tumbled into the room: "Come you two, eat. I work hard this. You must eat and grow strong and fat so you have energy to tell priest he should not lie. You should hear *his* confession, maybe.'"

So it was that Anastasia Lilly and Richard McSherry met, and spent the evening conspiring about how they were going to get even with their favorite priest.

7

Fr. Cahill had no designs on being a matchmaker. Yet in the case of Richard McSherry and Anastasia Lilly, having listened to both their confessions over time, it seemed natural, if not Providential, that they should meet and forge a friendship, if not something more. In the end, Fr. Cahill was pretty sure angels were involved; he just happened to be the arrow in Cupid's bow.

But his arrow flinging didn't end with their introduction. Over the coming months Anastasia continued to come to confession twice a month; and with Anastasia's presence in Hagerstown, Richard appeared at Magdala not once every two months, but often twice a month. Consequently, Fr. Cahill would hear Richard's confession more frequently and they would talk as friends. As a priest, he felt ignorant of the mysteries between men and women, though he attempted to offer the love birds advice of a spiritual nature. As Richard's friend, however, he was vicariously enjoying the drama and bewilderment of courtship.

Richard told Fr. Cahill that he had never seriously pursued a relationship with a woman, although doing so had been his eventual intent. He had rather been consumed with establishing his land holdings, building a secure asset base, and a stabilized revenue stream. He did not think that such could be done while courting a woman; they seemed mutually exclusive. Courtship would drain him emotionally and no doubt intellectually, resulting in foolish decisions, not just about land acquisitions, but about the woman as well. Though his parents were good examples he had learned much by observing the lives of sailors and revolutionaries in the islands. Now, having been so deceptively introduced to Anastasia, he found that his assumptions were right. Anastasia occupied his mind nearly every hour of the day and every day of the week, and thus he grappled with priorities. Was it business or the woman he was to pursue? Fr. Cahill could not make that decision for him. For Richard, the last few years was all business. He liked stability, and this woman business unnerved him, although he found the unnerving delightful and he longed for it more and more.

Anastasia had told Fr. Cahill several times that in her young life she had encountered more than her fair share of suitors. It started when she turned fourteen, at which time her parents had invited older men to come by and look over the merchandise. Her shock at their cavalier attitude forced her to compile a list of what she disliked in men. It was an easy list to compile because it was simply a list of what she despised in the men she was introduced to by her parents and those she lived with. Her perfect list was simply the opposite of all the men she had met. While she became stubborn about what she wanted in a man, her parents became impatient with her stubbornness.

This explained to Fr. Cahill why Anastasia was mature beyond her years regarding the opposite sex. She wanted consistency; she hated surprises, and a man who was indecisive, uncertain, confused, or given to vacillations was quickly put aside. She had explained to Fr. Cahill why she prioritized her relationship with the Church. There was no uncertainty in what the Church, and God by extension, demanded of her. But she went further. While the Church may not have codified what traits a man must have to respectably court a young Catholic woman, she had. The man had to be selfless and not given to irrational decisions. He needed to have in his possession natural habits of appearance, cleanliness, and orderliness. He must demonstrate commonsense, which to her meant a deep fear for the consequences of ignoring what the church taught. As she explained it, the Church didn't punish you for doing stupid things... nature and society did. Only such a man, in her eyes, could possibly attain the good life...of which she would gladly participate. It was at times like this that Fr. Cahill felt he was back in seminary hearing a lecture on moral theology, with seventeen-year-old Anastasia as the instructor. Without directly saying so, Fr. Cahill noted that her actions around Richard indicated he fit her criteria.

So it was, late one night, with a bottle of sherry mostly empty, that Richard finally came around and asked his friend, Denis (the priest known to others as Fr. Cahill) just how he might put away all this bafflement and propose marriage.

Denis joked. "In seminary the courses on proposing marriage were few. But here's an idea, why don't you ask her?"

"What!?" said Richard. "As if she wants tea or coffee with her porridge?"

"How would I know?" asked Denis. "You see, there are somethings priests aren't supposed to know. Tell you what, once you figure it out, come tell me. I'll pass it on."

"She has baggage, you know," said Richard.

"That she tells me. Hat boxes, I think she said."

"Hat boxes? She didn't tell me that."

"She has a weakness for fancy hats. I'm sure she told me that outside of confession, so I can tell you. You'll need a spare room for hat boxes."

"I'm not talking about hats. The baggage I'm talking about is her father."

"You mean if you marry, the father of the bride comes too?"

"No, no, no. She doesn't think her father will give me permission to marry her."

"Wait! So, you've already talked to Anastasia about marriage?"

"Well, yes."

"I thought you were asking about how to propose to her, as if the subject had never come up."

"Oh, no, no. She brought it up within a month of that deceitful supper arranged by our unscrupulous priest."

"She proposed to you?"

"Not exactly."

"What does that mean?"

"I guess her parents have been trying to get her married for years."

"That much is obvious. It's a miracle she isn't. So?"

"So, it's been on her mind and she hasn't been interested, but now she is. Or, at least she's open to the idea, as I am, although with a great many doubts."

"Don't enter marriage with doubts; it could invalidate the marriage."

"Evidently the doubts she has have to do with Mister Lilly, who is also a Richard, by the way."

"Great! That should make things all the more understandable. But why would any father not want you, of all people, a rich, Irish bachelor, and a good Catholic, as a son-in-law?"

"She tells me her father has issues."

8

Christmas, 1790.

Richard Lilly of Conewago was annoyed that his wife, Mary Ellen, had planned an unwieldy Christmas celebration—she had invited their six adult children and their families home for Christmas. In spite of the impending disruption, he did his duty and slaughtered the fatted calf, literally. Admittedly, it would be good to see all the kids in one place, as long as they didn't stay long. Farming *Good Luck*'s 200 acres with their remaining five inattentive boys and two indolent slaves was hard enough. But now the house and barn would be overrun by a horde of past children, spouses, and who knew how many grandkids. Added to the commotion it would be his job to clean up the mess left behind...and there would be a mess. This was not the good luck for which he had bargained. At least it would keep him busy most of the time and he wouldn't have to engage in small talk and gossip. *Give me a rake and a hoe; I'd rather talk to potatoes.*

Adding to his consternation, Anastasia was expected to arrive late on Christmas Eve with her Virginia dandy, or so he interpreted her letter in which she described the man's sizable land holdings, accomplishments, and appearance. Considering how hard he had labored to eke out an existence at Good Luck, it was obnoxious how a man twenty years his junior could accumulate a thousand times more and be called Richard at the same time. At least the dandy was not related to the McSherrys in Hanover—bumbling fools that they were.

Anastasia had written that she and Richard would arrive in his closed carriage, which had the luxury of a hot-coal foot warmer that worked well if they stopped every few hours at a tavern and bargained for fresh hot coals. He doubted Anastasia had ever seen the closed carriage or the foot warmer. She might be surprised if this McSherry chap showed up in an open buggy and the foot warmer was a horse blanket. No doubt Anastasia was dragging this man along so he could ask for her hand in marriage. He and Mary Ellen had been through this a dozen times before, if he counted right, and he could count. Anastasia had turned them all down, pigheaded girl. But let her leave home for a year and suddenly she's made up her mind, or so it seems. If he, Richard Lilly, was any judge of men, Anastasia's dandy was likely a leech looking for a dowry to feed his hag horse. Lilly prided himself as his daughter's gate keeper, and now was no time to let down his guard.

When the couple arrived, Richard Lilly was mortified. Indeed, they had arrived in a closed, upholstered carriage, driven by a warmly appareled coachman, and pulled by two blanketed, handsome, chestnut mares. Were the Lillys to put up the coachman as well? Yes, it seemed so. *He could eat with the help.*

When she alighted from the carriage, Richard Lilly marveled at how Anastasia's face and demeanor had matured in the year since he had last seen her. She looked older and more confident. She was warmly attired with her hair curled and framing her face under a large fancy hat with what looked like fox tails wrapped around the top. She greeted her father and mother with enthusiasm and smiles, and she rained kisses on her siblings, especially her younger brothers.

Mister Lilly's evaluation of the forty-something Richard McSherry was also in need of adjustment. McSherry was dignified, not given to flamboyance or exaggeration. He greeted everyone with respect and court appointed deference. Neither was this McSherry chap a brutish ogre, or greedy layabout. But first impressions were misleading. *What kind of hook and crook dandy travels in a heated carriage?*

Having arrived just at sundown, and after a full day of travel, the two were fed a warm meal, visited a little, and thereupon retired to separate rooms for the night.

The next morning the entire family and slaves rose, dressed for church, and bundled off in a collection of horses, buggies, and one closed carriage, for Christmas Mass at Conewago Chapel. After Mass, which was celebrated by *Fr. James Pellentz, they returned to Good Luck for a Christmas meal which Hannah and Mary Ellen, with help from the girls, had prepared. It was a raucous but enjoyable celebratory event with plenty of food, carol singing, and the first gift exchange of the twelve days of the Christmas season.

Richard Lilly was glad when it was mostly over. He longed for the peace and quiet of his fields. Beans never made as much noise when they were growing, only after you ate them.

But the day wasn't over. There was one more thing to attend to. Thus, he invited Richard McSherry into the parlor. There he poured two glasses of his favorite wine, an obscure vintage he could not name, gave one to his guest, and closed the door.

"Mister McSherry," began Mister Lilly, "My wife and I have been through this too many times to count." Taking a sip of his wine, Lilly sat in a worn leather chair across from McSherry who, Lilly noticed, had sniffed his glass of wine, and quickly put it aside. *Ungrateful snit.* He also noted that McSherry chose to sit on an uncushioned chair, place both feet squarely on the floor, sit erect, and give Lilly his undivided attention. *Arrogant, too.* "You probably don't know how many men have asked for my daughter's hand, and all were sent packing."

"Twenty-eight, I believe Ana said," McSherry added.

"That many?" asked a spurned Lilly. He was reacting not only to Anastasia's rejection of her father's many recommendations—he thought there had been only twelve—but to McSherry calling his daughter Ana. His daughter was too fastidious, and the man was too familiar.

McSherry continued: "I share a number of values with your daughter, Mister Lilly. We both love the Church; and I must say, Conewago Chapel is an impressive new structure. Fr. Pellentz must be a wonderful priest to have attracted so large a congregation as we saw today."

"Been with us for over twenty years," said Mister Lilly. "Baptized Anastasia and her younger brothers. Before him it was *Fr. Framback who baptized her older sisters and brothers. But Pellentz did the wedding Mass of Anastasia's older sisters, as no doubt he will do for Anastasia."

"You should know sir," said McSherry, "Ana and I are determined to raise Catholic children faithful to the Church."

Lilly stiffened again at McSherry's use of a nickname for Anastasia, as if his daughter were already the man's handmaid.

McSherry continued: "She is interested in working with the poor and disadvantaged, in which I am already involved. And..." At this point, McSherry stopped short. "Well, there are other ways in which we seem to be compatible."

He's hiding something, thought Lilly, *and he's probably never walked behind a plow, milked a cow, delivered a calf, or dirtied his riding boots in a field of mud.* "Please do go on, Mister McSherry. I'm interested to know exactly why you think you and my daughter are compatible."

"Social concerns, mostly," said the suitor, trying to avoid the detail.

"Such as?" pushed the Father.

McSherry sat up straighter, if that was possible, and caught Lilly's eye.

"Well, Mister Lilly, I hope you'll understand. We both oppose slavery. And your daughter has agreed to support the abolitionist movement which my brother I were part of in Jamaica, and now here in the United States."

"You don't say," said Lilly heavy with scorn.

"William and I were hardware merchants in Kingston for twenty years before coming to the United States four years ago. Sixty percent of Jamaica's population were African slaves and twenty percent were freed Africans. One group of freed slaves was led by a man called *Three Fingered Jack—Jack Mansong, until his unfortunate murder about ten years ago. He was killed ironically by another African free group, the Maroons. But Jack's community, just northeast of where we were in Kingston, continued to thrive and we were glad to extend them credit and trade with them; they honored our trust by keeping short accounts. They were industrious and proved themselves productive and constructive, farming sugar cane and beets."

"Not my experience," shot back Lilly. "I got me a Jack and he's an indolent bastard."

McSherry was startled at the description. "Perhaps, Mister Lilly, because he's not motivated. He's lost hope."

"Anastasia says you're a land speculator. That right?"

"Don't think I've ever used that word. I have invested in land throughout the Shenandoah Valley, some are rental properties in towns, some are farms with tenant farmers, and, yes, I've done a little speculation. But I'm not in it for the big payoff. I'd rather have a stable income."

"Like farm revenue?" challenged Lilly.

"Town properties are more stable if the tenants don't skip town. But farm revenues can be good if the crops don't fail. In a few instances, when the crops and harvest are strong, I share in the profits."

"Well, there you are," said Lilly as if he had stumbled onto hidden treasure.

"How's that?"

"You're not much different than me, except you don't farm, do you? Never hoed a field, have you? Have you ever walked behind a team of oxen for fourteen hours a day and plowed a field?"

"No, sir, I haven't. But I've financially helped many a tenant farmer who has done those things, extending them credit in hard times."

"You mean until their luck turns around? Yes, that's what it is that bothers me about you," concluded Lilly.

"Sir? What is that?" inquired McSherry.

"You're a hypocrite," jabbed Lilly.

McSherry's calm demeanor jumped at the assertion. "Sir!? Why would you lay such a claim? I am a devout Catholic man who holds short accounts with both God and my fellow man."

Lilly had touched a nerve. "Mister McSherry, you are a hypocrite and a liar. You're just clever enough to hide what you do from my naive daughter."

"Sir, you violate my honor by this frivolous and fraudulent insult."

Got him, the bastard. Backed into a corner and he's stupid to it. Look how irritated he is. "You're a liar about being against slavery because there is no way to farm and have any luck at it, unless you have slaves at your command to help you."

"I do not farm."

Lilly smiled at his guest, for he saw that he was getting to the quick of Mister McSherry's deceit. He had pricked deep enough to draw blood. It was not fair that a dandy like him should get rich off the labor of farmers like himself, slaves or not. Lilly grit his teeth and charged ahead with the truth as he saw it. "No, but you earn income from tenant farmers, and the money you collect is due to the productivity of slave labor, though I admit it could be more if the damn slaves worked like they're told."

"Mister Lilly, you are treading on quicksand, and I beg you to retract such dishonorable claims of which you have no evidence."

"Well, I'm right, aren't I? Admit it? Your income, just like mine, is off the backs of black Africans who according to the Constitution aren't even fully human. Look, I know Anastasia is against slavery, but for you to tell her you're against it too to woo her is a prevarication, boy. She just doesn't know you're profiting off slaves as we should and must do. You have courted her under false pretenses."

"Mister Lilly, you are a villain. I would be a fraud if one farthing of my earnings are the consequence of slave labor. I am confident it never has, nor will be."

Lilly knew no one could farm profitably without slaves. That had been proven time and again, and if he could afford a few more slaves he would see a good profit rather than just getting by.

McSherry attempted a defense: "The *Mansongs didn't own slaves; they didn't enslave their own. But they were able to build homes, feed their families, and enjoy the bounty of their labor. Further, there are hundreds if not thousands of farmers in the northern states that have families large enough to assist, or even hire day laborers."

"And they're poor because of the wages they have to pay."

Richard McSherry shot up from his chair and raised his voice. "No, that is where you're wrong. They're profitable because they are more productive. The laborers have freedom, hope, they're innovative, they find better ways to do the work with less effort. Of my tenants I charge less rent than most, which means they keep for themselves more of what is produced by their own labor. They're motivated. Slaves are not motivated to do that. Slavery robs African men and women of their God given dignity, they lose hope, and do only what's demanded of them. It's neither morally right, nor practically efficient."

Lilly was as mad now as McSherry, and raised his voice, lapsing into sarcasm: "No, of course not! You don't *own* African slaves, you *own* an Irish priest, who works for you like a slave, going around to these cities where Ana says you've started Catholic societies, collecting the pewage and giving it to *you* so you can create the appearance of riches with your fine carriage, blanketed horses, and a coachman."

At this point the parlor door swung open and Lilly's' wife, Mary Ellen, and Anastasia burst into the room. Lilly glared at his wife and daughter, turned back to McSherry, and lowered the boom. "You're a double liar and a hypocrite. I'll say it again for the sake of our audience. You're startin' these churches to collect pewage and pay this priest bond servant of yours a pittance. You're a sham. You're rich because of the labor of hundreds of slaves on the land you own, and you know it. No, you cannot marry my Anastasia, which is her name to you by the way, not Ana. She is too good for you, and I suggest you depart these premises immediately without her, for she's not going back to Hagerstown with you, so help me God."

Richard McSherry was too angry and too heart-broken to speak. He turned to Anastasia, clenched his jaw, lifted his head, and calmly strode out of the room. Mary Ellen openly sobbed as she dramatically wrung her hands.

And what of Anastasia? Likewise, she was stunned into an uncharacteristic silence. But if looks could kill, her father would have dropped dead.

Nor should we forget Richard Lilly. He pompously smirked at his wife and daughter, and with smug satisfaction laughed. It was as if he had just fought a duel with pistols and was the only one left standing save the seconds. He was right for once: Richard McSherry was a total fraud. Feeling deep pleasure at his excellent judge of character, he picked up his glass of an unknown vintage, and gulped downed the balance in celebration.

9

Anastasia scowled at her father as he took a victory lap around the parlor with his empty wine glass held high. Never had she witnessed such a blatant display of murderous envy. In an instant it was so obvious. Her father wasn't just jealous of Richard McSherry's success, he didn't just want to be as wealthy, he didn't just want a carriage with two fine horses and a coachman, he didn't want to learn how Richard had worked and saved for decades. No, Richard Lilly wanted to deny Richard McSherry success by denying Richard McSherry reputation, companionship, and love. That was the price of envy. *If I can't have it, then you can't have it either. Further, because I can't have what you've earned, you're the hypocrite and liar for having earned it and possessing it.* Jealousy she could tolerate, but she had no tolerance for envy, especially when she was the pawn.

Her mother reached out for Anastasia, begging her daughter to understand and forgive her father who worked so hard to supply the family with food, shelter, and clothing. But Anastasia was done with her mother's tolerance of evil. Too often growing up her mother had held out an olive branch to her husband not for justice but for peace at any cost. Anastasia would have none of it. She went in search of her hope.

She found Richard packing his bag. His eyes were moist, and his hands shook.

"Where's Eric?" she asked, her voice wavering.

"Insightful lad. He heard the argument, quickly packed his bag, and met me outside the parlor. He's on his way to ready the carriage. I will depart immediately. Eric says he can find the way to a nearby inn. I will stay there until morning and then home. What of you, my dear? I am so deeply sorry for this."

Anastasia stared at Richard with disbelief.

"'What of me, my dear?' Is that all you can say?" She started to cry, the disaster breaching her composure. "What of me, Richard?" She sobbed, "What of us!?"

Richard turned to her. "My dear, I am unworthy of you, it seems. I was without defense. No words would come from my heart or mind to change your father's opinion of me. To tell him the truth of my work would have been useless. I fear he was set on some strange course of revenge before we ever arrived. Why I cannot fathom...but my inability to mount a defense makes me a rude excuse of a man."

"And what does that make of me, a naive, brainless fool? What of our goals and work? What of our family, of God, and the poor? Are we not to fulfill our destiny on earth and fulfill our vocation as we so longingly have prayed?" She gazed at him—he seemed to harbor no doubts about what he was about to do, but he also appeared to be distraught about doing it. Their lives, their hopes, their dreams were suddenly in jeopardy and their future muddled.

There was a long silence between them. He reached for her, and she fell into his arms and cried. "I thought you were going to fight a duel," she sobbed.

He tightened his grip about her. "My dear, the Church has forbidden duels. But had I the pistols, I would have willingly met him in the glen. And yet, I could not kill your father, as despicable a man as he is, and as you tried to warn me."

She sucked in her breath: "Well, I don't suppose there will be a dowry." At that they both chuckled through their tears.

He pushed her away to look at her tear-stained face. With the ruffled cuff of his sleeve, he wiped her face dry, and with some doubt asked, "After I have failed so miserably in seeking your father's blessing, you would still marry me?"

She instinctively stiffened and put him at arms-length. "What do you mean? Still?"

"I've been ordered off the premises, without you."

"And did it ever occur to you to ask me?"

Richard narrowed his eyes and tilted his head as if to ask her meaning.

"Richard dear, there is no way you are leaving tonight...without me. I'm with you, for better or worse."

"But..." Richard began.

She released him, wiped her eyes, stepped back, and addressed him as she might one of her younger brothers. "Get ready. I'll meet you in the carriage. I know the way to the closest inn. It's quite nice. A cozy fireplace and bottle of sherry, Mister McSherry, will do us good."

And with that she walked out feeling free and purposeful once again, although somewhat less fashionable. Her heart raced. There would be no dowry, no exchange of land for bride. If she was to marry Richard McSherry, it would not be to strengthen familial politics, but to enrich the common good with charity, children, love, and God.

10

Christmas evening Richard and Anastasia did cozy up to a fire and drank an entire bottle of wine, of unknown vintage, at the modestly comfortable Fort Hanover Inn. After a long talk they retired to separate rooms. The next morning, after a warm breakfast, Eric drove them back to Hagerstown, returning Anastasia to her uncle. During the day-long trip they made rest-stops at taverns for food, beverages, and hot coals. On the road, sitting close but not embracing one another, they talked a great deal about their future and what their lives might be like together or apart, as Providence might will. Because it was the fashion of the time, they avoided the direct expression of their love or passion for the other, and instead talked as business owners might discuss a partnership of mutual benefit and how their companionship over the coming years might benefit the common good, the raising and education of children, and how each might support the other in works of charity.

Similarly, in some detail and honest conversation they confessed their faults one to the other. Richard confessed his impatience with the intemperate, the opinionated, the unwashed, and his preference for starched shirt collars, cuffs, and table linens—also starched. He also confessed his obsession with securing a livelihood for himself, and family, should he marry, and pleaded forbearance for his expected absence due to travel and obligations which would not make him a very good husband or father. He told her these things were "despicable weaknesses" of which he was "eternally embarrassed," but which were "not likely to depart his character."

For her part, Anastasia confessed very strong opinions on everything from siblings to slavery, from the poor to politics. Of such opinions she was very sorry, but she was unduly mortified about her curly hair which is why she was always trying to hide it behind big fancy hats, and that "no man should have to put up with such vanity."

It took hours and a great profusion of language to confess all these things one to the other. In the end, there were neither acts of contrition nor pronouncements of absolution. No doubt, in the minds of the angels who clung to the roof of the carriage on its bumpy journey and eavesdropped on the human conversation, Richard and Anastasia were two imperfect individuals who in the final analysis were perfect for each other.

What was not spoken of was perhaps more significant. No mention was made of their falling-out with Anastasia's father, nor of their abrupt dismissal from her father's inaptly named farm—Good Luck. Nor did they directly address how to bring about a reconciliation with her family, how wedding banns would be published in Conewago, nor where and how they were to be married. Trivial matters, really.

They did, however, talk at length and in detail of their shared concern for widows and the poor. Richard had quietly been helping farming families cope financially when crops had failed as well as finding homes for women in distress; and Anastasia had been volunteering at the German Reformed Church's widows' shelter hand-stitching clothes. So, upon arriving back in Hagerstown they went to Fr. Cahill and Immacolata with a proposition to start a Catholic charity at Magdala. The operation would collect food and clothing and be distributed to those who had fallen on *bad luck*. Fr. Cahill would oversee the charity, Immacolata would administer the hand-outs, and Anastasia, along with Richard when he came to town, would canvas the community, collect donations, and organize them at Magdala for distribution.

Although Anastasia returned to work at her uncle's factory and Richard returned to his business travels, which now included more frequent stops in Hagerstown, their free time was given to the charity. It was an instant success, and Magdala's second floor, root cellar, and rear yard quickly filled with sacks of grain, vegetables, clothing, discarded tools, and household supplies. Soon Anastasia and Richard were so busy organizing the coming and going of donations that they had stopped talking about their future together. About the same time, however, while claiming that they had found satisfaction in their work, Fr. Cahill noticed that there were minor disagreements and subtle tensions between them. He thought little of it until Immacolata observed: "Father, they fight like lovers, but they aren't lovers. They should be lovers, then they can fight."

In early March, as she always did, Anastasia came to confession. But this time she confessed to the sin of presumption. Fr. Cahill had to wonder if it was presumption or simply the expression of a repressed need. The way she told it: A week earlier Adam Livingston had brought his processed flax to Hagerstown Textiles to sell. After last year's depressed market, Anastasia was happy to see Mister Livingston return, for she was able to buy his wagonload at a much more favorable price. But, in her enthusiasm she let it slip that she was soon going to be his neighbor, for she realized the Livingstons' farm was only a few miles from Richard McSherry's Retirement in Leetown. She had never been to Leetown, but she had heard much of Richard's home, even from Fr. Cahill who had described the Rosary garden. After Mister Livingston had departed with his sack of Spanish half-doubloons, Anastasia realized her mistake. She was not yet betrothed to the handsome, generous, and kind Mister McSherry. Her presumption of marriage was all wishful thinking. Fr. Cahill assured her she was forgiven and gave her absolution. But he also decided it was time for a remedy.

Within a fortnight Richard showed up in Hagerstown. As he had been doing, he camped out in a corner of one of the Magdala guest rooms which was piled high with donations. Soon after he arrived Fr. Cahill invited Richard to evening supper. "Arnold Elder and his niece are coming, so put on some nice clothes."

"You mean like last time? Are we to expect *you*?" asked Richard.

"I'll be there. Immacolata made Spanish chicken stew, my favorite. She's also drafted a letter to the pope demanding I leave the priesthood if I don't show up. And if that's not enough she's threatened to hear my confession."

"Should I know anything about this little get together, or will it be a surprise?"

"You're getting married," said Fr. Cahill.

That got Richard's attention: "Does my prospective bride know this?"

"I'll tell her," said Fr. Cahill.

"Will you tell her father, too?" asked Richard. "And will you tell Fr. Pellentz. He's the Lilly family priest at Conewago who baptized and confirmed Anastasia. Will you tell him to marry us?"

"He'd never listen to me," said Fr. Cahill. "I know of the man. He's a Jesuit. Somehow he avoided the repression of his order and hid out here in the U.S. with a few others until the Constitution was passed. Now they've come out from hiding. No one tells a Jesuit, let alone one with over a thousand members and a brand-new chapel, what to do. I hear his chapel is the largest Catholic Church in the States. Have you seen it?"

"Yes, I told you. We attended Christmas Mass there...with the Lilly family."

"Oh, yes, you did," said Fr. Cahill.

Richard went on: "It's a large and beautiful building. I was jealous."

"As long as you're not envious," cautioned Fr. Cahill. "No, Fr. Pellentz would never listen to me, and I doubt he even listens much to our new bishop."

"Bishop Carroll?" asked Richard.

"The same. Bishop John Carroll, S.J. I need to confess something to you. Perhaps I should have told you earlier, but I kept waiting for an opportune time...perhaps this is it. Let's go into the parlor and have some sherry, first.

When they were settled and Fr. Cahill had emptied his half glass of sherry he cast some light on the political rumblings and court whisperings within the nascent United States Church. "Bishop Carroll no doubt knows about our work here, but I have held off writing him until we are better established, and I can give a good report, even one that could rival what is going on in Conewago. I hope you feel the same."

"Go on. I'll keep it between us," promised Richard.

"When I first came to the United States I did not think there was a superior or a bishop over Catholics in the United States. The American captain of the ship, a devout Catholic man himself, told me that. He thought that advantageous for Catholics and for me. Carroll wasn't bishop then, but he was the superior, I just didn't know it. Thus, I did not present myself to him. That may have been my first mistake. Then you and I met in those most unfortunate circumstances in Sharpsburg. You rescued me, swiftly carried me along, and in short order, thanks to you, I was riding a circuit and establishing societies in several towns. I am convinced to this day it was all in God's strange Providence. I found out only later when he was appointed bishop that Carroll had been appointed superior some years earlier. But not being the prolific letter writer, I put off writing and informing him of our work here in the west." Fr. Cahill paused to collect his thoughts.

"There's more?" asked Richard.

"Oh yes. In the late summer after you helped establish me here and after I started my circuit, I received a letter from the very same Fr. Pellentz in Conewago asking if I'd add my name to a petition to Pius VI to elevate Fr. Carroll from Superior of the Church in the United States to become our first bishop. Well, I didn't sign it. I had heard too many stories about Jesuits in Louisiana, when I was there, and how they had been expelled years earlier for their obstinance not just to civil authorities, but even to the pope. That explains why the Jesuits were dissolved in France. There was something, too, about the tone of the request from Pellentz. It was like an order demanding obedience. It was not a request giving reasons why Carroll deserved the position. That confused me for a while, but then I understood it. The letter was signed by Fr. Pellentz with S. J. after his name, just as we have recently seen the S. J. after Carroll's name. I suspect they only started adding the order's initials since the Constitution was ratified. You see, they are both Society of Jesus—Jesuits. So, of course, they're going to promote their own. Much later, after Carroll was confirmed as bishop last August, I found out that I was the only one of twenty-five priests active in the United States that had not added my name to that petition. Perhaps my second mistake. So, I apologize for what this means for your marriage to Anastasia in her home parish, which is where she should be rightly married. But for me to write Fr. Pellentz, as you now know, would not do you and Anastasia any favors."

Fr. Cahill let the story sink in before continuing. "But I have a solution."

"Ah...I have suspected," said Richard.

Fr. Cahill smiled. "Anastasia has not attended the Conewago parish for nearly two years. She attends here; I am her priest. Not Fr. Pellentz. And likewise, I am your priest."

It took but a moment for Richard to catch on, and when he did his eyes grew bright. "Is this what you are going to tell Anastasia at supper?"

"Well, I thought you might like to do that, not the stuff about me, Carroll, and Pellentz. But just that you both have my permission and blessing to marry, and I'd be honored if you'd let me officiate at your Wedding Mass. We can announce the banns starting anytime you two decide."

"And what about her father? Is he to be no part of this?"

"As far as I'm concerned, her father for the last two years has been Arnold Elder, her uncle. He's coming to supper tonight as well."

So it was that on Saturday, May 28, 1791, Fr. Cahill celebrated Mass and married Richard McSherry of Leetown, Virginia and Anastasia Lilly of Hagerstown, Maryland, formerly of Conewago, Pennsylvania. It was a grand celebration for the whole town as over 100 came to the outdoor Mass which, at Jonathan Hager's suggestion, was held in the Hagerstown Town Square.

By the way, the bride wore white.

In the weeks that followed, volunteers were appointed to carry on the Hagerstown Catholic Charity that operated out of Magdala with Fr. Cahill and Immacolata at the helm. But with Anastasia moving to Leetown and becoming the mistress of Retirement, the marriage only served to expand the ministry into Virginia. While Uncle Arnold lost a very accomplished account manager, he was happy for Anastasia. In turn, she promised to send him customers and suppliers from Virginia and nurture the factory's relationship with her new neighbor, Adam Livingston.

11

My Much Despised Cyn:

We now know something of how Anastasia Lilly fits into the Livingston-Cahill mix. She seems to be a linchpin of some sort, since she is the only one that knows all the major players. This is very disappointing, for she is as devout and robust in her faith as her husband and Cahill. The three create a formidable triumvirate. I suspect that some archangels are at work here. You may need reinforcements unless you get back your physical presence.

You did about as well as you could in alienating Anastasia from her father—a spineless soul easily manipulated with his arms around both a corrupt Church led by slave holding Jesuits and his own slaves. There's no wonder his other children left home as soon as they were of age. As much as I love conceit, Richard Lilly is not someone I'd like to be assigned to. He's primed for Perdition I suspect, maybe sooner than we think.

Human marriage is such an overrated cult. All those empty promises made, only to be broken. Why bother?

I peculiarly like the irony of "for better or worse." *Worse is better I say,* provided we're invited into the union. The fools continue along their course blindly accommodating their weakness, forgiving the sin, and essentially welcoming the next encounter. It's so duplicitous, but oh, how I enjoy it.

You were right to conjure up arrogant envy in the father, for that is his weakness, and each time we can stir the pot, our targets dig deeper their grave and their path to our eternal home of unrest. Envy is so much more savage than petty jealousy, which is almost not worth our time, except it can lead to what is grave. (I so love puns. But I must stop using that damnable word "love" for it is the bane of our existence.)

You have managed to further erode one family, the Lillys. Congratulations! But you have also resolutely solidified the marriage of the McSherrys. Although we cannot see into the future, there are signs that this is not good...for us. We must look for a way to undermine their union for a devout Catholic can do much damage to our cause.

Explore ways we can undermine McSherry's relationship with Cahill, who continually beleaguers us.

Yours for Eternity,
Master of Schisms

Chapter 22
Along for the Ride

1

Wednesday, June, 1, 1791.

Eve followed her mother along a stony path under a granite overhang and behind a waterfall. The roaring cascade of water fell to her right as she slid her left hand along a wall of smooth granite over which a thin sheet of water flowed. With water falling to her left and right, a cool mist dampened her face. All the while streaks of sunshine jetted through the waterfall to cast a kaleidoscope of color along the path.

Happily emerging from the other side of the waterfall, damp from head to toe, she walked into a bright beam of sunlight. It was beautiful and peaceful. The fresh smelling water, the rushing sound of the waterfall onto moss-covered boulders, and the spring flowers that surrounded the basin into which the water fell made Eve vow to return to this place often. But suddenly the dampness on her face felt rough, her nose tickled, and the sun nearly blinded her closed eyes. *Closed eyes? Why were they closed?*

That's when she woke to see rainbow-colored Calico licking her cheek with a wet, rough tongue, tickling her nose with cat whiskers, and lying down next to her face allowing the early morning sun that beamed through her window to fall directly into Eve's eyes. It was time to get up. But for a moment Eve just lay there trying to reconstruct the dream...only to realize, sadly, that in the dream she never caught sight of Mama's face.

Immediately, Eve clamped her eyes tight and prayed, "Dear God. Thank you for the lovely dream about Mama. At least I think that was her enjoying the waterfall and flowers. I hope I can really be with her someday. Please protect us today. Mama, pray for us. We'll pray for you."

It had been nearly three years since eleven-year-old Eve Livingston, Papa, and Henry her nine-year-old brother had arrived at their new farm in Smithfield, Virginia. Adam had named it Flax Haven, but it was anything but a haven to Eve without her dear mama.

In that time, with help of many individuals, including a construction team, Papa had built their new two-level frame house with a cellar, summer kitchen and woodshed. They had also finished an innovative three-level barn, plus multiple small out sheds and pens for chickens, pigs, sheep, a couple of privies, a smoke house, and a garden. There was also Sam and Bethany's cabin and woodshed tucked under the trees that backed into the wood.

They had fenced off four three-acre pastures near the barn, and had torn down the original Mayfield cabin and stable, and finally plowed under and started in rotation the planting of their five crop fields. With a borrowed surveyor's chain, she and Henry helped Pa survey the fields. They ranged in size from 29–40 acres, 175 tillable acres in all. That nearly quintupled the size of their tillable fields in Pennsylvania.

This past spring was the first time all five fields had been mostly cleared, plowed under, and planted. They had the help of migrant workers, who set up camp next to the Darks' cabin. She was happy for Pa. He had in the ground two fields of flax, and a field each of soybean, corn, and sweet potatoes. There was still a lot of work to be done, like building up rock and wood fencing, and building better water lifting pumps to get the water from the Opequon Creek into the irrigation ditches of the fields; with those she couldn't help. So, she bided her time keeping the house clean, the fireplaces supplied with wood, and keeping Henry out of trouble by helping him tend the pigs, chickens, and the weaned lambs which her pa had just purchased. One of their chores was to herd the lambs in and out of pasture. They might have some lamb-wool next spring to spin into yarn.

Papa was normally out and about the farm, and at night he would catch up on his reading of old newspapers brought from town to help her and Henry improve their reading and figures. When they first arrived in Virginia there was too much work to bother with schooling. Adam would say she was getting educated enough just by doing so much to build out and improve the farm. But there came a time, especially that first winter, when he purchased new readers and figure books and tried to help keep up their education. But at the end of the day he was often too tired. Sam and Bethany at first could not read or write, and so Eve spent a lot of time teaching them. They were getting pretty good at it now. But they needed more readers and practice books.

She missed Mama, who was well-educated and seemingly knew just how to help her and Henry learn more. She also missed Mama's hugs and conversation, although Bethany was very good at being a grown-up friend. When they cooked together, Bethany knew all sorts of ways to cook things. She learned a new word from Bethany—recipe—although she didn't know exactly how to spell it for a while. She found it by chance in one of Papa's newspapers. Bethany knew all sorts of recipes, and she would teach them to Eve as they made the food together. She liked that about Bethany; she learned stuff from her.

In some ways Bethany was much like Mama, especially when it came to religion. With Papa's permission, Eve had kept Mama's Bible and would bring it out now and then when teaching Bethany to read. Although Bethany couldn't read the Bible very well, she knew a lot of Bible stories, and would often tell them to Eve and Henry after supper and before she went to her cabin to be with Sam. Sometimes Sam would come and sit by the fireplace with them and listen to Bethany's Bible stories. She would tell the stories with different voices for the characters and all the drama she could muster. When Bethany pretended to talk like an evil king, or the giant Goliath, Sam would often laugh loudly, which to Eve and Henry sounded more like Goliath than Bethany's pretend voice. It was great fun. But Pa didn't like the stories and would often leave the gathering hall and go to the parlor where he would find something to read.

Eve also missed going to church. She missed seeing her friends and singing hymns, and hearing stories from the Bible told by the preacher with his raspy voice. But the most memorable times were to hear the preacher pray. It was as if God was standing in front of him listening. Sometimes the preacher would get mad about something and prayed to God as if he was rebuking the Almighty. That's when Eve got scared thinking God might strike him dead for losing his temper. Sam would say, "You's can't box wid God." But the preacher never died. Eve thought that was a near miracle.

Esther taught both Eve and Henry to pray, and she prayed with them every night before they went to sleep. But since they moved to Virginia, Papa never prayed with them. She'd ask, but he'd mutter something about how God doesn't answer prayer and would leave her room somewhat angry. Eve didn't like Papa angry, so she stopped asking him to pray. But Eve still prayed...every day. She prayed to Mama a lot, like when she was confused or scared about things. She didn't get scared often. She'd have a bad dream and wake up breathing hard. It's then she would whisper, "Mama, pray for me. I miss you," hoping Mama could hear her and was indeed praying for her up in heaven.

Eve often took long walks in the cool of the evening through the fields, or along the creek. She'd see ground hogs, squirrels, deer, muskrats, an occasional river otter, and what looked like wild dogs. Birds were everywhere, of course. When she saw a hawk or eagle soaring on the wind she would look up and follow them as long as she could. She would crane her neck and wonder how God made all the animals, and birds, and trees, and mulberry bushes, let alone the crops Papa planted and harvested. It was all amazing to her. She especially liked wildflowers that blossomed in the spring.

After Bethany went home in the evening, Eve would seek out Papa and get him to read the newspaper to her, or explain things about the government, or what was happening in the world. He was a good papa in that way, and he never got wrongly mad at either Henry or her. But she noticed he was often sad at night. He seemed lonely, for he, too, missed Mama. "*Oh, Mama. Pray for Papa,*" she would pray.

Once the planting was in, she noticed that Papa spent hours working at his desk. She thought this summer he might start reassembling the loom, but that didn't happen, and he seemed terribly distracted. One evening she came into his office. "Papa, what are you doing? Is something wrong? I'm worried. Normally after the planting you spend time with Henry and me, and help me read newspapers or letters or play games."

Her papa turned over the papers to hide what he was writing and turned to her. "It's a letter to someone about something very difficult. I can't tell you about it, just yet. In fact, I don't even know how to write what I'm writing, what I'm thinking."

"I can help, I'm good with words, even you have said so," Eve said, hoping to be let in on the secret.

Adam put down his quill and tried to wipe off the black ink on his fingers. But it was no use. The black stain would be there for several days. He checked that his writing was hidden, and invited Eve into his arms. She walked between his legs as he sat in his chair and let him embrace her with his massive arms. He hugged her tenderly. "No, with this you cannot help, although you help in so many other ways. When this is all over I will tell you, but not now."

She hugged him back. "Bethany is going to tell us a story. Do you want to come hear it?"

"No, you go ahead. I must work at this some more. I'll see you to bed tonight, though." He kissed her forehead and gave her another hug then gently scooted her out of the office.

Eve noticed that her papa's writing, and his frustration with it, went on every night for a week. During that time, even during the day, he fell into a terrible mood and seemed tired all day long. At night, if he didn't like what he wrote, he'd burn it in the fireplace and start over. Oh, how Eve wanted to take out the ashes and read those letters. She asked several more times if she could read what he had written before burning it, but he always said no. He was also unusually brusque with her, which was not his natural way with her. She noticed that if he didn't burn the unfinished letter he'd hide it away in his lock box. It was very mysterious and frustrating to her. She asked Bethany and Sam, but neither of them had any idea what occupied her father.

2

Adam was relieved when at last he finished the letter. It was the hardest thing he had done in a long time, and he was glad to have it over with. Late one night after everyone was in bed, Cleopatra demanded to curl up on Adam's lap, purr loudly, and repeatedly tried to interrupt his writing, begging for attention. It was unusual. Adam managed to read over what he had written and decided it was the best he could do.

Although the first few pages were days old and the ink dry, he nonetheless powdered and blotted every page carefully, folded the pages together with his bone knife, tucked it together, and sealed it with red lacquer. It was a heavy letter. It would cost more than normal to post. But it was what it was and it had to be. He addressed the front, and then hid it in a leather satchel before he went to bed.

Early the next morning he skipped breakfast and rode alone on Calvin into Charles Town to the tavern, paid the postage, and dropped the letter that could change his life into the mail pouch.

On the way home he contemplated the past week. Dreams had haunted him. One could call them nightmares. That he lost sleep, did not make him a happy farmer. He had been rude to everyone around him. Nothing seemed to satisfied him. He would apologize but that didn't make it right. He nursed a foreboding that the nightmares and the letter were connected, but he could not make any sense of how. Now that the letter was written and posted, maybe he would get some sleep.

As Calvin trotted towards the farm, Adam tried to connect the dreams with the premonitions he had experienced over the years. The nighttime dreams and the daytime premonitions were different in some ways, but similar in others. Both were extraordinary, mysterious, and seemingly unconnected with reality as he knew it. It wasn't until much later that the premonitions made sense.

He tried to reconstruct the past week. There were five dreams that he could remember. They were all about different things, except they were all the same in a very surreal way. His surroundings in the dreams were dramatically enhanced in size, color, sound, and speed. If there was a chair, or a door, or a horse, or another person, whatever it was, it was gigantic in size. The door to a house zoomed to be as tall as a tree, a stook of flax standing in the field became twenty feet high and ten feet wide instead of just a few feet high and a foot wide. Tables zoomed upwards through roofs, foods like an apple were too big to lift let alone eat. The Opequon Creek became a roaring river a hundred feet wide and too dangerous to cross for even the most robust ferry.

If he tried to move or someone near him moved, everything around him would move so quickly he became dizzy and afraid. Someone taking a step seemed to be a break-out run. If, in the dream, he turned his head, it seemed the world would spin out of control and cause him to fall. He couldn't seem to turn his head slow enough. The texture of cloth became rough bark on a log, pebbles on the ground became boulders, and firewood was too big for even two men to carry.

Then there was the sound: Everything was deafening. Horse hoofs entering the yard were like explosions, a spoon falling on the floor would force him to cover his ears, someone talking quietly would sound like they were yelling into his ears from only inches away. In short, everything was supernatural. There was nothing of normal size, speed, or sound that he could live with comfortably.

One night Eve woke him from the dream, and got him to sit on the side of his bed, but she kept moving around so quickly he fell over and had to lie down. But he kept his eyes open and watched her. She seemed to be running back and forth across the room, but she said she hadn't moved. Her voice was too loud and she spoke too quickly. He told her that and she tried to speak soft- ly and slowly. It didn't help much. He was awake, he thought, but the bed, the chairs, and walls were super large. Eve spoke to him again. But he had to clamp his hands over his ears. He asked her not to yell. She began to whisper. But her whispers became whirlwinds. Cleopatra jumped on his lap, but she felt like a mountain lion, her claws tearing open his night clothes and drawing blood. But there wasn't any blood, really, he just imagined it. And yet all this, in his dream, was real and he couldn't fully wake up. Eve tried to talk him down from wherever he was, but the hallucination would continue for a good hour before he fell back asleep, or so she would say the next day. Of course, she never sensed any of what he saw, felt, and heard. It scared him.

Each night's dreams were different in another way. The first night he had to cross the threshold of a door, but when the door opened, it opened so quickly, and it was so tall, the wind of the door opening knocked him over, he fell back off a cliff. When he got up he couldn't reach the threshold it was so high above him. He desperately tried to climb over the threshold, but rather than a narrow piece of timber against which the door would close, the threshold was higher than his head and he had no ladder.

The second night he went fishing for supper in the Opequon Creek that was now a roaring river. Somehow he caught a fish, but when he was able to bring it home it was too big to go through the door. Once he got it inside—how he was unsure—the fish was bigger than the supper table, and it began to flop about madly. It was still alive and its big eyes and mouth threatened to devour him and the whole family. In the process the furniture was destroyed and even the fireplace stones came loose and flew across the room.

The third night there was a tall table, covered with colorful linens. He had seen dyed linens before, but nothing this bright and colorful. Around the table men in robes stood and passed things back and forth to each other like they were eating supper. But they were so tall, and they moved so fast, and the table was so big, he could never see on top of it. He tried jumping, and climbing, and begging to see. But he never could. The men just ignored him.

The fourth night Esther was pulling bread out of a stone oven. But as the round loaf of bread was pulled out it suddenly expanded to fill the entire room to every corner, and no one could move. The bread was warm and delicious smelling, but the crust was hard as rock and though he tried, he was never able to bite and taste it.

The fifth night he had to cross the Opequon Creek in a boat. But the creek was like a roaring ocean surf, and one could not see the other side. The boat was too big to steer, and he capsized over and over again. He never got to the other side, which he never even saw.

He could make no sense of any of it. And yet it was there awaiting him every night. In a way, everything in the dreams was what he saw and dealt with every day in his house and around the farm. There were horses, but bigger than he could ever mount. There was a pitchfork, so long he could never wield it, there were flax fibers too big to spin, and the weft and warp of cloth that came off Esther's loom were as round as ten-inch logs. The scenes were all natural things, but they were so large and fast and intense they overwhelmed him and left him very much afraid.

But the letter. He finally figured out what to write and it was mailed.

3

Flax Haven, Smithfield, Virginia
June 15, 1791
Mrs. Mary Ann Babbitt
Apple Ridge Road
Winchester, Virginia

My Dear Mrs. Babbitt:

I hope this letter finds you in good health and surrounded by good friends.

Mrs. Mary Valens Gates, wife of General Horatio Gates, suggested I write and introduce myself. She and Gen. Gates moved to New York this past winter and in selling their farm at Travelers Rest invited me to their estate sale where I picked up a few items. In our conversation she suggested I write you. My farm work, however, is very busy in the winter processing flax, and then spring planting kept me so busy I did not find the time. But now, with the seed in the ground, I have time to think of myself and my family, and less of farm work.

I am Adam Livingston, a 52-year-old farmer in good health and strength. My farm, Flax Haven, is in Smithfield, Virginia, about 8 miles southwest of Travelers Rest and 20 miles from you, or two hours in a buggy. I have a reputation of being honest, industrious, and of fair intelligence.

I am the first American-born son of German immigrants Johann and *Susan Lieberstein. Before I was born, my father obtained a British court's permission to change the last name of his children to Livingston. I was born on my father's farm not far from Lancaster, Pennsylvania, where he grew a variety of crops including flax. After establishing my own modest Plantation not far from Lancaster in York, Pennsylvania, I married my dear wife, Esther. She bore me a daughter, Eve, now 11, and a son, Henry, now 9. Three and a half years ago Esther suddenly passed away of an ailment the doctor said was unknown. We buried her on my farm in Pennsylvania in the family plot where there also lie three small children, one died in infancy, the other two failed to survive birth.

Shortly thereafter, my father revealed that he had purchased 350 acres of prime farmland in the Shenandoah Valley. Kindly, he sold them to me fairly, so that I could start a new life. My children and I have been here in Virginia for two and one-half years.

I have a foreman and a housekeeper-cook, husband and wife, Sam and Bethany Dark. They were slaves of General Gates. But with Mary Valens' help, and encouragement from former minister to England, John Adams, General Gates sold to me Sam and Bethany, and I immediately manumitted them. I detest slavery.

They are good people and help me a great deal. They live on my land in their own dwelling. I also have a team of day laborers that come when I am in need to plant, harvest, or build. They either live nearby or camp on our land during planting and harvest.

My dear Madam, Mrs. Gates told me of your valiant and late husband, the honorable Col. Alvin Babbitt. She told me how he fought bravely under General Benedict Arnold and General Gates in the Battle of Saratoga, and how he was witness to Burgoyne's surrender, although he later succumbed to his injuries and died. I am so very sorry for your loss of so great a man. But from what I hear of that battle, his sacrifice, and yours, were not in vain, for the war turned our way thereafter.

I do not know your present state, but if you are alone, Mary Valens said you will not consider me too forward nor presumptuous to inquire if you are open to remarrying a man such as myself.

Madam, I am aware that you are not wealthy, but that you do possess a small farm that Mrs. Gates says you rent out for some "meager" income. She tells me you are well-educated, that you write, are wise to the world of politics, and the military, and that you are industrious, a good friend, and willing to entertain guests. I am not wealthy, either, although I have some small wealth to keep my family secure, and I do have hope of future wealth from industrious work, and expect many good years ahead, if the markets hold.

My daughter, Eve, is also industrious and intelligent. She can read and do figures well. I hope to teach her to weave like her mother when she is older. My son Henry, in honesty, is a lively boy, who is not as diligent as his sister, but he is loyal and keeps us alert.

Mrs. Gates says you have no children, but that you have longed to be a mother. May I offer my children to you? They need a mother and a teacher of things in the world and beyond, which I do not have the time to attend to. For myself, I am sadly in need of female companionship. Perhaps you long for a good male companion as well who can be your close friend in conversation. It is lonely at times when the children are in bed and the workers home. Perhaps we can be for each other—the half that makes the other whole?

I must also write that I am far from a perfect man. I am headstrong and determined to a fault. When I should give up and try another path, I persevere when all is otherwise lost. I am brusque when I am tired, impatient when confronted with difficult problems, and I must confess that the death of my devout Christian wife has turned me against religion of all kinds—I have no use for any of it. But I am good at business, keep good records, and do well at market when the crops are ready. Farming has been good for me and I have been good to the land.

Knowing all this, would it be acceptable if I traveled to Winchester to visit you and determine if there is a future with us as companions, friends, parents, and lovers?
Your devoted servant,
Adam Livingston

4

A week or so later Eve happened to greet the postal express rider as he rode onto the farm and handed her a letter for Papa. She looked at the writing on the outside, but couldn't decide where it was from. There was only one transit stamp at the bottom from the mail stop in Charles Town. The rider wanted to be paid for the delivery, but she had no money. So, she handed the letter back to him and went off to find Papa.

When Adam came, he paid the rider, and told Eve to go back to her chores. But she just stepped back, folded her arms, and glared at him. He was a bit miffed at her obstinance, and she at him for not telling her what was in the letter. He chuckled, cracked open the seal, unfolded the letter, and read it. After reading it once, he read it again. Then he carefully folded it and put it inside his shirt. She asked about it, but he just smiled and shook his head, and walked off to the barn. It was all very mystifying because he had often let her read business correspondence to advance her education. Of course, Henry didn't care one bit since at the time he was busy mucking out a stall.

5

Winchester, Virginia - June 19, 1791

Dear Mister Livingston:

I was surprised at your June 15 letter. It is most kind of you to write in such a gentlemanly way of introduction. Of course, I know Mary Valens quite well, even before she was conjoined with Gen. Gates. I visited her many times at Travelers Rest and there met the new owners Felicity and Stephen Randal who invited me to stay with them if ever I wanted to get away from Winchester. I am still in writing contact with Mary Valens, as they have settled at Rose Hill Farm in New York. It is a terrible thing that Gen. Washington has done to as valiant a solider as Gen. Gates, who has worked hard to restore his reputation since the war. I do believe Gen. Gates at Saratoga was significantly responsible for the victory over the British and should be rewarded for the surrender of Howe's forces, not Gen. Washington. I fear the latter's political connivance, and tolerance of division with the country's leadership will lead our new nation into tragedy greater than what was our state before the war.

While that is not why you have written, it informs you somewhat of my obstinacy at times and is what remains of my sentiment toward our government in losing my Alvin.

That Mary Valens suggested you write, you should know, is an endorsement of your person. She would not recommend someone to me for my detriment, nor would I to hers.

I am a baker's daughter, educated by my British mother. I enjoyed working in my father's shop in Boston. Then came along, when I was 18, Mister Babbitt, Jr., son of a successful English merchant. We married and moved west because we both sought the solitude of a fertile valley here in Winchester to start a small farm and live self-sufficiently. We came believing that the Indians had all moved west. It wasn't true, and there were raids that disturbed our peace.

Colonel *Daniel Morgan recruited a force to protect us, and Alvin, enamored with military life, joined his band on occasion after planting and harvest. It was a hard life. Alvin longed for adventure, and I longed for his companionship, which was often naught, due to his desire for my safety and his devotion to Colonel Morgan. Then came the war in 1775, and Alvin left with a hundred others. They called themselves *"Morgan's Sharpshooters." I'm told General Washington ordered them to attack the English in Boston. Alvin was paid little or nothing at all, though I believe he sent to me everything he was paid or thereabouts. I was left here with a few neighbors to scrape by. I've worked as a laborer for others doing odd tasks and I rented out our 60 acres to a farmer who paid me only when the crop was harvested and sold at market and then only if the crop and the market were good. They were not always.

Alvin and I had no children, though we tried. I have long desired motherhood.

At times I received letters from Alvin. He was happy to fight, but I was not, being alone. I thought many times of returning to Boston to be with my family there, but the dangers of the war in the East persuaded me to be independent, poor, and safe. Then I got word that Alvin was wounded and died after the surrender of Howe's forces at Saratoga.

After the war my younger sister, Helen, came to live with me and together we made our existence as I did before. Except, with the war over, and harvests more abundant, we did not starve, but enjoyed the other's company. An occasional traveler would stop to stay a night or two and pay us room and board. Helen was courted by one of those travelers on his way ever further west. They married and she left for adventure, like Alvin. I have not seen or heard from my dear sister in three years.

I am sorry to burden you with these stories of woe, which are not unlike your own, which must be enough.

I found your telling of Sam and Bethany agreeable, for I do not find value in keeping slaves, neither did Alvin. Since you have manumitted them, they must return their loyalty to you. I would like to meet them, and your children. And yes, I would very much like to meet you too, Mister Livingston. You are but two years older than my Alvin, and that you are not about to go off to war is agreeable to me.

I too have no place for religion as my father was a Catholic and mother a Quaker, and never did they see eye-to-eye about religion or attend either. They came to agree not to bother and tried, more successfully than not, to live in harmony, like the yeast added to flour and water contributes to goodness of bread and not to its division.

I'll say this about the Quakers that live near me along Apple Ridge Road that runs north out of town. They taught me to make good apple pies. During the war Hessian soldiers and then Colonial soldiers, who were camped in the vicinity, would come to Apple Ridge Road to buy and eat the Quaker apple pies. I made some money that way during the war, and still sell an apple pie or two to friends.

Part of my disagreement with religion, however, has to do with its presence in our government. According to the new Bill of Rights, should it be added to the Constitution, the two are not to mix. As I read the letters and speeches of General Washington, now in first position in our nation, he must not agree. That is worrisome to me. It was just last year in the Virginia Gazette that he praised the Catholic religion for the role papists played in defeating the English. One might think Washington sees religion as an indispensable element required to make our government and courts accountable. This is nonsense. Common sense is all that is needed. Perhaps it's because I have no use for Gen. Washington, who took my husband from me, that I also have no use for his opinion on the role of religion or God in the governance of our country. I have the least use for papists. It is all distasteful to me, as is the ownership of hundreds of slaves by the Jesuits in Maryland, Catholic priests that they claim to be. They are hypocrites; should one come to boarder with me, they would not cross my threshold. If this be a weakness of mine, well there it is. But it has served me well in my independence.

I write plainly sir. If this offends, I am sorry, but I am set in my ways, as no doubt you are in yours. Yet if it is agreeable to you, my weaknesses, vices, and my past, it would be good to receive you and meet you. Perhaps we can be companions, and perhaps also friends, parents, and lovers.

You may call on me at your leisure. My little farm, Deep Furrow, is just north of Winchester on the Main Wagon Trail which is Apple Ridge Road in these parts.

Affectionately,
Mary Ann Babbitt

6

Eve watched from afar as a week later Papa paid the postal express rider for yet another letter. As soon as the rider departed, Papa quickly opened the letter and read it over several times. He seemed to be lost in thought for a long time after. Later, when she asked about it, he said he would tell her later...maybe... then hid the letter away in the strong box along with his gold. This frustrated Eve and created hours of discomfort, as if the stability of her life was threatened. If only the letters were from her mama, she thought, then she could relax. Of course, she knew that was irrational, so she returned to something that made more sense—worry.

A few days later on a cool morning, Henry, in fulfilling his chores, brought an armload of wood into the gathering hall and dumped it near the fireplace. Eve noticed that he was walking funny and acting a bit strange. But she was helping Bethany with something in the pantry and didn't keep an eye on Henry, which was never a good idea. A moment later she noticed that he was feeding the fire with some small pieces of wood, something he almost never did. Normally, he left feeding the fire up to Eve, Bethany, or her papa.

About the time Henry was done stoking the fire, Adam came down from his bedroom and walked into the gathering hall for breakfast.

Henry saw his pa first: "What's with the duds? We goin' to church? It ain't Sunday...is it?"

Bethany and Eve looked up at the sight. It was to behold. Neither one of them had ever seen Adam dressed in a ruffled shirt, cravat necktie, waist coat, breeches, stockings...and polished bucketed shoes, no less.

"My good Lord," said Bethany, "Mister Livingston, where you go in dat git-up?"

Henry was on his game, "Can I come with you, Pa?"

Eve took a whiff of the air that had swirled into the room with her papa's entrance. He had splashed on some of Mama's lavender oil. Suddenly, Eve's observations of his strange behavior over the past weeks made sense. Between giggles she teased, "You can't go with him, Henry. He's goin' courtin', aren't you Papa?"

"Now, who told you that?" Adam snapped with a smile on his face.

"What he do wrong?" asked Henry.

"Wh-what?" stuttered Adam, glaring at his son.

"Henry, he's not going to court," Eve said. "He's going courting. It's something very different." Thinking about the consequences of some marriages she quickly added, "...or maybe not."

"Like what?" Henry asked.

"You'll see," said Eve with a grand smile.

Bethany circled Papa lightly touching the fine-looking clothes as if to sample their texture. "You do look mighty handsome, Mister Livingston. I should git me Samuel some of those duds. Oooeeee! They'd get my attention, yes sir!" she said with flirting eyes.

Henry finally caught on. "Yer gonna corral and lasso us a mother, aren't ya?" But the tone of his voice said he didn't think this was a good idea.

Bethany turned to Eve, "Why, I do believe he not like our cooking. He wants some new recipes."

"I'm not sure what's to happen," Adam said. "We'll see. Now is there something I can eat before I take the buggy to Winchester. I don't want to be too hungry before I get there."

With a twinkle in her eye and a ready answer Eve said, "We've got Bethany's egg and sugarcane porridge in the pot. Last week you said you liked it."

"Milk or coffee, Mister Livingston?" asked Bethany as she put a bowl and mug on the table.

"Coffee, if it's hot, please."

Eve took Papa's bowl and with a ladle stepped toward the fireplace and the pot of porridge. But at that very moment, Henry quickly backed away from the fireplace, his eyes fixed on the fire."

Adam suddenly grabbed Eve's arm to pull her away, "Eve!" Then, almost immediately "HENNN-RR-Y!?"

But it was too late. Before Eve could be yanked away, "BANG! BANG! Then a long sequence—BANG! BANG! BANG!...BANG! Embers and sparks flew from the bottom of the fireplace and across the room.

Scared to death, Eve SCREAMED. As Papa pulled her away from the fireplace the ladle in her hand caught the handle of the pot, tipping it, and spilling several servings of hot porridge into the fire with a sizzle.

Henry laughed his fool head off, even as Adam let go of Eve and walloped his son solidly on his backside.

But there was more.

"MISTER Livingston," Bethany screamed, "YER SHIRT'S ON FIRE!"

A spark had landed on the sleeve of Adam's white linen shirt and was smoldering a hole into his upper arm. Bethany quickly whetted a towel and slapped at the small flame and smoke, putting it out. Pulling off the towel, they all gazed at his arm. The flying ember had burned a hole as big as a Spanish piece of eight in his one and only dress shirt. Adam pulled on his sleeve, looked at his shirt and grabbed for his son, "Damn you, son. What's got into ya, a demon?"

Henry immediately stopped laughing.

Bethany and Eve grabbed some rags and started to clean up the spilled porridge on the hearth, even as Adam tried to tag Henry once more, but Henry dodged his pa's every grasp and the chase was on...through the gathering hall, into the foyer, and back, with Henry landing behind Bethany's apron,

"Papa's going to get married. Papa going to get married," Henry teased.

"He is not," said Eve. "Stop it. I'm sure we'll meet her before there's a wedding."

Pa danced around Bethany to get at his son, but Henry evaded ever grasp.

Bethany said, "Eve's right, Henry. Why before there's a weddin' they hav'ta post banns in the newspaper, and they hav'ta make announcements at church for three Sunday in a row, and the minister has'ta approve them. That right, ain't it, Mister Livingston?" Bethany was obviously pleased with herself. She smiled at Adam even as she tried to protect Henry from his flailing father.

Adam stopped and frowned at Bethany, who was still smiling up at him as if to pacify the bear of a man twice her size. It was a stand-off, both physically and intellectually as the family waited for the patriarch to respond. There was something ironic and challenging to Bethany's light-hearted attempt to quiet things down.

After an awkward moment, Adam spoke, mostly to himself, "I doubt that."

Eve wondered, "You ain't getting married?"

Her papa looked at her, almost apologetically, but then spoke frankly. "I doubt there will be a church wedding, if there is one...a wedding, I mean. The lady in question, which I'm supposed to meet today for the first time, ain't too fond of ministers or their churches." He paused. "Like myself."

Bethany turned serious. "Mister Livingston, ya always tell me ta speak plainly. So, I'm gonna do as ya asked." She paused. "You'd be wise ta seek a minister's blessing fer such a thing, and ya'll gonna need *his* blessing."

"I don't need no preacher's blessing."

"I's speaking of da Almighty," said Bethany.

"Bethany!" said Adam with resolve, "Yes, I told you to speak plainly. But let me speak plainly. You tend to the cookin'. Let me tend...to my affairs."

There was a pause as Bethany, Henry, and Eve turned solemn.

Bethany spoke first, for all of them, it seemed, as if she was a humble slave once again: "Sir, I am sorry, I don't mean to pry." She put her arms around both Henry and Eve, "Sam and me we'll watch the young-ins, while you gone. Don't you worry on account of them none."

"Just as long as you keep this one," Adam jabbed a finger toward his son, "tied up. I don't want to find my house burned down when I return. And have Sam stay close to the house after he eats, until I return. Understand? I'll be back this evening. Maybe after sunset."

"Yes, sir. I tell 'im. He be here shortly."

Adam turned to Henry, still cowering behind Bethany, "And before you eat young man, two more armfuls of wood, no more chestnuts, and feed those pigs of yours."

"Yes, Papa," Henry squeaked.

"I'll help him, Papa," said Eve.

Adam, satisfied, nodded a few times, looked down at the hole in the arm of his shirt. "I was going to wear a coat. Guess I'll go git it."

"Sir, I kin darn that for ya," said Bethany.

"When I return, thank you," said Adam, upon which he went upstairs, came down with his top hat and tail coat, and hurried out the front door.

Eve turned to Bethany, "He didn't eat any porridge, did he?"

Bethany thought for a moment, "No he sore didn't, Miss Eve. Guess his heart done shoved his stomach aside."

Fifteen minutes later, Eve watched as the buggy, pulled by Calvin, trotted out of the yard and onto the road headed south. Her destiny went along for the ride.

7

My Despised Cyn:

We clearly have competition trying to counter our efforts. We can't know what was in the little snit's dream except what she prayed out loud to the Almighty...whatever it was about her mother and a waterfall and something else I'm trying to forget. But clearly, it was not a dream you had inspired. I don't remember there being a waterfall in Glory. Sounds like the figment of some wayward angel's imagination. It just doesn't do us any good to have the little snit wake up and immediately start praying. For hell's sake, you must learn to create dreams for her that don't send her running to heaven. We want to scare Glory out of her, not Hades. We want her to believe that hell is her ally, not heaven, and definitely not her mother.

But then came that monstrous sequel that your mark experienced, if only we knew what it involved. Thankfully, and who are we to thank, certainly not the Almighty although whom else is there?...we know something of what your mark was exposed to due the little snit getting him out of bed and babysitting him. Evidently, he was having a vision of material objects and persons being way too big, too loud, and too fast. Whatever that was about. The problem with the Almighty is his mysteriousness and deliberateness. I would never have the patience. What that has to do with your strategic plans for the Babbitt woman we may never know, but I assure you it is going to throw a clunker or two into our works at some point. We need to be alert.

Taking your inspiration from Cahill's matchmaking with McSherry and Lilly, and transmogrifying it with Livingston and Babbitt seems to be working. Mary Ann Babbitt is a fine choice. She hates religion, more than Livingston. Should they marry, as is surely your intention, you will have a bulwark against the triumvirate of Cahill and the two McSherrys.

Don't let Livingston back down about there not being a church wedding. There can't be if this Mary Ann Babbitt is to reinforce our cause.

Another thing: Continue to dissuade Livingston from involving that daughter of his or the Darks in the decision. Keep Babbitt from them. They all have religion, and they are to be denied an opinion.

Eternally yours,
Master of Stupidity

Chapter 23
That was Delicious

1

August, 1791.

Mary Ann Babbitt never sought obscurity, but it came upon her like the cannon blast that ultimately killed her husband. She was content being the wife of Colonel Alvin Babbitt. Yes, there was the prestige she wore on her sleeve when among friends, but she also cherished what Alvin had expressed so often in his letters, that her mere existence gave him something to live for. She just didn't realize she also gave Alvin something to die for. That became shockingly clear when the letter with the black lacquer seal came from General Arnold. She knew instantly what it was, and she hadn't opened it until Alvin's letters ceased coming, along with the cessation of his irregular pittance of pay. As he had lived in the glories of war for her, so now she lived in the obscurity of death for him.

She did not put on her first black dresses out of some obscure social obligation, but out of true grief. That first year she wore black out of remembrance. In the second year she wore black out of honor. Black dresses, black hats and ribbons, black overcoats, black stockings and shoes had all become her hallmark, her solace, her lover. She even made several black nightgowns from cloth purchased in town. She didn't spin or weave, having neither the equipment nor anyone to pass the knowledge down to her. Her sister called the black night gowns "maudlin vestiges of hope lost." But when she curled up at night in the darkness of her bed, she somehow felt closer to Alvin, as if she could accompany him into the darkness of his descent.

Until Helen came to live with her at Deep Furrow, she didn't realize how different she was from her sister. Helen was aggressive on the outside, but very adaptive on the inside, like an angry barking dog that when approached would stop barking, turn tail, and run away. Of course, when Mark came to stay for a few days on his way to St. Louis in the Spanish territory, Helen turned and ran with him. Mary Ann considered that Helen had left with the adventurous Mark to distance herself from the stubborn-stuck-in-her-ways-and-unadventurous Mary Ann. No matter. Mary Ann was happier being her own person. Adventure and new things for her had meant disappointment and death, not life.

On the other hand, after Alvin and Helen had both left her, and loneliness came to stay, she wondered if there might be a middle ground. Some adventure or something new that would not result in disappearance. Something that might erase her obscurity without a cannon blast. There had been a few men since Alvin who dared engage her in friendship. But each was a backward type, not the kind she could rely on.

Then came a letter from an obscure man of whom she had never heard. He was a widower as she was a widow. He appeared to be a man of self-initiative who could be relied on, someone like herself. There was also the added credibility of Mary Valens' recommendation, her distant and socially unobscured friend—the newest light on the New York social scene. This just might be, Mary Ann thought, the middle ground she longed for, though it had waited until the middle of her life—fourteen years after Alvin, and three years after Helen.

Mary Ann was not physically strong enough to farm, but she was diligent during those years. It was Alvin's idea to rent the land out to a neighbor. The income was barely enough to keep their tiny house from falling down. But living along Ridge Road among the Quakers had brought in some money baking apple pies and selling them to soldiers. It was strange; they ate them practically on her doorstep, refusing to take them back to camp where the pies would be confiscated, they said. Then, after the war her education and penmanship found her regular work in the courthouse as a clerk, a scribe, a reader, and an interpreter of contracts.

Finally, though she hadn't considered her hand-made black dresses that stylish, she had been asked to make dresses similarly styled for women in town...for which she was paid. Only once had she made one in black, and not for the man's death but rather for their separation—she to the house and he to the barn. The animals, he had said, were easier to talk to. The woman purchased the cloth, and she, taking her size from one of the woman's other dresses, styled the new dress to the woman's liking. She never thought she was good with needle and thread; she would have much preferred to have someone else do the sewing and let her do the cooking. This is where her mother's exhortation on hard work, prudence, and virtue paid off. Oh, that her mum had survived that foul illness—she would have gone home the instant she heard of Alvin's death. But her mum was dead and her father, well, she had no idea where he was, having disappeared before even mum had died. Thus, Mary Ann had survived and done reasonably well for her station.

Although her body gave no sign that she was infertile, she doubted she could bear children. She was forty-four and had never heard of a woman her age having a child, except for an odd report in the local newspaper. Because she knew most of the people in Winchester, she had come to believe only half of what she read and held the other half with suspicion. She always suspected that Alvin's seed was the problem, not hers. But who was to know? She certainly wasn't going to give herself to a stranger just to find out. Clearly Mister Livingston was not of the infertile category. He and his wife had had five children, though only two survived, or so he had said. She had heard that men were fertile for at least a week after they were buried. Such a morbid thought. She had not thought much about getting pregnant until his letter arrived. Now, she was intrigued. If she did not bear him children, he had two already that needed a mother. That excited her—a man and his children who needed her. Something to chase the obscurity into obscurity.

They had exchanged several letters before they agreed on a date to meet. She was anxious to meet this man, but she was determined not to wear black when she did, so she delayed the encounter to make a new dress out of a muted grey with a matching parasol. She didn't want to make too drastic a change from black for fear she would not be recognized when they attended the summer fair. There were foot races, food contests, dancing, livestock competition, and the finale of a horse race...which was just coming back into vogue after the Continental Congress had forbidden them during the war.

She worried though, wondering if he be would be pleased to see her for the first time. Men could be such temperamental visual beasts. When she put on the muted grey dress that morning, she had her doubts, although at the time she had only one other choice—black. She had decided it wasn't a *muted* grey; it was a *drab* grey, or maybe the grey of *dawn*. A bit of sun, that's what she needed. She found a red silk sash to put about her waist and a white pancake hat with a matching red ribbon. The hat would strategically hide most of her unruly brown hair that matched her deep-set eyes. Hopefully he could see her eyes.

He had written that he would come in a buggy. So, when she heard a buggy turn off the road, she came out into the yard to greet him—drab (or dawn) grey dress, red sash, white pancake hat and all. Just as he had said, he arrived mid-morning in a one-horse buggy. The horse was what she saw first. The large, beautiful, black shire stallion with white feathering above its hoofs, and a white diamond on its forehead did not seem winded or even hot. If this was one of his plow horses, the hour or two to trot down from Smithfield was probably a relaxing jaunt. Adam put down the reins and stepped out of the buggy. He was indeed taller than she, broad-shouldered, with a full black beard and grey at the temples. His eyes were blue and gentle. He wore a riding cap which he took off to greet her. His hair was black, full, and long. He moved gently, not in a hurry or rude.

"Missus Babbitt?" he asked with a straight face and a bow.

"Mister Livingston, I presume. Yes, I'm Mary Ann," she said with a smile and then a curtsy.

Evidently her directions and map were sufficient. She figured the house was easy to find due to the wide stand of birch along the road and the drive in the midst of them. "Did you stop and ask directions?" she had asked.

He had replied, "No. There was no need. Your directions were precise and clear."

And while these pleasantries were being exchanged the question still raged in her mind, *will he like the way I look?* She had always considered herself of normal height. But now, looking up at Adam made her reconsider that perhaps she was short. She felt like a pony next to his shire. Alvin was about her size. But this man...was...well...big, and he was exceedingly handsome. Her heart raced as she reconstituted her smile, hoping to appear pleased while hoping he would be pleased as well. Keeping up with her racing heart were her doubts.

Then he smiled. It was a big, broad, genuine smile. Yes, he was pleased with her, even in drab grey. She relaxed—*the race was off.*

He kept adjusting his outer tail coat, which appeared to not fit him quite right, making him appear uncomfortable and awkward. Finally, she took note of what he was wearing, and she almost laughed out loud—a black top hat, a brown tail coat, a forest green waist coat, a white frock shirt with block print cravat, tan breeches, white stockings, and polished buckle shoes. He was dressed for a New York ball or the opera. She had not seen such things on a man since visiting Mary Valens years ago at Travelers Rest. Instantly, she wondered if he would have dressed more comfortably if they had made plans to plow a field instead of attending the fair. Thankfully, he was not wearing a powdered wig—how she despised such frivolity.

But all that was put aside as he helped her into the buggy with her picnic basket and off to the fair they trotted behind the proud shire that pulled them so swiftly and easily along.

The day went well. They talked a great deal and laughed, enjoyed the wandering minstrels, the foot races (they did not participate), table games (they played two games of checkers, tied at one all), the circus performers, and animal showcases, and the final horse race (neither placed bets). The only odd thing about the whole day was that Adam was very hot and was constantly seeking shade, or a cool drink. But he refused to take off his tail coat. No one else was dressed as he was. One man approached Adam assuming he was an official from Gen. Washington's staff. No, he was a farmer from Smithfield. The man looked at Adam as if Smithfield had some strange farming customs. Adam finally started to laugh at himself and his failed attempt to impress Mary Ann. Thereafter, his laugh and smile were beguiling.

Over the next couple of weeks Adam made other trips to Deep Furrow, but at no other time did he come dressed for a ball or opera. Discovering she owned a chestnut mare he rode down one time on Calvin and they spent the day riding horseback around the countryside, getting as far east as the southern fork of Opequon Creek, where they watered their horses and he explained that this was the same creek that ran past his farm. She thought about that—the same water that flowed past Winchester today, would flow past Flax Haven tomorrow. It was a good omen.

So, they set a date, and she sold her quaint farm to the neighbor who had been renting it for over a decade, cleaned out the house, got rid of her black dresses, bought some new clothes, and packed up what she wanted to keep.

On Tuesday morning, August 30, 1791, Adam showed up with his covered wagon pulled by his two shires. At noon, the Mayor of Winchester licensed, officiated, and registered their marriage. It was a simple event, the only witness being the Mayor's secretary. They spent the rest of the day packing the wagon with her assortment of crates, bags, and chests. That night, with a new bottle of wine, Mary Ann spent the last night in her old house consummating her new life with Adam. She wasn't sure if it was the wine or the man, but something agreed with her. She slept through the night for the first time in years and woke in his arms, and in a good mood.

Within an hour they were sitting next to each other on a blanket spread across the wagon's drive bench. Luther and Calvin pulled the wagon north along Apple Ridge Road. Mary Ann's mare, a palomino quarter horse she had named Apple, was tethered behind the wagon. She watched the two shires pull them and the heavy wagon easily along the often hilly road. She asked, "Why would a farmer who has little use for religion name his horses after the founders of two major Christian denominations?"

He chuckled a bit. "Well, there are two reasons, but they are really the same. I acquired Luther and Calvin after I was married to Esther. I had been raised Lutheran, and she was raised Presbyterian, the founder of which was John Calvin, of course. Although the leaders of our churches hated each other, Esther and I were determined to show that Christians could get along and work together toward the same purpose. These two shires do just that, as they are doing right now. They have worked side-by-side for years and never squabbled. They're good friends. They have done much good for me and my family. When Esther died, I gave up religion entirely. She was devout, but I've always thought that if there was any truth to Christianity, then it had to be capable of doing some good, of changing bad things that were wrong and making them better for the common good, just like Calvin and Luther here. But if all Christians do is squabble, and they can't fix problems or make them go away, then I figure they're worthless."

"That seems right," she said. But she wasn't convinced. She had been expecting a much simpler answer. Had she married a philosopher as well as a farmer? Perhaps this man was deep as well as good. She smiled and said, "Let's change the subject, shall we? We have a couple hours to go. Tell me all about my new children, whom I am anxious to meet. Especially my daughter, Eve. She sounds like a lovely and very smart girl."

2

Eve had been praying, and Bethany, too. It was Wednesday, August 31, 1791, about noon. Over the past months Papa had continued to get the mysterious letters, reading each with greater interest than the one before. Then came the fateful evening at supper, this past Saturday. He invited Bethany and Sam to eat with the family that night, which was unusual. After Eve offered grace, a practice Adam tolerated and which Sam and Bethany encouraged, Pa broke the news that he was getting married. This of course had long been the suspicion since weeks earlier he had left dressed for a ball and returned sweating like a horse. But, no, there would be no chance for the family, meaning Eve and Henry, to meet their new stepmother beforehand, any more than they had had a chance to meet Esther before they were born. Eve considered the current situation a bit different, but there didn't seem to be any room for debate.

Adam was sure Mary Ann Babbitt, with her experience and knowledge of working in the clerk's office, would greatly advance Eve and Henry's education. But his final comment to Eve and Henry that evening created a problem for Eve. Evidently, Missus Mary Ann and her first husband were unable to have children, which meant, according to Papa, that Mary Ann would love to have Eve and Henry as her children, and they were to call her *mother*. Eve decided that was not likely to happen.

Except for the "mother" part everything sounded okay, but then Eve asked the all-important question.

"Are you getting married in a church?"

Adam did not hesitate. "No, neither I nor your new mother have much use for religion." He went on to explain that they (the children) would learn to love Mary Ann much like a young lady learns to love her new husband without meeting him until the wedding, as was rumored to have occurred in so-called arranged marriages.

Except, Eve knew that wasn't the case these days. It certainly wasn't true in Papa's case with Mama, nor was it true in the current case since Papa had been exchanging letters with Mrs. Babbitt, whom he had visited on six earlier occasions—Eve had kept track. She knew the difference between Papa going to Charles Town for supplies and going courting. He dressed differently, acted differently, and he never took the wagon...until yesterday morning, and with the hooped cover no less.

Her papa had explained there would be a few rules to make the new Mrs. Livingston feel welcome as soon as she crossed the threshold. The children were to address her as Mama or Mother, and hopefully they would grow to love her as such over time. Sam and Bethany were to address her as Madam, or Mrs. Livingston, or Mary Ann if she gave them permission. He acknowledged that there would be some getting used to her and she to them, as personalities, habits, and customs of the household and farm were learned. He asked that they treat her with the respect she was due as the mistress of his home. In turn, he said, Mary Ann had promised to respect them as well.

Eve had her doubts and prayed to herself: *Oh, Mama, send angels. I think we're going to need help.*

It was getting close to noon. Eve and Bethany were putting the finishing touches on the big meal of the day, expecting Papa and Mary Ann to be home any time. Bethany asked Eve to go to the garden and fetch some spearmint leaves to use as a garnish on the peach compote. Eve had expected to find Henry there, weeding, which was one of his morning chores. But he wasn't there, so she assumed he had gone inside to wash and change clothes before Pa returned with Mary Ann. But as she picked spearmint leaves she saw growing weeds where she should have seen fresh up-turned earth. Henry was mostly her responsibility and she felt a mild panic rise. *Where is Henry?*

Sam was walking from his cabin past the garden to the house. He had cleaned up from fixing something in the pig pen earlier in the morning and was ready to meet the new mistress of the farm.

"Sam, have you seen Henry?" asked Eve. "He was supposed to be here, weeding but..." She stopped, for out of the corner of her eye she saw the covered wagon pull into the yard. *Too late! I'm in trouble now.* She quickly took the leaves to Bethany. "Pa's here. Just pulled in. And Henry's missing."

"Thank you dear, I'll be out in a moment," Bethany said.

Eve ran out to the yard. Sam was there and took Calvin and Luther's bridles in hand as the wagon pulled up to the house with its rear near the front steps of the porch.

"Sam," said Adam, "why don't you unhitch Calvin and Luther and just leave the wagon here until we unload it later. They need feed and water."

"Yes, sir, Missta Livingston. Howdy, Mrs. Babbitt," Sam said with a smile to the pretty lady in the blue dress and bonnet sitting next to her Mister Livingston.

"Hello. You must be Sam," Mary Ann said with a big smile. "But I must politely inform you, I'm Missus *Mary Ann Livingston now."

Sam laughed as did Pa. "Yes, Madam, you's right. My apologies," said Sam.

"You may call me Mary Ann, Sam. No need for formality with me."

"Thank you, ma'am," said Sam, as he began to unhitch Calvin and Luther.

Adam helped Mary Ann climb down from the wagon bench and the two walked to Eve who was standing alone a few feet away. "Mary Ann, this is my very grown-up daughter, Eve."

"How do you do, Madam?" curtsied Eve.

Mary Ann stuck out her hand and offered it to Eve. "I'm so very glad to meet you Eve. I've heard much about you."

Eve took her hand but didn't know what to do with it. So, Mary Ann just squeezed it and pulled Eve close and gave her a polite hug.

"Where is your brother, Eve?" asked Mary Ann.

"Yes, where is Henry?" echoed Adam as he scanned the horizon.

"Papa, I know you told me to make sure he was clean and waiting, but I was helping Miss Bethany with dinner, and when I went out to the garden to tell him to clean up, he wasn't there."

"Sam?" asked Adam.

"No sir, I's not seen 'im since early dis mornin'. He helped me for a bit with da pen, but den he took off," said Sam.

"Which way?" asked Adam.

"Mister Livingston, I think you knows, but I don't want'a be a tater tale," said Sam while rolling his head and eyes toward the Opequon.

Adam just nodded and then shook his head.

Just then Bethany came out the front door in her apron. Everyone looked up to her on the porch, which she quickly descended. "Let me welcome you, Missus Livingston. I'm Bethany, Mister Livingston's cook, and Sam's wife. We live over yonder." She pointed toward their cabin tucked under the shade of the wood. "I've got a big dinner for you after your trip, complete with pork, fish, sweet potatoes, fresh garden greens, peach compote, and Mister Livingston's favorite wine."

"Thank you, Bethany. It sounds wonderful, and I'm honestly hungry, although it may be the excitement of all this, too," said Mary Ann as she looked around taking in the farm buildings. "Adam, I'm so looking forward to a tour of my new home...and farm."

"Sam," called out Adam, "take care of Mary Ann's mare. That's Apple."

"Does Apple like apples, Missus Mary Ann?" asked Sam with a big smile.

"She sure does," said Mary Ann.

"Good. I get her one."

"Thanks, Sam," said Adam.

Sam tilted his eye and headed toward the creek. "Ah, Missta Livingston?"

Before her pa moved around the wagon to look, Eve saw Henry sauntering barefoot along the wagon path next to the pastures toward the house. He was caked in mud; one shoulder strap of his bib overalls unfastened to form a pouch in which he seemed to be cradling something.

"Oh, no," said Eve to herself.

Adam stared at his very unpresentable son, who by now was running toward them with a big smile on his face and working hard to protect his cargo. "Mary Ann," said a perturbed Adam, "I'm afraid this is my son you're about to meet, along with his recent pastime."

Mary Ann, apparently intrigued, stepped toward Henry.

Momentarily, Henry arrived, looked up with a wicked smile at his new stepmom and said, "Hi! I brought you somethin'" and spread open his bib to let her look down and inside the pouch it created.

Mary Ann looked down. Eve could not see what Mary Ann saw, but Eve knew what Mary Ann was looking at.

Inside Henry's soaking wet bib, lined with mud, were a dozen large, brown, squirmy crustaceans resembling small lobsters with two big claws, black eyes, and a flashing flat tail. "They're crawdaddies," said Henry with delight.

"Indeed, they are," said Mary Ann. "Have you ever had crawdaddies?"

"Sure do, I got a bunch right here."

"No. No, I mean have you ever eaten crawdaddies?"

"Uck! No way," revolted Henry.

"Oh, no son, they're quite delicious." Mary Ann looked up at Bethany, "Bethany, dear, would you get me a pan or pot. We're going to boil us some crawdaddies."

"Oh, my," exclaimed Bethany, "I do know about that." Bethany ran back into the house giggling and waving her hands as if the best thing in the world had just happened.

Eve skewed up her face and looked at Papa with disgust.

Henry's eyes opened super wide. "You're gonna eat 'em?"

"Why sure!" said Mary Ann. "You went to all the trouble to catch them, that couldn't have been too easy. It's just a little bit of extra effort to cook 'em."

Henry looked down at the disgusting critters as Bethany came out with a boiling pot and held it next to Henry's bib. Without hesitation or flinching Mary Ann reached into Henry's bib, picked up each squirmy ten-footed bottom fish and dropped it into the pot.

"Now, Bethany," said Mary Ann, "I am sure you have a lovely dinner prepared. But this will be our after-dinner snack. Can you wash off these fine creatures? I've got the perfect recipe for the dip." Mary Ann turned to Henry's father. "Adam, how do you wash off your son after such adventures?"

"We usually tie him to the well pulley and dunk him a few times," Adam said with a straight face. He was enjoying how Mary Ann was taking charge. "Come. I'll show you something you may not have seen in a farmhouse. Come along Son."

"Oh, Pa, not again!" squirmed Henry.

"Son, you can choose to do what you want, but you have no choice over the consequence."

Adam took his son's hand and led him into the house. Mary Ann and Eve followed along with Bethany and the pot of crawdaddies. They walked through the foyer, around and behind the central staircase, to an open trap door that led to steps into the cellar. On a small table next to the trap door was an always lit lantern, several unlit lanterns, and a tinderbox with wood slivers for matches. "Eve, grab a towel for Henry, will you?" Her papa then turned up the wick on the already lit lantern, lit a match from it and then passed the flame to the two other lanterns which he handed to Eve and Bethany. He then led the group down the steps into the dark cellar.

3

The cellar was familiar territory for Eve; she wondered what her new stepmother would think of it. The cellar walls formed the large rectangle foundation upon which the perimeter of the house rested. The walls themselves were constructed of stacked and mortared fieldstone, which rested on a two-foot-wide footing of fieldstones that were laid and mortared together in a trench two feet below the cellar floor. The walls were two feet wide at the bottom where the wall rested on the footings. They rose to a height of seven feet above the footings and were slowly narrowed to only sixteen inches wide at the top on which woodsill planks were installed. Spanning the walls were large wooden beams upon which wooden planks were nailed to form the subfloor of the main house.

Eve had watched with great interest as the house was built. Papa explained that key to the cellar's function was that the house was built into the side of a hill so that the entire rear wall was underground. This required a lot of digging and hauling of dirt, of course. The hill naturally sloped down toward the front of the house where only four feet of the cellar was underground. That meant the front cellar wall rose three feet above ground. By the time the front porch was added, a five-step stoop was required to climb onto the porch before entering the front door of the house.

The cellar floor was also made from fieldstones that were split to create a flat surface; the gaps in the floor stones were filled with mortar. To manage the inevitable leaks in the below-grade wall, the floor was sloped slightly to the west to allow for drainage through a weep hole at the bottom of the west wall into a dry stone well.

Built into both side walls of the cellar, near the front, were two small windows for light and ventilation. There were no windows at the rear, which was all underground; and there were no windows at the front, because that wall was under the front porch.

Adam had explained to her that the cellar was supposed to be a cold and dark place for the storage of food like sweet potatoes, carrots, and other vegetables. Yet for a unique reason their cellar would be colder than most, and that was good.

When the group got to the bottom of the stairs, Bethany said, "Follow me, Missus Mary Ann, you'll like this." Bethany led the way to the southern corner where there was a spring-fed cistern. "Mister Livingston found this spring on the land and built his house atop it. The water come into the cellar here...." She pointed to a continuous stream of cold, clear water falling from a carved stone spout cemented into the rear wall of the foundation. "It flow like a waterfall over these stones that comes out of the wall, into this large stone cistern." She held the lantern so Mary Ann could see clearly that the top of the cistern was about five feet above the cellar's floor. "When the cistern full, like now, water comes out this second spout and drain into this lower stone basin."

At this point Bethany dumped the pot of muddy crawdads into the one-foot-deep basin which was about three feet off the floor and big enough for a pile of clothes or a young boy. The flow of water from the cistern immediately began to clean the mud off the crawdads. Bethany continued: "From the basin, which you can plug to make a deep pool, the water fill up this shallow trough. It catch the mud and dirty, then it overflows and drain outside of the house to a underground channel of split fieldstone which comes out in the cistern next to the vegetable and herb garden. You probably saw that outside."

Mary Ann was obviously impressed. "This is amazing, Adam. I had no idea you were so clever."

"Wasn't my idea," he said. "The founder of Hagerstown, Jonathan Hager, built his first house, called it Hager's Fancy, on top of two springs. They cooled his cellar and provided safe drinking water. I just improved on the idea by adding the cistern and wash tub. But this water flows year-round, even in the summer like right now, and it keeps the cellar cooler. We can easily store a year's supply or more of roots and even some meats."

"It's a torture chamber," complained Henry.

"How's that?" asked Mary Ann.

"Because," said Eve pointing to the tub, "that's where Henry is put to be washed off when he gets this dirty."

"It's cold," said Henry.

Adam ignored his son for the moment and pointed to a plug at the bottom of the cistern. "You can also take water from the cistern even when the water gets low, through this plug. It's still high enough off the floor to put a bucket under."

Mary Ann shook her head in amazement. "I've never seen anything like this."

Under her breath Eve whispered, "Thank you, Mama, keep praying for us."

Mary Ann turned to Eve, "What was that?"

"Oh," said Eve, "I was just saying how nice this is...for us."

"Yes, it is," Mary Ann said.

Bethany proceeded to rinse out the pot, fill it part way with water, and then one by one she rinsed the crawdaddies and put them back into the pot of water.

"Okay, ladies," said Adam, "now that that's done, young man, strip. You're next."

"Pa!" Henry objected and glanced at the women standing all around waiting to be entertained.

"Son, they're not going to hurt you, now strip."

"They'll see me naked, Pa!"

"So, what?" Adam teased.

And with that Henry began to tear up.

"All right! All right! Ladies do you mind? Take the critters upstairs; we'll be along shortly. Give me the towel, Eve."

Robbed of the show, the women made some jokes, but trudged up the steps, leaving behind a man, a lantern, a towel, and one soon-to-be-naked boy. Once to the top of the stairs they heard Henry's screams as Adam put his son on the stone altar and began to wash the mud from his son's naked body. As the howls from Henry continued, a short-haired, black house cat showed up, rubbed against Mary Ann's ankles, looked up, greeted her with a meow, then scampered down the stairs to investigate the noise.

"That's a good sign, Missus Mary Ann," said Bethany. "That there is Bombay. He a stray cat claimed us as his own while back. He' probably hungry. Goin' to hunt mice if Cleopatra doesn't have them all by now. Cleopatra's our other cat. Sometime you go down there with the lantern, all you sees of him is two big yellow eyes. But don't ya be scared. He like everyone just dis same."

4

A short time later, after everyone had a chance to wash their hands and faces, and in Henry's case put on some clean clothes, it was time to eat. An extra place was made for Sam, who usually ate in his cabin well after the Livingstons ate. Bethany and Eve had laid out an abundance of food on the large gathering hall table which had been covered with a linen cloth Esther had woven years earlier. Then came the time Eve was looking forward to, but with some trepidation.

It was the family's custom when coming to dinner or supper to stand behind their place at table until a prayer of thanksgiving was said. Before Mama died, Papa would often pray. But when Mama died, Papa stopped praying. Yet he would let Eve recite the prayer Esther had prayed at mealtimes. Later, when they came to be part of the family, Bethany or Sam would sometimes pray. Eve especially liked it when Sam prayed. His deep, resonant voice made the chairs and table shake.

She wondered how this was going to happen today with her new stepmother who evidently wanted nothing to do with religion. If Papa allowed, she was ready, so before Adam or Mary Ann came down from washing up, Eve was sure to stand behind her place first and tug Henry to do the same. Bethany took her normal position behind a chair at the foot of the table nearest the kitchen, and Sam stood behind a chair around the corner next to Bethany. To Sam's right was an empty spot for Mary Ann which was around the corner from where Adam would sit at the head of the table.

When her papa and stepmother came into the room, Eve caught Papa's eye as if to ask, *may I pray tonight?* She noticed that Mary Ann was watching. Papa stared at Eve and grimaced just a bit but stood behind his chair. Mary Ann, looking around, wondering what to do, then stood behind her chair as well. Without smiling, Adam nodded at Eve.

Eve smiled back, then without looking at anyone else she bowed her head and prayed: *"Dear God. Thank you for this special day that has seen my father's marriage to this special lady, our new stepmother. We ask you to bless them and us in our new family."* And then Eve recited Mama's favorite prayer, *"O Lord our God and heavenly Father, which of Thy unspeakable mercy towards us hast provided meat and drink for the nourishment of our weak bodies, grant us peace to use them reverently, as from Thy hands, with thankful hearts. Let Thy blessing rest upon these Thy good creatures, to our comfort and sustenance, and grant, we humbly beseech Thee, good Lord, that as we do hunger and thirst for this food for our bodies, so our souls may earnestly long after the food of eternal life, through Jesus Christ, our Lord and Savior, Amen."*

Eve immediately glanced up at Mary Ann and smiled. Mary Ann threw a challenging glare at Eve over what could only be called an acquiescence. It lasted but a moment, but Eve caught the meaning: *This won't go on for long, my dear girl.* Mary Ann then glanced at Adam, who avoided everyone's look before sitting down. "Thank you, Bethany," he said, "and Eve for preparing this obvious feast for this important meal with my new bride." He smiled politely at Mary Ann and squeezed her hand, and she in return obliged him with a modest smile and a tight lip.

Eve was content that Papa's extended family enjoyed their first meal together amicably.

Immediately afterwards, Mary Ann kicked into gear. "All right, Bethany, the peach compote was good. But now for the real treat. Where's that pot of crawdaddies?"

"Why they've been in a pot of water over the fireplace cooking all this time."

"Oh, excellent, you're ahead of me. Where are the spices and cheese?" Mary Ann jumped up from the table.

Bethany got up as well. "I'll show you," and headed out the back door for the cooking kitchen.

Mary Ann grabbed a hot pad at the hearth, lifted the crawdad pot out of the fire and brought it around for Adam and Henry to look inside. "Look here gents. Don't they smell yummy?"

Eve looked over Henry's shoulder. The once dark brown and wiggly crawdaddies were bright orange and they had ceased to move. The fishy smell wasn't exactly what she'd call "yummy," and instinctively she wrinkled her nose.

"We'll be right back," Mary Ann said, and hauled the pot out the back door and down into the kitchen.

Adam began to chuckle. "Son, you have met your match."

Sam spoke up, "Henry, you's like these. I ate crawdads long ago. What you do..." and Sam mimed the action "...is grab de head in one hand 'en de tail in de odder, twist 'en snap off de tail, pull de meat out of de shell, dip it in de sauce, 'en suck it into yours mouth."

Henry threw Sam a disbelieving look: "You mean you don't eat the whole thing?"

"Oh, dear me, no. Pinchers, boney tail, those long feelers, buggy black eyes, and the whole head? On, no," Sam said shaking with laughter. "Only the devil would eat the whole thing."

Adam laughed, too. But Eve didn't even smile.

In a few minutes Mary Ann returned, her eyes dancing with mischief. Bethany was right behind licking her fingers. In front of Henry, Adam, and Eve, Mary Ann placed a large round plate on which the boiled, orange-red crawdaddies lay in a circle—their long feelers and pincher claws elbow-to-elbow pointed outward, and their tails pointing toward the center where there was a small bowl of spicy looking dip.

"Now Henry, do you know what to do?" asked Mary Ann.

Henry looked up at Sam, who leaned back, smiled, and nodded at Henry as if to say, "*Sure do!*" Behind Mary Ann's back, Sam held up his hands to again mime picking up the crawdad with the fingers of both hands, twisting the tail off the body, pulling out the meat, sliding it in the dip, then sucking it into his mouth.

Henry laughed at Sam, but then did it. He picked up a crawdad, twisted off the tail, pulled out the meat, dipped it into the dip, and sucked it into his mouth.

The table erupted in applause and cheers at Henry's perfect demonstration of eating crawfish. Henry smiled but twisted his mouth as if the taste wasn't all that agreeable to him.

But Mary Ann just stared at Henry, and with a sinister tone said, "Henry, I don't know who taught you how to do that, but it's all wrong, and you're missing the best part. Let me show you, dear, and then you can try it again." Mary Ann then picked up the biggest of the crawdads, held it up for Henry to see as she smirked at him with her piercing brown eyes, then dipped the entire crustacean tail in the dip, turned it around, and dipped one claw in the dip, then the head and the other claw. Holding it up with the dip dripping onto the plate she said, "Now doesn't this look better?" Without taking her eyes off him, she opened her mouth wide, and slid the entire ten-footed creature, feelers, bug eyes, claws, body, and tail into her mouth. Then she clamped down: CRUNCH! while her fingers pushed the parts that tried to escape from her mouth back in. CRUNCH! CRUNCH! CRUNCH!

Eve instantly felt like she was going to retch. She put her hands over her mouth. No one else said a word. The only noise in the room was Mary Ann's teeth, mouth, and lips crunching and smacking on the shell, and stuffing the claws, long feelers, or tail that kept trying to get out, back in between her lips. CRUNCH! CRUNCH! CRUNCH! For Eve, the sound and the sight were revolting.

After a few minutes, Mary Ann swallowed several times, smiled broadly, wiped her mouth with one of the linen napkins, took a sip of wine, and said, "Now, that was delicious."

And at that moment, Eve could hold it down no longer. She turned sideways...and very much involuntarily, bent over and retched several times, regurgitating her entire supper onto the floor.

5

My Despised Cyn:

Well played my thrice-over condemned Cyn. You have plotted the caper out well. You were able to keep Babbitt from the children and the Darks until it was too late. She immediately took charge with the crawdads. A courageous and smart woman. She will do well up against our foes whenever and however they meet, and at this juncture I am sure they will, but I have no idea how.

Indeed, only the devil would eat the whole thing. I suspect you, Cyn, made that happen.

Good work. Your temporal presence deserves to be set free... hope that is in the works.

Eternally yours,
Master of Grotesqueness

Chapter 24
Toads

1

Thanks to Henry and his crawdads Mary Ann had quickly accomplished her first objective as stepmother—to wield dominance. Although she had never raised children of her own, she remembered being the brat prodigy and what it took to get her in line. As an adult she had studied enough families to know that children respond best to a certain type of stimuli—*fear*.

As a parent it was important to be responsible and accountable, which meant being in control and coming out on top. As long as Eve and Henry had a fear of what she was capable, she would be in control.

It was a small thing, but it had worked. She had never eaten a whole crawdad before but seeing the disbelief and shock on their faces was worth the indignity. She just never thought the effect would be so powerful as to cause sweet, innocent Eve to toss her dinner. But the feeling of supremacy that came over her when Eve upchucked was marvelous. It established her as top dog so quickly she could hardly believe her luck. Beforehand, Adam had tried to alleviate her doubts about being a stepmother. "Just take charge," he had said. "I'll back you up. Don't worry. They had a good mother before, I'm sure you can be a good mother now, if not better. They learned some things from Esther, now they'll learn more things from you."

After she had swallowed the decapod and seeing the reaction of his children, Adam granted her that beguiling, confident, go-get-'em smile she liked so much. She had found herself sitting taller in her chair as if ascending the throne of queen mother. She just hoped her body was up to digesting a large, chewed-up crustacean.

She now had the confidence to pursue her next goal—social status. It was something that had eluded her in Winchester, no doubt due to her fourteen-year obsession mourning Alvin's death. A recluse, that's what she had become until Adam showed up and provided an escape from her coffin. He had taken her to the fair, stuffed-artichoke he appeared to be at the time, and proved he was a fair catch. His faux pas didn't cause him to disengage or retreat, but to charge forward. On another visit they went horseback riding, and the next time dancing. He had never been to a hall dance before, and he was a bit clumsy, but he didn't shy away. He plunged ahead. That shillelagh must give him confidence—so simple and humble looking, but in his hands, a confidence builder. She still shivered with glee remembering the time a drunk decided she was his wife. The man would not go away until Adam adroitly stuck his shillelagh between the man's already confused legs causing the gent to stumble off the boardwalk, down a hill, and into the mud. She felt safe around Adam, and he nourished her confidence to enter society.

A recluse no longer, or so she hoped. On her second day at Flax Haven, she suggested they hold an open house to introduce her and their marriage to society. For pretext, they could show off his new and beautiful house and his innovative barn. She also suggested to Adam that the open house would be an opportunity to establish himself in the farming community. It would accelerate them both into society, and likewise society with them. Adam readily agreed, and together they put together a list of who to invite.

In going over his list with her he explained who each invitee was and his relationship with them. One couple that heightened her interest was a man and his new wife living nearby in Leetown—Richard and Anastasia McSherry. Adam had never met Richard McSherry, but he had done business with Anastasia at Hagerstown Textiles before she married. After the McSherrys' wedding, which was only a month ago, Adam had received an invitation from Anastasia for his family to visit them in Leetown with directions to their home. But as of yet, Adam had not taken her up on the offer. There were two things about this couple that intrigued Mary Ann. First, it was Anastasia telling Adam that she was getting married, and that she was going to be living near him that had started Adam thinking about getting married again himself. Mary Ann had Anastasia to thank for Adam seeking her out and rescuing her from obscurity. Second, Adam had asked around and discovered that Richard McSherry was one of the largest landholders in the Shenandoah Valley. Although he had no holdings as far south as Winchester, he was well known from Charles Town north all the way to Chambersburg and very well known in Hagerstown and Fredrick, where she imagined Richard and Anastasia were the epitome of high society.

This excited her. It was one thing to be the mistress of a large and successful farm, but to be connected to such important people could only enhance one's prestige and stature. The prospects gave her new-found optimism, and she began to make plans to entertain the McSherrys...and, of course, others who were sure to come. It would be a grand day and one that would elevate her in the opinion of the entire region.

They scheduled the open house for the last Sunday afternoon in September, the 25th. That would give them time to prepare the house for visitors. Mary Ann asked Adam if the large, disassembled loom that dominated a front corner of the gathering hall, and the spinner that sat next to it, could be removed to the barn.

"I don't weave, Adam, dear," Mary Ann said.

"I do," he replied.

"When will you have time?" she asked.

"It's here for Eve to learn in her mother's place. I will assemble it when I find time."

"But why? We can buy commercial linens, cottons, or wool that are likely to be of finer quality than Eve can produce."

"I'm a flax farmer, Mary Ann. My family has always spun and woven. It's part of who we are, and Eve will carry on that tradition, or so she says she wants to."

Mary Ann could tell that the spinner and loom were part of Adam's soul, as was the linen that came from his crops, so for the time being she let it go. She would focus on the food to be prepared.

Adam knew about the apple pies she baked for the soldiers camped near the ridge north of Winchester, but he didn't know about all the recipes stored in her head or her passion for cooking. He probably didn't think she was a glutton, for she was trim and filled out only in the right places, even for a woman in mid-life. Perhaps it was the horseback riding, or the gardening and the occasional dancing that kept her body looking youthful. She didn't know, but she did know food, and for the open house, she intended to impress.

In that regard, Mary Ann worked with Bethany to plan and prepare the food and beverages for the event, and together they made several trips to stores in Charles Town. She decided they would make and serve gingerbread cookies, her famous apple pie with Ceylon cinnamon, apple pudding with nutmeg and mace, nuts, dried apricots, prunes, raisins, and deviled eggs if the store in Charles Town stocked cayenne pepper. She would buy some lemons and with sugar, fresh cream, and egg whites she'd show Bethany how to make lemon honeycomb, always a favorite, especially with lemon zest on top. Finally, there would be one more apple dish: apple tansey, if the Mexican vanilla was available. To drink there would be small beer, port beer, wine, perhaps raspberry tea, and water from their spring with spearmint leaves. That will shock folks, imagine drinking water that doesn't make you sick. She wished she had time to make cheese, as she had brought her cheese press from Winchester, but she liked it sharp, and it would require months of curing to get it right. Next time. In the meantime, she'd buy a cheese wheel from the shop in town. Mary Ann loved ice cream, but the ice vendor in town was almost out; it was September and ice won't keep forever, even in the best ice houses. Just thinking about all these things kept Mary Ann happy and busy in the kitchen with Bethany the entire week before the big day.

Meanwhile, Eve and Henry kept busy with their various chores around the house and farm. At Adam's insistence, Mary Ann and the children took time each afternoon to work on reading and vocabulary and doing figures. For the most part it was Mary Ann teaching Eve, then Eve taught Henry.

Adam placed a public invitation in both the Charles Town and Winchester newspapers. It read: "Adam Livingston of Smithfield invites the pubic to an open house and farm in honor of his new bride, Mary Ann (Babbitt) Livingston. Flax Haven Farm, Half-Mile North of Smithfield on the Charles Town Road. - Sunday After Noon, September 25, 1791." He had also taken personal invitations to those he and the children had met shortly after arriving in Virginia, except the McCulloughs. Included were the Smiths, the local livery owner Feltsbarron, the Randalls, who were the new owners of the Plantation at Travelers Rest, and the McSherrys of Leetown.

In Leetown, Adam followed the directions to the McSherrys' home that Anastasia had included in her recent letter. He was surprised to discover it was the marvelous stone house he and the children had visited years earlier when they first arrived in town and visited neighbors with loaves of fresh bread. It was the house with the garden of hedges in the shape of a cathedral or cross and the rose arbors which were now in bloom. Anastasia and Richard were both home when he dropped by with the invitation. Ana was delighted to see Adam again and confirmed that they would "not miss the open house for Mary Ann under any circumstances, save death." After returning to Flax Haven, Adam had told Mary Ann that he found Richard to be an Irish gentleman of refined deportment, but that the house, while very nice and expertly built entirely of stone, was not as lavishly appointed as he had expected for one of the richest men in the region. "It was very humble and simple," Adam had said.

In the days before the Sunday open house, Adam, Henry, and Sam worked at cleaning up and improving the barn and other out-buildings. They also posted a road sign at the farm's drive that read "FLAX HAVEN - THE LIVING-STONS."

Mary Ann and Bethany made the final food preparations, while Eve straightened everything in the house, did some dusting, mopped the wood-planked floors, and put linen coverings on the main table in the gathering hall, and smaller linens on the various smaller tables and game tables in the gathering hall and parlor. Eve found a chess set for the game table in the parlor, dominoes for the foyer table, and checkers for the game table in the gathering hall. Now, Mary Ann wondered, if she could just do something with that eye sore of a loom, stashed in parts in the corner. She spoke to Adam once again about it, but stubbornly, he would not move it and he had no time to assemble it. It was too big to easily move herself, or it would have been in his office-storeroom days ago.

2

The open house turned out to be a major summertime event. On Sunday, their guests started to arrive shortly after noon. At first, Adam and Mary Ann greeted them in the yard as they dismounted their horses, buggies, or wagons. Eve stationed herself on the porch to usher everyone inside where the food was laid out in the gathering hall. Henry kept looking for boys his own age to run around with and a few came much to his delight. Sam cared for the horses and conveyances that collected in the yard. By Adam's direction, Sam was to always meet guests eye-to-eye and introduce himself as Sam Dark, Flax Haven's foreman, in an attempt to forestall any false conclusions that Sam was any longer a slave. Bethany, who tended to the food table in the gathering hall did the same, but introduced herself as cook and house manager.

After a while Mary Ann and Adam found themselves greeting guests in the gathering hall where all the food was, but soon, the food table, chairs, stools, and game tables were so besieged that the newly married couple were driven into the parlor. There they settled down to receive their guests in comfort as they crossed Flax Haven's threshold. Among their guests was the son of the founder of Smithfield—Jon Smith, Jr., and his sons; and the founder of Charles Town—Charles Washington, who was the youngest brother of General George Washington.

Most surprising, however, was Brigadier General *Daniel Morgan from Winchester. As soon as he crossed their threshold Mary Ann recognized him and bitterness stabbed her heart. On his arm was a woman about his age, early fifties, probably his wife. Mary Ann was glad they would have to wait in line a few moments before she was face-to-face with a man she had hated for years. Things were different now, but still she struggled with her emotions that at once conjured up both disgust of the man and humility that he had come all the way from Winchester to honor her re-marriage. Years before the war it was then Colonel Morgan who had recruited Alvin to join the Sharpshooters, which were subsequently marched to Canada and into battle. It was Morgan along with Generals Washington, Gates, and Arnold that she blamed for her loss, and over a decade of mourning Alvin's death.

The thought came to her that she should be honored that the slightly rotund General Morgan came dressed in a formal Continental Army uniform—a dark blue officer's frock coat, polished steel buttons, medals, black cocked hat with gold trim (no wig), and sword, though he seemed to suffer from a hip ailment. His wife, Abigail Curry Morgan, was comfortably dressed also for a formal reception in a light-green dress with stomacher and white chiffon kerchief and pancake hat over her grey curls. *They went to some trouble for us,* she thought. Thankfully, Mrs. Morgan came without hoops under her dress, which Mary Ann had always considered ridiculous. After the war, General Morgan retired in Winchester with his wife and children. He built a large house on his estate that was rumored, by now, to be more than 200,000 acres. He named the estate Saratoga after his victory over General Burgoyne and the British at Saratoga, New York, with Generals Horatio Gates and Benedict Arnold. It was the battle where Alvin was mortally wounded.

When the general and his wife were finally introduced to Adam and Mary Ann, it was *Abigail who spoke first. She told Mary Ann that after the war, when the general was building their house in Winchester, he, not she, sent two Hessian prisoners of war under his command to Apple Ridge to buy three apple pies from her—two for the prisoners he had employed to build their house, and one for their family. "My dear Missus Livingston," said Abigail, "I will never forget how delicious that pie was."

When Mary Ann heard this, a flood of nostalgia and tears came over her. It was years ago, but she remembered vividly the Hessian soldiers who had bought the three pies, the last of a recent batch. Without thinking she found herself gracing the general's wife with a curtsy. *It was probably the Ceylon cinnamon,* thought Mary Ann.

Abigail then leaned in with a mischievous smile and said, "My dear, I hope I'm not too presumptuous to think there might be a slice or two of your apple pie in the next room?"

Mary Ann was smitten. "Not at all. I made it just for you, but you might hurry before they're gone."

"We will," replied Abigail.

"By the way," said Mary Ann, "you look marvelous in that dress, and you have my compliments for leaving the hoops at home."

Abigail laughed out loud. "Missus Livingston, panniers are the most cumbersome and immobilizing things."

"I very much agree," smiled Mary Ann.

"But I have an excuse, as well," said Abigail. "The general suffers from a pain in his hip from riding a horse into battle for so many years. Forgoing the hoops allows me to support him when a spasm hits." Then she whispered with a smile, "I'm not on his arm, my dear, he's on mine."

"Thank you for coming," said Mary Ann, "and if the pies are gone, I promise to make you one and send Adam or Sam to Winchester with it."

It was then that the general, warrior that he was celebrated to be, found the courage to speak. "My dear Abigail, let me get a word in with Missus Livingston, will you?" At once, Abigail took the general's arm, and helped him shift his weight to address Mary Ann directly. "Missus Livingston," the general began with all seriousness.

Mary Ann stiffened, and hoped he was not going to accuse Alvin of something while under his command, for surely, as much as she liked Abigail for her candor, she could not have her day ruined by criticism of Alvin by one of his former generals.

"Missus Livingston, I am very happy to meet you after all these years you were in Winchester and we never met. I am deeply sorry for that. When we saw the advertisement inviting citizens of Winchester to come today, despite my dear Abigail's taste for your pies, and mine as well, I insisted we make the journey. I wanted to come to pay my respects to your former husband, Colonel Babbitt. Your husband was one of the best sharpshooters in my company. He was very instrumental in helping us defeat General Burgoyne at Saratoga. When we named our home Saratoga, I thought often how brave your husband fought and died. Your husband was standing not ten feet from me when I accepted the swords of General Burgoyne's officers. And I had the honor of being in Alvin's burial party where he received military honors. Your great loss contributed to our country's great gain."

Mary Ann was a mix of emotions. No one had ever said anything to her so affectionately about Alvin's military service, not even in the letter that came to her from Washington's staff informing her of Alvin's death. She felt flushed when General Morgan finished and stepped back and bowed to her. Again, she responded with a deep and extra-long curtsy.

"General Morgan and Missus Morgan," said Adam. "I am very grateful to you for coming and expressing these honorable and touching sentiments to my wife. I am in your service, and I thank you for your service to our country."

As the Morgans entered the gathering hall for some of Mary Ann's apple pie with the Ceylon cinnamon, she felt as if years of bitterness had been lifted and, with Adam at her side, she felt whole.

Indeed, the Morgans could have been the most memorable guests of the afternoon, but Mary Ann had grander designs. Designs that involved Anastasia McSherry. For it was the McSherrys that were known in society throughout the region and were no doubt invited to all the important events and outings held in Charles Town, Hagerstown, and Fredrick. Mary Ann was determined to be part of that scene, and marrying a successful and innovative farmer like Adam was her invitation to move up in society. *Where were the McSherrys,* she wondered? What a tragedy if she had missed them. All her exquisite and expensive food preparation would have been for nothing. One taste of her lemon honeycomb or apple tansey, and she was sure Anastasia would want Mary Ann Livingston to come to every event she hosted or where she had influence. Although Hagerstown, where Mary Ann had heard the McSherrys were established socially, was a three-hour buggy ride, it would be worth it. She was sure Adam could spare Sam for a day now and then to drive her. She would persuade Adam of the prestige he would gain by such trips. Why, he could double the price of his flax just because of her fame. At least that was what she thought, although she had never taken a wagon load of anything to market and had no idea how prices were set. She imagined how Anastasia would brag about her exquisite cooking to the point that Mary Ann would become the favorite guest at fair and ball. Why, it wasn't but a year ago that she won the top prize for her apple pies at the Fredrick County fair. The Morgans had even recounted her fame in that regard. The only reason she didn't enter the contest this year was because Adam was courting her. So it was but a small step, she was sure, before she would be celebrated and honored everywhere she went. It all depended on Anastasia's falling in love with her lemon honeycomb, apple tansey, or yes, her Ceylon cinnamon apple pie. Anastasia would be her close friend. Why had she not seen her?

Later in the afternoon, the reception line disappeared, the crowd thinned, and Adam and Mary Ann came into the yard to see a couple off in their buggy. Mary Ann was depressed as she came to believe the whole reason for this day had been lost—the McSherrys. Sam was holding the bridle of the horse hitched to the couple's buggy. "Sam?" asked Mary Ann, "you know Anastasia McSherry. Has she or her husband been here? Did I miss them?"

"No, ma'am. They rode in on horses some minutes ago," Sam said. "When they come, some man hailed Mister and Missus McSherry from the barn. I think they're over there," as he pointed toward the barn. "That's der horses tied outside."

Mary Ann looked toward the barn. On the hitching post was a large chestnut stallion with an astride saddle and a smaller chestnut mare with a side-saddle. "Thanks, Sam," said Mary Ann. Her heart raced a bit. *All was not lost.* She hoped that there was ample food left, but she didn't want to take the time to check. As soon as the buggy pulled out she tugged on Adam's arm toward the barn. A few men and a woman were standing at the east entrance. Mary Ann knew Adam was proud of the post-and-beam constructed barn. The improvements it incorporated were the best that he could afford from the many barns he had examined over the years, but what a distraction it was from her food, she thought.

Only 300 feet southwest of the house the new 120-foot by 80-foot barn was also built into the side of the same hill. Each of its three levels had wagon access by earthen ramps. The builders said it was the only barn they knew of in the region like that.

Hay and straw were stored on the third level and dropped through trap doors in the floor to the second level livestock stalls. Likewise, waste from mucked out stalls was dropped through one of several trap doors in the main aisle to the cellar. When enough collected, the manure would be carted to a pasture where it would be spread out to dry, and then collected as fertilizer.

The barn had one other innovative feature. The roof was peaked in the center and gabled at the 80-foot ends. Along the 120-foot dimension, at the bottom of the roof shakes, troughs, carved from cedar, caught rainwater from the roof and funneled it to a cedar-planked cistern positioned between the second and third level. The cistern had a drain plug that allowed water to be drained into other cedar troughs that fed small drinking troughs in each of the stalls. When it failed to rain, water would have to be carried into each stall with a bucket from the well or creek.

It was these innovations that engrossed the group that now stood in the door of the barn. Adam pointed out Richard and Anastasia in their riding clothes who were among the group. When Mary Ann and Adam approached, Richard and Anastasia broke off from the group and made their greetings. Richard was most interested in the barn, along with the other men who had many questions for Adam. But Anastasia rolled her eyes humorously at Mary Ann as if there were better things to talk about or do. Mary Ann thought: *Good. She's of the same mind as mine. It's about food, not barns.* Although this was the first time Mary Ann and Anastasia had met, they seemed to be old friends, no doubt because of Adam's previous business relationship with Anastasia, and the short time Adam spent with Richard and Anastasia when he visited their house to drop off the invitation.

3

"Come into the house, Anastasia," said Mary Ann, "and let these men talk about farm stuff...unless you want to inspect the flax processing stations he's set up on the third level."

"I've already been there," Anastasia laughed as she gave Mary Ann a hug. "Let's leave the flax, horses, and manure to the men. What have you got to eat?"

"Good," said Mary Ann and she took the younger woman's arm and they walked off.

"I just hope there's food left," said Mary Ann. "We've had a gang of people here today, and I'm not sure we made enough." *I better be wrong,* she thought.

Anastasia explained their late arrival: "Richard wanted to ride out and look at some land he recently purchased, and said we'd stop here on the way home. I told him we should eat first and then ride, but not Richard: It's land first, then food." She giggled. "Men! You can never figure them out."

"Adam is the same way. He gets up before dawn and works the fields, or in the barn for several hours before he comes in for breakfast." Mary Ann paused, then dared to be personal. "Ana...can I call you that?"

"Oh, sure," Ana said, as they both squeezed each other's arms, as if it was a joy for old friends to finally see one another.

As they climbed the front stoop, Sam came out of the house with a piece of pie in his hand. "Sorry, Missus Mary Ann, I just wanted to get some of your pie all day but waited till almost everyone was gone." He then looked at Anastasia. "Oh, my goodness, Miss Anastasia. Hello! Hello! It's so good to see you again."

"Oh, Sam, so good to see you, too," said Anastasia, as she gave him a hug as well. "Wouldn't miss it. How are you?"

"I be fine once I eat Missus Mary Ann's pie. Do you think Mister McSherry would want me to water or feed your horses? I didn't get a chance to ask when ya'll rode in."

"I'm sure that would be fine, Sam. Just go ahead. The stallion is Romeo, and my horse is Persnickety, but she isn't. She'll eat anything."

As Mary Ann and Ana walked into the house, Sam dashed off with a slice of pie in his mouth.

Once across the threshold, Mary Ann steered Ana to the gathering hall. "The food's in here. I'll show you the rest of the house after."

"Good, I'm famished," said Ana.

Bethany and Eve were removing the empty dishes and cleaning up the table, but there was food left, evidenced by Henry, who was hovering over the fruit and nut bowls with his dirty hands and face.

"Henry!" said Mary Ann when she saw her stepson digging into the raisins. "We don't know where those have been."

"But, Madam. Eve just put them here to eat," Henry begged, pulling his hands out of the raisins.

"I'm not talking about the raisins, Henry," said Mary Ann. "I'm talking about your hands. Now go wash them and your face before you eat any more, but come here first. Eve. Bethany, you too. I want to introduce you to an important guest."

"Anastasia, this is our cook and house manager, Bethany Dark; you met her husband, Sam." Anastasia bowed to Bethany who responded with a curtsy.

"Very glad ta meet ya Madam," said Bethany.

"And this is Adam's daughter Eve, and his son, Henry."

Eve curtsied and Henry waved, then added, "You probably don't want to eat any of the raisins, they're dirty," and he left the room and trotted upstairs.

Anastasia smiled and called after him, "Thank you Henry, I'll save some for you."

"Bethany, do you have any spring water left? Can you wash off the raisins and dry them?"

"Yes'm, I'll do that."

"Now, look here...," said Mary Ann as she guided Ana to the large table that was arrayed with dishes of the food treats Mary Ann and Bethany had prepared. Each dish was under a tent of sheer linen with hand embroidered designs of tiny colorful flowers at the top and edges. Mary Ann didn't like the tents because they obscured the appeal of her food, but it was still warm enough that the windows needed to be open to allow the late September breeze to pass through the room. Of course, with the breeze and the scent of sugary treats came barnyard flies. The sheer linen tents kept the flies off the food.

"I see we still have...let me recommend my lemon honeycomb and apple tansey. I see we've got one piece of each left. Oh, I'm so glad. Eve, would you serve Ana the last of each? I'll finish up the apple pie."

"Yes'm," said Eve as she carefully removed each tent and put the last serving of each dessert on a plate and handed it to Anastasia with a fork. "The lemon honeycomb is my favorite," said Eve. "Would you like some wine, cider brandy, or spring water with spearmint?"

"Oooo, thank you, Eve. The cider brandy sounds perfect," said Anastasia.

"Me, too," said Mary Ann.

Mary Ann made a plate of the last of the apple pie and some nuts, and the two ladies sat in chairs by the hearth and the unlit fireplace. There was a small side table between them, on which Eve sat two tankards of brandy.

From the corner of her eye, Mary Ann watched Anastasia as she took her first forkful of the lemon honeycomb, and glanced at the apple tansey. Mary Ann expected her guest to study the tasty dessert, pick at it a bit, say how delicious it was, how unique and delightful, and then ask how it was made. But Anastasia's eyes were not on her food, nor did she pick at it. In fact, before the fork got anywhere near her mouth, her eyes seemed to wander over the table of food. *She must be hungry,* Mary Ann thought, *to be longing for more food when the best is inches from her mouth.* Finally, Anastasia put down her fork back on the plate, took a sip of brandy, and spoke. "Mary Ann, this is exquisite."

Mary Ann was thrilled; finally a judgment of her good taste and talent.

Putting her plate down on the side table, Ana stood and walked over to the table.

Mary Ann came along side. "Did you want something else, Ana?"

"Oh, no. I have plenty. I was just caught by the intricate designs and delicate sheer of these food tents. Where did you ever get them?"

Mary Ann was flabbergasted. *Food tents?! What did they have to do with... my food?* "I have no idea." She glared at Eve.

"My mother made them," said Eve. "My mama and papa that is. He made the wire frame; mama wove the linen sheer and hand-embroidered the flower designs."

Mary Ann was baffled that Ana had ignored her food entirely and was now looking ever closer at the hand-embroidery on the food tents. Every food tent featured a different abstract detail of flower blossoms in pastel yellows, pinks, blues, violets, and greens. "She obviously was very talented and had exquisite taste. The embroidery is amazing, and that it was sown into this sheer without gathering the weft or warp threads is even more amazing. In my time working in textiles I've never seen anything so beautiful."

Eve was smiling broadly now. "My mama also wove the linen table covering. Did you see the corner embroidery, here?" Eve lifted a corner of the large, thick, near-white table covering to reveal what was easily lost in the corner-folds. Indeed, Mary Ann had not even noticed. Explained Eve: "On each corner is a different design." Eve walked around the table lifting each corner and spread it out in her hand for Anastasia, and now Mary Ann, to see. The first corner depicted a country church with a tall spire and a simple cross on top. "This is the church she grew up in. I don't know where it is." The next corner was a detailed image of a white bird with a light blue background, its wings spread and its head erect. "And this is the Holy Spirit." The next corner displayed an elaborate letter "A" stitched in light green, overlapping an upside down "U" that looked more like a horseshoe, in dark green. "This represents God the Father, Mama said, who has no beginning and no end. These are Greek letters, I think she said, alpha and omega, the first and last letters in Greek." The last corner was the letter "P" with a big "X" through the stem. "And this is more Greek. I think it's the letters Chi and Rho, which together means Jesus the Christ, and I guess the "X" is also supposed to remind us of Christ's crucifixion."

"That is exactly what it means, Eve," said Anastasia as she passed her hand over the weave of the linen. "The weave of this cloth is remarkable as well. And the stitching of the edge hem, with that colorful thread that matches the corner embroideries. How delightful this all is. You should be proud of your mother. She was very talented. I don't think the full-time weavers back at my uncle's factory could do as well."

Mary Ann was stunned. She hated anything to do with religion, especially

Christianity, and here was *her* food set upon a table covering with all this symbolic rubbish stitched into it getting all the attention and praise. Eve had set the table, Bethany had found the food tents, and she felt chagrined that she had not looked closely at either. She was already frustrated by her agreed tolerance before every supper allowing Eve to recite that demented prayer. She vowed to confront Adam about it, as well as Bethany's Bible stories she told the children almost every evening after supper. She had said nothing, however, understanding that she was the outsider coming into an established family, but she was going to lose her mind if this didn't stop. Here were neighbors to impress, and yet her efforts at doing that were failing. How could someone of Anastasia's stature like all this religious foolery?

"You've been a good student, Eve." Anastasia went on. "Your mother is no doubt smiling down from heaven on you. What a wonderful legacy she left you. And it fits this table perfectly."

"Mama made it for a table the same size as this one, that's why, on that loom right over there," said Eve, pointing to the corner where a lifeless pile of parts sat that Adam claimed was a loom—an udder eyesore to Mary Ann.

"Eve, I think your mama is wanting you to learn to weave and embroider just like her. And there sits the loom for you to learn on. You just have to put it together, I think. Are you going to do that?"

"Papa had promised to do that and teach me. Someday I will learn, I'm sure."

It was all Mary Ann could do to restraint her anger at the turn of events. Every muscle in her trim body was on edge and tight with tension. She wondered if Anastasia would notice her quiet dissent to all this. How could she get attention back to her food and more practical things? She smiled, hard as it was... and then, a fly buzzed her nose. A fly of all things. *Where in hell did that come from?* But wait. Could a pesky house fly be her ally? "Oh, my! Look at this," she suddenly blurted out as she stepped toward Ana's dish of food on the side table. Mary Ann flapped her hands over the dish of food. "Go away flies. You're eating Ana's food. Oh, there are so many."

"Oh, nothing to worry over, my dear," said Ana. "They won't eat much."

"But I made this for you, not these flies." Then she instinctively added what she would later regret. "For all we know they've come straight from the pasture, and we all know what's there."

"Oh, Mary Ann," exclaimed Anastasia "I never thought of that. How absolutely disgusting. I'm so sorry, but you are right, I shan't have another bite."

If Mary Ann had been a cow's udder she would have burst. A whirlwind's destruction of her house and barn together could not have stunned her worse than Anastasia's promise not to eat a bite of what Mary Ann wanted her to inhale. After a few moments of shock, Mary Ann reminded herself to breathe; she had put herself and her dessert plate on a high pedestal only to have Anastasia nonchalantly push it off. Mary Ann was left speechless, sanctioned, and shattered.

Anastasia McSherry never took a single bite of Mary Ann's lemon honey-comb or apple tansey. The day was a nauseating disaster, especially since only Mary Ann knew that there were no flies whatsoever anywhere near Ana's dish. Mary Ann couldn't blame anyone but herself...but she did.

She blamed Esther and everything associated with her. Mary Ann never imagined that she would be competing with a corpse buried a hundred miles away, but that was what she was doing. The linens and the embroidery were there in her place and there wasn't room in the house for both Mary Ann and Esther.

Envy is a dreadful and deadly force, and it possessed Mary Ann from that moment on. Her heart quivered with rage and her blood ran cold. In the presence of others she willed stiff rods of iron to replace muscle, tendon, and bone; but when left by herself, her arms and legs trembled and quaked.

Mary Ann and Adam saw the McSherrys off. As soon as they cantered off the property, Adam turned to Mary Ann, "My dear, you're upset. What's wrong?"

Evidently, the iron rods concealed little...she deflected. "I'm not sure. I think I expected too much of myself. Been tense all day, hoping it would go well, and now that it's over, I'm still tense."

Adam put his arms around her and gave her a manly hug. "Mary Ann, you're shaking. You sure you're all right?"

She tried to look Adam in the eye, but she was afraid he'd see Esther looking back at him, so she just looked away. "Would it be too much to ask to saddle Apple with an astride saddle and us trot back to Turkey Creek and unwind?"

Adam smiled big. It was unusual for a woman to ask to ride astride, but he knew it was safer and would allow her to go beyond a trot, even to gallop. "You sure you'll be safe?"

"I've ridden that way a lot before you came along," she said finally looking up at him.

"I'll do it right away," he said. "You want to change into your riding clothes and boots? I'll bring Apple to the house."

Still stiff and shaking a bit, she fell into another of his hugs.

He took her face in his hands and kissed her. "My dear, it's warm out and you're freezing cold!" Adam rubbed her arms with his big hands.

His hands felt good. Somehow, she had to keep this man and live with herself. "Riding will get the blood flowing again," she said. "I'll be all right, promise." He nodded, released her, and walked briskly to the barn. She watched him go, determined to keep him close. She climbed the stoop and entered the house. It was a good mile-and-a-half back to Turkey Creek. If she circled the fields on the wagon and creek paths, it would be several miles and she'd never have to leave the farm. If someone saw her riding astride it might start a scandal. Yet, at this point, she didn't care. She had to rethink and reckon with her new life. Or perhaps she just had to remember Adam's words weeks ago: "Just take charge," he had said. "I'll back you up. Don't worry. They had a good mother before, I'm sure you can be a good mother now, if not better. They learned some things from Esther, now they'll learn more things from you. They'll be better for it."

That night after everyone had turned in for the night, she cuddled up to her man in bed and told him a version of what had happened with Anastasia and Eve. It had been a month since she had come to Flax Haven. Wasn't it time for her to be the stepmom, and not a disregarded guest?

Yes, he agreed. It was time.

4

Bethany had a bad feeling about Mister Livingston getting married without his children's approval of the woman. One day he announced he was getting married, and a few days later Missus Mary Ann Livingston showed up with a wagon full of possessions. Just like that Bethany had a new boss and the children a stepmother. Bethany knew her place, however. She did her job and didn't meddle.

Missus Mary Ann was a short, compact woman with alert, fierce eyes. She always wore a linen dress with buttons up the front, and a high collar. She never wore one of those sheer, silky kerchiefs that covered the neckline so indelicately like so many women whose bosoms were ready to spill over the top of their stomachers. Although quiet and soft-spoken, she was autocratic, independent, and demanding. Mister Livingston was just the opposite, aggressive on the outside, but he could be easily persuaded with just a word.

She suspected there was a reason Mister Livingston didn't bring Mary Ann around to get acquainted with the children before they married. When Esther died Mister Livingston gave up his faith. He blamed God for not healing Esther, and he drew battle lines. He had exchanged what little faith he had for revenge. Bethany wasn't exactly sure how a human being takes revenge on God, at least not successfully. It was a foolish way to go about your life, but that's what Mister Livingston did. His sweet, smart, and insistent daughter, on the other hand, had not lost her faith. Rather, Eve sought to understand God's purpose in her mother's death. Eve, however, was a child, and her father did not consider her faith of consequence.

As a consequence, Mister Livingston searched out and married a woman sympathetic to his revenge plot. Now Missus Mary Ann didn't blame God for her husband's death, but she did blame the authorities who were over Alvin when he died. That was about the same thing as Mister Livingston's anger at God. Like him, Missus Mary Ann wanted revenge on those that could have prevented Alvin's death. So, here was a man and woman who were both angry at an authority for the death of their spouses over which they had no control. They both wanted revenge, and they got married to wage a war; it was as simple as that. As far as Bethany could tell, it was a marriage made in hell.

From the time Missus Mary Ann took up residence at the farm, Eve brought her problems and questions to Bethany, whose faith was strong like Esther's, and perhaps stronger because of her life as a slave. This put Bethany in a strange way, for she was not the child's mother, nor did she have any authority. So Bethany and Sam worried for the children and prayed with them.

Since Eve was teaching Bethany how to read and since they both liked to use the Bible for practice, they would often do it on Bethany's porch or in her cabin. The Bible they used had been Esther's and it was the only Bible on the farm, so when Eve realized her stepmother's antagonism toward the faith, the Bible found a permanent home in Bethany's cabin. There was no use aggravating Missus Mary Ann more than she was already aggravated.

The day following the open house, which Bethany thought went well, things began to change, but not for the better. Normally, at the noon meal, Bethany and Sam would both eat with the Livingstons. Ever since she and Sam had arrived at Flax Haven, either she, Eve, or Sam would say a prayer before sitting down to eat. It was clear that Missus Mary Ann didn't like the prayers, especially the prayer Eve often recited of her mother's, but this day was different. It started as always with everyone standing behind their place at table. Mister Livingston would often nod to Eve, giving her permission to pray. On this day, however, he shook his head, and he and Mary Ann immediately sat down and began to serve themselves. Awkwardly, Eve, Henry, Bethany, and Sam remained standing behind their chairs.

"Papa, we must pray first," said Eve staring at her father with a bit of irritation, though she sensed this moment was coming from the looks of displeasure her stepmother had leveled at her over the past month.

"Eve," said Mary Ann, making eye contact, "there's no reason to pray."

"Of course, there is," Eve shot back. "We didn't make the potatoes, beans, and meat. God did, and we need to say our thanks."

Mary Ann smiled at her stepdaughter, but replied firmly: "Eve, your father, Bethany, and you, with a little help from Henry when he hoes, grew this food and brought it into the house. God didn't do that. We all did. God didn't peel the potatoes or cut up the beans or wash them, butter, salt, and cook them. Bethany and I did, with the fire and the wood that Sam cut and split. God didn't do any of that work."

Eve was angry now, and she didn't hold back. "But none of us made the seeds for all this, none of us made the soil in which it grew. None of us brought the sun or rain. None of us grew the trees from whence the wood came. And none of us invented the fire. God did all of that."

"Child, God does not exist. It's only in your imagination. I've never seen God. Have you? Now sit down and eat."

"I will not, until I thank God for it."

"Fine," said Mary Ann. "Thank your imaginary friend, quietly, to yourself, if you must, and then tell him to go away and leave the rest of us in peace."

Mary Ann seemed to have the last word, as Bethany and Sam looked on and Adam continued to pile food onto his plate. When his plate was full, he turned to Eve. "Eve, I tell you. Be kind and respectful to your stepmother. She is your mother now, and what she says goes in this house. Is that clear?"

At this, Eve started to shake with fear and sadness, as if God was about to strike the table with lightning and destroy them all. She began to sob, and through her tears spoke softly to her father: "Papa, can't I at least pray out loud for myself...and for Henry, and Sam, and Bethany, and for you, too...and...Missus Mary Ann before I sit and eat?"

Her father, disgruntled, put a forkful of potatoes in his mouth and chewed.

Frustrated, Eve closed her eyes, bowed her head, and blurted out, "Mama, please, look down on us and pray for us. Please!"

Adam swallowed and gazed at his daughter still standing behind her chair; she was bent over with grief and crying. Tears dropped onto her plate. He said: "Well, if you must, but...."

"Husband, you gave me your word you would back me up," seethed Mary Ann.

Adam had become the iron striker, and this woman the flint. He put down his fork, and spoke firmly but softly: "Daughter, your mama, bless her heart, is no longer with us. I doubt if she is truly looking down on us. Be kind to your stepmother...will you? Respect her as the Bible, which you claim to believe, tells you to honor. Pray to yourself if you must, but...we don't want to hear it." He frowned at Mary Ann with a mixture of grief and irritation.

Mary Ann smiled back at him, momentarily dipping her head to him in thanksgiving.

Bethany glanced at Sam who stared back at her, his mouth firmly shut. Finally, he bowed his head and seemed to pray silently, in resignation.

Adam continued: "Keep yer faith to yourself if you think it will do you any good, but we'll not be praying before meals out loud, just as we've not been goin' to church. Now, Daughter, be obedient. Sit down..." and he looked around the table at Henry, Sam, and Bethany who were still standing..."all of you, and eat the good food..." he paused to looked at Mary Ann, "...your mama with Bethany's help have prepared...out of love for you."

There was a long pause. Henry sat down. "Pa, can I have some meat and potatoes?"

"Yes, Son, as much as you want." Henry was sitting next to his father, so with his long arms Mister Livingston reached across the table and stabbed some meat, put it on Henry's plate, and then spooned some potatoes and then gravy on his plate as well.

As soon as Henry, who had been somewhat oblivious to the discussion all along, began to eat in earnest, Sam and Bethany sat down. Eve, still standing with head bowed, watched the others. Bethany caught Eve's eye and threw her a smile. Bethany then bowed her head with Sam. After a moment they raised their heads and served themselves portions of food and began to eat.

Eve closed her eyes, and in silence thought through the words of her mother's prayer, added a prayerful thought for everyone else, then sat down, served herself dinner, and ate...in silence.

Bethany felt a deep sadness. It was as if a spiritual slavery had enveloped the table with irons...not leg irons, but irons that pierced and chained the heart. Although the food was warm, her body chilled as she ate. Under the table, Sam's big hand reached over and gripped his wife's thigh and squeezed it long and hard as if to say, *We're together. We're not enslaved. God will protect us.*

The rest of the meal was one of the quieter ones in Livingston history, although Mister Livingston tried to make light-hearted comments about the coming harvest and how he expected the weather to cooperate and the year would be a good one at market. Sam would occasionally pipe up and say, "Yes, sir, it will be good, you'll see," or something like that, but otherwise, no one said anything, until they were done.

Before she took the last bite from her plate, Bethany asked: "Eve, help me clean up?"

Eve smiled at Bethany, "Yes'm."

"Before you all go," said Mister Livingston, "I have something more to say."

Bethany noticed that in saying this, he looked sideways at Missus Mary Ann. Bethany had a sense of what was coming. She tried to remain still, though she took a deep, slow breath to calm her nerves. As she did so, Mister Livingston did somewhat the same, except his breaths were fast and shallow. Her years of slavery told her that what was coming next was not good.

"Bethany," Mister Livingston began, "you have been faithful in teaching my children, entertaining them, and even preparing them for bed, as I have worked late into the evening so often to provide for this house and with Sam to farm this land. I have left that up to your discretion, I guess as their nanny. You've done a good job." He paused before continuing, glancing at Mary Ann for permission to continue. "Mary Ann and I ask that you to continue to do that."

Bethany suddenly let out her breath, which she unconsciously had been holding. He was not going to say what she feared, that going forward she was to have no contact with the children. This was a great relief. She never had children, and she loved being a surrogate mother to Eve and Henry, even when Henry was being a brat. In her eyes, he was a good brat, and she suspected that he knew she loved him, but there had to be more. She reined herself in.

Mister Livingston continued. "But now, after these last few weeks of transition, Eve and Henry have a new mother, one that loves them and has good designs for their future. Before she accepted to be my wife, she accepted and, in fact, looked forward to her other role as a teacher of our children. She acknowledges that your rich background can teach them a lot, too, about tolerance and getting along in very rough times. Both you and Sam provide gravity to our family by having been enslaved for most of your lives. You are strong, good people. We think you are good examples to Eve and Henry, and to me. Mary Ann appreciates you and looks forward to working with you and the children, but there needs to be a change in one small way. Please honor my wife with this request."

Here it comes, thought Bethany. She looked at Sam, who raised his eyebrows and shrugged his muscular shoulders, as if to say, "I have no idea what's coming."

"No more Bible stories," said Mister Livingston. "We'd like you to continue to tell them stories before bed if you like. You and Sam are good storytellers, but please, it is their new mother's wish that you avoid the Bible stories. And I agree. They're not needed. It gives them wrong-headed ideas." He paused and looked between Bethany and Sam. "Will you agree to that?"

"Papa, that's unfair," Eve said with bitterness. "Henry and I like those stories, especially the ones of battles and giants that Sam tells."

"Aw, c'mon," groaned Henry. "Some of those stories are getting boring. They haven't changed for years. I always know what's going to happen."

"There, you see?" said a smiling Mary Ann. "There is much more to learn about history and this country than what you can find in any archaic Bible. Bethany, I think you might tell the children stories of your days as a slave. I'm sure you won't glamorize them, but tell the truth, to awaken their hearts to how slavery is so wrong. You can form their moral life with such stories that are... well, true."

Bethany was sad for a host of reasons, not the least was the curse such a prohibition would bring upon the family. His request, though, was not nearly as severe as she feared. Mister Livingston had not said: "Don't pray with the children." He had not said: "Don't give them spiritual counsel." He had not even told her, "Don't read the Bible to them." Of course, reading the Bible was something Eve did a lot better than she did. Was she to interpret, "Don't *tell* them Bible stories" as "Don't *read* them Bible stories"? She decided the two were different...and she was *not* going to ask for a clarification.

"Missta' Livingston, Missus Mary Ann," began Bethany, "I'm sorry you're asking me not to tell 'em those good Bible stories. They'd teach your chil'en to be a man and a woman of strong moral character, but I will comply wit' your request. I liked Missus Mary Ann's idea 'bout telling 'em stories of when Sam and me was slaves. There are other stories that I can tell, too. They do same thing and help establish themselves to be good people." At that point Bethany said no more, and she threw a smile at the other end of the table to Mister Livingston and Missus Mary Ann who were both looking at her and listening intently. She forced the smile with her lips pressed tightly together—because, about the Bible stories she was lying through her teeth.

After dinner Mister Livingston and Missus Mary Ann retired to the parlor while Eve and Henry helped Bethany clear the table and Sam excused himself to get back to work outside. Once in the cooking kitchen where Bethany had a tub of water for washing the dishes and hot water over the fireplace for rinsing them, she quietly told both Eve and Henry, "Chil'en, the good book tell us all to honor our parents so your days will be long on dis here earth. Eve, you read that to me just last week from Exodus."

"Yes'm, I remember that. You can read that now, can't you?"

"Yes'm, I can, thanks to you 'n' Henry. Now you look forward to some good stories I got ta tell you. They be almost Bible stories. Well, they be Bible stories, but they won't sound like it. You both know that Mister Sam and I be prayin' for you both. You come to us any time you want. God put us here for you. That for sure. We love both of you's. Ya'll right with that?"

"And I'm going to keep saying my mama's prayer before I eat," said Eve. "I just won't say it out loud. God will still hear me, I'm sure. Henry, how 'bout you? You gonna still pray?"

"Yeah, I guess so, but can I make up my own?"

"Of course," both Bethany and Eve said in unison.

"Do I have to tell you what I prayed?"

"No," they both replied in unison, again.

"Okay, now that's settled, we done?" Henry asked with a grin. "I wanna take the pail of somethings I caught this mornin' to Missus Mary Ann and see what she'll do with 'em."

Bethany pulled up short. "What you got in your pail now, boy?"

Henry turned to Bethany and displayed a sinister smile. "Toads."

5

My Despised Cyn:

 The subtlety of your scheme to enrage Babbitt over the Christian embroidery is genius. It looks innocent and innocuous, but the ramifications can be extraordinary, especially with Babbitt's innovative and twisted mind. The sequel should be entertaining.

 Otherwise, you're making progress...no more prayers at dinner, and no more Bible stories. This is a woman after our own heart. Are there more where she came from? We could use them.

Eternally yours,
Master of Unbelief

Chapter 25
Lick the Bowl Dry

1

Several days after Adam proclaimed the cessation of prayer before meals and Bible stories after supper, Eve and Henry were at the Darks' cabin for their thrice weekly reading lesson. This gave Mary Ann time to hunt through the house for the linen table covering Eve had produced for the open house, which had infuriated Mary Ann by destroying her plans to impress Anastasia McSherry. It wasn't just that Ana had not sampled Mary Ann's food, it was the religious trappings that had distracted Ana from the food. She would have none of it inside her house, especially since Adam had finally established her as *Mistress of the Mansion*, so to speak.

There were just so many places one could store linens. She first looked in the three drawers of the hutch in the gathering hall. The first drawer she pulled open was at the bottom. Sure enough, here was a collection of linens, both table size and small napkins. They were all tightly woven, neatly folded, and each was a slightly different shade and color of the natural flax that distinguished a particular harvest from which they were woven. Some were dark grey with a tinge of yellow, others were a light tan, and one was nearly white. Also unique to each was the color and thickness of the hand stitching that finished the edges; all were strong cloth that would last a lifetime. She took each one out and examined it. Not finding embroidery on the first table size cloth, she laid in on the floor next to her.

After examining the third table covering, and not finding any corner embroidery, she went to lay it onto of the pile already started, but Cleopatra was laying on the pile with her head and eyes tracking Mary Ann's every move. When Mary Ann went to put the linen on the pile and shove Cleo off the pile, the cat resisted and lifted a front paw to push back on the linen, as if to say, *"Put the cloth back where you found it. It doesn't belong on the floor."* So Mary Ann simply started another pile next to the first. With each successive linen removed, Cleo's eyes and head followed Mary Ann's every move. This was odd. Cleo was affectionate to the children but usually paid her no attention. The cat would often sit on Eve's lap when Bethany told one of her Bible stories. She remembered one where the kids pretended Cleo was the main character in the story because the character had a coat of many colors, and Cleo's hair was white, black, and orange. But Cleo had never shown any affection for Mary Ann. Why suddenly this attention? Not finding the embroidered covering, Mary Ann put all the linens back in the drawer. Cleo didn't object. Mary Ann opened the next two drawers above. There were no linens in these drawers. Meanwhile, Cleo never left her place on the floor and judicially kept Mary Ann within sight.

When Mary Ann walked to the other side of the room to search in the chest of drawers, Cleo followed. Except this time the cat jumped on top of the chest, sat upright, and looked down on Mary Ann like a sphinx. Mary Ann removed linens she found here and again piled them on the floor. Of various colors and thicknesses, these were unfinished cloths as if they had just come off the loom. *This must be their cache of experimental weaves. Still too valuable to burn. Nothing here.* She put all the cloths back in the drawers and shut them. Cleo didn't budge.

Ignoring the cat, Mary Ann looked in the parlor where there was a hutch. Cleo followed and stood apart. Evidently, the cat somehow knew there were no linens in the parlor's hutch.

Next. Mary Ann went upstairs. Cleo followed, bounding up the stairs ahead. Mary Ann was familiar with what was in her own bedroom, so it was time to look in Eve's. At the foot of Eve's bed was a bedding box. She lifted the waterfall top. Sure enough, there on top was the large table covering with those cursed Christian symbols on the corners.

Instantly, Cleo jumped into the box and laid on top of the covering. Mary Ann went to remove the covering, but Cleo rebuffed her by turning on her back, raising all four paws, extending her claws and aggressively hissing and batting at Mary Ann.

"Protecting your mistress' linens, are you?" Mary Ann said to the cat. "Well, she's dead, and I'm not. And if you're not careful, you can join her." She grabbed the edge of the linen and pulled it out from under Cleo then tried to close the lid on the cat, crushing her, but Cleo scampered out before the lid slammed shut.

Mary Ann opened Eve's armoire. From a shelf she removed a light green dress she had recently seen Eve wear. Cleo was now stalking Mary Ann at close quarters. She kicked Cleo away with her foot, but the cat just jumped back and hissed all the more, though now at a distance.

Mary Ann wished she had the time and place here in the house to execute her plan. But she didn't. Someone else would have to do it for her. She carried the table linen and the dress to her bedroom and spread the table cover out on her bed. Instantly, Cleo jumped on top of the linen with all fours, arched her back and growled at Mary Ann with her long, sharp teeth. That was it for Mary Ann.

She left the cat and the linen covering on her bed, marched out of her bedroom to the small closet at the back of the upstairs hall, and removed a long handle broom. Returning to the bedroom she swatted Cleo off the bed. Cleo landed on all fours but turned to face Mary Ann again and screeched with her back arched high. Angry, Mary Ann went after the rebellious cat with the broom, swatting at the feline, chasing it out of the bedroom, into the hall, down the stairs, and all the way to the front door. Opening the door, Mary Ann didn't relent until the cat was on the porch, and then it was but a single, mighty swat that connected and sent Cleo flying off the porch, down the stoop, and into the dirt. Having clearly gotten the message, Cleopatra ran for the woods. *Good riddance. I wish ridding the house of Esther was as easy.*

Back in her bedroom, Mary Ann studied Esther's table covering spread out on her bed one last time. From her sewing chest, she retrieved a favorite pair of scissors brought from Winchester, ruthlessly hacked off the embroidered corners, and set them aside. Folding the remaining yards of cloth, she wrapped them in the light green dress, and the combination in a couple yards of burlap saved for the occasion. She then tied the bundle with string to create a tight but plain package. Taking the package and the clipped corners downstairs, she first went to the cooking kitchen where the only fire in the house was sure to be burning.

Laying on the hearth, curled up in a ball, was their black short-haired cat, Bombay. Mary Ann crouched next to Bombay and stroked the cat's back as she placed each of Esther's fancy embroidery corners on the fire. With a poker she ensured the corners were quickly consumed, disappearing up the chimney in a column of smoke. "Well, Bombay, it's up to you now. Your competitor has been banished. All the mice are yours. Maybe you can do something for me in return?" Bombay sat up and rubbed against Mary Ann's thigh, purring loudly. "How about something that is entirely mine, not Esther's. Can you arrange that?" The cat purred louder. "Yes, you're tired of the competition, too. I can tell."

As soon as the ash left by the linen corners was indistinguishable from the rest, Mary Ann took the burlap package containing what was left of the linen cover and Eve's dress to the barn where she knew Adam was working. She held the package out to him.

"Here's what we talked about," said Mary Ann.

"You sure about this?" Adam said.

She glared at him, "You promised."

Adam still hesitated...but finally took the package with a grimace. "I'll see it to town this afternoon."

2

The next day, Eve was using a hand pitchfork to loosen the dirt around a row of carrots to pull them from the ground. Toward the end of the row, Cleopatra wandered up to her, and purring, rubbed against her hands with an occasional meow.

"Cleo, where have you been? Have the mice in the cellar not been enough for your ravenous appetite?" Eve stroked Cleo's back, found a few burrs, and pulled them out; nothing unusual there. Both cats now and then got tired of the house and had to hunt elsewhere, if not for food, then for adventure. She had seen both Bombay and Cleo bring a mouse up from the cellar and play with it before the mouse keeled over dead, either from being beaten by those menacing paws, or a bite to the back of the neck and the subsequent violent shaking. One thing no one could stand, however, was the mess the cats left behind of rodent fur, blood, and bone after tearing apart and devouring their meal. So, whenever possible, whoever saw said cat playing with said mouse was required to put both cat and mouse outside for the finale. But today, Cleopatra was mouseless, so Eve invited her back into the house.

"I'm done here, Cleo, want to come in with me?" Eve put the small pitchfork aside, picked up her basket of carrots, walked to the front of the house, and climbed the first few steps of the stoop. Cleo followed her as far as the steps, but then held back, sat on her haunches, and stared at the top of the steps. Eve stopped halfway up the steps and followed Cleo's gaze to the top. There, Bombay was on the edge of the porch hunched over, his legs cocked under him, staring down at Cleo as if stalking prey. "Come on, Cleo," said Eve. "Bombay won't hurt you. He just wants to play." Cleo looked up at Eve, and taking the hint padded carefully across the front of the stoop to get behind her. Yet all along Cleo kept her gaze fixed on Bombay. At the same time Bombay shifted his focus to stalk Cleo as she moved behind Eve. "It's okay, Cleo, come on." Cleopatra gazed plaintively up at Eve, let out a weak meow, then extended a front paw to rest it on the step behind Eve.

Suddenly, Bombay snarled like an enraged mountain lion and catapulted its taut, black body at Cleopatra, flying across all five steps in a vicious leap, his front legs and sharp claws extended for the kill.

Cleopatra didn't hesitate. She turned in a flash and ran as fast as she could into the woods. Bombay landed with a thud on the ground exactly where Cleo had crouched, his back arched high, his hair on edge, his mouth hissing, his sharp teeth flashing.

"BOMBAY!" screamed Eve. "NO!" It was obvious that Bombay didn't want to play. He wanted to kill or at least keep sweet Cleopatra out of the house. Eve was stunned by the attack. She didn't know what to think. Cleopatra had disappeared and Bombay was standing guard, as if never to let the calico across the threshold of the house again.

After washing off the carrots in the cooking kitchen and laying them out to dry, Eve sought out her father who was in the pasture checking Apple's hoofs.

"Papa, I don't know what's got into Bombay, but she just attacked Cleopatra and chased her away from the house. I don't think Cleo's been in the house for days. Do you know why?"

Her father put down Apple's front hoof, patted the mare's neck and looked at Eve. "I have no idea, daughter. Where did Cleopatra go off to?"

"She ran into the woods. She was scared."

He looked toward the woods. "Ask Bethany, maybe she knows something. I'll keep a lookout for her. Have you ever seen them get into a scrap before?"

"No, never. They play-fight sometimes, but it's nothing like they're mad. Just now, I thought Bombay was going to kill Cleo. I was scared."

Papa just shook his head. "I'm sorry, Eve. I don't know. Let's keep our eyes open. I'll ask Mary Ann, too."

Two weeks passed since Cleopatra's disappearance and no one knew why. To Eve Cleo represented her mother for, in fact, Cleo was her mother's cat. When her mother was alive the two were always together. Cleo would spend hours at Mother's feet, or in her lap, and always slept atop a comforter at the foot of Mother's bed.

That afternoon while teaching Bethany a reading lesson on her porch, Eve took note of Sam returning from town with a load of supplies. Among the items he brought was a package wrapped neatly in linen with a bright red ribbon tied around it in a bow and he took it to her papa in the barn. She also noticed that her Papa was reluctant to take the package from Sam but finally did with a slight nod. She wondered, *what was in that package underneath that pretty red bow?*

3

An hour later Mary Ann was in her bedroom changing the bedsheets and spreading up the comforter when Adam came into the room with the linen wrapped package with the red bow. "I think this is the dress you ordered."

"Oh, thank you. I hope she likes it."

"We'll see," said a doubtful Adam. He was anxious to leave and did.

Mary Ann finished smoothing the bed covers, then quietly shut her bedroom door before she opened the package. Inside was the original light-green dress she had selected for a pattern, and the new dress made from the table covering. She held up the new dress. It was just what she had ordered. Made from the sturdy table covering, it was a fancy dress with waist gathering around which was a broad, bright red ribbon belt which provided the perfect accent to the distinctive brown-grey linen. There was a delicate white lace border at the bottom of the skirt and around the bottom of the sleeves. Around the neckline was a broad white lace collar. It was a stunning achievement. Eleanor Radcliff was very good. Making sure Eve was out of the house, Mary Ann took the already neatly folded light-green dress and put it back on a shelf in Eve's armoire. She then repackaged the new dress inside the linen packaging, which, Mary Ann now realized, was made from the leftover material of the dress. She then tied the red ribbon as it was before, to present to Eve.

4

After supper Eve was in her bedroom folding washed and dried clothes.

Mary Ann came into her room. "Daughter, I have a present for you. Would you like to open it? Eve was a bit surprised since her stepmother had barely made any kind of overture to her since her arrival. Eve took the package, forced a smile, and said, "Thank you, what is it?"

"It's something I bought for you. Think of it as a motherly gift, a harvest-time gift."

Eve relaxed a bit, sat down on the blanket box at the foot of her bed, and opened the package. She was very surprised. It was a new dress, from fine linen, with lace, white buttons down the front, and a red ribbon belt. Her real mother, Esther, had always made her dresses by hand. Eve had never owned a store-bought dress before, especially one as beautiful as this. She was overcome with emotion. It looked exactly the right size. *How did she find the right size without the need for alterations?* She started to weep tears of joy at the generous and wonderful gift.

"Why don't you change into it and come down to show us all how pretty it is on you?"

"Oh, thank you...Mother. I will." Getting the "mother" out was a bit tricky, but such a gift demanded such a concession, she thought.

Ten minutes later, Eve anxiously came downstairs. There was a looking glass in her father's office and that's the first place she went. The office was empty. The looking glass was inside the door of an armoire. She opened the door and looked at her reflection. She was amazed at how well the dress fit and how nice it looked on her. It was dressy, and not something she could wear every day, but rather to someplace special...like church. But on that thought she turned sad. They didn't go to church anymore. Maybe someday they would, but by then she would have outgrown this dress. Why then did Mary Ann buy this dress for her? It was a mystery. Well, she had to show the others.

She stood erect, trying to look proper like a lady should and walked into the gathering hall where everyone was sitting around the large table eating one of Mary Ann's desserts.

Henry was the first to see her: "Wow, look at you, will you? Where you goin' all dressed up?"

Everyone else turned to see what Henry was startled at. They all fell silent for a moment. Suddenly, there was a flurry of compliments about how beautiful Eve looked and how well the dress fit, and everything else one might imagine. Her papa had her turn around several times, and said she looked like a much older woman, not a little girl anymore. She didn't think of herself as a little girl, but she smiled at Papa nonetheless and curtsied to his comment.

In her innocence, Eve came to Mary Ann, gave her a hug and a kiss on her cheek. "Mother..." There's that word once more, "...thank you, again. I'm wondering, just where would I wear such a nice dress like this? Why, in a year, I will grow out of it. Perhaps I could wear it to church Sundays? Maybe Sam and Bethany could take me?" She looked over at Sam. She had not planned on asking that question, but after she had, she realized that neither Sam nor Bethany went to church. She was chagrined for saying something that didn't make a whole lot of sense.

"I'm sorry, Sam, I forgot you didn't have a church to go to."

Sam spoke quietly and with a touch of sorrow. "Dat's right, Miss Eve. No place we's knows 'round here would let us freed slaves in der church. We'd gladly go, but we's hear dat folk like us aren't entirely welcome. There are some free church we's do heard of, but they're nos whah nearby. If'n there was we'd be glad to take ya."

Eve then turned to Papa and her stepmother. "I'm sorry, Papa and Mother, I was not asking to go to church, although that would be nice. I was just asking where I could wear this nice dress." She tried her best to be genuine and earnest and not difficult. "It's just that it's too nice to wear around the farm for my chores, or even to cook in. Why a spark from the fire could singe this beautiful lace. And I'm too young for gentlemen to be calling."

Mary Ann's face twisted in confusion, and Eve saw that. She turned to her father, "Papa? Do you know?"

Adam turned his gaze on her stepmother and looked at her as if to say, "*Woman what were you thinking? Have I just spent good money on something that can't be used?*" No one said anything for a long time, and Eve stood quietly and respectfully, her head slightly bowed, her hands clasped in front of her below her waist, waiting for an answer.

"I suppose," her stepmother finally said, "we might have another open house." Her face said she was joking, and everyone chuckled. "That dress on you would have been the perfect complement as the reception's hostess."

Eve imagined herself wearing this dress, welcoming guests as they arrived, and ushering them into the gathering hall and to the table of food. She giggled and then the thought hit her. She said, "You're right, this dress would have been perfect. Why it almost perfectly matches the table covering that we used and that Miss Anastasia liked so much. Imagine me standing next to the table of your good food pointing out the lemon honeycomb, apple tansey, and your delicious apple cinnamon pie. All I'd need is some of my mother's flowery embroidery to perfectly match." Delighted with the idea, Eve twirled to give everyone a picture of what that might have looked like.

At that moment Bethany came over to look closely at the dress and finger the material. When she did her mouth hung open, her eyes narrowed, and her countenance fell. Suddenly discomforted, she turned away, walked to the table, picked up a few empty dishes and carried them into the cooking kitchen. Eve thought Bethany's behavior very odd. Then she looked to Mary Ann, again half-expecting a more reasonable answer to her question. It was at that moment that Mary Ann's face turned discontented, and she too turned away and started to clear the table of food.

Her father then spoke up, and he too had lost his glee at seeing her all dressed up. He acted as if there was something wrong with the dress and that no one wanted to ever see it on her again: "Eve, why don't you take off the dress, fold it neatly, and place it your armoire for the appropriate time to wear it. We'll think of a time. Please go now and change into something more suitable to help clean up."

The sudden change of climate perplexed Eve, but she didn't know what else to do but follow Papa's advice.

In her room she opened her armoire and from a shelf took down the light-green dress that was easily washed when it got dirty. It was folded, but in an odd way, not like she folded her other clothes. She laid it on her bed and proceeded to take off the new dress, fold it, and put it on a high shelf in her armoire where it wouldn't get squished by the removal or placement of other clothes. Returning to her bed, she picked up the light-green dress and shook out the folds before putting it on over her chemise. Surprisingly, six pieces of brown-grey linen fell from the folds of the green dress to the floor. Puzzled, she put the dress aside and picked up the linen pieces and laid them out on her bed. There were six altogether, one-to-two-feet in length. It appeared that each had been cut by shears into very strange shapes. What were these? Why were they folded up in her dress? Then she saw the straight, hemmed edge on one of the pieces. Her heart jumped and she sucked in her breath. The hand stitching of the colorful thread was immediately recognizable. It was the finished edge of her mother's table covering that Eve had used for the open house. The colorful edge stitching purposely matched the corner embroidery she had shown to Mrs. McSherry. She ran to the armoire and yanked down the new dress and threw it on her bed next to the pieces of linen. They matched, the same tight weave of brown-grey linen. She went to her bedding box and opened it. The table covering was not on top where she had last put it. She dug through the box like a mad child, pulling out everything that was in it, scattering it across the floor and her bed. The covering was not there.

Suddenly there was no air in the room; she couldn't breathe. Her heart stopped and her arms clutched frantically at her chest. Her hands went cold and her fingers began to tremble. Had her mother's sacred relic been cannibalized and profaned to make the dress? Where were the corner embroideries, the very embodiment of her mother's skill and faith? Eve went back to the pieces of linen on her bed. Sure enough, there was what remained of a corner of the table covering, its colorful hem stitching coming from two directions at right angles toward a corner, except the corner had been crudely chopped from the cloth, the exquisite embroidery expunged. No doubt that is what had been done to all four corners before the remaining linen had been sent to a seamstress to make the dress. Her old green work dress was used as the pattern.

Eve now recalled her stepmother's distressed expression as Miss Anastasia waxed with eloquent praise about the Christian symbols. The dress was no gift for a special occasion. It was an explicit expression of enmity and envy. It was an attack on her mother...and she, Eve, was being asked to wear the dress as a symbol of her stepmother's revenge against her real mother that loved her still.

Eve SCREAMED at the top of her lungs. For an eleven-year-old she surprised herself. She SCREAMED again, and again. She slammed the bedding box cover so hard the top was torn off its leather hinges. Then she grabbed the new dress and with all her might tore off the red belt, and then the lace, grabbed the edges, and with all her might ripped the new dress to shreds. She didn't have to look in a looking glass to know that her face was red, that blood covered her hands from tearing at the strong linen, and that tears poured down her face.

One last SCREAM...at which her father, Mary Ann, Henry, Sam, and Bethany all poured into her room and stood in shock at what she had done to her room, herself, and her new dress—a dress that would never, ever be worn again.

She grabbed a remnant of the dress in her fist and flew at her stepmother in a rage shrieking in her face: **YOU ARE NOT MY MOTHER AND YOU WILL NEVER BE. YOU. ARE. EVIL!** Overcome with anger and grief, Eve collapsed on the floor in great sobs of despair and hatred. "Mama, pray for us! Mama, pray for me! Mama, pray! Please pray!"

Adam was stunned at his traumatized daughter. He tried to grab her and hold her lovingly, but she hit him so hard he backed away. Her father ushered Mary Ann out of the room as Sam and Henry stood clear of the door in fright. Finally, Bethany came to her, sat on the floor next to her, held her, prayed for her, and over the next hour let Eve cry herself to sleep.

5

Over the last year of building up Flax Haven, Adam had made repeated trips to his buried strong box to retrieve the gold he needed to pay laborers and buy supplies. Another harvest was almost in, and with market prices rising he had the cash flow to cover on-going expenses. Winter was approaching, which would freeze the ground and make getting at his buried gold more difficult. Since he now had a good house with a cellar into the wall of which he had built a hidden lock box, it was time to move the gold.

Immediately after supper and before dusk, Adam grabbed his shillelagh, left the house dressed in a lightweight canvas coat, a cocked hat and leather gloves, stopped by the barn for a shovel and ventured into the woods alone.

He was glad for the gold and silver he had hidden. Each time he dug up the strong box a feeling of security came over him. He vowed to curtail his spending, however, and not spend the last of his gold unless an emergency arose.

As he came near the elm with the twisted limb that pointed toward the colony of maple leaf shrubs beneath which his gold was buried, he heard the plaintive whine of a cat's meow.

Looking up he saw Cleopatra sitting atop the twisted limb. She was huddled against the trunk and crouched on all fours. The hair on the back of her neck stood up in fright and she was shaking.

Adam walked over to the elm and beneath the limb. "Cleopatra!" he called out. "Where have you been? Why are you up there?"

Cleopatra gazed at Adam longingly, but she was too high to reach and she made no movement indicating she wanted to come down. Instead, she raised up on her legs, backed away from him an inch, arched her back and meowed as if begging for protection.

Her contrary behavior raised Adam's sense of a threat. Instinctively, he froze and glanced about. Nothing at first, but then, at the base of the elm, behind a mulberry shrub a shadow moved...and then a deep throated growl. Adam immediately dropped the shovel and raised his shillelagh across his body, his hands instinctively grasping both ends.

A second later a yowling coyote leaped from the shrub at Adam's throat, its snarling jaws unsheathing its razor-sharp incisors. At first an intense fear gripped Adam, but quickly his reflexes kicked in and he jammed the shillelagh crosswise into the mouth of the leaping beast.

The coyote chewed on the stick for a moment, then released it and fell back. A second later its agile body jumped at Adam again. Adam again tried to fend off the creature's frothing mouth with the stick, but the coyote's twisting was too fast. It dodged the stick and snapped viciously and repeatedly at Adam's hands, arms, and face. Scared that he might lose the battle, Adam jumped back far enough to wave the knob end of the stick back and forth in front of the coyote's nose to disorient the wild dog. At the same time Adam slipped his right hand into the thick leather loop at the shillelagh's base and tightened his fist about it. The coyote moved right, then left, as it looked for a way to parry the waving stick. Adam danced left, then right, countering the animal's feigned attacks. He waited for animal to lunge at him again thus exposing its vulnerable side. As he jogged left and right he feared he might miscalculate and expose his own ribs, except he relished the excitement. Farming can otherwise be such a bore. Adam smiled, as he played with his prey waiting for the right moment.

The opportunity came. The animal lunged and Adam purposefully stepped aside allowing it closer. Fear gave way to confidence as energy surged into Adam's limbs. His legs bent, his shoulders ducked, and with a flick of his muscular wrist the shillelagh suddenly swung over his head and down at the coyote's legs, snapping one of the animal's front legs and sweeping the other three off the ground. The animal whelped, whimpered, and stumbled backward.

In a flash it got back up, the broken leg dangling and useless. It was mad as ever, and seemingly faster than before. Hopping on its one front leg, it stalked Adam looking for an opportunity to attack again. It did...with a vengeance. Adam found it unbelievable that with one of its legs broken, the animal possessed such strength and determination. It was otherworldly.

A primal reflex to survive filled Adam's limbs. Repeatedly, he turned sideways to dodge one attack and then another. On the next attack, Adam flipped the shillelagh's knob end into his left hand and with his right grabbed the stick. As the animal came again, Adam lunged at the attacking coyote head-on and with the pointed end of the shillelagh speared the brute in its chest. The animal shrieked and fell back. Adam had hoped to pierce the animal's chest and put an end to the fight, but his thrust seemed only to knock the air out of the beast.

Moments later it was back on its three legs, hopping and stalking Adam again; froth now dripped from its mouth. Opting for a more conservative attack, the animal circled Adam widely, running as best it could to attack from the rear. Surprisingly, it did, and suddenly lunged at Adam's feet, successfully burrowing its teeth into the heel of Adam's right boot. With its hind legs dug into the earth, the coyote tried to pull and shake the man off his feet. At this Adam was emotionally relieved. Adam stopped evading and just looked down at the animal's futile efforts to topple the much heavier man. Adam put more weight on the boot pushing it firmly into the soil ensuring that the boot and the coyote's head would stay in one place. Adam knew that the coyote's instinct now was to never let go.

With his target firmly fixed in place, and his hand still in the shillelagh's leather loop, Adam took his time to skillfully swing the knob end of the stick over his head, carving a figure eight in the air, picking up speed. Then...with all his might he brought the knob of the shillelagh down across his body and behind his leg to connect perfectly with the coyote's skull, smashing it instantly. With barely a whimper the coyote fell to the ground, spasmed several times, and expelled its last gasp of breath.

Gasping for breath himself, Adam looked quickly around to fend off a possible second animal if there was one, but none appeared. He looked down at the coyote, its mouth still attached to his boot, its skull caved in several inches behind the ear. Turning the shillelagh around and grasping the knob end, he used the pointed end to pry the coyote's mouth off his boot. Only then did he relax. The battle was over.

Regaining his bearings, Adam looked around. Cleopatra was still in the tree. She meowed, a bit more courageously this time. He tramped to the tree, reached up with his shillelagh and propped it against the truck near the limb on which Cleopatra sat. With his other arm, he formed a cradle against his chest. "Come down, Cleopatra. It's okay now." Cleopatra crept along the limb to the trunk, jumped down, ricocheted off the shillelagh, fell against Adam's up-stretched arm, padded down to his shoulder, flopped into his cradled arm, and began to purr.

Still collecting his breath, but now with Cleopatra purring in his arm, Adam retrieved the dropped shovel and maneuvered his way behind the maple leaf shrubs. Boosting Cleo to his shoulder, Adam knelt and removed the surface field stones. He dug a little with his shovel and pried the strong box out of the ground. The box had rusted over the years and was nearly useless now. Opening the cover he confirmed that the gold he had last left was still inside, about ninety gold-doubloons. Also inside was an old leather drawstring bag that contained the fourteen double-doubloons he acquired from careless George. Removing the box from the ground, he filled up the hole with dirt and stones and headed back to the house with Cleopatra lounging on his shoulder.

When the house came into view, he could feel Cleopatra becoming unnerved, as if she was getting ready to jump off his shoulders. He didn't want that, so he headed into the barn, which was closer. Once in the barn, Cleopatra calmed and jumped from his shoulders to the ground, but stayed by his side, her back arched, her body on edge. He put away the shovel and put aside the strong box. Taking Cleopatra in his arms he tried to get her to purr and be comfortable, but she would not purr. When he stood in the barn doorway and took steps toward the house, she tensed and tried to stand as if to take flight. So he went back into the barn. Sitting on a milking stool he stroked the calico until she rolled onto her back and let him pet her belly. Cleopatra would be a good barn cat he decided. Putting her down next to a small pail of left over milk from Moon Beam's last milking, she immediately lowered herself onto her haunches and began to lick the bowl dry. When she was done, she glanced up at Adam, wandered over to the straw in Moon Beam's pen and lay down. The cat was there to stay.

6

My Despised Cyn:

What a lovely mess you've gotten us into. Wasn't it sufficient to let the personification of our charm in Livingston's house settle down to subtly influence his decisions? Did you have to totally alert the patriarch to the fact that his new bride is clearly, and is in fact, an evil witch set on destroying what faith his daughter has left? It's a nice thought, but not very strategic. Though, I must admit, it is amazing to me and my peers that you were able to get the old man to marry Colonial Babbitt's overly mournful widow. But for his devout daughter to declare that her stepmother is evil is not how we go about things. Denial and deceit are more to our liking.

Well, at least you've managed to brew hatred, which is always good for destroying what functionality may exist.

But we must stop this child from praying to her mother. Or is she praying to the Queen Mother? Neither is good, the former not as bad as the latter. Where did she learn that the Saints in the heavenlies pray for those left behind? That's a dangerous concept to let persist. Can you do something to undo that? Perhaps get her back to her mother's Protestant roots?

But on to more exciting things.

Previously, you successfully managed to get Livingston to steal a fair amount of gold from that idiot George Eshelman. What if Livingston becomes more possessive over what gold he has left?

We both know it's the love of money that's proven to be a bulwark of our success.

Your notion of Mary Ann taking shears to the linen has some significance. For most of history linen has represented to humans something deeply spiritual, useful, and eternal. There's a way that linen is sacred to many and no doubt flax is the foundation of Livingston's life. Attacking the linen as you've inspired Mary Ann to do with the shears may be a genius I didn't think you possessed. Undermining Livingston's attachment to his flax and the products that come from it may be key to annihilating any vestige of his faith, resulting in the achievement of your goal—his translation to Perdition.

And the coyote thing? Was that you, or was the coyote just hungry for domestic cat? I can't figure that one out. Nonetheless, Mary Ann's Bombay is to be preferred over Esther's Cleopatra.

Eternally yours,
Master of Evil

Chapter 26
Comforts of the Underworld

1

It was April, 1794. Prices for Adam's harvested crops, including flax, had risen steadily over the past three years. Then, last month, the demand for flax suddenly dropped. The cause was Eli Whitney's improvements to the cotton gin. The Indian roller cotton gin, also known as the *churka* gin, had been around for centuries with only limited improvements. But the churka was only good at deseeding long-fiber cotton that grew in Europe, Asia, and a few places on America's Atlantic coast. The short-fiber cotton, which was easily grown throughout the southern states, had to be manually deseeded. The process was time consuming and made southern cotton expensive. When Whitney came up with a solution, suddenly the southern plantations were turning out cotton so cheaply that it seemed only a matter of years before flax would become an obsolete crop, or so some in the textile industry claimed.

Adam believed, however, that the best flax would never go out of style. For short-fiber cotton could not produce the smooth feel or the robust strength of the extremely long flax fiber. Nonetheless, flax prices had recently dropped and there was no reason they were going to rebound anytime soon. This depressed Adam and made him irritable for months. In the end, he decided to experiment with different long-fiber seeds from different sellers in Europe. He was determined to develop a new, specialty strain of flax that would find a market niche and demand yet a higher price. He would prove to the world that his perseverance, determination, and innovation, even in the face of obstacles like Whitney's gin, did not rely on religion or God.

His marriage to Mary Ann suited Adam's goal to take revenge on God for ripping Esther from his life. He had not loved Esther because she was a Christian, but because she was a good cook, a seamstress, a gardener, and very beautiful and generous. She also gave him two healthy children, although there were the earlier tragedies. He had tolerated her strong faith.

If God existed, the Almighty was surely to be repudiated, and Mary Ann was the ticket. Mary Ann reinforced his independence of the supernatural because she was so fiercely independent herself, although he wished she was a bit more reliant on her husband. He overlooked the irony. Then again when he thought of her independence, he often smiled without knowing that he was smiling, for he enjoyed watching her work without doubt or guidance. If only he could find workers like that, who would work hard without supervision. In that regard Eve took after both her mother and stepmother. Who Henry took after was anyone's guess.

Adam had, however, miscalculated his daughter's reaction to her new step-mother. He thought children were adaptable; Henry certainly was. Eve, how-ever, was as religiously devout as her mother. Yet unlike her mother, Eve was savagely stubborn. At first he avoided the inevitable confrontation between Eve and Mary Ann by not introducing them until after the wedding, such as it was. Bad decision. Eve did not adapt. In fact, she refused to adapt, especially after the dress affair. Neither did Adam foresee that Esther's linens, which were ev-erywhere in the house, would constantly remind Mary Ann of Esther, nor did Adam foresee that the linens would make Mary Ann jealous. He felt chagrined for not introducing Eve and Mary Ann earlier, but every time he thought it through, he came to the same conclusion: either way Eve would have rejected Mary Ann.

Eve made it clear to her father that his decision to bring an "Evil Witch" into the family had also brought a curse, and that Eve had no intention of par-ticipating. That was nearly three years ago, and Eve had held strong to her con-viction to stand firm against Mary Ann. Eve made it clear she looked forward to the day when she could leave home. There was a sadness in all this for Adam, but it was balanced by his umbrage with God over Esther's death.

When Adam married Mary Ann, he was aware that she had not been able to conceive a child with Alvin. She thought it was Alvin's problem, not hers... and she was right. Though she was forty-four when she and Adam married, she conceived almost immediately. Adam wondered if the new child might fill the breech between Mary Ann and Eve. This gave him hope and brightened his life. As soon as he discovered that Mary Ann was with child, he privately told Eve the news and made a concession to his daughter—he suggested that she pray for a healthy and robust birth without Mary Ann knowing. Adam was not rediscovering his faith but trying to appease his daughter. He wondered if she'd take his suggestion to pray for the new child as a way of apologizing for his part in their breech. If so, that was fine with him.

Nine months later, on May 28, 1792, they experienced a rare occurrence. A child was not born to them, but rather fraternal twins. Mary Ann insist-ed on naming them George and Martha. To Adam this was bizarre; she hated George Washington, and by extension his wife, Martha. At the same time, she told Adam that naming the twins as she did was a way to amend her attitude and remember her former husband in an honorable way. She loved little George and Martha and doted over them. Martha took after her mother—strong willed and stubborn. If Martha needed to nurse and Mary Ann wasn't ready, the infant cried and struggled and sometimes lost her temper. In some ways like Adam, George was laid back and acquiesced to nearly every situation, although his eyes went wide and a smile erupted if something out of the norm was set upon him, like getting his diaper changed.

Strangely enough, their cat, Bombay, also doted over the twins. From the instant they were born Bombay could invariably be found following Mary Ann and the twins around, and when possible, cuddling up to them. It was as if the cat was their guardian angel, except it was black and liked to sharpen its claws on the hearth's granite next to a blazing fire. Adam watched the cat guardedly when the children were near.

Adam suspected, however, there was an unspoken and twisted reason for the names—they reminded Mary Ann to persist in her hate for the general and by extension the religion which the general promoted as a necessity if the country's experiment with democracy was going to work. Adam shunned Washington's sentiments; yet when he heard them, a rejoinder came to mind: *If God is good and in control, why does he allow the good to die and evil to live?* That was an irony or a paradox he couldn't reconcile.

With the arrival of the twins Eve had more reason to protest—Mary Ann increased her demands on Eve—to care for the twins. This repressed Eve's spirit and interest in the world around her. More and more she withdrew from conversation and found interest in fewer things except her own solitude. But she was trapped—she had a great fondness for the twins and she enjoyed taking care of them. If Martha didn't want to play, Eve made a game out of it and before Martha knew it, the "little Madam," as Eve called her, was smiling. George was always ready to smile at Eve's attention and would laugh so hard he could turn blue from not breathing right. All Eve had to do was look at him funny and George would crack a smile and giggle.

These observations convinced Adam it was time, way past time, to assemble the loom and teach Eve to weave. She was twelve at the time of the twin's birth and was now old enough and tall enough to reach the treadles. Perhaps the loom could reunite the women. The linens Eve wove would not be Esther's, they would be Eve's, or even Mary Ann's if Mary Ann would take Eve's fabric and make garments of her own design, possibly for the twins. Over time their combined products would replace Esther's, of which there were many in drawers, at the foot of beds, in armoires, hutches, and crates still in storage.

At least that was the idea two years ago when Adam reassembled the loom. It took longer than he expected since a few of the parts that had been damaged during the trip to Smithfield had to be remade. It was a large loom with a flying shuttle, four treadles, and a rocker beater that could produce cloth forty-eight inches wide. It was an unusual loom, and of value to him. Over the months Eve learned to make plain weave cloth, and some of her linens began to replace those of her mother's, such as napkins.

Mary Ann, however, was not easily soothed. She still believed she was competing with a corpse buried in York. When Eve began to weave larger cloths, albeit still plain weave, Mary Ann began to make excuses for not sewing garments even for George and Martha—the weave wasn't suitable, it was too loose, it was too tight, or the color of the cloth was not pleasing. Adam realized much too late that Mary Ann wasn't just *jealous* of Esther, she was *envious*, and the envy extended to Eve, the loom, and the weave. This frustrated Adam and he was running out of options. He thought of putting Eve to work in the fields, but that was backbreaking work unsuitable for young women.

Doubts about marrying Mary Ann rose in Adam's mind. But she was kind to him and supported his long hours of work as long as he supported her running of the house and children. She was also very skilled at organizing, cooking, cleaning, and when needed she would come to the barn and process flax. She was not afraid of work. She was a good farmer's wife. He kept reminding himself that farmers like him, at this time, did not get married out of love for one another but because they needed one another to survive—there was too much death, otherwise. Consequently, he went out of his way to ignore the conflict with Eve and found ways to praise Mary Ann.

But reality had a way of sneaking up and destroying his best intentions.

One day Eve came to Adam to report that a heddle frame of the loom was fractured, which prevented the reed from operating properly, and consequently the shuttle could not pick through the shed. Eve said when she left the loom the day before it was fine. When Adam examined the loom, he found several connecting rods broken, as well. Why these parts were broken was a mystery. They were made from sturdy pieces of oak and chestnut. It seemed mechanically impossible that such breaks were the result of the loom's misuse, which is what Mary Ann said must have happened. Mary Ann also said that while she knew nothing of the problem, she wasn't sad about the loom being inoperative. It was a noisy and nerve-rattling contraption which put the twins in an irritable mood.

Adam was not happy about the conflict between Mary Ann and his daughter. Every time a conflict arose, the hair on the back of his neck stood on end. He felt like Cleopatra after being treed by that rabid coyote. Except in this case, his shillelagh could not solve the problem. He decided that a broken loom might lead to peace in more than one way. He was only partly right. While Mary Ann was happier and the house quieter without the clicker-clack of the flying shuttle and squeaks of the beater arm and treadles...not fixing the loom only served to elevate Eve's resentment. Nonetheless, the loom remained damaged and inoperable.

2

Adam found Mary Ann's continued interest in the McSherrys odd—it waxed and waned. At the Charles Town summer fairs, it waxed. Mary Ann insisted on seeking out Anastasia strolling in the hat parade wearing one of her fancy hats, and Mary Ann would attempt to again entice Anastasia with one of her baking entries. Although neither woman won anything in either contest, they would chat for a few minutes in an aisle between cattle pens and the cockfights. After talking with Anastasia, Mary Ann would glow the rest of the day. But then Mary Ann's interest in Anastasia waned. On three occasions Anastasia invited the Livingstons to an open house at the McSherry Retirement mansion in Leetown. The first invitation came in early May, 1792, when the McSherrys' first child, Richard, Jr., named after his father, was christened. Mary Ann was anxious to go, although she was heavily pregnant with the twins. Eve was anxious to go too, but for entirely different reasons. Mary Ann wanted to roam and ogle at the furnishings of the richest man and woman in northern Virginia, or so she had ascertained. Eve wanted to go because it was the McSherrys who had the large garden of hedges and roses in the shape of a cathedral. Adam also took it for granted that Eve was attracted to Anastasia because he had heard the story of how Anastasia had brightened when Eve showed off the symbols of Christian embroidery on her mother's table covering—the covering that Mary Ann had destroyed.

After their first visit to the McSherrys, Mary Ann's interest in Anastasia disappeared. Her reasons? First, the house was not adorned with the luxurious appointments Mary Ann considered proper; and second, the house *was* appointed with Christian crosses, paintings of Christ, and small porcelain statues of saints. Then there was that awful toast to saints, and the coup de grâce—a Rosary prayer in the rose garden. Mary Ann walked out on that. Eve, on the other hand, found everything about the house and especially the Rosary prayer fascinating. Adam was afraid to ask, but he was pretty sure Eve would have moved in with the McSherrys as their maid had she been asked or if she had been bold enough to solicit the position. Privately, and somewhat excited at the discovery, Eve told him that she had learned that Jesus had a mother in heaven to which Catholics prayed, just as Eve prayed to her mama. Adam cringed at the idea but said nothing. Eve rattled on, however, about how she had never been taught about praying to saints to intercede for us; she had just started doing it. Eve was vindicated by the realization, he brushed it aside as idolatry, and Mary Ann found it disgusting.

There were two more open house parties at the McSherrys' to which the Livingstons were invited. One was in May, 1793, for the christening of their second son, William, who was born exactly a year later and named after Richard's twin brother. The most recent open house was just a few months ago, in March, 1794, for the christening of their third son, Dennis. But Adam never found out who Dennis McSherry was named after.

Mary Ann would have nothing to do with the second and third open houses. Her tolerance for anything religious and especially Christian had fully matured into intolerance. In hindsight Adam was glad the priest that had christened, or baptized, the McSherrys' children was not at the open houses. Mary Ann would have insulted the man to his face. Adam agreed that the McSherrys were super religious, but they didn't try to convert anyone. They appeared to be polite and respectful of all, regardless of their worldviews. He had also heard that Richard's land tenants gave him good reports, as did the citizens of Hagerstown for some unknown reason. Eve, however, begged to go to the open houses and Adam took her, for he found Richard a man of good taste and intelligent conversation, and his imported sherry was marvelous.

3

In the meantime, work at Flax Haven continued. Now that it was the beginning of May, and the seed was in the ground, it was time to catch up on repairs and the never-ending job of clearing the fields of stones and stumps to expand the tillable land. Adam decided they would finally clear the foundation stones of the old Mayfield cabin and stable. The stones would make a good wall along the Charles Town Road. Adam, Sam, and Henry hitched Luther to the farm wagon, piled on shovels, pick-axes, a leverage bar, and sledge hammer, pulled the wagon to the site, and set to work. It took most of the day prying up the field stone foundations of Mayfield's cabin and stable, and carting them to a clearing near the road. There, they dumped the stones for later construction of the wall.

Thinking their job was done, they jumped into the wagon and started back to the barn. On the way Adam saw the small cairn near what apparently was once a stand of small trees. The trunks had fallen years before and the stumps were so rotten they disintegrated with a hoe. The cairn reminded him of an obscure memorial; perhaps the stones were stacked atop the grave of an Indian warrior a century ago. He would not disturb the bones if that were true. They would just remove the stones and use them for the new wall. They diverted the wagon to the cairn, tossed the surface stones into the wagon, dug up the six foundation stones, and hauled them all to the clearing by the road where they were unceremoniously dumped.

It was dusk when they finished, and they were tired for good reason. So, it's doubtful that either of the men or the boy took notice of what happened after they left the clearing by the road. One of the cairn's foundation stones that ended up on top of the pile by the road was a black rectangular box-like obsidian stone with chiseled contours. It suddenly trembled a bit and cracked open. From within, a jet of black vapor escaped, coalesced into a spinning funnel, and drilled itself into the earth and the comforts of the underworld.

4

My Despised Cyn:

Congratulations are in order! You have done well in learning the patience of fools befitting your nature and have managed to escape the coffin of your quarantine.

I expect more from you, now...some real progress.

There is no time like the present, for a challenge approaches that can profit from the obnoxious presence of your physical re-constitution.

A sojourner will soon find his way to Livingston's farm. You have an opportunity of turning Flax Haven into Flax Hell. The sojourner, however, is indeed a rogue, for some of your peers have pestered him for more than twenty-seven years since he refused to obey his pope and return to Italy when his order was suppressed in Louisiana. He travels incognito as one of our greatest enemies. We fear he might greatly hinder our cause if he makes his way east to Baltimore. There, John Carroll, the new bishop, will likely give the sojourner an important assignment. We must prevent this. The sojourner is to be feared. It seems your physical presence has returned just in time. Don't mess this up. All of Hell is counting on you. He must not reach Baltimore.

Eternally yours,
Master of Peril

Part Five:
Stranger

Let the charity of the brotherhood abide in you.
And hospitality do not forget;
for by this some, being not aware of it,
have entertained angels.

(Hebrews 13:1–2)

Chapter 27
Politically Dangerous

Tuesday, May 13, 1794.

Bishop John Carroll, S.J., was portly and polite, but fancied himself a rebel. Although he had a generous and relaxed mouth, it was centered on a square and serious jaw. His long, aristocratic nose always appeared sunburned, though its owner spent most of his days indoors. The bishop's round, alert eyes were inviting and modestly set under a broad, smooth brow from which his hair had fully retreated. Soft grey curls fell gently over his temples and smallish ears.

Enjoying lunch on the verandah of his Baltimore residence, the bishop was joined by three Jesuit colleagues and his older brother, Daniel Carroll. During the past hour John Carroll had listened intently to his guests and spoken little, but now wished that his three Jesuit guests would take a clue from the servant clearing the table that the meeting, like the lunch, was over.

Yet the three priests were insistent that the bishop do something that seemed to the bishop not only politically dangerous, but repugnant. For emotional support, Bishop Carroll had invited his politically dangerous brother to the gathering. Daniel Carroll was a rich plantation owner in Maryland who had financially supported the Revolutionary War. As a delegate to the Philadelphia Convention of 1787, he was a signer of both the Articles of Confederation and the Constitution. It didn't help that everyone else around the table was also dangerous, but also stubborn, except the servant who wisely kept moving.

The bishop's Jesuit guests were Fr. Jean Baptiste and Fr. Louis, both originally from France, and Fr. Augustin, an immigrant from Germany. Rebelliously, they all wore the long robes of Jesuit missionaries in public even though Rome had officially repressed the Jesuits from the continent; and though local public sentiment was decidedly anti-Catholic, yet they persisted.

The bishop, a Jesuit himself, considered the Jesuit Suppression ill-conceived and an example of the papacy's weak spine when confronted by tyrannical kings and queens. Albeit the pope had been faced with a life or death dilemma which ultimately persuaded him to promulgate the repression. Charles III of Spain (King Carlos), through a secret commission, ordered governors of *all* Spanish territories to arrest *all* Jesuits and confiscate *all* their goods. The last statement of the order read: * *"If a single Jesuit, even though sick or dying, is still to be found in the area under your command after the embarkation, prepare yourself to face summary execution."*

Few knew that Bishop Carroll was seriously considering restoring the Jesuit order in the United States and not telling Rome or Spain. Carroll had precedent for such rebellion—his own. In 1773, when Pope Clement XIV ordered the

Society of Jesus suppressed, Jesuits were ordered out of the New World and into exile on an island near Italy. But *Carroll refused to sail to that "God-forsaken island under Rome's drippy nose." Instead, he quietly left France where he had been educated, ordained, and was teaching, and sailed *to* the New World. Home was in the British colony of Maryland, where his family owned a large plantation. There, on his own authority, he became a Jesuit missionary priest and didn't hide the fact. Further, in defiance of Maryland's anti-Catholic penal laws, he built a small chapel on his mother's land and celebrated Mass each week with his family and friends.

Rebellion ran in the Carroll family. John Carroll's cousin was Charles Carroll of Carrollton, a wealthy Maryland planter, and early advocate of independence from Britain. Charles was the *sole Catholic signer of the Declaration of Independence, the wealthiest man in the colonies, and also an underwriter of the war effort.

In 1776, at the request of the Continental Congress, John Carroll traveled with his cousin Charles and Benjamin Franklin to Canada to persuade the French Canadians to join the revolution against the British. The effort failed, but it forged a firm relationship with Franklin, and endeared John Carroll to Congress and others like George Washington.

Such relationships did two things: First, it gave Carroll an important political audience when he campaigned hard for the First Amendment and religious freedom. Second, in 1789 when the Constitution went into effect, Benjamin Franklin and twenty-four of the twenty-five priests practicing in the new country nominated John Carroll for the newly-created United States episcopacy. Pope Pius VI agreed, and named John Carroll its first Roman bishop.

The one priest that refused to sign and support Carroll for the position was Fr. Denis Cahill.

Bishop Carroll felt sympathy for the servant clearing the table. The job had become nearly impossible as the servant balanced dirty china and maneuvered around the wild gestures of frustrated priests unfamiliar with the bishop's political disposition.

"Your Grace must not realize," said Fr. Augustin, "the superb bearing of these thirty-five acres of land. It is from God."

Fr. Louis followed. "It is just to the west of the undeveloped territory, yet well within Virginia's borders."

Bishop Carroll grew impatient. "Why do you fail to understand? What you suggest may be in some sense legal, but it's political suicide." Shaking his head, he gazed at his statesman brother for assistance.

Daniel Carroll leaned back to let the servant take away his place setting, then leaned forward across the table and spoke to the robed Jesuits. "Gentlemen, it is true that a tract of land not properly deeded may be transferred to the Church for its use. The courts have recognized such common law precedent. But this is a new country, and Maryland and Northern Virginia are states, with deep anti-Catholic bias. In spite of our new Constitution and the First Amendment that voids the anti-Catholic penal laws, the public sentiment has *not* changed. It may be a generation or more before sentiment and violence against us will...."

Fr. Jean Baptiste interrupted. "But surely, as one of the signers of the Constitution, you have the influence to acquire this land for our ministry. The man who holds deed to it now has hundreds of acres more than he needs. It is only one small part that is, by common law, not rightfully his."

"But to invoke this so-called right," said Daniel, "would require a public trial in which the Protestants would portray the Church as attempting to take land from a man that *does* hold rightful deed, has improved it, and is farming it for the greater benefit of the country."

"Reverends," pleaded the bishop, "I have labored now nearly thirty years for the religious freedom we now enjoy. President Washington and I have publicly commended each other for staying out of each other's business. I fear that for the Church to take advantage of the government's courts would invite public sentiment to turn against us, and once again, in this very state, we would see our property that we now do occupy, own, and enjoy, ripped from us. And you, my dear brothers, may be chased down, deported, or hanged as the *ten were in New York not that long ago."

The bishop paused to let that sink in. Then he continued with a firm declaration: "No, we will be the Church of Jesus Christ. We will not take land from a man who thinks it is his and risk public ridicule. This is not a matter of doctrine or civil legality. It is a matter of common sense." The bishop stood, announcing that the meeting was over.

The three priests saw the opportunity slip from their grasp and stood as well, bowing to their bishop.

"Your Grace, what should we then do?" asked Fr. Augustin.

Bishop Carroll thought for moment, then gazed up at the large crucifix that hung on the wall. "We pray, of course. If God wants the church to have that land, he will give it to us...in his time, not ours."

The priests nodded their reluctant approval.

"Reverends," said Carroll, "Just, as...ah, a matter of prayer. Where did you say this land was?"

"In the Virginian, Shenandoah Valley, your Grace," said Fr. Louis.

"Is the owner, this farmer, you say a man of faith?" asked Carroll.

The priests looked to each other. Finally, Fr. Louis shrugged. "Word is that he is not. He has rejected what he otherwise knows to be true and has turned against God with some degree of belligerence."

Bishop Carroll looked sadly at the three men, and then to Daniel. "May God have mercy on his soul."

Chapter 28
Starving for a Good Meal

1

May 27, 1794.

Adam Livingston lit a lantern and made his way into the cellar of his farmhouse. He needed time alone to move some coin and reconcile accounts. Sam, Henry, and a few day laborers were tending to the irrigation channels in the southwest forty. Mary Ann was weeding their vegetable and herb garden by the side of the house. Behind the summer kitchen in the shade Bethany paired vegetables, while nearby on the edge of the wood Eve played tag with George and Martha—a challenge all of its own. The twins would be two years old tomorrow and could toddle along at a good pace. George loved to be tagged and purposely ran in circles hoping he would get knocked down and caught, giving him a reason to laugh. He also loved hugs and kisses. Martha on the other hand was strong as a bull and often acted like it. If George or Eve tried to catch her, and she was sure to be caught because she could not run that fast; she would suddenly turn and with a stern face slam both her pudgy little arms and hands into her pursuer. Of course, Martha was only tall enough to shove her hands into Eve's thighs. Nonetheless, Eve would pretend to fall down and be hurt, which would elicit a smile from Martha. But when Martha turned and knocked George over, George would not smile but actually cry until Eve picked him up and hugged him for a few minutes. During such times Martha would stand aloof nearby with a scowl, glaring at her brother as if she were the victim.

Content that everyone was out of sight and mind, Adam went into the cellar with a lantern, walked to the wash basin and picked up a wooden crate used as a step for the children. Maneuvering behind the stairs to the southeast wall he put the crate down. Standing on the crate he reached up and removed a facade of stones on top of the wall just beneath the sill plate.

After the foundation and cellar walls had been erected and the sill plate, summer beams, and floor joists installed, Adam came alone one day and removed a few stones from under the sill plate. In the cavity he installed a metal strong box with a lockable front door. After the box was mortared in place, he placed a facade of stones loosely in front to make it appear as if the wall was continuous. Only Adam knew that the facade stones could be removed, allowing access to the strong box.

Now, with the facade stones removed, he unlocked the strong box with a key and quickly performed a cursory inventory of the contents. There were papers, like the deed to his property, and leather sacks of gold and silver coin.

He removed a small sack of silver he would need before the fall harvest and put it into his pants' pocket. Then he withdrew the small sack of gold he had requisitioned from George Eshelman years earlier. Opening the drawstring sack, he quickly confirmed that it still contained fourteen gold double-doubloons. He felt rich when he looked at this gold. It was his emergency stash, and it warmed his heart to know that fate had rewarded his diligence with George's carelessness. He put the *crisis gold,* as he called it, in his pocket as well and patted his pants to ensure the coin sacks had not fallen though some undiscovered hole in his pocket.

By rote he began to replace the facade stones. That's when it hit him. The cavity in the wall, into which the strong box was mortared, suddenly receded deep into the wall. The wall at that point was about sixteen inches thick, but the face of the strong box suddenly seemed to recede dozens of feet into a dark tunnel. It looked like a very deep grave with a metal coffin at the bottom. So frightening and real was the premonition that Adam fell off the crate, and landed on the hard stone floor, bruising his left hip. *That hurt.* Looking up at the hole in the wall, he was stunned to see black smoke pour from it, as if the cavity was a chimney expelling a fume from a fireplace burning wet wood. The smoke rose to the floor joists and seeped in between the boards of the subfloor. Stunned, Adam thought there was a fire in the vault even though field stones don't burn. He scrambled to his feet and climbed back onto the crate. He tried to peer into the tunnel but the smoke was too thick. At the same time he was surprised that there was no heat nor smell of smoke associated with a fire. He waved the smoke away from the vault cavity to see where it came from, but the fume of smoke paid no heed to his waving hand. It would not be brushed aside but continued its path upwards. He tried again to brush the smoke aside, but it was impossible; his hand did nothing and felt nothing. It was as if the smoke didn't exist except in his mind's eye. No matter what he did, the blackness flowed *through* his hand, not around it, up to the joists above him, where it seemed to dissipate into the subfloor. It left behind no residual stain or soot. It was an apparition of some foreboding. Then, just as suddenly as it appeared, it disappeared. Adam peered into the vault cavity. There was nothing unusual. He reached in and touched the cold surface of the metal strong box. It was there as it should be. What his mind retained was the appearance of the deep, dark cavity with a metal coffin at the end.

Catching his breath and trying to calm down, he replaced the facade stones to cover the strong box's location. He stepped down from the crate and returned it to the wash basin. Shaking from the encounter he washed his face and neck with cold water from the spring. Returning to the vault area, he checked the floor beneath the vault to ensure that there were no tell-tale signs of his presence. Finally, once more, he examined the bottom of the subfloor above and saw no trace of black soot or vapor. Up the stairs he took his lantern to the first floor, where he walked over the floor just above the vault. There also he saw no sign of black vapor or residue, but he was still frightened, and his shaking continued as he climbed the main staircase to his bedroom.

2

Mary Ann was enjoying the coolness of the late afternoon. Occasionally peaking from behind clouds, the sun warmed her back as she weeded the garden southwest of the house. Nearby, Bombay jumped and batted flying insects when he wasn't staring at the barn where Cleopatra had finally settled-in as the barn queen.

All of a sudden Bombay stopped batting at flies and padded to Mary Ann, who was on her knees. The cat backed into Mary Ann as if to get her attention and hissed. Mary Ann smirked at Bombay whose gaze was riveted at the wagon path that came in from the Charles Town Road. Seeing nothing, Mary Ann went back to loosening the dirt around her parsley, sage and rosemary herbs and up-rooting alien vegetation. Bombay hissed louder. Mary Ann frowned at the black tomcat whose back now was arched and its hair standing on end. She put down her hand-hoe, stood up, and took a studied look toward the road. After a moment she quickly turned toward the house and called out.

3

Adam was in his bedroom on his knees pulling out a stack of old clothing from the floor of his armoire. Putting the stack of overalls and shirts aside he reached back into the dark corner and lifted out an old wooden sea chest. Putting it on his bed, he unlocked it with a key kept hidden in his office, opened the chest, and dropped in the small sacks of silver and "crisis" gold. That's when he heard Mary Ann's call through the open window.

"Adam? Adam! We have a visitor."

Sensing tension in her voice, Adam reacted with alarm. He hurriedly went to the window and looked out.

A bedraggled, thin *Stranger, probably in his late fifties or sixties, with longish white hair, a beard, and a dirty cloth bundle strapped to his back plodded toward the house from the road. There was something about the man that said he was not a beggar but a sojourner. Dressed in clean grey trousers that were not frayed or torn as many beggars' clothes were, the man wore a long-sleeve white linen shirt, and a black felt cocked hat. His pace was strong and sure, his back erect and his head held high. Although still at a distance, Adam detected the Stranger's clear blue eyes under the hat's brim. He could not see around the corner of the house to the garden, but the man obviously did. He looked up, smiled, and waved a greeting in the direction where Mary Ann worked. Nothing to worry about, Adam concluded, so he took his time to close and lock the sea chest, return it in the bottom of the armoire, cover it with the stack of old clothes, and closed the armoire doors.

Over the years, only a few strangers had ambled onto their property, so few in fact that Adam could not recall one in the past year. The appearance of this sojourner, although he looked safe enough, kept Adam on alert. The old man's gait, smile, and baggage, however, told Adam that this was a man of some reputation or credit, perhaps in need of a place to stay for the night. Although the room next to their bedroom was used mostly for storage, in it was a bed, small table, and wash basin suitable for guests. They would accommodate the sojourner, if Mary Ann was agreeable. Adam grabbed his shillelagh and went downstairs to meet the visitor.

4

Eve saw an older man approach her stepmother from the wagon path. He dipped his hat, and stopped a respectful distance from her. He said something, but Eve could not hear. Adam shortly appeared carrying his shillelagh, walked directly to the smiling man, and offered his hand. They chatted for a minute, then Adam introduced Mary Ann, who walked up and curtsied, the man bowing as if he was at court. The three (Adam, Mary Ann, and the Stranger) engaged in amicable conversation. Eve so wished she could have heard what they were saying, but they were too distant.

"Seems we may have a guest to supper," said Bethany as she picked up another potato from the bucket of water and began to peel it.

"I wonder where he's from?" said Eve. "He looks thin, like he's walked a long way."

"Be glad to fatten him up," giggled Bethany, "we's got plenty of taters. No use let'em rot."

Just then Adam turned toward Eve and motioned for her to come to him. "Papa wants me. Can you watch George and Martha?"

"Of course," said Bethany, as she turned to see where the twins were.

Eve walked briskly to her father, somewhat excited to meet someone new. As she did she took stock of her appearance and preened her hair, but then felt embarrassed because of her dirty house dress, but took some consolation after glancing at her stepmother who was covered in dirt from her garden work. The Stranger was dressed for a ball, compared to them. She was quick to notice that he had alert eyes

Adam introduced Eve. "Xavier, this is my daughter, Eve."

"Happy to make your acquaintance, Eve," said the articulate Stranger with a rich baritone voice and delicate French accent.

No sluggard here, thought Eve. Whomever he was, his clothes did not represent his station. She locked eyes with the man; there was a resonance that agreed with her...like a long-lost uncle who had traveled the world and could tell stories by the fireplace for hours on end. But her father interrupted her reverie.

"Eve, the tavern in Smithfield is full. Mister Xavier will be our guest at supper and stay the night with us before he travels on to Baltimore. Please inform Bethany to set another place at table. But before that, please check that our guest bed is suitably drawn, and fill the pitcher with fresh water and lay out clean linens, if you please. Go now and attend to that. I'll show him to the room in a minute."

Eve curtsied to Mister Xavier. "Glad to meet you, sir."

The man smiled, nodded back, but said nothing more, as she ran off to prepare his room.

5

Eve helped Bethany set the table for the late supper while Mary Ann fed the twins with food from the kitchen, and then nursed them in the master bedroom to a sound sleep. Bethany agreed that supper with the Stranger was a good time to break out the fine linen, although doing so depressed Eve as she remembered her mother's embroidered covering that Mary Ann had shamefully destroyed. Eve would never forgive Mary Ann for that.

The Stranger came down from the guest room cleaned up, with a clean linen shirt. He was a frail, gentle, and good-spirited man. His eyes gleamed with appreciation at a well-served table of meat and vegetables. Although his appetite was evident, he ate slowly. Eve thought he needed fattening up. He talked little; supper at their table had never been a time of conversation, but of consuming. Work on a farm was hard, so food was devoured seriously.

Near the end of supper when the Stranger was asked a question, he politely stopped eating, addressed the questioner directly, and spoke clearly. But his answers were not very good as much as Eve could tell.

"Where specifically have you come from?" asked Mary Ann.

"Considerably west of here, Madam. Yet nowhere specific that I can describe," came the Stranger's strange answer.

Mary Ann pressed: "And where is it that you're headed?"

"East, near Baltimore, to some friends. I hope—if they are still there, after the war."

"You don't know?" asked Mary Ann.

"It's been thirty years. I doubt very much they know I'm alive." He wiped his mouth with his napkin. "My thanks and blessings on you for sharing your food and hospitality. I have been in need of a good meal for days. Thank you so much."

"You are most welcome," said Mary Ann.

Eve grew anxious, not wanting the conversation to stop. "Did you see any Indians when you were west? What were they like?"

"Oh, yes, my dear. I've seen many Indians, and most were very kind and considerate," answered the Stranger forthrightly.

Henry asked, "You saw real Indians and they didn't kill you?"

Adam laughed, as did the Stranger, who patted his body down as if checking for his own death. "No, I guess not. I'm still alive it seems."

Henry was not to be denied, "I'll bet they tried to kill you, though, didn't they?"

"Ah, if you only realized," said the Stranger, "the people that really hate us. No, the Indians I lived with—"

"You LIVED with Indians?" cried Henry.

That got Eve's attention, and seemingly everyone else's. It suddenly got quiet.

"For many years, in fact," their guest said. "They were quite peaceful. Though they did need to defend themselves from time to time, but not from white men, but from other Indian tribes."

There was a pause for a moment as that thought soaked in. Bethany spoke. "If you'd all like to retire to the parlor or porch I'll clean up and we'll bring ya'll coffee, or lemonade. Eve, help me?"

"Yes'm," said Eve.

Moments later in the summer kitchen, Bethany, with a sly smile on her lips asked Eve, "Did you notice anything strange about our Stranger just before we began to eat?"

Eve felt ashamed. She had not noticed anything different, but she knew Bethany well enough to know Eve had missed something and she now wanted to know what it was. "No, what? About the Stranger?"

Quietly Bethany explained. "He was very sly about it, but as we began to pass the dishes he bowed his head, closed his eyes, his lips moved a little, and then, as if he was scratching an insect bite on his forehead, and adjustin' his shirt, crossed himself, like a Catholic does when they pray."

Eve was in shock. A Catholic at their supper table? Mary Ann would be furious.

"It just may be," Bethany continued, "that it wasn't noticed because we all do the same. You, me, and Sam, except we don't cross ourselves, exactly. But he did it." Bethany had the biggest smile on her face.

Eve felt her eyes grow wide. She put her hand over her mouth to suppress a scream of delight. She locked eyes with Bethany, and in joy they both hugged and jumped up and down a little. "I can't wait until tomorrow. I must talk to him and tell him to pray for us, and to tell him about Mama and what we've been through."

Bethany frowned a bit at that. "Now, child, you don't want Missus Mary Ann to find out 'en ruin the good man's visit. You probably won't have a moment alone with him, unless...unless you walk with him to Baltimore after he leaves, and you know you can't do that."

"No, but Sam could, and then Sam could tell us."

Bethany thought about that for a moment. "Yes, I suppose he could. In fact,

Sam could give Missta Stranger a ride as if he was going to town in the wagon, and they could talk."

"Bethany, Baltimore's in the opposite direction...isn't it?" asked Eve.

"No, actually, Baltimore is in the direction of Charles Town. Have I taught you nothing? I think I'll make a shopping list for Sam."

Eve nodded her head with delight.

But Bethany was still thinking. "Eve, who's ta say you'd like to do some shopping yourself?"

"Oh! Bethany, that's the greatest idea. The list, the list. We have to make a list. But it has to be a good one, so Papa will believe it."

"Leave it to me, child. Now let's get that coffee served. I suspect your father and Mister Stranger will be on that porch talkin' for hours. Tomorrow's a new day, 'day say."

6

After supper, in the cool of the evening, Adam and Xavier had enjoyed a hot cup of coffee on the porch. Adam had hoped to wrangle out of their guest a bit more of his background and wanderings, but that wasn't to be. Xavier was polite and grateful for the Livingstons' hospitality, but specifics of his past were mostly hidden behind answers that were innocuous, oblique, ambiguous, or just plain evasive. Adam was not sure if Xavier kept his past a secret out of shame or some political intrigue involving the French and Spanish.

Adam did discover, however, that Xavier had been sent to French Louisiana with French explorers as interpreter, peacemaker, and guide. Gifted in languages, he acted as an intermediary between the French who wanted furs and various Indian tribes, some who wanted to live in peace. Then there were various other factions who were out for revenge wherever they could find it. The continuous political upheaval between French explorers, then the Spanish, and then the British was intense. After a while Xavier decided to live among a group of farming Indians and hire himself out to Europeans as guide and interpreter. After the Treaty of Fontainebleau, when the territory was ceded to Spain, French settlers and explorers were given eighteen months to get out and move to French territories elsewhere in the world. Xavier decided to stay and live among the Indians where he had found a home. But when the tribe he had lived with decided to migrate south, Xavier, with advancing age, decided he needed to seek out old friends in Baltimore. It was a long walk, and he would continue it tomorrow.

During their porch visit Xavier thanked Adam several times for the good meal and the good fortune of a soft bed. Of this, Adam was happy to oblige their guest. Adam still worried for the man, however. Although his skin was rugged from living out of doors, he was thin and frail, as if a good meal and a good night's rest had been an uncommon experience. It did not pass Adam's notice, or Bethany's, as far as Adam could tell, that Xavier had eaten enough for three men. It was ironic that despite the man's evident ravenous appetite he took pains to be temperate by taking small bites. He was not gluttonous, but slow and deliberate. Xavier also had taken particular delight in Mary Ann's lemon honeycomb, of which he raved, but politely refused seconds. He said that if he ate his fill the children would not have servings tomorrow after he left. He had winked at Mary Ann as if he knew she had been starving for compliments as much as Xavier had been starving for a good meal.

They had not talked long before Xavier excused himself to bed, for he needed rest, which Adam could plainly see. Shortly thereafter, Mary Ann and the children turned in for the night, and Sam came for Bethany. Adam, however, still had not completed the reconciliation of his accounts, and so for another two hours he labored in his office until midnight, when he trudged up the stairs and fell soundly asleep next to slumbering Mary Ann.

7

Most Feared Master of Grotesqueness,

Pursuant to your request this is the first of what I hope will be many provocative field reports in our effort to entrap and condemn Adam Livingston and his family to Perdition, the destiny for millions.

Since the time of my release from the confines of physical exile (materialism can be so limiting), I have taken up your challenge to make progress with the honorable malfeasance due our kind. I know my duty to rile up disturbances that lead to Perdition—my happy occupation. At once I am proud that in my own right I too am a disturbance. All of this disturbs me and I trust disturbs you as well, my Master.

While there is much here to report, what undergirds my thorny thicket is that Livingston continues to experience premonitions that not only mock my haunts but alert the man to the reality that something beyond his materialistic self exists. That is not good, in a bad way. I know, from your eons of tutoring, that we are most effective when our targets are kept in the dark. The recent demonic councils on the invention of Post-Modernism are genius. I cannot wait for such thinking to pervade human society. Nonetheless, without much assistance on our part, Livingston is adopting the idea that everything spiritual or supernatural is to be distrusted—a lusciously devouring idea.

His recent premonition, however, is not good for us. It has reminded me that such visions have an origin—possibly a guardian. I must step up my attacks gradually to avoid detection; perhaps

I can seduce Livingston and his clan slowly and thus wean them from the Almighty's idolatry. Yes, my confinement has taught me an important lesson—not to run off uncontrolled as I did when I physically provoked Cain to kill Mayfield. I agree that was a mistake.

What scares me the most, if a despised entity as myself can be scared, is that I cannot see guardians except for their trailing artifacts when they move quickly and twist the dimensional universe. Lucky for us, Livingston has been stubborn enough not to think critically about his premonitions, no doubt because he has grown used to them since childhood. He's come to believe everyone has premonitions as part of everyday life. Still the guardian's presence is unsettling. Why does the Almighty persist to be interested in this little man when he and his wife have made repeated and strong repudiations of the Almighty, his Son, and His religion?

Nonetheless, the Stranger of whom you have warned has arrived, and now it is time that I act in the service of all we hold true.

At your sinful service,
Cyn Namrasit, OPSD

Chapter 29
Sudden Death

1

May 28, 1794.

In the master bedroom, Adam was fast asleep with Mary Ann at his side and the twins in their cribs. Framing partly open windows, sheer curtains floated effortlessly into the room on a light breeze. A great horned owl hooted in excitement having spied its prey—a vulnerable snowshoe hare far from its rabbit hole. Although the sky was cloudless, there was no moon, it being the night of a new moon. Thus, the Livingstons did not notice the swiveling black fume of vapor that wafted by their windows on its way to the open windows of their guest's bedroom.

Yet deep sleep and peace prevailed, until....

George and Martha both awoke and began to cry. Adam woke but refused to get out of bed, thinking they would go back to sleep. He wondered what had wakened them. For months they had slept through the night. Were they hungry? Mary Ann was still nursing although he didn't think she needed to. Was there something wrong with her milk? Were they preparing for another growth spurt? But then he heard the terrible thunder, followed by Mary Ann's groan. *Good, she's awake now*, he thought. *She'll take care of the kids.* But suddenly the thunder was so loud it sounded as if it was coming from the next room. It struck again, this time accompanied by a loud scream, and Mary Ann's kick, so powerful he jumped from fright, fell out of bed, and landed on the wood floor, injuring again his left hip. Lying on the floor and nursing a bruise, he tried to gather his wits. There was thunder for sure, or something pounding very loud. He looked up—Mary Ann leaned over the side of the bed and yelled at him. "DO SOMETHING, HUSBAND. GET UP!" As he sat up, dazed, he realized the noise was not thunder but pounding coming from the common wall of their bedroom with their guest room. Then he heard the muffled screams through the wall amidst the pounding.

It was their visitor, crying out for help. "NO! NO! NO! NOT YET. MISTER LIVINGSTON. HELP ME."

The commotion stunned Adam.

Mary Ann was waving her arms. "What are you waiting for?"

The Stranger wailed all the more: "I'M NOT READY, I'M NOT READY. No! Please!"

Adam still didn't move. It seemed surreal; he knew not what to make of it all.

But Mary Ann was not stunned or absent of mind. She bounded from the bed, lit the lantern on her side table, stepped past the crying twins in their cribs and dashed out of the bedroom.

Adam finally got to his feet, and though his limbs were half asleep and his hip in pain, followed his wife.

In the hall, Mary Ann cautiously opened the guest room door. But Adam was right behind her and reached over her and thrust the door open. Mary Ann held up her lantern, frozen in the hallway, but Adam took her lantern and pushed on into the room, holding the lantern high.

The guest room was also used for storage of miscellaneous items, including an odd assortment of crates, boxes, and unused furniture. It was not an attractive room, or even decorated with any intent. Set aside was a double bed, its headboard against the common wall with the master bedroom, a side table with wash basin, pitcher, linens, and a mirror on the wall.. Across from the bed was a chair and a writing table on which the Stranger had unfolded his bundle and a change of clothes and what appeared to be a well-used leather-bound book next to an unlit lantern.

Now inside the room, Adam quickly stepped to the man's bedside. The Stranger's frightened howls continued. His writhing body was on its back, half under a bed sheet. His limbs shook uncontrollably. He wore what appeared to be long underwear that now was thoroughly soaked with sweat. He looked like he had just been rescued from a shipwreck. His face perspired heavily, his eyes were wild as if seeing a vision of hell, and his mouth was parched as he gasped for life.

Mary Ann finally entered the room cautiously and stood somewhat shaken several feet from the side of the bed, but each time the Stranger screamed, or his limbs jerked, she backed away. The man was clearly mad. The twins in the next room cried all the more.

Over the withering protests of the man Adam tried to get his attention: "Xavier, what is it? What's wrong?"

Breathing heavily, Xavier's eyes, wild and bloodshot, focused on Adam and momentarily stopped his torment. He gawked at Adam as if seeing a ghost of frightening proportions. From quivering lips the Stranger exhaled repeatedly, trying to speak, but all that came out was spittle. Finally, he took a deep breath, focused, and begged Adam, "No! No! Please! Don't take me, I'm not done, there's so much to do, don't you understand. Please, please help me."

Henry entered the room and cowered behind his stepmother. Mary Ann glanced down and pulled Henry against her with one arm. The other she wrapped tightly about her own waist. Deep shadows slid across walls and ceiling from the one lantern Adam still held over Xavier.

Adam finally requisitioned his courage, leaned over the Stranger, and gently shook the man, trying to wake him from a nightmare. "Wake, old man. Wake up. You're nightmarin'!"

The Stranger, still shaking but not as wildly, gazed up at Adam, his face etched in pain as tears streamed from his bloodshot eyes. His shaking hands reached out for Adam, which Adam quickly took hold of.

"Oh, dear, dear host, my dear Mister Livingston, gracious, merciful you are to me, a sinner, a lost soul, I am," cried the Stranger. "He comes for me, I am lost, please help my poor soul."

Adam gently shook the man's hands and arms in encouragement, "Nonsense man. No one has come for you. You're safe here in this bed. Wake from your dream, I say."

The Stranger's fright-filled gaze bounced from Adam to Mary Ann and then to Henry, who had now crept closer to the foot of the bed, their shadows enlarged, dark and brooding on the wall behind them. The Stranger's voice was now calmer, but still filled with fright. "My dear, dear man and Madam," the Stranger said. "My dark, dark past has caught up with me…a fool I a…a lost fool, for eternity."

Mary Ann, showing some compassion, tried to help, "Please, listen to my husband. You are no fool. Sick perhaps, but you are here with us. Safe. Not lost."

"No, no, it is true. We are all lost, all lost, even now, without, without—"

"Without what, old man?" Adam asked. "How can I help you when you blather on?"

As if that was the one question he did not want to hear, the Stranger fell into a fit of uncontrolled grief, crying with deep sobs.

"I am dying. I know it. I've known it for some time, but didn't know when, and I put this off. Oh, I should not have put it off. It is tonight, I am sure. Please, please, Mister Livingston, fetch a priest, a priest, a Roman priest for me before I die. I must confess…"

It was as if the air had suddenly been sucked from the room. Mary Ann's compassion abruptly vanished. Adam backed away, reflecting his wife's reaction. But he didn't know the half of it.

Mary Ann, no longer fearful or compassionate stepped sharply forward. Venom dripped from her every pore. "A priest! A priest? You want a Catholic priest? The priests are all gone, gone to hell. Burned them, we did."

Adam, being no fan of religion or Catholics, was first taken back by Xavier asking for a priest, but Mary Ann's response unnerved him. Religion or not, here was a man, their guest, in obvious mental if not physical distress, and mocking him was wrong. Adam was speechless not knowing what to do or say, caught between a bitter woman and a dying man.

"Oh, sister," said the Stranger. "Such a thing, meaningless, I've seen real men burned, burned alive for their goodness."

"Who are you, man, really," said Adam. "Where did you come from?"

Xavier found it difficult to speak, still in a state of fear, his breath short, his limbs trembling. "I was a Jesuit missionary from France to the Yazoos and Choctaws, North Louisiana. We were suppressed. Exiled. My friends killed. I stayed, but failed. Please. Last Rites, the Church's Last Rites, I beg of you. Find a Roman priest for me, I need to—"

Mary Ann screamed at the Stranger as if the dying man was the devil himself, "HOW DARE YOU! ADAM, HE IS A GODDAMNED ROMAN PRIEST!"

Adam, wondering how he had got into this fix, in his own house in the middle of the night no less, finally turned on the Stranger. "Xavier, or whatever your name is, you have come to us falsely. I do not know if you are dying or not, but I swore an oath and so did my wife that no Roman priest would ever cross the threshold of this house. God be dammed and you, too, for your fraud and bringing a curse to this house. We know of no priest in these parts, and if there were, we doubly swear he should never pass the threshold of our home."

"Oh, Mister Livingston," the Stranger pleaded, "have mercy on me, a poor man who begs your forgiveness. My soul, my soul—"

"Such rubbish," said Mary Ann. "Let him die." She turned to the shaking man whose perspiration had soaked through the linens of her guest bed. "I hope you die. Be gone with you. Tonight!" She turned rabid on Adam. "Get him out of my house. Throw him out, now. I demand it."

But Adam, upset with his guest as he was, had his limits and rebuked Mary Ann for her assault on their guest. "It is my house, too, woman. I hate religion as much as you, but common decency says we wait till daybreak, if he lives that long."

Mary Ann seethed at Adam but held her tongue.

The Stranger, breathless, implored again, "Will you not find me a Catholic priest?"

Adam, now backing away from the sick man, spoke quietly, but firmly. "No! Never!"

"Burn in hell, priest," Mary Ann snarled.

"Mary Ann!" snapped Adam. "That's enough! Let him die in peace if he must."

Mary Ann seethed at Adam as if horns protruded from his forehead. In turn, Adam stared at Mary Ann wondering what had come over her. She was not herself. He was quick to notice that Henry had backed away from his stepmother and now cowered in the hall beyond the door. Eve curiously enough was nowhere to be seen, though surely she heard the goings-on.

To Adam's shame, Mary Ann was not done. Turning on their guest she launched her most vicious, scathing attack. Adam cringed at its demonic timbre: "I want to watch you die, I want to see Hell tear out your soul, I want to hear you scream in terror, for no doubt you have brought a curse upon our land, our country with your insufferable religion."

As Mary Ann raged on, the Stranger gazed at her, it seemed to Adam, with astonishing compassion. He marveled how her vociferous hatred appeared to heal their ill guest—his breathing settled down, his shaking stopped, and his bloodshot eyes became clear as they became transfixed on Mary Ann's face. The transformation must have affected Mary Ann as well, for suddenly she stopped her harangue and stared back at the Stranger.

As if by some supernatural endowment the Stranger's face, still moist with perspiration, glowed. Then, without the aid of arms or hands his torso peculiarly flexed at his waist and gradually he sat upright in the bed. The otherworldly movement frightened Adam and he backed away. The Stranger suddenly scowled at Mary Ann, a tremor on his lips. But when Mary Ann attempted to reprise her verbal assault, she could not speak. Try as she might, her lips would not open. Forbidden by some supernatural power to speak, her body also froze. She could neither turn her head, nor move her arms and legs. Immobile, frozen in place, she was forced to stare at the Stranger sitting up strangely in her guest bed staring back at her. Then, suddenly, reality shifted for Adam Livingston.

In a cacophonous voice the Stranger pronounced his malediction:

> *I curse you woman by the power of the Almighty. I curse the children of your womb for their guardians will take leave. By the transcendence of the heavens above they will die young, and by the depths of hell below you will die estranged and shamed.*

Sharply turning to Adam, Xavier continued the malediction:

> *Adam Livingston, my ungracious host, I curse you and all you so proudly call your own. Your house will be possessed and become a laughingstock of demons. Torn asunder it will be, destroyed, and erased forever. I curse your crops, they will fail. Your livestock will die grotesquely, and your barn will be consumed by heaven's fire. All you have will cease to be, but never will it be forgotten. Yet, the children of Esther's womb will thrive and be blessed forever more because they love Him who created them. Truly, you have spoken rightly that you hate religion, and the grace and mercy gifted you, none of which you deserved, will be removed. A curse brought on by you alone, in the Name of Him who gives me strength and judges all.*

Adam was afraid; he had never told this man the name of his first wife. But being an intensely proud and self-made man, Adam was even more resentful. That God would take Esther from him was reason enough to hate the Almighty, but to repay his efforts to live honestly and labor for the good of his family with a curse from a Stranger who took advantage of his hospitality was more than a good man could stand. There would be revenge, and it would be without mercy on his part. God be damned.

And then, as if by some supernatural oath, the Stranger suddenly turned from his wrath to great sorrow, and the tremors and shaking began anew. Pangs of sadness seized his demeanor. His tear-filled eyes transformed his features from that of a seething beast ready to devour Livingston to a woeful beggar seeking forgiveness from heaven.

"Oh, my God, my Jesus," cried the man. "What have I done? My anger! Lord, I have brought disaster upon this man. Forgive me. Forgive him, for we are but vapor, sooty ash. Mercy! Mercy! Sinners all. Forgive me, forgive us, Lord. Be merciful...remember their children, Spirit of saints. Shall they die, too? Oh, most merciful Mother, pray for us at the hour of our death."

As he prayed with great sorrow, his ability to speak with any clarity fell to broken words and mumblings. Finally, he fell back onto the bed and his body went limp except for his arms that were raised up to heaven as it were. Then his tremors and shaking ceased and his eyes became transfixed, or so it seemed, on something beyond the room. Tears continued to flow, and speech softened to a whisper. "*O me Iesu, indulge peccata nostra, conserva nos ab igne inferni, duc omnes ad caeli gloriam, pracecipue tua misericordia indigentes.*"

Adam, filled with trepidation, glanced sideways at Mary Ann, whose eyes were fixed on the Stranger.

After a brief moment, their guest's arms fell to his side, he exhaled a slight breath, and his eyes glazed over.

A moment later a gust of wind came through the windows and extinguished the lantern. The sudden darkness inside matched the pitch-black outside.

It was then that a soft glow floated into the doorway followed by Eve with a lit lantern, its flame flickering but bright. In a sad voice she simply asked, "Is he gone, now?"

Adam looked at the wall next to the bed. On it hung the large mirror that years ago, during Esther's burial preparation, hung behind her casket. Except now the mirror was not covered. He stared at the room's reflection in the mirror. It seemed that black vapor rushed across the floor from under the bed to the door, coalesced behind Eve, and dissipated into the floorboards. As it did, Eve appeared to shudder.

For a good two minutes the family made no movement but watched to see if the old man would move, or speak, or show signs of life. But the man neither moved nor made any sound. Although the twins still cried, Mary Ann, ramrod straight, continued to stare at the man as if she was waiting for Hell to open up and swallow him in some sort of apocalyptic spectacle.

Finally, Adam took Eve's lantern and held it over the man's eyes. The bright light did not affect the man's pupils; they were fully dilated. The man's chest was still; there was no breath. Adam felt for a pulse; there was none. But most sobering was the man's face. A moment ago, his translucent skin was tinged with the blood-red of life; now it was drained and white as death should be. Adam closed the Stranger's eyes and pulled the sweat-soaked sheet over his head. He had died, as he expected.

Adam turned to his wife. She didn't look too happy; evidently Hell was not going to cooperate. And yet the twins cried. Finally, Adam spoke: "George and Martha."

Without looking at him Mary Ann simply said, "It's after midnight—their second birthday." With that she turned from the bed and left the room. A few moments later the twins' crying ceased. *Somethin' about women,* Adam thought—*even in times of trauma, they're still mothers. She's right. Why wean them? She's nursing both at once.*

He sensed Eve looking at him. He turned to her. She had that innocent, begging look when at table she was asking him if she could pray. *Why was it that people wanted to pray at the dying of people? Mary Ann was out of the room...*he nodded.

As if she was in church, Eve stepped to the foot of the bed, folded her hands on top of the frame like it was an altar, and prayed aloud but quietly, probably so Mary Ann would not hear:

"Most gracious God. We thank you for the privilege to know Fr. Xavier briefly, to feed him, and to give him a bed to lie in. We do not understand why you have taken him from us, but we trust you, for there is no one else to trust. God, please give Fr. Xavier the eternal rest he deserves in his love for you. May your kind light shine upon him; may his soul, now departed from this world, find joy with you in heaven, and with the angels, the saints, and our mothers. Amen."

When she finished Adam said, "I'll go get Jacob to stay up with our guest until we can bury him in the morning."

"Papa, I'll stay until you return. Put the lantern there," and she pointed to the writing desk next to the bundle of the man's belongings. Adam did as she asked. She then took the chair at the writing table, turned it around, and sat in it facing the bed, whereupon she bowed her head.

Adam left the room, speaking to his son as he did. "Okay, Henry, back to bed. It's over."

Without hesitation, Henry obeyed.

2

Eve had heard the Stranger when he began to scream for help and pound on the wall. She had a sense that something was about to happen which would prevent her from talking with the man in the morning as she and Bethany had planned. Not wanting to jeopardize the possibility, she didn't want to be in the middle of another fight with Mary Ann. So Eve stayed in her room and listened by her door. When she heard the Stranger beg Papa for a priest before he died, that confirmed Bethany's suspicion that the man was a Catholic. *How deliciously ironic that was,* she thought. God was not going to let Papa or her stepmother cut God out of their family quite as easily as Papa and Mary Ann hoped. Eve concluded that the many prayers she had offered up to her mother in heaven were being answered. But how exactly she didn't fully know. It seemed that a grand adventure was afoot.

Then, as she listened to more of the conversation, his identity was confirmed. The man was not just a Catholic but a *Catholic priest...and a missionary, no less*. That put him in an entirely different class of people, like the McSherrys and their Rosary garden. When it seemed inevitable that the man was going to die, she quickly devised a risky mission. A mission that if Papa or Mary Ann found out, hell would be to pay.

Judging her entrance carefully, she walked into the guest room just after the man had died. As soon as she rounded the corner and came into the guest room, she quickly scanned the room. She was surprised that her lantern was the only one lit.

"Is he gone?" she had asked. But no one answered. It was as if they were not sure and kept up their gaze at the man for the longest time, as if they expected him to rise from the dead. Eve knew the man was dead. How she knew, she wasn't sure. Perhaps it was the cold chill she felt standing there in the door. It was odd because the twins were crying up a storm and yet neither did she feel the urge to go quiet them down nor did their mother make any gesture as if Eve should. The room was stopped in time, and her parents frozen in place.

She took the time to look around. The man's bundle of possessions was on the writing table. It sat behind her father's back, and luckily it was in the shadows. Like a gift from God the item she sought sat on top of the bundle.

Her heart raced. How would she ever accomplish this? Her father, stepmother, and little brother were all there. She was outnumbered. *Patience* was the thought that came to mind. So when Papa and Mary Ann seemed not to know what to do, Eve prayed to herself...for patience, for wisdom, and for the success of her quest.

Then the most amazing thing happened; well, several things. Her papa took her lantern and held it over Xavier's body to see if he was really dead, she guessed. Then Mary Ann left to feed the twins. Suddenly, with her stepmother out of the room, she felt the urge to pray for Fr. Xavier, but dared not without Papa's permission. She looked up at him, hoping he would know what she was asking. He looked at her as if trying to discern her request. Then he closed his mouth tightly and nodded his head. She smiled inside, walked reverently to the foot of the bed, and prayed aloud but quietly—her stepmother need not hear.

When she was done, Papa decided to go and get Mister Foster to sit up with the Stranger's body, as was the custom. Most people would be afraid to do it. There was no chance Mary Ann would. And her father would have other things to do in preparation for the man's burial. But she, Eve, the daughter of her mother, was not afraid, especially since the man was a missionary priest. "Papa, I'll stay with him until you return. Put the lantern there." She pointed to the writing desk next to the Stranger's bundle.

Would he take her suggestion? He did. Would he take Henry to bed? *Please Papa take Henry to bed; he won't listen to me.* Papa did that, too.

So Eve took the chair at the writing table, turned it, and sat in honor of the man before her. She would be left alone with him. She could hardly contain her excitement.

But she wasn't really alone.

When her father put Henry back to bed and had left to get Jacob Foster, Mary Ann was still awake feeding the twins. Papa would not be gone long. How long would the twins feed before they fell asleep? Eve sat in the chair before Xavier's body and prayed. *Mama, pray for me. You know what I should do. God has sent me a gift. Please let me acquire it safely.* She hoped Mary Ann would go to sleep after feeding the twins. But that was not to be.

Eve heard the twins settle down, stop feeding, and her stepmother put them down in their cribs. But Mary Ann didn't lie down. Instead, she put on her boots. *What's going on now?* A moment later Mary Ann stood in the guest bedroom doorway.

"Eve," said Mary Ann, "I'm going to tell Sam what's going on. I'll be back shortly."

"Yes'm," said Eve, with only a glance at her stepmother.

As Mary Ann walked down the stairs, Eve listened closely for other sounds; there were none. Henry was asleep, and the twins, too. She had to move quickly and quietly.

As soon as Mary Ann shut the front door and walked off the porch, Eve got up from her chair and turned around. She smiled that she had been so clever as to ask Papa to put her lantern on the writing table behind her. She was glad he didn't insist on putting it next to Xavier's bed. On top of the man's folded clothes was a thick leather book. She grabbed it and opened it. It appeared to be in two different languages, perhaps Latin on the left-hand page, and another language on the right, maybe a translation. She turned to the title page: there was a line that read, "Latin Et François." So, the other language was probably French. But she couldn't read either. She remembered Michael McCoy telling her about such a book when she attended Mass in Conewago. He called the book a Roman Missal. She put it aside, and quickly and carefully dug her hands into the man's bundle. She felt strange pilfering a grown man's luggage, but the man was dead, and she needed what he had. It didn't take long. Momentarily she pulled out a second book, this one not as thick, but it was in English. The cover said, "Christian Prayers." She opened it. It was all in English with some Latin. This was what she wanted. She put the book of Christian Prayers on top of the missal and dug further—just clothes, nothing more inside. Then she noticed that the top flap to the bundle had an inside pocket and there was something lumpy inside. She opened the top, put in her hand, and pulled out a cross with a small statue of Jesus nailed to it. It was a crucifix, she thought it was called. Priests used this to bless people. But what was this other thing. It was a string of beads, and at the end of it was another cross...or rather another crucifix. It was but a moment before she recalled several people at the McSherrys' used beads like this when they were praying the Rosary in the garden. This was a Rosary carved in wood. She could use this to pray to her mother in heaven, like Catholics used it to pray to Jesus' mother Mary.

Her heart was beating rapidly now, and she felt her face flush. Dare she take all of this? It is what she had planned to do, but should she? Where would she put them so her stepmother could not find them? That was going to be a problem. She wasn't sure what to do. She picked up the two books, the crucifix, and the Rosary, turned around and stood over Xavier's body. Reverently, she bowed her head and prayed aloud, but softly. "Fr. Xavier, may I have these sacred items that were yours in this life. I have a long life ahead of me and many problems for which I need God's help. I think my mother in heaven would want me to have these. What do you say? What do I do? I don't know even where to keep them where they will be safe. Please help me."

She had barely stopped praying when she heard a quiet but very clear voice. "Eve, you must for sure take them. It is God's will and no doubt your mother's, too."

Eve whirled around to face the door. It was Bethany, wearing her night dress and a long shawl. "Quickly, child," said Bethany. "Give me what you have. I will keep them safely in our cabin with your Bible. I'll explain them all to you. Mary Ann is taking her time to tell Sam all that has happened. I heard just a bit and then excused myself to come check on you and the children. God is good, child."

Eve cried for joy—her prayer had been answered—and so quickly. She gave over the two books, the crucifix and the Rosary beads to Bethany, who, too, seemed to understand that her unannounced appearance had been guided by Providence. Bethany wrapped the items in the folds of her shawl and quickly left. Eve tidied up Xavier's belongings and promptly sat down to pray again. The adventure was heating up.

3

Shortly thereafter, Adam rode into the yard with Jacob Foster, an older man, slight in stature, and solemn in demeanor. Jacob lived but a mile down the road in Smithfield. Waiting for them was Sam, who came off his porch and took the reins of the two horses. No words were exchanged as Adam and Jacob Foster dismounted and entered the main house.

Once inside, Adam lit two lanterns and led Jacob up the stairs. Upon entering the room, Eve rose from her chair and curtsied to her father and Jacob.

"Thank you, Miss Livingston," said Jacob.

Eve picked up her lantern and quietly left the room.

Jacob put his lantern on the writing table where hers had been. He took the chair, moved it slightly away from the bed, and sat down. Adam placed the second lantern on the side table and stepped back. But as soon as he did, both lanterns went out leaving behind pitch darkness. Eve reentered the room with several candles and put them around the room on tables. She lit the candles with a spare candle and stepped back. But no sooner had she done so than one by one the candles flickered and extinguished themselves. She and Adam re-lighted them, but with the same result. Only Eve's lantern stayed lit.

"Mister Foster," said Eve, "I will leave you my lantern; it will stay lit." She set it on the writing table behind him.

"Thank you, Miss Livingston."

With that, Adam and Eve backed out of the room and left Jacob Foster to sit with the corpse until daylight, as was the custom.

Suffice to say, the Stranger's death and curse rattled both Adam and Mary Ann, and neither could sleep. In their bedroom, Adam paced and Mary Ann fidgeted. For two people who didn't believe in the supernatural, their souls were restless, confused, and left in some degree of fear for their future. Finally, they both went downstairs. Adam made a fire. Mary Ann heated up the coffee pot, and there they sat, wide awake, without a word between them until dawn broke.

With the rising sun, Adam brought Sam to the room to size up the Stranger for a box, then went off looking for a place to bury the body. There was no way he was going to bury a Catholic in the family plot next to Nwanne and contaminate their sacred burial ground. Eve suggested that burying a Christian next to Nwanne would sanctify the land, but Adam would have none of it. Instead, he chose the small clearing in the wood far behind the barn, where no roots would obstruct the digging and no one would notice the disturbed ground afterwards.

It took but a few hours to make the box from scraps of wood Sam had stored in the barn. There would be no ceremony or remembrance of the man's life, for no one knew much of it. Good riddance, thought Adam. Mary Ann kept out of the proceedings entirely. Eve insisted that the body, out of human decency, be wrapped in linen, so Adam found an old grey cloth that was soiled and about to be cut up for rags. The men took the box to the guest bedroom and set it on the floor next to the bed. Eve lined the box with the grey linen, and Sam and Jacob then put the body inside and nailed the lid shut. Sam and Jacob dug the grave, throwing aside the small rocks they came upon. There was no wagon path to the clearing, so the three men and Henry were pallbearers to the grave site. As soon as the box was in the hole, Adam gave Sam instructions to fill in the grave and make it obscure. He didn't want anyone stumbling across it any time in his lifetime.

Hours later, after the deed was done, and after Jacob had been paid and trotted off, Adam could not find Eve in the house. Mary Ann took no notice of his daughter's absence and Bethany was setting the table for supper. It would be dark soon, the wind was blowing gustily, and rain threatened. Adam lit a lantern, went out, and walked through the darkening wood to the Stranger's grave site. Eve was not there, but it was evident that she had been well after the men had left. At the head of the grave a foot-high triangular cairn of stone had been erected. Around the perimeter of the grave, which had been only slightly rounded and would settle flat in the coming months, was a neatly placed row of round stones like a fence, and on top of the grave, most conspicuously, were larger stones in the shape of a Christian cross.

This was Eve's work. Adam was peeved, but he loved his daughter. She had not made a scene about praying for the man on his death bed, nor had she argued about the linen; and although he had told the men there was to be no grave markers, he had said nothing to Eve. She was a young woman now, fourteen, old enough to marry.

Movement caught his eye. He looked up. Eve was sitting on the edge of the clearing at the base of an elm, her knees pulled up to her chin and her dress pulled down over her knees to her ankles. The off-white dress was now covered with brown earth, for she had been kneeling to place the stones that the men had dug up. It was getting cold and no doubt rain would soon fall. Eve was watching her father. He walked the twenty or so feet to the elm and his daughter sitting on the ground and stared at her as if to ask something.

"Mama told me to do it," she said.

Adam glanced back at the stones that marked, outlined, and decorated the grave. He was not happy about what she had done, but he also knew that Mary Ann would never venture back to this clearing, nor would she ride Apple back here. There was no path, even for a horse. The wind began to howl in the tree tops and the breeze that maneuvered through the trees turned cool and fresh.

"What does your mother tell you to do now?" said Adam.

"Papa, she's prayin' for us—against the Wizard."

"The Wizard?"

Adam crouched down and lifted his lantern to look into his daughter's eyes. She stared back. They were beautiful turquoise eyes, clear, wide-open, and unblinking. Whiffs of her hair blew across her face. She made no effort to pull them out of the way. She didn't smile, but neither did she frown. She was at peace.

Adam turned back to look once more at the grave, and that's when he saw what else she had done. She had gathered handfuls of rich, green moss and transplanted it around the perimeter stones and over the entire top of the grave. It was a natural grave blanket; no doubt it would take root and spread. At the same time, the earth surrounding the grave was barren, as it had been under the heavy canopy of the trees.

He would let it be.

4

Most Feared Master of Shadows,

I am relieved that my hastening the passing of this so-called Stranger (who was anything but a Stranger, and rather a feared enemy) has not brought my further confinement. After all, it was you, Dragon Master, who worried that this Incognito would join with the renegade Jesuit. Although there was little I had to do insofar as the man was already on the verge of death from exposure and malnutrition—the work no doubt of my celebrated peers. All I had to do was suggest that Mary Ann, behind the slave woman's back, add a bit more butter, salt, and sugar to the food. The starving man ate more than he could digest, and natural law (the Almighty's invention) took care of the rest.

Now that the sojourner is out of the way, and you seem to be pleased, although one more soul in Glory is never reason for celebration, perhaps I can concentrate on my target as you have charged.

There are weaknesses. I can attack the Livingstons at the very source of their trust and effort—their self-sufficiency. But I must be creative and subtle. Fun and games, seduction, persistent and pervasive; that should be my framework.

Alas, I have forgotten the Fire-Breather in the room, for the Incognito has opened wide the gates for the haunting arts by cursing Livingston and all he owns, thus demanding that the Almighty allow my presence. I am thus assured barrier-free access to corrupt and destroy his fantasy of work and family. The Almighty is so foolish in this, thinking that ushering me into Livingston's life will somehow save his soul. It is as if we have deluded the Creator, for which I will gladly accept credit.

But there is no time to waste except to ensure that we are able to waste what time remains.

At your sinful service,
Cyn Namrasit, OPSD

Chapter 30
To Create What Others Want Destroyed

1

June 27, 1794.

Everyday Bethany's cooking would generate two buckets of food scraps. Into one bucket she tossed scraps for the pigs and in another scraps to be composted, which would decompose and be used as fertilizer for the vegetable garden. The pigs loved the scraps and would nearly run Henry down when he showed up. Perhaps that was why Henry was shy about feeding his pigs...they might feed on him, which was one reason Bethany never put meat scraps in the pig feed bucket.

Eve was peeved. Before Papa left to supervise his day laborers in the fields, he made a point of asking her to supervise Henry's feeding of his pigs. She wondered why Papa didn't just tell Henry to do it. But she knew Papa had, and that Henry had said he would...but he hadn't.

So Eve followed her twelve-year-old brother, who carried the pig scrap bucket from the summer kitchen to the pigs' quarters just beyond the barn.

"Do as Papa says, Henry. We want meat, not fat."

"I told you. I know what I'm doing," said Henry.

"Well, yesterday it didn't look like it," said Eve.

"Leave me alone."

"I promised Papa I'd help you."

Henry stopped in his tracks, turned and held the pail out to his sister. "Then you do it. You're such an expert."

"They're your pigs."

"Then why does everyone else eat what I raise. Seems everybody should be helping with the slop."

Eve admitted to herself she didn't have an answer for that.

Henry looked at her as if to say, *Finally something shut you up.* He turned and carried the pail to the pen.

"Scatter the scraps all over the pen, not just in the trough," Eve said. "They need exercise."

"If I do that, we'll be eating mud. You want mud in your meat?"

"There be no mud in my food, maybe mud in your eye. And give them plenty of water. Did you carry water to their trough today? Papa says..."

"Stop it already," said Henry. "They can drink from their wallow."

"Uck," said Eve as she faked a puking incident.

Henry opened the gate to the pig pen, walked in with the pail held above the pigs that quickly gathered around him, and shut the gate. Eve stepped up on the lower rail of the fence and watched over the top. He put half the scraps in the trough and tossed the rest around the pen. When he finished he turned back toward the barn. "You hear that?"

Eve twisted around and listened. The open door at the east end of the barn faced them. Coming from inside the barn was a reverberating noise that sounded like a metallic bird's chirping.

"We got crows in the loft again," said Henry as he shook out the pail of the last few scraps, maneuvered around a few pigs that were gorging on mud-covered scraps, and left the pen. Eve stepped down from the fence and they walked to the barn.

Once inside the barn they craned their necks, expecting to see large, black birds fluttering between rafters, chattering, looking for a way out of their entrapment. But there were no birds in sight, yet the chirping continued.

Trying to follow the sound that echoed in the large interior, they were finally drawn to a wool horse blanket lying on scattered hay in a corner. The blanket seemed to be moving up and down as if something was under it trying to get out. Black smoke seeped from the edges of the blanket in seductive pulses in sync with the blanket's undulations and slithered into the hay. Henry crept closer with Eve just behind him. As they closed in they heard the muffled but ominous growl of a cat battling something still unseen.

Suddenly the middle of the blanket, on its own, bulged up toward them. The shock was automatic. Eve shrieked and jumped back. At the same moment Henry's curiosity got the better of him and he grabbed the corner of the blanket and jerked it back to reveal Cleopatra, who screeched, jumped out of the blanket's folds, and scurried away.

"What was she doing under there?" Eve wondered aloud.

Once the kids settled from the scare, Henry folded the blanket and put it back on the saddle rack where it should have been.

2

That night at supper, Henry relayed the experience in the barn with the bird sounds and finding Cleopatra under the horse blanket. Adam thought nothing of it and scowled at this son. "Henry, if you were doing your job your mind wouldn't wander so much."

"Papa," Eve said, "I was with Henry the whole time, and he was feeding the pigs just like you told him. Remember you sent me to help him?"

"And did you hear the birds like Henry says?" Adam asked his daughter.

Eve paused. "Yes, I did. It was most strange. We looked everywhere and the birds kept chirping. I've never even heard a bird make such a noise, and it was strongest where that horse blanket was on the hay. But when we found Cleopatra, she ran away, and the bird sounds suddenly stopped."

Adam found himself listening carefully to Eve, who was more believable. "Did the birds come back?"

"We never saw any birds, Papa. Not then or after. But they could've flown away and we just didn't see them."

Adam glanced at Mary Ann, who just shrugged her shoulders and that was the end of the bird chirping story...until bedtime.

Mary Ann usually turned in to bed an hour before Adam who made the rounds, sometimes with Sam, of all the outbuildings, the pens, and the barn to ensure doors were closed and gates shut, and no foul play involving a coyote was evident on the property.

Adam came into the house, shut the door, checked on the summer kitchen coals, then climbed the stairs, changed into his bedclothes, cracked the window for ventilation, and turned down his bedside lantern. But no sooner had he closed his eyes than he heard birds chirping outside his window. It was the oddest sound of a bird, however, he could ever recall, for it didn't sound like a bird at all, but rather a mechanical clanging of two piece of steel. Yet it was familiar, as if he had heard it a thousand times before, but many years ago. The sound and his own curiosity prevented him from dozing off.

At first he tried to locate the sound without ever moving from his bed. Was the sound outside his window? In the hall? In his armoire? The attic? It was also odd because the sound didn't fade in and out, as if a bird was flying around outside. It was steady and constant: "CLINK. CLINK. CLINK."

"What is that noise, husband?" Mary Ann was now awake.

"I don't know. It just started. It woke you?"

"It would wake the dead."

They listened for a moment. "CLINK. CLINK. CLINK. CLINK. CLINK. CLINK." It seemed it would never stop.

"It's not a bird that I have ever heard," said Adam.

"Nor I," said Mary Ann. "Sounds like metal."

"Like two large nails, or a hammer hitting a nail lightly like...or a knife being sharpened."

"Can't you stop it?" Mary Ann asked.

"I'm sure I could if I knew what it was and if it wasn't a bird flying about."

Just then a glow appeared in the hall visible through their open door. Eve, in a long white nightgown appeared holding a lantern. "Papa, what's that noise?"

Mary Ann suddenly sat up. "Scissors! They're scissors—shearing cloth, that is what it is. But who?" Mary Ann stared at Eve, who obviously was holding a lantern, not scissors. Mary Ann swung out of bed and hastened to her sewing chest by the window. She reached in and withdrew her scissors, the same ones she used to cut up Esther's table covering. She opened and closed the scissors several times. The sound was exactly what they were hearing. But the sound was coming from outside their window.

Mary Ann turned to Adam. "Well, what are you doing in bed?"

That miffed Adam. *She's already up, why doesn't SHE go out and stop it?* he thought.

But after a moment, he swung his legs out of bed, struck a flint and lit his lantern, grabbed his shillelagh, put on his boots, and traipsed out of the room.

"It's the same sound we heard in the barn," said Eve.

Adam lifted his lantern to see her clearly. "Is it now! Are you sure?"

"Oh, yes. Very sure.

They stopped and listened. "CLINK. CLINK. CLINK. CLINK. CLINK. CLINK." It was unabated, although now it sounded as if it came from downstairs. He turned, gripped his shillelagh tight, swore to himself to beat the person who was making the sound, and descended the stairs. At the bottom, he glanced up to see Eve at the top, content for now to stay put.

In the foyer he stopped to listen and discern from what direction the sound came. At first it sounded as if it came from whence he came, back up the stairs. But when he started back up the stairs, the sound seemed to shift to the gathering hall. He stepped into the gathering hall and stood next to the inoperative and partially disassembled loom. He listened. The regular CLINK, CLINK, CLINK, like a cold heartbeat, was still there, but now it came from behind him. Whipping around, his stick at the ready, the sound surrounded him, but also seemed to fade as if the noise was now coming from outside.

Losing no time, and anxious as ever to stop the teasing of the infernal nuisance, he threw open the entrance door and stepped onto the porch. As soon as he did the CLINKING sound was off the porch and into the yard, drawing Adam further and further into the night. Standing on the ground a good rod in front of the porch, the sound was now suddenly softer, and he wondered if indeed it was some strange bird, now flying off never to be heard from again. It became quiet except for the crickets, frogs, the wind rustling leaves, and the occasional flutter of a bat feasting on flying insects. He gripped and swung his shillelagh, planning to hit something. Looking about the sky for the "scissors bird," he stared at the dim light of a thin, waning crescent moon, but saw nothing, not even a bat.

3

About two weeks later, Adam began to craft a replacement cradle for one of his harvesting scythes. He wanted to craft it himself, not trusting any of the hired help or even Sam to complete the woodcraft to his standards. As it happened, he found himself working into the night in a corner of his woodshop in the barn. When he was done, he made doubly sure that the lanterns were fully extinguished. The barn with its contents of dry hay, straw, and wood, along with its voluminous nature was easily susceptible to fire. Replacing a barn, its livestock, and feed would be significantly more difficult than a cabin. Whenever he thought of such things, his heart and mind reached out to Nwanne and his own need for revenge on the McCulloughs.

A little after midnight he headed for the house. There was a full moon, and its brightness fully illuminated the farm. Halfway across the wide yard between barn and house he stood for a moment and admired the moonlit buildings. Here it was dead of night and everything was brightly lit. He glanced up at the bright orb hanging overhead. As he squinted at the bright round light, it immediately began to rapidly dim. Was he witnessing a lunar eclipse? He remembered a lunar eclipse from years ago, which took hours to darken as it passed into and then out of the earth's shadow. What he was seeing now was much different and faster. In a matter of seconds the moon went from full to half to a thin crescent and then it was fully extinguished. It stayed dark for a while before the shadow of something (like the earth) moved off revealing a bright white crescent, then a half, and then full. Then the occulting repeated. He stood frozen in place, mesmerized and scared by the astronomical phenomenon, not knowing what to make of it. When the eclipse began the third time, Adam began to shake with fear as if the end of the world was upon him. He realized he was vulnerable, standing alone in the large yard without protection; and yet he could not move nor take his eyes from the sight.

Then it happened. When the moon went dark for the third time, it stayed that way, and all the stars of heaven seemed to burst from the blackness surrounding him. It was indeed a cloudless night. Suddenly, there was a roll of thunder and the sound of a thunder CRACK. It was so loud it nearly knocked Adam to the ground. He looked all around. Stars were clearly visible to the horizon in every direction. He gazed back in the direction of where the full moon had shown. In its place were stars, bright stars. The moon had disappeared.

Adam's heart beat hard and a deep dread fell upon him. Just as there was no moonlight, so there was no sound. Everything went still. He was suddenly in a mysterious realm where rubbing cricket wings, croaking frogs, rustling leaves, fluttering bats, and howling coyotes were banned. But there was a sound—CLINK, CLINK, CLINK—the faint opening and closing of shears that had haunted them weeks ago. Unlike any time before, he became frightened and afraid to move. Afraid of what was next. He listened carefully. The sound was not loud. It was gentle. No, it wasn't the sound of scissors cutting cloth, it was something else, something even more familiar, something warm and lovely and yet contentious. This was the sound of something he longed to hear again in spite of the problems it would reawaken. It was the rhythm of making cloth. CLACK. CLACK. CLACK.

4

In the middle of the night, Eve woke from a dream. It had been weeks since she and Henry had heard the CLINK, CLINK, CLINK noise in the barn. In Eve's dream, she was conversing with Esther, her mother, about how she needed to learn to weave because it would provide a counter impulse to the destructive forces present in her life. Eve agreed with her mother (in the dream) that she (Eve) should begin again to weave and learn the art. But in some ways Eve had very little sway over Papa, especially since Mary Ann was so set against the loom's presence in the house. In the dream, Eve told her mother, Esther, that she, Esther, needed to tell Papa to fix the loom because Papa would not listen to her, Eve, that is. And so, as it was left (in the dream), Esther agreed to talk to Adam, but she was unsure exactly how so that he would listen. Eve told her mother that she should then talk to the angels and they would know how. To that Mama was silent, then leaned over and kissed her daughter goodbye, for in her dream, Eve was laying on her bed and Mama was standing next to it. As soon as her mother left, Eve woke up. At least she thought she woke up. It was the middle of the night, the moon was bright, and she felt exhausted even though she had never left her bed. She glanced around her room, listened to the sounds of crickets and frogs in the distance, then closed her eyes and went back to sleep.

Hours later she woke up to daylight and the sound of CLINK, CLINK, CLINK. She had slept in, which she wasn't used to doing. Recognizing the sound, her heart jumped in fear as if the scissors bird, as Papa called the sound, had returned. But then she listened more carefully and her heart jumped again, this time in excitement. Eve jumped out of bed and hurried down the stairs to the rhythm of CLACK, CLACK, CLACK.

There, in the gathering hall Papa sat at the loom. He was working the shuttle, testing it out, she guessed, for there was no yarn or thread in the loom, and there were still parts of the loom lying about with Papa's tools. Shyly she entered the room in her bare feet and long white nightgown and stared at her father. "Does it work?"

"It will," said Papa. "Perhaps, by the end of the day. You'll be weaving by tomorrow, I promise. I still have to make a new beater bar and heddle beam."

Eve turned and looked around the room with concern.

"She's in the kitchen with Bethany. You missed breakfast, but they saved some for you."

"She's not going to like that you fixed this for me."

"We had a talk...leave it at that. One rule. Don't weave when the twins are trying to sleep or feed."

Eve thought about that. Sleeping and feeding was about all they did. That also meant she couldn't weave after they went to bed. She looked over the loom. It was big. "Can we move this to the barn someplace?"

Her papa thought about that for a moment. "That's not a bad idea in one respect. But the dust generated in the barn would make your finished cloth very dirty, and the new woven cloth would absorb the smell of manure." He shook his head. "You need a weaving hut. Maybe next year."

Eve decided it was time to be grateful. "Thank you, Papa. I will do my best."

Adam hugged his daughter.

While in his hug she said, "I had a dream. Mama wanted me to weave. I told her she had to talk to you about that. Did she?"

Adam quickly released his grip on Eve and held her out at arms length. "When was that?"

"Last night."

Eve never did understand the look on Papa's face at that moment, nor did she understand why he suddenly began to cry. She decided not to ask.

5

July 26, 1794.

It had been a month since Adam and his family had experienced the snipping sounds of scissors. At least that is what they thought the sound was. But since that had been weeks in the past, they had nearly forgotten it. At the time, Adam had insisted that their lives return to normal. The Stranger's visit and death, and then the various events that followed, had threatened to throw Flax Haven's operations into chaos. Adam had to fight to get Mary Ann, Sam, and his children to ignore the past and look toward the future—the children had to be educated, the fields tended to, and there was the everyday upkeep of the buildings and care of the livestock.

Since Mary Ann was more of a social animal than he, Adam suggested they invite Jack and Linda Stuart to a Sunday mid-day meal. Jack and Linda were the older merchants of the general store in Charles Town from whom Adam purchased many of their everyday supplies and tools. The Stuarts had raised four children, now all adults; two had moved on, and two remained behind and ran the day-to-day operation of the store. Adam also knew that the Stuarts were not particularly religious people, so inviting them to Sunday mid-day meal would not be an inconvenience with church attendance. They kept their store open on Sundays, although there was little business done on that day as most citizens avoided work and shopping due to religious obligations. While the Stuarts visited them, their children would mind the store.

Adam was glad to invite the Stuarts to Sunday dinner, although for Adam it wasn't just friendship; he had ulterior motives. One was to gain a favored trading relationship with Jack. Another was to mend his relationship with Mary Ann after the recent events had created tension between them. He knew that Mary Ann looked up to Linda as one of the matrons of the town, although, unlike Hagerstown, Charles Town enjoyed little social activity. But simply suggesting the idea of the Stuarts' visit to Mary Ann had cheered her up and given her something to look forward to. She would again enjoy making her favorite desserts and entertaining guests, all the while attempting to impress women whose social standing Mary Ann considered higher than her own, although in regard to Linda Stuart such wasn't the case.

When the Stuarts arrived, Mary Ann welcomed Linda into the house and Adam gave Jack a quick tour of the farm, but Adam did not want to leave Mary Ann, Eve, and Bethany alone with Linda for long. There were too many layers of tension between the women and Adam wanted to be sure to be present to smooth over any disagreement that might arise.

Having recently made the loom operational again, and knowing that Jack had an affinity for woven textiles, Adam brought Jack back to the gathering hall where the loom sat and where the women were preparing to serve the food. The loom was unique and perhaps the largest farm-based loom in the area. In Pennsylvania, Esther could compete with commercial looms with its forty-eight inch beam, flying-shuttle, and rocker-beater. Jack was clearly impressed with the loom, on which Eve had begun to weave a plain linen table covering the entire width of the loom. It was a test weave, as Eve was learning and Adam made adjustments. So Adam was able to let Jack try his hand at the breast bar and treadles. Jack had never seen a flying-shuttle, rocker-beater loom. Most flying-shuttle looms used an overhead pivot for the beater, and an overhead sling mechanism for picking or throwing the shuttle left and right through the shed. This required that the loom be seven feet high. The rocker-beater mechanism, however, sat on the floor, and the levers used for throwing the shuttle along its race were rigged under the shuttle race. This brought down the height of the loom to about five feet, so it could be more easily disassembled and moved. The rocker-beater also produced a finer and tighter fell and thus a smoother cloth.

As Adam demonstrated all this to Jack, especially the speed of the flying-shuttle and how it was kept from flying clear across the room, he noticed Mary Ann looking his way with displeasure. The noise irritated her and she thought it irritated the twins as well, although Adam had caught the twins bouncing with joy to the loom's rhythm on more than one occasion. Nevertheless, he tempered the demonstration with only an occasional throw of the shuttle (*CLACK*) and not the *CLACK, beat-beat, treadle, CLACK, beat-beat, treadle, CLACK, beat-beat, treadle*, of the loom at full speed.

"Eve," said Mary Ann, "would you set the table? Use some of your papa's linen."

Adam knew Mary Ann meant Esther's linens, but would never use Esther's name. Mary Ann's envy of Esther saddened Adam still. There was no reason for it. Nonetheless, Adam kept an eye on the table setting operation, hoping that Eve would cooperate without creating a scene from which Mary Ann could not escape without embarrassing herself in front of Linda.

Eve went to the linen cabinet and pulled open a drawer, but then froze, staring into the drawer. "Madam?" Eve whispered.

Mary Ann glanced at Eve, then looked in the direction of Eve's gaze. Adam glanced at Linda, who was busy ladling up stew at a side table. Henry was stoking the fire, which gave Adam added concern. And then he heard it. It must have begun when Eve opened the linen drawer. Over the sound of the crackling fire, and Jack operating the treadles trying to throw the shuttle without it going airborne, Adam heard the faint CLIP, CLIP, CLIP sound of scissors opening and closing. Adam froze.

6

Eve heard the CLIP, CLIP, CLIP, but that's not what froze her in her tracks. It was the stacks of linen in the drawer. Just like the horse blanket the stack of linen was pulsing in sync with the clipping sound, except this time there was no room for Cleopatra under the cloth. She called to Mary Ann in a whisper, but Mary Ann, engaged in conversation with Linda about the apple pie, waved Eve off as if to say *get on with it, child. Set the table.*

Miffed, Eve gazed back at the drawer. The stack of cloth was pulsing with the sound of the scissors. Instinctively, Eve SLAMMED her hand down on the linen to squash whatever animal was underneath. The clipping noise instantly stopped.

At the sound of Eve smashing the folded linen, both Linda and Mary Ann turned sharply to look at Eve. Mary Ann snapped, "Eve, spread out that linen, now."

Now, more than a tad upset with her stepmother, Eve grabbed the edges of the top linen and yanked it from the drawer. As Eve held one end, the nearly white luxurious cloth billowed up from the drawer, opened fully, and floated down onto the floor for all to see. It was eight-feet long and four-feet wide, one of the largest that her mother had woven on the loom from bleached linen yarn. Eve and Mary Ann were stunned at what they saw, and Adam, clear across the room, bolted up from the bench at the loom. The cloth was riddled with holes one to three inches in length and each in the shape, more or less, of a crescent moon. After the cloth settled, the cut-out crescent moon shapes drifted to cover the cloth and the floor.

Mary Ann and Eve stared at the cloth speechless, but Linda...

"My goodness, Mary Ann! That's interesting, even beautiful. Where did you get such a thing?"

Linda took the edge of the cloth and looked at it closely. Mary Ann and Eve gazed at each other, too scared to move.

Burdened with reticence, Eve said: "My mother, Esther, wove it."

"Eve, it's exquisite," said Linda.

"Let me see that!" said Adam, stepping forward and grabbing the linen, and fingering the crescent-shaped holes. Trying to suppress the anger in his voice but unable to, he demanded of Mary Ann, "How did this happen? Did you do this?"

Jack, too, took an interest in the fascinating cloth, taking a corner of the linen and examining it. "Adam, this isn't woven. The warp and the weft have been cut or eaten through. It would hardly stand a washing, no backing or seam. See here." He held out a cut crescent that he had easily pulled from the weave.

Adam looked at what Jack had done, as a matter of curiosity, and took it from him.

"Husband, how could I have done this? And when, and but...why, would I?"

Adam had nearly lost it by now. "Because you...." Adam abruptly stopped, but his bodily movements told all that he was mighty upset. "This...was...was one of my wife's...my *first* wife's finest creations. Is this some kind of joke? Who did this?" Adam fondled the cloth as if he was looking for Esther in the folds.

Eve didn't know if Papa was going to explode in anger or cry in despair. She looked at her stepmother, who was busily and clumsily gathering up the cloth, ripping it out of Adam's hands, trying to salvage what she could. "Yes, but it's far too delicate for us to be using today. Forgive me, Linda. Adam, let's talk about this later, shall we. Eve! Put that away. Find one without...the...design."

"Mary Ann," said Linda, "be not so envious. It is yours now."

Mary Ann, trembling, quickly and awkwardly folded the linen, and shoved it into Eve's arms as if it was a contagion. Eve stuffed the cut cloth into the drawer, closed it, and opened a second drawer to withdraw a sold linen, although not nearly as white. Inspecting it quickly, she nodded nervously to Mary Ann and together they spread it out over the table.

"Well, I'm a bit disappointed," said Linda. "But I was absolutely delighted to see it, Adam." It was a polite attempt to chastise Adam for not liking what to her was beautiful.

Eve was emotionally turned inside out. She loved and would defend her mother's woven linen, but the crescent moons, while horrible in one way, were beautiful in another, and she knew that Mary Ann had not cut them. The crescent holes were perfectly smooth as if some otherworldly device had made them, perhaps like a very sharp cookie-cutter. But why would anyone do that, and why leave behind the cut-out shapes that now littered the floor.

She looked up at her father who was still upset.

"Jack," said Adam, "I have no idea...."

Jack held up his hand, even as he knelt to retrieve several of the cut-out moon shapes from the floor. "Adam, I have no idea either, but seeing that cloth, and these cut-outs is, fascinating. Do you mind if I take these?" He held out his hand with half-dozen cut-outs in his palm.

"Of course not. Perhaps you can find out what cut that."

"I'll tell you right now. I have no clue."

"Eve," said Adam, "pick up these clippings and save them."

"Yes, Papa." Eve wasn't too happy about the request. She suspected they were part of the curse and she wanted to burn them...perhaps later she thought.

Supper got underway...without prayer, Eve sadly noted. Well, without her parents praying. But she did, to herself, as she always did. And then she added under her breath, "Mama, pray for us. We need you."

Eve tried her best to be the obedient daughter and not embarrass her fa-

454 ○ *Stanley D. Williams*

ther and Mary Ann in front of the Stuarts. But she was scared. Between nearly every bite she begged her mother...(her real mother, silently)...to intercede on their behalf. Eve was convinced that the crescent cut-outs were the direct consequence of the sounds of the scissors. She just wondered why the wool blanket in the barn was not also cut up into moon shapes. *Was it because it was wool?* As she thought about it, she didn't think the horse blanket was made by her mother from wool harvested by her father. *Was there some connection?*

Mary Ann and Papa were trying their best to act natural in front of the Stuarts, but she could tell they were play acting, and they weren't very good. Mr. Stuart would crack a very dull joke and Papa would laugh at it with great amusement. Her stepmother, likewise, was fawning over Linda, or over her dress, or a broach, or the salad...which to Eve was absolutely terrible. Why would anyone make a salad out of bitter weeds? Eve wasn't sure what was in it, but they looked like weeds, and they were bitter. Next time she'll suggest to Bethany to put more sugar in the dressing.

After the main courses were finished, Eve was looking forward to dessert— Eve's favorite, Mary Ann's lemon honeycomb, although the apple pie was there as an alternative. But first they would clear the table.

While she and Bethany cleared the table, Linda and Mary Ann played with the twins who were toddling about, and Jack persuaded Adam to let him operate the loom to see if he could get the flying shuttle machine working at speed. Eve took an interest in this because it was her practice weave that was on the loom. If she learned well, she could continue and make good cloth for their home, but for now the weave was anything but tight or well done. Letting Jack in on the exercise was fine by her. But what would Mary Ann say?

As Jack was trying to get Adam to let him try out the loom, Adam raised an eyebrow in Mary Ann's direction. Eve smiled and watched Mary Ann's reaction. Surprisingly, her stepmother nodded approval...as if to say *just this once.* So Jack sat on the bench and Adam provided some instruction regarding the treadle sequence and how to trigger the picker sticks to fly the shuttle. Then Adam made a tension adjustment to the warp beam ratchet and told Jack to go at it. Jack started off slow: *CLACK...beat...beat...treadle...CLACK...beat...beat... treadle,* but after a few minutes of coordinating his limbs he got the loom working at a good cadence—*CLACK, beat-beat, treadle, CLACK, beat-beat, treadle, CLACK, beat-beat, treadle, CLACK, beat-beat, treadle.*

While that was going on, Eve noticed that the twins were enjoying the rhythm and began to bounce in sync with the racket, much to Linda's entertainment and Mary Ann's angst. Mary Ann turned to Eve who was watching the circus and motioned with her hands to speed up the dessert so the noise could stop. Eve nodded, and got back to helping Bethany. In a few minutes Bethany took a large spoon and struck the coffee kettle that had been warming over the fire, to signal that dessert was served.

Eve watched Mary Ann as she sighed relief when the loom stopped.

Jack was upbeat from working a flying-shuttle rocker-beater and Eve was thrilled that the loom was working so well that even an inexperienced visitor could weave on the unique loom. She glanced at Papa, who appeared happy at providing some constructive entertainment to Mister Stuart. He must also feel good, Eve thought, that his repairs to the loom were successful.

The *CLACK, beat-beat, treadle—CLACK, beat-beat, treadle—CLACK, beat-beat, treadle* cadence stayed with the group for some moments after the loom stopped. It seemed as if everyone in the room was moving in jerks, as if the loom was still operating, for they could still "hear" the hypnotizing *CLACK, beat-beat, treadle* in their minds.

There was also the happy chatter and the twins baby-talk, and everyone complimenting Mary Ann on how appetizing the pie and honeycomb looked, and how they couldn't wait to taste one, the other, or both. There was all that, and the *CLACK, beat-beat, treadle*, in their minds. It wasn't until they were all sitting at the table with their mouths full of Mary Ann's tasty delights that they noticed the loom was still making noise. At least that is what Eve at first thought. It wasn't a loud noise. It was soft. But it wasn't a *CLACK - CLACK - CLACK* of the shuttle smacking the end of its race. No, it wasn't that at all. It was *CLIP-CLICK, CLIP-CLICK, CLIP-CLICK, CLIP-CLICK, CLIP-CLICK.*

Everyone heard it, but no one said anything about it. At first, it was if there were birds just outside the window tweeting a courting cadence. It should have been a sweet song. But Eve noted that the smiles of delight at Mary Ann's pastries turned slowly flat, and then sour, as heads turned to look about as if they all were being watched by a stern parent or despot. Then, when the plates of pie and honeycomb were clean there was an odd and awkward silence, and no one asked for seconds. And all the while *CLIP-CLICK, CLIP-CLICK, CLIP-CLICK, CLIP-CLICK* they heard scissors cutting cloth. Even the twins stopped chattering and looked with apprehension to the faces of the adults for assurance.

Adam finally broke the human silence: "It's our scissors bird...pay no mind."

"It definitely sounds like shears," said Linda, "don't you think so, Mary Ann?"

"If you say so," Mary Ann said, although it was clear to Eve that her stepmother was not being agreeable. The veins in her neck were showing, which meant it was time to stay clear of disagreements with her.

"I never heard of a scissors bird," said Jack. "What does it look like?"

"We're not sure," said Mary Ann.

"It could be our teasing neighbors," said Adam with a smile. "They're jokesters." Papa was trying to make light of something that had them all spooked.

"It's something more, Papa," Eve said.

"Nonsense," Adam snapped, then apologized. "I'm sorry, I didn't mean to be upset, it's just..." Turning to Jack and Linda, "...well, it's really nothing more."

But the *CLIP-CLICK, CLIP-CLICK, CLIP-CLICK* was louder now.

Henry had been watching the give-and-take with interest. "Papa, it's the same sound we heard in the barn, isn't it? But it was just Cleopatra."

"Cleopatra?" asked Linda.

"Our barn cat," answered Mary Ann. "Henry, that's enough," chastised Mary Ann.

Henry turned to Eve. "You heard it. Tell them."

Eve bowed her head as if to hide. "Papa, when I opened the drawer to get out the table cloth a little while ago...the first time...I heard the clipping. And the cloths in the drawer were moving up and down as if there were scissors under the cloth...cutting it. It scared me. I hit the cloth and the clipping stopped, but you saw what the cloth looked like when I took it out. The clipping sound is what cut the cloth."

Adam got up and went to the drawer where the clipped cloth had been returned. He opened it, and tore through the drawer's contents. Searching with his hand all around and under the folded linens. "There's no scissors here, daughter."

"I don't suppose there ever were," answered Eve, "but, see there?" She gestured to the floor around the drawer which Adam had opened. There were crescent moon cutouts all over the floor which had fallen from the drawer when Adam began rummaging around in it.

At that the twins began to fuss. They must have sensed the tension that was in the room, and all the while the *CLIP–CLICK, CLIP–CLICK* continued.

Jack suddenly pushed back his dish and got up from his chair. "Adam, Mary Ann, the food was delicious, especially the lemon honeycomb, but we must be leaving."

"But you must stay for coffee," insisted Mary Ann.

Jack looked around the room for the source of the *CLIP–CLICK, CLIP–CLICK*. "Thank you very much, but...Linda, dear, we've bothered these kind folks enough. Can we go...now?

Eve noticed the Stuarts were uncomfortable and eager to leave the strange events that had haunted their stay.

Jack awkwardly reached into his pocket and removed all the clippings of the cloth he had taken and put them on the table. Clearly, he wanted to distance himself from them as if they were cursed. Eve was sure they were. Very much in a hurry, and without lingering for even belabored good-byes as folks often did who had enjoyed their stay, and in spite of Mary Ann's continual encouragement to stay for coffee and apple pie, the Stuarts quickly left the house, got in their carriage, and trotted out of the yard without so much as a good-bye wave.

7

It was mid-afternoon when Adam followed the Stuarts out of the house and into the yard. He could understand their hasty departure, but his business sense kicked in and he tried to smooth over their discomfort.

Jack was polite, but he was nonetheless curt and upset…as was Linda, who asked Adam to relay her apology to Mary Ann and appreciation for the good food. It was clear to Adam, however, that Linda was glad to be pulled away by her doting husband. Indeed, something beleaguered Flax Haven and she wanted nothing to do with it. Adam wondered how he might be treated next time he walked into the Stuarts' store. Would they even want to do business with him?

Adam tore back into the house and stood still, listening. Bethany was cleaning up. He watched her suspiciously and listened carefully.

"'Tis not her, Adam," said Mary Ann sternly with her arms crossed; her eyes firing daggers at him, as if he had failed her.

The clipping sound was gone. He went to the drawer where Eve had stuffed the clipped cloth, yanked open the drawer, removed the cloth and spread it open. It was one of Esther's weaves, all right. Probably a full loom's width of forty-eight inches, and about eight-feet long. He could almost remember when it was woven and hemmed. It was a tight, herringbone weave…and the clips… he was speechless. How could these be cut out of the cloth so plainly, as with a razor? They were all about the same size, about an inch-and-a-half by one-half, and randomly positioned and rotated about the cloth. The whole cloth was littered with the holes. Where the cloth had been bent, after the clipping, the threads of the weave would come loose; if handled much the whole cloth would disintegrate. He was devastated, and he gripped the cloth as if he was holding Esther tight to stop her from disintegrating into eternity.

"What is it, Adam? What is that damn cloth?" demanded Mary Ann.

"It is a treasured heirloom, now destroyed," said Adam.

"What good is it then?" she said.

Adam kneeled on the floor, caressed the cloth, and held it to his face as if to dry his tears. But there were no tears, just a deep, obsessive rage.

"It's no good," said Mary Ann. "It's cursed."

Mary Ann's attack of anything related to Esther angered Adam, but he was more obsessed with what was going on with the cut-up cloth and the scissors noise. *Someone despised him. Who was it? Was it Esther's God? Her spirit? And what was that damn clipping noise?*

Adam broke out of his reverie, put the clipped cloth aside, and searched through the drawer for more clipped linen. He opened the other drawers and searched them as well. Nothing more! It was this one cursed cloth. Hurriedly he bundled the clipped linen in his arms, grabbed a flint box by the front door, and left the house.

Behind the barn Sam had established a rubbish burn pit, and there Adam burned the clipped cloth, standing over it, prodding it with a stick until it was ash, and then mixed the ash with the soil.

Now, where is that damn scissors bird? For the rest of the day Adam wandered his property with his shillelagh tightly in his grip, listening for the scissors bird, or for some mechanism in his house, the barn, the well, the gates, anything that might make the clipping noise. After supper, in the dark, he went out and cased the farm buildings, looking and listening for some clue, some sign of what had plagued their afternoon with the Stuarts. But all he found was a crescent moon hanging low in the sky above the barn...the same shape as the cloth cut-outs that he had burned.

When he slipped into bed later, Mary Ann was wide awake and was still grousing.

"All that food wasted," she said.

"And I've looked everywhere," he said.

"At least they could have shown some appreciation."

"Yeah, know what you mean. I found nothing."

"Bethany did everything I asked of her."

"Sam was thorough as usual."

"The pie was barely touched."

"Found nothing."

"Yes, honeycomb was gone."

"Those cuts...in such a tight weave, I'll never know."

"Why invite anyone ever again?"

"Normal. We need to get back to it."

"We have any neighbors that are that..."

"...normal?"

"Yes."

Adam thought for a long time...."No."

"Think they'll talk?"

"No doubt."

"What shall we do?"

"Find it and kill it."

"Find what?"

Another long pause.... "I don't know."

Eventually, sleep found them.

8

Eve never slept. Frightened? A little. But she was not confused. All she could think about was how her mother was now being attacked not by her step-mother, but by an invisible force brought on by the curse of Fr. Xavier. She wasn't sure if she should blame Fr. Xavier, God, or the Devil. The clipped table cloth was clearly of supernatural origin. Eve was also convinced that the scissors sound was supernatural. She had heard the sounds, watched the table cloth moving as if someone was cutting it, and then there were the holes. The three were connected.

And now, laying in bed, all she could think of was how the herringbone cloth that Papa had burned that afternoon needed to be replaced; and she was the only person likely to do it.

It was the middle of the night when Eve lit her lantern and descended the stairs ever so lightly so as not to wake Papa or Mary Ann. In her going down she decided that she would remake her mother's plain herringbone tablecloth. This would not be an easy or small project. But Mama and Papa had taught her enough over the years…and now she had motivation. She must try.

As she entered the dark gathering hall with her lantern, the two lantern sconces on the corner walls adjacent to the loom suddenly ignited, illuminating the room. Eve froze, afraid to move. She looked around, but of course no one was there. She stood facing the loom's bench, shaking in her nightshirt as if she was cold. But it wasn't cold. The embers in the fireplace a few feet away warmed the room. At the same time a thought clearly entered her mind, allowing her a vision of her mother. Mama was sitting cross-legged on the loom bench, her relaxed hands folded in her lap, facing her daughter. She was wearing a floor-length white satin wrap-around gown. The double-hemmed edges crossed beneath her full breasts and wrapped tight about her waist. Over her gown was a matching floor-length white satin robe with billowy sleeves that reached the palms of her hands. About her waist was a wide, satin-sash belt that contoured the ensemble as it flowed in a light breeze over her body. Eve recognized the gown's material at once. It was the satin-linen her father had woven for Mama's burial. But now it was a tailored gown, robe, and sash. Mama's hair was wrapped neatly on top of her head and held in place with strands of pink lily of the valley blossoms woven in and out of her long auburn hair. Mama's eyes were clear, blue and piercing; her thin lips glistened with dew as she smiled at her daughter.

It was as if Mama was waiting for a passing coach to pick her up and take her to a distant land. "What are you waiting for, my dearest Eve? Do you doubt your destiny or are you just beginning to understand it? Yes, you must create what others seek to destroy. That is your calling, for now. Beauty will save you. It will be hard. You will struggle. There will be persecution. But in your labor you will find meaning. Do not fear."

Eve stared at her mother's apparition for a few moments. Esther smiled back, and then, slowly the vision of her mother dissolved into thin air.

Eve shook from head to toe. She stood facing the loom for a long time, sobbing at the vision, wanting her mother to really be there, contemplating Mama's appearance and words. After a few minutes a deep but gentle euphoria enveloped her. There was no doubt now about her goal, her life.

She stared at the loom for a long time and took an inventory of its various parts: the square bench, the eight treadles, the four heddle harnesses and hundreds of wire heddles, the beater frame, the shuttle box and race, and the warp beam, paw and ratchet—all bespoke the task ahead of her. She would need to clear the loom of the training warp and cloth and reclaim the yarn on the flying shuttle spindle which would now be nearly useless, a scrap end. Then she would prepare an eight-foot warp on her mother's spinning warp rack that Papa had only recently reassembled after the move.

She went to Papa's office, sat at his desk, and with quill and paper sketched out a weaving pattern and treadle-heddle-frame sequence for the pattern she wanted to create. Up close it would look like a herringbone but from a distance a secret design would be evident. She then applied the mathematics she had learned. A 48-inch wide fabric for a table covering would require a set of 18 ends per inch (epi). This was the warp density. That meant she would need 864 warp threads, each 8 feet in length. She doubted that the warping board could hold 864 warp lines at once. She would need to prepare the warps for 12 inches of weft at a time. She multiplied 18 epi times 12 inches to get 216. So she'd create four warp bundles of 216 threads, each 9 feet long. *Wow,* she thought, *how much yarn is that? Do we have enough?* She multiplied again, 216 times 4, times 8 feet, equals 6,912 feet or 2,304 yards. And that was just for the warps. She would need at least twice that by the time she wound up her weft shuttles, or a total of approximately 4,600 yards. That sounded like a lot.

Eve quietly took her lantern and went back upstairs and slipped into the storage room, which was also the guest room where Fr. Xavier had died. She easily found the crate Papa had brought down from Pennsylvania with her mother's inventory of skeins. It had been only a short time ago that she and Papa had opened the crate and chosen yarn to dress the loom for practice. Inside the crate was a large, light-weight linen sack which protected the skeins from the rough wooden sides of the crate. Most of the skeins of yarn held 800 yards each. Holding her lantern above the crate she was delighted to discover that there were dozens of skeins of various weights and colors. Most were linen, but there was wool, cotton, and a few silk skeins as well. She would need approximately six skeins of bleached linen yarn. She dug around a bit and pulled out what she believed would work. There was plenty. Mother had often embarked on a weaving project for large cloths.

Again trying to be as quiet as a mouse, she replaced the crate's lid and tiptoed back downstairs. She placed the six skeins in a weaving basket next to the loom and set about removing and saving the practice warp and weft ends. Some would find dressing and undressing loom tedious work, but Eve loved working with her hands and feeling the soft yarn in her hands. It felt as if she was participating in some ancient sacred work, saving and carefully spooling the warp ends.

About daybreak she finished putting the warps and weft threads on spools to be taken back to the skein crate in the storage room. Putting the salvaged yard ends in a basket, she took three skeins of the bleached linen and returned to the storage room.

9

Mary Ann thought she had slept remarkably well, considering the disturbing events of the day before when the Stuarts came for supper. She had fed the twins at midnight and they were still asleep in their cribs. Yet, in spite of the sound sleep she was still unnerved. The sounds of Adam's scissors bird was still ringing in her head, and the sight of the clipped linen was haunting. Was this the curse that damn priest had leveled on them? It seemed hardly likely. The incessant bird sounds were bad enough, but then the linen table cloth cut to shreds...well, that frightened her. Her old insecurity came back almost full strength. That table cloth was woven by Esther, and clearly Adam was remembering Esther through her beautiful, damnable as it was, creation. Oh, how she'd like to burn all the linen in the house as if eradicating a plague. As long as anything resembling Esther was around, Adam would not give himself to her completely; and that noise, it kept on...if she could just get it out of her head.

Adam was already up and gone from the house, no doubt. A farmer's life doesn't allow for much sleep. She got out of bed, looked in on her darlings still sleeping soundly in their cribs by the windows, spread up the bed, and walked to the wash basin. It was then that she realized the clipping sound wasn't in her head, but coming from the hall. The door to her bedroom was half open; *couldn't men remember to shut doors behind them?* She stood just inside the door and listened, her mind trying to decide between flight or fight. She breathed deeper, her heart beat faster, then her mind started to analyze the sound: *Click-whirl-whirl-whirl-thump.* She had never heard anything like it before. The sound repeated: *Click-whirl-whirl-whirl-thump.*

"How many is that?" she heard Adam ask.

Mary Ann immediately opened the door all the way and stepped out. The sound was coming from the storeroom.

"Two-hundred-ten," said Eve.

Mary Ann stepped quickly to the storeroom door that was open and peered in. Adam was leaning against the writing desk watching Eve guide a strand of white yarn up around the outside of a spinning rack in a spiral design. The strand was unraveling from a pile of yarn on the floor, the remains of a skein. Eve stopped the rack from spinning with her hand (thump), looped the strand of yarn over a wood peg at the top, spun the rack (CLICK) in the other direction (whirl-whirl-whirl) as she guided the unbroken strand of yarn down along the same spiral path to a peg at the bottom, where she would stop the rack (thump), loop the yard around the peg and repeat the process.

"What are you doing?" Mary Ann asked clutching her night dress at her waist as if unsure whether the rack was going to attack.

"Spinning warps. She only has 600 or so to go," Adam said with a raised eyebrow and a touch of cynicism.

Eve kept working, murmuring to herself with each spin...215...216.

"She's going to weave a new table covering to replace the one that was, ah... clipped...and which I burned. These are the warps, each revolution is eight feet long."

Eve cut the yarn thread separating the yarn on the rack from the skein on the floor, and using small pieces of string began to tie off sections and the crossing of the yard on the rack. "I have to do three more of these each with 216 threads, but I'm going to dress the loom with this first, to see how it goes," Eve said.

"You should be more concerned with how it was clipped in the first place," said Mary Ann.

Adam looked away. "It's quiet now."

Mary Ann kept her voice low for fear of waking the twins: "For how long?"

Adam helped Eve remove the warp wrap from the rack and chain it, hand-over-hand, until she could carry the eight-foot length without it dragging on the floor. Eve then went downstairs and Adam followed her.

When they got to the gathering hall Mary Ann saw that the loom was clear of the practice dressing, and the space around it cleaned up and orderly. "When did this happen?"

"I couldn't sleep," said Eve.

Adam helped Eve attach the end of the warp bundle to the stick near the back of the loom and subdivide the 216 warps evenly on another stick. Mary Ann didn't know how to dress a loom, but it was clear that Eve was learning.

"Is this the source of our troubles?" Mary Ann brazenly asked, still keeping her voice down.

Adam kept his attention on Eve. It seems as if they were counting individual threads. "Nonsense," he said to Mary Ann.

"Adam, look at you. You have not yet given over Esther. You're hanging on to her; she haunts us. The riddled cloth all came from this loom, didn't it. And now, the very next day, you're trying to duplicate it."

Adam put his hand on Eve, but looked up to Mary Ann. He was miffed, and he didn't like be interrupted from his work, and Mary Ann knew that.

"Answer me, husband. That table covering was woven on this loom. Isn't that right?"

Adam shrugged and went back to directing Eve's counting of the warps so as to keep them in order.

Mary Ann kept it up. "Don't defend her. She's dead, gone, forever, forgotten."

Adam finally gave his full attention to Mary Ann. "My dear, Mary Ann. Esther excelled at the weave because she learned it from my parents, the most successful linen merchants in the colonies. This I have told you. And as she learned it from the generation before us, so Eve will learn from me. This is what we do."

That was no explanation that Mary Ann could endure. It wasn't about weaving, or history, or generations, it was about whether or not she was going to rule her home or be a pawn in it, subjected to always being second rate to the more talented, and luckily first. "I want it out of this house."

To Mary Ann, it was surprising that Adam was not angry at her demand. Perhaps he didn't take it seriously.

"So. We are to go naked?" he asked mocking her.

"Haven't so far. We can buy our clothes now. I will not learn it, and would have everything of hers gone. She haunts us."

"This is fancy," said Adam. "It's the...the Wizard, as Eve calls it, that haunts us. Besides, nearly everything in the house Esther touched, made, or molded. Shall we rid ourselves of everything but the walls?" He stared at Mary Ann, waiting for a response, but she had none.

She felt belittled, stunned at his rebuke, and embarrassed that she didn't have a better answer than the envy she so very clearly felt but of which she could not rid herself.

"Mary Ann," Adam continued, "I love you. The memory of Esther does not haunt us but endears us to one another."

"You still love her."

"Of course, I still love her. But I cannot love her the way I love you. You are here. Esther is gone."

Eve touched her father's arm as they were both sitting on chairs dressing the loom at the warp beam. "No, Papa. She *is* here. She spoke to me, even last night. She sat on the bench right there." Eve pointed to the weaver's bench which now was between her and Mary Ann.

At hearing this, a sour taste entered Mary Ann's mouth, as if her stomach had turned on her and was ready to vomit yesterday's food. Her knees went weak, and she longed to flee and be alone.

Adam turned sharply to his daughter, even as Mary Ann gazed anew at her.

"She told me to do this. To weave a cloth, to create what other want destroyed.

"Who wants to destroy?" barked Mary Ann.

"It's the Wizard," said Eve, then hurriedly added, "Papa, please keep mother's loom. I will learn to use it. She taught me some, and she can...that is, you can teach me the rest."

"Who is this Wizard? Do you know him?" asked Mary Ann.

But Eve turned away and refused to answer.

Adam shook his head at Mary Ann but he spoke to his daughter. "Daughter, I cannot teach you much. But, well and good. Apply thyself. The loom is part of who we are, who you will become. The loom will stay. You will weave... Wizard or no Wizard."

Mary Ann steeled herself. At once she felt confused, mad, and impotent to say or do anything. She was very much alone and isolated, her chin quivered.

Adam lowered his head and showed Eve how to count off the warp threads from the cross, eighteen at a time, and spread them evenly across the stick.

Henry came down the stairs. He had been listening. "You'll never do it, you know. It's just junk."

"No, it isn't," said Eve, defiantly staring up at him. I will learn to weave like mother and make beautiful things like her and grandpa.

"I don't think so," said Henry in a very grown up and unusual voice, so much so that Mary Ann turned to him surprised. Henry continued, "Your playing with it will only bring more haunts. It's bad."

Eve stared at her brother as if he was a horned devil, but she spoke to her father. "Papa, show me again how to dress these warp threads; I have hundreds more to do before the end of the day."

Mary Ann felt her heart sink deep and her chest go hollow, even as shivers ran down her spine. Hell was about to break loose, and there was nothing she could do about it.

At that moment the twins woke and began to cry. She thought, *how fitting*.

10

Most Feared Master of Death,

As you have insisted, I am persistent. My low-grade sorcery of cutting linen and the noise of my so-called "scissor-craft" at first irritated the Livingstons. It humored me that they thought I used scissors. But in recent months the family has grown accustomed to the haunts as if the sounds were some unobserved bird's mating call, or the clicking of bats, the crackling of grasshoppers, the rattling of cicadas, or that it was a delusional blue jay. I hope you noticed that I have followed a previously successful strategy of persistence to induce moral fatigue, and that it has worked in many cases. There is a limit, however, to such activity. Being the peculiar servant of the moon-demon restricts my haunts to the days and nights just before and after a new moon, when life on earth is the darkest and hope among humans is the bleakest.

Of course, I am proud of my prowess of cutting holes in cloth using only my teeth. By off-setting my jaw and clamping down quickly, my top and bottom incisors puncture the cloth and out comes the shape, much cleaner than I would have thought. The size is easily adjusted simply by how far I suck the cloth into my grimy gullet. That my teeth and cloth when rubbed together deceptively sound like a pair of shears was a benefit I did not expect. The only downside is that the dead flax fibers taste bitter; my taste is better suited for blood-spiked mucus and flesh. Regardless, I have found satisfaction in honing my cutlery skills. If only my chortling didn't sound like a frog. It frightened no one; instead they laughed and ran for a broom.

I am also confounded by the enemy that invisibly surrounds Livingston's daughter, Eve. With a name like hers she should be on our side, but alas that is not the case. You should know that her loyalty to the Almighty angers me. There is nothing I can do to entice her away from her irritating, pious obedience. Consequently, the daughter is successfully working on the large weaving, and I am unable to position myself to taste that new cloth when it's on the loom. Worse, the pattern looks like a herringbone to her father, but in fact it contains a cleverly integrated cross over which she prays and asks the mothers in heaven to protect it. This is very frustrating. I also observe her father and even our collaborator, Livingston's wife, heaping admiration on the daughter for her perseverance, although the latter is infrequent and insincere. Oh, how I want to devour and riddle that cloth. It will replace the earlier one I had chewed up and spat out. All I could manage to chew were a few smaller linens left unguarded—bitter delicacies they were. I am of the opinion that I need to branch out.

Most of my attention has been on Livingston's family, but I still brood over the dark specter of Denis Cahill's possible catastrophic influence on our efforts. Please note that I have not been entirely negligent of my duties to undermine and discredit Cahill's future, though my earlier efforts had met with only modest success. To my credit you should note the restriction of Cahill's duties I was able to influence in New Orleans; then there was the Gulf of Mexico storm aboard the Eagle and the death of that seaman. José Gaspar and my Florida pirates gave Cahill some fright I expect, and Will Canning's mugging near Sharpsburg made Cahill question his calling, if not his life. Canning is a favorite of ours, I know. May our Lord curse him forever more.

I had also hoped to entice Cahill's lust for the beautiful, virginal, and innocent Anastasia. There were many opportunities to foster Cahill's lust when she came regularly to confession and was alone with him. Yet again, I found it impossible to impregnate the relationship with lasciviousness, not because Cahill is so pious— he isn't—but because Anastasia is literally surrounded with that ghastly aura of chastity.

I am persistent, however, and am making progress on the flanks. Five years earlier I was successful enough to entice Richard McSherry with enough greed and Cahill with enough insecurity that the two agreed to that ridiculous contract for McSherry's support of Cahill on a five-year plan of declining support. Thus, over the last five years, McSherry's financial support of Cahill has slowly declined. Now it is up to Cahill to raise offerings in his

466 ○ *Stanley D. Williams*

parishes to make up the difference. Except the difference is never made up and Cahill is getting desperate. At first the collections had increased, but now, five years later, with waning enthusiasm, there is barely enough money to keep his belly full, let alone build the obnoxiously large edifices I put into his head. I calculated that Catholics were never going to compete with the ostentatious display of Protestant wealth.

McSherry knew, of course, that Cahill was in need of support and so he suggested that Cahill write Bishop Carroll and request support for the five parishes Cahill had founded. McSherry is pretty sure the bishop knew nothing about Fr. Cahill, and it is time he did. I'm counting on Cahill's blunt awkwardness and his hatred of authority to create a dispute where before there was none. I've been working on this in Cahill's mind since New Orleans. I don't think we'll be disappointed.

At your sinful service,
Cyn Namrasit, OPSD

Chapter 31
It is Nothing

1

Bishop John Carroll, S.J., was having a rough time of it. In 1774, when Pope Clement XIV dissolved the Jesuits, Carrol returned from England to his mother's home in Maryland rather than submitting to exile on an island off Italy's coast. In Maryland he began a Catholic mission and supported the American Revolution with his prayers and diplomacy. In 1784 he was appointed Superior of the American mission by the pope, and in 1790 he was consecrated as the first United States bishop. But his desire for the spread of authentic Catholicism throughout the United States was only as good as the priests that labored under him. Priests needed to be men of integrity and good will aside from being men of faith, and defenders of the faith with smart, agile minds. But there were few men that fit such common sense criteria. Thus Carroll and his associates were having difficulty finding priests for the western settlements where the population was spread out.

Of course there seemed to be no shortage of "priests" that wanted the assignments. Men would arrive in the country and present themselves to Carroll but soon were discovered to be charlatans and not priests at all. Some, in fact, had been ordained but had caused so many problems in their former position that they had been dismissed without references. Carroll began to require extensive written references and recommendations. Spanish Capuchin friar *Andrew Nugent was a case in point. The "friar" created a scandal in New York with his excesses that Carroll was still negotiating. In retrospect, Carroll suspected Fr. Nugent's written references and letters of recommendation were forged. But there were others, like *Father Smyth, whose coming and going from his parish were a mystery to his parishioners. In retrospect, there were unstated objectives in the man's letters of reference that smacked of intrigue. Carroll wondered if the man wasn't actually a British spy. On it went. Carroll rarely knew who he could trust.

Thus, it was little wonder that Carroll's suspicions rose when in January of 1795 he received a letter from a Father Denis Cahill who had apparently appeared in the backcountry of Maryland in 1788, and without Carroll's knowledge and certainly without Carroll's authorization, began missionary work of his own design. For Carroll it was one more headache he didn't need. The letter was blunt and, in Carroll's mind, began with a greeting that was twenty-one years late (he had been in America that long) and a defense that was seven years overdue (he had been the Catholic Superior in America for that long).

*January 24, 1795 - Hagerstown
My Lord,

I congratulate you on your happy arrival back to America and your appointment as bishop of these parts. The attention necessary for my various appointments prevents me the pleasure of waiting on you in person. For I have been successful since I came to these parts as a missionary in 1788, after being rescued from villains by a Catholic gentleman from Leetown. The congregations I have developed since then have grown very numerous, and the members of each mostly very exemplary and pious. I attend at Hagerstown, Martinsburg, Shepherd's Town, Winchester, Fort Cumberland, and Chambersburg, the four former more frequently than the latter two. Mr. Hager has given land to build a chapel in his town. Mr. Sheppard also gives a four-acre lot and ten pounds toward a chapel at Shepherd's Town. Mrs. McGuire has given one lot at Winchester, Mr. Bell one at Fort Cumberland, and Mrs. Lodsdon another at Martinsburg. Mr. Hartley, one at Chambersburg. I expect to have four chapels built by this time in twelve months. Please to prolong my faculties, and send to me at Hagerstown by the post my regular emoluments as my sponsor is no longer able to pay me for my ministries. I will need the money prior to Lent.

Your Lordship's most respectful, humble servant.

Rev. Denis Cahill

P. S. If you'd deign to visit us at any time you would make the people happy, and so that they may receive the sacraments of confirmation from your Lordship.

Bishop Carroll was left befuddled by the letter. He knew nothing of this man, although he had heard rumblings of Catholic societies being formed in the area. He had no inkling that a priest, if indeed the man was a priest, was behind the activity. He was tempted to get in a carriage that afternoon and head for the western territories, but he was not free to do such a thing. Traveling 100 miles west was no easy afternoon jaunt for tea, and he had other responsibilities which were more pressing. Priests for the western territories was a priority, and he was close to ordaining such a man for such a place. Ironically, the soon-to-be-ordained man would later play a part of this tale, but, alas, that is later.

2

By March 1795 spring seeding was well underway, and Adam and Mary Ann were much relieved that a month had passed without an increase in Wizardly affectations. There were, however, the occasional shredding of stored linen and the nightly noise of their yet unseen scissors bird. Neither Adam nor Mary Ann were superstitious by nature, but otherwise they could not account for the vexation. Infestations of unknown origins were always the bane of farmers, and some just had to be tolerated. Eve, Bethany, and Sam had other ideas, but kept their thoughts mostly to themselves, for the sake of the family's peace, Adam reasoned.

Thus it was that Mary Ann returned to her somewhat normal routine of cooking with Bethany, gardening, teaching a willing Henry and reluctant Eve, and mothering the twins. Adam continued to be grateful for Sam and Bethany and let them know it. He worried what would happen when their manumission contract expired in two years. Would they leave? Could he persuade them to stay? Sam had a quiet confidence about him which along with his fearlessness of work encouraged Adam and inspired their day laborers. Adam wondered if it wasn't Sam's size that motivated the workers, yet Sam never gave indication of any harsh treatment or even the threat of violence. Adam noted that all Sam had to do was look disappointed, and the effort of those under him seemed to pick up. Likewise, Bethany had adjusted well under Mary Ann's direction. Mary Ann was often overly nervous or worried about issues Adam considered insignificant; but Bethany's calm demeanor helped Mary Ann cope with her many responsibilities of being the mistress of the farm, setting menus, preparing new dishes, and nursing the now two-year-old toddlers and the increasing mischief they got into. The math and reading lessons continued for Eve and Henry from Mary Ann, then several times a week Eve would spend evenings at the Darks' cabin teaching Sam and Bethany to read. Adam was pleased with their progress; they could actually get through the occasional newspaper that he brought from town.

As far as the loom was concerned, Eve and Mary Ann had worked out an arrangement. Eve would only work the loom when Mary Ann wasn't in the gathering hall, parlor, or the their bedroom. The noise was just too great for Mary Ann's nerves. The arrangement, of course, slowed down Eve's work on the new table covering. Each day Eve worked the loom Adam would take a minute to examine his daughter's work. He was increasingly impressed with the herringbone pattern visible only upon close inspection. Otherwise, the cloth appeared plain and strong.

Of some concern was Bombay's curiosity of Eve's weaving. Whenever the loom started up, Bombay would scamper; but when the loom was quiet Adam noticed the black cat stalking the loom and staring up at either the warp beam or the finished cloth.

After the months of intermittent labor, including finishing the cloth's ends, Eve finished the large weaving. Adam and Mary Ann were both glad, but for different reasons. The celebrated herringbone table covering, Eve's first major project, found a home in the chest at the foot of her bed. She had no intention of exposing it to the Wizard's designs. In Adam's proud mind, Eve was now a weaver.

3

Friday, March 22, 1795.

Mary Ann was glad to have visitors once again at Flax Haven, but she was feeling apprehensive. Her visits to Charles Town and to the Stuarts' store were no longer friendly, chatty visits. Linda and Jack were kind but distant; they weren't cold toward her, but the warmth had left, and Mary Ann felt alienated every time she patronized their store. This was not what she had planned; infamy was not to her liking. She had been there before and it was not pleasant.

Now the Hendershots had come for the day, ostensibly to help Adam finish building the Charles Town Road stone fence. On his many trips to Charles Town Adam had admired Mannheim Hendershot's fence and the way the field stones were stacked in an intricate, interlocking fashion. Not only did it look stronger, but it was aesthetically pleasing. Adam had told Mary Ann how he had stopped one day to make acquaintances with Mannheim and Ruth. They had some German ancestry in their blood as well, with some strong young boys. When Adam had asked too many questions about the fence, Mannheim suggested he bring his boys up for the day to show Adam how to do it. Next thing Mary Ann knew, the whole clan was on their way up with, no less, a wagon full of field stone Mannheim could not use.

The plan was to have Mannheim, his two boys—Matt, sixteen, Eve's age, and the other, Terrance, much older, Adam, Sam, and Henry work on the fence. Meanwhile, Ruth, their daughter Natalie, age five, Bethany, and Eve would prepare supper. It would be a big evening supper rather than a big noon dinner. When they arrived in the early afternoon, the men immediately got to work on the fence, while the women prepared the food.

Ruth was talkative and curious, too curious for Mary Ann's comfort. Ruth joked about having come from a city-bred family and how long it took her to get used to the sounds and happenings around their farm. Had Mary Ann struggled to get used to the sounds and things around a farm? Mary Ann was immediately put on defense, although she tried not to show it. Being the suspicious type, Mary Ann was pretty sure Ruth Hendershot and Linda Stuart were still chatty friends, and Linda had told Ruth everything that had happened at Flax Haven when the Stuarts had come for dinner a month ago. It was as if Ruth was expecting some strange occurrence to entertain her. Mary Ann surmised that by nature Ruth was given to gossip and likely to take any frivolous event and make an evening's entertainment out of it. To Mary Ann, Ruth seemed artificially happy and nervous—making frivolous conversation and then giggling over what she had said. Mary Ann wondered why the twenty years she had spent with Mannheim farming had not mellowed the petite woman with curly hair that was always flopping into her face.

It was late in the afternoon when the men returned from work on the fence and right away Mary Ann sensed something was wrong. Adam would normally have made Mannheim and his sons at home, offering them something to drink, and showing them where to clean up, although the barn trough was the first step. But when the men and boys came into the gathering hall and stood behind each other as if afraid to say a word, Mary Ann noticed right away that none of them had bothered to visit the trough or wipe the grime from their faces or clothes. Mary Ann was curious why Bethany hadn't chastise the men for their grungy appearance, but then she noticed her husband's discomfort and that he was staring at her as if she was guilty of some great transgression. He offered no explanation at first as if she knew what had happened. Henry stayed by the door, ready to escape. Behind Adam a bit to one side was Hand, whose eyes darted about as if he expected to be attacked by an unseen villain; his two boys were uneasy as they rocked back and forth on their dirty boots. Mary Ann suddenly felt ill. First it was Ruth's jitters, and now it was Adam's gloom.

Mary Ann stopped setting the table, looked at Adam, and tilted her head to ask the meaning of his despondent display.

"The winter wheat field is…destroyed," said Adam finally.

"What do you mean?" Mary Ann said.

Adam was silent. He just took a deep breath and looked to Mannheim.

"Your field of winter wheat," said Mannheim, "has been pulled up by the roots, out of the ground." Mannheim stopped to look to Adam for help.

"Well, not everywhere," said Adam, "but enough."

Mannheim continued. "It looks like someone came with a large hoe and dug up the plants, in the shape of…crescents. Maybe four or five feet long and a couple feet wide. The whole field is like that."

Mary Ann felt her heart leap into her throat.

"Ooooooo!" said Ruth. "Let's go see, Mary Ann."

Mary Ann stared at Ruth as if a great insult had been hurled at her, but then untied her apron, threw it on a chair, and stormed out the front door. Ruth was right behind her.

Once into the yard, Mary Ann met up with Sam, who was watering the Hendershots' horses that were harnessed to the wagon they had used to come to Flax Haven from their farm. Nearby was a second wagon filled with shovels, pick axes, crow bars, and chisels; it was harnessed to Luther, who was inching toward the water trough in front of the house.

"Sam, can I drive Luther back to see our winter wheat?" said Mary Ann.

"You mean what's left of it? Yes ma'am, you can. Go right ahead."

472 ○ Stanley D. Williams

And with that Mary Ann climbed up into the rig. Right behind her was a smiling, even excited, Ruth. Mary Ann waited for Ruth, but wasn't too happy about entertaining her guest with the mysterious events that evidently Flax Haven had become known for.

The winter wheat field was a quarter-mile southwest of the barn. She could tell even before pulling up along side it, that something was amiss. The field looked like a battle field, with crops destroyed throughout. She walked into the field to examine up close what had happened. Indeed, the wheat stalks had been pulled out of the ground and were laying, roots bare, flat, the holes where the plants had been clearly visible. But no hoe, rake, or shovel had been involved. Instead these plants had been plucked straight up and out without the ground being disturbed, and that disturbed Mary Ann a great deal.

But evidently not Ruth, who was all smiles, as if she had just won the cake baking contest at the county fair. "Oh, Mary Ann! Isn't this amazing? Just imagine what did this? Can you?" Ruth crouched down and picked up a ripe green wheat stalk that had been pulled out. She looked at it up close. "Funny, the stem and foliage has not been grasped by hands or a tool. Nothing is crushed. It's like the stalks just popped out of the ground by themselves."

"Doesn't that concern you in the least?" barked Mary Ann.

Ruth didn't hesitate. "No. It's not my field or Mannheim's. But as sure as I get back to our farm at Wild Oats, I'm going to check on our wheat. Isn't this just wild? Why aren't you excited?"

Mary Ann grunted at her guest, being careful not to say something that would offend, but was she ever tempted. She wanted to level a curse on her visitor, like the visitor a few months back had leveled on them. It had to be a curse. The areas where the plants had been pulled out of the ground were indeed in the shape of crescent moons. The size varied a bit, about three to five feet long and a foot to two feet wide. She walked in between the uprootings and looked for boot depressions. This had to be the work of the McCulloughs or some other slave owner upset over Sam and Bethany's manumission. That was Adam's far-flung conclusion that came out of the scissors bird and linen clippings.

Mary Ann wondered if they could get back to normal. She wondered if the Hendershots, Ruth in particular, would rattle on them to everyone in town. No doubt she would. *Damn*, Mary Ann thought.

Mary Ann suppressed her confusion that was working its way toward anger. She had to get away from the field. She had to force life back to normal. She felt her breath coming deep and uneven and her face becoming red. She concentrated; sheer will power would get her through this, or so she hoped. She didn't consider herself an actor, but there was no better time to start. "Ruth, dear, let's go back and feed our menfolk," she said and started back to Luther and the wagon.

"But don't you want to know *what* did this?" said Ruth.

"No," snapped Mary Ann at her guest. "I want to know *who* did it."

Picking up their bustles, minimal as they were, they hustled back up and into the wagon. Mary Ann whipped Luther into a trot and they were back to the house in a few minutes, where they handed over the wagon and its steed to Sam, who said nothing but did his duty.

Mounting the porch, Mary Ann stared at her husband and the other clueless males wandering about as if lost sheep. "Well!" said Mary Ann. "Do you want to eat inside or are you going to wait for me to throw feed out for ya?"

Adam said nothing but motioned for the men to follow him off the porch to begin their clean-up routine.

It was minutes later that everyone, subdued in action and speech, but trying to act as if some fit of normality was required of them, gathered around the table that Bethany had served hot and steaming, except for the spearmint lemonade, of which she had prepared a couple gallons.

Adam was first to pull out his chair and sit down, but neither Mannheim, Ruth, or their child moved. Mary Ann looked at her guests with a forced pleasantry. "Ruth, Mannheim, we want to thank you and your brood for your kindness in helping Adam build that fence. Won't you sit down and replenish your bodies?"

But neither Mannheim nor Ruth moved, nor did their children. "We're glad to do it, Mary Ann," said Ruth with a forced but genuine spirit. "That is what neighbors are for. Right, Mannheim?"

By this time Henry and Adam were reaching for bowls of food to heap on their plate and looking to pass the food to Mannheim or Ruth or the children. Mary Ann glanced at Bethany, who kept a straight face, but Eve was smiling ear to ear. *More resistance, I see,* thought Mary Ann.

Still standing behind his chair, Mannheim finally spoke. "Adam, would you mind if I say a prayer of thanks for this good food the ladies have cooked, and for the success in building your fence?"

"'Twas not God's labor but ours," said Adam.

Already disturbed by the crop destruction, Mary Ann was primed: "And why should he, or she, or it...have buried the rocks you used for the fence and not put them in a useful place to begin with? Why is that, if there be a god? Foolishness!!"

Mannheim and Ruth were speechless.

Adam, embarrassed by Mary Ann's rant, offered a humble reply: "Mannheim, Ruth, please forgive us for offending your faith. Please go ahead and pray, if you must."

After a beat to collect their thoughts, Mannheim and Ruth bowed their heads. Eve was quick to follow. But Adam, Mary Ann, and Henry just stared at their guests as the toddlers in high chairs babbled their demand for food.

Quietly but clearly, Mannheim prayed. "Be present at our table, Lord. Be here and everywhere adored. These mercies bless and grant that we may feast in fellowship with Thee, for Christ's sake. Amen."

Mary Ann noticed she had mellowed toward this praying fiasco, as these were her guests and not her charges. Yet her mellowing was parried by what otherwise caught her eye. As Mannheim prayed, a sooty vapor streamed up from between the floor boards and into the hutch of pottery, stoneware, and china. Mary Ann's immediate response was to yell "Fire!" but the vapor wasn't the consequence of fire, but something else, and it was that something else that stopped her outburst. It was the sound of clipping shears. At first Mary Ann's eyes were fixed on the black vapor, but it soon dissipated, forcing her eyes to flit about the room looking for their elusive scissors bird.

"Mary Ann, what sound is that?" Ruth asked when Mannheim finished praying.

"What sound?" said Mary Ann, trying to hide an oncoming panic. "Oh, that? Ignore it, 'tis nothing, really. These parts have such strange noises, after a while we hear nothing. Isn't that right, Adam?"

Adam had stopped chewing, looked about, and then stared at Mary Ann as if he was about to lop off her head for speaking. While staring at Mary Ann he answered Ruth and no doubt Mannheim's inquiry. "It is our neighbors that haunt us. I will skin them if they be caught," Adam said in a joking manner.

Sensing something awry, Ruth glanced dumbfounded at Mannheim, who turned down his eyes as if not to make more of the situation. He grimaced at Ruth as if to say, *do not let curiosity overcome our peace.*

Mary Ann saw the non-verbal exchange between her guests and appreciated Mannheim's discretion. But there would be no peace. Something caught her attention high up on a shelf of the dish hutch that stood against the stairway wall. Behind a stack of rare china the black vapor congealed into the shape of a hand and with a quick flick sent a stack of china dishes crashing to the floor, shattering the plates into thousands of pieces.

Mary Ann jumped before the dishes hit the floor, but at the sound Bethany, Adam, and Mannheim all leapt from their chairs. Mary Ann doubted that anyone but her saw the hand. Its appearance added to her jitters. "Bethany, get a broom. Oh, I'm so sorry for this."

"What happened?" asked Adam.

"I don't know," lied Mary Ann. "They just suddenly were shoved off the shelf."

"Shoved off?" said Adam. "What does that mean? What shoved them off?"

"Does it matter? Bethany, hurry, clean this up...please. Adam, get a basket for me." Mary Ann then knelt among the mess and began picking up large pieces of china and dropping them into the basket that Adam had found. The china was rare and beautiful, but she didn't much like it. It had been collected by her predecessor, Esther. Its breakage was a happy occasion, and its future absence a blessing. In fact, she wished the rest of the china would come crashing down off those shelves. It was a terrible thought, but one she had nourished since coming to Flax Haven. Unlike the loom, the china didn't rattle her nerves, so she let it be, although she rarely chose to use them, favoring the clay pottery she had used today. But now, a secret wish was being fulfilled. But how?

The scissors bird was really busy now. The clipping sound was slower but louder. Was she the only one that heard it?

Suddenly, while on her knees picking up the broken pieces of Esther's china and happily throwing them in the basket, it happened again. She didn't see it this time.

Ruth shouted, "MARY, LOOK OUT!"

Before Mary Ann could look up, another stack of china fell down from the hutch, this time directly on top of her bent-over back. A sharp pain exploded through her body. The pain was excruciating, and the impact of the falling china knocked Mary Ann flat to the ground.

Adam was quick to help her up, but now the sounds of multiple scissors clanking filled the room. George and Martha, trapped in their highchairs, began to fuss, or actually Martha began to fuss. Little George just looked about the room with wide-eyed curiosity. Ruth, no longer smiling, tried to comfort Martha, but to no avail, until Eve came to her rescue and lifted her step-sister from the chair and carried her off to the parlor.

Suddenly, the front door to the house swung open with a BANG, but no one was there. It opened on its own. A moment later, the Hendershots' horses neighed loudly and she could hear their carriage being rattled. Henry, the men, and the Hendershot children, mostly freaked by the sounds and the falling china, ran from the table to see what the problem was outside. Mary Ann got back up on all fours and again picked up pieces of china and put them in the basket that was now getting full.

Mary Ann was alone except for Ruth, who looked as if she had seen a ghost. Her face was frozen in fear. Gone was the smile and the flitting about. *The excitement finally got the better of her,* Mary Ann thought. But Ruth, distracted now by the rumblings, neighing, and shouting of men trying to calm two horses in their carriage harnesses, finally dragged herself from the room. Mary Ann gazed after her.

"It okay, Missus Livingston," said Bethany, who had acquired a broom and was sweeping up the mess. "I clean this up; you go be with your guests."

Mary Ann got up, although the sharp pain in her back kept her bent over, and headed for the front door with everyone else.

As soon as she walked through the front door, which was still flung wide open, she was faced with a yard full of confusion. The Hendershots' buggy and its two horses jostled and jumped as if trying to escape a pit of snakes, though there was nothing under their feet but dry dirt.

Mannheim dared to grab the reins of his spooked team and calm them down, but it was difficult. Holding the reins in front of them, he worked them around the yard away from whatever had spooked them, the carriage following in their path. They pranced in place, less wild now, their eyes wide with fear, clearly anxious to get away.

"Ruth!" Mannheim yelled out. "Get the children. Adam, glad to help, and thank you for your hospitality, but it's time we leave. Ruth! Hurry!"

With that Ruth herded her children to the wagon and in an instant the Hendershots were gone.

Mary Ann felt utterly defeated. They hadn't touched a bit of her food. The china was destroyed, however. No loss there. She looked to Adam, who was standing to the side near Sam who had been caring for the horses. He only stared at her, as if she was to blame for the whole mess. She wasn't, of course, but that didn't help matters. She felt guilty...but for what? For her part, the day was a disaster and no doubt rumors would spread that Flax Haven was to be avoided at all costs. Her goal of being a favored hostess in the community was dashed.

It was late in the day, approaching dusk, after Mary Ann, Bethany, and Eve cleaned up from the dinner that never happened, and Adam wet-mopped the floor to remove the remaining slivers of china.

Dusk had fallen when Mary Ann walked outside for some fresh air and gazed into the sky. There, just above the horizon, was a crescent moon exactly in the shape of linen clippings, and apparently, if there was a hawk cruising above and looking down, the shapes of the destroyed winter wheat crop.

4

That night, well after the sun had set, and the house cleaned up, Adam sat on the edge of Henry's bed. Henry was tucked in, but far from going to sleep. Eve, dressed for bed in a long gown, sat on Adam's lap.

Henry looked up at his father with watery eyes. "Papa, I'm scared.".

"I know, son. So am I. I'm sorry."

Eve got off her papa's lap and sat next to Henry, taking his hand in hers. "Henry," she said. "Let's pray to Mama."

"No," said Henry. "Papa doesn't want us to."

"Why is that, Henry?" said Eve.

Adam said nothing, and Eve clearly had no intention of involving him. This was between her and Henry. Henry shrugged his shoulders and stared at Eve as if begging for an answer.

Eve glanced around the room, Adam presumed, to check that Mary Ann was not present. "Okay," Eve said, "I'll do it." With that Eve, still holding Henry's hand, bowed her head and closed her eyes. "Mama, Oh, Mama. You know everything. We know very little. We're a little scared right now because of the Wizard. He's trying to get us scared. But we know you want us to trust God. Please be kind to the Hendershots, and bless Bethany, Sam, our workers, and especially Papa and Mary Ann. Please help Papa to know what to do to make us safe, in Jesus' name. Amen." Then she quickly added, "And please help Henry not to be afraid and make him sleepy so he'll have sweet dreams. Amen, again." Eve then leaned over and kissed Henry on the forehead like their mother used to do when they were little and she put him to bed with a prayer.

Adam watched, eyes wide open with awe at the maturity of his daughter, who was acting more and more like Esther each day. She had to be scared, a little, but she seemed calm and reflective.

Henry had been quiet and just looked up at Eve, even after she kissed him and let go of his hand. "Thank you," he said. "Good night, Papa." With that Henry rolled over and closed his eyes.

"Goodnight, Papa," said Eve. She kissed him on the forehead too, and in her bare feet padded out of the room to her own bedroom.

Adam looked after her and the open doorway for a solid minute after she had left. When he turned back, Henry was sawing logs. Adam was in awe of his daughter, but he still had no use for God, and he certainly didn't believe in some Wizard. Childish imaginations.

After ensuring the house was shut up for the night he joined Mary Ann in bed and pulled a sheet over them. He looked at the sheet twice; there were no holes. Why did he do that? Was he expecting every piece of cloth in the house to be cut up? *A ridiculous thought.* Mary Ann was awake and cuddled up next to him. He put an arm around her and held her close. Her soft breasts under her nightgown felt warm against his chest, but making love to her was far from his mind, and hers.

"What will you do?" she asked in a whisper.

"Nothing," Adam said. "It will pass. Nothing. It is nothing. Go to sleep, my dear."

5

Most Feared Master of Brokenness,

I am not a happy sub-demon. I am broken. You have done this to me. Yes, I know that I should always hate myself, detest what I do, and glory in it at the same time. Irony is my loin cloth. But where is the satisfaction?

Here I am working my fool heart out trying to edge Livingston and his whole clan toward desperation and damnation, but my only reward is a prayer of faith to a saint before the Almighty, and a declaration that what I am doing is "nothing...it will pass."

Then there is the indignity of being called a "Wizard," which I do not appreciate. Wizard translated poorly, but unequivocally means "Gutless Inbu" or "him without genitalia." It is an insult. I'm no eunuch, although there is some similarity.

I did prompt Cahill, however, to cast the first stone and impudently ask the bishop in his ivory tower for money. The eventual consequences, I predict, will be rewarding...for us, not Cahill.

I must step up my game. Let's call out the cavalry.

At your sinful service,
Cyn Namrasit, OPSD

Chapter 32
Momma Told Me To

1

April 19, 1795.

After the Hendershots' visit the haunts had persisted for a few days and then diminished. The family enjoyed several weeks of normalcy and quiet.

One night, before he came to bed, Adam looked over the twins in their cribs. They slept soundly.

"I nursed them just before I laid down," Mary Ann said from under their bed covers.

"One day these cribs will be too small. I'll have to make bigger ones."

"If they live that long," she said.

"Why would you say that? They're almost three. Have they been sickly? You said the longer you nurse them the stronger they'll be. However you know that, I know not."

There was a long pause as Mary Ann turned over in bed. "Ruth told me that two children, healthy children, a boy and a girl about the ages of George and Martha, a family they know in Winchester, died in their sleep last month."

Adam said nothing as he sat on the edge of their bed and put his head in his hands. He got back up and made sure the twins were covered, touching them softly, checking their breathing, then he crawled into bed next to Mary Ann who had turned her back on him. Sleep did not come; their nerves were frayed. A gentle breeze drifted through an open window.

"Adam, what is going on?" Mary Ann said. "Things have not been right since you let that Stranger stay in the house."

"And who was it that invited him in?" Adam said.

"He cursed us, he did, and you've done nothing about it."

"Tell me what to do, and I be doing it."

They lay there for a while in silence, close but not touching, with only the sounds of crickets and night-owls keeping them company in their estrangement.

But that was not to be for long.

"You hear it?" said Adam.

"Yes," she said.

It was faint, but the sound was instantly recognized. In the distance, scissors clanking, nervously, insistently, even haphazardly. Adam froze, afraid to breathe. He felt Mary Ann beside him stiffen, too.

Suddenly they both twitched.

"Stop that," she said sharply.

"What?" he said.

"Quit shaking," she said. "You're making me nervous."

"I haven't moved."

Adam held perfectly still, but at his feet the bedspread and linen sheets that covered them were moving, undulating...with the sounds of the scissors opening and closing.

"Adam! Do not tease."

"Then stop your squirming, woman."

"'Tis not me."

Adam slid his bare feet away from his wife, but his big toes caught themselves in what felt like large holes...in the sheet which was under the bedspread.

In anger, Adam pulled back the bedspread and flung it to Mary Ann's side.

"What're you doing?" Mary Ann chafed, "I'm not cold."

Adam said nothing as he wiggled his toes. He couldn't see clearly in the dark, but it felt as if his toes were poking through holes that should not exist in the linen sheet. The sheet was not threadbare in the least. Linen didn't wear out. It lasted a lifetime, unlike cheap cotton. He shook his feet loose of whatever had entangled them and swung them out of the bed.

"Where you 'bout?" whined Mary Ann.

But Adam refused to speak. His mind was focused. He reached for the tinder box, struck a flint, and lit his side table lantern. Turning back to the bed, he pulled the bedspread off Mary Ann and the bed.

"Stop it," she snapped.

Standing by the side of the bed he lifted the lantern high and gazed at the foot of the bed. The foot of the linen sheet that lay atop their bodies had been cut to shreds, apparently in the shape of crescent moons. "Look!" he said. Her naked toes stuck through the holes in the sheet.

Mary Ann rose up and looked in fright at what she must have also felt.

Angry, Adam ripped the sheet entirely from the bed. Hundreds of small linen crescent moons fell from the sheet to the bed and floor.

Suddenly, the lower sash of the window flew up, opening the window wide to the outside. In swept a wind that whirled about, catching up the cut-out crescent shapes in a funnel and sucked them out the window. The whirlwind pulled at Adam and Mary Ann's bedclothes, tossed their hair, and extinguished the lantern Adam held aloft.

Mary Ann screamed. It was a blood-curdling scream filled with full-on fear and horror. She shook uncontrollably and kicked her feet wildly to get the shredded sheet off her legs. Adam sat on the bed and held her. Taken with fright she beat on him, as if he was the enemy who had to be destroyed.

As soon as it had come, the whirlwind disappeared, along with the cut-out crescents. Just as the window had slammed up, now it slammed closed with a bang. Mary Ann's body trembled. She grabbed Adam and hugged him for dear life.

Filled with rage and not a little fear, Adam was not one to flee, but to fight. The clipping sounds now came from outside the bedroom door, which was open. He gazed into the hall. Nothing there to see, but the sounds were definitely coming from that direction. He untangled himself from Mary Ann's arm, rotated out of bed, put on his boots, grabbed his shillelagh, and marched out of the bedroom. Suddenly, he stopped. Eve, holding a lit lantern, and Henry, both in their nightgowns, stood there staring at him. Henry's arms clung to his sister's. Adam stared at them, almost threatening them with his swinging fighting stick. The sounds of clipping scissors became louder, more insistent. Clearly they were coming from downstairs. The children watched him with wide eyes but no questions. Grasping his shillelagh in a tighter, more determined grip, he turned from the children and descended the stairs. He could hear Eve behind him. He glanced back; Henry had gone into his stepmother's room.

Adam descended the stairs to the foyer and stepped into the archway of the gathering hall. He stopped and listened. The clipping was close at hand but as soon as he entered the gathering hall it stopped.

Behind Adam, on its own, the front door latch lifted. Adam turned to the sound and watched the door creak open on its own allowing a gust of wind to enter.

Eve, who had been standing halfway up the stairs with her lantern, quickly ran down the stairs and hit the partially open door, slamming it shut. She relatched the door and put her back to it.

Adam stared at his daughter and she at him as they both listened. In a moment the clipping resumed...at the side of the gathering hall where the hutch stood with their dishes, pottery, and a drawer of linen.

2

Eve Livingston knew that the chest of drawers near the fireplace contained unfinished linen scraps, but the cloths in the hutch were much different. She turned quickly to the hutch and set her lantern on the counter top. The top two drawers contained centerpiece decorations and rarely used serving bowls and utensils, but the clipping sounded came from the top drawer. She pulled it open. No linens of course, just centerpiece decorations. The clipping intensified and shifted to the drawer below. Fearless, Eve pushed the top drawer closed and pulled open the second drawer...utensils and bowls. She stopped and listened. More clipping...cat and mouse...the sound shifted again to the bottom drawer. Closing the middle drawer she quickly pulled open the bottom drawer where finished and neatly folded linens were stored. There, to the side, the stacked pile of linen table coverings bulged up and down in sync with the clipping sound. It was as if a hand was under the cloth with a pair of shears. Eve frantically ripped out the folded material, one after the other, until she got to the bottom where the up and down movement of the bottom cloth was pronounced.

For just an instant she glimpsed a black translucent vapor of what appeared to be a small amorphous head chewing on the cloth. But the vapor dissipated and the clipping stopped as soon as it was exposed to the light, dim as it was. She pulled the cloth out and opened it up. Indeed there were holes in the cloth in the shape of crescent moons of various sizes and randomly spaced.

Adam came with his lantern and stood over her. She glanced up at his face filled with concern and frustration, but she didn't wait for him to tell her what to do. Frantically, Eve piled all the linens from the drawer, including the partially clipped cloth, in a pile. She tried to pick them up, but the pile was too heavy and unwieldy.

"Papa, pick these up. Take them to my room," Eve said somewhat breathlessly. Eve saw the question on Papa's face. "I'll take the lanterns. Follow me." She stood up and took his lantern, which he freely handed over, and she led him up the stairs with his load of linens all woven by her mother. She was protecting her mother's legacy, she knew it, and she suspected Papa knew it, too.

In Eve's bedroom were two heirloom chests. The one by the foot of her bed was full, but there was a second by the fireplace where she kept childhood wooden toys, dolls, and other keepsakes. Walking briskly to the second keepsake chest, she opened it and unceremoniously emptied its contents onto the floor between the fireplace and her bed. Then as her father stood by, she took each linen and put it reverently in the bottom of the chest.

When that was done, with the lid still wide open, she hurried to the heirloom chest at the foot of her bed, opened it, and dug deep along the front, pulling out a dark wooden object. She studied it momentarily. Bethany had suggested she keep it in her bedroom, mostly hidden, as a guard against evil spirits. Eve had no hesitation to do as Bethany suggested. Now that she had revealed the object's presence to her father, who stood a few feet away watching, she sensed that he would say nothing to her stepmother.

Carrying the object to the keepsake chest, she knelt down in front of the chest, held the wooden object close to her heart, bowed her head, and prayed: "Oh, Mama, Oh, Mama. A frightful Wizard from the depths of hell is after us. Please pray for us. Save us, Mama. Tell Jesus and the angels we need their help and protection. Oh, Mama. Oh, Mama, pray for us. Amen."

When she was done, she took the Stranger's crucifix and laid it on top of the stack of linens. Her father knelt beside her and started handing her dolls, toys, and keepsakes to put back in the chest on top of the crucifix and linens.

"Thank you, Papa," Eve said.

"Thank you, Eve."

No sooner had Eve shut the keepsake chest than they heard the front door rattle downstairs. Eve's eyes popped open and her heart raced. She stood and ran for the door, but Papa grabbed her and pulled her back.

"I got this, Eve. You go help Mary Ann with the twins and Henry."

Eve wasn't so sure she wanted to do that, but considering what had just happened, and what she had done, and with her father's tacit approval, she said, "Yes, Papa. I will pray for you."

Her father nodded and quickly left the bedroom, his shillelagh gripped tightly in hand.

Eve watched from the top of the stairs as Papa descended to the front door that rattled violently as if an angry bear were on the other side demanding entry. Approaching the door with his shillelagh raised and ready to strike, Adam reached for the latch and lifted it.

But before he could pull the vibrating door open, an explosion of air from outside forced the door open, shoving him back until he collapsed at the foot of the stairs. In rushed a thick whirlwind of black vapor that sought out every corner of the foyer, gathering hall, and parlor. So thick was the vapor that Eve lost sight of Papa for a few moments. It totally engulfed him. Then, as soon as it had entered, the black vapor was hastily sucked out the way it came.

In the process Papa's lantern was extinguished. Eve ran down the stairs. "Here, Papa, take mine." She wasn't sure why her lantern always stayed lit but it did.

Adam took her lantern and ventured onto the porch. As he did, Henry came down the stairs and stood behind Eve one step with a lantern. Eve was glad for that...because now she was in the dark, her lantern now outside with Papa. Henry edged past Eve to the now wide open door and watched his father; Eve took up a station behind her brother.

What greeted Adam outside was a windstorm that encircled the house. It created a cloud of intense dirt and dust and blocked the view of anything beyond, even though the moon was visible. So vicious was the encircling wind that it sounded like a stampede of horses in full gallop.

Adam, his shillelagh raised high, careened on the edge of the porch looking for something to hit. Eve thought Papa looked a bit like Moses on the edge of the Red Sea with his staff held high, but nothing to command.

Henry and Eve cautiously ventured onto the porch just behind their father.

"Look, Papa!" yelled Henry above the noise of the wind. He pointed to the ground under the whirling dirt just beyond the porch steps. Adam looked down as did Eve. What she saw surprised her and caused her to fear. Horse hoof prints could easily be seen stomping in the dirt. These were not hoof prints of shod horses but wild horses. And the louder the sound became, the more hoof-marks were stamped into the dirt, kicking up a cloud of dirt.

The three watched in awe and fear for some minutes as the spectacle played out in front of them. They were wordless. Nothing prepared them for that moment.

Eve went back into the house, lit a fresh lantern that was by the cellar stairs and came out next to her father on the porch. As she did, and more light was cast on the phenomenon, the whirlwind, the noise of galloping horses and the stamping of hoof prints in the dirt slowly abated.

When calm had returned to the farm, Adam descended the stoop steps and crouched down to examine the worn path of hoof prints. Eve and Henry came with him. The marks were of horses all right, but only the front of the hoofs were clearly struck into the dirt, leaving behind what appeared to be the shapes of crescent moons.

Adam stood and looked up. The crescent moon hung high in the sky. He glanced at his children, then back to the sky. "Have you noticed? These things only happen just before, during, or just after the new moon."

"Why?" said Henry looking up at the crescent.

"Don't know, son."

"It's a Wizard from hell, Papa," said Eve. "It's the Stranger's curse."

Adam looked down at his daughter and shook his head. "No daughter, it's not that, but I'll be stuck to know what it is."

Chapter 33
Three Months to Investigate

My Lord Maréchal,

The haunts that Mister Livingston, his family, and acquaintances experienced, I, too, would experience. Let me retrace how I came to the Livingston affair.

After my ordination, Bishop Carroll sent me to the Jesuit Manor house on the upper banks of the Potowmack at Port Tobacco to recover my health. Seminary life to me was most beautiful and edifying. Yet in my earnestness to completely fulfill my vocation to Christ, I neglected my delicate constitution and willingly submitted to the severe rule of the seminary. In my youthful enthusiasm—I was but twenty-five at the time of my ordination—I rejoiced whenever my confessor gave me additional penance and mortification. I was very sensitive to my failings and wanted to eradicate them completely. The mortifications and sedentary life of seminary, however, drained me of my youthful vigor. I could no longer jump easily onto a horse, or fence a friendly duel, both of which were passions of mine before.

In Europe I was an expert horseman, but after seminary the seventy-five mile trip on horseback to Port Tobacco, which should have taken two days, took me nearly four, more because of my seminary-induced malaise than anything due to the horse who trotted easily and without complaint.

After a much too short stay at the Manor, and some obstinate communication with Bishop Carroll, who wanted me to begin my circuit out of Conewago, I was assigned to assist the bishop in Baltimore as a translator for him with his German clerics. After a few months I relented to my bishop's wishes and was installed at Conewago with a number of other priests. We brought the sacraments to numerous settlements including the Allegheny mountains, which would eventually be my home, and from where I write you now.

It was during those first years attending those towns with the sacraments that I learned the desperate situation Mister Livingston would be in when he began to search for spiritual assistance. I found in my sacramental travels and teaching that among the American common man (I wanted to call them peasants) the greatest ignorance prevailed, along with prejudice, bigotry, and persecution. My former tutor, who as a priest accompanied me from Germany, Mr. Brosium, was likewise installed at Conewago. Already a priest who came to America as a missionary, he escaped from anti-Catholic ruffians one time, only because his horse was faster. In my own case, I faced many dangerous journeys. Now you may think that the ignorance and ideology were true only of the unreligious populace, but I assure you, it was also true of many foreign priests (Mr.

Brosium excepted) who came as missionaries. Bishop Carroll was faced with many difficulties in taming 20–30 priests that had come to America before him, and were developing parishes without the authority or guidance of a bishop and often with a weak or wrong understanding of Catholic teaching. This, of course, was Carroll's problem with Fr. Denis Cahill. Fr. Cahill knew the faith, and he was robust in it, even more so than my own at the time, but Bishop Carroll had his difficulties reining in the Irish renegade.

I can now vouch for Fr. Cahill as a man of powerful nerve and hearty faith, but at the time could not. I do not have a copy of Bishop Carroll's response, but I did come to know the tenor of it. Bishop Carroll informed Fr. Cahill that he needed to come to Baltimore and present himself and whatever credentials Cahill possessed. If the credentials satisfied the bishop, and if Cahill demonstrated a subordinate attitude, Carroll would accept him as a priest in good standing. But in so doing, Fr. Cahill must pledge obedience to Carroll's complete authority and be willing to be appointed where he was most needed, which may remove him from his current work.

As will become evident as my narrative continues, that did not sit well with Fr. Cahill, who, it turned out, was truly not only a priest of robust faith, but also a man of independent and temperamental spirit. Fr. Cahill ignored the bishop's request to appear in Baltimore and later explained to me that his experience with prelates was often contrary to his discernment of God's will.

My view in coming to Virginia in 1797 and remaining there three months was to investigate those extraordinary facts at the Livingstons, of which I had heard so much at Conewago, and which I could not prevail upon myself to believe; but I was soon converted to a full belief of them. No lawyer in a court of justice did ever examine or cross-examine witnesses more strictly than I did all those I could procure.

Your Servant,
Fr. Smith

Chapter 34
Pouch of Cold

1

May, 1795.

Richard McSherry was grappling with a problem of his own creation, or so he was telling himself. As Fr. Cahill's patron he was satisfied that Fr. Cahill had well established Catholic societies in Martinsburg, Shepherd's Town, Winchester, Fort Cumberland, Chambersburg, and of course in Hagerstown where Fr. Cahill lived at Magdala. Richard always received good reports that in each of these towns Fr. Cahill had faithfully administered the sacraments and provided instruction in the faith. To Richard it seemed clear that Fr. Cahill was a priest above reproach, a gentle confessor, and readily available for baptisms and attending to the sick if he was in town. When the two men met to share a meal and an evening together, as they did at least once a month, Fr. Cahill repeatedly complained about his congregations' woeful knowledge of the faith and the moral life. He had wondered how so many people had been so poorly catechized and had ever been confirmed. Verifying his congregants' history with the Church was difficult, as few had baptism or confirmation certificates. This was something Fr. Cahill was diligent in correcting, at least for those that he confirmed and baptized. Richard had witnessed, too, that Fr. Cahill's homilies were considerably longer than most—an attempt to instruct the faithful in their faith.

But there was one thing Fr. Cahill was not very good at, and this created a serious problem for Richard. It was Fr. Cahill's practice of placing a collection box at the back of the room where Mass was held and encouraging congregants to deposit their tithes on the way out. Richard much preferred the Protestant practice of passing a basket down the rows of the congregation, which created some peer pressure to put something in and not be outdone by others watching. Not all forms of pride were evil. Trying to outdo one another in generosity was a virtue according to St. Paul, but Catholics were not good tithers. In fact, they were bad tithers. Richard thought that some of the hesitancy to drop money in the offering box was the simple financial state in which most found themselves. He reasoned: even if each at least gave a widow's mite there might be enough to fully support their priest, and even build a small chapel. But no, that did not seem to be in the offing.

Without the full support of the rich, and Richard knew he fell into that category, the Church would wither on the vine. There were practical limits to Richard's coffers and his generosity, yet both men had designs to build chapels in each town, and even structures with tall steeples that would challenge the Protestant edifices. Fr. Cahill, however, was not persuasive in getting his parish members to give money. Richard had to finally admit that converting the stingy into the generous was not Fr. Cahill's gift.

Yet the well-being of the community, Richard believed, was tied to the physical growth of the Church and its visibility. While he would prefer to see a cathedral, a small chapel would suffice, at least at first. The physical presence of a building would provide Catholics with an identity and roots. There would be a visible place to pray and worship, and a permanent building would elevate the status of Catholicism among the non-Catholics, who just might take more seriously Church teachings of what is good and true.

But the offerings were paltry and barely met Fr. Cahill's personal expenses, let alone enough to start a building fund. At the same time, per their agreement, Fr. Cahill's allowance from Richard was waning, and while Richard could easily extend his allowance to support Fr. Cahill, such extension did not solve the basic problem of getting the parishes to support themselves.

Richard was pretty sure that smoothing over the riff between Fr. Cahill and Bishop Carroll might bring financial support from the bishop, but Richard was not sure that was a good fix. If Fr. Cahill's trouble motivating his parishes to be financially responsible was any indication, Richard could only imagine how difficult it was for the bishop. It was entirely possible that the bishop was expecting support from Cahill, and not the other way around, and that disappointed both Richard and his hired priest.

2

Adam had finally made the connection between the supernatural manifestations and waning and waxing of a new moon. As the moon ebbed and its crescent became less pronounced, the manifestations about the house and barn increased, reaching their peak when the moon went completely dark.

During this time Eve's collection of linens in both her bedroom keepsake chests grew until the chests were full and could hold no more. Except for the linens that Eve hid and thus protected, all other linens in the house had been destroyed.

This left Adam emotionally tortured. There was something special about his daughter, but he refused to accept that it had anything to do with her religious faith, so hardened he was over Esther's death.

For a time he worried that the clipped material was somehow a wicked prank Mary Ann played on him in another attempt to rid the loom from her gathering hall. Her emotional response to the clipping and the loom had their similarities, a general disgust and blaming him for both, as if the loom was the cause of the intrusions. He found himself unknowingly taking on Eve's attitude and thinking that what they were dealing with was an entity with an intelligence, a spiritual entity or Wizard as Eve referred to it. But he so hated the idea of not being in control of his life and farm that he became angry at himself for becoming superstitious. Others he had met were like that, and he so disrespected them he avoided their company. Ghosts didn't exist. At least, he concluded, an intelligent and disciplined mind was the surest way to guarantee they didn't exist.

But what then of his problem? How did he explain the activity that seemingly required an embodied entity to do the things that were being done? Most recently he had discovered marks on the leather harnesses, saddles, and tack in the barn. When he pointed this out to Mary Ann she instantly blamed the McCulloughs. At one point she suspected some of the day laborers, but Adam disregarded the theory; he pointed out that his day laborers were only in the barn when Sam or he was present.

Adam had become extra alert to Calvin's and Luther's behavior. Although the shire breed was regarded for their easy-going temperament, Adam knew his Calvin and Luther well, and that the presence of a stranger in the barn at odd times would make the horses anxious. Mary Ann's Apple would be agitated more quickly than the shires, but not nearly as easily as her mistress.

Mary Ann also did not believe in ghosts, so she took out her anger on Adam whenever new clippings were discovered. They would hear the sound of shears, but only later find a towel, sheet, or curtains shredded, as if an eclipse of moths had suddenly come and gone, devouring the materials in a night. Adam worried that their clothes might be next on the shredding docket.

3

Mary Ann Livingston was trying hard to balance her life, to find some meaning in the chaos that surrounded their farm. She had always felt that society was her place, but her hopes had been dashed several times, and the recent disturbances had isolated her even more. When she went to town people avoided her. It was annoying and made her sad. It was not easy to fall back into the rejected part of society as she was before she met Adam. She felt horrible when shopping in town to have old friends turn away instead of engaging her. She tried to ignore it and pretend she had no need of that particular individual. Yet her entire being longed for feminine friendship, conversation, and acknowledgment that she existed.

Mary Ann had never hit it off with the elite of the nearby towns. Not that she hadn't tried, Anastasia McSherry notwithstanding. She kept hoping, and diligently prepared for the opportune unscheduled visit. She hid, burned, or buried every scrap of clipped cloth or broken pottery that confirmed the rumors that strange spirits roamed her husband's farm. Consequently, the house was bare of table linens. Then she waited. Each day she secretly hoped someone would call on her, just to visit and be friendly, not suspicious or paranoid. But the suspicious and paranoid did come, always feigning some far-fetched ambiguous errand.

She felt like putting up a sign at the road saying, "Visitors Welcome… during full moons." But that sounded dangerous and she feared even more unwelcome curiosity seekers.

Eventually her efforts paid off…sort of.

Late one afternoon, while the men were off in the field working and Eve and Henry had taken the twins exploring, Bethany alerted Mary Ann that a closed carriage, driven by a coachman, had pulled into the yard. Mary Ann hurried up from the cellar where she was picking out sweet potatoes. The ladies of the house arrived on the front porch as the coachman opened the carriage's door and helped down a middle-aged woman in a fancy dress complete with sashes, scarves, a parasol, and a silk reticule.

Mary Ann was stunned. This was obviously a woman of distinction, a woman of society and rank. But where could she have come from, and how could Mary Ann, in her dirty work clothes and soiled apron, greet such a woman?

Alighting from the carriage, the woman walked briskly in her full skirt to the bottom of the porch stairs from which Mary Ann had descended.

"Missus Livingston?" the woman happily inquired.

Mary Ann was taken aback by the woman's ostentatious appearance. This was a working farm, not a governor's ball. "Yes, how can I be of service, Madam?"

"I am *Missus Henrietta Argyle. "My husband is an influential county official in Martinsburg."

"You came all the way from Martinsburg?" asked Mary Ann, very surprised, for Martinsburg was hours away by horse and further by carriage.

"We have close acquaintances in Charles Town," said Mrs. Argyle as she started up the steps as if on an errand of urgent importance. "Do you have any tea for a weary traveler?" Mrs. Argyle was shorter than Mary Ann, but not short in confidence as she lifted her skirt and twirled on her white leather, high-top button shoes to take in the landscape from atop the porch. "My, what a lovely farm and home you have." Her bright hazel eyes took in the wood planking as if she were counting ring patterns in the slats.

Bethany stepped away and caught Mary Ann's eye and whispered, "Shall I brew tea?"

"Why, that would be lovely, thank you," said Mrs. Argyle before Mary Ann could reply. "May I go in?" said the visitor to the mistress.

Mary Ann was startled at Mrs. Argyle's boldness, but also smitten by a confidence that Mary Ann envied. She opened the door for the *influential* official's nosy wife, then nodded approval to Bethany, who scampered away to prepare refreshments.

As soon as Mrs. Argyle stepped into the foyer Mary Ann noticed the woman's happy eyes turn to worry as they darted in every direction as if not to be caught unawares of some hidden trickery. At the same moment Mrs. Argyle's confident step turned staid, as if those pretty white boots were nailed to the foyer rug. Mary Ann noted with some confidence that the rug was still in one piece. The table coverings, doilies, towels, and curtains were all gone, but the rugs were amazingly still in tack. Mrs. Argyle had entered the inner sanctum, or so she must have surmised, and responded accordingly. Instantly, Mary Ann understood Mrs. Argyle's surprise appearance. It wasn't neighborly cordiality, but prying curiosity. While Mary Ann appreciated the attention of a society madam, she also lamented the motivation. But she had considered such a situation and had calculated a response.

"So, Missus Argyle," began Mary Ann, "you've never been in a haunted house before?"

Mrs. Argyle suddenly turned to Mary Ann with a blank, shocked gaze as if she had just been caught in the act of stealing a crystal bowl.

"What?! Whatever do you mean?" Mrs. Argyle asked with a subtle but uncontrollable quiver in her voice.

"Please come into the parlor and sit for a while. Bethany will bring us refreshments," Mary Ann said and led the suddenly petrified Mrs. Argyle to a cushioned chair, which Mary Ann also noted had not yet met the Wizard's curse. *All the better, more ammunition,* thought Mary Ann. "Please, sit here on this pretty cushioned chair. It's my favorite." Mary Ann watched as Mrs. Argyle tip-toed into the parlor, gazed down at the teal silk pillow with tassels on the four corners, and ran her gloved hand over the flawless weave. "You won't hurt it. Please make yourself comfortable."

Mrs. Argyle sat down carefully on the silk pillow and looked across to Mary Ann who sat on a plain wooden chair across from a round table on which a book and lantern sat. "I'm sorry for my effrontery, Missus Livingston. It's just that...." her voice trailed off.

Mary Ann completed the sentence for her: "You've heard that our house was visited by ghostly spirits and you just had to see for yourself." It was a matter-of-fact reply that rolled off her tongue.

At that point Bethany entered with a tray and set it on the table between the two ladies. On the tray was a clay dish of apple croissants, two pewter mugs of steaming jasmine tea, a small bowl of sugar, and a miniature pitcher of cream. None of the vessels matched in color, style, or material.

Mrs. Argyle gawked at the tray. She couldn't help herself. "No porcelain tea set?"

"This is a working farm, Missus Argyle, not the center of society."

"Yes, I see," replied the guest.

"Jasmine," said Bethany as she handed a mug to Mrs. Argyle, who tried to hold it like she might a delicate china tea cup with her thumb and finger, allowing her pinkie to point skyward. But pewter mugs defy such finger gymnastics and she finally plunged all four fingers through the handle and took the mug from Bethany's hand, turning up her nose at the sugar and cream and sipping the hot brew.

The tea seemed to bring Mrs. Argyle back to herself, and she smiled once again at her host. "You're right, Missus Livingston, I have not been in a haunted house, nor have I met a ghost. But rumors have it that is what besets you."

"Nonsense, Missus Argyle. Nothing could be further from the truth."

At this Bethany stared at Mrs. Livingston for a moment, until Mary Ann glanced back at Bethany with a sly smile and blinked her eyes. Bethany in turn raised her eyebrows, tipped her head back as if to laugh, but kept her mouth closed, pivoted, and left the room.

"You see, Madam," continued Mary Ann, "we are in the business of planting, growing, harvesting, and selling a variety of produce and flax. My husband is expert at what he does. But for some of us, farming is all work and no play. So, at times the children and I...well, actually, Mister Livingston and the help play at this as well, have made it a game of playing pranks on one another, and admittedly on our guests as well. What we didn't count on was the seriousness of how others would take it."

"Pranks?!" Mrs. Argyle was taken aback.

"Yes, I'm afraid so, just pranks," said Mary Ann. "And I'm sorry I can't demonstrate them to you for my compatriots in the business are all out right now." Mary Ann smiled, and chuckled at the joke, feeling like quite the actor and smiling continuously at her guest.

Mrs. Argyle looked around. "The rumors have it that all your linens have been destroyed or clipped to shreds. Where are your table coverings and doilies, if...."

"Never had any," interrupted Mary Ann. "Have you ever tried to dust table tops with those flimsy doilies getting in your way?"

"No, we have servants that do that," said Mrs. Argyle.

"Well, there you are, we have not servants."

"But...." Mrs. Argyle pointed out the door through which Bethany had left moments earlier.

"Bethany?" said Mary Ann. "Oh, Bethany's no servant. She's a free woman. Hired help along with her foreman husband, Sam. Good people. Have you ever tried to wash and iron table linens?"

Mrs. Argyle shook her head slowly.

"It's a hell of a job," said Mary Ann. "Not having them is much easier. And you can enjoy the character of the wood grain as you eat or work at the table."

At times during their conversation Mary Ann heard the Wizard's scissors bird quietly at work. But it was so soft that it did sound like a far-off bird chirping for a mate. Mary Ann said nothing, and Mrs. Argyle seemed not to notice. *Just as well,* thought Mary Ann. But she wondered just what was going to show up next...shredded.

It was late afternoon when the conversation in the parlor ended. Mary Ann was feeling proud of herself for not being a nervous wreck, and being inventive and entertaining at the same time. If she was honest, however, she did miss her porcelain tea set. Mary Ann saw the smiling Mrs. Argyle out to the front porch. Her coachman readied the carriage, harnessed the horse which had been grazing just east of the house, and brought the conveyance near the porch steps.

"Missus Livingston, it was a delight to meet you after all this talk and to understand your brood's sense of humor. It sure has livened up the gossip in recent months."

"Likewise, Missus Argyle. I'm sorry to disappoint you. But there are no ghosts, no clipping wizards. Just us dowdy farm folk."

"I am greatly embarrassed that for one moment I believed such vicious rumors about...well, you know how things get blown out of proportion."

At that moment Mary Ann gathered up the hem of her apron, which she had been wearing the whole time, and wiped her hands of nervous perspiration. In the process she felt something strange on the underlying skirt. She glanced down to see what it was. Her dark blue linen skirt of which she was so fond had dozens of crescent moons clipped out of it. She caught her breath and quickly dropped the apron in front of the shredded clothing. The perspiration suddenly returned, not just to her hands, but her face and neck as well. The smile also left her countenance and she suddenly became anxious to see Mrs. Argyle off and gone. But Mrs. Argyle wasn't paying attention to Mary Ann. *Thank goodness.*

Mrs. Argyle had descended the stairs and was fully back to her happy self, laughing as she twirled her expensive dress to show Mary Ann. "Look, my dear, my beautiful dress is all in one piece. I have to admit I worried that it might be 'clipped' as they say. But look, not a thread out of place. Thank you for your hospitality. I shall tell the ladies what a gracious host you are."

Mary Ann curtsied, careful not to reveal her own clipped skirt just discovered. "Why, thank you, Missus Argyle."

Mrs. Argyle opened her reticule and held it up for Mary Ann to see. Giggling, she said, "But just in case, I protected my very expensive Parisian silk scarf right here in my reticule." She pulled out the silk scarf as a magician might. "It's so beaut...."

Well, it *was* beautiful, thought Mary Ann. The multi-colored scarf was shredded by a hundred crescent shapes as it dangled like a dreaded disease from Henrietta's fingers. That's when Mrs. Henrietta Argyle let out a blood-curdling scream.

So frightening was the socialite's scream that it spooked her carriage horse that jumped left and right, trying to throw off its harness, and pulling the carriage in circles. The coachman ran after the conveyance, but Henrietta continued to scream and shriek in short uncontrolled bursts.

Mary Ann found the sight amusing, as if there was justice after all in the world. But after a few moments she worried that the woman might fall over dead in her yard and she, Mary Ann, would be charged with the killing.

Bethany, in shock and not a little fear, ran out onto the porch and stood next to Mary Ann watching Mrs. Argyle waving her shredded scarf in fright and running after the coachman, who was running after the carriage being pulled chaotically about the yard.

At the risk of being trampled, the coachman finally grabbed the spooked horse's harness, but the carriage continued to jump hither and yon. Finally, Mrs. Argyle, in a fit of panic, threw open the carriage door, jettisoned her body inside, and flopped onto the floor. A moment later she pulled her feet in and yanked the door shut. Only then were her frightened screams muffled by the upholstery of the carriage, no longer spooking the horse. The coachman, now out of breath, gathered up the reins, doffed his cap to Mary Ann and Bethany, climbed onto the drive bench, and gave the wide-eyed steed rein to trot out of the yard. As it did, silk crescent moons streamed from the carriage window, hovered in the air, then fell like rose petals marking the path to the Charles Town Road.

Muddied-up from field work, Adam ran from the barn to the front of the house to see the carriage leave in a gallop down the path. Mary Ann stood on the porch with her arms folded next to Bethany who held her hands over her mouth in astonishment.

"Society just paid us a visit," said Mary Ann as she looked down the steps at Adam.

Just then a yellow silk crescent moon floated onto Adam's chest where it stuck to the mud on his shirt. He picked it off and stared at it.

"She came to offer her husband's legal services in case we wanted to sue our neighbors...or our ghost," said Mary Ann.

"Who's her husband?" said Adam.

"Jordan Argyle, the county magistrate in Martinsburg."

4

Adam and Mary Ann came to the consensus that the older the linen was the more likely it was going to be found at some point destroyed. By this time, all older linen used for towels, table coverings, doilies, or clothing that Esther had made, sewn, or darned had been clipped or shredded. Unless, that is, Eve had squirreled the item away in her chests and protected them with some religious object.

There also seemed to be some unexplained disregard for newer items; and what was clipped was in proportion to the cloth's size. A full size table cloth, for instance, took at least a month to chew up, whereas Mrs. Argyle's silk scarf took but an hour or two.

A peculiar twist on the situation occurred when a traveling salesman of farm implements arrived. Wilkins Jenkins was his name. He drove a fair-sized wagon fully enclosed by wood panels drawn by two horses. Inside the wagon, accessible by steps that dropped down in back revealing a door, were samples of every kind of farm tools a farmer could imagine. He was a quiet man. The goods he hawked did the talking, because they were otherwise hard to come by and often a farmer had to hire a blacksmith to custom make a plow blade or harvesting broom or scythe. He also sold an odd assortment of hand tools for every situation.

On both sides of Mr. Jenkins' wagon was painted a fancy sign in red and yellow letters that read: "Smith-Jenkins-Roberts, Farm Implements and Farm Goods."

Mister Jenkins visited the area every year or so, spending a few days in a town and offering a discount to the farmer that put him up for those days—feeding him, providing a soft bed, at least one hot bath, and feed and water for his horses. During the days of those stays Jenkins would pull his wagon to other farms, and when he had visited all the farms in an area he would make his gracious good-byes and travel to the next town on his circuit.

Adam was always glad to welcome Jenkins to his farm, if not for the discount in goods, then for exchanging information and news, and most importantly being briefed on and trying out the latest farming inventions and techniques.

There was only one thing very odd about Wilkins. Like many city dudes, he was always dressed in a blue striped three-piece suit with cuffs, spats, and a blousy tie. How the man could demonstrate the latest plow design and exchange blades on a three-furrow-pull-behind always amazed Adam. Jenkins never seemed to step in mud or get his spats dirty.

It was a few hours after Mrs. Argyle left the farm flopping on the floor of her carriage and screaming her head off about her fancy now-shredded French silk scarf that Wilkins Jenkins and wagon pulled into Flax Haven's yard. It was late in the day, just before sundown. Adam had dismissed his day workers, and Sam and he, along with Henry and Eve were herding the livestock into the barn for the night.

Mary Ann heard the wagon pull up and came out to see who had arrived. She waved to Wilkins and pointed to Adam who was walking toward the house from the barn. Before Adam could engage Wilkins, Mary Ann jogged to Adam and spoke to him quietly. "Do you think it's wise to put up Wilkins right now?"

At first Adam seemed not to understand Mary Ann's concern. He scanned the sky. "The new moon was two days ago," he said.

"Well, we've had a minor disturbance today, if you'll remember the magistrate's wife, and I'm afraid of what could happen with Mister Jenkins."

"We've always boarded him. It's almost too late in the day to tell him no. What reason would I give? It's not like his plow blades are going to get clipped, is it?" Adam laughed at his own joke, but it hurt to do so. They were dealing with a wicked time and he found himself fearful of making decisions when it came to strangers entering his house. "Let me put it to him to decide," he said.

Adam and Mary Ann walked over to greet Wilkins who had climbed down from his wagon and led his horses to the yard trough by the house where they were lapping up their fill.

"Greetings, Mister Livingston and Missus. Good to see you. How are things? How is Flax Haven?"

Adam put out his hand and shook Wilkins' hand to welcome him. "Good to see you Mister Jenkins. Things have been better."

"Sorry to hear, sir. Perhaps my arrival is well timed. I have several improved implements that may be of service to you."

Adam glanced at Mary Ann who stood nearby. "No, I wish it were that simple. I assume you're looking for a place to stay for a few days?"

"Yes, that I am. You've been mightily gracious and helpful in the past, and of course I'm offering our discount on anything you may like to purchase in exchange."

"Yes, well, here is our predicament, and it's entirely up to you, of course. We do have our guest bedroom available, and you are more than welcome to board with us as well. But, well, I'm not sure how to put this, but things are not normal in our house, and we're not sure why. It's possible that in the middle of the night...you may be awakened by...ah, noises—horses, wagons, and strange sounds. And we have no towels or sheets. Only wool blankets."

Adam stopped, expecting Wilkins to climb back up on his wagon and trot off to another farm.

"Sounds mighty strange, sir. I'm sorry for your misfortune. But I'd still be appreciative of staying with you. I remember your wife's cooking and Bethany's. Is she still with you?"

"Yes, the food is still very good, thanks to Mary Ann and Bethany's spirit."

"I'd appreciate that, Mister Livingston, and Madam. And if I can get a bath tonight I'll be happy to drip dry, although I do have linens of my own I can use."

"Fine, Mister Jenkins. Do you need Sam to help you with your horses?"

"No, sir, I'll water, feed, and pasture them myself. Thank you. I'll just unload my suitcase here on the porch and come inside in a few minutes. Thank you, thank you very much." Wilkins slid his suitcase out from under his driver's bench and set it on the porch. Then he walked his team to the corral.

With that, although a bit nervous and apprehensive, Adam took Mary Ann's arm and helped her up the steps into their house, looking back at Wilkins, wondering how he cared for his horse and wagon without getting spot or wrinkle on his suit or spats. He watched from a distance and decided the man was more coordinated that most, including himself. Adam had great appreciation for Wilkins, even though his goods were expensive and Adam rarely purchased anything from him. Most of the implements he sold could be acquired in town at one of several outlets for less money. He wondered how his business fared.

That night Bethany, Eve, and Mary Ann put out a great spread of food that they all enjoyed along with Sam. After supper, around the fire, they listened to a few tales Jenkins had picked up along his travels, one with bandits that were going to rob him of his goods until they opened up the back of his wagon and didn't know what to do with a plow blade and a rake. Wilkins laughed hard about that as the thieves let him be, so surprised by their find they didn't bother to search for his hidden strong box.

After some hot coffee and a slice of Mary Ann's apple cinnamon pie, over which Wilkins raved, they all tottered off to bed.

That night in bed Adam and Mary Ann were troubled by the sounds of scissors clipping. Twice Adam checked the integrity of the wool blanket that covered them. He was thankful it was still in one piece, but he wondered what wouldn't be in the morning.

Whenever anyone stayed in the guest room, after the death of Xavier, Adam was always a bit nervous, hoping Xavier's experience would never be repeated. Sometimes the slightest noise would startle Adam awake and he would lay in bed for some minutes analyzing every little sound, hoping it didn't turn into a cacophony and unforeseen tragedy. Fortunately, Wilkins Jenkins was a quiet guest and Adam was hard pressed to assure himself that anyone was in the guest room at all. Adam heard neither footsteps, bed creaking, or even the pouring or splashing of water from the basin.

But all that changed in the morning. Wilkins had told Adam and Mary Ann that he was at times a late riser, especially after a day of travel, so Adam was up and out of the house before Mary Ann or anyone else was out of bed, and only came back in the house after sunrise for breakfast. He sat down at the table to eat.

"Has our guest risen?" Adam asked Mary Ann, who was putting out boiled eggs, ham, and jam with rolls. Bethany came mid-morning well after breakfast, Mary Ann being content with fixing breakfast with what Bethany had prepared the day before.

"No, haven't heard a peep," Mary Ann said. "Do you suppose he's alive?" She asked the question quietly even as she heard the twins being roused up by Eve, who was chatting with them and Henry, all still upstairs". But Mary Ann's question was not a joke. Her morose side had revealed itself ever since Xavier had come and gone; and with the Wizard's spooking the house she was not her former happy and confident self.

"Mister Livingston?" came a whisper from the foyer. "Might I have a word with you?"

Adam turned from the table in the gathering hall and looked toward the foyer. It was Wilkins, with only his head sticking around the corner. Adam got up from the table while still chewing a roll with jam and walked to the man.

Wilkins Jenkins stood at the base of the stairs in his sleeping gown, his face red with either embarrassment or anger, Adam couldn't tell which. Clutched in his arms was a ravel of blue cloth that had been cut into ribbons. It took but a moment for Adam to recognize the materials as the suit Mister Jenkins had arrived in yesterday, or what was left of it. Adam's face fell as he grabbed for the shredded material and pulled at it in his hands, the entire suit cut to pieces in the shape of crescent moons. He felt terrible for his guest...and for his own reputation that such a catastrophe would breed.

"What is this about, sir?" asked Mister Jenkins, the tremble and anger in his voice now evident, although he spoke as quietly as the emotions would allow. "I came to your home in good will. What sort of hospitality is this that you would mutilate my good clothing while I slept? You warned me of strange things but this, sir, is a perversion. There was no mention that my possessions would be destroyed."

At that moment Mary Ann walked around the corner into the foyer. Upon seeing Mister Jenkins in his bed clothes, she turned and backed away quickly, "Oh, I'm so sorry, sir." But she had not seen the source of Mister Jenkins' discontent.

Adam took the shredded suit from Wilkins and stepped back into the gathering hall to show Mary Ann. "This was the beautiful suit our guest arrived in yesterday."

"Oh, no!" exclaimed Mary Ann, and doubled over, taking the shredded suit down to the floor with her.

Adam turned back to the foyer.

"My suit, sir," said Wilkins his hand out. "I'm going to need it."

Adam was in no mood to argue with the irrational request, for what could Wilkins want with his shredded suit? Adam didn't argue or question. Leaning over he gently took the mass of blue scraps from Mary Ann's clutch, swiveled and took the bundle of useless rags to his guest. Adam felt defeated and at a loss as to how to stem the flow of disturbances, destruction, and loss of reputation.

Wilkins took the shredded bundle and climbed back up the stairs. A few minutes later he returned with his case, wearing another suit that was intact, and without speaking to Adam or Mary Ann left the house. Adam followed him out of the house and watched as Sam helped him harness his horses, climb into his wagon, and drive his team out of the yard, never to return Adam assumed. But he was wrong.

The next day Wilkins Jenkins returned, wearing the same suit he had worn when leaving. But alongside Jenkins, on his own horse, was a professional man, or so Adam assumed because the man was dressed in a dark suit, with a top hat, blousy white shirt, and a leather case strapped to the back of his saddle.

The two men dismounted their conveyances and approached Adam, who had come out onto his porch with Mary Ann at his side.

"Mister Livingston," said Jenkins, "this is my attorney, Zeke Matheson." Jenkins was all business. No smiles or how-do-you-dos this visit.

"Mister Livingston," said Matheson, "my client, here, Mister Jenkins, is prepared to file a suit over the loss of his very expensive designer suit while residing on your premises. He claims your negligence and disregard for his person and

lack of respect toward his honorable request to stay on your premises in return for a discount of his farm goods...resulted in this." At that point Matheson
produced a handful of Jenkins' shredded suit and threw them into the air for
dramatic flair. "His potential law suit, which we have drafted and are prepared
to file in Berkeley County Court, claims he is due compensation not only for
the loss of his suit, but that he should also be compensated for the distress he
has suffered, and is entitled to damages for loss of peace of mind and enjoyment
of his property and the deprivation of professional reputation. This comes to a
considerable sum, which he claims, and I happen to agree with him, is entirely
your liability. You have a choice to settle up immediately or suffer the consequences of greater penalty in a court of law which will no doubt force you to pay
court costs as well. Which will it be?"

Adam stepped down the porch stairs and glanced at the clippings of Jenkins' suit as they blew across the yard in the morning breeze. "Mister Matheson," began Adam, "I am indeed sorry for what happened to Mister Jenkins' suit
while sleeping in our guest bedroom. But I assure you no member of my family
sneaked into Mister Jenkins' bedroom and spent the night cutting up his suit.
It's much more likely Mister Jenkins sat up the whole night by himself with a
pair of shears and cut his own suit up, and then claimed it was me, or my wife,
or children, who done it." Adam paused and noticed Jenkins and Matheson
exchanging looks. Adam continued, "And why would he do that? Perhaps he
had retained you even before he came to my premises having concocted a plan
that is now playing out before us. You see you're missing something important.
What would be my motivation to cut up his suit? What could I possibly gain by
such a stunt...if I could do it? On the other hand there is motivation on Mister
Jenkins' part to blackmail me. You see his business is suffering and he needs
money. So, what evidence do you have that Mister Jenkins did not cut up his
own suit?"

During Adam's rebuttal, he noticed Sam was casually walking behind Jenkins' wagon. Jenkins' suitcase was sitting beneath the driver's bench as it had
when he first arrived the day before. Adam was surprised at what he saw Sam
doing out of the corner of his eye and behind Jenkins' and Matheson's back. But
he decided to not let on that he saw anything. Sam had quietly removed the
suitcase from under the bench and had laid it on the ground behind the wagon,
where no one, not even Adam, could see what he was doing.

"Mister Livingston," said Matheson, "those are serious accusations, which
I am sure an impartial judge would find slanderous of an upright businessman
known throughout the state as a man of impeccable integrity. You do yourself
harm, sir. You'd be well advised to pay up now and avoid additional legal entan-
glement and embarrassment."

Adam was getting curious. "And just what would you consider a fair settlement, if I might inquire," asked Adam, "assuming we do not hinder the courts?"
As soon as he asked the question, he caught the quick satisfying glance between

the two men, which confirmed his suspicion.

"Four Spanish silver dollars would buy Mister Jenkins a new suit, although the tailor is in London, and there is the inconvenience and time to acquire such a unique blue suit specifically tailored to Mister Jenkins' high standards; and then there is the emotional and mental distress, pain and suffering he has incurred, economic loss from his inability to call on customers, loss of peace of mind, his professional reputation, and of course my fee for negotiating this justice. Fifteen pounds sterling would be a fair and just settlement."

Adam did some fast figuring in his head, "Or, I suppose twenty gold doubloons, or forty silver dollars. Is that including the four silver dollars for the suit as well? That seems kind of stiff."

"No sir, not at all," said Matheson. "We're just interested in fairness, and justice, as I am sure you are, sir."

"And what should be the penalty, if you are wrong, and I am right, that Mister Jenkins is a crook of the highest order, a swindler, and you are his able mouth grifter? What am I due if such is the case?"

At this Matheson turned angry and Jenkins' entire body stiffened. "That, sir, is an outrage, and we would indeed drag your body into court and sue you for the farm if we are able. For you would totally ruin the reputation of this fine gentleman."

"Well, Mister Matheson, if that is really your name, I guarantee you his reputation is already ruined, and I intend to see that everyone in the surrounding towns knows of this blackmail and fraud you pursue."

"Sir, that is scandal of the highest order," screamed Matheson.

"Oh, is it?" said Adam.

At that, Mary Ann, who was standing at the top of the porch steps, began to laugh, and the three men below her looked up at her, as if to ask what was so funny. Mary Ann said nothing, but covered her mouth, nodded her head, and pointed behind them.

It was then that Wilkins Jenkins and Zeke Matheson turned and saw what Adam saw. Sam stood behind Jenkins' wagon holding aloft on a tailor's hanger a perfectly intact blue suit, and from the other hand he let drop the clippings which Jenkins had shown to Adam and Mary Ann the morning before. Indeed, it appeared as if he had not stayed up clipping his suit, but had brought along in his suitcase a bag of clippings cut from similar material as the suit.

Jenkins ran at Sam. "Damn slave, I'll have you whipped for getting into my private property. Give me that." At the same time, Matheson turned to Jenkins, "Damn idiot. I told you this wouldn't work. Let's get out of here." Jenkins was insistent on getting Sam and whipping him within an inch of his life. But Sam, being much bigger and smarter than the con artist, held the suit high over his head and threw the clippings in the man's face, back-pedaling and side-stepping just enough that Jenkins could do nothing.

"Wilkins," yelled Adam. "Give it up. Sam is a freeman, and he's more likely to whip you than you him...and he has my permission if I need give it."

At that Sam laughed as well. Jenkins, seeing his open suitcase lying on the ground, scampered to close it up, latch it as best he could, slide it under the drive seat of his wagon, climb up on it, and whip his team out of the yard. It was only after the wagon disappeared that Adam realized the attorney had disappeared before the wagon even got underway.

When the two con artists had vamoosed, Sam was still hanging onto the very much intact and expensive designer blue suit and a few clipping scraps. *It almost worked,* thought Adam. But almost wasn't good enough, and his admiration for Sam Dark soared.

In the midst of a very dark time, with the Wizard seemingly having his way with Adam and his family, it was nice to see Mary Ann smiling and waving her arms above her head in celebration. By now Bethany had joined Mary Ann on the porch and watched as Mary Ann descended the steps and hugged big Sam as hard as she could. She then took the blue suit on the tailor's hanger and dragged it in the dirt over to Adam. "Husband, I think I know what you should do with this. It's not clipped, but it is from the pit of hell."

"Indeed, wife. Sam and I will take care of it. But there is something I must do first." He immediately went to his office, obtained a hidden key, ran upstairs to his bedroom and retrieved his sea chest from his armoire. He put it on his bed and unlocked it feeling elated that they had so aptly defeated a visible enemy who had sought his financial ruin. Four silver dollars they said the suit was worth. Opening the sea chest Adam counted out four silver dollars, put them in his palm...but suddenly stopped.

Something was missing. He moved items around in the sea chest. The leather bag of his crisis gold—the fourteen double-doubloons—was gone. Adam racked his brain, wondering if he had moved it from the sea chest, but he was sure he hadn't. His mind was suddenly conflicted. He was elated on the one hand at their victory a moment ago, but now distressed, terribly so. Where was the gold? Where moments ago he had avoided being cheated out of twenty gold doubloons, now he was missing fourteen gold double-doubloons, the equivalent of twenty eight gold doubloons.

The juxtaposition of events was uncanny. He replayed Wilkins Jenkins' coming and going in his mind. Could he have stolen into the sea chest while Adam was downstairs with Mary Ann? He replayed the neatness of the stack of old coveralls that were heaped on top of and hid the sea chest on the floor of his armoire. No, they were unfazed, neat as always. Besides, he had the key to the sea chest that was never in the bedroom. Flustered, he slammed the sea chest shut, locked it, and replaced it in the bottom of his armoire.

Rushing downstairs, he first went to his office, and re-hid the key, then walked briskly out the front door and to Sam who was cleaning up the scattered clippings from the fake suit. "Sam, I have something for you." Adam palmed the four silver dollars into Sam's hand.

Sam opened his hand and stared at the silver coins, not understanding.

"Your quick wit and courage just saved me a small fortune in gold. This was how much those two scallywags claimed Wilkins' suit was worth, four Spanish silver dollars. Consider this a token of my thanks for your honesty and loyalty.

Sam fingered the silver coins. Bethany was on the porch watching, but didn't see or hear what Adam had said or given to her husband. "Look here, Beth'ny." Sam climbed the steps and held out his hand for her to see the four silver coins. While Adam paid them each a weekly wage, it was nothing close to the value of these four coins.

"Don't spend it too quickly, now," Adam said. "Save it for when you really need it."

Bethany hugged Adam and he hugged her back. Sam was all smiles, but didn't know what to say other than "Thank'in ya sir. Thank ya. Thank ya." But he was smart enough to give the coins to Bethany. "Dear wife, you's keep dese safe for whens we need 'em, like Missta say."

Bethany took the coins and closed them in her fist. "Yes, dear husband. And thank you again Mister Livingston."

"Sam," said Adam, "let's go burn this suit and clippings."

"Yas, sir. I think we's need to h've a burnin' party."

Gathering up the pieces of the shredded suit along with the suit on the tailor's hanger, they walked behind the barn to the refuse dump and had themselves a first ever effigy burning.

After the suit was well into flames, Sam spoke. "Missta Livingston, dat dere Wizard, or wad'ever demon spirit it is, didn't cut up dis suit, but those disturbances are still happenin' aren't dey?"

Adam's countenance turned from celebration to sobering. "That's right."

Neither man spoke for a while as they watched the suit and clippings go up in flames.

"Missta Livingston, sir, I knows you's don't really like to talk about such things, but Beth'ny and I...well, we's think der a solution fer you's, if I kin speak me mind."

Adam peered at Sam, wondering what he might be thinking. "Go ahead, then."

"Beth'ny and me be learning ta read, you's knows. En de Good Book says dat ministers of the Lord have power over evil spirits. Dat is what Beth'ny 'n' me think dis here Wizard is. Eve think dat too. We's knows you's don't like ministers none, but maybe you's like dis Wizard not so much. Beth'ny think a true minister of God could get rid of dis spirit. Dat wad the Good Book says."

Sam said no more, as he poked around in the fire making sure the last of the suit and clips were fully consumed.

Adam wasn't ignorant about what could be found in the Bible. He was just rebellious living by any of it. Though he could not quote or find exactly where it was written, he admitted to himself that a legitimate minister of the Gospel would have powers over evil spirits. He remembered stories of Jesus giving the twelve disciples power over spirits in all manner of ways, and how they could cast out demons, pick up serpents, and even drink poison. He wasn't about to do any of that nonsense. He wasn't going to be handling no snake, although there were two times he had come up on one in his path. The first time he struck the serpent dead with his shillelagh, the second time the rattler got a head full of lead from his Kock pistol. "You may be right, Sam. But don't tell Mary Ann I said that."

"They be stories of people b'n prayed o'er and evil spirits comin' out of 'dem. 'En picking up serpents, castin' out demons, even raisin' de dead. But you's need a real one. Minister, dat is. Beth'ny 'en me been goin' to dat church near town on Sundays. It's all dark folk. But dey pray up a good storm. Beth'ny say our preacher he could come up here 'en pray fer yer place."

"Sam," said Adam. "I appreciate your concern, but Mary Ann would rather live with the disturbances than let a Christian minister into our house."

"Well, jist a suggestion, if you's don't mind. I keep me thoughts to myself, then."

"That's fine, Sam. You're a good man, and I'm glad you're my friend as well."

5

Later than night, after nursing the twins, Mary Ann lay down next to Adam in bed. She curled into his arms, and hugged him tight as if he might disappear suddenly. He felt the press of her soft breasts and thighs against his. If only he felt like making love to her instead of worrying about what might happen that night in their sleep. They had not made love for weeks, it seemed, so distracted they were by the clippings and noises in the middle of the night. He was thinking about what Sam had said when Mary Ann actually brought it up.

"Adam, Bethany said something to me today that I immediately disregarded. But I've been thinking about it."

She said nothing more. Adam finally said, "Let me guess. Sam says Bethany been telling him about getting his church's preacher to come and pray over our house." As soon as he spoke those words, he could feel Mary Ann stiffen, as if she wanted to turn away from him. But he held her tight.

Mary Ann whispered, "Bethany says a true minister of Christ would exorcise the demon from the house, once and for all."

"Do you believe that?" said Adam.

There was a long silence. "I don't know," she said.

There was another long silence, as Adam risked changing subjects, for something else was on his mind and sleep was likely to escape him if he didn't find a resolution.

"Something is missing," Adam said.

"What?"

"A small pouch of gold. Our reserves."

Adam felt Mary Ann stiffen further and pull away from him slightly. *There will be no love making tonight,* Adam thought.

"Well! I am glad to know that we *had* reserves. But, I am not happy to know that I did not know it. And where 'bouts did such reserves find themselves gone, husband?"

Adam went cold. It was as if he had just been served a plate of beef steak that had gone cold and rotten days ago. It was now or later, he determined. Rising from bed, he lit his bedside lantern and with it walked toward the door.

"Where you goin'?" called Mary Ann.

"To find what is missing."

Adam went into Henry's room and sat on the side of his bed, holding the lantern in Henry's face and shook him awake. He heard Mary Ann come into the room behind him.

"What are you doing? He's asleep," growled Mary Ann.

Adam kept shaking Henry's shoulder until the boy mostly woke up, "Where is it?" Adam demanded.

"Wha-a-t?" said Henry mostly asleep.

"You know what I'm looking for."

Henry, now frightened as if he was still in a nightmare, tried to sit up, but his father pushed him back flat onto the bed and into his pillow. "Where is it?!"

Henry teared up and began to cry like a little boy, although he was a strapping fifteen year old. Still his father was much bigger, and it was night.

Mary Ann came up behind him and pulled on Adam's shoulder to get him to stop, "Adam, you're scaring him."

"Scare the devil out of him, I will," said Adam to Mary Ann. Then back in his son's face: "You took something from my sea chest."

Henry was now choking up and crying large tears. "What...Papa? I didn't take nothin'."

At that point Eve came into the room with her lantern. "What are you doing, Papa?"

"One of you children took a bag of gold from my sea chest, and I want it back, now. Not in the morning, now," he said in anger.

Henry pleaded with his father through tears, "I didn't take it, honest."

Eve jumped to their defense: "Papa, never would either of us take your money. We don't even know where you keep it. How would we?"

Mary Ann grabbed Adam's arm and held onto it as if he was ready to strike his son, which he wasn't. "Adam! Stop this madness. It's the middle of the night. None of us know anything about any gold that is missing. We'll look for it in the morning."

"There's nothing to look for, I tell you, it's gone. It's not where it should be."

"Fine. I believe you," said Mary Ann. "But now is not the time. As it is with this craziness of yours, we're going to be hard pressed getting back to sleep."

Both kids were crying out of fear. Adam, seeing what he had done and sorry for it, stalked out of Henry's room.

"Children, I'm sorry," said Mary Ann. "Your father had a bad day, and it's catching up to him. Go back to sleep, if you can. We'll talk in the morning." With that, she also marched out of the room, leaving Eve and Henry to resettle themselves in their beds.

The next day Adam mended a fence in the chicken coop while Mary Ann, in an apron with crescent moons cut from it, scattered seed on the ground at which the flightless birds pecked.

"The only time gold disappears is if someone steals it. Have we had any visitors I know not of, wife?" said Adam.

"Husband. That I would tell you," snapped back Mary Ann.

"Then it is Henry."

"Or, your daughter."

Adam glowered at his wife. She stared back, defiant.

"And when were you last in my locked chest?"

"Adam Livingston, don't you dare accuse me of taking something I didn't even know existed. And what would I do with it?"

"You have your designs."

"Ah, that I would. Surely! And how do you suppose I gain access to this gold and my designs?"

Adam stopped his work to study her.

"Is there but one key to your locked chest? And where do you keep it?"

"It is not always with me."

"Aye, and you are not always with yourself, husband. By god, whom I do not believe, I have never seen your key, or what is in this chest of yours, nor the gold that I wished I had known was there...or somewheres."

6

Most Feared Master of Ruinous,

I should take more encouragement from the long-term effect of our work in the Americas. I had no idea how encouraging Catholic's woeful knowledge of their faith would be so discouraging to priests. Apathy toward religion is evidently a good thing; one need not be against it, just not care about it. The consequences are the same. Either way the Almighty is diminished or rejected and Perdition is in the cards. Alleluia, as the devout would say.

Greed, too, seems to work much generously in our favor. I don't mind helping Protestants build large edifices that attract the curious, for once under their influence full truth is belittled and muted. Of course there are some Protestant groups that actually worship the Almighty...but they typically go for the plain, flat, monotonous architecture that ultimately entraps with mediocrity. Bring it on, I say. The grand Gothic Catholic edifices in Europe attract thousands. We must somehow work to change that, to neutralize the art and grandeur. Burn them all down, I say.

The Post-Modern idea may yet have some usefulness. But that is not my charge so I must leave Europe to others. I'm not too worried here; there is such need for money just to eat, that I'm sure Cahill's offering box will remain empty. We just don't want Cahill to start building edifices; they are too grand and point too effectively to the Creator who is above all.

Isn't it grand that Livingston still does not believe in us? I think that's wonderful. It gives us so much freedom. Although, I was not impressed with Mary Ann's defense of having no linen in the home. I trust she won't seriously embrace such a minimalist worldview—such will inhibit our objectives—but lying as she did was joyous to observe.

It is true I did not see the Jenkins' swindle coming. My congratulations to my peers who contrived such a devious rout...though it ultimately failed, perhaps due to my own lack of attention to the Darks, whose faith in the Almighty is as strong as Livingston's Eve. I need to spend more time undermining the Darks' confidence in religion. Especially, since Livingston's wife nearly believes Bethany that a true minister of Christ could get rid of me. That is not going to happen. Yet, just letting Mary Ann entertain such a thought is dangerous. I'll work on that.

I do find the missing gold a point of pure enjoyment. Livingston doesn't have a clue, although he should. Don't you just love how he blames his kids for his own sinfulness? This is what we're about, isn't it? I adore it when humans blame others while ignoring the natural consequences of their own actions. Gold goes missing...the gold he stole...he blames the kids...but he's the guilty one. Great fun. I knew we could twist the greed in Livingston's heart to our advantage. But where the gold went, I have no idea. He must have just misplaced it.

Now I have some major surprises in store, for the Stranger has opened myriad of opportunities to achieve our goal of condemnation...and my quiver is full. I will make you proud—ah, pride...the source of all sin.

Cheers for the bad guys.

At your sinful service,
Cyn Namrasit, OPSD

Part Six: Ministers

For our wrestling is not against flesh and blood;
but against principalities and power,
against the rulers of the world of this darkness,
against the spirits of wickedness in the high places.

(Ephesians 6:12)

Chapter 35
Hoop Skirts

1

Fr. Cahill had written home several times a year. In return he received short but happy responses from his mother, who always signed her letters *Alice Hannah (MacGuffin) Cahill*. But in June of 1795 he received a most unexpected but delightful letter from home. It was from his fifteen-year old sister, *Catharine, whom he knew only as a toddler two years of age before he left home.

Although the penal laws in Ireland had greatly relaxed over the past decade, his parents' life was still difficult. Francis, his father, still worked in the mine, but his lungs were getting worse and he was considering hiring out to a farmer for a much smaller wage.

Denis, who was been shuttled away to seminary as soon as the law allowed, had no choice in his departure. His younger sister, Catharine, had the wanderlust. She had read all of Denis' letters and had on occasion written him back, enclosing her letter with Mama's. In Denis' letters home he had told of his time in New Orleans, the journey from there to Baltimore and then to Leetown, and finally to Hagerstown. His letters described the freedom he enjoyed in America, in spite of the anti-Catholic sentiment that pervaded the country. Nonetheless, he was well and confident of God's will in his life. Thus the letter Fr. Cahill received, although it was from his sister directly, clearly conveyed his parents' sad permission for her writing.

> From: Catharine Cahill
> To: Denis Cahill
> Dublin, Ireland
> April 2, 1795
>
> Dear Brother now a Father,
>
> As Mama has told you several times in her letters, I miss you, although I barely remember you. I was only two when you left home. There is no one else that I can look up to and trust. All the boys here are rude and mean. I am very thankful that Mama and Papa will not let any of them visit. I will be sixteen this time next year and old enough to marry. But I cannot imagine anyone here I would want to spend an evening with, let alone the rest of my life. So I plan to come to America next year, although it saddens Mama and Papa for me to leave.
>
> I am very proud of your being a priest in America and helping

510 ○ *Stanley D. Williams*

so many. I want to come to America and attend Mass that you celebrate. Of course, I've never gone to you for confession...not that I
would really want to. If I did I could not be honest. When I left the
confessional I would have to return right away. My sin would be so
great, having not told you all, then lying that I had.

I have been saving my little money for several years in working for the Haggertys as a servant and nanny, and Papa is going to
talk to someone at the shipping brokerage to take me to America
without indenturing myself. He says that if I work hard the rest
of this year I will be able to pay my way to America in the spring,
although perhaps I will have to work on the ship as a cabin girl.
Do they have cabin girls? I never heard of one. But I'm sure I could
do the job.

Can I stay with you at the church where you are? Papa says
that would not look right for a young girl to stay with a priest, even
if they are brother and sister. But it would be fine with me. What
will I do?

Maybe you can find me a kind and generous husband? Please
write back and tell me what to do. I can't wait to see you.

Your little but growing sister,
Catharine

Denis Cahill wasted no time answering his sister's letter.

From: Denis Cahill
To: Miss Catharine Cahill
Hagerstown, Maryland
May 16, 1795

Dearest Catharine,

I am very happy to receive your letter of April 2, '95 this very
day. I have not hesitated to return this to you. I am most happy that
you are coming, for I miss the family as our mother must have told
you, but I am sad that Mother and Father will be without you and
me. You must know from my letters to Mother than I am fulfilling
her deepest desires for me, and while not everything is good, I am
happy and productive in my vocation for which our parents gave
me over to God. I will say Mass many times for your safe arrival,
although some time away. I travel my circuit quite a bit. You would
be welcome to stay in Magdala our rectory, but, as our papa says, it
would not look right. I know a good Catholic family that may take
you in. They, the McSherrys, are the ones that helped me. Now

as to a husband, that is a fine task to ask your brother priest to arrange. It would be laughable, except I seem to have already done well in that department several times, and will pray and look for you. There are many, many rogues here that I would not permit you to even meet, but there are a few, very few, whom I respect. We will see what God offers up. I am excited to see you. Perhaps I can find another priest for you to hear your confessions, although I am the only one I know nearby. Will you travel alone? On ship it may be fine for you, but depending on where you land, I might worry how you'll safely find your way to Hagerstown.

Brothe'y love,
Den

2

June 16, 1795.

Adam and Mary Ann had no more fallen asleep in their bed than they were suddenly awakened. Their bed began to shake and pound up and down on the floor; it lasted several seconds.

"Did you feel that?" said Mary Ann.

"I heard it," replied Adam.

"An earthquake?"

"Never heard of such in these parts."

"Nor have..." But she was interrupted when the quaking returned.

Adam turned his head to look at the lantern on the table next to the bed. It wasn't moving, and neither was the side table. But he was and so was the bed. He glanced about the room. Nothing else moved, it was only their heavy wood bed bouncing off the floor like a rubber ball. Adam jumped out of bed and grabbed hold of the headboard, but he could not stop the bed from jumping around. "The house isn't moving. It's just the bed," he said.

At that, Mary Ann, too, jumped out of bed. The bed continued to shake and bounce on the floor.

"Papa?" came Eve's cry from the other room. "What's that noise?"

Adam, too frightened to speak, said nothing as air pumped in and out of his lungs.

Suddenly the bed stopped jumping and fell back to the floor. Within seconds Adam heard a herd of horses and dozens of wagons surround the house, and now the entire house shook—so numerous were the horses and wagons that stampeded around the foundations. The building's posts and beams vibrated, rocking the flooring, causing Adam and Mary Ann to lose their balance and fall to the floor. Adam scrambled to his feet, grabbed his shillelagh, and headed toward the stairs. As he did the twins began to cry.

"I'm staying with the twins," said Mary Ann. She picked up Martha, who was fussing the most, then George, and fell back into the rocker near the bed, cradling, rocking, and trying to comfort both. It was a difficult task since they were three and getting heavier, and the rocker was more than rocking...it was bouncing.

Adam rushed downstairs; Eve and Henry were on his heels. When he got to the foyer, Mary Ann screamed from the bedroom, "It's started. The clipping! It's everywhere!" Adam heard it, too. It wasn't just in their bedroom; it seemed to come from every wall and the cellar, too. The house was literally shaking on its foundations. He feared it might collapse on top of them. He had to stop it, but how? The shaking floorboards, now in the foyer, sent shock waves up Adam's legs. He was scared and he felt his face go flush with blood. Henry ran to his side and grabbed his arm; Eve held onto the banister. It was dark in the house. He had not brought a lantern with him, nor had either of the children, although a dim light slithered through the windows from a crescent moon.

Adam dared to open the front door and step out with his shillelagh ready, but he was ill equipped. The galloping horses and the wagons in an apparent stampede about the house were invisible. Only the vibrations and noise could be felt and heard. There was nothing to see except clouds of dirt and dust that the ghosts kicked up. Adam was lost. He trembled. He could find no words, nor did he know what to do. He stood on the porch with his children holding on to both of his arms, the shillelagh hanging useless at his side. Tears fell from his eyes and mixed with the wraiths' dust, as he faced the encircling whirlwind from hell.

So overwhelming was the poltergeist that he struggled to stand and found himself balanced between his two teens who stood ramrod straight at his sides. They gripped his arms as if to squeeze blood from his pores. He wondered only briefly if the experience was but a phantasm, existing only in his mind, but one look at his children, who stared bewildered into the dark clouds of dust, told him this was no dream. It was as real as they were.

Speechless, he was scared dumb and useless.

But not Eve. "MAMA, PRAY FOR US," she screamed over the noise. "GOD, COME DOWN TO HELP US. MOTHER ALL KIND, ALL BEAUTIFUL, THE WIZARD HAUNTS US. PRAY FOR US! MAMA, PRAY FOR US!"

The haunting poltergeist didn't cease right away, but Eve's outburst stemmed the noise. As she continued mumbling her invocation, slowly the sound dissipated and the disturbance disappeared.

Adam didn't know what to make of the horrifying noise and wraiths' subjugation at Eve's prayer. It was miraculous. At once he hated it, loved it, was confused by it, and thankful for it. One thing was becoming clear: What they were battling was spiritual, not physical. It was a depressing thought, because if it was spiritual it was beyond his control. This angered him. Nothing ever before in his whole life was out of his control. But, of course, that was not entirely true.

Esther's death, and the deaths of his other children were all out of his control. At once he rejected both his impotency and some phantasmal control over this life. He couldn't really have it both ways, but he embraced the contradiction as the reality he had to live with.

3

That night no one went back to sleep. It took Mary Ann hours to get the twins to lie quietly after the trauma in the dark. And while Mary Ann talked soothingly to the twins, Adam and Mary Ann said barely a word to each other.

In the morning light they were crushed to discover that their comforter was sliced to shreds. So bad was the clip job that there was no hint of a pattern or neat cutouts of crescents that had been evident when their other linens were clipped. Whomever or whatever had cut up the comforter, the quaking of the bed had overcome the provoker's precision. Adam was devastated; his life was unraveling. The only thing that kept the farm operating was Sam's industry and reliability...and that his day laborers showed up fully ignorant of what the Livingstons had endured. Something had to be done.

That morning, Adam experienced a subtle shift of sorts in Mary Ann's attitude. When he told her that it was Eve's prayer that had dissipated the disturbance, Mary Ann refused to believe it. When Adam pressured her to accept the idea as a possibility, she became incensed. She told him she refused to believe that prayer or God was real or could have any good in it. It was something else she insisted, or it was a coincidence. But when Adam reminded her of the advice they had both received from Sam and Bethany, Mary Ann suddenly clammed up and said nothing more—she was as mute as a fence of well-fitted field stone.

Sam and Bethany marveled at the hoof and wagon tracks in the dirt. The apparent stampede of horses and wagons had even destroyed part of Mary Ann's herb and vegetable garden. Sam remarked how the hill into which the house was built had evidently not slowed down the ghostly horse and wagon train. Up one side and down the other they had stormed, apparently unimpeded. Yet both Sam and Bethany said they had heard nothing during the night and had slept soundly.

Sam again suggested that his church minister might be able to stem the ghost's enthusiasm, but Adam held up his hand and nodded. "After breakfast I intend to recruit a minister of my own from Charles Town."

"Well, sir, if you's needin' him, I tell you's how to find ours minister, but he don't have a church building," offered Sam.

Adam thanked Sam and let the subject drop.

Breakfast of porridge, toast, and milk was served as normal as could be expected thanks to Bethany's stable disposition. Mary Ann was so frazzled that she refused to leave their bedroom where she fed, nursed, and cared for the twins. Eve brought them food, more out of concern for the twins than her stepmother.

Meanwhile, Adam began to saddle up Calvin, then changed his mind and saddled Luther instead, considering where he was headed. He rode into Winchester. It was a Thursday, so he wasn't sure if he could find the person he sought. It had been years since he had been to church and never had he attended in Winchester. If he had been back in York County he would have sought out Frederick Brauer, the minister who knew his family. That was too far away, and Adam was glad, because he didn't want to face Brauer after chasing him out of his house the night Esther was buried.

Winchester was not big, and Adam knew few of the influential men in town, but with Mary Ann's advice he easily tracked down *Rev. Christian Streit at his large cabin just south of town. Streit, a little younger than Adam, was well known in the area. He had preached throughout the Shenandoah Valley, finally settling down in Winchester, where he founded the Grace Evangelical Lutheran Church. Mary Ann told Adam that his first two wives had died. When Adam arrived, Streit's third and much younger wife, Susannah, greeted him and brought tea, then left the men alone on the back porch overlooking their garden, a pond, and a milk cow that grazed lazily in a meadow beyond. Rev. Streit had three living children (two, six, and eleven) and one on the way, but he had lost four children and two wives, so he well understood Adam's frustration with the Almighty.

Rev. Streit was a handsome but short man with thin lips, a pointed nose, docile eyes, a high forehead and thinning brown hair that fell around his ears and over his collar in the back. Although he was born in New Jersey, he spoke fluid German as well as English. He wore a dusty black suit, now a little big for his thin frame.

Rev. Streit listened quietly as Adam emotionally related the events of the night before, and the history of his life, Esther's death, the coming to Virginia, the manumission of Sam and Bethany, Nawanne's death, the Stranger's coming, curse, and death, and then the recent hauntings, their losses since, and the on-going manifestations.

"Mister Livingston, I am so sorry to hear of this, ah, plight and difficulty that you're in. It's mighty unsettling. You have my deepest sympathies, but why are you coming to me?"

"You are a minister of Jesus Christ, are you not?"

"I am."

"Is it not true that Jesus gave power to his ministers to cast out demons?"

"Oh, Mister Livingston, that was centuries ago. I have no such power, nor does any other minister in this age."

"But the Bible clearly says that you do."

"No, no, you're mistaken. Christ gave that power to his apostles, not to ministers today."

"Why would Christ give that power only to his apostles? Do you not pray for the sick and for evil to be overcome yet today?"

"We do not understand the ways of God, sir. There is much that is a mystery and beyond our reach."

Adam was deeply disappointed and offended that a man with training as a minister of God did not believe what the Bible taught. After Streit's revelation, Adam just stared at the minister for an uncomfortably long time without saying a word. If Rev. Streit didn't have the power, then Adam wondered if he was a true minister of God.

Adam tried one more time: "Would you nonetheless come to my home and say some prayers and ask God, who does have the power, to remove this influence from our lives?"

"I'm not sure that would do any good," said Rev. Streit.

Adam persisted. "Please come. I beg you, for I am confident you do have the authority, but you must exercise it. Let us both see if you have the power or not. Perhaps this demon or whatever it is will leave us."

Rev. Streit said nothing and looked to Susannah, who had returned and joined them, for affirmation.

"Christian," she said, "I could ask some of the ladies from the guild to come with you. And, of course, I would come, too. I'll ask Sharon Fritz to watch the children."

"What if I make a sizable donation to your church?" said Adam. "Would that convince you that I'm sincere and not asking to inconvenience you for nothing in exchange?"

"Mister Livingston, God would gift me with a terrible disease if I were to let money motivate me, for God's blessings to us are freely given."

"But you must live off of offerings, I presume, given in exchange for your prayers and services."

Streit mulled over the offer.

4

Adam returned home late that morning to tell Mary Ann, the children, Sam, and Bethany what was about to transpire. Despite Rev. Streit's claim, Adam was confident that the defrauding spirit would be expelled.

Early in the afternoon two buggies pulled into the yard. The first one contained Rev. Streit in his dusty black suit with parson's hat, and Susannah in the same morning dress and bonnet. The second buggy ferried three ladies from the church, all dressed in finery including hoops, fancy hairdos and hats, and parasols as if attending a Sunday parade. Adam was not pleased with the ostentatious display. It portended insincerity.

Adam helped Rev. Streit and Susannah from their buggy. He left the three women, clearly of pretentious penchant, on their own.

"Mister Livingston," said Rev. Streit, "again, I'm not sure what I'm doing

516 ◯ *Stanley D. Williams*

here. And from what you said this morning, your wife doesn't want men like me visiting."

"This is true," said Adam quietly. "She's not taken kindly to religion. My doing, I reckon, since I blame God for taking my first wife from me. A godly woman she was, and I've been mighty mad about it."

"That's an understandable sort of thing. I've been mad at the Almighty myself a few times. But it don't serve me well."

"Now, if you're able, about payment for your services," said Adam.

"My dear, dear man. No one has ever paid me to preach or pray, although some might pay to have me die, though I'm unsure who that may be. Nonetheless, someday when I do die, and I'm sure it will come sooner than later, what I was paid will be left behind. Do not offend me with your money or grain. I want neither."

"I am sorry; nevertheless, it was because of such a promise that you have come."

"Nonsense, Mister Livingston. I did not come because of your promises." At that, Rev. Streit turned and glanced at his wife. Adam followed the glance to Susannah who had gathered the three women from their buggy and had assembled them near the front porch of the house. Susannah's back was to the house where she appeared to be briefing the women on etiquette and decorum. Meanwhile, the three women amused themselves by staring wide-eyed at the house's plain architecture, as if it was a palace of mirrors.

"Nonetheless, sir, contrary to my wife's insistence, I do hope my presence may provide some comfort. We will see, shan't we? Is your wife within?"

Adam nodded and took the Rev. Streit's arm to assist him up the porch steps. Streit shook off Adam's hand, however, and climbed the steps on his own, one at a time, as if mounting a steed for battle.

As they climbed the stairs side-by-side, Adam looked up. Mary Ann was standing on the front door's threshold, one hand on her hip and the other above her head bracing her body inside the jam, blocking their entrance. Her apron was shredded with clipped crescent moons. Adam gestured Streit to hold back as he approached Mary Ann and spoke softly to her: "You have harassed me to do something. And this is what I am doing. This man...this preacher...comes sincerely. We are besieged by what this man is against. Let him try, as I am attempting to protect you. Be kind, wife, you are capable and your desires are mine, and his, I trust."

In a huff, Mary Ann straightened her cut-up apron and dress, turned, and climbed the stairs to their rooms on the second floor.

At the foot of the stairs Henry stood ready to watch the proceedings. Just inside the gathering hall Eve stood with a warp of yarn in her hands preparing to dress the loom. When her father entered with Rev. Streit and the women, Eve stopped what she was doing and stood to the side of the room respectfully.

In the fireplace, Bethany was warming stew in a stone pot over a small fire and hot coals. When the entourage entered, she swung the stew pot away from the direct flames, spread out the fuel logs so they would not burn too quickly, and moved back to the kitchen door to sit on her chair at the supper table.

Rev. Streit entered the room cautiously, and the women behind him more so. "Mister Livingston, is this the room in which the spirit or spirits appear most frequently?"

"The clipping has occurred in every room, upstairs and down, but one." Adam glanced at his daughter. "It, the clipping that is, has occurred in this room most frequently, because it was here, in these drawers, that we kept our linen… no longer, however. The drawers are empty, except for this." Adam opened up a drawer and withdrew a towel that had been severely cut into crescent ribbons, the scalloping holes alternating back and forth, evenly like a weave. Adam handed the sliced-up towel to Rev. Streit, who took it and showed it to the women, who quickly but cautiously gathered around, thought it was difficult to "gather around" with their wide, round, hoop skirts.

As they fingered the shredded towel, it began—the clipping sounds. They all heard it and looked about in wonder.

"Yes, that's it," said Adam. "And during a new moon the house will be surrounded at night by the sounds of stampeding horses and wagons, which are always invisible except for their tracks that we find in the morning."

The clipping grew louder and the visitors gathered close together for protection.

Rev. Streit decided it was high-time to do something. "Ladies, let's pray." The preacher knelt in the middle of the gathering hall around which his wife and the ladies, spread out in their hoop skirts, also knelt. Streit took a prayer book from his suit jacket. Adam stood aside and watched.

No sooner had Streit opened his prayer book, but his hands began to shake. "Let us pray, ladies." After looking around for the source of the clipping, Streit bowed his head and began to read a selected prayer. It was not easy, for his hands shook, as did his voice. "Almighty God, the Father of our Lord Jesus Christ, who desires not the death of sinners, but rather that they turn from their wickedness and live. We pray that you exercise the power you gave to the Apostles to declare and pronounce…."

As Streit prayed the Wizard's clipping grew louder, and Adam could only wonder what materials the crescents were being cut from. The more Streit prayed, the less Adam heard the prayer and the more he heard the clipping.

Nonetheless, Streit prayed on and, prompted by his wife's "Amens," the three women also joined in: "…to his people, being penitent, the absolution and remission of their sins…," read Streit, "…the Lord truly pardons and absolves the penitent who with a sincere heart believes the holy Gospel."

Adam watched with increased interest. The longer Streit prayed, the more involved the women became, to the point of shedding tears and crying out loud in praise and petition for God to swoop down and cast the evil spirits asunder.

Adam had considered the women in hoop skirts imposters by their appearance, but their loud wailing and the intensity of their responses to Streit's calls had all the signs of sincerity. The call and response was well practiced.

Rev. Streit read a line:

"Blessed are thou, O, Lord."

And the women would respond with equal fervor, "O Lord, teach us thy statutes."

"With my lips have I declared...."

"...all the judgments of thy mouth."

The call and response ritual headed for a crescendo...when...

Suddenly the entire house shook violently as if by a mighty earthquake. Tremor after tremor rattled the floor and walls. So violent was the shaking that the fire in the fireplace went out. Then yet another tremor jolted the room, loosening a boulder from the stone fireplace and causing it to be catapulted across the room...directly at Rev. Streit, who ducked at the last second. Instead of flying straight and hitting the wall, however, the boulder turned in flight, rounded the room in a swift orbit, and flew again at Streit, who was by now on his feet and staring in horror at the orbiting rock. A second time Streit dodged the rock, and yet the boulder continued in its orbit, and came at him a third time.

By now, Adam came alive and threw his body at the rock, wrestling it with both arms to the ground, where it bounced erratically like a wild burro.

At this the women began to weep and bawl, calling on God and the angels for divine, supernatural help, as if their previous prayers had been purely perfunctory. But as the women called on the Almighty, the fireplace responded with repeated cannon blasts of grapeshot, except the grapeshot consisted of red-hot coals. It was as if invisible hands from hell were flinging the hot coals at the women with impunity. The three women in their wide hoop skirts, found it impossible to avoid the missiles—they were on their knees and their wide skirts, wedged against each other and the furniture, allowed for no lateral movement. They were perfect targets, sitting ducks with large fluffy tails fixed on a shelf of hell's shooting gallery. One after another the hot coals landed on their hooped skirts and burned through the thin cotton dresses, starting small fires of the flammable material that was draped on the whalebone frames.

Seeing all of this, the children screamed in terror. Bethany ran to the kitchen and returned with a bucket of water, heaving it in several swings at the burning and smoldering skirts and the women with their fancy hats and dos. The parasols might have done some good protecting them from the water, but they had long been put away and left by the door. The three women, helped by Susannah, quickly removed their outer dresses now destroyed by the coals. Once removed, the underlying petticoats that lay on top of the whalebone hoops were revealed. It was then that Adam turned away in great anguish, for the women's petticoats were clipped to shreds in thin crescent ribbons.

Strikingly, Susannah's clothes were neither burned or apparently clipped.

She hustled the three women out of the gathering hall and house amid shrieks of panic and holy fear, only returning to gather their earlier discarded parasols.

When the women had left the house, Adam turned back to find Rev. Streit fuming. "Livingston, I told you I had not the power to eradicate your damn spirits, and now you have brought holy hell upon my life and these up-standing parishioners of my fellowship. I have no idea what you have done, or what is going on here, but you, sir, are in a bucket of trouble and on your way to hell."

With that, Streit stomped out of the house and down the stairs to meet Su-sannah, who had already seen the other women off in their buggy. Together the Streits left in a hurry, not bothering to look back or offer condolences or even a prayer in parting.

Later that night, by lantern light, amidst a darkening interior depression, Adam and Sam finished cementing the rock back in its rightful place in the fireplace. It didn't fit right even after attempts to chisel it back into shape. After a while Adam told Sam it would have to do. Sam took the tools to the barn and Adam cleaned up the mess before heading up the stairs to bed. He doubted he would sleep at all, so disturbing were the events of the past twenty-four hours. As he undressed, put on his bed clothes, and lay down, still in the background were the distant sounds of clipping shears and the sobbing of a young boy...his Henry.

5

Most Feared Master of Bigotry,

I am bored. Gnashing cloth with my teeth is also wearing off my hellish enamel, and even the whirlwind bit is getting old. Yes, I know all about the daughter, but what can I do? She's innocent and wise. I have no leverage to tempt, bedevil, or deceive. Give me someone to work with, some fallible soul susceptible to sin. Do not criticize when you have no power to do better.

I can't go on like this forever. Livingston's will must be bro-ken; perhaps I'm not up to the task. Livingston's claim he doesn't believe in a God is nothing but foul snake oil. It's a diversion; it's not true. He always believed. I think he believes now; he's just bel-ligerent. Such rants do not count against the backdrop of eternity. Grace is bigger and you know it. Livingston must be brought to the point of cursing the Almighty in some vile, deeply personal way... and then drop dead.

I'm not sure whose idea it was to chomp up cloth as a means to that end, but it doesn't seem to be working. Livingston hasn't budged one way or another except in anger. In fact, the Almighty whisking his wife off to Glory was more effective in moving him

520 O *Stanley D. Williams*

toward us than all this indigestion over dead flax. Can't we kill the kids? That might work.

You have severely criticized me for allowing Livingston to recently seek out Christian ministers in an attempt to exorcise me from his presence. But I think you're assuming too much. It was our luck (I'm prohibited from invoking Providence) that the Lutherans in this neck of the earth were as useless as ever. Well, I can't claim that generally...Dr. Luther was of great benefit to our cause, but that was a few hundred years ago, and this is now.

Even though Livingston is now searching out a minister you don't give me the credit I deserve. I do hope the farcical visit by Streit and his ladies in waiting demonstrates my capacity to mock such efforts...Denis Cahill aside.

Speaking of the damn priest, I need to get him out of the picture. Yes, I have a plan, but it will take a while...remember, patience. Don't dismiss the malicious scandal that's coming. It will clearly put Cahill out of the running, although the tangible effects are still a year away. I'm persistent but patient. Are you?

At your sinful service,
Cyn Namrasit, OPSD

Chapter 36
No Condition to Ride

1

July, 1795.

Gregory McCullough looked forward to his monthly trek into Charles Town. It was a break from the grind of managing a farm and the supervisors that oversaw his slaves. Thinking of overseers, he rarely looked forward to the reconciliation of his accounts that were overseen by his accountant and audited by this banker, but such were the terms he had agreed to for the mortgage on his plantation. He was sure his banker didn't trust him any more than he trusted his slaves.

The trip to Charles Town passed Adam Livingston's farm, an irritation to McCullough ever since Livingston had manumitted Nwanne. McCullough felt justified in setting to flames the Darks' cabin. Livingston deserved to be intimidated and forced into conformity with community standards of respect for one's neighbor. The stability and prosperity of the whole region was at stake. McCullough had not intended to burn the Darks alive, but that Nwanne died in the fire was justice served, he concluded. He felt neither responsibility nor guilt. He intended it as a warning to Livingston but also to slaves who were tempted to rebel. His efforts had had a good effect—Livingston had not purchased or manumitted any more slaves, as far as he could tell.

His trip past Livingston's farm provided an opportunity to look in on his neighbor and see if there was evidence of further abolition activity. If there was, he was more than prepared to take additional action.

As his buggy approached the Livingston drive there appeared before him a new three-inch thick *rope stretched across the road preventing a conveyance, such as his horse and buggy, from continuing. His horse came to an abrupt halt. What was the meaning of this, he wondered? Is Livingston resorting to tolls? But there was no gate or toll taker. Besides, taking tolls on this public road would be illegal, as was this obstruction that crossed the road, held tight on both sides by stout trees.

McCullough dismounted from his buggy and walked to one end of the rope which was wrapped around a tree. Whatever this was about he would just untie it and go on his way. But when he arrived at the rope's end, there was no knot to untie. Further, the rope was not just securely wrapped around a tree and tied, but looped around the tree and woven back into itself seamlessly. So tight was the weave that the frayed ends of the rope were perfectly hidden within the rope's root. He walked to the other end, marveling how tightly the rope was pulled across the road, leaving no slack. When he got to the other end of the rope barrier it too was wrapped around the girth of a large tree and perfectly woven back into the rope's root.

McCullough was angry. The rope was thick, no thin piece of twine that could be broken or cut through, which he would have done in an instant. This had to be Livingston's doing. As much as he hated to do so, he now had an excuse to take a closer look at Livingston's operation and demand that the rope be removed.

2

Adam was standing next to his barn in the midst of handing out assignments to his dozen day laborers when Sam nudged him in the side and pointed to the wagon path that led to the Charles Town road. Adam looked to see Gregory McCullough striding toward them. No horse, no buggy, no wagon, just McCullough looking as mean as ever, but alone this time, and clearly with another grievance.

Adam separated himself from the group, indicating that Sam should carry on and get the day's work going. Adam met McCullough halfway across the yard. Adam noticed that McCullough was clearly more interested in his day laborers, although he walked directly to Adam in a huff, as if there was a thunder cloud overhead threatening a lightning strike—something Adam would have been glad to see; the man had it coming.

Glaring at the day laborers but avoiding Adam's eyes, McCullough made clear his love. "You've been nothing but trouble, Livingston. What's the meaning of roping off the road to Charles Town. You after tolls or some other goddamn tax? Ghosts won't let you sell your flax? Is that it? What's the idea of blocking the road?"

For a moment Adam wished he had grabbed his shillelagh before he left the house. Just seeing McCullough on his property was enough to raise his wrath. To Adam, McCullough was a murderer and was due some justice, but Adam also respected the law...at least that's what he told himself. "What do you want, Greg? Aren't you satisfied with oppressing your own slaves, you must come here and spew your belligerency?"

"I'm talking about the goddamn rope you have stretched across the road preventing man and beast from coming and going by your property. Do you think you now own the road?"

"If I did own it, would it stop you from passing this way?"

"You nigger lovin' fool. Given the chance I'd use that rope to string *you* up."

"What rope?"

"The one you lassoed across the *public* road."

"There's no rope or anything else blocking your free passage by my farm. In fact I'd rather not detain you, preferring you to pass quickly."

"That goes for both of us, but you've rigged a rope that no man can untie and which prevents my passage."

"I have not, nor has Sam or anyone else."

"Come with me, then."

Adam looked around to ensure that Sam was getting the workers assigned without an issue, then followed McCullough at a distance out the wagon path to the road.

Once to the road, Adam saw Greg's horse and buggy stopped before what looked like a thick hemp-woven rope.

"There! Just as I told ya. Call me a liar, will you? Seems like you intend to impede progress. I ain't paying no toll for a public thoroughfare. Now get that there thing out of my way."

Adam stared at the rope and looked to his left and right where the rope was attached to two trees. The sight was strange and surreal, as the rope did not dip in the middle from its own weight. Within seconds Adam discerned that this was the Wizard's sense of humor, although this was of an unexpected nature, and not in the least way funny. He walked to one end of the rope to see how it was tied around the tree only to discover it was woven into itself. Unseen by McCullough, Adam grabbed the rope to test its firmness. It was as he expected.

Coming from behind the tree Adam examined closely the stretch of the rope across the road without touching it. He came up next to McCullough who was standing next to his buggy. "Greg, there is no barrier to your impediment except your own belligerence pulling me away from my work. Be gone with you."

Adam walked back toward the wagon path, but McCullough jumped in front of him. McCullough wasn't as tall as Adam, but he was bulkier.

"Hell, you say," said McCullough. "You cotton mouth, lying son of the breach, *remove that rope.* I've lost me patience, I have." McCullough raised his fists as if to strike Adam. At first all Adam thought about, again, was his own naiveté in leaving his shillelagh behind, and how he'd like to use it on this rotten waste of flesh. But then he decided to do one better. As if he had his shillelagh in hand, Adam twirled his body, out-stretched his hand, and slapped the rear of McCullough's horse with a loud WHACK!

Immediately, the horse squealed and jumped at a run pulling the buggy through the rope apparition and continuing down the road at a gallop.

"Damn, you," McCullough yelled. "Look what you've gone done." Immediately McCullough ran after his horse and buggy, but when he came to the rope and tried to run through it, the rope stopped him dead, dropping McCullough to the ground. Now scared, Greg McCullough scrambled under the rope and ran after his buggy yelling obscenities.

Adam watched McCullough chase after his horse and buggy until they disappeared over a rise in the road. It was the first time he appreciated to any extent the Wizard's wizardry. Turning toward the wagon path once again, he walked back toward the house, never looking back at the rope which suddenly dissolved into black vapor and disappeared.

3

It was early in August, 1795, after attending to the towns and villages to the north, that Fr. Cahill returned to Magdala to find *Francis Bodkin, another priest, slightly older and significantly thinner, in the guest quarters across the hall from his own. The priest was a Dominican friar from Ireland, no less. Fr. Bodkin had arrived just days earlier. He related how he was greeted enthusiastically by the "priest keeper" and how she had provided bedding, linens, wine, much fine food, and more wine.

Their initial conversation in Magdala's upstairs hall was short, as Immacolata, full of excitement, told the men to come down for a feast that she had spent the day preparing.

"I must ask," said Fr. Cahill with childlike enthusiasm, "is your family from Galway, or is it Limerick? Perhaps you have detected in my voice that I am from Dublin."

"My dear man, Galway indeed is where I was born and raised, and I miss the land of my fathers deeply, as I am sure you do as well. But Europe and even England is in such a terrible straits for us Catholics. I fear it will be worse before it gets better."

"Please tell me about your life and what brings you here to America," pleaded Fr. Cahill.

"I am afraid my life to this point is somewhat of a restless journey in search of my place in the world. Dear Missus Rosso says that you had somewhat of a journey yourself, coming up lastly from Spain and New Orleans?"

"That is true, but I have been here now nearly seven years and have been satisfied that God has led me to this point. For a number of marvels and feats of chance, which might not pass scrutiny for miracles, have nonetheless secured my place. But tell me more of yourself."

They were interrupted again by the priest keeper who poured burgundy into their goblets and told them to drink and eat for she had labored for their health, and then added that they were both too skinny to enter God's sanctuary and needed fattening.

After a toast to America, Fr. Bodkin continued. "I felt the call to be a priest from my early years, although I may have been seeking a rebellious adventure. Being Catholic in Ireland, as you know, meant either exile or execution. In secret my parents managed to scuttle me off to Spain at the age of ten, to an Italian, Catholic family that to this day I know not how my mother or father knew. A few years later the family returned, with me, to Italy. My stepfather, as he was Italian, had longed to return to his home in Naples where I attended school and Mass almost daily. The divine call was strong, and so it was natural that I eventually entered seminary in Rome. When ordained, by Pius the Sixth, I was not in good health. I was always weak, and still am though it has been fifteen years now. I served at a parish in Spain for a few years, but longed to return to a language I knew. My Spanish is fair but not good. I tried to settle in London, but the accommodations with a private family fell through. The damp weather in London was not to my benefit at any rate. I had a brother in the West Indies, so I negotiated a berth aboard an American-bound vessel and ended up in Baltimore, where I planned to change ships that would take me to Kingston. But I was not well from the crossing and ended up paying a visit to Bishop Carroll who found a place for me to stay and recuperate before I continued to the islands. That was a year ago. He provided me with a room and good food. After a month he decided I was well enough to earn my keep and sent me out to local parishes to administer the sacraments and preach. One thing led to another and so here I am in Hagerstown."

Fr. Cahill found Fr. Bodkin's story interesting, but the abruptness of its ending, "...here I am in Hagerstown," left him cold. *Just what IS he doing in Hagerstown?* he wondered. "That's not what I thought you were going to tell me," said Fr. Cahill.

"Oh, what were you thinking?"

"When you mentioned Kingston, for there must be a lot of Irish there, I thought you were going to tell me how the McSherry brothers had found you and brought you here. Richard McSherry, who lives south of here in Leetown, Virginia, was particularly instrumental in helping me establish multiple Catholic societies in these parts."

"No, I have not heard of the McSherrys."

"Were you sent here, then, by Bishop Carroll?"

"I was. He said that the church in Hagerstown needed a priest and asked if I would be willing to see if ministering here agreed with me, rather than going south. But I am equally surprised to meet you, a priest well-established here, as you are no doubt surprised at seeing me."

Fr. Cahill began to put the pieces together. Bishop Carroll had judged him unsuitable for the ministry and perhaps even considered him an interloper, an intruder, and a pretender at best. "So, you have been sent here," concluded Fr. Cahill, "to be the pastor of my parish?" He asked the question in a perturbed way. Either he had to submit to the bishop or suffer the consequences of being unceremoniously dismissed from the ministry. *Bishop Carroll underestimates me,* thought Fr. Cahill.

But the question went unanswered, for at that moment Immacolata brought washed greens, shelled nuts, cheese chunks, fruit slices, dressing, and more wine. Fr. Cahill marveled at how fresh the greens appeared, from Magdala's garden no doubt, and looked forward to Immacolata's very spicy dressing.

"Did Bishop Carroll make any mention of me in sending you here?"

Francis Bodkin thought for a moment. "No. He did not. He did say there were Catholics in the area that needed a priest, but he…" Fr. Bodkin paused to think. "That is very odd, he was indirect. You might say restrained or circumspect. I understood that there was no priest anywhere nearby. And yet here you are. What do you make of that?"

Fr. Cahill smirked and shook his head. *So it evolves.* "The bishop and I have never met, and yet we have exchanged letters, but not cordially. He knows I am here and active in establishing a number of parishes, although for lack of money we have not built any church, and this building, technically a rectory, is owned by the local society which Richard McSherry heads, although I am on the board. The problem between myself and Bishop Carroll may be this. When I came to America from New Orleans, I had been told by the American captain of the ship that brought me, a devout Catholic man by the way, that there wasn't a bishop or superior in America but that the land needed missionary priests. He gave me free passage for my services as a chaplain, and told me to follow God's leading into the interior and start churches. That I have done. I bring the sacraments to no less than six societies now, although not as regularly as both I and my congregations would like. It was Richard McSherry's plan to have several priests live here at Magdala and be of service to the surrounding villages and towns. I thought you might be another, like myself, which Richard had saved from thieves. But I am now of the opinion that Richard knows nothing of you."

"You talked of this Richard McSherry as if he was a bishop or pope."

"He'd make a good one or the other," said Fr. Cahill. "But his calling is land and farm management, and, with his wife, cares a great deal for the poor. I was fortunate enough to oversee their courtship and marriage, here in Hagerstown."

"I've been told my health would improve in a southern climate. Do you think that may be true of New Orleans?"

"New Orleans? No, no. I do not. Kingston, possibly. Richard would know about that. He and his brother William were the proprietors of a successful hardware business there, which William continues to operate in Baltimore by the wharf. New Orleans does get fresh airs from the Gulf, but it's surrounded by humid swamps, infectious mosquitoes, and then there are hurricanes and fires."

"I've heard there are ships there that depart regularly for Kingston."

"That's true, but it's true of Baltimore, too. I'm also not sure how a Dominican friar would fair with the New Orleans Capuchin rector of the church there—Père Antoine, a strict and disagreeable man.

Bodkin paused to consider what he was just told. "Might we find a way to work together?" asked Fr. Bodkin.

"Let us get to know each other better," said Fr. Cahill. "Certainly, the local populace, although only a dozen or less, would like to attend daily Mass. We have fifty on Sundays depending on the weather. When comfortable with each other I can make my circuit more frequently and you can attend to the faithful in Hagerstown. Do you ride?"

"I do, but not well. My strength has not fully returned, I fear."

"I pray you regain your strength. You will want to meet Richard and Anastasia, his wife."

4

It was only weeks later (August, 1795) that Richard McSherry, having visited Hagerstown in his usual course, met Fr. Bodkin. Having been briefed by Fr. Cahill as to the sudden appearance of Bodkin, and the possible political ramifications, Richard was happy but skeptical to meet the new priest. Two priests in Hagerstown, while giving Catholicism more credibility, now, under the presumptuous circumstances, also raised the specter of scandal. Conversely, Richard considered Fr. Bodkin's arrival a good omen that possibly, just possibly, the bishop might find reason to begin funding the work in Hagerstown, relieving Richard from his on-going sponsorship. Yes, he could still afford it, but the goal was to make the church self-sustaining by adding souls to the rolls. No doubt Bodkin would receive a stipend from the bishop.

Richard persuaded Fr. Cahill and Fr. Bodkin to travel to Leetown for a day and a night to meet his growing family. By the time they did, early in September, 1795, Anastasia had become the doting mother of three boys: Richard Jr., three, William, two, and Dennis, one. Any traveling more than a quick trip into Charles Town and back was something Anastasia did not relish, but they had servants, not slaves, and entertaining two priests for a day and a night in their large two-story stone home was a comfortable event. The visit was refreshing for all, and Richard was satisfied that the informal arrangement, which made it appear that Bodkin was the Hagerstown pastor, was workable. Although Bodkin would always be around town because Fr. Cahill traveled the circuit and Bodkin did not, in truth, Fr. Cahill, not Bodkin, held the reins of local authority, finances, and was on the society's board.

Richard did have a concern, however, with Carroll's assignment of Bodkin to Hagerstown, and he shared that with Fr. Denis. It appeared that Carroll wanted to dispense with Cahill and install Bodkin as Hagerstown's sole pastor. Richard appreciated the Church hierarchy, but after meeting and talking with Bodkin, Richard could see that Cahill was the robust, missionary, adventurous priest, and Bodkin was not healthy enough to ride but one leg of a circuit without needing an extended rest. Time would tell. He told himself to stay out of the administration of the church and let the priests and bishops battle it out. On the other hand, Richard was not willing to relegate the situation to others when he had so much invested.

So, Richard traveled to Baltimore to visit his brother William. It had been nearly a year since his last visit and the brothers were overdue for a rendezvous. One evening, over supper at an opulent restaurant, one of the few luxuries William allowed into his life, Richard explained the uncertain situation between Cahill and Bodkin and the investment he, Richard, had put into the Catholic effort in Western Maryland. Richard explained that he suspected that Bishop Carroll would not welcome a face-to-face visit from Richard because Richard's private sponsorship of a priest for these many years no doubt appeared to be usurping the bishop's authority. Did William know anyone on the inside of the bishop's administration that could discover Carroll's true intentions?

William said that he was good friends with a man who headed up the local business consortium, a Fred McCracken, who advised the bishop on political and civil matters. Whether or not he was close enough to the bishop to dig up dirt on Bodkin, William did not know. That was enough for Richard.

After meeting with McCracken, and confident that he had done all he could to protect Fr. Cahill and his own business and religious interests, Richard returned home without telling either priest that he had a spy on the inside of the bishopric.

5

While riding his circuit, Fr. Cahill could not get out of his mind some of the ideas Richard had raised about the bishop's purpose in sending Bodkin to Hagerstown. Fr. Cahill decided he should write Bishop Carroll and set a few things straight...and suggest that he too should receive a stipend.

*From: D. Cahill
To: J. Carroll
Sept. 27, 1795
Hagerstown

My Lord,

Desirous to let you know my conduct and motives regarding Rev. F. Bodkin, who came here at your request in early Aug.

I am forced to make the following report. I have forbid him the use of any of the remote churches, of which I have the possession and care, as I fear for his health. He is in no condition to ride the circuit. Indeed, he nearly begged to stay in Hagerstown where we live together in a converted home owned by the Shenandoah Catholic Society. This seems agreeable to him and he regularly officiates in Hagerstown with my blessing as it allows me to attend in the six other villages and towns more regularly with the sacraments.

I discharge what I think my duty and the good of our common cause compels me to inform you that I have justification to fear that he is not fit to be trusted with the care of souls. Should you require it, I can substantiate the cause of my fear, but I would rather not, to avoid any scandal that might arise from my dispute between him and me; be it optional with you to continue him in

Hagerstown, and, when he is well enough, to Chambersburg & Fort Cumberland, or send me another in his place.

I am glad to see that some of my people are desirous to have church oftener than I could attend them, which Fr. Bodkin facilitates.

I have advanced forty pounds on the Church building in Hagerstown. I hope to be repaid it, by a designation of Mr. J. Carroll's subscription to me of ten pounds a year 'til such sum be paid; and the officiating clergyman will collect such sum from the people for himself.

I am with due respect your humble servant.

D. Cahill

To this letter Fr. Denis received no reply.

Chapter 37
Squandered Integrity

1

January 9, 1796.

Regina Robinson was old, but she wasn't sure how old. In 1732, as a very young woman in her teens, she was captured from her African village during a war between rival kingdoms. Along with most of the able-bodied men and a few other young girls, the warriors took Regina and the other prisoners by boat down a long river to a *large white, stone castle on the African west coast. There she was herded into a stone room with ten other women. After several weeks of confinement she was traded to European slave traders that brought her to the French island of Martinique and sold her to a French planter. *The Code Noir (or The Black Code) instituted by Louis XIV in 1685 required her new owners to baptize her within eight days of arrival and instruct her in the Roman Catholic religion. Later she was to hear that the rationale for her baptism was that if she were to die due to the severe life she was to experience, she would go to heaven, and thus the French king and slave owners believed they were doing some good for the Africans they enslaved. That was the first she had ever heard of the white man's religion, or heaven. To her new owner she carried herself like a queen, and so he gave her the Christian name Regina. Of course, the baptism didn't make sense to her at first, but the Christian instruction in Catholicism slowly did.

On Martinique she became the nanny to the children her owner had sired from other young slave women like herself. The only reason the owner never forced himself on her was due to the jealousy of the other women who would send Regina away when he was around, which wasn't often. Some years later, she was sold to a trader who shipped her to Virginia. There she was sold to a kind plantation owner who cared well for his several dozen slaves who worked the fields. It was there that she met Matthew Robinson, an older, large and gentle man that towered over Regina's diminutive frame. After a short courtship they married with their plantation owner's permission. In fact, their owner married them in a Christian wedding and allowed them a Sunday reception. With Matthew, she bore a single child, Wallace, who took up his daddy's passion—Sunday preaching. Their owner allowed the slaves Sundays off and to hold Sunday services. Ten years ago Matthew died of a fever. He was buried in the plantation cemetery after a Christian funeral service on a Sunday afternoon, at which young Wallace preached.

Because Matthew, Regina, and young Wallace were hard-working, loyal slaves, their owner, in a fit of recompense, which the other slaves had never seen, set Regina and Wallace free. She eventually settled in a rural village called *Freetown established by former slaves who bought the land from *Merrell Bastone in two-acre lots. Little by little, as former slaves joined them, the village grew to eighty acres. Located between Charles Town and Harper's Ferry, the community of thirty former slaves sold their farm goods at the Charles Town market. Regina never married again, but found a place in the Freetown Free Church that Wallace started. All of the inhabitants of Freetown attended Wallace's Free Church, but on any Sunday the population of Freetown doubled, as free and some still indentured slaves were allowed to travel and attend his services. Sam and Bethany Dark attended twice a month. Although Wallace was the pastor, Regina was the queen mother.

Bethany had told Regina about the hauntings at Flax Haven and had asked for advice. At first Regina suggested Bethany and Sam pray for the Livingstons. That was the simplest and safest advice. But every other week when they showed up at Free Church, Regina asked, and Bethany or Sam would tell of another disruption. The Darks told her that their home was free of the effects, for which they were glad, but that the Livingstons were good employers and the Darks worried for them. Some months after Regina had heard her first detailed account of the Livingstons' clippings, rumblings, and crop destruction, she felt she needed to offer more than just advice. She asked Bethany to get the Livingstons' permission, for her and Wallace to come to the farm and pray over the house that the evil spirit might depart.

Thus, on January 9, one day before the new moon, they visited the Livingston farm. Regina dressed as if she was going to church. She wrapped her head in a white tignow, or headwrap, which she turned into a modest fashion statement with a floppy bow in front. The tignow bow matched the bow and brooch at her neckline, which held together the folds of a sheer white shawl pulled over a white linen gown and petticoats. With naturally alert eyes, her smile was her signature; it lit up her face and the entire room wherever she entered.

When Regina and Wallace arrived, in the early afternoon, Bethany and a reluctant Mary Ann met them in the yard. "Hello, Missus Robinson," said Mary Ann who offered her hand. "You needn't have come. No need to be polite on my behalf. I'm a tired woman and I don't believe in ghosts, holy ones or otherwise." Even as she greeted Regina, Mary Ann was distracted, nervously looking at a point in the western sky just below the sun.

As Mary Ann led them inside, Bethany tugged on Regina's sleeve and pointed to the thin crescent moon above the western horizon where Mary Ann had been staring. "The hauntings only come just before and after a new moon," Bethany said. "You see the moon is waning. Sometime tomorrow the new moon will occur when the hauntings will peak. My mistress is scared of what may happen in the next couple days.."

That piece of information pricked Regina's imagination and memory. As a young girl in Africa she recalled the incantations, dances, and portents their village Sangoma, or healer, would invoke when a crescent moon appeared. The man seemed possessed for a week; he would not eat, but drank monkey's blood to sustain his energy, or so her mother told her. Regina always disliked that time of the month. It reminded her of her own monthly cycles which had impaired her self-confidence until an older and kinder woman in Martinique befriended her. Bethany's pointing out the crescent moon brought an instant shiver to Regina's spine. She began to understand what the Livingstons might be facing. Despite her advanced age and tendency to stoop, she straightened her spine, and prepared for a fight.

As she stepped into the house, Regina asked Mary Ann what exactly was going on. It was clear to Regina that Mary Ann was not exactly thrilled at their coming, but to answer Regina's question she took Regina and Wallace on a short tour of the house. Whenever they entered a room, Mary Ann's eyes darted warily about and Regina and Wallace did the same, because wherever in the house they went they all heard the Wizard's chirp.

"You hear it?" Mary Ann asked. "It's cutting something up, but we won't know what for a while."

"What's cuttin' what up?" asked Regina.

They were in the parlor at the time. Mary Ann pulled open a drawer and withdrew a linen cloth that had been ravaged by holes in the shape of crescent moons. "You hear it now?" Pointing to the cloth in Regina's hands, "That's what it's doing somewhere. I'm surprised your petticoat is in one piece."

Regina glanced down at her petticoat; it was in one piece. Then, she saw the dozen or so small crescent-shaped holes in Mary Ann's apron.

Throughout the tour Regina watched Wallace's reaction. He was tall like Matthew and towered over her petite frame. Wallace had grown into a formidable man and she felt well-protected whenever they traveled. No roadside thief would think of even approaching her when Wallace was around. He was equally intimidating, in a strange, loving way, when he preached. The people loved his gentle, authoritative personality. He rarely showed anger; he was always in control of his faculties, but to hear him preach the pure Word of God…well, it scared the hell out of folks.

The incessant chirping was giving Regina a headache. Yet, as she watched her son's reaction, she was surprised, for she saw fear creep into his eyes. The confidence she normally associated with his personality ebbed the longer the tour lasted. When Mary Ann showed them the Wizard's clippings she had saved against Eve's advice, Wallace literally backed up and refused to touch the riddled cloth, although Regina thought nothing of the useless rag and turned it over and over in her hands to examine it.

As they stood in the gathering hall Mary Ann confessed her feelings: "I doubt very much if your presence will do anything. What you're hearing happens every month just before and after the new moon. Adam has tried to rid our lives of it but…life's miserable."

"Missus Livingston," said Regina, "I hear all about dis here demon Wizard ya got, and I got to tell ya, y'all got to fight fire wid fire."

Mary Ann glanced at the small fire in the fireplace. "I don't catch your meaning."

"You pray ta God much, Missus Livingston?" said Regina.

"Don't believe in God. Husband did. He'd say God *preys* on us."

"All I can really do is pray fer ya 'en try to rid yer home of ya's spook."

"Do as you please, but don't expect me to pray."

"Might help if ya did. Dis yer home, right?"

Mary Ann sighed deeply and shook her head. "Would you like tea while you pray?"

Regina recognized that Mary Ann was trying to be pleasant, but it was just as clear that Mary Ann did not relish a prayer meeting in her gathering hall. She already said it would do no good, but from Regina's perspective, the *word of God did not return void.*

"Missus Robinson," said Mary Ann, "you and your son go ahead with whatever you do. Bethany, would you make me some tea?"

Bethany looked to Regina, as if to ask permission.

"Missus Livingston," said Regina, "it'd be mighty helpful if those with the ability to pray, do pray. We's not playing Ringing the Bull here. We's asking God Almighty to ring out Satan 'en his demons who's afflicted dis house. Bethany a prayer warrior, and I's need her in dis fight, especially if'en you're running scared."

"Missus Robinson, that is impolite," said Mary Ann.

"When we come, Missus Livingston, you says 'No need to be polite on my behalf.' So, I's not. I's being truthful. Bethany, you pray, darlin'. This house needs you prayin'." Regina stopped and looked toward Mary Ann. "Missus Livingston?"

"All right, all right…fine," said Mary Ann. "Do what you have to do. I'm going to have some tea." With that Mary Ann walked down into the summer kitchen.

"We best kneel," said Regina. "Wallace, you pray, then Bethany, then me." The three got on their knees facing each other in the center of the room and bowed their heads and raised their arms in prayer.

No sooner had they done this, without ever saying a word, than the floor began to vibrate. Regina looked sharply to Bethany, who simply nodded her head as if to say, *yes this is part of it.* They both looked to Wallace. "Wallace," said Regina, "that's your sign to begin."

But Wallace was shaking like a leaf in a gale, and it wasn't the vibrating floor that was making him shake. His eyes bugged out and looked about the room for the devil while taking sharp shallow breaths. Perspiration began to form on his brow, and he shook his head at his mother as if to say, *no not me…you start.*

Regina slouched in disappointed at her son, but after a moment straightened, closed her eyes tight, and began to pray in tongues, as was their custom, as loud and forcefully as she could: "*Ngọzi na -adịrị onye na -adịghị eje ije. Na ndụmọdụ ndị ajọ omume, anaghịkwa eguzo n'ụzọ ndị mmehie. Ma ọ bụ gị na ndị na -akwa emo anọkọ.*" *Liko, iwu nke Onye -nwe bụ ọnụ ya; Ọ na -atụgharịkwa uche n'iwu ya ehihie na abalị. Ọ dị ka osisi kụrụ n'akụkụ iyi mmiri, nke na -amị mkpụrụ ya n'oge ya.*"

She paused. The sound of the clipping and the vibrating floor were more pronounced than when she began. She prayed harder: "*Akwụkwọ ya adịghị akpọnwụ; ihe ọ bụla ọ na -eme na -aga nke ọma. Ma ọ bụghị otú ahụ ka ndị ajọ omume dị, ọ bụghị otú ahụ! Ha dị ka igbogbo ọka nke ifufe na -ebugharị.*"

Now the table and chairs were added to the cacophony and were bouncing off the floor. The loom, that large and heavy contraption in the corner near the entrance, was moving about as if it was a feather in the wind.

Regina Robinson intensified her efforts: "*Ya mere, ndị ajọ omume agaghị ebili n'oge ikpe, ọ bụghịkwa ndị mmehie na nzukọ ndị ezi omume. N'ihi na Onye -nwe -ayi mara ụzọ ndi ezi omume, ma ụzọ ndị ajọ omume na -eduba ná mbibi.*"

But there was more. Suddenly there was a large BOOM in the fireplace as if a large chimney stone had shaken loose and fallen into the fire, sending flying sparks and burning embers into the room. Strangely, the burning embers hovered over the three that were still on their knees, floating and slowly revolving in a circle just above their heads. Regina was surprised—she immediately thought of the tongues of fire that came to rest above the Apostles in Acts 2 when they first spoke in tongues. Was this a sign from God, or were they being mocked by the spirit they were trying to expel? She stopped praying and stared at the floating embers and flames. Suspicious, she tried to grab one of them, but it slipped through her hands. Whatever it was, it wasn't hot. Was it a specter, an apparition, a ghost? Or, was it like everything else that had been rumored—a hoax? What brought it on or how it was done, she had no idea, and she wasn't sure she wanted to know.

Regina looked about the room. Bethany was becalmed and stared wide-eyed at the floating fire as if she had never seen anything like it before. Wallace was a different story. He had reached his limit. Very spooked and frightened, and finding it hard to catch his breath, Wallace tried to stand but instead stumbled and tripped over his own feet before he literally tumbled and rolled out the front door in a panic.

Regina noticed that as soon as she stopped praying...or was it when Wallace left in fright, the rumbling floor stopped vibrating and the burning embers dissipated into thin air. The chirping continued, suggesting their prayers had little or no effect, and with Wallace running scared she doubted there was much benefit in continuing.

Disheartened at her son's cowardice, and angry at the Livingstons' for staging a hoax to gather attention, Regina barely had the energy to stand. But stand she did. She looked at Bethany, then turned her gaze at Mary Ann who sat calmly at the supper table sipping her tea, as if nothing had happened. "Missus Livingston, dis is an elaborate trick you's playin' on us, though I know not how. 'Tis sad how you's fool my dear sister, Bethany." She glanced at Bethany who now shook her head at the church mother as if to say, *No, this is real, it's not a trick.* But Regina wasn't fooled. She turned to Bethany, "My dear, I hope we sees you at services this Sunday. I will pray for you's until then." When Regina said the words "for you" she was careful to be staring directly at Mary Ann.

Regina was mad. She had been fooled by these heathens, and poor Bethany was trapped in a situation where she had to make nice to these awful people. Regina could not understand why the Livingstons were so intent on fooling folks with this clipping non sense. She didn't know how they made the sounds or made it seem like there was fire floating 'round d'her heads, but they did. She couldn't wait to get out of there. Tricks people play on other folk is not good for the community. You kin't be a liar and be respected. Well, she was certain that the Livingstons' days were numbered if they kept this up.

She got quickly into her buggy. "Wallace, let's git outa-here. But what's got into you?" Wallace was still shaking even as he drove the buggy out of the Livingston yard. Regina carried on for some time, however, as they traveled down the road. "That was a prank they played on you, my dear boy, and me, I suppose. But I see through it. It weren't real. Stuff like that don't happen in real life. We's hav'ta pray for dear Bethany and Sam. They kind-a stuck."

2

Mary Ann watched in silence as Regina Robinson stomped out of the room and descended the porch stairs. A befuddled Mary Ann and a silent Bethany followed the esteemed so-called church mother out onto the porch. They watched as Regina hurried into Wallace's buggy, and he, still shaking, drove them both off without a word or goodbye.

Moments later, Adam and Sam came around the side of the house and stopped at the foot of the steps. "What happened?" asked Adam.

"Nothing as far as I can tell," said Mary Ann.

"What?" asked Adam.

"They were praying in some gibberish language," Mary Ann said, "when suddenly they stopped. Her son ran out of the house shaking like a he'd seen a ghost. Angry she was. Said something to me about me playing a trick on them. That's it!"

"You didn't see?" asked Bethany.

"See what?" Mary Ann replied.

"The shaking and the fire?"

"What shaking and fire?" asked Mary Ann.

"As soon as we started to pray," Bethany said, "the floor started to shake somethin' fierce, and after a bit more praying in mother's angelical tongue—which I'm sure probably scared them demons—there was an explosion in the fireplace, and pieces of burnin' wood flew out of the fireplace and flew around our heads. Just like when the Holy Ghost came on the Apostles with tongues of fire—and that fire stayed over our heads until we stopped prayin' and then it all went away, sudden like."

Mary Ann stared in disbelief at Bethany, but she could see that Bethany must have really experienced what she had described, for Mary Ann had never known Bethany to lie or make up some outlandish tall tale. Adam, however, didn't take the time to stare at Bethany, but jumped up the steps and into the house.

"You didn't see any of that?" asked Bethany.

Mary Ann shook her head, frustrated but confirmed in her belief that prayer to an unseen "god" had no effect.

Sam ran after Adam into the house and then Mary Ann and Bethany after them.

In the gathering hall Adam examined the fireplace. There was nothing out of place, and there was no fire in the room or any evidence of burning.

But the Wizard's clipping, their scissors bird, chirped away.

3

Later in January, 1796, Fr. Cahill was resting at the McSherrys' Retirement home in Leetown after Hagerstown Christmas and New Year festivities. He had planned this break from his duties and had notified the societies on his circuit that he would return to them by the middle of January. Meanwhile in Hagerstown, he had given over all the Masses in early January to Fr. Bodkin. What a relief that was to have an assistant pastor to allow him some much needed rest.

Shortly after his arrival, Richard, who was in an unusually serious mood, invited Fr. Cahill into the parlor to talk. Richard revealed that over a month ago, in November, he had received a letter from Baltimore that concerned them both but that it was so disturbing he had held off saying anything about it until now, after the busyness and celebrations of the holidays. Saying nothing more, Richard produced a letter and handed it to Fr. Cahill to read.

From: F. Bodkin
To: J. Carroll
October 1, 1795
Hagerstown

My Lord,

As you requested I arrived in Hagerstown and assumed the role of pastor to the small number of Catholics here.

I have been unable to travel to outlying villages and towns because my duty is to the devout souls here who are most zealous, even demanding, for daily availability of the sacraments, which I attend to. They have much appreciated my devotion to them.

But there are few souls here. It seems that there were more in the recent past but reports are that they emigrated to seek their fortune in Kentucky where the soil is reported much better than here in this valley.

My recommendation is that Hagerstown should be made a mission of Emmitsburg, the former Jesuit mission, where I believe you said Rev. Matthew Ryan has erected a church on land bestowed by James and Joseph Hughes.

As you suspected, there is no church building here, but rather a poor excuse for one. We meet in a run-down rental and I keep a room on the second floor. A local lady has agreed to provide food and light housekeeping during my stay.

While I am amenable to serve your lordship in this capacity, my health has not improved as I would have hoped. Perhaps it was the journey here from Baltimore where my strength was recovering, no doubt due to the proximity of the coastal waters. As I originally related to you, my physician in London recommended the southern coastal waters of America which have reportedly been free of the miasma that ails me.

I will continue to minister here, at your pleasure, until spring, when I should resume my journey to the south, even to Kingston if God wills.

I thank you for the stipend that has arrived. I will save much of it for my further journeys.

Your Servant,
F. Bodkin, O.P.

Until Fr. Cahill started to read he was in good spirits, but his countenance fell as he first scanned the letter, then read it closely. The letter sent shock waves through his brain and body. He felt his anger rise, and a cold sweat along his spine. He whispered under his breath, "Lord, make me an instrument of your peace..." Putting down the letter he gazed across the small table at his friend. "Would you mind if I had another glass...a full glass this time."

"Not at all," said Richard as he uncorked the bottle and poured Fr. Cahill a full glass of the amber spirit. Said Richard: "When I first read that a great fury rose within me. You are the pastor at Hagerstown, not Francis Bodkin. I'm not sure if the sin sits with the bishop or Bodkin. By omission and pertinence they have squandered any integrity either might have earned in my estimation. I have always vowed to respect the Church's hierarchy, but that letter destroys any respect I had. Though it was not the bishop that omitted our accomplishments these past years. The presumption is depressing. We established true Catholic societies in six towns and villages. Several hundred have been baptized, and what twenty-four, twenty-five marriages? Confessions are offered monthly, if not weekly. Catholics are better respected wherever there is a society, and many poor are served through our charity. True, there is no church building, not even a chapel that could compete with the Protestant edifices, but Bodkin's sins of omission, ignoring your presence, work, and contribution, were blatant and somehow need to be corrected. And the bishop needs to be put in his place. The gall is unforgivable."

"How did you come upon this?" asked Fr. Cahill. "Is it authentic? This does not look like Francis' hand."

"It is a copy, attested to be verbatim. How it came to me must remain private for the time being, to protect you, as well as the source."

From the moment Fr. Cahill arrived at Retirement a few days ago he had sensed that all was not well. Richard normally smiled when greeting friends, but the smile on his lips when he had arrived had been short lived, which put Fr. Cahill on edge. This letter was the reason.

"What do we do now?" asked Fr. Cahill, sipping his Madeira.

"I wish it was...we," said Richard. "I can only advise, but this is a delicacy you need to own. It seems that Carroll had seriously poisoned your place as a priest. Perhaps he's told Bodkin to displace you, or act as if you do not exist. No doubt your previous communication with the bishop and your refusal to gallop to Baltimore and kiss his ring played a part."

"At times I've had doubts about my calling. This is one such time."

"No, that's not it. Would it help to make amends with the bishop and come under this authority?"

"He'd cast me out, and erase all we've done."

"It would seem. But perhaps not."

"That he would send a less than adequate priest to replace me speaks simply. Am I too bold, too confident?"

"To do what you've done, one needs to be," said Richard.

"I was hoping Bodkin's presence was going to be beneficial. I guess not. He seemed content to stay in Hagerstown and not ride the circuit. He's made no comment or commitment otherwise, nor has he even asked to share in the meager offerings. That's probably because he's received at least one stipend from the bishop."

"Yes, I believe that is true," said Richard. "Clearly, he does not intend to stick around. Also, recall his occasional references to New Orleans and Kingston. And he does not look well, even with Immacolata's fatty diet."

"I've tried to tell him that New Orleans would not improve his health. Is Kingston's air fresh and cool?"

"Rarely. It is usually hot, oppressive, windy, and overcast. A native born to it can adapt, as can the robust and young. William and I did. You get used to it. But a weak man, like Bodkin, would deteriorate in no time. The advice he received was not from experience."

"My experience in New Orleans is that the South is a place where fevers are epidemic. The man would be better served if he returned to Ireland."

"He can do that today," said Fr. Cahill. "Haven't you heard? There's even a *Catholic seminary there now, at St. Patrick's College in Maynooth. The government even helped build it, just this year. Can you believe that?"

"I had not heard that," said Richard. "Aren't you concerned that the bishop considers Bodkin the pastor at Hagerstown and your work these past years may be dismissed and come to naught? This mention of Emmitsburg makes it seem that Hagerstown has been dismissed as insignificant."

Cahill took a long swig of wine. "Perhaps the wine is affecting my thinking, but I fear if I go to Baltimore I will be prevented from returning, and you would never hear from me again."

"Write Carroll again. Make the point that you are in control, not Bodkin, and that Bodkin can't even travel a circuit because of his health. You can't demand it, but you should let the bishop know what he doesn't know. In the end he may appreciate your candor and dedication to the ministry. Clearly Bodkin lacks it."

Fr. Cahill thought for a moment. "I'm not of the opinion that the bishop cares a hoot for my candor. As shorthanded for priests as he is, he should be celebrating our successes and paying me a stipend, not Bodkin."

"Set the record straight. If you don't the bishop will launch a more robust way to put you to pasture."

Fr. Cahill could find little with which to disagree. Bodkin was not a robust man. In fact, he had nearly begged to stay in Hagerstown and not travel at all. That was hardly the kind of missionary priest one would send into the West to take over. But the culprit here wasn't Bodkin, who had worked with Cahill amicably. The demon was Carroll. It seemed that Captain Johns of the Eagle was right: "You put a bishop in charge anywhere and everything falls apart."

*From Denis Cahill
To John Carroll
January 21, 1796

My Lord,

At the sole leading of our sovereign Savior I was led to come to the United States as a missionary priest in 1788. Since then, I have labored without rest on behalf of the Church and without due compensation. I have done more to establish the Church in western Maryl'd, Penn, and Virgn'a than most could even dream. In response to my dedication you send a totally incapable and inept priest to replace me. What do you take me for? A fool? Most new priests are lucky to establish a single parish. I have begun six. Where is my equal? And yet you would cast me and the souls I have nourished aside as rubbish and replace me with a man who cannot even ride a circuit he is so sick. I believe you are jealous, even envious, while I have the zeal of a hundred, working in the wilderness for the king, while you are content to sit in your tower and demand respect and obedience. You have cast onto me a cruel injustice, sir, and by your venomous breath have dared to blast the fruits of my labor. No doubt the rumors are true that you have bought your miter from other disenfranchised Jesuits. Perhaps your behavior is why the pope suppressed your order. I take note that you disobeyed and remained here in the New World. To date I have done my own suppression of the scandals including Rev. John Ashton's tasty arrangement with his doll Sukov, and his claim that you, yourself, have fathered children in Virginia. Do not suppose that I will continue to keep my silence when you so publicly disrespect me. I am due a stipend, not Bodkin who does little work. Three hundred dollars should be good for a start.

Yours,
D. Cahill
Magdala in Hagerstown.

4

Most Feared Master of Manipulation,

Who is my equal? Of course I jest. For you, O Dragon Master, are the true Master of Manipulation. Yet as your doting apprentice, I'm saddened over your lack of appreciation for my proficiency with hemp. "Fooled you, made you look," could be my motto. It's as if I've rediscovered the joy of pranking humans; so gullible and stupid they are about what they call supernatural—of course it's a false dichotomy between what is physical and what is spiritual. We know it as *one*...as the Creator made it. I guess we should thank Him for human blindness that makes our job so much easier. But sending "Thank You" greetings to Glory is forbidden, I suspect. I digress. It was, dear Master, a delightful diversion—the hemp for flax, I mean. I hope you noticed that my time hovering over that dreg in the Gulf of Mexico was not a complete waste. I did learn something—I've been anxious to practice my marlinspike skills ever since.

So, how do you like the commotion I've created around Cahill and Bodkin-the-wretch? Such angst must at least be entertaining to your peers. That game still needs to play out, as I play with the priest and his arrogant bishop. Yes, yes, the plot thickens. I wasn't able to keep McSherry from visiting Baltimore, but at least we've added the potential for more scandal with McSherry's so-called spy. I wonder what he'll discover. I'm not sure much more is needed than Cahill's arrogant letter to the bishop demanding $300. Can you imagine? Why the bishop hasn't seen that much money since he scampered home to mother after the repression. And then Richard comes up with the Bodkin letter to Carroll. Oh, this is rich. Sparks will fly. Count on it.

I whooped and hollered at Wallace Robinson and his verbose mother attempting to impress Livingston's household with a so-called angelic tongue. If on one hand they don't believe in spirits then in the next breath they're attempting to imitate them. Humans are so confused...thanks to our presence.

I realize you're getting thirsty for a little blood letting. I'll see what I can do.

At your sinful service,
Cyn Namrasit, OPSD

Chapter 38
Dire Consequences

1

Monday, February 8, 1796.

After breakfast, Adam and Sam packed the wagon for a trip to Charles Town for trading and purchase of supplies. They had finished processing the fall's harvest of flax seed and planned to take the barrel of seed to the miller to make oil. Mary Ann planned to go with them to shop for food stuff, or so she said. Adam knew, however, that she wasn't really that low. Rather, she was always looking for a way to be away from the farm during the new moon and the Wizard's haunts that disturbed her, perhaps more than anyone else in the family.

Meanwhile, Bethany and Eve took the twins to Bethany's cabin for the morning. Mary Ann had nursed them earlier, and Bethany and Eve seemed more than ready to let them eat real food.

Sam brought the wagon hitched with both Calvin and Luther around to the house. Adam helped Mary Ann load in a few items when his now sixteen-year-old daughter, Eve, came out to see them off.

"I wish you'd go with us," said Adam. "It's a new moon. Bethany can handle the twins by herself."

"I know," said Eve, "but this afternoon when the twins nap I was hoping to work on the loom."

"I see," said Adam. "It's just that this time of month I don't like to leave you alone."

"Papa, I'm practically a grown woman. At least I'm old enough to marry. I can take care of myself."

"Sure you'll be all right?"

"Father," she said using the more formal address to get his attention, "the Wizard's a toothless nuisance. It's scary at times, but it's never hurt us. And somehow I think it fears the linens Mama or I have woven. So, if I can weave like Mama did, maybe the Wizard will leave us. Does that make sense?"

Adam stared at his daughter and wondered how such a mature and fearless young woman came from his loins. But then he realized she was Esther's daughter as well. He saw his first wife's countenance in Eve, which gave him confidence and pride. She had completed several projects on the loom, a large table covering that had yet to be used for fear of it being clipped, and was preparing to start another table covering having recently prepared another eight-foot long warp on the spinning rack in his office. She was developing into a beautiful young woman. He began to wonder if some young men might not discover her and begin to call. That would create new challenges, but it was inevitable, he told himself. "Okay, stay if you must. We will hurry back." Adam helped a bundled up Mary Ann into the wagon. Henry crawled in the back where bundles of straw made riding comfortable. Up front on the bench sat Adam, Mary Ann, and Sam, driving the team.

"We're all set, Sam," said Adam, and with that Sam slapped the reins a bit, spoke softly to Calvin and Luther to "git up," and the team pulled the wagon out to the road and on to Charles Town.

Once on the road Mary Ann picked up on a conversation she and Adam had begun earlier. "Mister Livingston, you misunderstand me on this subject. I am not an absolute skeptic. I believe in the unseen. It's just that anything that can't be seen is something to which I give no quarter, no attention. You can trust it for no good. It is bad because it is secret. I don't like secrets. Secrets are evil—and that is our problem."

"Dear wife, that is why I married you. You're predictable. I like looking at you. I can see you." He smiled at Mary Ann and gave her a hug. "Sam, isn't that a good reason to marry a woman?"

"Yas, sir," said Sam. "Ya kin trust what ya sees…as fer as ya kin sees it. But ya jist kin't always sees what's a comin."

"Husband, you give quarter to this Wizard as if he were real, and that only encourages him. It's just like these fool religious who talk on and on about praying to beings they can't see. Whether or not they exist, their hallucinations take over. But there be no foundation for reality. And our condition is the same." Adam noticed she was glancing at Sam a bit as she spoke. It appeared he wanted to butt in. Mary Ann said, "Sam, you keep out of this, ya hear."

"Ya right 'bout that, Ma'am," said Sam. "I sees what ya saying about seeing. I not gittin' involved in hallucinatin' things. But, like I says, ya kin't always sees what's a comin."

Adam said, "I don't want to believe in God. It's not done me good to believe. But you confuse me, as if Henry was the one in broad daylight cutting up our curtains and bed linens."

Rising up off the straw in back, Henry pipped: "Papa, I didn't do none of that. Don't you know that?" Then appealing to his stepmother, "Mama?!"

"Henry," said Mary Ann, "you know yer papa has reason to believe your done some of that. It's in yer nature."

"You ain't seen me."

It was quiet for a moment as Adam and Mary Ann exchanged glances.

Sam slapped the reins and pulled Calvin and Luther back on the path. "I don't like dis not seeing. But tis always seems to be a comin."

"That's it, exactly," said Mary Ann. "If you can't see it, it's not good. Henry, everything you do that can't be seen is not to be done."

Henry thought about that, then said, "You mean like takin' a pee?"

Adam and Sam laughed.

Mary Ann didn't think it funny, "Henry!"

To himself, Sam said, "I don't wants to sees that."

"What I'm saying," Adam continued, "is that we've never seen the Wizard, but we see what he done, and it's bad. And while we've never seen the U.S. Constitution, most think it's good. And what about those Continentals? We had thousands of them, we could see them, but they were worthless. Might as well been invisible."

"Yas, sir," said Sam. "Ya could sees worthless. It be a blessing that some of 'dem actually bought some's freedom when 'dey was seesable."

"Esther, she held onto the unseen," said Adam. "But it was what we couldn't see that took her, I figure."

"You see," said Mary Ann. "Give it no quarter. Ignore it and its power will be robbed like a thief without arms or legs."

"Don't want ta sees dat," said Sam quietly.

"Dear wife. I cannot ignore what I see. The problem is that what I see coming is from what I can't see."

"Exactly," said Mary Ann. "Just ignore it."

"What I'm seeing?"

"Yes."

Sam bowed his head, "Didn't sees dat a comin.'"

2

That afternoon Eve made progress tying off the warp yarns on the spinning rack and chaining them to carry to the loom for attaching to the warp beam. She had begun to attach one end of a warp yarn to the beam when she heard voices in the yard. She wondered who they belonged to, but she was dressing the warp and couldn't stop to even look out the window. After a moment the voices became louder, and she did stop to look out a window toward the porch and yard. Three teen boys, without horses, meandered toward the front porch. One was a little older than she, perhaps seventeen, and the youngest was perhaps Henry's age, all dressed in winter coats. Some of the coats had large brown burrs on them as if they had been traipsing through the woods. The windows were closed so she couldn't hear what they were saying, but the older one was motioning for the two younger ones to be quiet. She heard him tell the others to "Hush!"

Eve did not want to be interrupted, just when she was at the delicate point of wrapping the warp beam with eight feet of linen warp containing hundreds of warp yarns. A moment later she heard the three pairs of teen male legs and boots unsteadily step onto the porch among whispers and hushes.

Eve was a mix of curiosity and disappointment. Boys had never come calling before. The only people her age or younger that had visited Flax Haven were with parents.

Suddenly, there was a banging on the front door. Eve groaned, carefully draped her warp on the beam, and went to the foyer.

Eve lifted the door latch and opened the door, but stood in the gap so as to not invite the apparent delinquents inside. She said nothing, but just stared at them for a few moments, sizing them up. "Who are you and what do you want?" she finally inquired.

The tallest, with unruly blonde hair, started to say something, but the short kid with wavy brown hair elbow-ribbed the blonde and spoke first. "We just come to call on ya, that's all. Just come to call."

"Oh, yeah? What your names?" shot back Eve. She had no more asked the question than she realized the two older boys were unsteady on their feet, and both had trouble focusing. They were both inebriated. A deep breath confirmed her suspicions. They had come across some strong beer or wine and had more than a nip. The shortest and youngest, a baby-faced boy who looked much younger than he was, stood apart from the other two. He was steady on his feet and appeared disgusted with his compatriots and tried to apologize with his eyes by looking down at the deck.

The tall blonde kid started to talk again, but hiccupped real strong. He grabbed his chest and bent over. The wavy brown-haired kid said, with a confident smile, "I'm Dick Cuth-ber—Cuth-bert-son." He had trouble getting it out as he tried to secure his footing. Pointing to the baby-faced teen, "That's Thomas Swath-more-ham."

"Am not," said the baby-faced teen, with hair cut so short he looked bald.

Dick stopped and looked at his friends, first to the baby-faced kid and then the tall blonde. Finally, pointing to the blonde he said, "No, no, ah, this is Thomas, and..." pointing to the short kid, "...that's...what's your name anyway?"

"Ben Williams, at your service, Madam," he said bowing deeply to Eve, clearly chagrined at being in the company of two inebriates.

Thomas, the tall blonde, if they had it right, was the best looking of the three, Eve thought. But he was also the most ill-kept and unsteady on his feet. A few times she almost reached out to stop him from falling to the deck, but she didn't. She wanted to see, if he did fall, if he could get back up again. She doubted it.

Dick, the pack's leader, had a crooked nose, deep-set eyes, and a mud-caked coat and pants. His face was dirty and scratched, but he didn't care. He seemed to know who he was regardless of what he looked like.

Ben captured her admiration, however. Here was a kid who was dressed neatly, kept his face clean, and probably his honor as well. What he was doing with the other two skunks only heaven knew.

"Where did you find the moonshine, boys?" asked Eve, staring at Dick and Thomas.

Neither of them answered. Ben piped up, "Mister Swathmoreham's still.

He's going to whip Tommy when he finds out."

Thomas leaned over, stared at Ben and shook his head, "Will not."

Ben smiled at Eve, and shrugged his shoulders, but he had nothing more to say.

"Okay, Tom, Dick, and Ben, what do you want? Why did you come calling. My father is not home, or do you know that already?"

No one had an answer, it seemed. But she caught them all looking at her like deer at the end of a muzzle.

Finally, Dick spoke. "We just come to call on ya, that's all. Just come to call."

"They knew your Pa had gone to town with your mom. Thomas likes you. That's why he can't look at you straight," Ben said with thick disgust.

Eve had been told she was pretty, but this was the first evidence outside her family that it just might be true. She wasn't sure what to do. She was sure of one thing. If her father was here, there would be, in short order, at least two hides skinned and drying in the smoke house. Ben would be polite, apologize, and just disappear.

"Yeah," said Thomas with a smile that was still missing that front tooth, "I just wanted to get...to...ah...know you, ya know."

"But he doesn't talk so good," said Dick. "So, I do the talking for him."

"And what's Ben do," Eve asked winking at Ben who turned away with a smile.

"We're not sure," said Dick.

The three amigos just stared at Eve, who still stood firmly in the door gap, holding tight to the latch on the inside if she suddenly had to slam the door shut and latch it. She decided a curtsy would be too much, but perhaps a sign of appreciation was in order. "My, my, that's very nice of you all," she managed to push out between tight lips.

Suddenly, Ben was emboldened, and like a sophisticated gentleman said, "Would you like to go riding?"

Eve looked out beyond them. "That might be nice. On what do you suggest I ride?"

Ben quickly looked behind him, then back. "My mother has a pony. Would that suit you?"

Eve stared at the baby-faced gentleman. "Ben, we ain't goin' riding. You know that. What you saying?"

There was a long pause as the two taller ones tried to stand in one place, and Ben looked to his pals. Finally, Dick confessed. "Yea, okay. So, we came to check you out. I mean your place. We heard it's haunted."

Suddenly, Thomas jumped toward Eve, and yelled, "BOO!" Then he turned to Dick, bent over, and screamed as if he'd been stabbed in the gut with a knife. "I'M BLEEDING. HELP ME."

Dick laughed at Thomas and egged him on. "OOOO, I'M SACRED...OH, DON'T DO THAT. ARE YOU HURT, TOMMY? I'M SO SORRY."

Eve knew she was being mocked, but the two were such sorry cases of humanity she felt sorry for them. She turned to Ben, who just shook his head and backed away from the other two. He said to Eve, "I came to see you. I don't believe the rumors about the haunts. I'm sorry."

But Thomas and Dick could not stop laughing at Eve as they took a step closer, intimidating her.

Eve backed away and thought about closing the door on them, when Thomas said, "Yeah, we came to see the ghosts everybody been talking about. Aren't you *scared?*" he chuckled. "But we was wondering if they were white ghosts or darkie ghosts." Thomas slapped Dick on the back and almost knocked him over.

"Yeah," Dick said, "we's wondering if they like berry-fine, moonbeam-shine, or dandelion-wine," all the while laughing.

Ben backed off away from the two jerks, and mouthed to Eve, "I'm really sorry. I didn't know."

She threw Ben a shallow smile, and whispered a prayer: "Mama. Mama. Mama. Deliver me…."

But before she could finish the spontaneous request, the porch suddenly tilted. It tilted away from the house and the two inebriates lost their footings and slid toward the steps. Suddenly, they were overcome with drunken fear. Ben grabbed an upright post and looked about in fright.

Eve jumped back, too, and stared at the tilted porch. It was as if supports beneath it along the front edge were suddenly gone, adding to her guests' rubbery legs.

Then, just as suddenly, it tilted back, then forward, then to the side, then to the other side. Ben adeptly stepped down the steps onto solid ground and watched his comrades dance like Mexican jumping beans.

Thomas and Dick didn't know which way was up, principally due to their soused state. Dick screamed and tried to reach a railing for support, but about the time he got to one side, the porch tilted hard to the opposite and shook both teens silly.

Ben, now feeling sorry for his friends, tried to come up the steps and grab them, but as he did they slid past him down the steps and landed hard on their rumps on the ground. They sat stunned, their legs sprawled.

Eve stood in the doorway and stared as if to say, "Serves you right."

Thomas and Dick gazed back at Eve, afraid to move, the porch now straight and solid once again.

Suddenly the busy sound of scissors clipping—CLIP! CLIP! CLIP! CLIP! CLIP! CLIP! CLIP! CLIP! CLIP!

Eve opened the door and stepped out onto the porch. She looked down at the three: "Boys! What have you done to your overalls?"

The boys gazed at their overalls. Not only were they shredded in crescent shapes from their waists down, leaving very little to the imagination, but they had also wet their pants.

"You are so rude!" she screamed at them.

Dick and Thomas put their hands over their privates, turned, and ran nearly buck naked. But it's hard to run with pants ripped to shreds and said shreds obstructing sprinting legs.

"I'm sorry, Miss Livingston," said Ben, still by the porch steps. "I ought to be getting my friends home."

Eve smiled at Ben, as he dragged his friends into the nearby wood.

When they were all out of sight, Eve stepped back inside, and shut the door and leaned up against the door posts. She was actually more scared than she let on. "Thank you, Mama." She was pretty sure that it *was* her mother and not the Wizard.

In the next moment she realized where she had seen Ben before. A few months ago, when she had accompanied her father to Charles Town, Ben was in the street handing out flyers. He was the son of the pastor of a new Methodist church there. Actually, it was a small chapel. At the time Ben, although younger than she, had impressed her. And now, he impressed her even more. She wondered if his father might be able to do anything about the Wizard, but she doubted it. Over the last year since Xavier had died and the house had been overcome with hauntings, she had spent a lot of time with his prayer book and Rosary while visiting Bethany's cabin. She had a sense that no Protestant minister was going to be able to do anything. Yet Ben, being such a nice lad, she would have to try. Maybe it was her Presbyterian mother who had sent Ben, but she doubted it—Ben was Methodist.

3

The stew between Fr. Cahill and Bishop Carroll continued to boil through the exchange of letters through the spring of 1796. It is true that John Carroll was dealing with multiple renegade priests who had not been under the authority of a bishop for most of their priestly lives and had suddenly come under John Carroll's. There had been little or no relationship established before the conflicts. The conflict with Denis Cahill was not as serious as some, for Cahill was faithful to the Church's teachings, except for the canonical law that stipulated priests be subject to an ordinary—a bishop. Of course, that had not been true until recently, and had it, it's entirely possible that Denis Cahill would not be part of this story, if any priest could be. The conflict, nevertheless, would have dire consequences.

*From, John Carroll
To, Denis Cahill

March 2d, 1796

I received on the 18th of Feb your letter of Jan 21st. So unexpected, extraordinary, & undeserved from you especially are its contents, that it cannot be accounted for otherwise, that supposing it to have been written under the impression of circumstances unknown to me, & which, to certain degree, may apologize for, tho they cannot justify such a letter. I deferred till this time making any answer, hoping that in their turn, shame & duty would operate on your mind & draw from it some reparation for language so criminal & calumnies so atrocious. Hitherto I have waited in vain but am resolved still to wait & send these few lines, that you may reflect on your proceedings, & weigh its consequence. If after a reasonable delay, I should not hear again, & in a different style, the presumption will be that you refuse to retract your most false & malignant imputations. This will reduce me to the necessity & impose on me the duty of taking such farther steps as are required for the preservation of good order, subordination, & the general advantage of religion in the diocese committed to my care. In the meantime, you may rest assured that your silence will not be purchased by paying any orders, which have been, or may be addressed to me.

I am,
Yrs JC.

Fr. Cahill wasted no time in responding.

*My Lord,

Yours of the 2nd current came to hand. On the 21st Jan, my last, I remonstrated to you only the unjust treatment I received from you. My motives for leaving in the W. Marsh part and what I advanced in it, I know by watchful inference. It is the best I have heard from credible people, some of whom I candidly named to you. This knowledge, I presume, is common to all men. Still it appears to you malignant and abrasive. I require of you but what every one who believes he is answerable to God for his conduct is bound to do. I am ready and willing to make every effort wherewithal in my power to God, to you, or any other person if I knew the motive of the offense for which I am charged. If I have been amiss in my duty, or criminally transgressed it, I invoke you to come forward and show wherein—I have and do require of you, to impact my character, that you endeavor to display wherewithal even a shadow of grounds, or the public good beginning it, and show a consideration for my labors from the start. Awaiting your application. I am with reasonable obedience your humble servant,

Den Cahill
Winchester 23 March '796.

Richard did not see the correspondence between Fr. Denis and Bishop Carroll. He didn't want to, but he knew something had changed. Cahill had always been clean shaven. But during the last few months, since this latest correspondence with Carroll, Cahill had let his beard grow, and only very recently had begun to trim it back. He kept it short, maybe one to two inches of woolly redness. While the beard looked good on him, and while it did give him a more mature and mystical appearance, he worried. Fr. Denis had not been the best at communicating delicate ideas in writing. At the same time, communicating with the bishop was not Richard's place. He just prayed while walking in his Rosary garden that good would come out of conflict between priest and bishop and not something intolerable. Richard cared deeply for Fr. Denis and knew his heart to be pure, his soul faithful, and his countenance robust. Whatever the disagreements, he prayed they would pass and be resolved sooner than later. Richard also worried that the bishop did not understand the necessary strength and will to persevere which a circuit rider in this time and place must possess. Fr. Denis was clearly the man called to do what was being done, whether or not the bishop understood or agreed.

As so often happens when grappling with God or the Church, events take too long and solutions are eons in coming. Richard, being the twice successful entrepreneur, was accustomed to making decisions quickly, then making adjustments as time advanced. It was better to make a decision, and then back away from it, than to delay and risk the consequences of dilatoriness or vacillation.

So, it was with great relief that upon visiting Hagerstown in April of 1796 that he found Fr. Bodkin's room empty, and Fr. Denis in good spirits. Fr. Denis later reported that Bodkin's health had not improved and quite suddenly the restless priest found passage along the western road to the Mississippi, and reportedly was on his way to New Orleans. That, at least, is what Fr. Bodkin told Fr. Denis the morning he left. Fr. Denis wished the sickly priest God's good fortune and waited with him on Magdala's porch until an agent came in a buggy to pack Fr. Bodkin away to a waiting wagon train. At least he would not be traveling alone.

In reflecting on the "Bodkin Affair" as he and Fr. Denis would later refer to it, Richard concluded that Fr. Denis was a unique and stalwart man, who let neither thief nor bishop get in God's way. So be it, thought Richard as he again opened his purse and advanced Fr. Denis an additional month's allowance, hoping the future would be better than today.

Chapter 39
Obscure Incantation

1

Back in February, Eve Livingston had told her father what had happened when the three boys came calling, how the porch shook, and how two of the boys left with their pants clipped to shreds. She omitted that they had also peed their pants. In retrospect, she thought it funny, but Papa was furious. Something terrible could have happened to her. She dismissed it, of course, since two of the boys could hardly stand up. Telling her father that, however, only infuriated him the more.

Then she told him about Ben Williams and how polite and gentlemanly he was in spite of his inebriated cohorts, and how Ben had helped his friends home, or at least away from the Livingston farm. She also told her father how she had met Ben briefly on the street in Charles Town last summer handing out handbills for his dad's new church.

Upon hearing about the porch's instability, Adam immediately went out to check on its structure. Eve accompanied him. The porch was sound. No nails were out of place and nothing seemed disturbed.

Her papa asked for clarification: "Did you see the porch bouncing and tilting as you described, or were the boys reacting to what they thought was happening?"

That stumped Eve. At the time she was pretty sure the porch was going to fall apart, but now, after seeing how the porch was still intact, she wasn't so sure, and that's what she told Papa. "I think you should go talk to Ben's father. Maybe he can help with our ghost. Ben seemed very down to earth, smart, and polite."

In April, Adam arranged to visit Rev. Jeremiah Williams in Charles Town, and Eve went along. She kind of wanted to meet Ben again, even if he was younger.

It was a warm day when they arrived at Rev. Williams' home on the outskirts of the town. They sat in summer chairs outside under a maple tree and Emily Jane Williams, his wife, served them lemonade that Eve thought was every bit as good as Mary Ann's.

Rev. Williams was a thin man of average height with a wide forehead, pointed chin, thin down-turned mouth, and large ears that stuck out from his head like an elephant. He wore a white shirt and creased black pants with suspenders. He was clean shaven, with salt and pepper hair that was relatively thin for his middle age. Ben joined them, and he was as polite as he was before. Ben's slightly rotund figure came from his mother, but his gentlemanly nature came from his father.

"Ben told me about what happened at your farm and the shaking porch," said Rev. Williams, "although I'm inclined to believe there was some exaggeration on his part. I apologize for that; he's not normally given to it." Rev. Williams studied his son as he spoke, and Ben stared back, looking a little sad that his father didn't believe him. Ben did not appear to be the argumentative type, and was willing to let people believe what they wanted even if his own reputation was thrown into question. Rev. Williams continued, "But I must say that when he is with his cousin, I do not necessarily approve of his activities. But that was probably our fault." Rev. Williams smiled at his son as if there was a secret between them. Ben smiled back at his father, somewhat sheepishly, then looked down at the ground to avoid eye contact. Eve could tell they had a good relationship, but that Rev. Williams did not take to misbehavior. Rev. Williams went on: "On that particular day, Ben was in Smithfield, near your place, visiting his cousin, Richard. Emily Jane was trying to help her sister, Adrian, by sending Ben up there for a few days. Their behavior at your farm was typical of what happens when Ben spends time with Richard. Adrian thinks Ben's a good influence on her son, but I think her son is not a good influence on Ben." Rev. Williams looked at Ben. "What do you think, son?"

Eve glanced at Ben, who just shrugged his shoulders.

Eve could see that Ben was embarrassed, and his father was not being entirely fair. Rev. Williams had not been on her porch that day to see exactly what had happened. So Eve spoke up: "Rev. Williams? Please do not take me for being rude." She peeked at Ben who was looking at her with wide, astonished eyes as if whatever Eve said was going to get him in even deeper trouble. "That day Ben was the absolute gentleman. He was the only one of the three that—well, you would have been proud of Ben. He acted like a real Christian…and the porch did shake, quite a bit, actually."

This clearly shocked Rev. Williams, but within seconds he cracked a big smile that he directed in Ben's direction. Ben blushed, which Eve could see even in the shade of the sun. Ben bit his lips but smiled at Eve as if he had met an everlasting friend. Eve nodded back at Ben and sat up straight. Then she said what was really on her mind, "That is why I wanted to come today. I wanted to see my friend, Ben, again."

Ben's eyes got big again. Eve wondered if that was the first time a girl, a pretty girl, had said anything that nice to him. Well, enough of that, Eve thought, she could see Ben's complexion turning red. Now, it was Eve who was embarrassed…for flirting in front of Papa and Rev. Williams. She could be too bold at times. She looked away.

It took a few seconds before the men resumed their conversation. Adam had shared with Rev. Williams a general outline of their ghost problem and how it began with the death and curse of a Catholic stranger. Rev. Williams listened quietly and respectfully. At one point he hinted that the Smithfield Ghost, as he put it, had a fairly wide reputation in Charles Town and Smithfield, as his wife and her sister were members of the region's gossip cartel.

What surprised Eve was that Rev. Williams did not ask about the ghost, but asked about their family. Did they go to church? Did they read their Bible and pray as a family? Did they pray before meals thanking God for food, shelter, and clothing? To each of these, Adam reluctantly, and with decreasing volume, admitted they did not. Adam explained that they did once, and that Eve still prayed silently to herself, but now his wife forbade praying aloud before meals.

"Mister Livingston," said Rev. Williams, "I'm not sure I can help you with your ghost problem. I live for the spiritual battles, but I suspect your problem isn't so much with the ghost as with you."

"But I'm not cutting up our linens," said Papa, "or driving wagons and horses about our house in the middle of the night, or throwing dishes to the floor."

"No, but you're giving permission for someone, or something else to do it for you."

Eve's father was not pleased with the advice, but he was still listening.

"May I make a suggestion?"

Adam nodded.

"Invite my family for dinner, on a new moon. Let's see what happens."

Adam took a deep breath and thought about that. "You may be sorry. We've invited others to dinner. The results have not been pleasant."

But Rev. Williams said no more and Adam said he would talk with Mary Ann and send an invitation...or not.

Weeks later, on Saturday, May 7, 1796, during the new moon, Rev. Jeremiah Williams, his wife Emily Jane and son Ben came to Flax Haven for noon dinner. Eve, Papa, and her stepmother admitted that they were nervous about what the Wizard might do. The clipping noises, while sounding like chirping birds surrounding the house, had intensified throughout the morning, and there were sporadic but light vibrations in the floor.

They had abolished guest dinners after the Hendershots, but Bethany had encouraged Mary Ann to serve a good meal with the best table covering (one that Eve had recently woven) and something special. Bethany suggested, and Mary Ann agreed, to serve a cold chicken salad with greens, nuts, and fruits as the main course, followed with Eve's favorite dessert. So that morning Bethany went to the chicken coop, selected a particularly fat bird she had been feeding extra scraps, slaughtered it, cleaned it, cooked it, and then Eve helped her pick off the meat for the salad.

Eve was nervous, however, for a different reason. The prerequisite for the dinner was that Rev. Williams be allowed to pray before they sat down to eat. Mary Ann was not pleased, but she had come to the point of allowing whatever might work to rid them of the Smithfield Ghost.

When they showed up, Adam gave Rev. Williams, Emily Jane, and Ben a quick tour of the farm and house. Eve and Henry joined them. Once in the house Adam noticed that the disturbances had picked up a little, perhaps to intimidate the minister that was present. When Adam pointed these out to Rev. Williams, in particular the small tremors, their guest suggested something Adam had not thought of before.

"In college I took a course in geology," said Rev. Williams. "These tremors almost feel as if your farm is located on a fault line. With the Appalachian Mountains so close and the presence of the Potowmack River Valley and Opequon, you know, that might be what you're feeling."

Ben gazed at Eve and without his father seeing it, slowly shook his head. Eve nodded her agreement. His father's explanation did not explain the vibrating porch; but then Rev. Williams was not there for that.

Before dinner was served, Eve managed to give Rev. Williams a hand printed copy of her mother's favorite prayer. She told Rev. Williams that her mother was a devout Christian who prayed this prayer nearly ever meal when they lived in Pennsylvania. Would he pray it as part of his prayer before the meal? Rev. Williams took great interest in the suggestion.

When it came time before dinner to pray, with everyone standing behind their seats, Rev. Williams prayed a long and extemporaneous prayer of his own, asking God to bless the food, the family and the farm; and then he read Esther's prayer, which made Eve very happy. But he prayed nothing about the disturbances, the Wizard, or a ghost, or possibly a demon. Eve could tell her father was disappointed about that, and that her stepmother was upset about praying about anything, especially Esther's prayer that Eve had managed to slip in. Well, Eve thought, *I've done what I thought was right.*

As they ate, Eve watched her stepmother closely. Any little noise distracted her almost to tears. The longer the dinner went on, the more uptight Mary Ann became.

But nothing more happened. In fact, by the time the Williams left Charles Town, and even the rest of the night, there were no disruptions. There was no haunting. No clipping sounds. No falling and shattering china. No rattling wagons and horses. Could it be that the solution was so simple...to simply pray before the meals? Eve didn't think so. It could not be that simple. But yet, it was. Adam even double checked the Almanac. Was it the new moon? Yes, it was. The ghost had vanished.

For one night.

2

The next morning, Mary Ann was feeling good. The family had successfully entertained a family without incident or disruption from their so-called ghost. True, she had given in and let the minister pray before the meal. It was also true that she was upset when Rev. Williams read Eve's mother's prayer. But the outcome of all that was good. Perhaps the Wizard was gone for good. She could only hope, but for now she would enjoy. Imagine, a day in the new moon cycle without clipping noises, charging horses, circling wagons, and new cloth being destroyed. Speaking of new cloth, she sat at the table with the entire family calmly eating breakfast of ham, eggs, and grits off the new table covering Eve had woven. Amazingly, it was not clipped. She might actually come to like it.

After they had begun breakfast, Eve had mentioned that they had not prayed before breakfast and perhaps they should have because of yesterday's success. Mary Ann was quick to demur the thought and was sure now it was not necessary. She noted that they were eating in peace, and could return to their normal practice. Eve began to argue with her, but Adam shut her down. Mary Ann smiled broadly as if to say, "*Thank you, husband. I need you to back me up like that.*"

So, the subject was dropped, although out of the side of her eye she could see Bethany looking disapprovingly, or did she look sad? Exhausted was probably it. After all, Bethany had worked hard yesterday preparing that scrumptious chicken salad, having slaughtered the bird, boiled it, cleaned it, and everything else. Poor bird. But then they had plenty of others to collect eggs from or to cook. Adam was certainly a good provider. Mary Ann felt rich, even pampered.

All of a sudden, things changed. There was a new sound, which nonetheless sounded eerily familiar, though at a lower pitch. It wasn't the high-pitched chirp of a bird, or the clip of scissors. It was a CLANK! A deep hollow CLANK! And only one, not repetitive sounds like the clipping of scissors on cloth. After a minute there was another CLANK!

A cold shiver ran up Mary Ann's spine. Everyone around the table stopped eating and looked about; even George and Martha turned at the sound. Intuitively, Mary Ann knew it was the Wizard. Her disappointment was thick. They were entering a new phase, one more ponderous and threatening. She exchanged looks with Adam. His eyes steeled over. In hers she could feel tears. What could this mean? Whatever it was, she didn't want to know.

Suddenly, they heard Sam in the distance as he ran toward the house and up the front steps. Sam was not someone who was easily upset. His emotions were always in check...except this morning. Sam burst into the house and ran into the gathering hall. Everyone had already stopped eating, but now turned and stared up at the intrusion. "Missta Livingston! Missta Livingston! Come quick! Come quick!" Sam said. "You's gotta come quick like, you's gotta to see. Oh, Lordy, Lordy! Come quick. I dunno what to do, sir. I dunno what to do." Sam's forehead was all knotted up, and his face was perspiring.

"What's wrong, Sam?" asked Adam.

"Jist come quick, sir. I don't knows how to tell you's. Jist come."

Adam jumped up along with the rest of the family.

"Bethany, stay with the twins," said Mary Ann as she got up and threw down her napkin.

"Yes'm," Bethany said.

The family immediately left the table and followed Sam out of the house, down the front porch steps, and around the house by the garden to the chicken coop situated at the top of the hill behind the summer kitchen. It was placed there so Bethany, Eve, or Mary Ann could quickly gather morning eggs.

*What greeted Mary Ann and the rest of the family would never be forgotten. This early in the morning the chickens could be expected to be pecking the ground fairly close to the coop as they waited for Bethany to scatter scraps from the kitchen. But on this morning the birds were scattered far and wide. The reason became quickly apparent. Half a dozen birds were flopping wildly about on the ground, on their side, trying to stand, then falling over, and running into each other. Their heads were missing, but still they were clucking up a racket. Red blood oozed from their severed necks. A quick scan of the ground revealed the heads lying on their sides, immobile on the ground, their blue eyes wide open looking up at the sky. As Mary Ann approached the scene she heard low-pitched CLANK and watched as another chicken's head, by some invisible means, was severed and fell to the ground. The wiggling body, spastic legs, and flapping wings accompanied the feathered body as it flopped around wildly. Then another CLANK, and another hen's head fell off. Mary Ann was not unaccustomed to taking a knife to a chicken's neck; she had slaughtered hundreds of chickens in her life, but this was different. There was no human hands holding a knife. There was, in fact, no knife.

Adam flew into action and tried to grab a chicken with its head in tact and get it safely into the coop, but herding chickens was like herding cats. "Quick," Adam yelled, "get the birds into the coop." Everyone tried, but it was nearly impossible; the birds were scared silly. Adam finally grabbed a bird, but as soon as he did there was a CLANK and the head fell off, blood falling across his hands. The bird began to twist and flap insanely. The same thing happened to Sam, and Mary Ann, Henry, and Eve. CLANK! CLANK! CLANK! CLANK! Soon there were more chicken heads lying on the ground than there were whole chickens, and not stepping on a severed head was out of the question.

Mary Ann was frightened and stared wide-eyed in disbelief. Seeing the hen's necks severed easily caused the hair on the back of her neck to lift, and sent more shivers down her spine. Unconsciously she rubbed the back of her own neck as if to protect it from the Wizard's knife, gigantic scissors, or whatever it was. Seeing this many hens die by invisible hands was doubly scary. It seemed that no life was safe. If helpless chickens today, could their *lives* be next? What about George and Martha? The more she thought about it the more afraid she became. Panic set in. Terror struck; she stood frozen in place and screamed.

A moment later, Adam was in front of her, grabbing her shoulders, and shaking her. "Mary Ann, snap out of it. Settle down. It's okay. Stop yelling. Look at me, LOOK AT ME!"

She couldn't imagine why he would shake her so violently. Why would he yell at her? What was wrong? But then a searing pain over took her throat, and she heard herself screaming, uncontrollably amidst her paralysis—as if her blood had turned to ice. She saw George and Martha running around without their heads, blood flowing like a fountain from their open necks. She tried to catch them, but she couldn't move. She ordered her legs to run after her twins, but her muscles refused to obey—a paralyzing panic, brain fog, she couldn't think which way was up. The Wizard was coming after her with a large razor sharp knife. And all she could do was SCREAM…SCREAM…SCREAM!

Suddenly she tripped to the ground and curled up in a tight ball on the dusty ground. She so badly wanted to get away from the killing and spilled blood. Then she let herself cry…cry…cry….uncontrollably.

3

Adam shook Mary Ann. "Mary Ann! Mary Ann! Stop it. You're all right! Please! Stop crying!" But she wouldn't…she couldn't. She just curled up in a ball on the ground and sobbed, her tears choking her throat and her eyes, so watery, he was sure she could not focus. He decided the best thing he could do was just to hold her and let her feel his body close to hers on the ground. He turned his attention back to the coop. It was not long before every bird was decapitated, and vultures began to circle.

By now, Bethany had emerged from the summer kitchen to survey the disaster. Adam watched her from a distance. Nothing seemed to phase her. She had seen it all. Two dozen decapitated chickens was probably nothing. With disgust Adam wondered if Bethany had seen owners murdering their slaves, perhaps even slitting their throats. He shivered to think of it. From just behind the summer kitchen Bethany stared in unbelief. Many of the birds were still fluttering around without their heads, although some had stopped and lay still on the ground. He could see the deep concern on Bethany's face, and then the resolve not to let headless chickens go to waste if she could help it. He watched as Bethany searched among the dead poultry, picked up four chickens by their wings, and carried them to the summer kitchen door and set them on the ground. She had selected the fattest of the birds. He knew she would boil and clean them. In the cool cellar the meat would last a while.

While he watched Bethany, a vulture had landed in the yard. It looked about and then picked up a chicken's head and flew off. He looked aloft as other vultures were closing in. Sam, Eve, and Henry all backed away to let the professional scavengers do what they did best—clean up bloody messes.

But the trial was far from over. Adam helped Mary Ann back into the house. She could not stand on her own; her robust vigor exorcised. Still frantic and crying out in bursts of anguish, she could not move and lay quietly on the parlor floor. He covered her with a coat, and sat next to her on the floor…and waited.

Finally, she turned to him. "Adam, take me and the twins to the Randalls.

They told me to come if ever I wanted." Adam remembered the Randalls. They were the new owners of Travelers Rest, and Mary Ann had known them before she knew Adam. He had met them once when the Gates were departing for New York. Their large house had several guest rooms. Yes, indeed, he would take her there. She needed to rest and he hoped the Randalls were home and were able to care for his wife, especially if he would pay them to do so. As he considered how to get her and the twins there, she curled up on his chest and sobbed softly.

He heard Eve in the gathering hall. "Eve?"

She came to him in the parlor and looked down at Mary Ann with compassion. It was a disposition he had not seen in Eve's eyes since bringing Mary Ann home as his wife. "Yes, Papa."

"Go find Sam, wherever he is. Tell him to hitch up Calvin and Luther to the buggy. I need him to drive your stepmother, the twins, and me to Travelers Rest. And while he's doing that, please pack a week's worth of clothing and toiletries for your step-mom and the children. She needs a rest."

"Yes, Papa, I will, right away. Do you think she would like some warm milk before you go?"

"Yes, that would be good. And coffee for me—hot."

With that Eve busied herself getting a tankard of hot coffee for her father and warmed milk for her stepmother, taking them both to her father who had not moved from his place on the parlor floor. Then she wiped her hands on the towel she was carrying, removed her apron, and ran out the front door to look for Sam.

Thirty minutes later Sam drove the buggy with Adam, Mary Ann, the twins, a box of supplies and a suitcase out of the yard to Travelers Rest.

4

As Adam returned to Flax Haven, his mind was on Mary Ann and her situation at the Randalls. The Randalls had welcomed Mary Ann with open arms, and indeed they did have a spare bedroom where she could recuperate. But the Randalls were plantation owners and slave holders. Travelers Rest was a large plantation that required a large workforce. When Gates and his wife, Mary Valens, moved to New York, evidently they had not freed all their slaves as John Adams had encouraged. Or, if he had, the Randalls brought their own.

Shortly after getting Mary Ann settled in a room and Adam offering to pay Mary Ann's expenses for her stay with the Randalls, a young slave girl was assigned to tend to his wife's needs. Adam wasn't so sure how that was going to work with Mary Ann who hated slavery, but in her current condition she accepted it. This was the first time Adam had visited Travelers Rest since the Randalls had taken over. It appeared that Randalls' slaves were decently cared for. That eased his mind a bit, for it gave him an indication of how well Mary

Ann might be cared for.

That night, Adam slept fitfully. His mind worried and wandered. He ruminated about Rev. Williams' visit. It had seemed that Williams' presence had vanquished the ghost, but as soon as he had left, the hauntings returned. It wasn't just the catastrophic loss of all his chickens, but it was the first time in years he had slept alone. It reminded him of the weeks after Esther died. He was fine being alone when he worked around the farm, but he got lonely in the evenings and at night. But sleep he did...and dream he did.

It was hot, dark, foggy, and muggy. He was surrounded by trees and walking was difficult since the floor of the forest was thick mud. A crescent moon provided little light through the fog and thick underbrush. Every step strained his muscles as he strained to pull his boots out of the muck only to plunge them back into the sucking mire. Where he was going he wasn't sure, but onward he trudged over fallen and rotten logs. He felt as if his destination was as important as life and death, but progress seemed impossible. There was a lighted clearing ahead, but brush and hanging moss obscured his vision. His clothes were covered in mud and burrs. He reached for a low-hanging branch to push it out of the way, only for a thorn to scratch his arm. His shirt had crescent-shaped holes in it; blood oozed from the wound. He felt a cold breeze on his legs. He couldn't see his legs, yet it felt like his pants had holes in them too.

He struggled forward, toward the lighted clearing. Suddenly, he broke through. The light seemed to emanate from six candles that circled the clearing. The ground was soft but not mucky. He heard sounds like a shuttle loom. The fog cleared and there before him was his loom, the shuttle and beater moving faster than humanly possible. He looked down at the cloth being woven, but it was obscured.

Beyond the loom in a dense flog was a man. The image was blurry. The man wore a black gown that reached to the ground. He was performing some indistinct incantation, a ritual, waving his arms, turning, bowing, arms raised, kneeling and such. Adam tried to see the man's face but it was obscured, and what the man was doing was hidden. Adam struggled to get around the loom and closer to the man, but suddenly the floor of the clearing became mud, and Spanish moss created a curtain that was impassable. Adam tried to separate the hanging moss and step beyond it to get to the man, and finally he did. He reached out and touched the man's cloak. The man turned and looked at Adam...the image lasted but a second...before everything went blank.

Adam woke up sweating head to toe. It was dark and he was alone.

5

Most Feared Master of Slavery,

I'm not sure what went awry. It seemed such a bad idea (i.e., good for our side) to suggest that Tom and Dick dupe Ben into joining their escapade. I obviously miscalculated.

To Tom and Dick, Eve was to be exploited, but to Ben, Eve was to be respected. Ben is such a virtuous kid I just assumed he could easily be soiled. No one is that good, I thought, and what better way than to pair him up with a couple of peers who are actually idiots. To enhance the plot, who of us could resist not involving Swathmoreham's unguarded still. What could possibly go wrong?

It's just hard for me to fathom the corruption of youth these days; all some of them want to do is align themselves with what is good and true, and no amount of peer pressure can scuttle their judgment. So disappointing. Boys will be boys, I thought, and thus their vile decisions can often be excused—that was the plan.

I should have known, but didn't, that Jeremiah Williams had at least one virtuous kid. Somewhere in this formula there must be a way to undermine Eve Livingston's dignity and confidence in the Almighty. Until we figure that out she continues to be a galling obstacle.

I also thought we were going to get more out of Bodkin instead of a single nasty letter and a cowardly scramble to the South, incognito no less. Why is it that we keep aligning ourselves with the desperate, sick, and weak? Is there a way you can assign a S.D. under your control to undermine McSherry's financial holdings? I was hoping he'd run out of money, but he keeps giving more and more to Cahill. Such generosity and persistence is disheartening, except for Cahill.

The Devil save me, but don't complain about the effect Jeremiah Williams had on me during his short and unassuming visit to Livingston's abode. I scrambled about looking for a sliver of doubt or sin in the man that would allow some leverage to undo the effect of his presence. Robust faith like that is nearly impossible to thwart. I need a toehold, a dark alley, a moral abscess...even venial.

At least I was able to fulfill your desire for blood, although it was chicken of me to resort to helpless chickens. Yet, the effect did its job, although it's bittersweet that Livingston's wife, although she succumbed to our harassment, is now miles away with a generous and carrying soul...and with her twins. Such unintended consequences torment my intentions and give way to Natural Law. Is there no way to negate it? Yes, I know we've been through this centuries before.

Did you recognize my contrivances in Livingston's midnight adventure? My best designs, however, did not avoid the dream's wrong turn—another unattended consequence. Just as I invaded Livingston's dream-state, an interloper appeared—a Guardian I suppose if I read the artifacts right. I struggled to imbue a deep psychological fear in Livingston's subvertical cortex. What I encountered was a residual sediment of faith. His subconscious was grasping onto a sliver of hope and the Guardian latched on to it before I could fill the void with fear. But all is not lost. What the Guardian attempted to communicate I contaminated with fear, at least for now.

At your sinful service,
Cyn Namrasit, OPSD

Chapter 40
The Intrigue of Mystery

1

Fr. Denis Cahill was owned by no man and beholden only to one—Richard McSherry, who, in an entirely temporal way, had become Cahill's bishop. A natural self-starter, Fr. Cahill easily took initiative, but he rebelled at orders that contradicted his conscience. He expected an answer from the bishop to his last missive but nothing came…until Monday, June 20, 1796 when an express rider arrived at Magdala.

> *From John Carroll
> To Denis Cahill
> Hagerstown, Maryland
> June 11, 1796 (a Saturday)

> An almost invincible reluctance to push matters to an extremity has withheld me till this day from taking such notice of your letters of Jan. 21st & March 23d., as my duty perhaps required. A hope still was harbored in my bosom, that after the declaration made in your last of your readiness to make every reparation in your power to God, or in any person, if the nature of the offense really required it, you would see your letters in their true light and offer an apology for them. But having expected so long in vain, it is a matter of obligation & not of choice to call upon you, by the obedience & reverence which you swore to your ordinary at your consecration, to appear at Baltimore on or about the 5th day of July, there to answer to the following charges. 1ly, of having falsely and most irreverently reproached your bishop with traducing your character, and otherwise maltreating you & of having deprived you unjustly of monies and temporal relief to which you had a right and title. 2ly, of having asserted, that the bishop obtain a petition to Rome for a miter by a sacrifice of property to his Brethren. 3d, of having pretended to have heard, & endeavored to give a credit to infamous imputations on the bishop's character of traducing, in an outrageous manner, the character of the other Clergymen; & 4ly, casting odious imputations on many of them, whose merits and services have been of the highest value to the increase of the Catholic faith. 5ly, of aiming to induce the bishop to purchase silence respecting the imputations aforesaid, by paying you a large

sum of money.

These are matters which you are called to answer. The inquiry will be committed to Messr. Nagot, president, & Tessier & Garnier, Professors in the Seminary of Baltre. If one of them should not be able to attend, the Rev. Dr. Caffrey will be appointed in his stead. They will hear the charges, & your defense; and on their report, will depend the sentence on you.

I am, Yrs J.C.

Fr. Cahill read the letter quickly then put it away and tried to put it out of mind. It was not John Carroll who had sent him to Maryland. John Carroll had not supported him, although Fr. Cahill had labored long and hard and in places and ways that the bishop no doubt would never dare to do himself. The bishop did however *make an appearance in Hagerstown when Cahill was miles away on his circuit and unaware that the bishop was coming. Had the bishop come when Cahill was present it would have done wonders to acknowledge and validate his ministry—the work that God had so clearly directed. Appearing in Hagerstown, as the bishop did, reinforced the bishop's opinion of Denis' labor as non-existent or irrelevant.

He could not ignore the letter, however, and it greatly discouraged the missionary priest. It was as if God Himself had delivered the letter on his death bed and had written: "*don't bother presenting yourself at the pearly gates. You will be told, 'I do not know you.' Your sacrifice has not been accepted. Although you are indeed a priest of the Church with all the faculties such a position requires, you are unfit.*" Denis did not believe that God thought that, but he was sure the bishop did.

2

Monday, June 27, 1796

Immacolata had spent the morning helping Fr. Denis prepare to depart for this southern circuit to Winchester when an unexpected coach and four pulled up in front of Magdala and began to unload baggage and two women. The priest keeper, who had eyes in the back of her bonnet, went onto the front porch to see who might be visiting. Presently, two women in poor peasant dress, albeit with large drawstring linen hand bags, descended from the compartment and presented themselves in front of the house. They were young women, no more than seventeen to eighteen years of age, and they were thin, so thin Immacolata thought them unhealthy. Both had bright blue eyes and wet hair tucked under their peasantry bonnets. The slightly shorter one was a bit nervous. She had bright but thin red hair, not unlike Fr. Denis, and a face that resembled the priest. The other, slightly taller, was more relaxed, and had thick, auburn hair.

No doubt they had found a stream to bathe in hours earlier, although their dresses were dirty, as if they had just stepped off a boat after a long and frightful voyage. Meanwhile, the coachman carried onto the porch two modest sized but beat-up travel trunks, the type one might use when crossing an ocean.

The shorter young woman curtsied to Immacolata Rosso and said, "Is this the residence of de Reverend Denis Cahill?" She had a distinct Irish lilt that sounded very much like Fr. Denis'.

Immacolata was not at a loss for words. She had in fact anticipated this encounter. Immacolata had teased Fr. Denis many times about his Irish lilt and was well practiced in the imitation arts. "Well, lassies, you's look like ye jist fell off de boat firm Dublin, did ya?"

"Yes, Madam," the young woman said with a smile, for she seemed to know a heavy set Spanish woman had not a lick of Irish blood in her.

"Whom may I say is inquiring?" the priest keeper asked as if she didn't know.

"I am his sister, Catharine," the young woman said. "And dis is my friend, *Letitia McCartney. We 'ave jist arrive' we did firm Ireland."

"Ye, don't say, now!" the priest keeper kept it up. "And who might this Reverend Denis Cahill, as ye call him, be?" Immacolata, standing on the porch several steps higher than the girls looked down on them with a stern face.

The girls laughed. The first one, the apparently less confident of the two, looked to the taller who put on a cunning grin and said to the priest keeper, "We're so sorry to 'ave bot'ered ya. We were told t'ere be a *Spanish* priest keeper here who could fatten us up...not an Irish Madam."

Suddenly, from inside the house, came Fr. Denis' voice, "Catharine! Catharine!" The door flew open and out ran Fr. Cahill with a big smile on his face, when he suddenly stopped dead in his tracks halfway down the steps...and stared at the two young women, first at Catharine and then...at...Letitia.

3

Fr. Cahill had been in his room packing when he heard the coach and four stop in front of Magdala. Hearing coaches and teams of horses pass the house throughout the day was common, so at first he thought nothing of it. Then he realized the coach had stopped in front of Magdala. He heard Immacolata go out onto the porch and talk to someone. He also heard her mocking Irish lilt, although he could not understand what she was saying. When he had packed his saddle bags, he slung them over his shoulder and came down the stairs. In the foyer he peeked out a corner of a window to see what was occupying his priest keeper. That's when he saw Catharine. He had never met Catharine as a grown woman, but she looked exactly like his mother; his mother's face had never left his mind since leaving home at sixteen. Instantly, he knew who she was, especially when he saw the two travel trunks on the porch. But through the corner of the window he had not seen Letitia McCartney standing next to his sister...until he ran onto the porch.

For an instant Denis did not know what to do, but it was only for an instant. Collecting his thoughts he quickly went to his sister and embraced her. His mind, however, was embracing the other woman. Her stunning beauty and thick, luscious auburn hair shocked him. All his training as a priest, all his years of disciplined chastity, the habit of turning his eyes and thoughts away from enchanting women...evaporated in an instant. Catharine must have felt his distraction. His embrace was perfunctory, not familial. He felt an odd guilt. It was a strange and alien feeling which he could not recall in all his years of priestly devotion. Even Anastasia McSherry, before she was married, as attractive as she was and still is, even when he was alone with her in the confessional did not affect him the way this maid standing next to Catharine did. He felt he needed to apologize to Catharine for being distracted, but how does one go about doing that? *Catharine, I'm glad you made it, but I'm not really interested in you, or what you have to say, nor do I care to hear a wit about your trip. I only want to know, who is this beguiling young woman with you?*

Of course that would never do. I'm a priest; such thoughts are dangerous.

Denis backed away and held his sister at arms length, forced himself to look into her eyes and see his mother. Catharine smiled big. He kissed her on the forehead. She hugged him and kissed him on the cheek. They stared into each other's eyes. Her eyes teared up. His eyes wandered.

Catharine spoke: "Den...oops, sorry...*Fr. Cahill,* this is my best friend..." she turned to Miss Auburn... "Letitia McCartney."

Denis turned to Letitia. Up close, Letitia looked older than Catharine, more mature, refined. "Did you come across with Catharine?" he asked her. His voice quivered slightly. He hoped it wasn't noticeable. *Were his hands cold? Doesn't matter, she's wearing gloves. Did he squeeze too tightly? No, his grip was too weak, too effeminate.*

"Yes," Letitia said, "Catharine, or rather your parents, insisted she not make the trip alone. Perhaps I was a bit responsible for instigating the idea. I always wanted to come to America." Letitia lowered her brow as she told him this. She was quiet, almost humble, and persuasive. But it was also the confident and upright posture that told Denis that the trip was all Letitia's idea, not Catharine's. She intrigued Denis; here was a mature, clever, and wise woman, older than her years probably, and thus needing to be held at arm's length.

Denis turned to his sister. "Is that true? Was this, ah, Miss McCartney's idea of adventure?"

Letitia smiled at Denis and looked to Catharine, who was slow to respond, "That might be true, but I wasn't without purpose, dear brother. The men in Dublin are all rakes."

Denis raised his eyebrows at the comment. He was from Dublin.

"Present company excluded?" asked Letitia.

Catharine bobbled her head about. "Well, yes!" She threw a prissy, condescending look at Letitia. "It's not like he's available."

To that Letitia gave Fr. Cahill a once over, and raised her eyebrows at Catharine as if to say, *he looks like an unmarried man to me.*

"Denis...sorry, Father, if you must know...." She paused here, making it clear that she didn't want to reveal what she was bound to reveal if he'd only be patient a few more seconds. "Letitia is older than me, by two years, and with her family and brothers she has traveled to England, France, and Italy, all by sea, of course. So Mum and Pa agreed that she was a good companion because...of all that."

Indeed, it made more sense to Denis now. His baby sister had an experienced chaperone. Catharine wasn't proud of that fact, but that was how she managed to make the trip.

"I promise not to tell a soul," Denis said quietly to Catharine.

"Thank you, brother," with which Catharine leaned in and kissed her priest brother again. Letitia and Denis exchanged looks. It was a quick glance, but it carried a willingness to further the acquaintance.

Months ago he asked Richard and Anastasia if an Irish immigrant, his kid sister, could live with them. Without hesitation they both agreed. But now there were two. Fr. Cahill was due to leave within the hour for Winchester. Leetown was not far out of the way, but for the girls to leave right away after their long trip was out of the question. He turned around. Immacolata was on the porch. He wondered if the priest keeper would be willing to be an immigrant keeper until he returned.

Over the next two weeks Fr. Cahill arranged with Richard for both girls to live at Retirement in Leetown with Richard's growing family. Anastasia, especially, was excited to have two slightly younger, well-educated women at Retirement. They were sixteen and eighteen, and Anastasia was twenty-four. They were close enough in age that soon Anastasia was as close to them as Catharine and Letitia had been close most of their lives, Fr. Cahill learned. Both were born on January 21, two houses apart in Dublin. The young women were glad to help with the McSherrys' three boys (Richard 4, William 3, and Denis 2) which were a handful now that all three were walking and jabbering. Anastasia realized that she and the boys could now go on more outings, since she had two nannies to help—one woman per boy, which seemed just about right, she told Fr. Cahill.

Anastasia recalled how at nineteen she had married Richard, and how Catharine and Letitia were approaching that same age. That the girls had come to America seeking husbands was all the more exciting for no other reason than the romance involved. Perhaps she could be the matchmaker—how exciting this was for Anastasia, she told Fr. Cahill. Richard, too, was welcoming, especially since they brought news of the home country, and how so much had changed since he had left thirty-three years ago.

Catharine was disappointed, however, that she would not see her brother everyday, or even once a week, as his circuit only brought him to Shepherd's Town, where the McSherrys attended Mass, but twice a month. Richard promised, however, to have Fr. Cahill stay at Retirement either the day before or day after the Shepherd's Town Mass, and the priest agreed.

But for Fr. Cahill, there was a problem with the arrangement, namely Letitia McCartney. He found her attractive, not just physically but intellectually as well. In the coming weeks, whenever he stayed at the McSherrys' he sought out Richard more than Catharine. Catharine was upset by this, but the reason was simple. Wherever Catharine was, Letitia was almost always close at hand, and if he was going to stay true to his vows, he could not allow himself to be near her for long.

The problem was compounded when Richard was traveling away from Retirement, or when the family came to Shepherd's Town for confession. He did not want to hear Letitia's confession. He did not want to know her inner thoughts nor did he desire to know more about her. The less he knew about her the less he'd be attracted to her, or so he told himself. However, he had not counted on the power of curiosity, unprompted fantasies, or the intrigue of mystery.

The real problem, however, was deeper than hearing Letitia McCartney's intimate thoughts. Since coming to Hagerstown there was no priest for him to confess to. By Church edict it was required that he participate in the Rite of Reconciliation at least once a year. For Capuchins, and he was still technically a member of the order, going to confession was required four times a year, and he had not been to confession once since leaving New Orleans nearly nine years ago. With Miss McCartney around, the need for confession was only going to escalate.

As he contemplated this dilemma he recalled the Bodkin letter to Carroll and the mention of Rev. Matthew Ryan whom Carroll had sent to Emmitsburg to establish a parish. Emmitsburg, forty miles east of Hagerstown, was not far from Fr. Cahill's backwoods circuit. At a trot it was but a day there and back. He would have to see if once a quarter Fr. Ryan would hear his confession.

Chapter 41
Imposters

My Lord Maréchal,

It was July, 1796, and still many citizens in the area of Livingston's farm, and those a day's journey or more away, believed that pranksters were responsible for the hauntings at Flax Haven. Yet, to old man Livingston and those that experienced the manifestations, all were convinced that the disturbances had their origin in the supernatural. Such is the belief that I finally came to as well.

To speed our story along, there were other accounts of manifestations that I will not belabor. In one, *three men of good reputation, who were deacons of Rev. Streit's Grace Evangelical Lutheran Church, had heard Rev. Streit tell of his encounter with the ghost. These three well intentioned souls came from Winchester in order to free the house from what troubled it, even if it were the Devil himself. Yet, as soon as they entered the farmhouse, a large stone was jettisoned from the fire place and flew at them. It rolled around on the floor for many minutes apparently attacking the men where they stood, and yet, upon examining the chimney later, Livingston found no stone was missing from it. The gentlemen sneaked away and were not heard from again.

Mister Livingston had also tried to obtain help from a chaplain in the Revolutionary Army, who later married a near relative of President Madison. The man's name was *Rev. Alexander Balmain, an Episcopal Minister, who had come from Scotland and was a tutor to the family of Richard Henry Lee, grandfather of Robert E. Lee. Neither his patriotism, nor his courage, nor his social status saved him from embarrassment. Rev. Balmain's attempted exorcism of Livingston's premises was famously abused by the scornful spirit, so much so that the prayerbook he used was found subsequently in the chamber pot of one of the rooms. Such was the respect shown by the ghost for the Episcopal Church's Sacred Liturgy.

Throughout all these enterprises Adam Livingston began to wonder if Christ no longer had any true ministers on earth, and that those who pretended to be such were a set of imposters. He was determined, henceforth, never to apply to any again who called themselves ministers of Christ.

But then Hoover Horace Hhoats made an appearance.

Your Servant,
Fr. Smith

Chapter 42
Like an Indian War Drum

1

On a Wednesday near dusk, early in August, 1796, a stout, middle-aged man dressed like a pioneer preacher rode onto the Livingston homestead on the back of a mule. Incongruously, the man wore a white suit, white shirt, and black bow tie. His suit was not entirely clean. There were dirt smudges scattered about the white pant legs above his brown boots, and along the sleeves and skirts of his suit coat. The white shirt was a bit wrinkled but not so bad as to offend. The black bow tie, however, was immaculately tied and straight. He was clean shaven, although long white hair fell from under a straw hat with a wide flat brim. The man sat upon a saddle designed more for a large horse than a modest-sized mule. Over the back of the seat was tied a fat saddle bag, a canteen, and a bed roll.

Adam was standing with Sam near the barn when the man rode into the yard. Adam looked to Sam as if to ask who was this wanderer, but Sam shrugged. Adam walked toward the house where the man was headed, but the man saw Adam and turned his ride in Adam's direction. When they closed, the man dismounted, retrieved a large but worn Bible from his saddle bag, and tucking it in his arm, bowed low before Adam, doffed his hat, and spoke.

"My good sir," said the man, "We meet again. You may remember, I am the Reverend Hoover Horace Hhoats. H. H. O. A. T. S., the second "H" is silent." Hhoats' speech was full and rounded, his vowels slurred, but each syllable articulated as if he was preaching on a hillside to a large outdoor congregation. "I believe you claimed to be in need of my services?"

Adam paused and looked the man over. He suspected he knew why the man had suddenly showed up, but he decided to play along. "Thank you muchly for coming, sir. And just what might your services be that I am in sore need of? I don't recall."

Hhoats turned away from Adam, spread his feet apart to steady his stout form, and studied the house as if he was a likely purchaser. "Muchly, indeed. Indeed. Indeed. Tell me, sir, where is this that you want dismissed?" Hhoats turned back to Adam. "Ah, but first, if you please, the down payment we agreed upon."

Adam stared at the man for a moment wondering if "Huckster" was a middle name the man had forgotten to include in his litany. Adam was ready to wave his shillelagh and chase the quack off his property, when he remembered. It was several months earlier that he had heard of a traveling preacher and exorcist of evil spirits from North Carolina. The man had an honest although flamboyant reputation. Adam recalled sending a message to the preacher to come to Smithfield with a promise to pay him up front to rid his farm of a distressing spirit. But they had never met in person, but by other means...yes, they had met. "Indeed. Yes, indeed. Here," said Adam as he reached into his pocket and produced a silver crown.

Hhoats took the coin, tried to bite it, after which he put the coin into his coat pocket and patted his pocket to hear the sound of coin against coins.

"Hope that coin doesn't wear a hole in that there pocket," said Adam.

"It does. But I carry needle and thread," said Hhoats. "Where is this here ghost? I came as you requested on a new moon."

Adam hadn't checked his almanac lately but Hhoats was right. The disturbances had increased the last few days.

Sam tended to Hhoats' mule while Adam ushered the preacher into the house. A fire burned in the fireplace of the gathering hall where Bethany sat shelling peas. Mary Ann was still at Travelers Rest. The clipping of shears could be heard faintly as if coming from the cellar.

"You hear that?" asked Adam.

"Scissors," said Hhoats.

"That's our ghost, though he seems to be sleeping at the moment."

"Well, let's wake him, it, or her up," said Hhoats.

Bethany spoke up: "Be not anxious, Mister. You be sorry."

"Reverend," said Adam, gesturing toward Bethany, "this is Bethany Dark. Bethany, this is Reverend Hhoats."

Bethany didn't bother to look up or stop shucking her peas, "Glad to meet you, Mister Oats."

Hhoats turned to Bethany without walking over to her. "Madam, I am the Very Reverend Horace Hoover Hhoats. H.H.O.A.T.S. First H is silent. Good to meet you, madam." He nodded in her direction.

Bethany looked between Hhoats and Adam wondering how she might respond to all the H's, as if they might be a substitute for the clipping noise.

With a bit of concern Hhoats turned back to Adam. "Is she the one of which you spoke, an unbeliever?"

"No. No. My wife, Missus Livingston is, ah...away today. Bethany is our cook, among other things."

"Sir, I know my job and the spirits obey me."

"If you reckon you can restore our life to normal, and vanquish our haunting spirit then please do it."

"Just lead me to this Wizard of yours and I'll exorcise your living quarters and make it again a warm abode fit for king, queen, prince and, ah mistress. Where? Where? Lead me." Hhoats paused for a moment, sniffing the air. "Is dinner to come?"

"We ate already," said Bethany.

Hhoats relinquished a sigh of disappointment.

The faint clipping persisted.

"You hear it?" she asked.

Hhoats cocked his head. "Ah, yes, I do. This is new," he said. He turned to Adam, "From whence or where does it rise?

Said Adam, "from whence or wherever it wants. It clips our linens."

Adam stepped to a wooden chair and lifted the blanket covering for Hhoats to examine. It was riddled in precisely cut crescent moons.

"Odd. May I sit to examine this?" Hhoats said.

Adam gestured to the chair. Hhoats took the blanket and sat, but the chair suddenly moved away from him. Hhoats caught himself and stood again. "What's the meaning of this? Why did you do that?"

But before Adam could answer, Hhoats put Adam in his line of sight, backed to the chair, and again committed his weight. Again, the chair moved back, but this time Hhoats fell hard on his rump, jamming his inners into his throat causing a hoarse gasp for air.

Suddenly and speedily between his outstretched legs, just above his boots, thick charcoal smoke streamed up from between the floor boards, quickly congealed into a naked human foot and stomped down hard on Horace's overlapping pant cuffs, effectively nailing the cuffs and Hhoats to the floor so he could not hover. Adam was caught off guard. This *was* something new. Hhoats' tried to lift his legs, but he could not. Adam then heard the sound of heavy iron shears— CLANK, CLANK. At each clank a crescent moon several inches tall was cut from the bottom of each immobilized pant leg.

Hhoats thrashed and babbled incoherently. He tried to crawl away from the black foot that held his pants to the floor, but he couldn't move. He was a prisoner of his own doubts, subject to what he claimed to have power over, and victim of something neither of them could imagine.

Adam grabbed his shillelagh and instinctively struck at the black foot and ankle that rose above Hhoats' boots. Adam felt no resistance as the shillelagh swept through the black foot, but when it did the foot dissipated and the smoke vaporized into thin air.

Shaking with anger, and a smidgen of fear, Hhoats scrambled to his feet and gazed down at the crescent holes in his pants. "Sir, you are a rude devil. I have never been treated this way my entire ministry."

"Sorry about your pants, Reverend."

"Most ill mannered of you, sir. Most unprofessional."

"'Twas not I but the spirit you promised to rid us of," Adam said.

"'Twas not a spirit but a rapscallion, a sheezicks, a wagpastie, a scattermouch...such cannot be removed without the proprietor's permission."

"But I gave you permission."

You falsified the commodity, sir. I'm a respected minister of the pulpit, and you have brought me here under false pretenses. A badger, a barker, a peddler or pigman you are. You should be ashamed. Deserving of these haunts you are, sir."

With that Hhoats pulled himself together, looked quickly about for the door, and marched out of the house still fuming at Adam's supposed deception. As he went he sputtered. "There are others that will better respect my skills, sir, and I must attended to them as my priorities and responsibilities dictate, in hopes that I can reclaim my reputation that you so callously have sullied, stained, and...and...besmirched."

Hhoats scampered across the porch and down the steps, then turned and looked up at Adam who had followed him out of the house. "Before I leave do you know of any other ghost that I might render helpless?"

"You mean, like you did ours?" said Adam.

"No sir, a real ghost. A spirit that will obey a minister of the Gospel such as myself."

"No, Reverend, I know of no one that would take you for a minister of any Gospel whether he be a real man or real ghost."

Ignoring the reproof, Hhoats gave Adam a snort, untied his mule, pulled himself into his oversized saddle, and trotted out of the yard.

Bethany, coming onto the porch, gathered her wits, for she too was shaking just a bit. Her strong but trembling voice asked, "You paid him already, didn't you?"

Adam simply nodded and shuffled off to the barn to close it up.

2

Sunday, August 7, 1796.

Over the last year the congregation in Shepherd's Town had outgrown Gabriel and Ruth Menghinis' accommodations. As he had promised, Thomas Shepherd, Jr., deeded over the four-acre parcel of land to the St. Agnes Catholic Society of Shepherd's Town. The lot was on top of that hill that overlooked the town and the Potowmack River. In July, laymen of the society began construction on a weather-boarded chapel with an adjoining apartment or rectory for a traveling priest. It was a simple building with two outside entrances, one to the small rectory and one to the chapel proper, over which they erected a simple cross. There was also a door inside connecting the chapel with the rectory. The idea was that the foyer to the priest's quarters could be also used as a confessional and sacristy.

Despite the lack of support from Bishop Carroll, Fr. Cahill was very happy with the progress of the Shepherd's Town chapel, but progress on the chapel's construction was slow because the men building it did so only in their spare time. Consequently, services, confession, and classes still took place at the Menghinis' home, which was only crowded when regular Masses were offered.

It was Fr. Cahill's practice when staying at the Menghinis' in Shepherd's

Town to hear confessions in the hours prior to the noon Mass, with a potluck supper for the congregants after. Having arrived the afternoon before, he established himself in the parlor with a makeshift screen Gabriel had fabricated from lumber left over from renovations at his boarding house, and a scrap of sheer linen Ruth had left over from a long-forgotten sewing project.

Confessions, as in most places, were hardly concealed, as the screen was but a modesty prop. Fr. Cahill turned his face away from the parlor door when a penitent entered as a matter of courtesy, but the penitent's identity was never actually concealed. Fr. Cahill had come to relish his role as a confessor, but not out of any thought of pride, power, or prejudice. As he had been trained, it was typical that within an hour of the penitent finishing the reconciliation rite Fr. Cahill had conveniently forgotten what was confessed by whom. But there were times when he believed what was confessed would never leave his memory, and in that he lamented. Some sins, as murder, or other sins of bloodshed, brutality, abuse, or assault would haunt him for years.

On this day, however, he hoped to avoid a particular penitent for entirely different reasons, but he suspected his desires of avoidance were in vain. Richard and Anastasia McSherry always came to confession once a month when his Mass was held in Shepherd's Town on a Sunday, as was the case today. Today would be the first time they came, no doubt with his sister Catharine, and her friend, Letitia. He looked forward to his sister's confession. This expectation was not out of any grotesque curiosity of his sister's sin-laden secrets, but purely because he cared greatly for his sister's spiritual well-being. He desired for her conscience to be free of guilt and remorse so she could live in peace and happiness.

What he wanted to sidestep, prevent, forestall, and entirely head off was hearing the confession of Letitia McCartney. This was especially true if she had any inclination or disposition to confess thoughts or actions of a romantic or sexual nature. He was a priest, but he was still very much a man. While he had been blessed with the capacity to live a chaste life, there had always been the lure, although short of an inclination, to entertain thoughts about what it would be like to be married, to know a woman carnally, and have children. Such thoughts came regularly to his mind, but he had been able to quickly set them aside, focus his mind on spiritual things, avoid the escalation to lust, and God forbid to act on the lust to any degree. Thus, over the years, he had been careful in how he came in physical contact with women. There was never a problem in holding the hand or embracing an elderly woman, but the more attractive the lady, he was inclined to become more distant. In Letitia McCartney's case he had already wished her return to Ireland.

On the other side of the coin, however, it was entirely possible that listening to Letitia's confession, just one time, could dramatically change his opinion of her. The depth of a woman's outward beauty was measured by her integrity, intelligence, and the imagination of her inward mind. Would she be delicate or coarse? Prideful or humble? Articulate or stammering? Worldly or spiritual? Indeed, listening to confessions this morning would tell a tale.

Anastasia, as was usual for the saint she was, had nothing significant to confess. Getting upset with the boys was perhaps a virtue and a good thing, not a weakness or a sin. She still spent too much on hats, but this was a venial contrivance better suited for the general confession, thought Fr. Cahill. She was perhaps a bit vain but keeping Richard's attention was perhaps a wifely duty. She wasn't trying to attract the untoward attention of others. Fr. Cahill was pleased that their marriage seemed to be matched in heaven and that he had played a part.

Richard was another case altogether, but not a disappointment. A lustful thought here and there when traveling, but seemingly only fleeting and not pursued. Fr. Cahill gave Anastasia credit for that and granted her clemency for her vanity, which no doubt Richard found a virtue insofar as his eyes did not wander far. Unlike some confessors Fr. Cahill knew, he did not expect some sins would diminish over the years. He had heard too many confessions of men in the autumn of their lives who longed for youthful feminine beauty to grace their lives. It wasn't going to happen, but the fantasies were always there. Richard did have a problem with expecting perfection of his debtors. He lacked mercy when money was due and not paid. No doubt this lack of mercy contributed to his wealthy attire.

Richard left and Catharine came and lowered herself to the kneeler. Her brother, the priest, was anxious. This would be the first time he heard her confession, and the beginning he hoped of a long relationship and connection to his mother and father.

"Denis, we need to talk," she began without any of the preliminaries.

"Catharine!" her brother admonished. "This is a sacred time. Have you come to gossip or confess?"

Catharine let out a long sigh. "When else can we talk in private? It's not fair. You avoid me. Why is that?"

Denis knew very well why he avoided his sister. He was actually avoiding his sister's companion, but he could hardly tell her that. At least he would avoid lying, or so he hoped.

"I agree," he began, "that we need to spend time in private and talk about Mum, Pa, and…well, many things. I apologize. But you have not been, how do I say it, alone. Letitia is always at your elbow as if a hovering nanny. You may feel comfortable speaking frankly in her presence, but it does not seem the right way to talk about private things in the presence of another. Let us plan to do that, perhaps today when others leave after supper." He paused for her response.

"I think you're being too sensitive. If I cannot confide in Letitia, I…this will sound condescending… if I cannot confide in Letitia, I don't see how I am to confide in my brother. Letitia is like part of my brain. I find it hard to explain things. She helps. I wish she was here now, but I know that's not allowed."

Fr. Denis was glad *it was not allowed*. "So then, let us begin," he said. "In nomine Patris, et Filii, et Spiritus Sancti. Amen. May God, who has enlightened every heart, help you to know your sins and trust in his mercy."

"It has been a long time since I was last at confession," Catharine said.

"Longer than a year?" said Fr. Denis.

"No. Not that long. Since maybe a month before the voyage, until today. Maybe six months. There was no priest on board the Carolina."

"Did you attend Mass before departure?"

"Aye. Mum said that when you left home, Mass was illegal. That is changed. We now have a church in Dublin. Many come."

"That is good to hear, but have you sinned in being absent from Mass?"

"There was none that I could attend since leaving Mum and Pa."

"I understand. That is not something you could have avoided. It is not a sin. What else?"

"I was angry with Mum...not Pa, about she not wanting me to come to America. Pa said it was all right if I traveled with someone older. That be Letitia. I was mad at her, Mum I mean, she forbade me. Pa talked to her. I am sorry I was angry. But then I am here, now, and feel bad that I was angry. I miss her now."

"Aye, we talk 'bout that later, we can." her brother said.

Catharine said nothing for a few moments, and he heard her sobbing.

"What's wrong, Catharine?"

"I did somethin' very bad...when I was mad at Mum."

Fr. Denis said nothing. He waited and tensed up.

"I knew a boy...in Dublin."

It was like a kick to Fr. Denis' stomach. Emotions raged through his limbs. A great sadness fell over him like a heavy blanket for his sister. A murderous hatred rose in his loins for the boy. For a moment he forgot he was hearing a confession: "Did he force himself on you? What did Pa do?"

"Pa and Mum don't know. I ain't told them nothing."

"Did..." Fr. Denis started in again, but she interrupted him.

"No. He didn't make me. I wanted to. I wanted to get even with Mum for keepin' me home all the time, being protecting."

"How long ago was this? Are you with child."

"No. Letitia says I'm not with child. I still have me bleed every month. I am sorry...Father. I am. I shan't do it again."

Denis could not see her face, but he heard her tears; they were real.

"Did this go on? How often did you know this boy?"

"Jest once. I was scared. I didn't love him, or anything. I ask him. He didn't want to."

Denis said nothing for a long time. The shock of it took away the words he was supposed to say.

Catharine spoke again. "He was another reason I wanted to leave home. I shan't want to see him again. He might expect me...I dunno, marry him."

It was enough for Fr. Denis. He wanted to hear no more. His innocent sister was no longer his kid sister but a woman he would look at differently. He didn't despise her or hate her, but he was sad, and sad for her. He wanted to take her in his arms and comfort her. Indeed, they would talk privately...later; and he would ask Letitia to leave them alone for a while.

"Is there anything else, my dear sister you want to tell...the Lord? Does Letitia know this?"

"Letitia knows and was angry at the boy. She knows him. He's her age. He liked Letitia, but she didn't like him."

Fr. Denis wondered if the boy's reason for taking his sister's innocence was in reprisal at Letitia. "Anything else, Catharine...that God needs to know?"

"Does he not know everything?" she said.

"Yes, he surely does. But he also wants to know your sorrow."

"Then he knows I lied to Mum and Pa about earnin' the money ta come to America. I stole some of it. I shan't be indentured, you knows."

If it had been anyone else, his job would be perfunctory. But this was his flesh and blood. His heart ached. "You must pay it back."

"But they be in Ireland. How do I do that?"

"With a bank transfer. You must earn the money here, save it up, go to a bank and send it to the person you stole it from with an apology. You do know who you stole it from, do you not?"

There was a pause. Then quietly, "Yes, I know them. They be the family I nannied fer."

"What else, Catharine? God is merciful. He desires for you a clean heart."

"That's enough, isn't it?"

"I hope so, but I don't know. Only you and our heavenly Father knows."

"Is it wrong that I want to marry?"

"That is not a sin but I suspect, for you, it is God's will. You must pray and trust Him to lead you to the right man."

"I was hoping *you* would."

"Yes, I recall you asking that. I have thought little about it since, but I promise I will keep my eyes open...and pray as well."

"Then, that is all I can remember."

"Then tell God of your heart's contrition."

This was always the difficult part for Fr. Denis. Somehow, by God's grace, he had to discern if the person on the other side of the screen was contrite. Just how did they intone their act of contrition? Was it sincere? Was there at least the appearance of sorrow? Some of course could pour on the tears as easily as closing a door with squeaky hinges. It wasn't entirely up to him to discern the penitent's true heart, but he was at least responsible for the general appearance of contriteness.

"Lord Jesus, Son of God, have mercy on me, a sinner. Help me not to ever sin again. I'm truly sorry for my sins, and desire to do better. Please forgive me."

"Good, Catharine. Now, here is the Father's absolution: Dominus noster Jesus Christus te absolvat...*God, the Father of mercies, through the death and resurrection of his Son has reconciled the world to himself and sent the Holy Spirit among us for the forgiveness of sins; through the ministry of the Church may God give you pardon and peace, and I absolve you from your sins in the name of the Father +, and of the Son +, and of the Holy Spirit +. Amen. Go in peace, my good sister.*"

"Amen," said Catharine, who then lifted off the kneeler. Fr. Denis felt a great burden lift from his heart. His sister was mortal, but now she was off to a better start than when she left Ireland.

No sooner, however, had his sister walked out than Fr. Denis' heart sank, for it was Letitia who came next and sank to her knees. She was wearing a scent, an intoxicating scent that distracted his otherwise chaste mind. He could only see an obscure image of her body behind the screen, but the delicate bouquet filled in for her beauty. Her presence was worse than he imagined, and he did imagine.

Might as well get on with it, perhaps her heart will sully her beauty. He would search it out. "In nomine Patris, et Filii, et Spiritus Sancti. Amen. May God, who has enlightened every heart, help you to know your sins and trust in his mercy."

"Hello, Father Denis."

He said nothing at first. But then neither did she. "How long has it been since your last confession, my sister?" he finally intoned.

"Oh, 'twas perhaps two months before we left fair Dublin."

"And what transgressions has God revealed to you to confess since then?"

"Well, I missed Mass for the seven weeks we were on board. There was no priest with us."

"Yes, I have heard. That is regrettable, but that is no sin. It was not your intention and you could do nothing else. Did you hold God close to your heart in your daily prayers during the crossing?"

"Oh, yes, Father, I do that every day upon waking and at night I examine my conscience for faults, which are many."

"Perhaps we can start there? For what do you need to ask the Lord for forgiveness?"

"I have not put God first in my thoughts. Especially during the crossing, I was in awe of the sea, the waves, and the fish that we saw. When during a storm, I was frightened at the wind and lightening. It was very frightening at night when the storm lasted for so long."

"How is that a sin, my sister? The fear of the Lord is the beginning of wisdom."

"I feared the sea and the storm."

"You feared what God created. That is a good thing. Did your fear cause you to reject God and curse Him?"

"Oh, no. I would never do that."

"Then that is not a sin."

"But the discomfort of the boat during the storm made me very sick. It was most embarrassing."

"Perhaps you were filled with pride? Was it pride that made you embarrassed?"

"I can't rightly say. I believe my sickness made others near me discomforted and I feared they might get sick because of me, or get the sickness from me."

"Were you concerned what others thought of you?"

"Oh, no. I don't care what others think of me. I didn't want them to get sick, too."

Fr. Denis sighed quietly to himself. This was going to be difficult. "Then, neither is that a sin, for you were thinking of the well-being of others."

"I guess."

She paused for a moment. Fr. Denis could hear her catching her breath, and unfortunately the image of her doing so was not a virtuous image. He whispered a "Hail! Mary" under his breath.

"Father, Denis, I did not honor my father and mother."

"Having her say his first name, even reverently with the formal address did not help. "How did you do that?"

"They did not want me to make the trip to America. They feared they might never see me again. I am their oldest daughter." She fell silent.

"Did you disobey them in coming? Or did they give you their blessings before you departed? Did you grieve them?"

"It was at first they didn't want me to go. But it was...oh, aye two weeks 'fore the boat was to depart that Pa told me though it was hard on Mum, he understood that I was of an age and mind that I could not stay. Pa, and Mum too, had tried to find me a suitable suitor. But their every suggestion was not met with even their enthusiasm let alone mine. The men were all haughty, lazy, or non-religious. I spent evenings with many in our parlor and could not wait for each evening to end. I don't think any of them had been to Mass in the last year, since the last Christ Mass. So, they gave me their blessing before I left. I do miss them."

"My sister, neither is that a sin. You did not disobey. And if you had, you are of age that you are due them respect but not literal obedience in matters of the heart and mind which of themselves are not mortal sins...venial perhaps, but that is not a matter for confession."

Fr. Denis was worried. His attraction to this woman's mind was building. He had hoped for the opposite.

"Well, I guess I should confess ––" She was silent for a several moments. Then very tentatively she said: "I've had bad thoughts...about...a man."

"Like you want to kill him?"

"No. Like I want to marry him."

"Marriage is a sacrament. God loves marriages. How is that a sin?"

Fr. Denis could hear that suddenly Letitia held her breath. Then very softly: "He's a priest."

Now it was Fr. Denis' turn to be silent…except his heart began to bang like an Indian war drum.

"I don't think he should be a priest," she said.

Fr. Denis had no idea what to say. For, in fact, she had just said aloud what he had been thinking since his fall-out with Bishop Carroll.

3

Most Feared Master of Hatred,

Pay attention. Hell, I am delivering on my promises. Hate me all you want, but there is love in the air which, under the current circumstances, is something to celebrate. Okay, it's not love, it's lust, but I ask you now, what could be grander? There must be some reward when the hideous likes of yours truly stimulates the sexual appetite of a chaste Catholic priest. Is this not an achievement celebrated in the halls of Hades for millennia? Have I not demonstrated my persistence and patience with this ironic result? Okay, nothing has happened just yet, but it will. You're right, it's no great accomplishment for other Catholic rites, or even Protestant denominations. But for the arrogant Romans who pride themselves with chastity, as if *it* alone will guarantee immortality, it is a pretentious if not paramount, principled, and primordial achievement, if I do say so myself…and I do. Chaste Roman priests always have a better chance at Glory than other clerics, or any man for that matter. But who am I to speak of chastity, since I want nothing of it. Chastity serves no useful purpose where our kind is concerned. Give me lust, adultery, fornication…even homosexuality, although we don't need to go that far. In my estimation those five cities of the Jordan Plain got what they deserved. But I can almost guarantee that I have found the key to Cahill's heart, and I intend to twist, twist, twist. Watch me now!

At your sinful service,
Cyn Namrasit, OPSD

Chapter 43
I Remember Well

1

October 24, 1796.

Adam, along with Sam, Henry, and their day laborers had just finished a day of harvesting crops. It had been a mediocre reaping with less rain than a farmer would have wanted, and there were diseased sections of the fields and, of course, the near total loss of winter wheat from the wizardly destruction. Adam was feeling neither spry nor confident. He kept telling himself that there was always going to be good years and bad years. It wasn't a drought, but it wasn't a bumper, either. Despite all his work, experimentation, and diligence he still had to contend with nature. He wondered if someday someone would figure out how to make it rain on demand, or stop if floods threatened.

After the day laborers had left, Adam went into the barn to look over the scythes and other tools for damage. Sam came to him.

"Missta Livingston, do you's 'ave time to talk a bit?" said Sam.

"Of course. Did you repair that plow harness? We're going to need it next week."

"Yas, sir, all ready to go." Sam seemed hesitant to go on, but Adam stopped what he was doing and gave his full attention to the man who was responsible for keeping the day laborers productive. Sam had a way about him that men respected. "Well, sir, it's been eight years comin' up next week."

Adam waited for more. But Sam stopped talking and seemed to be waiting for Adam to remember. But Adam had no clue; his mind was on the hard day's work they had just put in without a whole lot to show for it. "Eight years? What's that mean, Sam?"

"Me 'en Bethany we's wondering if you's...well, our indenture ta works fer ya as freeman...well, it be done next week."

Adam was stunned that he had overlooked this important date. He was good at numbers, accounting, and dates, but he had totally forgotten about the labor indenture he, Sam, and Bethany had signed, and which was witnessed by John Adams and Mary Valens Gates. "Has it really been that long, Sam?"

"Dis here is 1796 and we signed ours indenture wid you's in 1788. Me and Bethany were reading it last night, now dat we's kin read. We could't read den, when we's put our marks on it." Sam's voice was shaking a bit. He wanted to say something more, but he seemed hesitant

"Sam what's wrong? Go on, say what you're thinking," said Adam.

"Are you's going ta honor de indenture, sir, and set us free from it?"

"Sam, I have never reneged on any agreement with anyone. That goes for you and Bethany, too. But..." Adam was nearly at a loss for words. "I will be unhappy when you leave. I've depended on you for so much."

"That's jist it, sir," said Sam. "Wad happens to us'n next? Now that de indenture is over, wad me 'en Beth'ny to do? Whas we goin'? We don't know nobody. Dis here's is all we's know."

Adam sat down on a stool, and gestured for Sam to do the same. He was taken off guard by this revelation and he felt stupid for not knowing, but Sam was right, the indenture was up. Sam and Bethany had fulfilled every requirement of the agreement; they were free to leave him. That scared Adam. What would he do without Sam and Bethany? They had become part of his family. It was like he had been hit in the stomach by a plow handle that had suddenly hit an underground root, knocking the wind out of him.

"Sir, I thinking dat we's have to leave not only you's, but the state of Virginia. Dere a law, or so we's been told, dat say freed slaves must leave Virginia. They say we's got to be enslaved or under indenture to stay, or they arrest you and kin enslave you's again."

Adam knew that to be true, but he had never thought about it. He had never thought what he would do when the indenture was up and Sam and Bethany would have to leave or be jailed, or chased like escaped chattel.

"What I don't understand," said Sam, "is Bethany...she not scared. She think everythin' all right. But I'm scared dat something like de McCulloughs dey come 'ere and sudden' we's either dead or enslaves again."

"What did Bethany say?"

"She not make sense. You know how women be sometime."

"Where is she now?" asked Adam.

"She at the house gettin' dinner ready, I think."

"Yes, I guess I am hungry. Let's go. Henry?!"

2

Bethany had told Eve she didn't need to help with dinner, since she was busy on the loom. Bethany set the table, although there was no table covering and just rags for napkins, when the men showed up.

As was her habit, Bethany hustled to the front door, and stuck her head out. "No, don't you dare bring all that mud 'en muck into this house. I jist cleaned it. Take off those boots and scrape off dat mud from your overalls. And don't come to the table all dirty, like. Wash up!"

If Bethany had given that speech once, she had repeated it a hundred times. But she felt she always had to say it, else she'd been cleaning up the mud and stuff into the night, long after supper was supposed to be over and she be home with Sam.

After a bit she had the food ready, and the cleaned-up men came to the table. There was no prayer, although she and Sam always stopped and bowed their heads for a moment, and she noticed Eve doing the same. Someday, perhaps, there would be prayer again at this table.

After satisfying their initial hunger, she noticed Sam looking repeatedly at Mister Livingston, who nodded to Sam as if they had planned somethin'. Bethany looked at Sam. "You got somethin' to say?"

Sam looked up at Mister Livingston, and gestured his head toward Bethany.

"Bethany," said Mister Livingston, "I guess you know that your labor indenture with me is up next week."

"Yes, Mister Livingston. Sam and I was readin' de indenture last night."

"Sam is worried where you're going to go."

She turned to Sam. "Husband, why you asking Mister Livingston *dat* question? That's not what we talked about." She turned back to Mister Livingston. "Didn't he ask you properly?"

"Ask me what?"

"What he's supposed to ask you."

"What was it I supposed to ask him?" said Sam.

"Mister Livingston," said Bethany, "are you gonna honor the indenture? Are we goin' to be free to leave?" Bethany was careful to smile when she said that.

Mister Livingston's face turned sad. He was disturbed. "I told Sam I have never dishonored any agreement I've made, at least not willingly. If you must leave, now that our agreement is over, then please tell me so I can start looking for someone to replace both of you. But I suspect it will be mighty hard."

"Mister Livingston," said Bethany, "we don't want to leave you. Besides that, we have no place other to go to."

"That presents a problem, though, doesn't it?" said Adam. "You are freemen, and now that the indenture is up, by law you have one week, from October 31, I guess it is, to leave the state. You can't stay here or else the constable from Martinsburg will come and jail you."

"Pa," said Eve, "that doesn't have to be."

"What do you know about all this?" said Adam, turning to his daughter.

"Ask, Bethany," Eve said.

"Confound it people," said Adam, "what is going on? Bethany is smiling like a cat, Sam is scowling like a coyote, my daughter is telling me my servants know more than me, and...." he turned to Henry, "do you have anything you want to contribute?"

Henry looked at Eve and said, "Pa, why do they have to leave? Can't they still work for you and live in their cabin?"

"It's fine with me," said Adam, "but others seem to think that they have to go to New York or someplace other than Virginia."

"Mister Livingston," said Bethany. "I'm sorry for the confusion, but the solution may not be difficult, if you would like, as we would like, for us to stay."

"And what is that?" asked a very frustrated and impatient farmer.

Bethany sat up straighter and squared her shoulders. "'We could sign another indenture to continue working fer you. That way we kin stay. We won't be entirely free to leave, although we will still be freemen.'"

Adam thought about that for a full minute as he played with his food and kept looking between his plate and the expectant faces around the table. Finally, he said, "That might work. What's wrong with the old one?"

"It's expiring, Pa," said Eve.

"Aside from that?" Adam said.

Bethany changed her disposition, and became a bit more businesslike. "Well, I don't think the *new* indenture...." she put an emphasis on *new*, "... should require us to tell you when we go out for evenings, or what time to get back to our cabin, or that we need to ask your permission to go where we want to go when we not working. And we need to have a day where we not have to work. We don't really have that now. Except a few on Sunday."

Adam thought about that. "But during harvest there is no time to take off. We've got to work all day, every day."

"Agreed," said Bethany. "But during the growing season and winter?"

"Perhaps."

Bethany continued. "The present indenture says we were working to pay you for the indebtedness you incurred for our purchase. If that be true, and we've now paid you for that with our work, you could now pay us the difference over the wage you have paid us."

"But what would you do with the extra?"

"Pa!" interrupted Henry. "Let'em buy whatever they want."

"Why, thank you, Henry," Bethany said. "Sam and me want good Sunday clothes for church. That we can buy. You can provide us work clothes like you do now."

Adam was getting tense. "What else?"

"That be enough, Mister Livingston," said Bethany.

Adam was glad she didn't demand that they pray before meals, or that he go to church with them. Suddenly, he realized that the anxiety of the last few minutes, since Sam reminded him that the indenture was going to expire, had evaporated. In fact, he felt good...that Sam and Bethany would be around for yet a long time.

3

Monday, October 31, 1796.

Over the past few months Adam had made frequent trips to Travelers Rest to visit Mary Ann and the twins. He brought them clean clothing, fresh produce from the farm, and news. It was during her time at Travelers Rest that Mary Ann fully weaned four-year old George and Martha. Mary Ann later conceded she had Felicity Randal to thank for that. For, as soon as the twins arrived at

Travelers Rest, Felicity took them into her heart and made it her goal to help Mary Ann fully wean the children. It would help Mary Ann heal, if for no other reason than she would get more rest. So, Felicity fixed nutritious food for the twins that they would crave more than their mother's breast.

While there was this success with the twins, Adam was disappointed that there was still failure with his daughter. Eve never once visited her stepmother, and Adam didn't push it. Henry traveled with him on occasion, riding Mary Ann's Apple. Adam considered that Henry's desire to go along had nothing to do with visiting his stepmother, and everything to do with riding a horse. Henry was growing into a strong and surprisingly reliable teen boy, becoming more and more helpful around the farm. Adam got the sense that as soon as he had put Henry on a horse and taught him to ride, the boy suddenly matured, as if riding was a mark of manhood. But even more so, Adam figured that not having to deal with Mary Ann, who still demonstrated a mental barrier to accepting Eve and Henry as her own, had helped Henry become the young man of whom Adam could be proud. Mary Ann was not there to constantly correct or belittle him, and so the boy grew in confidence and reliability, and became a true asset around the farm.

Now it was time for Mary Ann to return home. The Randalls were not kicking her out. Adam had not only supplemented the Randalls' food supplies, thanks to Bethany's industriousness, but he paid them a stipend as well. Looking after a sick woman was not easy. The Randalls had several dogs and cats, which George and Martha adored and gave the children, now running everywhere, plenty to do. The dogs, too, took to the children and protected them like nannies. Whenever Adam visited he marveled at how dogs, both large and small, were gentle in playing with George and Martha, and even allowed George to pick up the smaller ones and carry them about like straw dolls. Strangely, the dogs seemed to like it, licking George's face as they toddled along. Martha wasn't so careful or kind with the animals, however. One time a cat scratched her. Martha didn't cry; she just kicked the cat away.

Mary Ann was sure she wanted to return to Flax Haven, even though Adam warned her that not much had changed as far as the haunts were concerned. By now there was very little linen left to clip, except what Eve protected in her keepsake chests. For special occasions, when the occasion did not correspond to a new moon cycle, Eve would bring out a new cloth she had woven for supper, but after she would return it quickly to her cloth sanctuary. Adam was nervous about Mary Ann returning because it was clear that Mary Ann was still envious of Eve's ability to produce new cloth.

When Adam brought Mary Ann home, and before she even let herself down from the wagon with George and Martha, he heard the working loom. At once he noticed Mary Ann stiffened, and as soon as they let themselves down from the wagon, Mary Ann picked up the kids and held them tight as if to protect them from ravenous wolves. Adam was immediately disappointed. He had hoped she was over her paranoia. When they entered the front door, Eve was busy at the loom, the flying shuttle and treadles making their characteristic rhythmic racket. Perhaps because their mother was gripping them so tight, but more so because they sensed their mother's discomfort like an animal senses a human's fear, the kids began to cry and fuss. That was all that was needed to set Mary Ann off on a rant, as if she had never left the farm months earlier.

"Adam Livingston!" she began. "You curse us again with that demonic contraption. We don't need it, I tell you. Get rid of it, or the devil himself will. Can't you see what it does to your children?" ...and she shook George and Martha as if they were inanimate objects, which only made them cry all the more and try to escape their mother's iron grip.

Eve, hearing and seeing the commotion, wide-eyed and worried, instantly stopped weaving, got up, and took George and Martha from Mary Ann's arms and climbed the stairs to the bedrooms. Before she got halfway up the stairs the children were hugging Eve, their crying and fussing diminished to faint sobs and tears. Mary Ann scowled after Eve but said nothing.

Adam could see the jealousy caused by the children's attraction to their step-sister instead of their mother. He was mostly at a loss, except for the calmness of mind to take Mary Ann into his arms and tenderly hold and rub her back. "It will be fine, my beautiful bride. Just let 'em be. They are but innocent children who don't understand the world within which we must live. Let them get reacquainted."

As the evening progressed, Adam could see that Mary Ann was not entirely healed in mind, so he asked Bethany to treat Mary Ann asif she was still severely in need of comfort and tolerance. Bethany agreed, and served up, without Eve's help, a wonderful meal with many of Mary Ann's favorites. It heartened Adam's heart to hear Mary Ann compliment Bethany several times, although Mary Ann's tone was reserved and reticent. Nonetheless her mind seemed to be on the right track, and Adam had reason to relax.

In the back of his mind, however, was the loom. In a spare moment, Eve had shared with him that she would not weave when Mary Ann was in the house, and he thanked Eve for that. When he had time he examined the finished cloth Eve was creating. He was surprised to see a very complicated but structured herringbone pattern he had never seen before. The finished cloth was two feet wide. The warps were beamed in alternating shades of natural fiber in ten-thread blocks, and she was weaving with two different shuttles, also in contrasting shaded threads. The effect in the finished cloth was startling; he had never seen a weave so elegant or engaging to the eye. How she had learned this he did not know, but he was proud of his daughter's enterprising spirit. The loom was indeed a good thing. Somehow Mary Ann would have to understand its importance. As he left the loom to attend to his chores he glanced back and was impressed that Eve, too, continued in her organized way. There was nothing about the loom's setup or the basket of yarn, the warp beam or the cloth beam, or the heddles that was disarrayed. Eve even kept the shed closed to give a more neat appearance. Like the tightly woven cloth, the loom and its environs were neat and tidy, and swept, too. Except he expected it was Bethany that kept the area swept, not Eve.

That evening, Adam completed his bookkeeping and came to bed well into the night. His mind was worried. The disturbances in the house had affected the yield of his fields, if for no other reason than his own lack of attention to giving his farm hands the attention they required to cultivate, irrigate, and maintain the feed and watering of livestock. Sam was an immense help with all this, but he was only one man, and he could not oversee everything. So it was with a weary heart and mind that Adam came to bed and extinguished his lantern for what he hoped would be a sound sleep. But his hopes were misplaced.

4

Adam dreamed.

Again, Adam found himself in an enchanted swamp. It was dark and muggy. He slugged through the underbrush, trying to work his way out of a fog that lay before him. Pushing brambles, burrs, and brush out of his way, he struggled forward, slashing his arms on buckhorn spikes…blood dripping from the wounds. He willed himself on. At least the floor of the forest was not a foot deep in mud, but there were vines that caught his boots threatening to tip him, and the waning crescent moon provided little light.

Suddenly ahead he heard the sound of a loom's flying shuttle and the double-thump of a beater bar. His heart quickened and he eagerly crawled through the vines and shrubs toward the source of the sound. There, in a clearing, though partly obscured by hanging Spanish moss, was a loom with a specter sitting on the bench jerking the shuttle launch chords, alternating the treadles, and pulling on the beater. Pushing the Spanish moss and buckthorn aside he came face-to-face with the weaver. It was Esther.

She worked tirelessly, effortlessly. She turned toward him and smiled, but never stopped her rhythm. He looked down at her finished cloth. It was a pure white, plain weave, the warp and weft, perfectly even and tight. She looked up, and beyond the loom. He followed her gaze.

Beyond the loom was the same man he had seen last time, but this time the fog and vision was clear. Adam struggled to move around the loom. The man, his back to Adam, was dressed in the same long, black gown over which he wore a shorter white tunic, and a green stole over his shoulders. The man raised his arms and he turned to the right and left. Then he bowed low and finally kneeled. It was the same ritual, the same incantation as before, but exactly what he was doing Adam had no idea. Adam drew closer. This time the man turned and gazed sternly at Adam. With both hands the man extended his arms towards Adam, and offered him a loaf of bread. The man did not speak, but Adam heard a voice. It was an otherworldly voice, that originated from within his mind. It was not loud but its intimate presence scared him: "This is the man who can relieve you."

Suddenly, he felt someone shaking him. He awoke, and looked around. It was still the middle of the night. Pitch dark. No moon.

"Adam, wake up," Mary Ann said, shaking his shoulder. "What's wrong? Stop your groanin'. You woke me up."

Adam turned toward her. "Sorry. It was a dream." He looked around to get his bearings. It was his bedroom, not the swamp, but the dream haunted him. In the distance he still heard the loom's flying shuttle, the treadles working, and a beater arm compacting the finished cloth, just like his dream. He sat up, listened, and softly said to Mary Ann, "Do you hear that?"

"What?"

"The loom. Is Eve up working?"

"In the middle of the night? I hope not. I don't hear anything."

Adam was spooked. It was probably the dream. But he would not be able to sleep unless he looked around.

5

Adam carried a premonition that the dream was not over. Yet Mary Ann had shaken him awake and now he was standing by the side of his bed with a lit lantern in his hand. It was pitch black outside, and yet he clearly heard the loom working at a furious pace in the gathering hall below. It was a faster rhythm than he had ever heard, and he worried that Eve was going to break something rocketing the shuttle back and forth so fast and stomping on the treadles. He'd have to stop her.

But he also felt fear, a dark foreboding. In his bed clothes and barefoot, he grabbed his shillelagh and headed for the stairs.

As he crept down the steps the sound of the loom intensified. It was indeed their loom he heard. It was not some phantom of a dream. Descending a few steps he stepped on a pebble. It hurt and he jerked his foot up and then swept the stair step with his foot. The pebble went flying and hit the floor below. He was definitely awake now and not dreaming.

Yet, there was no lantern light coming from the gathering hall. He descended a few more steps, the sound grew louder, and his bare feet felt the vibrations as the beater slammed against the finished cloth. Why was Eve weaving in the dark? It was possible, but the energy he felt wasn't coming from a sixteen-year-old girl.

The further down the stairs Adam crept the more frightened he became. By the time he reached the bottom tread he was shaking. Stepping away from the staircase, he lifted his lantern and gazed towards the loom in the dark gathering hall.

*The bench of the loom was closest to him. No one sat on it. The loom, however, was working at breakneck speed. The yoke of the flying shuttle chords were pulled in strong jerks, left and right, by an invisible hand. The treadles moved smartly up and down as if invisible feet had been doing the requisite pattern for years. There was no hesitation as to what treadle combination was next. As Adam stared mesmerized at the treadle patterns, he was dumbfounded. There were not just one or two treadles being depressed at once, but three, and at one point there appeared to be four. Just as mystifying was the beater beam. It slammed so hard against the woven weft that the entire loom shuddered, sending vibrations across the floor board to his feet. But it was when Adam dared to get close enough to the autonomously operating loom to see what was being woven that he panicked. The warp threads appeared to be tight-spun black silk, as was the weft on the shuttle that flew back and forth at lightning speed. He lifted his lantern and looked closely at the cloth. *It was black, in a tight weave with two-inch wide crescent moons already cut out; the warp and weft went missing to create the mysterious hole.*

For a few seconds Adam froze in fear. His heart raced, his breath became shallow, his chest tight. His entire body broke out in a sweat. His fist grew tight around his shillelagh. After he set his lantern on the floor, what he did next was involuntary. His muscles jolted with uncontrolled hostility. He raised his shillelagh and let it rip across the loom's heddles, the most vulnerable part of the loom. One strong swipe of his stick and the string heddles tore into pieces. A second swipe and the warp that had been threaded through the heddles fell into a rat's nest of threads which prevented the treadles from lifting or dropping the warp. The loom came to a dead stop, but Adam didn't. Repeatedly, he slammed his shillelagh into the loom and tried to break anything that his shillelagh, his hands, and his arms could hit. It was a blind rage. But there were limits to his strength. The warp and the take-up beams were too thick. When struck, the shillelagh only transferred the beam's strength to Adam's hands, arms, and shoulders, thrusting Adam back against the floor or the wall. On his hands and knees he crawled under the loom's bench, threw his arms around the treadles and tried to pull them off their support beam, but on the second or third tug the edge of the end treadle tore into Adam's arm causing a deep bruise and bleeding beneath the skin. He got up, still furious, and circled the loom's structure and kicked at its supports. At the warp beam he grabbed the black warp threads and tried to pull them off the loom, but they too cut into his hands; the tight-spun silk was sharp as a knife. He fell back and tucked his bleeding hands under his arm pits...put his head between his legs...and cried.

The noise Adam created roused Mary Ann, Eve, and Henry. They came hurriedly down the stairs with lanterns. They found Adam curled up laying on his side, nursing his hands and arms, trying in vain to restrain cries of despondency. They also found the loom utterly destroyed.

"What is this? What have you done, husband? Have you gone mad?" said Mary Ann. Adam looked up and searched the eyes of his family. Eve was sitting on the floor crying. Henry was back against the wall afraid to move. But Mary

Ann was on her feet and none the worse for wear. "Are you crazy? Look what you've done. All that work Eve has been doing, and you've destroyed it. Why did you do such a thing? I hate the loom but this is madness."

Adam found it hard to believe that Mary Ann was defending Eve. But it wasn't Eve's weaving that he destroyed; it was the devil's own. Eve got up off the floor, tears pouring down her face, walked and fell down among the loom's ruins and caressed what remained of her herringbone pattern of white and natural colored yarns entangled in the now broken parts of the loom. In tears Eve looked at her father, also on the floor, "Why, Papa? Why? Why did you do this?"

Adam was in shock. The black silk, crescent moon weave was gone. In its place was what was on the loom when he had gone to bed—Eve's beautiful woven creation that he had so much adored. He was speechless. He just shook his head, realizing that his nightmare had turned into a nightmare for his whole family. He felt a great sadness. He had been tricked by the Wizard into harming the one person he wished never to hurt. He crawled over to where Eve sat on the floor crying and opened his arms to embrace her, but she recoiled and stared at him as if he was the devil incarnate. The palms of his hands were bloody, and the arms of his night gown were stained with blood that flowed from underneath where he had injured his arms.

"Pa, what happened to you?" cried Eve.

Immediately, Mary Ann came over and examined Adam's wounds. "Let me get bandages," she said, as she got up to leave.

"It was black," Adam said. "It was black, like silk, with crescents cut out... woven that way. It was weaving itself. It was weaving itself. There was no one. Just...just...there was no one."

Adam labored that morning to clean up the mess he had made of the loom. He hated himself for what he had done—for destroying Eve's beautiful weave. He knew that the finished cloth on the take-up beam could be salvaged, but it would have to be hemmed into the rest of the cloth, a scar. Of course, such an assumption was dependent on him repairing the loom and helping Eve continue her pattern. He wondered if he could meticulously rethread the loom so there would be no seam, no scar. Probably not without insane attention to re-threading the warp in reverse, with the partially finished cloth wrapped securely on the take-up beam. The thought gave him a headache to match his daughter's heart ache. But the repair was not going to happen soon. The parts he had destroyed would take days, if not weeks, to fabricate. But he would do it.

He tried to apologize to Eve and say he would fix it, but she would have nothing to do with him, and in tears she ran up the stairs to her room.

6

Adam was desperate to rid his life of his damn Wizard, but all his efforts had failed. The nightmarish vision suggested he needed to struggle through a thicket, perhaps even a muddy swamp. A normal man would ignore the nightmare, but Adam could not. His life had been punctuated with too many visions that were true in some odd and disturbing sense.

He remembered that Mary Ann had not too long ago made a snide comment that she would rather he apply to a rumored conjurer who lived in the mountains south of Winchester. The picture she painted, from rumors, was that the man lived in a thicket surrounded by a swamp. Could that be what his dream was telling him? Was that the man who could relieve him? Mary Ann really knew nothing about this hermit or whatever he was, but some of her friends claimed the recluse could perform miracles, or perhaps he was some kind of faith healer, she supposed.

Adam was convinced he was dealing with something of a religious nature, but he also concluded that any godly power did not exist in Christian ministers. They were all talk but had no practical use. In his mind they only pretended to be ministers of God. They were imposters. He decided he would never again approach them. Perhaps, however, the conjurer in the mountain thicket, which matched his dream, was worth a try.

The area of the country that Mary Ann indicated from which rumors arose was around Massanutten. There were Germans in that region, and being a mountainous area, Adam wondered if this conjurer was a practitioner of "braucherei" or "powering," as he had once heard. It seemed that he had heard tales from his father, grandfather, or their friends going to a braucherei to get a curse removed. If that was the case, tracking down this braucherei might be worth the effort.

It was early in the morning, October 31, All Hallow's Eve, when Adam packed some food in Calvin's saddle, along with his father's Mayntz pistol, slid his shillelagh into his saddle's scabbard, and rode off for Winchester. Mary Ann told him the general store to inquire at, and sure enough the proprietor, Alister Sinclair, knew of the man Adam was seeking. Sinclair said the hermit, who didn't even know his own name, did however claim to banish evil spirits, for a certain sum of money. "Appleton, we calls him," said Sinclair. But Sinclair could not attest to it, nor did he know anyone that could. "A weird sort, if you ask me," said Sinclair. "But what do I know. I do know nails. But about all the good that will do me is to seal my coffin properly."

After obtaining an odd assortment of directions to Appleton's cottage, Adam walked Calvin along a narrow wooded trail—up a mountain, across a stream, across a rock slide, back across the stream, and through a high meadow. Adam found the place, at least he could see it several hundred yards ahead. It was a strangely shaped cabin, not rectangular, but with multiple sides, none of them truly vertical, of mismatched logs and chink, built atop a rock outcropping. The trail came to an end next to a brook with the remains of a hitching post. Adam dismounted and let Calvin's reins drop so the animal could feed and drink as he saw fit. He took his shillelagh and set off on a foot path that led behind the outcropping and up the backside of the hill. The last hundred feet or so Adam attempted to dodge wind chimes and spinning gargoyles hanging low from branches or tall sprawling shrubs. He supposed the chimes would alert Appleton of approaching visitors as he could not help but brush against them. The miniature gargoyles carved from wood were to frighten off fiendish specters too vaporous for the touch-off chimes, or so Adam surmised.

He expected Appleton to be a gaunt, shriveled up old man with long, tangled grey hair and a burr-encrusted beard hanging to his waist. From the tales told of him he'd have a crooked spine leaning on an equally crooked walking stick. When Adam was about a hundred feet from the back the cabin, for that is where the walking-path took him, a short fat man with a bald head, near middle-age, with a straight spine and piercing eyes, waddled around the side of the cabin and gazed down at his visitor.

Adam stopped when he saw the man. If this was Appleton, Adam thought, it was a fitting name. The man's body was round like an apple. His neck was thin and stuck out of his shoulders at an angle like an apple's stem. The man's cheeks were neither sunken nor anemic, but rosy like a polished apple. "I'm sorry to invade your solitude," Adam said. "I'm looking for a man named Appleton, possibly a braucherei." Adam waited, looking up at the man hopefully.

After perhaps a minute of sizing up his intruder, the man spoke in a high-pitched voice: "Your name and business?"

Leaning on his shillelagh, Adam looked up at the man. "I am Adam Livingston, a farmer from Smithfield. My farm has been infested it seems by a spirit that disturbs us—day and night. If you're Appleton, some folks claim you might help me rid ourselves of our menace."

After a moment of consideration, Appleton waved Adam up the hill and led him inside his odd-shaped abode. Eccentric decor would be an understatement. The resident was clearly a pack-rat at heart, but selective. Nothing artificial hung from the walls, but rather stringed collections of dried oak leaves, herbs, gourds, roots, and vegetables. It was a one-room affair. An alcove with bedding to one side, on another side a fireplace and cooking, on another a table with knives lying next to a collection of what looked like weeds with incense burning, on yet another side a divan with crudely stuffed pillows and old, torn blankets, and in the middle a triangular table and three chairs made from branches of a birch tree, the seats woven from rush fibers.

Up close Appleton's face was deeply pock-marked, an earlier aliment. He continued to study Adam as if divining his visitor's true intent. He glanced around the wood slate floor, moved to take a position behind the triangular table and looked up at Livingston. "Mister Livingston, I do indeed banish spirits, both the good and the bad. I'm very good at it. If I trust you and if you pay me what I ask on the spot, you can consider the deal done. If not, you can leave the way you came."

Adam considered Appleton's proposal. "And what is it that you asked to be paid on the spot, and how do you make good on your promise?"

"How I make good on my promise is not for me to decide. But without payment, why should I bother to trust you?"

Adam didn't hesitate, "And why should I trust you if payment is made before the deed? How much do you ask?"

"Three British pounds sterling."

Adam tried not to react. That was a lot of coin, essentially worth two double gold doubloons. He hesitated, but then he considered how good it would be to be rid of the Wizard. Yes, it would be worth two double doubloons. "Mister Appleton, that is a lot of money. But it may be worth it if you can do as you say."

"I can, put your money on the table and we will get started."

Adam made eye contact with the man. Appleton's eyes shifted back and forth, as if looking for a way out. Adam didn't trust men whose eyes shifted. "No, I shan't do it. I will, however, make you this offer. Do the deed, and then I will pay you six-pounds sterling. But if you cannot, I will owe you nothing." Adam maintained eye contact and kept his lips firmly together as if to say, "This is who I am; work with it or no deal." He figured the man was hard up for money. What he was offering, six-pounds, was probably a wind-fall for him. He may be too anxious, but Adam needed a solution, not another big talker who was unable to walk straight.

Appleton looked about the room again. He turned, retrieved a clay jar from a high shelf behind him, removed a well-worn deck of playing cards, replaced the jar, and sat down at the table. "Please be seated, Mister Livingston. Let's see what the spirits have in store for us."

Adam, still dressed in his traveling clothes, sat down and pulled his hat down over his forehead. The brim shielded his eyes from Appleton's, but he would see the table clearly.

Appleton held the deck over the middle of the table. He cut the deck seven times, counting in a strange tongue with each cut. He then placed the deck face down in front of him and ceremoniously picked the top card off the deck and looked at its face. Adam tilted up his head to see Appleton's expression. There was none, as Appleton set the card face up on the table. It was a deck of tarot cards, but Adam knew little or nothing about them. "What does that mean?" he asked.

"That is the moon. It is reversed. You are confused and in fear. You do not know what you are dealing with. Deception is occurring." Appleton looked up at Adam.

Adam nodded his head. "That's right."

Appleton closed his eyes and placed both hands over the deck in front of him. After a moment of murmuring under his breath, he picked up the next card, looked at it, and placed it on the table next to the moon card. "This is the Judgment. It is upright. You are approaching a reckoning, an awakening. It may not be what you expect."

Appleton quickly turned over the next card and placed it next to Judgment. "This is Eight Swords. It is upright. You are imprisoned and the victim of something you have done to yourself. Your curse is not of someone else's doing but your own." Appleton stared at Adam...Adam stared back. "What have you done to bring this onto yourself, Mister Livingston?"

"I don't know what you mean," said Adam. "I've done nothing."

"Nonetheless, the cards do not lie. This is of your own doing." Appleton stared at the four cards on the table, then more cautiously lifted the next card and placed it next to the Eight Swords. It was a picture of a juggler. Appleton was reluctant to speak. His eyes flicked between Adam's face and the face of the card. "This is The Fool." He paused again. "It is reversed. There is either chaos in your life now, or there will be. If there is now, the chaos will increase. That it appears right after Judgment is ominous, very ominous. It says poor judgment has been involved and...stupidity." Appleton looked back down at the cards. As he lifted his hand to draw the next card from the deck, his hands began to shake. It shook so hard and fast that he could not steady his hands to pick up the card. Finally, he thrust his hands into his lap. He was breathing deeply. Without looking up at Adam he said, "Mister Livingston, I am sorry, but I am unable to lift the next card. Can you, sir, turn it over and place it on the table next to The Fool?" In saying this Appleton was reticent, as if he knew what was coming next.

Adam, reticent as well, reached across the table and picked up the next card. He looked at it without showing it to Appleton. It was the picture of a man sitting on a throne with his hand raised, but the man's legs and head were those a goat. At the bottom of the card were the words "The Devil." Adam carefully placed the card next to The Fool.

As soon as Adam pulled his hand back revealing the card's identity, Appleton gasped and jumped up from his chair, backing away from the table. His eyes stared wide-eyed at the cards on the table. Adam looked at the man. Blood seeped from Appleton's furrowed brow. His lips quivered.

In a flash, Appleton gathered up the cards, covered them with a fringed cloth he produced from thin air, placed the cloth containing the cards in a tin container and slammed the lid shut. "This is not for me to do," he said, his suddenly bloodshot eyes glaring at Adam.

"But I will pay you...in gold," Adam said.

This got the man's attention. "Perhaps..." he stuttered, still shaking. Then... "No. No. I cannot. Not me. Not this."

"I will pay you twice your normal rate. Just come and see."

"Ah, but I can see from here, and what I see..." the seer said shaking his head.

Adam stood to make his case, "Please, my family is in dire need. Is there no way?" Adam was standing now, a bit flustered. The man had obviously seen something Adam had not.

The seer's eyes now glossed over. "Please leave me. Quickly, go. Do not come back. I can help you not."

Adam scrutinized the man in whom he had put his last hopes.

Suddenly, the seer spoke to Adam in an otherworldly, resonate voice that shook Adam to the core as if the supernatural had suddenly invaded the room of hanging gourds, dried fruit, and roots.

> Leave me.
> Do not return.
> A curse you are.
> Condemned.
> Dread, death, and
> Despair surrounds you there.
> Leave me.
> Leave me be.
> Never fair.
> Only darkness hearkens there.
> What you need.
> You must heed.
> A rod.
> A staff.
> A robust man of God.

Appleton suddenly grabbed Adam's shillelagh that Adam had left leaning against the table, and attacked Adam with the fighting stick, pushing and shoving Adam out of the strange cabin, and then heaving his shillelagh after him.

7

It was late when Adam returned to Flax Haven. He expected Mary Ann to be in bed, but when he came into the house she was sitting in the gathering hall by the fire cuddling a sleeping George, who at four years was almost too big to be cuddled. She laid George on the rug by the hearth and came to embrace Adam.

"You traveled safe?" she asked, burying her face in his chest.

Adam noticed she had been crying. He kissed her tears. "Yes. What's wrong?"

"Damn spirit scared me out of bed. The bedsheets were moving, clipping, felt something with my feet. Scared me stiff. Couldn't get back to sleep. George began to cry; he normally doesn't. Usually it's Martha. I came down here an hour ago." She backed off and wandered back toward the fire and sat in her rocker, George at her feet.

Adam doffed his coat, gloves, and boots, and leaned his shillelagh in the corner. He sat near her on a stool by the fire, warming his hands.

"Did you find the hermit, or braucherei or whatever you call him?"

Adam shook his head as if to say no, but instead said, "Yes,..." and he told her all that had happened, which was, in the end, a resounding "no." When he was done, she looked to him as if she might fall asleep. "Let's get to bed," he said. "I'll take Georgie up."

As they entered the foyer, Mary Ann took Adam's shillelagh before mounting the stairs. "You may need this. Eve's Wizard has been around tonight."

Not happily, Adam nodded and they climbed the stairs—George in Adam's arms, and the shillelagh in Mary Ann's.

No sooner had Adam settled George in his bed and Mary Ann crawled under her covers than Adam heard someone, it sounded like Eve, descending the stairs. Taking up his shillelagh, Adam left his bedroom and glanced down the stairs. It was Eve in her nightgown and winter coat. She carried a lantern. She stopped at the landing, glanced at the wrecked loom, stepped into her boots, and walked quietly out the front door.

What could she possibly be doing this time of night? He looked back at Mary Ann who seemed to be already fast asleep.

Adam quietly descended the stairs, slipped on his coat and boots, and followed Eve out the front door. He doubted she was up to anything nefarious, but he was curious. He carried no lantern, and there was no moon. It was the night after the new moon. Keeping his distance from Eve, he followed her lantern in the dark. Off the porch steps Adam expected her to walk across the yard to the Darks' cabin. That would have made sense since Bethany had become Eve's surrogate mother. But she turned left, walked past the garden and headed for the barn. He kept his distance. Was she going to the barn to check on Cleopatra or one of the animals? Had she forgotten to water or feed one of them? Or was she checking on Henry to see if he had fulfilled his chores? When she got most of the way to the barn, Adam stepped off the porch and descended the stairs and slowly followed her lantern as she neared the barn.

But Eve did not go in the barn. She walked past it, toward the sheep pen. There was a hill behind the barn from which a ramp was built into the barn's third level, but Eve stayed on the ground level and walked past the barn and the sheep pen and into the wood. As she made her way into the wood, her lantern was occulted by the trees she walked behind. She was following the path to the heart of it, and now he knew where she was headed. Yes, it made sense now. He followed her more closely, but stopped along the path when she did.

She put her lantern down next to the Stranger's grave. The cross she had laid out on top of the grave was still there, but some animals had nudged some of the stones out of alignment. She straightened them. At the head of the grave, she re-stacked the cairn of stone that had partially fallen over. Then, she knelt before the grave, and began to pray out loud. Adam could not hear her, but he wanted to. In fact, he was surprised at himself—he wanted to pray, too.

In the dark, he turned away from her and spoke loudly, to give Eve a sense that he was farther away than he actually was. "Eve. This is your Papa. Are you in the wood?" He turned back around to see what she would do. She turned toward him, although he was sure she couldn't see him. She looked in the darkness at him for a moment, then she spoke loud enough for her voice to reach him. "Yes, Papa. I'm here—at Xavier's grave."

Adam waited for her to turn away from him again, which she did after a moment. He waited a moment longer, then made noise with his boots along the path and walked to where she knelt. He stood next to her. She turned to look up at him.

"Mama woke me," Eve said. "Said I should come here and pray for us...and against the Wizard."

Adam lowered himself to his knees next to her. What he said next to her was hard for him to say in a way, but it was from his heart, and he knew Mary Ann would not hear him, although he did turn and look back toward the barn as if to check that she was not following him as he had followed Eve. "Will you pray for me, too, daughter?"

"Mama says we need to pray for a robust man of God to help us."

Adam froze. A strong shiver jumped up his spine, and he broke out in an instant sweat. "What did you say?"

"It's what Mama said." She hesitated. "We need to pray...for a robust man of God to relieve us."

A second shock jolted Adam's spine. "Why did you say that?"

"Say, what, Papa?"

"What you just said, a man...a robust man to relieve us?"

"That's what Mama said. 'We need a robust man of God to relieve us.'"

Adam tried to hold back his tears. The words of the conjurer flooded back into his mind. "*You need a robust man of God*," and then the voice from his dream: *This is the man who can relieve you.* He asked Eve, "Did I tell you this?"

"Tell me what, Papa?"

Adam's voice shook, "Those words about a robust man and a man to relieve us."

"Papa, what's wrong? Are you okay? You're scaring me."

"I don't know. Those words are what I heard in a dream and then from the man I went to Winchester to find. I was to find a man to relieve us, and then we needed a robust man of God. Those were the words, and just now you said those very words. Are you sure you didn't hear that from me or your stepmother?"

Even said nothing for a moment. Adam looked at her. She was staring down at the ground thinking, he supposed.

"No, Papa. Like I said, Mama told me very clearly to come here and pray for a robust man of God to come and relieve us."

"Then you better pray."

Eve began to pray out loud. "Dear God..."

As she prayed, Adam thought he should close his eyes tight to stop his tears from being shed and Eve seeing them. But as Eve prayed, he realized his eyes were closed very tight—he, too, was praying.

8

Eve was intimidated and surprised that her father had followed her into the woods and found her praying before Xavier's grave. Mama had appeared to her again in a dream. It didn't happen all the time, but it was often enough that Eve paid attention. She was sure Papa loved Esther but being mad at God like he was, she hardly ever told Papa about Mama appearing to her. She was sure he'd get upset with her because Mama's dreams were always about Eve's need to pray for her family, and for all practical purposes Papa had outlawed prayer. But tonight's dream was special, or at least different. Mama was specific. She told Eve to pray for a "robust man to relieve them." When she told Papa what Mama had said he acted strange. She was surprised that he had heard those very words also in a dream and from that conjurer in the southern mountains. Eve knew that going to a fortune teller, seer, or conjurer was wrong, but she also knew that her father didn't want to be preached to by his teen daughter.

Eve prayed a lot, but God never seemed to do anything. Where was God? Why didn't he answer? Who was this robust man that could relieve them? The only robust man as far as she knew was dead and buried in the grave she now knelt before. She knew that her father had not killed Xavier, but she also knew that Xavier's death was somehow Papa's fault. That's why she came tonight to the grave to pray for the robust man. She hadn't been here in a while, but the near destruction of the loom because of what Papa claims he saw—it weaving on its own—frightened her. They definitely needed relief, but all she could do was pray.

Her heart leapt for joy when Papa gave her permission to pray, and in fact told her to pray for him; that was astonishing. She guessed he felt pretty bad about the loom. She hoped it was something more than that. Could he really be turning back to God? She didn't know, but she would gladly obey Papa this night, and pray for her family, the farm, and Papa as he knelt by her side at Xavier's tomb.

But there was one more thing, a secret. She worried a little about what Papa would say or do. She needed courage. No, she needed faith. To herself she whispered a prayer. "Dear God, don't let Papa be mad at me, or take this from me." That gave her the confidence she needed, just that little prayer.

She loosened her coat and carefully removed Xavier's Christian prayer book. Weeks earlier Bethany had given it back to her and told her to hide it, but to use it every night before she went to sleep. The book had half a dozen colored ribbons she could use as bookmarks. She had the red one in a page of one of her favorite prayers. It was a hymn of victory that Moses sang after crossing the Red Sea. She put the book on the ground so her lantern could light the pages. Then she read the prayers.

"Dear Mama, pray for us.

> *I will sing to the Lord, for he is gloriously triumphant; horse and chariot he has cast into the sea. My strength and my courage is the Lord and he has been my savior. He is my God. I praise him; the God of my fathers, I extol him. The Lord is a warrior, Lord is his name! Pharaoh's chariots and army he hurled into the sea....Who is like you among the gods, O Lord? Who is like you, magnificent in holiness? O terrible in renown, worker of wonders, when you stretched out your right hand, the earth swallowed them! I cry to you O Lord, for you are my refuge. You are all I desire in the land of the living; for you are my refuge. Glory to the Father and the Son and the Holy Ghost. As it was in the beginning, is now, and ever shall be, Amen.*

"Oh Mama, pray for us." Eve turned to a yellow ribbon in the book and read another prayer.

> *He who dwells in the shelter of the Most High and abides in the shadow of the Almighty says to the Lord: 'My refuge, my stronghold, my God in whom I trust!' It is he who will free you from the snare of the fowler who seeks to destroy you; he will conceal you with his pinions and under his wings you will find refuge. You will not fear the terror of the night nor the arrow that flies by day, nor the plague that prowls in the darkness nor the scourge that lays waste at noon.*

Eve glanced at her father. His eyes were open and looking at her. He nodded to her as if giving her permission to continue. She turned again to a purple ribbon and read more.

> *Hear, O Israel! The Lord is our God, the Lord alone! Therefore, you shall love the Lord your God with all your heart, and with all your soul, and with all your strength. Take to heart these words which I enjoin on you today. Drill them into your children. Speak of them at home and abroad, whether you are busy or at rest. Into your hands, Lord, I commend my spirit. Protect us, Lord, as we stay awake; watch over us as we sleep, that awake, we may keep watch with Christ, and asleep, rest in his peace.*

Eve turned one last time to a green ribbon.

> *Lord, we beg you to visit our house and banish from it all the deadly power of the enemy. May your holy angels dwell there to keep us in peace, and may your blessing be upon us always. We ask this through Christ our Lord...May the all-powerful Lord grant us a restful night and a peaceful death. Amen.*

Eve was done. She closed the book and concealed it again in her coat, but she didn't get up off her knees. She just stayed where she was for several minutes, praying silently for God to help her father get rid of the ghost, or the Wizard, or the demon, or whatever it was.

Finally she stood. "I'm done now, Papa. Will you walk me back to the house?"

With help from his shillelagh Papa got up off his knees, "Yes, daughter. Those were good prayers."

Eve almost cried when he said that. That was an answer to a prayer for sure, his endorsement. Perhaps she could not pray at dinner yet, for his fear of making her stepmother mad, but she was pretty sure he'd come here with her again, in the dead of night, and pray with her. That was enough…for now, and it was good.

But not everything was good.

As they came out of the woods and rounded the barn, she immediately heard a commotion across the open yard near the house, yet it was too dark for her to see what it was. It sounded like wagons and horses.

"This does not sound safe, daughter," said Papa. "Your prayers may have stirred up the demon that we're trying to eradicate. Stay close." With that he offered his hand and she took it. By the light of her lantern she saw that he had taken up his shillelagh in his other hand and gripped it tight like a fighting stick. He gripped her hand even tighter. She did not object.

As they got closer the sounds of wagons and horses grew louder. She thought of what she had just prayed about, Pharaoh's horses and chariots being cast into the sea. Oh, she thought, if we were only near the sea into which they could be cast. When the Israelites crossed the Red Sea and Pharaoh's army came after them, it must have been very noisy just like this. As they got closer, and Papa held onto her hand ever tighter, a huge dust cloud could be seen totally obstructing their view of the house, although the only light they had was her lantern. She also felt the ground vibrating with the stampede of animals that appeared to be circling the house with the cargo wagons. They came from the left, crossed in front of the house to the right, then up the hill behind the house, then back down the other side and repeated the circuit.

Suddenly, Eve thought of the garden that was to the right of the house. She started toward it, but Papa held her back. She was sure the garden was going to be destroyed. "Don't worry about the garden," Papa said. "Everything's been picked from it for the season. Better it get trampled than you."

Eve felt sick to her stomach. This was both horrible and frightening. She looked toward the Darks' cabin, and saw a lantern or two being lit inside. Momentarily, Sam and Bethany, in coats over their bed clothes, both holding lanterns, came out the front door and walked quickly toward them. Now there were three lanterns, and a cloud of dust enveloping the house could easily be seen. In the dust were wagons, and large black wild horses. They circled the house at a ferocious pace.

"What dis?" said Sam. "Is this you's Wizard, Miss Eve? I never seen anything like dat in my whole life."

Bethany came next to Eve and put her arm around the teen and pulled her close. Quietly, Bethany prayed: "O, God, please deliver us. The devil, he after us. Come Lord Jesus, save us."

Her papa, seeing that Bethany had hold of Eve, dropped Eve's hand. "Sam, give me your lantern."

"Yas, sir." Papa took Sam's lantern, held it high, and moved closer to the surreal stampede of horses and empty cargo wagons. With the lamp her father now held high, Eve could see that what they thought was dust was really dark swirling smoke. For a second she wondered if the house was on fire, but there was no such light or fire in the house, although a moment later the front door opened and she could see Mary Ann with a lantern, and hiding behind her were Henry, George, and Martha.

Papa was now whipping his stick in a circle, stalking ever closer to the mysterious mayhem.

"Missta Livingston," Sam yelled above the cacophony, "we's don't need you's trampled."

But Papa was not ready to back down. He got closer and closer. The whirling smoke began to obstruct what she could see of him.

Bethany suddenly yelled, "Sam, Eve, pray wid me. Now!" Bethany started to pray and Sam and Eve joined in. "Our Father, who are in Heaven. Hallowed be thy name. Thy kingdom come, they will be done, on earth as it is in Heaven…"

They prayed as loud as they could as Papa engaged the wild wraith and swung his shillelagh at the swirling specters.

"And lead us not into temptation, but deliver us from evil."

Papa waded deeper into the morass, swinging his shillelagh violently at the thicket of evil. Tensely, Eve watched as he jumped out of the way of a wagon or a horse, but as they passed he would ruthlessly strike, swipe, and thrust at them. At one point he shoved his shillelagh into the rotating spokes of a wagon wheel. The wheel suddenly shattered, the spinning parts flying in all directions. Yet as soon as the wheel disintegrated, so did the rest of the wagon. It just disappeared. But there were many wagons. He struck at the head of a stampeding horse. The horse reared up to trample Papa, but he dodged its deadly hoofs and stabbed the wraith in the chest like a spear. Instantly the horse exploded into a cloud of black smoke. The cloud rushed at Eve, Sam, and Bethany and enveloped them. It was hot, and carried an obnoxious smell like that of a privy pit under a noonday sun…minus the horde of flies.

9

Adam was unaware that something had changed in him. He was no longer afraid or frustrated. He was provoked, angry, and mad. He no longer believed that he was in control of the universe, or even his farm. The mediocre harvest was evidence of that. But he *was* in control of himself. He could not attack a spook that hid beneath the floor boards, or cowered in dark drawers, or with invisible hands shoved stacks of dishes to the floor. This spectacle of specters, however, that encircled his house and kept him from entering it to protect his wife and children was something else.

Fearlessly, he entered the swirling mass of smoke, horses, and wagons. Wielding his shillelagh like Saint Michael's sword, he slashed, stabbed, and struck with severity. Like a swashbuckler he scrambled wheel spokes, hobbled horses, sliced the sinews of equine elbows and stallion shins, and liberally freed his fury at the fiends. With each strike the specters splintered and fell sundered. While the wraiths were vulnerable ghosts, horse hoofs nonetheless bruised and bloodied his body, and wagons waged war with his legs, arms, and his shillelagh. One by one, however, strike-by-strike, the devices of the belligerent demon dissolved and disappeared until there was none. He had won, but for how long? He knew they would return.

As bold as he had become, the battle bludgeoned him. When the smoke cleared, Adam collapsed unconscious amidst the fresh wagon ruts and hoof hollows at the foot of his porch.

Adam found himself being carried through the dark swamp of his previous dreams. Through the thicket, thorns, and tangles he was pushed, pried, and plowed until at last he came again to the man in the black gown, white tunic, green stole, and the stern face. The man nodded at Adam, held out a gold chalice, even as the same otherworldly voice resonated in his mind: "This is the man who can relieve you." The man leaned close, reached out, and laid his open hand on top of Adam's head.

It was Mary Ann's hand. He was lying on his back and his body ached, as if he had fallen and rolled down a rock-strewn cliff. He had been carried up the porch steps, through the foyer, up the staircase, into his bedroom, and laid on his bed. A wash basin was on the side table. Mary Ann was bathing his head and face with a warm wash cloth. His face stung from open cuts, so did his arms and legs. "What happened?" he asked her.

"We're not sure," she said.

Adam looked about. Around the bed looking down at him were Sam, Bethany, Eve, Henry, and the twins. Mary Ann said, "You're okay now, we think. Can you move your arms and legs?"

He could and he did, but they hurt.

"It's gone now," she said.

"What?" he said.

"The horses and wagons…and the smoke."

"It was the Wizard, Papa," said Eve. "Don't you remember? We had just returned from…." she hesitated "…from the woods."

Adam looked admiringly at his daughter for a few moments. Tears formed in his eyes. "Yes, I remember. I remember well."

10

Most Feared Master of Disasters,

No doubt you are trembling in your heeled spats that I have utterly failed once again. You have seen Livingston praying, of all the grotesque things, at the Stranger's grave site with his pious daughter. You think this indicates some mystical conversion of heart. Don't believe everything you see, and only half of what I tell you. Yes, I'm a liar like the best of you. Have nothing to fear, but love itself. Do not lose heart. Livingston following his daughter and then kneeling at the grave site is not extraordinary. It is the action of a weak man entirely under my control. I'm just letting out a little line, giving him some slack. In a moment I'll yank it back hard, and hook him for good. Besides, the injuries he sustained battling my wraiths will not only slow him down but give him pause of ever physically assaulting me again. He will always lose.

As evidence that what I tell you is true (although we both are obligated to honor falsehoods), look at his mediocre harvest that I inflicted, and consider what happened to the loom after my grand artistic apparition. I fooled him, made him look, and the loom suffered the consequences. That pugnacious device we've come to hate was once again destroyed...at Livingston's own hands no less. Don't doubt my resources.

And once again I obscured his midnight vision, although the vision *does* concern me because I did not instigate it, but only obscured it. It's his Guardian again I suspect, attempting to give guidance, toward what I do not know.

On the other hand, consider how the Darks were suddenly going to leave Livingston and the glorious slave state of Virginia upon the expiration of their indenture. But what happened? Bethany Dark had the bold idea to renew the contract. And whose idea was that? Don't think for a moment I don't have this under control. Yes, yes, I realize the new indenture comes with expanded physical freedoms and an increase in pay, but they are still slaves in my book. Don't think either that I haven't taken into account that their absence from Livingston would have set him spiritually adrift and made him more vulnerable to us. Perhaps. But consider that now Livingston is not motivated to change anything. He's relaxed, his guard is down, he'll embrace the status quo and that makes him all the more vulnerable.

In Cahill's case, do you see how I'm advancing his deformation? The idea I put into McSherry's head to ask the bishop for money has escalated just as I planned. The bishop is not someone who likes to be challenged, especially if the challenger is right.

But my proudest accomplishment is how the confessional was converted so easily into a psychological brothel. I expect a promotion after I deliver. I'll be bringing not only Cahill but a few others, I suspect. Trust me; he'll remember nothing. Here's to ghosts, gallows, and graveyards.

At your sinful service,
Cyn Namrasit, OPSD

Part Seven:
Priests

For the invisible things of Him,
from the creation of the world,
are clearly seen, being understood by the things
that are made—his eternal power and divinity:
so that they are inexcusable.
Because they knew God, but
have not glorified Him as God,
or given Him thanks;
but became vain in their thoughts,
and their foolish heart was darkened.
For professing themselves to be wise,
they became fools.
Wherefore God gave them up
to the desires of their heart...

(Romans 1:20-24)

Chapter 44
Unfortunate and Unforeseen

My Lord Maréchal,

The juxtaposition of Adam's unforeseen time praying with Eve at Xavier's grave, and then battling the swirling wraith that encircled his house, presented him with a serious dilemma. He had deliberately weaned himself of faith, and schooled himself in skepticism. It was not reasonable that a man, least of all a stubborn German like Adam Livingston, could fluidly plunge from one to the other. He had his integrity to protect, and peace with an agnostic wife to preserve. It is true that he felt at peace kneeling and praying with Eve, but if you had asked, he wasn't really praying. He was letting Eve do it. He didn't feel he had the right or capacity to pray, not from his heart at least.

He had found a balance with Mary Ann that allowed him to love her, to be intimate with her, and he felt respected in his own house because of their accord. In spite of the apparent supernatural nature of the Wizard's haunts, she refused to acknowledge God or even the underworld. She had said to him more than once, "If God exists, and is all benevolent and powerful as some claim, why the war that caused us so much sorrow, and why this spirit that brings fear, loathing, and discomfort to our lives. We have no need for whatever realm it is that disrupts us so." Adam didn't argue with her. He accepted it for the sake of living peaceably with a woman who brought order to his life, and even love to his bed.

He had arrived at an age when he realized he could not have everything he wanted. The harvest had been pathetically wretched by his former standards, but then he imagined what it might have been had he not worked so hard at making it otherwise. Life was a delicate balance between good and evil, both of which he decided he had to live with and accept. He would find peace where he could find it here and there. If that means getting up in the dead of night and kneeling next to a grave with Eve to live at peace, although a secretive event, so be it. It was a paradox—he could not explain it, but perhaps he could live it.

Deep down he still could not accept God's sovereignty regarding Esther's death. He still could not qualify it. He wasn't a bad person, so if there was a God and he was just, how could he accept the punishment that her sudden death represented? He couldn't. So, he didn't understand prayer, or why Eve found solace in it. Perhaps she had to experience some catastrophe in her life before she accepted the contradiction that life proposed. But wasn't the death of her much beloved mother a catastrophe?

It was going to take more than a prayer or a swirling mass of ghosts to bring such a stubborn man to a full understanding of reality.

So it was that the winter of '96–'97 was spent for the most part processing flax, for though the harvest was inferior by Livingston's standards, its produce was not unappreciated. He still had to work hard, for failure to do so would only mean more trouble.

Then there was the loom. Parts had to be fabricated, and its repair facilitated. Mary Ann claimed she did not need it and she was glad to see it out of commission, but Adam knew she enjoyed and appreciated its output. In truth, he wasn't sure of his true motivation for the long hours required to effect the repair. His love for Eve and her loyalty during these difficult times was part of it, for she had learned to mitigate her stepmother's anger in the use of the loom. He suspected, however, that the true motivation for an operative loom was seeing finished cloth taken up on the cloth beam. It made his labors in the field complete. Linen cloth produced by the loom was the purpose of planting flax in the first place.

Fixing the loom required perseverance and not a little concentration, but he had it done before Christmas. His daughter thanked her papa with a hug, and immediately began to prepare a fine white wrap for plain weave table linens and napkins. She wasn't sure why she chose such a simple project, but she felt good about it. She planned to weave a large cloth, and then cut and hem it into different sizes. There would be a large cloth for the entire table and then smaller pieces for napkins and placemats—all white, all very pure and simple. She also decided that she would work hard during the non-haunting days of the month to finish and remove the cloth from the loom so when the new moon approached all the finished cloth would be safe in her protected heirloom chest. She was surprised by the strength of her motivation, but she persevered. She would be rewarded, but it would be months later.

Adam had not forgotten his nightmares of the robust man who could relieve him, but in his dalliance did nothing to find such a man. He no doubt assumed that he had done his bit asking those various ministers to come and exorcise his house. Yet the ministers were all spiritually impotent and nothing changed. It is for the likes of men like Adam Livingston that God is eternally patient, desiring them to come to him.

At the same time, there is a difficulty that God's patience creates when men close to him fall away. Such was the case of Fr. Denis Cahill. It was during this same time, the winter of '96–'97, that two prongs of attack by the enemy found purchase.

The Shepherd's Town laymen finished their weather-boarded chapel before winter set in providing Fr. Cahill a place to stay whenever he came. Conveniently, he could arrive anytime of day or night and know that there was a place ready. Because of this convenience he could schedule Masses, confessions and classes at anytime without worry that his schedule would conflict with the goings and comings of the Menghinis. It was unfortunate and unforeseen, however, that progress on the Shepherd's Town chapel, placed Fr. Cahill on a dangerous path.

Your Servant,
Fr. Smith

Chapter 45
Entirely Forgotten

1

It was the middle of the night in the middle of June, 1797, when Eve undertook her monthly prayer vigil at Fr. Xavier's grave. After the one and only time Papa followed her to the grave site and knelt with her, he never came again. She guessed the aftermath of battling the Wizard's specters had scared him off. It had taken a good two weeks for his battle wounds to heal. She was proud of her father for his courage to do physical battle, but she wished he was more open to doing spiritual battle. Since that night, months ago, she had hoped he might really change and turn back to God. But nothing happened and her hope faded like a moonless night.

On this night, while walking back to the house after praying at Xavier's grave, an idea occurred to her. While she did not know any robust Christian men that might relieve them of the Wizard, although Sam might partly qualify, it occurred to her that she did know a robust Christian woman—Anastasia McSherry. Eve remembered that Anastasia was an outspoken Christian and having such an acquaintance who was both rich and beautiful inspired Eve.

She had not seen or heard anything of the McSherrys since the last invitation to their third son's christening open house. That was more than three years ago. The McSherrys' boys would have grown since then. What were they like, she wondered. She hoped they weren't like Henry. That would be a handful for Anastasia. Yet she wondered: Would her father ride with her to the McSherrys' for a visit, *just a friendly visit* she would say? And while there, while Papa talked with Mister McSherry, perhaps she could persuade Anastasia to walk with her through the Rosary garden and pray with her.

Later that day, when she found her father in the barn and away from her stepmother, she asked him if he would go with her to the McSherrys' to visit with Anastasia and her boys. She was quick to remind him that he might like to talk with Mister McSherry. Adam agreed and they decided to drop in a few days later. She was excited, but she said nothing to Mary Ann, Bethany, or Henry for fear some objection would be lodged and the visit canceled.

She wasn't sure exactly how her father had finagled it, but two days hence, right after lunch, Sam rigged a sidesaddle for Eve on Sizemore, and with her father on Calvin they set off to visit the McSherrys. She hoped they were home. What if they weren't? In that case she would ask her father to walk through the Rosary garden with her, and she would pray, hoping he would join her.

But the McSherrys were home, at least there were people milling around the shaded garden patio behind the house where a table was set for eating. As they rode up she counted three women and three boys. The boys were chasing each other all over the place. She hastily recalled the dates of the christening open houses to recall the boy's names. The tallest boy, waving a stick in the air like a sword, must be Richard, Jr., who was five. Chasing him with a "sword" of his own was William, who would have to be four. The smallest was ignoring his older brothers and was chasing a pair of white geese. That was probably Dennis, age three. Good! They were receiving guests, so she and her father would not be an interruption.

As soon as they dismounted, Anastasia came to the side yard and the hitching rail to greet them. She remembered them both. She asked Papa about the harvest; it was not good, and she was sorry to hear that. She asked Eve if she was weaving, to which Eve replied that she was.

Standing in the garden patio looking after Anastasia, while also keeping one or more eyes on the rambunctious boys, were two young women. Eve noticed they didn't look as if they were visiting. They were wearing house dresses, and seemed to be keeping tabs on the boys as if they were nannies. Could Anastasia have hired *two* nannies for her boys? They were rich, but Eve had never heard of such a thing.

Anastasia drew Eve and her father to the patio: "Mister Livingston, Eve, I'd like you to meet two close friends of mine who are living with us these days." She took the hand of the younger of the two women, and pulled her close. "This is Catharine Cahill"; then, gesturing for the older but still youthful and beautiful woman to join them, "and this is her friend Letitia McCartney. Both came from Ireland to live in the United States just a year ago now."

The women offered their hands to both her and Papa, but Eve felt like a curtsy and so she did and the young women, giggling, curtsied in response, but, *oh, so much finer,* Eve thought.

"Catharine," Anastasia continued, "is the sister of our priest, Fr. Denis Cahill, and Letitia, well, she's Catharine's friend as I said. They both came from Ireland...oh, I said that already. Anyway, that's where Fr. Denis is from, and where Richard was born as well. Come, have some tea with us. We're letting the boys wear themselves down before their afternoon nap."

"Is Mister McSherry around?" asked Eve. "My father would love to visit with him."

"Oh! I'm sorry he's not. He's on a four-day trip to Hagerstown and his rentals in that area, trying to collect rents and check on harvests. I'm sorry you missed him. But thank you for coming. Eve, it's so wonderful to see you," Anastasia put her arm around Eve and pulled her along to the garden table and tea.

Catharine leaned into Anastasia and quietly asked, "Do you think it is time?"

Anastasia scanned the yard for the boys' whereabouts. "Yes, it's time. Thank you."

And with that Eve saw that indeed Anastasia had two nannies. Catharine and Letitia gently corralled their charges, took the sticks from their fists, brushed off their shorts and tops, ushered them to a door in the house, removed their shoes, and they were off to their naps.

"Come, have some tea," said Anastasia suddenly turning somber. She gestured to two chairs at the table in which Eve and her father sat. Anastasia produced two clean tea cups and saucers of exquisite imported china, and poured hot tea into them. "Tell me what's been happening at Flax Haven. How is Mary Ann? Trust me, I'm not a gossip. But Felicity Randall is a close friend, and she told me Mary Ann and the twins had stayed with her at Travelers Rest for a while. I am so glad Mary Ann is back home. Tell me what's going on. Can I or Richard be of any assistance?" With that she placed the cups and saucers before Eve and Papa, "Sugar?" She opened a container of sugar, put a silver spoon in it, and placed it near their cups.

Eve had never seen a silver spoon before, or the exquisite china. She was stunned. She carefully took hold of the tiny sugar spoon and shoveled a spoonful into her cup.

"Oh, I'm sorry," said Anastasia, "here's a spoon to stir in your sugar and perhaps cool the tea. Letitia just brought it out before you came." Anastasia handed Eve a much larger spoon, also silver, and placed a second one on her father's saucer.

"Thank you," both Eve and her father said at once.

Anastasia refilled her own cup, ignored the sugar, and sat down to listen.

Eve and her father were silent at first. They were not expecting such a receptive and ready ear. Her father looked at Eve as if to ask if she wanted to speak first.

Eve did want to talk with Anastasia and tell her what was going on, but she had figured Papa would have been with Mister McSherry and her conversation with Anastasia would be private. Now what? She looked at her father one last time. He smiled at her and nodded, as if to give her permission to speak. She smiled at Papa, said a prayer under her breath, and spoke: "Perhaps you've heard. We've been beset by a haunting—a terrible haunting. It's cut up almost all our linens, it's killed our chickens, keeps us awake at night, and all kinds of horrible other things. My Papa doesn't know what to do. I pray, but God doesn't seem to hear."

Very softly and quite tenderly Anastasia said, "I'm sorry. I have heard. It seems many know all about your trials."

Eve looked up at her downcast papa, his head was bowed in defeat. She didn't suppose this is what he was expecting when he agreed to come. Like many times in the past he was silent and let her talk for them both.

"Did I hear right that some ministers came and prayed over you and your house?" Anastasia inquired.

This time Eve looked to her father for an answer.

"Yes," said Adam. "Several. From different churches. Every time the spirits, or the Wizard as Eve calls it, scared them away, or cut up their clothes, or heaved fire and rocks at them. That's what caused Mary Ann to dispose herself to Travelers Rest. The Randalls were perfect hosts for her, by the way. I was so appreciative of their care for her and the twins."

"Tell her about the dream, Papa," said Eve.

"No, I don't think..."

"Please," begged Eve.

Her father looked kindly at her. He was warming his hands around the delicate cup. He shook his head slightly, pulled his mouth taut, and glanced up at Anastasia as if to ask permission.

"What about your dream, Mister Livingston? I'm not an interpreter of dreams, but I am curious. I can share it with Richard when he returns, if you want."

Adam nodded, took a sip of the sweet tea, and began. "At times, throughout my life, I see or hear things that no one else does. They're like nightmares except they usually happen during the day. I never know what they mean, exactly. But later something happens that relates. I was working in my barn late one night and suddenly I saw an inferno of flames, and I heard animals bellowing as if trying to escape. I thought my barn was on fire. I checked but it wasn't. Yet, days later I heard that a neighbor's barn had burned down...that same night. I also had visions on two separate occasions of infant deaths in either tragic or horrific situations that scared me deeply. They came true when my first wife, Esther, had two miscarriages. And then, the most terrifying of all after our little Amy, she was only month old, our first child..."

Adam had to stop as he began to sob. Eve was riveted, she had never heard these stories of her siblings. She remembered her siblings' graves, she remembered her mother telling her about the deaths, but she had no idea that Papa had foreseen them in these frightening ways.

Adam collected himself and continued. "Then there was Amy, the joy of our life. She was beautiful and sweet and her laugh...she laughed every time I came in from the fields and she saw me. Her little arms and legs would shake with excitement because she knew I was going to pick her up. I can still hear her today. She was starting to talk. We loved her so much." Adam took out a handkerchief and wiped his eyes and nose. "When she was about seven months old, I had another premonition. It was of a child's funeral. There were people at the funeral but I couldn't see their faces. And the child in her beautiful casket, her face was blocked from me as well. I didn't recognize anyone, but I knew I was alone. Esther wasn't there. I kept looking for her but she had disappeared. When the vision ended, I somehow knew the funeral was for Amy. But I couldn't bear to tell Esther. Then, three days later..."

Eve watched as suddenly her father broke down in tears and deep sobs. He buried his face in his hands and handkerchief. She leaned over to him and hugged him. She suddenly realized how important she was to him.

After a minute, "…she died in her sleep. At the funeral Esther was so devastated, three dead children she had given me, that she could not attend the funeral. She cried for days after."

"Mister Livingston," began Anastasia, "I am so sorry to hear this." She looked up with a thin smile at Eve. "Is Eve the child that came after that?"

Eve turned to her father. She knew the answer, but this was a special moment. He nodded his head vigorously. "Yes, and we were so happy, and I still am." And he let out another burst of tears, turned, and hugged Eve tightly for a long time.

Finally, Adam regained his composure. "I'm sorry for this…this unmanly behavior. I'm not sure why I'm like this. It was so long ago." He straightened up and wadded his damp handkerchief into a ball in his folded hands. "So, I've had these premonitions or visions and I never know what they're about until it's too late. And I'm afraid to tell others about them because it will scare them, or me."

He stopped talking as if he was being reminded not to say anything more. Eve turned to Anastasia with a pleading look on her face. Anastasia caught her meaning, and turned to Adam. "Mister Livingston, I think you need to tell us, Eve and me. Now would be a good time."

Eve spoke up, "It was something to do with the Wizard, you'll see. Papa has had the vision or dream several times now. Right, Papa?"

Adam collected himself yet again and began, "The dream is always pretty much the same. Sometimes it starts from the beginning as I'm clawing my way through a dense forest or jungle. It's night, although there is some moon light. I'm driven to get somewhere but I'm not sure where I'm going. Eventually, I see a light in the distance, and I push the thickets aside, pull my boots out of deep mud, and I climb over fallen tree trunks. I get cut up in the process. There's a clearing, and a man in the clearing. He's wearing robes, and he's performing some kind of incantation, waving his arms up and down, he turns to the right and the left. He kneels, then he stands up and turns around. He's wearing a long black robe, sometimes with a white bib-like covering and a green stole. I get close enough, usually, that I can touch his robes, but as soon as I do, he disappears. Except…except the last few times as I reach out to touch him, he turns and looks at me even before I can touch him. His face is always stern, he has red stubble for a beard. One time he held out a loaf of bread to me, and another time it was a gold chalice. Sometimes he lays his hands on my head, and then I hear a voice. It's not the man's voice, it's an otherworldly voice and it says, 'This is the man who can relieve you.'"

Eve had never heard the whole of his dream or the part about the bread or the gold chalice, but there was something oddly familiar about it. She had only heard about the voice, the part about: *This is the man who can relieve you.* As he talked his eyes were cast down and at times even closed as he re-envisioned what he had seen.

Where Anastasia before had been relaxed and even sat back in her chair sipping her tea, now she was sitting ramrod straight, even leaning forward a bit, her eyes wide and her mouth agape. "Mister Livingston," Anastasia said in a quiet but astonished voice, "the image you paint sounds very much like...the Mass."

"The what?" asked Papa.

Instantly, Eve recognized what her father had described. "Papa, it's a Catholic Mass, like the one I attended with Mister Charles in Conewago years ago."

"Yes," said Anastasia, "that's what I meant. It sounds like a Catholic Mass. The man in your dream is a Catholic priest celebrating Mass."

"Oh, I *know* it is," said a confident Eve.

Her papa turned to Eve, "Just how do you know daughter? You only went that one time."

"But I paid attention. And I've been reading about it in that prayer book from Fr. Xavier."

"So, that's where you got that book. You stole it from our guest."

"Our *dead* guest, yes. Mama told me to take it after he died."

"The bread and the gold chalice did it for me," said Anastasia.

"Papa, do you know why I go to Fr. Xavier's grave to pray?"

Adam stared down at his daughter and slowly shook his head.

"Because Mama said we need a robust man to relieve us and then she told me to pray at Fr. Xavier's grave. I think he's the robust man who can relieve us."

"Excuse me," said Anastasia. "Who is Fr. Xavier and who is Mama you're talking about?"

2

Sunday, June 25, 1797.

The following Sunday was a special day for Anastasia McSherry. After her tea with Adam Livingston and Eve, she had invited them to attend Mass with her family. She had told them to come to the house early Sunday and ride in one of the two open carriages. It would mean Richard would have to hire an extra carriage and driver from Charles Town. She, Richard, Eve, and Adam would ride in one and the boys would ride with Catharine and Letitia in the second. Mass was scheduled for noon. The chapel at Shepherd's Town was twenty miles from the McSherrys, so it would take about two hours trotting for the carriages to get there.

Anastasia told Eve and Adam there was no need to get dressed up, as many of those who attended Mass were farmers and didn't have formal wear. Anastasia was surprised then when Eve showed up in a long dress nearly suited for a ball. It had a fluffy white choker-collar, long sleeves, made from blue and white linen that reminded her of the flax blossom. She had put up her hair and dressed up an everyday white bonnet with a blue ribbon tied in a bow below her chin. For his part, Adam came in natural canvas trousers that laced up his calves for wearing his knee-high riding boots, but he wore no boots, only shoes without buckles. He wore a high-collar white shirt and black bowtie, but the shirt was all but covered by a blue woolen waistcoat. She thought it kind of hot for the weather, though the carriage ride would be breezy.

Anastasia wore her lime green dress with white lace trim, and a dark green fancy hat with peasant feathers for trim. Richard, as usual for Sundays, put on his buckle shoes over white silk stockings, mustard breeches, a white ruffled shirt, a matching mustard waist coat with brass buttons that were unbuttoned from the top half down to show off his shirt's ruffle.

In the carriage Anastasia and Eve sat with their backs to the front and Richard and Adam faced forward. Richard had returned Friday from his tour of the northern Virginia and Maryland communities so there had been little time for him to catch up on why their neighbors would be joining them for Mass, although Anastasia had told him some of the stories Felicity had shared with her of the Livingstons' plight. Anastasia felt sorry for the Livingstons, but Richard was irritated that she had invited them to attend Mass. He explained to her that while he found Mister Livingston an innovative farmer with a good head on him, this haunting business was suspicious. Being skeptical of the rumors, he didn't believe as others did, but he acquiesced to Adam and his daughter riding along to meet Fr. Cahill.

"*Relieve you!* Those were the words used?" asked Richard.

"Aye," said Adam.

Richard turned to Anastasia, "Again, my dear, what made you think it was a Catholic Mass he was seeing?"

Anastasia began to answer, but Richard, who was irritated about the inconvenience, cut her off. It was not like him, but she had decided to be tolerant. Richard was wise to the ways of the world far more than she, and his standing in the surrounding communities was proof of it. She was in his debt and still very much in love with the former Irish bachelor.

"Oh yes, I remember…the robes, the bread, and the brass goblet, "Richard said.

"Gold," said Anastasia. "Right, Mister Livingston, it was gold, not brass?"

"Yes, Madam. It appeared to be gold, not brass."

"Well," continued Richard, "Father Denis is persnickety and wary. The man has battled bigots, thieves, murderers, and the devil himself. He suffered the same in Ireland and New Orleans. Once he arrived in the United States you must add 'priests' and 'bishops' to the list. Sir, you should know that many in Shepherd's Town have heard of your clipping ghost. Best keep a low profile. They say it is your well-deserved fate."

Anastasia cringed at Richard. He saw her look, but turned to watch the passing scenery. *The poor man,* Anastasia thought of her husband, *all he seems to know is his own opinion.*

"That it may be," said Adam, "but I'm unsure how it is."

There was an awkward lull in the conversation.

"I do wish Missus Livingston could have joined us," said Anastasia changing the subject.

"She would have nothing to do with this," said Adam.

"Has that always been the case?" asked Anastasia.

"The former Missus Livingston, my wife Esther, and Eve's mother, would have come cheerfully. But if that were the case…" Adam seemed to have lost his train of thought. It appeared to Anastasia as if he was experiencing a moment of grief remembering his first love.

Glaring at Richard who was staring out the window aimlessly, she said, "Put your mind at ease, Mister Livingston. That you should go with us today, I have no doubts."

In an attempt to coax some tolerance from Richard, who sat across from her, Anastasia nudged his boot. He nudged back, kept his face turned outward, and smiled. That was enough; he got the message, or so she hoped.

3

Adam grew more anxious and alert as they drew closer to Shepherd's Town. He gazed attentively ahead, studying the faces of men that came into sight. Perhaps he was naive, but he wanted to believe that a man in Shepherd's Town would look like the stern man in his dream, the man Anastasia claimed was a Catholic priest. Others would not suppose that the image in a dream could be faithfully reproduced in reality, but Adam Livingston was of a different persuasion. His years of exposure to dreams that came true in peculiar and frightful ways had him on edge and observant.

Before they arrived in the village of Shepherd's Town their steeds pulled the two carriages up a slopping hill. At the top, with a view of the town and the sharp bends in the Potowmack River, was a white weather-boarded chapel. A sign over the entrance read, "St. Agnes Catholic Chapel." The main building featured a high gabled roof with a cross at the peak. There was a large wood-planked porch surrounding the French door entrance. The porch was only a few inches off the ground, so no steps were necessary. But over the porch and half the height of the main roof was an extended roof that also provided some protection for the entrance. Either side of the entrance were two large, plain, rectangular windows. To the east side of the church proper was a lean-to addition with a second entrance and a very small porch and roof, as well as a few windows facing east. It was not an architectural marvel like many of the Protestant edifices, but it appeared solidly built and practical. Along the wagon path leading to the chapel were carriages, buggies, and horses hitched to posts as well as in an adjacent field.

The carriage drivers stopped near the chapel entrance and the Livingstons,

McSherrys, Catharine, Letitia, and the boys joined others walking to the entrance.

Anastasia walked with Adam. "Fr. Cahill will greet us following Mass, but there will usually be many that will want to chat with him, so we will have to be patient."

"I understand," said Adam. "I just hope I can persuade him to pay us a visit."

"Be content," said Anastasia, "Richard and I will testify of your need. Won't we, Richard?"

"Aye, as sure as the sea is calm," said Richard.

Anastasia scowled at her once-Irish bachelor, then smiled at Adam, but Adam got the message—Richard was wary of Adam's mission and his spook.

Inside two dozen couples and children sat quietly on split-log benches. Some prayed and others chatted quietly. At the front there was a modest platform. To one side there was a lectern. Against the back wall was an altar with six lighted candles already burning and in the center an open book resting on a stand. On the back wall above the altar was a three-foot high crucifix. The cross was carved from a dark wood, and the body of Christ that hung on it appeared to be cast in white plaster.

Adam hung back. Richard headed up the center aisle to a bench near the front. Anastasia, however, gestured for Catharine and Letitia to herd the boys into a rear bench. She followed, tugged Eve's coat sleeve to follow her, and with her eyes beckoned Adam to follow Eve. Richard meanwhile had walked to a bench near the front when he realized that his entourage had not followed him. He turned to see his family and friends settling into the rear bench. Adam saw Richard's face register disappointment, whereupon Richard returned to sit next to Adam. As he did, some of the women and men who were already settled turned and gawked at the McSherry clan—sitting in the rear. Adam figured sitting in the rear was unusual for the McSherrys and the others were curious as to why. Perhaps it was his imagination, but the curious eyes seemed to lock onto him and Eve, then turn back to one another and whisper astonishment.

Remembering Richard's advice to keep a low profile, Adam pulled the brim of his hat down over his eyes to hide. But Richard nudged Adam in the side and shook his head. Adam glared at Richard not understanding his meaning. In response, Richard grimaced sternly, reached up and yanked Adam's hat off his head and put it in his lap. No longer able to hide, Adam stared back at two ladies who were still turned around staring at him. As soon as he made eye contact with the women, they averted their gaze and turned back towards the front.

When Adam turned his attention back to his companions he noticed that everyone in his row was kneeling and praying except himself. Even Eve was kneeling, with her hands folded in prayer. He looked around the congregation, a few others were so postured, but most were sitting, so he did the same. Sitting looked a lot more comfortable than kneeling on a hard wood floor.

After a few minutes Richard, Anastasia, and the others got up off their knees and sat quietly, except for the boys, who could hardly sit still in spite of the adult women sitting between them, which didn't seem to stop them from trying to tease and poke each other.

After exercising some patience, a bell rang at the back of the room and things got underway. Everyone stood, and an unseen man began singing a hymn; everyone joined in with him, but it was in Latin, so Adam understood nothing; all he could do was be patient again and wait.

While they were singing, a man in a black cassock with a raised collar, and a square black hat walked up the center aisle. This was probably the McSherrys' priest, Fr. Denis Cahill. A white tunic over the cassock hung to his thighs. A green stole lay across the back of his neck. Adam could not take his eyes off the priest's back. The black cassock and white tunic were identical to the gowns from his nightmares. Adam caught himself holding his breath and forced himself to breathe.

When Fr. Cahill arrived at the front of the church, he bowed, crossed himself, and stood with his back to the congregation until the hymn ended. Then, he turned to the congregation his arms outstretched and said, "Dominus vobiscum."

Adam suddenly gasped. It was the man from his dreams—same face, same blue eyes, and same trimmed red beard. The green stole that hung on his neck was crossed in front before it draped to the floor. The cassock had an up-turned collar and was buttoned down the front. Fr. Denis Cahill was the man from his dream. As the congregation responded to Fr. Cahill, "Et cum spiritu tuo," Adam grabbed hold of Richard's arm and blurted out, "That's the man...the man from my dream. He's the one who can relieve me."

The Mass suddenly came to an abrupt although temporary halt as everyone in the nave turned around, and in pregnant silence gaped at Adam. But Adam continued to cry out, this time to Fr. Cahill: "Please! You must help me."

Richard threw a cynical smile at Anastasia, then took firm hold of Adam's hand and arm and whispered: "In due time, Mister Livingston. In due time."

Adam was shaking from the shock of it all as Richard eased him down to the bench.

A moment later Fr. Cahill continued celebration of the Mass, which would have been otherwise unremarkable except Adam experienced a premonition during the Bible readings. He had heard before the story of the Israelites crossing the Red Sea, but when the story was read this time he suddenly had a vision.

A pillar of fire flew down from the sky. At first it separated the Egyptian Army from the Israelites, but then it bloomed outward and enveloped both the Egyptians and the Israelites, torching everything in sight. Egyptian chariots and the Israelite wagons burned like dry kindling. Egyptian war horses evaporated in whirlwinds of fire, and lightning hit Israelite cows which exploded in grotesque ways. The conflagration came without warning, leaving behind the burned, blackened ruins of spears, chariot wheels, and wagon decks.

The vision was over in a flash, but it was nonetheless vivid. For the rest of the Mass he thought of nothing else, and wondered what it meant. In the past his premonitions had warned of something bad in the future, yet the vision and the intended message were never clear. It was as if the premonitions were messages intended only for him, but the messenger had been obstructed or the vision corrupted.

4

When Papa blurted out his astonishment that Fr. Cahill was the man in his dream, a shot of excitement flew through Eve's body. Her face went flush and broke out in perspiration. That the man in Papa's dreams was a Catholic priest was astonishing. She could see Papa was shocked to come to that realization, as was Mister McSherry. She could not tell what was to follow, but suddenly there was hope for her family and Papa. Her papa was shaking violently, but Mister McSherry quieted him down and managed to get him to sit on the bench under a semblance of composure. Mister McSherry put his arm around Papa and held him gently and still on the bench so that Mass could continue. But what was next?

At the conclusion of Mass everyone stood for the recessional hymn, also in Latin. Fr. Cahill walked back down the aisle and as he passed their bench he smiled and nodded at Richard and Adam. Then he went out the front door, propping it open for everyone else to leave. Her papa was eager to talk with Fr. Cahill, but this time Anastasia reached across Eve and tugged on Papa's coat sleeve.

"Adam, he'll talk to you, but let everyone else leave first and have their time with him, otherwise you'll be continuously interrupted."

Papa nodded, but clearly he was anxious.

Eve put her arm through Papa's and pulled it against her body. "Can you sit with me and wait?"

"No, daughter, I can't. Let's go out. I can walk around at least. But I can't sit still."

Hearing that, Richard spoke: "Let's go outside a different way and we can avoid the crowd and curiosity seekers." At that Richard leaned over to Anastasia, "Have the girls and boys leave through the rectory door and then outside. It will be faster."

Anastasia maneuvered herself around the boys, Catharine, and Letitia to the far end of the bench and managed to get them to follow her. She led them down the side aisle of the nave to a door and through it.

When Eve entered the door she saw that they had entered a small foyer that, to the right, led through an exterior door and outside which is where Anastasia was leading them. To the left, however, the foyer led to what appeared to be a small apartment where a quick glance told her there was a fireplace, a food preparation counter, and beyond that a bed and some storage. No doubt this is where Fr. Cahill stayed when he came to Shepherd's Town. Directly in front of her was a piece of furniture she had never seen before. It was a stand-alone wooden partition perhaps five feet tall and three feet side. To the left of the partition was a chair and a small table with a book that had colored ribbons coming out of the spine. The book looked just like Fr. Xavier's prayer book. On the other side of the partition was nothing but an upholstered kneeler that faced the partition with a small rectangular hole in it that was draped with white linen. She wondered what it could be.

Eve followed Anastasia and exited the foyer and went outside, thus circumventing the crowd at the church's main entrance that was engaged with Fr. Cahill who gave everyone that wanted it his attention.

Once outside, Anastasia spoke with Catharine and Letitia who corralled the boys and took them to the side of the church where they could run around safely.

Meanwhile, Eve held onto Papa's arm as he went to Richard. "Richard, I am very sorry for my outburst in there. It was such a shock to me. Fr. Cahill's red hair and beard, his blue eyes, the shape of his face, it was exactly what I saw in my dreams, two times. I've had dreams and visions before, but nothing was ever so clear than today. I am properly shocked and overwhelmed."

"Yes," said Richard, "it must be a real shock. I can't say I know how you feel. I rarely dream. I'm sure Fr. Cahill will give us all the time we need once everyone leaves. As you see, people have come from far away to attend Mass. He's a good priest. But he's not given to superstitions. He may not understand your situation."

"We will see," said Adam, who then turned to Eve and whispered, "Pray he does."

Eve nodded.

One by one the congregants said goodbye to their priest, mounted their horses, buggies, or carriages and departed. Behind and to one side an older man, and a woman who appeared to be his wife, waited patiently, as if he was to take Fr. Cahill off to dine with them. The last in line were the McSherrys' three boys and their nannies, Catharine and Letitia. The boys quickly shook Fr. Cahill's hand then ran off. The young women lingered. After chatting a bit, Eve was surprised to see the one young woman kiss Fr. Cahill on the cheek and give him a long hug, but then Eve realized they were brother and sister. The other woman, Letitia, tried to hug Fr. Cahill, but he held her off and gave her a nary but friendly look. Eve caught Mister McSherry watching the interaction between Fr. Cahill and Letitia and he didn't look too happy about it.

After the boys and the nannies stepped aside, Anastasia ushered Papa to Fr. Cahill and made introductions. Eve was sure to hang on her father's arm as she didn't want to miss anything said.

"Fr. Denis," said Anastasia, "this is our neighbor, and one of my former customers from Uncle Arnold's factory in Hagerstown, Adam Livingston."

Fr. Cahill put out his hand. I'm glad to make your acquaintance, Mister Livingston." Adam took Fr. Cahill's hand and shook it heartily.

"And this is his eldest daughter, Eve," continued Anastasia.

Eve curtsied. "Pleased to meet you, Father. My Papa has a request to make of you."

"Yes, so I gathered," said Fr. Cahill. "Mister Livingston, what is it that I can help you with?"

Her papa explained, as briefly as he could, the situation at Flax Haven, although he left out the part about not getting a priest for Xavier before he died. Papa also left out the part about the curse, which Eve thought was a most important part of the story. But he did explain that the hauntings only occur around the time of the new moon, which was yesterday, so the spirit was currently active. "Rev. Cahill, everything I've told you is true," said Papa, "and it was you I saw in my dreams. A voice from the dreams said you are the man who can relieve us from this curse and cast this…this frightful thing from our lives."

Adam finally stopped and waited for Fr. Cahill to reply. Smiling and looking Papa in the eyes, Fr. Cahill said, "Mister Livingston, I'm very sorry for your situation. I have heard vague and distant rumors of your predicament, but not from the McSherrys. I doubt it is really, as you say, an evil spirit. Probably…yes, I am sure it is your neighbors who are playing tricks on you. Stay up and watch for them. You do not need me."

"Are you suggesting that our neighbors are in our linen drawers, and under the coverlet of our bed, while we are in it? Do you suggest that our neighbors are dislodging stones from our fireplace and flinging them with fire across our gathering hall injuring guests? Or that our neighbors are shoving stacks of pottery off our supper shelves with invisible hands as we watch?" Eve thought her father's rebuttal convincing and effective.

Anastasia spoke up: "Fr. Denis, I have known Mister Livingston in a business capacity for several years before you married Richard and me. He is a very honest and trustworthy man, and respected in the farming community. He and his family have visited our home, and although neither Richard nor myself have witnessed these hauntings first hand, we have heard from many who have. The reports we hear are not the tricks of neighbors, and I assure you, he's not crazy."

"Richard, what say you of this?" asked Fr. Cahill.

"Ana will tell you, I am a skeptic. But I can vouch for Mister Livingston's good reputation otherwise, in business and farming. He is one of the most innovative farmers in the region. If others are involved, they are jealous of his competencies."

Eve noticed that while this conversation was carried on, the older man who waited patiently behind Fr. Cahill had moved closer to hear what was being discussed. Fr. Cahill noticed this, and finally introduced him to Papa. "Mister Livingston, may I introduce Gabriel Menghini, and…" he gestured a greeting to the woman standing a short distance away, "...his wife, Ruth. They have been close associates of mine during my years here in Mecklenburg, or Shepherd's Town as the folks now choose to call it. Gabriel is president of the Catholic Society here and, quite honestly a faithful advisor of mine, along definitely with Richard who started me on this local adventure of which I am deeply indebted."

Gabriel stepped close enough to offer his hand to Papa, "I'm glad to meet you, Mister Livingston, I'm, as Father says, Gabriel Menghini. Ruth and I have lived here in town for twenty-five years. I own a boarding house and some other properties."

The men shook hands.

"Mister Livingston," Gabriel said, "may I ask, are you Catholic?"

"No, sir, I am not. Which is, no doubt, the reason we have not met before here at your fine chapel. I was raised Lutheran, but not a very good one, I admit. My first wife, Esther, was a devout Presbyterian until she suddenly died prior to my moving to Smithfield. We're originally from York, Pennsylvania. This is my daughter Eve..." at which Eve curtsied her greeting "...she is the religious one in our family. She makes a habit of prayer."

Eve was proud of Papa's honesty.

Anastasia had more to say. "Father, I must testify on behalf of my friends, although they are not believers...well, Eve is, and her birth mother clearly was. The current Mrs. Livingston is very much antagonistic to our faith. But Adam's heart has softened of late, and become even contrite, if I can be so bold as to presume on his behalf. When he described his dream to me, it was clear that who he saw was you, Fr. Cahill, not just any priest, but you...and, in his dream, you were celebrating Holy Mass. That is very noteworthy and honestly in my estimation, a miracle. Perhaps it's a call upon you to exercise your priestly duties for the benefit of our community, Catholic or not."

Fr. Cahill stopped smiling and looked among the group gathered. Eve glanced at her father and saw tears in his eyes. Clearly he was desperate and she prayed softly to her mother for Fr. Cahill's compassion. She clung hard to her father's arm, which she noticed Fr. Cahill took note. Surprisingly, Anastasia put her arm through Papa's other arm, and everyone looked to Fr. Cahill for an answer. At the same time, Richard, being good at holding his tongue, looked away.

Gabriel stepped close to Fr. Cahill and spoke softly to his priest, but loud enough for all to hear. "Father Denis, perhaps it is just me, but I'm curious. Ruth and I were to have you as our guest for dinner, but perhaps she will pack us a lunch and I can drive you to Smithfield this afternoon; we...err, you can see for yourself."

Fr. Cahill turned to Gabriel. "You believe this?"

"I am curious."

"You must realize," Fr. Cahill said to Gabriel, if this does have credibility, that without the bishop's permission I cannot attempt any sort of exorcism for fear I create a scandal for which the Church is blamed, especially for a family that is not Catholic."

"That is true. But as a priest, you are not limited to exorcisms."

Fr. Cahill stared at Mister Menghini for a few moments. Fr. Cahill then turned to Mister McSherry. "Richard, would you attend us if we undertake this...this...curiosity?"

Richard scanned the sky and glanced at Anastasia, who firmly nodded her support. Richard twisted his mouth, nodded a half-hearted agreement with his wife, and glanced about for the whereabouts of his boys. They were with their nannies near the carriages, no doubt ready to go.

But Fr. Cahill still had doubts and Eve saw this.

Her papa, too, must have concluded the same, because quickly and surprising to all, Papa faced Fr. Cahill, untied his black bow tie, unbuttoned his waist coat, and pulled it open for the priest to see the white linen shirt beneath— riddled with dozens of small but precisely cut holes in the shape of crescent moons. Eve was very surprised, for Papa's bare chest was visible through the clipped holes. "This is what our neighbors have done," said Adam, "while we slept, with our linens folded and kept neat and clean in drawers and armoires. Our neighbors are very clever, don't you think?" Eve knew Papa was being sarcastic, for no man or woman could cut such precise holes in shapes like these in any cloth. Richard and Anastasia also looked at the shirt and their mouths fell open.

Fr. Cahill looked closely as well. He kept his mouth shut, jaw grinding as if regurgitating his cud. Eve noticed something telling. Fr. Cahill appeared to recognize something familiar in what Papa revealed. In fact, there was a bit of fear and caution that rapidly spread across Fr. Cahill's face. All of a sudden Fr. Cahill was taking Papa seriously.

With a firm change in attitude and in all seriousness, Fr. Cahill looked at Adam, but spoke to his friend: "Very well, Mister Menghini. Let us grace Ruth with our presence and then leave for Smithfield this afternoon...as soon as we are able." To Richard and Adam he said, "It will take you a couple hours to get home, will it not? And you should have something to eat."

Anastasia spoke: "We brought a picnic lunch we planned to eat on the way home. "Come to our place; it's on the way. Richard knows Mister Livingston's farm, and can lead you there."

"Late this afternoon then?"

Everyone nodded in agreement. Richard in particular was silent and re-flective. Papa re-buttoned his waistcoat and gave Eve a big side-hug as if to say, *Thank you for praying. Your mother came through for us.*

5

Fr. Cahill had not been skeptical about the existence of evil; he had experienced his share. Some would say he had experienced more than his share.

Nor was he skeptical about the existence of prowling demons who sought the destruction of human souls, Catholic priests, or even the Catholic Church. How else could one explain the killing of the priest that baptized him as an infant, the burning of the St. Louis Church in New Orleans, the Guy Fawkes movement, the Suppression of the Jesuits, his mugging and near death in Sharpsburg, or last year's French invasion of the Papal States and the rumors that some obscure French general, by the unlikely name of Napoleon Bonaparte, was laying siege to the Vatican? No, none of that entered his mind. Instead, it was that this particular, non-religious, insignificant farmer was important enough to garner the attention of the netherworld. *That* he could not believe. But once he saw the crescent moons in Adam's shirt, cut out more precisely than any human could produce with the sharpest of shears, his skepticism dissipated like a vanquished specter. Adam Livingston had somehow aroused the attention of a moon-god, a demon, a spirit worshiped since antiquity. Fr. Cahill had encountered the same in the ruins of the St. Louis church in New Orleans after the 1788 fire. This was nothing to be trifled with. Suddenly cautious, Fr. Cahill was also intensely curious. *Adam Livingston was somehow more important to human history than it appeared.*

He and Gabriel Menghini indeed did get a lunch basket from Ruth, and a short time later rode to Leetown in the Menghinis' buggy. They stopped at McSherrys' Retirement, where they turned down the obligatory goblet of Madeira. From Retirement they followed Richard and Anastasia, both on horseback, to Livingston's Flax Haven farm. As the group tied up at the house's hitching post, Adam and a teenage boy came from across the yard to greet them. Also accompanying Adam was a large black man, who, Fr. Cahill noted, was dressed too well to be a slave.

"Fr. Cahill," said Adam, "thank you for coming. This is Sam Dark, a freeman and foreman of my plantation. He will care for your animals. And this is my son, Henry, Eve's brother by my first wife."

Fr. Cahill greeted both. He was still dressed in his full length cassock but without the white surplice (tunic). He draped a thin purple stole over his shoulders, crossed it in front with a button, then removed from his satchel a small book of rituals, a bronze pail (an aspersorium) with a relief of an angel on the side, and a liturgical wand (aspergillum) with a wooden handle on one end with a porous metal ball on the other end used to sprinkle Holy Water. He handed the latter items to Gabriel.

At that moment, Eve came out of the house and down the porch steps to her father. She spoke quietly but loud enough for Fr. Cahill to hear, "Mary Ann is on the war path."

"I suspect so," Adam said.

A moment later a compact woman in a house dress and apron exited the front door in a fury and stormed across the porch to the top of the steps. This was probably Adam's wife, Mary Ann, of whom he had been forewarned. She was clearly upset at the collection of people staring up at her from the yard. Following Mary Ann was a black woman, perhaps the cook the way she was dressed, who was much reserved and quietly stood back.

Attempting to forestall the tempest, Adam spoke first. "Mary Ann, my lovely and temperate wife, I'd like you to meet Fr. Denis Cahill and Gabriel Menghini; they've come to relieve us, or so we hope. Father Cahill, this is my wife Mary Ann, and our cook, Bethany, a free woman who is Sam's wife."

He and Gabriel bowed slightly to Mary Ann and Bethany and made polite greetings to both, hoping to please Adam's wife. But Mary Ann's temper was not tempered.

She glared down and assailed them: "Adam, why must you continue to violate your sacred oath, bringing destruction and desolation to our family? Why, why, why Adam?! You know every time you bring some damn minister to pray in our house…or do whatever they do, things get worse. More of our belongings and peace are destroyed, the children cry endlessly. We're kept awake at night by stampeding cattle and runaway wagons, and our guests run away in fright. Why do you insist? Prayer to who knows what has never and will never do any good."

Bethany approached Mary Ann and put an arm around her. At first, Mary Ann rejected Bethany's comfort and brushed off the arm, but Bethany gently insisted. Moments later Mary Ann finally relented. Sobbing, she pleaded: "Enough of this! We are tired, broken, and now poor."

After a moment of silence, Fr. Cahill felt the need to speak: "Missus Livingston, be comforted. We are not here to bring disruption to your family, which I do believe you've experienced. You should know that I am forbidden an attempt to exorcise your house. I do not have the authority without my bishop's permission."

That seemed to catch Mary Ann's attention.

"What then?" Mary Ann shot back. "Why have you come? How can you possibly help, or are you damn curiosity seekers come again to harass us?"

"We will leave if you so ask," he said. "But I beg you, patience for a bit." He paused for a moment to consider what might be said next. "I believe I know the disrupting spirit with which you have been cursed, or at least its kind. And while I do not know why it is here, or what God's will may be in my role to assist you, I ask your permission to examine your home and at least impart a blessing. Perhaps that will relieve you of the spell…for a spell."

He stopped talking and prayed silently that God would give Mary Ann peace for a time so he might examine and bless the premises and see if he could be of any benefit.

Bethany held a sobbing Mary Ann in one arm and whispered something in her ear. With barely a nod, Mary Ann came down the steps with Bethany.

"I'll get the twins, and bring them to you…Mother," said Eve as she ran up the steps and into the house. Fr. Cahill noticed that when Eve called Mary Ann "mother," Mary Ann turned in surprise and watched Eve go into the house. Mary Ann then looked at Adam in astonishment, and Adam at her, shrugging his shoulders as if to say, *I have no idea.* Moments later, a young boy and girl, perhaps four or five, came out of the house and down the steps holding Eve's two hands. Eve turned to her brother. "Henry, will you help us?" Whereupon the four children walked to the bench under a nearby oak tree where Mary Ann and Bethany had settled.

"Mister Livingston," said Gabriel, handing Adam the aspersorium, "can you fill this with water and bring it back to Father along with a handful of salt?"

"Just the water, sir," Fr. Cahill said, "I have brought a cache of salt. Thank you."

As Adam ran into the house with the aspersorium, Fr. Cahill reached into his cassock's pocket and produced a small cloth sack tied closed with string and handed it to Gabriel. "Consecrated salt."

Gabriel nodded, took the small sack, and untied the string.

A minute later Adam returned with the aspersorium filled with water. Gabriel, with the bag of salt in one hand, took the aspersorium of water in the other, and held them both in front of Fr. Cahill. Opening the small book he carried, Fr. Cahill read a prayer in Latin and, while doing so, took pinches of the salt and dropped the grains into the water in the sign of the cross. Then there were more Latin prayers, some to which Gabriel responded, also in Latin.

After the ritual, Gabriel slid the aspergillum into the aspersorium of water with the handle sticking out the top.

Fr. Cahill turned to Adam, "We're going to bless you and your home." He turned to the McSherrys. "Do you have your Rosaries?"

"I don't," said Richard.

"I do," said Anastasia and opened her palm to show him.

He turned to Richard. "Use your fingers. Pray silently the Sorrowful Mysteries, stay close."

Grasping the aspergillum and pulling it from the aspersorium of Holy Water that Menghini held, Fr. Cahill liberally doused Menghini, the McSherrys, and Livingston, "In nomine Patris, et Filii, et Spiritus Sancti." He then handed the aspergillum to Gabriel, folded his hands in prayer, and bowed slightly.

Gabriel took the aspergillum and lightly sprinkled his priest.

Fr. Cahill objected. "More. Do not take this lightly."

Gabriel dunked the aspergillum deep into the aspersorium and shook it hard over Fr. Cahill's head, soaking the priest front and back.

"That's enough," Cahill said.

Taking back the aspergillum, Fr. Cahill walked to the bench under the oak. Sam was standing some distance away. Fr. Cahill gestured for Sam to join the group under the oak, which Sam did. Charging the aspergillum with water, and without asking, Fr. Cahill sprinkled Sam, the children, a disgruntled Mary Ann, and an agreeable Bethany, "In nomine Patris, et Filli, et Spiritus Sancti."

Returning to the house, and before ascending the porch steps, he began to read in Latin from his book of rituals, "Pax huic dómui...*Peace be unto this home.*"

Menghini responded, also in Latin, "Et ómnibus habitántibus in ea...*And unto all who dwell herein.*"

Fr. Cahill then doused the porch steps with Holy Water. As soon as droplets fell on the porch steps, the porch began to vibrate and bounce erratically. There was a terrible rumbling as if the wood planks might come loose. It surprised him, that Holy Water, a transient sacramental, would have such an immediate effect. The infestation was greater than he had imagined. Valor was needed. Without hesitation he boldly ascended the steps and doused more Holy Water on the porch, reading from his book of rituals, now more loudly: "Exáudi nos, Dómine sancta...*Hear us, holy Lord and Father, almighty everlasting God, and in your goodness send your holy angel from heaven to watch over and protect all who live in this home, to be with them and give them comfort and encouragement, through Christ our Lord.*"

Immediately the vibrations diminished, and before Adam had stepped onto the porch they had ceased.

Entering the foyer, he heard the distant sound of shears at work. He flicked the aspergillum about, sprinkling the walls and floor and reciting a Psalm in Latin: "Miserere mei Deus...*Have mercy on me, O God, according to thy great mercy. And according to the multitude of thy tender mercies blot out my iniquity.*" Nothing changed, the clipping noise continued. Perhaps it was coming from the parlor.

Entering the parlor, the clipping noise was louder. He looked about curiously. Plunging the aspergillum into the bucket he threw Holy Water in every direction, as he read more of the Psalm. "Quoniam iniquitatem meam ego...*For I know my iniquity, and my sin is always before me.*" The clipping noise diminished but it didn't cease. "What is above here?" he asked Adam.

"Bedrooms," said Adam.

"Let's go there," he said.

Up the stairs they climbed. Along the way Fr. Cahill doused the stairs and walls.

Eve's bedroom was remarkably quiet, but Fr. Cahill sprinkled and prayed in it nonetheless. In Henry's room the sounds returned but sprinkling and praying in the room didn't help. A bit frustrated, he was determined to satisfy his curiosity and confront whatever haunted the dwelling. Shortly, his desire was fulfilled.

As soon as he entered the master bedroom he felt an unmistakable sense of dread. Charging the aspergillum with an extra load of water, he began again the Latin prayer and drenched the walls, floors, and furniture with sacramental water: "Cor mundum crea in me Deus...*Create a clean heart in me, O God: and renew a right spirit within me.*"

As he prayed and sprinkled, the clipping sounds intensified, and with it the abrupt appearance of black smoke that jetted up between the floorboards. The sooty vapor didn't seem to be real smoke; there was no burnt smell to it. But, as he prayed and moved about the room with the aspergillum, the smoke quickly coalesced into a semi-transparent form of a naked upper male torso that loomed over Cahill and Menghini. Fr. Cahill sneered at the personification, attacked it viciously with a fully charged aspergillum, hitting it on the head and yelling: "Ne proicias me a facie tua…*Cast me not away from thy face; and take not thy holy spirit from me. Restore unto me the joy of thy salvation and strengthen me with a perfect spirit.*"

With each strike of Holy Water, with each word of Latin, and with each advance Fr. Cahill made into the vapor, the form of what could only have been the demon attempting entry into the physical realm, reverted to a fog. It then settled on the floor, and either dissipated or was sucked back into the cracks between the floorboards, leaving behind only the noise of the clipping.

"What's below?" asked Fr. Cahill.

"The gathering hall, Father," said Adam.

"Go there, immediately. Quickly now," and he turned around to the McSherrys and said, "Pray all the more earnestly, now."

In the gathering hall, indeed the clipping noise was the loudest, but so was the sound of stampeding horses, racing carriages, and wagons. The room vibrated with the cacophony of sound that came from every direction, evidently emanating from outside and around the house. Fr. Cahill knew he was on a mission and making progress. The demon was on the run and feared being caught. Gabriel had a hard time keeping up with Fr. Cahill charging about the room, flinging Holy Water wherever there seemed to be black vapor attempting to occupy the space by seeping down the walls from above. Holy water and Latin prayers filled the room. Fr. Cahill imagined himself preaching on a platform hovering above the earth with demons surrounding him on every side. He cried to heaven and invoked St. Michael to wield his sword and summon the angelic host to battle.

But Fr. Cahill didn't wait for St. Michael. Instead, he soaked every nook and cranny of the room with Holy Water flying off the tip of his aspergillum as fast as Menghini could make the aspersorium available: "Libera me de sanguinibu Deus…*Deliver me from blood, O God, thou God of my salvation and my tongue shall extol thy justice. O Lord, thou wilt open my lips: and my mouth shall declare thy praise.*"

No sooner would the black vapor appear at the front of the room hovering above the loom, than he would chase the disturbance to the rear where it slid into the pottery hutch, shaking the shelves and causing the hutch to tilt and vibrate. Covering the cabinet with sprays from his aspergillum he yelled: "Sacrificium Deo spiritus…*A sacrifice to God is an afflicted spirit: a contrite and humbled heart, O God, thou wilt not despise.*" Dousing every shelf he cried,

"Redde mihi laetitiam salutaris...*Restore unto me the joy of thy salvation and strengthen me with a perfect spirit.*" Keeping it up, Fr. Cahill chased the specters and sounds repeatedly about the room, exhausting himself but not letting up.

Finally, the clipping sounds began to stutter, as if the demon was sticking its tongue out at the priest. With the stuttering, the black vapor fell to the floor as precipitate where, little by little, it disintegrated. As the vapor disappeared, so the vibrations and sounds of horses and carriages faded and finally ceased.

Quite suddenly and surprisingly, all was quiet.

Fr. Cahill froze in place, the aspergillum glued to his hand. His heart beat rapidly, his respiration deep. Yet, he was tense and alert.

Suddenly the floor began to vibrate wildly, jostling everyone and the furniture in the room. Porcelain fell from the cabinet, crashing and shattering on the floor.

Quickly, Cahill grabbed the aspersorium from Menghini and flung the Holy Water across the floorboards while proclaiming at the top of his lungs: "GLORIA PATRI ET FILLO ET SPIRITUI SANCO. SICUT ERAT IN PRINCIPIO ET NUNC ET SEMPER, ET IN SAECULA SAECULORUM. AMEN."

Suddenly the vibrations stopped with a thud, as if the house's posts and beams were forcibly reset on its stone footings.

Fr. Cahill's cassock was soaked with Holy Water and sweat, but something had happened. He looked about and listened, as did the others.

All was quiet.

After another long moment Fr. Cahill walked about mumbling beneath his breath in Latin, until he finally fell back into a chair to rest.

6

Adam was astonished. The priest had not faltered, hesitated, run off, nor had he responded with anything but unflinching fervor and dedication to the task. From Adam's perspective, it was as if Fr. Cahill was living up to his calling. There was no doubt, no hesitancy. He was fully, even robustly applied. "Father Cahill, you have done what no one else has been able."

The exhausted priest handed the empty aspersorium and aspergillum to Menghini. He motioned for Adam to sit across from him. "Mister Livingston, it is not I, but the power of God. While it may look like we have succeeded in chasing your spirit off, I sense it is only for a short while. It is likely to return with a vengeance. In fact, I predict it will. Your house must be exorcised properly. In the meantime, my advice is to forsake your unbelief, come into the Church, be baptized, and partake regularly of the sacraments. They will be life to your soul and solace to your family. Otherwise, there are no promises."

Adam nodded weakly and shared a glance with Richard McSherry who was emotionally preoccupied with a permanent look of bewilderment that had seized his countenance. It was as if the experience had made him a believer all over again. Richard and Anastasia both wore expressions of contrition and confusion, if not fear. Gone was Richard's skepticism. Anastasia, often aloof and self-confident, held tight to Richard's arm as if to let go would cast her into hellfire.

"I must confess," Fr. Cahill continued, "I am now fully convinced of your predicament, and I sincerely apologize for not believing you earlier." Fr. Cahill paused to collect his thoughts. Adam was listening. "Here is what I propose. In the next day or so, as soon as I can get back to Hagerstown and adjust my responsibilities, I will personally go to Baltimore and petition Bishop Carroll for permission to exorcise your home. Unfortunately, the bishop and I are of different mindsets so, I am not sure what he will say regarding your situation and my involvement. Regardless, I will ask on your benefit and return as soon as I know something. In the meantime, pray that you are content and your family safe, and consider seriously what I suggest."

As Fr. Cahill prepared to leave, they walked to the foyer. Adam opened the hinged cover of a small wooden box near the front door and withdrew a scrap of linen that had been riddled with crescent moon cutouts. "Here, take this. We burn most of what is clipped, but we keep some to show skeptics what we're fighting. Show this to your bishop."

Fr. Cahill took the scrap of linen, examined it with great interest, then folded it carefully and put it in a pocket. "I will do that, thank you."

With that Fr. Cahill stepped toward the front door which had been left open since they first entered the house. As he stepped on the threshold he momentarily lost his balance. Looking down, Adam saw that Fr. Cahill's boot was resting on a small *drawstring bag.

"What's this?" said Fr. Cahill. He picked up the bag and weighed it in his hands. It sounded as if there were coins inside. He handed it to Adam. "Something misplaced...of value?"

Adam froze when he saw the bag. It was very familiar. *How did this get here?* He opened the bag and poured out the contents into his hand—fourteen gold coins. "It, ah,...our savings, lost months ago, after these hauntings began. Was it just lying there on the threshold?"

"It appears so," said Fr. Cahill.

Adam knew that the fourteen double-doubloons was the money he had inadvertently and then purposely stolen from George Eshelman, but no one else knew that. He suddenly felt convicted of the theft, began to weep, and fell on his knees before Fr. Cahill. He held the bag of gold up to the priest. "Father, this is for you. It has long been lost and now it appears on the threshold to my home. The threshold that I swore a priest would never cross. You are clearly a man of God, I have been wrong, and this must be your reward." He continued to extend the bag of gold to Fr. Cahill.

Fr. Cahill did not seem for a moment to consider taking it, and by this time Mary Ann, Bethany, Sam, and the children had gathered on the porch around

Adam, who was still on his knees before Fr. Cahill.

After a moment Fr. Cahill said, "Is this your confession? If it is, it is not complete. And I implore you to finish before God finishes it for you."

Adam could not believe what he heard. It was as if this Catholic priest could suddenly read his heart. Everyone was silent as Adam bent over in contrition and yet again extended his hand with the bag of gold and offered it for Fr. Cahill to take.

"It is my offering to the Church for benefit received. It is your reward I...I offer it ..."

Fr. Cahill interrupted, "Nonsense, Mister Livingston. This is filthy lucre. I know not how you came upon it, but it is not yours or mine, is it?"

Adam bowed low, hid his face, and clutched the bag.

"The reward we will all receive is for you to rectify its place and set it right," said Fr. Cahill. "Whose money is this? Who did it belong to long ago?"

Adam had trouble getting the words out, but eventually they came...although he was greatly embarrassed that his family and friends could hear his confession. "George Eshelman. He accidentally overpaid to buy my farm in Pennsylvania. Later, he asked if I had found this gold hidden in the satchel he had gifted me. I had. But I lied, and I kept the gold."

"Obedience to the law, good works, and the sacraments, sir. That is your salvation. For you and for your household," said Fr. Cahill without much hesitation and looking about to the others gathered around.

Fr. Cahill made the sign of the cross over Adam and then repeated it toward the others nearby. When he came to Mary Ann to bless her, she broke loose of Eve and darted up the stairs. Of the group only Menghini and the McSherrys crossed themselves, just before Fr. Cahill stepped off the porch and down the steps.

7

The night after Fr. Cahill blessed the house, it was unusually quiet. Since the hauntings began, it was the first time during a new moon cycle that it had been quiet apart from the time Rev. Williams had visited. At the same time, Mary Ann, the ever skeptic, refused to believe what Adam said had happened. It was some manipulative trick of a popish cleric, she claimed. Time would tell.

The next day, Monday, June 26, Adam took the fourteen-double-gold-doubloons to the Charles Town bank where they were weighed. The value of the coins had increased over the years. Instead of twenty-one pounds sterling they were now worth twenty-three pounds sterling. According to his word, Adam ordered the bank to send the money, all of it, via bank transfer to George Eshelman. With his conscience now clear, Adam hoped the future would be kind.

Sometimes, however, when a correction is made, it is too little and too late.

That night Adam and Mary Ann lay in bed staring at the ceiling. The bed-

632 O *Stanley D. Williams*

spread was riddled with the clipped holes of crescent moons, but it was quiet. They heard only crickets, hoot owls, and the rustle of leaves in the breeze.

The next morning the family enjoyed boiled porridge with fruit, milk, and sugar. No one spoke for fear that the blessings would expire and the curse return. And yet, there were no other sounds or manifestations. By now, of course—three days past the new moon—it would be quiet. But there seemed to be a deeper peace that had settled on the farm as if they would never again have to worry about the next new moon. In the fields the flax crop was growing and waving in the wind, and that evening there was a luxurious red sunset that held promise of calm days ahead.

A few nights later, by lantern light, Adam and Mary Ann sat in rockers on the front porch. She knitted—a quiet compromise to the rattling loom which sat dormant. He stared peacefully across the tranquil yard to the lantern light in the Darks' cabin. Eve and Henry came out in their bed clothes. Each hugged their father and stepmother, said their good-nights, and returned to the house to scale the stairs to their slumber.

That night Mary Ann slept soundly in bed as Adam removed the small sea chest from his wardrobe, set it on a table, opened it, and under the light of his lantern placed in the chest the empty bag that had contained the fourteen double-gold-doubloons. He quietly shut the chest, locked it, and returned it to the floor of his armoire.

In the days that followed, Adam, Sam, Henry, and a few day laborers cleaned up the neglected barn. When they were done, Adam took inventory of his industry. He was proud of the barn and what they had accumulated in it—the animals, the feed and seed, the tools, and processing apparatus. The next day he slaughtered Henry's fattest pig and the family, with the Darks, celebrated with a feast their new life.

Unfortunately, Adam had entirely forgotten Fr. Cahill's warning.

8

Most Feared Master of Evil,

It may appear to those who have denounced my campaign that I have lost control. While pessimism is our aspiration along with dread and horror, there is reason for optimism. Recent events only serve to expand our influence and attract our enemy's affection. Be reminded that my arsenal of pretense, persuasion, and poltergeist phenomena is far from being plundered. For there still is much to pillage.

For example, Richard McSherry is strongly opinionated, greedy, and susceptible to our way of thinking. He is suspicious by nature and doubts the authenticity of any thing which he does not control. This plays into our perverse delights and depraved plans and will draw him deeper into our deception—one of the reasons I quickly retreated from Livingston's dwelling when Cahill became obsessed with flinging water about and muttering abusive Latin.

As proof of this, you will soon see McSherry turn against his friend. This will confound Livingston's efforts to exorcise my charm and advance our efforts to terrorize his future. Further, allowing the introduction of Livingston to Cahill, while it may have been our objective to prevent, provides potential to distract and even corrupt Cahill.

I admit, however, that my attempt to muddle Livingston's dream state, initiated I'm sure by a Guardian, fell short of my goal; yet, it may still serve to cast doubt in Livingston's mind on the priestly art. For my intrusion amplified his fear and dislike of his premonitions. Surely his wife thinks this way about anything associated with priests. When this campaign is complete, we need to give her a participation ribbon for running off her mouth at the slightest provocation. She's always a joy to behold.

In the end, Livingston is further down our intended path, for he forgot everything about which Cahill warned, and that sets both of them up for the coming fall...and great will be the fall of them both.

As to the reappearance of the gold...I have no idea where it went, from whence it returned, or why; and I am disappointed that he returned the gold to Eshelman. Livingston's guilt in the matter was something I often leveraged, reminding him to disregard such feelings, thus indebting him to me and our deceptive arts.

As to the farm's lack of haunts these past days...patience is a virtue the enemy claims, a memorable contrivance takes time, and Livingston is due a cataclysm.

At your sinful service,
Cyn Namrasit, OPSD

Chapter 46
Nothing is Forever

1

It was late in the day when Gabriel Menghini drove Fr. Cahill back to the Shepherd's Town chapel. The next morning Fr. Cahill rode Sassafras back to Hagerstown and made arrangements for taking a week off for the trip to Baltimore. He debated why he was willing to appear before Bishop Carroll now and not earlier. He didn't think the experience at the Livingstons' was a turning point in his life, though it was memorable. He had confronted personified evil many times as a priest, but this was the first time a spirit from the netherworld had made a direct assault instead of by human proxy or nature. He was not so shocked as he was angry. Yes, yes, he had heard or read theologians explain how control of earth had been given over to Lucifer. But what then was he to make of Christ's coming and dying if not to defeat the dark powers? As Christ's vicar he had overcome evil numerous times, and his time at Livingston's house was clearly one of them, although different. What he encountered at Livingston's was not a mad man, a bandit, or a Catholic-hating adulterating bigot. It was a demonic spirit itself. While Livingston may think that he had defeated the specter, he knew differently. In times past when he was spit upon, threatened, put in his place by a superior, beat within an inch of his life, tossed about by a storm, or even attacked by pirates, none of those times scared him. His lack of fear in those situations was not because he had been prepared for the confrontation. No, that wasn't it. He accepted such attacks as part of his duty as a vicar of Christ. They were bound to happen, and did.

But Livingston's Wizard was different. It had scared him. It had frightened him. It had shaken his faith. Yet in the midst of the battle to bless Livingston's home the thought never occurred to him to turn and run. Such behavior made no sense. Fight, yes. Flight, no. He was called to fight evil. That's all a priest was, after all. The simplest definition of the Catholic priesthood was to confront evil and do away with it using the Sacramental tools of the Church as ordained by Christ. Never, ever, had he in all his priestly life while administering sacraments, or sacramentals, felt fear. But this time he did. It was confronting the real thing, the real evil, in its raw form, not some human proxy, that changed his mind.

Going to see Bishop Carroll was not something he had thought through. He had not analyzed the pros and cons or what he might say or not say to Carroll in his defense of their tense communiques. Yes, Carroll wanted him to answer charges for maligning his character, although such denigration appeared only in a private letter. And yet, the bishop had maligned the priest's character. At the same time he felt the claims against the bishop of simony were just. If what he had heard were only rumors, then it was up to the bishop to prove otherwise, not to ignore them and malign the messenger. Surely the promotion of some priests who had favored the bishop's elevation were worthy of being challenged. Especially since it seemed that the bishop, from one of the richest and politically most powerful families in the country, had purchased his office through political connections and pretense. Are not ministers and priests worthy of their pay? Carroll had never sent one shilling to him. If the bishop was not willing to pay priests for their labor, why should the priest pretend to come under the bishop's authority?

But all that, which before were reasons not to give Carroll homage and trot off to Baltimore for a chance to kiss his ring, now seemed paltry in comparison. The decision to go was now instinctive. There was no need to reason, or weigh the pros and cons. There was now a visceral battle which he did not feel equipped to wage. He was out of his league. He needed the authority of something or someone with greater agency. Until he met the Wizard, or whatever it was or pretended to be, Cahill felt self-reliant and autonomous. He had felt no guilt in leaving Spain and coming to the New World. He felt no shame in leaving New Orleans. He felt no fear in getting on Captain Johns' creaky vessel and sailing through storms and pirates. He was eager to journey across America alone even though there was the chance of death at the hands of bandits. But the Wizard had imbued fear.

Yet there was one other thing that scared him. There was something else that had threatened to change him, to upend all he had learned and worked toward. Yes, he was afraid of one other thing, and perhaps it scared him more than the demon.

Thus, on his way to Baltimore, although it was out of his way, he traveled through Emmitsburg, Maryland, and sought out the founder of St. Joseph's parish, *Rev. Matthew Ryan. It was Fr. Bodkin that told him that Fr. Ryan was an immigrant from Ireland. Unlike himself, Fr. Ryan had the bishop's endorsement. Fr. Cahill would rather have found an independent priest like himself, but he knew of no one that shared his experience or credentials. He could only hope that Fr. Ryan was a man of compassion and held sacred the seal of confession.

2

"How long has it been," asked the rotund Irish priest.

"Nearly nine years," said Fr. Denis.

"That's a long time."

"I knew no other priest—that was close, or that I trusted."

"I was here," said Fr. Ryan.

"I only knew that maybe two years ago."

"Who was your ordinary?"

"Originally, Andrés José Barco Espinosa. I was ordained in Salamanca, Spain, college and seminary. But most recently, Fr. Antoine, New Orleans, Capuchin."

"Are you Franciscan?"

"Never made final vows. I left to come to the United States in 1788. I've been a pioneering priest here since then."

"Who appointed you?"

"God led me here. There was no superior when I came."

"John Carroll was superior in 1788."

"There was no sign at the wharf telling me that. I was told by the Catholic captain of my American merchant ship that there was no bishop or superior and that the country was better because of it."

"Hmm! That much I understand. I have heard of your parish in Hagerstown. Where do you circuit?"

"I've founded and attend in Martinsburg, Shepherd's Town, Winchester, Chambersburg, and occasionally visit Fort Cumberland and Leetown."

"I had a visit from a Fr. Bodkin, I believe, who claimed he was priest in Hagerstown."

"A liar and interloper sent by Carroll to dislodge me. Bodkin lasted a few months and went south. He came late without invitation and left early." Fr. Cahill paused as if to start the rite fresh. "Perhaps I should start there."

Fr. Ryan donned his confessional stole and with the sign of the cross began: "In nomine Patris, et Filii, et Spiritus Sancti. Amen. May God, who has enlightened every heart, help you to know your sins and trust in his mercy."

"I have been critical of our bishop, perhaps unjustly," began Fr. Cahill. "When Bodkin attempted to usurp my faculties in Hagerstown, he, Carroll, refused to recognize my service and sacrifice these nine years. I am sure I have sinned in not acknowledging his leadership and have found it embittering. I am on a trek now to Baltimore to correct said rebellion, although with trepidation and doubt. In the process, I may have falsely and irreverently reproached our bishop for his treatment of me and withholding monies due me for my service."

"The diocese is very poor," said Fr. Ryan. "You should know that even I, although I assume I am in the bishop's good graces, have not received half what I am officially due."

"That is where I have been intolerant. I have also accused him of simony."

"Publicly?"

"No! Only in private letters to him. For which he took great offense."

"Yes, I presume he would," said Fr. Ryan.

"His family is not poor," said Fr. Cahill.

"No, indeed they are not."

"In the process I have judged others in the bishop's circle of not being truthful, when I do not know beyond speculation."

"I hope you have not included myself in such accusations; I am in the bishop's orbit we might say."

"Your name has not come up, one of the reasons I came to you. Finally, I threatened the bishop with exposure of the simony rumors if he didn't start paying my subscription. He didn't like that, although I'm unsure if it was my threat or what I requested that upset him." Fr. Cahill was silent for a while.

"I suspect there is more," said Fr. Ryan. "None of this is terribly scandalous but actually quite common among our ranks, as you must know."

"Oh, yes. Nine years needs unpacking. There was a slaver in New Orleans that demanded absolution for his cruel bigotry that I witnessed first hand. I considered killing him. It would have been justified. When I refused him forgiveness, he persuaded the governor to persuade my superior to have me removed from ministry. That is one of the reasons I left the Capuchins in New Orleans and came here."

"I'm not sure wishing death on a slaver is a sin."

"I agree. But that is not the reason for my need of reconciliation," said Fr. Cahill reluctantly. "It is a great fear that I have never encountered before. It is a young Catholic woman on the hunt. She has entered my life and has captured my imagination and lust. She is the close friend of my younger sister who immigrated not too long ago. Both are living with my sponsor's family. They come together to confession. It is nearly impossible to avoid her. Never before has such an occasion presented itself with so strong a temptation. It has come about, in part, because I am faltering in confidence of my call to the priesthood. Until now I have harbored no doubts. But this woman weakens me. The bishop's rejection of me has added fuel to the fire. It is as if I plot revenge against the bishop and God, which grieves me." Fr. Cahill paused. "That is my confession... and fear."

Fr. Ryan contemplated his brother's heart. "This is most difficult. May God guide you with confidence, faith, and obedience...wherever the spirit leads."

The rite concluded without further grave revelations and a promise of Fr. Ryan's prayers for Fr. Cahill.

Continuing on his journey to Baltimore, Fr. Cahill felt a dark cloud was following him. Finding reconciliation with Fr. Ryan had confirmed in Fr. Cahill's heart his peaceful resolution to come fully under the obedience of Bishop Carroll, regardless of what that meant. Confronting evil can have that effect on a priest. Yes, the future of his ministry and his reputation with hundreds of parishioners, especially the McSherrys, worried him. Depending on Bishop Carroll's judgment, his entire ministry as a pioneering priest may come to an abrupt halt.

3

Bishop John Carroll had a full schedule ahead of him. Most important was a late morning meeting on the shores of the Potowmack with the new president, John Adams, who had driven down in a carriage from Philadelphia the day before to settle a dispute between Congress and architect *Pierre Charles L'Enfant. While completing the new Capitol's construction was now only a matter of formality, there were past irritations that had inflamed the architect, Congress, the city commission, to say nothing of the political sensitivities of elites like Washington and Adams. It had not helped that L'Enfant, years earlier, had unceremoniously *torn down one of his commissioner's homes to make way for New Jersey Avenue SE. The home belonged to Daniel Carroll of Duggington—a distant cousin of Charles Carroll of Carrollton, perhaps the wealthiest colonist at the outbreak of the Revolutionary War and a signer of the Declaration of Independence. Charles Carroll of Carrollton was also first cousin of Bishop John Carroll which led to the bishop's involvement in the current legal escapade. The demolition of Daniel Carroll of Dugginton's home (only recently constructed) had led President Washington to fire L'Enfant, although by then much of the design and construction of the new Capitol was well underway. Meanwhile, L'Enfant attempted to be paid for this design and construction oversight by seeking over $95,000 dollars from Congress. Mister Adams, more in line with what Congress had set aside, considered $3,800 a more suitable fee. Of course, this enraged L'Enfant and thus there were to be discussions between attorneys, commissioners, and politicians that morning in an effort to find a compromise. John Carroll had been asked to referee the discussions, an assignment the bishop did not savor. He desired to be a man of the cloth and keep politicians at arm's length, but he could not deny the blood lines that connected him to the new government, or this rich heritage that put him in carriages with ministers and presidents.

As the bishop was leaving his Baltimore residence to share a carriage to the Potowmack, William Zane, the bishop's secretary and seminarian, drew him aside.

"Bishop Carroll, you have an unannounced visitor."

"They are all unannounced, Mister Zane. Who is it this time?"

"He says his name is Fr. Denis Cahill. He's waiting in your parlor."

The bishop pulled up short at his naive secretary. "Denis Cahill, the meddler priest from Hagerstown? Who put him in the parlor?"

"I suppose he did, your Excellency. Your agenda and the parlor were both empty per your instructions…at least until moments ago."

The bishop took a deep breath as he stepped to the foyer windows and looked out across the house's garden and entrance. Just beyond, in the recently bricked street, was a carriage waiting for him. The carriage contained an impatient solicitor who was to brief Carroll on the negotiations with L'Enfant. The bishop drew William further aside and lowered his voice, realizing the parlor was within hearing. "Most inconvenient, but of this gentleman I have no high expectations. Are you familiar with the gentleman priest and his situation?" the bishop asked.

"No, your Excellency, I am not."

"Then do this. First keep my whereabouts this day confidential. Father Cahill is here to answer serious charges of which I demanded he appear...oh, it must have been two years ago, now. And he has finally come. I have no time for him today. Let him sit in the parlor for the morning. On your own, reference my letter file under his name and parish in Hagerstown, Maryland. Familiarize yourself with our exchange. There must be three or four letters between us. I forget who I assigned to assist in this case, but take it upon yourself to contact the parties I mention in my letters, arrange for a hearing between Fr. Cahill and I believe President Nagot, John Tessier, and others. Let them review my letters demanding Cahill answer charges. Over the next few days, arrange for the parties to meet in confidence at the seminary, not here. I will not be available until tomorrow morning at the earliest. And I do not want to meet Cahill, but only Nagot or Caffrey, and only after they have had their hearing with this priest. Now, that is a lot for you to burden, but I am confident that you can arrange it. The bottom line here is this: Denis Cahill needs to answer to others before I am involved. Keep me out of it. Find a place for Cahill to stay at the seminary. Feed him; he's traveled some days to get here. You and I will talk tomorrow upon my return. Questions?"

"No, your Excellency. I know Monsignor Nagot, of course, and Professor Tessier I will find after his morning classes. I will collect your letters over the situation and brief them. Enjoy your trip."

4

Fr. Denis Cahill did wait in the parlor most of the morning. William Zane, who introduced himself as a third-year seminarian, was overly kind in providing tea and some pastries (although stale). To Fr. Denis, however, Zane appeared too pale and thin for his own heath—perhaps he had taken up self-mortification as a past-time—and Fr. Cahill felt a tad guilty eating the pastries when it was the secretary that needed the nourishment.

Late in the morning Zane told Fr. Cahill that the bishop would be unable to see him today but that others would attend to his concerns, although it would be the next day at the earliest. Fr. Cahill had expected nothing else, insofar as the bishop had many other responsibilities aside from reacting to the complaints of a rebellious and errant priest. The secretary made arrangements for Fr. Cahill to stay in a room at the seminary, just down the hall from the chapel.

The next afternoon William Zane ushered Fr. Cahill to a small classroom and introduced him to the president of the seminary, *Monsignor Charles Nagot, a tall gangly man in his sixties with a thin face, high cheek bones, and long aristocratic nose. Clean shaven and bald, Nagot's eyebrows were white as clouds on a sunny day and matched the wavy white hair that was combed over his ears. Mister Zane introduced Monsignor as a Sulpician order priest from France whom Bishop Carroll had called upon to establish St. Mary's seminary in Baltimore and a prep school for boys. Nagot's eyes were watery, which he wiped repeatedly with a dirty white hankie. Fr. Cahill worried that the president was not in the best of heath, until he spoke. His voice resonated with a rich French accent, although the man had clearly mastered several other languages, including English and Spanish. His tone resonated through the room as if he were used to preaching to large outdoor gatherings. There was no doubt who was in charge.

Professors Tessier and Garnier were slightly younger but also French. They played the part as witnesses to the interrogation.

"Fr. Cahill," said Monsignor Nagot, "the three of us have been asked by his Excellency, Bishop Carroll, to inquire of your credentials, your past, and to ask you to answer charges that our bishop has levied against you, now two years ago. Most curious to him, and myself, is why you have not responded to his demands that you show yourself accountable here in Baltimore before now. It has been most difficult for Bishop Carroll to administer the Church given the brief history and tumult he has encountered especially with numerous so-called clerics who claim to be priests but have no traceable or verified credentials. I am not sorry for bringing this challenge to the forefront insofar as over the past few years the credibility and authority of Bishop Carroll has been continually challenged by men who have suddenly shown up on this country's docks pretending to be priests, demanding money, authority, and respect, when in fact they have no credentials, and their self-serving attitudes make a mockery of the institution with which Pius VI has entrusted John Carroll. So, why don't we start by asking you to defend you credentials, of which we have no letter, endorsement…in short nothing of who you are or reasons why you should be the parish priest of not one but several outlying congregations in the west as you claim.

Nagot certainly knew how to draw the lines. Fr. Cahill was disappointed. He was expecting a more congenial reception. Nonetheless, he immediately produced his certificate of ordination from Archbishop Andrés José Barco Espinosa, and his credentials from the college and seminary in Salamanca, Spain. It was certainly not of his doing that he possessed no baptism certificate, although he might have negotiated for such when he was in seminary. But then, just where was he to find his baptismal records when the priest that had baptized him was murdered only minutes afterward?

Over the next two hours, Fr. Cahill, as humbly as his temperament allowed, told his story—from Ireland as a young lad, to Spain, to New Orleans, to America. He dropped as many names as he could remember. When Professor Tessier cast doubt on his accomplishments and why the bishop knew little of them except by rumor, Fr. Cahill was quick to enumerate the baptisms, marriages, confirmations, and congregants that numbered in the hundreds altogether. He rattled off the names of his society officers and where they met. Then he challenged Tessier to deny or show that his work was anything but what he claimed. To Fr. Cahill it was clear that the interrogators were trying to pick holes in his story, to find inconsistencies, and convince themselves that Cahill was an impostor like so many others that came calling on the bishop. But Fr. Cahill stuck to his story. He reminded Nagot that unlike the so-called Fr. Bodkin, he, Fr. Cahill, had not deserted his post for lack of salary, nor had he lied about his ministry or intentions as Bodkin had conveniently done. That, Fr. Cahill saw, struck a note of credibility.

He also asked just how he was supposed to know Carroll was Superior when he had first arrived in Baltimore in 1788. There was no cathedral, no school, no organization of any sort that could be called Catholic, and the captain of his ship, who made Baltimore his home port, also claimed there was no Catholic organization or leadership. Was there a parish established anywhere near the docks? In fact, William McSherry, whom the men did know, although not personally, was the one that arranged for him to connect with layman and Church planter Richard McSherry, who could vouch for his sincerity, loyalty, and Catholic conduct. William McSherry was not a Catholic, but it was nonetheless this faithless man that set Fr. Cahill on a journey that did establish no less than six parishes. By logic, it was Fr. Cahill that was establishing the Church in the United States, not John Carroll. That sort of reasoning, of course, did not go over well, but then Fr. Cahill was tired of playing the defend-or-disappear game.

Fr. Cahill also described in some detail the charity that Richard and Anastasia began in Hagerstown over which he supervised with the able help of his "Priest Keeper," Immacolata Rosso. The charity today was well established both in Hagerstown, Maryland, and Charles Town, Virginia.

Fr. Cahill finally dropped Fred McCracken's name, the local business consultant to the bishop on civil commerce matters. That got an immediate rise from President Nagot, but when asked how he knew McCracken, Cahill had to admit he didn't. It was but a connection through the McSherrys in an attempt to protect his ministry in Hagerstown from being usurped by Bodkin.

When the matter turned to Carroll's enumerated charges of Cahill's irreverence toward the bishop, demand for money, and charges of simony, Fr. Cahill pulled back completely. He pointed out that his complaints and charges were of a personal nature in an attempt to rescue his fledgling parishes from financial devastation, and that while he felt entitled to due payment to keep his work functioning, he apologized and explained that he had recently sought reconciliation.

Finally, Nagot asked the pivotal question. Why had he come to Baltimore now, and not two years earlier when requested. Regardless of the reason, Nagot pointed out, his delay undermined the bishop's authority and threw into question Cahill's suitability to obey the bishop, which was foundational to the work of the Church.

"Gentlemen," said Fr. Cahill, "my reasons for not coming sooner were the very reasons I stated in my letter. I did not trust the bishop due to his attempts to ignore me and undermine my good ministry. Then there were the rumors that questioned his authority. But I hope that is all in the past. As I have explained several times, I am guilty of such judgments. I have asked the Church for forgiveness, and particular events have brought me to the full realization that I am accountable to Bishop Carroll. There is a matter of deep spiritual importance in Western Maryland that is beyond my ability and authority. Without the bishop's authorization and direction, there is the potential of great spiritual loss to several families in the Shepherd's Town, Leetown, and the Smithfield vicinity. By comparison, the points of conflict between the bishop and myself are insignificant; I hope you and the good bishop will agree they are. I throw myself at the bishop's mercy, not for my sake but for my neighbors and parishioners."

"Mister Cahill," said Monsignor, purposefully avoiding the title of Reverend or Father, "we are meeting today on account of very serious accusations you have made against the Church's utmost authority this side of the Atlantic. And because of those accusations the bishop is close to making sure your priestly credentials are immediately removed and your ministry here, as such, will abruptly come to an end. Insubordination, even if a private matter, cannot be tolerated, and will not be. The bishop has removed several from priestly ministry already, although it is debatable if such individuals were ever priests to begin with, which makes null their removal. So what could possibly be more important than a priest showing obedience to his ordinary?"

Fr. Cahill realized he was on very shaky ground. What he was about to reveal may have no bearing whatsoever on the spiritual need for exorcism as he understood it. For what good is authority to exorcise evil spirits when it is the priest that needs to be exorcised and removed? This he had not considered. It had never crossed his mind—that Adam Livingston's demonic disturbances may somehow be sourced in the ministry of Fr. Denis Cahill. He had not considered that his refusal to come under the bishop's authority was directly related to the demonic presence refusing to come under the Church's authority. Removing Fr. Cahill from the picture may in fact solve Adam Livingston's problem, and the more Fr. Cahill insisted on his involvement in exorcising the spirit, the worse the situation for Livingston and his family could become. But it was too late to back down now. Livingston and McSherry had come to Cahill under remarkable circumstances, especially Livingston's dreams. The disturbances at Livingston's house were real and of supernatural origin, and of such a character that Denis Cahill had never experienced. He must remember the fear he felt. Perhaps that motivation was proof that he was indeed a priest and not an impostor. He understood evil well, and his relationship as a priest to it.

Fr. Cahill continued.

"This past Sunday, after services at Shepherd's town, I was approached by a local farmer, who, although he is not Catholic, was surrounded with support by the very Catholic family that has sponsored my ministry since 1788 and helped establish my parishes. The farmer is Adam Livingston, a man of good reputation and innovation who is known in the territory as a man of integrity. He told the story of how his farm and family these past three years have been cursed. The curse came about when he refused to find a priest for a dying Stranger who stayed the night in his home. The Stranger was by some indications an incognito Jesuit making his way to reunite with John Carroll after the Jesuit Suppression and this Stranger's secret years of ministry among the Indians in the far West. Well, he died that night in the Livingstons' home, and Livingston and his wife, avowed anti-Catholics, refused to find him a priest for Last Rites. It may be worth noting that neither Livingston nor his wife knew any Catholics at the time, our religion still undergoing persecution from the likes of Guy Fawkes and anti-clerics that as I have described who prey upon many of us pioneering priests.

"The curse personified itself by cutting all linen on the premises into ribbons or the cut-out shapes of crescent moons. There was also the incessant noise of shears that evidently were doing the cutting, but never seen. Visitors were scared from the premises. Pottery was shoved off shelves by invisible hands. The house would shake, fireplace stones cemented in place would come loose and be thrown, again by invisible hands, at visitors, catching their clothes on fire. There was the sound of wagons and galloping horses that would surround the house and keep the family awake. The wife, Mary Ann Livingston, suffered a nervous breakdown because of these haunts and spent a few months recuperating at a friend's quarters some miles away. In his effort to stop the disturbances, Mister Livingston called on Lutheran, Presbyterian, and Methodist ministers, including a spiritualist from the Winchester mountains. Strangely the spiritualist, a known conjurer, would not come but told Livingston he needed a true Christian minister. I am told that in every situation these various ministers could do nothing and often ran off scared, unable to mitigate the disturbances.

"Evidently, Mister Livingston in recent months had several dreams in which he was told that the man he saw in his dream could relieve him. He told the dream to the McSherrys who told him that the man in his dream was a Catholic priest. The McSherrys brought Mister Livingston and his daughter, ironically a devout Christian young woman, to my Mass in Shepherd's Town this past Sunday. As soon as I greeted the congregation, Mister Livingston, who was in the back with the McSherrys, yelled out, 'That is that man who can relieve me.' I was obviously shocked because I knew nothing of the situation. After Mass, however, several parishioners whom I know and trust convinced me to visit the Livingston farm and see for myself. I was duly skeptical and actually laughed at the man originally, telling him his neighbors were pranking him. But my closest laymen disputed with me, and suggested I go. Without the bishop's approval I cannot perform an exorcism over the house, especially when the owner is not Catholic, and, as others claim, Mister Livingston is not a believer or congregant at any Christian church.

"But I went with others that I trusted. Evidently these hauntings only occur during the days just before and after the new moon. There may be some connection with the monthly cycle of the moon and the cut-out crescent moons of the linen which I have seen.... Oh, yes, I almost forgot. I have brought a sample."

At that, Fr. Cahill produced the sample of the cut-up linen that Adam had given him. "This is a linen scrap from Mister Livingston's house. Most of the linen in the house, and only the linen, not the wool or cotton, looks like this."

Monsignor Nagot took the one-foot square scrap of linen with at least a dozen crescent cut-outs in it and examined the holes closely. Professors Tessier and Garnier crowded in. Fr. Cahill was glad to see how interested, even reverently, the men examined the cloth, turning it over, and touching the edges of the holes.

"Notice how precisely the crescent shapes have been cut. No one seems to know how they were made, for the sharpest scissors or even a barber's razors could not produce such crispness without the warp and weft unraveling. There is a supernatural aspect to this that I do not understand other than to say it's real and not of this world."

His interrogators, unable to look away from the cloth, nodded. "Can I keep this and show it to the bishop?" asked Nagot.

"Yes, of course." After a moment, Fr. Cahill continued. "The crescent moons are shockingly similar to what I have seen among the spiritualists in New Orleans. It is the same, a demon related to the ancient moon god. Since I was not authorized to say the prayers of exorcism over the house, my good lay ministers suggested I bless the house with Holy Water and the salt of exorcism. I was very skeptical until I stepped onto the porch of the house and doused the premises with Holy Water. With the first sprinkle the porch began to shake to the point that I expected the wood slats to fall off the risers. We entered the house and blessed every room; there were noises, vibrations, coalescing smoke in the shape of a human torso, and the very loud rumbling of wagons and horses that encircled the home. I aggressively used the sacramental water and in Latin repeated the prayers of blessing that I could. There were with me Mister Livingston, Mister and Missus McSherry, and my most trusted layman from Shepherd's Town, Gabriel Menghini. The apparitions, the disturbances were very real. I was not tempted to run, but to fight. I am a priest called by God to combat evil. That is my only job. The tools at my disposal are only those of the church, the sacraments, and sacramentals, and of course prayer and fasting. There is more to relate, but let me conclude with this. The blessing of water and salt halted the activity. When I left, the house was at peace and Mister Livingston was amazed that a Catholic priest could do what no other minister could. But it was evident, every evident to me, that the spirit will return with a vengeance unless the house is properly exorcised.

"That is why I have come now. I seek the bishop's authority to exorcise the house with the prayers of exorcism. I explained to my accomplices I had no authority to perform such without the bishop's express approval and direction. I also need the assistance of a second priest. I also warned Mister Livingston that to avoid that sort of activity in the future he and his family must fully convert, be baptized, and enter a life of obedience, sacraments, and prayer. This experience convinced me that I was under the bishop's authority and could do no more without my obedience to the bishop and his permission. At the same time, the entire area surrounding Livingston's farm is very much aware of the Wizard Clip, as they call this spirit, and by now have heard that the blessing of a Catholic priest has been effective, at least for a time. They are looking to the Church for relief. I am prepared to give that relief, but only with Bishop Carroll's express approval."

With that Fr. Cahill fell silent.

It was some minutes before any of the three men stirred. Fr. Cahill did not shy from watching his inquisitors in the meantime. Throughout his tale each of the men paid close attention. There were no yawns, or distractions. Their tea cups sat idle, and their postures were unflinching. If they were uncomfortable with the story and its spiritual implications, none gave any indication.

"Father Cahill," said Monsignor, finally. "That is an astonishing story of which I have heard similar, but I have never experienced."

Fr. Cahill was partially relieved to hear Monsignor use his informal title— Father. Perhaps there was hope that his ministry might actually be recognized and his apology accepted.

The Monsignor looked to his associates. "Gentlemen, do you have any questions at this juncture?" Both shook their heads no.

"In that case, Fr. Cahill, let us adjourn for now. We will excuse you and discuss what you have told us among ourselves. When the bishop returns to town we will meet with him, and then, no doubt, he with you. Please enjoy your stay in our fine city. Mr. Zane will be in touch with you."

With that Fr. Cahill excused himself, leaving behind three bemused academic professors to discuss his fate, that of his ministry, and the clipped linen.

5

It was two days later that William Zane escorted Fr. Cahill to Bishop Carroll's office and offered the visitor one of two chairs facing the bishop's modest, beat-up desk. It looked as if its planks were taken from a war ship. *The truth was not far off, for the desk was a gift from Jesuits who had repurposed the wood of a Huron War Canoe nearly 100 years earlier.

Monsignor Nagot was also there. He sat at the side of the room like a distant visitor in one of a row of chairs under a large woven tapestry of the United States and the vast western plain bounded by the Mississippi River. It was a woven artistic wall hanging, not intended for accuracy.

"Father Cahill," began the bishop.

It was a good start, thought Fr. Cahill. *He called me "father."*

The bishop continued without pause. "Someone said against the backdrop of eternity that some things are better late than never. I note that may be true in your case. I am glad you have come to your senses, found reconciliation with the Church through Fr. Ryan's ministry, and have accepted the fallible but nonetheless authority of your bishop. But it has also been said that too often accommodations are made too little too late. That may also be true. Time and eternity will tell. I am going to ask you to reaffirm the promises you made at your ordination. I assume you made them and thus these will be provisional. Then, there will be a test."

Fr. Cahill sat still and kept his eyes respectfully on Bishop Carroll. He sensed that all was not going to end well even though it may have started out that way. The bishop had a written document in front of him on his desk, which he kept looking at as he talked.

"Monsignor Nagot, Professors Tessier, Garnier, and I reviewed your case and your testimony. My purpose has been to be objective of their findings, although that cannot be entirely true because of the blunt way you and I began our relationship. I am glad, however, that you have found reconciliation over our earlier situation, and I accept that. I am also envious of your service to the Church which has evidently been sacrificial and effective. However, I hope you sincerely realize that the Church in America is very poor and that we have no intention of petitioning Congress, any political facility, or institution of any kind for taxation or financial support. Many disagree with me on this, but I intend to maintain the religious freedom our Constitution so far has afforded, particularly under the First Amendment for which I have fought long and hard. I expect that battle will continue for the rest of my life and no doubt beyond. The forces fighting to bring the Church under the control of the government are still very strong. That means the only support we can expect financially is from our parish constituents or private donations. It is a fact of political survival in my estimation. We have every intention of completely decoupling the Church and the State to avoid the unmitigated disaster that France and the Church in France has been through these past years."

"Now regarding practical matters," continued the bishop; he was deliberate and unhurried. "I have in front of me the three promises from our rite of Holy Orders. These are the promises that all diocesan priests will make as part of their ordination. We are pretty sure you made these promises to Andrés José Barco Espinosa when you were originally ordained. There is also a matter of your penance, which I will cover separately."

At the mention of a penance, Fr. Cahill felt disappointed, although he was quick to remind himself of his earlier promise to himself to come under the bishop's authority. The battle for independent priests needed to come to an end, even if he disagreed with the bishop.

"Let's make this as formal as possible," said the bishop as he stood and came from behind his desk and gestured for Fr. Cahill to stand, which he did. Monsignor and William then came and stood along side.

"Reverend Denis Cahill," said Bishop Carroll, "in the presence of God and these witnesses are you resolved, as a sign of your complete and unreserved dedication to Christ and His Church, to remain celibate for the sake of the kingdom and give your life in lifelong service to God and mankind? If so, answer, 'I do so promise.'"

The bishop was correct. Denis Cahill had made three promises to Bishop Andrés years ago. He did not hesitate. "I do so promise."

"Are you resolved to maintain and deepen a spirit of prayer appropriate to your way of life and in keeping with what is required of you, to celebrate faithfully the Liturgy of the Hours for the Church and for the whole world, and celebrate Mass daily?"

"I do so promise."

"Do you promise respect and obedience to your ordinary and his successors in all matters of liturgical correspondence, uniformity, and assignment of place?"

"I do so promise."

"Fr. Denis Cahill, I welcome you to the service of the Catholic Church in America."

At that Bishop Carroll glanced at Monsignor and then held out his ring. Fr. Cahill hesitated, but then dropped to one knee, took the bishop's hand, and kissed his ring.

Thereupon, Bishop Carroll lifted both hands and placed them on Fr. Denis' head, and Monsignor opened a book of rites to a ribbon, and held it for the bishop to read:

> *O Jesus, our great High Priest, hear our humble prayers on behalf of your priest, Father Denis Cahill. Give him a deep faith, a bright and firm hope, and a burning love which will ever increase in the course of his priestly life. In his loneliness, comfort him; in his sorrows, strengthen him; in his frustrations, remind him that it is through suffering that his soul is purified. Show him that he is needed by the Church and the souls he serves for the work of redemption. O loving, Blessed Virgin Mary, Mother of us all, take into your heart your son, Denis Cahill, protect him, validate the power that Christ has given him to effectuate the sacraments and to carry on the work of Christ in a world that needs the Savior*

*and your loving care. Be his comfort, joy, strength, and help him
to live and to defend the meaning of being a priest of Jesus Christ
here in America. In nomine Patris, et Filii, et Spiritus Sancti.
Amen.*

At that point Bishop Carroll took Fr. Cahill's arms, raised him up, and embraced him. Monsignor came and embraced Fr. Cahill as well.

"Fr. Cahill be seated," said the bishop. "We are not yet done, although what we have just concluded is a good first step and it goes a long way to heal the breach that has separated us these years. The Church is stronger because of our ministry and work together. However, there is, as I said, a test. And this is it. With grace and mercy I implore you to take upon yourself the following penance to fully heal the breach. It will strengthen the Church, but it may be, I suspect, hard for you to embrace. I ask this of you in loving obedience to your bishop who means only your good, as it will mend the breach of trust between us.

"I am assigning you to the parish you have established at Shepherd's Town for at least six months. While there you may continue your parish duties to the people of that town and district as priest, confessor, and teacher, but otherwise you are to submit yourself to prayer, fasting, and the practice of humility. I prohibit you from all other ministries involving Hagerstown, Martinsburg, Winchester, Chambersburg, and Fort Cumberland. We will make arrangements to have priests from Taneytown, Conewago, and Emmitsburg provide the sacraments and administration in those towns for the time being."

Fr. Cahill's heart burst. The bishop had just cut him off from nine years of intimate relationships, hard work, and his passion for service. What would he say to Immacolata and Richard? He bowed his head in resignation. He felt broken inside but forced himself to reestablish eye contact with Bishop Carroll, whom he felt was being vindictive.

The bishop continued: "It will be good of you to share the specifics of your circuit with Mister Zane and your other responsibilities so we are able to fulfill the expectations of the parishioners. There is no need to explain to them your reassignment, except to say your bishop has requested this of you and being an obedient servant you will comply."

Fr. Cahill felt like a broken man, a man without a ministry and without purpose, but he was also robust and focused on the important things that had brought him originally to Baltimore. "I am disappointed," said Fr. Cahill, "and I fear there are numerous things that will need looking after that I will not even remember. There are building plans in several of my parishes, although nascent in most. There is the charity work in Hagerstown that will need oversight several times a week, although it is true that Missus Rosso is competent to direct and assist whomever you send to oversee that. Mister Hager will need to be informed; he has been very generous, as, of course, has been Richard McSherry.

Will you allow me to travel to my parishes, celebrate Mass one last time at each location, and at least secure the Church's interests before I cloister myself in Shepherd's Town?"

"Yes, of course, please do," said the bishop. Take several weeks if you need. Your transition needs to be orderly and not harsh or appear regressive. And so that you understand fully my well-meaning and God's mercy, before you leave, Mister Zane will advance you a stipend to carry you through this transition."

"What shall I tell Mister McSherry, my sponsor these past years, whose introduction and backing has secured these parishes? I may have been the priest, but it is Mister McSherry who is administratively responsible and is in fact an officer of the Catholic society in more than one location. He is also the landlord over Magdala, the rectory and meeting place in Hagerstown, and it is his wife who is the functional heart of the charity for the poor we have established there and in Charles Town."

"I suspect," said the bishop, "if Mister McSherry is half the businessman you have made him and his brother out to be, he will easily transition to working with the new administrators. But tell him that I welcome his calling on me here in Baltimore anytime, although some advance notice to ensure my presence would be best. Please tell him, as delicately as you can, that your reassignment is no reflection on him, but is out of respect for his sacrifice to you these many years."

Fr. Cahill was surprised at the offering of the stipend. He could immediately suspect that would cover little if anything of the expense involved in moving his possessions from Hagerstown to Shepherd's Town, but as a sign of normalized relationships with the bishop it went a long way. "What of the exorcism concerns of the Livingston plantation, and those of other practicing Catholics in the Smithfield vicinity who are relying on the Church's authority over this spiritual domination that has so disrupted the area."

The bishop wavered. "The first thing that comes to mind is that what you have reported is a delicate issue that is outside the immediate concern of the Church. For us to intervene risks raising anti-Catholic sentiment among those we have worked hard to appease."

"But Livingston came to us," said Fr. Cahill. "We did not go to him. And it was evident through the faithful Catholics present that the presence of a Catholic priest, even with just Holy Water, was effective. I have promised Mister Livingston I would return with word from you as to what steps we or he should take other than baptism and conversion, which is obvious."

"That is what concerns me the most," said the bishop. "For the Church to barge in and start baptizing those who have not actively sought the Church and conversion on their own. This is a particularly sensitive matter because of my political connections with the new government. If word gets out that somehow I am involved, gave permission, or the order that these pagans should be converted and brought into the church, I fear reprisals and a political reaction in

Congress that I could not, and the Church may not, be able to contain. I must demand, therefore, that you do not perform an exorcism of his premises or attempt to convert him or his family. On the other hand, I will do this: In the next few weeks I will send an emissary to look in on the Livingston premises to ensure that there isn't something we should be doing, although exorcism of a non-Catholic's domicile seems extreme to me. While your report to us of the situation is useful, it is not complete, and another's examination is required for my satisfaction."

"Again," said Fr. Cahill, "if my discernment is right, Mister Livingston's faith, which has been absent these many years, is now tenderly ajar. I was skeptical, but am no more, either to the spirit's activity or of Mister Livingston's receptivity. I must return to him and give him the news that you are...what, should I tell him?"

"That I care for his soul and that of his family, and will send someone soon to meet with him, and minister to their needs. Do not convey my doubt about how that is to be accomplished. The Holy Spirit will direct in God's own time, which is rarely my own." The bishop turned to Monsignor. Perhaps, God will reveal a solution to Monsignor, or even Mister Zane. But for now, we offer only our prayers for their well-being."

Fr. Cahill wanted to continue the argument, but he saw it as futile. The bishop was in control, as he should be, although Fr. Cahill felt rejected and cast out. He viewed himself as a man with a passion but suddenly without a mission, a ship adrift on a storm-tossed sea without a shred of sail to brace and guide it.

6

Fr. Denis Cahill left Baltimore and headed directly to Leetown to talk to Richard McSherry, who would need to know what just happened. Perhaps Richard would know what to do, if there was anything to do. He also needed to visit Adam Livingston and convey the bishop's plans or lack of them. He took two days to ride to Retirement. All the way he found it difficult to focus. Until now he had been unaware of the many relationships and responsibilities he had accumulated over the last nine years and how many people and parishioners had relied on him to bring them the sacraments, listen to their confessions, baptize their babies, and marry their sons and daughters. He felt like his entire ministry had been lashed crudely together in rotten canvas like a corpse and tossed unceremoniously overboard to be buried at sea without so much as a buoy to mark the memory. He felt as if five of his six parishes had suddenly been banned, made illegal, the property snatched by an illegitimate authority.

In short he felt betrayed and could not shake the sense that the bishop's action were contrary to natural law and order. As the priest in question, he was saddened by his consent to the arrangement. He had not fought back at the demonic attack but fled like a scared kitten. He concluded he was without will or mission and a complete failure. He had failed to fight and instead fled. He tried to find some consolation and reason for what had happened. He admitted he was at fault for attacking the bishop in his early letters, but he contested that the punishment did not fit the crime.

William Zane and Monsignor Nagot now had his latest circuit schedule. They promised to see that Masses, confessions, and instruction carried on with the least amount of interruption. Some of that depended on Fr. Cahill maintaining the circuit for the next few weeks and alerting leaders to the transition. But what had been most disconcerting is that the bishop had told him parish assignments would not revert to what they had been. Fr. Cahill's ministry, as he and Richard had imagined and constructed it, was at an end. What would happen in six months was unknown. It was the unknowable that distressed Fr. Cahill the most.

Why should that bother him, he wondered, when his life for the most part had been in transition? When he left Ireland as a teenager he had no idea what awaited him in Spain. The same when he was ordained and had made temporary promises to the Capuchins in New Orleans. Certainly he knew nothing beforehand of the great fire and destruction of the Church there, or how his relationship with Fr. Antoine would be hindered and disintegrated. Had he known what was in store for the voyage aboard Captain Johns' Eagle? When he arrived in Baltimore even William McSherry had no idea what to do with a stray priest that was no better off than a street urchin. Surviving anti-Catholic thieves was a miracle, as was connecting with Richard McSherry. He recalled the dedication and loyalty of Immacolata Rosso, his priest keeper. Who could have known her value? Would she take care of the next priest as well as she cared for him? He was surprised by his latent wish that she would not. But the incertitude he now faced was beyond all that. In retrospect, his life as a pioneering priest seemed like a beautiful tapestry, its ratty short ends of the yarn hidden from view behind the colorful and artistic facade. In his present state he could not decipher the front from the back of the tapestry. It was now a tangled mess, and confusion swirled though his mind. Fr. Cahill's soul was in great turmoil, and once again he questioned his calling.

7

Letitia McCartney rode McSherrys' mare, Hopscotch, hard along the trails that crisscrossed the 5,000 plus acres of farmland and woodland of the Retirement estate. Most of the land was wooded, but Richard rented out the tillable acreage to tenant farmers who planted a variety of crops including radishes, corn, and potatoes. It was a sunny, pleasant day and Letitia relished the few hours she had alone each week to walk, canter, and even gallop astride Hopscotch. The mare seemed to enjoy the exploration as much as Letitia. The never-ending trails and wagon paths connected the rich farm land with irrigation ponds and the often raging water of the Opequon Creek a half-mile to the west.

Catharine and Anastasia also enjoyed riding and exploring, but with three active boys to care for it was rare that the three women could get away by themselves. Anastasia rarely wanted to leave the boys' side, so she was content to stay around the homestead when Letitia and Catharine wanted to get away for a few hours. But most often it was Letitia, the more adventurous, who rode off by herself in the cool of the morning.

She returned to the estate mid-morning and handed off Hopscotch to Hank Paulson, an older local man with white hair and a long-handled mustache who cared for their five horses, maintained their stable, and kept up with the estate's maintenance.

As soon as she turned from the stable and walked toward the house she saw Sassafras tied up at the house by the water trough. The gelding was loaded down with traveling bags and looked as if it needed a rub down.

"I'm gettin' to her, Miss McCartney," Hank yelled after Letitia. "Father just rode in a few minutes ago. Looks like he's been travelin' a bit."

"Thanks, Hank," said Letitia. *What was Fr. Cahill doing here,* she wondered? She got in front of the gelding, held out her gloved hand for the horse to smell, then stroked the horse's neck. Sassafras was a smart and loyal steed to its owner. They were a good match. When she first met Fr. Cahill in Hagerstown she was impressed with his poise and presence, but when she later heard the story of his perilous journey from New Orleans to Leetown, she became enamored with his adventurous, never-say-die character. Too bad he was a priest, she had thought. "But then, miracles do happen, don't they, Sassafras?" she said as she stroked the gelding's nose. The horse responded by rubbing its nose gently along Letitia's neck.

Her heart skipped a beat as she realized she would see him in a moment. She slapped the dust off her riding skirt, brushed her auburn hair away from her face, moistened her dry lips, and reminded herself that the riding boots would have to come off before she went inside. She had not avoided that pile of fresh horse muck at the stable…careless of her. Then she noticed Fr. Cahill's riding boots set aside outside the back door. She took hers off and purposely set them close to his.

On the south side of the kitchen was the family's supper room. It was a circular space with windows all around, and in the center was a round table. There was enough room for the entire family to sit together and enjoy a meal. When Letitia entered the room, Anastasia was pouring lemonade, Catharine was laughing, and the three boys had decided that Fr. Cahill, who was sitting at the table, was a mountain that needed to be conquered. She had never seen Fr. Cahill laugh or tease young children, but there he was, seemingly having the time of his life tickling and rough-housing with three rambunctious boys who cared nothing for Fr. Cahill's reverent priestly calling. He was one of them… and it was playtime.

Letitia stopped in her tracks and just watched. She could not remember, ever, witnessing a priest playing roughly with boys. All four were laughing their heads off and screaming with delight, and Anastasia and Catharine were no exceptions. The only one not laughing or giggling was Letitia. She was stunned. Her heart ached—what a great father—to young children—he would be.

She knew Fr. Cahill was there to see Richard and she suspected it had something to do with Adam Livingston and the hauntings at Flax Haven. She had not been at Flax Haven when Fr. Cahill blessed the house, but she heard all about it that evening from a very surprised and subdued Richard and Anastasia. She had also heard that Fr. Cahill was going to Baltimore to speak to the bishop, and that Richard didn't feel easy about the audience but understood why Fr. Cahill had to go.

Here it was nearly a week later, and Fr. Cahill had just returned from Baltimore, but Richard was traveling and was not expected back for a couple days. Priests did not call on single women or on married women whose husbands were away. But something here was different.

When at last the boys were distracted and sent outside to play, she heard the tale, along with Catharine and Anastasia, of Fr. Cahill's trip to Baltimore. It was not a good story, and the three women sat in silence as he told them the highlights of what had happened and how he had been removed from his ministry at all but Shepherd's Town. Anxious as he was to talk with Richard, Fr. Cahill had not even stopped at Shepherd's Town on the way to Leetown, although he passed within sight of his hilltop chapel. Letitia could see that the man was depressed and lost. Her heart reached out to him. If only her arms could also embrace him, but that was not to be. As socially awkward as it seemed, Anastasia made up the guest bedroom and told Fr. Cahill that he was welcome to stay until Richard returned. Fr. Cahill quickly said yes, and that he would spend the time in prayer and reflection.

Over the next two days Fr. Cahill did spend long hours alone in his room. He prayed the Liturgy of the Hours, he took long walks around the property, and he walked in the garden praying his Rosary. He also celebrated Mass with the ladies and the boys, once in the Rosary garden, and once at night after the boys had been tucked into bed. But what Letitia remembered the most about those two days were the playtimes Fr. Cahill gave to the boys—chasing each other around the yard, collecting rocks, examining the skeletons of dead birds, traipsing through the muddy creek, and at night the stories he told the boys of sailing ships and pirates. The stories seemed so real that afterward, when he was alone, Letitia had to ask if the stories were true.

"Did you want them to be?" he asked, and he winked at her.

The two days were an eternity for Letitia. Whenever she had a moment and he was alone, she could not help herself but to find an excuse to sit, walk, and talk with him. When she first approached him, when they were alone in the garden, he avoided her look. Her heart said that he needed to talk to someone.

654 O Stanley D. Williams

Having one's life work ripped out from under him had to be a severe blow. He had to be hurting. She asked about his family back in Ireland. He liked talking about his mum and pa, and sister, Catharine. He asked how she and Catharine had become friends. She told him. He asked after his mum and pa, how they were, how they felt about their children being the other side of the ocean. She told him and he listened carefully, watching her talk. When she told him about her own family and her mum and pa he watched her even more intently, she thought. She liked him watching her more than when he avoided her gaze. She asked about Spain and his time at seminary. He wasn't so open about those times. He seemed unsure about how it all happened. Was he afraid to go on a long and dangerous passage across the ocean? A little, but it was an adventure. When did he decide to be a priest? It just happened. Did his parents always expect him to be a priest? He didn't think so, but they were both surprised and happy when he wrote them that he was ordained. They were also sad that he was sailing to the New World and New Orleans.

One afternoon they walked to the stables to feed the horses apples that had fallen from the trees and were too far gone to be made into pies. She was quiet for a while. There was a question she wanted to ask but feared his reaction. Finally, she collected the courage. "Did you ever think about getting married instead of being a priest? Was there ever a girl…you wanted to marry, instead?" She glanced at him sideways when she asked it. She could see he didn't want to answer. He curled his lips over his teeth and bit down. He appeared stumped and he didn't look at her or say anything for a long time.

Finally, when they got to the stables and Hank was out of earshot, he looked at her. In a quiet and serious tone he said, "Not until after I was a priest. By then it was too late." It was a joke, but he didn't smile or laugh. He just stared at her as if trying to see through her. It was as if he wanted to know why she had asked that question. They looked at each other for what seemed like a long time. Finally, she lifted the basket of apples and presented them to him. He took an apple, and she took one, and they fed them to the horses who gobbled up the juicy fruit as if they had not eaten in days.

Going back to the house, neither of them spoke to each other the rest of the day. The next day, Richard returned.

8

Richard was eager to get back to Leetown. He had left Retirement to visit tenants in the west the same day that Fr. Cahill had left for Baltimore. Richard knew how fluid the situation was between Fr. Cahill and the bishop, and he was not at peace about them meeting, although he did understand the need for Fr. Cahill to make things right with the bishop. After spending an hour with Fr. Cahill and Gabriel Menghini blessing Flax Haven, Richard's attitude toward the bishop had changed. What he saw that day, and what Fr. Cahill accomplished, convinced him that something very wrong was going on at Flax Haven and it wasn't Adam Livingston's imagination. Perhaps Fr. Cahill had a special calling. Far be it from Richard to stand in the way of that. But Richard was not so sure about Bishop Carroll. Yes, Richard knew that in the past Fr. Cahill had not handled his relations with the bishop in the best of ways. He also knew that the bishop was eager to put Denis in his place. That made Richard nervous. The bishop probably had no idea of the work and money he and Fr. Cahill had put into the Catholic societies in the towns and villages of western Maryland and Virginia. Unfortunately, he had no idea when Fr. Cahill might return, although he did remember Adam Livingston being promised by Fr. Cahill that as soon as he returned he would report what the bishop had said.

On the way back to Leetown, Richard reined Romeo to swing past Flax Haven and pay Adam a visit. But the visit was in vain. Adam had not heard from Fr. Cahill, although Richard was very happy to find that Flax Haven had been a quiet place of refuge during the last week and the disruptions were apparently a thing of the past. That lightened his heart, and he turned Romeo toward home, a few miles northeast along the Leetown Road.

It was early afternoon when he arrived home at Retirement. He turned over Romeo to Hank and unpacked his saddle bags. "Thank you again, Hank, for being around in my absence. Is everything and everyone okay?"

"As far as I know, Mister McSherry. Although two days ago Fr. Cahill arrived. He's waiting for you inside if he's not wanderin' the property."

"Two days ago? I'm eager to talk to him. How did he appear to you? Is he okay?"

"Can't rightly say. My guess is he's not exactly a happy priest."

"Thanks for the warning."

Richard found his family, Catharine, and Letitia feeding themselves in the round supper room. He kissed Anastasia and greeted the rest at a distance. The boys' faces, bibs, and hands were so covered in food he simply patted each on the head, and he did that carefully as they all reached out for him from their strapped-in child chairs.

He turned to Anastasia. "Where's Fr. Denis?"

With her hands full of various eating implements in vain attempts to shovel nutrients into young hungry mouths, she pointed with her elbow out the window.

Fr. Cahill was sitting alone on a bench at the far end of the Rosary garden. "He hasn't eaten since this time yesterday," Anastasia said. "He's been waiting for you."

Richard went out the side door and headed for the garden. Fr. Cahill saw him. They greeted each other, embraced, and occupied a nearby bench. Over the next hour Fr. Denis told Richard all that had happened since they had last been together. He explained how the bishop had come to accept Fr. Cahill as a credentialed priest, which for Fr. Cahill was a relief. But he also explained how the bishop had removed him from his circuit of parishes, except at Shepherd's Town. That was a grave disappointment with which Fr. Cahill was still struggling. The decision was for at least six months, but perhaps much longer

"So, you have not been to see Livingston?" asked Richard.

"That's right."

"Do you want me to go with you to Livingston's?"

"Not for my sake. It might help him. I fear it will seem that the bishop's decision will appear as if the Catholic Church, like every other church, has abandoned him."

"But you said the bishop would send someone."

"Maybe, but who knows when or who that will be."

When they were done, Richard offered no alternative to the bishop's edict, and for the sake of the Catholic societies they had founded they decided it was best to follow the bishop's directives. Richard could see, however, how this disappointed Fr. Cahill deeply and how he was led again to question his calling. Yet, short of starting another protesting sect, there was nothing else to do. At last they consoled each other that they would celebrate Mass together regularly each week in Shepherd's Town. They also both agreed that having Fr. Cahill in Shepherd's Town would actually encourage the parishioners there and no doubt grow the Church.

Fr. Cahill would leave in the morning, visit Livingston, then go on to Hagerstown and begin the transition. In several weeks he would settle down in Shepherd's Town and give it all over to God.

That evening, Fr. Cahill sat on a porch swing and read his breviary. Letitia came and sat next to him. Richard noticed but thought nothing much of it as he and Anastasia prayed with and put the boys to bed. Catharine sat in the parlor and knitted.

When Anastasia and Richard were coming down the stairs from the boys' second floor bedroom, Anastasia leaned into Richard, kissed him and said, "There's been some romance in the air, if you haven't noticed."

"Who?"

"*Philip Field has been calling on Catharine, coincidentally while you've been gone."

"Was he here of late?"

"Yes, the evening before Fr. Cahill came. I don't think Fr. Cahill is aware of Philip, but…."

"…he should be," finished Richard. "How serious is it?"

"Let's just say, I expect a giggling young woman any day now."

Richard said nothing, but suddenly began to wonder what his patriarchal responsibilities toward Catharine might be. He was interrupted by Anastasia's further observation.

"By the way, my dear husband, you have not witnessed this, but I should tell you. Miss McCartney and Fr. Denis, if I should be that informal, except for late last night and today, have been nearly inseparable, as they are right now out on the porch."

Richard turned to his wife in surprise.

She continued, "Nothing untoward I might add, as I've kept a close eye on them. But she has essentially taken our depressed priest under her mindful care, and raised his spirit to something respectful and endearing."

"Just what are you suggesting?" he asked.

"Well, if you recall, Miss McCartney did not come to America simply to protect Catharine from hounds and scoundrels." Anastasia paused and looked at her husband suggestively.

Richard caught it. "Right. She's looking for an 'Irish bachelor' is how I think she put it."

"Like you, my dear. But you're already taken, thank goodness."

"I have not looked twice at Miss McCartney, I hope you should know."

"I do, and I thank you husband. But..." and she let it linger in the air that he might catch her meaning.

"Fr. Denis is not an Irish bachelor," snapped Richard.

"Richard, dear. If he wasn't a priest he would be a very eligible Irish bachelor, and quite a catch for any woman looking for one. Is that frank enough?"

"Oh, God! Anastasia! How could you think of such a thing?"

"My dear, I'm not thinking it. But a woman's instincts tell me that someone is."

At that moment laughter of a man and a woman erupted from the porch swing not twenty feet away through a screen door.

A moment later Richard came onto the porch, where Fr. Denis sat on the porch swing with Letitia. They were still smirking from whatever had made them laugh moments earlier, as if trying to quell a private joke. But as soon as Richard made his presence known, they stopped their friendly prattle and Letitia, seeing Richard's serious and concerned demeanor, excused herself and left the porch somewhat embarrassed.

Richard looked quizzically at Fr. Denis as if catching him doing something he shouldn't, then glanced after the retreating Letitia. "Richard," said Fr. Denis. "You need to get her married off."

"Me? I'm not her father." Richard sat down next to his priest friend on the unstable swing.

"Well, I'm not either. But if I wasn't one..." and he let that hang for a moment.

"Denis!" snapped Richard.

"Well, then, find her a man!"

Richard fairly missed a beat. "Like Philip Field, perhaps?"

Fr. Denis thought for a moment. "Why, that's an excellent prospect. Has he been calling?"

"Yes, he has," said Richard.

Fr. Denis' face lit up. "Why, they would make an excellent couple. Should I...encourage it perhaps like I did with you and Anastasia?"

"From what I hear you're too late. But it's not Letitia Mister Field is calling on." He let that sink in.

Fr. Denis tried to make out his meaning. "Not Letitia? Then....? Oh, my goodness! Are you serious? Why didn't I know about this?"

"My guess is you will know soon, or so says my instinctive wife who has welcomed Mr. Field here when I've been gone."

"And it's not Letitia?"

"No. Although I wonder for your sake if it should be."

"Yes, for my sake. Well, no danger yet. But I'll reiterate. The woman in question has some personable qualities."

Fr. Denis got up from the swing, leaving Richard literally in the lurch. "Catharine! Catharine! Wherefore art thou, Catharine, my dear sister to me?" With that, Fr. Denis disappeared into the house and shut the screen door behind him.

9

Catharine did not mind for an instant that Letitia had interrupted her knitting. She was getting bored knitting scarfs in the middle of summer, and was much more interested in what her best friend was thinking, having spent so much time the last few days with her brother—the priest, of all people. Catharine was young but she was not in the least bit naive.

Letitia had somewhat skipped into the parlor and flopped down next to Catharine on the sofa and was still snickering. "Fr. Denis just told me the most marvelous story. I had no idea he was such a trickster."

"My brother? Well, it's possible. What did you hear?"

"Have you ever heard the story about how Anastasia and Richard met and began to court?"

Catharine thought for a moment. She had not heard, and she suddenly felt left out of what must have been a grand story. "You heard this from my brother?"

"Yes. Yes, your brother. Oh, Catharine it's marvelous. I had no idea priests could be romantic cupids."

"Oh, I guarantee you, he's no angel, if he's anything like our papa. Tell me. Tell me, what did he say?"

Just then, they heard the porch door swing shut and latch and Fr. Denis bellow: "Catharine! Catharine! Wherefore art thou, Catharine, my dear sister to me?"

"Oh, no," said Letitia. "He's found out that I know."

"Know what? What do you know? Tell me!"

Just then Fr. Denis walked into the parlor and stood over his sister and Letitia sitting close together on the sofa. Letitia was giggling like a teenager, even as both her hands gripped Catharine's hands and knitting needles including the balled-up, partially finished scarf. Catharine looked at her brother standing in the doorway with a very serious and disturbed look on his face. Then he turned his attention to Letitia who burst out laughing, jumped up, and ran past Fr. Denis out of the room.

Catharine, with no smile or her face, dared to look up into her brother's eyes. "Will someone please tell me what's going on? What did you just tell my best friend that has her running about and giggling like a child?"

"When were you going to tell me?" inquired the stern-faced priest.

"What?" cracked Catharine. "Tell you what?"

"About Philip Field."

Catharine guffawed. "When there's something to tell, I suppose."

The brother and sister stared at each other for a minute or so. It was a stand-off. Catharine had no intention of telling her brother anything that wasn't true, and Fr. Denis finally gave up the contest and went back to the porch.

No sooner was Catharine left alone than she was assaulted once again by Letitia, who slithered back into the parlor and took up her seat on the sofa next to her best friend.

"And when were you going to tell me?" Letitia whispered.

"About what?" snapped Catharine.

"About that cute little boy, Philip?"

"Oh, Letitia, stop it. You know as much as I do. Perhaps more, the way you hang around when he comes. So let's turn the tables. When were you going to tell me?"

"About what?" asked Letitia.

"Don't be coy. It doesn't work with me. About your diabolical designs."

"I have no idea what you're talking about," said Letitia.

"Okay, let me put it to you this way. If Philip proposes and I accept, what will you do?"

Letitia studied her friend's face for a moment, then looked down at the unfinished scarf betwixt and between the pointed needles.

Catharine pressed. "Letitia, there are no secrets between us. We've gone over this at least dozen times. Once and for all...." Catharine lowered her voice to a whisper. "You can't marry my brother. He's a priest...forever."

Letitia fingered Catharine's unfinished scarf. "Speaking of designs, this is a lovely design you've got going in this scarf." Letitia slowly pulled Catharine's working yarn. It came off the point of a needle, and as Letitia slowly pulled, the design of the scarf came unraveled. "Nothing is forever, Catharine."

10

Most Feared Master of Peril,

It appears I've been unnecessarily defending my campaign to haul off to Perdition my target, Adam Livingston. Perhaps it's been the case that my tactics require long suffering to develop. Most recently, however, I'm encouraged to see the progress my toil has secured.

It is our long established custom to keep Christians from confessing their sins, and particularly to keep Catholics from the confessional. In the case of Denis Cahill, this being his first time seeking reconciliation in many years, I found my despised self reveling in our success. Sins pile up, humans forget about them, and subconsciously are weighed down with an unresolved, unrepentant, and unmindful backlog of sin. It's the presence of conscious guilt, of course, that drives them to confession. I feel accomplished when I can suggest to souls that they need not concern themselves with guilty feelings, and that guilty pleasures are much more in vogue. *Distraction, Deflection, and Denial* I think is the slogan we were taught in conflagration training. Such good ideas are so bad, and valued.

I'm not sure what to think about Cahill going to Baltimore from the scare I gave him. That's not the way it's supposed to work. Cowardice is preferred. He does exhibit shards of robustness, but all humans, especially priests, have their thorn. I expected Cahill to retreat to his arrogance and independence, not grovel before an uppity-up closet Jesuit. Still he ran; he did not stand and fight. Cheers for the bad guys.

Notice how subtle my tactics can be. I'm still chortling over the success of my campaign. Cahill admits he hasn't thought through his visit to Carroll while at the same time thinking Carroll purchased his office. It's good to know that simony is still alive and well in the Church, or at least we can provoke scandals with the suspicion of it. Nothing like creating a scandal where none actually exists. Yes, yes—Distract, Deflect, and Deny—such useful rubrics.

And then there is our luscious Letitia, our all grown up little darling. To see my salacious suggestions take root is so sweet. Did you notice how Cahill is actually frightened of the nymph? Rightly so, although on the downside such fear has sent him to Ryan, the priest with the salacious first name—Matthew (that's the sorrow).

My ultimate aim to sideline Cahill has actually occurred, in part. Pure irony—Cahill goes to confession and kisses the bishop's golden slippers, expecting not only forgiveness but money, and what happened? He's nearly removed from the priesthood and confined to a pathetic chapel on a hill to nowhere. That he's removed from Western Maryland's citadel of Catholicism, Hagerstown, is even more sweet and Bodkin has gone south (pun intended) leaving Hagerstown without the sacraments. I am so good at what I do—Cahill's other parishes will now flounder allowing us inroads in many places and hearts. The plan is moving along so well.

At your sinful service,
Cyn Namrasit, OPSD

Chapter 47
Bandages

1

Friday, July 7, 1797.

The next morning Fr. Cahill departed Retirement and headed down the road to Smithfield and the Livingstons' plantation. During the short ride he was a mix of emotions. He felt confident that there had been no supernatural disruptions since his last visit not quite two weeks ago. He was feeling chagrined, however, in bearing the bishop's news that there would be no exorcism...at least for now.

When he rode into the yard day laborers were already at work in the fields. Turning Sassafras toward the house he saw Adam descending the porch steps leaving for work. Just above him on the porch was Mary Ann. He stayed astride Sassafras, rode to the porch, and tipped his galero.

Adam lit up with a smile when he saw Fr. Cahill.

Adam lit up with a smile when he saw Fr. Cahill.

Mary Ann, however, backed away and prepared to re-enter the house. There seemed to be a permanent scowl on her face. Fr. Cahill wondered if the Wizard had been active in his absence.

"Priest! Welcome to Flax Haven," said Adam in greeting.

"Good morning, Adam...Mary Ann," and Fr. Cahill tipped his hat again. "Good to see you both. How are things these last two weeks?"

Adam turned to glance at his wife. Fr. Cahill followed the look to Mary Ann's scowl that seemed no longer permanent but cemented onto eternity's backdrop. Turning back to Fr. Cahill, Adam gloated. "*Things,* as you put it, couldn't be better. We've had a very peaceful and undisturbed two weeks. You really are a miracle worker, Father. We thank you dearly, we do."

"I'm glad to hear that," said Fr. Cahill. "You recall I promised to ride to Baltimore and seek my bishop's permission to come and exorcise the premises to assure that you are never disturbed again." Fr. Cahill had intended to continue with the bishop's full answer, but Adam interrupted him.

"Father, I don't think that'll be necessary." Adam glanced at Mary Ann, whose glare centered on Fr. Cahill as if he was the problem and therefore unwelcome.

Hearing Adam's response, Fr. Cahill was taken back; it wasn't what he expected.

Adam continued, "We've heard or seen nothing since you blessed our house. As I said at the time, you did what no one else wanted to do or could. We hold you in our debt. But the miracle, if you want to call it that, is done, and...." this time Adam was interrupted by his wife, who in very terse tones addressed Fr. Cahill.

"You can leave now. We are fine and finally at peace, for whatever reason."

Adam quickly turned back to Mary Ann. "My dear wife, please be kind to the man who has relieved us. There is no need to speak that way to the priest for any reason."

"You forget husband," snarked Mary Ann, "they bring evil, eventually. We've had weeks of peace before especially between the new moons. Let us wait for the month to be up. Who knows what evil lurks because of his maledictions. You trust too quickly." With that Mary Ann entered the house and closed the door firmly behind her.

Adam, downcast, turned back with regret to Fr. Cahill. "We, or ah, at least I appreciate you looking in on us, Father. As you witness, I'm in a pickle. If it was up to me, you'd be welcome at my table anytime. Peace, however, must be cultivated and at times the harvest cannot be discerned from the thistles. Forgive me."

Fr. Cahill thought for a moment. "Yes, I understand. I stopped by to see how you were doing, of course, but also to fulfill my promise and convey my bishop's concern for you. Ironically, you might tell your wife that my bishop is of the same opinion as she, that an exorcism of your premises at this time is perhaps not best. Although, I must tell you, I disagree with my bishop. But since I'm trying to be an obedience priest I will abide by his wishes...and your wife's, of course."

Sassafras seemed to think it was time to go, and turned away from the house. Fr. Cahill was not done, however, and turned the horse back. "Mister Livingston, a couple more things may be important for you to hear. First, Bishop Carroll said he would send an emissary, other than myself, to visit you some time in the not too distant future. Please consider it a courtesy call when he comes. I assume it will be a priest, but I know not who. As you may recall, I said the bishop and I are not on the best of terms and he wants a second opinion.

Second, from myself, on your behalf, I implore you again to seek shelter in the Catholic Church. Be converted, baptized, and partake of the Church's sacraments. And pray. Do pray for mercy. Pray heartedly and seriously. Not just for your farm and these premises, but for your soul, for I fear it is in peril."

"Thank you for your concern, Father. But as you see, we are fine now." Adam turned slightly sheepish. "I would offer you the gold that mysteriously appeared when you were here last, but I have returned it to its owner as you requested."

"That is good to hear, Mister Livingston. Very good to hear. I bless you. But it was not me. It was God and the authority he extends through the Church that has put you at peace. I pray it lasts." At that, Fr. Cahill made the sign of the cross over Adam and his house with a Latin blessing: "In nomine Patris, et Filii, et Spiritus Sancti." Then, with another tip of his galero, he turned Sassafras, trotted out of the yard, and headed for Hagerstown.

Over the next two weeks, Fr. Cahill completed his transitional circuit and moved his belongings to Shepherd's Town and the St. Agnes Chapel rectory-apartment. All the time he thought how he would miss his priest keeper, Mrs. Rosso, and how he would have to learn how to cook. Once settled, he canvassed the town, door-to-door, and posted hand bills of the new Mass schedule and times for confession, instruction, and daily Mass. Since he had long been established in the town as their circuit riding priest, and since he enjoyed a strong turnout for Sunday Mass, he expected at least a half-dozen to come to daily Mass. Yet, during the first two weeks at St. Agnes no one came. He was used to celebrating Mass everyday alone, yet after inviting the entire town to join him and with no one coming, he again questioned his calling. Further disheartening was the difference between Shepherd's Town's St. Agnes and Hagerstown's Magdala. St. Agnes was on a hill and isolated from the town, although most of the town could be seen from St. Agnes' porch. Nonetheless, the chapel was not on a street like in Hagerstown by which traffic and commerce passed throughout the day. Effectively, now, in Shepherd's Town Fr. Cahill was cloistered, and he had never signed up to be a monk. A Capuchin friar? Sure! Friars were supposed to be out and about, mingling and caring for regular people in the community. Monks were called to hide away and pray and sometimes would go for days without talking to anyone. They claimed it brought them closer to God. Fr. Cahill wasn't so sure about that. He knew himself well enough to know he was not called to be a monk.

2

Sunday, July 23, 1797.

It was just over two weeks later and the Livingstons had enjoyed a quiet Sunday evening. In fact, it had been quiet and peaceful for the past month. Fr. Cahill's blessing of the house with Holy Water had been very effective, or so thought Adam Livingston. Life was getting back to normal. The Wizard's disruptions had been disturbed, for good.

Adam, however, had still not taken Fr. Cahill's warning seriously that if the house was not exorcised and Adam and his family did not come into the Church, be baptized, and partake regularly of the sacraments, the demonic manifestations would likely return with a vengeance. Compared to his peers, Adam was normal in many respects. Humans have many weaknesses, and one of them is sentimentality—the reliance on feelings as a guide to truth, or at best a shallow reliance on emotions at the expense of reason.

So it was that Adam and Mary Ann Livingston fell asleep in their beds confident that their good life was going to continue...forever. But few things are forever.

Just after midnight Adam woke. He sat up in bed, listened carefully, and looked about in the dark. He wondered what had stirred him from a sound slumber. Outside the window there was a cool breeze in the trees along with the normal nighttime sounds of insects eating, mating, or attempting such. There were no clipping sounds, nor stray wagons or stampeding horses encircling the house. It was perfectly peaceful. But Adam was aware that something was wrong. His body tensed as if a guillotine was about to drop on his neck. Sweat began to pour from his forehead and the soles of his feet. His heart beat wildly, his breath came shallow and short, and he felt a hopeless, bottomless dread. He turned to Mary Ann sleeping next to him. So deep was her sleep that she was actually snoring. He had never heard her snore before, but it was soft like a cat purring. He could not shake the idea that something terrifying and life-threatening had occurred...or was about to.

Then it began.

In the distance he heard the frightened, throaty hiss of several screech owls. It sounded like the clashing of rusty scythes or swords battling for dominance. But soon there was something more, like a divided parliament of owls growling, hooting, and squabbling over the skin of a snake. Then, at once the fowl feuding stopped, and with a fierce flutter was suddenly replaced with a dull, muffled explosion. Moments later the house reverberated. Mary Ann's peaceful breathing stopped and she jolted awake.

"What was that?" she said, sitting up.

"I don't know," said Adam, who was now out of bed and putting on clothes and boots.

There was a second muted explosion, and a moment later the house shook again. Adam realized the eruption, or whatever it was, was not that far away. He leaned down and looked out his bedroom window. The only structure in his line of sight was the Darks' cabin, but that was enough. There, he saw Sam step out onto his porch with a lit lantern and turn toward the barn.

At that moment there was a flash of yellow light that momentarily illuminated the Darks' cabin from the direction of the barn, then there was a third dull explosion—a moment later the house shook again. Sam jumped back with the flash of light. Something was happening in the barn.

Adam ran downstairs, grabbed a lantern, and followed Sam as they ran toward the barn. Adam was more angry than fearful. The darkness of the night reminded him that it was a new moon. If the Wizard was going to attack, this was the first prime night after Fr. Cahill's blessing with Holy Water. Mary Ann was right...wait a month.

A black cloud hovered over the barn with sooty tentacles that laced the perimeter of the building allowing black vapor to stream into the structure through cracks around windows and under doors. Adam heard the frightened animals inside, kicking at stall walls. Sam opened the door but it was Adam who dashed in first. Black fog filled the barn like an evil menace. Suddenly there was a fourth dull explosion accompanied by a flash of light that momentarily turned the black fog as yellow as an egg yolk. It came from the cow stalls. It wasn't like a sudden gunpowder explosion but something more gradual, like expanding leather.

The men quickly moved to the stalls and lifted their lanterns. The horses were wide-eyed and rousting about, anxious and unnerved. In the cow stalls across the aisle, the floor was covered with the remains of their four milk cows, their carcasses blown wide open, their intestines, excrement and entrails strewn everywhere. Hide was plastered to the floor and walls, legs and heads had been torn from the bodies by some god-awful monster. Broken bones, blood, guts, and slime covered everything and mixed in with bedding straw and feed. Adam crouched down and wiped his hand against what was left of Moon Beam's hide. It was still warm. His hand was covered in body tissue, liquid, and blood.

"N'er seen anythin' like 'dis before," said Sam. "Wad you's suppose did 'dis?"

The intense smell of slaughter and carnage made Adam cough. "The Wizard, that's who—or what."

Adam's heart had not stopped beating through his chest since rising from bed. Now he was in shock. He found it hard to breathe. His hands, arms, legs and torso shook almost uncontrollably. He forced himself to move. "Let's get the other animals outside to the pasture and clear out this air."

They turned to the horse stalls. Suddenly, there was a guttural sound as if one of the horses was finding it hard to breathe. Sam lifted his lantern as did Adam. It was Apple, Mary Ann's prized palomino mare, with its gold coat and white mane, a truly beautiful animal. It stood in its stall unable to move, its body convulsing, as black fog streamed into the Apple's nostrils and mouth. She tried to exhale, snort, and stomp her feet, but she couldn't move, yet her chest and abdomen grew larger second by second. It was a grotesque sight, the horse's body growing ever larger, inflating beyond recognition. Instinctively, Adam and Sam backed away from the stall, when suddenly the mare exploded with that same dull blast Adam had heard four times before. Entrails, bones, hide, sinews, splattered everywhere and covered both him and Sam.

Behind them, Mary Ann, who had come to see what was happening, let loose a blood-curdling scream at the moment her prized quarter house burst into unrecognizable organic fragments.

Adam turned to see his wife's body frozen in space and time, her distorted head and mouth wide open in shock with no air in her lungs to yell any longer. Adam rushed to her and caught her folded body before it hit the floor. Picking up his rag-doll wife, Adam carried her outside and laid her next to a fence far from the barn.

He turned to see Sam chase the other horses from the barn, letting them run wild and hopefully to safety. Adam noticed each as they came through the door, streaming black fog behind them, but apparently breathing freely—Calvin, Luther, Pickles, and Sizemore. He didn't worry about Cleopatra; the cat had no doubt escaped at the first screeching of owls. Sam returned and opened all the doors to the barn to let it air out, then joined Adam and Mary Ann, who were now joined by Bethany. Adam looked around for his children but evidently they were all safe in their beds...but no, in the starlight he saw four small figures hovering on the house porch. Mary Ann was still collapsed at his feet, staring at the barn.

"Bethany," said Adam, "go back to the house and see that the children are safe. Stay with them."

"Yes, sir, on my way," she said.

As Adam watched Bethany run to his house, he failed to notice something else that was quickly making its way to Flax Haven.

To anyone gazing into the clear night sky, the point of light would have looked like any one of a thousand stars. But it quickly grew larger, flew across the sky at an alarming rate, then detonated into a fireball that turned the dead of night into day. That's when Adam, Sam, and even Mary Ann looked up to see the ball of fire streak low across the horizon, turn and come directly toward them...then, swooping up to the zenith above them, it paused for a moment, then fell with frightening speed directly onto the barn. The direct hit produced a horrifying explosion. In a blinding flash the barn was ripped to shreds. Eyelids of man and beast snapped shut and turned away. Adam, Mary Ann, and Sam quickly ran from the intense conflagration back toward the house. The light and heat were beyond imagining. In an instant, any life in or near the barn was extinguished. Burning debris from the scattered remains ignited small fires throughout Flax Haven's compound, although none reached the house. The two out-buildings near the barn—the sheep shed and pig shack—were engulfed in the apocalypse.

Adam, Mary Ann, and Sam stopped halfway back to the house and watched as the fire ravaged their three-tiered barn, farming implements, flax processing equipment, wagons, straw, hay, and tackle. Everything was ablaze, and there was nothing they could do to stop it.

Mary Ann finally became coherent. "You and your damn priests. Doom and destruction is all religion brings. Wars, hatred, bigotry, greed, envy, and strife of every kind. Listen to me? No! Never! Cursed we live, and cursed we die."

Suddenly Adam, remembered the premonition he experienced during Mass in Shepherd's Town, the whirlwind of fire, the exploding cows and the burned wreckage. He fell to his knees on the ground, covered his ears, and cried.

3

Bethany Dark had experienced darker times. So had Sam. While shocked by the destruction of the barn and animals, the next day she kept reminding Sam to tell Mister Livingston to start praying and be careful not to curse the Almighty. Sam wasn't so sure Mister Livingston wanted to hear such tidings, but Bethany held nothing back from Missus Livingston. Of course, Mary Ann was not very receptive, but she listened to Bethany's soft words: "God will take care of us, Missus Livingston, you just wait and see."

Bethany knew that the Almighty was somehow involved in the disaster and that he meant it for good. Although on the surface and out in the barnyard it looked very different. How this was all going to work out was beyond her, and when Mary Ann challenged her, Bethany admitted she didn't know. "I'm sorry, Missus Livingston, God don't tell me these things. We just got 'ta wait and see."

When the fireball hit the barn, all the children watching from the porch screamed and cried from fright, including Eve. Bethany's breath was knocked out of her at first, so explosive was the fireball's impact. Within minutes, however, she came to the conclusion that something bigger than all of them was happening and they were eyewitnesses. She had a hard time explaining that to the children, but Eve came to the rescue.

"Henry," said Eve trying to recover from a bout of crying as she watched the barn go up flames. "Do you remember the story Bethany told us of how her tribe in Africa, the Togosantes, were trapped on a beach between the blue ocean and the green jungle and how the Jaga Marauders with all their horses, soldiers, chariots, spears, and arrows were just about ready to surround and kill them all?"

Henry stopped sobbing for a moment and said, "Yeah, but the blue ocean opened up and they escaped."

"That's right, but there was something that happened just before, in the middle of the night. What was it?"

"I dunno," said Henry.

"Adora, the god of her tribe, created a pillar of fire all the way to the sky, and put it between the Togosantes and the Jaga Marauders. But the pillar of fire was turned so the Togosantes had light all night long so they could see to pack up their tents and belongings and prepare to cross the ocean in the morning. But all night long *not* one beam of light from the pillar fell on the Jaga Marauders' army. They were in the dark. They couldn't see and they were confused."

Bethany was thrilled that Eve had remembered this detail from the story of the Israeli Exodus from Egypt which she had modified to satisfy Mary Ann and Adam. "Eve," said Bethany, "are you sayin' the fire we're seeing burning up the barn is like 'dat pillar of fire?"

"Could be," said Eve. "We'll have to wait and see."

Now, it was Bethany's turn to shed some tears, of joy, for her efforts had not gone to waste.

The burned ruins of the barn sat and smoldered all the next day, Monday, July 24, 1797. A few day laborers, not knowing what had happened during the night, showed up for work. Sam kept them busy. Where it was possible and the coals had cooled, they began to pull out of the ruins what could be salvaged, which wasn't much.

The next day, Bethany was surprised by the number of neighbors that came with wagons and carriages. The wagons carried spare farming implements, plows, scythes, shovels, tools and the like. Bethany saw that Adam was speechless at first, then humbled. Sam was not so surprised and undertook organizing the gifts in places where they could be protected. One group of four men from Smithfield, including the founder's son, John Smith, Jr., and David Feltsbarron, the livery proprietor and part-time blacksmith, brought in a load of scavenged lumber, erected a temporary forge, and over the next two days built a sturdy three-sided shed to protect the material and equipment being donated. Bethany was also busy with what the carriages brought them—food from as far away as Charles Town. As hardened as Mary Ann had become, the unsolicited kindness and generosity of neighbors reduced her to tears several times over the days.

4

Anastasia McSherry got word of Livingston's barn fire late morning, Tuesday, July 25. She immediately wanted to go and help the Livingstons, but Richard was gone for the day and the boys were off on an adventure into the woods with Catharine and Letitia in a buggy that Hank had rigged up. When the regular mail courier came just after noon, she sent a message to Fr. Cahill in Shepherd's Town to come the next day if he could and go with them to the Livingstons'.

The next morning, Fr. Cahill, wearing work clothes, arrived on Sassafras. Anastasia wanted both Catharine and Letitia to stay with the boys, but when Fr. Cahill arrived and the situation was explained, Catharine took charge and Letitia went with Anastasia, Fr. Cahill, and Richard on horseback to Flax Haven.

Anastasia was surprised by the immensity of the burned-out ruin of the barn and the number of people that had come to help. There were horses, wagons, and carriages throughout the yard. Around what used to be the barn, a dozen men pulled apart and sorted timbers that could be salvaged, and with hammers and pry bars decoupled the iron joints that had been used in the barn's post-and-beam construction.

Richard and Fr. Cahill rode directly to the hollowed-out barn that in places was still smoldering. Sam was directing the work and Adam was making decisions about what to trash or salvage. Anastasia and Letitia rode to the house where Mary Ann was sitting on the porch steps with a few women trying to occupy George who refused to sit still with so much activity around them. Bethany, Eve, and two others were busy putting out food and drink on the edge of the porch for the workers. Of course George, who was getting pudgier by the day, thought the food was all for him. Martha occupied herself against the back wall of the porch grooming Bombay.

Anastasia and Letitia dismounted and tied up their horses at the oak tree since the hitching rail was occupied. As soon as Anastasia turned toward the house she caught Mary Ann's eye and suddenly had doubts about their coming. A moment before, Mary Ann was surprisingly happy and smiling as she teasingly poked George in his abdomen with her finger. But when Mary Ann saw Anastasia the silliness turned to spite. Mary Ann's eyes jumped to scan the workers near the barn. She caught sight of something and leapt back to stare at Anastasia. Handing off George to a woman sitting next to her, Mary Ann rose and marched to cut Anastasia and Letitia off before they got closer.

Mary Ann nodded respectfully to Anastasia but her voice was loaded with indignation. "Missus McSherry, how kind of you to come and bring your men folk with you to clean up the destruction your kind has caused."

Anastasia noticed Mary Ann had tried to keep her voice low, but several of the women surrounding the porch steps heard the attack and what glee there had been moments earlier vanished in an instant.

Before Anastasia or Letitia could react, Mary Ann pivoted and marched toward the barn where men were lifting timbers and kicking up black dust as they cleared the barn's debris. Anastasia, shocked at the reception, stood frozen in place and watched Mary Ann walk off. Letitia, however, followed quickly behind Mary Ann in a march to destiny.

5

It did not take Letitia but seconds to figure out that Mary Ann Livingston blamed Denis Cahill and all Catholics that surrounded him for the barn's destruction. Mary Ann's accusation hurled recklessly at Anastasia was not the first clue. She recalled clearly the reports from Richard, Anastasia, and Fr. Denis of what had happened when Fr. Denis had blessed the Livingstons' premises. Mary Ann Livingston, for whatever reasons, harbored a deep prejudice against all religion, and most significantly toward Catholic priests. The only thing that made sense to Letitia was the rumor that the Stranger who had cursed the house was also rumored to be a Catholic priest, but no one seemed to know if that was true. Yet from what Letitia had heard from Anastasia and what she was observing now, Mary Ann Livingston hated Catholics and disliked overly religious folk long before the Stranger visited their house. But blaming Fr. Denis for the curse was too much for Letitia. Yes, she had grown to love the man, even if he was a priest, and defend him she was prepared to do, regardless of what others said or how they defamed her. This man, this priest, this Denis Cahill, was the most courageous, daring, intelligent, worthy, and handsome man she had ever known, and she was not about to let him be demeaned for doing what was good, true, and beautiful.

Letitia was on Mary Ann's heels when she got in front of Fr. Denis, who was carrying a burnt-out oak beam to the salvage pile.

"You, mister, are not welcome," Mary Ann barked at Fr. Denis and with both hands shoved him back.

The confrontation was so unexpected Fr. Denis lost his balance and fell, the oak beam cantilevering against the ground and grazing his head.

Workers nearby suddenly stopped to watch the confrontation.

Letitia was having none of this. Without hesitation she jumped between Fr. Denis and Mary Ann and shoved Mary Ann away. The shoving battle would have continued except Fr. Denis jumped to his feet, grabbed Letitia, and held her back, unconsciously using her as a shield.

Mary Ann was not deterred and kept at Fr. Denis even if she had to go through Letitia. "He's the one that caused all this. Look at it! Our lives are destroyed because of him." She turned to Richard and Anastasia who were there by now. "All you damn Catholics, putting your nose into other people's business and bringing hell down on them. GET OUT! GET OUT ! LEAVE US ALONE!. Please! Leave us alone!"

Adam now got in front of Mary Ann and ushered her into the arms of two women who put their arms around her and led her back to the house. Adam then turned to Richard and Fr. Cahill. "I'm so sorry about this, Mister McSherry...Father. Your kindness and generosity are always appreciated. All I can do is say I'm sorry for my Mary Ann. She's not in her right mind. One of the animals we lost here was her favorite palomino."

Richard stepped forward. "We understand, Mister Livingston. This is quite the tragedy. I doubt any of us would be in our right mind if it happened to us. If there's anything we can do without upsetting your wife, please let us know."

Adam reached out with both his hands, grasped Richard's right, and shook it heartily. Adam did the same with Fr. Cahill, who was still somewhat stunned by his fall and was being steadied from behind by Letitia.

Anastasia stepped in. "Richard, perhaps we need to go. Shall I get the horses?"

Richard nodded to his wife and turned to Adam. "I hope to see you around, sir. Best of luck here."

"Thank you, Mister McSherry," said Adam. "You're a good neighbor."

Fr. Denis turned to go and came face-to-face with Letitia. He grasped her forearms in gratitude. "Thank you, Letitia." She held his look for a moment. He was distraught and saddened. He tried to hide it, but she saw the tears in his eyes—the response when evil is returned for good.

Anastasia brought the horses. Richard helped Anastasia up in her side saddle, and Fr. Denis helped Letitia into hers, and out of the yard the four rode together.

When they arrived back at Retirement's stables about noon, Anastasia said, "Fr. Denis, please come in and eat with us. Perhaps you might suggest what we can do to rectify this pitiful situation."

"Darling," said Richard, "I think it's best to just forget the Livingstons and let them lie in their own manure."

"Oh, Richard! That is so unchristian of you."

"Perhaps," he said, "but I see no sense in rushing into the Colosseum to save the Romans who are finally being attacked by the lions. What do you say, Father?"

Fr. Cahill was still sitting on Sassafras and made no attempt to dismount. "Don't know what to make of it." His voice trembled as he spoke. "The very thing I warned him about happened. Vengeance. But worse than I imagined. Black vapor, bloating animals exploding, and then the fireball from hell. It was clearly revenge for our blessing his house. But as clearly as we showed him the solution, the man did not take our advice. He must fear his wife more than hell. A superior in Spain used to say, 'There will always be fools and they will always be lost.' It's so discouraged me. I can do nothing right, and when I do, they call it wrong."

"Fr. Denis," said Anastasia, "please don't say things like that."

"My dear wife, sometimes bad things happen and there's nothing we can do to correct it. Fr. Denis has learned that many times over. What happened today will only strengthen his resolve as a priest to serve those who will listen. He can do nothing else."

"I hope that's true," said Fr. Denis. "Well, I need to get going. Thank you. Hopefully I'll see you Sunday." With that, Fr. Denis pulled on Sassafras' reins and trotted off the property toward Shepherd's Town.

As Fr. Denis rode away, Hank took the reins of Romeo and Persnickety, then reached for the reins of Letitia's mare, Hopscotch, but she pulled them back.

"Anastasia. Mister McSherry," call out Letitia. "You can't let Fr. Denis ride off like that. He's not in his right mind. Didn't you see how sad and disappointed he was? Why, back at the Livingston farm he was in tears when that wicked woman was yelling and shoving him around. He's not in any condition to be left alone. He should stay and have supper with us, and maybe stay the night."

"He'll be fine," said Richard. "Let it go, Letitia. You are not Fr. Denis' guardian, nor are we. He's under the bishop's care now. We need to back away and let him be."

"How can you say that?" challenged Letitia. "You mean he's being guided by a blind bishop and a pagan planter. That's suicide! Mister McSherry, you sacrificed a lot of money to establish Fr. Denis. You've told me you cosigned for multiple properties. He's the man that saw, before either of you, that you were perfect for each other. He matched you, he married you, and you named sweet little Dennis after him. You love and care for him that much. He's welcome to stay with you anytime. He's family. You can't just send him off in the dark night of his soul and expect him to survive. He's encouraged you all your married life. Now it's time for you to encourage him, and not let him out of your sight until he knows he's valuable and needed, just as he did for both of you." She was about to add, "...and me," but thought the better of it.

"He's gone now, Letitia," said Richard. "Let him be."

"Richard," said Anastasia, "you could easily catch him and bring him back."

"Yes, you could," repeated Letitia.

"Possibly," said Richard, "but I'm not going to."

There was a long pause.

"Well, I am," said Letitia. With that she swung herself into Hopscotch's saddle. "Set another place for supper. We'll be back." Letitia dug her heels into the mare's flank and in an instant she was gone, galloping after the man they all loved, but differently.

It was hours later near dusk when Letitia returned. Dinner and supper had both been cleared. Hank had long ago gone home. Letitia saw Anastasia watching her from the window. Richard did not come out to stable the horse, which he often did. That was a signal that she had slighted her host. She rubbed the mare down, fed and watered her, left her in her stall, and closed up the stable.

When she came inside, Anastasia simply asked, "Do you want anything to eat?"

Letitia shook her head sadly, and said, "He wouldn't come back."

"How is he? asked Anastasia.

Letitia carefully kept her thoughts to herself and simply said, "Better, I think. I'm going to bed. Is Catharine up?"

"She's knitting in the parlor."

"She's good at that," said Letitia. "I'm on breakfast duty in the morning. See you then." It was dark by the time Letitia put away her riding clothes and washed the dust and perspiration off her body. The bedroom she shared with Catharine was a welcome sight. Later, when Catharine came to bed, Letitia never stirred. She slept soundly that night. Fr. Denis, not so well.

6

Sunday, August 6, 1797.

Richard McSherry brought his extended family to confession once a month an hour before Mass. It was a comforting habit, but today was different. Today was the first time they had come to confession since the Livingston barn fire and Letitia's conspicuous pursuit of Fr. Denis but failure to bring him back. Alone, Letitia's concern for a depressed priest might not have troubled Richard, but there was Anastasia's direct warnings that Letitia and Fr. Denis might be romantically linked. Further, since Philip Field had been calling on Catharine regularly, there was Catharine's teasing of Letitia about her having a hard time finding an Irish bachelor. Most disturbing to Richard, however, was Letitia's behavior when Fr. Denis was anywhere close. Her eyes never left him, and her attempts to mimic Catharine's acts of *sisterly* affection on Fr. Denis were abject failures—the woman was obviously besotted if not smitten with their priest. It wasn't unusual for a single woman to be attracted to a young, good looking, confident priest. But closely watching Fr. Denis suggested the feelings were reciprocal, and that kept Richard awake at night.

If publicly Fr. Denis and Letitia were romantically linked, Richard's reputation would instantly sink. Richard had established Fr. Denis at St. Agnes, and in a legitimate and charitable way they were still business partners. Richard had underwritten several of the Catholic societies over which Fr. Cahill had presided; and, as if to add fuel to the fire, Letitia, along with Fr. Cahill's sister, lived with his family. For his entire life Richard had carefully guarded his reputation, thus a moral scandal involving Fr. Denis and Letitia terrified him.

That Sunday, his family and other parishioners waited on benches in the back of the St. Agnes Chapel's nave for Fr. Denis to hear their confessions. In turn, each would enter the side door to the rectory and kneel before the confessional screen. Fr. Cahill, sitting on the other side, would lead them through the rite, provide counsel, give them a penance, and then grant absolution. After the blessing, the confessed would exit the same way they had come, leaving the rectory door ajar as a sign for the next person to enter. The confessed would then either leave the church and wait outside, or sit in the nave and pray until Mass began.

Catharine exited the rectory door after her confession and sat in the nave to pray her penance. Letitia was next in line. As soon as the door closed, Richard wrinkled his brow at Anastasia, who responded by peering back at her husband with amusement and a smile. That his wife found the amorous relationship between their priest and a beautiful single girl living with them funny was maddening.

For the next few minutes while Letitia and Fr. Denis hid behind a shut door, Richard's imagination ran wild, and his sense of accountability waged war with his sense of propriety. He wanted to burst in on them and catch them in the act. But what if there was nothing untoward between them? What if she was dutifully kneeling behind the screen and Fr. Denis was making the sign of the cross over her giving her absolution? If that were the case, his act of overbearing pride and presumption would *only* engulf him in a scandal that would exile him from family and the church. He was meant to be sitting quietly, examining his own conscience, not someone else's. He was obligated to be preparing for a good confession by accurately accounting for *his* sins, not adding to them.

Unable to bear the suspense, Richard quietly left the bench he was sitting on and his place in line. He glanced back to see Anastasia watch him leave the building and shut the entrance behind him. Hopefully, she would not follow.

Fortunately, there was no one outside to see him. Discreetly, and casually, as if just passing the time with no purposeful intent, he walked past the rectory's outside entrance and around the side of the apartment. He felt chagrined pretending to be inconspicuous. If caught, he would need a good excuse, something that seemed reasonable. He was a land speculator, after all, a man who spent time evaluating property and buildings as investment opportunities, and just as often found himself inspecting buildings he owned for needed repairs and improvements. Then again he was a member of the local Catholic society's board of directors who needed to ensure their investment in the St. Agnes structure was secure. *Yes, the foundation looked secure here, and the weather boards were secure and not flapping in the breeze.*

Having granted himself a reasonable alibi, he pretended now to confidently study the structure's detail. In so doing, he quickly moved behind the building. There he found the window that had been built into the side of the apartment just above a food preparation counter. If his remembrance was correct, that window was in line of sight of the apartment's entrance and the foyer where the confessional screen was located. He crouched down and pretended to examine the foundation stones that were dry fit and elevated above the grade on which the joists for the apartment and church flooring rested. By design they had to be above where water would run off the hill, else the joists would rot and the building would collapse. Indeed, the foundation stones were solidly fit, above grade, and the ends of the joists, which were tucked behind the weather boards, were dry.

In order to reinforce his legitimacy in case someone was watching, Richard lifted a loose rock lying next to the foundation and weighed it in his right hand as if evaluating its resiliency and strength. At the same time he raised up slightly and looked into the corner of the window toward the foyer, the front entrance, and the confessional. Fr. Denis and whomever was confessing to him would be silhouetted against the windows in the apartment's entrance. Of course, his view could be obscured by crockery, a stewpot, or potted plant sitting on the counter, but that was not the case. There was nothing to obstruct his view, except daylight glare in the window pane.

Using his hand to negate the glare he looked a second time.

It took but a moment.

Quickly and rashly Richard moved aside from the window, stood up, and angrily heaved the rock in his hand as hard as he could down the hill toward the Potowmack. A small mound of dirt nearby also took an uncharacteristic kick from his boot. He was mad and he didn't care who saw him. A moment later he felt a sharp pain in his right hand. He looked down. There was a long gash along his index finger, and blood flowed freely from it. Abruptly, his attention turned from what he had seen through the window to stopping the blood that had already dripped onto his pants and was being soaked up by his shirt sleeve. He needed to find a bandage. But where? He didn't think there was any in the Church, and there was none in the carriage in which he, Anastasia, and the boys had ridden. The girls, however, Catharine and Letitia, had decided to ride horses. Perhaps he could ride one into town and find aid for his now profusely bleeding hand.

He rounded the front of the apartment and headed toward the hitching posts, but as he came to the front of the church, stepping out of the church having left confession was Letitia. They locked eyes. Richard was in shock that he would see her at that moment as if she knew he had just spied on her through the back window. But the look on her face was not of anger, which he expected, but one of sincere compassion for his injury. For the blood now covered his entire hand, wrist, and had soaked well up into his linen shirt sleeve.

"Mister McSherry," she said, "what happened?"

Richard was in too much pain to respond as he gripped his right wrist as tightly as he could to stem the flow of blood.

"Here!" Letitia cried. "Sit down here on the porch."

Richard stumbled to the church porch and sat down.

Letitia sat on his right side and lifted her outer skirt revealing a beautifully embroidered linen white petticoat with a scalloped hem. As if Letitia had done so a hundred times, she grabbed the hem between two scallops with both hands and ripped the petticoat several feet up her side, revealing her chemise. Grabbing the hem again, a few scallops over, she ripped the petticoat on a parallel path and then ripped the top, creating a long, white, clean bandage. "Hold out your hand," said Letitia. "Where's the cut exactly?"

Richard pointed along the gash.

"Oh, I see it now. That's nasty. How did that happen?"

"I was throwing a rock," he said truthfully. "Must've been a sharp edge."

"You're shaking; hold still a moment."

Without thinking of keeping her own outer skirt clean, Letitia took Richard's bloody wrist and clamped it between her knees so that his hand was held steady and outstretched into the air away from her. With a deftness reserved but for a surgeon, she expertly wrapped his finger and hand in a figure-eight pattern that stopped the blood and held the wound closed.

But she wasn't done. She lifted her outer skirt again, and tore off another long bandage. With it she quickly wrapped his hand and wrist. "I don't want to wrap your hand too tightly because you still need blood flow or you'll get gangrene. Now we need some cold water to clean up."

"There's a well in the park, at the bottom of the hill," he said.

At this point people were starting to arrive and gather around the hitching posts for Mass. Catharine came out of the church, saw the bloody mess and ran back inside to get Anastasia with the boys. When they came out of the church Catharine took the boys under her care and Anastasia looked down at Letitia and her husband sitting on the church porch with blood all around them.

"You want to explain this?" Anastasia said.

"Later?" queried Richard. "Can you drive us to the well at the bottom of the hill in the carriage so we can clean up?"

"I can do that, Missus McSherry," said Letitia. "You stay with your boys and Catharine. We'll be back in a bit. Comin' Mister McSherry. Let's get you cleaned up."

"Where'd you get the bandages?" asked Anastasia.

Letitia pointed at the hem of her outer-skirt and lifted it a foot into the air while smiling.

"Of course you did," said Anastasia. "Bless you, and thank you for taking care of the *man* in our family."

"My pleasure," Letitia said with a quirky smile. "We'll be back in a jiffy."

With that Letitia helped Richard off the church porch and they walked to the carriage.

Needless to say, Richard and Letitia missed Mass, although Richard had his own reasons for not going and it wasn't the cut on his hand. By the time they were cleaned up, Letitia's skirts were soaking wet in an attempt to get the blood stains out of them, so she was content to sit in the carriage, soak up the sun, and try to dry out.

Later, Letitia and Catharine rode Hopscotch and Persnickety home while Anastasia drove the carriage, since Richard's bandaged hand was useless. On the way home, Anastasia interrogated her husband as to why he left the chapel before going to confession, what happened with his hand, and how Letitia happened to be right there when he needed her to bandage him up. Richard, however, stayed true to his alibi, and waxed eloquent about how well the chapel had been built upon its firm foundation.

7

Most Feared Master of Stupidity,

It is true, although I like fabrications much better, that my campaign to bring Livingston to condemnation is showing promise beyond what I imagined. The past few days have proven yet again that we're on the brink of success. I feel as if Livingston at any moment could fall on his pitch fork, curse God, and die.

Did I not tell you? Livingston has conveniently forgotten everything he was warned about, and is no closer to baptism, obedience to the Creator, or the sacraments. Cahill even comes and says the bishop won't allow the exorcism. You see, success on every front from the bishop on down, and the one person who could be a danger to us, Cahill, is banned from the priestly arts most dangerous to us. And you doubted me? Human arrogance and lack of knowledge of reality is a beautiful thing. On such ignorance we thrive. Pride reigns. They never have needed the Almighty—Oh how we will need a different name when He is defeated.

Livingston's wife never ceases to amaze as she universally assigns evil to Christian ministers and priests. "They bring evil eventually..." she says. How rich is that?

Hovering over Shepherd's Town as I do from time to time, I was a whirlwind of excitement when no one came to Cahill's daily Mass, even after he literally canvassed the entire town. Not one person showed up! Of course, this led to the logical conclusion

I've been suggesting to him all along—he was never called to be a priest. It was all his parents' doing and his respect for them that led him down the primrose path—a path that leads to damnation. It's just glorious, although I don't like to use that word. Forgive me.

This field report should be put on display, for I am obliged to tip my horn-tipped cap to Cahill for warning Livingston that the haunts would return with a vengeance. So true. With such a prediction I just had to go to the ends of the Earth. I wouldn't want to let a robust priest down. Thus, the sucker punch, the conflagration, the fireball from hell, which ironically appeared to fall from the heavenlies. Yes, the last will be greater than the first...and I'm not done yet. Either he commits to visiting hell, or hell will continue to visit him.

At your sinful service,
Cyn Namrasit, OPSD

Chapter 48
A Great Prejudice

My Lord Maréchal,

I hesitate at this juncture like other men who hesitate to enter the confessional. At once the man knows that he must fulfill his commitment to the Immortal One and reveal his weaknesses to one who is mortal. The irony is seldom lost on any.

Likewise, it is with much humility and not a little shame that I relate the following events when I traveled to Smithfield at the request of Bishop Carroll. Pray for my redemption as my faltering through this valley of shadows becomes evident. But the truth must be told.

Perhaps you are not fully aware of my *background which will make my involvement in this tale even more ironic. I was born December 22, 1770, into a Russian family as Prince Dmitri Dmitrievich Gallitzin. At the time my parents resided in The Hague. My father, Dimitri Alexeievich, served as Russian minister plenipotentiary from the court of Catharine II. Father was also an intimate friend of Voltaire. My mother, a Prussian Countess was a friend of Empress Catharine, whom I am told held me in her arms whenever my mother visited the palace.

I was raised somewhat indifferent to religion, although my family were nominal members of the Russian Orthodox Church. In 1786, my mother, Princess Amalia von Gallitzin, converted to Catholicism much against my father's wishes. In turn, a year later, I made confession and first communion in my seventeenth year and took the name Augustine, the great seeker of truth.

It was traditional that a young man of my lineage continue his education by travel throughout Europe, but the mood in France leading up to the French Revolution was not safe for Catholics, especially a royal, as I was considered. So, in 1792 my parents sent me to the United States with my tutor where I took the name Augustine Schmet or Smith. This avoided the awkwardness of being a Russian prince in a fledgling country that had rejected the trappings of European royalty. The name Smith also honored my mother's family name—Adelheid Amalia von Schmettau.

Through my mother's friendship with the Empress, who was also Catholic, I was given letters of introduction to your predecessor, Bishop John Carroll. Arriving in Baltimore October 28, 1792, my desire to serve the Church in this country grew rapidly. Soon, I entered the new Sulpician Seminary in Baltimore established by Monsignor Nagot. Three years later, March 18, 1795, I was ordained by Bishop Carroll. I was the first priest to complete all my seminary training in the United States and be ordained.

Bishop Carroll soon sent me as a missionary priest to Conewago Chapel, Pennsylvania. From there I served in many towns in Maryland, Virginia, and Pennsylvania. Eventually, that led to my founding of the town of Loretto in the Allegheny Mountains, where I am today.

But the bishop had a problem with my service. I found the Catholics I was sent to serve incredibly ignorant of their faith, and the surrounding community severely bigoted against us. It was demoralizing and frustrating. They were thick-headed and nearly unteachable. In looking back, I believe they were unduly influenced by the heretical and often pagan beliefs of Protestants who called themselves Christians but rejected basic Christian understanding of the Scriptures and the sacraments, especially the Eucharist.

This was all very hard on me. I was not raised in America where freedom of thought and action is held fastidiously. I was raised and educated by philosophers, princes, military leaders, and kings. I had then, and have today, very little patience for the lazy indifference that makes a mockery of reason and natural law. I was, therefore, and am still today a firm, devout, and plain-spoken defender of reality and Catholic teaching. In my stern approach to those in my district who disregarded my clear teaching, I would reproach, correct, and assail my opponents, often publicly. It was difficult for them to accept what to me was a unequivocal truth, and it was equally true that it was difficult for me to accept them.

The result was that Bishop Carroll received letters from civic leaders in my district to either replace me or discipline my unbridled criticism of those that opposed me. I was of the mindset that if my superior in the royal guards told me to do such and such, I did it, without deviation and especially without hint of subjective interpretation. This lack of reason continues to haunt and motivate my work to this day. Daily I pray to come upon intelligent souls unsullied by the devil's lies.

It was therefore the bishop's wisdom that I should learn the art of gentle persuasion and forego the use of authority. He temporarily relieved me of my mission in Conewago and asked me to spend several months in Virginia to investigate reports of a demonic spirit's infestation of a non-believer's farm. The infestation, I was told, resulted in several years of persecution and the destruction of some crops and his barn. Fr. Denis Cahill, as I have described, had been involved with the McSherrys for some years, and then, just before I became involved, had come to bless the Livingston premises with Holy Water. The bishop had explained to me his reservations of Fr. Cahill's ministry and involvement and so I came with a great prejudice against Fr. Cahill. But as I was to discover in the coming months, Fr. Denis Cahill was bluff and hearty, a man of powerful nerve and hearty faith. In arrogance and naivety into that setting, I arrived.

At the time I was not aware of how significant that day was, but I suspect Bishop Carroll knew. It was on August 22, 1797, a new moon, when I rode into the yard at Adam Livingston's plantation, Flax Haven.

Your Servant,
Fr. Smith

Chapter 49
Shooting Gallery

1

Tuesday Morning, August 22, 1797.

It was evident to Adam that the Wizard was still active, and that a new moon was at hand. It was two days earlier on Sunday, August 20, that the clipping noises had begun again, and the last couple of nights there had been occasional incursions of circling wagons, runaway livestock, and minor house quakes. Even so, the family had grown somewhat used to the hauntings and managed to get some sleep.

During the day, however, there was a conscious effort to get away from the spooked house. Bethany cooked more in her cabin, and sometimes would feed the family on her porch rather than everyone gathering in the main house. Mary Ann and Bethany had gone shopping to Charles Town. They had taken Luther with donated tackle and a wagon spared in the fire. Eve watched the twins, taking them on a hike through the woods and teaching them to read. She had pieces of paper on which she had written the name of small mammals and insects. When they saw a squirrel or butterfly, the children tried to select the piece of paper with the right name. Sam was in the field cultivating crops with a handful of laborers. Adam and Henry, now fifteen, were in the largest of the three-sided sheds sorting through the donated goods neighbors had gifted them after the fire. There was also a team of workmen nearby preparing to erect a new but smaller barn.

Henry did not have the focus on work that Adam wished, but he did what he was asked, and it was satisfying to have his son working alongside him. Easily distracted, Henry called out across the shed: "Pa, someone's here."

Adam looked up and out the open side of the shed. A man on a sleek, black stallion had entered the yard and had stopped halfway between the house and the sheds. He was looking around for signs of life.

"Over here," yelled Adam, as he walked out of the shed's shadow to be seen in the daylight. The horseman looked like a Catholic priest. He was wearing a black cassock over a thin and slight frame. Like Fr. Cahill's cassock it had an up-turned collar and was buttoned down the front. On his head was one of those funny round black hats. He had deep-set eyes, a long up-turned nose, high cheek bones, broad forehead, and was clean shaven. He sat erect and poised in the saddle like a field marshal surveying his troops. Clearly he wasn't a farmer or anyone from around the area. He looked out of place. The large horse and the man's posture gave the impression that he was not in the least bit lost, but in command.

Seeing Adam, the man reined his stallion toward the shed and let his eyes scan the scene—the piles of burned out timbers and salvaged goods, the construction team working on the new barn, the laborers in the nearby fields, the several sheds sheltering piles of donated goods…and the house upon which his gaze lingered. Approaching Adam and Henry the man tipped his hat and spoke with a thick European accent: "Adam Livingston, I presume?"

"Yes," said Adam. "Greetings, sir."

The horseman dismounted with an effortless leap, bowed to Henry and said, "Hello, young prince." Now standing almost at attention by his steed that reminded Adam of a knight on a chess board—its head held high, proud, and alert—the man turned to Adam and said, "Mister Livingston, I am a Catholic priest, Father Smith."

Adam removed his work glove and shook Fr. Smith's hand, and with a smile said, "Smith, huh? That's an American name, but you're not American, are you?"

The man replied without hesitation, in perfect German, "Es tut mir leid, Herr Liebenstein."

That got Adam's attention. His German was rusty. His parents spoke it enough that he could be somewhat conversant, but it had been years since he had lived with his parents. Amused, and smiling broadly, Adam replied in German, *"You know I am German? How is that possible? But you aren't German, are you?"*

The man lapsed back into English with a smile, although the accent was still thick. "Sir, my name here in America is Smith, it is common enough, yes? But my given name is Demetrius Augustine Gallitzin. I am at your service." He snapped his boots together and bowed, again. "My father was Prussian, my mother German. I was born in Berlin, although more recently I departed for America from the Hague where my father was, ah…employed, shall I say. I apologize for my accent, I am still learning the American way of speaking."

"Do you speak Russian, too?"

"Oh, yes, and French and Dutch, but not Spanish. American English is the most difficult. Hard are the idioms; they make no sense to me. Like, 'ignorance is bliss,' which does not sound like a happy state."

Adam laughed. "If that was a joke, it is a good one. You'll make a good American, I think."

"Thank you, I am trying," said Fr. Smith, "but I am new, even a new priest. The American bishop, his Excellency John Carroll, only a few years ago ordained me."

"Then you really are here…an immigrant…and an American, now."

"That is what I am told, and it is my wish."

"But how did you know I was German?"

"Ah, that is a bit of a story, perhaps for another time. But…you think, no… ah yes, you are a *chip off the old block*. Did I say that right?"

"I'm not sure, what do you mean?"

"Your father, Johann Georg Liebenstein was known by the Catholic Church in Conewago, where I was most recently stationed. I did not know your father, but others in my association did. Although he was Lutheran and did not think kindly of us Roman Catholics, he had no problem selling us the finest linens for vestments, altar linens, and purificators for our Mass celebrations. I think I have used them, although I am not entirely sure."

"That is true, but years long ago," said Adam. "Now, what do I call you? You have too many names."

"Father Dimitri, if you wish, but I am officially a Smith, the judge tells me. *Smith* I am told, will help me blend in, is that how you say it?"

"With your accent, Father, that's not going to work."

Fr. Dimitri laughed. "Yes, that I am told also."

"What kind of horse is that?" asked Henry.

"I'm sorry, Fr. Dimitri, this is my able-bodied and soon-to-mature son, Henry."

"I'm glad to make your acquaintance, Prince Henry."

"I'm not a prince."

"Oh, but you are," gesturing to his father. "You are the son of this farm's ruling monarch, Herr Livingston. From now on you should be known as Prince Henry. I so decree."

Henry, a little shy from the attention and pronouncement of his new name, again pointed to Fr. Dimitri's horse, "So what kind of horse is that?"

"Ah, this is Count Samuel." Fr. Dimitri stroked Count Samuel's neck and the horse raised and lowered its powerful head in acknowledgment. I named him after my grandfather who was a Prussian Field Marshal. He is a Kabarda, bred over hundreds of years in Russia for their endurance and adaptation to different climates. He's got some Arabian in him, I think, from long ago."

Adam stepped forward and let Count Samuel smell his hand and then stroked the horse's nose. "I've never seen a Kabarda here in the States. Did you bring him with you?"

"Oh, no, he was a gift on my ordination from my godmother, Empress Catharine of Russia, a close friend of my mother. When I came to America they both pondered what might happen to me. So they were very happy when they heard I was in seminary to became a priest. Empress Catharine died just last year, but my mother still worries for me."

"Well, Fr. Dimitri," said Adam, "what brings you and Count Samuel here?"

Fr. Dimitri turned and surveyed the yard, the house, and the rebuilding of the barn. "I was sent here by Bishop Carroll. He knows of your plight from a haunting spirit, and heard of your barn's destruction. He asked me to investigate and see if I can be of any help."

Adam hesitated. "Then you must know Fr. Cahill."

"Only by name. Bishop Carroll and Fr. Cahill are not on the best of terms."

"And do you know the McSherrys?" asked Adam.

"I met them yesterday. The bishop arranged that I might stay with them during this trip."

Adam said: "Fr. Cahill told me he asked the bishop for permission to exorcise our house, but the bishop said no."

"Yes," said Fr. Dimitri. "The bishop wanted another priest's opinion. So he has sent me. If I come to the same conclusion as Fr. Cahill, the bishop has given me permission to perform the solemn exorcism."

"Alone? You, alone with no others?"

"Mister Livingston, it is not complicated. It's just a series of prayers. I have the rite in my saddle bag. It should not be that hard."

"Fr. Dimitri, I do not think you realize what you're up against. A layman, the McSherrys, and I were with Fr. Cahill when he blessed the house with Holy Water, and it was not an easy task. But what he accomplished was more than the half-dozen other ministers who tried."

"With all due respect to Fr. Cahill, the McSherrys, yourself...and others...as I have said, everything is not right with Fr. Cahill, or else the bishop would have agreed with him and not sent me."

"What could be the difference between you and Cahill, then?" asked Adam.

Fr. Dimitri stood a bit more erect, if that was possible. "I do not know, exactly, sir. But the bishop did not feel comfortable allowing the exorcism to proceed with Fr. Cahill, if, in fact, it is at all needed. Perhaps you do not know, Fr. Cahill's education and credentials are somewhat in question. He was not educated here, but in Spain, I believe. Myself, on the other hand, have been completely educated here under Bishop Carroll's authority. It may be that the bishop believes I am better suited for the task. It is also likely that because of my aristocratic and royal upbringing the bishop believes that my temperament may be more suited to command this deranged spirit to be expelled. In short, Fr. Cahill may not have been the best priest to have called on. There can be little doubt, looking at the destruction you have sustained, that could well be the reason. You needed a real priest."

Adam had first been impressed by Fr. Dimitri. The man cut an impressive figure on his Kabarda when he first arrived. His aristocratic presence was obvious just in the way he sat on his horse and the gentlemanly and authoritative way he conducted himself. But there was also something deeply naive about him that was absent in Fr. Cahill's practical, down-to-earth demeanor. Yes, Fr. Cahill was skeptical at first, but Adam never forgot the way Fr. Cahill's attitude abruptly changed when Adam opened his waistcoat to reveal his clipped shirt. The skepticism turned instantly to an informed fear. Fr. Dimitri seemed to be of a different breed. Could it be that Fr. Cahill had repeatedly confronted the kind of demonic evil that haunted his farm, but Fr. Dimitri had never experienced it even once? Was Fr. Dimitri telling the truth or was he flaunting the pompous pretensions of an arrogant aristocrat? There was only one way to find out, and it was convenient that Mary Ann was not at home but the Wizard was.

"So, you think I need a real priest, like you? asked Adam.

"Sir, it may be so," said Fr. Dimitri, who then turned around, reached into his saddle bag and withdrew a book of rites, holding it up as a badge of honor for Adam to see. "Would you show me your dwelling? I alone have been authorized by His Excellency to perform an exorcism of it, if such is required."

Adam was not sure he wanted to commit to this without McSherry and Cahill also present, but his curiosity got the best of him. "Well, by all means, Fr. Dimitri Augustine Gallitzin Smith, let's get to it," and Adam gestured toward the house. "Henry, take Count Samuel here and give him some water and hay."

"Aw, Pa, I want to watch," objected Henry.

"You can, just take the horse over to the stable first."

Henry did as he was asked, and Count Samuel seemed to know there was a treat in store, for the steed followed Henry willingly.

Adam yelled after his son, "And Henry? Find Eve and the twins and keep them away from the house for a while."

"Pa! You said…"

"All right! All right! But keep an eye out for them. I don't want them in the middle of this."

"You're in good hands," said Fr. Dimitri. "There's nothing to worry about."

It was at that moment that Adam knew he had a rookie priest in tow. He could not imagine Fr. Cahill saying such a thing. There was nothing worse than a man who believes he knows what he doesn't. Adam had lived with the Wizard's haunting now for three years. There was plenty to worry about, as if the rubbish pile from the burned-out barn wasn't evidence enough.

The shed where they stood talking was far enough from the house that any disturbances in the house at the time would not have been seen or heard. When they began their walk to the house, Fr. Dimitri was all smiles as if he was about to banish a demonic despot by simply brandishing his book of rites.

But as they came closer the profundity of the problem became apparent, and even Adam was surprised. When Adam had left the house in the morning there was some faint clipping noise. The wagon and wild beast sounds seemed to come out at night and faded in the daylight. It was true that even during the day the house would occasionally shake, but nothing very violent, and nothing would break, or so it seemed. But now, with Fr. Dimitri walking next to him, the hauntings were more pronounced. It suddenly occurred to Adam that the mere presence of a Catholic priest…even a greenhorn priest…could be sensed by the Wizard and the manifestations magnified as a defense. Certainly that happened with Fr. Cahill when he blessed the house, and only with Fr. Cahill's aggressive persistence with Holy Water and Latin prayers had the Wizard's antics been subdued.

They were even closer to the house now.

"What is that constant snipping noise I hear? Is it a new kind of bird nesting near the house?" asked Fr. Dimitri.

"No, Father, that is the Wizard warming up. That's the sound of his invisible shears that have cut to ribbons pretty much every piece of linen that has come close to our premises. We wear mostly cotton in summer and wool in winter these days. Are you wearing any linen, possibly this outer garment? It does look like a linen weave."

"I don't know," said Fr. Dimitri. "It's called a cassock."

"Well, we'll soon find out," said Adam mostly to himself.

When the men, and now Henry for he had caught up to his father and the Father, stepped onto the steps that led to the porch, Adam could feel the steps tremble. "Do you feel that, Fr. Dimitri? That trembling?"

"No, nothing, really," said the still smiling priest.

When they reached the top of the steps and put their full weight on the porch, the floor boards suddenly shifted, right, then left.

"What was that?" cried the priest, while at the same time losing his smile.

"Oh, that's just the Wizard's way of welcoming us to his abode," said Adam.

The porch shifted again. Adam and Henry, used to it, barely faltered. Fr. Dimitri, however, suddenly crouched low so he didn't fall over. Adam helped him back up, but Fr. Dimitri was unsteady after that. "Courage, Father."

Fr. Dimitri asked Adam to hold his book of rites, which Adam did. The priest reached into a cassock pocket and pulled out a thin purple stole, draped it over his neck, crossed it in front, secured the overlapping tails with a cassock button and took back his book of rites.

They walked into the foyer. Adam removed both work gloves and laid them aside. In the corner by the door was his shillelagh which he now took into his hands. On the floor near the door was a wooden box about one-foot square with a hinged cover. With the tip of his shillelagh Adam opened the box lid.

"Papa, let me show him," said Henry.

Adam stepped back and Henry reached in and pulled out a piece of linen cloth about as tall as he. "This was a table covering for our game table," Henry said holding the covering up. It was cut in ribbons of small crescent moons. The cutouts were precise cuts, far finer than any human could do by hand with shears. "We keep some of these to show visitors. It's our *sample box*. We burn the rest."

Fr. Dimitri reached out and took the cloth and studied it. His hand was shaking a bit. "Is this what happens with that snipping noise?" he asked nervously. "How is it done?"

"We have no idea," said Adam. "I'd watch the bottom hem of your cassock. It's likely to get some holes in it before you leave."

Fr. Dimitri glanced at his cassock's hem. Adam followed his gaze. No holes yet. Adam noticed that Fr. Dimitri's smile had been replaced with a twitching in his left eye. Fr. Dimitri held the book of rites close to his chest with both hands. Adam glanced at his grip on the book. His fingers hadn't turned white yet, but he didn't expect it would be too much longer before they did.

The floor in the foyer shuddered more strongly than Adam had remembered. Yes, the presence of a priest…a Catholic priest…was a threat to this ghost. Adam needed to be careful. Either this priest needed to take effective action like Fr. Cahill, or Adam needed to get him out of the house before something catastrophic occurred.

It was with that thought that Adam had reason to panic. The barn apocalypse, which he was convinced was the Wizard's retribution, had nothing to do with the barn. The barn suffered because the Wizard was chased out of the house, if only for a fortnight. Either Fr. Dimitri needed to really and truly exorcise the spirit from their house, or Adam needed to get Fr. Dimitri to safety. It was also at that moment that Adam wondered why the house had not been destroyed instead of the barn. Could it have been that the house somehow provided a necessary habitation for the spirit, and destroying the house would leave the spirit without a home? Or did it have something to do with Eve and her sacred keepsakes? Adam shivered at both thoughts. His home may surely be possessed in a literal sense. Adam turned to Fr. Dimitri, hoping this apprentice priest had something up those billowy sleeves of his.

Fr. Dimitri wandered into the gathering hall and Adam became more alert. There was no fire in the fireplace, although there were no doubt hot coals in the summer kitchen fireplace. *Good, at least there would be no inside fireballs for Fr. Dimitri to dodge.* There was black vapor, however, and it did not come from the fireplace. It was coming up through the floorboards.

"Your house is on fire, Mister Livingston," yelled the panicky priest. Fr. Dimitri turned to run from the room, but Adam grabbed his cassock sleeve and pulled him back.

"It's not a fire. There is no smell of fire is there? There's no heat."

Fr. Dimitri took a deep breath. "No…what is it, then?"

Adam waved his shillelagh through the vapor which swirled around the stick as it passed through. Instantly, Adam knew there was something different going on. Before, the stick would pass through without the vapor being disturbed. Now, however, there was resistance. The vapor had density—it swirled about the shillelagh. That worried Adam.

Fr. Dimitri must have seen the look on Adam's face. "What is it, Mister Livingston?"

"I was going to say there's nothing to be afraid of. This vapor or smoke is often hovering through the house. But it's heavier this time. We must be careful not to antagonize our resident ghost too much." Adam paused to look about and wave his stick through the vapor as it came up from the floorboards. "What do you think, Father? Is this a spirit you can exorcise?"

"I'm not sure…." Fr. Dimitri began, but then he stopped. For at that moment the entire floor began to shake. It wasn't a quaint shift of the floorboards as had happened on the porch. This was a tremor that felt like a real earthquake.

The whole house shook along with every thing and every body in it.

"Papa!?" exclaimed Henry. "What's that?"

"I don't know, son. Hold on." Adam grabbed his son's shoulders and held him close. "Fr. Dimitri, what do you say? Our spirit may just be celebrating that it has managed to scare us and snag a priest. It may soon tire…but this might be a good time to exorcise the beast. Now that we know it is here, you can confront it."

Fr. Dimitri nodded dubiously and opened his book of rites. But as soon as the book was opened the shaking intensified and the sound of stampeding horses and runaway wagons assaulted their ears.

Fr. Dimitri's whole body was now shivering as if a blast of cold air had enveloped him. His trembling made it difficult if not impossible to turn the pages of the book. Consequently, he could not find the rite of exorcism. In fact, he was having a hard time just standing. Suddenly he dropped to his knees to find stability, but he still struggled to turn the pages—his quivering hands and arms would not cooperate. Adam knelt next, Fr. Dimitri and tried to hold his arms steady. That helped, but not enough. He started to pray extemporaneously in Latin, hoping to find some traction: "In nomine — Patris — et Filii — et Spiritus Sancti…" but his voice quavered and his body trembled. The rumbling wagons, the clipping shears, and the room's vibrations continued to intensify and Fr. Dimitri's condition continued to worsen. Finally, he found it impossible to hold the book in his hands and it fell, sprawled open on the floor. Fumbling, he picked it up and held its open pages so tightly against his chest that his fingers turned white. Closing his eyes he prayed in Latin from memory: "Sicut deficit fumus—deficiant; sicut—fluit cera a facie—ignis, sic…*Let God arise—let His enemies be scattered—them that hate Him—flee.*"

But so violent was the haunting that, even on his knees, it was hard to stay upright. Fr. Dimitri's voice finally trailed off. His hands were shaking so badly that he could barely hold onto the open book, its pages now being scrunched and wrinkled against his chest. Raising his quivering voice above the cacophony, he leaned against Adam. "I cannot go on. This is beyond me."

Adam, more than a bit perturbed, helped the shaking priest to stand, teeter out of the house, stumble over the porch, and nearly tumble down the steps. Back on solid ground, Adam looked up. There was a small crowd of laborers and Sam standing not twenty feet away watching them and the house. The disturbance was so loud that it attracted everyone in the vicinity. Standing next to Sam, his big arms around her, was Eve, who on either side of her held George and Martha close.

"What is the trouble, Father?" said Adam.

Fr. Dimitri, still shaking now from fear, said, *"You need a more robust priest than I, sir."

"Indeed!" exclaimed Adam. "Father, look at the hem of your cassock."

Fr. Dimitri looked down. Near the bottom of his cassock, scattered about the lower foot, several dozen crescent moons about two inches long had been cleanly cut out of the cloth. Fr. Dimitri shrieked and his whole body jerked in an attempt to get away from the clipped cloth.

Adam steadied the priest's arms and talked him down. "It's all right now. They won't hurt you. But they will remind you. Show that to his excellency, the bishop."

At that point, Fr. Dimitri relaxed his arms and lowered the book of Latin rites from his chest. He didn't look at the book, but Adam did. While Adam could not read Latin, the large text at the top of the one wrinkled page was in English. The book had fallen open to the "ROMAN RITUAL OF SOLEMN EXORCISM."

All of that happened before noon.

Fr. Dimitri soon left Flax Haven completely exhausted. Adam wondered if he was strong enough to ride Count Samuel the four miles down the road to the McSherrys, but the beast must have sensed his rider was not well and responded gently. Fr. Dimitri promised to return when he could, but Adam wasn't sure he would, or if he did, what good it would do?

After the priest was gone Adam reflected on what had just happened. He was both disappointed and relieved. When Fr. Cahill had chased the spirit off, there were repercussions that Adam and his family had badly suffered. Now that the spirit had defeated a priest would there would be relief, not reprisal? Either way, Adam feared what he did not know.

Sam and the workers returned to the field, but there was much chatter among them for the rest of the day. For some had only heard the gossip that had spread through the county. Now, however, they had seen and heard what had been rumored. They were eyewitnesses. They all saw the house shake, and heard the phantom horse stampede and runaway wagons, although none actually appeared as they had done frequently at night. Some of the workers even claimed to have seen the black vapor on the porch and through the windows. Two of the workers were so spooked they refused to work anymore and left without being paid.

Adam was left with Eve, Henry, and the twins, all of whom had retreated to the bench near the oak tree. They too had seen and heard the fiasco that Fr. Dimitri had brought on, at least that is how Adam saw it. He was sorry he had mocked the priest and then encouraged him. In retrospect he should have appeased the over-confident cleric and let him wander about to satisfy his curiosity, leaving the property and the Wizard unaffected.

"Papa," said Eve, "I think I shall take George and Martha to Bethany's cabin for the rest of the day until their mother returns. I don't think it will be a good idea to go back into the house until perhaps tomorrow. Look, there is still black vapor just inside the front door."

Adam looked toward the house. When he had helped Fr. Dimitri out, he had left the front door open, and indeed there was vapor still swirling about inside, vapor that had substance to it. Strangely enough, Bombay sat on his haunches at the top of the porch steps staring at them. Adam had come to dislike the cat, and yet there it was, as comfortable as a bear in its den waiting to be provoked. "I agree, Eve. Thank you for being alert and keeping the children safe. I just hope their mother has as much sense."

2

Late Afternoon.

For Eve, the days of hauntings that occurred once a month around the new moon were bittersweet. On the one hand, getting out of the house to avoid the Wizard's disturbances precluded her from working on the loom, which she loved. Leaving the house also interrupted her reading and school work routine, both which she relished. It also meant she would be helping Bethany in her small cabin kitchen, which was difficult. On the other hand, the haunting days were usually when Mary Ann left for a day to go shopping or visit friends, leaving Eve to her own devices, which almost made up for the difficulties. But with Mary Ann's absence there was another good thing that occurred which was almost its own reward—caring for the twins, George and Martha.

Eve had grown to love the children for themselves, and they her. Martha was a bit of a handful, but when Eve remembered to treat her like an adult and not a five-year-old brat they got along much better. What was a constant trial for Eve's patience and bargaining skills was that Martha really was the quintessential little terror, and pretending to treat her as an adult in as effort to trick her into compliance was wearing. Georgie, as Eve had begun to call Martha's brother, was just the opposite. You just had to look at him, and he knew what he was supposed to be doing, and he did it. In the end, Eve adored them both and felt like a mother to them. Perhaps that is why they came to Eve when they had a problem rather than to Mary Ann. Eve listened to them and tried to negotiate, explaining to them the pros and cons of their decisions. Mary Ann demanded obedience and didn't take the time to explain the situation. Eve had always been thankful that Mama Esther was the listener. Her papa listened too, but not as much. She could not imagine having a mother like Mary Ann.

After Fr. Dimitri had left, the haunts in the main house were not just present, but worse. Especially scary was the black vapor that her papa said now had substance. Eve was thus content to keep the twins in or near Bethany's cabin. She found snacks there and was even prepared to fix them supper if Bethany and Mary Ann didn't return in time.

But they did.

Now Eve was faced with a dilemma. When Mary Ann and Bethany left for Charles Town the house was inhabitable. Yes, there were disturbances but they were mild and for practical purposes could be ignored. But that was not the case after Fr. Dimitri had left. At one point in the afternoon, while the twins were napping, Eve approached the house and stepped onto the porch and opened the front door. The vibrations were too intense and continuous to ignore, and there was black vapor flowing *up* the staircase. Eve did not investigate further. She shut the door and went back to the safety of the Darks' cabin. But what to tell Mary Ann?

From the Darks' porch, Eve watched as Mary Ann and Bethany pulled up in their wagon stacked with supplies to the house's porch steps. As soon as they did, they stopped and stared at the porch. *They see it,* Eve thought. She was sure they saw and heard the porch quaking every few seconds. Then Mary Ann climbed the steps, stood on the porch a moment, but then beat a hasty retreat back down to the ground. Mary Ann looked around and saw Eve on the Darks' porch. They waved at each other. At that moment George and Martha came out of the cabin and trotted across the yard to their mother. Eve followed. She hoped she did not have to explain what took place earlier and why the haunts had intensified beyond what was expected during a new moon. She was relieved when Adam and Henry came from the shed.

"Something happen while we were gone?" Mary Ann asked Adam.

Looking a bit chagrined, Adam nodded, but he didn't offer an explanation. Mary Ann glared at him, demanding one.

Henry came to her rescue, if you could call it that. "A priest was here. And he really screwed things up."

Eve glanced at Papa. He scowled at Henry as if to say, *"Thanks buddy, you just made the rest of my day hell."*

Mary Ann stood her ground and stared at her husband, waiting for him to supply the missing narrative.

Bethany broke the silence. To Mary Ann she said, "Should I start to take these goods into the kitchen?"

Mary Ann ignored Bethany and continued to gaze at Adam, who answered Bethany.

"It might be better if we put them in your cabin for now," said Adam.

"Wait!" said Mary Ann, holding out her hand to Bethany. "What happened, husband?"

Adam was very reluctant, but finally caved: "Remember, Fr. Cahill told us that his bishop forbade him to exorcise our house."

"I agree with the bishop," said Mary Ann.

"This morning, the bishop sent a newly ordained priest, a man named Smith, to see if the haunts were real, and if this Fr. Smith decided they were real, he had permission from the bishop to perform an exorcism on our premises. You weren't here, so I let him try, but he couldn't do a thing. As he got close to the house the haunts intensified. Once up the porch steps, the vibrations were so strong he almost fell over. In the foyer, and then in the gathering hall, the clipping, the stampeding horses and the wagons, they were all very loud, and the black vapor was different this time. It was solidifying, and it's still circulating in the house. It's much worse that ever before."

"What were you possibly thinking?" Mary Ann challenged.

"All right, hear me out. It is this, dear wife. There is something about these Catholic priests that scares the Wizard. If these priests were nothing unusual the haunts wouldn't intensify when they came around. But the closer this Fr. Smith got in the house, and especially when he opened his prayer book, the disturbances became severe. But this Fr. Smith, he was too scared. It was not like Cahill, who aggressively went after the spirit and chased it away for weeks. Smith might have been a danger to the Wizard, but he was weak, the Wizard was stronger, and the poor man left shattered. Even the bottom of his cassock was clipped into crescent shapes."

"You're crazy, Adam," said Mary Ann. "This is all in your mind. These priests are useless. They have no power."

"If that's so," said Adam, "how do you explain the weeks of peace we had after Fr. Cahill left? Don't you recall…no, maybe he said it only to me. He warned me: Either we convert and be baptized and go to Mass every week, and have the house exorcised, or the evil would come back with a vengeance. That is what he said. And it happened. Look at our barn, your horse, Apple, our four milk cows. It happened just like the priest said. That was Cahill. But the priest that came today…well, he *was* a real priest but not a strong one. For sure the Wizard was scared and tried his best to scare off this Smith priest, and he succeeded. But it was not *nothing*. It is *something*. And these Catholic priests know what it is. We just need a more robust priest to go after it. Damn bishop. Fr. Cahill was right. He should have been here, not this rookie."

Eve was proud of Papa. He was actually beginning to see what was really going on. When he stopped his rant, Mary Ann was crying softly to herself. She wouldn't look at Papa, but turned away and stared at the house for a long time. She finally burst into tears. Bethany was near her at that moment, and took Mary Ann into her arms. Eve was surprised. She had never seen her stepmother break down like this. She cried openly, as if Bethany was her long-lost mother. Her spirit was truly broken.

Eve wasn't sure if the tears were from Papa being mad at her, or if she too was realizing that a Catholic priest could relieve them, provided it was the right one. Was she tearing up because she knew she had been wrong all this time? Or was it something else?

Mary Ann whispered something to Bethany, who nodded and then released Mary Ann, who turned away from the house, and climbed into the driver's seat of the wagon. Bethany gestured to Eve, who with Bethany followed the wagon to the Darks' cabin. Once there, with Adam and Henry's help, they unloaded the food and household supplies onto the Darks' porch. Henry then led Luther and the wagon to a shed and the stable where he and Adam unloaded the feed for the livestock and a few items for Sam and the field work.

That evening the Livingstons and the Darks ate supper on the Darks' porch, but throughout those hours Mary Ann said nothing but stared at the house across the yard—so close but so forbidden. Martha pestered her mom for attention, but got little. The little girl turned to Eve, who put Martha to work helping Bethany organize her small cabin with the extra supplies. Eve was surprised at Martha's willingness and industriousness in helping. Perhaps the little girl would mature into a responsible young woman. George, meantime, was sweetly content to play with wooden blocks Adam had made for him. It would soon be dark and Papa and Sam would be back after making improvements to the pen in the livestock shed for the new milk cow, yet to be named.

At one point, Mary Ann came into the cabin, took an empty crate and started to put into it a few items.

"Can I help you get somethin' Missus Mary Ann?" said Bethany.

"Yes, before it gets darker, I'm going to take the twins and go sleep in our own house. I appreciate your hospitality, Bethany, but Nwanne's old room is not really going to be big enough for all six of us. Besides, there's only one bed in there."

"You sure about that, goin' to sleep with that Wizard still flyin' around and making a racket like it does? You gonna be able to sleep?"

"We've managed in the past," said Mary Ann.

After a bit of fussing, she convinced Martha and George to follow her across the yard to the main house.

Seeing his wife and twins walk across the yard with a box, and Eve tagging along behind carrying a sack, Adam came from across the yard and intercepted the convoy before it got to the house steps.

"You think this is wise?" asked Adam as gently as he could.

"I think it is necessary," she said. "Adam, we have worked too hard to give possession of this wonderful house over to a damn spirit we can't even see or kick out like we can anyone or anything else. I think we have to fight it, and not let it disturb our lives."

"Isn't that what I've been trying to do? What implements of war do you suggest we attempt? Simple defiance or just denial?"

Mary Ann was frustrated by Adam's questions. Her chin quivered, and her eyes flicked about. She was on the verge of tears again. "I just don't want to let go, to give in."

Eve had come to see that her stepmother was driven by a belief that *reality* was what she *wished* it to be, not what had been demonstrated through experience. Regardless of what happened to her, the children, her husband, or the farm, she was the one in control, or should have been if only by force of will. To act otherwise was foolish and a lie. Of course, the lie was to believe that such foolishness was true. Eve could see that this thinking had in part attracted her to Papa, who embraced a similar mindset—that the world revolved around him. Of course, in recent years Papa had begun to change.

Mary Ann charged up the steps to the porch, but she dropped the crate.

Adam, right behind her, caught it and carried it up the rest of the way. She turned around to Eve. "Eve, bring that sack to me." Mary Ann opened the door and went into the house. Adam carried the crate in and put it down on the foyer floor, which every few seconds quaked. Eve came behind them. Around them swirled the black vapor that Eve could feel like a wind on her skin.

Adam felt it too. "This is not a good idea, Mary Ann."

"Give me that sack, Eve," she said.

Eve did.

Opening the sack, Mary Ann pulled out a brand new white linen table cloth she had purchased in Charles Town. It was for a small game table and around the edges there was delicate embroidery. She held up the pristine cloth. "There's one thing you haven't tried, and I intend to try it tonight. Where's your Mayntz pistol and the Knox rifle?"

"What you gonna do?" said Adam. He thought for just a moment. "Oh, no, you're not."

Mary Ann said, "Oh, yes I am. I'm going to lay out this beautiful cloth here in the foyer, on top of that there crate, and I'm going to sit on the stairs and wait for the damn whatever-it-is to start clipping, and then I'm going to blast it with both guns at close range."

"Now who's crazy? Those guns haven't been fired for a year."

"Well, go get them and fire'em up before nightfall. I'm going to kill me a Wizard."

Eve could not believe the conversation. She had only seen Papa fire his rifle a couple times when he did some hunting shortly after they arrived in Virginia. He didn't like guns, and preferred trapping his meat when they couldn't buy it.

Adam and Mary Ann argued for a long time, but in the end Papa got the guns and told Eve and Henry to take the twins and stay with the Darks until they got back. Then he and Mary Ann walked into the woods behind the house. In the distance Eve could hear the guns being fired. Both she and Henry wished they had not missed out on that.

3

Adam had grave doubts about letting Mary Ann use his guns, let alone try to shoot a ghost with them. He knew it was an idiotic idea, but he had long ago learned that what was idiocy to him was perfectly rational to others. Reason can rarely compete with a stubborn will.

Mary Ann was not ignorant of flint-lock firearms, but Adam nonetheless took her through a refresher course and safety ritual. He adjusted the flint so it struck the frizzen just right. He cleaned the barrels, primed the pan, compressed the gunpowder, wad, and ball into the bottom of the barrel, and he half-cocked the firing mechanism so the frizzen captured the priming powder. As he worked over the guns he saw that nothing worried Mary Ann about such things, and that worried him. He thought it wise to fear anything that could kill you, even by accident. His patience won out and she finally gave in to his concerns and took the process more seriously.

They picked out a tree trunk to shoot at. He reminded her several times never to point a gun, loaded or not, at anything living if she didn't intend to kill it. The gun might accidentally discharge. More than once, while she handled the pistol, Adam grabbed the barrel and pointed it away from some part of his body. Since she would be discharging the guns in succession, he had her practice picking up the pistol, firing it, putting it down, picking up the rifle, firing it, and putting it down...always pointing the guns away from herself and him. As her competence rose in safely handling the guns his fear lessened.

The real fright came when she started shooting. He took a position behind her and to one side. She picked up the pistol and took careful aim at the tree trunk. Suddenly, he experienced a flash premonition. It scared the wits out of him, and he yelled, "STOP!"

Mary Ann put the gun down aimed away from them, and turned to Adam, "Why? What's wrong?"

Adam peered downrange at the target and all around the area. Making sure she had the pistol pointed away from the range, he walked to the tree trunk and looked behind it. He also looked behind and around the trees nearby. He saw nothing unusual, which confirmed that what he saw was a premonition and not real. He returned to her, apologized, and asked her again take aim and discharge the weapon.

She did. BAM! A direct hit.

Altogether, Mary Ann discharged the pistol and the rifle a total of six times, but the shooting practice was interrupted twice more by Adam's premonitions. Just before Mary Ann squeezed the trigger of either the pistol or rifle, Adam saw something that scared him and he yelled, "STOP!"

After the second time she'd demanded: "What am I doing wrong?"

Adam looked all around them and at the gun in her hands and said, "Nothing, let's try again."

The third time he yelled at her to stop, she ignored him and discharged the gun anyway. She had a calm grip and she rarely missed her target.

When they were done and were packing up the armory kit, she asked again, "Adam, what was wrong? Why did you keep yelling at me to stop?"

"I didn't want you to kill something alive." Then he lied. "There was a rabbit, or a squirrel, or a bird in your line of fire."

She thought back. "I didn't see any thing like that, and there's nothing wrong with my eyesight."

"Well, I thought I did. I'm sorry."

Adam knew he was a terrible liar, but this was no time to tell her the truth. If she thought he was a bit strange or overly cautious, so be it. He would keep the secret to himself.

On the walk back to the house he thought about what he had seen and it disturbed him even more than the Wizard's best haunts. In the past the premonitions had been longer in duration, maybe several seconds. But the premonitions he had just experienced were no longer than the time it took for the primer powder to flash and the gun to discharge. The first time Mary Ann took aim, he saw their little girl, Martha, playing hide-n-seek behind the tree at which Mary Ann was aiming. Martha's face and upper body leaned out from behind the tree and smiled at them. Mary Ann's pistol was pointed directly at Martha's face. He shivered at the vision, even in recalling it. The second time it was Georgie peeking from behind the other side of the tree but looking directly at them down Mary Ann's rifle barrel. The third time Martha suddenly appeared behind one tree, Georgie from behind another, and she chased him giggling all the way into the brush. As Adam played the visions back in his mind, his heart beat more rapidly than normal. He was truly scared.

There was something else about these premonitions that struck him as different. As he thought back, he could not recall an earlier premonition in which he recognized a real person. That he quickly recognized Martha and George in these premonitions made him very nervous. His premonitions had always come true, but in odd ways that defied easy connections. These three visions felt very close and more accurate than anything before. It was as if the messenger, hindered before, was finally getting through.

4

Eve was glad when she heard the distant firing stop, and Papa and her step-mother returned from gun practice. It was dark now, and reluctantly the family moved into the house and into their bedrooms for the night. Eve wasn't overly concerned because her room was fairly immune to the haunts, although she heard what was going on elsewhere. Henry asked if he could sleep in her room. She said yes, and they made up a bed for him on the floor near her armoire.

The twins still used their small beds located in Papa's and Mary Ann's bedroom. There had been plans, once weaned, to make them larger beds and move them into Eve's and Henry's rooms, but Mary Ann couldn't stand a night without them near her.

That night Adam and Mary Ann prepared the twins for bed, but Papa and Mary Ann stayed dressed.

From their conversation, even as they were readying for bed, Eve could hear the argument. Adam didn't feel comfortable giving loaded flint-lock guns to his wife, but he was going to do it. The twins would be in their beds, Mary Ann would aim the guns at the crate and cloth below her on the stairs. That way the spent balls would end up safely either in the crate or the foyer floor. Papa would sit or sleep on the landing at the top of the foyer stairs. He wasn't going to let his guns far out of his sight. They lit two lanterns in the foyer so Mary Ann could see, and they settled down until the shooting began. The last thing Adam said to Mary Ann was, "Wife, I want you to remember that while this is crazier than those Catholic priests you object to, I'm helping you do this fool thing. I hope you don't kill any of us. Thinking you can shoot a ghost with a gun is like pretending I'm a woman and you're a man. It's nuts. So, tonight you go ahead and shoot your ghost, and tomorrow I'll suckle the twins."

"They're already weaned," she said.

"Perhaps, but I just felt my milk drop."

At that point Eve heard something hit the wall as if it had been thrown across the room. There was a groan and that was it.

As Eve lay down and pulled the cotton sheet over her, she took note of the haunts. There were the usual sounds and quakes, but tonight they were more intense, and the black vapor which swirled through the lower rooms and up the stairs before returning into the floor boards did feel like a light wind on the skin. That was different and a bit alarming. She felt safe in her bedroom, convinced that Xavier's crucifix in her heirloom chest and his Roman Missal in the second chest would protect her mother's linens, and that Fr. Xavier's prayer book, which was under her pillow, would this night protect her and Henry, too.

5

Mary Ann was both exhausted and mad, but finally she was doing something that Adam had failed to do—use lethal force against their tormentor. She understood Adam's doubts, but inviting priests to stir up tragedies didn't sound smart either.

Everything was set. The guns were loaded and resting on the step behind her. She had pillows with her on the steps, although after the day traveling to and from Charles Town she wondered if she would be able to stay awake—even with the pillows the wooden stairs were hard and uncomfortable. She had checked the oil in the two lanterns set in the corners of the foyer; they would burn all night if they had to. Adam kept watch from the landing behind her, and the children were all safe in their beds. Nothing to do now but wait.

Mary Ann did doze off, but around midnight she was stirred slowly awake. Half asleep, it sounded to her as if the clipping sounds that always seemed to be with them had become more frequent, or faster. She jolted fully awake, remembering where she was and what was resting on the step just behind her back.

"Adam?" she called out softly.

"Yeah, I'm here. It's started. Take a look."

Mary Ann raised her head and focused her eyes. Indeed the beautiful linen table covering she had purchased with great care in Charles Town was moving. It was as if there was a hand underneath the cloth. She looked closer. All at once a two-inch long hole appeared in the cloth—in the recognizable shape of a crescent moon. The pure linen cloth had been the perfect bait. Like ants attracted to sugar the Wizard could not help but clip linen. One hole after another sponta-neously appeared around the edges and in the center of the cloth.

The Wizard had never been shy about its vexing performances. Adam and Mary Ann could be running around the room and their bedspread would still move and get clipped. Outside, Adam could attack the wraiths in his rage with his shillelagh, and even that would not deter them from stampeding about the house. But for some reason, now, Mary Ann moved slowly, so as not to scare off the prey she had lured into her deadly trap.

Proud she was of her cleverness as she reached carefully behind and picked up the pistol and then the rifle. With Adam's help, both were loaded with pow-der, a wad, and a ball. The firing mechanisms were both half-cocked with prim-ing powder already in the pans held in place by the closed frizzens. She laid the rifle in her lap with its barrel pointed toward the front door. Then she grasped the pistol in her right hand, pulled the hammer back to the fully cocked posi-tion, carefully aimed the barrel at the moving cloth…and slowly squeezed the trigger. The hammer holding the flint flew forward, struck the frizzen, and at once shoved it out of the way and threw sparks into the primer pan. The primer ignited and sent an explosive charge through the flash hole into the barrel where the main charge, the wad, and a ball was packed and waiting. A half-second lat-er the gun fired. BAM, and the ball flew out of the barrel toward its target. She looked up quickly to check her aim. It was right on target. The cloth still lay on top of the crate, but now there was a black hole in the middle of it from the ball. Quickly, she put down the pistol and repeated the sequence with the rifle. BAM! The ball this time was larger, and so was the second black hole in the cloth. No one would claim she could hit the broadside of a barn at twenty yards, but she wasn't too shabby at hitting a table cloth at ten feet.

"Good shots!" exclaimed Adam from the landing behind her. "You hit it twice. Perfectly."

She gazed at the crate and the cloth that still sat in the middle of the foyer on the crate, but now with two bullet holes clearly in the middle. But what was more exciting to her was that the clipping sound had stopped. All of it. In fact, the floor stopped vibrating, and the other sounds ceased as well. The cloth was not moving. Crescent shaped holes were no longer dropping out of the cloth. She could not believe her idea had worked. You *can* shoot a ghost with a gun.

She sat still. Everything was quiet, except the twins fussing, and the sound of Eve and Henry padding in their bare feet coming down the steps to the land-ing where their father sat applauding his wife's marksmanship.

She turned around and smiled at Adam and the children.

"Did it stop?" asked Eve.

"It seems so," said Adam. "Amazing! I owe your stepmother an apology. This is wonderful."

The whole house was quiet, except for the fussing of George and Martha who obviously did not know what was going on except for two very loud noises that had awakened them in the middle of the night.

Mary Ann, feeling very proud and successful, put down the guns, stretched, and climbed the stairs: "Better see to the little ones, poor things. I probably scared them out of their minds." As she passed Adam on the landing step and Eve and Henry who stood next to him, she kissed Adam on the cheek, and patted Eve and Henry on their heads.

At the top of the stairs Mary Ann walked down the short hall to her bedroom door which had been shut. The lit lantern in the hall reminded her that they had also left a lit lantern in their bedroom so the kids wouldn't be left in the pitch dark. But Mary Ann suddenly became worried—George and Martha's child like fussing had turned into a raspy, congestive, howl. She suddenly shuddered, quickly opened the bedroom door, and stepped into the room. What met her forced her to shriek, take a breath, and fall to the floor. Her eyelids slammed shut. It felt like abrasive ash had been blown into her eye sockets. At the same time she gasped for air but couldn't breathe. She called out, "Adam!" but all she could get out was a searing, painful cough. Her throat felt as if it had been shredded by a razor. The room was filled with what looked like the Wizard's black vapor, but this was not the innocuous black fume they had grown accustomed to over the years. This was the thick, nearly opaque, noxious exhaust of a raging fire but without the heat and flame. There was no fire, just a thick wall of black, poisonous gas. She tried calling out again "Adam!" but she could find no air in her constricted lungs to force out the word. She banged on the floor with her fist, she hacked out a few coughs, and finally felt the tremor of Adam's foot steps running up the stairs. She tried again to take a breath but it felt like the long, sharp spikes of a hawthorn tree had been shoved down her wind pipe and into her lungs. She couldn't see or breathe, but she could still hear George and Martha, faintly. Their cries now diminished to grating, hacking coughs punctuated by airless screams.

She was being dragged away from the door, carried down the steps, pulled through the foyer, down more steps, and laid on the ground away from the house. She kept trying to fill her lungs with air, and finally did, but breathing came only with searing pain as if her chest, throat, and nostrils were being sliced open with a butcher's cleaver. When she finally was able to speak, all that came to her mind and lips were the names of her dear little five-year-olds—"Georgie...Martha. Georgie...Martha. How are they? Did they get out? Where are they? Adam? Adam? Find them. Save them."

But Adam didn't reply. It was silent, and Mary Ann cried...for a very long time.

6

It all happened too fast for Eve: One second they thought the Wizard had been killed or scared away by Mary Ann's lead balls, the next Papa was carrying

Mary Ann to safety down the stairs and yelling at her and Henry to get out of the house. Papa was coughing when he carried Mary Ann down the stairs. Eve breathed some of the smoke that trailed after him. It stung her eyes and nose but she managed to hold her breath until she got outside. Henry was mostly already down the steps looking at Papa's guns that Mary Ann had left behind, so he ran out unaffected.

Once they were all outside, Papa handed Mary Ann off to Sam, who, with Bethany, had come into the yard when they heard the gunshots. Evidently Adam had told Sam what Mary Ann was going to do, and Sam, in his wisdom, had gone to bed with his clothes and boots on. Sam carried Mary Ann back to his porch with Bethany at his side. At the same time Papa ran back into the house. Eve followed him, but only as far as the front door. The black smoke was cascading down the stairs. At the door she took a breath. The substance had thinned but what was in the air instantly burned her eyes and nose, and her mouth stiffened at the corrosive taste. She managed to grab one of the lanterns that was just inside the front door, then ran back into the yard and fresh air. Her papa wasn't far behind. He had only gotten halfway up the stairs before he, too, had to back down.

His voice was shaking, and his eyes were watering from the smoke and fear. "I can't hear them anymore," he cried. "I heard them a little when I picked up Mary Ann, but now there's nothing. They aren't crying, or coughing. O, God, what have we done?" He looked up at the front of the house, and sobbed, "We even shut the windows when we put them to bed. Damn it! Damn it! What have we done?"

Her papa kept trying to go back into the house and up the stairs. Each time he got a little further before he had to run back out.

Many minutes later, when the smoke had cleared, Papa got all the way to his bedroom and carried out little Georgie and Martha into the fresh air. He laid their limp, lifeless, pale bodies on the ground near the house. Mary Ann saw this and came running and wailing. She lifted her only children from the cold ground and hugged them, but their pudgy little arms hung limp at their sides and didn't hug back She kissed their cold, ashen faces but they didn't smile or giggle back. As much as she tried her actions only triggered more grief and distress, not just in Mary Ann but in Adam and the rest who watched the tragic scene.

Eve was weak watching her stepmother frantically try to bring Georgie and Martha back to life with an abundance of love and attention. *Too little, too late,* thought Eve. The thought shamed her, and she ran to her father and buried her tear-sodden face in his chest. Henry was shaking and stunned to silence; he didn't cry but kept looking to his father for courage and direction. Adam gave his shaking son a lantern to hold, which the boy did although the light shook as well.

Papa curtailed his own sobs long enough to ask, "Eve, do you have an intact linen sheet or blanket or anything to cover them up. Your stepmother can't go on like this."

Sam was there and said, "If'n Miss Eve has a sheet, I get a wagon, and we's kin put dem in the wagon 'en cover dem up."

"Thanks Sam, let's do that."

"Henry!" Sam called. "Come with me."

Henry, glad to have something to do, handed the lantern to Papa, then trotted with Sam to the stables. Eve ran into the house and up the stairs. At the top of the stairs she avoided the temptation to look into Papa's bedroom and instead turned sharply to her own. She immediately opened the heirloom chest at the foot of her bed, moved the crucifix aside, lifted out a sheet that the Wizard had not touched, returned the crucifix, shut the lid, and ran back downstairs and outside.

Her papa, with Bethany's help, was carrying a grieving Mary Ann back to the Darks' cabin and away from George's and Martha's bodies. Sam and Henry brought a small wagon. Sam was pulling and Henry was pushing it across the yard in the dark. They had not taken the time to hitch up Luther or Calvin. The wagon had raised sides and a tailgate and in it Sam had spread out a layer of clean straw. Sam removed the tailgate, reverently picked up each of the bodies in turn and laid them on the straw. Then he took the unsoiled white linen cloth Eve had brought and covered the bodies, then replaced the tailgate.

Sam and Henry rolled the wagon beside their cabin, but around the corner where it could not be seen easily from the porch. "Henry," said Sam, "we's got ta guard dis wagon as long as it's outside. Otherwise we's have animals 'en vultures all ov'r yer brother 'n' sister before de sun come up. You, me, and Miss Eve, we gotta take turns guarding dem until yer papa decides wad we's gonna do. Now, you 'en Eve go inside, see if ye can get any sleep. I'll get me's a stick to chase off any animals or birds that come. If'n I get too tired, I's come 'en git one of ya."

Adam had just returned from closing up the main house. "Here, Sam," said Adam, "take this. Almost left it in the house." It was Papa's shillelagh.

Sam took it and nodded his appreciation, "Dat'll work." He grabbed a wicker chair, a lantern, and sat on the corner of the porch where he could see the tail end of the wagon.

Inside the cabin, Papa went into the spare bedroom where Bethany sat next to Mary Ann resting on the bed. He excused Bethany, and laid next to Mary Ann and took her into his arms.

"Come children," said Bethany. "We'll make you comfortable out here by the fire."

Bethany put a couple of logs on the fire and laid down some cushions by it for Eve and her brother to sleep on after perhaps the most harrowing night of their lives. Henry fell asleep quickly. Eve, however, stayed awake the rest of the night, part mourning the death of her step-siblings, and part wondering what the Wizard would be up to in the morning, and who or what would truly get rid of it forever.

7

August 23, 1797.

In the morning, Adam, unable to sleep in an unfamiliar bed and fully clothed, was up early, but he couldn't beat Bethany. She was used to getting up in the dark, starting fires, and cooking breakfast before empty stomachs knew they needed food. When Adam came out of the spare bedroom he saw that Eve was on the porch guarding the bodies. Henry had been moved away from the fire, and Bethany had cooked up big helpings of eggs, bacon, and cheese. She first made up a bowl for Eve and took it out to her, then for Adam and Sam. The men had breakfast and coffee on the porch.

"I kin make caskets fer 'da children dis morning," said Sam. The workers don't need me's today. 'Dey kin work on 'der own."

"Let's get a couple of them to dig graves, though," said Adam.

"Yea, we do that, first thing. Up next 'a Nwanne?"

"That be fine, Sam. For my wife's sake I'd like to get this over with quickly."

Mary Ann was sound asleep in the spare bedroom. Adam went to Bethany and asked her to keep Mary Ann in her cabin and somehow occupied for the day, if that was possible. Bethany agreed. There were things he needed to do at the main house before they tried to move back in, if that was possible.

Henry was up by now, had breakfast, and took over guard duty. Eve curled up in a corner of the spare bedroom and took a nap.

Adam went to the main house and checked on its condition and most immediately the Wizard's status. This was the first day after the new moon, and he expected, or rather hoped, that the haunts would have diminished enough to reoccupy the house. But after last night's tragic events, he wasn't sure if anyone would want to stay in the house ever again. The house was mostly quiet, but not entirely. In the foyer there were very faint clipping sounds, and almost unnoticeable floor quakes, but they were enough to convince him that the Wizard had not been killed. He removed the crate and the linen cloth with the two bullet holes in it. He would secretly burn both with rubbish. He wanted no evidence to remind him or Mary Ann of last night. But, the crate had not stopped the balls. He dug the lead out of the floor boards which would be marred until he could replaced the planks.

With some trepidation he climbed the stairs and went into his bedroom. He had been there last night when he carried the bodies out, but now he could see better in the light of day. Looking at the two small beds he first wondered if the wood in them could be used for their coffins. He would suggest that to Sam. When he looked into the beds he was shaken. On both cotton mattress covers where the children had lain there was evidence of coughed blood and mucus. They probably had not struggled very long, but it had to be very painful based on what he and Mary Ann had experienced during their escape. He would burn the mattresses and covers. Most discouraging, however, was that when he stood over the beds, the floor was quaking, and the sounds of clipping and a rushing wind were more intense than usual. Thank goodness the vapor that had turned into deadly smoke was gone, but clearly the Wizard was alive, and malevolent as ever. He would return tomorrow and see if another day from the new moon would allow the room to be inhabited. He would ask Eve to come and clean out all the children's spare clothes and toys and anything that might remind Mary Ann of her children. He would burn them all.

Sam liked the idea of making the caskets from the beds, and said he would do that immediately. Eve likewise, although very sad about the assignment, agreed to clean out the bedroom and the rest of the house of anything that might remind Mary Ann of George or Martha and take it all to the rubbish pile.

When the workers came, Sam assigned two to remove the beds and take them to the tool shed where he would make the coffins. Then he asked them to dig the graves where Mister Livingston directed. Adam hoped they could complete the task by dusk. If they stayed one more night with the Darks, perhaps they could move back into the house tomorrow morning.

Now that the house had been surveyed and the tasks assigned, Adam had time to ponder the last twenty-four hours. Clearly the flash premonitions he experienced in the woods with Mary Ann shooting his guns at tree trunks had come true. He racked his brain—*was there a way he could have connected the visions with his children's death? Could he have prevented it?* His frustration was layered with dread.

There was something else eating at his soul. He walked about the farm trying to clear his mind. He checked on Mary Ann and Eve—both were asleep; he watched Henry play with small pebbles as he guarded the wagon and bodies—there had been no animals or birds. He inspected the grave digging—there were the typical rocks and roots the men had to dig out and cut through; and he looked in on Sam in the tool shed—there would be sufficient wood from the beds to make coffins.

Then it came to him.

Without explaining what or where he was going, except that he would be gone for an hour or so, he saddled up Calvin and rode out of the yard. At the Charles Town Road he turned right, and a half mile later at the junction in Smithfield, he turned left and headed northeast toward Leetown.

The Wizard's vengeance that Fr. Cahill had warned him about was now fully realized. He felt a deep guilt. Had he believed Fr. Cahill, the barn and the children would still be with them. Mary Ann might be upset, but she would not be permanently wounded. As Calvin cantered along the Leetown Road, Adam was not high in his saddle. He was bent over, his head bowed, and he did not prohibit the tears. There was part of him that wanted to die. He had failed himself, his wife, his children, and especially poor little George and Martha, but his German stubbornness forced him on. He wondered how many more mistakes he would make before his life ended. Well, perhaps today he could do one thing right.

When Adam arrived at Retirement, the McSherrys invited him in and handed him a time-honored glass of Madeira. He asked to speak with Fr. Dimitri, but they could listen if they wanted. Subdued, Adam suspected his eyes were still red and wet from his tears. They all gathered in the parlor, Fr. Dimitri, Anastasia, Catharine, Letitia, and Richard who was wrapped up in a blanket. His eyes were red and he looked ill, but he sat on the edge of his chair and listened.

"Last night," Adam began, "our two small children, George and Martha died."

His hosts gasped and Anastasia began to weep.

"How, Adam?" asked Fr. Dimitri.

Adam hesitated. He did not want to blame Mary Ann and her gun fantasy, for he knew that *he* was the one to blame for rejecting what the only effective minister against the Wizard had warned.

"After Fr. Dimitri left yesterday, the Wizard's haunts intensified. It became clear to me that it, the Wizard that is, feared Catholic priests, for something similar occurred when Fr. Cahill came and blessed the house. Mary Ann and I decided that we didn't need a priest, but that we could fight it alone. We tried, in the middle of the night…and for a few moments we thought we had succeeded. The hauntings suddenly stopped. For the first time during the time of a new moon there was no clipping, stampeding horses, or wagons, or vibrations, and there was no black vapor. Everything was peaceful. We were elated. But the twins were crying from the noise we had made, so Mary Ann went to their beds. Except she couldn't get to them. The bedroom was filled with a thick, black, acid smoke that seared our lungs and burned our eyes. It was like the intense smoke from a house fire, except there was no fire. Just the smoke. Martha and George were in the middle of it. They couldn't breathe…and they died."

Anastasia, who had three boys the twins' ages and younger broke down and cried. She turned to Richard and held onto him as if her boys' life had just ended. Richard held her close, but gazed at Adam. "Oh, Adam. How horrible," but otherwise he was speechless. Catharine began to tremble and gripped Letitia's arm in fear, while Letitia froze where she sat as tears fell from her eyes.

Adam continued, "It was the Wizard attacking us, warning us not to try to expel it. The same thing with the barn. And the only common thing between the barn and our children's death is the presence of a Catholic priest." At that point Adam turned and looked at Fr. Dimitri.

"Mister Livingston," said Fr. Dimitri, "I assure you that every thought I had when I was with you was against this spirit. I am so very sorry. Surely, had I known anything like this were to happen, I would not have tried. I know what I should have done, but I could not. I'm so sorry."

"I have not spoken clearly," said Adam. "*You* did not kill my children. It is not your fault. The fault lies only with *me*. For I did not listen to Fr. Cahill and his warning to convert, be baptized, take the sacraments, and exorcise the house. After his blessing and warning I even had the gall to tell him he wasn't needed anymore. I am at fault. My arrogance has killed two of my children. I need a Catholic priest. I know now that only a Catholic priest can relieve us. We are desperate."

Fr. Dimitri was very subdued. "I am devastated at this news, Mister Livingston. What can I do for you now?"

"You must come with me and bury my children. I was just going to bury them myself, but you must pray over them and ask God to forgive me and protect their souls, even if their bodies are in the ground. We are digging graves right now, and Sam is making caskets from the wood of the beds they died in. Won't you please come and bury them?"

"But your wife, what will she say?"

Adam suddenly turned angry. "She has nothing to say in this. This is my decision. I know you and Fr. Cahill to be men of God, empowered to fight evil. You, Fr. Dimitri, need more courage, and perhaps Fr. Cahill can help you with that. But you should be able to bless my dead children and bury them. Will you come with me?"

Fr. Dimitri immediately stood. "I will come with you immediately." He turned to Richard. "Do you see it, Richard? Our prayers, my prayer has been answered. God is at work." He turned back to Adam. "Let me get my book of rites and my riding boots." He turned back to Richard, again. "When I return, Richard, we must talk about what should be done next for Mister Livingston."

"I will tell you what we need next," said Adam. "We need Fr. Denis Cahill, and he needs permission to exorcise our house like he wanted to do in the first place."

"I don't think you need Fr. Cahill," said Richard, who interrupted and spoke with an uncharacteristically weak voice. "The man is not to be trusted."

This got Adam's attention.

"Richard!" exclaimed Anastasia, "why would you say such a thing?"

"I'm not willing to say," Richard said, "but it would be best if none of you would consider him any longer a trustworthy priest. If Fr. Dimitri is not courageous enough, then go back to the bishop and find another."

As Richard said that, Adam caught Richard's sideways glance at Letitia, who glared back at Richard as if there was some secret animosity between them. It was only for an instant, but it made Adam curious. On the surface, Adam could not believe what he was hearing, for Adam's faith in Fr. Cahill was strong. Something perhaps demonic must have come over Richard McSherry for him to say something like this. Adam spoke up: "Mister McSherry, you know that I respect your opinion and person, but it was only Fr. Cahill that chased the spirit from our house for a time. Even Fr. Dimitri said we need a more robust priest. Do you know of anyone else?"

Richard shook his head, and spoke softly. "No, I do not."

There was a lapse in the conversation.

"Mister Livingston," said Fr. Dimitri, "let us go bury your children. I am most eager to do something constructive for you." Turning to Richard he said, "Please get some rest. I hope you're feeling better when I return."

Richard appeared bewildered but he nodded at Fr. Dimitri. "Aye, that I will do, Father. God speed."

Adam and Fr. Dimitri were out the door when Richard called after them, "Adam?"

Adam stopped and stepped back inside.

"Will you come back with Father after you bury your dear children? I want to talk with you."

"Of course," said Adam, and he left.

Adam and Fr. Dimitri rode back to Flax Haven. When they arrived, the graves were dug, but the caskets were not finished. It would be a couple of hours before Sam and the caskets would be ready. So Fr. Dimitri hung out with Sam in the tool shed and handed him tools or helped as he could. When the caskets were ready they put straw in the bottom of each and with Luther in a harness brought the wagon with the children's bodies to the tool shed. Eve came along as did Henry. They wrapped the children in white linen that Eve had procured from her heirloom chests and laid the bodies in the caskets. The lids were left off to be nailed shut at the grave site. Luther then pulled the wagon to the top of the hill and the family grave site where the fresh graves had been dug.

Mary Ann had still been with Bethany in the Darks' cabin. Adam took time to be with his wife. Did she want to be present when they buried the children? She shook her head. Then Adam said, "I have gone to the McSherrys' and brought back Fr. Dimitri to pray over them before we bury them. He's going to perform a solemn burial rite and to bless them. Are you sure you don't want to be present?"

She turned to him, "Isn't he the man you told me who tried to exorcise the house, and failed. Isn't he the man who is responsible for our children's deaths?"

"Mary Ann, listen to me. It is because of his power as a Catholic priest that the Wizard became so afraid that it attacked and killed our children. It is with these priests that we *can* rid ourselves of these malicious spirits. But we have to do what they say, not as we want. We have to be converted and baptized and take the sacraments, and, yes, have our house exorcised by a courageous and robust priest. I did not do that. But I am going to do it now, and Fr. Dimitri is here to bury our children. Will you come? I want you to come."

"Adam, I am tired. I understand what you are saying, but so far we have lost our barn, almost our livelihood, and George and Martha. And it is only because Catholic priests were involved. Either they have the power or not. It can't rest in any way on you, whether you do this or I do that."

"My dear wife. Much of this is *my* fault. True, it is my farm and our children. But we cannot blame priests for a bad yield if I do not rotate my crops. Priests are the intermediaries between us and the Creator who created the land on which we farm and allows flax to grow from flaxseed instead of radishes.

There is a natural way to work and live, and these priests know what that is and how best to do it. We can follow their directions or not. We have a choice. But when we make a bad choice we cannot blame others for the natural consequences we suffer. Priests hold the power, God's power, to relieve us. But to get that relief we have to do what they say. And I ignored it."

Mary Ann hesitated, then said, "I am sure I am not going to convert. But I will come with you. I do want to see our dear children buried properly."

Mary Ann was weak, but she came to the top of the hill behind the house. Henry and Eve were there along with the Darks. Adam could see that Eve was stunned that her stepmother would stand by a grave while a Catholic priest read prayers and they buried her children. Mary Ann said nothing the whole time, and there were no haunts to interrupt them. At the end Fr. Dimitri read prayers:

> *Lord Jesus Christ, by your own three days in the tomb, you hallowed the graves of all who believe in you and so made the grave a sign of hope that promises resurrection even as it claims our mortal bodies. Grant that our brother and sister, Martha Livingston and George Livingston, may sleep here in peace until you awaken them to glory, for you are the resurrection and the life. Then they will see you face to face and in your light will see light and know the splendor of God, for you live and reign forever and ever. Amen.*
>
> *O God, by whose mercy the faithful departed find rest, send your holy Angel to watch over this grave. Through Christ our Lord. Amen.*

Sam's workers filled the graves in over the small caskets. Sam had made simple crosses, and after Mary Ann had left Eve carefully erected the crosses at the heads of the graves with a cairn of stones for support.

It was late afternoon by the time they left the hill top grave site. Adam inspected the house again. The Wizard was growing weaker as the new moon passed into history, but he asked his family to settle down with the Darks another night. He then rode back to the McSherrys' with Fr. Dimitri. Adam was intent on involving Fr. Cahill, and he felt the need to convince Richard of that, regardless of Richard's sudden dislike for the man. On their ride back, Adam told Fr. Dimitri about his dreams and how Fr. Cahill matched the man in his dreams that the voice said could relieve him. Fr. Dimitri did not doubt Adam, and acknowledged that Adam's dreams were likely brought to him by an angel and he needed to heed what he was told. Fr. Dimitri had no problems admitting to his fear and that the story of Fr. Cahill aggressively blessing Adam's house and leaving it peaceful for weeks convinced him that Fr. Cahill was their man. By the time they had returned to Leetown, Fr. Dimitri was eager to meet Fr. Cahill. They decided there was some special, perhaps miraculous reason that Fr. Cahill must be involved.

7

Fr. Cahill was tending his small vegetable garden next to St. Agnes Chapel's rectory, when a horse galloped into the yard. When he saw Letitia riding astride Hopscotch his heart stopped. Letitia and the horse were a handsome pair, and Letitia was in perfect control of the large steed. She had no fear, only focus and poise. But for her to show up alone at the chapel made him wary. At first he wondered if anyone had seen her arrive. No doubt someone had. He would have to be careful.

When she dismounted near him, he held up his hands to make sure they did not embrace even in a sister-brother way, but she needed no warning. Before she hit the ground she started to tell him that Adam Livingston had just come to Retirement to inform them that his twins, George and Martha, had suddenly died. At that she had his full attention.

She had come to ask him to come to Retirement right away and to tell him that another priest, sent by the bishop, was there. She wasn't sure of his name; it might be Smith, Gallitzin, or Dimitri—he had a strange accent. Anyway, this priest had tried to exorcise the Livingston house but couldn't. Then somehow in the hours after the priest left the children had died. She said Mister Livingston was convinced that the deaths were in retribution by the spirit for the presence of the priest and his attempted exorcism.

Fr. Cahill was at once shocked and distressed by this news. So many thoughts flooded his mind. The barn's destruction was one thing, but the lives of two little children was something entirely different and serious. All over again, he got mad at the bishop for not taking him seriously about the need to exorcise the Livingston farm. But listening to Letitia's worry and concern warmed his heart. She was a fascinating woman full of compassion and intelligence.

Winded from her ride, she was eager to know if he could come immediately to Retirement and see Adam and this other priest. Fr. Cahill didn't think for long. Yes, he would come immediately. He quickly brushed the dirt from his knees, washed his hands, donned a clean shirt and his riding boots, saddled Sassafras, packed his priest kit into a saddle bag, and they rode off to Leetown together.

When Fr. Cahill and Letitia arrived at Retirement it appeared that two other riders had just arrived and were handing their reins over to Hank.

"That's the other priest, Smith or something, with Mister Livingston," said Letitia as they reined their horses to a stop.

Adam immediately came and stroked Sassafras' neck. "Fr. Cahill, how is it that you're here? I so need to talk with you."

Fr. Cahill and Letitia dismounted and handed Hank their reins.

"I brought him," said Letitia. "After the two of you left here to bury the twins, Mister McSherry very strangely asked me to quickly ride to Shepherd's Town and fetch Fr. Denis." She glanced at Fr. Denis: "He even made a point that

I return *immediately.*" She shared a weak smile with Fr. Cahill who momentarily glared back at her. She quickly recollected herself and continued: "Richard thought that because of the circumstances you should talk to Fr. Denis, and that Fr. Denis should meet Fr. Dimitri…or is it Prince Gallitzin…or Mister Smith. I'm not sure what we should call you."

Fr. Dimitri grinned. In his amalgamated European accent he said, "It's all three actually. Call me whatever you want. I'll explain later."

"Good," said Fr. Cahill. "I want to hear that story, too. Adam, I am truly sorry about your children. Miss McCartney filled me in a little on the way here."

"You warned me," said Adam. "Twice you warned me, and I did not listen. I'm the one that needs to apologize. I am desperate and full of remorse."

Fr. Cahill studied Adam's eyes for a moment, then turned to Fr. Dimitri. "Father, I'm Denis Cahill. I understand Bishop Carroll sent you to investigate the Livingston infestation. Is that true? Can you fill me in?"

At that moment Anastasia came from the house. "Gentlemen, and lady, let me interrupt you. Supper will not be for at least an hour, but if you care to make yourselves comfortable on the garden patio I'll bring you tea and something to nibble on. Richard is resting; he'll join us for supper. Mister Livingston, can you join us for supper?"

"Probably not, Anastasia, but thank you for asking. I should get back as soon as I can."

"I understand," said Anastasia. "Letitia, you've had a hard ride. Just relax and get something to drink. Catharine will help me if I need it."

"Yes, Madam, thank you," Letitia said.

The men sat down around the garden table. When Anastasia brought out the tea, sugar, and lemon slices, Letitia served it up, then sat with Anastasia to listen.

Fr. Dimitri explained to Fr. Cahill and Adam what the bishop had told him about forbidding Fr. Cahill's performing an exorcism of the Livingston premises.

"That sounds about right," said Fr. Cahill. "So Carroll gave you permission to perform an exorcism?"

"Yes, if I felt the infestation was real."

"What happened then?" asked Anastasia.

"I was very skeptical about the whole affair," said Fr. Dimitri.

"As was I, at first," said Fr. Cahill.

"Evidently," continued Fr. Dimitri, "when I arrived at Flax Haven, the haunts intensified. Is that right Adam?"

"Yes. It was the same as when Fr. Cahill came to bless the house, but worse. I think the Wizard fears Catholic priests. As a defense the haunts get worse."

"I quickly saw that the infestation was real," said Fr. Dimitri, "and decided to go ahead and perform the exorcism. Perhaps it was my lack of faith, but the house shook so much, and the noise was beyond anything I had experienced. I could hardly stand. Even finding the right page to read was impossible. It was bizarre and maddening. Frankly, I was scared out of my mind. I utterly failed."

"Do you think," Fr. Cahill asked, "your presence had anything to do with the children's deaths?"

"I don't know. What do you think, Mister Livingston?"

"Most definitely," said Adam. "It's the presence of a Catholic priest that has this spirit scared, and now it has turned murderous. After Fr. Dimitri left the property, the haunts intensified far beyond what we have come to expect. I'm embarrassed to tell you this, but last night Mary Ann tried to kill the ghost with a couple of guns, luring it with a new linen cloth. I nearly laughed at her. 'You can't kill a ghost with a gun,' I said. But she went through with it, and we thought she *had* killed it, because after she shot at the linen cloth—we actually saw it being clipped—suddenly all the haunts, the clipping sounds and other noises, the shaking, and the black vapor disappeared. But the vapor had not disappeared; it had simply amassed in our bedroom where Georgie and Martha slept and turned into a poisonous smoke. It was so thick and bad we couldn't even get into the room to get them out until it was too late."

"That's horrifying," said Fr. Cahill as he glanced at Anastasia who was wiping her eyes, and at Letitia who stared at Adam in disbelief.

"Is there no way you can exorcise our house, Fr. Denis?" asked Adam. "Can Fr. Dimitri possibly help you?"

"It doesn't work that way. My power to do such a thing begins and ends with the bishop. If he says no to my performing an exorcism then I lose my authority and ability to do it. It sounds strange, I know, but that's the way it works. It's all about obedience. Humph! Maybe we should get the bishop down here. Let him do it."

After a few moments, Fr. Dimitri stirred. "Adam, earlier at the grave site, when we buried precious George and Martha, but before you nailed on the coffin covers, did I see whole, unclipped linen lining the coffins and shrouding the children's bodies?"

"Yes. Eve brought it from her heirloom chest where she keeps her mother's woven linens."

Anastasia spoke up: "Eve impresses me as a girl of strong Christian faith. Is she?"

Adam bowed his head, clearly embarrassed at his own lack of faith. "Yes, she is. Like her mother, Esther, Eve is very devout. Prays to her mother all the time. In fact, after she visited here during one of your christening receptions, I think it was for Richard Jr., she watched a group of you pray in the Rosary garden."

"Yes," said Anastasia, "I remember her standing with us and listening. She was very attentive. I thought she'd make a good Catholic."

Adam continued: "She came home convinced that if Catholics can pray to their Mother in Heaven, she can pray to hers."

"Good for her," said Anastasia.

"She prays a lot, does she?" asked Fr. Dimitri.

"Yes, I think so," Adam continued: "But, of course, her praying, particularly at meals, got her in trouble with her stepmother who hates all things religious. To counter that Eve has a chest in her bedroom filled with her mother's heirloom woven linen—the only linen cloths in the house that the Wizard has been unable to clip. They are in perfect condition." He paused, embarrassed, perhaps, to go on.

"Why do you suppose that is?" asked Fr. Cahill.

"I don't suppose. I know," said Adam. "The hauntings began when a Stranger stayed overnight with us. In the night he became deathly ill. He asked me to find a Catholic priest to give him last rites or something like that. Mary Ann and I refused and she especially raged at him. Of course, we didn't know any Catholic priests, but even if we had we had promised each other that a Catholic priest would never cross the threshold of our home. Well, the man died in our guest bed…as we watched. But before he died, he cursed my wife and the children of her womb, and said they would die young."

Letitia gasped, "How terrible!"

"The twins were two years old at the time," said Adam. "Then he cursed me and all I call my own, my farm, the house, our crops. He said our livestock would die grotesquely and the barn would be consumed by heaven's fire. Then he said the children of my first wife, Esther, would thrive and be blessed for they loved God. The haunts began immediately after that. After the Stranger died and before we buried him, Eve took from his belongings a crucifix about a foot long, some beads—Rosary beads I think you call them—and two books—a Roman Missal and a book of Christian Prayers. The Stranger's name was Xavier, not sure if that was his first or last name. Because of what Eve requisitioned from the man's belongings, Eve thinks he was a Catholic priest. I think she's right. He was traveling incognito for some reason. Oh, and another thing. Just before he passed he said something like a prayer, I think in Latin."

Adam continued. "Anyway, Eve uses the prayer book everyday. And although she can't read or understand Latin, she tells me she enjoys trying to read the Roman Missal and pronouncing the words she finds there. It reminds her of a Mass she once attended years ago in Conewago."

"Conewago?" asked a surprised Fr. Dimitri.

"Why, yes," said Adam.

"When was this?"

Adam thought for a moment. "Let' see, we were migrating from our home in York to Smithfield. We had a layover in Hanover, and one of our Teamsters was Catholic and wanted to attend Mass at the new chapel there. Eve asked to go to the service with him, so I let her. It was about nine years ago. She would have been seven or eight."

"Conewago is where I am currently stationed," said Fr. Dimitri. "I say Mass there all the time. But I've only been there a year."

Fr. Cahill interrupted, "So, Adam, you were telling us that she reads, or tries to read the missal in her bedroom?"

"Yes, I got the sense that she stands in front of her window and pretends she's the priest."

Fr. Cahill guffawed. "Don't let Bishop Carroll hear that. I'm sure he's not ready for women at St. Mary's Seminary."

"Why not?" asked Letitia teasing.

"Oh, my dear," said Anastasia, "don't go there. We're outnumbered."

The women laughed, but the two priests just glared at them.

"Please, Adam," said Fr. Cahill, "please continue."

"I was almost done," said Adam. "I think what keeps the linens safe, now that I think about it, is the crucifix that lies on top of them inside one chest, and the Roman Missal that lies on top of other linens in a second chest of hers. My daughter is an angel and I have wretchedly disregarded her faith." At that he stopped talking and lowered his head in shame.

Fr. Cahill was astonished at this report. He looked at Fr. Dimitri who also appeared dumbfounded at this young bastion of faith who had flourished in the midst of a rabid anti-Christian home. There was little doubt now about what had protected Adam from even worse calamities, and perhaps what had drawn two Catholic priests together to fight the presence of evil.

"Adam," said Fr. Cahill, "did you say a Roman Missal was protecting cloth in a second chest?"

"Yes, that's right," said Adam.

Fr. Cahill sat up straighter. He noticed that Fr. Dimitri did the same.

Fr. Dimitri turned to Fr. Cahill and quietly said: "Are you thinking what I'm thinking?"

"Perhaps," said Fr. Cahill. "I think we've just been schooled by a sixteen-year old Protestant...ah, woman."

"You know, there is one prayer that is far more powerful than the exorcism rite...or any other for that matter."

"And the bishop has not forbidden it of me...or you," said Fr. Cahill. "Is that your understanding?"

"It is," said Fr. Dimitri. "Has the bishop prohibited you from Livingston's farm?"

"Not exactly," said Fr. Cahill. "In fact, I have been back there at the bishop's express direction to tell Adam of the bishop's restrictions on me."

"Prohibiting you from performing the *exorcism rite* was his only restriction?

Fr. Cahill began to smile, shook his head no, and then said, "Yes."

After a long moment of silence, Fr. Cahill spoke softly. "Adam, Fr. Dimitri and I think we can help you, and we may have a way to exorcise your demon without directly violating my bishop's directives. But there's something you and your family must do beforehand."

Adam looked up, wiped his wet eyes, and gazed at the robust priest sent to relieve him.

8

Most Feared Master of Cynicism,

That these Catholics don't seem to give up is entertaining. The bishop should know better, but evidently he doesn't. For all their education, Jesuits can be so dumb at times. First, he sends Bodkin, a near invalid, to Hagerstown to replace Cahill, perhaps the most energetic and efficacious priest in all the Americas. Of course, that move fails and Bodkin leaves the field of combat. Then, the bishop ignores Cahill's report and evidence, and demeans the poverty-stricken priest for asking to be paid for his work. Then, he sends a failed Russian prince so full of arrogance and so green behind the ears that he can't see straight and is scared off—too easily, I might add. I hardly had to raise a barbed tail. That's good because I don't have one, and don't want one. My peers that are so equipped, if you can call them peers, find the pointed appendages cumbersome, useless, and vulnerable to snagging and tearing just like the bungling bishop. I've come to see him as our ally; every decision he makes works in our favor.

Now, as to Livingston's wife. I suppose I need to address her as Mary Ann Babbitt, or is it Baker? Nevertheless, her ploy to shoot me with a gun as I chewed on fresh linens was a farce and void of common sense. Livingston was remarkably tolerant of the folly. But the violence she expressed toward my person was galling. I could no longer count her as a comrade, and like a petulant child there are consequences for such rebellion. Hopefully, my torturous murder of her children will cause her to repent. You bet humans can repent to their demon overlords, the same way a freedom-loving slave repents to a cruel taskmaster. They do or they die.

Now, I am faced with a challenge, although an innocuous one. Naïve Dimitri has joined with pagan Livingston, sickly McSherry, and an immorally corrupted Cahill to challenge me, even against the bishop's will. Never before have I faced such a collection of misfits who have blissfully dared to challenge my reign.

I have but one option and it should be entertaining. If Cahill is willing to be a martyr for his cause, I will be for mine.

Do or die! Bring it on.

At your sinful service,
Cyn Namrasit, OPSD

Chapter 50
Water's Edge

1

After George and Martha's burial, while Adam rode to the McSherrys' with Fr. Dimitri, Bethany fed every one on the Darks' porch. There was little talk as everyone contemplated the tragic events of the past night and day.

Eve thought about how often she had been in the Darks' cabin for reading practice and would read aloud to Bethany and Henry from her mother's Bible and from Xavier's Christian Prayers book. She was surprised by Henry's openness to prayer and spiritual things, and wondered if it was his growing older, or if it was listening to Bethany's engaging stories about her life with Sam. Eve could almost always recognize the Bible story that Bethany intended, but the modern day detail somehow made the stories more interesting. Her favorite prayer, which Bethany liked a lot too, was the beginning of Psalm 139. With the barn burning and now the twins' death, it seemed especially true:

> *Lord, behind and before you encircle me and rest your hand upon me. Such knowledge is too wonderful for me, far too lofty for me to reach. Where can I go from your spirit? From your presence, where can I flee? If I ascend to the heavens, you are there; if I lie down in Sheol, there you are…your right hand holds me fast…darkness is not dark for you, and night shines as the day.*

But Eve worried about what was next for their family. Two priests had come to Flax Haven and had failed to get rid of the Wizard's haunts. It was good that Fr. Dimitri returned to bury George and Martha, and that her stepmother stood and listened to all the prayers he read. That was really amazing. But closely watching her stepmother during the burial told Eve nothing much was going to change. It was clear by Mary Ann's grimaces, furrows in her forehead, and sidelong glances that she didn't like the prayers or the priest. It was hard for Eve to hang onto hope, in spite of Psalm 139.

Her papa returned from the McSherrys but said little about why he had gone. He revisited the house alone and reported back that the hauntings had almost disappeared. He hoped that by tomorrow the house would be habitable, at least until the next new moon. But there was something more he wanted to say.

"Sam. Bethany. Thank you for letting us stay with you these days and nights. Your generosity is deeply appreciated. Henry, Eve, and Mary Ann, I need to also deeply apologize to you for my lack of courage in dealing with the infestation in our home. I have not done what I should have done. I rejected most of the good advice I was given." Her papa looked at Mary Ann. "I did so for Mary Ann's sake, for I thought it would bring peace to our home." Eve saw that her stepmother didn't appreciate Papa's roundabout blame for any of this. She was biting her lip, trying not to argue.

Her papa continued: "But the events of the last month, which have nearly destroyed us, have brought me to my senses. At least I hope so. What has happened has been far worse than anything I thought I was protecting us from. So some things are going to change."

Mary Ann could not be silent. "Just keep the priests away. No priest is a good priest. The ministers you brought a while back caused a bit of havoc, but these Catholic priests have brought nothing but destruction and death. You can't deny that, husband."

Eve could see Papa suppressing the urge to get angry with her stepmother. He took the gamble and spoke anyway. "So, you're saying any Catholic priest is worthless, and no priest is a good thing?"

"Isn't it obvious?" Mary Ann snapped.

Eve glanced at Sam and Bethany. They stared at Papa and Mary Ann as if a brawl was about to erupt, but Papa seemed to have found his footing.

"It's not that simple, my dear. Look, you're sitting on a chair right now. Is it better that you have a chair, or no chair?"

"A chair is a lot different than a damn priest, Adam. What kind of argument is that?"

"You're right a chair and a priest are very different. That's my point. Some things in life are very simple. The opposite of having a chair is *not* having a chair. That's a simple idea. It's a simple truth. But not everything is that way. Not everything that is good or bad is a matter of having it or not. Some things that seem useless become more valuable when we keep them and use them the way nature intends. For example, what do you do with the food scraps from the kitchen? Their presence seems useless. They rot and smell and attract flies and vermin. If you let them sit around they will grow mold and fungus and ruin good food nearby and perhaps make us sick. So what do you do with them? Do you get rid of them?"

Papa waited for her stepmother to answer, but Mary Ann refused.

"Can I answer that, Mister Livingston?"

"Sure, Bethany," said Papa.

"You's keep the kitchen scraps and compost them to make fertilizer to make the vegetables grow better."

Even Eve knew that. Her stepmother was being stubborn.

Her papa continued: "Or give it to the chickens or pigs so they can grow fat. Right? So, the presence of some things we don't like can have a greater value, or a deeper truth, when we keep them and use them correctly."

"Here's my favorite example." Adam reached into his pocket and removed a hand full of flax seeds. "When I put these flax seeds into the ground, nothing happens for a while. It's as if the seeds were worthless. But if we are smart enough to plant them in a field that's been rotated, and if there is the right amount of sun and rain, in time we have a flax plant. So the opposite of having the seed is having the plant. To some folk, who are not flax farmers like us, the flax plant may look like a weed, and they might tear it out or cut it down and burn it. But the deeper truth is that if we use the harvested plant the way nature intends, what do we get?

"Baking flour and cooking oil," said Bethany.

"And yarn for linen and clothes," said Eve.

"That's right," said Papa. "So we might say that the opposite of this seed could be oil, flour, yarn, or even linen cloth, couldn't we? None of those things *are* seeds, but they are only possible because we kept the seeds. They are the transformed opposites. It's not like the opposite of Mary Ann's chair, which is either here or not. With flax seeds the opposite is more useful than what they were before, but getting there is very hard work. It's hard to see the value of a flax seed until we do the work. We plow the fields, sow the seeds, let the stalks grow, cultivate the fields, pull out the stalks by their roots, dry them in stooks, and rip out the seeds that we grind into flour and press for oil. Then we ret the remaining stalks and let them decompose. We process them with a flax break, we scutch them, hackle them, and finally we have flax fibers. The fibers we spin into yarn, then weave the yarn into cloth for clothes. So, in the end, the flax seed is very valuable, but to get all the benefits of the seed requires discipline, perseverance, and especially that we follow the rules of how the world and we are made, or we don't have oil, flour, or cloth."

"Okay, husband, we know all that, what's the point?" snarked Mary Ann. "If you go on much longer we're going to be ready for breakfast."

"As you pointed out, dear wife, the Wizard's attacks were trivial when other ministers came to pray it away. But when the Catholic priests showed up, we lost much. Remember my dreams? I was told this man, which turned out to be Fr. Cahill, could relieve us. You say he didn't, but rather made things worse. But recall, he did chase the spirit away during that new moon without any destruction. However, here's the mistake I made. Right after he chased the demon out, Fr. Cahill told me what to do to keep it out...but I didn't do it. It was like being told that to get oil, flour, or yarn I needed to plant the seed and do the work, but I was unwilling to do it. I was arrogant and lazy. We have suffered much because I threw out the kitchen scraps and didn't compost them. I threw out the flax seed and didn't plant them, or I thought the flax plant was a weed and didn't do the work to process it. Well, now, I've decided I am going to do the work. We're going to keep the scraps and compost them, or feed them to the pigs, and we're going to keep the seeds and plant them and let them grow and do the work, and likewise we're going to keep the priests and let them guide us."

Adam paused for a moment to let all that sink in. Then he continued.

"Starting immediately, I'm going to follow the rules. Beginning this Sunday

I'm going to Mass and I'm going to take instruction to become a baptized Catholic. Fr. Cahill and Fr. Dimitri have figured out a way to exorcise our house, but Fr. Cahill says it will only work if we are instructed in the faith, are baptized, and go to Mass and confession regularly. He assures us that if we follow the Church's rules, the Wizard will leave us."

Eve had not expected any of this. It was an answer to her prayers that were beyond belief. Her mama in heaven really came through. In her mind she kept repeating, "*Thank you, Mama. Thank you, Mama. Thank you, Mama.*" She could hardly contain herself. She blurted out: "Father, can I come with you, take instruction and be baptized…a Catholic?"

"Yes, of course," he said, at which point Eve cried out and jumped for joy into her papa's arms.

Adam managed to speak in spite of Eve's bear hug, "I want you all to come. The more of us, including Sam and Bethany, who follow this advice, the sooner and more thoroughly we may be able to rid ourselves of this plague."

"And you're expecting this of me?" challenged Mary Ann.

"Yes, my dear. I'm praying…yes, that's right I'm praying…that you will come and get instruction. Fr. Cahill says he will hold classes for us the next three Sundays, and then baptize us on the fourth. That will be just three days before the next new moon. On that day, I think it's a Wednesday, Fr. Cahill and Fr. Dimitri will both come and celebrate the Mass in our house. They hope, although they cannot be sure, that with our baptisms, and by celebrating Mass in our house, the Wizard will permanently flee from us. Recall, this is what Fr. Cahill warned us about after he blessed the house, and it worked, remember? He told me that if we didn't do this, the demon would bring vengeance upon us. I ignored the warning, and destruction followed. It is my fault, but no longer."

"Can I come, too, Papa?" asked Henry.

"Yes, son, I certainly hope so."

Sam and Bethany had been whispering to each other. "Missta Livingston," said Sam, "Bethany 'en I wanna come, too."

"That's wonderful, Sam."

Eve finally backed away from her father, but still stood directly in front of him, afraid that if he got out of her sight her dream might evaporate. "Does this mean I can pray again at dinner and supper?"

"It means we will all pray whenever we eat together. I expect to hear your mother's prayer coming from your lips first thing in the morning at breakfast."

Eve beamed from ear to ear.

"Hallelujah!" said Bethany.

"Amen!" echoed Sam.

Eve glanced at her stepmother. Mary Ann was not happy. She sat stiffly with arms folded, legs crossed, jaw clenched, and a glare that shot daggers at Eve's beloved papa.

"Papa," said Eve, "I'm afraid. The Wizard will know this, and it won't like what we're doing. Is something else going to happen to us?"

Adam was quiet for awhile.

"Most certain it will," said a troubled Mary Ann. "You can't defeat evil without a fight."

2

True to his word, Adam took his children, Sam, Bethany, and even Mary Ann to Shepherd's Town the next four Sundays, which were all-day affairs. There was a short instructional time before Mass, then Mass in the late morning, followed by a picnic lunch that Bethany and Eve had packed, after which Fr. Cahill and Fr. Dimitri had them meet in the nave of the St. Agnes Chapel for a full afternoon of instruction.

There were a few others from Shepherd's Town who also wanted to be baptized, so altogether Adam counted ten that were going to be in the class: his family of four, the Darks, and four others from town. Gabriel Menghini also came to class—during breaks he was available for participants to ask questions; he also ran errands for the priests and made sure the nave was straightened and cleaned up.

Before Mass on the first Sunday, Fr. Cahill explained that at this point they were to be called Catechumens, for none of them had been baptized nor had they been confirmed as Catholics. Baptism and confirmation would all happen on the fourth Sunday. Until then they could not partake of communion during the second half of the Mass. Otherwise, they should participate in the Mass as much as they could, listen carefully to the Scripture readings that would be all in English, along with the creed, which they would memorize, and learn the hymns, for there were no hymnals.

Since so much of the Mass would be in Latin, every Sunday before Mass Fr. Dimitri would lead the group in recitation practice of the Latin responses, provide a verbal translation, and explain their meaning. Adam wished that there was a book written in English for him to follow along, but the only missals that existed were in Latin and some other language. Each Sunday, Eve brought Fr. Xavier's missal and Christian Prayers book to instruction with her. Fr. Cahill and Fr. Dimitri took an active interest in both. Fr. Dimitri read French, so he identified Eve's missal as a 1718 edition of the Roman Missal, in Latin and French, printed in Paris and authorized by King Louis the XV. He said, "You will want to keep this missal safe. Someday it will be valuable as a collector's item. Most certainly the owner was a French missionary priest."

Each afternoon the instruction was broken into three separate sessions, and each session was divided into two parts. In the first, Fr. Cahill gave a talk about a topic, and in the second Fr. Dimitri answered the group's questions on what Fr. Cahill had talked about. The first Sunday the three sessions covered the Creeds, the Ten Commandments, and the History of the Church and the Bible.

The second Sunday they covered the Mass and Liturgy, the Eucharist and Miracles, Confirmation, and Baptism. On the third Sunday the instruction finished up with sessions on Vocations and Civic Responsibility, Sin and Confession, and Christian Prayer.

Adam was chagrined at his lack of understanding of the Christian faith, but proud of what his daughter Eve had retained from her mother. He was further annoyed at himself for his misunderstanding of Catholicism. There was so much he had misunderstood. He was embarrassed to the point that the first Sunday he was afraid to ask any questions. He still didn't understand everything, especially about the Virgin Mary, but because only Fr. Cahill and Fr. Dimitri had the power he expected true ministers of God to possess, he had to believe that the Church was right about everything else.

Eve, however, was not shy in the least. She always had a question on the tip of her tongue. He noticed that Henry, who sat next to Eve, would lean over occasionally and whisper something to Eve. She would nod, or whisper something back to him. Adam suspected Henry was letting Eve ask his questions.

Bethany was confused at times about things she had been told by Protestants about what Catholics believed or did. Fr. Dimitri always had an explanation that satisfied her and which Adam thought insightful—Fr. Dimitri was gifted at such explanations. Later, Adam discovered that Fr. Dimitri had gotten in trouble with the bishop because he was always arguing with Protestants up in Pennsylvania. That was funny, thought Adam.

Sam almost never spoke up, but when Adam looked at him, Sam was fully engaged and listening. Adam decided that Sam was a very good foreman of his farm because he listened well and intuitively understood how things worked given only minimum information.

Mary Ann, on the other hand, although she appeared attentive, for which Adam was glad, never had a question, nor did she engage Adam in any discussion about Catholicism between Sundays. She seemed to be just going through the motions for the sake of peace. That disappointed Adam. Although he was glad for the peace, he worried it might end.

When the second and third Sunday instructions came along, Adam was full of questions, and although he didn't always understand the answers, he understood enough and found such a consistency in the answers that he decided to trust what he didn't understand. It was a good strategy, because as the instruction continued, he was able to piece together what at first he didn't understand. By the third Sunday, he felt confident that his decision to be baptized was right, but would Mary Ann agree? At the end of the third Sunday's instruction, Fr. Cahill told the class to meet him next Sunday morning at *Packhorse Ford and to bring a change of clothes.

3

Packhorse Ford was a bit more than a mile east of Shepherd's Town. It was where Fr. Cahill and Richard McSherry had crossed the Potowmack River when escaping from Sharpsburg years earlier. The ford was possible because the river widened at that point as it flowed over a relatively flat ledge of rocks that extended from Maryland south to the Virginia embankment. Depending on the time of year the water was anywhere from ankle to shin deep all the way across. Thus, the ford became the major crossing of the Potowmack River for the Philadelphia Wagon Road. Use of the ford had declined in the last few decades because an easier route through the Appalachian Mountains had been opened further north which crossed the Potowmack by ferries at Williamsport, Maryland. There was also a ferry at Shepherd's Town, but for those travelers that were local or didn't want to pay the ferry fees, the Old Philadelphia Wagon Road and Packhorse Ford was still convenient and passable.

On either side, the bank sloped gently to the water's edge, making it possible for wagon, buggy, horse, individuals, and even large herds of livestock to approach the river and wade across. The embankments were covered with clover and short grass and scattered trees which made the site convenient for a picnic or for people just to sit and relax.

Adam was eager to be baptized, but it was to be a bitter sweet day. That morning Mary Ann told Adam she would come with him to Shepherd's Town, but she would not allow Fr. Cahill to baptize her. She didn't believe or understand most of what she called the "religious mumbo-jumbo" Fr. Cahill had talked about. Adam was not surprised by this, but he was deflated because of it, and it took the joy out of the day. Fr. Cahill and Fr. Dimitri, too, were disappointed by Mary Ann's decision, but they encouraged Adam to trust God that things would work out.

It was mid morning, Sunday, September 17, 1797, when Fr. Cahill and Fr. Dimitri, both wearing their cassocks and a green stole, arrived at the ford along with the class of nine catechumens—Adam, Henry, Eve, Sam, Bethany, and the four others from the St. Agnes Chapel. Others came as well: Anastasia, Letitia, and Catharine brought the boys, although Richard was still sick in bed back at Retirement. There were also about a dozen family and friends of the other catechumens including Ruth and Gabriel Menghini, and of course Mary Ann. The group made their way down the grassy bank to the river's edge and made themselves comfortable. Those that were being baptized sat near the water's edge.

Standing on the edge of the water, Fr. Cahill addressed the catechumens. "Today you are making a life-changing commitment. You have been instructed in the basics of the Catholic faith, but be assured that as much as you think you know now, you will only grow in knowledge and faith in the years ahead. The sacrament you are about to receive, however, is most important. It is your initiation into the Christian faith and Holy Mother Church. Let me read to you from First Peter."

Fr. Cahill opened his Bible and read:

> *In the days of Noah during the building of the ark, in which a few*
> *persons, eight in all, were saved through water…*

Fr. Cahill broke from the reading and smiled at the row of catechumens: "We have nine today, one more than in the days of Noah. We're making progress." A few on the river bank chuckled, whereupon Fr. Cahill went back to his Bible:

> *This prefigured baptism, which today saves you. It is not a remov-*
> *al of dirt from the body that saves you, but an appeal to God for*
> *a clear conscience, through the resurrection of Jesus Christ, who*
> *has gone into heaven and is at the right hand of God, with angels,*
> *authorities, and powers subject to him.*

"You may remember from our instruction the story of Nicodemus who comes to Jesus and asks how one is born again. Jesus answers 'one cannot enter the kingdom of God without being born of water and the Spirit.' Today you will take the first step and be reborn through the waters of baptism. In the book of Acts Peter tells his catechumens, 'Repent and be baptized, every one of you, in the name of Jesus Christ for the forgiveness of your sins; and you will receive the gift of the Holy Spirit.' Now you must all remember that what you are going through today is not because of any righteous deeds you have done. It is a sacrament and a free gift that you earnestly desire, for through this water you will be birthed into the Church. Then, going forward, you will be renewed continually by the Holy Spirit through your discipline to avoid sin, coming to confession when you do sin, attending Mass and taking the Eucharist, and through your private daily prayers. This baptism is a first step; it is not the final step. It does not guarantee your admission into heaven, but it does initiate you into the body of Christ, which opens the doors to God's mercy and grace.

"Let's begin, now, by asking you to stand and answer each of these questions from the Apostles' Creed as we talked about during instruction."

The nine catechumens stood, and Fr. Dimitri handed a book of rites to Fr. Cahill to read. In turn Fr. Cahill read off each of the catechumen's names, then asked, "Do you renounce Satan and all his works and all his empty show?"

The nine responded together, "I do."

"Do you believe in God, the Father Almighty, Creator of heaven and earth?" "I do."

"Do you believe in Jesus Christ, his only Son, our Lord, who was born of the Virgin Mary, suffered death and was buried, rose again from the dead and is seated at the right hand of the Father?"

"I do."

"Do you believe in the Holy Spirit, the Lord, the giver of life, who came upon the Apostles at Pentecost and today is given to you sacramentally in Confirmation?"

"I do."

"Do you believe in the Holy Catholic Church, the communion of saints, the forgiveness of sins, the resurrection of the body, and life everlasting?"

"I do."

"This is our faith. This is the faith of the Church. We are proud to profess it in Christ Jesus our Lord."

And the entire group said, "Amen."

Fr. Dimitri took the book of rites back and held it open in front of Fr. Cahill to read. "Let us pray." Fr. Cahill held his hands high over the heads of the catechumens and read: "All-powerful God, Father of our Lord Jesus Christ, by water and the Holy Spirit you freed your sons and daughters from sin and gave them new life. Send your Holy Spirit upon them to be their helper and guide. Give them the spirit of wisdom and understanding, the spirit of right judgment and courage, the spirit of knowledge and reverence. Fill them with the spirit of wonder and awe in your presence. Amen."

"Adam," said Fr. Cahill. "I believe you wanted to be first."

At that Fr. Dimitri handed the book of rites to Gabriel Menghini and waded into the water until it was thigh deep.

Adam waded out into the water to Fr. Dimitri who was facing the embankment. Adam faced upstream and kneeled in the water and with one hand held his nose closed and with his other hand gripped the wrist of his other arm. Fr. Dimitri put one hand behind Adam's back for support, and with his other hand held onto Adam's topmost wrist.

Ensuring that Adam was firmly in his grasp, Fr. Dimitri said, "Adam Livingston, I baptize you in the name of the Father..." at which point Fr. Dimitri leaned Adam's body backwards and immersed his head under water and bringing him back up right away to take a breath,..."the Son," ...again Adam's body and head were immersed,..."and the Holy Spirit,".... and the third time Adam was immersed and brought up. Adam stood up, Fr. Dimitri embraced him for a moment, and helped him start back to Fr. Cahill.

Adam came out of the river onto the shoreline and stood before Fr. Cahill who tipped an open vial and wetted his right thumb with oil, then made the sign of the cross on Adam's forehead, saying, "With this Chrism Oil, be sealed with the gift of the Holy Spirit."

"Amen!" said Adam.

"Peace be with you," said Fr. Cahill.

"And with your spirit," said Adam.

As Adam climbed back up the embankment, the group applauded.

Henry was next. When he came out of the water he broke out in a wide smile and raised his fists in celebration. Eve followed Henry, and started to cry even before Fr. Dimitri immersed her the first time. When she came up on shore she sat in Papa's lap and hugged him for several minutes, all the time softly saying, "Thank you, Mama. Thank you, Mama." Sam and Bethany walked into the water holding hands. Sam stood by as Bethany was baptized, and she stood by as he was. Then they embraced and left the water holding hands. They held hands as Fr. Cahill confirmed both with the Chrism Oil. So it went for the rest.

When all were out of the water, Fr. Cahill said, "While those that want to change out of their wet clothes behind the sheets that the Ladies Guild have erected between the trees in the back, it is customary that the rest of us recite the Litany of the Saints.

The women lined up at the modesty sheets, but the men had decided to wear their wet clothes back to the Chapel where they would change in Fr. Cahill's apartment.

While the women changed, Fr. Cahill started the litany that called out the names of one hundred saints after which those in attendance responded "Pray for us." Adam thought it would never end—calling on the names of one-hundred saints to pray for us. By the end he wished he had changed from his wet clothes, for even though the weather was mild he was shivering in the shade of the maple under which they sat. Finally the litany stopped. Or at least he thought it had.

Eve had changed her clothes and was sitting next to him on the grass. When Fr. Cahill at last intoned the final amen, Eve spoke up: "But Father Cahill, you forgot someone."

Fr. Cahill gazed at Eve, "Who is that?"

Eve bowed her head and said real loud for everyone to hear, "Mama! Saint Esther...."

And the entire group yelled out, "Pray for us."

Chapter 51
Vernacular

My Lord Maréchal,

I am coming to the most important part of my tale. You will see that I have followed your suggestion. You told me that you intend to share this account with others and in particular those that have not been raised in the Catholic faith. You know my life-long ministry to those outside the Church and the many *letters I have written to them defending the Church. You also know my love of the Mass and its sacred language that lends force to the Church's most powerful and effectual rite.

So, you presented to me a dilemma in recounting those parts of what comes next. For the devil hates Latin and loves the vernacular, and yet our countrymen, who would like to understand the end of this tale, while they may not despise Latin may only understand the vernacular. Consequently, they will not be able to comprehend the formidable strength the sacred language imparts to our most sacred liturgy—the work of the people.

You are, no doubt, familiar with those influences in the Church that want to weaken this great celebration by muttering it entirely in the vernacular and even remove many solemn prayers. You know I have written against this. It will be a tragedy if these dreadful influences ever have their way and weaken the Church's sacred fabric.

Nonetheless, for those who may read this account and not understand its nominative form and thus miss the effect it had on Livingston's haunting wizard, I will acquiesce to your wise suggestion. I will recount the liturgy beginning with Latin and then lapse into the vernacular, as my writing has already done in a few places. Hopefully that will recall to your reader's mind the power of our religion.

May the ancient language of the Church never be squandered, mislaid, or forgotten.

Your obedient servant,
Fr. Smith

Chapter 52
Bones Will Have To Wait

1

Wednesday, September 20, 1797 - New Moon.

Fr. Denis Cahill was up early. He was going to need the help of all the angels in heaven he could persuade to come to his aid. Donning a fresh cassock he went into the chapel and read the Morning Office and said a Rosary before the Blessed Sacrament. His breakfast consisted of cooked oatmeal, nuts and honey; he would eat no more until that evening. Checking the contents of his large leather satchel, he added to it a purple stole and surplice. When he was ready he left his apartment and sat on the bench outside the St. Agnes Chapel and recited parts of Psalm 139:

> *If only you, God, would slay the wicked!*
> *Away from me, you who are bloodthirsty!*

Shortly, Gabriel Menghini came with his buggy. Fr. Cahill put the large satchel in the back, and the two set off for Leetown.

2

Anastasia had gathered her family around the supper table and was feeding them a brunch. Fr. Dimitri had been up earlier and eaten lightly, then he went out to saddle up Count Samuel and tie him up at the hitching post near the house.

When Fr. Denis arrived she greeted him and Gabriel. Their stop at Retirement would be short but important.

Gabriel had brought in the aspergillum and aspersorium which Anastasia filled with water. Gabriel held the aspersorium for Fr. Denis who added sacred salt and prayed in Latin over it. He then took the aspergillum and liberally sprinkled the family sitting around the table and blessed them.

"Now Richard," he said.

"In his bedroom," said Anastasia, who led the way, although she didn't want Fr. Denis to see Richard, who appeared close to death. The last few days she had come to fear for his life.

Richard was in bed, and Fr. Denis was surprised at his condition. "Richard, I expected you to be out of bed by now. What is wrong, man?"

"Nothing, nothing," Richard said very weakly.

Anastasia thought, *The man is certainly capable of lying, but to a priest it's a bad idea.*

"Why are you here?" said Richard.

"We're going to Livingston's…"

"Oh, yes, yes. I pray you are successful."

"We came to anoint you and your household with Holy Water for protection while we're at Flax Haven."

"Good, did you get my boys good and wet?"

"He did," said Fr. Dimitri, chuckling.

"Good," said Richard.

"And now you," said Fr. Denis, who grabbed the aspergillum from the aspersorium of water…

But Richard raised his hand, saying: "Let Fr. Dimitri. I've gotten to know him pretty well lately."

Fr. Denis appeared to be taken aback, but handed the aspergillum to Fr. Dimitri, who reluctantly took it and sprinkled Richard from head to toe: "In nomine Patris, et Filii, et Spiritus Sancti. Amen."

"Thank you," said Richard with a cough. "What about Anastasia and the girls?"

"We are all staying here," said Anastasia, "We'll be praying a Rosary for Fr. Denis and Fr. Dimitri.

"We're off, now," said Fr. Dimitri. "We'll be back after."

"Good! God speed," said a feeble Richard as he tried to smile.

Anastasia led the men back to the hall. As Fr. Dimitri grabbed his packed satchel by the door, Fr. Denis turned to Fr. Dimitri. "What was that all about? Tell me he's going to be alive when we return. Has a doctor been here?"

"He has been very stubborn lately," said Fr. Dimitri.

"No, he won't see a doctor," said Anastasia. "He says he's fine, but obviously he's very sick. I can't get anything out of him."

"We should anoint him when we return," said Fr. Denis.

"If we make it back," said Fr. Dimitri, half joking.

"Which reminds me," said Fr. Denis. "I have one more thing to attend to. Go on out and put your satchel in the back of the buggy with mine. I'll be there in a minute."

Fr. Dimitri went out the door and Fr. Denis came into the supper room where the ladies were clearing the table. "Excuse me. Can I borrow Letitia for a moment?"

Everyone turned with surprise, especially Letitia.

Fr. Denis ushered Letitia out the far door that led toward the Rosary garden and closed the door behind him. Anastasia wondered what was up; she watched through the window. Once in the garden, the two stood apart and Fr. Denis turned his back to the house which allowed Anastasia to clearly see Letitia's face. Letitia stared at Fr. Denis fearful of what he might say. Fr. Denis spoke quickly and emphatically. Anastasia wished she could hear, but Fr. Denis clearly had not wanted anyone but Letitia to hear what he had to say. Letitia nodded a few times and looked sad, biting her lips. Fr. Denis kept talking. All at once Letitia's eyes got wide with surprise and anticipation. Then she nodded strongly with affirmation and smiled, but covered her mouth with both hands as if utterly embarrassed. She nodded her agreement a few more times, then dropped her hands and held them tightly together in a nervous gesture. She gazed at Fr. Denis as if he had just told her the world was coming to an end. Suddenly, Fr. Denis left Letitia seemingly stunned and standing alone in the garden. He rushed around the outside of the house to the buggy entrance where Fr. Dimitri unhitched Count Samuel's reins, leaped into the saddle, trotted out of the yard, and turned left on the Leetown road. Fr. Denis hopped in the buggy with Gabriel and they followed Fr. Dimitri, presumably, thought Anastasia, on the short trip to Flax Haven.

3

Adam was apprehensive. He had picked up his shillelagh more out of nervousness than thinking he needed it. The fighting stick had become both his psychological and physical crutch. It gave his hands, which were usually manipulating farm implements, something to do when he was not farming.

He had gathered his family—Mary Ann, Henry, and Eve, on the Darks' porch in anticipation of Fr. Cahill and Fr. Dimitri's arrival. Mary Ann had been displaying an unusual repugnance at having two priests cross the threshold of their house. Bethany, the epitome of patience and compassion, assured Adam she would keep Mary Ann company, but Adam could take just so much.

He was relieved when Rev. Jeremiah Williams' buggy pulled into the yard. Fr. Dimitri, in consulting with Fr. Cahill, had suggested that Adam invite one or two Protestant ministers who had previously been on the property to come and pray with them. Adam could only think of one that he respected. He relayed to the two priests how Rev. Jeremiah Williams and family had come to supper, and not to exorcise the house as all the others had. Rev. Williams' only demand was that he be allowed to pray before the meal, which he did. As a result, a short-term exorcism had occurred. There were haunts when the Williams family arrived, but none after he had prayed for the meal, although only for a day. That impressed Adam and Fr. Cahill and Fr. Dimitri as well. They invited Adam to invite Rev. Williams to come pray with them. So while Mary Ann was being consoled by Bethany, Adam was standing under the oak tree talking with Rev. Williams.

"Mister Livingston," said Rev. Williams, "I'm still not sure you want me here. I've heard the rumors of your ghost all right, and I see the pile of ruins over yonder of your barn that burned, and I'm still in shock over the deaths of your beautiful children. But it's hard to believe all that was the work of a demon. When we enjoyed the gracious meal your wife and cook prepared, there were the tremors and the birds chirping, but those didn't last long. I still think your house is on a fault line. By the time we left I didn't hear or feel a thing."

"That's true," said Adam. "It may have been your heartfelt prayer that chased it away for most of a day. I invited you today because I think you're one of the few true Christian ministers in the area."

"But how do you expect me to pray with a Catholic priest? And it's hard for me to reconcile that you've just been baptized Catholic. Now, don't get me wrong, I believe you, but only because you have a reputation for being an honest man. I've just never heard of such a thing. Are you sure you know what you're doing?"

"We will just have to wait and see," said Adam. "Look here, they've arrived."

Fr. Dimitri on Count Samuel and the buggy with Fr. Cahill and Gabriel entered the yard. Hitching their horses to the Darks' hitching post, they left enough rein so the horses could water at the trough and nibble on the hay Sam had scattered on the ground. Adam and Rev. Williams walked over to greet them.

Adam introduced them to Rev. Williams, who held a book of Common Prayer at his side. After the men all greeted one another, Fr. Cahill took note of Rev. Williams' Common Prayer book and said, "It's good that you brought that. We're going to need a lot of prayer."

"Well, I doubt they're the same prayers as you may have, and mine are not in Latin," teased Rev. Williams.

Fr. Cahill smiled graciously at the Methodist and said, "My understanding is that the Almighty has big ears and is good at interpreting the desires of our hearts."

Rev. Williams visibly relaxed at this. "Yes, that is very true."

"Well, Adam," said Fr. Cahill, as he stared at the house, "what do we have today?"

"We have a haunting spirit that is very much aware that there are priests and a minister nearby. The usual for this time of month: frequent house quakes, clipping sounds, and an occasional wagon rumble. But they are more intense now that you are here. It knows you don't have its good will in mind."

"Oh, but we do," said Fr. Cahill. "It's just that it probably doesn't like what we think is good."

Adam glanced at Rev. Williams, curious how the Methodist would react to what they were about to do and experience.

"Adam, before we go into the house we need to protect your family." Gabriel handed Bethany the aspersorium and she went off to fill it with water. While she did, the priests went to their satchels in the back of the buggy and donned white surplice vestments and purple stoles. The stoles draped around their necks, crossed in front, and were secured with a button from their cassocks that was accessed through a slit in the middle of their surplices.

Bethany brought the filled aspersorium and handed it to Gabriel. Fr. Cahill added the salt to the water and prayed in Latin over it. Adam noticed Rev. Williams watching with great interest.

Fr. Dimitri then faced Fr. Cahill, closed his eyes, held his hands together in prayer, and bowed. With the aspergillum Fr. Cahill sprinkled him with water three times:

In nomine Patris, et Filii, et Spiritus Sancti.

Fr. Cahill then gave the aspergillum to Fr. Dimitri, and Fr. Dimitri likewise sprinkled Fr. Cahill. Fr. Cahill took back the aspergillum and turned to the porch. "Who is going to pray with us, even though you may stay here on the porch? Let me protect you with this Holy Water." Eve, Henry, and Bethany, who were on the porch, came to the porch rail. Gabriel, Adam, and Sam stood on the ground next to the rail. All were in front of Fr. Cahill. Mary Ann stayed seated behind Bethany, and Rev. Williams, who stood behind Fr. Cahill, backed shyly away.

Fr. Cahill bowed to the group and they bowed back. Before he sprinkled them with the aspergillum, Fr. Cahill caught Bethany's eye and motioned for her to scoot a little to the side. She did.

Adam wondered what that was about, but he kept his eye on Fr. Cahill, who then liberally doused the group with Holy Water three times:

In nomine Patris, et Filii, et Spiritus Sancti.

"Hey, you're getting me all wet," yelled out Mary Ann who was sitting behind the group.

Adam caught Fr. Cahill and Bethany exchanging smiles, and then Fr. Cahill said loud enough for everyone to hear, "That was the idea."

As if he had eyes in the back of his head, Fr. Cahill said, "Rev. Williams?" then whirled to the minister who had ducked behind.

"Yes?" said Rev. Williams.

"Sir, are you a minister of the Gospel of Christ?"

"Indeed, I am," said Rev. Williams..."baptized and sanctified in the Lord Jesus Christ, sir."

"And do you pray?" asked Fr. Cahill.

"Indeed, I do, sir."

"Of course you do," said Fr. Cahill raising the aspergillum to douse the Methodist.

"But," said Rev. Williams gesturing to the aspergillum, "...that ain't gonna help much here."

"Don't be too sure," said Fr. Cahill, as he shook the aspergillum over the Methodist minister three times drenching his head; "In the name of the Father, the Son, and the Holy Ghost. Amen." Adam wondered if Rev. Williams had been baptized. Probably so, but if not, he was now, by a Catholic priest no less.

Without missing a beat, Fr. Cahill reached over, took Adam's shillelagh, and dipped one end and then the other into the aspersorium, intoning:

In nomine Patris, et Filii et Spiritus Sancti.

...and handed the dripping implement back to its speechless owner, and returned the aspergillum to the aspersorium.

"Sam?" called Fr. Cahill, handing the aspersorium to him, "Will you carry these into the house when we go. We will need them inside."

Sam nodded and carefully took the aspersorium of Holy Water in his big hands.

Fr. Cahill then said to the entire group, "Let us pray." He bowed his head and said, "O glorious Archangel St. Michael, Prince of the heavenly host, defend us in battle, and in the struggle which is ours against the Principalities and Powers, against the rulers of this world of darkness, against spirits of evil in high places. In the name of the Father, and of the Son, and of the Holy Ghost. Amen."

Raising his head, Fr. Cahill addressed the group. "Now, who will be going in with us?" Adam, Sam, Eve, Gabriel, and Rev. Williams raised their hands. "Bethany and Henry," said Fr. Cahill, "even though you're staying here with Missus Livingston, it's still important that you pray for us and our protection as well as for your own. So this next instruction I'm going to give to the others applies to you as well. Okay?"

Bethany put her arm around Henry, "Yas, sir, Frather Denis, we will be prayin.'"

"Good," said Fr. Cahill as he turned to the others. "It's important that while we are inside, regardless of what transpires, you remain constantly in prayer if you're not doing something to physically assist us. Rev. Williams came prepared with his prayer book, and Eve has one as well...where is it, Eve?"

"It's in my room, but I'll get it," said Eve.

"Sam," asked Fr. Cahill, "you know some prayers by heart?"

"I sure knows how 'ta pray. Do it all da time."

"Do you know the 'Our Father' or 'Lord's Prayer'?"

"Yas, sir."

"Keep it on your lips the whole time. Just keep repeating it."

"Yas, sir."

"Adam," said Fr. Cahill, "what about you?"

"Sorry, I just don't know any prayers by heart," said Adam.

"You know the Lord's Prayer?"

"I suppose I can stumble through it, sure."

"Sam, you pray it out loud so Adam can hear you. Adam, you repeat whatever Sam says. Keep it up. Or, Adam, if you're nearer Eve and Eve can pray out loud, repeat whatever prayer she's reading. You all must keep your minds on God and pray for us."

The group responded that they would.

"Fr. Dimitri and I have one more short but important ritual to perform in private, and then we will be ready to enter the house." He turned to Eve. "The linen table cover you said you had woven?"

"Yes, Father. It's in my heirloom chest."

"When we enter the house bring it to the gathering hall."

Adam watched as the two priests walked about ten paces away, faced each other, and turned slightly so they could whisper in each others' ears. It seemed like an urgent conversation. At one point when Fr. Dimitri was listening and Fr. Cahill talking, Fr. Dimitri reared up and looked at Fr. Cahill with surprise, if not shock. There was a lull in their conversation before Fr. Cahill began talking again, and Fr. Dimitri nodded briefly but sadly. When they were done each made the sign of the cross over the other, and then laid hands on each others' heads and evidently prayed one for the other. Finally, they briefly embraced.

Returning to the group Fr. Cahill nodded to Gabriel and led the group to the rear of Gabriel's buggy, where Fr. Cahill removed items from the priests' satchels. To Gabriel he handed a thurible (a metal censer suspended from chains), and to Adam a pair of small tongs.

Gabriel and Adam entered Bethany's cabin and crouched down at the fireplace. Gabriel lifted the thurible's lid, and with tongs Adam placed several burning embers into the crucible in the bottom of the thurible. They brought it back outside, where Fr. Cahill opened a small metal cannister and spooned incense onto the burning coals. The incense immediately began to smoke. Gabriel then lowered the thurible's lid which had holes in it to allow the fragrant smoke to waft into the air as he swung it lightly back and forth on its chains. Fr. Cahill returned the small tongs to the buggy, but gave the incense cannister to Gabriel to hold. Fr. Cahill then retrieved a smaller leather case from his satchel and a leather book that to Adam looked like Xavier's Roman Missal. Fr. Dimitri was already holding a crucifix perhaps a foot tall with a flat base for sitting on a table.

Fr. Cahill said, "We're ready now. Follow us. Fr. Dimitri will lead with the cross, followed by Gabriel with the incense, then the rest of you. I'll be last."

Holding the crucifix in front of him, Fr. Dimitri led the procession to the steps of the house. Gabriel followed, swinging the thurible that swirled smoke about them. Adam noticed that the closer they came to the house the clipping chirped crisper, the quakes caused yard dirt to jump an inch into the air and hover for seconds at a time. As soon as Fr. Dimitri's foot landed on the front steps the porch floor boards began to vibrate intensely. That caused a terrified Rev. Williams to pull back from climbing the stairs, but Adam took his arm and pulled him along, "C'mon Jeremiah," said Adam with a smile, "this is what you've lived for; remember what you told me? Spiritual battles."

When Fr. Dimitri stepped onto the porch the rumbling of wagon sounds circling the house commenced. Adam glanced behind him but no wagons were in sight. Suddenly, the porch shook so violently that the ends of a half-dozen wood planks which made up the porch flooring sprang up, causing the nails, which held the ends down, to pop up and protrude into the air. Adam instinctively flipped his shillelagh and with the knob end whacked the nails and the planks back into place, daring another nail to show itself.

As if the shaking porch wasn't strange enough, when Eve stepped onto it, the shaking suddenly stopped, leaving the entire porch level again. Ignoring her effect, she hurried into the house and up the stairs to her bedroom.

Adam, in a protective mood, dashed up the stairs behind her.

Eve walked quickly into her bedroom, lifted the lid to the heirloom chest at the foot of her bed, removed the hand-carved wooden crucifix, set aside several linen napkins, and took up the larger linen cloth that lay on top of the others and handed it to her father. She replaced the crucifix, closed the chest, and from under her pillow pulled out Fr. Xavier's prayer book.

Adam descended the steps with Eve behind him and entered the gathering hall. Earlier, Adam had cleared the hall of extraneous items like the rug, chairs, the game table, loose decor items, and Eve had unthreaded the loom, which was a difficult task. She also moved the baskets of yarn to her bedroom. That left just the large empty table in the center of the room, which Fr. Cahill would need.

It was obvious that the Wizard was likewise going all out preparing for battle, and Eve's presence did nothing to quiet the disorder. The snipping shears, the terrestrial tremors, the whomping of wagons, and now a thin, dark vale of vapor confirmed the enemy's deployment of forces for combat.

To establish battle lines, Fr. Cahill, assisted by Sam, liberally sprinkled Holy Water around the room while praying loudly in Latin.

> *Aspérges me, Dómine, hyssópo, et mundábor...Sprinkle me, O Lord, with hyssop, and I shall be clean.*

The floor still shook and the noises were still present, but the Holy Water seemed to temper and keep the haunts at bay. Gabriel placed the thurible on the hearth. When Fr. Cahill finished sprinkling the room, Sam set the aspergillum and aspersorium next to the thurible.

Adam put the folded linen on the supper table, but almost immediately he heard the sounds of clipping shears intensify, as if the linen was fair game and the Wizard was coming for it. He suddenly feared that Eve's cloth may be destroyed before it could be used.

Fr. Cahill must have also sensed the linen's vulnerability. He quickly picked up the folded cloth and handed it to Eve. "Hold this close to your body until we're ready. It looks beautiful, by the way. We don't need it clipped before we can prepare the altar."

Eve smiled, took the linen in her arms, held it close to her body with Xavier's prayer book, backed out of the way and stood next to the empty loom.

Fr. Cahill took a position in the center of the room, his back to the fireplace, and pointed at the opposite wall. "That is approximately east, so let's place the table here in front of me as I stand."

"Sam, help me," said Adam.

Sam tried to lift one end of the table and Adam the other, but it felt as if the table was nailed to the floor. Struggle as they might the table would not budge.

Fr. Cahill saw this and asked, "Is it fastened to the floor?"

"No," said Adam, "but we can't lift it."

Fr. Cahill grabbed the aspergillum and liberally wet down each of the table's four legs as well as the top of the table, and then invoked a blessing.

"Try it now," said Fr. Cahill.

The table immediately was freed. Adam and Sam rotated the table and placed it in front of Fr. Cahill as he faced east. Moving quickly, Fr. Cahill opened the small case he had brought and removed a vial of Chrism Oil used at the Potowmack baptisms. He handed the case to Gabriel. Sprinkling the oil liberally onto the table, he then rubbed it thoroughly into the grain with his bare hands while reciting a Latin prayer:

> *Sancte Michael Archangele, defende nos in proelio…Saint Michael, the Archangel, defend us in battle. Be our protection against the wickedness and snares of the devil; May God rebuke him, we humbly pray; And do thou, O, Prince of the Heavenly host, by the power of God, thrust into hell Satan and all evil spirits who wander through the world for the ruin of souls. Amen.*

"The devil hates Latin," said Fr. Dimitri, who stood nearby still holding the crucifix.

"Now the altar cloth," said Fr. Cahill. "It should be protected now."

Eve put the linen on the table and Adam helped her spread the cloth. It was obviously made for this table as it evenly draped a foot over all four sides. Fr. Dimitri then placed his crucifix on its stand at the front and center on the table.

Adam noted that once the table had been anointed with oil, the cloth in place, and the crucifix placed, the clipping sounds did not intensify as they had moments earlier.

"Adam, the candles…and let's light them," said Fr. Cahill.

Amidst the continued but reduced torments of noises and vibrations, Adam gestured for Fr. Dimitri and Eve to go to the side of the room where the dish and pottery hutch stood. At that moment Adam realized he had not cleared the room as well as he had hoped. The hutch was full of plates, bowls, serving dishes and containers of various sizes. He would have to keep an eye on this. On the hutch's counter were six candle sticks with white candles in each. He handed two each to Eve and Fr. Dimitri, and took two himself, putting them on the table. Fr. Dimitri then spaced the six candles evenly left to right.

They had an altar.

Adam took down the tinderbox from above the fireplace and knelt on the hearth to strike a flint and light a match, but when his striker produced a spark off the flint and lit the tinder, there was a sudden burst of flames from under several smoldering logs left in the fireplace. Just as suddenly the flames went out. Surprised, he held his hands over the logs. As expected they were warm but there were no flames. Had he just experienced a premonition? Like the dish hutch he realized he had not cleared out the fireplace of logs, but at the time they were too hot to handle. Could they instantly combust and be used by the Wizard? He didn't think so, but the sudden burst of flames, imagined or real, was fair warning.

Lighting a match stick, he took the flame to the table and tried to light the candles, but as soon as he was within a foot of the table a cool, quick draft of wind blew out his match. The tinder was still burning, so this time he picked up the tinder box, protecting it with his hand from another gust of wind, held it over the table next to each candle and lit them. But after all were lit, a cold gust of wind swept the table and the candles were extinguished.

Seeing this, Fr. Cahill gestured for the thurible, which Gabriel retrieved and produced the incense cannister from a pocket. Fr. Cahill scooped a generous amount of incense into the thurible's crucible producing the sweet-smelling smoke, then double-swung the thurible around, above, and below the altar. He then incensed Fr. Dimitri. Fr. Dimitri then incensed Fr. Cahill and Gabriel. Gabriel took the thurible and incensed Adam, Rev. Williams, Sam, and Eve, finally retiring the thurible to the hearth. When they were done the room was filled with incense. Adam noted that this whole process had dramatically reduced the Wizard's manifestations, and that the Wizard's veil of black vapor had been displaced to the edges of the room by the incense, which rose to the ceiling as it wafted through the room.

Adam stood amazed at the miracle, but suddenly he experienced a premonition that this would not always be the case. Appearing before him for a split second was a personified human-like specter that came aggressively at him. He reacted by gripping his shillelagh, but the vision dissipated quickly and he relaxed, only to remember the candles were still not lit. He quickly tried to light the candles again and this time he was successful. There was no draft, and the candle flames stood upright on their wicks.

Surveying the room, Adam gazed at Jeremiah who stood in the archway from the foyer, his eyes bulging as he took in the room and the ritual of preparing the altar. Adam was sure the Methodist preacher had never gone to so much trouble.

Fr. Cahill laid his missal on the altar and Fr. Dimitri unpacked Fr. Cahill's small case and produced several altar linens, a corporal, purificators, finger towel, a pall, a small gold chalice, a gold paten (or flat dish), and two small cruets, one that contained wine and the other water. Fr. Cahill reached into the case and removed a container of small, round communion hosts, counted out five, and placed them on the paten. Then, opening a round gold case with a cross on top, he removed a much larger communion wafer, which he placed on top of the smaller ones on the paten.

While Fr. Cahill made final adjustments to the items on the altar, Fr. Dimitri turned and gestured for everyone to line up behind Fr. Cahill who faced the altar and east. Adam ended up at the far left. Next to him was Sam, then Eve, then Rev. Williams, and finally Gabriel on the far right.

Fr. Cahill turned toward them, raised his hands in greeting and said, "We will now celebrate the Holy Sacrifice of The Mass, the Church's most efficacious prayer for our salvation. Let us pray."

…and the floor began to shake a little bit more. Clearly, Adam thought, the Wizard did not like praying on its premises.

4

Fr. Cahill and Fr. Dimitri turned their backs to the group and faced the altar, genuflected and made the sign of the cross.

Adam felt a cool wind blow through the room. Normally, that would make sense since the windows were open, but the breeze felt colder than it should for this time of year. The wind also had a sharp bitter edge to it that put Adam on edge.

With his hands raised, Fr. Cahill began in Latin,

> *Exáudi nos, Dómine sancte, Pater omnípotens, ætérne Deus…*
> *Hear us, O Holy Lord, almighty Father, eternal God, and deign to send your holy Angel from heaven to guard, foster, protect, visit, and defend all those who live in this dwelling, through Christ our Lord.*

In the middle of Fr. Cahill's prayer Adam heard the hauntings begin—there was aggressive clipping and a rebellious increase in the sounds of rumbling wagons circling the house. His body naturally tensed and he wondered exactly what he should do. He recalled Fr. Cahill plunging both ends of his shillelagh into the container of Holy Water. From Fr. Cahill's previous visit to Flax Haven, Adam understood the power of Holy Water. He kept his shillelagh close.

The clipping and the wagon manifestations escalated.

Gripping his shillelagh, Adam intently watched Fr. Cahill.

Both priests backed away from the altar several steps and dropped to their knees. They both crossed themselves again as Fr. Cahill began…

> *In nomine Patris, et Filii, et Spiritus Sancti. Amen.*

Bringing their hands together in prayer they began to recite a prayer or Psalm antiphonally.

Fr. Cahill began:

> *Introíbo ad altáre Dei…I will go to the altar of God.*

Fr. Dimitri responded:

> *Ad Deum qui lætíficat juventútem meam…To God, who gives joy*

to my youth,

Júdica me, Deus...Judge me, O God, and distinguish my cause from an unholy nation; from the evil and fraudulent man, deliver me.

Quia tu es, Deus...For you, O God, are my strength. Why have you cast me off, and why do I go forth sorrowful, while my enemy afflicts me?

While they continued the liturgy Adam's attention was drawn to the priests' feet where he saw what he dreaded—streams of black vapor snaking up from cracks in the floorboards. The streams of smoke surrounded Fr. Cahill's kneeling body and formed a tottering train of crescent moons that boldly flowed over Fr. Cahill's ankles. To Adam it appeared like a chain that enslaved Africans. His face hardened. He was instantly disgusted. Taking up his shillelagh he swung the tip through the chain of coalescing vapor. The vapor swirled when the tip of his fighting stick passed through it, but then the vapor wrapped itself around the stick, took hold, and tried to lever it from Adam's tight fist. But Adam would not give up that easily. He slammed the stick against the floor, scraped the vapor off with his boot, then stomped at the smoke. The vapor finally retreated below the floorboards...except, that is, for a remnant that lurked just above the floor as if waiting for a new opportunity. This vapor's substance told him it was the same that occupied his house the night George and Martha died. It wasn't harmless vapor. He took deep careful breaths, his body grew tense, and he worried what would come next. In spite of the distraction, Fr. Cahill and Fr. Dimitri kept steadfast at prayer.

Adjutórium nostrum in nómine Dómini...Our help is in the name of the Lord," said Fr. Cahill.

Fr. Dimitri responded:

Qui fecit cælum et terram...Who made Heaven and earth.

Fr. Cahill followed:

Confíteor Deo omnipoténti...I confess to almighty God, to blessed Mary ever Virgin, to blessed Michael the Archangel, to blessed John the Baptist, to the holy Apostles Peter and Paul, to all the Saints, and to you, my brothers and sisters.

Adam's attention was divided between wishing to understand what Fr. Cahill was saying and watching the vapor pulsate through the seams of the floorboards around the legs of the altar. He dared not try to hit or stomp on the vapor so close to the priest's feet. It was as if the Wizard was teasing him. If he took his eyes off the vapor for a split second he imagined it coming out of the floor, wrapping itself around both Fr. Cahill's boots and carrying him off. Vigilance was called for.

Fr. Cahill continued:

> *May the Almighty and merciful Lord grant us forgiveness, absolution, and the remission of our sins.*

"Amen," said Fr. Dimitri.

Adam had been so concentrating on the vapor that he hadn't noticed Gabriel bring the thurible to the altar along with the cannister of incense. Fr. Cahill stepped up to the altar, took the incense cannister from Gabriel, and liberally spooned the brown grains into the thurible producing thick white smoke. He then incensed the altar again, double and triple swinging the thurible under and over the altar as he walked around its circumference. When he was done, Gabriel took command of the chains and incensed Fr. Cahill, then Fr. Dimitri, and then Adam and the group, finally returning the thurible to the hearth. Adam looked back at the altar. It was now shrouded in white, sweet smelling incense. The black vapor had been chased out of sight beneath the floorboards. This did not make Adam comfortable. It was like sweeping sand under the rug—the dirt was still there and would find a way to slither out.

The Wizard, of course, was not lacking imagination. During the past few minutes, while the clipping and wagon rumbling continued, there was a rapping beneath the floor as if the vapor had coalesced and was banging to get out. It was a soft rap, like a thump that sounded an irregular rhythm as if it were alive, perhaps a trapped animal banging its head against an empty pail. At the same time, the cool breeze that blew through the window now carried the scent of a frightened skunk, the one scent he had not smelled since leaving Pennsylvania. Odd, he thought, that he had not seen a skunk in Virginia. What was not odd was that the Wizard had found a fragrance to block the smell of the sweet incense, and of course the breeze helped to waft away the incense, leaving the skunk smell behind. Adam thought of closing the windows, but realized that could play into the Wizard's hands by restricting a draft of fresh air.

The thumping from the cellar got the best of him. Taking his shillelagh, he left the gathering hall and went down to the cellar with a lantern. The sound was now more distinct and had a direction. He followed it to the wash tubs. As he approached the basins he stepped into a puddle of water, and just as soon as he did, a clump of water spilled from the basin onto the floor and into a metal pail, which was now overflowing. There was the thumping he had heard. But why was the sink overflowing? He raised his lantern. In the mud trough was an animal sloshing about as if it was playing in bathwater. It was Bombay clogging the drain and making a mess, occasionally splashing water out and into the pail. Adam had never seen a cat take a bath. They had always seemed to have an aversion to water. Adam went to grab the cat and pull it out of the trough with his right hand, but Bombay would have nothing of it. It snarled at Adam and swiped at his hand, scratching it. He pulled his hand away but not quickly enough before the cat's nails left a deep cut. Adam held his hand up to the lantern. It was bleeding. He forced it to bleed more profusely to clean the wound. He would have to bandage it, but first the cat had to go. Taking the knob end of his shillelagh in his left hand, he pried Bombay out of the mud-trough and to the floor. The cat landed in the pail full of water, and stayed there. *Convenient,* thought Adam. He whirled his shillelagh around and hooked the stick's knob under the pail's handle and carried the pail and cat up the stairs and across the hall, where he threw open the rear door. Stepping onto the back porch, he took the pail in both hands and swung it as hard as he could, tossing the water and the cat as far as he could into the woods. *"Never did like that cat,"* he murmured to himself.

After closing the door, he set the pail down in the hall, stepped into his office and found some cotton bandages. At that moment Eve came into the office.

"What's wrong, Papa?"

"Bombay made a mess in the cellar and clawed me. See?" He held out his hand and the bandages. "Tie this on for me, nice and tight."

Eve didn't hesitate. She bandaged her father's hand as good as any surgeon. "Let's get back," he said.

When they slipped back into the gathering hall, Fr. Cahill faced the altar and had his hands together in prayer. As he prayed he glanced at Adam and nodded his approval, as if the prayer he was reading was perfect for the moment.

> *Dixi Domino: Deus meus es tu...I say to the LORD: You are my God; listen, LORD, to the words of my pleas. LORD, my master, my strong deliverer, you cover my head on the day of armed conflict. LORD, do not grant the desires of the wicked one; do not let his plot succeed.*

Fr. Cahill, Fr. Dimitri, and Gabriel began to antiphonally chant and with one hand beat their breasts:

> *Kýrie eléison,...Lord, have mercy...Christ have mercy...Lord have mercy.*

Whatever they were saying it must have bothered their ghost, for in rhythm with their hands beating their breasts the floor vibrated a bit more intensely, each time trying to drown out the words. This was no common house quake as they had experienced before, for it sounded as if hell was coughing up phlegm. It was a repulsive sound, as if the house was on the verge of a vast vomit. It had the effect, in Adam at least, of making him want to regurgitate. But before he could assume the position the sound of rumbling wagons along with stampeding livestock suddenly became intense, and his attention and his body were drawn out the front door.

5

When Adam arrived on the porch what greeted him was not just sounds, but specters much like those he had battled the night he came back from praying with Eve at Xavier's grave. His body tensed and he tightened his grip on the shillelagh. The black smoke swirled from underneath the house and formed ghost-like wagons and an occasional free-running horse that circled the house at breakneck speed. Adam knew that the horses and wagons had to be apparitions, but the noise was thunderous, and the dust kicked up was absolutely real, for it irritated his mouth and eyes.

Yet, as the seconds ticked by, the ghostly shapes became more concrete and the vibrations he felt through the porch deck doubled in severity.

Gripping his shillelagh in his right hand, Adam jumped off the porch and threw himself into the path of a wagon as it came around the north corner of the porch. He thought it was pure vapor and entirely harmless, but it had partly solidified and the impact, while somewhat cushioned, nonetheless knocked Adam back ten feet to the ground. His presence, however, had an effect. It had disrupted the specter's trajectory. As it attempted to turn around the west corner of the porch, the wagon's front left wheel caught the corner. The rim and spokes shattered, the bed tilted, hit the porch, and broke apart, sending the pieces into the air where they disintegrated, leaving the porch intact.

Seeing this, Adam gathered his courage and advanced toward the havoc creating column of circling wagons and horses. Bracing himself near their path, he waited for the right moment, then thrust the tip of his blessed shillelagh into the spokes of a passing wheel. His shillelagh spasmed as the specter became entangled with it, but instantly the wagon's wheel broke apart, throwing the wagon bed into the dirt. He watched mesmerized as the wagon shattered, flew into the air and disintegrated into nothingness.

But his back was turned to the advancing column and seconds later he was run over by a wraith of horse and wagon which knocked him to the ground. Successive wagons, steel rims, and horse hoofs pummeled his body into the earth. Each time he tried to get up the mayhem knocked him left and right, up and down. Crawling to the outside, he struggled to his feet. Being more careful this time, he gauged his opportunities and repeatedly thrust his shillelagh into one wheel, and then another, and between the legs of the horses. Spokes were stripped from wheel hubs as wagon beds crashed into the soil and each other, while the horses disintegrated as soon as their legs kicked the shillelagh. His effort was wild and chaotic, but by sheer perseverance Adam transformed the wagons into smoky smithereens, and simultaneously muted many, but not all of the wagon and horse bedlam. There was a price to pay, however. Adam teetered up the steps and back into the gathering hall. He was dirty, bruised, beat-up, and exhausted.

6

Adam glanced up. All eyes were on him, except Fr. Cahill who was standing at the left side of the altar reading from the missal in English, which certainly got Adam's attention.

> *And I say to thee, thou art Peter; and upon this rock I will build my church, and the gates of hell shall not prevail against it. And I will give to thee the keys of the kingdom of heaven. And whatsoever thou shalt bind upon earth...*

From the corner of his eye, Adam noticed Rev. Williams wrestling with his prayer book. It was a strange sight as the Methodist twisted and turned in an effort to prevent the prayer book from flying out of his hands.

Suddenly, Adam jabbed the knob end of his shillelagh directly at Fr. Cahill's head. It seemed outrageous, even to Adam, but an instant later, the shillelagh's knob intercepted Rev. Williams' prayer book that had been hurled like a bullet at the back of the priest's head. The book ricocheted off the knob, into the air, and fell into Fr. Dimitri's hands. Stepping forward, Adam took the wayward book from Fr. Dimitri and returned it to the Methodist.

"Pray harder," said Adam to the scared minister.

Williams, whose forearms and hands were shaking even more than the flooring, nodded, and took the book back.

Within moments, Fr. Cahill, together with Fr. Dimitri and Gabriel began a recitation of the creed:

> *Reo in unum Deum, Patrem omnipot-éntem...I believe in one Lord Jesus Christ, the Only Begotten Son of God, born of the Father before all ages. God from God, Light from Light, true God from true God, begotten, not made, consubstantial with the Father; through him all things were made...*

Almost immediately, the dish hutch began to rattle. This is what he feared. If only he had been more thorough in clearing the room. But it was too late. There were too many items to move now, or was there still time? As the Latin recitation continued...

> *For us men and for our salvation he came down from heaven, and by the Holy Spirit was incarnate of the Virgin Mary, and became man.*

...Adam gestured to Eve to help him. Together they carried stacks of dishes and jars of pottery to the parlor, but after only one trip a dish suddenly flew out of the hutch and headed for the altar. Quick as lightning Adam caught it and tossed it to Eve, who took it to the parlor. The hutch began to shake even more. A jar vibrated off a shelf, fell, and broke into pieces.

Apparently oblivious to everything happening around him, Fr. Cahill focused on the liturgy. He lifted the paten with the large Host into the air and held it reverently before his breast and prayed,

> *Súscipe, sancte Pater...Receive, O holy Father, almighty everlasting God, this spotless Host,...*

When that prayer began, stacks of plates, cups, and saucers jumped in place as if they had been impregnated with an illicit energy that needed release.

> *...which I, thine unworthy servant, offer unto thee, my living and true God, for my innumerable sins, offenses and negligences...*

Adam, who was between the front of the altar and the hutch, had glanced back at Fr. Cahill, curious as to what he was doing when suddenly a plate whizzed past Adam's head and flew at Fr. Cahill's face. Fr. Cahill ducked just in time. The plate hit the hearth and broke with a crash. Fr. Cahill stopped his ritual, put his hand over the paten to protect the Host, and stared at Adam. Adam turned back toward the hutch and wrapped the leather strap in the tip of his shillelagh around his right wrist.

Fr. Cahill picked up the liturgy...

> *...and for all who stand here around, as also for all faithful Christians, both living and departed, that to me and to them it may avail for salvation unto life everlasting.*

Suddenly, it began en masse. A stone tankard shot out of the hutch and flew toward the altar. Adam two-handed the fighting stick and with the knob-end knocked the tankard to the ground. One by one other dishes, cups, saucers, jars and tankards flew from the hutch, all aimed for Fr. Cahill or Fr. Dimitri. Adam concentrated and hit most of the pottery missiles with his shillelagh's knob; some he missed and the priests had to duck. He wondered if they had learned that skill in seminary.

Courageously, through it all, Fr. Cahill continued the celebration.

> *We offer unto thee, O Lord, this chalice of salvation, begging your clemency....*

In defiance, Fr. Cahill offered up the chalice. He was relying on Adam's deft skill at shattering the Wizard's missiles, but not all the splintered fragments fell short. Some hit Fr. Cahill and Fr. Dimitri. Debris also fell on the altar, which Fr. Dimitri cleared off as fast as he could. Some china pieces, when hit by the shillelagh, burst into bits and pieces, the sharp edges flying into Adam and cutting his arms and face. He refused, however, to stop until all the serving ware that had been in the hutch ended up as rubble on the floor.

Nearly exhausted from the effort, Adam dropped to his knees to catch his breath. He looked up at Fr. Cahill...the liturgy continued:

> *...that in the sight of your divine majesty, it may rise up with the odor of sweetness for our salvation and that of the whole world.*

Fr. Cahill smiled at Adam. "*Amen.*"

At the right side of the altar, Fr. Dimitri took the two cruets of wine and water and emptied the wine into the chalice. After adding a few drops of water he passed the chalice to Fr. Cahill, who held it in the air before him.

> *Deus, qui humánæ substántaiæ...O God, who wondrously created the dignity of our human nature and more wondrously restored it, grant that through the mystery of this water and wine we may come to share in the divinity of him who humbled himself to share in our humanity...*

Eve knelt next to her father and nudged him. In her hands were cotton bandages from his office, and next to her was Sam who brought a container of water. Together they washed and bandaged Adam. Before they could finish, however, a strong, cold wind blew through the room creating a dust storm. Adam glanced at the altar. Amazingly, the candles stayed lit in the wind, although the flames laid over on their sides and flickered wildly. Sam jumped up and closed the windows and checked the doors, but the wind was not coming from the windows. It was circulating in the room on its own, creating a whirlwind of debris around the altar.

Despite the whirlwind and debris, Fr. Cahill did not stop.

Adam sensed that Fr. Cahill understood that the only way to stop the Wizard was to *not* stop the Mass. He watched as Fr. Cahill made the sign of the cross three times over the paten and chalice and pressed on with the liturgy by raising his voice:

> *Veni, Sanctificátor omnípotens ætérne Deus...Come, O Sanctifier, almighty and eternal God, and bless this sacrifice prepared for the honor of your holy name.*

In response, out of the wind came a demonic, otherworldly, mocking voice that ridiculed Fr. Cahill's prayer: "*Yes, papist scum. Bless this cursed sacrifice, spat upon and rejected, a flawed, brutalized, offending offering.*" The voice finished with a sinister laugh that trailed into silence.

Everyone in the room heard the voice and looked about. Rev. Williams nervously shifted his eyes and bit his lip. Sam looked positively scared as if he was about to be whipped at the pleasure of a malevolent master. Eve's eyes got big and stared at Papa for assurance, but Adam could offer none. Fr. Dimitri retreated to the hearth, grabbed the aspergillum and shook Holy Water over the group and Fr. Cahill. Gabriel then took the aspergillum and doused Fr. Dimitri. The voice receded. Gabriel returned the wand and Fr. Dimitri turned back to the altar. And so it continued. The further Fr. Cahill invoked Latin and approached the consecration of the elements, the harder the Wizard worked to invalidate them. *We're in for a long hard ride*, thought Adam.

7

Minutes later, Adam notice how fervently Fr. Cahill reverenced the large Host that now lay on the white linen cloth in the center of the altar. Adam thought things couldn't get much worse, but he was wrong. He reminded himself that when battling evil, evil always fights back. That's when he noticed that the altar had literally lifted off the floor and was being jostled about as if it were on a river ferry crossing turbulent rapids. Instinctively he knelt next to one of the four legs, grabbed hold, and tried to bring it back down to earth. Following his lead, Sam, Eve, and Gabriel did the same.

Rev. Williams just looked on in horror. Adam thought he was a good example of a man caught between fight and flight—going with the flow was so much easier. Adam stared at the man. He held his prayer book close and his lips moving, and if he wasn't wiping debris from his eyes he was watching Fr. Cahill, who at that moment made the sign of the cross over the large Host and the chalice together.

> *Quam oblatiónem tu, Deus...Be pleased, O God, we pray, to bless, acknowledge, and approve this offering in every respect; make it spiritual and acceptable, so that it may become for us the Body and....*

All at once, the chalice, on its own, lifted off the altar and began to tip, as if an invisible hand intended to pour out the contents. Fr. Cahill was reading from the missal and didn't see what was happening, but Fr. Dimitri did. He grabbed the base of the chalice and held it to the altar. Yet the altar was still shaking even as Sam, Eve, Gabriel, and Adam attempted to weigh down the legs and keep it on the floor amidst the whirlwind and everything else.

Adam fought despondency and wondered if what Fr. Cahill was doing was doing any good at all. While he literally held down his part of the bargain, he looked up at Rev. Williams. Jeremiah's lips were moving but his eyes were glazed over staring at the struggle around the sacred table that involved everyone but him.

Carefully pronouncing his words, Fr. Cahill completed a prayer:

> *...et Sanguis fiat dilectíssimi Fílii tui Dómini, nostri Jesu Christi... the Blood of your most beloved Son, our Lord Jesus Christ.*

Fr. Cahill then joined his hands together.

Oh, thought Adam, *if I could only understand what was being said.* Fatigue was setting in from holding down the altar, which fought back with upward jerks. Adam was sure the others were tired as well, especially Eve.

Then, when Fr. Cahill put his hands together, there was a sudden and thunderous thunderclap that came from high above the house. The sound resonated repeatedly as if a large gong was being struck over and over.

Whatever that was, thought Adam, *it certainly had an effect…and none too soon.* With the thunderclap the altar fell to the floor, once again becoming a fixture in the room. After a moment the leg handlers got off their knees, stood and lurched back to their places behind Fr. Cahill. Standing again, Adam noticed that the wind, too, had dropped to a gentle breeze, although all the windows were shut tight.

Collecting himself, Fr. Cahill took a moment to straighten the altar cover, the linens, chalice, center the paten and adjust the missal. Then he continued, reverently holding the Host in his hands,

> *Qui prídie quam paterétur,…On the day before he was to suffer, he took bread in his holy and venerable hands…*

Eve abruptly whispered to her father, "Papa, look!" She pointed behind the altar to the table next to the kitchen door. On the table was a wooden breadbox with two hinged doors; behind each they stored loaves of bread. The top door had popped open to form a shelf. As Adam looked, the loaf that was behind the door flew out and rolled onto the floor behind the altar. At the same time a *banshee screamed*. It was the wail of impending death. Adam hastily went to recover the bread that had fallen to the floor, but decided to take the whole breadbox out of the room. As soon as he picked up the box the bottom door flopped open and the second loaf fell to the floor. Adam glanced at Eve, who came to his aid, picked up both loaves and opened the door to the summer kitchen. Adam took the bread box and the loaves down the stairs, set them on a counter, and returned, shutting the door firmly behind him.

Fr. Cahill lifted his eyes to heaven,

> *…et elevátis óculis in cælum…and with eyes lifted up to heaven unto thee, God, his almighty Father…*

A flash of blinding light emanated from inside the room and temporarily blinded Adam. Then another crack of thunder, it too inside the room, although this thunderclap sounded weaker than the one outside. It was accompanied by another *banshee scream*. Adam thought the Wizard was mimicking the Almighty, which Adam now thought was the source of the former thunderclap.

Cahill bowed his head,

> *Deum Patrem suum omnipoténtem…O God, his almighty Father, giving you thanks he said the blessing,* …

As Fr. Cahill made the sign of the cross over the Host, Adam heard what sounded like gravel being scraped off a roadbed. He turned to the hearth behind him to see a large oblong stone break from its cemented place in the hearth's wall and fly at Fr. Cahill. Without thinking of the consequence, Adam jumped in front of the stone, which hit him in the shoulder and fell to one side. Thankfully, it missed Fr. Cahill but fell on Fr. Dimitri's foot, causing him to fall to the floor in pain. Fr. Cahill stopped the liturgy and knelt next to Fr. Dimitri, who gripped and massaged his foot.

"Can you continue?" asked Fr. Cahill.

"I will," said Fr. Dimitri as he limped to his feet.

Sam picked up the stone and carried it out the front door.

Fr. Cahill came to Adam, who was nursing his shoulder, laid a hand on it and prayed silently. Adam was appreciative of the priest's attention, "Thank you, Father, but I've suffered worse. Keep going. Don't stop for me."

Fr. Cahill returned to the altar and picked up where he had left off signing over the Host,

> *...benedixit, fregit...he said the blessing, broke the bread and gave it to his disciples, saying: Take this, all of you and eat of it.*

Bowing profoundly over the altar, Fr. Cahill was about to say something when there was a third *banshee scream*. But this one was pitched much lower: It sounded like a large, starving, predatory cat on the prowl. Suddenly, Adam doubled over in pain. It felt as if a knife had sliced open his gut. He took a deep breath and felt a sharp pain in his lungs and abdomen, but there was no wound nor was there blood, just the specter of it. Could the Wizard now attack their bodies from within? This was new if it was that. He was tempted to panic, but he stayed still for a moment, then he stretched out what must have been a muscle spasm. He felt like a crippled old man with wounds everywhere.

The loud, low scream continued, obstructing his ability to think. He was tired but determined, distressed but hopeful. Something within him told him to hang on, to persist, and to pray.

He looked about, as did the others, for the source of the blood-curdling scream, but there was nothing to see. Adam was amazed that through it all Fr. Cahill stayed intent on the liturgy. At that moment, Fr. Cahill stared with particular solemnity at the Host and spoke quietly and slowly,

HOC EST ENIM CORPUS MEUM...FOR THIS IS MY BODY.

As Fr. Cahill genuflected and then raised the Host high in the air to reverence it, what sounded like a large gong in the sky above the house sounded three times. The room shook with such strength that Adam was sure the house would collapse. It was hard for everyone to maintain their footing, and Adam fell, but quickly got back up. He began to understand the violent reaction. According to Catholic teaching, at the consecration of the Host, Jesus Christ became present, and the devil cannot stand in the presence of God who Christ is. He knew what was coming next—the consecration of the cup. If the Wizard didn't like the Host becoming divine, he would hate the blood.

Fr. Cahill read from the missal...

> *Símili modo postquam...In a similar way, when supper was ended,*
> *he took this precious chalice in his holy and venerable hands, and*
> *once more giving you thanks, he said the blessing and gave the*
> *chalice to his disciples, saying: Take this, all of you, and drink from*
> *it.*

...and took the chalice in both hands. As soon as he did the room was filled with the otherworldly screams of pain, but this time at a higher and more frantic pitch.

Fr. Cahill made the sign of the cross over the chalice, and as he did the room shook again with great strength and persistence. The banshee scream was there as well, and louder. Fr. Cahill bowed to the chalice, lowered his head and stared deeply into it at the wine, soon to be the sacramental blood of Christ. Again he spoke quietly and slowly,

> *HIC EST ENIM CALIX SÁNGUINIS MEI...FOR THIS IS THE*
> *CHALICE OF MY BLOOD, THE BLOOD OF THE NEW AND*
> *ETERNAL COVENANT, THE MYSTERY OF FAITH, WHICH*
> *WILL BE POURED OUT FOR YOU AND FOR MANY FOR*
> *THE FORGIVENESS OF SINS.*

Fr. Cahill set the chalice on the altar and genuflected, then stood and raised the chalice above his head. The gong, high in the heavens, or so it seemed, sounded again three times.

> *Hæc quotiescúmque...As often as you do these things, you do them*
> *in memory of me.*

That's when all hell broke loose. The room shook so violently that everyone fell to the floor, including the priests. Fr. Cahill fell to his knees while still elevating the chalice but could not maintain his balance. Fr. Dimitri and Adam crawled to Fr. Cahill. Staying on their knees they gripped his waist, one man on each side, and lifted him up, allowing Fr. Cahill to stand while keeping the chalice elevated high above the altar.

> *This pure victim, this holy victim, this spotless victim...*

But the Wizard wasn't done.

Behind him, Adam heard a fire crackling and air rushing up the chimney. Still holding onto a shaky Fr. Cahill, Adam looked back at the fireplace. Before there had been no fire, but now the fireplace hosted flames that fed off the charred, mostly spent logs. The intensity of the flames grew second by second until there was a blazing inferno, which coalesced into a...

"Watch out!" yelled Adam.

As if from a cannon, a fireball shot out of the fireplace. It flew across the room, barely missing Eve who was on all fours trying to keep from sprawling flat. The fireball struck Adam in the chest, knocking him down, then it shattered into hundreds of flaming embers that ignited his clothes. With half his support gone, Fr. Cahill fell back to his knees onto the floor, which continued to shake violently. He managed to set the chalice on the altar and hold it upright.

Rev. Williams and Eve tried to slap out the flames burning Adam's clothes when he felt water being poured on the flames. Gabriel had grabbed the aspersorium and was appropriating the Holy Water. Along with Eve and Rev. Williams' handy attention, the flames were extinguished. He was left with a charred shirt and trousers but no serious burns. Adam thought, *I'll bet the Vatican never thought Holy Water could be so used to literally to extinguish the devil's work.*

He decided that he had to get the now-smoldering logs out of the fireplace, but exactly how he wasn't sure. The three logs were too big for the fireplace tongs. He would need a bucket of sand to smother them. Then the logs would need to cool before they could be carried out.

Meantime, Fr. Cahill had raised himself up by holding onto the edge of the altar, and although unsteady, reverenced the Host and chalice:

> …*the holy Bread of eternal life and the Chalice of everlasting salvation.*

Adam regained his feet on the vibrating floor by steadying himself on the altar, but an explosion ripped apart one of the logs in the fireplace. Hot coals flew into the air like a fireworks display, raining burning embers everywhere, including on top of the altar cloth. Adam reached across the altar to brush the embers away, but Fr. Cahill put out his hand and stopped him. Adam, confused, backed away and watched as the hot embers were suddenly extinguished by an unseen force, and then flicked off the cloth and hurled harmlessly against the far wall, by…what was it, invisible fingers? Adam looked back at the altar cloth. There was no sign of the cloth being singed, scorched, or burnt. To witness such miracles left him at once humbled and feeling useless.

Fr. Cahill extended his hands over the Host and chalice, continuing the liturgy:

> …*so that all of us who through this participation at the altar receive the most holy Body and Blood of your Son, may be filled with every grace and heavenly blessing. Through the same Christ our Lord. Amen.*

Fr. Cahill's "Amen," however, was like iron striking flint in a tinder factory. The two remaining logs in the fireplace burst into flames and rocketed into the room, flying in a circle eye-level about the altar. Adam felt the blood drain from his face and his breath quicken. He stared intently at the logs, wanting to grab them and smash them over the devil's head.

The blazing timbers came at Eve. "Eve!" yelled Adam.

Fortunately, Eve had seen the logs and ducked as they flew past, one on each side. Unfortunately, the lit logs landed on the loom. Fortunately, at her father's direction, she had unthreaded the entire loom and removed the yarn basket. Unfortunately, the densely packed string heddles incinerated in seconds, which in turn ignited the smaller timbers.

"Sam," yelled Eve, "Water!"

Sam was already on it. He had rushed to the cellar and brought up a pail of water. Adam recognized the pail: he had left it in the back hall after deposing Bombay out the back door.

Eve ran and grabbed an armful of the clipped linen from the sample box by the front door and gave some to Adam and some to Sam. Each of them soaked the linen scraps in the pail of water and proceeded to wipe down the loom's timbers, smothering the flames. But the fiery logs were at their feet and beginning to scorch the floor. Carefully, Sam took the pail and poured water over the logs, suffocating the flames. When the loom fire was extinguished, Adam and Sam soaked their cloths again and grabbed the logs to take them out the front door.

Adam felt terrible about the loom. It had been the object of repeated reprisals and repairs. In some ways he was not sad about the repairs he had made, for each time he took the opportunity to improve the loom's mechanics, but there was something mystical about the loom. Several times it had fallen to disrepair, damage, or nearly destroyed. Yet each time it was resurrected. It seemed to him that the loom had become a symbol of what is true. Constantly attacked, wounded, destroyed, and maligned by something, it managed each time to return and create good things that enhanced life. The loom was like his fields of crops: They died in winter, but bloomed in the spring, and in spite of drought, floods, pestilence, or fire, they sustained life and became an ongoing source of beauty.

Upon returning to the gathering hall, Adam took what was left of the water and poured it over the embers in the fireplace. It made a mess, but it was a safe mess. He looked back at the loom. It was a sad sight. If it was to be used again, there would be hours spent by him and Eve reconstructing the hundreds of heddles. It was a tedious job of knot tying, but rewarding too, for the time spent with his daughter.

Adam took note that the disturbances had been significantly muted, as if something had changed. He thought that perhaps the successful consecrations of the Host and chalice, which clearly had provoked the Wizard, were the reason. While the floor quaked—but moderately— and the whirlwind had subsided, but was still present—Adam wondered if the Wizard was regrouping to attack their flank. Or, perhaps, it was waiting for reinforcements.

He was weary when he noticed that while the black vapor had been suppressed by the incense, it was now seeping back into the room.

This was not over.

Eve came to him and whispered so as not to disturb Fr. Cahill, who somehow carried on with the liturgy. "Papa, are you all right? Your face is bloody and covered in soot. And look at your clothes, they're burned and torn."

"I can see and hear, daughter, and I am alive and alert. All is well. And soon will be very well. My faith is strong. This Wizard is losing."

Eve said nothing more, but surrendered a smile. He noticed her eyes were wet and she was shaking a bit, but her shaking wasn't because of the still-vibrating floor. She was scared. The loom represented everything she loved about her beloved but deceased mother. Every time the loom was disabled, it was as if her mother had died all over again, along with Eve's future. All they could do was persevere.

Eve pulled her papa back to the altar and together they knelt behind the priests, who were also on their knees reciting prayers.

> *Súpplices te rogámus, omnípotens Deus...We humbly beseech thee, almighty God: command these offerings to be brought by the hands of thy holy Angel to thine altar on high, in sight of thy divine majesty: that all we...*

Cahill kissed the altar.

> *...who at this partaking of the altar shall receive the most sacred Body and Blood of thy Son may be filled with all heavenly benediction and grace, through the same Christ our Lord. Amen.*

While the priests prayed, Adam speculated. The haunts were definitely subdued. Had they won the battle? He didn't think so. The Wizard was regrouping. This was the calm before the storm. He looked about, and steeled himself. *Where's my shillelagh?* It was lying on the floor at the altar's left. He got up, retrieved it, and returned to kneel again next to Eve, but rested on the upright fighting stick.

He was ready.

Then, something unexpected happened.

Fr. Cahill uncovered the chalice, genuflected, and took the Host between his right thumb and forefinger. Holding the chalice firmly on the altar with his left hand, he signed the cross three times over the top of the chalice with his right hand that held the Host. Like a cloud quickly revealing the sun behind it, beams of pure, intense, white light emerged from the Host as well as from the inside of the chalice and illuminated white clouds that had suddenly formed above the altar. With each signing of the cross there was a deluge of bright light from the clouds that flooded the room along with a modest rumble of thunder. It was a response to the offering of the Body and the Blood, an acceptance of the sacrifice, a sign of hope to persevere.

Adam put his arm around Eve and held her tight. *Have hope my child. God is here.*

> *Through him, and with him, and in him. O God, almighty Father,*
> *in the unity of the Holy Ghost,...*

said Fr. Cahill as he elevated the chalice with the Host high above the altar for all to see.

> *All honor and glory are thine for ever and ever.*

"Amen," said Fr Dimitri, Gabriel, and belatedly Adam, Sam, and Eve.

> *Orémus...Let us pray.*

Everyone bowed their heads and closed their eyes, thus they failed to notice that the white light from the Host and chalice disappeared. Nor did they see the thick, black, vapor storm that seeped into the room from the ceiling joists. The menacing vapor collected above the altar and displaced the white fluffy clouds.

8

Fr. Cahill extended his hands in prayer:

> *Pater noster, qui es in caelis, sanctificetur...Our Father, who art*
> *in heaven, hallowed be thy name; thy kingdom come; thy will be*
> *done on earth as it is in heaven. Give us this day our daily bread,*
> *and forgive us our trespasses as we forgive those who trespass*
> *against us. Lead us not into temptation...*

Suddenly, an eerie silence and palpable feeling of oppression filled the room. Everyone but Fr. Cahill stopped praying, opened their eyes, and gazed about.

Oblivious to the sudden absence of other voices, Fr. Cahill continued:

> *...sed libera nos a malo,...but deliver us from evil.*

With the dread came a distant, frightful, otherworldly groan that surrounded the house from outside, or so it seemed, but the fright resonated nonetheless inside the room. At the same time the black vapor that had collected above the altar solidified and descended like a curtain between Adam and the altar, cutting him off from the Mass and others.

Isolated, he feared.

Beyond the curtain Adam could still hear Fr. Cahill, but only faintly.

> *Deliver us, O, Lord, we beseech thee, from all evils, past, present,*
> *and to come....*

On Adam's side of the veil something entirely different was taking place. The veil was quickly becoming an opaque curtain of black vapor out of which materialized a large, emaciated skeletal figure. It wasn't human, but rather a grotesque personification with two arms, two legs, and a head. As it solidified, the dark skin appeared to be hairless and singed with blisters. At first it whipped about as if to orient itself after a long journey. Its spine stuck through the shinny, creosote-soaked skin like lethal spikes on a silk-floss tree. An elaborate, full-body tattoo wrapped around its back and chest made up of black, intricately shaped crescent moons. Its neck was doubly thick, the head was large and hex-agonally shaped and soared two feet over Adam. It was afflicted with a nauseat-ingly long and thin nose, a small, oval-shaped, lipless mouth behind which was a full set of razor-sharp white teeth. There were egg-sized indentations for ears, large deep-socketed eyes with red eye balls and black irises. The skin on its bald head was pulled so tight Adam could make out the cranial cracks in the skull beneath. It was naked. The genitalia appeared to be male, but the scrotum and phallus had receded mostly inside the pelvic cavity, no doubt for protection. Its legs, like the arms, were skeletal except for abhorrently protruding muscles. It had more than five toes on each of its large feet, but Adam could not make out how many. The arms terminated in large hands with opposing thumbs on either side of five fat fingers. But most intimidating was how the massive hands gripped a large and lethal-looking guandao weapon, a fighting pole with a steel spear on one end and a razor sharp, crescent moon-shaped blade on the other. After the beast had fully personified, the curtain became hazy, as if the beast's embodiment was comprised of the vaporous resources.

Adam felt the hair on the back of his neck rise and his bowels drop. His breath quickened and his heart beat through his rib cage. Although bandaged, he looped his right hand through his shillelagh's leather loop and with his left hand gripped the other end just below the knob. He had waited years for this moment. The Wizard, personified, had come to fight. Adam was ready.

Eve was close at hand; he pushed her toward Sam. She looked back at him, irritated, and Sam looked at him quizzically, as if neither could see what he could. Fr. Cahill, also unaware of the personified demon behind him, raised the Host above the altar and proclaimed,

> *Behold the Lamb of God, behold him who taketh away the sins of the world.*

Soot shot from the beast's sweaty pores. In a rage, it whirled toward Fr. Ca-hill, raised its guandao, and in an otherworldly voice proclaimed, *"God damned, whoring papist. I am Cyn Namrasit, hell's enforcer, and you're on your way to the pit of hell as my guest."*

9

Adam reacted intuitively and swung his shillelagh at the specter's back but the knob missed and only scraped the surface. Nonetheless, the swipe caused Namrasit's skin to distort and swirl. It was enough.

Instantly, Namrasit whirled from Fr. Cahill to Adam. It was the raging face of a drug-fueled reveler, the red eyes drawing a bead on the farmer as if he were an infectious pest in need of eradication.

Namrasit swung the guandao's razor sharp blade at Adam's neck. Adam ducked under the blade and readied his shillelagh, but the demon was faster and quickly rounded the guandao's shaft, whacking the back of Adam's head and knocking him to the floor. Adam considered that the specter's body was not fully solidified, but the guandao's shaft was solid wood, and the blade no doubt was made of lethal steel.

Adam on the floor, his hands cut and bleeding, took both hands as best he could and swung his shillelagh at the vaporous legs. But the shillelagh passed harmlessly through, even as the demon's visage sputtered from the swipe. That gave Adam a moment to get to his feet...but as soon as he did his chest was caught by the sweep of the guandao's pole, which smashed against his chest and threw him back against a low cabinet under a window.

Laughing, Namrasit snarled in Adam's face, *"You're next, goddamned fool!"* Adam recoiled at the demon's sulfur-ladened breath and glanced at Fr. Cahill. Adam figured he only had to keep the demon occupied and away from the altar where Fr. Cahill was administering communion. Holding a small Host between his thumb and forefinger, Fr. Cahill laid it on a kneeling Gabriel's tongue.

At that moment the demon twirled the guandao and thrust the spear end at Adam's neck, but, in a blink of an eye, Adam deflected the thrust with his shillelagh and the spear penetrated the cabinet's wooden drawers and got stuck.

As fast as he could, Adam dropped below the stuck shaft, rolled into the clear, got to his feet, and with all his strength swung the knob end of his shillelagh into the demon's back. The knob connected this time with the protruding spine from which black vapor exploded. Clearly feeling the pain, Namrasit arched away from the strike and his form dissipated and completely disappeared.

Adam was elated, but as soon as he thought it was time to celebrate, he felt the demonic dread behind him. He turned in time to see the vapor coalescing until the hellish beast was again fully constituted and raring to fight.

But for Adam there was hope. The ghostly malevolent was vulnerable. Instantly, not waiting for Namrasit to attack, Adam did. He jabbed the shillelagh's pointed end into one of the demon's eye sockets. It was not entirely vapor and Adam felt the substance give way when he shoved his stick even deeper.

Deep red vapor poured out like blood, a deep wound. Namrasit whirled away from Adam and with its mouth open attempted to suck in the expelled nutrients that were lost. The hemorrhage and the demon's reaction revealed a key vulnerability to Adam.

Adam glanced back at Fr. Cahill who, oblivious to Adam's battle with the ghost, walked to a kneeling Rev. Williams and, pinching a small Host between his thumb and forefinger, presented it to the Methodist minister.

Fr. Dimitri stepped forward and registered his objection about giving communion to a Protestant.

Cahill glared at Dimitri, shook his head, and turned back to Williams. Adam could faintly hear the exchange.

"May the Body of our Lord Jesus Christ preserve thy soul unto everlasting life."

Williams put out his hand.

"Your tongue, pastor," said Fr. Cahill.

Williams opened his mouth and presented his tongue, upon which Cahill deposited the Host, and Rev. Williams consumed the Body of his Lord.

With the demon occupied and perhaps fatally wounded, Adam made a move to kneel before Cahill. But Namrasit, with one wounded eye, suddenly rematerialized in front of Adam and blocked his path. Without hesitation, the demon swung its guandao blade at Adam's chest, slicing open his shirt and slicing the skin beneath, drawing blood.

Adam backed away, wiped his chest, and saw on his hand the blood, now rapidly soaking his shirt. The demon's recovery and Adam's wound only served to embolden Adam. If he was to die, then it would not be for nothing. He would take this cursed entity with him and send him home to hell. With renewed strength, from whence it came he knew not, Adam backed Namrasit up with repeated swings and thrusts of his shillelagh, persistently passing the stick through parts of the violent visage, apparently causing its dark essence in the form of thick black fumes to leak from the specter's innards.

Gathering its energy, Namrasit was able to dodge many of Adam's thrusts, and when the opportunity rose, retaliated and speared Adam in the side, drawing the human's red blood, and again soaking his shirt.

Fr. Cahill was administering communion to Eve and Sam. Namrasit saw this as well and parried Adam's shillelagh in an effort to get to Cahill.

Adam, however, worked to position himself between the demon and the priest, hoping to avoid yet another wound. Adam smashed, slugged, and slammed his shillelagh into the beast, often extracting and dissipating small snatches of black essence. Namrasit, expertly turning the guandao end-for-end, stabbed, swiped, and sliced the farmer, adding to the blood already absorbed by his clothes.

By the constant parry and crossing, shifting and backing, attacking and retreating…Adam, unknowingly, backed himself into a corner. At that point, Namrasit made a hard connection with Adam's legs, causing him to fall to his back and land on the sharp edges of broken pottery.

Namrasit, now weakened, but seeing the advantage, loomed over the wounded and equally weakened Adam, who was leaning on his side, his neck fully exposed—a clear invitation for the razor-sharp blade of Namrasit's guandao. Seeing the opportunity, the demon shifted to its right to get a clear shot at delivering the lethal blow, decapitating Adam and ending his earthly existence. Adam, unable to move due to his multiple wounds, saw this. His only thought was a quiet prayer: *Lord have mercy.*

Suddenly, Eve appeared at his side, seemingly unaware of the visage. "Papa, what's wrong?" She tried to help him up, but her hand came in contact with the blood draining from his side. She stopped and gazed at the blood on her hand. Suddenly, her expression changed as she became fully aware of the danger.

At the same time Adam, still lying wounded on the floor amidst broken china and pottery, watched Namrasit with its guandao rear up above them both, ready to strike. Quickly, he pushed Eve out of the blade's strike zone, but in doing so she wiped her blood-covered hand across his face. She looked at him. Overwhelmed by the blood on his face that came from her hand, she fell back and looked up.

For the first time she saw their scourge, the being she had called the Wizard, preparing his guandao for the lethal blow. His lipless mouth widened into a mischievous grin and revealed the razor sharp teeth that had gnawed and clipped their linens for the last three years.

Adam knew what she was seeing, and wondered why her reaction was so reserved. She lay still next to him among the splintered pottery and pools of his blood, and just stared up at the demon that had summoned hell into their home. And then...

SHE SCREAMED!

But the scream was not a scream of fear. She was not afraid. It was an attack, a willful shriek, a righteous shout, a loud and purposeful solicitation, a prayer of intense supplication. Her assault was so loud that Adam momentarily forgot the sorrow he had accepted for his failure as a man and his looming execution.

Time abruptly came to a halt, and in that short moment of eternity the scream was answered.

Namrasit balked in his down-swing, swiveled his guandao blade to the side, and leaned in close to "see" from whence the scream emanated.

At first Adam thought that it was perhaps instinct, but later he realized that it was more likely part of the eternal answer that the scream invoked. Still on his back, the fear and acceptance of his plight vanished and anger took hold. It was a righteous anger, a confident strength he had never felt before. With it came a calm assurance that although he was on his back and moments from certain death, he was at a great advantage.

Without thinking, his two hands found the shillelagh, pointed it at their visitor from hell, and thrust it into the demon's good eye, shoved it all the way through the back of Namrasit's virtual skull.

The eye exploded in a massive, thick plume of red and black vapor. In shock, as before, the specter whirled about and with its mouth began to suck in the remnant of its substance, but it was clear that the demon could no longer see as it flailed about seeking to reconstitute its demonic presence.

Adam, the bloody mess that he was, wasted no time. With Eve's help he crawled out of the corner to Fr. Cahill. The floor still quaked, the black vapor still swirled with the whirlwind, wagons and stampeding horses still circled the house, and back in the corner of the room the demon known as Cyn Namrasit scurried blindly to save its unholy honor.

Awkwardly, Adam kneeled before his priest, who presented a Host to the farmer: "May the Body of our Lord Jesus Christ preserve thy soul unto everlasting life."

"Amen," said Adam. He opened his mouth and presented his tongue.

Very slowly and reverently, Fr. Cahill laid the unblemished Host on the tongue of the blemished farmer who sought redemption.

At the moment the Host landed on Adam's tongue, the demon in the corner turned blindly to Adam and in the otherworldly voice, strained and raging against the forced confession, declared:

> *Cursed this land not long ago*
> *Stranger's mad oath neglected*
> *Mayfield murdered now below*
> *Toil for his soul rejected*
> *Bones beneath the cairn lo*
> *Eventually extracted*
> *Sanctify the land and sow*
> *His holiness requested.*
> *I go.*

Suddenly, the swirling, searching specter of vapor denigrated in a silent explosion, the wagons and stampeding horses no longer circled the house, the black vapor dissolved into nothingness, the whirlwind ceased, and the floor no longer quaked.

The exorcism was complete.

10

Namrasit's declaration wasn't exactly a premonition, but Adam knew exactly what it meant, and it required action. He had long thought the haunting manifestations were the sole consequence of the Stranger's curse because he and Mary Ann refused to find the dying man a priest. In some way that may have been true, for the hauntings began shortly thereafter. But the Stranger's curse was evidently not the only reason. The soil of his land, namely the thirty-five acres that were under contention in the land office years ago, had been cursed long before he arrived. There was in that soil, under the last cairn he, Sam, and Henry removed, the bones of a murdered man—a man named Mayfield who owned a deed to the land before him. The demon had murdered the man and somehow buried him on the property, cursing it. It just needed the right conditions, a second curse from a priest, to trigger everything. As soon as they cleaned up the gathering hall, he would need Fr. Cahill to perform one more blessing.

After Fr. Cahill and Fr. Dimitri finished the liturgy and the group attempted to clean up the destruction, Adam experienced another premonition. Although he was only arms length from the others, they neither saw nor heard any of it. Yet they knew something was happening. For suddenly, as he held a small crate of broken pottery, Adam fell into a trance of some minutes long. It was not a flash but a transcendent translation.

When the trance released him, he told his friends that he saw something disturbing and he heard a Voice. It was not the otherworldly Voice of the demon, but a gentle, loving, angelic voice. No one else heard it, just as no one else but Eve saw the Wizard. But the Voice told him something no one else could have known, and with the message came an urgency.

Mayfield's bones would have to wait.

Chapter 53
A Priest Forever

1

Richard McSherry knew he was dying. He did not envy Adam Livingston's problems with haunting ghosts, but it seemed to Richard that his own life was haunted just the same. It had been over six weeks since he had cut his hand in a fit of anger. The hand wound had not healed. It had become infected and the infection had spread, contributing he was sure, to the serious decline of his health. Ironically, the worsening illness provided an excuse to avoid Mass and confession, for which he was thankful. How he was going to resolve this in the long run, since he still considered himself a man of devout faith, he knew not. Further, how he was going to attend to his investments, which required travel of which he had done none over the past month, was another problem he had put off.

Anastasia had insisted he have a doctor call, but he had no faith in the so-called medical profession. Over the years in Jamaica and a few times here in the States, when he had ushered a doctor to the bedside of a sick friend or associate the results were pretty much the same—the patient got sicker and sometimes died. Doctors claimed to be on the cutting edge of science, but to him they were cutting open their patients and bleeding them to death. He would have nothing to do with them. Let God do with him as the Almighty pleased, but please keep doctors away. They were no benefit *to* him, but they always sought benefits *from* him—whether a pence, a shilling, or a pound.

Of course, the haunting of his illness was related to the haunting which caused it—the secret relationship of his close friend, priest, and ecclesial partner Fr. Denis Cahill with Letitia McCartney, who was now his wife's close friend, nanny, and boarder. He had seen Fr. Denis and Letitia passionately embracing next to the confessional. It was not a brotherly-sisterly embrace by any means. Their wandering hands and lips repulsed him. The glimpse was burned into his memory. It was something he could not not see, and recalling the image late at night strangled his sleep. Confirmation of their illicit romance had led to the cut on his hand. It had also angered him to the point of rejecting anything and everything associated with Mister Denis Cahill. Thus, Richard, in avoiding the man, avoided Cahill's Mass and his confessional.

Confounding the haunting of Denis and Letitia's failings was Richard's grasp of their uncommon strengths. Letitia had proven time and time again her loyalty and willingness to sacrifice her time and personal resources for the care and compassion of others. Denis was like that as well, and no doubt that was one reason for their attraction to each other. Letitia was unusual in this regard. While she was more attractive than most women her age, and while she was attentive of her appearance and cleanliness, there was no pretense to protect herself when another was in need. She was at once self-assured and sacrificial. Anastasia had remarked on this several times and he had witnessed it as well. She would don a pretty dress and do her hair to perfection, then think nothing of being dirtied and soiled when tending joyfully to the needs of their boys. He was reminded of this, and guilt ridden, when without hesitation she ripped her expensive petticoat and bloodied her Sunday dress to tend to his wound. In this way he understood Denis' attraction to her character. Although there was a naturalness to their attraction, the impropriety of it gave him no peace.

Denis also created a haunting that Richard could not resolve. Here was a man, a priest, and a resolute champion of the Church. He also took little, if any, regard for himself. Yes, he presented himself well. He was orderly, dignified, friendly, and a man of devout faith, knowledge, and natural intelligence (although he was only a fair homilist). He was persevering and confident, sometimes to a fault, but rarely. Richard understood how women could be attracted to such a man. He was, after all an Irish bachelor, and, in the romantic sense of the word, much like himself. Anastasia had confided in Richard that had Denis not been a priest when she met him she would have easily considered an offer of marriage from him, had one been forthcoming. She said he was adventuresome (like Richard), handsome (like Richard), and was even a bit cute with his red hair and stubble beard. Richard, however, was not cute, as she put it. He was a gentleman, suave, and debonair—a much better combination for her fancy hats. She also told Richard she was much happier with Richard than she could have been with Denis. When he asked why, she said, "Because, my dear, you're rich and he's not." And then she giggled, sat on his lap, and kissed him. All of that aside, Denis was, as Fr. Dimitri said, a man of robust and uncommonly stout faith. Richard saw this firsthand when Denis chased off the Livingston demon. It was a scary episode that Richard would never forget. The image left in Richard's mind was of Denis hitting the demon on the head with his aspergillum, as if Denis Cahill was a strict school headmaster and the demon was a belligerent rapscallion. There was no doubt who was in charge. Richard had great respect for Fr. Dimitri. But when confronting evil, as Denis had done many times in his life, Fr. Dimitri held no candle to Denis. Regardless of his virtues, that this robust man of God was in an illicit relationship with a beautiful maiden, who lived in his house no less, bothered him greatly.

Richard heard two buggies and several horses come into the yard. "Anastasia," he called out weakly. "Have they returned?"

After a moment she came into the bedroom. "It appears so, and Adam Livingston is with them."

"Are there two buggies? It sounds like two buggies and several horses."

"Yes, it's Gabriel and Fr. Denis in one, and Fr. Dimitri drove a second buggy with Adam Livingston. Count Samuel was reined behind."

"Do give them some Madeira. Then have them come see me," he said.

"Of course, dear."

Richard was eager to know what had happened. He heard the men come into the house and the various greetings and voices of the women and his boys. Their tone was reserved but genuine and polite, as if the venture had been successful, or nearly so. There was the usual shuffling of feet, the removal of boots, the clinking of goblets, silence, and compliments on the beverage.

Soon Anastasia entered the small room with a smile on her face, and behind her crowded in Fr. Dimitri and Denis, both in their black cassocks, and Adam Livingston. Each of the men held a half-consumed goblet of Madeira, but none of them were smiling.

They gazed down at him with the most serious and even deathly appearances. Well, he thought, he felt about as good as they looked. He knew he was not well. His head throbbed, his skin was feverish, his throat was raw, which made it difficult to talk, and he was so fatigued that Anastasia had to bring him a pan, since there was no way he could even get out of bed.

Denis worked his way to the side of the bed and sat on it. "Richard, how are you?"

"What kind of question is that to ask of a man in my condition?" said Richard in a strained whisper. "You can see how I am, can't you?"

"Yes, but...."

"But nothing," interrupted Richard. "How did it go? Adam, tell me, what happened?" Richard suddenly opened his eyes wide and took a second long look at Adam. His hand and face were bandaged, and he was stooped over.

"Mister Livingston," said Fr. Dimitri pulling up a chair, "here, sit down." Fr. Dimitri turned to Richard. "We had a battle of sorts, and Adam took a beating."

"And...?" said Richard waiting for the blow-by-blow account.

"It appears we were successful," said Denis. "Time will tell."

"But what happened to you, Adam?" asked Richard.

Adam looked weary but eager. "I'm not sure how to explain it."

Fr. Dimitri interrupted. "His gathering hall was practically destroyed by the haunting spirit who tried to stop the liturgy. Mister Livingston placed himself repeatedly between the demon and the altar where Fr. Denis celebrated. And, well...it departed, maybe it's even destroyed. We don't know; like Father says," and he gestured at Denis, "only time will tell."

"Richard," said Adam in a much more robust voice than his appearance called for, "they are being modest. The Wizard is gone. I know so, and in one very significant way. And that's the reason I've come to see you."

It was as if Adam had just delivered the preface for a Greek play. Denis rose from the side of the bed where he had been seated, and moved with Fr. Dimitri aside, giving Adam the stage, so to speak.

Adam sipped his wine and put the goblet down on a side table. Although shaky, he stood, hobbled to the foot of the bed, and gripped the brass bed rail. "Richard, I don't think I've told you this, but most of my life, even as a child, I've been plagued with premonitions. Some folk call them visions. I never talked about them because I was embarrassed. The few times I told my parents or a friend, they thought I was nuts. The visions were always strange and some I couldn't even describe. But one thing about them never changed. They always preceded some event that in looking back predicted what was to happen. I had one before my first wife died. I saw my neighbor's farm burn one time in a vision, but I didn't know it was my neighbor, or that his farm was in danger. The same thing before my barn burned. I could not have told you it was a barn burning or that it was mine. I had several surrounding the Wizard's hauntings, and one very scary one before Martha and George died. I saw all these things, but they weren't that clear. You remember when I told you, or was it Anastasia, about the dreams I had of a man in robes performing some kind of incantation. That was a premonition I had about Fr. Denis, as you know now. It was one of the few times when I saw a clear face in the dream, and it matched a real person. Only in looking back did I see the connection. It was as if God were trying to warn me and tell me something was going to happen, or that I should do something. It was like an angel was sent to tell me something, but he was blocked, or he spoke to me, but there was too much noise for me to hear the message clearly. Now I know this is true, and I know that the Wizard is gone...because...after the hauntings disappeared today, because of Fr. Denis' liturgy, I had another premonition. But it wasn't mysterious, or vague. Nor was it obscured like all the others. It happened while we were cleaning up the gathering hall. There was no trigger. But suddenly I was at a funeral. Before I would have visions of people but their faces were obscured. But what happened a little while ago was much different. Like I said, I was at a funeral, and I recognized everyone. Anastasia was there, your three boys were there. Fr. Denis and Fr. Dimitri were there. I was there with my family. It was very scary and very real."

"Whose funeral was it?" asked Richard.

Adam hesitated. "It was yours. I saw you laid out on a table. They were getting ready to put you in a coffin and nail on the lid. Everything was perfectly clear."

Richard froze. As weak as he felt, he believed what Adam was telling him. It is what he had been feeling for days. He was going to die.

"And then a voice came to me," Adam continued. "It was very clear. It was a soft, kind, and gentle...a man's voice. And it said to me,

> *Now that the resistance is gone from your life, Adam Livingston,*
> *and I am no longer obstructed, I can speak to you clearly. Go*
> *immediately to Richard McSherry, for he is close to death. Tell*
> *him that he must confess his sins to his priest, else he shall die and*
> *bring great sorrow on his family. He has neglected the sacraments.*

He must neglect them no more. Do not hesitate. Do not doubt me. Richard McSherry is at death's door, but he can be saved if he does this.

And then it was gone. The voice and the vision left me standing…holding a crate of broken pottery. We came right away, so I could tell you this."

Richard was awestruck. He said nothing for a long time, although his lips quivered as if he wanted to speak. Although this was the first time he had been admonished for neglecting the sacraments, he did not need to hear it to know it was true. For his conscience had convicted him weeks ago.

But hearing the admonition was new for Anastasia. After a moment she broke down in tears, hurried to Richard's bedside and buried her face in the crook of his neck. "Oh Richard. Richard. My dear, dear Richard. Oh, how I love you, Richard. Thank you, God Almighty, for my Richard." She sobbed for some few minutes as the three men looked on. Then, slowly, she raised up. Her eyes were red as they looked down on him and said through her sobs, "God is so good, Richard. Not only did he tell you this, but he sent not one, but two priests to you."

By now, Richard also had tears in his eyes. There was no debate. He had been conflicted, convicted, and found out. He would obey. "Anastasia, my dear, I love you. Please leave us now. Fr. Dimitri? Will you hear my confession?"

Fr. Dimitri was taken aback. He turned and stared at Denis, who looked as if he had just been betrayed by a good friend. Denis, however, only shrugged, lowered his head, and said, "Adam. Anastasia. Let's give them some privacy," and gestured to the door for them to leave. After they left the room, he left as well, and shut the door behind him.

Richard lowered his eyes and said to Fr. Dimitri, "I'm ready, Father."

Fr. Dimitri wavered. "No, you're not," he said and then nonchalantly sipped his Madeira. "I am not going to hear your confession."

"But, you just heard…."

*"I heard that you need to confess, but not to me. Rather to *your* priest, *your* confessor, who is familiar with your weaknesses and can counsel away your weaknesses and guide you to spiritual strength."

"There is no rubric that I must confess to the same priest. It can be any priest."

"Perhaps. Why will you not confess to Fr. Denis?"

"He's no longer a priest."

"Really? Is this something you've decided? Have you told God? Maybe the Almighty would like to know what you know and he doesn't. He's not real happy being left out, you know."

"I know what I know."

"Based on what I just saw at Livingston's he's a more priest than I am."

Richard clammed up, miffed at the opposition. Finally, "Why won't you hear my confession?"

"Because I know something you don't know, and I think you need to let Fr. Denis know what you think you know, so he can know it, and give you absolution."

They stared at each other for a few moments.

"Or," continued Fr. Dimitri, "you can die in your sins."

"You would let me do that?"

"I have no say in it, really. It's ultimately between you and God. I'm only the messenger." Fr. Dimitri let that sink in, then... "Shall I go get *your* priest so you can do this properly?"

"He's a sinner, Father. He's abdicated his office. My confession to him would be invalid."

Fr. Dimitri glared at the man on his death bed. "Richard," said Fr. Dimitri holding up his wine goblet, "whose wine glass is this?"

"What does that mean?"

"Humor me. Whose wine glass, and whose wine is this?

Richard wasn't into playing word games. Annoyed, he said, "It's my wife's glass and I suppose your wine now that you've tasted it."

"And it's good wine, too. Madeira, is it?"

"Yes," replied the miffed man on his death bed.

Fr. Dimitri finished off the wine. "I don't want to make too much of a mess, but..." and he dropped the goblet on the floor where it shattered.

"Holy Mary," blasphemed Richard. "Why did you do that?"

"Whose glass is it now?" said Fr. Dimitri

"I shall make you pay for that. But until you do, it's still my wife's and the wine is clearly and wholly yours now that it's in you."

"So the wine is consumed and the glass is broken. Neither exist in their prior state. But their ownership and substance is still the same. Even if it's broken, and now out of service, the glass is Anastasia's."

"Yes, so what's your point?" demanded Richard.

"Just this, and forgive me a little, for analogies all break down at some point. Whether or not the goblet appears unblemished and is put into the cook's service, or dirty and in need of washing, scratched and in need of burnishing, or broken and out of service, the glass is still a goblet, even if a broken goblet. Likewise, a priest is a priest forever, even if he appears blemished, or if his life seems dirty and in need of confession, or scratched and in need of discipline, or if he breaks and is no longer in service. Regardless, the goblet is still the goblet, and the priest is still a priest. If that weren't so, there would be no priests. For, like Fr. Denis, I too am a sinner.... He paused. "And so is the pope. Amen."

"So you're still not going to hear my confession?" asked Richard wearily.

"Nope...but Fr. Denis will."

There was a long pause as Richard tried to sit up in bed a bit more. He coughed a couple of times, looked out the window in disgust, stared back at Fr.

Dimitri, and finally dropped his head in defeat.

"All right, all right. You've worn me out…even more than I was. But I don't think it's going to help."

"Time will tell," said Fr. Dimitri as he knelt down, picked up the larger pieces of broken glass in his fingers, brushed the smaller pieces into his hand, and left the room.

A few minutes later—enough time for Richard to examine his conscience—Fr. Denis entered the bedroom and closed the door behind him. A confessional stole was draped about his neck and he was holding a cruet of oil. "Sorry," said Fr. Denis, "but Fr. Dimitri didn't have his stole with him."

"How could that possibly be so?" said Richard, "He lives here and all his vestments with him."

Fr. Denis shrugged his shoulders, pulled over the chair Adam had been sitting in, and sat down next to Richard's bedside. "Richard, since you have missed quite a few Masses, I need to hear your confession. Then I want to anoint you with oil for your sickness. And finally, I have brought you the Eucharist. Shall we begin?"

"Yes, let's begin," said Richard, fully surrendering and closing his eyes, for he was exhausted from the verbal and mental gymnastics.

Richard's confession was fairly benign, except he confessed missing Mass during the early part of his illness when he could have attended. He confessed being repeatedly short-tempered with Anastasia this past month; he confessed harboring bitterness toward a close friend and business partner; and he confessed holding back his tithe from the Church.

"Did you apologize to your wife for your short temper and make it up to her in some sacrificial way so that her days go smoother?"

"I will, Father."

"Does your business partner know of your bitterness toward him? Did you do anything unfair or untoward to him that there is a need to personally face him and ask his forgiveness?"

"Probably. Must I?"

"Let's be thorough about it for the sake of eternity. Yes, you should."

Richard took a deep breath. "I will, Father."

"Have you made up your tithe to the Church?"

"I'll give it to you before you leave."

"Is there anything else you'd like to confess?"

"No, Father."

"Good, now make a good Irish act of contrition."

"Aye, Father. O my God, I am heartily sorry for having offended Thee: and I detest my sins most sincerely because they displease Thee, my God, Who art so deserving of all my love for Thy infinite goodness and most amiable perfections; and I firmly purpose by Thy holy grace never more to offend Thee."

Fr. Denis extended his hands over Richard's bowed head and said,

> *"Deus, Pater misericordiárum...God, the Father of mercies,*
> *through the death and resurrection of his Son has reconciled the*
> *world to himself and sent the Holy Spirit among us for the for-*
> *giveness of sins; through the ministry of the Church may God give*
> *you pardon and peace, and I absolve you from all your sins in the*
> *name of the Father, and of the Son, and of the Holy Spirit,"*

At the end, Fr. Denis made the sign of the cross over Richard.

"Amen," said Richard.

"Now, let me anoint you with oil for your sickness," said Fr. Denis and he retrieved the cruet of oil he had brought into the house.

But Richard stopped him. "Wait!" A sudden rush of warmth flowed through Richard's body. It started in his head and flowed quickly to his toes. His headache evaporated, he cleared his throat. There was no pain. "I feel better, suddenly," he said. With a shiver up and down his spine his skin chills disappeared. His malaise and fatigue faded. Richard put out his hand and gripped Fr. Cahill's forearm. His strength was back. He had not been able to get out of bed for weeks, and suddenly he found himself throwing off his covers and swinging his legs out of the bed. Fr. Cahill jumped off the chair and stood up.

"Yes, I know," said Richard. "I need a bath. But look...I don't need to be anointed." He stood up and stretched. His voice was back. "ANASTASIA," he yelled with joy, "COME HERE." Anastasia rushed into the room, along with Fr. Dimitri and Adam. "I'm well." He was not surprised that they were stunned. He was stunned. "Adam," he said. "You saved my life. Thank you, and you, too, Fr. Dimitri." He turned to Anastasia. "My darling, I am famished; it feels like I haven't eaten in days."

"Well, look at you," cried Anastasia, "you haven't. You're skinny as a sapling. I'll fix you something right away."

"No, don't," said Richard. "I need to do it, for you. I've treated you badly these past weeks. I can make it up to you a little. I'll fix supper for all of us."

"Fr. Cahill," said Anastasia, "don't put away that oil. We may need it yet."

"Okay, now leave me alone to get dressed," said Richard.

"How about I first bring you a wash basin?" said Anastasia.

"Okay, okay. Now you all leave, except Fr. Denis, I need to talk to him a bit more."

Everyone left except Fr. Denis, who remarked, "In all my days of hearing confessions, I have never seen anything like this."

"Do not tease me, Father. Neither have I. But I am sure I'm okay. When you came I could barely talk and when I did, my throat burned. I could not sit up. I haven't been out of bed for weeks. I'm healed. Adam Livingston must be someone very special."

"Yes, I think you are right."

"Now, I need to make a confession to you as a man, not my priest. You are the business partner I have been embittered toward."

Fr. Denis was surprised. "I did not know that. I heard you had cut yourself, of course, and that the infection took over your body."

"But you need to know how I cut myself."

"Okay, how?"

"I am embarrassed to tell you this. But maybe you already knew. I suspected that you and a certain lady..."

Fr. Denis held up his hand to interrupt. "Yes, it is true. But how did you know, or how did you cut yourself?"

"The answer is one and the same," said Richard. "Six weeks ago, when I was in line for you to hear my confession, there in the St. Agnes rectory foyer, it was Letitia's turn and she went in before me. I had been suspecting that the two of you were romantically involved. She couldn't take her eyes off you whenever you were near, and you seemed to enjoy her attention. But I didn't know for sure. So, that Sunday, while she was in confession with you, I went outside and sneaked around the rectory pretending to examine the foundation of the building. I'm a trustee, you know. I looked through that window in the back and saw the two of you embraced, kissing, and...you know. That confirmed my suspicion, and I instantly became very angry and bitter with you. That is why at first I refused to come to confession, come to Mass, and earlier today not let you bless me with Holy Water. I didn't believe you were any longer a priest. After all we had been through together, in anger I threw a rock down the hillside. It had a sharp edge to it, and I sliced open my hand. Do you know who bandaged it up without knowing how it happened?"

"Yes, she told me," Fr. Denis said, then paused and hung his head. "I'm very sorry you saw that. It was wrong for me in many ways. I violated my promise to be chaste. If it is any consolation to you, I have already confessed this to Fr. Dimitri and received absolution. He knows. But I need to have a longer session with him. There is more detail I need to get off my conscience."

"Will you forgive me for my bitterness toward you?" asked Richard.

"Of course I do," said Fr. Denis. "Can you forgive me for my violation of a sacred trust?"

"Yes, I do."

The two men briefly embraced. When they released each other, Richard noticed that Fr. Denis was holding his breath.

"What are you going to do?" asked Richard.

"I don't know, exactly...but you need to bathe."

Richard laughed.

"I need to talk with Fr. Dimitri," said Fr. Denis. "Let me do that now. Then you need to eat. Your time of fasting is over."

Richard did indeed *fix supper that night for the entire family and their guests, although it was Anastasia that supervised and hovered over the operation—stirring and seasoning the stew and taking the apple pie out of the oven before the crust burned. Present around the table were the three McSherry boys, Richard, Fr. Dimitri, and Fr. Denis. Sitting next to Fr. Denis was Letitia, then Adam, Gabriel Menghini, and Catharine, who rarely sat down as it was her turn to serve. As they were finishing up the apple pie, which was delicious, although Adam thought it needed a bit of Ceylon cinnamon, Fr. Denis made an announcement:

"My time with you and working especially with Richard has been rewarding in many ways. One particular reward has been seeing you three boys grow up. You know if it wasn't for me, you three wouldn't be here."

The boys looked at Fr. Denis like he was nuts. "Is that true, Mama?" asked Richard, Jr.

Anastasia smiled, took a deep breath, winked at Richard and said, "Yes, dear, Father is quite right. I'll explain later."

Fr. Denis continued. "God has blessed and protected me here." He looked to Adam, "and given me experiences that I will never forget but never want to experience again."

The men who were at the Livingston house for Mass laughed.

"But it is time to move on."

The room went silent...and everyone stared at their favorite family priest. Fr. Denis smiled broadly at the boys.

"Tomorrow I will write Bishop Carroll and resign from the priesthood. Day after tomorrow, Letitia and I will make a visit to the Berkeley County courthouse and post our *marriage bond."

There were gasps around the table. He took Letitia's hand under the table and smiled at her. Embarrassed but happy, she gazed back at him, then dipped her head and blushed

"You are the first to know, and we hope you'll come to our wedding. Plans to be announced."

2

William Zane rushed into his boss's office with a diplomatic pouch fresh off a ship from the docks.

Bishop John Carroll sat at his desk talking with Monsignor Nagot. In the bishop's hands were two letters, which William recognized as having been placed in the bishop's mail stack earlier that morning.

"Mister Zane," said the bishop. "You'll find this interesting, even scandalous. You recall how we sent Fr. Gallitzin to Smithfield to investigate Fr. Cahill's so-called haunted house, and how we prohibited Cahill from performing the exorcism, which, of course, we didn't really believe was needed. Well, we've got two sneaky priests to deal with. In this letter," the bishop held up his left hand, "Gallitzin not only confirms Cahill's claim of a demonic spirit that possessed this Protestant's house, but recounts a horrific exorcism Mass in the Livingston gathering hall, celebrated by Cahill with Gallitzin as deacon."

The bishop shook his head in disgust.

"Evidently, it nearly destroyed the house in the process. I called Monsignor in here to figure out how we're going to deal with this. We were talking about ways to isolate Cahill before he gets us into more trouble. And then, I glance at my desk and here's a letter from the rogue himself. I just opened it up. Are you ready for this? Cahill writes:

> My Dear Lord Carroll,
>
> I am compelled to address your Reverence because a continu-ation of silence on my part regarding the point of this letter would be criminal. Thanks to divine Providence it seems right and good to inform you that I resign my obligations as priest in Shepherd's Town and will in the coming weeks take the hand of a compas-sionate and supportive woman in marriage...

"This is hard to fathom," said the bishop. "Why does the Almighty in his omni-science and potency do this to me? Not one scandal but two, and at the hands of the same malignancy."

"But your Excellency," said William, "he's solved your problem. He's no lon-ger a priest if he resigns and gets married."

"My dear young man, you don't understand. Denis Cahill is a priest forever. Even if he's no longer active in a parish he can oblige us more trouble."

Monsignor interrupted. "Unless he goes back to Ireland and there's no re-cord as to why."

"That's Monsignor's solution," said the bishop. "Sweep it all under the car-pet, put his return to Ireland in the official history, and pretend neither hap-pened."

"Well, you can't erase the exorcism," said Monsignor. "According to Gallitz-in there were plenty of witnesses over the past years to the "disruptive spirit," as he puts it, and there were witnesses at the exorcism Mass. But you might be able to obscure the marriage as a footnote in history."

"What do you think, William?" asked the bishop.

"Might work. Shall I have Dr. Faucette come see you? He's the historian that keeps the archives up to date."

"Yes, why don't you do that." The bishop reached for the diplomatic pouch. "Now what have you here? Another scandal?"

William handed the pouch to his bishop, who opened it up and read the document inside. After a moment...

"Monsignor," said the bishop. "Remember how we were joking a minute ago...wondering where the Livingston demon had been dispatched, now that it's no longer wanted in Smithfield?"

"Yes, what is it?"

"This is from Cardinal Krupp of the Vatican Diplomatic Corp. He's seeking our help. I think we know where Livingston's demon absconded. William, get my carriage. I must see General, ah, President Washington immediately. Vatican City has been occupied by Napoleon's forces. Pius the Sixth has been imprisoned."

Chapter 54
Some Will Scoff at You

My Lord Maréchal,

My story is concluded, but of course the lives of the actors continued. Several days after these events, I joined Adam Livingston and Sam Dark as they found the location of the final cairn they had disassembled, having used the stones for a wall along the Charles Town Road. They did not have to dig far before they came upon the bony remains of a man with remnants of clothes and boots still intact. The man's skull had been crushed as if hit by a large object. Adam believed they belonged to Alexander Mayfield, who was listed on his deed as a previous owner of the disputed thirty-five acre parcel. They carefully removed the bones, whereupon I blessed the ground with Holy Water. We then reverently reburied the remains in a new grave next to the Stranger's in the woods. We then honored the man with a brief burial rite that I conducted.

When I returned to Conewago, *I took with me samples of the clippings from the sample box next to Livingston's front door. They were the center of intense interest for awhile, until my *superior found fit to burn them. They had become a distraction, if not an invitation for the influence of evil in our ministry.

For several years after we had celebrated the exorcism Mass in Livingston's house, Adam and his family were visited by a *disembodied Voice that was almost always accompanied by a bright light. The Voice catechized the family in the Roman faith. Who belonged to this gentle, kind, but insistent Voice is open to speculation. Some believe it was Fr. Xavier who had returned from the dead, for the Voice claimed to have once been in the flesh like Adam. Among other things, the Voice told them "all the sighs and tears of the whole world put together were not worth so much as one Mass in which a pure God was offered up to God," and "one Mass was more acceptable to God than if the whole world was in sackcloth and ashes." The Voice also warned them of impending world events, or the illness or death of neighbors, or how a particular person was still suffering in the flames of purgatory over some sin in their life. The Voice would lead the family in prayers for hours at a time for the person's release. It was not uncommon for the Voice to tell Adam of people in need and urge him and his family to tend to the need, which Adam always did.

Mrs. Livingston, however, was of a different character. Although she was present at Fr. Cahill's instruction, at the baptisms, witnessed the results of the blessing and the exorcism, and heard the Voice as often as the others, she played both the victim and villain to Adam's heroism. This made her unpopular with those that knew about the manifestations, which was just about everyone within a day's ride. About a year after the exorcism, Mrs. Livingston was publicly excoriated in the Potowmack Guardian with a letter written by *Rev. Lawrence Sylvester (L. Silo) Phelan, who had been installed by Bishop Carroll in Hagerstown after Fr. Cahill's removal. As you will read, Fr. Phelan was of the opposite persuasion to my own; and no, he never talked with me or Fr. Cahill nor asked of our experience.

*August 29, 1798

> Few there are in Martinsburg or Winchester but have heard of Livingston's ghosts and revelations. In returning to my Hagerstown parish from Martinsburg, it was mere curiosity to visit the little town called Wizard Clip (also known as Smithfield), where I visited Livingston and his wife. The visit was instructive. I concluded that over these past years the unaccountable events had been imposed upon the man, who was simple in appearance, by his wife, who in my opinion is the ghost herself, along with the assistance of some other knavish hussies of the neighborhood. She has played on the poor old man, her husband. The whole affair was an imposture. Whatever may have been the motive of the actors, they have been discovered, and are now made public as an homage due to truth. Let the public now judge who was the devil that burnt L's barn and played so many wicked pranks on his family. For my part, I am now satisfied that L's wife, and not Gorman the adulterer and the hussy he keeps, was the chief actor in this unfavorable plot.

> —Fr. Lawrence Sylvester Phelan, Catholic Priest of Hagerstown

Two weeks later the Potowmack Guardian published this letter from Mrs. Livingston:

*September 12, 1798 (Published)

> Ask Mr. Phelan why he said, when he visited us, that he was sent by the bishop to visit Livingston's family in this troubled situation, and now states in his piece, "it was mere curiosity" that brought him from his business in Martinsburg to "the little town called Wizard Clip." For my part, whatever the one who sent him might have said, whether true or false, I believe it to be from one well instructed in the pernicious doctrines of the Romish tenet. I now take the liberty of stating to the Public, that the trouble still remains in Livingston's family, at times, in a greater or less degree, in spite of the priestly art. Whatever it is, it is wonderful and unaccountable to the most penetrating mind. Aided by priestcraft,

the affair has been most unhappy for me. It has been the means of secluding me from the business of my family, the embraces of an affectionate husband, and fixed me as an object of public contempt. However, it is finally thought, if Priests and Spirits could frighten me to relinquish my claim to my lawful thirds of Adam Livingston's estate, the Public ear would be no longer thus amused, but this I leave for time to prove.

—Mary Ann Livingston, Smithfield, Sept 6, 1798.

I am well convinced that Mrs. Livingston's reference to "the trouble still remains" refers to the Voice that continued to instruct them in the Catholic faith, for she endeavored by every means in her power to falsify it. She used to say she was the Judas, for the haunts of Namrasit were no more. The Voice told her, *"If she would not submit to the rules of the Roman Catholic Church, she would open up her eyes in Hell." The Voice also told her that she would die in her own house. She was so often rebuked by it that she would not stay at home, but went to the house of a Quaker family. While there she became ill and to prove the voice wrong positively refused to be taken home. But, afterwards, she was forced to beg to be carried back, and died in her own house, as predicted.

Eve and Henry both died a few years ago, still young in years and heart. How they passed I do not know. I am told, however, that both lived exemplary Christian lives of service to the Church and community. Until her death, Eve continued to weave. The linens she wove and bleached are used throughout the American Catholic Church as altar cloths, corporals, purificators, finger towels, and pall covers.

As an act of penance and thanksgiving to God for his conversion, Adam Livingston attempted to give to the Church thirty-five acres of land for the support of a priest. It was the same parcel that had been originally contested and on which Alexander Mayfield's remains had been found. But the laws in the state of Virginia required that his wife give her consent, since she held right over one-third of all his possessions. Mrs. Livingston refused, as evidenced in the letter above. I am unsure what finally convinced her to do so, but a few years later she relinquished her hold on the property and the thirty-five acres were *deeded to the Catholic society of that area for the keeping of a priest. *The priest named was Denis Cahill, for whom Livingston had great respect. The deed was co-signed by Richard McSherry, Joseph (Gabriel) Menghini, and Clement Pierce. Yet Fr. Cahill never took possession of the land. The deed nonetheless states that Livingston was *"conscious to bestow on the said Reverend Denis Cahill some lasting proof of his esteem for him and the religion, the principles of which he inculcates and enforces by his example." If it was not possible for Fr. Cahill or another priest to reside on the land, the deed stipulates that "the land be rented and the profits thereof are to be applied towards building and repairing a church or chapel thereupon." But Adam had another reason for donating the thirty-five acres, which was a ten percent tithe of his land holdings. The Voice, which had accurately predicted future events, told him, *"Before the end of time, this land will be a great place of prayer and fasting and praise!"

Before his conversion, Mr. Livingston bore his losses very impatiently, but after his conversion, he never complained. Years later, Adam Livingston traveled to Baltimore and met Bishop John Carroll. After their visit, *Carroll reported that he had never met a layman who was better educated in the faith than was Adam Livingston.

A final note is no doubt necessary about Gregory McCullough. A few years after the Livingston exorcism, in the early 1800s, his slaves staged a successful revolt. He and his henchmen were killed. Most of the slaves escaped to the north into free territory. The girl that loved Nwanne came to the Livingstons looking for Nwanne, and ended up living and working with the Darks. I do not know what happened to the Darks, but Livingston made sure they were well cared for after he retired.

*After his children and wife died, Mr. Livingston sold the remainder of his farm and moved from Virginia to Bedford County, Pennsylvania, about twenty miles from here (Loretto) where he died in the Spring of 1820, just a year ago. I had Mass at his house repeatedly. He continued to the last very attentive to his duties as a Christian, but did not receive the last rites of the Church due to his last illness, which carried him off too quickly to afford any chance of sending for a priest.

*A final warning came from the Voice to Adam: "Many people will not believe these things. Some priests, ministers, and bishops will scoff at you because of them. They will believe things that are not true, just as you have done. When what is clearly known through creation is repeatedly rejected, the Almighty will give them over to their own desires, whereupon evil, death, and destruction will descend upon them, just as it did upon you, for they rejected the truth that surrounds them. When that happens, do not try to convince them, for the spirit of deception will be present until the end of times."

Likewise, my mother told me repeatedly what Empress Catharine had told her—that we can make any decision we want, and take any action within our capacity, but we have no choice over the consequence—what is true cannot be changed.

I must also offer this final salute to my friend Fr. Denis Cahill. Regardless of his failings, *he was bluff and hearty, a man of powerful nerve and strong faith, a robust priest for sure.

I remain in your service,
Rev. Demetrius Augustine Gallitzin (Fr. Smith)

The Moral Premise

Rejecting the authority and hierarchy of natural order
leads to dysfunction, chaos, and death;

BUT

Respecting the authority and hierarchy of natural order
leads to function, progress, and life.

~ ◯ ~
AMDG - PS 19

Afterword

Author's Notes

As a work of historical fiction, this novel incorporates a great deal of my imagination in a historical setting. Since truth is often *stranger than fiction*, my wife, who listened patiently to my reading aloud many chapters, kept asking which parts were true and which were imagined. She wanted me to somehow highlight the true parts for the reader. But I declined except for the asterisk notation, as explained on the front matter's title page. The line between fiction and history in my own mind was often muddled, and attempting to delineate for the reader would weaken the story as entertainment.

Even the best historian cannot faithfully represent life in times past. One has to live it, and even then the dilemma for the writer is finding a balance between historical realism and the fantasy that will carry the reader along. As much as I've researched and attempted to include historical details, the fact is that I am unsure of their factual nature. For instance, I have in my files (both paper and electronic) perhaps thirty different versions of the Adam Livingston, Wizard Clip, Fr. Cahill, and Fr. Gallitzin story. The accounts span a time period of their authorship from the mid 1800s to the late 1900s. In one way or another, they all relate the events and details *differently*.

Attesting to this historical problem is perhaps the most comprehensive and earliest attempt to document the story. In 1879 Rev. Joseph M. Finotti, S.J., published a 143-page monograph simply titled: "The Mystery of the Wizard Clip" (Baltimore: Kelly, Piet and Company). One might hope for a cogent, chronological telling from start to finish, but Fr. Finotti's research, which consisted of a compilation of accounts and remembrances by anyone that had any close knowledge of the Wizard Clip events, resulted in numerous replies that were as divergent as we find today. The first pages of the monograph acknowledge the difficulty of knowing what to believe:

> No preface seems needed to a compilation of documents which are laid before the people without a determined intent to force a conclusion upon the mind of the reader. My aim has been, simply, to gather information about events which occurred more than three-quarters of a century ago lest they perish from the memory of the third and following generations.

I hope the truth of the story can be found in the theme (or Moral Premise) it conveys, for I disavow that you should trust in any of the detail except to be entertained even as I believe a good part of the story and the detail are true and factual.

Rev. Prince Demetrius Augustine Gallitzin (1770-1840), a.k.a. Fr. Smith, whom I have chosen to narrate this tale, is today honored by the Roman Catholic Church as a Servant of God, the first of several steps toward canonization. While he was yet alive, he became known as the Apostle of the Alleghenies, where he spent a good deal of his royal Russian inheritance to establish the town of Loretto, Pennsylvania. In researching this tome I was privileged to have visited his grave site in Loretto. It is a fenced-off shrine outside the Basilica of St. Michael the Archangel, which he founded. I was also able to visit and interview the champions of Fr. Gallitzin's cause, Betty and Frank Seymour, in their home. They live not a hundred yards from the Basilica property and Fr. Gallitzin's grave. Betty is a Lilly, that is a descendant of Anastasia (Lilly) McSherry's brother, Samuel-Joseph Lilly.

The Voice's prediction concerning the thirty-five acres donated for the keeping of a priest was this: "Before the end of time, this land will be a great place of prayer and fasting and praise!" This has certainly come true. Today the land is known as Priest Field. As I write this, their website claims:

> Priest Field is a center for Christian life where people can walk with Jesus and experience Him through personal and group retreats, authentic community, and the beauty of our creek-side cedar forest in wild, wonderful West Virginia. It is located on 40 acres of wooded property along the Opequon Creek in the Shenandoah Valley.

In 2014, when my curiosity about Denis Cahill's destiny got the best of me, I took a research trip to Pennsylvania, Maryland, and West Virginia to see what I could discover. The story took place in an area that was Virginia until the Civil War, when in 1863 it became West Virginia. During my research and travel in the area I stayed at Priest Field for several days. There are hiking and wilderness trails; thirty-nine guest rooms with double beds, private baths, and an outdoor balcony or patio; five conference rooms with audio-visual support and one with digital video-conferencing; an on-site commercial kitchen and dining facility with views of the woods; two chapels; several cabins and apartments leased to tenants who work at Priest Field; and two bunk houses for large families and groups. Outside the main entrance is a shrine of sorts to Adam Livingston with a 4/5ths scale wood carving of the farmer. The bronze plaque beneath reads: "In Memory of ADAM LIVINGSTON, who donated this land to the Church in 1802 to sustain a priest." The hiking trails will take you to the Stranger's Grave, but I believe it is only symbolic.

My research also took me to the Archdiocese of Baltimore archives in search of information about Denis Cahill. With the help of Tricia Pyne, Head Archivist, and Allison Foley, Assistant Archivist, I copied hundreds of pages of documents, including letters between Cahill and Bishop John Carroll. I was surprised at their contentious relationship, but I discovered little about Cahill after Carroll removed him from Hagerstown. The historical accounts of the time only make passing mention that he returned to Ireland around 1806 and there died around 1827, but there was no evidence of such travel. As I was leaving the archives, Tricia Pyne asked if I had found what I was looking for. I said, "not really," and explained that I had been looking for the final disposition or account of Fr. Denis Cahill's ministry. That is, after the Wizard's exorcism, what happened to Fr. Cahill? He seems to have disappeared from the face of the earth. Ms. Pyne said she wasn't sure, but that several years ago an elderly journalist and historian by the name of Edythe Darrow had visited them. The librarian told me that Edythe was memorable because of the unique spelling of her first name, and of what she revealed about Fr. Cahill—that he had left the priesthood and married. How Edythe knew this Pyne had no idea. I was very surprised by this, but realized truth is often more interesting than fiction. "Do you think Ms. Darrow is still alive?" I asked. The librarian doubted it. At the time of her visit to the archives Darrow was writing for *The Journal* in Martinsburg.

In my van I pulled out my iPhone, accessed the Internet, and was about to call The Journal's editor and ask if Edythe Darrow was still with the living. But on a hunch I typed into Google's Search engine: "Edythe Darrow"—the spelling was unique enough. Immediately a phone number came up for Martinsburg, just twenty minutes away. I called. A man named Eddie answered. I later found out Eddie was Edythe's nephew. I explained who I was and why I was calling. A moment later Edythe came on the line. A rush of excitement came over me. That night I took her out to supper and we had a good talk. She was articulate and had a fabulous memory. She told me where to look. The next day I visited the Berkeley County courthouse. No, they no longer had marriage certificates for that time period. They were all in Richmond, Virginia. As I was leaving, the secretary for the county clerk came running down the outside steps to catch me. While they didn't have the actual certificates, they did have a book that alphabetically listed "Marriage Records of Berkeley County, Virginia, 1781–1854," compiled by Guy L. Keesecker. It was a one-of-a-kind hard-bound book of a hundred pages documenting on one line each the marriage records for seventy-three years. The pages were manually typed, single spaced, one line each, meticulously listing thousands of marriage bonds and marriages. I laid the book on a work counter in the file room of the clerk's office surrounded by hundreds of years of deeds and other legal documents in metal and cardboard file cases that lined the walls to the twelve-foot high ceiling. I felt like I was in a movie. The room had to be over 200 years old.

In no time I found the following, here expanded from the abbreviated text columns found in the book:

> *Sept 25, 1805 Denis Cahill paid a bond to guarantee the marriage commitment of Catharine Cahill to Philip Field.*

The line below read, notice the earlier date:

> *April 30, 1805, Cornelius Kelly paid a bond to guarantee the marriage commitment of Denis Cahill to Letitia McCartney.*

Notice the spelling of "Denis" not "Dennis" which reflects, I believe, the honor Denis Cahill's parents gave to St. Denis of Paris, a Christian martyr of the third century. But the above were typed. I needed a signature to compare with Fr. Cahill's letters signed to Bishop Carroll. Once home in Michigan, again thanks to Google, I found a photocopy of the actual bond certificate for Philip and Catharine's marriage. It is signed by Philip Field and Denis Cahill, and Denis Cahill's signature matches the signatures on the letters he sent to Bishop Carroll.

Did he and Letitia return to Ireland after they married? Edythe said she didn't think so. She had discovered that Denis became a farmer with Philip further south; she didn't know where exactly. Further, Denis and Letitia ended up in Pittsburgh, where he died, or so Edythe believed.

On a separate trip I visited the only Catholic cemetery of that time in Pittsburgh, Pennsylvania. I found a grave plot belonging to Denis Cahill, but there was no Cahill tombstone to confirm it. Back in my office, researching on line ancestry records, I discovered an 1850 Pittsburgh census listing for Letitia Cahill (age seventy, born in Ireland), living with a Denis Cahill (age twenty-two, born in Pennsylvania), but no Denis senior, who would have been 82–84 at the time of the census. Letitia and young Denis were living with Robert Kief (age thirty, born in Ireland), his wife Catharine (age twenty-six, born in Pennsylvania), and their child, Mary Kief (age two, born in Pennsylvania). This Pittsburgh Letitia, age seventy, matches the age of Letitia McCartney in the Wizard Clip story. That couples of the time named their first boy after the father would make the Pittsburgh Denis Cahill (age twenty-two) born in 1828 probably the son of Fr. Denis Cahill. This also means Letitia was forty-eight years of age and Fr. Denis was sixty when Denis, Jr., was born. That's a bit old for a woman to bear children, but it's not impossible. Perhaps it's only coincidence that the wife of Robert Kief has the same first name, and spelling, as Catharine Cahill, Letitia's best friend from Ireland. Nothing here is proof that Denis Cahill left the priesthood and married Letitia McCartney, but there's plenty for the basis of a novel.

As I write this in 2022, I came across Edythe Mary Darrow's obituary online. She died in 2018 at the age of ninety, four years after we met. In part it reads:

> She lived an adventurous life, touring Europe and living in the Vatican for six years as a journalist. She authored several books and worked as a vocational therapist. She was a member of St. Joseph Catholic Church and the director of the Christian Life Community CLC. Her hobby was to help others by bringing them together through the research of their genealogy.

Thank you, Edythe. You certainly helped me bring Denis Cahill to life. I might also add: Edythe was at first hesitant to tell me what she had learned by Denis Cahill. Although advanced in age she wanted to write a version of the book that you hold in your hands.

One geographical note that I should make is that the original deed to Adam

Livingston's land notes that the land was in three parcels, all east and south of Opequon Creek and bounded by Turkey Run Creek. Given those landmarks, the novel describes a 350-acre land that is mostly rectangular and that runs parallel to Opequon (southwest to northeast) for one-and-a-half miles, and is 0.3 to 0.4 miles wide. Priest Field is in the very northern corner alongside the Opequon and Charles Town Road. Deciphering the deed to determine the exact lay of the parcels has been difficult and there does not seem to be a plat map in existence. I've been told, however, that the present day Charles Town Road (Route 51) did not exist in Livingston's time, and that the main road through town (Smithfield) was what is today Grace Street and Bunker Hill Road, crossing the Opequon three-quarters of a mile further southwest from where the Charles Town Road today crosses on a bridge. I do not doubt what I've been told but the narrative I've woven and history would seem to require that the Priest Field land would have road access in 1797 as it does today. Therefore, I have left the exact location of Livingston's farm house a mystery.

Yes, many things in this story have been fictionalized. But many things too are factual parts of history.

Acknowledgments

I am deeply thankful to the many people that motivated me to tell this story and to those who contributed their time, knowledge, and suppositions of history and of the characters that populated history. Hopefully the story is enriched by their contribution and not defrauded by my interpretation.

No doubt I will neglect to name someone who was critical in the writing of this tome, but let me try, for the work of a storyteller and amateur historian such as I am is impossible without the contribution of many others to whom I extend my deep appreciation.

Jaime Sotelo must be near the top of my list. Jaime is a Filipino living in Australia. He called me on the phone in 2012. He had been a customer of my distribution company, Nineveh's Crossing, and knew I was also a filmmaker of some modest reputation. Jaime thought I should make a movie based on The Mystery of the Wizard Clip, details which he had scoured off the Internet. I listened patiently and jotted down some notes and website addresses, but being involved in numerous other projects, I did not think much more about it. Later, Jaime sent me an airmail package of documents he had acquired and again encouraged me to make a movie…possibly with Mel Gibson's Australian-based brother whom Jaime claimed to know. With such promptings, a year later I drafted a screenplay about Livingston and the Wizard that interested several individuals in Hollywood, but no one with the wherewithal to make the movie. So, thank you, Jaime, for the motivation.

During my research travels I met many helpful individuals in addition to those already mentioned. Jon Gilot of the Wheeling, West Virginia Diocese Archives hosted me for a day and later sent me a large envelope full of helpful historical news clippings and even later put up with my email questions. At beautiful Priest Field, Susan Kersey and her staff were gracious, the accommodations comfortable, and the trails around Livingston's former land next to the Opequon Creek inspiring. In Middleway, West Virginia, James Grantham, of The Middleway Conservancy, showed me through his historic home, The Daniel Fry House, and let me take pictures while he answered many questions. Larry Myers, Priest Field Historian, allowed me to pepper him with questions by phone. In Shepherdstown at St. Agnes Church I sat with secretary Kate Diservio who faced a stained glass mural that contained a nearly life-size representation of Fr. Cahill on horseback. When I told St. Agnes priest Fr. Mathew Rowgh the disposition of Fr. Cahill, he laughed and shook his head in surprise. Cathy Miller of West Virginia Division of Culture and History sent me copies of numerous historical newspaper articles. Jeff Bowers of the Harper's Ferry National Historical Park Service answered questions regarding the ferry's actual location. I learned the ancestries and developed family trees for the Lillys of Conewago, the Hagers of Hagerstown, the Carrolls of Washington and Philadelphia, the

Washingtons of Charles Town, the McSherrys of Leetown, and the Gates near Kearneysville through the helpful resources of Ancestry.com, MyHeritage.com, and LegacyTree.com.

There has been, also, a finite list of reference books and documents aside from the Baltimore Diocese Associated Archives at St. Mary's Seminary and University, Baltimore, Maryland, that were invaluable. These include:

- *Gallitzin's Letters*, Angelmodde Press, Loretto, PA, 1940
- *The Mystery of the Wizard Clip*, 143-page monograph by Rev. Joseph M. Finotti, S.J., 1870. The manuscript I have was a gift from Jon-Erik Gilot of the Catholic Diocese of Wheeling-Charleston archives
- *The Mystery of the Wizard Clip: Supernatural Visitations in Old Virginia and their Remarkable Legacy*, by Raphael Brown and Rev. Msgr. John L. O'Reilly, Catholic Diocese of Wheeling-Charleston, 1990
- *St. Mary Church (Hagerstown, Maryland) 1758–2000: A History for the Millennium and Mother of Churches*, both by Rita Clark Hutzell, 2000
- *St. Agnes Church, Shepherd's Town, West Virginia, 2008*, a memory book and a manuscript of the church's history upon the dedication of their new church
- *Adam Livingston and The Wizard Clip and The Voice: A Historical Account*, by A.L. Marshall, 1978. Somehow I acquired both an early manuscript of this booklet and the final published edition, available at the Priest Field gift shop.
- *Basic Seamanship Brigantines Exy Johnson and Irving Johnson*, by Douglas Corey, of the Los Angeles Maritime Institute, 2002.
- *Demetrius Augustine Gallitzin Prince and Priest*, by Sara Brownson. Google Books via the Harvard College library, 1873.

Jeff Wiitala, former proofreader for a well-known book publisher, should get special credit. Jeff proofed the entire manuscript and made *thousands* of corrections and suggestions. Of course, after I made his changes I did not give the manuscript back to him to correct my revisions of his corrections.

To the rescue came my sister, Hope Smith, the professional editor and proofreader in the family, who did her usual excellent job finding the *hundreds* of mistakes I had added back in after Jeff's effort. Hope also made numerous editorial suggestions for which I was very thankful. We are all sure there are still errors in the book, for which I must take full responsibility. Either that or it's Livingston's ghost.

There were other early readers, too, who graciously pointed out room for improvement and to them I am also grateful—Jan Swedorske and Monica Miller, thank you. A few others reminded me that Mass was not celebrated on Good Friday in New Orleans in 1788, although none of us are really sure if it was or not, although if it was celebrated early that morning, God was not pleased and the church burnt down.

Last on this list, but first in my heart, is my lovely, beautiful, and eternally patient wife, Pamela Sue, who listened to me read to her aloud every page of this story several times over. Her comments were not always received graciously, but they were always spot on and filled with insight that eventually convinced me to make the necessary revisions. Pam has been a heavenly gift to me, our children, grandchildren, and many others.

Brownson on Gallitzin

During my research into the history and legends surrounding this tale, I acquired a Google Books copy from the Harvard College library of Sarah Brownson's 444-page biography *Demetrius Augustine Gallitzin Prince and Priest*. It was published in 1873, not quite 100 years after the events around which this novel is based. The reader may find this source document of interest in terms of authenticating parts of the story which I have clearly and without apology fictionalized. Of the many versions I have read or heard, this is as trustworthy as any.

Demetrius Augustine Gallitzin Prince and Priest
by Sarah Brownson
excerpt pages 99-107

Fr. Gallitzin remained in Baltimore until some time in the year 1796, when he fulfilled the bishop's original design by taking an active part in what was called the Conewago mission, visiting from this central point Taneytown, Pipe Creek, Hagerstown, and Cumberland in Maryland, not far from the Pennsylvania border; Chambersburg, Path and Shade Valley, Huntingdon, and even the Allegheny Mountains in Pennsylvania. In Maryland his congregations were mainly English-speaking people, which forced him to a greater fluency in the English language. In Pennsylvania, especially in the neighborhood of Chambersburg, the greatest ignorance prevailed, accompanied, as usual, by prejudice, bigotry, and persecution. Mr. Brosius attending the same mission, was looked upon with such horror, being known to be a Catholic priest, that he was in danger of his life at one time and only saved himself from a party of pursuing bigots by the superior speed of an excellent horse, which enabled him to take refuge at the house of Mr. Michael Stillinger, a good Catholic residing at Chambersburg in whose home the priests often said Mass before a church could be built. Mr. Gallitzin, "timid Mitri" (also Dimitri), accustomed to the quiet and orderly vicinity of Muenster and Angelmodde, had many a dangerous journey to face upon his missions.

In the summer of 1797 reports accumulated at Conewago of mysterious, perhaps diabolical performances in Virginia. Fr. Gallitzin was relieved for a time of his laborious mission in Conewago (by Bishop Carroll) and deputed to visit the scene and investigate the truth of the reports in Smithfield. He did so with readiness, not having the least faith in them, and no belief whatever in any but a natural cause for all that, since then, has become familiar cultish practice under the general head of Spiritism. He remained in Virginia from September until Christmas, dividing his time between the houses of Mr. Livingston and Mr. Richard McSherry.

Years later he wrote Mrs. Boll, daughter of Mr. McSherry:

> Ten lawyers in a court of justice never examined and cross-examined all the witnesses I could procure more than I did. I spent several days in penning down the whole account, which, on my return to Conewago, was read with the greatest interest, and handed down from one to another, till, at last (when I wanted it back), it could no longer be found.

These things caused the greatest excitement at the time and many accounts, more or less mingled with reports and recollections of those who knew the original persons concerned, have since been published.

Father Gallitzin spent many happy days in the pious and agreeable society of the Catholic families mentioned and bore witness to these manifestations. He very soon came to a full belief in the presence of the evil spirit, and possibly it was from this early contest with the devil in such material form that he received, and never afterwards could overcome, a nervous dislike of ever again encountering him.

This occurred in Jefferson County [today Berkeley County], at a village called Middleway, since changed, on account of what there took place, to Cliptown, near Martinsburg, Virginia. Some seven or eight years previously, Mr. Adam Livingston, a Pennsylvanian by birth, of Dutch descent, and a Lutheran in religion, an honest, industrious farmer, moved with his large family from Pennsylvania to Middleway, and soon acquired a handsome property there. He was kind, generous, and hospitable.

It was said that a poor Irish traveler, a Catholic, being ill while in Livingston's neighborhood, was taken into his house, carefully nursed and attended through his last sickness, and properly buried. The only thing Mr. Livingston refused to do for the sick man was to send for a priest for him; Mr. Livingston had never seen one, and in common with the generality of his class had probably very extraordinary ideas of Catholic priests, many actually believing that they were the living emissaries of Satan, that they had horns like their master, and various other equally enlightened fancies. Nothing, therefore, could induce any of the Livingstons to accede to the dying man's entreaty; and this through no hardness of heart, it must be understood, for they were all of kindly disposition; but because to them the request was absurd, of no consequence, and a great deal better disregarded.

Soon after this death, and this refusal, Mr. Livingston appeared to be given over to the buffetings of Satan in good earnest. His barns got on fire and burned down, nobody knew how; his horses and cattle died; his clothing and those of his family, their beds and bedding were either burnt up, or cut into strips so small they could never be mended or put together again, generally in little pieces in the shape of a crescent. Boots, saddles, harnesses, all shared the same fate; chunks of fire rolled over the floors without any apparent cause; all conceivable noise tormented their ears; their furniture was banged about at the most inconvenient times, their crockery dashed to the floor and broken to atoms. These things, depriving them of sleep, torturing their nerves, and terrifying their very souls, very soon reduced the family to the depths of physical and mental distress, while they aroused the whole neighborhood to horror and sympathetic advice.

Livingston sent far and wide for ministers of all persuasions, for conjurors of all kinds, to come and slay the devil, but the evil one gave each a most inhospitable reception, mingled with a malice so minute, and yet so overpowering that it actually seemed as if the demon and all his imps were laughing at them. The ministers' tracts and the conjurors' riddles were flung about the house and treated one with as little respect as the other, and when it was thought the reverend gentlemen had talked long enough, a great stone, apparently kicked down the fireplace, brought their exhortations to a sudden end, and so terrified them that they unceremoniously departed.

Less meddlesome visitors, as they might have been considered, were hardly any better treated. One old Presbyterian lady having heard of the clipping at a tea party went to Livingston's house to satisfy her curiosity. However, before entering it, she took her new black silk cap off her head, wrapped it up in her silk handkerchief, and put it in her pocket, to save it from being clipped. After a while she stepped out again to go home, and having drawn the handkerchief out of her pocket and opened it, she found her cap cut into ribbons.

In this hopeless misery, Mr. Livingston was permitted, we may, perhaps, be allowed to fancy on account of his hospitality to the poor traveller, to have a dream so remarkable and so vivid that it was more like a vision. He dreamed he had toiled up a rugged mountain, climbing it with the greatest difficulty. At the top of the mountain he saw a beautiful church, and in the church a man dressed in a style he had never seen before. While he was gazing upon this person, a voice said to him: "This is the man who will bring you relief." He related this dream to his wife and many other persons, one of whom told him that the dress described worn by the minister of his dream was precisely that worn by Catholic priests, and advised him to try one of them. But Livingston, discouraged at so many failures, paid little attention to this advice until importuned by his wife, who made enquiries to learn where one such priest could be found. Somebody knew of a Catholic family named McSherry living near Leetown, where he would be likely to find a priest. Livingston's troubles increasing, and his wife entreating, a conviction forced itself into his own head that a Catholic priest could not work him much more evil than he was already enduring, thus induced Livingston to go to Mr. McSherry's and try. Mrs. McSherry met him at the gate of her residence, and asked him his errand. He told her he would like to see the priest, to which she replied that there was no priest there, but one would be at Shepherd's Town to say Mass the next Sunday. Mr. Livingston went to Shepherd's Town at the time she told him, and the moment the priest, Rev. Denis Cahill, came out upon the altar to say Mass, Mr. Livingston was so affected that he cried out before the people: "The very man I saw in my dream!" He remained during the service in the greatest agitation, and as soon as the priest had retired into the sacristy, followed him, accompanied by Mr. Richard McSherry, and an Italian gentleman, Mr. Menghini, who kept a boarding house at Sulphur Springs, who were among the prominent men of Mr. Cahill's mission, who had heard the exclamation and knew something of the circumstances. No sooner had Mr. Livingston, with tears in his eyes and choking in his throat, made known his errand, than the bluff and hearty priest laughed at him, and told him his neighbors were teasing him; to go home, to watch them closely, and they would soon get tired of the amusement. The other gentlemen, however, took up his case most earnestly, and insisted upon the priest's compliance. Fr. Cahill very reluctantly yielded to them at last, assured that it was all nonsense, loss of time, and a very unnecessary journey.

When he reached the house, and heard and saw pretty clear proofs of Livingston's story, however, he sprinkled the house with Holy Water, at which the disturbances ceased, for a time. At the moment the priest was leaving, having one foot over the door-sill, a purse of money, which had disappeared some time before, was laid between Fr. Cahill's feet.

When Father Gallitzin arrived at Bishop Carroll's request, the disturbances having recommenced, he (Fr. Gallitzin) intended to exorcise the evil spirits for good and all. But as Fr. Gallitzin commenced, the rattling and rumbling, as of innumerable wagons outside the house worked so upon his nerves that he could not command himself sufficiently to read the exorcism. He was obliged to go for Rev. Cahill, a man of powerful nerve and hearty faith, who returned with Fr. Gallitzin to Livingston's, and bidding all to kneel down, commanded the evil spirits to leave the house without doing any injury to any one there; after a stubborn resistance on the part of the devil, they were finally conquered and compelled to obey the priest.

Afterwards, Rev. Cahill said Mass there, and there was no more trouble. Father Gallitzin carried a trunk full of clothing, which had been cut to pieces during this period of destruction, back to Conewago, where they have been seen, even of late years, by eminent priests, who have added their testimony to the truth of these occurrences. Among these clothes, however, are said to have been one or two garments marked in quite a different manner, one bearing the impression of a hand burnt in the cloth, the other an I.H.S. made in the same manner. For scarcely had the Livingston family been relieved from the torments of the devil than they were visited by a consoling voice, which remained with them for seventeen years. It has been supposed that this voice came from some soul suffering in purgatory, for some reason permitted to visit, console, and, finally, to instruct the family. This may, perhaps, have been in return for the hospitality shown the poor Catholic who died at their house.

In gratitude, perhaps, for the relief he had received at the hands of a Catholic priest, and with perfect submission of his will to the truth of the Church which alone could cast out devils, Mr. Livingston desired, with a portion of his family, to be made a member of it, and after giving the Livingston family the rudiments of instruction which were absolutely necessary, Mr. Cahill received them into the Church. Mrs. Livingston complied with this, but she was never sincerely converted, and always said she was Judas. They had scarcely made their profession of faith, and heard one or two

Masses, before a bright light awoke Mr. Livingston one night, and a clear, sweet voice told him to arise, call his family together and to pray. He did so; the hours passed as a moment, for the voice prayed with them, leading their prayers. Then it spoke to them, in the most simple yet eloquent manner of all the great mysteries of the Catholic faith to which they had assented, and which, as far as they could, vaguely understanding them, they sincerely and firmly believed. But now these truths, dimly guessed at before, and accepted because the Church gave them, became clear, intelligible, fascinating, ever and ever more plain and more beautiful.

Among other things which they could remember to repeat to others, the Voice said that all the sighs and tears of the whole world were worth nothing in comparison with one Mass in which a God is offered to a God. It exhorted to boundless devotion to the Bless-ed Virgin Mary, continually implored them to pray for the suffer-ing souls in purgatory, whose agony the voice could never weary of describing, and once, in illustration of their pains, a burning hand was impressed upon some article of clothing, directly under the eyes of the family, while it was speaking. It also urged to hospi-tality, and to simplicity in dress; it would reprove the least extrav-agance in which any of them might indulge, and induced them to many voluntary penances, to long strict fasts, to unbounded charity, and to continual prayer.

Mr. Livingston, to whom the voice more particularly ad-dressed itself, was made its agent for innumerable good works; he would be called up at night to undertake long journeys to persons taken suddenly ill or in affliction miles away; he would receive messages without any explanation, which he was enjoined to give at once to different people, to whom they would prove of immense relief, of amazing prophecy, of timely warning. It foretold events which were always verified, and explained the meaning of many others. It is said that while Father Gallitzin was investigating these matters, and was much concerned if they were of God or a delusive spirit, that startling proofs were given him that, at least, they were not of man, and that he was told of terrible trials, of slander, perse-cution, denunciation, of bitterest deception and desertion in store for him, even circumstantial details, so far from anything he was likely to meet, that he could hardly understand, but did not fail to remember them, and, afterwards, they were verified to the letter.

As the evil spirits cannot foresee the future, it evidently was from this Voice that he received the communication. Upon one occasion, Mr. Livingston and his family were together in one room when there appeared among them a young man very poorly clad, and, though it was a bitterly cold day, barefooted. They asked him where he came from; he answered: "From my father." "Where are you going?" "I'm going to my father," he said, "and I have come to you to teach you the way to him. He stayed with them three days and three nights, instructing them on all points of Christian doctrine. They asked him if he was not cold, offering him a pair of shoes; he replied that in his country there was neither heat nor cold. When he left the house, the same idea occurred to each of them, that, as they had not noticed when he came in, they would watch and see what direction he took when going away. They saw him go into a lot in the front of the house and then disappear. At that time there was no priest settled in the neighborhood, and very few Catholic books to be had even in the large cities. But Bishop Carroll, Mr. Gallitzin, Mr. Brosius, Mr. Cahill, and Father Pellentz, and other clergymen who conversed with Mr. Livingston, were astonished at his knowledge of the Catholic religion, and were all convinced that he had been instructed from above.

Mrs. Livingston heard the Voice oftener than the others and endeavored by every means in her power to falsify it. Among other things, it is said she would die in her own house; she was so often rebuked by it that she would not stay at home, but went to the house of a Quaker family; while there she became ill, and, to prove the Voice wrong, positively refused to be taken home; but, afterwards, she was forced to beg to be carried back, and died in her own house, as predicted.

Fourteen persons were converted in one winter by these things, which were well knowns and widely discussed; others, influenced by the account of them, received clearer impressions of the reality of another world, of the close proximity of the evil one, and of the intimate union between the Church Militant and the Church Suffering, from which they were moved to the serious practice of virtue and to endeavor to live as they wish to die.

Prince Gallitzin, having fully and thoroughly satisfied himself of the nature of these different manifestations, returned to Conewago and took up again the burden of his missions.

Stan Williams is a writer and filmmaker, based in Michigan with occasional forays to Los Angeles and Europe. He's known as a story and screenplay consultant and workshop leader due to his book *The Moral Premise: Harnessing Virtue and Vice for Box Office Success.* The Wizard Clip story came to him from an ex-pat Filipino and emigrant to Australia who thought the Wizard Clip would make a good movie. Stan agreed, but figured he'd better write the book first. He and his wife, Pam, have three children and ten grandchildren. Stan holds degrees in Physics (BA), Mass Communications (MA), and Film Studies/Narrative Theory (PhD). www.stanwilliams.com

also by Stanley D. Williams
available at Amazon.com and NinevehsCrossing.com

*THE MORAL PREMISE: Harnessing Virtue and Vice
for Box Office Success*
(Michael Wiese Productions publisher)

The quintessential book on story structure for screen-
writers, novelists, and all storytellers, used as the basis
of his Storycraft Training workshops throughout the
film industry.

MoralPremise.com
MoralPremise.blogspot.com
StorycraftTraining.MoralPremise.com

~

*GROWING UP CHRISTIAN: Searching for a
Reasonable Faith in the Heartland of America.*

"Reads like pure Americana" (M.K.)

"Wicked humor, subversive satire, and brutal honesty."
(Y.W.)

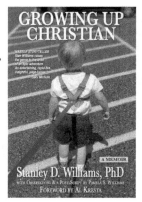

"Hardly a page can be turned without laughing out
loud or nodding over a similar experience or even
blinking away a tear or two at God's tender mercy. An
absolute delight to read!" (Fr. J.B.)

"A delightful, sentimental, and insightful 'romp'
through American Christianity" (D.A.)

Printed in the USA
CPSIA information can be obtained
at www.ICGtesting.com
LVHW021229021123
762556LV00029B/267/J